HENRY JAMES

HENRY JAMES

NOVELS 1881–1886

Washington Square
The Portrait of a Lady
The Bostonians

THE LIBRARY OF AMERICA

The paper used in this publication meets the
minimum requirements of the American National Standard
for Information Sciences—Permanence of Paper for
Printed Library Materials, ANSI z39.48–1984.

Distributed to the trade in the United States
and Canada by the Viking Press.

Library of Congress Catalog Card Number: 85–5207
For Cataloging in Publication Data, see end of *Notes* section.
ISBN 0–940450–30–5

Second Printing
The Library of America—29

Manufactured in the United States of America

WILLIAM T. STAFFORD
WROTE THE NOTES AND SELECTED THE
TEXTS FOR THIS VOLUME

Grateful acknowledgement is made to the National Endowment for the Humanities and the Ford Foundation for their generous financial support of this series.

Contents

WASHINGTON SQUARE

I

DURING A PORTION of the first half of the present century, and more particularly during the latter part of it, there flourished and practised in the city of New York a physician who enjoyed perhaps an exceptional share of the consideration which, in the United States, has always been bestowed upon distinguished members of the medical profession. This profession in America has constantly been held in honour, and more successfully than elsewhere has put forward a claim to the epithet of "liberal." In a country in which, to play a social part, you must either earn your income or make believe that you earn it, the healing art has appeared in a high degree to combine two recognised sources of credit. It belongs to the realm of the practical, which in the United States is a great recommendation; and it is touched by the light of science—a merit appreciated in a community in which the love of knowledge has not always been accompanied by leisure and opportunity. It was an element in Dr. Sloper's reputation that his learning and his skill were very evenly balanced; he was what you might call a scholarly doctor, and yet there was nothing abstract in his remedies—he always ordered you to take something. Though he was felt to be extremely thorough, he was not uncomfortably theoretic, and if he sometimes explained matters rather more minutely than might seem of use to the patient, he never went so far (like some practitioners one has heard of) as to trust to the explanation alone, but always left behind him an inscrutable prescription. There were some doctors that left the prescription without offering any explanation at all; and he did not belong to that class either, which was after all the most vulgar. It will be seen that I am describing a clever man; and this is really the reason why Dr. Sloper had become a local celebrity. At the time at which we are chiefly concerned with him, he was some fifty years of age, and his popularity was at its height. He was very witty, and he passed in the best society of New York for a man of the world—which, indeed, he was, in a very sufficient degree. I hasten to add, to anticipate possible misconception, that he was not the least of a charlatan.

He was a thoroughly honest man—honest in a degree of which he had perhaps lacked the opportunity to give the complete measure; and, putting aside the great good-nature of the circle in which he practised, which was rather fond of boasting that it possessed the "brightest" doctor in the country, he daily justified his claim to the talents attributed to him by the popular voice. He was an observer, even a philosopher, and to be bright was so natural to him, and (as the popular voice said) came so easily, that he never aimed at mere effect, and had none of the little tricks and pretensions of second-rate reputations. It must be confessed that fortune had favoured him, and that he had found the path to prosperity very soft to his tread. He had married at the age of twenty-seven, for love, a very charming girl, Miss Catherine Harrington, of New York, who, in addition to her charms, had brought him a solid dowry. Mrs. Sloper was amiable, graceful, accomplished, elegant, and in 1820 she had been one of the pretty girls of the small but promising capital which clustered about the Battery and overlooked the Bay, and of which the uppermost boundary was indicated by the grassy waysides of Canal Street. Even at the age of twenty-seven Austin Sloper had made his mark sufficiently to mitigate the anomaly of his having been chosen among a dozen suitors by a young woman of high fashion, who had ten thousand dollars of income and the most charming eyes in the island of Manhattan. These eyes, and some of their accompaniments, were for about five years a source of extreme satisfaction to the young physician, who was both a devoted and a very happy husband. The fact of his having married a rich woman made no difference in the line he had traced for himself, and he cultivated his profession with as definite a purpose as if he still had no other resources than his fraction of the modest patrimony which on his father's death he had shared with his brothers and sisters. This purpose had not been preponderantly to make money—it had been rather to learn something and to do something. To learn something interesting, and to do something useful—this was, roughly speaking, the programme he had sketched, and of which the accident of his wife having an income appeared to him in no degree to modify the validity. He was fond of his practice, and of exercising a skill of which he was agreeably conscious, and it was so patent a truth that if he were not a doctor there was nothing else he could be, that a doctor he persisted in being, in the best possible conditions. Of course his easy domestic situation saved him a good deal of drudgery, and his wife's affiliation to the "best people" brought him a good many of those patients whose symptoms are, if not more interesting in themselves than those of the lower orders, at least more consistently displayed. He desired experience, and in the course of twenty years he got a great deal. It must be added that it came to him in some forms which, whatever might have been their intrinsic value, made it the reverse of welcome. His first child, a little boy of extraordinary promise, as the Doctor, who was not addicted to easy enthusiasms, firmly believed, died at three years of age, in spite of everything that the mother's tenderness and the father's science could invent to save him. Two years later Mrs. Sloper gave birth to a second infant—an infant of a sex which rendered the poor child, to the Doctor's sense, an inadequate substitute for his lamented first-born, of whom he had promised himself to make an admirable man. The little girl was a disappointment; but this was not the worst. A week after her birth the young mother, who, as the phrase is, had been doing well, suddenly betrayed alarming symptoms, and before another week had elapsed Austin Sloper was a widower.

For a man whose trade was to keep people alive he had certainly done poorly in his own family; and a bright doctor who within three years loses his wife and his little boy should perhaps be prepared to see either his skill or his affection impugned. Our friend, however, escaped criticism: that is, he escaped all criticism but his own, which was much the most competent and most formidable. He walked under the weight of this very private censure for the rest of his days, and bore for ever the scars of a castigation to which the strongest hand he knew had treated him on the night that followed his wife's death. The world, which, as I have said, appreciated him, pitied him too much to be ironical; his misfortune made him more interesting, and even helped him to be the fashion. It was observed that even medical families cannot escape the more insidious forms of disease, and that, after all, Dr. Sloper had lost other patients beside the two I have mentioned; which constituted an honourable precedent. His little girl remained to him, and though she was not what he had desired, he proposed to himself to make the best of her. He had on hand a stock of unexpended authority, by which the child, in its early years, profited largely. She had been named, as a matter of course, after her poor mother, and even in her most diminutive babyhood the Doctor never called her anything but Catherine. She grew up a very robust and healthy child, and her father, as he looked at her, often said to himself that, such as she was, he at least need have no fear of losing her. I say "such as she was," because, to tell the truth—— But this is a truth of which I will defer the telling.

II

WHEN THE CHILD was about ten years old, he invited his sister, Mrs. Penniman, to come and stay with him. The Miss Slopers had been but two in number, and both of them had married early in life. The younger, Mrs. Almond by name, was the wife of a prosperous merchant and the mother of a blooming family. She bloomed herself, indeed, and was a comely, comfortable, reasonable woman, and a favourite with her clever brother, who, in the matter of women, even when they were nearly related to him, was a man of distinct preferences. He preferred Mrs. Almond to his sister Lavinia, who had married a poor clergyman, of a sickly constitution and a flowery style of eloquence, and then, at the age of thirty-three, had been left a widow, without children, without fortune—with nothing but the memory of Mr. Penniman's flowers of speech, a certain vague aroma of which hovered about her own conversation. Nevertheless, he had offered her a home under his own roof, which Lavinia accepted with the alacrity of a woman who had spent the ten years of her married life in the town of Poughkeepsie. The Doctor had not proposed to Mrs. Penniman to come and live with him indefinitely; he had suggested that she should make an asylum of his house while she looked about for unfurnished lodgings. It is uncertain whether Mrs. Penniman ever instituted a search for unfurnished lodgings, but it is beyond dispute that she never found them. She settled herself with her brother and never went away, and when Catherine was twenty years old her Aunt Lavinia was still one of the most striking features of her immediate *entourage*. Mrs. Penniman's own account of the matter was that she had remained to take charge of her niece's education. She had given this account, at least, to every one but the Doctor, who never asked for explanations which he could entertain himself any day with inventing. Mrs. Penniman, moreover, though she had a good deal of a certain sort of artificial assurance, shrank, for indefinable reasons, from presenting herself to her brother as a fountain of instruction. She had not a high sense of humour, but she had enough to prevent her from making this mistake; and her brother, on his side, had enough to excuse her, in her situation, for laying him under contribution during a considerable part of a lifetime. He therefore assented tacitly to the proposition which Mrs. Penniman had tacitly laid down, that it was of importance that the poor motherless girl should have a brilliant woman near her. His assent could only be tacit, for he had never been dazzled by his sister's intellectual lustre. Save when he fell in love with Catherine Harrington, he had never been dazzled, indeed, by any feminine characteristics whatever; and though he was to a certain extent what is called a ladies' doctor, his private opinion of the more complicated sex was not exalted. He regarded its complications as more curious than edifying, and he had an idea of the beauty of *reason*, which was on the whole meagrely gratified by what he observed in his female patients. His wife had been a reasonable woman, but she was a bright exception; among several things that he was sure of, this was perhaps the principal. Such a conviction, of course, did little either to mitigate or to abbreviate his widowhood; and it set a limit to his recognition, at the best, of Catherine's possibilities and of Mrs. Penniman's ministrations. He, nevertheless, at the end of six months, accepted his sister's permanent presence as an accomplished fact, and as Catherine grew older perceived that there were in effect good reasons why she should have a companion of her own imperfect sex. He was extremely polite to Lavinia, scrupulously, formally polite; and she had never seen him in anger but once in her life, when he lost his temper in a theological discussion with her late husband. With her he never discussed theology, nor, indeed, discussed anything; he contented himself with making known, very distinctly, in the form of a lucid ultimatum, his wishes with regard to Catherine.

Once, when the girl was about twelve years old, he had said to her—

"Try and make a clever woman of her, Lavinia; I should like her to be a clever woman."

Mrs. Penniman, at this, looked thoughtful a moment. "My dear Austin," she then inquired, "do you think it is better to be clever than to be good?"

"Good for what?" asked the Doctor. "You are good for nothing unless you are clever."

From this assertion Mrs. Penniman saw no reason to dissent; she possibly reflected that her own great use in the world was owing to her aptitude for many things.

"Of course I wish Catherine to be good," the Doctor said next day; "but she won't be any the less virtuous for not being a fool. I am not afraid of her being wicked; she will never have the salt of malice in her character. She is as good as good bread, as the French say; but six years hence I don't want to have to compare her to good bread and butter."

"Are you afraid she will be insipid? My dear brother, it is I who supply the butter; so you needn't fear!" said Mrs. Penniman, who had taken in hand the child's accomplishments, overlooking her at the piano, where Catherine displayed a certain talent, and going with her to the dancing-class, where it must be confessed that she made but a modest figure.

Mrs. Penniman was a tall, thin, fair, rather faded woman, with a perfectly amiable disposition, a high standard of gentility, a taste for light literature, and a certain foolish indirectness and obliquity of character. She was romantic, she was sentimental, she had a passion for little secrets and mysteries—a very innocent passion, for her secrets had hitherto always been as unpractical as addled eggs. She was not absolutely veracious; but this defect was of no great consequence, for she had never had anything to conceal. She would have liked to have a lover, and to correspond with him under an assumed name in letters left at a shop; I am bound to say that her imagination never carried the intimacy farther than this. Mrs. Penniman had never had a lover, but her brother, who was very shrewd, understood her turn of mind. "When Catherine is about seventeen," he said to himself, "Lavinia will try and persuade her that some young man with a moustache is in love with her. It will be quite untrue; no young man, with a moustache or without, will ever be in love with Catherine. But Lavinia will take it up, and talk to her about it; perhaps, even, if her taste for clandestine operations doesn't prevail with her, she will talk to me about it. Catherine won't see it, and won't believe it, fortunately for her peace of mind; poor Catherine isn't romantic."

She was a healthy well-grown child, without a trace of her mother's beauty. She was not ugly; she had simply a plain, dull, gentle countenance. The most that had ever been said for her was that she had a "nice" face, and, though she was an heiress, no one had ever thought of regarding her as a belle. Her father's opinion of her moral purity was abundantly justified; she was excellently, imperturbably good; affectionate, docile, obedient, and much addicted to speaking the truth. In her younger years she was a good deal of a romp, and, though it is an awkward confession to make about one's heroine, I must add that she was something of a glutton. She never, that I know of, stole raisins out of the pantry; but she devoted her pocket-money to the purchase of cream-cakes. As regards this, however, a critical attitude would be inconsistent with a candid reference to the early annals of any biographer. Catherine was decidedly not clever; she was not quick with her book, nor, indeed, with anything else. She was not abnormally deficient, and she mustered learning enough to acquit herself respectably in conversation with her contemporaries, among whom it must be avowed, however, that she occupied a secondary place. It is well known that in New York it is possible for a young girl to occupy a primary one. Catherine, who was extremely modest, had no desire to shine, and on most social occasions, as they are called, you would have found her lurking in the background. She was extremely fond of her father and very much afraid of him; she thought him the cleverest and handsomest and most celebrated of men. The poor girl found her account so completely in the exercise of her affections that the little tremor of fear that mixed itself with her filial passion gave the thing an extra relish rather than blunted its edge. Her deepest desire was to please him, and her conception of happiness was to know that she had succeeded in pleasing him. She had never succeeded beyond a certain point. Though on the whole he was very kind to her, she was perfectly aware of this, and to go beyond the point in question seemed to her really something to live for. What she could not know, of course, was that she disappointed him, though on three or four occasions the Doctor had been almost frank about it. She grew up peacefully and prosperously, but at the age of eighteen Mrs. Penniman had not made a clever woman of her. Dr. Sloper would have liked to be proud of his daughter; but there was nothing to be proud of in poor Catherine. There was nothing, of course, to be ashamed of; but this was not enough for the Doctor, who was a proud man and would have enjoyed being able to think of his daughter as an unusual girl. There would have been a fitness in her being pretty and graceful, intelligent and distinguished; for her mother had been the most charming woman of her little day, and as regards her father, of course he knew his own value. He had moments of irritation at having produced a commonplace child, and he even went so far at times as to take a certain satisfaction in the thought that his wife had not lived to find her out. He was naturally slow in making this discovery himself, and it was not till Catherine had become a young lady grown that he regarded the matter as settled. He gave her the benefit of a great many doubts; he was in no haste to conclude. Mrs. Penniman frequently assured him that his daughter had a delightful nature; but he knew how to interpret this assurance. It meant, to his sense, that Catherine was not wise enough to discover that her aunt was a goose—a limitation of mind that could not fail to be agreeable to Mrs. Penniman. Both she and her brother, however, exaggerated the young girl's limitations; for Catherine, though she was very fond of her aunt, and conscious of the gratitude she owed her, regarded her without a particle of that gentle dread which gave its stamp to her admiration of her father. To her mind there was nothing of the infinite about Mrs. Penniman; Catherine saw her all at once, as it were, and was not dazzled by the apparition; whereas her father's great faculties seemed, as they stretched away, to lose themselves in a sort of luminous vagueness, which indicated, not that they stopped, but that Catherine's own mind ceased to follow them.

It must not be supposed that Dr. Sloper visited his disappointment upon the poor girl, or ever let her suspect that she had played him a trick. On the contrary, for fear of being unjust to her, he did his duty with exemplary zeal, and recognised that she was a faithful and affectionate child. Besides, he was a philosopher; he smoked a good many cigars over his disappointment, and in the fulness of time he got used to it. He satisfied himself that he had expected nothing, though, indeed, with a certain oddity of reasoning. "I expect nothing," he said to himself, "so that if she gives me a surprise, it will be all clear gain. If she doesn't, it will be no loss." This was about the time Catherine had reached her eighteenth year; so that it will be seen her father had not been precipitate. At this time she seemed not only incapable of giving surprises; it was almost a question whether she could have received one—she was so quiet and irresponsive. People who expressed themselves roughly called her stolid. But she was irresponsive because she was shy, uncomfortably, painfully shy. This was not always understood, and she sometimes produced an impression of insensibility. In reality she was the softest creature in the world.

III

A s a child she had promised to be tall, but when she was sixteen she ceased to grow, and her stature, like most other points in her composition, was not unusual. She was strong, however, and properly made, and, fortunately, her health was excellent. It has been noted that the Doctor was a philosopher, but I would not have answered for his philosophy if the poor girl had proved a sickly and suffering person. Her appearance of health constituted her principal claim to beauty, and her clear, fresh complexion, in which white and red were very equally distributed, was, indeed, an excellent thing to see. Her eye was small and quiet, her features were rather thick, her tresses brown and smooth. A dull, plain girl she was called by rigorous critics—a quiet, ladylike girl, by those of the more imaginative sort; but by neither class was she very elaborately discussed. When it had been duly impressed upon her that she was a young lady—it was a good while before she could believe it—she suddenly developed a lively taste for dress: a lively taste is quite the expression to use. I feel as if I ought to write it very small, her judgment in this matter was by no means infallible; it was liable to confusions and embarrassments. Her great indulgence of it was really the desire of a rather inarticulate nature to manifest itself; she sought to be eloquent in her garments, and to make up for her diffidence of speech by a fine frankness of costume. But if she expressed herself in her clothes it is certain that people were not to blame for not thinking her a witty person. It must be added that though she had the expectation of a fortune—Dr. Sloper for a long time had been making twenty thousand dollars a year by his profession and laying aside the half of it—the amount of money at her disposal was not greater than the allowance made to many poorer girls. In those days in New York there were still a few altar-fires flickering in the temple of Republican simplicity, and Dr. Sloper would have been glad to see his daughter present herself, with a classic grace, as a priestess of this mild faith. It made him fairly grimace, in private, to think that a child of his should be both ugly and overdressed. For himself, he was fond of the good things of life, and he made a considerable use of them; but he had a dread of vulgarity and even a theory that it was increasing in the society that surrounded him. Moreover, the standard of luxury in the United States thirty years ago was carried by no means so high as at present, and Catherine's clever father took the old-fashioned view of the education of young persons. He had no particular theory on the subject; it had scarcely as yet become a necessity of self-defence to have a collection of theories. It simply appeared to him proper and reasonable that a well-bred young woman should not carry half her fortune on her back. Catherine's back was a broad one, and would have carried a good deal; but to the weight of the paternal displeasure she never ventured to expose it, and our heroine was twenty years old before she treated herself, for evening wear, to a red satin gown trimmed with gold fringe; though this was an article which, for many years, she had coveted in secret. It made her look, when she sported it, like a woman of thirty; but oddly enough, in spite of her taste for fine clothes, she had not a grain of coquetry, and her anxiety when she put them on was as to whether they, and not she, would look well. It is a point on which history has not been explicit, but the assumption is warrantable; it was in the royal raiment just mentioned that she presented herself at a little entertainment given by her aunt, Mrs. Almond. The girl was at this time in her twenty-first year, and Mrs. Almond's party was the beginning of something very important.

Some three or four years before this, Dr. Sloper had moved his household gods up town, as they say in New York. He had been living ever since his marriage in an edifice of red brick, with granite copings and an enormous fanlight over the door, standing in a street within five minutes' walk of the City Hall, which saw its best days (from the social point of view) about 1820. After this, the tide of fashion began to set steadily northward, as, indeed, in New York, thanks to the narrow channel in which it flows, it is obliged to do, and the great hum of traffic rolled farther to the right and left of Broadway. By the time the Doctor changed his residence, the murmur of trade had become a mighty uproar, which was music in the ears of all good citizens interested in the commercial devel-

opment, as they delighted to call it, of their fortunate isle. Dr.
Sloper's interest in this phenomenon was only indirect—
though, seeing that, as the years went on, half his patients
came to be over-worked men of business, it might have been
more immediate—and when most of his neighbours' dwellings (also ornamented with granite copings and large fan-
lights) had been converted into offices, warehouses, and
shipping agencies, and otherwise applied to the base uses of
commerce, he determined to look out for a quieter home.
The ideal of quiet and of genteel retirement, in 1835, was
found in Washington Square, where the doctor built himself
a handsome, modern, wide-fronted house, with a big balcony
before the drawing-room windows, and a flight of white marble steps ascending to a portal which was also faced with
white marble. This structure, and many of its neighbours,
which it exactly resembled, were supposed, forty years ago, to
embody the last results of architectural science, and they remain to this day very solid and honourable dwellings. In front
of them was the square, containing a considerable quantity of
inexpensive vegetation, enclosed by a wooden paling, which
increased its rural and accessible appearance; and round the
corner was the more august precinct of the Fifth Avenue, taking its origin at this point with a spacious and confident air
which already marked it for high destinies. I know not
whether it is owing to the tenderness of early associations,
but this portion of New York appears to many persons the
most delectable. It has a kind of established repose which is
not of frequent occurrence in other quarters of the long, shrill
city; it has a riper, richer, more honourable look than any of
the upper ramifications of the great longitudinal thoroughfare—the look of having had something of a social history. It
was here, as you might have been informed on good authority, that you had come into a world which appeared to offer
a variety of sources of interest; it was here that your grandmother lived, in venerable solitude, and dispensed a hospitality which commended itself alike to the infant imagination
and the infant palate; it was here that you took your first
walks abroad, following the nursery-maid with unequal step
and sniffing up the strange odour of the ailantus-trees which
at that time formed the principal umbrage of the square, and

diffused an aroma that you were not yet critical enough to dislike as it deserved; it was here, finally, that your first school, kept by a broad-bosomed, broad-based old lady with a ferule, who was always having tea in a blue cup, with a saucer that didn't match, enlarged the circle both of your observations and your sensations. It was here, at any rate, that my heroine spent many years of her life; which is my excuse for this topographical parenthesis.

Mrs. Almond lived much farther up town, in an embryonic street with a high number—a region where the extension of the city began to assume a theoretic air, where poplars grew beside the pavement (when there was one), and mingled their shade with the steep roofs of desultory Dutch houses, and where pigs and chickens disported themselves in the gutter. These elements of rural picturesqueness have now wholly departed from New York street scenery; but they were to be found within the memory of middle-aged persons, in quarters which now would blush to be reminded of them. Catherine had a great many cousins, and with her Aunt Almond's children, who ended by being nine in number, she lived on terms of considerable intimacy. When she was younger, they had been rather afraid of her; she was believed, as the phrase is, to be highly educated, and a person who lived in the intimacy of their Aunt Penniman had something of reflected grandeur. Mrs. Penniman, among the little Almonds, was an object of more admiration than sympathy. Her manners were strange and formidable, and her mourning robes—she dressed in black for twenty years after her husband's death, and then suddenly appeared, one morning, with pink roses in her cap—were complicated in odd, unexpected places with buckles, bugles, and pins, which discouraged familiarity. She took children too hard, both for good and for evil, and had an oppressive air of expecting subtle things of them; so that going to see her was a good deal like being taken to church and made to sit in a front pew. It was discovered after a while, however, that Aunt Penniman was but an accident in Catherine's existence, and not a part of its essence, and that when the girl came to spend a Saturday with her cousins, she was available for "follow-my-master," and even for leap-frog. On this basis an understanding was easily arrived at, and for several years Catherine fraternised with her young kinsmen. I say young kinsmen, because seven of the little Almonds were boys, and Catherine had a preference for those games which are most conveniently played in trousers. By degrees, however, the little Almonds' trousers began to lengthen, and the wearers to disperse and settle themselves in life. The elder children were older than Catherine, and the boys were sent to college or placed in counting-rooms. Of the girls, one married very punctually, and the other as punctually became engaged. It was to celebrate this latter event that Mrs. Almond gave the little party I have mentioned. Her daughter was to marry a stout young stockbroker, a boy of twenty; it was thought a very good thing.

IV

M RS. PENNIMAN, with more buckles and bangles than ever, came of course to the entertainment, accompanied by her niece; the Doctor, too, had promised to look in later in the evening. There was to be a good deal of dancing, and before it had gone very far, Marian Almond came up to Catherine, in company with a tall young man. She introduced the young man as a person who had a great desire to make our heroine's acquaintance, and as a cousin of Arthur Townsend, her own intended.

Marian Almond was a pretty little person of seventeen, with a very small figure and a very big sash, to the elegance of whose manners matrimony had nothing to add. She already had all the airs of a hostess, receiving the company, shaking her fan, saying that with so many people to attend to she should have no time to dance. She made a long speech about Mr. Townsend's cousin, to whom she administered a tap with her fan before turning away to other cares. Catherine had not understood all that she said; her attention was given to enjoying Marian's ease of manner and flow of ideas, and to looking at the young man, who was remarkably handsome. She had succeeded, however, as she often failed to do when people were presented to her, in catching his name, which appeared to be the same as that of Marian's little stockbroker. Catherine was always agitated by an introduction; it seemed a difficult moment, and she wondered that some people—her new acquaintance at this moment, for instance—should mind it so little. She wondered what she ought to say, and what would be the consequences of her saying nothing. The consequences at present were very agreeable. Mr. Townsend, leaving her no time for embarrassment, began to talk with an easy smile, as if he had known her for a year.

"What a delightful party! What a charming house! What an interesting family! What a pretty girl your cousin is!"

These observations, in themselves of no great profundity, Mr. Townsend seemed to offer for what they were worth, and as a contribution to an acquaintance. He looked straight into Catherine's eyes. She answered nothing; she only listened, and looked at him; and he, as if he expected no particular reply, went on to say many other things in the same comfortable and natural manner. Catherine, though she felt tongue-tied, was conscious of no embarrassment; it seemed proper that he should talk, and that she should simply look at him. What made it natural was that he was so handsome, or rather, as she phrased it to herself, so beautiful. The music had been silent for a while, but it suddenly began again; and then he asked her, with a deeper, intenser, smile, if she would do him the honour of dancing with him. Even to this inquiry she gave no audible assent; she simply let him put his arm round her waist—as she did so it occurred to her more vividly than it had ever done before, that this was a singular place for a gentleman's arm to be—and in a moment he was guiding her round the room in the harmonious rotation of the polka. When they paused, she felt that she was red; and then, for some moments, she stopped looking at him. She fanned herself, and looked at the flowers that were painted on her fan. He asked her if she would begin again, and she hesitated to answer, still looking at the flowers.

"Does it make you dizzy?" he asked, in a tone of great kindness.

Then Catherine looked up at him; he was certainly beautiful, and not at all red. "Yes," she said; she hardly knew why, for dancing had never made her dizzy.

"Ah, well, in that case," said Mr. Townsend, "we will sit still and talk. I will find a good place to sit."

He found a good place—a charming place; a little sofa that seemed meant only for two persons. The rooms by this time were very full; the dancers increased in number, and people stood close in front of them, turning their backs, so that Catherine and her companion seemed secluded and unobserved. "*We* will talk," the young man had said; but he still did all the talking. Catherine leaned back in her place, with her eyes fixed upon him, smiling and thinking him very clever. He had features like young men in pictures; Catherine had never seen such features—so delicate, so chiselled and finished—among the young New Yorkers whom she passed in the streets and met at parties. He was tall and slim, but he looked extremely strong. Catherine thought he looked like a statue. But a statue would not talk like that, and, above all, would not have eyes of so rare a colour. He had never been at Mrs. Almond's before; he felt very much like a stranger; and it was very kind of Catherine to take pity on him. He was Arthur Townsend's cousin—not very near; several times removed—and Arthur had brought him to present him to the family. In fact, he was a great stranger in New York. It was his native place; but he had not been there for many years. He had been knocking about the world, and living in far-away lands; he had only come back a month or two before. New York was very pleasant, only he felt lonely.

"You see, people forget you," he said, smiling at Catherine with his delightful gaze, while he leaned forward obliquely, turning towards her, with his elbows on his knees.

It seemed to Catherine that no one who had once seen him would ever forget him; but though she made this reflection she kept it to herself, almost as you would keep something precious.

They sat there for some time. He was very amusing. He asked her about the people that were near them; he tried to guess who some of them were, and he made the most laughable mistakes. He criticised them very freely, in a positive, off-hand way. Catherine had never heard any one—especially any young man—talk just like that. It was the way a young man might talk in a novel; or better still, in a play, on the stage, close before the footlights, looking at the audience, and with every one looking at him, so that you wondered at his presence of mind. And yet Mr. Townsend was not like an actor; he seemed so sincere, so natural. This was very interesting; but in the midst of it, Marian Almond came pushing through the crowd, with a little ironical cry, when she found these young people still together, which made every one turn round, and cost Catherine a conscious blush. Marian broke up their talk, and told Mr. Townsend—whom she treated as if she were already married, and he had become her cousin—to run away to her mother, who had been wishing for the last half-hour to introduce him to Mr. Almond.

"We shall meet again!" he said to Catherine as he left her, and Catherine thought it a very original speech.

Her cousin took her by the arm, and made her walk about.

"I needn't ask you what you think of Morris!" the young girl exclaimed.

"Is that his name?"

"I don't ask you what you think of his name, but what you think of himself," said Marian.

"Oh, nothing particular!" Catherine answered, dissembling for the first time in her life.

"I have half a mind to tell him that!" cried Marian. "It will do him good. He's so terribly conceited."

"Conceited?" said Catherine, staring.

"So Arthur says, and Arthur knows about him."

"Oh, don't tell him!" Catherine murmured imploringly.

"Don't tell him he's conceited? I have told him so a dozen times."

At this profession of audacity, Catherine looked down at her little companion in amazement. She supposed it was because Marian was going to be married that she took so much on herself; but she wondered too, whether, when she herself should become engaged, such exploits would be expected of her.

Half an hour later she saw her aunt Penniman sitting in the embrasure of a window, with her head a little on one side, and her gold eye-glass raised to her eyes, which were wandering about the room. In front of her was a gentleman, bending forward a little, with his back turned to Catherine. She knew his back immediately, though she had never seen it; for when he left her, at Marian's instigation, he had retreated in the best order, without turning round. Morris Townsend—the name had already become very familiar to her, as if some one had been repeating it in her ear for the last half hour—Morris Townsend was giving his impressions of the company to her aunt, as he had done to herself; he was saying clever things, and Mrs. Penniman was smiling, as if she approved of them. As soon as Catherine had perceived this she moved away; she would not have liked him to turn round and see her. But it gave her pleasure—the whole thing. That he should talk with Mrs. Penniman, with whom she lived and whom she saw and talked with every day—that seemed to keep him near her, and to make him even easier to contemplate than if she herself had been the object of his civilities; and that Aunt Lavinia should like him, should not be shocked or startled by what he said, this also appeared to the girl a personal gain; for Aunt Lavinia's standard was extremely high, planted as it was over the grave of her late husband, in which, as she had convinced every one, the very genius of conversation was buried. One of the Almond boys, as Catherine called them, invited our heroine to dance a quadrille, and for a quarter of an hour her feet at least were occupied. This time she was not dizzy; her head was very clear. Just when the dance was over, she found herself in the crowd face to face with her father. Dr. Sloper had usually a little smile, never a very big one, and with his little smile playing in his clear eyes and on his neatly-shaved lips, he looked at his daughter's crimson gown.

"Is it possible that this magnificent person is my child?" he said.

You would have surprised him if you had told him so; but it is a literal fact that he almost never addressed his daughter save in the ironical form. Whenever he addressed her he gave her pleasure; but she had to cut her pleasure out of the piece, as it were. There were portions left over, light remnants and snippets of irony, which she never knew what to do with, which seemed too delicate for her own use; and yet Catherine, lamenting the limitations of her understanding, felt that they were too valuable to waste, and had a belief that if they passed over her head they yet contributed to the general sum of human wisdom.

"I am not magnificent," she said, mildly, wishing that she had put on another dress.

"You are sumptuous, opulent, expensive," her father rejoined. "You look as if you had eighty thousand a year."

"Well, so long as I haven't——" said Catherine illogically. Her conception of her prospective wealth was as yet very indefinite.

"So long as you haven't you shouldn't look as if you had. Have you enjoyed your party?"

Catherine hesitated a moment; and then, looking away, "I am rather tired," she murmured. I have said that this entertainment was the beginning of something important for Catherine. For the second time in her life she made an indirect answer; and the beginning of a period of dissimulation is certainly a significant date. Catherine was not so easily tired as that.

Nevertheless, in the carriage, as they drove home, she was as quiet as if fatigue had been her portion. Dr. Sloper's manner of addressing his sister Lavinia had a good deal of resemblance to the tone he had adopted towards Catherine.

"Who was the young man that was making love to you?" he presently asked.

"Oh, my good brother!" murmured Mrs. Penniman, in deprecation.

"He seemed uncommonly tender. Whenever I looked at you, for half an hour, he had the most devoted air."

"The devotion was not to me," said Mrs. Penniman. "It was to Catherine; he talked to me of her."

Catherine had been listening with all her ears. "Oh, Aunt Penniman!" she exclaimed faintly.

"He is very handsome; he is very clever; he expressed himself with a great deal—a great deal of felicity," her aunt went on.

"He is in love with this regal creature, then?" the Doctor inquired humorously.

"Oh, father," cried the girl, still more faintly, devoutly thankful the carriage was dark.

"I don't know that; but he admired her dress."

Catherine did not say to herself in the dark, "My dress only?" Mrs. Penniman's announcement struck her by its richness, not by its meagreness.

"You see," said her father, "he thinks you have eighty thousand a year."

"I don't believe he thinks of that," said Mrs. Penniman; "he is too refined."

"He must be tremendously refined not to think of that!"

"Well, he is!" Catherine exclaimed, before she knew it.

"I thought you had gone to sleep," her father answered. "The hour has come!" he added to himself. "Lavinia is going to get up a romance for Catherine. It's a shame to play such tricks on the girl. What is the gentleman's name?" he went on, aloud.

"I didn't catch it, and I didn't like to ask him. He asked to be introduced to me," said Mrs. Penniman, with a certain grandeur; "but you know how indistinctly Jefferson speaks." Jefferson was Mr. Almond. "Catherine, dear, what was the gentleman's name?"

For a minute, if it had not been for the rumbling of the carriage, you might have heard a pin drop.

"I don't know, Aunt Lavinia," said Catherine, very softly. And, with all his irony, her father believed her.

V

H E LEARNED what he had asked some three or four days
later, after Morris Townsend, with his cousin, had
called in Washington Square. Mrs. Penniman did not tell her
brother, on the drive home, that she had intimated to this
agreeable young man, whose name she did not know, that,
with her niece, she should be very glad to see him; but she
was greatly pleased, and even a little flattered, when, late on
a Sunday afternoon, the two gentlemen made their appearance. His coming with Arthur Townsend made it more natural and easy; the latter young man was on the point of
becoming connected with the family, and Mrs. Penniman had
remarked to Catherine that, as he was going to marry Marian,
it would be polite in him to call. These events came to pass
late in the autumn, and Catherine and her aunt had been sitting together in the closing dusk, by the firelight, in the high
back-parlour.

Arthur Townsend fell to Catherine's portion, while his
companion placed himself on the sofa, beside Mrs. Penniman.
Catherine had hitherto not been a harsh critic; she was easy
to please—she liked to talk with young men. But Marian's
betrothed, this evening, made her feel vaguely fastidious; he
sat looking at the fire and rubbing his knees with his hands.
As for Catherine, she scarcely even pretended to keep up the
conversation; her attention had fixed itself on the other side
of the room; she was listening to what went on between the
other Mr. Townsend and her aunt. Every now and then he
looked over at Catherine herself and smiled, as if to show that
what he said was for her benefit too. Catherine would have
liked to change her place, to go and sit near them, where she
might see and hear him better. But she was afraid of seeming
bold—of looking eager; and, besides, it would not have been
polite to Marian's little suitor. She wondered why the other
gentleman had picked out her aunt—how he came to have so
much to say to Mrs. Penniman, to whom, usually, young men
were not especially devoted. She was not at all jealous of Aunt
Lavinia, but she was a little envious, and above all she wondered; for Morris Townsend was an object on which she

found that her imagination could exercise itself indefinitely. His cousin had been describing a house that he had taken in view of his union with Marian, and the domestic conveniences he meant to introduce into it; how Marian wanted a larger one, and Mrs. Almond recommended a smaller one, and how he himself was convinced that he had got the neatest house in New York.

"It doesn't matter," he said; "it's only for three or four years. At the end of three or four years we'll move. That's the way to live in New York—to move every three or four years. Then you always get the last thing. It's because the city's growing so quick—you've got to keep up with it. It's going straight up town—that's where New York's going. If I wasn't afraid Marian would be lonely, I'd go up there—right up to the top—and wait for it. Only have to wait ten years—they'd all come up after you. But Marian says she wants some neighbours—she doesn't want to be a pioneer. She says that if she's got to be the first settler she had better go out to Minnesota. I guess we'll move up little by little; when we get tired of one street we'll go higher. So you see we'll always have a new house; it's a great advantage to have a new house; you get all the latest improvements. They invent everything all over again about every five years, and it's a great thing to keep up with the new things. I always try and keep up with the new things of every kind. Don't you think that's a good motto for a young couple—to keep 'going higher?' That's the name of that piece of poetry—what do they call it?— *Excelsior!*"

Catherine bestowed on her junior visitor only just enough attention to feel that this was not the way Mr. Morris Townsend had talked the other night, or that he was talking now to her fortunate aunt. But suddenly his aspiring kinsman became more interesting. He seemed to have become conscious that she was affected by his companion's presence, and he thought it proper to explain it.

"My cousin asked me to bring him, or I shouldn't have taken the liberty. He seemed to want very much to come; you know he's awfully sociable. I told him I wanted to ask you first, but he said Mrs. Penniman had invited him. He isn't

particular what he says when he wants to come somewhere!
But Mrs. Penniman seems to think it's all right."

"We are very glad to see him," said Catherine. And she
wished to talk more about him; but she hardly knew what to
say. "I never saw him before," she went on presently.

Arthur Townsend stared.

"Why, he told me he talked with you for over half an hour
the other night."

"I mean before the other night. That was the first time."

"Oh, he has been away from New York—he has been all
round the world. He doesn't know many people here, but
he's very sociable, and he wants to know every one."

"Every one?" said Catherine.

"Well, I mean all the good ones. All the pretty young
ladies—like Mrs. Penniman!" And Arthur Townsend gave a
private laugh.

"My aunt likes him very much," said Catherine.

"Most people like him—he's so brilliant."

"He's more like a foreigner," Catherine suggested.

"Well, I never knew a foreigner!" said young Townsend, in
a tone which seemed to indicate that his ignorance had been
optional.

"Neither have I," Catherine confessed, with more humility.
"They say they are generally brilliant," she added, vaguely.

"Well, the people of this city are clever enough for me. I
know some of them that think they are too clever for me; but
they ain't!"

"I suppose you can't be too clever," said Catherine, still
with humility.

"I don't know. I know some people that call my cousin too
clever."

Catherine listened to this statement with extreme interest,
and a feeling that if Morris Townsend had a fault it would
naturally be that one. But she did not commit herself, and in
a moment she asked:—"Now that he has come back, will he
stay here always?"

"Ah," said Arthur, "if he can get something to do."

"Something to do?"

"Some place or other; some business."

"Hasn't he got any?" said Catherine, who had never heard of a young man—of the upper class—in this situation.

"No; he's looking round. But he can't find anything."

"I am very sorry," Catherine permitted herself to observe.

"Oh, he doesn't mind," said young Townsend. "He takes it easy—he isn't in a hurry. He is very particular."

Catherine thought he naturally would be, and gave herself up for some moments to the contemplation of this idea, in several of its bearings.

"Won't his father take him into his business—his office?" she at last inquired.

"He hasn't got any father—he has only got a sister. Your sister can't help you much."

It seemed to Catherine that if she were his sister she would disprove this axiom. "Is she—is she pleasant?" she asked in a moment.

"I don't know—I believe she's very respectable," said young Townsend. And then he looked across to his cousin and began to laugh. "Look here, we are talking about you," he added.

Morris Townsend paused in his conversation with Mrs. Penniman, and stared, with a little smile. Then he got up, as if he were going.

"As far as you are concerned, I can't return the compliment," he said to Catherine's companion. "But as regards Miss Sloper, it's another affair."

Catherine thought this little speech wonderfully well turned; but she was embarrassed by it, and she also got up. Morris Townsend stood looking at her and smiling; he put out his hand for farewell. He was going, without having said anything to her; but even on these terms she was glad to have seen him.

"I will tell her what you have said—when you go!" said Mrs. Penniman, with an insinuating laugh.

Catherine blushed, for she felt almost as if they were making sport of her. What in the world could this beautiful young man have said? He looked at her still, in spite of her blush; but very kindly and respectfully.

"I have had no talk with you," he said, "and that was what

I came for. But it will be a good reason for coming another time; a little pretext—if I am obliged to give one. I am not afraid of what your aunt will say when I go."

With this the two young men took their departure; after which Catherine, with her blush still lingering, directed a serious and interrogative eye to Mrs. Penniman. She was incapable of elaborate artifice, and she resorted to no jocular device—to no affectation of the belief that she had been maligned—to learn what she desired.

"What did you say you would tell me?" she asked.

Mrs. Penniman came up to her, smiling and nodding a little, looked at her all over, and gave a twist to the knot of ribbon in her neck. "It's a great secret, my dear child; but he is coming a-courting!"

Catherine was serious still. "Is that what he told you?"

"He didn't say so exactly. But he left me to guess it. I'm a good guesser."

"Do you mean a-courting me?"

"Not me, certainly, miss; though I must say he is a hundred times more polite to a person who has no longer extreme youth to recommend her than most of the young men. He is thinking of some one else." And Mrs. Penniman gave her niece a delicate little kiss. "You must be very gracious to him."

Catherine stared—she was bewildered. "I don't understand you," she said; "he doesn't know me."

"Oh yes, he does; more than you think. I have told him all about you."

"Oh, Aunt Penniman!" murmured Catherine, as if this had been a breach of trust. "He is a perfect stranger—we don't know him." There was infinite modesty in the poor girl's " we."

Aunt Penniman, however, took no account of it; she spoke even with a touch of acrimony. "My dear Catherine, you know very well that you admire him!"

"Oh, Aunt Penniman!" Catherine could only murmur again. It might very well be that she admired him—though this did not seem to her a thing to talk about. But that this brilliant stranger—this sudden apparition, who had barely heard the sound of her voice—took that sort of interest in her that was expressed by the romantic phrase of which Mrs.

Penniman had just made use: this could only be a figment of the restless brain of Aunt Lavinia, whom every one knew to be a woman of powerful imagination.

VI

M<small>RS. PENNIMAN</small> even took for granted at times that other people had as much imagination as herself; so that when, half an hour later, her brother came in, she addressed him quite on this principle.

"He has just been here, Austin; it's such a pity you missed him."

"Whom in the world have I missed?" asked the Doctor.

"Mr. Morris Townsend; he has made us such a delightful visit."

"And who in the world is Mr. Morris Townsend?"

"Aunt Penniman means the gentleman—the gentleman whose name I couldn't remember," said Catherine.

"The gentleman at Elizabeth's party who was so struck with Catherine," Mrs. Penniman added.

"Oh, his name is Morris Townsend, is it? And did he come here to propose to you?"

"Oh, father," murmured the girl for all answer, turning away to the window, where the dusk had deepened to darkness.

"I hope he won't do that without your permission," said Mrs. Penniman, very graciously.

"After all, my dear, he seems to have yours," her brother answered.

Lavinia simpered, as if this might not be quite enough, and Catherine, with her forehead touching the window-panes, listened to this exchange of epigrams as reservedly as if they had not each been a pin-prick in her own destiny.

"The next time he comes," the Doctor added, "you had better call me. He might like to see me."

Morris Townsend came again, some five days afterwards; but Dr. Sloper was not called, as he was absent from home at the time. Catherine was with her aunt when the young man's name was brought in, and Mrs. Penniman, effacing herself and protesting, made a great point of her niece's going into the drawing-room alone.

"This time it's for you—for you only," she said. "Before, when he talked to me, it was only preliminary—it was to gain my confidence. Literally, my dear, I should not have the *courage* to show myself to-day."

And this was perfectly true. Mrs. Penniman was not a brave woman, and Morris Townsend had struck her as a young man of great force of character, and of remarkable powers of satire; a keen, resolute, brilliant nature, with which one must exercise a great deal of tact. She said to herself that he was "imperious," and she liked the word and the idea. She was not the least jealous of her niece, and she had been perfectly happy with Mr. Penniman, but in the bottom of her heart she permitted herself the observation: "That's the sort of husband I should have had!" He was certainly much more imperious—she ended by calling it imperial—than Mr. Penniman.

So Catherine saw Mr. Townsend alone, and her aunt did not come in even at the end of the visit. The visit was a long one; he sat there—in the front parlour, in the biggest armchair—for more than an hour. He seemed more at home this time—more familiar; lounging a little in the chair, slapping a cushion that was near him with his stick, and looking round the room a good deal, and at the objects it contained, as well as at Catherine; whom, however, he also contemplated freely. There was a smile of respectful devotion in his handsome eyes which seemed to Catherine almost solemnly beautiful; it made her think of a young knight in a poem. His talk, however, was not particularly knightly; it was light and easy and friendly; it took a practical turn, and he asked a number of questions about herself—what were her tastes—if she liked this and that—what were her habits. He said to her, with his charming smile, "Tell me about yourself; give me a little sketch." Catherine had very little to tell, and she had no talent for sketching; but before he went she had confided to him that she had a secret passion for the theatre, which had been but scantily gratified, and a taste for operatic music—that of Bellini and Donizetti, in especial (it must be remembered in extenuation of this primitive young woman that she held these opinions in an age of general darkness)—which she rarely had an occasion to hear, except on the hand-organ. She confessed that she was not particularly fond of literature. Morris Townsend agreed with her that books were tiresome things; only, as he said, you had to read a good many before you found it out. He had been to places that people had written books about, and they were not a bit like the descriptions. To see for yourself—that was the great thing; he always tried to see for himself. He had seen all the principal actors—he had been to all the best theatres in London and Paris. But the actors were always like the authors—they always exaggerated. He liked everything to be natural. Suddenly he stopped, looking at Catherine with his smile.

"That's what I like you for; you are so natural! Excuse me," he added; "you see I am natural myself."

And before she had time to think whether she excused him or not—which afterwards, at leisure, she became conscious that she did—he began to talk about music, and to say that it was his greatest pleasure in life. He had heard all the great singers in Paris and London—Pasta and Rubini and Lablache—and when you had done that, you could say that you knew what singing was.

"I sing a little myself," he said; "some day I will show you. Not to-day, but some other time."

And then he got up to go; he had omitted, by accident, to say that he would sing to her if she would play to him. He thought of this after he got into the street; but he might have spared his compunction, for Catherine had not noticed the lapse. She was thinking only that "some other time" had a delightful sound; it seemed to spread itself over the future.

This was all the more reason, however, though she was ashamed and uncomfortable, why she should tell her father that Mr. Morris Townsend had called again. She announced the fact abruptly, almost violently, as soon as the Doctor came into the house; and having done so—it was her duty— she took measures to leave the room. But she could not leave it fast enough; her father stopped her just as she reached the door.

"Well, my dear, did he propose to you to-day?" the Doctor asked.

This was just what she had been afraid he would say; and yet she had no answer ready. Of course she would have liked to take it as a joke—as her father must have meant it; and yet she would have liked, also, in denying it, to be a little positive, a little sharp; so that he would perhaps not ask the question again. She didn't like it—it made her unhappy. But Catherine could never be sharp; and for a moment she only stood, with her hand on the door-knob, looking at her satiric parent, and giving a little laugh.

"Decidedly," said the Doctor to himself, "my daughter is not brilliant!"

But he had no sooner made this reflection than Catherine found something; she had decided on the whole to take the thing as a joke.

"Perhaps he will do it the next time!" she exclaimed, with a repetition of her laugh. And she quickly got out of the room.

The Doctor stood staring; he wondered whether his daughter were serious. Catherine went straight to her own room, and by the time she reached it she bethought herself that there was something else—something better—she might have said. She almost wished, now, that her father would ask his question again, so that she might reply:—"Oh yes, Mr. Morris Townsend proposed to me, and I refused him!"

The Doctor, however, began to put his questions elsewhere; it naturally having occurred to him that he ought to inform himself properly about this handsome young man who had formed the habit of running in and out of his house. He addressed himself to the elder of his sisters, Mrs. Almond—not going to her for the purpose; there was no such hurry as that—but having made a note of the matter for the first opportunity. The Doctor was never eager, never impatient nor nervous; but he made notes of everything, and he regularly consulted his notes. Among them the information he obtained from Mrs. Almond about Morris Townsend took its place.

"Lavinia has already been to ask me," she said. "Lavinia is most excited; I don't understand it. It's not, after all, Lavinia that the young man is supposed to have designs upon. She is very peculiar."

"Ah, my dear," the Doctor replied, "she has not lived with me these twelve years without my finding it out!"

"She has got such an artificial mind," said Mrs. Almond, who always enjoyed an opportunity to discuss Lavinia's peculiarities with her brother. "She didn't want me to tell you that she had asked me about Mr. Townsend; but I told her I would. She always wants to conceal everything."

"And yet at moments no one blurts things out with such crudity. She is like a revolving lighthouse; pitch darkness alternating with a dazzling brilliancy! But what did you tell her?" the Doctor asked.

"What I tell you; that I know very little of him."

"Lavinia must have been disappointed at that," said the Doctor; "she would prefer him to have been guilty of some romantic crime. However, we must make the best of people. They tell me our gentleman is the cousin of the little boy to whom you are about to entrust the future of your little girl."

"Arthur is not a little boy; he is a very old man; you and I will never be so old. He is a distant relation of Lavinia's *protégé*. The name is the same, but I am given to understand that there are Townsends and Townsends. So Arthur's mother tells me; she talked about 'branches'—younger branches, elder branches, inferior branches—as if it were a royal house. Arthur, it appears, is of the reigning line, but poor Lavinia's young man is not. Beyond this, Arthur's mother knows very little about him; she has only a vague story that he has been 'wild.' But I know his sister a little, and she is a very nice woman. Her name is Mrs. Montgomery; she is a widow, with a little property and five children. She lives in the Second Avenue."

"What does Mrs. Montgomery say about him?"

"That he has talents by which he might distinguish himself."

"Only he is lazy, eh?"

"She doesn't say so."

"That's family pride," said the Doctor. "What is his profession?"

"He hasn't got any; he is looking for something. I believe he was once in the Navy."

"Once? What is his age?"

"I suppose he is upwards of thirty. He must have gone into the Navy very young. I think Arthur told me that he inherited a small property—which was perhaps the cause of his leaving the Navy—and that he spent it all in a few years. He travelled all over the world, lived abroad, amused himself. I believe it was a kind of system, a theory he had. He has lately come back to America, with the intention, as he tells Arthur, of beginning life in earnest."

"Is he in earnest about Catherine, then?"

"I don't see why you should be incredulous," said Mrs. Almond. "It seems to me that you have never done Catherine justice. You must remember that she has the prospect of thirty thousand a year."

The Doctor looked at his sister a moment, and then, with the slightest touch of bitterness:—"You at least appreciate her," he said.

Mrs. Almond blushed.

"I don't mean that is her only merit; I simply mean that it is a great one. A great many young men think so; and you appear to me never to have been properly aware of that. You have always had a little way of alluding to her as an unmarriageable girl."

"My allusions are as kind as yours, Elizabeth," said the Doctor, frankly. "How many suitors has Catherine had, with all her expectations—how much attention has she ever received? Catherine is not unmarriageable, but she is absolutely unattractive. What other reason is there for Lavinia being so charmed with the idea that there is a lover in the house? There has never been one before, and Lavinia, with her sensitive, sympathetic nature, is not used to the idea. It affects her imagination. I must do the young men of New York the justice to say that they strike me as very disinterested. They prefer pretty girls—lively girls—girls like your own. Catherine is neither pretty nor lively."

"Catherine does very well; she has a style of her own—which is more than my poor Marian has, who has no style at all," said Mrs. Almond. "The reason Catherine has received so little attention is that she seems to all the young men to be older than themselves. She is so large, and she dresses—so richly. They are rather afraid of her, I think; she looks as if she had been married already, and you know they don't like married women. And if our young men appear disinterested," the Doctor's wiser sister went on, "it is because they marry, as a general thing, so young, before twenty-five, at the age of innocence and sincerity, before the age of calculation. If they only waited a little, Catherine would fare better."

"As a calculation? Thank you very much," said the Doctor.

"Wait till some intelligent man of forty comes along, and he will be delighted with Catherine," Mrs. Almond continued.

"Mr. Townsend is not old enough, then; his motives may be pure."

"It is very possible that his motives are pure; I should be very sorry to take the contrary for granted. Lavinia is sure of it, and, as he is a very prepossessing youth, you might give him the benefit of the doubt."

Dr. Sloper reflected a moment.

"What are his present means of subsistence?"

"I have no idea. He lives, as I say, with his sister."

"A widow, with five children? Do you mean he lives *upon* her?"

Mrs. Almond got up, and with a certain impatience: "Had you not better ask Mrs. Montgomery herself?" she inquired.

"Perhaps I may come to that," said the Doctor. "Did you say the Second Avenue?" He made a note of the Second Avenue.

VII

HE WAS, however, by no means so much in earnest as this might seem to indicate; and, indeed, he was more than anything else amused with the whole situation. He was not in the least in a state of tension or of vigilance, with regard to Catherine's prospects; he was even on his guard against the ridicule that might attach itself to the spectacle of a house thrown into agitation by its daughter and heiress receiving attentions unprecedented in its annals. More than this, he went so far as to promise himself some entertainment from the little drama—if drama it was—of which Mrs. Penniman desired to represent the ingenious Mr. Townsend as the hero. He had no intention, as yet, of regulating the *dénouement*. He was perfectly willing, as Elizabeth had suggested, to give the young man the benefit of every doubt. There was no great danger in it; for Catherine, at the age of twenty-two, was after all a rather mature blossom, such as could be plucked from the stem only by a vigorous jerk. The fact that Morris Townsend was poor—was not of necessity against him; the Doctor had never made up his mind that his daughter should marry a rich man. The fortune she would inherit struck him as a very sufficient provision for two reasonable persons, and if a penniless swain who could give a good account of himself should enter the lists, he should be judged quite upon his personal merits. There were other things besides. The Doctor thought it very vulgar to be precipitate in accusing people of mercenary motives, inasmuch as his door had as yet not been in the least besieged by fortune-hunters; and, lastly, he was very curious to see whether Catherine might really be loved for her moral worth. He smiled as he reflected that poor Mr. Townsend had been only twice to the house, and he said to Mrs. Penniman that the next time he should come she must ask him to dinner.

He came very soon again, and Mrs. Penniman had of course great pleasure in executing this mission. Morris Townsend accepted her invitation with equal good grace, and the dinner took place a few days later. The Doctor had said to himself, justly enough, that they must not have the young

man alone; this would partake too much of the nature of encouragement. So two or three other persons were invited; but
Morris Townsend, though he was by no means the ostensible,
was the real occasion of the feast. There is every reason to
suppose that he desired to make a good impression; and if he
fell short of this result, it was not for want of a good deal of
intelligent effort. The Doctor talked to him very little during
dinner; but he observed him attentively, and after the ladies
had gone out he pushed him the wine and asked him several
questions. Morris was not a young man who needed to be
pressed, and he found quite enough encouragement in the
superior quality of the claret. The Doctor's wine was admirable, and it may be communicated to the reader that while
he sipped it Morris reflected that a cellar-full of good liquor—there was evidently a cellar-full here—would be a
most attractive idiosyncrasy in a father-in-law. The Doctor
was struck with his appreciative guest; he saw that he was not
a commonplace young man. "He has ability," said Catherine's
father, "decided ability; he has a very good head if he chooses
to use it. And he is uncommonly well turned out; quite the
sort of figure that pleases the ladies. But I don't think I like
him." The Doctor, however, kept his reflections to himself,
and talked to his visitors about foreign lands, concerning
which Morris offered him more information than he was
ready, as he mentally phrased it, to swallow. Dr. Sloper had
travelled but little, and he took the liberty of not believing
everything this anecdotical idler narrated. He prided himself
on being something of a physiognomist, and while the
young man, chatting with easy assurance, puffed his cigar
and filled his glass again, the Doctor sat with his eyes quietly
fixed on his bright, expressive face. "He has the assurance of
the devil himself," said Morris's host; "I don't think I ever
saw such assurance. And his powers of invention are most
remarkable. He is very knowing; they were not so knowing
as that in my time. And a good head, did I say? I should
think so—after a bottle of Madeira, and a bottle and a half
of claret!"

After dinner Morris Townsend went and stood before
Catherine, who was standing before the fire in her red satin
gown.

"He doesn't like me—he doesn't like me at all!" said the young man.

"Who doesn't like you?" asked Catherine.

"Your father; extraordinary man!"

"I don't see how you know," said Catherine, blushing.

"I feel; I am very quick to feel."

"Perhaps you are mistaken."

"Ah, well; you ask him and you will see."

"I would rather not ask him, if there is any danger of his saying what you think."

Morris looked at her with an air of mock melancholy.

"It wouldn't give you any pleasure to contradict him?"

"I never contradict him," said Catherine.

"Will you hear me abused without opening your lips in my defence?"

"My father won't abuse you. He doesn't know you enough."

Morris Townsend gave a loud laugh, and Catherine began to blush again.

"I shall never mention you," she said, to take refuge from her confusion.

"That is very well; but it is not quite what I should have liked you to say. I should have liked you to say: 'If my father doesn't think well of you, what does it matter?' "

"Ah, but it would matter; I couldn't say that!" the girl exclaimed.

He looked at her for a moment, smiling a little; and the Doctor, if he had been watching him just then, would have seen a gleam of fine impatience in the sociable softness of his eye. But there was no impatience in his rejoinder—none, at least, save what was expressed in a little appealing sigh. "Ah, well, then, I must not give up the hope of bringing him round!"

He expressed it more frankly to Mrs. Penniman, later in the evening. But before that he sang two or three songs at Catherine's timid request; not that he flattered himself that this would help to bring her father round. He had a sweet, light tenor voice, and when he had finished, every one made some exclamation—every one, that is, save Catherine, who remained intensely silent. Mrs. Penniman declared that his manner of singing was "most artistic," and Dr. Sloper said it was "very taking—very taking indeed;" speaking loudly and distinctly, but with a certain dryness.

"He doesn't like me—he doesn't like me at all," said Morris Townsend, addressing the aunt in the same manner as he had done the niece. "He thinks I'm all wrong."

Unlike her niece, Mrs. Penniman asked for no explanation. She only smiled very sweetly, as if she understood everything; and, unlike Catherine too, she made no attempt to contradict him. "Pray, what does it matter?" she murmured softly.

"Ah, you say the right thing!" said Morris, greatly to the gratification of Mrs. Penniman, who prided herself on always saying the right thing.

The Doctor, the next time he saw his sister Elizabeth, let her know that he had made the acquaintance of Lavinia's *protégé*.

"Physically," he said, "he's uncommonly well set up. As an anatomist, it is really a pleasure to me to see such a beautiful structure; although, if people were all like him, I suppose there would be very little need for doctors."

"Don't you see anything in people but their bones?" Mrs. Almond rejoined. "What do you think of him as a father?"

"As a father? Thank Heaven I am not his father!"

"No; but you are Catherine's. Lavinia tells me she is in love."

"She must get over it. He is not a gentleman."

"Ah, take care! Remember that he is a branch of the Townsends."

"He is not what I call a gentleman. He has not the soul of one. He is extremely insinuating; but it's a vulgar nature. I saw through it in a minute. He is altogether too familiar— I hate familiarity. He is a plausible coxcomb."

"Ah, well," said Mrs. Almond; "if you make up your mind so easily, it's a great advantage."

"I don't make up my mind easily. What I tell you is the result of thirty years of observation; and in order to be able to form that judgment in a single evening, I have had to spend a lifetime in study."

"Very possibly you are right. But the thing is for Catherine to see it."

"I will present her with a pair of spectacles!" said the Doctor.

VIII

IF IT WERE true that she was in love, she was certainly very
quiet about it; but the Doctor was of course prepared to
admit that her quietness might mean volumes. She had told
Morris Townsend that she would not mention him to her
father, and she saw no reason to retract this vow of discretion. It was no more than decently civil, of course, that after
having dined in Washington Square, Morris should call there
again; and it was no more than natural that, having been
kindly received on this occasion, he should continue to present himself. He had had plenty of leisure on his hands; and
thirty years ago, in New York, a young man of leisure had
reason to be thankful for aids to self-oblivion. Catherine said
nothing to her father about these visits, though they had rapidly become the most important, the most absorbing thing in
her life. The girl was very happy. She knew not as yet what
would come of it; but the present had suddenly grown rich
and solemn. If she had been told she was in love, she would
have been a good deal surprised; for she had an idea that love
was an eager and exacting passion, and her own heart was
filled in these days with the impulse of self-effacement and
sacrifice. Whenever Morris Townsend had left the house, her
imagination projected itself, with all its strength, into the idea
of his soon coming back; but if she had been told at such a
moment that he would not return for a year, or even that he
would never return, she would not have complained nor re-
belled, but would have humbly accepted the decree, and
sought for consolation in thinking over the times she had already seen him, the words he had spoken, the sound of his
voice, of his tread, the expression of his face. Love demands
certain things as a right; but Catherine had no sense of her
rights; she had only a consciousness of immense and unexpected favours. Her very gratitude for these things had
hushed itself; for it seemed to her that there would be something of impudence in making a festival of her secret. Her
father suspected Morris Townsend's visits, and noted her
reserve. She seemed to beg pardon for it; she looked at
him constantly in silence, as if she meant to say that she said

nothing because she was afraid of irritating him. But the poor girl's dumb eloquence irritated him more than anything else would have done, and he caught himself murmuring more than once that it was a grievous pity his only child was a simpleton. His murmurs, however, were inaudible; and for a while he said nothing to any one. He would have liked to know exactly how often young Townsend came; but he had determined to ask no questions of the girl herself—to say nothing more to her that would show that he watched her. The Doctor had a great idea of being largely just: he wished to leave his daughter her liberty, and interfere only when the danger should be proved. It was not in his manner to obtain information by indirect methods, and it never even occurred to him to question the servants. As for Lavinia, he hated to talk to her about the matter; she annoyed him with her mock romanticism. But he had to come to this. Mrs. Penniman's convictions as regards the relations of her niece and the clever young visitor who saved appearances by coming ostensibly for both the ladies—Mrs. Penniman's convictions had passed into a riper and richer phase. There was to be no crudity in Mrs. Penniman's treatment of the situation; she had become as uncommunicative as Catherine herself. She was tasting of the sweets of concealment; she had taken up the line of mystery. "She would be enchanted to be able to prove to herself that she is persecuted," said the Doctor; and when at last he questioned her, he was sure she would contrive to extract from his words a pretext for this belief.

"Be so good as to let me know what is going on in the house," he said to her, in a tone which, under the circumstances, he himself deemed genial.

"Going on, Austin?" Mrs. Penniman exclaimed. "Why, I am sure I don't know! I believe that last night the old gray cat had kittens?"

"At her age?" said the Doctor. "The idea is startling—almost shocking. Be so good as to see that they are all drowned. But what else has happened?"

"Ah, the dear little kittens!" cried Mrs. Penniman. "I wouldn't have them drowned for the world!"

Her brother puffed his cigar a few moments in silence.

"Your sympathy with kittens, Lavinia," he presently resumed, "arises from a feline element in your own character."

"Cats are very graceful, and very clean," said Mrs. Penniman, smiling.

"And very stealthy. You are the embodiment both of grace and of neatness; but you are wanting in frankness."

"You certainly are not, dear brother."

"I don't pretend to be graceful, though I try to be neat. Why haven't you let me know that Mr. Morris Townsend is coming to the house four times a week?"

Mrs. Penniman lifted her eyebrows. "Four times a week?"

"Five times, if you prefer it. I am away all day, and I see nothing. But when such things happen, you should let me know."

Mrs. Penniman, with her eyebrows still raised, reflected intently. "Dear Austin," she said at last, "I am incapable of betraying a confidence. I would rather suffer anything."

"Never fear; you shall not suffer. To whose confidence is it you allude? Has Catherine made you take a vow of eternal secrecy?"

"By no means. Catherine has not told me as much as she might. She has not been very trustful."

"It is the young man, then, who has made you his confidant? Allow me to say that it is extremely indiscreet of you to form secret alliances with young men. You don't know where they may lead you."

"I don't know what you mean by an alliance," said Mrs. Penniman. "I take a great interest in Mr. Townsend; I won't conceal that. But that's all."

"Under the circumstances, that is quite enough. What is the source of your interest in Mr. Townsend?"

"Why," said Mrs. Penniman, musing, and then breaking into her smile, "that he is so interesting!"

The Doctor felt that he had need of his patience. "And what makes him interesting?—his good looks?"

"His misfortunes, Austin."

"Ah, he has had misfortunes? That, of course, is always interesting. Are you at liberty to mention a few of Mr. Townsend's?"

"I don't know that he would like it," said Mrs. Penniman.

"He has told me a great deal about himself—he has told me, in fact, his whole history. But I don't think I ought to repeat those things. He would tell them to you, I am sure, if he thought you would listen to him kindly. With kindness you may do anything with him."

The Doctor gave a laugh. "I shall request him very kindly, then, to leave Catherine alone."

"Ah!" said Mrs. Penniman, shaking her forefinger at her brother, with her little finger turned out, "Catherine has probably said something to him kinder than that!"

"Said that she loved him? Do you mean that?"

Mrs. Penniman fixed her eyes on the floor. "As I tell you, Austin, she doesn't confide in me."

"You have an opinion, I suppose, all the same. It is that I ask you for; though I don't conceal from you that I shall not regard it as conclusive."

Mrs. Penniman's gaze continued to rest on the carpet; but at last she lifted it, and then her brother thought it very expressive. "I think Catherine is very happy; that is all I can say."

"Townsend is trying to marry her—is that what you mean?"

"He is greatly interested in her."

"He finds her such an attractive girl?"

"Catherine has a lovely nature, Austin," said Mrs. Penniman, "and Mr. Townsend has had the intelligence to discover that."

"With a little help from you, I suppose. My dear Lavinia," cried the Doctor, "you are an admirable aunt!"

"So Mr. Townsend says," observed Lavinia, smiling.

"Do you think he is sincere?" asked her brother.

"In saying that?"

"No; that's of course. But in his admiration for Catherine?"

"Deeply sincere. He has said to me the most appreciative, the most charming things about her. He would say them to you, if he were sure you would listen to him—gently."

"I doubt whether I can undertake it. He appears to require a great deal of gentleness."

"He is a sympathetic, sensitive nature," said Mrs. Penniman.

Her brother puffed his cigar again in silence. "These delicate qualities have survived his vicissitudes, eh? All this while you haven't told me about his misfortunes."

"It is a long story," said Mrs. Penniman, "and I regard it as a sacred trust. But I suppose there is no objection to my saying that he has been wild—he frankly confesses that. But he has paid for it."

"That's what has impoverished him, eh?"

"I don't mean simply in money. He is very much alone in the world."

"Do you mean that he has behaved so badly that his friends have given him up?"

"He has had false friends, who have deceived and betrayed him."

"He seems to have some good ones too. He has a devoted sister, and half a dozen nephews and nieces."

Mrs. Penniman was silent a minute. "The nephews and nieces are children, and the sister is not a very attractive person."

"I hope he doesn't abuse her to you," said the Doctor; "for I am told he lives upon her."

"Lives upon her?"

"Lives with her, and does nothing for himself; it is about the same thing."

"He is looking for a position—most earnestly," said Mrs. Penniman. "He hopes every day to find one."

"Precisely. He is looking for it here—over there in the front parlour. The position of husband of a weak-minded woman with a large fortune would suit him to perfection!"

Mrs. Penniman was truly amiable, but she now gave signs of temper. She rose with much animation, and stood for a moment looking at her brother. "My dear Austin," she remarked, "if you regard Catherine as a weak-minded woman, you are particularly mistaken!" And with this she moved majestically away.

IX

IT WAS a regular custom with the family in Washington Square to go and spend Sunday evening at Mrs. Almond's. On the Sunday after the conversation I have just narrated, this custom was not intermitted; and on this occasion, towards the middle of the evening, Dr. Sloper found reason to withdraw to the library, with his brother-in-law, to talk over a matter of business. He was absent some twenty minutes, and when he came back into the circle, which was enlivened by the presence of several friends of the family, he saw that Morris Townsend had come in and had lost as little time as possible in seating himself on a small sofa, beside Catherine. In the large room, where several different groups had been formed, and the hum of voices and of laughter was loud, these two young persons might confabulate, as the Doctor phrased it to himself, without attracting attention. He saw in a moment, however, that his daughter was painfully conscious of his own observation. She sat motionless, with her eyes bent down, staring at her open fan, deeply flushed, shrinking together as if to minimise the indiscretion of which she confessed herself guilty.

The Doctor almost pitied her. Poor Catherine was not defiant; she had no genius for bravado; and as she felt that her father viewed her companion's attentions with an unsympathising eye, there was nothing but discomfort for her in the accident of seeming to challenge him. The Doctor felt, indeed, so sorry for her that he turned away, to spare her the sense of being watched; and he was so intelligent a man that, in his thoughts, he rendered a sort of poetic justice to her situation.

"It must be deucedly pleasant for a plain, inanimate girl like that to have a beautiful young fellow come and sit down beside her and whisper to her that he is her slave—if that is what this one whispers. No wonder she likes it, and that she thinks me a cruel tyrant; which of course she does, though she is afraid—she hasn't the animation necessary—to admit it to herself. Poor old Catherine!" mused the Doctor; "I verily believe she is capable of defending me when Townsend abuses me!"

And the force of this reflection, for the moment, was such in making him feel the natural opposition between his point of view and that of an infatuated child, that he said to himself that he was perhaps after all taking things too hard and crying out before he was hurt. He must not condemn Morris Townsend unheard. He had a great aversion to taking things too hard; he thought that half the discomfort and many of the disappointments of life come from it; and for an instant he asked himself whether, possibly, he did not appear ridiculous to this intelligent young man, whose private perception of incongruities he suspected of being keen. At the end of a quarter of an hour Catherine had got rid of him, and Townsend was now standing before the fireplace in conversation with Mrs. Almond.

"We will try him again," said the Doctor. And he crossed the room and joined his sister and her companion, making her a sign that she should leave the young man to him. She presently did so, while Morris looked at him, smiling, without a sign of evasiveness in his affable eye.

"He's amazingly conceited!" thought the Doctor; and then he said aloud: "I am told you are looking out for a position."

"Oh, a position is more than I should presume to call it," Morris Townsend answered. "That sounds so fine. I should like some quiet work—something to turn an honest penny."

"What sort of thing should you prefer?"

"Do you mean what am I fit for? Very little, I am afraid. I have nothing but my good right arm, as they say in the melodramas."

"You are too modest," said the Doctor. "In addition to your good right arm, you have your subtle brain. I know nothing of you but what I see; but I see by your physiognomy that you are extremely intelligent."

"Ah," Townsend murmured, "I don't know what to answer when you say that! You advise me, then, not to despair?"

And he looked at his interlocutor as if the question might have a double meaning. The Doctor caught the look and weighed it a moment before he replied. "I should be very sorry to admit that a robust and well-disposed young man need ever despair. If he doesn't succeed in one thing, he can try another. Only, I should add, he should choose his line with discretion."

"Ah, yes, with discretion," Morris Townsend repeated, sympathetically. "Well, I have been indiscreet, formerly; but I think I have got over it. I am very steady now." And he stood a moment, looking down at his remarkably neat shoes. Then at last, "Were you kindly intending to propose something for my advantage?" he inquired, looking up and smiling.

"Damn his impudence!" the Doctor exclaimed, privately. But in a moment he reflected that he himself had, after all, touched first upon this delicate point, and that his words might have been construed as an offer of assistance. "I have no particular proposal to make," he presently said; "but it occurred to me to let you know that I have you in my mind. Sometimes one hears of opportunities. For instance—should you object to leaving New York—to going to a distance?"

"I am afraid I shouldn't be able to manage that. I must seek my fortune here or nowhere. You see," added Morris Townsend, "I have ties—I have responsibilities here. I have a sister, a widow, from whom I have been separated for a long time, and to whom I am almost everything. I shouldn't like to say to her that I must leave her. She rather depends upon me, you see."

"Ah, that's very proper; family feeling is very proper," said Dr. Sloper. "I often think there is not enough of it in our city. I think I have heard of your sister."

"It is possible, but I rather doubt it; she lives so very quietly."

"As quietly, you mean," the Doctor went on, with a short laugh, "as a lady may do who has several young children."

"Ah, my little nephews and nieces—that's the very point! I am helping to bring them up," said Morris Townsend. "I am a kind of amateur tutor; I give them lessons."

"That's very proper, as I say; but it is hardly a career."

"It won't make my fortune!" the young man confessed.

"You must not be too much bent on a fortune," said the Doctor. "But I assure you I will keep you in mind; I won't lose sight of you!"

"If my situation becomes desperate I shall perhaps take the

liberty of reminding you!" Morris rejoined, raising his voice a little, with a brighter smile, as his interlocutor turned away.

Before he left the house the Doctor had a few words with Mrs. Almond.

"I should like to see his sister," he said. "What do you call her? Mrs. Montgomery. I should like to have a little talk with her."

"I will try and manage it," Mrs. Almond responded. "I will take the first opportunity of inviting her, and you shall come and meet her. Unless, indeed," Mrs. Almond added, "she first takes it into her head to be sick and to send for you."

"Ah no, not that; she must have trouble enough without that. But it would have its advantages, for then I should see the children. I should like very much to see the children."

"You are very thorough. Do you want to catechise them about their uncle?"

"Precisely. Their uncle tells me he has charge of their education, that he saves their mother the expense of school-bills. I should like to ask them a few questions in the commoner branches."

"He certainly has not the cut of a schoolmaster!" Mrs. Almond said to herself a short time afterwards, as she saw Morris Townsend in a corner bending over her niece, who was seated.

And there was, indeed, nothing in the young man's discourse at this moment that savoured of the pedagogue.

"Will you meet me somewhere to-morrow or next day?" he said, in a low tone, to Catherine.

"Meet you?" she asked, lifting her frightened eyes.

"I have something particular to say to you—very particular."

"Can't you come to the house? Can't you say it there?"

Townsend shook his head gloomily. "I can't enter your doors again!"

"Oh, Mr. Townsend!" murmured Catherine. She trembled as she wondered what had happened, whether her father had forbidden it.

"I can't in self-respect," said the young man. "Your father has insulted me."

"Insulted you?"

"He has taunted me with my poverty."

"Oh, you are mistaken—you misunderstood him!" Catherine spoke with energy, getting up from her chair.

"Perhaps I am too proud—too sensitive. But would you have me otherwise?" he asked, tenderly.

"Where my father is concerned, you must not be sure. He is full of goodness," said Catherine.

"He laughed at me for having no position! I took it quietly; but only because he belongs to you."

"I don't know," said Catherine; "I don't know what he thinks. I am sure he means to be kind. You must not be too proud."

"I will be proud only of you," Morris answered. "Will you meet me in the Square in the afternoon?"

A great blush on Catherine's part had been the answer to the declaration I have just quoted. She turned away, heedless of his question.

"Will you meet me?" he repeated. "It is very quiet there; no one need see us—toward dusk?"

"It is you who are unkind, it is you who laugh, when you say such things as that."

"My dear girl!" the young man murmured.

"You know how little there is in me to be proud of. I am ugly and stupid."

Morris greeted this remark with an ardent murmur, in which she recognised nothing articulate but an assurance that she was his own dearest.

But she went on. "I am not even—I am not even——" And she paused a moment.

"You are not what?"

"I am not even brave."

"Ah, then, if you are afraid, what shall we do?"

She hesitated awhile; then at last—"You must come to the house," she said; "I am not afraid of that."

"I would rather it were in the Square," the young man urged. "You know how empty it is, often. No one will see us."

"I don't care who sees us! But leave me now."

He left her resignedly; he had got what he wanted. Fortunately he was ignorant that half an hour later, going home with her father and feeling him near, the poor girl, in spite of her sudden declaration of courage, began to tremble again. Her father said nothing; but she had an idea his eyes were fixed upon her in the darkness. Mrs. Penniman also was silent; Morris Townsend had told her that her niece preferred, unromantically, an interview in a chintz-covered parlour to a sentimental tryst beside a fountain sheeted with dead leaves, and she was lost in wonderment at the oddity—almost the perversity—of the choice.

X

CATHERINE received the young man the next day on the ground she had chosen—amid the chaste upholstery of a New York drawing-room furnished in the fashion of fifty years ago. Morris had swallowed his pride and made the effort necessary to cross the threshold of her too derisive parent—an act of magnanimity which could not fail to render him doubly interesting.

"We must settle something—we must take a line," he declared, passing his hand through his hair and giving a glance at the long narrow mirror which adorned the space between the two windows, and which had at its base a little gilded bracket covered by a thin slab of white marble, supporting in its turn a backgammon board folded together in the shape of two volumes, two shining folios inscribed in letters of greenish gilt, *History of England*. If Morris had been pleased to describe the master of the house as a heartless scoffer, it is because he thought him too much on his guard, and this was the easiest way to express his own dissatisfaction—a dissatisfaction which he had made a point of concealing from the Doctor. It will probably seem to the reader, however, that the Doctor's vigilance was by no means excessive, and that these two young people had an open field. Their intimacy was now considerable, and it may appear that for a shrinking and retiring person our heroine had been liberal of her favours. The young man, within a few days, had made her listen to things for which she had not supposed that she was prepared; having a lively foreboding of difficulties, he proceeded to gain as much ground as possible in the present. He remembered that fortune favours the brave, and even if he had forgotten it, Mrs. Penniman would have remembered it for him. Mrs. Penniman delighted of all things in a drama, and she flattered herself that a drama would now be enacted. Combining as she did the zeal of the prompter with the impatience of the spectator, she had long since done her utmost to pull up the curtain. She, too, expected to figure in the performance—to be the confidant, the Chorus, to speak the epilogue. It may even be said that there were times when she lost sight alto-

gether of the modest heroine of the play, in the contemplation of certain great passages which would naturally occur
between the hero and herself.

What Morris had told Catherine at last was simply that he
loved her, or rather adored her. Virtually, he had made
known as much already—his visits had been a series of eloquent intimations of it. But now he had affirmed it in lover's vows, and, as a memorable sign of it, he had passed his
arm round the girl's waist and taken a kiss. This happy cer-
titude had come sooner than Catherine expected, and she
had regarded it, very naturally, as a priceless treasure. It may
even be doubted whether she had ever definitely expected to
possess it; she had not been waiting for it, and she had
never said to herself that at a given moment it must come.
As I have tried to explain, she was not eager and exacting;
she took what was given her from day to day; and if the
delightful custom of her lover's visits, which yielded her a
happiness in which confidence and timidity were strangely
blended, had suddenly come to an end, she would not only
not have spoken of herself as one of the forsaken, but she
would not have thought of herself as one of the disappointed. After Morris had kissed her, the last time he was
with her, as a ripe assurance of his devotion, she begged him
to go away, to leave her alone, to let her think. Morris went
away, taking another kiss first. But Catherine's meditations
had lacked a certain coherence. She felt his kisses on her lips
and on her cheeks for a long time afterwards; the sensation
was rather an obstacle than an aid to reflection. She would
have liked to see her situation all clearly before her, to make
up her mind what she should do if, as she feared, her father
should tell her that he disapproved of Morris Townsend. But
all that she could see with any vividness was that it was terribly strange that any one should disapprove of him; that
there must in that case be some mistake, some mystery,
which in a little while would be set at rest. She put off deciding and choosing; before the vision of a conflict with her
father she dropped her eyes and sat motionless, holding her
breath and waiting. It made her heart beat, it was intensely
painful. When Morris kissed her and said these things—
that also made her heart beat; but this was worse, and it

frightened her. Nevertheless, to-day, when the young man spoke of settling something, taking a line, she felt that it was the truth, and she answered very simply and without hesitating.

"We must do our duty," she said; "we must speak to my father. I will do it to-night; you must do it to-morrow."

"It is very good of you to do it first," Morris answered. "The young man—the happy lover—generally does that. But just as you please!"

It pleased Catherine to think that she should be brave for his sake, and in her satisfaction she even gave a little smile. "Women have more tact," she said; "they ought to do it first. They are more conciliating; they can persuade better."

"You will need all your powers of persuasion. But after all," Morris added, "you are irresistible."

"Please don't speak that way—and promise me this. To-morrow, when you talk with father, you will be very gentle and respectful."

"As much so as possible," Morris promised. "It won't be much use, but I shall try. I certainly would rather have you easily than have to fight for you."

"Don't talk about fighting; we shall not fight."

"Ah, we must be prepared," Morris rejoined; "you especially, because for you it must come hardest. Do you know the first thing your father will say to you?"

"No, Morris; please tell me."

"He will tell you I am mercenary."

"Mercenary?"

"It's a big word; but it means a low thing. It means that I am after your money."

"Oh!" murmured Catherine, softly.

The exclamation was so deprecating and touching that Morris indulged in another little demonstration of affection. "But he will be sure to say it," he added.

"It will be easy to be prepared for that," Catherine said. "I shall simply say that he is mistaken—that other men may be that way, but that you are not."

"You must make a great point of that, for it will be his own great point."

Catherine looked at her lover a minute, and then she said,

"I shall persuade him. But I am glad we shall be rich," she added.

Morris turned away, looking into the crown of his hat. "No, it's a misfortune," he said at last. "It is from that our difficulty will come."

"Well, if it is the worst misfortune, we are not so unhappy. Many people would not think it so bad. I will persuade him, and after that we shall be very glad we have money."

Morris Townsend listened to this robust logic in silence. "I will leave my defence to you; it's a charge that a man has to stoop to defend himself from."

Catherine on her side was silent for a while; she was looking at him while he looked, with a good deal of fixedness, out of the window. "Morris," she said, abruptly, "are you very sure you love me?"

He turned round, and in a moment he was bending over her. "My own dearest, can you doubt it?"

"I have only known it five days," she said; "but now it seems to me as if I could never do without it."

"You will never be called upon to try!" And he gave a little tender, reassuring laugh. Then, in a moment, he added, "There is something you must tell me, too." She had closed her eyes after the last word she uttered, and kept them closed; and at this she nodded her head, without opening them. "You must tell me," he went on, "that if your father is dead against me, if he absolutely forbids our marriage, you will still be faithful."

Catherine opened her eyes, gazing at him, and she could give no better promise than what he read there.

"You will cleave to me?" said Morris. "You know you are your own mistress—you are of age."

"Ah, Morris!" she murmured, for all answer. Or rather not for all; for she put her hand into his own. He kept it awhile, and presently he kissed her again. This is all that need be recorded of their conversation; but Mrs. Penniman, if she had been present, would probably have admitted that it was as well it had not taken place beside the fountain in Washington Square.

XI

CATHERINE listened for her father when he came in that evening, and she heard him go to his study. She sat quiet, though her heart was beating fast, for nearly half an hour; then she went and knocked at his door—a ceremony without which she never crossed the threshold of this apartment. On entering it now she found him in his chair beside the fire, entertaining himself with a cigar and the evening paper.

"I have something to say to you," she began very gently; and she sat down in the first place that offered.

"I shall be very happy to hear it, my dear," said her father. He waited—waited, looking at her, while she stared, in a long silence, at the fire. He was curious and impatient, for he was sure she was going to speak of Morris Townsend; but he let her take her own time, for he was determined to be very mild.

"I am engaged to be married!" Catherine announced at last, still staring at the fire.

The Doctor was startled; the accomplished fact was more than he had expected. But he betrayed no surprise. "You do right to tell me," he simply said. "And who is the happy mortal whom you have honoured with your choice?"

"Mr. Morris Townsend." And as she pronounced her lover's name, Catherine looked at him. What she saw was her father's still gray eye and his clear-cut, definite smile. She contemplated these objects for a moment, and then she looked back at the fire; it was much warmer.

"When was this arrangement made?" the Doctor asked.

"This afternoon—two hours ago."

"Was Mr. Townsend here?"

"Yes, father; in the front parlour." She was very glad that she was not obliged to tell him that the ceremony of their betrothal had taken place out there under the bare ailantus-trees.

"Is it serious?" said the Doctor.

"Very serious, father."

Her father was silent a moment. "Mr. Townsend ought to have told me."

"He means to tell you to-morrow."

"After I know all about it from you? He ought to have told me before. Does he think I didn't care—because I left you so much liberty?"

"Oh, no," said Catherine; "he knew you would care. And we have been so much obliged to you for—for the liberty."

The Doctor gave a short laugh. "You might have made a better use of it, Catherine."

"Please don't say that, father," the girl urged, softly, fixing her dull and gentle eyes upon him.

He puffed his cigar awhile, meditatively. "You have gone very fast," he said at last.

"Yes," Catherine answered simply; "I think we have."

Her father glanced at her an instant, removing his eyes from the fire. "I don't wonder Mr. Townsend likes you. You are so simple and so good."

"I don't know why it is—but he *does* like me. I am sure of that."

"And are you very fond of Mr. Townsend?"

"I like him very much, of course—or I shouldn't consent to marry him."

"But you have known him a very short time, my dear."

"Oh," said Catherine, with some eagerness, "it doesn't take long to like a person—when once you begin."

"You must have begun very quickly. Was it the first time you saw him—that night at your aunt's party?"

"I don't know, father," the girl answered. "I can't tell you about that."

"Of course; that's your own affair. You will have observed that I have acted on that principle. I have not interfered, I have left you your liberty, I have remembered that you are no longer a little girl—that you have arrived at years of discretion."

"I feel very old—and very wise," said Catherine, smiling faintly.

"I am afraid that before long you will feel older and wiser yet. I don't like your engagement."

"Ah!" Catherine exclaimed, softly, getting up from her chair.

"No, my dear. I am sorry to give you pain; but I don't like

it. You should have consulted me before you settled it. I have been too easy with you, and I feel as if you had taken advantage of my indulgence. Most decidedly, you should have spoken to me first."

Catherine hesitated a moment, and then—"It was because I was afraid you wouldn't like it!" she confessed.

"Ah, there it is! You had a bad conscience."

"No, I have not a bad conscience, father!" the girl cried out, with considerable energy. "Please don't accuse me of anything so dreadful." These words, in fact, represented to her imagination something very terrible indeed, something base and cruel, which she associated with malefactors and prisoners. "It was because I was afraid—afraid——" she went on.

"If you were afraid, it was because you had been foolish!"

"I was afraid you didn't like Mr. Townsend."

"You were quite right. I don't like him."

"Dear father, you don't know him," said Catherine, in a voice so timidly argumentative that it might have touched him.

"Very true; I don't know him intimately. But I know him enough. I have my impression of him. You don't know him either."

She stood before the fire, with her hands lightly clasped in front of her; and her father, leaning back in his chair and looking up at her, made this remark with a placidity that might have been irritating.

I doubt, however, whether Catherine was irritated, though she broke into a vehement protest. "I don't know him?" she cried. "Why, I know him—better than I have ever known any one!"

"You know a part of him—what he has chosen to show you. But you don't know the rest."

"The rest? What is the rest?"

"Whatever it may be. There is sure to be plenty of it."

"I know what you mean," said Catherine, remembering how Morris had forewarned her. "You mean that he is mercenary."

Her father looked up at her still, with his cold, quiet, reasonable eye. "If I meant it, my dear, I should say it! But there is an error I wish particularly to avoid—that of rendering Mr.

Townsend more interesting to you by saying hard things about him."

"I won't think them hard, if they are true," said Catherine.

"If you don't, you will be a remarkably sensible young woman!"

"They will be your reasons, at any rate, and you will want me to hear your reasons."

The Doctor smiled a little. "Very true. You have a perfect right to ask for them." And he puffed his cigar a few moments. "Very well, then, without accusing Mr. Townsend of being in love only with your fortune—and with the fortune that you justly expect—I will say that there is every reason to suppose that these good things have entered into his calculation more largely than a tender solicitude for your happiness strictly requires. There is, of course, nothing impossible in an intelligent young man entertaining a disinterested affection for you. You are an honest, amiable girl, and an intelligent young man might easily find it out. But the principal thing that we know about this young man—who is, indeed, very intelligent—leads us to suppose that, however much he may value your personal merits, he values your money more. The principal thing we know about him is that he has led a life of dissipation, and has spent a fortune of his own in doing so. That is enough for me, my dear. I wish you to marry a young man with other antecedents—a young man who could give positive guarantees. If Morris Townsend has spent his own fortune in amusing himself, there is every reason to believe that he would spend yours."

The Doctor delivered himself of these remarks slowly, deliberately, with occasional pauses and prolongations of accent, which made no great allowance for poor Catherine's suspense as to his conclusion. She sat down at last, with her head bent and her eyes still fixed upon him; and strangely enough—I hardly know how to tell it—even while she felt that what he said went so terribly against her, she admired his neatness and nobleness of expression. There was something hopeless and oppressive in having to argue with her father; but she too, on her side, must try to be clear. He was so quiet; he was not at all angry; and she, too, must be quiet. But her very effort to be quiet made her tremble.

"That is not the principal thing we know about him," she said; and there was a touch of her tremor in her voice. "There are other things—many other things. He has very high abilities—he wants so much to do something. He is kind, and generous, and true," said poor Catherine, who had not suspected hitherto the resources of her eloquence. "And his fortune—his fortune that he spent—was very small!"

"All the more reason he shouldn't have spent it," cried the Doctor, getting up with a laugh. Then as Catherine, who had also risen to her feet again, stood there in her rather angular earnestness, wishing so much and expressing so little, he drew her towards him and kissed her. "You won't think me cruel?" he said, holding her a moment.

This question was not reassuring; it seemed to Catherine, on the contrary, to suggest possibilities which made her feel sick. But she answered coherently enough—"No, dear father; because if you knew how I feel—and you must know, you know everything—you would be so kind, so gentle."

"Yes, I think I know how you feel," the Doctor said. "I will be very kind—be sure of that. And I will see Mr. Townsend to-morrow. Meanwhile, and for the present, be so good as to mention to no one that you are engaged."

XII

O N THE MORROW, in the afternoon, he stayed at home,
awaiting Mr. Townsend's call—a proceeding by which
it appeared to him (justly perhaps, for he was a very busy
man) that he paid Catherine's suitor great honour, and gave
both these young people so much the less to complain of.
Morris presented himself with a countenance sufficiently serene—he appeared to have forgotten the "insult" for which
he had solicited Catherine's sympathy two evenings before,
and Dr. Sloper lost no time in letting him know that he had
been prepared for his visit.

"Catherine told me yesterday what has been going on between you," he said. "You must allow me to say that it would
have been becoming of you to give me notice of your intentions before they had gone so far."

"I should have done so," Morris answered, "if you had not
had so much the appearance of leaving your daughter at liberty. She seems to me quite her own mistress."

"Literally, she is. But she has not emancipated herself morally quite so far, I trust, as to choose a husband without con-
sulting me. I have left her at liberty, but I have not been in
the least indifferent. The truth is that your little affair has
come to a head with a rapidity that surprises me. It was only
the other day that Catherine made your acquaintance."

"It was not long ago, certainly," said Morris, with great
gravity. "I admit that we have not been slow to—to arrive at
an understanding. But that was very natural, from the
moment we were sure of ourselves—and of each other. My
interest in Miss Sloper began the first time I saw her."

"Did it not by chance precede your first meeting?" the
Doctor asked.

Morris looked at him an instant. "I certainly had already
heard that she was a charming girl."

"A charming girl—that's what you think her?"

"Assuredly. Otherwise I should not be sitting here."

The Doctor meditated a moment. "My dear young man,"
he said at last, "you must be very susceptible. As Catherine's
father, I have, I trust, a just and tender appreciation of her

many good qualities; but I don't mind telling you that I have never thought of her as a charming girl, and never expected any one else to do so."

Morris Townsend received this statement with a smile that was not wholly devoid of deference. "I don't know what I might think of her if I were her father. I can't put myself in that place. I speak from my own point of view."

"You speak very well," said the Doctor; "but that is not all that is necessary. I told Catherine yesterday that I disapproved of her engagement."

"She let me know as much, and I was very sorry to hear it. I am greatly disappointed." And Morris sat in silence awhile, looking at the floor.

"Did you really expect I would say I was delighted, and throw my daughter into your arms?"

"Oh, no; I had an idea you didn't like me."

"What gave you the idea?"

"The fact that I am poor."

"That has a harsh sound," said the Doctor, "but it is about the truth—speaking of you strictly as a son-in-law. Your absence of means, of a profession, of visible resources or prospects, places you in a category from which it would be imprudent for me to select a husband for my daughter, who is a weak young woman with a large fortune. In any other capacity I am perfectly prepared to like you. As a son-in-law, I abominate you!"

Morris Townsend listened respectfully. "I don't think Miss Sloper is a weak woman," he presently said.

"Of course you must defend her—it's the least you can do. But I have known my child twenty years, and you have known her six weeks. Even if she were not weak, however, you would still be a penniless man."

"Ah, yes; that is *my* weakness! And therefore, you mean, I am mercenary—I only want your daughter's money."

"I don't say that. I am not obliged to say it; and to say it, save under stress of compulsion, would be very bad taste. I say simply that you belong to the wrong category."

"But your daughter doesn't marry a category," Townsend urged, with his handsome smile. "She marries an individual— an individual whom she is so good as to say she loves."

"An individual who offers so little in return!"

"Is it possible to offer more than the most tender affection and a lifelong devotion?" the young man demanded.

"It depends how we take it. It is possible to offer a few other things besides, and not only is it possible, but it's usual. A lifelong devotion is measured after the fact; and meanwhile it is customary in these cases to give a few material securities. What are yours? A very handsome face and figure, and a very good manner. They are excellent as far as they go, but they don't go far enough."

"There is one thing you should add to them," said Morris; "the word of a gentleman!"

"The word of a gentleman that you will always love Catherine? You must be a very fine gentleman to be sure of that."

"The word of a gentleman that I am not mercenary; that my affection for Miss Sloper is as pure and disinterested a sentiment as was ever lodged in a human breast! I care no more for her fortune than for the ashes in that grate."

"I take note—I take note," said the Doctor. "But having done so, I turn to our category again. Even with that solemn vow on your lips, you take your place in it. There is nothing against you but an accident, if you will; but with my thirty years' medical practice, I have seen that accidents may have far-reaching consequences."

Morris smoothed his hat—it was already remarkably glossy—and continued to display a self-control which, as the Doctor was obliged to admit, was extremely creditable to him. But his disappointment was evidently keen.

"Is there nothing I can do to make you believe in me?"

"If there were I should be sorry to suggest it, for—don't you see?—I don't want to believe in you!" said the Doctor, smiling.

"I would go and dig in the fields."

"That would be foolish."

"I will take the first work that offers, to-morrow."

"Do so by all means—but for your own sake, not for mine."

"I see; you think I am an idler!" Morris exclaimed, a little too much in the tone of a man who has made a discovery. But he saw his error immediately and blushed.

"It doesn't matter what I think, when once I have told you I don't think of you as a son-in-law."

But Morris persisted. "You think I would squander her money."

The Doctor smiled. "It doesn't matter, as I say; but I plead guilty to that."

"That's because I spent my own, I suppose," said Morris. "I frankly confess that. I have been wild. I have been foolish. I will tell you every crazy thing I ever did, if you like. There were some great follies among the number—I have never concealed that. But I have sown my wild oats. Isn't there some proverb about a reformed rake? I was not a rake, but I assure you I have reformed. It is better to have amused one-self for a while and have done with it. Your daughter would never care for a milksop; and I will take the liberty of saying that you would like one quite as little. Besides, between my money and hers there is a great difference. I spent my own; it was because it was my own that I spent it. And I made no debts; when it was gone I stopped. I don't owe a penny in the world."

"Allow me to inquire what you are living on now—though I admit," the Doctor added, "that the question, on my part, is inconsistent."

"I am living on the remnants of my property," said Morris Townsend.

"Thank you!" the Doctor gravely replied.

Yes, certainly, Morris's self-control was laudable. "Even ad-mitting I attach an undue importance to Miss Sloper's for-tune," he went on, " would not that be in itself an assurance that I should take good care of it?"

"That you should take too much care would be quite as bad as that you should take too little. Catherine might suffer as much by your economy as by your extravagance."

"I think you are very unjust!" The young man made this declaration decently, civilly, without violence.

"It is your privilege to think so, and I surrender my repu-tation to you! I certainly don't flatter myself I gratify you."

"Don't you care a little to gratify your daughter? Do you enjoy the idea of making her miserable?"

"I am perfectly resigned to her thinking me a tyrant for a twelvemonth."

"For a twelvemonth!" exclaimed Morris, with a laugh.

"For a lifetime, then! She may as well be miserable in that way as in the other."

Here at last Morris lost his temper. "Ah, you are not polite, sir!" he cried.

"You push me to it—you argue too much."

"I have a great deal at stake."

"Well, whatever it is," said the Doctor, "you have lost it!"

"Are you sure of that?" asked Morris; "are you sure your daughter will give me up?"

"I mean, of course, you have lost it as far as I am concerned. As for Catherine's giving you up—no, I am not sure of it. But as I shall strongly recommend it, as I have a great fund of respect and affection in my daughter's mind to draw upon, and as she has the sentiment of duty developed in a very high degree, I think it extremely possible."

Morris Townsend began to smooth his hat again. "I, too, have a fund of affection to draw upon!" he observed at last.

The Doctor at this point showed his own first symptoms of irritation. "Do you mean to defy me?"

"Call it what you please, sir! I mean not to give your daughter up."

The Doctor shook his head. "I haven't the least fear of your pining away your life. You are made to enjoy it."

Morris gave a laugh. "Your opposition to my marriage is all the more cruel, then! Do you intend to forbid your daughter to see me again?"

"She is past the age at which people are forbidden, and I am not a father in an old-fashioned novel. But I shall strongly urge her to break with you."

"I don't think she will," said Morris Townsend.

"Perhaps not. But I shall have done what I could."

"She has gone too far," Morris went on.

"To retreat? Then let her stop where she is."

"Too far to stop, I mean."

The Doctor looked at him a moment; Morris had his hand

on the door. "There is a great deal of impertinence in your saying it."

"I will say no more, sir!" Morris answered; and, making his bow, he left the room.

XIII

IT MAY BE thought the Doctor was too positive, and Mrs. Almond intimated as much. But as he said, he had his impression; it seemed to him sufficient, and he had no wish to modify it. He had passed his life in estimating people (it was part of the medical trade), and in nineteen cases out of twenty he was right.

"Perhaps Mr. Townsend is the twentieth case," Mrs. Almond suggested.

"Perhaps he is, though he doesn't look to me at all like a twentieth case. But I will give him the benefit of the doubt, and, to make sure, I will go and talk with Mrs. Montgomery. She will almost certainly tell me I have done right; but it is just possible that she will prove to me that I have made the greatest mistake of my life. If she does, I will beg Mr. Townsend's pardon. You needn't invite her to meet me, as you kindly proposed; I will write her a frank letter, telling her how matters stand, and asking leave to come and see her."

"I am afraid the frankness will be chiefly on your side. The poor little woman will stand up for her brother, whatever he may be."

"Whatever he may be? I doubt that. People are not always so fond of their brothers."

"Ah," said Mrs. Almond, "when it's a question of thirty thousand a year coming into a family——"

"If she stands up for him on account of the money, she will be a humbug. If she is a humbug I shall see it. If I see it, I won't waste time with her."

"She is not a humbug—she is an exemplary woman. She will not wish to play her brother a trick simply because he is selfish."

"If she is worth talking to, she will sooner play him a trick than that he should play Catherine one. Has she seen Catherine, by the way—does she know her?"

"Not to my knowledge. Mr. Townsend can have had no particular interest in bringing them together."

"If she is an exemplary woman, no. But we shall see to what extent she answers your description."

"I shall be curious to hear her description of you!" said Mrs. Almond, with a laugh. "And, meanwhile, how is Catherine taking it?"

"As she takes everything—as a matter of course."

"Doesn't she make a noise? Hasn't she made a scene?"

"She is not scenic."

"I thought a love-lorn maiden was always scenic."

"A fantastic widow is more so. Lavinia has made me a speech; she thinks me very arbitrary."

"She has a talent for being in the wrong," said Mrs. Almond. "But I am very sorry for Catherine, all the same."

"So am I. But she will get over it."

"You believe she will give him up?"

"I count upon it. She has such an admiration for her father."

"Oh, we know all about that! But it only makes me pity her the more. It makes her dilemma the more painful, and the effort of choosing between you and her lover almost impossible."

"If she can't choose, all the better."

"Yes, but he will stand there entreating her to choose, and Lavinia will pull on that side."

"I am glad she is not on my side; she is capable of ruining an excellent cause. The day Lavinia gets into your boat it capsizes. But she had better be careful," said the Doctor. "I will have no treason in my house!"

"I suspect she will be careful; for she is at bottom very much afraid of you."

"They are both afraid of me—harmless as I am!" the Doctor answered. "And it is on that that I build—on the salutary terror I inspire!"

XIV

H E WROTE his frank letter to Mrs. Montgomery, who
punctually answered it, mentioning an hour at which
he might present himself in the Second Avenue. She lived in
a neat little house of red brick, which had been freshly
painted, with the edges of the bricks very sharply marked out
in white. It has now disappeared, with its companions, to
make room for a row of structures more majestic. There were
green shutters upon the windows, without slats, but pierced
with little holes, arranged in groups; and before the house
was a diminutive yard, ornamented with a bush of mysterious
character, and surrounded by a low wooden paling, painted
in the same green as the shutters. The place looked like a
magnified baby-house, and might have been taken down from
a shelf in a toy-shop. Dr. Sloper, when he went to call, said
to himself, as he glanced at the objects I have enumerated,
that Mrs. Montgomery was evidently a thrifty and self-
respecting little person—the modest proportions of her
dwelling seemed to indicate that she was of small stature—
who took a virtuous satisfaction in keeping herself tidy, and
had resolved that, since she might not be splendid, she
would at least be immaculate. She received him in a little
parlour, which was precisely the parlour he had expected: a
small unspeckled bower, ornamented with a desultory foliage
of tissue-paper, and with clusters of glass drops, amid
which—to carry out the analogy—the temperature of the
leafy season was maintained by means of a cast-iron stove,
emitting a dry blue flame, and smelling strongly of varnish.
The walls were embellished with engravings swathed in pink
gauze, and the tables ornamented with volumes of extracts
from the poets, usually bound in black cloth stamped with
florid designs in jaundiced gilt. The Doctor had time to take
cognisance of these details; for Mrs. Montgomery, whose
conduct he pronounced under the circumstances inexcusable,
kept him waiting some ten minutes before she appeared. At
last, however, she rustled in, smoothing down a stiff poplin
dress, with a little frightened flush in a gracefully rounded
cheek.

She was a small, plump, fair woman, with a bright, clear eye, and an extraordinary air of neatness and briskness. But these qualities were evidently combined with an unaffected humility, and the Doctor gave her his esteem as soon as he had looked at her. A brave little person, with lively perceptions, and yet a disbelief in her own talent for social, as distinguished from practical, affairs—this was his rapid mental *résumé* of Mrs. Montgomery, who, as he saw, was flattered by what she regarded as the honour of his visit. Mrs. Montgomery, in her little red house in the Second Avenue, was a person for whom Dr. Sloper was one of the great men, one of the fine gentlemen of New York; and while she fixed her agitated eyes upon him, while she clasped her mittened hands together in her glossy poplin lap, she had the appearance of saying to herself that he quite answered her idea of what a distinguished guest would naturally be. She apologized for being late; but he interrupted her.

"It doesn't matter," he said; "for while I sat here I had time to think over what I wish to say to you, and to make up my mind how to begin."

"Oh, do begin!" murmured Mrs. Montgomery.

"It is not so easy," said the Doctor, smiling. "You will have gathered from my letter that I wish to ask you a few questions, and you may not find it very comfortable to answer them."

"Yes; I have thought what I should say. It is not very easy."

"But you must understand my situation—my state of mind. Your brother wishes to marry my daughter, and I wish to find out what sort of a young man he is. A good way to do so seemed to be to come and ask you; which I have proceeded to do."

Mrs. Montgomery evidently took the situation very seriously; she was in a state of extreme moral concentration. She kept her pretty eyes, which were illumined by a sort of brilliant modesty, attached to his own countenance, and evidently paid the most earnest attention to each of his words. Her expression indicated that she thought his idea of coming to see her a very superior conception, but that she was really afraid to have opinions on strange subjects.

"I am extremely glad to see you," she said, in a tone which

seemed to admit, at the same time, that this had nothing to do with the question.

The Doctor took advantage of this admission. "I didn't come to see you for your pleasure; I came to make you say disagreeable things—and you can't like that. What sort of a gentleman is your brother?"

Mrs. Montgomery's illuminated gaze grew vague, and began to wander. She smiled a little, and for some time made no answer, so that the Doctor at last became impatient. And her answer, when it came, was not satisfactory. "It is difficult to talk about one's brother."

"Not when one is fond of him, and when one has plenty of good to say."

"Yes, even then, when a good deal depends on it," said Mrs. Montgomery.

"Nothing depends on it, for you."

"I mean for—for——" and she hesitated.

"For your brother himself. I see!"

"I mean for Miss Sloper," said Mrs. Montgomery.

The Doctor liked this; it had the accent of sincerity. "Exactly; that's the point. If my poor girl should marry your brother, everything—as regards her happiness—would depend on his being a good fellow. She is the best creature in the world, and she could never do him a grain of injury. He, on the other hand, if he should not be all that we desire, might make her very miserable. That is why I want you to throw some light upon his character, you know. Of course, you are not bound to do it. My daughter, whom you have never seen, is nothing to you; and I, possibly, am only an indiscreet and impertinent old man. It is perfectly open to you to tell me that my visit is in very bad taste and that I had better go about my business. But I don't think you will do this; because I think we shall interest you, my poor girl and I. I am sure that if you were to see Catherine, she would interest you very much. I don't mean because she is interesting in the usual sense of the word, but because you would feel sorry for her. She is so soft, so simple-minded, she would be such an easy victim! A bad husband would have remarkable facilities for making her miserable; for she would have neither the intelligence nor the resolution to get the better of him, and yet she would have an exaggerated power of suffering. I see," added the Doctor, with his most insinuating, his most professional laugh, "you are already interested!"

"I have been interested from the moment he told me he was engaged," said Mrs. Montgomery.

"Ah! he says that—he calls it an engagement?"

"Oh, he has told me you didn't like it."

"Did he tell you that I don't like *him*?"

"Yes, he told me that too. I said I couldn't help it!" added Mrs. Montgomery.

"Of course you can't. But what you can do is to tell me I am right—to give me an attestation, as it were." And the Doctor accompanied this remark with another professional smile.

Mrs. Montgomery, however, smiled not at all; it was obvious that she could not take the humorous view of his appeal. "That is a good deal to ask," she said at last.

"There can be no doubt of that; and I must, in conscience, remind you of the advantages a young man marrying my daughter would enjoy. She has an income of ten thousand dollars in her own right, left her by her mother; if she marries a husband I approve, she will come into almost twice as much more at my death."

Mrs. Montgomery listened in great earnestness to this splendid financial statement; she had never heard thousands of dollars so familiarly talked about. She flushed a little with excitement. "Your daughter will be immensely rich," she said softly.

"Precisely—that's the bother of it."

"And if Morris should marry her, he—he——" And she hesitated timidly.

"He would be master of all that money? By no means. He would be master of the ten thousand a year that she has from her mother; but I should leave every penny of my own fortune, earned in the laborious exercise of my profession, to public institutions."

Mrs. Montgomery dropped her eyes at this, and sat for some time gazing at the straw matting which covered her floor.

"I suppose it seems to you," said the Doctor, laughing,

"that in so doing I should play your brother a very shabby trick."

"Not at all. That is too much money to get possession of so easily, by marrying. I don't think it would be right."

"It's right to get all one can. But in this case your brother wouldn't be able. If Catherine marries without my consent, she doesn't get a penny from my own pocket."

"Is that certain?" asked Mrs. Montgomery, looking up.

"As certain as that I sit here!"

"Even if she should pine away?"

"Even if she should pine to a shadow, which isn't probable."

"Does Morris know this?"

"I shall be most happy to inform him!" the Doctor exclaimed.

Mrs. Montgomery resumed her meditations, and her visitor, who was prepared to give time to the affair, asked himself whether, in spite of her little conscientious air, she was not playing into her brother's hands. At the same time he was half ashamed of the ordeal to which he had subjected her, and was touched by the gentleness with which she bore it. "If she were a humbug," he said, "she would get angry; unless she be very deep indeed. It is not probable that she is as deep as that."

"What makes you dislike Morris so much?" she presently asked, emerging from her reflections.

"I don't dislike him in the least as a friend, as a companion. He seems to me a charming fellow, and I should think he would be excellent company. I dislike him, exclusively, as a son-in-law. If the only office of a son-in-law were to dine at the paternal table, I should set a high value upon your brother. He dines capitally. But that is a small part of his function, which, in general, is to be a protector, and caretaker of my child, who is singularly ill-adapted to take care of herself. It is there that he doesn't satisfy me. I confess I have nothing but my impression to go by; but I am in the habit of trusting my impression. Of course you are at liberty to contradict it flat. He strikes me as selfish and shallow."

Mrs. Montgomery's eyes expanded a little, and the Doctor

fancied he saw the light of admiration in them. "I wonder you have discovered he is selfish!" she exclaimed.

"Do you think he hides it so well?"

"Very well indeed," said Mrs. Montgomery. "And I think we are all rather selfish," she added quickly.

"I think so too; but I have seen people hide it better than he. You see I am helped by a habit I have of dividing people into classes, into types. I may easily be mistaken about your brother as an individual, but his type is written on his whole person."

"He is very good-looking," said Mrs. Montgomery.

The Doctor eyed her a moment. "You women are all the same! But the type to which your brother belongs was made to be the ruin of you, and you were made to be its handmaids and victims. The sign of the type in question is the determination—sometimes terrible in its quiet intensity—to accept nothing of life but its pleasures, and to secure these pleasures chiefly by the aid of your complaisant sex. Young men of this class never do anything for themselves that they can get other people to do for them, and it is the infatuation, the devotion, the superstition of others, that keeps them going. These others in ninety-nine cases out of a hundred are women. What our young friends chiefly insist upon is that some one else shall suffer for them; and women do that sort of thing, as you must know, wonderfully well." The Doctor paused a moment, and then he added abruptly, "You have suffered immensely for your brother!"

This exclamation was abrupt, as I say, but it was also perfectly calculated. The Doctor had been rather disappointed at not finding his compact and comfortable little hostess surrounded in a more visible degree by the ravages of Morris Townsend's immorality; but he had said to himself that this was not because the young man had spared her, but because she had contrived to plaster up her wounds. They were aching there, behind the varnished stove, the festooned engravings, beneath her own neat little poplin bosom; and if he could only touch the tender spot, she would make a movement that would betray her. The words I have just quoted were an attempt to put his finger suddenly upon the place; and they had some of the success that he looked for. The tears sprang for a moment to Mrs. Montgomery's eyes, and she indulged in a proud little jerk of the head.

"I don't know how you have found that out!" she exclaimed.

"By a philosophic trick—by what they call induction. You know you have always your option of contradicting me. But kindly answer me a question. Don't you give your brother money? I think you ought to answer that."

"Yes, I have given him money," said Mrs. Montgomery.

"And you have not had much to give him?"

She was silent a moment. "If you ask me for a confession of poverty, that is easily made. I am very poor."

"One would never suppose it from your—your charming house," said the Doctor. "I learned from my sister that your income was moderate, and your family numerous."

"I have five children," Mrs. Montgomery observed; "but I am happy to say I can bring them up decently."

"Of course you can—accomplished and devoted as you are! But your brother has counted them over, I suppose?"

"Counted them over?"

"He knows there are five, I mean. He tells me it is he that brings them up."

Mrs. Montgomery stared a moment, and then quickly— "Oh, yes; he teaches them——Spanish."

The Doctor laughed out. "That must take a great deal off your hands! Your brother also knows, of course, that you have very little money."

"I have often told him so!" Mrs. Montgomery exclaimed, more unreservedly than she had yet spoken. She was apparently taking some comfort in the Doctor's clairvoyance.

"Which means that you have often occasion to, and that he often sponges on you. Excuse the crudity of my language; I simply express a fact. I don't ask you how much of your money he has had, it is none of my business. I have ascertained what I suspected—what I wished." And the Doctor got up, gently smoothing his hat. "Your brother lives on you," he said as he stood there.

Mrs. Montgomery quickly rose from her chair, following her visitor's movements with a look of fascination. But then, with a certain inconsequence—"I have never complained of him!" she said.

"You needn't protest—you have not betrayed him. But I advise you not to give him any more money."

"Don't you see it is in my interest that he should marry a rich person?" she asked. "If, as you say, he lives on me, I can only wish to get rid of him, and to put obstacles in the way of his marrying is to increase my own difficulties."

"I wish very much you would come to me with your difficulties," said the Doctor. "Certainly, if I throw him back on your hands, the least I can do is to help you to bear the burden. If you will allow me to say so, then, I shall take the liberty of placing in your hands, for the present, a certain fund for your brother's support."

Mrs. Montgomery stared; she evidently thought he was jesting; but she presently saw that he was not, and the complication of her feelings became painful. "It seems to me that I ought to be very much offended with you," she murmured.

"Because I have offered you money? That's a superstition," said the Doctor. "You must let me come and see you again, and we will talk about these things. I suppose that some of your children are girls."

"I have two little girls," said Mrs. Montgomery.

"Well, when they grow up, and begin to think of taking husbands, you will see how anxious you will be about the moral character of these gentlemen. Then you will understand this visit of mine!"

"Ah, you are not to believe that Morris's moral character is bad!"

The Doctor looked at her a little, with folded arms. "There is something I should greatly like—as a moral satisfaction. I should like to hear you say—'He is abominably selfish!'"

The words came out with the grave distinctiveness of his voice, and they seemed for an instant to create, to poor Mrs. Montgomery's troubled vision, a material image. She gazed at it an instant, and then she turned away. "You distress me, sir!" she exclaimed. "He is, after all, my brother, and his talents, his talents——" On these last words her voice quavered, and before he knew it she had burst into tears.

"His talents are first-rate!" said the Doctor. "We must find the proper field for them!" And he assured her most respectfully of his regret at having so greatly discomposed her. "It's all for my poor Catherine," he went on. "You must know her, and you will see."

Mrs. Montgomery brushed away her tears and blushed at having shed them. "I should like to know your daughter," she answered; and then, in an instant—"Don't let her marry him!"

Dr. Sloper went away with the words gently humming in his ears—"Don't let her marry him!" They gave him the moral satisfaction of which he had just spoken, and their value was the greater that they had evidently cost a pang to poor little Mrs. Montgomery's family pride.

XV

H<small>E HAD BEEN</small> puzzled by the way that Catherine carried herself; her attitude at this sentimental crisis seemed to him unnaturally passive. She had not spoken to him again after that scene in the library, the day before his interview with Morris; and a week had elapsed without making any change in her manner. There was nothing in it that appealed for pity, and he was even a little disappointed at her not giving him an opportunity to make up for his harshness by some manifestation of liberality which should operate as a compensation. He thought a little of offering to take her for a tour in Europe; but he was determined to do this only in case she should seem mutely to reproach him. He had an idea that she would display a talent for mute reproaches, and he was surprised at not finding himself exposed to these silent batteries. She said nothing, either tacitly, or explicitly, and as she was never very talkative, there was now no especial eloquence in her reserve. And poor Catherine was not sulky—a style of behaviour for which she had too little histrionic talent; she was simply very patient. Of course she was thinking over her situation, and she was apparently doing so in a deliberate and unimpassioned manner, with a view of making the best of it.

"She will do as I have bidden her," said the Doctor, and he made the further reflection that his daughter was not a woman of a great spirit. I know not whether he had hoped for a little more resistance for the sake of a little more entertainment; but he said to himself, as he had said before, that though it might have its momentary alarms, paternity was, after all, not an exciting vocation.

Catherine meanwhile had made a discovery of a very different sort; it had become vivid to her that there was a great excitement in trying to be a good daughter. She had an entirely new feeling, which may be described as a state of expectant suspense about her own actions. She watched herself as she would have watched another person, and wondered what she would do. It was as if this other person, who was both herself and not herself, had suddenly sprung into being, inspiring her with a natural curiosity as to the performance of untested functions.

"I am glad I have such a good daughter," said her father, kissing her, after the lapse of several days.

"I am trying to be good," she answered, turning away, with a conscience not altogether clear.

"If there is anything you would like to say to me, you know you must not hesitate. You needn't feel obliged to be so quiet. I shouldn't care that Mr. Townsend should be a frequent topic of conversation, but whenever you have anything particular to say about him I shall be very glad to hear it."

"Thank you," said Catherine; "I have nothing particular at present."

He never asked her whether she had seen Morris again, because he was sure that if this had been the case she would tell him. She had in fact not seen him, she had only written him a long letter. The letter at least was long for her; and, it may be added, that it was long for Morris; it consisted of five pages, in a remarkably neat and handsome hand. Catherine's handwriting was beautiful, and she was even a little proud of it; she was extremely fond of copying, and possessed volumes of extracts which testified to this accomplishment; volumes which she had exhibited one day to her lover, when the bliss of feeling that she was important in his eyes was exceptionally keen. She told Morris in writing that her father had expressed the wish that she should not see him again, and that she begged he would not come to the house until she should have "made up her mind." Morris replied with a passionate epistle, in which he asked to what, in Heaven's name, she wished to make up her mind. Had not her mind been made up two weeks before, and could it be possible that she entertained the idea of throwing him off? Did she mean to break down at the very beginning of their ordeal, after all the promises of fidelity she had both given and extracted? And he gave an account of his own interview with her father—an account not identical at all points with that offered in these pages. "He was terribly violent," Morris wrote; "but you know my self-control. I have need of it all when I remember that I have it in my power to break in upon your cruel captivity." Catherine sent him in answer to this, a note of three lines. "I am in great trouble; do not doubt of my affection, but let me wait a little and think." The idea of a struggle with her father, of setting up her will against his own, was heavy on her soul, and it kept her formally submissive, as a great physical weight keeps us motionless. It never entered into her mind to throw her lover off; but from the first she tried to assure herself that there would be a peaceful way out of their difficulty. The assurance was vague, for it contained no element of positive conviction that her father would change his mind. She only had an idea that if she should be very good, the situation would in some mysterious manner improve. To be good, she must be patient, respectful, abstain from judging her father too harshly, and from committing any act of open defiance. He was perhaps right, after all, to think as he did; by which Catherine meant not in the least that his judgment of Morris's motives in seeking to marry her was perhaps a just one, but that it was probably natural and proper that conscientious parents should be suspicious and even unjust. There were probably people in the world as bad as her father supposed Morris to be, and if there were the slightest chance of Morris being one of these sinister persons, the Doctor was right in taking it into account. Of course he could not know what she knew, how the purest love and truth were seated in the young man's eyes; but Heaven, in its time, might appoint a way of bringing him to such knowledge. Catherine expected a good deal of Heaven, and referred to the skies the initiative, as the French say, in dealing with her dilemma. She could not imagine herself imparting any kind of knowledge to her father, there was something superior even in his injustice and absolute in his mistakes. But she could at least be good, and if she were only good enough, Heaven would invent some way of reconciling all things—the dignity of her father's errors and the sweetness of her own confidence, the strict performance of her filial duties and the enjoyment of Morris Townsend's affection. Poor Catherine would have been glad to regard Mrs. Penniman as an illuminating agent, a part which this lady herself indeed was but imperfectly prepared to play. Mrs. Penniman took too much satisfaction in the sentimental shadows of this little drama to have, for the moment, any great interest in dissipating them. She wished the plot to thicken, and the advice that she gave her niece tended, in her own imagination, to produce this result. It was rather incoherent counsel, and from one day to another it contradicted itself; but it was pervaded by an earnest desire that Catherine should do something striking. "You must *act*, my dear; in your situation the great thing is to act," said Mrs. Penniman, who found her niece altogether beneath her opportunities. Mrs. Penniman's real hope was that the girl would make a secret marriage, at which she should officiate as brideswoman or duenna. She had a vision of this ceremony being performed in some subterranean chapel—subterranean chapels in New York were not frequent, but Mrs. Penniman's imagination was not chilled by trifles—and of the guilty couple—she liked to think of poor Catherine and her suitor as the guilty couple—being shuffled away in a fast-whirling vehicle to some obscure lodging in the suburbs, where she would pay them (in a thick veil) clandestine visits, where they would endure a period of romantic privation, and where ultimately, after she should have been their earthly providence, their intercessor, their advocate, and their medium of communication with the world, they should be reconciled to her brother in an artistic tableau, in which she herself should be somehow the central figure. She hesitated as yet to recommend this course to Catherine, but she attempted to draw an attractive picture of it to Morris Townsend. She was in daily communication with the young man, whom she kept informed by letters of the state of affairs in Washington Square. As he had been banished, as she said, from the house, she no longer saw him; but she ended by writing to him that she longed for an interview. This interview could take place only on neutral ground, and she bethought herself greatly before selecting a place of meeting. She had an inclination for Greenwood Cemetery, but she gave it up as too distant; she could not absent herself for so long, as she said, without exciting suspicion. Then she thought of the Battery, but that was rather cold and windy, besides one's being exposed to intrusion from the Irish emigrants who at this point alight, with large appetites, in the New World; and at last she fixed upon an oyster saloon in the Seventh Avenue, kept by a negro—an establishment of which she knew nothing save that she had noticed it in passing. She made an appointment with Morris Townsend to meet him there, and she went to the tryst at dusk, enveloped in an impenetrable veil. He kept her waiting for half-an-hour—he had almost the whole width of the city to traverse—but she liked to wait, it seemed to intensify the situation. She ordered a cup of tea, which proved excessively bad, and this gave her a sense that she was suffering in a romantic cause. When Morris at last arrived, they sat together for half-an-hour in the duskiest corner of a back shop; and it is hardly too much to say that this was the happiest half-hour that Mrs. Penniman had known for years. The situation was really thrilling, and it scarcely seemed to her a false note when her companion asked for an oyster-stew, and proceeded to consume it before her eyes. Morris, indeed, needed all the satisfaction that stewed oysters could give him, for it may be intimated to the reader that he regarded Mrs. Penniman in the light of a fifth wheel to his coach. He was in a state of irritation natural to a gentleman of fine parts who had been snubbed in a benevolent attempt to confer a distinction upon a young woman of inferior characteristics, and the insinuating sympathy of this somewhat desiccated matron appeared to offer him no practical relief. He thought her a humbug, and he judged of humbugs with a good deal of confidence. He had listened and made himself agreeable to her at first, in order to get a footing in Washington Square; and at present he needed all his self-command to be decently civil. It would have gratified him to tell her that she was a fantastic old woman, and that he should like to put her into an omnibus and send her home. We know, however, that Morris possessed the virtue of self-control, and he had moreover the constant habit of seeking to be agreeable; so that, although Mrs. Penniman's demeanour only exasperated his already unquiet nerves, he listened to her with a sombre deference in which she found much to admire.

XVI

THEY HAD of course immediately spoken of Catherine. "Did she send me a message, or—or anything?" Morris asked. He appeared to think that she might have sent him a trinket or a lock of her hair.

Mrs. Penniman was slightly embarrassed, for she had not told her niece of her intended expedition. "Not exactly a message," she said; "I didn't ask her for one, because I was afraid to—to excite her."

"I am afraid she is not very excitable!" And Morris gave a smile of some bitterness.

"She is better than that. She is steadfast—she is true!"

"Do you think she will hold fast then?"

"To the death!"

"Oh, I hope it won't come to that," said Morris.

"We must be prepared for the worst, and that is what I wish to speak to you about."

"What do you call the worst?"

"Well," said Mrs. Penniman, "my brother's hard, intellectual nature."

"Oh, the devil!"

"He is impervious to pity," Mrs. Penniman added, by way of explanation.

"Do you mean that he won't come round?"

"He will never be vanquished by argument. I have studied him. He will be vanquished only by the accomplished fact."

"The accomplished fact?"

"He will come round afterwards," said Mrs. Penniman, with extreme significance. "He cares for nothing but facts; he must be met by facts!"

"Well," rejoined Morris, "it is a fact that I wish to marry his daughter. I met him with that the other day, but he was not at all vanquished."

Mrs. Penniman was silent a little, and her smile beneath the shadow of her capacious bonnet, on the edge of which her black veil was arranged curtain-wise, fixed itself upon Morris's face with a still more tender brilliancy. "Marry Catherine first, and meet him afterwards!" she exclaimed.

"Do you recommend that?" asked the young man, frowning heavily.

She was a little frightened, but she went on with considerable boldness. "That is the way I see it: a private marriage— a private marriage." She repeated the phrase because she liked it.

"Do you mean that I should carry Catherine off? What do they call it—elope with her?"

"It is not a crime when you are driven to it," said Mrs. Penniman. "My husband, as I have told you, was a distinguished clergyman; one of the most eloquent men of his day. He once married a young couple that had fled from the house of the young lady's father. He was so interested in their story. He had no hesitation, and everything came out beautifully. The father was afterwards reconciled, and thought everything of the young man. Mr. Penniman married them in the evening, about seven o'clock. The church was so dark, you could scarcely see; and Mr. Penniman was intensely agitated; he was so sympathetic. I don't believe he could have done it again."

"Unfortunately Catherine and I have not Mr. Penniman to marry us," said Morris.

"No, but you have me!" rejoined Mrs. Penniman, expressively. "I can't perform the ceremony, but I can help you. I can watch."

"The woman's an idiot," thought Morris; but he was obliged to say something different. It was not, however, materially more civil. "Was it in order to tell me this that you requested I would meet you here?"

Mrs. Penniman had been conscious of a certain vagueness in her errand, and of not being able to offer him any very tangible reward for his long walk. "I thought perhaps you would like to see one who is so near to Catherine," she observed with considerable majesty. "And also," she added, "that you would value an opportunity of sending her something."

Morris extended his empty hands with a melancholy smile. "I am greatly obliged to you, but I have nothing to send."

"Haven't you a *word*?" asked his companion, with her suggestive smile coming back.

Morris frowned again. "Tell her to hold fast," he said, rather curtly.

"That is a good word—a noble word. It will make her happy for many days. She is very touching, very brave," Mrs. Penniman went on, arranging her mantle and preparing to depart. While she was so engaged she had an inspiration. She found the phrase that she could boldly offer as a vindication of the step she had taken. "If you marry Catherine at all risks," she said, "you will give my brother a proof of your being what he pretends to doubt."

"What he pretends to doubt?"

"Don't you know what that is?" Mrs. Penniman asked, almost playfully.

"It does not concern me to know," said Morris, grandly.

"Of course it makes you angry."

"I despise it," Morris declared.

"Ah, you know what it is, then?" said Mrs. Penniman, shaking her finger at him. "He pretends that you like—you like the money."

Morris hesitated a moment; and then, as if he spoke advisedly—"I *do* like the money!"

"Ah, but not—but not as he means it. You don't like it more than Catherine?"

He leaned his elbows on the table and buried his head in his hands. "You torture me!" he murmured. And, indeed, this was almost the effect of the poor lady's too importunate interest in his situation.

But she insisted on making her point. "If you marry her in spite of him, he will take for granted that you expect nothing of him, and are prepared to do without it. And so he will see that you are disinterested."

Morris raised his head a little, following this argument. "And what shall I gain by that?"

"Why, that he will see that he has been wrong in thinking that you wished to get his money."

"And seeing that I wish he would go to the deuce with it, he will leave it to a hospital. Is that what you mean?" asked Morris.

"No, I don't mean that; though that would be very grand!"

Mrs. Penniman quickly added. "I mean that having done you such an injustice, he will think it his duty, at the end, to make some amends."

Morris shook his head, though it must be confessed he was a little struck with this idea. "Do you think he is so sentimental?"

"He is not sentimental," said Mrs. Penniman; "but, to be perfectly fair to him, I think he has, in his own narrow way, a certain sense of duty."

There passed through Morris Townsend's mind a rapid wonder as to what he might, even under a remote contingency, be indebted to from the action of this principle in Dr. Sloper's breast, and the inquiry exhausted itself in his sense of the ludicrous. "Your brother has no duties to me," he said presently, "and I none to him."

"Ah, but he has duties to Catherine."

"Yes, but you see that on that principle Catherine has duties to him as well."

Mrs. Penniman got up, with a melancholy sigh, as if she thought him very unimaginative. "She has always performed them faithfully; and now do you think she has no duties to *you*?" Mrs. Penniman always, even in conversation, italicised her personal pronouns.

"It would sound harsh to say so! I am so grateful for her love," Morris added.

"I will tell her you said that! And now, remember that if you need me, I am there." And Mrs. Penniman, who could think of nothing more to say, nodded vaguely in the direction of Washington Square.

Morris looked some moments at the sanded floor of the shop; he seemed to be disposed to linger a moment. At last, looking up with a certain abruptness, "It is your belief that if she marries me he will cut her off?" he asked.

Mrs. Penniman stared a little, and smiled. "Why, I have explained to you what I think would happen—that in the end it would be the best thing to do."

"You mean that, whatever she does, in the long run she will get the money?"

"It doesn't depend upon her, but upon you. Venture to

appear as disinterested as you are!" said Mrs. Penniman ingeniously. Morris dropped his eyes on the sanded floor again,
pondering this; and she pursued. "Mr. Penniman and I had
nothing, and we were very happy. Catherine, moreover, has
her mother's fortune, which, at the time my sister-in-law married, was considered a very handsome one."

"Oh, don't speak of that!" said Morris; and, indeed, it was
quite superfluous, for he had contemplated the fact in all its
lights.

"Austin married a wife with money—why shouldn't you?"

"Ah! but your brother was a doctor," Morris objected.

"Well, all young men can't be doctors!"

"I should think it an extremely loathsome profession," said
Morris, with an air of intellectual independence. Then, in a
moment, he went on rather inconsequently, "Do you suppose
there is a will already made in Catherine's favour?"

"I suppose so—even doctors must die; and perhaps a little
in mine," Mrs. Penniman frankly added.

"And you believe he would certainly change it—as regards
Catherine?"

"Yes; and then change it back again."

"Ah, but one can't depend on that!" said Morris.

"Do you want to *depend* on it?" Mrs. Penniman asked.

Morris blushed a little. "Well, I am certainly afraid of being
the cause of an injury to Catherine."

"Ah! you must not be afraid. Be afraid of nothing, and
everything will go well!"

And then Mrs. Penniman paid for her cup of tea, and Morris paid for his oyster stew, and they went out together into
the dimly-lighted wilderness of the Seventh Avenue. The dusk
had closed in completely, and the street lamps were separated
by wide intervals of a pavement in which cavities and fissures
played a disproportionate part. An omnibus, emblazoned
with strange pictures, went tumbling over the dislocated
cobble-stones.

"How will you go home?" Morris asked, following this vehicle with an interested eye. Mrs. Penniman had taken his arm.

She hesitated a moment. "I think this manner would be
pleasant," she said; and she continued to let him feel the value
of his support.

So he walked with her through the devious ways of the west side of the town, and through the bustle of gathering nightfall in populous streets, to the quiet precinct of Washington Square. They lingered a moment at the foot of Dr. Sloper's white marble steps, above which a spotless white door, adorned with a glittering silver plate, seemed to figure, for Morris, the closed portal of happiness; and then Mrs. Penniman's companion rested a melancholy eye upon a lighted window in the upper part of the house.

"That is my room—my dear little room!" Mrs. Penniman remarked.

Morris started. "Then I needn't come walking round the square to gaze at it."

"That's as you please. But Catherine's is behind; two noble windows on the second floor. I think you can see them from the other street."

"I don't want to see them, ma'am!" And Morris turned his back to the house.

"I will tell her you have been *here*, at any rate," said Mrs. Penniman, pointing to the spot where they stood; "and I will give her your message—that she is to hold fast!"

"Oh, yes! of course. You know I write her all that."

"It seems to say more when it is spoken! And remember, if you need me, that I am *there*;" and Mrs. Penniman glanced at the third floor.

On this they separated, and Morris, left to himself, stood looking at the house a moment; after which he turned away, and took a gloomy walk round the Square, on the opposite side, close to the wooden fence. Then he came back, and paused for a minute in front of Dr. Sloper's dwelling. His eyes travelled over it; they even rested on the ruddy windows of Mrs. Penniman's apartment. He thought it a devilish comfortable house.

XVII

MRS. PENNIMAN told Catherine that evening—the two ladies were sitting in the back parlour—that she had had an interview with Morris Townsend; and on receiving this news the girl started with a sense of pain. She felt angry for the moment; it was almost the first time she had ever felt angry. It seemed to her that her aunt was meddlesome; and from this came a vague apprehension that she would spoil something.

"I don't see why you should have seen him. I don't think it was right," Catherine said.

"I was so sorry for him—it seemed to me some one ought to see him."

"No one but I," said Catherine, who felt as if she were making the most presumptuous speech of her life, and yet at the same time had an instinct that she was right in doing so.

"But you wouldn't, my dear," Aunt Lavinia rejoined; "and I didn't know what might have become of him."

"I have not seen him, because my father has forbidden it," Catherine said, very simply.

There was a simplicity in this, indeed, which fairly vexed Mrs. Penniman. "If your father forbade you to go to sleep, I suppose you would keep awake!" she commented.

Catherine looked at her. "I don't understand you. You seem to be very strange."

"Well, my dear, you will understand me some day!" And Mrs. Penniman, who was reading the evening paper, which she perused daily from the first line to the last, resumed her occupation. She wrapped herself in silence; she was determined Catherine should ask her for an account of her interview with Morris. But Catherine was silent for so long, that she almost lost patience; and she was on the point of remarking to her that she was very heartless, when the girl at last spoke.

"What did he say?" she asked.

"He said he is ready to marry you any day, in spite of everything."

Catherine made no answer to this, and Mrs. Penniman

almost lost patience again; owing to which she at last volunteered the information that Morris looked very handsome, but terribly haggard.

"Did he seem sad?" asked her niece.

"He was dark under the eyes," said Mrs. Penniman. "So different from when I first saw him; though I am not sure that if I had seen him in this condition the first time, I should not have been even more struck with him. There is something brilliant in his very misery."

This was, to Catherine's sense, a vivid picture, and though she disapproved, she felt herself gazing at it. "Where did you see him?" she asked presently.

"In—in the Bowery; at a confectioner's," said Mrs. Penniman, who had a general idea that she ought to dissemble a little.

"Whereabouts is the place?" Catherine inquired, after another pause.

"Do you wish to go there, my dear?" said her aunt.

"Oh, no!" And Catherine got up from her seat and went to the fire, where she stood looking awhile at the glowing coals.

"Why are you so dry, Catherine?" Mrs. Penniman said at last.

"So dry?"

"So cold—so irresponsive."

The girl turned, very quickly. "Did *he* say that?"

Mrs. Penniman hesitated a moment. "I will tell you what he said. He said he feared only one thing—that you would be afraid."

"Afraid of what?"

"Afraid of your father."

Catherine turned back to the fire again, and then, after a pause, she said—"I *am* afraid of my father."

Mrs. Penniman got quickly up from her chair and approached her niece. "Do you mean to give him up, then?"

Catherine for some time never moved; she kept her eyes on the coals. At last she raised her head and looked at her aunt. "Why do you push me so?" she asked.

"I don't push you. When have I spoken to you before?"

"It seems to me that you have spoken to me several times."

"I am afraid it is necessary, then, Catherine," said Mrs. Penniman, with a good deal of solemnity. "I am afraid you don't feel the importance——" She paused a little; Catherine was looking at her. "The importance of not disappointing that gallant young heart!" And Mrs. Penniman went back to her chair, by the lamp, and, with a little jerk, picked up the evening paper again.

Catherine stood there before the fire, with her hands behind her, looking at her aunt, to whom it seemed that the girl had never had just this dark fixedness in her gaze. "I don't think you understand—or that you know me," she said.

"If I don't, it is not wonderful; you trust me so little."

Catherine made no attempt to deny this charge, and for some time more nothing was said. But Mrs. Penniman's imagination was restless, and the evening paper failed on this occasion to enchain it.

"If you succumb to the dread of your father's wrath," she said, "I don't know what will become of us."

"Did *he* tell you to say these things to me?"

"He told me to use my influence."

"You must be mistaken," said Catherine. "He trusts me."

"I hope he may never repent of it!" And Mrs. Penniman gave a little sharp slap to her newspaper. She knew not what to make of her niece, who had suddenly become stern and contradictious.

This tendency on Catherine's part was presently even more apparent. "You had much better not make any more appointments with Mr. Townsend," she said. "I don't think it is right."

Mrs. Penniman rose with considerable majesty. "My poor child, are you jealous of me?" she inquired.

"Oh, Aunt Lavinia!" murmured Catherine blushing.

"I don't think it is your place to teach me what is right."

On this point Catherine made no concession. "It can't be right to deceive."

"I certainly have not deceived *you!*"

"Yes; but I promised my father——"

"I have no doubt you promised your father. But I have promised him nothing!"

Catherine had to admit this, and she did so in silence. "I don't believe Mr. Townsend himself likes it," she said at last.

"Doesn't like meeting me?"

"Not in secret."

"It was not in secret; the place was full of people."

"But it was a secret place—away off in the Bowery."

Mrs. Penniman flinched a little. "Gentlemen enjoy such things," she remarked, presently. "I know what gentlemen like."

"My father wouldn't like it, if he knew."

"Pray, do you propose to inform him?" Mrs. Penniman inquired.

"No, Aunt Lavinia. But please don't do it again."

"If I do it again, you will inform him: is that what you mean? I do not share your dread of my brother; I have always known how to defend my own position. But I shall certainly never again take any step on your behalf; you are much too thankless. I knew you were not a spontaneous nature, but I believed you were firm, and I told your father that he would find you so. I am disappointed—but your father will not be!" And with this, Mrs. Penniman offered her niece a brief good-night, and withdrew to her own apartment.

XVIII

CATHERINE sat alone by the parlour fire—sat there for more than an hour, lost in her meditations. Her aunt seemed to her aggressive and foolish, and to see it so clearly—to judge Mrs. Penniman so positively—made her feel old and grave. She did not resent the imputation of weakness; it made no impression on her, for she had not the sense of weakness, and she was not hurt at not being appreciated. She had an immense respect for her father, and she felt that to displease him would be a misdemeanour analogous to an act of profanity in a great temple: but her purpose had slowly ripened, and she believed that her prayers had purified it of its violence. The evening advanced, and the lamp burned dim without her noticing it; her eyes were fixed upon her terrible plan. She knew her father was in his study—that he had been there all the evening; from time to time she expected to hear him move. She thought he would perhaps come, as he sometimes came, into the parlour. At last the clock struck eleven, and the house was wrapped in silence; the servants had gone to bed. Catherine got up and went slowly to the door of the library, where she waited a moment, motionless. Then she knocked, and then she waited again. Her father had answered her, but she had not the courage to turn the latch. What she had said to her aunt was true enough—she was afraid of him; and in saying that she had no sense of weakness she meant that she was not afraid of herself. She heard him move within, and he came and opened the door for her.

"What is the matter?" asked the Doctor. "You are standing there like a ghost."

She went into the room, but it was some time before she contrived to say what she had come to say. Her father, who was in his dressing-gown and slippers, had been busy at his writing-table, and after looking at her for some moments, and waiting for her to speak, he went and seated himself at his papers again. His back was turned to her—she began to hear the scratching of his pen. She remained near the door, with her heart thumping beneath her bodice; and she was very glad that his back was turned, for it seemed to her that she could more easily address herself to this portion of his person than to his face. At last she began, watching it while she spoke.

"You told me that if I should have anything more to say about Mr. Townsend you would be glad to listen to it."

"Exactly, my dear," said the Doctor, not turning round, but stopping his pen.

Catherine wished it would go on, but she herself continued. "I thought I would tell you that I have not seen him again, but that I should like to do so."

"To bid him good-bye?" asked the Doctor.

The girl hesitated a moment. "He is not going away."

The Doctor wheeled slowly round in his chair, with a smile that seemed to accuse her of an epigram; but extremes meet, and Catherine had not intended one. "It is not to bid him good-bye, then?" her father said.

"No, father, not that; at least, not for ever. I have not seen him again, but I should like to see him," Catherine repeated.

The Doctor slowly rubbed his under lip with the feather of his quill.

"Have you written to him?"

"Yes, four times."

"You have not dismissed him, then. Once would have done that."

"No," said Catherine; "I have asked him—asked him to wait."

Her father sat looking at her, and she was afraid he was going to break out into wrath; his eyes were so fine and cold.

"You are a dear, faithful child," he said at last. "Come here to your father." And he got up, holding out his hands toward her.

The words were a surprise, and they gave her an exquisite joy. She went to him, and he put his arm round her tenderly, soothingly; and then he kissed her. After this he said—

"Do you wish to make me very happy?"

"I should like to—but I am afraid I can't," Catherine answered.

"You can if you will. It all depends on your will."

"Is it to give him up?" said Catherine.

"Yes, it is to give him up."

And he held her still, with the same tenderness, looking into her face and resting his eyes on her averted eyes. There was a long silence; she wished he would release her.

"You are happier than I, father," she said, at last.

"I have no doubt you are unhappy just now. But it is better to be unhappy for three months and get over it, than for many years and never get over it."

"Yes, if that were so," said Catherine.

"It would be so; I am sure of that." She answered nothing, and he went on. "Have you no faith in my wisdom, in my tenderness, in my solicitude for your future?"

"Oh, father!" murmured the girl.

"Don't you suppose that I know something of men: their vices, their follies, their falsities?"

She detached herself, and turned upon him. "He is not vicious—he is not false!"

Her father kept looking at her with his sharp, pure eye. "You make nothing of my judgment, then?"

"I can't believe that!"

"I don't ask you to believe it, but to take it on trust."

Catherine was far from saying to herself that this was an ingenious sophism; but she met the appeal none the less squarely. "What has he done—what do you know?"

"He has never done anything—he is a selfish idler."

"Oh, father, don't abuse him!" she exclaimed, pleadingly.

"I don't mean to abuse him; it would be a great mistake. You may do as you choose," he added, turning away.

"I may see him again?"

"Just as you choose."

"Will you forgive me?"

"By no means."

"It will only be for once."

"I don't know what you mean by once. You must either give him up or continue the acquaintance."

"I wish to explain—to tell him to wait."

"To wait for what?"

"Till you know him better—till you consent."

"Don't tell him any such nonsense as that. I know him well enough, and I shall never consent."

"But we can wait a long time," said poor Catherine, in a

tone which was meant to express the humblest conciliation, but which had upon her father's nerves the effect of an iteration not characterised by tact.

The Doctor answered, however, quietly enough: "Of course you can wait till I die, if you like."

Catherine gave a cry of natural horror.

"Your engagement will have one delightful effect upon you; it will make you extremely impatient for that event."

Catherine stood staring, and the Doctor enjoyed the point he had made. It came to Catherine with the force—or rather with the vague impressiveness—of a logical axiom which it was not in her province to controvert; and yet, though it was a scientific truth, she felt wholly unable to accept it.

"I would rather not marry, if that were true," she said.

"Give me a proof of it, then; for it is beyond a question that by engaging yourself to Morris Townsend you simply wait for my death."

She turned away, feeling sick and faint; and the Doctor went on. "And if you wait for it with impatience, judge, if you please, what *his* eagerness will be!"

Catherine turned it over—her father's words had such an authority for her that her very thoughts were capable of obeying him. There was a dreadful ugliness in it, which seemed to glare at her through the interposing medium of her own feebler reason. Suddenly, however, she had an inspiration— she almost knew it to be an inspiration.

"If I don't marry before your death, I will not after," she said.

To her father, it must be admitted, this seemed only another epigram; and as obstinacy, in unaccomplished minds, does not usually select such a mode of expression, he was the more surprised at this wanton play of a fixed idea.

"Do you mean that for an impertinence?" he inquired; an inquiry of which, as he made it, he quite perceived the grossness.

"An impertinence? Oh, father, what terrible things you say!"

"If you don't wait for my death, you might as well marry immediately; there is nothing else to wait for."

For some time Catherine made no answer; but finally she said—

"I think Morris—little by little—might persuade you."

"I shall never let him speak to me again. I dislike him too much."

Catherine gave a long, low sigh; she tried to stifle it, for she had made up her mind that it was wrong to make a parade of her trouble, and to endeavour to act upon her father by the meretricious aid of emotion. Indeed, she even thought it wrong—in the sense of being inconsiderate—to attempt to act upon his feelings at all; her part was to effect some gentle, gradual change in his intellectual perception of poor Morris's character. But the means of effecting such a change were at present shrouded in mystery, and she felt miserably helpless and hopeless. She had exhausted all arguments, all replies. Her father might have pitied her, and in fact he did so; but he was sure he was right.

"There is one thing you can tell Mr. Townsend, when you see him again," he said: "that if you marry without my consent, I don't leave you a farthing of money. That will interest him more than anything else you can tell him."

"That would be very right," Catherine answered. "I ought not in that case to have a farthing of your money."

"My dear child," the Doctor observed, laughing, "your simplicity is touching. Make that remark, in that tone, and with that expression of countenance, to Mr. Townsend, and take a note of his answer. It won't be polite—it will express irritation; and I shall be glad of that, as it will put me in the right; unless, indeed—which is perfectly possible—you should like him the better for being rude to you."

"He will never be rude to me," said Catherine, gently.

"Tell him what I say, all the same."

She looked at her father, and her quiet eyes filled with tears.

"I think I will see him, then," she murmured, in her timid voice.

"Exactly as you choose!" And he went to the door and opened it for her to go out. The movement gave her a terrible sense of his turning her off.

"It will be only once, for the present," she added, lingering a moment.

"Exactly as you choose," he repeated, standing there with his hand on the door. "I have told you what I think. If you see him, you will be an ungrateful, cruel child; you will have given your old father the greatest pain of his life."

This was more than the poor girl could bear; her tears overflowed, and she moved towards her grimly consistent parent with a pitiful cry. Her hands were raised in supplication, but he sternly evaded this appeal. Instead of letting her sob out her misery on his shoulder, he simply took her by the arm and directed her course across the threshold, closing the door gently but firmly behind her. After he had done so, he remained listening. For a long time there was no sound; he knew that she was standing outside. He was sorry for her, as I have said; but he was so sure he was right. At last he heard her move away, and then her footstep creaked faintly upon the stairs.

The Doctor took several turns round his study, with his hands in his pockets, and a thin sparkle, possibly of irritation, but partly also of something like humour, in his eye. "By Jove," he said to himself, "I believe she will stick—I believe she will stick!" And this idea of Catherine "sticking" appeared to have a comical side, and to offer a prospect of entertainment. He determined, as he said to himself, to see it out.

XIX

IT WAS for reasons connected with this determination that on the morrow he sought a few words of private conversation with Mrs. Penniman. He sent for her to the library, and he there informed her that he hoped very much that, as regarded this affair of Catherine's, she would mind her *p*'s and *q*'s.

"I don't know what you mean by such an expression," said his sister. "You speak as if I were learning the alphabet."

"The alphabet of common sense is something you will never learn," the Doctor permitted himself to respond.

"Have you called me here to insult me?" Mrs. Penniman inquired.

"Not at all. Simply to advise you. You have taken up young Townsend; that's your own affair. I have nothing to do with your sentiments, your fancies, your affections, your delusions; but what I request of you is that you will keep these things to yourself. I have explained my views to Catherine; she understands them perfectly, and anything that she does further in the way of encouraging Mr. Townsend's attentions will be in deliberate opposition to my wishes. Anything that you should do in the way of giving her aid and comfort will be—permit me the expression—distinctly treasonable. You know high treason is a capital offense; take care how you incur the penalty."

Mrs. Penniman threw back her head, with a certain expansion of the eye which she occasionally practised. "It seems to me that you talk like a great autocrat."

"I talk like my daughter's father."

"Not like your sister's brother!" cried Lavinia.

"My dear Lavinia," said the Doctor, "I sometimes wonder whether I am your brother. We are so extremely different. In spite of differences, however, we can, at a pinch, understand each other; and that is the essential thing just now. Walk straight with regard to Mr. Townsend; that's all I ask. It is highly probable you have been corresponding with him for the last three weeks—perhaps even seeing him. I don't ask you—you needn't tell me." He had a moral conviction that she would contrive to tell a fib about the matter, which it would disgust him to listen to. "Whatever you have done, stop doing it. That's all I wish."

"Don't you wish also by chance to murder your child?" Mrs. Penniman inquired.

"On the contrary, I wish to make her live and be happy."

"You will kill her; she passed a dreadful night."

"She won't die of one dreadful night, nor of a dozen. Remember that I am a distinguished physician."

Mrs. Penniman hesitated a moment. Then she risked her retort. "Your being a distinguished physician has not prevented you from already losing *two members* of your family!"

She had risked it, but her brother gave her such a terribly incisive look—a look so like a surgeon's lancet—that she was frightened at her courage. And he answered her in words that corresponded to the look: "It may not prevent me, either, from losing the society of still another."

Mrs. Penniman took herself off, with whatever air of depreciated merit was at her command, and repaired to Catherine's room, where the poor girl was closeted. She knew all about her dreadful night, for the two had met again, the evening before, after Catherine left her father. Mrs. Penniman was on the landing of the second floor when her niece came upstairs. It was not remarkable that a person of so much subtlety should have discovered that Catherine had been shut up with the Doctor. It was still less remarkable that she should have felt an extreme curiosity to learn the result of this interview, and that this sentiment, combined with her great amiability and generosity, should have prompted her to regret the sharp words lately exchanged between her niece and herself. As the unhappy girl came into sight, in the dusky corridor, she made a lively demonstration of sympathy. Catherine's bursting heart was equally oblivious. She only knew that her aunt was taking her into her arms. Mrs. Penniman drew her into Catherine's own room, and the two women sat there together, far into the small hours; the younger one with her head on the other's lap, sobbing and sobbing at first in a soundless, stifled manner, and then at last perfectly still. It gratified Mrs. Penniman to be able to feel conscientiously that this scene virtually removed the interdict which Catherine had placed upon her further communion with Morris Townsend. She was not gratified, however, when, in coming back to her niece's room before breakfast, she found that Catherine had risen and was preparing herself for this meal.

"You should not go to breakfast," she said; "you are not well enough, after your fearful night."

"Yes, I am very well, and I am only afraid of being late."

"I can't understand you!" Mrs. Penniman cried. "You should stay in bed for three days."

"Oh, I could never do that!" said Catherine, to whom this idea presented no attractions.

Mrs. Penniman was in despair, and she noted, with extreme annoyance, that the trace of the night's tears had completely vanished from Catherine's eyes. She had a most impracticable *physique*. "What effect do you expect to have upon your father," her aunt demanded, "if you come plumping down, without a vestige of any sort of feeling, as if nothing in the world had happened?"

"He would not like me to lie in bed," said Catherine, simply.

"All the more reason for your doing it. How else do you expect to move him?"

Catherine thought a little. "I don't know how; but not in that way. I wish to be just as usual." And she finished dressing, and, according to her aunt's expression, went plumping down into the paternal presence. She was really too modest for consistent pathos.

And yet it was perfectly true that she had had a dreadful night. Even after Mrs. Penniman left her she had had no sleep. She lay staring at the uncomforting gloom, with her eyes and ears filled with the movement with which her father had turned her out of his room, and of the words in which he had told her that she was a heartless daughter. Her heart was breaking. She had heart enough for that. At moments it seemed to her that she believed him, and that to do what she was doing, a girl must indeed be bad. She *was* bad; but she couldn't help it. She would try to appear good, even if her heart were perverted; and from time to time she had a fancy that she might accomplish something by ingenious concessions to form, though she should persist in caring for Morris.

Catherine's ingenuities were indefinite, and we are not called upon to expose their hollowness. The best of them perhaps showed itself in that freshness of aspect which was so discouraging to Mrs. Penniman, who was amazed at the absence of haggardness in a young woman who for a whole night had lain quivering beneath a father's curse. Poor Catherine was conscious of her freshness; it gave her a feeling about the future which rather added to the weight upon her mind. It seemed a proof that she was strong and solid and dense, and would live to a great age—longer than might be generally convenient; and this idea was depressing, for it appeared to saddle her with a pretension the more, just when the cultivation of any pretension was inconsistent with her doing right. She wrote that day to Morris Townsend, requesting him to come and see her on the morrow; using very few words, and explaining nothing. She would explain everything face to face.

XX

O N THE MORROW, in the afternoon, she heard his voice
at the door, and his step in the hall. She received him
in the big, bright front-parlour, and she instructed the servant
that if any one should call she was particularly engaged. She
was not afraid of her father's coming in, for at that hour he
was always driving about town. When Morris stood there before her, the first thing that she was conscious of was that he
was even more beautiful to look at than fond recollection had
painted him; the next was that he had pressed her in his arms.
When she was free again it appeared to her that she had now
indeed thrown herself into the gulf of defiance, and even, for
an instant, that she had been married to him.

He told her that she had been very cruel, and had made
him very unhappy; and Catherine felt acutely the difficulty of
her destiny, which forced her to give pain in such opposite
quarters. But she wished that, instead of reproaches, however
tender, he would give her help; he was certainly wise enough,
and clever enough, to invent some issue from their troubles.
She expressed this belief, and Morris received the assurance as
if he thought it natural; but he interrogated, at first—as was
natural too—rather than committed himself to marking out
a course.

"You should not have made me wait so long," he said. "I
don't know how I have been living; every hour seemed like
years. You should have decided sooner."

"Decided?" Catherine asked.

"Decided whether you would keep me or give me up."

"Oh, Morris," she cried, with a long tender murmur, "I
never thought of giving you up!"

"What, then, were you waiting for?" The young man was
ardently logical.

"I thought my father might—might——" and she hesitated.

"Might see how unhappy you were?"

"Oh, no! But that he might look at it differently."

"And now you have sent for me to tell me that at last he
does so. Is that it?"

This hypothetical optimism gave the poor girl a pang. "No, Morris," she said solemnly, "he looks at it still in the same way."

"Then why have you sent for me?"

"Because I wanted to see you!" cried Catherine, piteously.

"That's an excellent reason, surely. But did you want to look at me only? Have you nothing to tell me?"

His beautiful persuasive eyes were fixed upon her face, and she wondered what answer would be noble enough to make to such a gaze as that. For a moment her own eyes took it in, and then—"I *did* want to look at you!" she said, gently. But after this speech, most inconsistently, she hid her face.

Morris watched her for a moment, attentively. "Will you marry me to-morrow?" he asked suddenly.

"To-morrow?"

"Next week, then. Any time within a month."

"Isn't it better to wait?" said Catherine.

"To wait for what?"

She hardly knew for what; but this tremendous leap alarmed her. "Till we have thought about it a little more."

He shook his head, sadly and reproachfully. "I thought you had been thinking about it these three weeks. Do you want to turn it over in your mind for five years? You have given me more than time enough. My poor girl," he added in a moment, "you are not sincere!"

Catherine coloured from brow to chin, and her eyes filled with tears. "Oh, how can you say that?" she murmured.

"Why, you must take me or leave me," said Morris, very reasonably. "You can't please your father and me both; you must choose between us."

"I have chosen you!" she said, passionately.

"Then marry me next week."

She stood gazing at him. "Isn't there any other way?"

"None that I know of for arriving at the same result. If there is, I should be happy to hear of it."

Catherine could think of nothing of the kind, and Morris's luminosity seemed almost pitiless. The only thing she could think of was that her father might after all come round, and she articulated, with an awkward sense of her helplessness in doing so, a wish that this miracle might happen.

"Do you think it is in the least degree likely?" Morris asked.

"It would be, if he could only know you!"

"He can know me if he will. What is to prevent it?"

"His ideas, his reasons," said Catherine. "They are so—so terribly strong." She trembled with the recollection of them yet.

"Strong?" cried Morris. "I would rather you should think them weak."

"Oh, nothing about my father is weak!" said the girl.

Morris turned away, walking to the window, where he stood looking out. "You are terribly afraid of him!" he remarked at last.

She felt no impulse to deny it, because she had no shame in it; for if it was no honour to herself, at least it was an honour to him. "I suppose I must be," she said, simply.

"Then you don't love me—not as I love you. If you fear your father more than you love me, then your love is not what I hoped it was."

"Ah, my friend!" she said, going to him.

"Do *I* fear anything?" he demanded, turning round on her. "For your sake what am I not ready to face?"

"You are noble—you are brave!" she answered, stopping short at a distance that was almost respectful.

"Small good it does me, if you are so timid."

"I don't think that I am—*really*," said Catherine.

"I don't know what you mean by 'really.' It is really enough to make us miserable."

"I should be strong enough to wait—to wait a long time."

"And suppose after a long time your father should hate me worse than ever?"

"He wouldn't—he couldn't!"

"He would be touched by my fidelity? Is that what you mean? If he is so easily touched, then why should you be afraid of him?"

This was much to the point, and Catherine was struck by it. "I will try not to be," she said. And she stood there, submissively, the image, in advance, of a dutiful and responsible wife. This image could not fail to recommend itself to Morris Townsend, and he continued to give proof of the high estimation in which he held her. It could only have been at the prompting of such a sentiment that he presently mentioned to her that the course recommended by Mrs. Penniman was an immediate union, regardless of consequences.

"Yes, Aunt Penniman would like that," Catherine said, simply—and yet with a certain shrewdness. It must, however, have been in pure simplicity, and from motives quite untouched by sarcasm, that, a few moments after, she went on to say to Morris that her father had given her a message for him. It was quite on her conscience to deliver this message, and had the mission been ten times more painful she would have as scrupulously performed it. "He told me to tell you—to tell you very distinctly, and directly from himself, that if I marry without his consent, I shall not inherit a penny of his fortune. He made a great point of this. He seemed to think—he seemed to think——"

Morris flushed, as any young man of spirit might have flushed at an imputation of baseness.

"What did he seem to think?"

"That it would make a difference."

"It *will* make a difference—in many things. We shall be by many thousands of dollars the poorer; and that is a great difference. But it will make none in my affection."

"We shall not want the money," said Catherine; "for you know I have a good deal myself."

"Yes, my dear girl, I know you have something. And he can't touch that!"

"He would never," said Catherine. "My mother left it to me."

Morris was silent awhile. "He was very positive about this, was he?" he asked at last. "He thought such a message would annoy me terribly, and make me throw off the mask, eh?"

"I don't know what he thought," said Catherine, wearily.

"Please tell him that I care for his message as much as for that!" And Morris snapped his fingers sonorously.

"I don't think I could tell him that."

"Do you know you sometimes disappoint me?" said Morris.

"I should think I might. I disappoint every one—father and Aunt Penniman."

"Well, it doesn't matter with me, because I am fonder of you than they are."

"Yes, Morris," said the girl, with her imagination—what there was of it—swimming in this happy truth, which seemed, after all, invidious to no one.

"Is it your belief that he will stick to it—stick to it for ever, to this idea of disinheriting you?—that your goodness and patience will never wear out his cruelty?"

"The trouble is that if I marry you, he will think I am not good. He will think that a proof."

"Ah, then, he will never forgive you!"

This idea, sharply expressed by Morris's handsome lips, renewed for a moment, to the poor girl's temporarily pacified conscience, all its dreadful vividness. "Oh, you must love me very much!" she cried.

"There is no doubt of that, my dear!" her lover rejoined. "You don't like that word 'disinherited,'" he added in a moment.

"It isn't the money; it is that he should—that he should feel so."

"I suppose it seems to you a kind of curse," said Morris. "It must be very dismal. But don't you think," he went on presently, "that if you were to try to be very clever, and to set rightly about it, you might in the end conjure it away? Don't you think," he continued further, in a tone of sympathetic speculation, "that a really clever woman, in your place, might bring him round at last? Don't you think——"

Here, suddenly, Morris was interrupted; these ingenious inquiries had not reached Catherine's ears. The terrible word "disinheritance," with all its impressive moral reprobation, was still ringing there; seemed indeed to gather force as it lingered. The mortal chill of her situation struck more deeply into her child-like heart, and she was overwhelmed by a feeling of loneliness and danger. But her refuge was there, close to her, and she put out her hands to grasp it. "Ah, Morris," she said, with a shudder, "I will marry you as soon as you please!" And she surrendered herself, leaning her head on his shoulder.

"My dear good girl!" he exclaimed, looking down at his prize. And then he looked up again, rather vaguely, with parted lips and lifted eyebrows.

XXI

D R. SLOPER very soon imparted his conviction to Mrs. Almond, in the same terms in which he had announced it to himself. "She's going to stick, by Jove! she's going to stick."

"Do you mean that she is going to marry him?" Mrs. Almond inquired.

"I don't know that; but she is not going to break down. She is going to drag out the engagement, in the hope of making me relent."

"And shall you not relent?"

"Shall a geometrical proposition relent? I am not so superficial."

"Doesn't geometry treat of surfaces?" asked Mrs. Almond, who, as we know, was clever, smiling.

"Yes; but it treats of them profoundly. Catherine and her young man are my surfaces; I have taken their measure."

"You speak as if it surprised you."

"It is immense; there will be a great deal to observe."

"You are shockingly cold-blooded!" said Mrs. Almond.

"I need to be, with all this hot blood about me. Young Townsend indeed is cool; I must allow him that merit."

"I can't judge him," Mrs. Almond answered; "but I am not at all surprised at Catherine."

"I confess I am a little; she must have been so deucedly divided and bothered."

"Say it amuses you outright! I don't see why it should be such a joke that your daughter adores you."

"It is the point where the adoration stops that I find it interesting to fix."

"It stops where the other sentiment begins."

"Not at all—that would be simple enough. The two things are extremely mixed up, and the mixture is extremely odd. It will produce some third element, and that's what I am waiting to see. I wait with suspense—with positive excitement; and that is a sort of emotion that I didn't suppose Catherine would ever provide for me. I am really very much obliged to her."

"She will cling," said Mrs. Almond; "she will certainly cling."

"Yes; as I say, she will stick."

"Cling is prettier. That's what those very simple natures always do, and nothing could be simpler than Catherine. She doesn't take many impressions; but when she takes one she keeps it. She is like a copper kettle that receives a dent; you may polish up the kettle, but you can't efface the mark."

"We must try and polish up Catherine," said the Doctor. "I will take her to Europe."

"She won't forget him in Europe."

"He will forget her, then."

Mrs. Almond looked grave. "Should you really like that?"

"Extremely!" said the Doctor.

Mrs. Penniman, meanwhile, lost little time in putting herself again in communication with Morris Townsend. She requested him to favour her with another interview, but she did not on this occasion select an oyster-saloon as the scene of their meeting. She proposed that he should join her at the door of a certain church, after service on Sunday afternoon, and she was careful not to appoint the place of worship which she usually visited, and where, as she said, the congregation would have spied upon her. She picked out a less elegant resort, and on issuing from its portal at the hour she had fixed she saw the young man standing apart. She offered him no recognition till she had crossed the street and he had followed her to some distance. Here, with a smile—"Excuse my apparent want of cordiality," she said. "You know what to believe about that. Prudence before everything." And on his asking her in what direction they should walk, "Where we shall be least observed," she murmured.

Morris was not in high good-humour, and his response to this speech was not particularly gallant. "I don't flatter myself we shall be much observed anywhere." Then he turned recklessly toward the centre of the town. "I hope you have come to tell me that he has knocked under," he went on.

"I am afraid I am not altogether a harbinger of good; and yet, too, I am to a certain extent a messenger of peace. I have been thinking a great deal, Mr. Townsend," said Mrs. Penniman.

"You think too much."

"I suppose I do; but I can't help it, my mind is so terribly active. When I give myself, I give myself. I pay the penalty in my headaches, my famous headaches—a perfect circlet of pain! But I carry it as a queen carries her crown. Would you believe that I have one now? I wouldn't, however, have missed our rendezvous for anything. I have something very important to tell you."

"Well, let's have it," said Morris.

"I was perhaps a little headlong the other day in advising you to marry immediately. I have been thinking it over, and now I see it just a little differently."

"You seem to have a great many different ways of seeing the same object."

"Their number is infinite!" said Mrs. Penniman, in a tone which seemed to suggest that this convenient faculty was one of her brightest attributes.

"I recommend you to take one way and stick to it," Morris replied.

"Ah! but it isn't easy to choose. My imagination is never quiet, never satisfied. It makes me a bad adviser, perhaps; but it makes me a capital friend!"

"A capital friend who gives bad advice!" said Morris.

"Not intentionally—and who hurries off, at every risk, to make the most humble excuses!"

"Well, what do you advise me now?"

"To be very patient; to watch and wait."

"And is that bad advice or good?"

"That is not for me to say," Mrs. Penniman rejoined, with some dignity. "I only pretend it's sincere."

"And will you come to me next week and recommend something different and equally sincere?"

"I may come to you next week and tell you that I am in the streets!"

"In the streets?"

"I have had a terrible scene with my brother, and he threatens, if anything happens, to turn me out of the house. You know I am a poor woman."

Morris had a speculative idea that she had a little property; but he naturally did not press this.

"I should be very sorry to see you suffer martyrdom for me," he said. "But you make your brother out a regular Turk."

Mrs. Penniman hesitated a little.

"I certainly do not regard Austin as a satisfactory Christian."

"And am I to wait till he is converted?"

"Wait at any rate till he is less violent. Bide your time, Mr. Townsend; remember the prize is great!"

Morris walked along some time in silence, tapping the railings and gateposts very sharply with his stick.

"You certainly are devilish inconsistent!" he broke out at last. "I have already got Catherine to consent to a private marriage."

Mrs. Penniman was indeed inconsistent, for at this news she gave a little jump of gratification.

"Oh! when and where?" she cried. And then she stopped short.

Morris was a little vague about this.

"That isn't fixed; but she consents. It's deuced awkward, now, to back out."

Mrs. Penniman, as I say, had stopped short; and she stood there with her eyes fixed, brilliantly, on her companion.

"Mr. Townsend," she proceeded, "shall I tell you something? Catherine loves you so much that you may do anything."

This declaration was slightly ambiguous, and Morris opened his eyes.

"I am happy to hear it! But what do you mean by 'anything'?"

"You may postpone—you may change about; she won't think the worse of you."

Morris stood there still, with his raised eyebrows; then he said simply and rather dryly—"Ah!" After this he remarked to Mrs. Penniman that if she walked so slowly she would attract notice, and he succeeded, after a fashion, in hurrying her back to the domicile of which her tenure had become so insecure.

XXII

H E HAD slightly misrepresented the matter in saying that Catherine had consented to take the great step. We left her just now declaring that she would burn her ships behind her; but Morris, after having elicited this declaration, had become conscious of good reasons for not taking it up. He avoided, gracefully enough, fixing a day, though he left her under the impression that he had his eye on one. Catherine may have had her difficulties; but those of her circumspect suitor are also worthy of consideration. The prize was certainly great; but it was only to be won by striking the happy mean between precipitancy and caution. It would be all very well to take one's jump and trust to Providence; Providence was more especially on the side of clever people, and clever people were known by an indisposition to risk their bones. The ultimate reward of a union with a young woman who was both unattractive and impoverished ought to be connected with immediate disadvantages by some very palpable chain. Between the fear of losing Catherine and her possible fortune altogether, and the fear of taking her too soon and finding this possible fortune as void of actuality as a collection of emptied bottles, it was not comfortable for Morris Townsend to choose; a fact that should be remembered by readers disposed to judge harshly of a young man who may have struck them as making but an indifferently successful use of fine natural parts. He had not forgotten that in any event Catherine had her own ten thousand a year; he had devoted an abundance of meditation to this circumstance. But with his fine parts he rated himself high, and he had a perfectly definite appreciation of his value, which seemed to him inadequately represented by the sum I have mentioned. At the same time he reminded himself that this sum was considerable, that everything is relative, and that if a modest income is less desirable than a large one, the complete absence of revenue is nowhere accounted an advantage. These reflections gave him plenty of occupation, and made it necessary that he should trim his sail. Dr. Sloper's opposition was the unknown quantity in the problem he had to work out. The natural way to work it out was by marrying Catherine; but in mathematics there are many short cuts, and Morris was not without a hope that he should yet discover one. When Catherine took him at his word and consented to renounce the attempt to mollify her father, he drew back skilfully enough, as I have said, and kept the wedding-day still an open question. Her faith in his sincerity was so complete that she was incapable of suspecting that he was playing with her; her trouble just now was of another kind. The poor girl had an admirable sense of honour; and from the moment she had brought herself to the point of violating her father's wish, it seemed to her that she had no right to enjoy his protection. It was on her conscience that she ought not to live under his roof only so long as she conformed to his wisdom. There was a great deal of glory in such a position, but poor Catherine felt that she had forfeited her claim to it. She had cast her lot with a young man against whom he had solemnly warned her, and broken the contract under which he provided her with a happy home. She could not give up the young man, so she must leave the home; and the sooner the object of her preference offered her another, the sooner her situation would lose its awkward twist. This was close reasoning; but it was commingled with an infinite amount of merely instinctive penitence. Catherine's days, at this time, were dismal, and the weight of some of her hours was almost more than she could bear. Her father never looked at her, never spoke to her. He knew perfectly what he was about, and this was part of a plan. She looked at him as much as she dared (for she was afraid of seeming to offer herself to his observation), and she pitied him for the sorrow she had brought upon him. She held up her head and busied her hands, and went about her daily occupations; and when the state of things in Washington Square seemed intolerable, she closed her eyes and indulged herself with an intellectual vision of the man for whose sake she had broken a sacred law. Mrs. Penniman, of the three persons in Washington Square, had much the most of the manner that belongs to a great crisis. If Catherine was quiet, she was quietly quiet, as I may say, and her pathetic effects, which there was no one to notice, were entirely unstudied and unintended. If the Doctor was stiff and dry and absolutely indifferent to the presence of his companions, it was so lightly, neatly, easily done, that you would have had to know him well to discover that on the whole he rather enjoyed having to be so disagreeable. But Mrs. Penniman was elaborately reserved and significantly silent; there was a richer rustle in the very deliberate movements to which she confined herself, and when she occasionally spoke, in connection with some very trivial event, she had the air of meaning something deeper than what she said. Between Catherine and her father nothing had passed since the evening she went to speak to him in his study. She had something to say to him—it seemed to her she ought to say it; but she kept it back, for fear of irritating him. He also had something to say to her; but he was determined not to speak first. He was interested, as we know, in seeing how, if she were left to herself, she would "stick." At last she told him she had seen Morris Townsend again, and that their relations remained quite the same.

"I think we shall marry—before very long. And probably, meanwhile, I shall see him rather often; about once a week, not more."

The Doctor looked at her coldly from head to foot, as if she had been a stranger. It was the first time his eyes had rested on her for a week, which was fortunate, if that was to be their expression. "Why not three times a day?" he asked. "What prevents your meeting as often as you choose?"

She turned away a moment; there were tears in her eyes. Then she said, "It is better once a week."

"I don't see how it is better. It is as bad as it can be. If you flatter yourself that I care for little modifications of that sort, you are very much mistaken. It is as wrong of you to see him once a week as it would be to see him all day long. Not that it matters to me, however."

Catherine tried to follow these words, but they seemed to lead towards a vague horror from which she recoiled. "I think we shall marry pretty soon," she repeated at last.

Her father gave her his dreadful look again, as if she were some one else. "Why do you tell me that? It's no concern of mine."

"Oh, father!" she broke out, "don't you care, even if you do feel so?"

"Not a button. Once you marry, it's quite the same to me when or where or why you do it; and if you think to compound for your folly by hoisting your flag in this way, you may spare yourself the trouble."

With this he turned away. But the next day he spoke to her of his own accord, and his manner was somewhat changed. "Shall you be married within the next four or five months?" he asked.

"I don't know, father," said Catherine. "It is not very easy for us to make up our minds."

"Put it off, then, for six months, and in the meantime I will take you to Europe. I should like you very much to go."

It gave her such delight, after his words of the day before, to hear that he should "like" her to do something, and that he still had in his heart any of the tenderness of preference, that she gave a little exclamation of joy. But then she became conscious that Morris was not included in this proposal, and that—as regards really going—she would greatly prefer to remain at home with him. But she blushed, none the less, more comfortably than she had done of late. "It would be delightful to go to Europe," she remarked, with a sense that the idea was not original, and that her tone was not all it might be.

"Very well, then, we will go. Pack up your clothes."

"I had better tell Mr. Townsend," said Catherine.

Her father fixed his cold eyes upon her. "If you mean that you had better ask his leave, all that remains to me is to hope he will give it."

The girl was sharply touched by the pathetic ring of the words; it was the most calculated, the most dramatic little speech the Doctor had ever uttered. She felt that it was a great thing for her, under the circumstances, to have this fine opportunity of showing him her respect; and yet there was something else that she felt as well, and that she presently expressed. "I sometimes think that if I do what you dislike so much, I ought not to stay with you."

"To stay with me?"

"If I live with you, I ought to obey you."

"If that's your theory, it's certainly mine," said the Doctor, with a dry laugh.

"But if I don't obey you, I ought not to live with you—to enjoy your kindness and protection."

This striking argument gave the Doctor a sudden sense of having underestimated his daughter; it seemed even more than worthy of a young woman who had revealed the quality of unaggressive obstinacy. But it displeased him—displeased him deeply, and he signified as much. "That idea is in very bad taste," he said. "Did you get it from Mr. Townsend?"

"Oh no; it's my own!" said Catherine eagerly.

"Keep it to yourself, then," her father answered, more than ever determined she should go to Europe.

XXIII

IF MORRIS TOWNSEND was not to be included in this journey, no more was Mrs. Penniman, who would have been
thankful for an invitation, but who (to do her justice) bore
her disappointment in a perfectly lady-like manner. "I should
enjoy seeing the works of Raphael and the ruins—the ruins
of the Pantheon," she said to Mrs. Almond; "but on the other
hand, I shall not be sorry to be alone and at peace for the
next few months in Washington Square. I want rest; I have
been through so much in the last four months." Mrs. Almond
thought it rather cruel that her brother should not take poor
Lavinia abroad; but she easily understood that, if the purpose
of his expedition was to make Catherine forget her lover, it
was not in his interest to give his daughter this young man's
best friend as a companion. "If Lavinia had not been so foolish, she might visit the ruins of the Pantheon," she said to
herself; and she continued to regret her sister's folly, even
though the latter assured her that she had often heard the
relics in question most satisfactorily described by Mr. Penniman. Mrs. Penniman was perfectly aware that her brother's
motive in undertaking a foreign tour was to lay a trap for
Catherine's constancy; and she imparted this conviction very
frankly to her niece.

"He thinks it will make you forget Morris," she said (she
always called the young man "Morris" now); "out of sight,
out of mind, you know. He thinks that all the things you will
see over there will drive him out of your thoughts."

Catherine looked greatly alarmed. "If he thinks that, I
ought to tell him beforehand."

Mrs. Penniman shook her head. "Tell him afterwards, my
dear! After he has had all the trouble and the expense! That's
the way to serve him." And she added, in a softer key, that it
must be delightful to think of those who love us among the
ruins of the Pantheon.

Her father's displeasure had cost the girl, as we know, a
great deal of deep-welling sorrow—sorrow of the purest and
most generous kind, without a touch of resentment or rancour; but for the first time, after he had dismissed with such

contemptuous brevity her apology for being a charge upon him, there was a spark of anger in her grief. She had felt his contempt; it had scorched her; that speech about her bad taste made her ears burn for three days. During this period she was less considerate; she had an idea—a rather vague one, but it was agreeable to her sense of injury—that now she was absolved from penance, and might do what she chose. She chose to write to Morris Townsend to meet her in the Square and take her to walk about the town. If she were going to Europe out of respect to her father, she might at least give herself this satisfaction. She felt in every way at present more free and more resolute; there was a force that urged her. Now at last, completely and unreservedly, her passion possessed her.

Morris met her at last, and they took a long walk. She told him immediately what had happened—that her father wished to take her away. It would be for six months, to Europe; she would do absolutely what Morris should think best. She hoped inexpressibly that he would think it best she should stay at home. It was some time before he said what he thought: he asked, as they walked along, a great many questions. There was one that especially struck her; it seemed so incongruous.

"Should you like to see all those celebrated things over there?"

"Oh, no, Morris!" said Catherine, quite deprecatingly.

"Gracious Heaven, what a dull woman!" Morris exclaimed to himself.

"He thinks I will forget you," said Catherine; "that all these things will drive you out of my mind."

"Well, my dear, perhaps they will!"

"Please don't say that," Catherine answered gently, as they walked along. "Poor father will be disappointed."

Morris gave a little laugh. "Yes, I verily believe that your poor father will be disappointed! But you will have seen Europe," he added humorously. "What a take-in!"

"I don't care for seeing Europe," Catherine said.

"You ought to care, my dear. And it may mollify your father."

Catherine, conscious of her obstinacy, expected little of

this, and could not rid herself of the idea that in going abroad and yet remaining firm, she should play her father a trick. "Don't you think it would be a kind of deception?" she asked.

"Doesn't he want to deceive you?" cried Morris. "It will serve him right! I really think you had better go."

"And not be married for so long?"

"Be married when you come back. You can buy your wedding-clothes in Paris." And then Morris, with great kindness of tone, explained his view of the matter. It would be a good thing that she should go; it would put them completely in the right. It would show they were reasonable and willing to wait. Once they were so sure of each other, they could afford to wait—what had they to fear? If there was a particle of chance that her father would be favourably affected by her going, that ought to settle it; for, after all, Morris was very unwilling to be the cause of her being disinherited. It was not for himself, it was for her and for her children. He was willing to wait for her; it would be hard, but he could do it. And over there, among beautiful scenes and noble monuments, perhaps the old gentleman would be softened; such things were supposed to exert a humanising influence. He might be touched by her gentleness, her patience, her willingness to make any sacrifice but *that* one; and if she should appeal to him some day, in some celebrated spot—in Italy, say, in the evening; in Venice, in a gondola, by moonlight—if she should be a little clever about it and touch the right chord, perhaps he would fold her in his arms and tell her that he forgave her. Catherine was immensely struck with this conception of the affair, which seemed eminently worthy of her lover's brilliant intellect; though she viewed it askance in so far as it depended upon her own powers of execution. The idea of being "clever" in a gondola by moonlight appeared to her to involve elements of which her grasp was not active. But it was settled between them that she should tell her father that she was ready to follow him obediently anywhere, making the mental reservation that she loved Morris Townsend more than ever.

She informed the Doctor she was ready to embark, and he made rapid arrangements for this event. Catherine had many farewells to make, but with only two of them are we actively concerned. Mrs. Penniman took a discriminating view of her niece's journey; it seemed to her very proper that Mr. Townsend's destined bride should wish to embellish her mind by a foreign tour.

"You leave him in good hands," she said, pressing her lips to Catherine's forehead. (She was very fond of kissing people's foreheads; it was an involuntary expression of sympathy with the intellectual part.) "I shall see him often; I shall feel like one of the vestals of old, tending the sacred flame."

"You behave beautifully about not going with us," Catherine answered, not presuming to examine this analogy.

"It is my pride that keeps me up," said Mrs. Penniman, tapping the body of her dress, which always gave forth a sort of metallic ring.

Catherine's parting with her lover was short, and few words were exchanged.

"Shall I find you just the same when I come back?" she asked; though the question was not the fruit of scepticism.

"The same—only more so!" said Morris, smiling.

It does not enter into our scheme to narrate in detail Dr. Sloper's proceedings in the Eastern hemisphere. He made the grand tour of Europe, travelled in considerable splendour, and (as was to have been expected in a man of his high cultivation) found so much in art and antiquity to interest him, that he remained abroad, not for six months, but for twelve. Mrs. Penniman, in Washington Square, accommodated herself to his absence. She enjoyed her uncontested dominion in the empty house, and flattered herself that she made it more attractive to their friends than when her brother was at home. To Morris Townsend, at least, it would have appeared that she made it singularly attractive. He was altogether her most frequent visitor, and Mrs. Penniman was very fond of asking him to tea. He had his chair—a very easy one—at the fireside in the back-parlour (when the great mahogany sliding-doors, with silver knobs and hinges, which divided this apartment from its more formal neighbour, were closed), and he used to smoke cigars in the Doctor's study, where he often spent an hour in turning over the curious collections of its absent proprietor. He thought Mrs. Penniman a goose, as we know; but he was no goose himself, and, as a young man of luxurious

tastes and scanty resources, he found the house a perfect castle
of indolence. It became for him a club with a single member.
Mrs. Penniman saw much less of her sister than while the
Doctor was at home; for Mrs. Almond had felt moved to tell
her that she disapproved of her relations with Mr. Townsend.
She had no business to be so friendly to a young man of
whom their brother thought so meanly, and Mrs. Almond
was surprised at her levity in foisting a most deplorable engagement upon Catherine.

"Deplorable?" cried Lavinia. "He will make her a lovely
husband!"

"I don't believe in lovely husbands," said Mrs. Almond; "I
only believe in good ones. If he marries her, and she comes
into Austin's money, they may get on. He will be an idle,
amiable, selfish, and doubtless tolerably good-natured fellow.
But if she doesn't get the money and he finds himself tied to
her, Heaven have mercy on her! He will have none. He will
hate her for his disappointment, and take his revenge; he will
be pitiless and cruel. Woe betide poor Catherine! I recommend you to talk a little with his sister; it's a pity Catherine
can't marry *her*!"

Mrs. Penniman had no appetite whatever for conversation
with Mrs. Montgomery, whose acquaintance she made no
trouble to cultivate; and the effect of this alarming forecast of
her niece's destiny was to make her think it indeed a thousand
pities that Mr. Townsend's generous nature should be embittered. Bright enjoyment was his natural element, and how
could he be comfortable if there should prove to be nothing
to enjoy? It became a fixed idea with Mrs. Penniman that he
should yet enjoy her brother's fortune, on which she had
acuteness enough to perceive that her own claim was small.

"If he doesn't leave it to Catherine, it certainly won't be to
leave it to me," she said.

XXIV

THE DOCTOR, during the first six months he was abroad, never spoke to his daughter of their little difference; partly on system, and partly because he had a great many other things to think about. It was idle to attempt to ascertain the state of her affections without direct inquiry, because, if she had not had an expressive manner among the familiar influences of home, she failed to gather animation from the mountains of Switzerland or the monuments of Italy. She was always her father's docile and reasonable associate—going through their sight-seeing in deferential silence, never complaining of fatigue, always ready to start at the hour he had appointed over-night, making no foolish criticisms and indulging in no refinements of appreciation. "She is about as intelligent as the bundle of shawls," the Doctor said; her main superiority being that while the bundle of shawls sometimes got lost, or tumbled out of the carriage, Catherine was always at her post, and had a firm and ample seat. But her father had expected this, and he was not constrained to set down her intellectual limitations as a tourist to sentimental depression; she had completely divested herself of the characteristics of a victim, and during the whole time that they were abroad she never uttered an audible sigh. He supposed she was in correspondence with Morris Townsend; but he held his peace about it, for he never saw the young man's letters, and Catherine's own missives were always given to the courier to post. She heard from her lover with considerable regularity, but his letters came enclosed in Mrs. Penniman's; so that whenever the Doctor handed her a packet addressed in his sister's hand, he was an involuntary instrument of the passion he condemned. Catherine made this reflection, and six months earlier she would have felt bound to give him warning; but now she deemed herself absolved. There was a sore spot in her heart that his own words had made when once she spoke to him as she thought honour prompted; she would try and please him as far as she could, but she would never speak that way again. She read her lover's letters in secret.

One day, at the end of the summer, the two travellers

found themselves in a lonely valley of the Alps. They were crossing one of the passes, and on the long ascent they had got out of the carriage and had wandered much in advance. After a while the Doctor descried a footpath which, leading through a transverse valley, would bring them out, as he justly supposed, at a much higher point of the ascent. They followed this devious way and finally lost the path; the valley proved very wild and rough, and their walk became rather a scramble. They were good walkers, however, and they took their adventure easily; from time to time they stopped, that Catherine might rest; and then she sat upon a stone and looked about her at the hard-featured rocks and the glowing sky. It was late in the afternoon, in the last of August; night was coming on, and, as they had reached a great elevation, the air was cold and sharp. In the west there was a great suffusion of cold, red light, which made the sides of the little valley look only the more rugged and dusky. During one of their pauses, her father left her and wandered away to some high place, at a distance, to get a view. He was out of sight; she sat there alone, in the stillness, which was just touched by the vague murmur, somewhere, of a mountain brook. She thought of Morris Townsend, and the place was so desolate and lonely that he seemed very far away. Her father remained absent a long time; she began to wonder what had become of him. But at last he reappeared, coming towards her in the clear twilight, and she got up, to go on. He made no motion to proceed, however, but came close to her, as if he had something to say. He stopped in front of her and stood looking at her, with eyes that had kept the light of the flushing snow-summits on which they had just been fixed. Then, abruptly, in a low tone, he asked her an unexpected question—

"Have you given him up?"

The question was unexpected, but Catherine was only superficially unprepared.

"No, father!" she answered.

He looked at her again, for some moments, without speaking.

"Does he write to you?" he asked.

"Yes—about twice a month."

The Doctor looked up and down the valley, swinging his stick; then he said to her, in the same low tone—

"I am very angry."

She wondered what he meant—whether he wished to frighten her. If he did, the place was well chosen; this hard, melancholy dell, abandoned by the summer light, made her feel her loneliness. She looked around her, and her heart grew cold; for a moment her fear was great. But she could think of nothing to say, save to murmur gently, "I am sorry."

"You try my patience," her father went on, "and you ought to know what I am. I am not a very good man. Though I am very smooth externally, at bottom I am very passionate; and I assure you I can be very hard."

She could not think why he told her these things. Had he brought her there on purpose, and was it part of a plan? What was the plan? Catherine asked herself. Was it to startle her suddenly into a retraction—to take an advantage of her by dread? Dread of what? The place was ugly and lonely, but the place could do her no harm. There was a kind of still intensity about her father which made him dangerous, but Catherine hardly went so far as to say to herself that it might be part of his plan to fasten his hand—the neat, fine, supple hand of a distinguished physician—in her throat. Nevertheless, she receded a step. "I am sure you can be anything you please," she said. And it was her simple belief.

"I am very angry," he replied, more sharply.

"Why has it taken you so suddenly?"

"It has not taken me suddenly. I have been raging inwardly for the last six months. But just now this seemed a good place to flare out. It's so quiet, and we are alone."

"Yes, it's very quiet," said Catherine vaguely, looking about her. "Won't you come back to the carriage?"

"In a moment. Do you mean that in all this time you have not yielded an inch?"

"I would if I could, father; but I can't."

The Doctor looked round him too. "Should you like to be left in such a place as this, to starve?"

"What do you mean?" cried the girl.

"That will be your fate—that's how he will leave you."

He would not touch her, but he had touched Morris. The

warmth came back to her heart. "That is not true, father," she broke out, "and you ought not to say it! It is not right, and it's not true!"

He shook his head slowly. "No, it's not right, because you won't believe it. But it *is* true. Come back to the carriage."

He turned away, and she followed him; he went faster, and was presently much in advance. But from time to time he stopped, without turning round, to let her keep up with him, and she made her way forward with difficulty, her heart beating with the excitement of having for the first time spoken to him in violence. By this time it had grown almost dark, and she ended by losing sight of him. But she kept her course, and after a little, the valley making a sudden turn, she gained the road, where the carriage stood waiting. In it sat her father, rigid and silent; in silence, too, she took her place beside him.

It seemed to her, later, in looking back upon all this, that for days afterwards not a word had been exchanged between them. The scene had been a strange one, but it had not permanently affected her feeling towards her father, for it was natural, after all, that he should occasionally make a scene of some kind, and he had let her alone for six months. The strangest part of it was that he had said he was not a good man; Catherine wondered a great deal what he had meant by that. The statement failed to appeal to her credence, and it was not grateful to any resentment that she entertained. Even in the utmost bitterness that she might feel, it would give her no satisfaction to think him less complete. Such a saying as that was a part of his great subtlety—men so clever as he might say anything and mean anything. And as to his being hard, that surely, in a man, was a virtue.

He let her alone for six months more—six months during which she accommodated herself without a protest to the extension of their tour. But he spoke again at the end of this time; it was at the very last, the night before they embarked for New York, in the hotel at Liverpool. They had been dining together in a great dim, musty sitting-room; and then the cloth had been removed, and the Doctor walked slowly up and down. Catherine at last took her candle to go to bed, but her father motioned her to stay.

"What do you mean to do when you get home?" he asked, while she stood there with her candle in her hand.

"Do you mean about Mr. Townsend?"

"About Mr. Townsend."

"We shall probably marry."

The Doctor took several turns again while she waited. "Do you hear from him as much as ever?"

"Yes; twice a month," said Catherine, promptly.

"And does he always talk about marriage?"

"Oh, yes! That is, he talks about other things too, but he always says something about that."

"I am glad to hear he varies his subjects; his letters might otherwise be monotonous."

"He writes beautifully," said Catherine, who was very glad of a chance to say it.

"They always write beautifully. However, in a given case that doesn't diminish the merit. So, as soon as you arrive, you are going off with him?"

This seemed a rather gross way of putting it, and something that there was of dignity in Catherine resented it. "I cannot tell you till we arrive," she said.

"That's reasonable enough," her father answered. "That's all I ask of you—that you *do* tell me, that you give me definite notice. When a poor man is to lose his only child, he likes to have an inkling of it beforehand."

"Oh, father, you will not lose me!" Catherine said, spilling her candle-wax.

"Three days before will do," he went on, "if you are in a position to be positive then. He ought to be very thankful to me, do you know. I have done a mighty good thing for him in taking you abroad; your value is twice as great, with all the knowledge and taste that you have acquired. A year ago, you were perhaps a little limited—a little rustic; but now you have seen everything, and appreciated everything, and you will be a most entertaining companion. We have fattened the sheep for him before he kills it!" Catherine turned away, and stood staring at the blank door. "Go to bed," said her father; "and, as we don't go aboard till noon, you may sleep late. We shall probably have a most uncomfortable voyage."

XXV

T HE VOYAGE was indeed uncomfortable, and Catherine, on arriving in New York, had not the compensation of "going off," in her father's phrase, with Morris Townsend. She saw him, however, the day after she landed; and, in the meantime, he formed a natural subject of conversation between our heroine and her Aunt Lavinia, with whom, the night she disembarked, the girl was closeted for a long time before either lady retired to rest.

"I have seen a great deal of him," said Mrs. Penniman. "He is not very easy to know. I suppose you think you know him; but you don't, my dear. You will some day; but it will only be after you have lived with him. I may almost say *I* have lived with him," Mrs. Penniman proceeded, while Catherine stared. "I think I know him now; I have had such remarkable opportunities. You will have the same—or rather, you will have better!" and Aunt Lavinia smiled. "Then you will see what I mean. It's a wonderful character, full of passion and energy, and just as true!"

Catherine listened with a mixture of interest and apprehension. Aunt Lavinia was intensely sympathetic, and Catherine, for the past year, while she wandered through foreign galleries and churches, and rolled over the smoothness of posting roads, nursing the thoughts that never passed her lips, had often longed for the company of some intelligent person of her own sex. To tell her story to some kind woman—at moments it seemed to her that this would give her comfort, and she had more than once been on the point of taking the landlady, or the nice young person from the dressmaker's, into her confidence. If a woman had been near her she would on certain occasions have treated such a companion to a fit of weeping; and she had an apprehension that, on her return, this would form her response to Aunt Lavinia's first embrace. In fact, however, the two ladies had met, in Washington Square, without tears, and when they found themselves alone together a certain dryness fell upon the girl's emotion. It came over her with a greater force that Mrs. Penniman had enjoyed a whole year of her lover's society, and it was not a pleasure to her to hear her aunt explain and interpret the young man, speaking of him as if her own knowledge of him were supreme. It was not that Catherine was jealous; but her sense of Mrs. Penniman's innocent falsity, which had lain dormant, began to haunt her again, and she was glad that she was safely at home. With this, however, it was a blessing to be able to talk of Morris, to sound his name, to be with a person who was not unjust to him.

"You have been very kind to him," said Catherine. "He has written me that, often. I shall never forget that, Aunt Lavinia."

"I have done what I could; it has been very little. To let him come and talk to me, and give him his cup of tea—that was all. Your Aunt Almond thought it was too much, and used to scold me terribly; but she promised me, at least, not to betray me."

"To betray you?"

"Not to tell your father. He used to sit in your father's study!" said Mrs. Penniman, with a little laugh.

Catherine was silent a moment. This idea was disagreeable to her, and she was reminded again, with pain, of her aunt's secretive habits. Morris, the reader may be informed, had had the tact not to tell her that he sat in her father's study. He had known her but for a few months, and her aunt had known her for fifteen years; and yet he would not have made the mistake of thinking that Catherine would see the joke of the thing. "I am sorry you made him go into father's room," she said, after a while.

"I didn't make him go; he went himself. He liked to look at the books, and at all those things in the glass cases. He knows all about them; he knows all about everything."

Catherine was silent again; then, "I wish he had found some employment," she said.

"He has found some employment! It's beautiful news, and he told me to tell you as soon as you arrived. He has gone into partnership with a commission-merchant. It was all settled, quite suddenly, a week ago."

This seemed to Catherine indeed beautiful news; it had a fine prosperous air. "Oh, I'm so glad!" she said; and now, for a moment, she was disposed to throw herself on Aunt Lavinia's neck.

"It's much better than being under some one; and he has never been used to that," Mrs. Penniman went on. "He is just as good as his partner—they are perfectly equal! You see how right he was to wait. I should like to know what your father can say now! They have got an office in Duane Street, and little printed cards; he brought me one to show me. I have got it in my room, and you shall see it to-morrow. That's what he said to me the last time he was here—'You see how right I was to wait!' He has got other people under him, instead of being a subordinate. He could never be a subordinate; I have often told him I could never think of him in that way."

Catherine assented to this proposition, and was very happy to know that Morris was his own master; but she was deprived of the satisfaction of thinking that she might communicate this news in triumph to her father. Her father would care equally little whether Morris were established in business or transported for life. Her trunks had been brought into her room, and further reference to her lover was for a short time suspended, while she opened them and displayed to her aunt some of the spoils of foreign travel. These were rich and abundant; and Catherine had brought home a present to every one—to every one save Morris, to whom she had brought simply her undiverted heart. To Mrs. Penniman she had been lavishly generous, and Aunt Lavinia spent half-an-hour in unfolding and folding again, with little ejaculations of gratitude and taste. She marched about for some time in a splendid cashmere shawl, which Catherine had begged her to accept, settling it on her shoulders, and twisting down her head to see how low the point descended behind.

"I shall regard it only as a loan," she said. "I will leave it to you again when I die; or rather," she added, kissing her niece again, "I will leave it to your first-born little girl!" And draped in her shawl, she stood there smiling.

"You had better wait till she comes," said Catherine.

"I don't like the way you say that," Mrs. Penniman rejoined, in a moment. "Catherine, are you changed?"

"No; I am the same."

"You have not swerved a line?"

"I am exactly the same," Catherine repeated, wishing her aunt were a little less sympathetic.

"Well, I am glad!" and Mrs. Penniman surveyed her cashmere in the glass. Then, "How is your father?" she asked in a moment, with her eyes on her niece. "Your letters were so meagre—I could never tell!"

"Father is very well."

"Ah, you know what I mean," said Mrs. Penniman, with a dignity to which the cashmere gave a richer effect. "Is he still implacable?"

"Oh, yes!"

"Quite unchanged?"

"He is, if possible, more firm."

Mrs. Penniman took off her great shawl, and slowly folded it up. "That is very bad. You had no success with your little project?"

"What little project?"

"Morris told me all about it. The idea of turning the tables on him, in Europe; of watching him, when he was agreeably impressed by some celebrated sight—he pretends to be so artistic, you know—and then just pleading with him and bringing him round."

"I never tried it. It was Morris's idea; but if he had been with us, in Europe, he would have seen that father was never impressed in that way. He *is* artistic—tremendously artistic; but the more celebrated places we visited, and the more he admired them, the less use it would have been to plead with him. They seemed only to make him more determined—more terrible," said poor Catherine. "I shall never bring him round, and I expect nothing now."

"Well, I must say," Mrs. Penniman answered, "I never supposed you were going to give it up."

"I have given it up. I don't care now."

"You have grown very brave," said Mrs. Penniman, with a short laugh. "I didn't advise you to sacrifice your property."

"Yes, I am braver than I was. You asked me if I had changed; I have changed in that way. Oh," the girl went on, "I have changed very much. And it isn't my property. If *he* doesn't care for it, why should I?"

Mrs. Penniman hesitated. "Perhaps he does care for it."

"He cares for it for my sake, because he doesn't want to injure me. But he will know—he knows already—how little he need be afraid about that. Besides," said Catherine, "I have got plenty of money of my own. We shall be very well off; and now hasn't he got his business? I am delighted about that business." She went on talking, showing a good deal of excitement as she proceeded. Her aunt had never seen her with just this manner, and Mrs. Penniman, observing her, set it down to foreign travel, which had made her more positive, more mature. She thought also that Catherine had improved in appearance; she looked rather handsome. Mrs. Penniman wondered whether Morris Townsend would be struck with that. While she was engaged in this speculation, Catherine broke out, with a certain sharpness, "Why are you so contradictory, Aunt Penniman? You seem to think one thing at one time, and another at another. A year ago, before I went away, you wished me not to mind about displeasing father; and now you seem to recommend me to take another line. You change about so."

This attack was unexpected, for Mrs. Penniman was not used, in any discussion, to seeing the war carried into her own country—possibly because the enemy generally had doubts of finding subsistence there. To her own consciousness, the flowery fields of her reason had rarely been ravaged by a hostile force. It was perhaps on this account that in defending them she was majestic rather than agile.

"I don't know what you accuse me of, save of being too deeply interested in your happiness. It is the first time I have been told I am capricious. That fault is not what I am usually reproached with."

"You were angry last year that I wouldn't marry immediately, and now you talk about my winning my father over. You told me it would serve him right if he should take me to Europe for nothing. Well, he has taken me for nothing, and you ought to be satisfied. Nothing is changed—nothing but my feeling about father. I don't mind nearly so much now. I have been as good as I could, but he doesn't care. Now I don't care either. I don't know whether I have grown bad; perhaps I have. But I don't care for that. I have come home to be married—that's all I know. That ought to please you, unless you have taken up some new idea; you are so strange. You may do as you please; but you must never speak to me again about pleading with father. I shall never plead with him for anything; that is all over. He has put me off. I am come home to be married."

This was a more authoritative speech than she had ever heard on her niece's lips, and Mrs. Penniman was proportionately startled. She was indeed a little awe-struck, and the force of the girl's emotion and resolution left her nothing to reply. She was easily frightened, and she always carried off her discomfiture by a concession; a concession which was often accompanied, as in the present case, by a little nervous laugh.

XXVI

I F SHE HAD disturbed her niece's temper—she began from
this moment forward to talk a good deal about Catherine's
temper, an article which up to that time had never been mentioned in connection with our heroine—Catherine had opportunity, on the morrow, to recover her serenity. Mrs.
Penniman had given her a message from Morris Townsend,
to the effect that he would come and welcome her home on
the day after her arrival. He came in the afternoon; but, as
may be imagined, he was not on this occasion made free of
Dr. Sloper's study. He had been coming and going, for the
past year, so comfortably and irresponsibly, that he had a certain sense of being wronged by finding himself reminded that
he must now limit his horizon to the front-parlour, which
was Catherine's particular province.

"I am very glad you have come back," he said; "it makes
me very happy to see you again." And he looked at her, smiling, from head to foot; though it did not appear, afterwards,
that he agreed with Mrs. Penniman (who, womanlike, went
more into details) in thinking her embellished.

To Catherine he appeared resplendent; it was some time
before she could believe again that this beautiful young man
was her own exclusive property. They had a great deal of
characteristic lovers' talk—a soft exchange of inquiries and
assurances. In these matters Morris had an excellent grace,
which flung a picturesque interest even over the account of
his début in the commission-business—a subject as to which
his companion earnestly questioned him. From time to time
he got up from the sofa where they sat together, and walked
about the room; after which he came back, smiling and passing his hand through his hair. He was unquiet, as was natural
in a young man who has just been re-united to a long-absent
mistress, and Catherine made the reflection that she had never
seen him so excited. It gave her pleasure, somehow, to note
this fact. He asked her questions about her travels, to some
of which she was unable to reply, for she had forgotten the
names of places and the order of her father's journey. But for
the moment she was so happy, so lifted up by the belief that

her troubles at last were over, that she forgot to be ashamed of her meagre answers. It seemed to her now that she could marry him without the remnant of a scruple or a single tremor save those that belonged to joy. Without waiting for him to ask, she told him that her father had come back in exactly the same state of mind—that he had not yielded an inch.

"We must not expect it now," she said, "and we must do without it."

Morris sat looking and smiling. "My poor dear girl!" he exclaimed.

"You mustn't pity me," said Catherine; "I don't mind it now—I am used to it."

Morris continued to smile, and then he got up and walked about again. "You had better let me try him!"

"Try to bring him over? You would only make him worse," Catherine answered, resolutely.

"You say that because I managed it so badly before. But I should manage it differently now. I am much wiser; I have had a year to think of it. I have more tact."

"Is that what you have been thinking of for a year?"

"Much of the time. You see, the idea sticks in my crop. I don't like to be beaten."

"How are you beaten if we marry?"

"Of course, I am not beaten on the main issue; but I am, don't you see, on all the rest of it—on the question of my reputation, of my relations with your father, of my relations with my own children, if we should have any."

"We shall have enough for our children—we shall have enough for everything. Don't you expect to succeed in business?"

"Brilliantly, and we shall certainly be very comfortable. But it isn't of the mere material comfort I speak; it is of the moral comfort," said Morris—"of the intellectual satisfaction!"

"I have great moral comfort now," Catherine declared, very simply.

"Of course you have. But with me it is different. I have staked my pride on proving to your father that he is wrong; and now that I am at the head of a flourishing business, I can deal with him as an equal. I have a capital plan—do let me go at him!"

He stood before her with his bright face, his jaunty air, his hands in his pockets; and she got up, with her eyes resting on his own. "Please don't, Morris; please don't," she said; and there was a certain mild, sad firmness in her tone which he heard for the first time. "We must ask no favours of him— we must ask nothing more. He won't relent, and nothing good will come of it. I know it now—I have a very good reason."

"And pray what is your reason?"

She hesitated to bring it out, but at last it came. "He is not very fond of me!"

"Oh, bother!" cried Morris, angrily.

"I wouldn't say such a thing without being sure. I saw it, I felt it, in England, just before he came away. He talked to me one night—the last night; and then it came over me. You can tell when a person feels that way. I wouldn't accuse him if he hadn't made me feel that way. I don't accuse him; I just tell you that that's how it is. He can't help it; we can't govern our affections. Do I govern mine? mightn't he say that to me? It's because he is so fond of my mother, whom we lost so long ago. She was beautiful, and very, very brilliant; he is always thinking of her. I am not at all like her; Aunt Penniman has told me that. Of course it isn't my fault; but neither is it his fault. All I mean is, it's true; and it's a stronger reason for his never being reconciled than simply his dislike for you."

" 'Simply?' " cried Morris, with a laugh. "I am much obliged for that!"

"I don't mind about his disliking you now; I mind everything less. I feel differently; I feel separated from my father."

"Upon my word," said Morris, "you are a queer family!"

"Don't say that—don't say anything unkind," the girl entreated. "You must be very kind to me now, because, Morris—because," and she hesitated a moment—"because I have done a great deal for you."

"Oh, I know that, my dear!"

She had spoken up to this moment without vehemence or outward sign of emotion, gently, reasoningly, only trying to explain. But her emotion had been ineffectually smothered, and it betrayed itself at last in the trembling of her voice. "It is a great thing to be separated like that from your father, when you have worshipped him before. It has made me very unhappy; or it would have made me so if I didn't love you. You can tell when a person speaks to you as if—as if——"

"As if what?"

"As if they despised you!" said Catherine, passionately. "He spoke that way the night before we sailed. It wasn't much, but it was enough, and I thought of it on the voyage, all the time. Then I made up my mind. I will never ask him for anything again, or expect anything from him. It would not be natural now. We must be very happy together, and we must not seem to depend upon his forgiveness. And Morris, Morris, you must never despise me!"

This was an easy promise to make, and Morris made it with fine effect. But for the moment he undertook nothing more onerous.

XXVII

THE DOCTOR, of course, on his return, had a good deal of talk with his sisters. He was at no great pains to narrate his travels or to communicate his impressions of distant lands to Mrs. Penniman, upon whom he contented himself with bestowing a memento of his enviable experience, in the shape of a velvet gown. But he conversed with her at some length about matters nearer home, and lost no time in assuring her that he was still an inflexible father.

"I have no doubt you have seen a great deal of Mr. Townsend, and done your best to console him for Catherine's absence," he said. "I don't ask you, and you needn't deny it. I wouldn't put the question to you for the world, and expose you to the inconvenience of having to—a—excogitate an answer. No one has betrayed you, and there has been no spy upon your proceedings. Elizabeth has told no tales, and has never mentioned you except to praise your good looks and good spirits. The thing is simply an inference of my own—an induction, as the philosophers say. It seems to me likely that you would have offered an asylum to an interesting sufferer. Mr. Townsend has been a good deal in the house; there is something in the house that tells me so. We doctors, you know, end by acquiring fine perceptions, and it is impressed upon my sensorium that he has sat in these chairs, in a very easy attitude, and warmed himself at that fire. I don't grudge him the comfort of it; it is the only one he will ever enjoy at my expense. It seems likely, indeed, that I shall be able to economise at his own. I don't know what you may have said to him, or what you may say hereafter; but I should like you to know that if you have encouraged him to believe that he will gain anything by hanging on, or that I have budged a hair's breadth from the position I took up a year ago, you have played him a trick for which he may exact reparation. I'm not sure that he may not bring a suit against you. Of course you have done it conscientiously; you have made yourself believe that I can be tired out. This is the most baseless hallucination that ever visited the brain of a genial optimist. I am not in the least tired; I am as fresh as when I started; I am good for fifty years yet. Catherine appears not to have budged an inch either; she is equally fresh; so we are about where we were before. This, however, you know as well as I. What I wish is simply to give you notice of my own state of mind! Take it to heart, dear Lavinia. Beware of the just resentment of a deluded fortune-hunter!"

"I can't say I expected it," said Mrs. Penniman. "And I had a sort of foolish hope that you would come home without that odious ironical tone with which you treat the most sacred subjects."

"Don't undervalue irony, it is often of great use. It is not, however, always necessary, and I will show you how gracefully I can lay it aside. I should like to know whether you think Morris Townsend will hang on."

"I will answer you with your own weapons," said Mrs. Penniman. "You had better wait and see!"

"Do you call such a speech as that one of my own weapons? I never said anything so rough."

"He will hang on long enough to make you very uncomfortable, then."

"My dear Lavinia," exclaimed the Doctor, "do you call that irony? I call it pugilism."

Mrs. Penniman, however, in spite of her pugilism, was a good deal frightened, and she took counsel of her fears. Her brother meanwhile took counsel, with many reservations, of Mrs. Almond, to whom he was no less generous than to Lavinia, and a good deal more communicative.

"I suppose she has had him there all the while," he said. "I must look into the state of my wine! You needn't mind telling me now; I have already said all I mean to say to her on the subject."

"I believe he was in the house a good deal," Mrs. Almond answered. "But you must admit that your leaving Lavinia quite alone was a great change for her, and that it was natural she should want some society."

"I do admit that, and that is why I shall make no row about the wine; I shall set it down as compensation to Lavinia. She is capable of telling me that she drank it all herself. Think of the inconceivable bad taste, in the circumstances, of that fellow making free with the house—or coming there at all! If that doesn't describe him, he is indescribable."

"His plan is to get what he can. Lavinia will have supported him for a year," said Mrs. Almond. "It's so much gained."

"She will have to support him for the rest of his life, then!" cried the Doctor. "But without wine, as they say at the *tables d'hôte*."

"Catherine tells me he has set up a business, and is making a great deal of money."

The Doctor stared. "She has not told me that—and Lavinia didn't deign. Ah!" he cried, "Catherine has given me up. Not that it matters, for all that the business amounts to."

"She has not given up Mr. Townsend," said Mrs. Almond. "I saw that in the first half-minute. She has come home exactly the same."

"Exactly the same; not a grain more intelligent. She didn't notice a stick or a stone all the while we were away—not a picture nor a view, not a statue nor a cathedral."

"How could she notice? She had other things to think of; they are never for an instant out of her mind. She touches me very much."

"She would touch me if she didn't irritate me. That's the effect she has upon me now. I have tried everything upon her; I really have been quite merciless. But it is of no use whatever; she is absolutely *glued*. I have passed, in consequence, into the exasperated stage. At first I had a good deal of a certain genial curiosity about it; I wanted to see if she really would stick. But, good Lord, one's curiosity is satisfied! I see she is capable of it, and now she can let go."

"She will never let go," said Mrs. Almond.

"Take care, or you will exasperate me too. If she doesn't let go, she will be shaken off—sent tumbling into the dust! That's a nice position for my daughter. She can't see that if you are going to be pushed you had better jump. And then she will complain of her bruises."

"She will never complain," said Mrs. Almond.

"That I shall object to even more. But the deuce will be that I can't prevent anything."

"If she is to have a fall," said Mrs. Almond, with a gentle

laugh, "we must spread as many carpets as we can." And she carried out this idea by showing a great deal of motherly kindness to the girl.

Mrs. Penniman immediately wrote to Morris Townsend. The intimacy between these two was by this time consummate, but I must content myself with noting but a few of its features. Mrs. Penniman's own share in it was a singular sentiment, which might have been misinterpreted, but which in itself was not discreditable to the poor lady. It was a romantic interest in this attractive and unfortunate young man, and yet it was not such an interest as Catherine might have been jealous of. Mrs. Penniman had not a particle of jealousy of her niece. For herself, she felt as if she were Morris's mother or sister—a mother or sister of an emotional temperament—and she had an absorbing desire to make him comfortable and happy. She had striven to do so during the year that her brother left her an open field, and her efforts had been attended with the success that has been pointed out. She had never had a child of her own, and Catherine, whom she had done her best to invest with the importance that would naturally belong to a youthful Penniman, had only partly rewarded her zeal. Catherine, as an object of affection and solicitude, had never had that picturesque charm which (as it seemed to her) would have been a natural attribute of her own progeny. Even the maternal passion in Mrs. Penniman would have been romantic and factitious, and Catherine was not constituted to inspire a romantic passion. Mrs. Penniman was as fond of her as ever, but she had grown to feel that with Catherine she lacked opportunity. Sentimentally speaking, therefore, she had (though she had not disinherited her niece) adopted Morris Townsend, who gave her opportunity in abundance. She would have been very happy to have a handsome and tyrannical son, and would have taken an extreme interest in his love affairs. This was the light in which she had come to regard Morris, who had conciliated her at first, and made his impression by his delicate and calculated deference—a sort of exhibition to which Mrs. Penniman was particularly sensitive. He had largely abated his deference afterwards, for he economised his resources, but the impression was made, and the young man's very brutality came to have a sort of filial value. If Mrs. Penniman had had a son, she would probably have been afraid of him, and at this stage of our narrative she was certainly afraid of Morris Townsend. This was one of the results of his domestication in Washington Square. He took his ease with her—as, for that matter, he would certainly have done with his own mother.

XXVIII

T HE LETTER was a word of warning; it informed him that
the Doctor had come home more impracticable than
ever. She might have reflected that Catherine would supply
him with all the information he needed on this point; but we
know that Mrs. Penniman's reflections were rarely just; and,
moreover, she felt that it was not for her to depend on what
Catherine might do. She was to do her duty, quite irrespec-
tive of Catherine. I have said that her young friend took his
ease with her, and it is an illustration of the fact that he made
no answer to her letter. He took note of it, amply; but he
lighted his cigar with it, and he waited, in tranquil confidence
that he should receive another. "His state of mind really
freezes my blood," Mrs. Penniman had written, alluding to
her brother; and it would have seemed that upon this statement she could hardly improve. Nevertheless, she wrote
again, expressing herself with the aid of a different figure.
"His hatred of you burns with a lurid flame—the flame that
never dies," she wrote. "But it doesn't light up the darkness
of your future. If my affection could do so, all the years of
your life would be an eternal sunshine. I can extract nothing
from C.; she is so terribly secretive, like her father. She seems
to expect to be married very soon, and has evidently made
preparations in Europe—quantities of clothing, ten pairs of
shoes, etc. My dear friend, you cannot set up in married life
simply with a few pairs of shoes, can you? Tell me what you
think of this. I am intensely anxious to see you; I have so
much to say. I miss you dreadfully; the house seems so empty
without you. What is the news down town? Is the business
extending? That dear little business—I think it's so brave of
you! Couldn't I come to your office?—just for three minutes?
I might pass for a customer—is that what you call them? I
might come in to buy something—some shares or some rail-
road things. *Tell me what you think of this plan.* I would carry
a little reticule, like a woman of the people."

In spite of the suggestion about the reticule, Morris appeared to think poorly of the plan, for he gave Mrs. Penniman no encouragement whatever to visit his office, which he

had already represented to her as a place peculiarly and unnaturally difficult to find. But as she persisted in desiring an
interview—up to the last, after months of intimate colloquy,
she called these meetings "interviews"—he agreed that they
should take a walk together, and was even kind enough to
leave his office for this purpose, during the hours at which
business might have been supposed to be liveliest. It was no
surprise to him, when they met at a street-corner, in a region
of empty lots and undeveloped pavements (Mrs. Penniman
being attired as much as possible like a "woman of the people"), to find that, in spite of her urgency, what she chiefly
had to convey to him was the assurance of her sympathy. Of
such assurances, however, he had already a voluminous collection, and it would not have been worth his while to forsake
a fruitful avocation merely to hear Mrs. Penniman say, for the
thousandth time, that she had made his cause her own. Morris had something of his own to say. It was not an easy thing
to bring out, and while he turned it over the difficulty made
him acrimonious.

"Oh yes, I know perfectly that he combines the properties
of a lump of ice and a red-hot coal," he observed. "Catherine
has made it thoroughly clear, and you have told me so till I
am sick of it. You needn't tell me again; I am perfectly satisfied. He will never give us a penny; I regard that as mathe-
matically proved."

Mrs. Penniman at this point had an inspiration.

"Couldn't you bring a lawsuit against him?" She wondered
that this simple expedient had never occurred to her before.

"I will bring a lawsuit against *you*," said Morris, "if you ask
me any more such aggravating questions. A man should
know when he is beaten," he added, in a moment. "I must
give her up!"

Mrs. Penniman received this declaration in silence, though
it made her heart beat a little. It found her by no means unprepared, for she had accustomed herself to the thought
that, if Morris should decidedly not be able to get her brother's money, it would not do for him to marry Catherine
without it. "It would not do" was a vague way of putting
the thing; but Mrs. Penniman's natural affection completed
the idea, which, though it had not as yet been so crudely

expressed between them as in the form that Morris had just given it, had nevertheless been implied so often, in certain easy intervals of talk, as he sat stretching his legs in the Doctor's well-stuffed arm-chairs, that she had grown first to regard it with an emotion which she flattered herself was philosophic, and then to have a secret tenderness for it. The fact that she kept her tenderness secret proves, of course, that she was ashamed of it; but she managed to blink her shame by reminding herself that she was, after all, the official protector of her niece's marriage. Her logic would scarcely have passed muster with the Doctor. In the first place, Morris *must* get the money, and she would help him to it. In the second, it was plain it would never come to him, and it would be a grievous pity he should marry without it—a young man who might so easily find something better. After her brother had delivered himself, on his return from Europe, of that incisive little address that has been quoted, Morris's cause seemed so hopeless that Mrs. Penniman fixed her attention exclusively upon the latter branch of her argument. If Morris had been her son, she would certainly have sacrificed Catherine to a superior conception of his future; and to be ready to do so as the case stood was therefore even a finer degree of devotion. Nevertheless, it checked her breath a little to have the sacrificial knife, as it were, suddenly thrust into her hand.

Morris walked along a moment, and then he repeated, harshly—

"I must give her up!"

"I think I understand you," said Mrs. Penniman, gently.

"I certainly say it distinctly enough—brutally and vulgarly enough."

He was ashamed of himself, and his shame was uncomfortable; and as he was extremely intolerant of discomfort, he felt vicious and cruel. He wanted to abuse somebody, and he began, cautiously—for he was always cautious—with himself.

"Couldn't you take her down a little?" he asked.

"Take her down?"

"Prepare her—try and ease me off."

Mrs. Penniman stopped, looking at him very solemnly.

"My poor Morris, do you know how much she loves you?"

"No, I don't. I don't want to know. I have always tried to keep from knowing. It would be too painful."

"She will suffer much," said Mrs. Penniman.

"You must console her. If you are as good a friend to me as you pretend to be, you will manage it."

Mrs. Penniman shook her head, sadly.

"You talk of my 'pretending' to like you; but I can't pretend to hate you. I can only tell her I think very highly of you; and how will that console her for losing you?"

"The Doctor will help you. He will be delighted at the thing being broken off, and, as he is a knowing fellow, he will invent something to comfort her."

"He will invent a new torture!" cried Mrs. Penniman. "Heaven deliver her from her father's comfort. It will consist of his crowing over her and saying, 'I always told you so!'"

Morris coloured a most uncomfortable red.

"If you don't console her any better than you console me, you certainly won't be of much use! It's a damned disagreeable necessity; I feel it extremely, and you ought to make it easy for me."

"I will be your friend for life!" Mrs. Penniman declared.

"Be my friend *now*!" And Morris walked on.

She went with him; she was almost trembling.

"Should you like me to tell her?" she asked.

"You mustn't tell her, but you can—you can——" And he hesitated, trying to think what Mrs. Penniman could do. "You can explain to her why it is. It's because I can't bring myself to step in between her and her father—to give him the pretext he grasps at so eagerly (it's a hideous sight) for depriving her of her rights."

Mrs. Penniman felt with remarkable promptitude the charm of this formula.

"That's so like you," she said; "it's so finely felt."

Morris gave his stick an angry swing.

"Oh botheration!" he exclaimed perversely.

Mrs. Penniman, however, was not discouraged.

"It may turn out better than you think. Catherine is, after all, so very peculiar." And she thought she might take it upon herself to assure him that, whatever happened, the girl would be very quiet—she wouldn't make a noise. They extended their walk, and, while they proceeded, Mrs. Penniman took upon herself other things besides, and ended by having assumed a considerable burden; Morris being ready enough, as may be imagined, to put everything off upon her. But he was not for a single instant the dupe of her blundering alacrity; he knew that of what she promised she was competent to perform but an insignificant fraction, and the more she professed her willingness to serve him, the greater fool he thought her.

"What will you do if you don't marry her?" she ventured to inquire in the course of this conversation.

"Something brilliant," said Morris. "Shouldn't you like me to do something brilliant?"

The idea gave Mrs. Penniman exceeding pleasure.

"I shall feel sadly taken in if you don't."

"I shall have to, to make up for this. This isn't at all brilliant, you know."

Mrs. Penniman mused a little, as if there might be some way of making out that it was; but she had to give up the attempt, and, to carry off the awkwardness of failure, she risked a new inquiry.

"Do you mean—do you mean another marriage?"

Morris greeted this question with a reflection which was hardly the less impudent from being inaudible. "Surely, women are more crude than men!" And then he answered audibly—

"Never in the world!"

Mrs. Penniman felt disappointed and snubbed, and she relieved herself in a little vaguely sarcastic cry. He was certainly perverse.

"I give her up not for another woman, but for a wider career!" Morris announced.

This was very grand; but still Mrs. Penniman, who felt that she had exposed herself, was faintly rancorous.

"Do you mean never to come to see her again?" she asked, with some sharpness.

"Oh no, I shall come again; but what is the use of dragging it out? I have been four times since she came back, and it's terribly awkward work. I can't keep it up indefinitely; she oughtn't to expect that, you know. A woman should never keep a man dangling!" he added, finely.

"Ah, but you must have your last parting!" urged his companion, in whose imagination the idea of last partings occupied a place inferior in dignity only to that of first meetings.

XXIX

HE CAME again, without managing the last parting; and again and again, without finding that Mrs. Penniman had as yet done much to pave the path of retreat with flowers. It was devilish awkward, as he said, and he felt a lively animosity for Catherine's aunt, who, as he had now quite formed the habit of saying to himself, had dragged him into the mess and was bound in common charity to get him out of it. Mrs. Penniman, to tell the truth, had, in the seclusion of her own apartment—and, I may add, amid the suggestiveness of Catherine's, which wore in those days the appearance of that of a young lady laying out her *trousseau*—Mrs. Penniman had measured her responsibilities, and taken fright at their magnitude. The task of preparing Catherine and easing off Morris presented difficulties which increased in the execution, and even led the impulsive Lavinia to ask herself whether the modification of the young man's original project had been conceived in a happy spirit. A brilliant future, a wider career, a conscience exempt from the reproach of interference between a young lady and her natural rights—these excellent things might be too troublesomely purchased. From Catherine herself Mrs. Penniman received no assistance whatever; the poor girl was apparently without suspicion of her danger. She looked at her lover with eyes of undiminished trust, and though she had less confidence in her aunt than in a young man with whom she had exchanged so many tender vows, she gave her no handle for explaining or confessing. Mrs. Penniman, faltering and wavering, declared Catherine was very stupid, put off the great scene, as she would have called it, from day to day, and wandered about very uncomfortably, primed, to repletion, with her apology, but unable to bring it to the light. Morris's own scenes were very small ones just now; but even these were beyond his strength. He made his visits as brief as possible, and, while he sat with his mistress, found terribly little to talk about. She was waiting for him, in vulgar parlance, to name the day; and so long as he was unprepared to be explicit on this point, it seemed a mockery to pretend to talk about matters more abstract. She had no airs and no arts; she never attempted to disguise her expectancy. She was waiting on his good pleasure, and would wait modestly and patiently; his hanging back at this supreme time might appear strange, but of course he must have a good reason for it. Catherine would have made a wife of the gentle old-fashioned pattern—regarding reasons as favours and windfalls, but no more expecting one every day than she would have expected a bouquet of camellias. During the period of her engagement, however, a young lady even of the most slender pretensions counts upon more bouquets than at other times; and there was a want of perfume in the air at this moment which at last excited the girl's alarm.

"Are you sick?" she asked of Morris. "You seem so restless, and you look pale."

"I am not at all well," said Morris; and it occurred to him that, if he could only make her pity him enough, he might get off.

"I am afraid you are overworked; you oughtn't to work so much."

"I must do that." And then he added, with a sort of calculated brutality, "I don't want to owe you everything!"

"Ah, how can you say that?"

"I am too proud," said Morris.

"Yes—you are too proud!"

"Well, you must take me as I am," he went on; "you can never change me."

"I don't want to change you," she said, gently. "I will take you as you are!" And she stood looking at him.

"You know people talk tremendously about a man's marrying a rich girl," Morris remarked. "It's excessively disagreeable."

"But I am not rich!" said Catherine.

"You are rich enough to make me talked about!"

"Of course you are talked about. It's an honour!"

"It's an honour I could easily dispense with."

She was on the point of asking him whether it were not a compensation for this annoyance that the poor girl who had the misfortune to bring it upon him, loved him so dearly and believed in him so truly; but she hesitated, thinking that this would perhaps seem an exacting speech, and while she hesitated, he suddenly left her.

The next time he came, however, she brought it out, and she told him again that he was too proud. He repeated that he couldn't change, and this time she felt the impulse to say that with a little effort he might change.

Sometimes he thought that if he could only make a quarrel with her it might help him; but the question was how to quarrel with a young woman who had such treasures of concession. "I suppose you think the effort is all on your side!" he was reduced to exclaiming. "Don't you believe that I have my own effort to make?"

"It's all yours now," she said. "My effort is finished and done with!"

"Well, mine is not."

"We must bear things together," said Catherine. "That's what we ought to do."

Morris attempted a natural smile. "There are some things which we can't very well bear together—for instance, separation."

"Why do you speak of separation?"

"Ah! you don't like it; I knew you wouldn't!"

"Where are you going, Morris?" she suddenly asked.

He fixed his eye on her a moment, and for a part of that moment she was afraid of it. "Will you promise not to make a scene?"

"A scene!—do I make scenes?"

"All women do!" said Morris, with the tone of large experience.

"I don't. Where are you going?"

"If I should say I was going away on business, should you think it very strange?"

She wondered a moment, gazing at him. "Yes—no. Not if you will take me with you."

"Take you with me—on business?"

"What is your business? Your business is to be with me."

"I don't earn my living with you," said Morris. "Or rather," he cried with a sudden inspiration, "that's just what I do— or what the world says I do!"

This ought perhaps to have been a great stroke, but it miscarried. "Where are you going?" Catherine simply repeated.

"To New Orleans. About buying some cotton."

"I am perfectly willing to go to New Orleans," Catherine said.

"Do you suppose I would take you to a nest of yellow fever?" cried Morris. "Do you suppose I would expose you at such a time as this?"

"If there is yellow fever, why should you go? Morris, you must not go!"

"It is to make six thousand dollars," said Morris. "Do you grudge me that satisfaction?"

"We have no need of six thousand dollars. You think too much about money!"

"You can afford to say that! This is a great chance; we heard of it last night." And he explained to her in what the chance consisted; and told her a long story, going over more than once several of the details, about the remarkable stroke of business which he and his partner had planned between them.

But Catherine's imagination, for reasons best known to herself, absolutely refused to be fired. "If you can go to New Orleans, I can go," she said. "Why shouldn't you catch yellow fever quite as easily as I? I am every bit as strong as you, and not in the least afraid of any fever. When we were in Europe, we were in very unhealthy places; my father used to make me take some pills. I never caught anything, and I never was nervous. What will be the use of six thousand dollars if you die of a fever? When persons are going to be married, they oughtn't to think so much about business. You shouldn't think about cotton, you should think about me. You can go to New Orleans some other time—there will always be plenty of cotton. It isn't the moment to choose—we have waited too long already." She spoke more forcibly and volubly than he had ever heard her, and she held his arm in her two hands.

"You said you wouldn't make a scene!" cried Morris. "I call this a scene."

"It's you that are making it! I have never asked you anything before. We have waited too long already." And it was a comfort to her to think that she had hitherto asked so little; it seemed to make her right to insist the greater now.

Morris bethought himself a little. "Very well, then; we won't talk about it any more. I will transact my business by letter." And he began to smooth his hat, as if to take leave.

"You won't go?" And she stood looking up at him.

He could not give up his idea of provoking a quarrel; it was so much the simplest way! He bent his eyes on her up-turned face, with the darkest frown he could achieve. "You are not discreet. You mustn't bully me!"

But, as usual, she conceded everything. "No, I am not discreet; I know I am too pressing. But isn't it natural? It is only for a moment."

"In a moment you may do a great deal of harm. Try and be calmer the next time I come."

"When will you come?"

"Do you want to make conditions?" Morris asked. "I will come next Saturday."

"Come to-morrow," Catherine begged; "I want you to come to-morrow. I will be very quiet," she added; and her agitation had by this time become so great that the assurance was not unbecoming. A sudden fear had come over her; it was like the solid conjunction of a dozen disembodied doubts, and her imagination, at a single bound, had traversed an enormous distance. All her being, for the moment, centred in the wish to keep him in the room.

Morris bent his head and kissed her forehead. "When you are quiet, you are perfection," he said; "but when you are violent, you are not in character."

It was Catherine's wish that there should be no violence about her save the beating of her heart, which she could not help; and she went on, as gently as possible, "Will you promise to come to-morrow?"

"I said Saturday!" Morris answered smiling. He tried a frown at one moment, a smile at another; he was at his wit's end.

"Yes, Saturday too," she answered, trying to smile. "But to-morrow first." He was going to the door, and she went with him, quickly. She leaned her shoulder against it; it seemed to her that she would do anything to keep him.

"If I am prevented from coming to-morrow, you will say I have deceived you!" he said.

"How can you be prevented? You can come if you will."

"I am a busy man—I am not a dangler!" cried Morris, sternly.

His voice was so hard and unnatural that, with a helpless look at him, she turned away; and then he quickly laid his hand on the door-knob. He felt as if he were absolutely running away from her. But in an instant she was close to him again, and murmuring in a tone none the less penetrating for being low, "Morris, you are going to leave me."

"Yes, for a little while."

"For how long?"

"Till you are reasonable again."

"I shall never be reasonable in that way!" And she tried to keep him longer; it was almost a struggle. "Think of what I have done!" she broke out. "Morris, I have given up everything!"

"You shall have everything back!"

"You wouldn't say that if you didn't mean something. What is it?—what has happened?—what have I done?—what has changed you?"

"I will write to you—that is better," Morris stammered.

"Ah, you won't come back!" she cried, bursting into tears.

"Dear Catherine," he said, "don't believe that! I promise you that you shall see me again!" And he managed to get away and to close the door behind him.

XXX

IT WAS almost her last outbreak of passive grief; at least, she never indulged in another that the world knew anything about. But this one was long and terrible; she flung herself on the sofa and gave herself up to her misery. She hardly knew what had happened; ostensibly she had only had a difference with her lover, as other girls had had before, and the thing was not only not a rupture, but she was under no obligation to regard it even as a menace. Nevertheless, she felt a wound, even if he had not dealt it; it seemed to her that a mask had suddenly fallen from his face. He had wished to get away from her; he had been angry and cruel, and said strange things, with strange looks. She was smothered and stunned; she buried her head in the cushions, sobbing and talking to herself. But at last she raised herself, with the fear that either her father or Mrs. Penniman would come in; and then she sat there, staring before her, while the room grew darker. She said to herself that perhaps he would come back to tell her he had not meant what he said; and she listened for his ring at the door, trying to believe that this was probable. A long time passed, but Morris remained absent; the shadows gathered; the evening settled down on the meagre elegance of the light, clear-coloured room; the fire went out. When it had grown dark, Catherine went to the window and looked out; she stood there for half an hour, on the mere chance that he would come up the steps. At last she turned away, for she saw her father come in. He had seen her at the window looking out, and he stopped a moment at the bottom of the white steps, and gravely, with an air of exaggerated courtesy, lifted his hat to her. The gesture was so incongruous to the condition she was in, this stately tribute of respect to a poor girl despised and forsaken was so out of place, that the thing gave her a kind of horror, and she hurried away to her room. It seemed to her that she had given Morris up.

She had to show herself half an hour later, and she was sustained at table by the immensity of her desire that her father should not perceive that anything had happened. This was a great help to her afterwards, and it served her (though

never as much as she supposed) from the first. On this occasion Dr. Sloper was rather talkative. He told a great many
stories about a wonderful poodle that he had seen at the
house of an old lady whom he visited professionally. Catherine not only tried to appear to listen to the anecdotes of the
poodle, but she endeavoured to interest herself in them, so as
not to think of her scene with Morris. That perhaps was an
hallucination; he was mistaken, she was jealous; people didn't
change like that from one day to another. Then she knew that
she had had doubts before—strange suspicions, that were at
once vague and acute—and that he had been different ever
since her return from Europe: whereupon she tried again to
listen to her father, who told a story so remarkably well. Afterwards she went straight to her own room; it was beyond
her strength to undertake to spend the evening with her aunt.
All the evening, alone, she questioned herself. Her trouble
was terrible; but was it a thing of her imagination, engen-
dered by an extravagant sensibility, or did it represent a clear-
cut reality, and had the worst that was possible actually come
to pass? Mrs. Penniman, with a degree of tact that was as
unusual as it was commendable, took the line of leaving her
alone. The truth is, that her suspicions having been aroused,
she indulged a desire, natural to a timid person, that the explosion should be localised. So long as the air still vibrated
she kept out of the way.

She passed and repassed Catherine's door several times in
the course of the evening, as if she expected to hear a plaintive
moan behind it. But the room remained perfectly still; and
accordingly, the last thing before retiring to her own couch,
she applied for admittance. Catherine was sitting up, and had
a book that she pretended to be reading. She had no wish to
go to bed, for she had no expectation of sleeping. After Mrs.
Penniman had left her she sat up half the night, and she
offered her visitor no inducement to remain. Her aunt
came stealing in very gently, and approached her with great
solemnity.

"I am afraid you are in trouble, my dear. Can I do anything
to help you?"

"I am not in any trouble whatever, and do not need any
help," said Catherine, fibbing roundly, and proving thereby

that not only our faults, but our most involuntary misfortunes, tend to corrupt our morals.

"Has nothing happened to you?"

"Nothing whatever."

"Are you very sure, dear?"

"Perfectly sure."

"And can I really do nothing for you?"

"Nothing, aunt, but kindly leave me alone," said Catherine.

Mrs. Penniman, though she had been afraid of too warm a welcome before, was now disappointed at so cold a one; and in relating afterwards, as she did to many persons, and with considerable variations of detail, the history of the termination of her niece's engagement, she was usually careful to mention that the young lady, on a certain occasion, had "hustled" her out of the room. It was characteristic of Mrs. Penniman that she related this fact, not in the least out of malignity to Catherine, whom she very sufficiently pitied, but simply from a natural disposition to embellish any subject that she touched.

Catherine, as I have said, sat up half the night, as if she still expected to hear Morris Townsend ring at the door. On the morrow this expectation was less unreasonable; but it was not gratified by the reappearance of the young man. Neither had he written; there was not a word of explanation or reassurance. Fortunately for Catherine she could take refuge from her excitement, which had now become intense, in her determination that her father should see nothing of it. How well she deceived her father we shall have occasion to learn; but her innocent arts were of little avail before a person of the rare perspicacity of Mrs. Penniman. This lady easily saw that she was agitated, and if there was any agitation going forward, Mrs. Penniman was not a person to forfeit her natural share in it. She returned to the charge the next evening, and requested her niece to lean upon her—to unburden her heart. Perhaps she should be able to explain certain things that now seemed dark, and that she knew more about than Catherine supposed. If Catherine had been frigid the night before, today she was haughty.

"You are completely mistaken, and I have not the least idea what you mean. I don't know what you are trying to fasten on me, and I have never had less need of any one's explanations in my life."

In this way the girl delivered herself, and from hour to hour kept her aunt at bay. From hour to hour Mrs. Penniman's curiosity grew. She would have given her little finger to know what Morris had said and done, what tone he had taken, what pretext he had found. She wrote to him, naturally, to request an interview; but she received, as naturally, no answer to her petition. Morris was not in a writing mood; for Catherine had addressed him two short notes which met with no acknowledgment. These notes were so brief that I may give them entire. "Won't you give me some sign that you didn't mean to be so cruel as you seemed on Tuesday?"—that was the first; the other was a little longer. "If I was unreasonable or suspicious, on Tuesday—if I annoyed you or troubled you in any way—I beg your forgiveness, and I promise never again to be so foolish. I am punished enough, and I don't understand. Dear Morris, you are killing me!" These notes were despatched on the Friday and Saturday; but Saturday and Sunday passed without bringing the poor girl the satisfaction she desired. Her punishment accumulated; she continued to bear it, however, with a good deal of superficial fortitude. On Saturday morning, the Doctor, who had been watching in silence, spoke to his sister Lavinia.

"The thing has happened—the scoundrel has backed out!"

"Never!" cried Mrs. Penniman, who had bethought herself what she should say to Catherine, but was not provided with a line of defence against her brother, so that indignant negation was the only weapon in her hands.

"He has begged for a reprieve, then, if you like that better!"

"It seems to make you very happy that your daughter's affections have been trifled with."

"It does," said the Doctor; "for I had foretold it! It's a great pleasure to be in the right."

"Your pleasures make one shudder!" his sister exclaimed.

Catherine went rigidly through her usual occupations; that is, up to the point of going with her aunt to church on Sunday morning. She generally went to afternoon service as well; but on this occasion her courage faltered, and she begged of Mrs. Penniman to go without her.

"I am sure you have a secret," said Mrs. Penniman, with great significance, looking at her rather grimly.

"If I have, I shall keep it!" Catherine answered, turning away.

Mrs. Penniman started for church; but before she had arrived, she stopped and turned back, and before twenty minutes had elapsed she re-entered the house, looked into the empty parlours, and then went upstairs and knocked at Catherine's door. She got no answer; Catherine was not in her room, and Mrs. Penniman presently ascertained that she was not in the house. "She has gone to him, she has fled!" Lavinia cried, clasping her hands with admiration and envy. But she soon perceived that Catherine had taken nothing with her—all her personal property in her room was intact—and then she jumped at the hypothesis that the girl had gone forth, not in tenderness, but in resentment. "She has followed him to his own door—she has burst upon him in his own apartment!" It was in these terms that Mrs. Penniman depicted to herself her niece's errand, which, viewed in this light, gratified her sense of the picturesque only a shade less strongly than the idea of a clandestine marriage. To visit one's lover, with tears and reproaches, at his own residence, was an image so agreeable to Mrs. Penniman's mind that she felt a sort of æsthetic disappointment at its lacking, in this case, the harmonious accompaniments of darkness and storm. A quiet Sunday afternoon appeared an inadequate setting for it; and, indeed, Mrs. Penniman was quite out of humour with the conditions of the time, which passed very slowly as she sat in the front-parlour, in her bonnet and her cashmere shawl, awaiting Catherine's return.

This event at last took place. She saw her—at the window—mount the steps, and she went to await her in the hall, where she pounced upon her as soon as she had entered the house, and drew her into the parlour, closing the door with solemnity. Catherine was flushed, and her eye was bright. Mrs. Penniman hardly knew what to think.

"May I venture to ask where you have been?" she demanded.

"I have been to take a walk," said Catherine. "I thought you had gone to church."

"I did go to church; but the service was shorter than usual. And pray where did you walk?"

"I don't know!" said Catherine.

"Your ignorance is most extraordinary! Dear Catherine, you can trust me."

"What am I to trust you with?"

"With your secret—your sorrow."

"I have no sorrow!" said Catherine fiercely.

"My poor child," Mrs. Penniman insisted, "you can't deceive me. I know everything. I have been requested to—a—to converse with you."

"I don't want to converse!"

"It will relieve you. Don't you know Shakespeare's lines?— 'the grief that does not speak!' My dear girl, it is better as it is."

"What is better?" Catherine asked.

She was really too perverse. A certain amount of perversity was to be allowed for in a young lady whose lover had thrown her over; but not such an amount as would prove inconvenient to his apologists. "That you should be reasonable," said Mrs. Penniman, with some sternness. "That you should take counsel of worldly prudence, and submit to practical considerations. That you should agree to—a—separate."

Catherine had been ice up to this moment, but at this word she flamed up. "Separate? What do you know about our separating?"

Mrs. Penniman shook her head with a sadness in which there was almost a sense of injury. "Your pride is my pride, and your susceptibilities are mine. I see your side perfectly, but I also"—and she smiled with melancholy suggestiveness—"I also see the situation as a whole!"

This suggestiveness was lost upon Catherine, who repeated her violent inquiry. "Why do you talk about separation; what do you know about it?"

"We must study resignation," said Mrs. Penniman, hesitating, but sententious at a venture.

"Resignation to what?"

"To a change of—of our plans."

"My plans have not changed!" said Catherine, with a little laugh.

"Ah, but Mr. Townsend's have," her aunt answered very gently.

"What do you mean?"

There was an imperious brevity in the tone of this inquiry, against which Mrs. Penniman felt bound to protest; the information with which she had undertaken to supply her niece was after all a favour. She had tried sharpness, and she had tried sternness; but neither would do; she was shocked at the girl's obstinacy. "Ah, well," she said, "if he hasn't told you! . . ." and she turned away.

Catherine watched her a moment in silence; then she hurried after her, stopping her before she reached the door. "Told me what? What do you mean? What are you hinting at and threatening me with?"

"Isn't it broken off?" asked Mrs. Penniman.

"My engagement? Not in the least!"

"I beg your pardon in that case. I have spoken too soon!"

"Too soon! Soon or late," Catherine broke out, "you speak foolishly and cruelly!"

"What has happened between you then?" asked her aunt, struck by the sincerity of this cry. "For something certainly has happened."

"Nothing has happened but that I love him more and more!"

Mrs. Penniman was silent an instant. "I suppose that's the reason you went to see him this afternoon."

Catherine flushed as if she had been struck. "Yes, I did go to see him! But that's my own business."

"Very well, then; we won't talk about it." And Mrs. Penniman moved towards the door again. But she was stopped by a sudden imploring cry from the girl.

"Aunt Lavinia, *where* has he gone?"

"Ah, you admit then that he has gone away? Didn't they know at his house?"

"They said he had left town. I asked no more questions; I was ashamed," said Catherine, simply enough.

"You needn't have taken so compromising a step if you had had a little more confidence in me," Mrs. Penniman observed, with a good deal of grandeur.

"Is it to New Orleans?" Catherine went on, irrelevantly.

It was the first time Mrs. Penniman had heard of New Orleans in this connection; but she was averse to letting Catherine know that she was in the dark. She attempted to strike an illumination from the instructions she had received from Morris. "My dear Catherine," she said, "when a separation has been agreed upon, the farther he goes away the better."

"Agreed upon? Has he agreed upon it with you?" A consummate sense of her aunt's meddlesome folly had come over her during the last five minutes, and she was sickened at the thought that Mrs. Penniman had been let loose, as it were, upon her happiness.

"He certainly has sometimes advised with me," said Mrs. Penniman.

"Is it you then that have changed him and made him so unnatural?" Catherine cried. "Is it you that have worked on him and taken him from me? He doesn't belong to you, and I don't see how you have anything to do with what is between us! Is it you that have made this plot and told him to leave me? How could you be so wicked, so cruel? What have I ever done to you; why can't you leave me alone? I was afraid you would spoil everything; for you *do* spoil everything you touch! I was afraid of you all the time we were abroad; I had no rest when I thought that you were always talking to him." Catherine went on with growing vehemence, pouring out in her bitterness and in the clairvoyance of her passion (which suddenly, jumping all processes, made her judge her aunt finally and without appeal), the uneasiness which had lain for so many months upon her heart.

Mrs. Penniman was scared and bewildered; she saw no prospect of introducing her little account of the purity of Morris's motives. "You are a most ungrateful girl!" she cried. "Do you scold me for talking with him? I am sure we never talked of anything but you!"

"Yes; and that was the way you worried him; you made him tired of my very name! I wish you had never spoken of me to him; I never asked your help!"

"I am sure if it hadn't been for me he would never have come to the house, and you would never have known what he thought of you," Mrs. Penniman rejoined with a good deal of justice.

"I wish he never had come to the house, and that I never had known it! That's better than this," said poor Catherine.

"You are a very ungrateful girl," Aunt Lavinia repeated.

Catherine's outbreak of anger and the sense of wrong gave her, while they lasted, the satisfaction that comes from all assertion of force; they hurried her along, and there is always a sort of pleasure in cleaving the air. But at the bottom she hated to be violent, and she was conscious of no aptitude for organised resentment. She calmed herself with a great effort, but with great rapidity, and walked about the room a few moments, trying to say to herself that her aunt had meant everything for the best. She did not succeed in saying it with much conviction, but after a little she was able to speak quietly enough.

"I am not ungrateful, but I am very unhappy. It's hard to be grateful for that," she said. "Will you please tell me where he is?"

"I haven't the least idea; I am not in secret correspondence with him!" And Mrs. Penniman wished indeed that she were, so that she might let him know how Catherine abused her, after all she had done.

"Was it a plan of his, then, to break off——?" By this time Catherine had become completely quiet.

Mrs. Penniman began again to have a glimpse of her chance for explaining. "He shrank—he shrank," she said. "He lacked courage, but it was the courage to injure you! He couldn't bear to bring down on you your father's curse."

Catherine listened to this with her eyes fixed upon her aunt, and continued to gaze at her for some time afterwards. "Did he tell you to say that?"

"He told me to say many things—all so delicate, so discriminating. And he told me to tell you he hoped you wouldn't despise him."

"I don't," said Catherine. And then she added: "And will he stay away for ever?"

"Oh, for ever is a long time. Your father, perhaps, won't live for ever."

"Perhaps not."

"I am sure you appreciate—you understand—even though your heart bleeds," said Mrs. Penniman. "You doubtless think him too scrupulous. So do I, but I respect his scruples. What he asks of you is that you should do the same."

Catherine was still gazing at her aunt, but she spoke, at last, as if she had not heard or not understood her. "It has been a regular plan, then. He has broken it off deliberately; he has given me up."

"For the present, dear Catherine. He has put it off, only."

"He has left me alone," Catherine went on.

"Haven't you *me*?" asked Mrs. Penniman, with much expression.

Catherine shook her head slowly. "I don't believe it!" and she left the room.

XXXI

THOUGH she had forced herself to be calm, she preferred practising this virtue in private, and she forbore to show herself at tea—a repast which, on Sundays, at six o'clock, took the place of dinner. Dr. Sloper and his sister sat face to face, but Mrs. Penniman never met her brother's eye. Late in the evening she went with him, but without Catherine, to their sister Almond's, where, between the two ladies, Catherine's unhappy situation was discussed with a frankness that was conditioned by a good deal of mysterious reticence on Mrs. Penniman's part.

"I am delighted he is not to marry her," said Mrs. Almond, "but he ought to be horsewhipped all the same."

Mrs. Penniman, who was shocked at her sister's coarseness, replied that he had been actuated by the noblest of motives—the desire not to impoverish Catherine.

"I am very happy that Catherine is not to be impoverished—but I hope he may never have a penny too much! And what does the poor girl say to *you?*" Mrs. Almond asked.

"She says I have a genius for consolation," said Mrs. Penniman.

This was the account of the matter that she gave to her sister, and it was perhaps with the consciousness of genius that, on her return that evening to Washington Square, she again presented herself for admittance at Catherine's door. Catherine came and opened it; she was apparently very quiet.

"I only want to give you a little word of advice," she said. "If your father asks you, say that everything is going on."

Catherine stood there, with her hand on the knob, looking at her aunt, but not asking her to come in. "Do you think he will ask me?"

"I am sure he will. He asked me just now, on our way home from your Aunt Elizabeth's. I explained the whole thing to your Aunt Elizabeth. I said to your father I know nothing about it."

"Do you think he will ask me, when he sees—when he sees——?" But here Catherine stopped.

"The more he sees, the more disagreeable he will be," said her aunt.

"He shall see as little as possible!" Catherine declared.

"Tell him you are to be married."

"So I am," said Catherine, softly; and she closed the door upon her aunt.

She could not have said this two days later—for instance, on Tuesday, when she at last received a letter from Morris Townsend. It was an epistle of considerable length, measuring five large square pages, and written at Philadelphia. It was an explanatory document, and it explained a great many things, chief among which were the considerations that had led the writer to take advantage of an urgent "professional" absence to try and banish from his mind the image of one whose path he had crossed only to scatter it with ruins. He ventured to expect but partial success in this attempt, but he could promise her that, whatever his failure, he would never again interpose between her generous heart and her brilliant prospects and filial duties. He closed with an intimation that his professional pursuits might compel him to travel for some months, and with the hope that when they should each have accommodated themselves to what was sternly involved in their respective positions—even should this result not be reached for years—they should meet as friends, as fellow-sufferers, as innocent but philosophic victims of a great social law. That her life should be peaceful and happy was the dearest wish of him who ventured still to subscribe himself her most obedient servant. The letter was beautifully written, and Catherine, who kept it for many years after this, was able, when her sense of the bitterness of its meaning and the hollowness of its tone had grown less acute, to admire its grace of expression. At present, for a long time after she received it, all she had to help her was the determination, daily more rigid, to make no appeal to the compassion of her father.

He suffered a week to elapse, and then one day, in the morning, at an hour at which she rarely saw him, he strolled into the back-parlour. He had watched his time, and he found her alone. She was sitting with some work, and he came and stood in front of her. He was going out; he had on his hat and was drawing on his gloves.

"It doesn't seem to me that you are treating me just now with all the consideration I deserve," he said in a moment.

"I don't know what I have done," Catherine answered, with her eyes on her work.

"You have apparently quite banished from your mind the request I made you at Liverpool, before we sailed; the request that you would notify me in advance before leaving my house."

"I have not left your house!" said Catherine.

"But you intend to leave it, and by what you gave me to understand, your departure must be impending. In fact, though you are still here in body, you are already absent in spirit. Your mind has taken up its residence with your prospective husband, and you might quite as well be lodged under the conjugal roof, for all the benefit we get from your society."

"I will try and be more cheerful!" said Catherine.

"You certainly ought to be cheerful; you ask a great deal if you are not. To the pleasure of marrying a brilliant young man, you add that of having your own way; you strike me as a very lucky young lady!"

Catherine got up; she was suffocating. But she folded her work, deliberately and correctly, bending her burning face upon it. Her father stood where he had planted himself; she hoped he would go, but he smoothed and buttoned his gloves, and then he rested his hands upon his hips.

"It would be a convenience to me to know when I may expect to have an empty house," he went on. "When you go, your aunt marches."

She looked at him at last, with a long silent gaze, which, in spite of her pride and her resolution, uttered part of the appeal she had tried not to make. Her father's cold gray eye sounded her own, and he insisted on his point.

"Is it to-morrow? Is it next week, or the week after?"

"I shall not go away!" said Catherine.

The Doctor raised his eyebrows. "Has he backed out?"

"I have broken off my engagement."

"Broken it off?"

"I have asked him to leave New York, and he has gone away for a long time."

The Doctor was both puzzled and disappointed, but he solved his perplexity by saying to himself that his daughter simply misrepresented—justifiably, if one would, but nevertheless, misrepresented—the facts; and he eased off his disappointment, which was that of a man losing a chance for a little triumph that he had rather counted on, by a few words that he uttered aloud.

"How does he take his dismissal?"

"I don't know!" said Catherine, less ingeniously than she had hitherto spoken.

"You mean you don't care? You are rather cruel, after encouraging him and playing with him for so long!"

The Doctor had his revenge after all.

XXXII

OUR STORY has hitherto moved with very short steps, but as it approaches its termination it must take a long stride. As time went on, it might have appeared to the Doctor that his daughter's account of her rupture with Morris Townsend, mere bravado as he had deemed it, was in some degree justified by the sequel. Morris remained as rigidly and unremittingly absent as if he had died of a broken heart, and Catherine had apparently buried the memory of this fruitless episode as deep as if it had terminated by her own choice. We know that she had been deeply and incurably wounded, but the Doctor had no means of knowing it. He was certainly curious about it, and would have given a good deal to discover the exact truth; but it was his punishment that he never knew—his punishment, I mean, for the abuse of sarcasm in his relations with his daughter. There was a good deal of effective sarcasm in her keeping him in the dark, and the rest of the world conspired with her, in this sense, to be sarcastic. Mrs. Penniman told him nothing, partly because he never questioned her—he made too light of Mrs. Penniman for that—and partly because she flattered herself that a tormenting reserve, and a serene profession of ignorance, would avenge her for his theory that she had meddled in the matter. He went two or three times to see Mrs. Montgomery, but Mrs. Montgomery had nothing to impart. She simply knew that her brother's engagement was broken off, and now that Miss Sloper was out of danger, she preferred not to bear witness in any way against Morris. She had done so before— however unwillingly—because she was sorry for Miss Sloper; but she was not sorry for Miss Sloper now—not at all sorry. Morris had told her nothing about his relations with Miss Sloper at the time, and he had told her nothing since. He was always away, and he very seldom wrote to her; she believed he had gone to California. Mrs. Almond had, in her sister's phrase, "taken up" Catherine violently since the recent catastrophe; but though the girl was very grateful to her for her kindness, she revealed no secrets, and the good lady could give the Doctor no satisfaction. Even, however, had she been able to narrate to him the private history of his daughter's unhappy love-affair, it would have given her a certain comfort to leave him in ignorance; for Mrs. Almond was at this time not altogether in sympathy with her brother. She had guessed for herself that Catherine had been cruelly jilted—she knew nothing from Mrs. Penniman, for Mrs. Penniman had not ventured to lay the famous explanation of Morris's motives before Mrs. Almond, though she had thought it good enough for Catherine—and she pronounced her brother too consistently indifferent to what the poor creature must have suffered and must still be suffering. Dr. Sloper had his theory, and he rarely altered his theories. The marriage would have been an abominable one, and the girl had had a blessed escape. She was not to be pitied for that, and to pretend to condole with her would have been to make concessions to the idea that she had ever had a right to think of Morris.

"I put my foot on this idea from the first, and I keep it there now," said the Doctor. "I don't see anything cruel in that; one can't keep it there too long." To this Mrs. Almond more than once replied that if Catherine had got rid of her incongruous lover, she deserved the credit of it, and that to bring herself to her father's enlightened view of the matter must have cost her an effort that he was bound to appreciate.

"I am by no means sure she has got rid of him," the Doctor said. "There is not the smallest probability that, after having been as obstinate as a mule for two years, she suddenly became amenable to reason. It is infinitely more probable that he got rid of her."

"All the more reason you should be gentle with her."

"I *am* gentle with her. But I can't do the pathetic; I can't pump up tears, to look graceful, over the most fortunate thing that ever happened to her."

"You have no sympathy," said Mrs. Almond; "that was never your strong point. You have only to look at her to see that, right or wrong, and whether the rupture came from herself or from him, her poor little heart is grievously bruised."

"Handling bruises—and even dropping tears on them— doesn't make them any better! My business is to see she gets no more knocks, and that I shall carefully attend to. But I don't at all recognise your description of Catherine. She doesn't strike me in the least as a young woman going about in search of a moral poultice. In fact, she seems to me much better than while the fellow was hanging about. She is perfectly comfortable and blooming; she eats and sleeps, takes her usual exercise, and overloads herself, as usual, with finery. She is always knitting some purse or embroidering some handkerchief, and it seems to me she turns these articles out about as fast as ever. She hasn't much to say; but when had she anything to say? She had her little dance, and now she is sitting down to rest. I suspect that, on the whole, she enjoys it."

"She enjoys it as people enjoy getting rid of a leg that has been crushed. The state of mind after amputation is doubtless one of comparative repose."

"If your leg is a metaphor for young Townsend, I can assure you he has never been crushed. Crushed? Not he! He is alive and perfectly intact, and that's why I am not satisfied."

"Should you have liked to kill him?" asked Mrs. Almond.

"Yes, very much. I think it is quite possible that it is all a blind."

"A blind?"

"An arrangement between them. *Il fait le mort*, as they say in France; but he is looking out of the corner of his eye. You can depend upon it he has not burned his ships; he has kept one to come back in. When I am dead, he will set sail again, and then she will marry him."

"It is interesting to know that you accuse your only daughter of being the vilest of hypocrites," said Mrs. Almond.

"I don't see what difference her being my only daughter makes. It is better to accuse one than a dozen. But I don't accuse any one. There is not the smallest hypocrisy about Catherine, and I deny that she even pretends to be miserable."

The Doctor's idea that the thing was a "blind" had its intermissions and revivals; but it may be said on the whole to have increased as he grew older; together with his impression of Catherine's blooming and comfortable condition. Naturally, if he had not found grounds for viewing her as a lovelorn maiden during the year or two that followed her great trouble, he found none at a time when she had completely recovered her self-possession. He was obliged to recognise the fact that if the two young people were waiting for him to get out of the way, they were at least waiting very patiently. He had heard from time to time that Morris was in New York; but he never remained there long, and, to the best of the Doctor's belief, had no communication with Catherine. He was sure they never met, and he had reason to suspect that Morris never wrote to her. After the letter that has been mentioned, she heard from him twice again, at considerable intervals; but on none of these occasions did she write herself. On the other hand, as the Doctor observed, she averted herself rigidly from the idea of marrying other people. Her opportunities for doing so were not numerous, but they occurred often enough to test her disposition. She refused a widower, a man with a genial temperament, a handsome fortune, and three little girls (he had heard that she was very fond of children, and he pointed to his own with some confidence); and she turned a deaf ear to the solicitations of a clever young lawyer, who, with the prospect of a great practice, and the reputation of a most agreeable man, had had the shrewdness, when he came to look about him for a wife, to believe that she would suit him better than several younger and prettier girls. Mr. Macalister, the widower, had desired to make a marriage of reason, and had chosen Catherine for what he supposed to be her latent matronly qualities; but John Ludlow, who was a year the girl's junior, and spoken of always as a young man who might have his "pick," was seriously in love with her. Catherine, however, would never look at him; she made it plain to him that she thought he came to see her too often. He afterwards consoled himself, and married a very different person, little Miss Sturtevant, whose attractions were obvious to the dullest comprehension. Catherine, at the time of these events, had left her thirtieth year well behind her, and had quite taken her place as an old maid. Her father would have preferred she should marry, and he once told her that he hoped she would not be too fastidious. "I should like to see you an honest man's wife before I die," he said. This was after John Ludlow had been compelled to give it up, though the Doctor had advised him to persevere. The Doctor exercised no further pressure, and had the credit of not " worrying" at all over his daughter's singleness.

In fact he worried rather more than appeared, and there were considerable periods during which he felt sure that Morris Townsend was hidden behind some door. "If he is not, why doesn't she marry?" he asked himself. "Limited as her intelligence may be, she must understand perfectly well that she is made to do the usual thing." Catherine, however, became an admirable old maid. She formed habits, regulated her days upon a system of her own, interested herself in charitable institutions, asylums, hospitals, and aid-societies; and went generally, with an even and noiseless step, about the rigid business of her life. This life had, however, a secret history as well as a public one—if I may talk of the public history of a mature and diffident spinster for whom publicity had always a combination of terrors. From her own point of view the great facts of her career were that Morris Townsend had trifled with her affection, and that her father had broken its spring. Nothing could ever alter these facts; they were always there, like her name, her age, her plain face. Nothing could ever undo the wrong or cure the pain that Morris had inflicted on her, and nothing could ever make her feel towards her father as she felt in her younger years. There was something dead in her life, and her duty was to try and fill the void. Catherine recognised this duty to the utmost; she had a great disapproval of brooding and moping. She had of course no faculty for quenching memory in dissipation; but she mingled freely in the usual gaieties of the town, and she became at last an inevitable figure at all respectable entertainments. She was greatly liked, and as time went on she grew to be a sort of kindly maiden-aunt to the younger portion of society. Young girls were apt to confide to her their love-affairs (which they never did to Mrs. Penniman), and young men to be fond of her without knowing why. She developed a few harmless eccentricities; her habits, once formed, were rather stiffly maintained; her opinions, on all moral and social matters, were extremely conservative; and before she was forty she was regarded as an old-fashioned person, and an authority on customs that had passed away. Mrs. Penniman, in comparison, was quite a girlish figure; she grew younger as she advanced in life. She lost none of her relish for beauty and mystery, but she had little opportunity to exercise it. With

Catherine's later wooers she failed to establish relations as intimate as those which had given her so many interesting hours in the society of Morris Townsend. These gentlemen had an indefinable mistrust of her good offices, and they never talked to her about Catherine's charms. Her ringlets, her buckles and bangles glistened more brightly with each succeeding year, and she remained quite the same officious and imaginative Mrs. Penniman, and the odd mixture of impetuosity and circumspection, that we have hitherto known. As regards one point, however, her circumspection prevailed, and she must be given due credit for it. For upwards of seventeen years she never mentioned Morris Townsend's name to her niece. Catherine was grateful to her, but this consistent silence, so little in accord with her aunt's character, gave her a certain alarm, and she could never wholly rid herself of a suspicion that Mrs. Penniman sometimes had news of him.

XXXIII

LITTLE BY LITTLE Dr. Sloper had retired from his profession; he visited only those patients in whose symptoms he recognised a certain originality. He went again to Europe, and remained two years; Catherine went with him, and on this occasion Mrs. Penniman was of the party. Europe apparently had few surprises for Mrs. Penniman, who frequently remarked, in the most romantic sites—"You know I am very familiar with all this." It should be added that such remarks were usually not addressed to her brother, or yet to her niece, but to fellow-tourists who happened to be at hand, or even to the cicerone or the goat-herd in the foreground.

One day, after his return from Europe, the Doctor said something to his daughter that made her start—it seemed to come from so far out of the past.

"I should like you to promise me something before I die."

"Why do you talk about your dying?" she asked.

"Because I am sixty-eight years old."

"I hope you will live a long time," said Catherine.

"I hope I shall! But some day I shall take a bad cold, and then it will not matter much what any one hopes. That will be the manner of my exit, and when it takes place, remember I told you so. Promise me not to marry Morris Townsend after I am gone."

This was what made Catherine start, as I have said; but her start was a silent one, and for some moments she said nothing. "Why do you speak of him?" she asked at last.

"You challenge everything I say. I speak of him because he's a topic, like any other. He's to be seen, like any one else, and he is still looking for a wife—having had one and got rid of her, I don't know by what means. He has lately been in New York, and at your cousin Marian's house; your Aunt Elizabeth saw him there."

"They neither of them told me," said Catherine.

"That's their merit; it's not yours. He has grown fat and bald, and he has not made his fortune. But I can't trust those facts alone to steel your heart against him, and that's why I ask you to promise."

"Fat and bald;" these words presented a strange image to Catherine's mind, out of which the memory of the most beautiful young man in the world had never faded. "I don't think you understand," she said. "I very seldom think of Mr. Townsend."

"It will be very easy for you to go on, then. Promise me, after my death, to do the same."

Again, for some moments, Catherine was silent; her father's request deeply amazed her; it opened an old wound and made it ache afresh. "I don't think I can promise that," she answered.

"It would be a great satisfaction," said her father.

"You don't understand. I can't promise that."

The Doctor was silent a minute. "I ask you for a particular reason. I am altering my will."

This reason failed to strike Catherine; and indeed she scarcely understood it. All her feelings were merged in the sense that he was trying to treat her as he had treated her years before. She had suffered from it then; and now all her experience, all her acquired tranquillity and rigidity, protested. She had been so humble in her youth that she could now afford to have a little pride, and there was something in this request, and in her father's thinking himself so free to make it, that seemed an injury to her dignity. Poor Catherine's dignity was not aggressive; it never sat in state; but if you pushed far enough you could find it. Her father had pushed very far.

"I can't promise," she simply repeated.

"You are very obstinate," said the Doctor.

"I don't think you understand."

"Please explain, then."

"I can't explain," said Catherine. "And I can't promise."

"Upon my word," her father exclaimed, "I had no idea how obstinate you are!"

She knew herself that she was obstinate, and it gave her a certain joy. She was now a middle-aged woman.

About a year after this, the accident that the Doctor had spoken of occurred; he took a violent cold. Driving out to Bloomingdale one April day to see a patient of unsound mind, who was confined in a private asylum for the insane, and whose family greatly desired a medical opinion from an eminent source, he was caught in a spring shower, and being in a buggy, without a hood, he found himself soaked to the skin. He came home with an ominous chill, and on the morrow he was seriously ill. "It is congestion of the lungs," he said to Catherine; "I shall need very good nursing. It will make no difference, for I shall not recover; but I wish everything to be done, to the smallest detail, as if I should. I hate an ill-conducted sick-room; and you will be so good as to nurse me on the hypothesis that I shall get well." He told her which of his fellow-physicians to send for, and gave her a multitude of minute directions; it was quite on the optimistic hypothesis that she nursed him. But he had never been wrong in his life, and he was not wrong now. He was touching his seventieth year, and though he had a very well-tempered constitution, his hold upon life had lost its firmness. He died after three weeks' illness, during which Mrs. Penniman, as well as his daughter, had been assiduous at his bedside.

On his will being opened after a decent interval, it was found to consist of two portions. The first of these dated from ten years back, and consisted of a series of dispositions by which he left the great mass of his property to his daughter, with becoming legacies to his two sisters. The second was a codicil, of recent origin, maintaining the annuities to Mrs. Penniman and Mrs. Almond, but reducing Catherine's share to a fifth of what he had first bequeathed her. "She is amply provided for from her mother's side," the document ran, "never having spent more than a fraction of her income from this source; so that her fortune is already more than sufficient to attract those unscrupulous adventurers whom she has given me reason to believe that she persists in regarding as an interesting class." The large remainder of his property, therefore, Dr. Sloper had divided into seven unequal parts, which he left, as endowments, to as many different hospitals and schools of medicine, in various cities of the Union.

To Mrs. Penniman it seemed monstrous that a man should play such tricks with other people's money; for after his death, of course, as she said, it was other people's. "Of course you will dispute the will," she remarked, fatuously, to Catherine.

"Oh no," Catherine answered, "I like it very much. Only I wish it had been expressed a little differently!"

XXXIV

IT WAS her habit to remain in town very late in the summer; she preferred the house in Washington Square to any other habitation whatever, and it was under protest that she used to go to the seaside for the month of August. At the sea she spent her month at an hotel. The year that her father died she intermitted this custom altogether, not thinking it consistent with deep mourning; and the year after that she put off her departure till so late that the middle of August found her still in the heated solitude of Washington Square. Mrs. Penniman, who was fond of a change, was usually eager for a visit to the country; but this year she appeared quite content with such rural impressions as she could gather, at the parlour window, from the ailantus-trees behind the wooden paling. The peculiar fragrance of this vegetation used to diffuse itself in the evening air, and Mrs. Penniman, on the warm nights of July, often sat at the open window and inhaled it. This was a happy moment for Mrs. Penniman; after the death of her brother she felt more free to obey her impulses. A vague oppression had disappeared from her life, and she enjoyed a sense of freedom of which she had not been conscious since the memorable time, so long ago, when the Doctor went abroad with Catherine and left her at home to entertain Morris Townsend. The year that had elapsed since her brother's death reminded her of that happy time, because, although Catherine, in growing older, had become a person to be reckoned with, yet her society was a very different thing, as Mrs. Penniman said, from that of a tank of cold water. The elder lady hardly knew what use to make of this larger margin of her life; she sat and looked at it very much as she had often sat, with her poised needle in her hand, before her tapestry-frame. She had a confident hope, however, that her rich impulses, her talent for embroidery, would still find their application, and this confidence was justified before many months had elapsed.

Catherine continued to live in her father's house in spite of its being represented to her that a maiden-lady of quiet habits might find a more convenient abode in one of the smaller dwellings, with brown stone fronts, which had at this time begun to adorn the transverse thoroughfares in the upper part of the town. She liked the earlier structure—it had begun by this time to be called an "old" house—and proposed to herself to end her days in it. If it was too large for a pair of unpretending gentlewomen, this was better than the opposite fault; for Catherine had no desire to find herself in closer quarters with her aunt. She expected to spend the rest of her life in Washington Square, and to enjoy Mrs. Penniman's society for the whole of this period; as she had a conviction that, long as she might live, her aunt would live at least as long, and always retain her brilliancy and activity. Mrs. Penniman suggested to her the idea of a rich vitality.

On one of those warm evenings in July of which mention has been made, the two ladies sat together at an open window, looking out on the quiet Square. It was too hot for lighted lamps, for reading, or for work; it might have appeared too hot even for conversation, Mrs. Penniman having long been speechless. She sat forward in the window, half on the balcony, humming a little song. Catherine was within the room, in a low rocking-chair, dressed in white, and slowly using a large palmetto fan. It was in this way, at this season, that the aunt and niece, after they had had tea, habitually spent their evenings.

"Catherine," said Mrs. Penniman at last, "I am going to say something that will surprise you."

"Pray do," Catherine answered; "I like surprises. And it is so quiet now."

"Well, then, I have seen Morris Townsend."

If Catherine was surprised, she checked the expression of it; she gave neither a start nor an exclamation. She remained, indeed, for some moments intensely still, and this may very well have been a symptom of emotion. "I hope he was well," she said at last.

"I don't know; he is a great deal changed. He would like very much to see you."

"I would rather not see him," said Catherine, quickly.

"I was afraid you would say that. But you don't seem surprised!"

"I am—very much."

"I met him at Marian's," said Mrs. Penniman. "He goes to

Marian's, and they are so afraid you will meet him there. It's my belief that that's why he goes. He wants so much to see you." Catherine made no response to this, and Mrs. Penniman went on. "I didn't know him at first; he is so remarkably changed. But he knew me in a minute. He says I am not in the least changed. You know how polite he always was. He was coming away when I came, and we walked a little distance together. He is still very handsome, only, of course, he looks older, and he is not so—so animated as he used to be. There was a touch of sadness about him; but there was a touch of sadness about him before—especially when he went away. I am afraid he has not been very successful—that he has never got thoroughly established. I don't suppose he is sufficiently plodding, and that, after all, is what succeeds in this world." Mrs. Penniman had not mentioned Morris Townsend's name to her niece for upwards of the fifth of a century; but now that she had broken the spell, she seemed to wish to make up for lost time, as if there had been a sort of exhilaration in hearing herself talk of him. She proceeded, however, with considerable caution, pausing occasionally to let Catherine give some sign. Catherine gave no other sign than to stop the rocking of her chair and the swaying of her fan; she sat motionless and silent. "It was on Tuesday last," said Mrs. Penniman, "and I have been hesitating ever since about telling you. I didn't know how you might like it. At last I thought that it was so long ago that you would probably not have any particular feeling. I saw him again, after meeting him at Marian's. I met him in the street, and he went a few steps with me. The first thing he said was about you; he asked ever so many questions. Marian didn't want me to speak to you; she didn't want you to know that they receive him. I told him I was sure that after all these years you couldn't have any feeling about that; you couldn't grudge him the hospitality of his own cousin's house. I said you would be bitter indeed if you did that. Marian has the most extraordinary ideas about what happened between you; she seems to think he behaved in some very unusual manner. I took the liberty of reminding her of the real facts, and placing the story in its true light. *He* has no bitterness, Catherine, I can assure you; and he might be excused for it, for things have not gone well with him. He has been all over the world, and tried to establish himself everywhere; but his evil star was against him. It is most interesting to hear him talk of his evil star. Everything failed; everything but his—you know, you remember—his proud, high spirit. I believe he married some lady somewhere in Europe. You know they marry in such a peculiar matter-of-course way in Europe; a marriage of reason they call it. She died soon afterwards; as he said to me, she only flitted across his life. He has not been in New York for ten years; he came back a few days ago. The first thing he did was to ask me about you. He had heard you had never married; he seemed very much interested about that. He said you had been the real romance of his life."

Catherine had suffered her companion to proceed from point to point, and pause to pause, without interrupting her; she fixed her eyes on the ground and listened. But the last phrase I have quoted was followed by a pause of peculiar significance, and then, at last, Catherine spoke. It will be observed that before doing so she had received a good deal of information about Morris Townsend. "Please say no more; please don't follow up that subject."

"Doesn't it interest you?" asked Mrs. Penniman, with a certain timorous archness.

"It pains me," said Catherine.

"I was afraid you would say that. But don't you think you could get used to it? He wants so much to see you."

"Please don't, Aunt Lavinia," said Catherine, getting up from her seat. She moved quickly away, and went to the other window, which stood open to the balcony; and here, in the embrasure, concealed from her aunt by the white curtains, she remained a long time, looking out into the warm darkness. She had had a great shock; it was as if the gulf of the past had suddenly opened, and a spectral figure had risen out of it. There were some things she believed she had got over, some feelings that she had thought of as dead; but apparently there was a certain vitality in them still. Mrs. Penniman had made them stir themselves. It was but a momentary agitation, Catherine said to herself; it would presently pass away. She was trembling, and her heart was beating so that she could feel it; but this also would subside. Then, suddenly, while she waited for a return of her calmness, she burst into tears. But her tears flowed very silently, so that Mrs. Penniman had no observation of them. It was perhaps, however, because Mrs. Penniman suspected them that she said no more that evening about Morris Townsend.

XXXV

H ER REFRESHED attention to this gentleman had not those limits of which Catherine desired, for herself, to be conscious; it lasted long enough to enable her to wait another week before speaking of him again. It was under the same circumstances that she once more attacked the subject. She had been sitting with her niece in the evening; only on this occasion, as the night was not so warm, the lamp had been lighted, and Catherine had placed herself near it with a morsel of fancy-work. Mrs. Penniman went and sat alone for half an hour on the balcony; then she came in, moving vaguely about the room. At last she sank into a seat near Catherine, with clasped hands, and a little look of excitement.

"Shall you be angry if I speak to you again about *him*?" she asked.

Catherine looked up at her quietly. "Who is *he*?"

"He whom you once loved."

"I shall not be angry, but I shall not like it."

"He sent you a message," said Mrs. Penniman. "I promised him to deliver it, and I must keep my promise."

In all these years Catherine had had time to forget how little she had to thank her aunt for in the season of her misery; she had long ago forgiven Mrs. Penniman for taking too much upon herself. But for a moment this attitude of interposition and disinterestedness, this carrying of messages and redeeming of promises, brought back the sense that her companion was a dangerous woman. She had said she would not be angry; but for an instant she felt sore. "I don't care what you do with your promise!" she answered.

Mrs. Penniman, however, with her high conception of the sanctity of pledges, carried her point. "I have gone too far to retreat," she said, though precisely what this meant she was not at pains to explain. "Mr. Townsend wishes most particularly to see you, Catherine; he believes that if you knew how much, and why, he wishes it, you would consent to do so."

"There can be no reason," said Catherine; "no good reason."

"His happiness depends upon it. Is not that a good reason?" asked Mrs. Penniman, impressively.

"Not for me. My happiness does not."

"I think you will be happier after you have seen him. He is going away again—going to resume his wanderings. It is a very lonely, restless, joyless life. Before he goes, he wishes to speak to you; it is a fixed idea with him—he is always thinking of it. He has something very important to say to you. He believes that you never understood him—that you never judged him rightly, and the belief has always weighed upon him terribly. He wishes to justify himself; he believes that in a very few words he could do so. He wishes to meet you as a friend."

Catherine listened to this wonderful speech, without pausing in her work; she had now had several days to accustom herself to think of Morris Townsend again as an actuality. When it was over she said simply, "Please say to Mr. Townsend that I wish he would leave me alone."

She had hardly spoken when a sharp, firm ring at the door vibrated through the summer night. Catherine looked up at the clock; it marked a quarter-past nine—a very late hour for visitors, especially in the empty condition of the town. Mrs. Penniman at the same moment gave a little start, and then Catherine's eyes turned quickly to her aunt. They met Mrs. Penniman's and sounded them for a moment, sharply. Mrs. Penniman was blushing; her look was a conscious one; it seemed to confess something. Catherine guessed its meaning, and rose quickly from her chair.

"Aunt Penniman," she said, in a tone that scared her companion, "have you taken *the liberty* . . . ?"

"My dearest Catherine," stammered Mrs. Penniman, "just wait till you see him!"

Catherine had frightened her aunt, but she was also frightened herself; she was on the point of rushing to give orders to the servant, who was passing to the door, to admit no one; but the fear of meeting her visitor checked her.

"Mr. Morris Townsend."

This was what she heard, vaguely but recognisably articulated by the domestic, while she hesitated. She had her back turned to the door of the parlour, and for some moments she kept it turned, feeling that he had come in. He had not spoken, however, and at last she faced about. Then she saw a gentleman standing in the middle of the room, from which her aunt had discreetly retired.

She would never have known him. He was forty-five years old, and his figure was not that of the straight, slim young man she remembered. But it was a very fine person, and a fair and lustrous beard, spreading itself upon a well-presented chest, contributed to its effect. After a moment Catherine recognised the upper half of the face, which, though her visitor's clustering locks had grown thin, was still remarkably handsome. He stood in a deeply deferential attitude, with his eyes on her face. "I have ventured—I have ventured," he said; and then he paused, looking about him, as if he expected her to ask him to sit down. It was the old voice; but it had not the old charm. Catherine, for a minute, was conscious of a distinct determination not to invite him to take a seat. Why had he come? It was wrong for him to come. Morris was embarrassed, but Catherine gave him no help. It was not that she was glad of his embarrassment; on the contrary, it excited all her own liabilities of this kind, and gave her great pain. But how could she welcome him when she felt so vividly that he ought not to have come? "I wanted so much—I was determined," Morris went on. But he stopped again; it was not easy. Catherine still said nothing, and he may well have recalled with apprehension her ancient faculty of silence. She continued to look at him, however, and as she did so she made the strangest observation. It seemed to be he, and yet not he; it was the man who had been everything, and yet this person was nothing. How long ago it was—how old she had grown—how much she had lived! She had lived on something that was connected with *him*, and she had consumed it in doing so. This person did not look unhappy. He was fair and well-preserved, perfectly dressed, mature and complete. As Catherine looked at him, the story of his life defined itself in his eyes: he had made himself comfortable, and he had never been caught. But even while her perception opened itself to this, she had no desire to catch him; his presence was painful to her, and she only wished he would go.

"Will you not sit down?" he asked.

"I think we had better not," said Catherine.

"I offend you by coming?" He was very grave; he spoke in a tone of the richest respect.

"I don't think you ought to have come."

"Did not Mrs. Penniman tell you—did she not give you my message?"

"She told me something, but I did not understand."

"I wish you would let *me* tell you—let me speak for myself."

"I don't think it is necessary," said Catherine.

"Not for you, perhaps, but for me. It would be a great satisfaction—and I have not many." He seemed to be coming nearer; Catherine turned away. "Can we not be friends again?" he asked.

"We are not enemies," said Catherine. "I have none but friendly feelings to you."

"Ah, I wonder whether you know the happiness it gives me to hear you say that!" Catherine uttered no intimation that she measured the influence of her words; and he presently went on, "You have not changed—the years have passed happily for you."

"They have passed very quietly," said Catherine.

"They have left no marks; you are admirably young." This time he succeeded in coming nearer—he was close to her; she saw his glossy perfumed beard, and his eyes above it looking strange and hard. It was very different from his old—from his young—face. If she had first seen him this way she would not have liked him. It seemed to her that he was smiling, or trying to smile. "Catherine," he said, lowering his voice, "I have never ceased to think of you."

"Please don't say those things," she answered.

"Do you hate me?"

"Oh no," said Catherine.

Something in her tone discouraged him, but in a moment he recovered himself. "Have you still some kindness for me, then?"

"I don't know why you have come here to ask me such things!" Catherine exclaimed.

"Because for many years it has been the desire of my life that we should be friends again."

"That is impossible."

"Why so? Not if you will allow it."

"I will not allow it!" said Catherine.

He looked at her again in silence. "I see; my presence troubles you and pains you. I will go away; but you must give me leave to come again."

"Please don't come again," she said.

"Never?—never?"

She made a great effort; she wished to say something that would make it impossible he should ever again cross her threshold. "It is wrong of you. There is no propriety in it—no reason for it."

"Ah, dearest lady, you do me injustice!" cried Morris Townsend. "We have only waited, and now we are free."

"You treated me badly," said Catherine.

"Not if you think of it rightly. You had your quiet life with your father—which was just what I could not make up my mind to rob you of."

"Yes; I had that."

Morris felt it to be a considerable damage to his cause that he could not add that she had had something more besides; for it is needless to say that he had learnt the contents of Doctor Sloper's will. He was nevertheless not at a loss. "There are worse fates than that!" he exclaimed with expression; and he might have been supposed to refer to his own unprotected situation. Then he added, with a deeper tenderness, "Catherine, have you never forgiven me?"

"I forgave you years ago, but it is useless for us to attempt to be friends."

"Not if we forget the past. We have still a future, thank God!"

"I can't forget—I don't forget," said Catherine. "You treated me too badly. I felt it very much; I felt it for years." And then she went on, with her wish to show him that he must not come to her this way. "I can't begin again—I can't take it up. Everything is dead and buried. It was too serious; it made a great change in my life. I never expected to see you here."

"Ah, you are angry!" cried Morris, who wished immensely that he could extort some flash of passion from her mildness. In that case he might hope.

"No, I am not angry. Anger does not last, that way, for years. But there are other things. Impressions last, when they have been strong.—But I can't talk."

Morris stood stroking his beard, with a clouded eye. "Why have you never married?" he asked abruptly. "You have had opportunities."

"I didn't wish to marry."

"Yes, you are rich, you are free; you had nothing to gain."

"I had nothing to gain," said Catherine.

Morris looked vaguely round him, and gave a deep sigh. "Well, I was in hopes that we might still have been friends."

"I meant to tell you, by my aunt, in answer to your message—if you had waited for an answer—that it was unnecessary for you to come in that hope."

"Good-bye, then," said Morris. "Excuse my indiscretion."

He bowed, and she turned away—standing there, averted, with her eyes on the ground, for some moments after she had heard him close the door of the room.

In the hall he found Mrs. Penniman, fluttered and eager; she appeared to have been hovering there under the irreconcilable promptings of her curiosity and her dignity.

"That was a precious plan of yours!" said Morris, clapping on his hat.

"Is she so hard?" asked Mrs. Penniman.

"She doesn't care a button for me—with her confounded little dry manner."

"Was it very dry?" pursued Mrs. Penniman, with solicitude.

Morris took no notice of her question; he stood musing an instant, with his hat on. "But why the deuce, then, would she never marry?"

"Yes—why indeed?" sighed Mrs. Penniman. And then, as if from a sense of the inadequacy of this explanation, "But you will not despair—you will come back?"

"Come back? Damnation!" And Morris Townsend strode out of the house, leaving Mrs. Penniman staring.

Catherine, meanwhile, in the parlour, picking up her morsel of fancy-work, had seated herself with it again—for life, as it were.

THE PORTRAIT OF A LADY

I

UNDER certain circumstances there are few hours in life more agreeable than the hour dedicated to the ceremony known as afternoon tea. There are circumstances in which, whether you partake of the tea or not—some people of course never do—the situation is in itself delightful. Those that I have in mind in beginning to unfold this simple history offered an admirable setting to an innocent pastime. The implements of the little feast had been disposed upon the lawn of an old English country-house, in what I should call the perfect middle of a splendid summer afternoon. Part of the afternoon had waned, but much of it was left, and what was left was of the finest and rarest quality. Real dusk would not arrive for many hours; but the flood of summer light had begun to ebb, the air had grown mellow, the shadows were long upon the smooth, dense turf. They lengthened slowly, however, and the scene expressed that sense of leisure still to come which is perhaps the chief source of one's enjoyment of such a scene at such an hour. From five o'clock to eight is on certain occasions a little eternity; but on such an occasion as this the interval could be only an eternity of pleasure. The persons concerned in it were taking their pleasure quietly, and they were not of the sex which is supposed to furnish the regular votaries of the ceremony I have mentioned. The shadows on the perfect lawn were straight and angular; they were the shadows of an old man sitting in a deep wicker-chair near the low table on which the tea had been served, and of two younger men strolling to and fro, in desultory talk, in front of him. The old man had his cup in his hand; it was an unusually large cup, of a different pattern from the rest of the set, and painted in brilliant colours. He disposed of its contents with much circumspection, holding it for a long time close to his chin, with his face turned to the house. His companions had either finished their tea or were indifferent to their privilege; they smoked cigarettes as they continued to stroll. One of them, from time to time, as he passed, looked with a certain attention at the elder man, who, unconscious of observation, rested his eyes upon the rich red front of his dwelling. The house that rose beyond the lawn was a structure to repay such consideration, and was the most characteristic object in the peculiarly English picture I have attempted to sketch.

It stood upon a low hill, above the river—the river being the Thames, at some forty miles from London. A long gabled front of red brick, with the complexion of which time and the weather had played all sorts of picturesque tricks, only, however, to improve and refine it, presented itself to the lawn, with its patches of ivy, its clustered chimneys, its windows smothered in creepers. The house had a name and a history; the old gentleman taking his tea would have been delighted to tell you these things: how it had been built under Edward the Sixth, had offered a night's hospitality to the great Elizabeth (whose august person had extended itself upon a huge, magnificent, and terribly angular bed which still formed the principal honour of the sleeping apartments), had been a good deal bruised and defaced in Cromwell's wars, and then, under the Restoration, repaired and much enlarged; and how, finally, after having been remodelled and disfigured in the eighteenth century, it had passed into the careful keeping of a shrewd American banker, who had bought it originally because (owing to circumstances too complicated to set forth) it was offered at a great bargain; bought it with much grumbling at its ugliness, its antiquity, its incommodity, and who now, at the end of twenty years, had become conscious of a real æsthetic passion for it, so that he knew all its points, and would tell you just where to stand to see them in combination, and just the hour when the shadows of its various protuberances—which fell so softly upon the warm, weary brickwork—were of the right measure. Besides this, as I have said, he could have counted off most of the successive owners and occupants, several of whom were known to general fame; doing so, however, with an undemonstrative conviction that the latest phase of its destiny was not the least honourable. The front of the house, overlooking that portion of the lawn with which we are concerned, was not the entrance-front; this was in quite another quarter. Privacy here reigned supreme, and the wide carpet of turf that covered the level hilltop seemed but the extension of a luxurious interior. The

great still oaks and beeches flung down a shade as dense as
that of velvet curtains; and the place was furnished, like a
room, with cushioned seats, with rich-coloured rugs, with the
books and papers that lay upon the grass. The river was at
some distance; where the ground began to slope, the lawn,
properly speaking, ceased. But it was none the less a charming
walk down to the water.

The old gentleman at the tea-table, who had come from
America thirty years before, had brought with him, at the top
of his baggage, his American physiognomy; and he had not
only brought it with him, but he had kept it in the best order,
so that, if necessary, he might have taken it back to his own
country with perfect confidence. But at present, obviously, he
was not likely to displace himself; his journeys were over, and
he was taking the rest that precedes the great rest. He had a
narrow, clean-shaven face, with evenly distributed features,
and an expression of placid acuteness. It was evidently a face
in which the range of expression was not large; so that the
air of contented shrewdness was all the more of a merit. It
seemed to tell that he had been successful in life, but it
seemed to tell also that his success had not been exclusive and
invidious, but had had much of the inoffensiveness of failure.
He had certainly had a great experience of men; but there was
an almost rustic simplicity in the faint smile that played upon
his lean, spacious cheek, and lighted up his humorous eye, as
he at last slowly and carefully deposited his big tea-cup upon
the table. He was neatly dressed, in well-brushed black; but a
shawl was folded upon his knees, and his feet were encased in
thick, embroidered slippers. A beautiful collie dog lay upon
the grass near his chair, watching the master's face almost as
tenderly as the master contemplated the still more magisterial
physiognomy of the house; and a little bristling, bustling
terrier bestowed a desultory attendance upon the other
gentlemen.

One of these was a remarkably well-made man of five-and-
thirty, with a face as English as that of the old gentleman I
have just sketched was something else; a noticeably handsome
face, fresh-coloured, fair, and frank, with firm, straight features, a lively grey eye, and the rich adornment of a chestnut
beard. This person had a certain fortunate, brilliant excep-

tional look—the air of a happy temperament fertilised by a high civilisation—which would have made almost any observer envy him at a venture. He was booted and spurred, as if he had dismounted from a long ride; he wore a white hat, which looked too large for him; he held his two hands behind him, and in one of them—a large, white, well-shaped fist—was crumpled a pair of soiled dog-skin gloves.

His companion, measuring the length of the lawn beside him, was a person of quite another pattern, who, although he might have excited grave curiosity, would not, like the other, have provoked you to wish yourself, almost blindly, in his place. Tall, lean, loosely and feebly put together, he had an ugly, sickly, witty, charming face—furnished, but by no means decorated, with a straggling moustache and whisker. He looked clever and ill—a combination by no means felicitous; and he wore a brown velvet jacket. He carried his hands in his pockets, and there was something in the way he did it that showed the habit was inveterate. His gait had a shambling, wandering quality; he was not very firm on his legs. As I have said, whenever he passed the old man in the chair, he rested his eyes upon him; and at this moment, with their faces brought into relation, you would easily have seen that they were father and son.

The father caught his son's eye at last, and gave him a mild, responsive smile.

"I am getting on very well," he said.

"Have you drunk your tea?" asked the son.

"Yes, and enjoyed it."

"Shall I give you some more?"

The old man considered, placidly.

"Well, I guess I will wait and see."

He had, in speaking, the American tone.

"Are you cold?" his son inquired.

The father slowly rubbed his legs.

"Well, I don't know. I can't tell till I feel."

"Perhaps some one might feel for you," said the younger man, laughing.

"Oh, I hope some one will always feel for me! Don't you feel for me, Lord Warburton?"

"Oh yes, immensely," said the gentleman addressed as Lord

Warburton, promptly. "I am bound to say you look wonder-fully comfortable."

"Well, I suppose I am, in most respects." And the old man looked down at his green shawl, and smoothed it over his knees. "The fact is, I have been comfortable so many years that I suppose I have got so used to it I don't know it."

"Yes, that's the bore of comfort," said Lord Warburton. "We only know when we are uncomfortable."

"It strikes me that we are rather particular," said his companion.

"Oh yes, there is no doubt we're particular," Lord Warburton murmured.

And then the three men remained silent a while; the two younger ones standing looking down at the other, who presently asked for more tea.

"I should think you would be very unhappy with that shawl," said Lord Warburton, while his companion filled the old man's cup again.

"Oh no, he must have the shawl!" cried the gentleman in the velvet coat. "Don't put such ideas as that into his head."

"It belongs to my wife," said the old man, simply.

"Oh, if it's for sentimental reasons——" And Lord Warburton made a gesture of apology.

"I suppose I must give it to her when she comes," the old man went on.

"You will please to do nothing of the kind. You will keep it to cover your poor old legs."

"Well, you mustn't abuse my legs," said the old man. "I guess they are as good as yours."

"Oh, you are perfectly free to abuse mine," his son replied, giving him his tea.

"Well, we are two lame ducks; I don't think there is much difference."

"I am much obliged to you for calling me a duck. How is your tea?"

"Well, it's rather hot."

"That's intended to be a merit."

"Ah, there's a great deal of merit," murmured the old man, kindly. "He's a very good nurse, Lord Warburton."

"Isn't he a bit clumsy?" asked his lordship.

"Oh no, he's not clumsy—considering that he's an invalid himself. He's a very good nurse—for a sick-nurse. I call him my sick-nurse because he's sick himself."

"Oh, come, daddy!" the ugly young man exclaimed.

"Well, you are; I wish you weren't. But I suppose you can't help it."

"I might try: that's an idea," said the young man.

"Were you ever sick, Lord Warburton?" his father asked.

Lord Warburton considered a moment.

"Yes, sir, once, in the Persian Gulf."

"He is making light of you, daddy," said the other young man. "That's a sort of joke."

"Well, there seem to be so many sorts now," daddy replied, serenely. "You don't look as if you had been sick, any way, Lord Warburton."

"He is sick of life; he was just telling me so; going on fearfully about it," said Lord Warburton's friend.

"Is that true, sir?" asked the old man gravely.

"If it is, your son gave me no consolation. He's a wretched fellow to talk to—a regular cynic. He doesn't seem to believe anything."

"That's another sort of joke," said the person accused of cynicism.

"It's because his health is so poor," his father explained to Lord Warburton. "It affects his mind, and colours his way of looking at things; he seems to feel as if he had never had a chance. But it's almost entirely theoretical, you know; it doesn't seem to affect his spirits. I have hardly ever seen him when he wasn't cheerful—about as he is at present. He often cheers me up."

The young man so described looked at Lord Warburton and laughed.

"Is it a glowing eulogy or an accusation of levity? Should you like me to carry out my theories, daddy?"

"By Jove, we should see some queer things!" cried Lord Warburton.

"I hope you haven't taken up that sort of tone," said the old man.

"Warburton's tone is worse than mine; he pretends to be

bored. I am not in the least bored; I find life only too interesting."

"Ah, *too* interesting; you shouldn't allow it to be that, you know!"

"I am never bored when I come here," said Lord Warburton. "One gets such uncommonly good talk."

"Is that another sort of joke?" asked the old man. "You have no excuse for being bored anywhere. When I was your age, I had never heard of such a thing."

"You must have developed very late."

"No, I developed very quick; that was just the reason. When I was twenty years old, I was very highly developed indeed. I was working, tooth and nail. You wouldn't be bored if you had something to do; but all you young men are too idle. You think too much of your pleasure. You are too fastidious, and too indolent, and too rich."

"Oh, I say," cried Lord Warburton, "you're hardly the person to accuse a fellow-creature of being too rich!"

"Do you mean because I am a banker?" asked the old man.

"Because of that, if you like; and because you are so ridiculously wealthy."

"He isn't very rich," said the other young man, indicating his father. "He has given away an immense deal of money."

"Well, I suppose it was his own," said Lord Warburton; "and in that case could there be a better proof of wealth? Let not a public benefactor talk of one's being too fond of pleasure."

"Daddy is very fond of pleasure—of other people's."

The old man shook his head.

"I don't pretend to have contributed anything to the amusement of my contemporaries."

"My dear father, you are too modest!"

"That's a kind of joke, sir," said Lord Warburton.

"You young men have too many jokes. When there are no jokes, you have nothing left."

"Fortunately there are always more jokes," the ugly young man remarked.

"I don't believe it—I believe things are getting more serious. You young men will find that out."

"The increasing seriousness of things—that is the great opportunity of jokes."

"They will have to be grim jokes," said the old man. "I am convinced there will be great changes; and not all for the better."

"I quite agree with you, sir," Lord Warburton declared. "I am very sure there will be great changes, and that all sorts of queer things will happen. That's why I find so much difficulty in applying your advice; you know you told me the other day that I ought to 'take hold' of something. One hesitates to take hold of a thing that may the next moment be knocked sky-high."

"You ought to take hold of a pretty woman," said his companion. "He is trying hard to fall in love," he added, by way of explanation, to his father.

"The pretty women themselves may be sent flying!" Lord Warburton exclaimed.

"No, no, they will be firm," the old man rejoined; "they will not be affected by the social and political changes I just referred to."

"You mean they won't be abolished? Very well, then, I will lay hands on one as soon as possible, and tie her round my neck as a life-preserver."

"The ladies will save us," said the old man; "that is, the best of them will—for I make a difference between them. Make up to a good one and marry her, and your life will become much more interesting."

A momentary silence marked perhaps on the part of his auditors a sense of the magnanimity of this speech, for it was a secret neither for his son nor for his visitor that his own experiment in matrimony had not been a happy one. As he said, however, he made a difference; and these words may have been intended as a confession of personal error; though of course it was not in place for either of his companions to remark that apparently the lady of his choice had not been one of the best.

"If I marry an interesting woman, I shall be interested: is that what you say?" Lord Warburton asked. "I am not at all keen about marrying—your son misrepresented me; but there is no knowing what an interesting woman might do with me."

"I should like to see your idea of an interesting woman," said his friend.

"My dear fellow, you can't see ideas—especially such ethereal ones as mine. If I could only see it myself—that would be a great step in advance."

"Well, you may fall in love with whomsoever you please; but you must not fall in love with my niece," said the old man.

His son broke into a laugh. "He will think you mean that as a provocation! My dear father, you have lived with the English for thirty years, and you have picked up a good many of the things they say. But you have never learned the things they don't say!"

"I say what I please," the old man declared, with all his serenity.

"I haven't the honour of knowing your niece," Lord Warburton said. "I think it is the first time I have heard of her."

"She is a niece of my wife's; Mrs. Touchett brings her to England."

Then young Mr. Touchett explained. "My mother, you know, has been spending the winter in America, and we are expecting her back. She writes that she has discovered a niece, and that she has invited her to come with her."

"I see—very kind of her," said Lord Warburton. "Is the young lady interesting?"

"We hardly know more about her than you; my mother has not gone into details. She chiefly communicates with us by means of telegrams, and her telegrams are rather inscrutable. They say women don't know how to write them, but my mother has thoroughly mastered the art of condensation. 'Tired America, hot weather awful, return England with niece, first steamer, decent cabin.' That's the sort of message we get from her—that was the last that came. But there had been another before, which I think contained the first mention of the niece. 'Changed hotel, very bad, impudent clerk, address here. Taken sister's girl, died last year, go to Europe, two sisters, quite independent.' Over that my father and I have scarcely stopped puzzling; it seems to admit of so many interpretations."

"There is one thing very clear in it," said the old man; "she has given the hotel-clerk a dressing."

"I am not sure even of that, since he has driven her from the field. We thought at first that the sister mentioned might be the sister of the clerk; but the subsequent mention of a niece seems to prove that the allusion is to one of my aunts. Then there was a question as to whose the two other sisters were; they are probably two of my late aunt's daughters. But who is 'quite independent,' and in what sense is the term used?—that point is not yet settled. Does the expression apply more particularly to the young lady my mother has adopted, or does it characterise her sisters equally?—and is it used in a moral or in a financial sense? Does it mean that they have been left well off, or that they wish to be under no obligations? or does it simply mean that they are fond of their own way?"

"Whatever else it means, it is pretty sure to mean that," Mr. Touchett remarked.

"You will see for yourself," said Lord Warburton. "When does Mrs. Touchett arrive?"

"We are quite in the dark; as soon as she can find a decent cabin. She may be waiting for it yet; on the other hand, she may already have disembarked in England."

"In that case she would probably have telegraphed to you."

"She never telegraphs when you would expect it—only when you don't," said the old man. "She likes to drop on me suddenly; she thinks she will find me doing something wrong. She has never done so yet, but she is not discouraged."

"It's her independence," her son explained, more favourably. "Whatever that of those young ladies may be, her own is a match for it. She likes to do everything for herself, and has no belief in any one's power to help her. She thinks me of no more use than a postage-stamp without gum, and she would never forgive me if I should presume to go to Liverpool to meet her."

"Will you at least let me know when your cousin arrives?" Lord Warburton asked.

"Only on the condition I have mentioned—that you don't fall in love with her!" Mr. Touchett declared.

"That strikes me as hard. Don't you think me good enough?"

"I think you too good—because I shouldn't like her to marry you. She hasn't come here to look for a husband, I hope; so many young ladies are doing that, as if there were no good ones at home. Then she is probably engaged; American girls are usually engaged, I believe. Moreover, I am not sure, after all, that you would be a good husband."

"Very likely she is engaged; I have known a good many American girls, and they always were; but I could never see that it made any difference, upon my word! As for my being a good husband, I am not sure of that either; one can but try!"

"Try as much as you please, but don't try on my niece," said the old man, whose opposition to the idea was broadly humorous.

"Ah, well," said Lord Warburton, with a humour broader still, "perhaps, after all, she is not worth trying on!"

II

WHILE this exchange of pleasantries took place between the two, Ralph Touchett wandered away a little, with his usual slouching gait, his hands in his pockets, and his little rowdyish terrier at his heels. His face was turned towards the house, but his eyes were bent, musingly, upon the lawn; so that he had been an object of observation to a person who had just made her appearance in the doorway of the dwelling for some moments before he perceived her. His attention was called to her by the conduct of his dog, who had suddenly darted forward, with a little volley of shrill barks, in which the note of welcome, however, was more sensible than that of defiance. The person in question was a young lady, who seemed immediately to interpret the greeting of the little terrier. He advanced with great rapidity, and stood at her feet, looking up and barking hard; whereupon, without hesitation, she stooped and caught him in her hands, holding him face to face while he continued his joyous demonstration. His master now had had time to follow and to see that Bunchie's new friend was a tall girl in a black dress, who at first sight looked pretty. She was bare-headed, as if she were staying in the house—a fact which conveyed perplexity to the son of its master, conscious of that immunity from visitors which had for some time been rendered necessary by the latter's ill-health. Meantime the two other gentlemen had also taken note of the new-comer.

"Dear me, who is that strange woman?" Mr. Touchett had asked.

"Perhaps it is Mrs. Touchett's niece—the independent young lady," Lord Warburton suggested. "I think she must be, from the way she handles the dog."

The collie, too, had now allowed his attention to be diverted, and he trotted toward the young lady in the doorway, slowly setting his tail in motion as he went.

"But where is my wife, then?" murmured the old man.

"I suppose the young lady has left her somewhere: that's a part of the independence."

The girl spoke to Ralph, smiling, while she still held up the terrier. "Is this your little dog, sir?"

"He was mine a moment ago; but you have suddenly acquired a remarkable air of property in him."

"Couldn't we share him?" asked the girl. "He's such a little darling."

Ralph looked at her a moment; she was unexpectedly pretty. "You may have him altogether," he said.

The young lady seemed to have a great deal of confidence, both in herself and in others; but this abrupt generosity made her blush. "I ought to tell you that I am probably your cousin," she murmured, putting down the dog. "And here's another!" she added quickly, as the collie came up.

"Probably?" the young man exclaimed, laughing. "I supposed it was quite settled! Have you come with my mother?"

"Yes, half-an-hour ago."

"And has she deposited you and departed again?"

"No, she went straight to her room; and she told me that, if I should see you, I was to say to you that you must come to her there at a quarter to seven."

The young man looked at his watch. "Thank you very much; I shall be punctual." And then he looked at his cousin. "You are very welcome here," he went on. "I am delighted to see you."

She was looking at everything, with an eye that denoted quick perception—at her companion, at the two dogs, at the two gentlemen under the trees, at the beautiful scene that surrounded her. "I have never seen anything so lovely as this place," she said. "I have been all over the house; it's too enchanting."

"I am sorry you should have been here so long without our knowing it."

"Your mother told me that in England people arrived very quietly; so I thought it was all right. Is one of those gentlemen your father?"

"Yes, the elder one—the one sitting down," said Ralph.

The young girl gave a laugh. "I don't suppose it's the other. Who is the other?"

"He is a friend of ours—Lord Warburton."

"Oh, I hoped there would be a lord; it's just like a novel!"

And then—"O you adorable creature!" she suddenly cried, stooping down and picking up the little terrier again.

She remained standing where they had met, making no offer to advance or to speak to Mr. Touchett, and while she lingered in the doorway, slim and charming, her interlocutor wondered whether she expected the old man to come and pay her his respects. American girls were used to a great deal of deference, and it had been intimated that this one had a high spirit. Indeed, Ralph could see that in her face.

"Won't you come and make acquaintance with my father?" he nevertheless ventured to ask. "He is old and infirm—he doesn't leave his chair."

"Ah, poor man, I am very sorry!" the girl exclaimed, immediately moving forward. "I got the impression from your mother that he was rather—rather strong."

Ralph Touchett was silent a moment.

"She has not seen him for a year."

"Well, he has got a lovely place to sit. Come along, little dogs."

"It's a dear old place," said the young man, looking sidewise at his neighbour.

"What's his name?" she asked, her attention having reverted to the terrier again.

"My father's name?"

"Yes," said the young lady, humorously; "but don't tell him I asked you."

They had come by this time to where old Mr. Touchett was sitting, and he slowly got up from his chair to introduce himself.

"My mother has arrived," said Ralph, "and this is Miss Archer."

The old man placed his two hands on her shoulders, looked at her a moment with extreme benevolence, and then gallantly kissed her.

"It is a great pleasure to me to see you here; but I wish you had given us a chance to receive you."

"Oh, we were received," said the girl. "There were about a dozen servants in the hall. And there was an old woman curtseying at the gate."

"We can do better than that—if we have notice!" And the

old man stood there, smiling, rubbing his hands, and slowly shaking his head at her. "But Mrs. Touchett doesn't like receptions."

"She went straight to her room."

"Yes—and locked herself in. She always does that. Well, I suppose I shall see her next week." And Mrs. Touchett's husband slowly resumed his former posture.

"Before that," said Miss Archer. "She is coming down to dinner—at eight o'clock. Don't you forget a quarter to seven," she added, turning with a smile to Ralph.

"What is to happen at a quarter to seven?"

"I am to see my mother," said Ralph.

"Ah, happy boy!" the old man murmured. "You must sit down—you must have some tea," he went on, addressing his wife's niece.

"They gave me some tea in my room the moment I arrived," this young lady answered. "I am sorry you are out of health," she added, resting her eyes upon her venerable host.

"Oh, I'm an old man, my dear; it's time for me to be old. But I shall be the better for having you here."

She had been looking all round her again—at the lawn, the great trees, the reedy, silvery Thames, the beautiful old house; and while engaged in this survey, she had also narrowly scrutinized her companions; a comprehensiveness of observation easily conceivable on the part of a young woman who was evidently both intelligent and excited. She had seated herself, and had put away the little dog; her white hands, in her lap, were folded upon her black dress; her head was erect, her eye brilliant, her flexible figure turned itself lightly this way and that, in sympathy with the alertness with which she evidently caught impressions. Her impressions were numerous, and they were all reflected in a clear, still smile. "I have never seen anything so beautiful as this," she declared.

"It's looking very well," said Mr. Touchett. "I know the way it strikes you. I have been through all that. But you are very beautiful yourself," he added with a politeness by no means crudely jocular, and with the happy consciousness that his advanced age gave him the privilege of saying such things—even to young girls who might possibly take alarm at them.

What degree of alarm this young girl took need not be exactly measured; she instantly rose, however, with a blush which was not a refutation.

"Oh yes, of course, I'm lovely!" she exclaimed quickly, with a little laugh. "How old is your house? Is it Elizabethan?"

"It's early Tudor," said Ralph Touchett.

She turned toward him, watching his face a little. "Early Tudor? How very delightful! And I suppose there are a great many others."

"There are many much better ones."

"Don't say that, my son!" the old man protested. "There is nothing better than this."

"I have got a very good one; I think in some respects it's rather better," said Lord Warburton, who as yet had not spoken, but who had kept an attentive eye upon Miss Archer. He bent towards her a little smiling; he had an excellent manner with women. The girl appreciated it in an instant; she had not forgotten that this was Lord Warburton. "I should like very much to show it to you," he added.

"Don't believe him," cried the old man; "don't look at it! It's a wretched old barrack—not to be compared with this."

"I don't know—I can't judge," said the girl, smiling at Lord Warburton.

In this discussion, Ralph Touchett took no interest whatever; he stood with his hands in his pockets, looking greatly as if he should like to renew his conversation with his new-found cousin.

"Are you very fond of dogs?" he inquired, by way of beginning; and it was an awkward beginning for a clever man.

"Very fond of them indeed."

"You must keep the terrier, you know," he went on, still awkwardly.

"I will keep him while I am here, with pleasure."

"That will be for a long time, I hope."

"You are very kind. I hardly know. My aunt must settle that."

"I will settle it with her—at a quarter to seven." And Ralph looked at his watch again.

"I am glad to be here at all," said the girl.

"I don't believe you allow things to be settled for you."

"Oh yes; if they are settled as I like them."

"I shall settle this as I like it," said Ralph. "It's most unaccountable that we should never have known you."

"I was there—you had only to come and see me."

"There? Where do you mean?"

"In the United States: in New York, and Albany, and other places."

"I have been there—all over, but I never saw you. I can't make it out."

Miss Archer hesitated a moment.

"It was because there had been some disagreement between your mother and my father, after my mother's death, which took place when I was a child. In consequence of it, we never expected to see you."

"Ah, but I don't embrace all my mother's quarrels—Heaven forbid!" the young man cried. "You have lately lost your father?" he went on, more gravely.

"Yes; more than a year ago. After that my aunt was very kind to me; she came to see me, and proposed that I should come to Europe."

"I see," said Ralph. "She has adopted you."

"Adopted me?" The girl stared, and her blush came back to her, together with a momentary look of pain, which gave her interlocutor some alarm. He had under-estimated the effect of his words. Lord Warburton, who appeared constantly desirous of a nearer view of Miss Archer, strolled toward the two cousins at the moment, and as he did so, she rested her startled eyes upon him. "Oh, no; she has not adopted me," she said. "I am not a candidate for adoption."

"I beg a thousand pardons," Ralph murmured. "I meant—I meant——" He hardly knew what he meant.

"You meant she has taken me up. Yes; she likes to take people up. She has been very kind to me; but," she added, with a certain visible eagerness of desire to be explicit, "I am very fond of my liberty."

"Are you talking about Mrs. Touchett?" the old man called out from his chair. "Come here, my dear, and tell me about her. I am always thankful for information."

The girl hesitated a moment, smiling.

"She is really very benevolent," she answered; and then she

went over to her uncle, whose mirth was excited by her words.

Lord Warburton was left standing with Ralph Touchett, to whom in a moment he said—

"You wished a while ago to see my idea of an interesting woman. There it is!"

III

M<small>RS. TOUCHETT</small> was certainly a person of many oddities, of which her behaviour on returning to her husband's house after many months was a noticeable specimen. She had her own way of doing all that she did, and this is the simplest description of a character which, although it was by no means without benevolence, rarely succeeded in giving an impression of softness. Mrs. Touchett might do a great deal of good, but she never pleased. This way of her own, of which she was so fond, was not intrinsically offensive—it was simply very sharply distinguished from the ways of others. The edges of her conduct were so very clear-cut that for susceptible persons it sometimes had a wounding effect. This purity of outline was visible in her deportment during the first hours of her return from America, under circumstances in which it might have seemed that her first act would have been to exchange greetings with her husband and son. Mrs. Touchett, for reasons which she deemed excellent, always retired on such occasions into impenetrable seclusion, postponing the more sentimental ceremony until she had achieved a toilet which had the less reason to be of high importance as neither beauty nor vanity were concerned in it. She was a plain-faced old woman, without coquetry and without any great elegance, but with an extreme respect for her own motives. She was usually prepared to explain these—when the explanation was asked as a favour; and in such a case they proved totally different from those that had been attributed to her. She was virtually separated from her husband, but she appeared to perceive nothing irregular in the situation. It had become apparent, at an early stage of their relations, that they should never desire the same thing at the same moment, and this fact had prompted her to rescue disagreement from the vulgar realm of accident. She did what she could to erect it into a law—a much more edifying aspect of it—by going to live in Florence, where she bought a house and established herself; leaving her husband in England to take care of his bank. This arrangement greatly pleased her; it was so extremely definite. It struck her husband in the same light, in a foggy square in

London, where it was at times the most definite fact he discerned; but he would have preferred that discomfort should have a greater vagueness. To agree to disagree had cost him an effort; he was ready to agree to almost anything but that, and saw no reason why either assent or dissent should be so terribly consistent. Mrs. Touchett indulged in no regrets nor speculations, and usually came once a year to spend a month with her husband, a period during which she apparently took pains to convince him that she had adopted the right system. She was not fond of England, and had three or four reasons for it to which she currently alluded; they bore upon minor points of British civilisation, but for Mrs. Touchett they amply justified non-residence. She detested bread-sauce, which, as she said, looked like a poultice and tasted like soap; she objected to the consumption of beer by her maid-servants; and she affirmed that the British laundress (Mrs. Touchett was very particular about the appearance of her linen) was not a mistress of her art. At fixed intervals she paid a visit to her own country; but this last one had been longer than any of its predecessors.

She had taken up her niece—there was little doubt of that. One wet afternoon, some four months earlier than the occurrence lately narrated, this young lady had been seated alone with a book. To say that she had a book is to say that her solitude did not press upon her; for her love of knowledge had a fertilising quality and her imagination was strong. There was at this time, however, a want of lightness in her situation, which the arrival of an unexpected visitor did much to dispel. The visitor had not been announced; the girl heard her at last walking about the adjoining room. It was an old house at Albany—a large, square, double house, with a notice of sale in the windows of the parlour. There were two entrances, one of which had long been out of use, but had never been removed. They were exactly alike—large white doors, with an arched frame and wide side-lights, perched upon little "stoops" of red stone, which descended sidewise to the brick pavement of the street. The two houses together formed a single dwelling, the party-wall having been removed and the rooms placed in communication. These rooms, above-stairs, were extremely numerous, and were painted all over exactly alike, in a yellowish white which had grown sallow with time. On the third floor there was a sort of arched passage, connecting the two sides of the house, which Isabel and her sisters used in their childhood to call the tunnel, and which, though it was short and well-lighted, always seemed to the girl to be strange and lonely, especially on winter afternoons. She had been in the house, at different periods, as a child; in those days her grandmother lived there. Then there had been an absence of ten years, followed by a return to Albany before her father's death. Her grandmother, old Mrs. Archer, had exercised, chiefly within the limits of the family, a large hospitality in the early period, and the little girls often spent weeks under her roof—weeks of which Isabel had the happiest memory. The manner of life was different from that of her own home—larger, more plentiful, more sociable; the discipline of the nursery was delightfully vague, and the opportunity of listening to the conversation of one's elders (which with Isabel was a highly-valued pleasure) almost unbounded. There was a constant coming and going; her grandmother's sons and daughters, and their children, appeared to be in the enjoyment of standing invitations to stay with her, so that the house offered, to a certain extent, the appearance of a bustling provincial inn, kept by a gentle old landlady who sighed a great deal and never presented a bill. Isabel, of course, knew nothing about bills; but even as a child she thought her grandmother's dwelling picturesque. There was a covered piazza behind it, furnished with a swing, which was a source of tremulous interest; and beyond this was a long garden, sloping down to the stable, and containing certain capital peach-trees. Isabel had stayed with her grandmother at various seasons; but, somehow, all her visits had a flavour of peaches. On the other side, opposite, across the street, was an old house that was called the Dutch House—a peculiar structure, dating from the earliest colonial time, composed of bricks that had been painted yellow, crowned with a gable that was pointed out to strangers, defended by a rickety wooden paling, and standing sidewise to the street. It was occupied by a primary school for children of both sexes, kept in an amateurish manner by a demonstrative lady, of whom Isabel's chief recollection was that her hair was puffed out very much at the temples and that she was the widow of some one of consequence. The little girl had been offered the opportunity of laying a foundation of knowledge in this establishment; but having spent a single day in it, she had expressed great disgust with the place, and had been allowed to stay at home, where in the September days, when the windows of the Dutch House were open, she used to hear the hum of childish voices repeating the multiplication table—an incident in which the elation of liberty and the pain of exclusion were indistinguishably mingled. The foundation of her knowledge was really laid in the idleness of her grandmother's house, where, as most of the other inmates were not reading people, she had uncontrolled use of a library full of books with frontispieces, which she used to climb upon a chair to take down. When she had found one to her taste—she was guided in the selection chiefly by the frontispiece—she carried it into a mysterious apartment which lay beyond the library, and which was called, traditionally, no one knew why, the office. Whose office it had been, and at what period it had flourished, she never learned; it was enough for her that it contained an echo and a pleasant musty smell, and that it was a chamber of disgrace for old pieces of furniture, whose infirmities were not always apparent (so that the disgrace seemed unmerited, and rendered them victims of injustice), and with which, in the manner of children, she had established relations almost human, or dramatic. There was an old haircloth sofa, in especial, to which she had confided a hundred childish sorrows. The place owed much of its mysterious melancholy to the fact that it was properly entered from the second door of the house, the door that had been condemned, and that was fastened by bolts which a particularly slender little girl found it impossible to slide. She knew that this silent, motionless portal opened into the street; if the sidelights had not been filled with green paper, she might have looked out upon the little brown stoop and the well-worn brick pavement. But she had no wish to look out, for this would have interfered with her theory that there was a strange, unseen place on the other side—a place which became, to the child's imagination, according to its different moods, a region of delight or of terror.

It was in the "office" still that Isabel was sitting on that melancholy afternoon of early spring which I have just mentioned. At this time she might have had the whole house to choose from, and the room she had selected was the most joyless chamber it contained. She had never opened the bolted door nor removed the green paper (renewed by other hands) from its side-lights; she had never assured herself that the vulgar street lay beyond it. A crude, cold rain was falling heavily; the spring-time presented itself as a questionable improvement. Isabel, however, gave as little attention as possible to the incongruities of the season; she kept her eyes on her book and tried to fix her mind. It had lately occurred to her that her mind was a good deal of a vagabond, and she had spent much ingenuity in training it to a military step, and teaching it to advance, to halt, to retreat, to perform even more complicated manœuvres, at the word of command. Just now she had given it marching orders, and it had been trudging over the sandy plains of a history of German Thought. Suddenly she became aware of a step very different from her own intellectual pace; she listened a little, and perceived that some one was walking about the library, which communicated with the office. It struck her first as the step of a person from whom she had reason to expect a visit; then almost immediately announced itself as the tread of a woman and a stranger—her possible visitor being neither. It had an inquisitive, experimental quality, which suggested that it would not stop short of the threshold of the office; and, in fact, the doorway of this apartment was presently occupied by a lady who paused there and looked very hard at our heroine. She was a plain, elderly woman, dressed in a comprehensive waterproof mantle: she had a sharp, but not an unpleasant, face.

"Oh," she said, "is that where you usually sit?" And she looked about at the heterogeneous chairs and tables.

"Not when I have visitors," said Isabel, getting up to receive the intruder.

She directed their course back to the library, and the visitor continued to look about her. "You seem to have plenty of other rooms; they are in rather better condition. But everything is immensely worn."

"Have you come to look at the house?" Isabel asked. "The servant will show it to you."

"Send her away; I don't want to buy it. She has probably gone to look for you, and is wandering about up-stairs; she didn't seem at all intelligent. You had better tell her it is no matter." And then, while the girl stood there, hesitating and wondering, this unexpected critic said to her abruptly, "I suppose you are one of the daughters?"

Isabel thought she had very strange manners. "It depends upon whose daughters you mean."

"The late Mr. Archer's—and my poor sister's."

"Ah," said Isabel, slowly, "you must be our crazy Aunt Lydia!"

"Is that what your father told you to call me? I am your Aunt Lydia, but I am not crazy. And which of the daughters are you?"

"I am the youngest of the three, and my name is Isabel."

"Yes; the others are Lilian and Edith. And are you the prettiest?"

"I have not the least idea," said the girl.

"I think you must be." And in this way the aunt and the niece made friends. The aunt had quarrelled, years before, with her brother-in-law, after the death of her sister, taking him to task for the manner in which he brought up his three girls. Being a high-tempered man, he had requested her to mind her own business; and she had taken him at his word. For many years she held no communication with him, and after his death she addressed not a word to his daughters, who had been bred in that disrespectful view of her which we have just seen Isabel betray. Mrs. Touchett's behaviour was, as usual, perfectly deliberate. She intended to go to America to look after her investments (with which her husband, in spite of his great financial position, had nothing to do), and would take advantage of this opportunity to inquire into the condition of her nieces. There was no need of writing, for she should attach no importance to any account of them that she should elicit by letter; she believed, always, in seeing for one's self. Isabel found, however, that she knew a good deal about them, and knew about the marriage of the two elder girls; knew that their poor father had left very little money, but that the house in Albany, which had passed into his hands, was to be sold for their benefit; knew, finally, that Edmund Ludlow, Lilian's husband, had taken upon himself to attend to this matter, in consideration of which the young couple, who had come to Albany during Mr. Archer's illness, were remaining there for the present, and, as well as Isabel herself, occupying the mansion.

"How much money do you expect to get for it?" Mrs. Touchett asked of the girl, who had brought her to sit in the front-parlour, which she had inspected without enthusiasm.

"I haven't the least idea," said the girl.

"That's the second time you have said that to me," her aunt rejoined. "And yet you don't look at all stupid."

"I am not stupid; but I don't know anything about money."

"Yes, that's the way you were brought up—as if you were to inherit a million. In point of fact, what have you inherited?"

"I really can't tell you. You must ask Edmund and Lilian; they will be back in half-an-hour."

"In Florence we should call it a very bad house," said Mrs. Touchett; "but here, I suspect, it will bring a high price. It ought to make a considerable sum for each of you. In addition to that, you *must* have something else; it's most extraordinary your not knowing. The position is of value, and they will probably pull it down and make a row of shops. I wonder you don't do that yourself; you might let the shops to great advantage."

Isabel stared; the idea of letting shops was new to her.

"I hope they won't pull it down," she said; "I am extremely fond of it."

"I don't see what makes you fond of it; your father died here."

"Yes; but I don't dislike it for that," said the girl, rather strangely. "I like places in which things have happened—even if they are sad things. A great many people have died here; the place has been full of life."

"Is that what you call being full of life?"

"I mean full of experience—of people's feelings and

sorrows. And not of their sorrows only, for I have been very happy here as a child."

"You should go to Florence if you like houses in which things have happened—especially deaths. I live in an old palace in which three people have been murdered; three that were known, and I don't know how many more besides."

"In an old palace?" Isabel repeated.

"Yes, my dear; a very different affair from this. This is very *bourgeois*."

Isabel felt some emotion, for she had always thought highly of her grandmother's house. But the emotion was of a kind which led her to say—

"I should like very much to go to Florence."

"Well, if you will be very good, and do everything I tell you, I will take you there," Mrs. Touchett rejoined.

The girl's emotion deepened; she flushed a little, and smiled at her aunt in silence.

"Do everything you tell me? I don't think I can promise that."

"No, you don't look like a young lady of that sort. You are fond of your own way; but it's not for me to blame you."

"And yet, to go to Florence," the girl exclaimed in a moment, "I would promise almost anything!"

Edmund and Lilian were slow to return, and Mrs. Touchett had an hour's uninterrupted talk with her niece, who found her a strange and interesting person. She was as eccentric as Isabel had always supposed; and hitherto, whenever the girl had heard people described as eccentric, she had thought of them as disagreeable. To her imagination the term had always suggested something grotesque and inharmonious. But her aunt infused a new vividness into the idea, and gave her so many fresh impressions that it seemed to her she had over-estimated the charms of conformity. She had never met any one so entertaining as this little thin-lipped, bright-eyed, foreign-looking woman, who retrieved an insignificant appearance by a distinguished manner, and, sitting there in a well-worn waterproof, talked with striking familiarity of European courts. There was nothing flighty about Mrs. Touchett, but she was fond of social grandeur, and she enjoyed the consciousness of making an impression on a candid and susceptible mind. Isabel at first had answered a good many questions, and it was from her answers apparently that Mrs. Touchett derived a high opinion of her intelligence. But after this she had asked a good many, and her aunt's answers, whatever they were, struck her as deeply interesting. Mrs. Touchett waited for the return of her other niece as long as she thought reasonable, but as at six o'clock Mrs. Ludlow had not come in, she prepared to take her departure.

"Your sister must be a great gossip," she said. "Is she accustomed to staying out for hours?"

"You have been out almost as long as she," Isabel answered; "she can have left the house but a short time before you came in."

Mrs. Touchett looked at the girl without resentment; she appeared to enjoy a bold retort, and to be disposed to be gracious to her niece.

"Perhaps she has not had so good an excuse as I. Tell her, at any rate, that she must come and see me this evening at that horrid hotel. She may bring her husband if she likes, but she needn't bring you. I shall see plenty of you later."

IV

MRS. LUDLOW was the eldest of the three sisters, and was usually thought the most sensible; the classification being in general that Lilian was the practical one, Edith the beauty, and Isabel the "intellectual" one. Mrs. Keyes, the second sister, was the wife of an officer in the United States Engineers, and as our history is not further concerned with her, it will be enough to say that she was indeed very pretty, and that she formed the ornament of those various military stations, chiefly in the unfashionable West, to which, to her deep chagrin, her husband was successively relegated. Lilian had married a New York lawyer, a young man with a loud voice and an enthusiasm for his profession; the match was not brilliant, any more than Edith's had been, but Lilian had occasionally been spoken of as a young woman who might be thankful to marry at all—she was so much plainer than her sisters. She was, however, very happy, and now, as the mother of two peremptory little boys, and the mistress of a house which presented a narrowness of new brown stone to Fifty-third Street, she had quite justified her claim to matrimony. She was short and plump, and, as people said, had improved since her marriage; the two things in life of which she was most distinctly conscious were her husband's force in argument and her sister Isabel's originality. "I have never felt like Isabel's sister, and I am sure I never shall," she had said to an intimate friend; a declaration which made it all the more creditable that she had been prolific in sisterly offices.

"I want to see her safely married—that's what I want to see," she frequently remarked to her husband.

"Well, I must say I should have no particular desire to marry her," Edmund Ludlow was accustomed to answer, in an extremely audible tone.

"I know you say that for argument; you always take the opposite ground. I don't see what you have against her, except that she is so original."

"Well, I don't like originals; I like translations," Mr. Ludlow had more than once replied. "Isabel is written in a foreign tongue. I can't make her out. She ought to marry an Armenian, or a Portuguese."

"That's just what I am afraid she will do!" cried Lilian, who thought Isabel capable of anything.

She listened with great interest to the girl's account of Mrs. Touchett's visit, and in the evening prepared to comply with her commands. Of what Isabel said to her no report has remained, but her sister's words must have prompted a remark that she made to her husband in the conjugal chamber as the two were getting ready to go to the hotel.

"I do hope immensely she will do something handsome for Isabel; she has evidently taken a great fancy to her."

"What is it you wish her to do?" Edmund Ludlow asked; "make her a big present?"

"No, indeed; nothing of the sort. But take an interest in her—sympathise with her. She is evidently just the sort of person to appreciate Isabel. She has lived so much in foreign society; she told Isabel all about it. You know you have always thought Isabel rather foreign."

"You want her to give her a little foreign sympathy, eh? Don't you think she gets enough at home?"

"Well, she ought to go abroad," said Mrs. Ludlow. "She's just the person to go abroad."

"And you want the old lady to take her, is that it?" her husband asked.

"She has offered to take her—she is dying to have Isabel go! But what I want her to do when she gets her there is to give her all the advantages. I am sure that all we have got to do," said Mrs. Ludlow, "is to give her a chance!"

"A chance for what?"

"A chance to develop."

"O Jupiter!" Edmund Ludlow exclaimed. "I hope she isn't going to develop any more!"

"If I were not sure you only said that for argument, I should feel very badly," his wife replied. "But you know you love her."

"Do *you* know I love you?" the young man said, jocosely, to Isabel a little later, while he brushed his hat.

"I am sure I don't care whether you do or not!" exclaimed the girl, whose voice and smile, however, were sweeter than the words she uttered.

"Oh, she feels so grand since Mrs. Touchett's visit," said her sister.

But Isabel challenged this assertion with a good deal of seriousness.

"You must not say that, Lily. I don't feel grand at all."

"I am sure there is no harm," said the conciliatory Lily.

"Ah, but there is nothing in Mrs. Touchett's visit to make one feel grand."

"Oh," exclaimed Ludlow, "she is grander than ever!"

"Whenever I feel grand," said the girl, "it will be for a better reason."

Whether she felt grand or no, she at any rate felt busy; busy, I mean, with her thoughts. Left to herself for the evening, she sat awhile under the lamp, with empty hands, heedless of her usual avocations. Then she rose and moved about the room, and from one room to another, preferring the places where the vague lamplight expired. She was restless, and even excited; at moments she trembled a little. She felt that something had happened to her of which the importance was out of proportion to its appearance; there had really been a change in her life. What it would bring with it was as yet extremely indefinite; but Isabel was in a situation which gave a value to any change. She had a desire to leave the past behind her, and, as she said to herself, to begin afresh. This desire, indeed, was not a birth of the present occasion; it was as familiar as the sound of the rain upon the window, and it had led to her beginning afresh a great many times. She closed her eyes as she sat in one of the dusky corners of the quiet parlour; but it was not with a desire to take a nap. On the contrary, it was because she felt too wide-awake, and wished to check the sense of seeing too many things at once. Her imagination was by habit ridiculously active; if the door were not opened to it, it jumped out of the window. She was not accustomed, indeed, to keep it behind bolts; and, at important moments, when she would have been thankful to make use of her judgment alone, she paid the penalty of having given undue encouragement to the faculty of seeing without judging. At present, with her sense that the note of change had been struck, came gradually a host of images of the things she was leaving behind her. The years and hours of her life came back to her, and for a long time, in a stillness broken only by the ticking of the big bronze clock, she passed them in review. It had been a very happy life and she had been a very fortunate girl—this was the truth that seemed to emerge most vividly. She had had the best of everything, and in a world in which the circumstances of so many people made them unenviable, it was an advantage never to have known anything particularly disagreeable. It appeared to Isabel that the disagreeable had been even too absent from her knowledge, for she had gathered from her acquaintance with literature that it was often a source of interest, and even of instruction. Her father had kept it away from her—her handsome, much-loved father, who always had such an aversion to it. It was a great good fortune to have been his daughter; Isabel was even proud of her parentage. Since his death she had gathered a vague impression that he turned his brighter side to his children, and that he had not eluded discomfort quite so much in practice as in aspiration. But this only made her tenderness for him greater; it was scarcely even painful to have to think that he was too generous, too good-natured, too indifferent to sordid considerations. Many persons thought that he carried this indifference too far; especially the large number of those to whom he owed money. Of their opinions, Isabel was never very definitely informed; but it may interest the reader to know that, while they admitted that the late Mr. Archer had a remarkably handsome head and a very taking manner (indeed, as one of them had said, he was always taking something), they declared that he had made a very poor use of his life. He had squandered a substantial fortune, he had been deplorably convivial, he was known to have gambled freely. A few very harsh critics went so far as to say that he had not even brought up his daughters. They had had no regular education and no permanent home; they had been at once spoiled and neglected; they had lived with nursemaids and governesses (usually very bad ones), or had been sent to strange schools kept by foreigners, from which, at the end of a month, they had been removed in tears. This view of the matter would have excited Isabel's indignation, for to her own sense her opportunities had been abundant. Even when her father had left his daughters for three months at Neufchâtel with a French *bonne*, who eloped with a Russian nobleman, staying at the same hotel—even in this irregular situation (an incident of the girl's eleventh year) she had been neither frightened nor ashamed, but had thought it a picturesque episode in a liberal education. Her father had a large way of looking at life, of which his restlessness and even his occasional incoherency of conduct had been only a proof. He wished his daughters, even as children, to see as much of the world as possible; and it was for this purpose that, before Isabel was fourteen, he had transported them three times across the Atlantic, giving them on each occasion, however, but a few months' view of foreign lands; a course which had whetted our heroine's curiosity without enabling her to satisfy it. She ought to have been a partisan of her father, for among his three daughters she was quite his favourite, and in his last days his general willingness to take leave of a world in which the difficulty of doing as one liked appeared to increase as one grew older was sensibly modified by the pain of separation from his clever, his superior, his remarkable girl. Later, when the journeys to Europe ceased, he still had shown his children all sorts of indulgence, and if he had been troubled about money-matters, nothing ever disturbed their irreflective consciousness of many possessions. Isabel, though she danced very well, had not the recollection of having been in New York a successful member of the choregraphic circle; her sister Edith was, as every one said, so very much more popular. Edith was so striking an example of success that Isabel could have no illusions as to what constituted this advantage, or as to the moderate character of her own triumphs. Nineteen persons out of twenty (including the younger sister herself) pronounced Edith infinitely the prettier of the two; but the twentieth, besides reversing this judgment, had the entertainment of thinking all the others a parcel of fools. Isabel had in the depths of her nature an even more unquenchable desire to please than Edith; but the depths of this young lady's nature were a very out-of-the-way place, between which and the surface communication was interrupted by a dozen capricious forces. She saw the young men who came in large numbers to see her sister; but as a general thing they were afraid of her; they had a belief that some special preparation was required for talking with her. Her reputation of reading a great deal hung about her like the cloudy envelope of a goddess in an epic; it was supposed to engender difficult questions, and to keep the conversation at a low temperature. The poor girl liked to be thought clever, but she hated to be thought book-ish; she used to read in secret, and, though her memory was excellent, to abstain from quotation. She had a great desire for knowledge, but she really preferred almost any source of information to the printed page; she had an immense curios-ity about life, and was constantly staring and wondering. She carried within herself a great fund of life, and her deepest enjoyment was to feel the continuity between the movements of her own heart and the agitations of the world. For this reason she was fond of seeing great crowds and large stretches of country, of reading about revolutions and wars, of looking at historical pictures—a class of efforts to which she had of-ten gone so far as to forgive much bad painting for the sake of the subject. While the Civil War went on, she was still a very young girl; but she passed months of this long period in a state of almost passionate excitement, in which she felt her-self at times (to her extreme confusion) stirred almost indis-criminately by the valour of either army. Of course the circumspection of the local youth had never gone the length of making her a social proscript; for the proportion of those whose hearts, as they approached her, beat only just fast enough to make it a sensible pleasure, was sufficient to re-deem her maidenly career from failure. She had had every-thing that a girl could have: kindness, admiration, flattery, bouquets, the sense of exclusion from none of the privileges of the world she lived in, abundant opportunity for dancing, the latest publications, plenty of new dresses, the London *Spectator*, and a glimpse of contemporary æsthetics.

These things now, as memory played over them, resolved themselves into a multitude of scenes and figures. Forgotten things came back to her; many others, which she had lately thought of great moment, dropped out of sight. The result was kaleidoscopic; but the movement of the instrument was checked at last by the servant's coming in with the name of a gentleman. The name of the gentleman was Caspar Good-wood; he was a straight young man from Boston, who had

known Miss Archer for the last twelvemonth, and who, thinking her the most beautiful young woman of her time, had
pronounced the time, according to the rule I have hinted at,
a foolish period of history. He sometimes wrote to Isabel,
and he had lately written to her from New York. She had
thought it very possible he would come in—had, indeed, all
the rainy day been vaguely expecting him. Nevertheless, now
that she learned he was there, she felt no eagerness to receive
him. He was the finest young man she had ever seen, was,
indeed, quite a magnificent young man; he filled her with a
certain feeling of respect which she had never entertained for
any one else. He was supposed by the world in general to
wish to marry her; but this of course was between themselves.
It at least may be affirmed that he had travelled from New
York to Albany expressly to see her; having learned in the
former city, where he was spending a few days and where he
had hoped to find her, that she was still at the capital. Isabel
delayed for some minutes to go to him; she moved about the
room with a certain feeling of embarrassment. But at last she
presented herself, and found him standing near the lamp. He
was tall, strong, and somewhat stiff; he was also lean and
brown. He was not especially good-looking, but his physiognomy had an air of requesting your attention, which it rewarded or not, according to the charm you found in a blue
eye of remarkable fixedness and a jaw of the somewhat angular mould, which is supposed to bespeak resolution. Isabel
said to herself that it bespoke resolution to-night; but, nevertheless, an hour later, Caspar Goodwood, who had arrived
hopeful as well as resolute, took his way back to his lodging
with the feeling of a man defeated. He was not, however, a
man to be discouraged by a defeat.

V

RALPH TOUCHETT was a philosopher, but nevertheless he knocked at his mother's door (at a quarter to seven) with a good deal of eagerness. Even philosophers have their preferences, and it must be admitted that of his progenitors his father ministered most to his sense of the sweetness of filial dependence. His father, as he had often said to himself, was the more motherly; his mother, on the other hand, was paternal, and even, according to the slang of the day, gubernatorial. She was nevertheless very fond of her only child, and had always insisted on his spending three months of the year with her. Ralph rendered perfect justice to her affection, and knew that in her thoughts his turn always came after the care of her house and her conservatory (she was extremely fond of flowers). He found her completely dressed for dinner, but she embraced her boy with her gloved hands, and made him sit on the sofa beside her. She inquired scrupulously about her husband's health and about the young man's own, and receiving no very brilliant account of either, she remarked that she was more than ever convinced of her wisdom in not exposing herself to the English climate. In this case she also might have broken down. Ralph smiled at the idea of his mother breaking down, but made no point of reminding her that his own enfeebled condition was not the result of the English climate, from which he absented himself for a considerable part of each year.

He had been a very small boy when his father, Daniel Tracy Touchett, who was a native of Rutland, in the State of Vermont, came to England as subordinate partner in a banking-house, in which some ten years later he acquired a preponderant interest. Daniel Touchett saw before him a life-long residence in his adopted country, of which, from the first, he took a simple, cheerful, and eminently practical view. But, as he said to himself, he had no intention of turning Englishman, nor had he any desire to convert his only son to the same sturdy faith. It had been for himself so very soluble a problem to live in England, and yet not be of it, that it seemed to him equally simple that after his death his lawful heir should carry on the bank in a pure American spirit. He took pains to cultivate this spirit, however, by sending the boy home for his education. Ralph spent several terms in an American school, and took a degree at an American college, after which, as he struck his father on his return as even redundantly national, he was placed for some three years in residence at Oxford. Oxford swallowed up Harvard, and Ralph became at last English enough. His outward conformity to the manners that surrounded him was none the less the mask of a mind that greatly enjoyed its independence, on which nothing long imposed itself, and which, naturally inclined to jocosity and irony, indulged in a boundless liberty of appreciation. He began with being a young man of promise; at Oxford he distinguished himself, to his father's ineffable satisfaction, and the people about him said it was a thousand pities so clever a fellow should be shut out from a career. He might have had a career by returning to his own country (though this point is shrouded in uncertainty), and even if Mr. Touchett had been willing to part with him (which was not the case), it would have gone hard with him to put the ocean (which he detested) permanently between himself and the old man whom he regarded as his best friend. Ralph was not only fond of his father, but he admired him—he enjoyed the opportunity of observing him. Daniel Touchett to his perception was a man of genius, and though he himself had no great fancy for the banking business, he made a point of learning enough of it to measure the great figure his father had played. It was not this, however, he mainly relished, it was the old man's effective simplicity. Daniel Touchett had been neither at Harvard nor at Oxford, and it was his own fault if he had put into his son's hands the key to modern criticism. Ralph, whose head was full of ideas which his father had never guessed, had a high esteem for the latter's originality. Americans, rightly or wrongly, are commended for the ease with which they adapt themselves to foreign conditions; but Mr. Touchett had given evidence of this talent only up to a certain point. He had made himself thoroughly comfortable in England, but he had never attempted to pitch his thoughts in the English key. He had retained many characteristics of Rutland, Vermont; his tone, as his son always noted with pleasure, was that of the more luxuriant parts of New England. At the end of his life, especially, he was a gentle, refined, fastidious old man, who combined consummate shrewdness with a sort of fraternising good-humour, and whose feeling about his own position in the world was quite of the democratic sort. It was perhaps his want of imagination and of what is called the historic consciousness; but to many of the impressions usually made by English life upon the cultivated stranger his sense was completely closed. There were certain differences he never perceived, certain habits he never formed, certain mysteries he never understood. As regards these latter, on the day that he had understood them his son would have thought less well of him.

Ralph, on leaving Oxford, spent a couple of years in travelling; after which he found himself mounted on a high stool in his father's bank. The responsibility and honour of such positions is not, I believe, measured by the height of the stool, which depends upon other considerations; Ralph, indeed, who had very long legs, was fond of standing, and even of walking about, at his work. To this exercise, however, he was obliged to devote but a limited period, for at the end of some eighteen months he became conscious that he was seriously out of health. He had caught a violent cold, which fixed itself upon his lungs and threw them into extreme embarrassment. He had to give up work and embrace the sorry occupation known as taking care of one's self. At first he was greatly disgusted; it appeared to him that it was not himself in the least that he was taking care of, but an uninteresting and uninterested person with whom he had nothing in common. This person, however, improved on acquaintance, and Ralph grew at last to have a certain grudging tolerance, and even undemonstrative respect, for him. Misfortune makes strange bed-fellows, and our young man, feeling that he had something at stake in the matter—it usually seemed to him to be his reputation for common sense—devoted to his unattractive *protégé* an amount of attention of which note was duly taken, and which had at least the effect of keeping the poor fellow alive. One of his lungs began to heal, the other promised to follow its example, and he was assured that he might outweather a dozen winters if he would betake himself

to one of those climates in which consumptives chiefly con-
gregate. He had grown extremely fond of London, and
cursed this immitigable necessity; but at the same time that
he cursed, he conformed, and gradually, when he found that
his sensitive organ was really grateful for such grim favours,
he conferred them with a better grace. He wintered abroad,
as the phrase is; basked in the sun, stopped at home when
the wind blew, went to bed when it rained, and once or
twice, when it snowed, almost never got up again. A certain
fund of indolence that he possessed came to his aid and
helped to reconcile him to doing nothing; for at the best he
was too ill for anything but a passive life. As he said to himself, there was really nothing he had wanted very much to do,
so that he had given up nothing. At present, however, the
perfume of forbidden fruit seemed occasionally to float past
him, to remind him that the finest pleasures of life are to be
found in the world of action. Living as he now lived was like
reading a good book in a poor translation—a meagre entertainment for a young man who felt that he might have been
an excellent linguist. He had good winters and poor winters,
and while the former lasted he was sometimes the sport of a
vision of virtual recovery. But this vision was dispelled some
three years before the occurrence of the incidents with which
this history opens; he had on this occasion remained later
than usual in England, and had been overtaken by bad
weather before reaching Algiers. He reached it more dead
than alive, and lay there for several weeks between life and
death. His convalescence was a miracle, but the first use he
made of it was to assure himself that such miracles happen
but once. He said to himself that his hour was in sight, and
that it behoved him to keep his eyes upon it, but that it was
also open to him to spend the interval as agreeably as might
be consistent with such a pre-occupation. With the prospect
of losing them, the simple use of his faculties became an exquisite pleasure; it seemed to him that the delights of observation had never been suspected. He was far from the time
when he had found it hard that he should be obliged to give
up the idea of distinguishing himself; an idea none the less
importunate for being vague, and none the less delightful for
having to struggle with a good deal of native indifference.

His friends at present found him much more cheerful, and attributed it to a theory, over which they shook their heads knowingly, that he would recover his health. The truth was that he had simply accepted the situation.

It was very probable this sweet-tasting property of observation to which I allude (for he found himself in these last years much more inclined to notice the pleasant things of the world than the others) that was mainly concerned in Ralph's quickly-stirred interest in the arrival of a young lady who was evidently not insipid. If he were observantly disposed, something told him, here was occupation enough for a succession of days. It may be added, somewhat crudely, that the liberty of falling in love had a place in Ralph Touchett's programme. This was of course a liberty to be very temperately used; for though the safest form of any sentiment is that which is conditioned upon silence, it is not always the most comfortable, and Ralph had forbidden himself the art of demonstration. But conscious observation of a lovely woman had struck him as the finest entertainment that the world now had to offer him, and if the interest should become poignant, he flattered himself that he could carry it off quietly, as he had carried other discomforts. He speedily acquired a conviction, however, that he was not destined to fall in love with his cousin.

"And now tell me about the young lady," he said to his mother. "What do you mean to do with her?"

Mrs. Touchett hesitated a little. "I mean to ask your father to invite her to stay three or four weeks at Gardencourt."

"You needn't stand on any such ceremony as that," said Ralph. "My father will ask her as a matter of course."

"I don't know about that. She is my niece; she is not his."

"Good Lord, dear mother; what a sense of property! That's all the more reason for his asking her. But after that—I mean after three months (for it's absurd asking the poor girl to remain but for three or four paltry weeks)—what do you mean to do with her?"

"I mean to take her to Paris, to get her some clothes."

"Ah yes, that's of course. But independently of that?"

"I shall invite her to spend the autumn with me in Florence."

"You don't rise above detail, dear mother," said Ralph. "I

should like to know what you mean to do with her in a general way."

"My duty!" Mrs. Touchett declared. "I suppose you pity her very much," she added.

"No, I don't think I pity her. She doesn't strike me as a girl that suggests compassion. I think I envy her. Before being sure, however, give me a hint of what your duty will direct you to do."

"It will direct me to show her four European countries—I shall leave her the choice of two of them—and to give her the opportunity of perfecting herself in French, which she already knows very well."

Ralph frowned a little. "That sounds rather dry—even giving her the choice of two of the countries."

"If it's dry," said his mother with a laugh, "you can leave Isabel alone to water it! She is as good as a summer rain, any day."

"Do you mean that she is a gifted being?"

"I don't know whether she is a gifted being, but she is a clever girl, with a strong will and a high temper. She has no idea of being bored."

"I can imagine that," said Ralph; and then he added, abruptly, "How do you two get on?"

"Do you mean by that that I am a bore? I don't think Isabel finds me one. Some girls might, I know; but this one is too clever for that. I think I amuse her a good deal. We get on very well, because I understand her; I know the sort of girl she is. She is very frank, and I am very frank; we know just what to expect of each other."

"Ah, dear mother," Ralph exclaimed, "one always knows what to expect of you! You have never surprised me but once, and that is to-day—in presenting me with a pretty cousin whose existence I had never suspected."

"Do you think her very pretty?"

"Very pretty indeed; but I don't insist upon that. It's her general air of being some one in particular that strikes me. Who is this rare creature, and what is she? Where did you find her, and how did you make her acquaintance?"

"I found her in an old house at Albany, sitting in a dreary room on a rainy day, reading a heavy book, and boring herself to death. She didn't know she was bored, but when I told her, she seemed very grateful for the hint. You may say I shouldn't have told her—I should have let her alone. There is a good deal in that; but I acted conscientiously; I thought she was meant for something better. It occurred to me that it would be a kindness to take her about and introduce her to the world. She thinks she knows a great deal of it—like most American girls; but like most American girls she is very much mistaken. If you want to know, I thought she would do me credit. I like to be well thought of, and for a woman of my age there is no more becoming ornament than an attractive niece. You know I had seen nothing of my sister's children for years; I disapproved entirely of the father. But I always meant to do something for them when he should have gone to his reward. I ascertained where they were to be found, and, without any preliminaries, went and introduced myself. There are two other sisters, both of whom are married; but I saw only the elder, who has, by the way, a very uncivil husband. The wife, whose name is Lily, jumped at the idea of my taking an interest in Isabel; she said it was just what her sister needed—that some one should take an interest in her. She spoke of her as you might speak of some young person of genius, in want of encouragement and patronage. It may be that Isabel is a genius; but in that case I have not yet learned her special line. Mrs. Ludlow was especially keen about my taking her to Europe; they all regard Europe over there as a sort of land of emigration, a refuge for their superfluous population. Isabel herself seemed very glad to come, and the thing was easily arranged. There was a little difficulty about the money-question, as she seemed averse to being under pecuniary obligations. But she has a small income, and she supposes herself to be travelling at her own expense."

Ralph had listened attentively to this judicious account of his pretty cousin, by which his interest in her was not impaired. "Ah, if she is a genius," he said, " we must find out her special line. Is it, by chance, for flirting?"

"I don't think so. You may suspect that at first, but you will be wrong."

"Warburton is wrong, then!" Ralph Touchett exclaimed. "He flatters himself he has made that discovery."

His mother shook her head. "Lord Warburton won't understand her; he needn't try."

"He is very intelligent," said Ralph; "but it's right he should be puzzled once in a while."

"Isabel will enjoy puzzling a lord," Mrs. Touchett remarked.

Her son frowned a little. "What does she know about lords?"

"Nothing at all; that will puzzle him all the more."

Ralph greeted these words with a laugh, and looked out of the window a little. Then—"Are you not going down to see my father?" he asked.

"At a quarter to eight," said Mrs. Touchett.

Her son looked at his watch. "You have another quarter of an hour, then; tell me some more about Isabel." But Mrs. Touchett declined his invitation, declaring that he must find out for himself.

"Well," said Ralph, "she will certainly do you credit. But won't she also give you trouble?"

"I hope not; but if she does, I shall not shrink from it. I never do that."

"She strikes me as very natural," said Ralph.

"Natural people are not the most trouble."

"No," said Ralph; "you yourself are a proof of that. You are extremely natural, and I am sure you have never troubled any one. But tell me this; it just occurs to me. Is Isabel capable of making herself disagreeable?"

"Ah," cried his mother, "you ask too many questions! Find that out for yourself."

His questions, however, were not exhausted. "All this time," he said, "you have not told me what you intend to do with her."

"Do with her? You talk as if she were a yard of calico. I shall do absolutely nothing with her, and she herself will do everything that she chooses. She gave me notice of that."

"What you meant then, in your telegram, was that her character was independent."

"I never know what I mean by my telegrams—especially those I send from America. Clearness is too expensive. Come down to your father."

"It is not yet a quarter to eight," said Ralph.

"I must allow for his impatience," Mrs. Touchett answered.

Ralph knew what to think of his father's impatience; but making no rejoinder, he offered his mother his arm. This put it into his power, as they descended together, to stop her a moment on the middle landing of the staircase—the broad, low, wide-armed staircase of time-stained oak which was one of the most striking ornaments of Gardencourt.

"You have no plan of marrying her?" he said, smiling.

"Marry her? I should be sorry to play her such a trick! But apart from that, she is perfectly able to marry herself; she has every facility."

"Do you mean to say she has a husband picked out?"

"I don't know about a husband, but there is a young man in Boston——"

Ralph went on; he had no desire to hear about the young man in Boston. "As my father says," he exclaimed, "they are always engaged!"

His mother had told him that he must extract his information about his cousin from the girl herself, and it soon became evident to him that he should not want for opportunity. He had, for instance, a good deal of talk with her that same evening, when the two had been left alone together in the drawing-room. Lord Warburton, who had ridden over from his own house, some ten miles distant, remounted and took his departure before dinner; and an hour after this meal was concluded, Mr. and Mrs. Touchett, who appeared to have exhausted each other's conversation, withdrew, under the valid pretext of fatigue, to their respective apartments. The young man spent an hour with his cousin; though she had been travelling half the day she appeared to have no sense of weariness. She was really tired; she knew it, and knew that she should pay for it on the morrow; but it was her habit at this period to carry fatigue to the furthest point, and confess to it only when dissimulation had become impossible. For the present it was perfectly possible; she was interested and excited. She asked Ralph to show her the pictures; there were a great many of them in the house, most of them of his own choosing. The best of them were arranged in an oaken gallery of charming proportions, which had a sitting-room at either end of it, and which in the evening was usually lighted. The light was insufficient to show the pictures to advantage, and the visit might have been deferred till the morrow. This suggestion Ralph had ventured to make; but Isabel looked disappointed—smiling still, however—and said, "If you please, I should like to see them just a little." She was eager, she knew that she was eager and that she seemed so; but she could not help it. "She doesn't take suggestions," Ralph said to himself; but he said it without irritation; her eagerness amused and even pleased him. The lamps were on brackets, at intervals, and if the light was imperfect it was genial. It fell upon the vague squares of rich colour and on the faded gilding of heavy frames; it made a shining on the polished floor of the gallery. Ralph took a candlestick and moved about, pointing out the things he liked; Isabel, bending toward one picture after another, indulged in little exclamations and murmurs. She was evidently a judge; she had a natural taste; he was struck with that. She took a candlestick herself and held it slowly here and there; she lifted it high, and as she did so, he found himself pausing in the middle of the gallery and bending his eyes much less upon the pictures than on her figure. He lost nothing, in truth, by these wandering glances; for she was better worth looking at than most works of art. She was thin, and light, and middling tall; when people had wished to distinguish her from the other two Miss Archers, they always called her the thin one. Her hair, which was dark even to blackness, had been an object of envy to many women; her light grey eye, a little too keen perhaps in her graver moments, had an enchanting softness when she smiled. They walked slowly up one side of the gallery and down the other, and then she said—

"Well, now I know more than I did when I began!"

"You apparently have a great passion for knowledge," her cousin answered, laughing.

"I think I have; most girls seem to me so ignorant," said Isabel.

"You strike me as different from most girls."

"Ah, some girls are so nice," murmured Isabel, who preferred not to talk about herself. Then, in a moment, to change the subject, she went on, "Please tell me—isn't there a ghost?"

"A ghost?"

"A spectre, a phantom; we call them ghosts in America."

"So we do here, when we see them."

"You do see them, then? You ought to, in this romantic old house."

"It's not a romantic house," said Ralph. "You will be disappointed if you count on that. It's dismally prosaic; there is no romance here but what you may have brought with you."

"I have brought a great deal; but it seems to me I have brought it to the right place."

"To keep it out of harm, certainly; nothing will ever happen to it here, between my father and me."

Isabel looked at him a moment.

"Is there never any one here but your father and you?"

"My mother, of course."

"Oh, I know your mother; she is not romantic. Haven't you other people?"

"Very few."

"I am sorry for that; I like so much to see people."

"Oh, we will invite all the county to amuse you," said Ralph.

"Now you are making fun of me," the girl answered, rather gravely. "Who was the gentleman that was on the lawn when I arrived?"

"A county neighbour; he doesn't come very often."

"I am sorry for that; I liked him," said Isabel.

"Why, it seemed to me that you barely spoke to him," Ralph objected.

"Never mind, I like him all the same. I like your father, too, immensely."

"You can't do better than that; he is a dear old man."

"I am so sorry he is ill," said Isabel.

"You must help me to nurse him; you ought to be a good nurse."

"I don't think I am; I have been told I am not; I am said to be too theoretic. But you haven't told me about the ghost," she added.

Ralph, however, gave no heed to this observation.

"You like my father, and you like Lord Warburton. I infer also that you like my mother."

"I like your mother very much, because—because——" And Isabel found herself attempting to assign a reason for her affection for Mrs. Touchett.

"Ah, we never know why!" said her companion, laughing.

"I always know why," the girl answered. "It's because she doesn't expect one to like her; she doesn't care whether one does or not."

"So you adore her, out of perversity? Well, I take greatly after my mother," said Ralph.

"I don't believe you do at all. You wish people to like you, and you try to make them do it."

"Good heavens, how you see through one!" cried Ralph, with a dismay that was not altogether jocular.

"But I like you all the same," his cousin went on. "The way to clinch the matter will be to show me the ghost."

Ralph shook his head sadly. "I might show it to you, but you would never see it. The privilege isn't given to every one; it's not enviable. It has never been seen by a young, happy, innocent person like you. You must have suffered first, have suffered greatly, have gained some miserable knowledge. In that way your eyes are opened to it. I saw it long ago," said Ralph, smiling.

"I told you just now I was very fond of knowledge," the girl answered.

"Yes, of happy knowledge—of pleasant knowledge. But you haven't suffered, and you are not made to suffer. I hope you will never see the ghost!"

Isabel had listened to him attentively, with a smile on her lips, but with a certain gravity in her eyes. Charming as he found her, she had struck him as rather presumptuous—indeed it was a part of her charm; and he wondered what she would say.

"I am not afraid," she said; which seemed quite presumptuous enough.

"You are not afraid of suffering?"

"Yes, I am afraid of suffering. But I am not afraid of ghosts. And I think people suffer too easily," she added.

"I don't believe you do," said Ralph, looking at her with his hands in his pockets.

"I don't think that's a fault," she answered. "It is not absolutely necessary to suffer; we were not made for that."

"You were not, certainly."

"I am not speaking of myself." And she turned away a little.

"No, it isn't a fault," said her cousin. "It's a merit to be strong."

"Only, if you don't suffer, they call you hard," Isabel remarked. They passed out of the smaller drawing-room, into which they had returned from the gallery, and paused in the hall, at the foot of the staircase. Here Ralph presented his companion with her bed-room candle, which he had taken from a niche. "Never mind what they call you," he said. "When you do suffer, they call you an idiot. The great point is to be as happy as possible."

She looked at him a little; she had taken her candle, and placed her foot on the oaken stair. "Well," she said, "that's what I came to Europe for, to be as happy as possible. Good night."

"Good night! I wish you all success, and shall be very glad to contribute to it!"

She turned away, and he watched her, as she slowly ascended. Then, with his hands always in his pockets, he went back to the empty drawing-room.

VI

ISABEL ARCHER was a young person of many theories; her imagination was remarkably active. It had been her fortune to possess a finer mind than most of the persons among whom her lot was cast; to have a larger perception of surrounding facts, and to care for knowledge that was tinged with the unfamiliar. It is true that among her contemporaries she passed for a young woman of extraordinary profundity; for these excellent people never withheld their admiration from a reach of intellect of which they themselves were not conscious, and spoke of Isabel as a prodigy of learning, a young lady reputed to have read the classic authors—in translations. Her paternal aunt, Mrs. Varian, once spread the rumour that Isabel was writing a book—Mrs. Varian having a reverence for books—and averred that Isabel would distinguish herself in print. Mrs. Varian thought highly of literature, for which she entertained that esteem that is connected with a sense of privation. Her own large house, remarkable for its assortment of mosaic tables and decorated ceilings, was unfurnished with a library, and in the way of printed volumes contained nothing but half-a-dozen novels in paper, on a shelf in the apartment of one of the Miss Varians. Practically, Mrs. Varian's acquaintance with literature was confined to the *New York Interviewer*; as she very justly said, after you had read the *Interviewer*, you had no time for anything else. Her tendency, however, was rather to keep the *Interviewer* out of the way of her daughters; she was determined to bring them up seriously, and they read nothing at all. Her impression with regard to Isabel's labours was quite illusory; the girl never attempted to write a book, and had no desire to be an authoress. She had no talent for expression, and had none of the consciousness of genius; she only had a general idea that people were right when they treated her as if she were rather superior. Whether or no she were superior, people were right in admiring her if they thought her so; for it seemed to her often that her mind moved more quickly than theirs, and this encouraged an impatience that might easily be confounded with superiority. It may be affirmed without delay that Isabel was probably very liable to the sin of self-esteem; she often surveyed with complacency the field of her own nature; she was in the habit of taking for granted, on scanty evidence, that she was right; impulsively, she often admired herself. Meanwhile her errors and delusions were frequently such as a biographer interested in preserving the dignity of his heroine must shrink from specifying. Her thoughts were a tangle of vague outlines, which had never been corrected by the judgment of people who seemed to her to speak with authority. In matters of opinion she had had her own way, and it had led her into a thousand ridiculous zigzags. Every now and then she found out she was wrong, and then she treated herself to a week of passionate humility. After this she held her head higher than ever again; for it was of no use, she had an unquenchable desire to think well of herself. She had a theory that it was only on this condition that life was worth living; that one should be one of the best, should be conscious of a fine organization (she could not help knowing her organization was fine), should move in a realm of light, of natural wisdom, of happy impulse, of inspiration gracefully chronic. It was almost as unnecessary to cultivate doubt of oneself as to cultivate doubt of one's best friend; one should try to be one's own best friend, and to give oneself, in this manner, distinguished company. The girl had a certain nobleness of imagination which rendered her a good many services and played her a great many tricks. She spent half her time in thinking of beauty, and bravery, and magnanimity; she had a fixed determination to regard the world as a place of brightness, of free expansion, of irresistible action; she thought it would be detestable to be afraid or ashamed. She had an infinite hope that she should never do anything wrong. She had resented so strongly, after discovering them, her mere errors of feeling (the discovery always made her tremble, as if she had escaped from a trap which might have caught her and smothered her), that the chance of inflicting a sensible injury upon another person, presented only as a contingency, caused her at moments to hold her breath. That always seemed to her the worst thing that could happen to one. On the whole, reflectively, she was in no uncertainty about the things that were wrong. She had no taste for thinking of them, but whenever she looked at them fixedly she recognized them. It was wrong to be mean, to be jealous, to be false, to be cruel; she had seen very little of the evil of the world, but she had seen women who lied and who tried to hurt each other. Seeing such things had quickened her high spirit; it seemed right to scorn them. Of course the danger of a high spirit is the danger of inconsistency—the danger of keeping up the flag after the place has surrendered; a sort of behaviour so anomalous as to be almost a dishonour to the flag. But Isabel, who knew little of the sorts of artillery to which young ladies are exposed, flattered herself that such contradictions would never be observed in her own conduct. Her life should always be in harmony with the most pleasing impression she should produce; she would be what she appeared, and she would appear what she was. Sometimes she went so far as to wish that she should find herself some day in a difficult position, so that she might have the pleasure of being as heroic as the occasion demanded. Altogether, with her meagre knowledge, her inflated ideals, her confidence at once innocent and dogmatic, her temper at once exacting and indulgent, her mixture of curiosity and fastidiousness, of vivacity and indifference, her desire to look very well and to be if possible even better; her determination to see, to try, to know; her combination of the delicate, desultory, flame-like spirit and the eager and personal young girl; she would be an easy victim of scientific criticism, if she were not intended to awaken on the reader's part an impulse more tender and more purely expectant.

It was one of her theories that Isabel Archer was very fortunate in being independent, and that she ought to make some very enlightened use of her independence. She never called it loneliness; she thought that weak; and besides, her sister Lily constantly urged her to come and stay with her. She had a friend whose acquaintance she had made shortly before her father's death, who offered so laudable an example of useful activity that Isabel always thought of her as a model. Henrietta Stackpole had the advantage of a remarkable talent; she was thoroughly launched in journalism, and her letters to the *Interviewer*, from Washington, Newport, the White Mountains, and other places, were universally admired. Isabel did not accept them unrestrictedly, but she esteemed the

courage, energy, and good-humour of her friend, who, without parents and without property, had adopted three of the
children of an infirm and widowed sister, and was paying
their school-bills out of the proceeds of her literary labour.
Henrietta was a great radical, and had clear-cut views on most
subjects; her cherished desire had long been to come to Europe and write a series of letters to the *Interviewer* from the
radical point of view—an enterprise the less difficult as she
knew perfectly in advance what her opinions would be, and
to how many objections most European institutions lay open.
When she heard that Isabel was coming, she wished to start
at once; thinking, naturally, that it would be delightful the
two should travel together. She had been obliged, however,
to postpone this enterprise. She thought Isabel a glorious
creature, and had spoken of her, covertly, in some of her letters, though she never mentioned the fact to her friend, who
would not have taken pleasure in it and was not a regular
reader of the *Interviewer*. Henrietta, for Isabel, was chiefly a
proof that a woman might suffice to herself and be happy.
Her resources were of the obvious kind; but even if one had
not the journalistic talent and a genius for guessing, as Henrietta said, what the public was going to want, one was not
therefore to conclude that one had no vocation, no beneficent
aptitude of any sort, and resign oneself to being trivial and
superficial. Isabel was resolutely determined not to be superficial. If one should wait expectantly and trustfully, one would
find some happy work to one's hand. Of course, among her
theories, this young lady was not without a collection of
opinions on the question of marriage. The first on the list was
a conviction that it was very vulgar to think too much about
it. From lapsing into a state of eagerness on this point she
earnestly prayed that she might be delivered; she held that a
woman ought to be able to make up her life in singleness,
and that it was perfectly possible to be happy without the
society of a more or less coarse-minded person of another sex.
The girl's prayer was very sufficiently answered; something
pure and proud that there was in her—something cold and
stiff, an unappreciated suitor with a taste for analysis might
have called it—had hitherto kept her from any great vanity
of conjecture on the subject of possible husbands. Few of the

men she saw seemed worth an expenditure of imagination, and it made her smile to think that one of them should present himself as an incentive to hope and a reward of patience. Deep in her soul—it was the deepest thing there—lay a belief that if a certain light should dawn, she could give herself completely; but this image, on the whole, was too formidable to be attractive. Isabel's thoughts hovered about it, but they seldom rested on it long; after a little it ended by frightening her. It often seemed to her that she thought too much about herself; you could have made her blush, any day in the year, by telling her that she was selfish. She was always planning out her own development, desiring her own perfection, observing her own progress. Her nature had for her own imagination a certain garden-like quality, a suggestion of perfume and murmuring boughs, of shady bowers and lengthening vistas, which made her feel that introspection was, after all, an exercise in the open air, and that a visit to the recesses of one's mind was harmless when one returned from it with a lapful of roses. But she was often reminded that there were other gardens in the world than those of her virginal soul, and that there were, moreover, a great many places that were not gardens at all—only dusky, pestiferous tracts, planted thick with ugliness and misery. In the current of that easy eagerness on which she had lately been floating, which had conveyed her to this beautiful old England and might carry her much further still, she often checked herself with the thought of the thousands of people who were less happy than herself—a thought which for the moment made her absorbing happiness appear to her a kind of immodesty. What should one do with the misery of the world in a scheme of the agreeable for oneself? It must be confessed that this question never held her long. She was too young, too impatient to live, too unacquainted with pain. She always returned to her theory that a young woman whom after all every one thought clever, should begin by getting a general impression of life. This was necessary to prevent mistakes, and after it should be secured she might make the unfortunate condition of others an object of special attention.

England was a revelation to her, and she found herself as entertained as a child at a pantomime. In her infantine excursions to Europe she had seen only the Continent, and seen it from the nursery window; Paris, not London, was her father's Mecca. The impressions of that time, moreover, had become faint and remote, and the old-world quality in everything that she now saw had all the charm of strangeness. Her uncle's house seemed a picture made real; no refinement of the agreeable was lost upon Isabel; the rich perfection of Gardencourt at once revealed a world and gratified a need. The large, low rooms, with brown ceilings and dusky corners, the deep embrasures and curious casements, the quiet light on dark, polished panels, the deep greenness outside, that seemed always peeping in, the sense of well-ordered privacy, in the centre of a "property"—a place where sounds were felicitously accidental, where the tread was muffled by the earth itself, and in the thick mild air all shrillness dropped out of conversation—these things were much to the taste of our young lady, whose taste played a considerable part in her emotions. She formed a fast friendship with her uncle, and often sat by his chair when he had had it moved out to the lawn. He passed hours in the open air, sitting placidly with folded hands, like a good old man who had done his work and received his wages, and was trying to grow used to weeks and months made up only of off-days. Isabel amused him more than she suspected—the effect she produced upon people was often different from what she supposed—and he frequently gave himself the pleasure of making her chatter. It was by this term that he qualified her conversation, which had much of the vivacity observable in that of the young ladies of her country, to whom the ear of the world is more directly presented than to their sisters in other lands. Like the majority of American girls, Isabel had been encouraged to express herself; her remarks had been attended to; she had been expected to have emotions and opinions. Many of her opinions had doubtless but a slender value, many of her emotions passed away in the utterance; but they had left a trace in giving her the habit of seeming at least to feel and think, and in imparting, moreover, to her words, when she was really moved, that artless vividness which so many people had regarded as a sign of superiority. Mr. Touchett used to think that she reminded him of his wife when his wife was in her

teens. It was because she was fresh and natural and quick to
understand, to speak—so many characteristics of her niece—
that he had fallen in love with Mrs. Touchett. He never expressed this analogy to the girl herself, however; for if Mrs.
Touchett had once been like Isabel, Isabel was not at all like
Mrs. Touchett. The old man was full of kindness for her; it
was a long time, as he said, since they had had any young life
in the house; and our rustling, quickly-moving, clear-voiced
heroine was as agreeable to his sense as the sound of flowing
water. He wished to do something for her, he wished she
would ask something of him. But Isabel asked nothing but
questions; it is true that of these she asked a great many. Her
uncle had a great fund of answers, though interrogation
sometimes came in forms that puzzled him. She questioned
him immensely about England, about the British constitution, the English character, the state of politics, the manners
and customs of the royal family, the peculiarities of the aristocracy, the way of living and thinking of his neighbours; and
in asking to be enlightened on these points she usually inquired whether they correspond with the descriptions in the
books. The old man always looked at her a little, with his fine
dry smile, while he smoothed down the shawl that was spread
across his legs.

"The books?" he once said; "well, I don't know much
about the books. You must ask Ralph about that. I have always ascertained for myself—got my information in the natural form. I never asked many questions even; I just kept
quiet and took notice. Of course, I have had very good opportunities—better than what a young lady would naturally
have. I am of an inquisitive disposition, though you mightn't
think it if you were to watch me; however much you might
watch me, I should be watching you more. I have been
watching these people for upwards of thirty-five years, and I
don't hesitate to say that I have acquired considerable information. It's a very fine country on the whole—finer perhaps
than what we give it credit for on the other side. There are
several improvements that I should like to see introduced; but
the necessity of them doesn't seem to be generally felt as yet.
When the necessity of a thing is generally felt, they usually
manage to accomplish it; but they seem to feel pretty com-

fortable about waiting till then. I certainly feel more at home among them than I expected to when I first came over; I suppose it's because I have had a considerable degree of success. When you are successful you naturally feel more at home."

"Do you suppose that if I am successful I shall feel at home?" Isabel asked.

"I should think it very probable, and you certainly will be successful. They like American young ladies very much over here; they show them a great deal of kindness. But you mustn't feel too much at home, you know."

"Oh, I am by no means sure I shall like it," said Isabel, somewhat judicially. "I like the place very much, but I am not sure I shall like the people."

"The people are very good people; especially if you like them."

"I have no doubt they are good," Isabel rejoined; "but are they pleasant in society? They won't rob me nor beat me; but will they make themselves agreeable to me? That's what I like people to do. I don't hesitate to say so, because I always appreciate it. I don't believe they are very nice to girls; they are not nice to them in the novels."

"I don't know about the novels," said Mr. Touchett. "I believe the novels have a great deal of ability, but I don't suppose they are very accurate. We once had a lady who wrote novels staying here; she was a friend of Ralph's, and he asked her down. She was very positive, very positive; but she was not the sort of person that you could depend on her testimony. Too much imagination—I suppose, that was it. She afterwards published a work of fiction in which she was understood to have given a representation—something in the nature of a caricature, as you might say—of my unworthy self. I didn't read it, but Ralph just handed me the book, with the principal passages marked. It was understood to be a description of my conversation; American peculiarities, nasal twang, Yankee notions, stars and stripes. Well, it was not at all accurate; she couldn't have listened very attentively. I had no objection to her giving a report of my conversation, if she liked; but I didn't like the idea that she hadn't taken the trouble to listen to it. Of course I talk like an American—I can't

talk like a Hottentot. However I talk, I have made them understand me pretty well over here. But I don't talk like the
old gentleman in that lady's novel. He wasn't an American;
we wouldn't have him over there! I just mention that fact to
show you that they are not always accurate. Of course, as I
have no daughters, and as Mrs. Touchett resides in Florence,
I haven't had much chance to notice about the young ladies.
It sometimes appears as if the young women in the lower
class were not very well treated; but I guess their position is
better in the upper class."

"Dear me!" Isabel exclaimed; "how many classes have they?
About fifty, I suppose."

"Well, I don't know that I ever counted them. I never took
much notice of the classes. That's the advantage of being an
American here; you don't belong to any class."

"I hope so," said Isabel. "Imagine one's belonging to an
English class!"

"Well, I guess some of them are pretty comfortable—
especially towards the top. But for me there are only two
classes: the people I trust, and the people I don't. Of those
two, my dear Isabel, you belong to the first."

"I am much obliged to you," said the young girl, quickly.
Her way of taking compliments seemed sometimes rather dry;
she got rid of them as rapidly as possible. But as regards this,
she was sometimes misjudged; she was thought insensible to
them, whereas in fact she was simply unwilling to show how
infinitely they pleased her. To show that was to show too
much. "I am sure the English are very conventional," she
added.

"They have got everything pretty well fixed," Mr. Touchett
admitted. "It's all settled beforehand—they don't leave it to
the last moment."

"I don't like to have everything settled beforehand," said
the girl. "I like more unexpectedness."

Her uncle seemed amused at her distinctness of preference.
"Well, it's settled beforehand that you will have great success," he rejoined. "I suppose you will like that."

"I shall not have success if they are conventional. I am not
in the least conventional. I am just the contrary. That's what
they won't like."

"No, no, you are all wrong," said the old man. "You can't tell what they will like. They are very inconsistent; that's their principal interest."

"Ah well," said Isabel, standing before her uncle with her hands clasped about the belt of her black dress, and looking up and down the lawn—"that will suit me perfectly!"

VII

THE TWO amused themselves, time and again, with talking of the attitude of the British public, as if the young lady had been in a position to appeal to it; but in fact the British public remained for the present profoundly indifferent to Miss Isabel Archer, whose fortune had dropped her, as her cousin said, into the dullest house in England. Her gouty uncle received very little company, and Mrs. Touchett, not having cultivated relations with her husband's neighbours, was not warranted in expecting visits from them. She had, however, a peculiar taste; she liked to receive cards. For what is usually called social intercourse she had very little relish; but nothing pleased her more than to find her hall-table whitened with oblong morsels of symbolic pasteboard. She flattered herself that she was a very just woman, and had mastered the sovereign truth that nothing in this world is got for nothing. She had played no social part as mistress of Gardencourt, and it was not to be supposed that, in the surrounding country, a minute account should be kept of her comings and goings. But it is by no means certain that she did not feel it to be wrong that so little notice was taken of them, and that her failure (really very gratuitous) to make herself important in the neighbourhood, had not much to do with the acrimony of her allusions to her husband's adopted country. Isabel presently found herself in the singular situation of defending the British constitution against her aunt; Mrs. Touchett having formed the habit of sticking pins into this venerable instrument. Isabel always felt an impulse to pull out the pins; not that she imagined they inflicted any damage on the tough old parchment, but because it seemed to her that her aunt might make better use of her sharpness. She was very critical herself—it was incidental to her age, her sex, and her nationality; but she was very sentimental as well, and there was something in Mrs. Touchett's dryness that set her own moral fountains flowing.

"Now what is your point of view?" she asked of her aunt. "When you criticize everything here, you should have a point of view. Yours doesn't seem to be American—you thought everything over there so disagreeable. When I criticize, I have mine; it's thoroughly American!"

"My dear young lady," said Mrs. Touchett, "there are as many points of view in the world as there are people of sense. You may say that doesn't make them very numerous! American? Never in the world; that's shockingly narrow. My point of view, thank God, is personal!"

Isabel thought this a better answer than she admitted; it was a tolerable description of her own manner of judging, but it would not have sounded well for her to say so. On the lips of a person less advanced in life, and less enlightened by experience than Mrs. Touchett, such a declaration would savour of immodesty, even of arrogance. She risked it nevertheless, in talking with Ralph, with whom she talked a great deal, and with whom her conversation was of a sort that gave a large licence to violent statements. Her cousin used, as the phrase is, to chaff her; he very soon established with her a reputation for treating everything as a joke, and he was not a man to neglect the privileges such a reputation conferred. She accused him of an odious want of seriousness, of laughing at all things, beginning with himself. Such slender faculty of reverence as he possessed centred wholly upon his father; for the rest, he exercised his wit indiscriminately upon his father's son, this gentleman's weak lungs, his useless life, his anomalous mother, his friends (Lord Warburton in especial), his adopted and his native country, his charming new-found cousin. "I keep a band of music in my ante-room," he said once to her. "It has orders to play without stopping; it renders me two excellent services. It keeps the sounds of the world from reaching the private apartments, and it makes the world think that dancing is going on within." It was dance-music indeed that you usually heard when you came within ear-shot of Ralph's band; the liveliest waltzes seemed to float upon the air. Isabel often found herself irritated by this perpetual fiddling; she would have liked to pass through the ante-room, as her cousin called it, and enter the private apartments. It mattered little that he had assured her that they were a very dismal place; she would have been glad to undertake to sweep them and set them in order. It was but half-hospitality to let her remain outside; to punish him for which,

Isabel administered innumerable taps with the ferrule of her straight young wit. It must be said that her wit was exercised to a large extent in self-defence, for her cousin amused himself with calling her "Columbia," and accusing her of a patriotism so fervid that it scorched. He drew a caricature of her, in which she was represented as a very pretty young woman, dressed, in the height of the prevailing fashion, in the folds of the national banner. Isabel's chief dread in life, at this period of her development, was that she should appear narrow-minded; what she feared next afterwards was that she should be so. But she nevertheless made no scruple of abounding in her cousin's sense, and pretending to sigh for the charms of her native land. She would be as American as it pleased him to regard her, and if he chose to laugh at her, she would give him plenty of occupation. She defended England against his mother, but when Ralph sang its praises, on purpose, as she said, to torment her, she found herself able to differ from him on a variety of points. In fact, the quality of this small ripe country seemed as sweet to her as the taste of an October pear; and her satisfaction was at the root of the good spirits which enabled her to take her cousin's chaff and return it in kind. If her good-humour flagged at moments, it was not because she thought herself ill-used, but because she suddenly felt sorry for Ralph. It seemed to her that he was talking as a blind and had little heart in what he said.

"I don't know what is the matter with you," she said to him once; "but I suspect you are a great humbug."

"That's your privilege," Ralph answered, who had not been used to being so crudely addressed.

"I don't know what you care for; I don't think you care for anything. You don't really care for England when you praise it; you don't care for America even when you pretend to abuse it."

"I care for nothing but you, dear cousin," said Ralph.

"If I could believe even that, I should be very glad."

"Ah, well, I should hope so!" the young man exclaimed.

Isabel might have believed it, and not have been far from the truth. He thought a great deal about her; she was constantly present to his mind. At a time when his thoughts had been a good deal of a burden to him, her sudden arrival, which promised nothing and was an open-handed gift of fate, had refreshed and quickened them, given them wings and something to fly for. Poor Ralph for many weeks had been steeped in melancholy; his out-look, habitually sombre, lay under the shadow of a deeper cloud. He had grown anxious about his father, whose gout, hitherto confined to his legs, had begun to ascend into regions more vital. The old man had been gravely ill in the spring, and the doctors had whispered to Ralph that another attack would be less easy to deal with. Just now he appeared tolerably comfortable, but Ralph could not rid himself of a suspicion that this was a subterfuge of the enemy, who was waiting to take him off his guard. If the manœuvre should succeed, there would be little hope of any great resistance. Ralph had always taken for granted that his father would survive him—that his own name would be the first called. The father and son had been close companions, and the idea of being left alone with the remnant of a tasteless life on his hands was not gratifying to the young man, who had always and tacitly counted upon his elder's help in making the best of a poor business. At the prospect of losing his great motive, Ralph was indeed mightily disgusted. If they might die at the same time, it would be all very well; but without the encouragement of his father's society he should barely have patience to await his own turn. He had not the incentive of feeling that he was indispensable to his mother; it was a rule with his mother to have no regrets. He bethought himself, of course, that it had been a small kindness to his father to wish that, of the two, the active rather than the passive party should know the pain of loss; he remembered that the old man had always treated his own forecast of an uncompleted career as a clever fallacy, which he should be delighted to discredit so far as he might by dying first. But of the two triumphs, that of refuting a sophistical son and that of holding on a while longer to a state of being which, with all abatements, he enjoyed, Ralph deemed it no sin to hope that the latter might be vouchsafed to Mr. Touchett.

These were nice questions, but Isabel's arrival put a stop to his puzzling over them. It even suggested that there might be a compensation for the intolerable ennui of surviving his genial sire. He wondered whether he were falling in love with this spontaneous young woman from Albany; but he decided that on the whole he was not. After he had known her for a week, he quite made up his mind to this, and every day he felt a little more sure. Lord Warburton had been right about her; she was a thoroughly interesting woman. Ralph wondered how Lord Warburton had found it out so soon; and then he said it was only another proof of his friend's high abilities, which he had always greatly admired. If his cousin were to be nothing more than an entertainment to him, Ralph was conscious that she was an entertainment of a high order. "A character like that," he said to himself, "is the finest thing in nature. It is finer than the finest work of art—than a Greek bas-relief, than a great Titian, than a Gothic cathedral. It is very pleasant to be so well-treated where one least looked for it. I had never been more blue, more bored, than for a week before she came; I had never expected less that something agreeable would happen. Suddenly I receive a Titian, by the post, to hang on my wall—a Greek bas-relief to stick over my chimney-piece. The key of a beautiful edifice is thrust into my hand, and I am told to walk in and admire. My poor boy, you have been sadly ungrateful, and now you had better keep very quiet and never grumble again." The sentiment of these reflections was very just; but it was not exactly true that Ralph Touchett had had a key put into his hand. His cousin was a very brilliant girl, who would take, as he said, a good deal of knowing; but she needed the knowing, and his attitude with regard to her, though it was contemplative and critical, was not judicial. He surveyed the edifice from the outside, and admired it greatly; he looked in at the windows, and received an impression of proportions equally fair. But he felt that he saw it only by glimpses, and that he had not yet stood under the roof. The door was fastened, and though he had keys in his pocket he had a conviction that none of them would fit. She was intelligent and generous; it was a fine free nature; but what was she going to do with herself? This question was irregular, for with most women one had no occasion to ask it. Most women did with themselves nothing at all; they waited, in attitudes more or less gracefully passive, for a man to come that way and furnish them with a destiny.

Isabel's originality was that she gave one an impression of having intentions of her own. "Whenever she executes them," said Ralph, "may I be there to see!"

It devolved upon him of course to do the honours of the place. Mr. Touchett was confined to his chair, and his wife's position was that of a rather grim visitor; so that in the line of conduct that opened itself to Ralph, duty and inclination were harmoniously mingled. He was not a great walker, but he strolled about the grounds with his cousin—a pastime for which the weather remained favourable with a persistency not allowed for in Isabel's somewhat lugubrious prevision of the climate; and in the long afternoons, of which the length was but the measure of her gratified eagerness, they took a boat on the river, the dear little river, as Isabel called it, where the opposite shore seemed still a part of the foreground of the landscape; or drove over the country in a phaeton—a low, capacious, thick-wheeled phaeton formerly much used by Mr. Touchett, but which he had now ceased to enjoy. Isabel enjoyed it largely, and, handling the reins in a manner which approved itself to the groom as "knowing," was never weary of driving her uncle's capital horses through winding lanes and byways full of the rural incidents she had confidently expected to find; past cottages thatched and timbered, past alehouses latticed and sanded, past patches of ancient common and glimpses of empty parks, between hedgerows made thick by midsummer. When they reached home, they usually found that tea had been served upon the lawn, and that Mrs. Touchett had not absolved herself from the obligation of handing her husband his cup. But the two for the most part sat silent; the old man with his head back and his eyes closed, his wife occupied with her knitting, and wearing that appearance of extraordinary meditation with which some ladies contemplate the movement of their needles.

One day, however, a visitor had arrived. The two young people, after spending an hour upon the river, strolled back to the house and perceived Lord Warburton sitting under the trees and engaged in conversation, of which even at a distance the desultory character was appreciable, with Mrs. Touchett. He had driven over from his own place with a portmanteau, and had asked, as the father and son often invited him to do, for a dinner and a lodging. Isabel, seeing him for half-an-hour on the day of her arrival, had discovered in this brief space that she liked him; he had made indeed a tolerably vivid impression on her mind, and she had thought of him several times. She had hoped that she should see him again—hoped too that she should see a few others. Gardencourt was not dull; the place itself was so delightful, her uncle was such a perfection of an uncle, and Ralph was so unlike any cousin she had ever encountered—her view of cousins being rather monotonous. Then her impressions were still so fresh and so quickly renewed that there was as yet hardly a sense of vacancy in the prospect. But Isabel had need to remind herself that she was interested in human nature, and that her foremost hope in coming abroad had been that she should see a great many people. When Ralph said to her, as he had done several times—"I wonder you find this endurable; you ought to see some of the neighbours and some of our friends— because we have really got a few, though you would never suppose it"—when he offered to invite what he called a "lot of people," and make the young girl acquainted with English society, she encouraged the hospitable impulse and promised, in advance, to be delighted. Little, however, for the present, had come of Ralph's offers, and it may be confided to the reader that, if the young man delayed to carry them out, it was because he found the labour of entertaining his cousin by no means so severe as to require extraneous help. Isabel had spoken to him very often about "specimens"; it was a word that played a considerable part in her vocabulary; she had given him to understand that she wished to see English society illustrated by figures.

"Well now, there's a specimen," he said to her, as they walked up from the river-side, and he recognized Lord Warburton.

"A specimen of what?" asked the girl.

"A specimen of an English gentleman."

"Do you mean they are all like him?"

"Oh no; they are not all like him."

"He's a favourable specimen, then," said Isabel; "because I am sure he is good."

"Yes, he is very good. And he is very fortunate."

The fortunate Lord Warburton exchanged a handshake with our heroine, and hoped she was very well. "But I needn't ask that," he said, "since you have been handling the oars."

"I have been rowing a little," Isabel answered; "but how should you know it?"

"Oh, I know *he* doesn't row; he's too lazy," said his lordship, indicating Ralph Touchett, with a laugh.

"He has a good excuse for his laziness," Isabel rejoined, lowering her voice a little.

"Ah, he has a good excuse for everything!" cried Lord Warburton, still with his deep, agreeable laugh.

"My excuse for not rowing is that my cousin rows so well," said Ralph. "She does everything well. She touches nothing that she doesn't adorn!"

"It makes one want to be touched, Miss Archer," Lord Warburton declared.

"Be touched in the right sense, and you will never look the worse for it," said Isabel, who, if it pleased her to hear it said that her accomplishments were numerous, was happily able to reflect that such complacency was not the indication of a feeble mind, inasmuch as there were several things in which she excelled. Her desire to think well of herself always needed to be supported by proof; though it is possible that this fact is not the sign of a milder egotism.

Lord Warburton not only spent the night at Gardencourt, but he was persuaded to remain over the second day; and when the second day was ended, he determined to postpone his departure till the morrow. During this period he addressed much of his conversation to Isabel, who accepted this evidence of his esteem with a very good grace. She found herself liking him extremely; the first impression he had made upon her was pleasant, but at the end of an evening spent in his society she thought him quite one of the most delectable persons she had met. She retired to rest with a sense of good fortune, with a quickened consciousness of the pleasantness of life. "It's very nice to know two such charming people as those," she said, meaning by "those" her cousin and her cousin's friend. It must be added, moreover, that an incident had occurred which might have seemed to put her good humour to the test. Mr. Touchett went to bed at half-past nine o'clock, but his wife remained in the drawing-room with the other members of the party. She prolonged her vigil for something less than an hour, and then rising, she said to Isabel that it was time they should bid the gentlemen good-night. Isabel had as yet no desire to go to bed; the occasion wore, to her sense, a festive character, and feasts were not in the habit of terminating so early. So, without further thought, she replied, very simply—

"Need I go, dear aunt? I will come up in half-an-hour."

"It's impossible I should wait for you," Mrs. Touchett answered.

"Ah, you needn't wait! Ralph will light my candle," said Isabel, smiling.

"I will light your candle; do let me light your candle, Miss Archer!" Lord Warburton exclaimed. "Only I beg it shall not be before midnight."

Mrs. Touchett fixed her bright little eyes upon him for a moment, and then transferred them to her niece.

"You can't stay alone with the gentlemen. You are not—you are not at Albany, my dear."

Isabel rose, blushing.

"I wish I were," she said.

"Oh, I say, mother!" Ralph broke out.

"My dear Mrs. Touchett," Lord Warburton murmured.

"I didn't make your country, my lord," Mrs. Touchett said majestically. "I must take it as I find it."

"Can't I stay with my own cousin?" Isabel inquired.

"I am not aware that Lord Warburton is your cousin."

"Perhaps I had better go to bed!" the visitor exclaimed. "That will arrange it."

Mrs. Touchett gave a little look of despair, and sat down again.

"Oh, if it's necessary, I will stay up till midnight," she said.

Ralph meanwhile handed Isabel her candlestick. He had been watching her; it had seemed to him that her temper was stirred—an accident that might be interesting. But if he had expected an exhibition of temper, he was disappointed, for the girl simply laughed a little, nodded good night, and withdrew, accompanied by her aunt. For himself he was annoyed at his mother, though he thought she was right. Above-stairs, the two ladies separated at Mrs. Touchett's door. Isabel had said nothing on her way up.

"Of course you are displeased at my interfering with you," said Mrs. Touchett.

Isabel reflected a moment.

"I am not displeased, but I am surprised—and a good deal puzzled. Was it not proper I should remain in the drawing-room?"

"Not in the least. Young girls here don't sit alone with the gentlemen late at night."

"You were very right to tell me then," said Isabel. "I don't understand it, but I am very glad to know it."

"I shall always tell you," her aunt answered, "whenever I see you taking what seems to be too much liberty."

"Pray do; but I don't say I shall always think your remonstrance just."

"Very likely not. You are too fond of your liberty."

"Yes, I think I am very fond of it. But I always want to know the things one shouldn't do."

"So as to do them?" asked her aunt.

"So as to choose," said Isabel.

VIII

As she was much interested in the picturesque, Lord Warburton ventured to express a hope that she would come some day and see his house, which was a very curious old place. He extracted from Mrs. Touchett a promise that she would bring her niece to Lockleigh, and Ralph signified his willingness to attend upon the ladies if his father should be able to spare him. Lord Warburton assured our heroine that in the mean time his sisters would come and see her. She knew something about his sisters, having interrogated him, during the hours they spent together while he was at Gardencourt, on many points connected with his family. When Isabel was interested, she asked a great many questions, and as her companion was a copious talker, she asked him on this occasion by no means in vain. He told her that he had four sisters and two brothers, and had lost both his parents. The brothers and sisters were very good people—"not particularly clever, you know," he said, "but simple and respectable and trustworthy;" and he was so good as to hope that Miss Archer should know them well. One of the brothers was in the Church, settled in the parsonage at Lockleigh, which was rather a largeish parish, and was an excellent fellow, in spite of his thinking differently from himself on every conceivable topic. And then Lord Warburton mentioned some of the opinions held by his brother, which were opinions that Isabel had often heard expressed and that she supposed to be entertained by a considerable portion of the human family. Many of them, indeed, she supposed she had held herself, till he assured her that she was quite mistaken, that it was really impossible, that she had doubtless imagined she entertained them, but that she might depend that, if she thought them over a little, she would find there was nothing in them. When she answered that she had already thought several of them over very attentively, he declared that she was only another example of what he had often been struck with—the fact that, of all the people in the world, the Americans were the most grossly superstitious. They were rank Tories and bigots, every one of them; there were no conservatives like American

conservatives. Her uncle and her cousin were there to prove
it; nothing could be more mediæval than many of their views;
they had ideas that people in England now-a-days were
ashamed to confess to; and they had the impudence, moreover, said his lordship, laughing, to pretend they know more
about the needs and dangers of this poor dear stupid old England than he who was born in it and owned a considerable
part of it—the more shame to him! From all of which Isabel
gathered that Lord Warburton was a nobleman of the newest
pattern, a reformer, a radical, a contemner of ancient ways.
His other brother, who was in the army in India, was rather
wild and pig-headed, and had not been of much use as yet
but to make debts for Warburton to pay—one of the most
precious privileges of an elder brother. "I don't think I will
pay any more," said Warburton; "he lives a monstrous deal
better than I do, enjoys unheard-of luxuries, and thinks himself a much finer gentleman than I. As I am a consistent radical, I go in only for equality; I don't go in for the superiority
of the younger brothers." Two of his four sisters, the second
and fourth, were married, one of them having done very well,
as they said, the other only so-so. The husband of the elder,
Lord Haycock, was a very good fellow, but unfortunately a
horrid Tory; and his wife, like all good English wives, was
worse than her husband. The other had espoused a smallish
squire in Norfolk, and, though she was married only the
other day, had already five children. This information, and
much more, Lord Warburton imparted to his young American listener, taking pains to make many things clear and to
lay bare to her apprehension the peculiarities of English life.
Isabel was often amused at his explicitness and at the small
allowance he seemed to make either for her own experience
or for her imagination. "He thinks I am a barbarian," she
said, "and that I have never seen forks and spoons;" and she
used to ask him artless questions for the pleasure of hearing
him answer seriously. Then when he had fallen into the
trap—"It's a pity you can't see me in my war-paint and feathers," she remarked; "if I had known how kind you are to the
poor savages, I would have brought over my national costume!" Lord Warburton had travelled through the United
States, and knew much more about them than Isabel; he was

so good as to say that America was the most charming country in the world, but his recollections of it appeared to encourage the idea that Americans in England would need to have a great many things explained to them. "If I had only had you to explain things to me in America!" he said. "I was rather puzzled in your country; in fact, I was quite bewildered, and the trouble was that the explanations only puzzled me more. You know I think they often gave me the wrong ones on purpose; they are rather clever about that over there. But when I explain, you can trust me; about what I tell you there is no mistake." There was no mistake at least about his being very intelligent and cultivated, and knowing almost everything in the world. Although he said the most interesting and entertaining things, Isabel perceived that he never said them to exhibit himself, and though he had a great good fortune, he was as far as possible from making a merit of it. He had enjoyed the best things of life, but they had not spoiled his sense of proportion. His composition was a mixture of good-humoured manly force and a modesty that at times was almost boyish; the sweet and wholesome savour of which—it was as agreeable as something tasted—lost nothing from the addition of a tone of kindness which was not boyish, inasmuch as there was a good deal of reflection and of conscience in it.

"I like your specimen English gentleman very much," Isabel said to Ralph, after Lord Warburton had gone.

"I like him too—I love him well," said Ralph. "But I pity him more."

Isabel looked at him askance.

"Why, that seems to me his only fault—that one can't pity him a little. He appears to have everything, to know everything, to be everything."

"Oh, he's in a bad way," Ralph insisted.

"I suppose you don't mean in health?"

"No, as to that, he's detestably robust. What I mean is that he is a man with a great position, who is playing all sorts of tricks with it. He doesn't take himself seriously."

"Does he regard himself as a joke?"

"Much worse; he regards himself as an imposition—as an abuse."

"Well, perhaps he is," said Isabel.

"Perhaps he is—though on the whole I don't think so. But in that case, what is more pitiable than a sentient, self-conscious abuse, planted by other hands, deeply rooted, but aching with a sense of its injustice? For me, I could take the poor fellow very seriously; he occupies a position that appeals to my imagination. Great responsibilities, great opportunities, great consideration, great wealth, great power, a natural share in the public affairs of a great country. But he is all in a muddle about himself, his position, his power, and everything else. He is the victim of a critical age; he has ceased to believe in himself, and he doesn't know what to believe in. When I attempt to tell him (because if I were he, I know very well what I should believe in), he calls me an old-fashioned and narrow-minded person. I believe he seriously thinks me an awful Philistine; he says I don't understand my time. I understand it certainly better than he, who can neither abolish himself as a nuisance nor maintain himself as an institution."

"He doesn't look very wretched," Isabel observed.

"Possibly not; though, being a man of imagination, I think he often has uncomfortable hours. But what is it to say of a man of his opportunities that he is not miserable? Besides, I believe he is."

"I don't," said Isabel.

"Well," her cousin rejoined, "if he is not, he ought to be!"

In the afternoon she spent an hour with her uncle on the lawn, where the old man sat, as usual, with his shawl over his legs and his large cup of diluted tea in his hands. In the course of conversation he asked her what she thought of their late visitor.

"I think he is charming," Isabel answered.

"He's a fine fellow," said Mr. Touchett, "but I don't recommend you to fall in love with him."

"I shall not do it then; I shall never fall in love but on your recommendation. Moreover," Isabel added, "my cousin gives me a rather sad account of Lord Warburton."

"Oh, indeed? I don't know what there may be to say, but you must remember that Ralph is rather fanciful."

"He thinks Lord Warburton is too radical—or not radical enough! I don't quite understand which," said Isabel.

The old man shook his head slowly, smiled, and put down his cup.

"I don't know which, either. He goes very far, but it is quite possible he doesn't go far enough. He seems to want to do away with a good many things, but he seems to want to remain himself. I suppose that is natural; but it is rather inconsistent."

"Oh, I hope he will remain himself," said Isabel. "If he were to be done away with, his friends would miss him sadly."

"Well," said the old man, "I guess he'll stay and amuse his friends. I should certainly miss him very much here at Gardencourt. He always amuses me when he comes over, and I think he amuses himself as well. There is a considerable number like him, round in society; they are very fashionable just now. I don't know what they are trying to do—whether they are trying to get up a revolution; I hope at any rate they will put it off till after I am gone. You see they want to disestablish everything; but I'm a pretty big landowner here, and I don't want to be disestablished. I wouldn't have come over if I had thought they were going to behave like that," Mr. Touchett went on, with expanding hilarity. "I came over because I thought England was a safe country. I call it a regular fraud, if they are going to introduce any considerable changes; there'll be a large number disappointed in that case."

"Oh, I do hope they will make a revolution!" Isabel exclaimed. "I should delight in seeing a revolution."

"Let me see," said her uncle, with a humorous intention; "I forget whether you are a liberal or a conservative. I have heard you take such opposite views."

"I am both. I think I am a little of everything. In a revolution—after it was well begun—I think I should be a conservative. One sympathises more with them, and they have a chance to behave so picturesquely."

"I don't know that I understand what you mean by behaving picturesquely, but it seems to me that you do that always, my dear."

"Oh, you lovely man, if I could believe that!" the girl interrupted.

"I am afraid, after all, you won't have the pleasure of seeing a revolution here just now," Mr. Touchett went on. "If you want to see one, you must pay us a long visit. You see, when you come to the point, it wouldn't suit them to be taken at their word."

"Of whom are you speaking?"

"Well, I mean Lord Warburton and his friends—the radicals of the upper class. Of course I only know the way it strikes me. They talk about the changes, but I don't think they quite realise. You and I, you know, we know what it is to have lived under democratic institutions; I always thought them very comfortable, but I was used to them from the first. But then, I ain't a lord; you're a lady, my dear, but I ain't a lord. Now, over here, I don't think it quite comes home to them. It's a matter of every day and every hour, and I don't think many of them would find it as pleasant as what they've got. Of course if they want to try, it's their own business; but I expect they won't try very hard."

"Don't you think they are sincere?" Isabel asked.

"Well, they are very conscientious," Mr. Touchett allowed; "but it seems as if they took it out in theories, mostly. Their radical views are a kind of amusement; they have got to have some amusement, and they might have coarser tastes than that. You see they are very luxurious, and these progressive ideas are about their biggest luxury. They make them feel moral, and yet they don't affect their position. They think a great deal of their position; don't let one of them ever persuade you he doesn't, for if you were to proceed on that basis, you would be pulled up very short."

Isabel followed her uncle's argument, which he unfolded with his mild, reflective, optimistic accent, most attentively, and though she was unacquainted with the British aristocracy, she found it in harmony with her general impressions of human nature. But she felt moved to put in a protest on Lord Warburton's behalf.

"I don't believe Lord Warburton's a humbug," she said; "I don't care what the others are. I should like to see Lord Warburton put to the test."

"Heaven deliver me from my friends!" Mr. Touchett answered. "Lord Warburton is a very amiable young man—a very fine young man. He has a hundred thousand a year. He owns fifty thousand acres of the soil of this little island. He has half-a-dozen houses to live in. He has a seat in Parliament as I have one at my own dinner-table. He has very cultivated tastes—cares for literature, for art, for science, for charming young ladies. The most cultivated is his taste for the new views. It affords him a great deal of entertainment—more perhaps than anything else, except the young ladies. His old house over there—what does he call it, Lockleigh?—is very attractive; but I don't think it is as pleasant as this. That doesn't matter, however—he has got so many others. His views don't hurt any one as far as I can see; they certainly don't hurt himself. And if there were to be a revolution, he would come off very easily; they wouldn't touch him, they would leave him as he is; he is too much liked."

"Ah, he couldn't be a martyr even if he wished!" Isabel exclaimed. "That's a very poor position."

"He will never be a martyr unless you make him one," said the old man.

Isabel shook her head; there might have been something laughable in the fact that she did it with a touch of sadness.

"I shall never make any one a martyr."

"You will never be one, I hope."

"I hope not. But you don't pity Lord Warburton, then, as Ralph does?"

Her uncle looked at her a while, with genial acuteness.

"Yes, I do, after all!"

IX

THE TWO Misses Molyneux, this nobleman's sisters, came presently to call upon her, and Isabel took a fancy to the young ladies, who appeared to her to have a very original stamp. It is true that, when she spoke of them to her cousin as original, he declared that no epithet could be less applicable than this to the two Misses Molyneux, for that there were fifty thousand young women in England who exactly resembled them. Deprived of this advantage, however, Isabel's visitors retained that of an extreme sweetness and shyness of demeanour, and of having, as she thought, the kindest eyes in the world.

"They are not morbid, at any rate, whatever they are," our heroine said to herself; and she deemed this a great charm, for two or three of the friends of her girlhood had been regrettably open to the charge (they would have been so nice without it), to say nothing of Isabel's having occasionally suspected that it might become a fault of her own. The Misses Molyneux were not in their first youth, but they had bright, fresh complexions, and something of the smile of childhood. Their eyes, which Isabel admired so much, were quiet and contented, and their figures, of a generous roundness, were encased in sealskin jackets. Their friendliness was great, so great that they were almost embarrassed to show it; they seemed somewhat afraid of the young lady from the other side of the world, and rather looked than spoke their good wishes. But they made it clear to her that they hoped she would come to lunch at Lockleigh, where they lived with their brother, and then they might see her very, very often. They wondered whether she wouldn't come over some day and sleep; they were expecting some people on the twenty-ninth, and perhaps she would come while the people were there.

"I'm afraid it isn't any one very remarkable," said the elder sister; "but I daresay you will take us as you find us."

"I shall find you delightful; I think you are enchanting just as you are," replied Isabel, who often praised profusely.

Her visitors blushed, and her cousin told her, after they

were gone, that if she said such things to those poor girls, they would think she was quizzing them; he was sure it was the first time they had been called enchanting.

"I can't help it," Isabel answered. "I think it's lovely to be so quiet, and reasonable, and satisfied. I should like to be like that."

"Heaven forbid!" cried Ralph, with ardour.

"I mean to try and imitate them," said Isabel. "I want very much to see them at home."

She had this pleasure a few days later, when, with Ralph and his mother, she drove over to Lockleigh. She found the Misses Molyneux sitting in a vast drawing-room (she perceived afterwards it was one of several), in a wilderness of faded chintz; they were dressed on this occasion in black velveteen. Isabel liked them even better at home than she had done at Gardencourt, and was more than ever struck with the fact that they were not morbid. It had seemed to her before that, if they had a fault, it was a want of vivacity; but she presently saw that they were capable of deep emotion. Before lunch she was alone with them, for some time, on one side of the room, while Lord Warburton, at a distance, talked to Mrs. Touchett.

"Is it true that your brother is such a great radical?" Isabel asked. She knew it was true, but we have seen that her interest in human nature was keen, and she had a desire to draw the Misses Molyneux out.

"Oh dear, yes; he's immensely advanced," said Mildred, the younger sister.

"At the same time, Warburton is very reasonable," Miss Molyneux observed.

Isabel watched him a moment, at the other side of the room; he was evidently trying hard to make himself agreeable to Mrs. Touchett. Ralph was playing with one of the dogs before the fire, which the temperature of an English August, in the ancient, spacious room, had not made an impertinence. "Do you suppose your brother is sincere?" Isabel inquired with a smile.

"Oh, he must be, you know!" Mildred exclaimed, quickly; while the elder sister gazed at our heroine in silence.

"Do you think he would stand the test?"

"The test?"

"I mean, for instance, having to give up all this!"

"Having to give up Lockleigh?" said Miss Molyneux, finding her voice.

"Yes, and the other places; what are they called?"

The two sisters exchanged an almost frightened glance. "Do you mean—do you mean on account of the expense?" the younger one asked.

"I daresay he might let one or two of his houses," said the other.

"Let them for nothing?" Isabel inquired.

"I can't fancy his giving up his property," said Miss Molyneux.

"Ah, I am afraid he is an impostor!" Isabel exclaimed. "Don't you think it's a false position?"

Her companions, evidently, were rapidly getting bewildered. "My brother's position?" Miss Molyneux inquired.

"It's thought a very good position," said the younger sister. "It's the first position in the county."

"I suspect you think me very irreverent," Isabel took occasion to observe. "I suppose you revere your brother, and are rather afraid of him."

"Of course one looks up to one's brother," said Miss Molyneux, simply.

"If you do that, he must be very good—because you, evidently, are very good."

"He is most kind. It will never be known, the good he does."

"His ability is known," Mildred added; "every one thinks it's immense."

"Oh, I can see that," said Isabel. "But if I were he, I should wish to be a conservative. I should wish to keep everything."

"I think one ought to be liberal," Mildred argued, gently. "We have always been so, even from the earliest times."

"Ah well," said Isabel, "you have made a great success of it; I don't wonder you like it. I see you are very fond of crewels."

When Lord Warburton showed her the house, after lunch, it seemed to her a matter of course that it should be a noble picture. Within, it had been a good deal modernised—some

of its best points had lost their purity; but as they saw it from
the gardens, a stout, grey pile, of the softest, deepest, most
weather-fretted hue, rising from a broad, still moat, it seemed
to Isabel a castle in a fairy-tale. The day was cool and rather
lustreless; the first note of autumn had been struck; and the
watery sunshine rested on the walls in blurred and desultory
gleams, washing them, as it were, in places tenderly chosen,
where the ache of antiquity was keenest. Her host's brother,
the Vicar, had come to lunch, and Isabel had had five minutes' talk with him—time enough to institute a search for
theological characteristics and give it up as vain. The characteristics of the Vicar of Lockleigh were a big, athletic figure,
a candid, natural countenance, a capacious appetite, and a
tendency to abundant laughter. Isabel learned afterwards
from her cousin that, before taking orders, he had been a
mighty wrestler, and that he was still, on occasion—in the
privacy of the family circle as it were—quite capable of floor-
ing his man. Isabel liked him—she was in the mood for liking
everything; but her imagination was a good deal taxed to
think of him as a source of spiritual aid. The whole party, on
leaving lunch, went to walk in the grounds; but Lord Warburton exercised some ingenuity in engaging his youngest visitor in a stroll somewhat apart from the others.

"I wish you to see the place properly, seriously," he said.
"You can't do so if your attention is distracted by irrelevant
gossip." His own conversation (though he told Isabel a good
deal about the house, which had a very curious history) was
not purely archæological; he reverted at intervals to matters
more personal—matters personal to the young lady as well as
to himself. But at last, after a pause of some duration, returning for a moment to their ostensible theme, "Ah, well," he
said, "I am very glad indeed you like the old house. I wish
you could see more of it—that you could stay here a while.
My sisters have taken an immense fancy to you—if that
would be any inducement."

"There is no want of inducements," Isabel answered; "but
I am afraid I can't make engagements. I am quite in my aunt's
hands."

"Ah, excuse me if I say I don't exactly believe that. I am
pretty sure you can do whatever you want."

"I am sorry if I make that impression on you; I don't think it's a nice impression to make."

"It has the merit of permitting me to hope." And Lord Warburton paused a moment.

"To hope what?"

"That in future I may see you often."

"Ah," said Isabel, "to enjoy that pleasure, I needn't be so terribly emancipated."

"Doubtless not; and yet, at the same time, I don't think your uncle likes me."

"You are very much mistaken. I have heard him speak very highly of you."

"I am glad you have talked about me," said Lord Warburton. "But, all the same, I don't think he would like me to keep coming to Gardencourt."

"I can't answer for my uncle's tastes," the girl rejoined, "though I ought, as far as possible, to take them into account. But, for myself, I shall be very glad to see you."

"Now that's what I like to hear you say. I am charmed when you say that."

"You are easily charmed, my lord," said Isabel.

"No, I am not easily charmed!" And then he stopped a moment. "But you have charmed me, Miss Archer," he added.

These words were uttered with an indefinable sound which startled the girl; it struck her as the prelude to something grave; she had heard the sound before, and she recognised it. She had no wish, however, that for the moment such a prelude should have a sequel, and she said, as gaily as possible and as quickly as an appreciable degree of agitation would allow her, "I am afraid there is no prospect of my being able to come here again."

"Never?" said Lord Warburton.

"I won't say 'never'; I should feel very melodramatic."

"May I come and see you then some day next week?"

"Most assuredly. What is there to prevent it?"

"Nothing tangible. But with you I never feel safe. I have a sort of sense that you are always judging people."

"You don't of necessity lose by that."

"It is very kind of you to say so; but even if I gain, stern justice is not what I most love. Is Mrs. Touchett going to take you abroad?"

"I hope so."

"Is England not good enough for you?"

"That's a very Machiavellian speech; it doesn't deserve an answer. I want very much to see foreign lands as well."

"Then you will go on judging, I suppose."

"Enjoying, I hope, too."

"Yes, that's what you enjoy most; I can't make out what you are up to," said Lord Warburton. "You strike me as having mysterious purposes—vast designs!"

"You are so good as to have a theory about me which I don't at all fill out. Is there anything mysterious in a purpose entertained and executed every year, in the most public manner, by fifty thousand of my fellow-countrymen—the purpose of improving one's mind by foreign travel?"

"You can't improve your mind, Miss Archer," her companion declared. "It's already a most formidable instrument. It looks down on us all; it despises us."

"Despises you? You are making fun of me," said Isabel, seriously.

"Well, you think us picturesque—that's the same thing. I won't be thought picturesque, to begin with; I am not so in the least. I protest."

"That protest is one of the most picturesque things I have ever heard," Isabel answered with a smile.

Lord Warburton was silent a moment. "You judge only from the outside—you don't care," he said presently. "You only care to amuse yourself!" The note she had heard in his voice a moment before reappeared, and mixed with it now was an audible strain of bitterness—a bitterness so abrupt and inconsequent that the girl was afraid she had hurt him. She had often heard that the English were a highly eccentric people; and she had even read in some ingenious author that they were, at bottom, the most romantic of races. Was Lord Warburton suddenly turning romantic—was he going to make a scene, in his own house, only the third time they had met? She was reassured, quickly enough, by her sense of his great good manners, which was not impaired by the fact that he had already touched the furthest limit of good taste in expressing his admiration of a young lady who had confided in his hospitality. She was right in trusting to his good manners, for he presently went on, laughing a little, and without a trace of the accent that had discomposed her—"I don't mean, of course, that you amuse yourself with trifles. You select great materials; the foibles, the afflictions of human nature, the peculiarities of nations!"

"As regards that," said Isabel, "I should find in my own nation entertainment for a lifetime. But we have a long drive, and my aunt will soon wish to start." She turned back toward the others, and Lord Warburton walked beside her in silence. But before they reached the others—"I shall come and see you next week," he said.

She had received an appreciable shock, but as it died away she felt that she could not pretend to herself that it was altogether a painful one. Nevertheless, she made answer to this declaration, coldly enough, "Just as you please." And her coldness was not coquetry—a quality that she possessed in a much smaller degree than would have seemed probable to many critics; it came from a certain fear.

X

THE DAY after her visit to Lockleigh she received a note from her friend, Miss Stackpole—a note of which the envelope, exhibiting in conjunction the postmark of Liverpool and the neat calligraphy of the quick-fingered Henrietta, caused her some liveliness of emotion. "Here I am, my lovely friend," Miss Stackpole wrote; "I managed to get off at last. I decided only the night before I left New York—the *Interviewer* having come round to my figure. I put a few things into a bag, like a veteran journalist, and came down to the steamer in a street-car. Where are you, and where can we meet? I suppose you are visiting at some castle or other, and have already acquired the correct accent. Perhaps, even, you have married a lord; I almost hope you have, for I want some introductions to the first people, and shall count on you for a few. The *Interviewer* wants some light on the nobility. My first impressions (of the people at large) are not rose-coloured; but I wish to talk them over with you, and you know that whatever I am, at least I am not superficial. I have also something very particular to tell you. Do appoint a meeting as quickly as you can; come to London (I should like so much to visit the sights with you), or else let me come to you, *wherever you are*. I will do so with pleasure; for you know everything interests me, and I wish to see as much as possible of the inner life."

Isabel did not show this letter to her uncle; but she acquainted him with its purport, and, as she expected, he begged her instantly to assure Miss Stackpole, in his name, that he should be delighted to receive her at Gardencourt. "Though she is a literary lady," he said, "I suppose that, being an American, she won't reproduce me, as that other one did. She has seen others like me."

"She has seen no other so delightful!" Isabel answered; but she was not altogether at ease about Henrietta's reproductive instincts, which belonged to that side of her friend's character which she regarded with least complacency. She wrote to Miss Stackpole, however, that she would be very welcome under Mr. Touchett's roof; and this enterprising young woman lost no time in signifying her intention of arriving. She had gone up to London, and it was from the metropolis that she took the train for the station nearest to Gardencourt, where Isabel and Ralph were in waiting to receive the visitor.

"Shall I love her, or shall I hate her?" asked Ralph, while they stood on the platform, before the advent of the train.

"Whichever you do will matter very little to her," said Isabel. "She doesn't care a straw what men think of her."

"As a man I am bound to dislike her, then. She must be a kind of monster. Is she very ugly?"

"No, she is decidedly pretty."

"A female interviewer—a reporter in petticoats? I am very curious to see her," Ralph declared.

"It is very easy to laugh at her, but it is not easy to be as brave as she."

"I should think not; interviewing requires bravery. Do you suppose she will interview me?"

"Never in the world. She will not think you of enough importance."

"You will see," said Ralph. "She will send a description of us all, including Bunchie, to her newspaper."

"I shall ask her not to," Isabel answered.

"You think she is capable of it, then."

"Perfectly."

"And yet you have made her your bosom-friend?"

"I have not made her my bosom-friend; but I like her, in spite of her faults."

"Ah, well," said Ralph, "I am afraid I shall dislike her, in spite of her merits."

"You will probably fall in love with her at the end of three days."

"And have my love-letters published in the *Interviewer*? Never!" cried the young man.

The train presently arrived, and Miss Stackpole, promptly descending, proved to be, as Isabel had said, decidedly pretty. She was a fair, plump person, of medium stature, with a round face, a small mouth, a delicate complexion, a bunch of light brown ringlets at the back of her head, and a peculiarly open, surprised-looking eye. The most striking point in her appearance was the remarkable fixedness of this organ, which rested without impudence or defiance, but as if in conscientious exercise of a natural right, upon every object it happened to encounter. It rested in this manner upon Ralph himself, who was somewhat disconcerted by Miss Stackpole's gracious and comfortable aspect, which seemed to indicate that it would not be so easy as he had assumed to disapprove of her. She was very well dressed, in fresh, dove-coloured draperies, and Ralph saw at a glance that she was scrupulously, fastidiously neat. From top to toe she carried not an ink-stain. She spoke in a clear, high voice—a voice not rich, but loud, though after she had taken her place, with her companions, in Mr. Touchett's carriage, she struck him, rather to his surprise, as not an abundant talker. She answered the inquiries made of her by Isabel, however, and in which the young man ventured to join, with a great deal of precison and distinctness; and later, in the library at Gardencourt, when she had made the acquaintance of Mr. Touchett (his wife not having thought it necessary to appear), did more to give the measure of her conversational powers.

"Well, I should like to know whether you consider yourselves American or English," she said. "If once I knew, I could talk to you accordingly."

"Talk to us anyhow, and we shall be thankful," Ralph answered, liberally.

She fixed her eyes upon him, and there was something in their character that reminded him of large, polished buttons; he seemed to see the reflection of surrounding objects upon the pupil. The expression of a button is not usually deemed human, but there was something in Miss Stackpole's gaze that made him, as he was a very modest man, feel vaguely embarrassed and uncomfortable. This sensation, it must be added, after he had spent a day or two in her company, sensibly diminished, though it never wholly disappeared. "I don't suppose that you are going to undertake to persuade me that *you* are an American," she said.

"To please you, I will be an Englishman, I will be a Turk!"

"Well, if you can change about that way, you are very welcome," Miss Stackpole rejoined.

"I am sure you understand everything, and that differences of nationality are no barrier to you," Ralph went on.

Miss Stackpole gazed at him still. "Do you mean the foreign languages?"

"The languages are nothing. I mean the spirit—the
genius."

"I am not sure that I understand you," said the correspondent of the *Interviewer*; "but I expect I shall before I leave."

"He is what is called a cosmopolitan," Isabel suggested.

"That means he's a little of everything and not much of
any. I must say I think patriotism is like charity—it begins at
home."

"Ah, but where does home begin, Miss Stackpole?" Ralph
inquired.

"I don't know where it begins, but I know where it ends.
It ended a long time before I got here."

"Don't you like it over here?" asked Mr. Touchett, with his
mild, wise, aged, innocent voice.

"Well, sir, I haven't quite made up my mind what ground
I shall take. I feel a good deal cramped. I felt it on the journey
from Liverpool to London."

"Perhaps you were in a crowded carriage," Ralph suggested.

"Yes, but it was crowded with friends—a party of Americans whose acquaintance I had made upon the steamer; a
most lovely group, from Little Rock, Arkansas. In spite of
that I felt cramped—I felt something pressing upon me; I
couldn't tell what it was. I felt at the very commencement as
if I were not going to sympathise with the atmosphere. But I
suppose I shall make my own atmosphere. Your surroundings
seem very attractive."

"Ah, we too are a lovely group!" said Ralph. "Wait a little
and you will see."

Miss Stackpole showed every disposition to wait, and evidently was prepared to make a considerable stay at Gardencourt. She occupied herself in the mornings with literary
labour; but in spite of this Isabel spent many hours with her
friend, who, once her daily task performed, was of an eminently social tendency. Isabel speedily found occasion to request her to desist from celebrating the charms of their
common sojourn in print, having discovered, on the second
morning of Miss Stackpole's visit, that she was engaged upon

a letter to the *Interviewer*, of which the title, in her exquisitely neat and legible hand (exactly that of the copy-books which our heroine remembered at school), was "Americans and Tudors—Glimpses of Gardencourt." Miss Stackpole, with the best conscience in the world, offered to read her letter to Isabel, who immediately put in her protest.

"I don't think you ought to do that. I don't think you ought to describe the place."

Henrietta gazed at her, as usual. "Why, it's just what the people want, and it's a lovely place."

"It's too lovely to be put in the newspapers, and it's not what my uncle wants."

"Don't you believe that!" cried Henrietta. "They are always delighted, afterwards."

"My uncle won't be delighted—nor my cousin, either. They will consider it a breach of hospitality."

Miss Stackpole showed no sense of confusion; she simply wiped her pen, very neatly, upon an elegant little implement which she kept for the purpose, and put away her manuscript. "Of course if you don't approve, I won't do it; but I sacrifice a beautiful subject."

"There are plenty of other subjects, there are subjects all round you. We will take some drives, and I will show you some charming scenery."

"Scenery is not my department; I always need a human interest. You know I am deeply human, Isabel; I always was," Miss Stackpole rejoined. "I was going to bring in your cousin—the alienated American. There is a great demand just now for the alienated American, and your cousin is a beautiful specimen. I should have handled him severely."

"He would have died of it!" Isabel exclaimed. "Not of the severity, but of the publicity."

"Well, I should have liked to kill him a little. And I should have delighted to do your uncle, who seems to me a much nobler type—the American faithful still. He is a grand old man; I don't see how he can object to my paying him honour."

Isabel looked at her companion in much wonderment; it appeared to her so strange that a nature in which she found so much to esteem should exhibit such extraordinary disparities. "My poor Henrietta," she said, "you have no sense of privacy."

Henrietta coloured deeply, and for a moment her brilliant eyes were suffused; while Isabel marvelled more than ever at her inconsistency. "You do me great injustice," said Miss Stackpole, with dignity. "I have never written a word about myself!"

"I am very sure of that; but it seems to me one should be modest for others also!"

"Ah, that is very good!" cried Henrietta, seizing her pen again. "Just let me make a note of it, and I will put it in a letter." She was a thoroughly good-natured woman, and half an hour later she was in as cheerful a mood as should have been looked for in a newspaper-correspondent in want of material. "I have promised to do the social side," she said to Isabel; "and how can I do it unless I get ideas? If I can't describe this place, don't you know some place I can describe?" Isabel promised she would bethink herself, and the next day, in conversation with her friend, she happened to mention her visit to Lord Warburton's ancient house. "Ah, you must take me there—that is just the place for me!" Miss Stackpole exclaimed. "I must get a glimpse of the nobility."

"I can't take you," said Isabel; "but Lord Warburton is coming here, and you will have a chance to see him and observe him. Only if you intend to repeat his conversation, I shall certainly give him warning."

"Don't do that," her companion begged; "I want him to be natural."

"An Englishman is never so natural as when he is holding his tongue," Isabel rejoined.

It was not apparent, at the end of three days, that her cousin had fallen in love with their visitor, though he had spent a good deal of time in her society. They strolled about the park together, and sat under the trees, and in the afternoon, when it was delightful to float along the Thames, Miss Stackpole occupied a place in the boat in which hitherto Ralph had had but a single companion. Her society had a less insoluble quality than Ralph had expected in the natural perturbation of his sense of the perfect adequacy of that of his cousin; for the correspondent of the *Interviewer* made him laugh a good deal, and he had long since decided that abundant laughter should be the embellishment of the remainder of his days. Henrietta, on her side, did not quite justify Isabel's declaration with regard to her indifference to masculine opinion; for poor Ralph appeared to have presented himself to her as an irritating problem, which it would be superficial on her part not to solve.

"What does he do for a living?" she asked of Isabel, the evening of her arrival. "Does he go round all day with his hands in his pockets?"

"He does nothing," said Isabel, smiling; "he's a gentleman of leisure."

"Well, I call that a shame—when I have to work like a cotton-mill," Miss Stackpole replied. "I should like to show him up."

"He is in wretched health; he is quite unfit for work," Isabel urged.

"Pshaw! don't you believe it. I work when I am sick," cried her friend. Later, when she stepped into the boat, on joining the water-party, she remarked to Ralph that she supposed he hated her—he would like to drown her.

"Ah, no," said Ralph, "I keep my victims for a slower torture. And you would be such an interesting one!"

"Well, you do torture me, I may say that. But I shock all your prejudices; that's one comfort."

"My prejudices? I haven't a prejudice to bless myself with. There's intellectual poverty for you."

"The more shame to you; I have some delicious prejudices. Of course I spoil your flirtation, or whatever it is you call it, with your cousin; but I don't care for that, for I render your cousin the service of drawing you out. She will see how thin you are."

"Ah, do draw me out!" Ralph exclaimed. "So few people will take the trouble."

Miss Stackpole, in this undertaking, appeared to shrink from no trouble; resorting largely, whenever the opportunity offered, to the natural expedient of interrogation. On the following day the weather was bad, and in the afternoon the young man, by way of providing in-door amusement, offered to show her the pictures. Henrietta strolled through the long

gallery in his society, while he pointed out its principal ornaments and mentioned the painters and subjects. Miss Stackpole looked at the pictures in perfect silence, committing
herself to no opinion, and Ralph was gratified by the fact that
she delivered herself of none of the little ready-made ejaculations of delight of which the visitors to Gardencourt were so
frequently lavish. This young lady, indeed, to do her justice,
was but little addicted to the use of conventional phrases;
there was something earnest and inventive in her tone, which
at times, in its brilliant deliberation, suggested a person of
high culture speaking a foreign language. Ralph Touchett
subsequently learned that she had at one time officiated as art-
critic to a Transatlantic journal; but she appeared, in spite of
this fact, to carry in her pocket none of the small change of
admiration. Suddenly, just after he had called her attention to
a charming Constable, she turned and looked at him as if he
himself had been a picture.

"Do you always spend your time like this?" she demanded.

"I seldom spend it so agreeably," said Ralph.

"Well, you know what I mean—without any regular occupation."

"Ah," said Ralph, "I am the idlest man living."

Miss Stackpole turned her gaze to the Constable again, and
Ralph bespoke her attention for a small Watteau hanging near
it, which represented a gentleman in a pink doublet and hose
and a ruff, leaning against the pedestal of the statue of a
nymph in a garden, and playing the guitar to two ladies
seated on the grass.

"That's my ideal of a regular occupation," he said.

Miss Stackpole turned to him again, and though her eyes
had rested upon the picture, he saw that she had not appre-
hended the subject. She was thinking of something much
more serious.

"I don't see how you can reconcile it to your conscience,"
she said.

"My dear lady, I have no conscience!"

"Well, I advise you to cultivate one. You will need it the
next time you go to America."

"I shall probably never go again."

"Are you ashamed to show yourself?"

Ralph meditated, with a gentle smile.

"I suppose that, if one has no conscience, one has no shame."

"Well, you have got plenty of assurance," Henrietta declared. "Do you consider it right to give up your country?"

"Ah, one doesn't give up one's country any more than one gives up one's grandmother. It's antecedent to choice."

"I suppose that means that you would give it up if you could? What do they think of you over here?"

"They delight in me."

"That's because you truckle to them."

"Ah, set it down a little to my natural charm!" Ralph urged.

"I don't know anything about your natural charm. If you have got any charm, it's quite unnatural. It's wholly acquired—or at least you have tried hard to acquire it, living over here. I don't say you have succeeded. It's a charm that I don't appreciate, any way. Make yourself useful in some way, and then we will talk about it."

"Well now, tell me what I shall do," said Ralph.

"Go right home, to begin with."

"Yes, I see. And then?"

"Take right hold of something."

"Well, now, what sort of thing?"

"Anything you please, so long as you take hold. Some new idea, some big work."

"Is it very difficult to take hold?" Ralph inquired.

"Not if you put your heart into it."

"Ah, my heart," said Ralph. "If it depends upon my heart——"

"Haven't you got any?"

"I had one a few days ago, but I have lost it since."

"You are not serious," Miss Stackpole remarked; "that's what's the matter with you." But for all this, in a day or two she again permitted him to fix her attention, and on this occasion assigned a different cause to his mysterious perversity. "I know what's the matter with you, Mr. Touchett," she said. "You think you are too good to get married."

"I thought so till I knew you, Miss Stackpole," Ralph answered; "and then I suddenly changed my mind."

"Oh, pshaw!" Henrietta exclaimed impatiently.

"Then it seemed to me," said Ralph, "that I was not good enough."

"It would improve you. Besides, it's your duty."

"Ah," cried the young man, "one has so many duties! Is that a duty too?"

"Of course it is—did you never know that before? It's every one's duty to get married."

Ralph meditated a moment; he was disappointed. There was something in Miss Stackpole he had begun to like; it seemed to him that if she was not a charming woman she was at least a very good fellow. She was wanting in distinction, but, as Isabel had said, she was brave, and there is always something fine about that. He had not supposed her to be capable of vulgar arts; but these last words struck him as a false note. When a marriageable young woman urges matrimony upon an unencumbered young man, the most obvious explanation of her conduct is not the altruistic impulse.

"Ah, well now, there is a good deal to be said about that," Ralph rejoined.

"There may be, but that is the principal thing. I must say I think it looks very exclusive, going round all alone, as if you thought no woman was good enough for you. Do you think you are better than any one else in the world? In America it's usual for people to marry."

"If it's my duty," Ralph asked, "is it not, by analogy, yours as well?"

Miss Stackpole's brilliant eyes expanded still further.

"Have you the fond hope of finding a flaw in my reasoning? Of course I have got as good a right to marry as any one else."

"Well then," said Ralph, "I won't say it vexes me to see you single. It delights me rather."

"You are not serious yet. You never will be."

"Shall you not believe me to be so on the day that I tell you I desire to give up the practice of going round alone?"

Miss Stackpole looked at him for a moment in a manner which seemed to announce a reply that might technically be called encouraging. But to his great surprise this expression suddenly resolved itself into an appearance of alarm, and even of resentment.

"No, not even then," she answered, dryly. After which she walked away.

"I have not fallen in love with your friend," Ralph said that evening to Isabel, "though we talked some time this morning about it."

"And you said something she didn't like," the girl replied.

Ralph stared. "Has she complained of me?"

"She told me she thinks there is something very low in the tone of Europeans towards women."

"Does she call me a European?"

"One of the worst. She told me you had said to her something that an American never would have said. But she didn't repeat it."

Ralph treated himself to a burst of resounding laughter.

"She is an extraordinary combination. Did she think I was making love to her?"

"No; I believe even Americans do that. But she apparently thought you mistook the intention of something she had said, and put an unkind construction on it."

"I thought she was proposing marriage to me, and I accepted her. Was that unkind?"

Isabel smiled. "It was unkind to me. I don't want you to marry."

"My dear cousin, what is one to do among you all?" Ralph demanded. "Miss Stackpole tells me it's my bounden duty, and that it's hers to see I do mine!"

"She has a great sense of duty," said Isabel gravely. "She has, indeed, and it's the motive of everything she says. That's what I like her for. She thinks it's very frivolous for you to be single; that's what she meant to express to you. If you thought she was trying to—to attract you, you were very wrong."

"It is true it was an odd way; but I did think she was trying to attract me. Excuse my superficiality."

"You are very conceited. She had no interested views, and never supposed you would think she had."

"One must be very modest, then, to talk with such women," Ralph said, humbly. "But it's a very strange type.

She is too personal—considering that she expects other people not to be. She walks in without knocking at the door."

"Yes," Isabel admitted, "she doesn't sufficiently recognise the existence of knockers; and indeed I am not sure that she doesn't think them a rather pretentious ornament. She thinks one's door should stand ajar. But I persist in liking her."

"I persist in thinking her too familiar," Ralph rejoined, naturally somewhat uncomfortable under the sense of having been doubly deceived in Miss Stackpole.

"Well," said Isabel, smiling, "I am afraid it is because she is rather vulgar that I like her."

"She would be flattered by your reason!"

"If I should tell her, I would not express it in that way. I should say it is because there is something of the 'people' in her."

"What do you know about the people? and what does she, for that matter?"

"She knows a great deal, and I know enough to feel that she is a kind of emanation of the great democracy—of the continent, the country, the nation. I don't say that she sums it all up, that would be too much to ask of her. But she suggests it; she reminds me of it."

"You like her then for patriotic reasons. I am afraid it is on those very grounds that I object to her."

"Ah," said Isabel, with a kind of joyous sigh, "I like so many things! If a thing strikes me in a certain way, I like it. I don't want to boast, but I suppose I am rather versatile. I like people to be totally different from Henrietta—in the style of Lord Warburton's sisters, for instance. So long as I look at the Misses Molyneux, they seem to me to answer a kind of ideal. Then Henrietta presents herself, and I am immensely struck with her; not so much for herself as what stands behind her."

"Ah, you mean the back view of her," Ralph suggested.

"What she says is true," his cousin answered; "you will never be serious. I like the great country stretching away beyond the rivers and across the prairies, blooming and smiling and spreading, till it stops at the blue Pacific! A strong, sweet, fresh odour seems to rise from it, and Henrietta—excuse my simile—has something of that odour in her garments."

Isabel blushed a little as she concluded this speech, and the blush, together with the momentary ardour she had thrown into it, was so becoming to her that Ralph stood smiling at her for a moment after she had ceased speaking.

"I am not sure the Pacific is blue," he said; "but you are a woman of imagination. Henrietta, however, is fragrant— Henrietta is decidedly fragrant!"

XI

HE TOOK a resolve after this not to misinterpret her words, even when Miss Stackpole appeared to strike the personal note most strongly. He bethought himself that persons, in her view, were simple and homogeneous organisms, and that he, for his own part, was too perverted a representative of human nature to have a right to deal with her in strict reciprocity. He carried out his resolve with a great deal of tact, and the young lady found in her relations with him no obstacle to the exercise of that somewhat aggressive frankness which was the social expression of her nature. Her situation at Gardencourt, therefore, appreciated as we have seen her to be by Isabel, and full of appreciation herself of that fine freedom of composition which, to her sense, rendered Isabel's character a sister-spirit, and of the easy venerableness of Mr. Touchett, whose general tone, as she said, met with her full approval—her situation at Gardencourt would have been perfectly comfortable, had she not conceived an irresistible mistrust of the little lady to whom she had at first supposed herself obliged to pay a certain deference as mistress of the house. She presently discovered, however, that this obligation was of the lightest, and that Mrs. Touchett cared very little how Miss Stackpole behaved. Mrs. Touchett had spoken of her to Isabel as a "newspaper-woman," and expressed some surprise at her niece's having selected such a friend; but she had immediately added that she knew Isabel's friends were her own affair, and that she never undertook to like them all, or to restrict the girl to those she liked.

"If you could see none but the people I like, my dear, you would have a very small society," Mrs. Touchett frankly admitted; "and I don't think I like any man or woman well enough to recommend them to you. When it comes to recommending, it is a serious affair. I don't like Miss Stackpole—I don't like her tone. She talks too loud, and she looks at me too hard. I am sure she has lived all her life in a boarding-house, and I detest the style of manners that such a way of living produces. If you ask me if I prefer my own manners, which you doubtless think very bad, I will tell you that I prefer them immensely. Miss Stackpole knows that I detest boarding-house civilisation, and she detests me for detesting it, because she thinks it is the highest in the world. She would like Gardencourt a great deal better if it were a boarding-house. For me, I find it almost too much of one! We shall never get on together, therefore, and there is no use trying."

Mrs. Touchett was right in guessing that Henrietta disapproved of her, but she had not quite put her finger on the reason. A day or two after Miss Stackpole's arrival she had made some invidious reflections on American hotels, which excited a vein of counter-argument on the part of the correspondent of the *Interviewer*, who in the exercise of her profession had acquired a large familiarity with the technical hospitality of her country. Henrietta expressed the opinion that American hotels were the best in the world, and Mrs. Touchett recorded a conviction that they were the worst. Ralph, with his experimental geniality, suggested, by way of healing the breach, that the truth lay between the two extremes, and that the establishments in question ought to be described as fair middling. This contribution to the discussion, however, Miss Stackpole rejected with scorn. Middling, indeed! If they were not the best in the world, they were the worst, but there was nothing middling about an American hotel.

"We judge from different points of view, evidently," said Mrs. Touchett. "I like to be treated as an individual; you like to be treated as a 'party.' "

"I don't know what you mean," Henrietta replied. "I like to be treated as an American lady."

"Poor American ladies!" cried Mrs. Touchett, with a laugh. "They are the slaves of slaves."

"They are the companions of freemen," Henrietta rejoined.

"They are the companions of their servants—the Irish chambermaid and the negro waiter. They share their work."

"Do you call the domestics in an American household 'slaves'?" Miss Stackpole inquired. "If that's the way you desire to treat them, no wonder you don't like America."

"If you have not good servants, you are miserable," Mrs. Touchett said, serenely. "They are very bad in America, but I have five perfect ones in Florence."

"I don't see what you want with five," Henrietta could not

help observing. "I don't think I should like to see five persons surrounding me in that menial position."

"I like them in that position better than in some others," cried Mrs. Touchett, with a laugh.

"Should you like me better if I were your butler, dear?" her husband asked.

"I don't think I should; you would make a very poor butler."

"The companions of freemen—I like that, Miss Stackpole," said Ralph. "It's a beautiful description."

"When I said freemen, I didn't mean you, sir!"

And this was the only reward that Ralph got for his compliment. Miss Stackpole was baffled; she evidently thought there was something treasonable in Mrs. Touchett's appreciation of a class which she privately suspected of being a mysterious survival of feudalism. It was perhaps because her mind was oppressed with this image that she suffered some days to elapse before she said to Isabel in the morning, while they were alone together,

"My dear friend, I wonder whether you are growing faithless?"

"Faithless? Faithless to you, Henrietta?"

"No, that would be a great pain; but it is not that."

"Faithless to my country, then?"

"Ah, that I hope will never be. When I wrote to you from Liverpool, I said I had something particular to tell you. You have never asked me what it is. Is it because you have suspected?"

"Suspected what? As a rule, I don't think I suspect," said Isabel. "I remember now that phrase in your letter, but I confess I had forgotten it. What have you to tell me?"

Henrietta looked disappointed, and her steady gaze betrayed it.

"You don't ask that right—as if you thought it important. You are changed—you are thinking of other things."

"Tell me what you mean, and I will think of that."

"Will you really think of it? That is what I wish to be sure of."

"I have not much control of my thoughts, but I will do my best," said Isabel.

Henrietta gazed at her, in silence, for a period of time which tried Isabel's patience, so that our heroine said at last—

"Do you mean that you are going to be married?"

"Not till I have seen Europe!" said Miss Stackpole. "What are you laughing at?" she went on. "What I mean is, that Mr. Goodwood came out in the steamer with me."

"Ah!" Isabel exclaimed, quickly.

"You say that right. I had a good deal of talk with him; he has come after you."

"Did he tell you so?"

"No, he told me nothing; that's how I knew it," said Henrietta, cleverly. "He said very little about you, but I spoke of you a good deal."

Isabel was silent a moment. At the mention of Mr. Goodwood's name she had coloured a little, and now her blush was slowly fading.

"I am very sorry you did that," she observed at last.

"It was a pleasure to me, and I liked the way he listened. I could have talked a long time to such a listener; he was so quiet, so intense; he drank it all in."

"What did you say about me?" Isabel asked.

"I said you were on the whole the finest creature I know."

"I am very sorry for that. He thinks too well of me already; he ought not to be encouraged."

"He is dying for a little encouragement. I see his face now, and his earnest, absorbed look, while I talked. I never saw an ugly man look so handsome!"

"He is very simple-minded," said Isabel. "And he is not so ugly."

"There is nothing so simple as a great passion."

"It is not a great passion; I am very sure it is not that."

"You don't say that as if you were sure."

Isabel gave rather a cold smile.

"I shall say it better to Mr. Goodwood himself!"

"He will soon give you a chance," said Henrietta.

Isabel offered no answer to this assertion, which her companion made with an air of great confidence.

"He will find you changed," the latter pursued. "You have been affected by your new surroundings."

"Very likely. I am affected by everything."

"By everything but Mr. Goodwood!" Miss Stackpole exclaimed, with a laugh.

Isabel failed even to smile in reply; and in a moment she said—

"Did he ask you to speak to me?"

"Not in so many words. But his eyes asked it—and his handshake, when he bade me good-bye."

"Thank you for doing so." And Isabel turned away.

"Yes, you are changed; you have got new ideas over here," her friend continued.

"I hope so," said Isabel; "one should get as many new ideas as possible."

"Yes; but they shouldn't interfere with the old ones."

Isabel turned about again. "If you mean that I had any idea with regard to Mr. Goodwood——" And then she paused; Henrietta's bright eyes seemed to her to grow enormous.

"My dear child, you certainly encouraged him," said Miss Stackpole.

Isabel appeared for the moment to be on the point of denying this charge, but instead of this she presently answered—"It is very true; I did encourage him." And then she inquired whether her companion had learned from Mr. Goodwood what he intended to do. This inquiry was a concession to curiosity, for she did not enjoy discussing the gentleman with Henrietta Stackpole, and she thought that in her treatment of the subject this faithful friend lacked delicacy.

"I asked him, and he said he meant to do nothing," Miss Stackpole answered. "But I don't believe that; he's not a man to do nothing. He is a man of action. Whatever happens to him, he will always do something, and whatever he does will be right."

"I quite believe that," said Isabel. Henrietta might be wanting in delicacy; but it touched the girl, all the same, to hear this rich assertion made.

"Ah, you *do* care for him," Henrietta murmured.

"Whatever he does will be right," Isabel repeated. "When a man is of that supernatural mould, what does it matter to him whether one cares for him?"

"It may not matter to him, but it matters to one's self."

"Ah, what it matters to me, that is not what we are discussing," said Isabel, smiling a little.

This time her companion was grave. "Well, I don't care; you have changed," she replied. "You are not the girl you were a few short weeks ago, and Mr. Goodwood will see it. I expect him here any day."

"I hope he will hate me, then," said Isabel.

"I believe that you hope it about as much as I believe that he is capable of it."

To this observation our heroine made no rejoinder; she was absorbed in the feeling of alarm given her by Henrietta's intimation that Caspar Goodwood would present himself at Gardencourt. Alarm is perhaps a violent term to apply to the uneasiness with which she regarded this contingency; but her uneasiness was keen, and there were various good reasons for it. She pretended to herself that she thought the event impossible, and, later, she communicated her disbelief to her friend; but for the next forty-eight hours, nevertheless, she stood prepared to hear the young man's name announced. The feeling was oppressive; it made the air sultry, as if there were to be a change of weather; and the weather, socially speaking, had been so agreeable during Isabel's stay at Gardencourt that any change would be for the worse. Her suspense, however, was dissipated on the second day. She had walked into the park, in company with the sociable Bunchie, and after strolling about for some time, in a manner at once listless and restless, had seated herself on a garden-bench, within sight of the house, beneath a spreading beech, where, in a white dress ornamented with black ribbons, she formed, among the flickering shadows, a very graceful and harmonious image. She entertained herself for some moments with talking to the little terrier, as to whom the proposal of an ownership divided with her cousin had been applied as impartially as possible— as impartially as Bunchie's own somewhat fickle and inconstant sympathies would allow. But she was notified for the first time, on this occasion, of the finite character of Bunchie's intellect; hitherto she had been mainly struck with its extent. It seemed to her at last that she would do well to take a book; formerly, when she felt heavy-hearted, she had been able, with the help of some well-chosen volume, to transfer the seat of consciousness to the organ of pure reason. Of late, however, it was not to be denied, literature had seemed a fading light, and even after she had reminded herself that her uncle's library was provided with a complete set of those authors which no gentleman's collection should be without, she sat motionless and empty-handed, with her eyes fixed upon the cool green turf of the lawn. Her meditations were presently interrupted by the arrival of a servant, who handed her a letter. The letter bore the London postmark, and was addressed in a hand that she knew—that she seemed to know all the better, indeed, as the writer had been present to her mind when the letter was delivered. This document proved to be short, and I may give it entire.

"MY DEAR MISS ARCHER—I don't know whether you will have heard of my coming to England, but even if you have not, it will scarcely be a surprise to you. You will remember that when you gave me my dismissal at Albany three months ago, I did not accept it. I protested against it. You in fact appeared to accept my protest, and to admit that I had the right on my side. I had come to see you with the hope that you would let me bring you over to my conviction; my reasons for entertaining this hope had been of the best. But you disappointed it; I found you changed, and you were able to give me no reason for the change. You admitted that you were unreasonable, and it was the only concession you would make; but it was a very cheap one, because you are not unreasonable. No, you are not, and you never will be. Therefore it is that I believe you will let me see you again. You told me that I am not disagreeable to you, and I believe it; for I don't see why that should be. I shall always think of you; I shall never think of any one else. I came to England simply because you are here; I couldn't stay at home after you had gone; I hated the country because you were not in it. If I like this country at present, it is only because you are here. I have been to England before, but I have never enjoyed it much. May I not come and see you for half-an-hour? This at present is the dearest wish of, yours faithfully,

"CASPAR GOODWOOD."

Isabel read Mr. Goodwood's letter with such profound

attention that she had not perceived an approaching tread on the soft grass. Looking up, however, as she mechanically folded the paper, she saw Lord Warburton standing before her.

XII

SHE PUT the letter into her pocket, and offered her visitor a smile of welcome, exhibiting no trace of discomposure, and half surprised at her self-possession.

"They told me you were out here," said Lord Warburton; "and as there was no one in the drawing-room, and it is really you that I wish to see, I came out with no more ado."

Isabel had got up; she felt a wish, for the moment, that he should not sit down beside her. "I was just going in-doors," she said.

"Please don't do that; it is much pleasanter here; I have ridden over from Lockleigh; it's a lovely day." His smile was peculiarly friendly and pleasing, and his whole person seemed to emit that radiance of good-feeling and good fare which had formed the charm of the girl's first impression of him. It surrounded him like a zone of fine June weather.

"We will walk about a little, then," said Isabel, who could not divest herself of the sense of an intention on the part of her visitor, and who wished both to elude the intention and to satisfy her curiosity regarding it. It had flashed upon her vision once before, and it had given her on that occasion, as we know, a certain alarm. This alarm was composed of several elements, not all of which were disagreeable; she had indeed spent some days in analysing them, and had succeeded in separating the pleasant part of this idea of Lord Warburton's making love to her from the painful. It may appear to some readers that the young lady was both precipitate and unduly fastidious; but the latter of these facts, if the charge be true, may serve to exonerate her from the discredit of the former. She was not eager to convince herself that a territorial magnate, as she had heard Lord Warburton called, was smitten with her charms; because a declaration from such a source would point to more questions than it would answer. She had received a strong impression of Lord Warburton's being a personage, and she had occupied herself in examining the idea. At the risk of making the reader smile, it must be said that there had been moments when the intimation that she was admired by a "personage" struck her as an aggression which she would rather have been spared. She had never known a personage before; there were no personages in her native land. When she had thought of such matters as this, she had done so on the basis of character—of what one liked in a gentleman's mind and in his talk. She herself was a character—she could not help being aware of that; and hitherto her visions of a completed life had concerned themselves largely with moral images—things as to which the question would be whether they pleased her soul. Lord Warburton loomed up before her, largely and brightly, as a collection of attributes and powers which were not to be measured by this simple rule, but which demanded a different sort of appreciation—an appreciation which the girl, with her habit of judging quickly and freely, felt that she lacked the patience to bestow. Of course, there would be a short cut to it, and as Lord Warburton was evidently a very fine fellow, it would probably also be a safe cut. Isabel was able to say all this to herself, but she was unable to feel the force of it. What she felt was that a territorial, a political, a social magnate had conceived the design of drawing her into the system in which he lived and moved. A certain instinct, not imperious, but persuasive, told her to resist—it murmured to her that virtually she had a system and an orbit of her own. It told her other things besides—things which both contradicted and confirmed each other; that a girl might do much worse than trust herself to such a man as Lord Warburton, and that it would be very interesting to see something of his system from his own point of view; that, on the other hand, however, there was evidently a great deal of it which she should regard only as an incumbrance, and that even in the whole there was something heavy and rigid which would make it unacceptable. Furthermore, there was a young man lately come from America who had no system at all; but who had a character of which it was useless for her to try to persuade herself that the impression on her mind had been light. The letter that she carried in her pocket sufficiently reminded her of the contrary. Smile not, however, I venture to repeat, at this simple young lady from Albany, who debated whether she should accept an English peer before he had offered himself, and who was disposed to believe that on the whole she could do better. She was a person of great good faith, and if there was a great deal of folly in her wisdom, those who judge her severely may have the satisfaction of finding that, later, she became consistently wise only at the cost of an amount of folly which will constitute almost a direct appeal to charity.

Lord Warburton seemed quite ready to walk, to sit, or to do anything that Isabel should propose, and he gave her this assurance with his usual air of being particularly pleased to exercise a social virtue. But he was, nevertheless, not in command of his emotions, and as he strolled beside her for a moment, in silence, looking at her without letting her know it, there was something embarrassed in his glance and his misdirected laughter. Yes, assuredly—as we have touched on the point, we may return to it for a moment again—the English are the most romantic people in the world, and Lord Warburton was about to give an example of it. He was about to take a step which would astonish all his friends and displease a great many of them, and which, superficially, had nothing to recommend it. The young lady who trod the turf beside him had come from a queer country across the sea, which he knew a good deal about; her antecedents, her associations, were very vague to his mind, except in so far as they were generic, and in this sense they revealed themselves with a certain vividness. Miss Archer had neither a fortune nor the sort of beauty that justifies a man to the multitude, and he calculated that he had spent about twenty-six hours in her company. He had summed up all this—the perversity of the impulse, which had declined to avail itself of the most liberal opportunities to subside, and the judgment of mankind, as exemplified particularly in the more quickly-judging half of it; he had looked these things well in the face, and then he had dismissed them from his thoughts. He cared no more for them than for the rosebud in his button-hole. It is the good fortune of a man who for the greater part of a lifetime has abstained without effort from making himself disagreeable to his friends, that when the need comes for such a course it is not discredited by irritating associations.

"I hope you had a pleasant ride," said Isabel, who observed her companion's hesitancy.

"It would have been pleasant if for nothing else than that it brought me here," Lord Warburton answered.

"Are you so fond of Gardencourt?" the girl asked; more and more sure that he meant to make some demand of her; wishing not to challenge him if he hesitated, and yet to keep all the quietness of her reason if he proceeded. It suddenly came upon her that her situation was one which a few weeks ago she would have deemed deeply romantic; the park of an old English country-house, with the foreground embellished by a local nobleman in the act of making love to a young lady who, on careful inspection, should be found to present remarkable analogies with herself. But if she were now the heroine of the situation, she succeeded scarcely the less in looking at it from the outside.

"I care nothing for Gardencourt," said Lord Warburton; "I care only for you."

"You have known me too short a time to have a right to say that, and I cannot believe you are serious."

These words of Isabel's were not perfectly sincere, for she had no doubt whatever that he was serious. They were simply a tribute to the fact, of which she was perfectly aware, that those he himself had just uttered would have excited surprise on the part of the public at large. And, moreover, if anything beside the sense she had already acquired that Lord Warburton was not a frivolous person had been needed to convince her, the tone in which he replied to her would quite have served the purpose.

"One's right in such a matter is not measured by the time, Miss Archer; it is measured by the feeling itself. If I were to wait three months, it would make no difference; I shall not be more sure of what I mean than I am to-day. Of course I have seen you very little; but my impression dates from the very first hour we met. I lost no time; I fell in love with you then. It was at first sight, as the novels say; I know now that is not a fancy-phrase, and I shall think better of novels for evermore. Those two days I spent here settled it; I don't know whether you suspected I was doing so, but I paid— mentally speaking, I mean—the greatest possible attention to you. Nothing you said, nothing you did, was lost upon me. When you came to Lockleigh the other day—or rather,

when you went away—I was perfectly sure. Nevertheless, I
made up my mind to think it over, and to question myself
narrowly. I have done so; all these days I have thought of
nothing else. I don't make mistakes about such things; I am
a very judicious fellow. I don't go off easily, but when I am
touched, it's for life. It's for life, Miss Archer, it's for life,"
Lord Warburton repeated in the kindest, tenderest, pleasantest voice Isabel had ever heard, and looking at her with eyes
that shone with the light of a passion that had sifted itself
clear of the baser parts of emotion—the heat, the violence,
the unreason—and which burned as steadily as a lamp in a
windless place.

By tacit consent, as he talked, they had walked more and
more slowly, and at last they stopped, and he took her hand.

"Ah, Lord Warburton, how little you know me!" Isabel
said, very gently; gently, too, she drew her hand away.

"Don't taunt me with that; that I don't know you better
makes me unhappy enough already; it's all my loss. But that
is what I want, and it seems to me I am taking the best way.
If you will be my wife, then I shall know you, and when I
tell you all the good I think of you, you will not be able to
say it is from ignorance."

"If you know me little, I know you even less," said Isabel.

"You mean that, unlike yourself, I may not improve on acquaintance? Ah, of course, that is very possible. But think, to
speak to you as I do, how determined I must be to try and
give satisfaction! You do like me rather, don't you?"

"I like you very much, Lord Warburton," the girl answered;
and at this moment she liked him immensely.

"I thank you for saying that; it shows you don't regard me
as a stranger. I really believe I have filled all the other relations
of life very creditably, and I don't see why I should not fill
this one—in which I offer myself to you—seeing that I care
so much more about it. Ask the people who know me well; I
have friends who will speak for me."

"I don't need the recommendation of your friends," said
Isabel.

"Ah now, that is delightful of you. You believe in me yourself."

"Completely," Isabel declared; and it was the truth.

The light in her companion's eyes turned into a smile, and he gave a long exhalation of joy.

"If you are mistaken, Miss Archer, let me lose all I possess!"

She wondered whether he meant this for a reminder that he was rich, and, on the instant, felt sure that he did not. He was sinking that, as he would have said himself; and indeed he might safely leave it to the memory of any interlocutor, especially of one to whom he was offering his hand. Isabel had prayed that she might not be agitated, and her mind was tranquil enough, even while she listened and asked herself what it was best she should say, to indulge in this incidental criticism. What she should say, had she asked herself? Her foremost wish was to say something as nearly as possible as kind as what he had said to her. His words had carried perfect conviction with them; she felt that he loved her.

"I thank you more than I can say for your offer," she rejoined at last; "it does me great honour."

"Ah, don't say that!" Lord Warburton broke out. "I was afraid you would say something like that. I don't see what you have to do with that sort of thing. I don't see why you should thank me—it is I who ought to thank you, for listening to me; a man whom you know so little, coming down on you with such a thumper! Of course it's a great question; I must tell you that I would rather ask it than have it to answer myself. But the way you have listened—or at least your having listened at all—gives me some hope."

"Don't hope too much," Isabel said.

"Oh, Miss Archer!" her companion murmured, smiling again in his seriousness, as if such a warning might perhaps be taken but as the play of high spirits—the coquetry of elation.

"Should you be greatly surprised if I were to beg you not to hope at all?" Isabel asked.

"Surprised? I don't know what you mean by surprise. It wouldn't be that; it would be a feeling very much worse."

Isabel walked on again; she was silent for some minutes.

"I am very sure that, highly as I already think of you, my opinion of you, if I should know you well, would only rise. But I am by no means sure that you would not be disappointed. And I say that not in the least out of conventional modesty; it is perfectly sincere."

"I am willing to risk it, Miss Archer," her companion answered.

"It's a great question, as you say; it's a very difficult question."

"I don't expect you, of course, to answer it outright. Think it over as long as may be necessary. If I can gain by waiting, I will gladly wait a long time. Only remember that in the end my dearest happiness depends upon your answer."

"I should be very sorry to keep you in suspense," said Isabel.

"Oh, don't mind. I would much rather have a good answer six months hence than a bad one to-day."

"But it is very probable that even six months hence I should not be able to give you one that you would think good."

"Why not, since you really like me?"

"Ah, you must never doubt of that," said Isabel.

"Well, then, I don't see what more you ask!"

"It is not what I ask; it is what I can give. I don't think I should suit you; I really don't think I should."

"You needn't bother about that; that's my affair. You needn't be a better royalist than the king."

"It is not only that," said Isabel; "but I am not sure I wish to marry any one."

"Very likely you don't. I have no doubt a great many women begin that way," said his lordship, who, be it averred, did not in the least believe in the axiom he thus beguiled his anxiety by uttering. "But they are frequently persuaded."

"Ah, that is because they want to be!"

And Isabel lightly laughed.

Her suitor's countenance fell, and he looked at her for a while in silence.

"I'm afraid it's my being an Englishman that makes you hesitate," he said, presently. "I know your uncle thinks you ought to marry in your own country."

Isabel listened to this assertion with some interest; it had never occurred to her that Mr. Touchett was likely to discuss her matrimonial prospects with Lord Warburton.

"Has he told you that?" she asked.

"I remember his making the remark; he spoke perhaps of Americans generally."

"He appears himself to have found it very pleasant to live in England," said Isabel, in a manner that might have seemed a little perverse, but which expressed both her constant perception of her uncle's pictorial circumstances and her general disposition to elude any obligation to take a restricted view.

It gave her companion hope, and he immediately exclaimed, warmly—

"Ah, my dear Miss Archer, old England is a very good sort of country, you know! And it will be still better when we have furbished it up a little."

"Oh, don't furbish it, Lord Warburton; leave it alone; I like it this way."

"Well, then, if you like it, I am more and more unable to see your objection to what I propose."

"I am afraid I can't make you understand."

"You ought at least to try; I have got a fair intelligence. Are you afraid—afraid of the climate? We can easily live elsewhere, you know. You can pick out your climate, the whole world over."

These words were uttered with a tender eagerness which went to Isabel's heart, and she would have given her little finger at that moment, to feel, strongly and simply, the impulse to answer, "Lord Warburton, it is impossible for a woman to do better in this world than to commit herself to your loyalty." But though she could conceive the impulse, she could not let it operate; her imagination was charmed, but it was not led captive. What she finally bethought herself of saying was something very different—something which altogether deferred the need of answering. "Don't think me unkind if I ask you to say no more about this to-day."

"Certainly, certainly!" cried Lord Warburton. "I wouldn't bore you for the world."

"You have given me a great deal to think about, and I promise you I will do it justice."

"That's all I ask of you, of course—and that you will remember that my happiness is in your hands."

Isabel listened with extreme respect to this admonition, but she said after a minute—"I must tell you that what I shall think about is some way of letting you know that what you ask is impossible, without making you miserable."

"There is no way to do that, Miss Archer. I won't say that, if you refuse me, you will kill me; I shall not die of it. But I shall do worse; I shall live to no purpose."

"You will live to marry a better woman than I."

"Don't say that, please," said Lord Warburton, very gravely. "That is fair to neither of us."

"To marry a worse one, then."

"If there are better women than you, then I prefer the bad ones; that's all I can say," he went on, with the same gravity. "There is no accounting for tastes."

His gravity made her feel equally grave, and she showed it by again requesting him to drop the subject for the present. "I will speak to you myself, very soon," she said. "Perhaps I shall write to you."

"At your convenience, yes," he answered. "Whatever time you take, it must seem to me long, and I suppose I must make the best of that."

"I shall not keep you in suspense; I only want to collect my mind a little."

He gave a melancholy sigh and stood looking at her a moment, with his hands behind him, giving short nervous shakes to his hunting-whip. "Do you know I am very much afraid of it—of that mind of yours?"

Our heroine's biographer can scarcely tell why, but the question made her start and brought a conscious blush to her cheek. She returned his look a moment, and then, with a note in her voice that might almost have appealed to his compassion—"So am I, my lord!" she exclaimed.

His compassion was not stirred, however; all that he possessed of the faculty of pity was needed at home. "Ah! be merciful, be merciful," he murmured.

"I think you had better go," said Isabel. "I will write to you."

"Very good; but whatever you write, I will come and see you." And then he stood reflecting, with his eyes fixed on the observant countenance of Bunchie, who had the air of having understood all that had been said, and of pretending to carry

off the indiscretion by a simulated fit of curiosity as to the
roots of an ancient beech. "There is one thing more," said
Lord Warburton. "You know, if you don't like Lockleigh—if
you think it's damp, or anything of that sort—you need
never go within fifty miles of it. It is not damp, by the way;
I have had the house thoroughly examined; it is perfectly san-
itary. But if you shouldn't fancy it, you needn't dream of living in it. There is no difficulty whatever about that; there are
plenty of houses. I thought I would just mention it; some
people don't like a moat, you know. Good-bye."

"I delight in a moat," said Isabel. "Good-bye."

He held out his hand, and she gave him hers a moment—
a moment long enough for him to bend his head and kiss it.
Then, shaking his hunting-whip with little quick strokes, he
walked rapidly away. He was evidently very nervous.

Isabel herself was nervous, but she was not affected as she
would have imagined. What she felt was not a great responsibility, a great difficulty of choice; for it appeared to her that
there was no choice in the question. She could not marry
Lord Warburton; the idea failed to correspond to any vision
of happiness that she had hitherto entertained, or was now
capable of entertaining. She must write this to him, she must
convince him, and this duty was comparatively simple. But
what disturbed her, in the sense that it struck her with wonderment, was this very fact that it cost her so little to refuse a
great opportunity. With whatever qualifications one would,
Lord Warburton had offered her a great opportunity; the situation might have discomforts, might contain elements that
would displease her, but she did her sex no injustice in believing that nineteen women out of twenty would accommodate
themselves to it with extreme zeal. Why then upon her also
should it not impose itself? Who was she, what was she, that
she should hold herself superior? What view of life, what design upon fate, what conception of happiness, had she that
pretended to be larger than this large occasion? If she would
not do this, then she must do great things, she must do something greater. Poor Isabel found occasion to remind herself
from time to time that she must not be too proud, and nothing could be more sincere than her prayer to be delivered
from such a danger; for the isolation and loneliness of pride

had for her mind the horror of a desert place. If it were pride
that interfered with her accepting Lord Warburton, it was singularly misplaced; and she was so conscious of liking him that
she ventured to assure herself it was not. She liked him too
much to marry him, that was the point; something told her
that she should not be satisfied, and to inflict upon a man
who offered so much a wife with a tendency to criticise
would be a peculiarly discreditable act. She had promised him
that she would consider his proposal, and when, after he had
left her, she wandered back to the bench where he had found
her, and lost herself in meditation, it might have seemed that
she was keeping her word. But this was not the case; she was
wondering whether she were not a cold, hard girl; and when
at last she got up and rather quickly went back to the house,
it was because, as she had said to Lord Warburton, she was
really frightened at herself.

XIII

IT WAS this feeling, and not the wish to ask advice—she had no desire whatever for that—that led her to speak to her uncle of what Lord Warburton had said to her. She wished to speak to some one; she should feel more natural, more human, and her uncle, for this purpose, presented himself in a more attractive light than either her aunt or her friend Henrietta. Her cousin, of course, was a possible confidant; but it would have been disagreeable to her to confide this particular matter to Ralph. So, the next day, after breakfast, she sought her occasion. Her uncle never left his apartment till the afternoon; but he received his cronies, as he said, in his dressing-room. Isabel had quite taken her place in the class so designated, which, for the rest, included the old man's son, his physician, his personal servant, and even Miss Stackpole. Mrs. Touchett did not figure in the list, and this was an obstacle the less to Isabel's finding her uncle alone. He sat in a complicated mechanical chair, at the open window of his room, looking westward over the park and the river, with his newspapers and letters piled up beside him, his toilet freshly and minutely made, and his smooth, speculative face composed to benevolent expectation.

Isabel approached her point very directly. "I think I ought to let you know that Lord Warburton has asked me to marry him. I suppose I ought to tell my aunt; but it seems best to tell you first."

The old man expressed no surprise, but thanked her for the confidence she showed him. "Do you mind telling me whether you accepted him?" he added.

"I have not answered him definitely yet; I have taken a little time to think of it, because that seems more respectful. But I shall not accept him."

Mr. Touchett made no comment upon this; he had the air of thinking that whatever interest he might take in the matter from the point of view of sociability, he had no active voice in it. "Well, I told you you would be a success over here. Americans are highly appreciated."

"Very highly indeed," said Isabel. "But at the cost of

seeming ungrateful, I don't think I can marry Lord Warburton."

"Well," her uncle went on, "of course an old man can't
judge for a young lady. I am glad you didn't ask me before
you made up your mind. I suppose I ought to tell you," he
added slowly, but as if it were not of much consequence,
"that I have known all about it these three days."

"About Lord Warburton's state of mind?"

"About his intentions, as they say here. He wrote me a very
pleasant letter, telling me all about them. Should you like to
see it?" the old man asked, obligingly.

"Thank you; I don't think I care about that. But I am glad
he wrote to you; it was right that he should, and he would
be certain to do what was right."

"Ah, well, I guess you do like him!" Mr. Touchett declared.
"You needn't pretend you don't."

"I like him extremely; I am very free to admit that. But I
don't wish to marry any one just now."

"You think some one may come along whom you may
like better. Well, that's very likely," said Mr. Touchett, who
appeared to wish to show his kindness to the girl by easing
off her decision, as it were, and finding cheerful reasons
for it.

"I don't care if I don't meet any one else; I like Lord Warburton quite well enough," said Isabel, with that appearance
of a sudden change of point of view with which she sometimes startled and even displeased her interlocutors.

Her uncle, however, seemed proof against either of these
sensations.

"He's a very fine man," he resumed, in a tone which might
have passed for that of encouragement. "His letter was one of
the pleasantest letters I have received for some weeks. I suppose one of the reasons I liked it was that it was all about
you; that is, all except the part which was about himself. I
suppose he told you all that."

"He would have told me everything I wished to ask him,"
Isabel said.

"But you didn't feel curious?"

"My curiosity would have been idle—once I had determined to decline his offer."

"You didn't find it sufficiently attractive?" Mr. Touchett inquired.

The girl was silent a moment.

"I suppose it was that," she presently admitted. "But I don't know why."

"Fortunately, ladies are not obliged to give reasons," said her uncle. "There's a great deal that's attractive about such an idea; but I don't see why the English should want to entice us away from our native land. I know that we try to attract them over there; but that's because our population is insufficient. Here, you know, they are rather crowded. However, I suppose there is room for charming young ladies everywhere."

"There seems to have been room here for you," said Isabel, whose eyes had been wandering over the large pleasure-spaces of the park.

Mr. Touchett gave a shrewd, conscious smile.

"There is room everywhere, my dear, if you will pay for it. I sometimes think I have paid too much for this. Perhaps you also might have to pay too much."

"Perhaps I might," the girl replied.

This suggestion gave her something more definite to rest upon than she had found in her own thoughts, and the fact of her uncle's genial shrewdness being associated with her dilemma seemed to prove to her that she was concerned with the natural and reasonable emotions of life, and not altogether a victim to intellectual eagerness and vague ambitions—ambitions reaching beyond Lord Warburton's handsome offer to something indefinable and possibly not commendable. In so far as the indefinable had an influence upon Isabel's behaviour at this juncture, it was not the conception, however unformulated, of a union with Caspar Goodwood; for however little she might have felt warranted in lending a receptive ear to her English suitor, she was at least as far removed from the disposition to let the young man from Boston take complete possession of her. The sentiment in which she ultimately took refuge, after reading his letter, was a critical view of his having come abroad; for it was part of the influence he had upon her that he seemed to take from her the sense of freedom. There was something too forcible, something oppressive and restrictive, in the manner in which he presented himself. She had been haunted at moments by the image of his disapproval, and she had wondered—a consideration she had never paid in one equal degree to any one else—whether he would like what she did. The difficulty was that more than any man she had ever known, more than poor Lord Warburton (she had begun now to give his lordship the benefit of this epithet), Caspar Goodwood gave her an impression of energy. She might like it or not, but at any rate there was something very strong about him; even in one's usual contact with him one had to reckon with it. The idea of a diminished liberty was particularly disagreeable to Isabel at present, because it seemed to her that she had just given a sort of personal accent to her independence by making up her mind to refuse Lord Warburton. Sometimes Caspar Goodwood had seemed to range himself on the side of her destiny, to be the stubbornest fact she knew; she said to herself at such moments that she might evade him for a time, but that she must make terms with him at last—terms which would be certain to be favourable to himself. Her impulse had been to avail herself of the things that helped her to resist such an obligation; and this impulse had been much concerned in her eager acceptance of her aunt's invitation, which had come to her at a time when she expected from day to day to see Mr. Goodwood, and when she was glad to have an answer ready for something she was sure he would say to her. When she had told him at Albany, on the evening of Mrs. Touchett's visit, that she could not now discuss difficult questions, because she was preoccupied with the idea of going to Europe with her aunt, he declared that this was no answer at all; and it was to obtain a better one that he followed her across the seas. To say to herself that he was a kind of fate was well enough for a fanciful young woman, who was able to take much for granted in him; but the reader has a right to demand a description less metaphysical.

He was the son of a proprietor of certain well-known cotton-mills in Massachusetts—a gentleman who had accumulated a considerable fortune in the exercise of this industry. Caspar now managed the establishment, with a judgment and a brilliancy which, in spite of keen competition and languid years, had kept its prosperity from dwindling. He had received the better part of his education at Harvard University, where, however, he had gained more renown as a gymnast and an oarsman than as a votary of culture. Later, he had become reconciled to culture, and though he was still fond of sport, he was capable of showing an excellent understanding of other matters. He had a remarkable aptitude for mechanics, and had invented an improvement in the cotton-spinning process, which was now largely used and was known by his name. You might have seen his name in the papers in connection with this fruitful contrivance; assurance of which he had given to Isabel by showing her in the columns of the New York *Interviewer* an exhaustive article on the Goodwood patent—an article not prepared by Miss Stackpole, friendly as she had proved herself to his more sentimental interests. He had great talent for business, for administration, and for making people execute his purpose and carry out his views—for managing men, as the phrase was; and to give its complete value to this faculty, he had an insatiable, an almost fierce, ambition. It always struck people who knew him that he might do greater things than carry on a cotton-factory; there was nothing cottony about Caspar Goodwood, and his friends took for granted that he would not always content himself with that. He had once said to Isabel that, if the United States were only not such a confoundedly peaceful nation, he would find his proper place in the army. He keenly regretted that the Civil War should have terminated just as he had grown old enough to wear shoulder-straps, and was sure that if something of the same kind would only occur again, he would make a display of striking military talent. It pleased Isabel to believe that he had the qualities of a famous captain, and she answered that, if it would help him on, she shouldn't object to a war—a speech which ranked among the three or four most encouraging ones he had elicited from her, and of which the value was not diminished by her subsequent regret at having said anything so heartless, inasmuch as she never communicated this regret to him. She liked at any rate this idea of his being potentially a commander of men—liked it much better than some other points in his character and appearance. She cared nothing about his cotton-mill, and the Goodwood patent left her imagination absolutely cold. She wished him not an inch less a man than he was; but she sometimes thought he would be rather nicer if he looked, for instance, a little differently. His jaw was too square and grim, and his figure too straight and stiff; these things suggested a want of easy adaptability to some of the occasions of life. Then she regarded with disfavour a habit he had of dressing always in the same manner; it was not apparently that he wore the same clothes continually, for, on the contrary, his garments had a way of looking rather too new. But they all seemed to be made of the same piece; the pattern, the cut, was in every case identical. She had reminded herself more than once that this was a frivolous objection to a man of Mr. Goodwood's importance; and then she had amended the rebuke by saying that it would be a frivolous objection if she were in love with him. She was not in love with him, and therefore she might criticise his small defects as well as his great ones—which latter consisted in the collective reproach of his being too serious, or, rather, not of his being too serious, for one could never be that, but of his seeming so. He showed his seriousness too simply, too artlessly; when one was alone with him he talked too much about the same subject, and when other people were present he talked too little about anything. And yet he was the strongest man she had ever known, and she believed that at bottom he was the cleverest. It was very strange; she was far from understanding the contradictions among her own impressions. Caspar Goodwood had never corresponded to her idea of a delightful person, and she supposed that this was why he was so unsatisfactory. When, however, Lord Warburton, who not only did correspond with it, but gave an extension to the term, appealed to her approval, she found herself still unsatisfied. It was certainly strange.

Such incongruities were not a help to answering Mr. Goodwood's letter, and Isabel determined to leave it a while unanswered. If he had determined to persecute her, he must take the consequences; foremost among which was his being left to perceive that she did not approve of his coming to

Gardencourt. She was already liable to the incursions of one suitor at this place, and though it might be pleasant to be appreciated in opposite quarters, Isabel had a personal shrinking from entertaining two lovers at once, even in a case where the entertainment should consist of dismissing them. She sent no answer to Mr. Goodwood; but at the end of three days she wrote to Lord Warburton, and the letter belongs to our history. It ran as follows.

"DEAR LORD WARBURTON—A great deal of careful reflection has not led me to change my mind about the suggestion you were so kind as to make me the other day. I do not find myself able to regard you in the light of a husband, or to regard your home—your various homes—in the light of my own. These things cannot be reasoned about, and I very earnestly entreat you not to return to the subject we discussed so exhaustively. We see our lives from our own point of view; that is the privilege of the weakest and humblest of us; and I shall never be able to see mine in the manner you proposed. Kindly let this suffice you, and do me the justice to believe that I have given your proposal the deeply respectful consideration it deserves. It is with this feeling of respect that I remain very truly yours,

                                        "ISABEL ARCHER."

While the author of this missive was making up her mind to despatch it, Henrietta Stackpole formed a resolution which was accompanied by no hesitation. She invited Ralph Touchett to take a walk with her in the garden, and when he had assented with that alacrity which seemed constantly to testify to his high expectations, she informed him that she had a favour to ask of him. It may be confided to the reader that at this information the young man flinched; for we know that Miss Stackpole had struck him as indiscreet. The movement was unreasonable, however; for he had measured the limits of her discretion as little as he had explored its extent; and he made a very civil profession of the desire to serve her. He was afraid of her, and he presently told her so. "When you look at me in a certain way," he said, "my knees knock together, my faculties desert me; I am filled with trepidation, and I ask only for strength to execute your commands. You have a look which I have never encountered in any woman."

"Well," Henrietta replied, good-humouredly, "if I had not known before that you were trying to turn me into ridicule, I should know it now. Of course I am easy game—I was brought up with such different customs and ideas. I am not used to your arbitrary standards, and I have never been spoken to in America as you have spoken to me. If a gentleman conversing with me over there, were to speak to me like that, I shouldn't know what to make of it. We take everything more naturally over there, and, after all, we are a great deal more simple. I admit that; I am very simple myself. Of course, if you choose to laugh at me for that, you are very welcome; but I think on the whole I would rather be myself than you. I am quite content to be myself; I don't want to change. There are plenty of people that appreciate me just as I am; it is true they are only Americans!" Henrietta had lately taken up the tone of helpless innocence and large concession. "I want you to assist me a little," she went on. "I don't care in the least whether I amuse you while you do so; or, rather, I am perfectly willing that your amusement should be your reward. I want you to help me about Isabel."

"Has she injured you?" Ralph asked.

"If she had I shouldn't mind, and I should never tell you. What I am afraid of is that she will injure herself."

"I think that is very possible," said Ralph.

His companion stopped in the garden-walk, fixing on him a gaze which may perhaps have contained the quality that caused his knees to knock together. "That, too, would amuse you, I suppose. The way you do say things! I never heard any one so indifferent."

"To Isabel? Never in the world."

"Well, you are not in love with her, I hope."

"How can that be, when I am in love with another?"

"You are in love with yourself, that's the other!" Miss Stackpole declared. "Much good may it do you! But if you wish to be serious once in your life, here's a chance; and if you really care for your cousin, here is an opportunity to prove it. I don't expect you to understand her; that's too much to ask. But you needn't do that to grant my favour. I will supply the necessary intelligence."

"I shall enjoy that immensely!" Ralph exclaimed. "I will be Caliban, and you shall be Ariel."

"You are not at all like Caliban, because you are sophisticated, and Caliban was not. But I am not talking about imaginary characters; I am talking about Isabel. Isabel is intensely real. What I wish to tell you is that I find her fearfully changed."

"Since you came, do you mean?"

"Since I came, and before I came. She is not the same as she was."

"As she was in America?"

"Yes, in America. I suppose you know that she comes from there. She can't help it, but she does."

"Do you want to change her back again?"

"Of course I do; and I want you to help me."

"Ah," said Ralph, "I am only Caliban; I am not Prospero."

"You were Prospero enough to make her what she has become. You have acted on Isabel Archer since she came here, Mr. Touchett."

"I, my dear Miss Stackpole? Never in the world. Isabel Archer has acted on me—yes; she acts on every one. But I have been absolutely passive."

"You are too passive, then. You had better stir yourself and be careful. Isabel is changing every day; she is drifting away—right out to sea. I have watched her and I can see it. She is not the bright American girl she was. She is taking different views, and turning away from her old ideals. I want to save those ideals, Mr. Touchett, and that is where you come in."

"Not surely as an ideal?"

"Well, I hope not," Henrietta replied, promptly. "I have got a fear in my heart that she is going to marry one of these Europeans, and I want to prevent it."

"Ah, I see," cried Ralph; "and to prevent it, you want me to step in and marry her?"

"Not quite; that remedy would be as bad as the disease, for you are the typical European from whom I wish to rescue her. No; I wish you to take an interest in another person—a young man to whom she once gave great encouragement, and whom she now doesn't seem to think good enough. He's a noble fellow, and a very dear friend of mine, and I wish very much you would invite him to pay a visit here."

Ralph was much puzzled by this appeal, and it is perhaps not to the credit of his purity of mind that he failed to look at it at first in the simplest light. It wore, to his eyes, a tortuous air, and his fault was that he was not quite sure that anything in the world could really be as candid as this request of Miss Stackpole's appeared. That a young woman should demand that a gentleman whom she described as her very dear friend should be furnished with an opportunity to make himself agreeable to another young woman, whose attention had wandered and whose charms were greater—this was an anomaly which for the moment challenged all his ingenuity of interpretation. To read between the lines was easier than to follow the text, and to suppose that Miss Stackpole wished the gentleman invited to Gardencourt on her own account was the sign not so much of a vulgar, as of an embarrassed, mind. Even from this venial act of vulgarity, however, Ralph was saved, and saved by a force that I can scarcely call anything less than inspiration. With no more outward light on the subject than he already possessed, he suddenly acquired the conviction that it would be a sovereign injustice to the correspondent of the *Interviewer* to assign a dishonourable motive to any act of hers. This conviction passed into his mind with extreme rapidity; it was perhaps kindled by the pure radiance of the young lady's imperturbable gaze. He returned this gaze a moment, consciously, resisting an inclination to frown, as one frowns in the presence of larger luminaries. "Who is the gentleman you speak of?"

"Mr. Caspar Goodwood, from Boston. He has been extremely attentive to Isabel—just as devoted to her as he can live. He has followed her out here, and he is at present in London. I don't know his address, but I guess I can obtain it."

"I have never heard of him," said Ralph.

"Well, I suppose you haven't heard of every one. I don't believe he has ever heard of you; but that is no reason why Isabel shouldn't marry him."

Ralph gave a small laugh. "What a rage you have for

marrying people! Do you remember how you wanted to marry me the other day?"

"I have got over that. You don't know how to take such ideas. Mr. Goodwood does, however; and that's what I like about him. He's a splendid man and a perfect gentleman; and Isabel knows it."

"Is she very fond of him?"

"If she isn't she ought to be. He is simply wrapped up in her."

"And you wish me to ask him here," said Ralph, reflectively.

"It would be an act of true hospitality."

"Caspar Goodwood," Ralph continued—"it's rather a striking name."

"I don't care anything about his name. It might be Ezekiel Jenkins, and I should say the same. He is the only man I have ever seen whom I think worthy of Isabel."

"You are a very devoted friend," said Ralph.

"Of course I am. If you say that to laugh at me, I don't care."

"I don't say it to laugh at you; I am very much struck with it."

"You are laughing worse than ever; but I advise you not to laugh at Mr. Goodwood."

"I assure you I am very serious; you ought to understand that," said Ralph.

In a moment his companion understood it. "I believe you are; now you are too serious."

"You are difficult to please."

"Oh, you are very serious indeed. You won't invite Mr. Goodwood."

"I don't know," said Ralph. "I am capable of strange things. Tell me a little about Mr. Goodwood. What is he like?"

"He is just the opposite of you. He is at the head of a cotton factory; a very fine one."

"Has he pleasant manners?" asked Ralph.

"Splendid manners—in the American style."

"Would he be an agreeable member of our little circle?"

"I don't think he would care much about our little circle. He would concentrate on Isabel."

"And how would my cousin like that?"

"Very possibly not at all. But it will be good for her. It will call back her thoughts."

"Call them back—from where?"

"From foreign parts and other unnatural places. Three months ago she gave Mr. Goodwood every reason to suppose that he was acceptable to her, and it is not worthy of Isabel to turn her back upon a real friend simply because she has changed the scene. I have changed the scene too, and the effect of it has been to make me care more for my old associations than ever. It's my belief that the sooner Isabel changes it back again the better. I know her well enough to know that she would never be truly happy over here, and I wish her to form some strong American tie that will act as a preservative."

"Are you not a little too much in a hurry?" Ralph inquired. "Don't you think you ought to give her more of a chance in poor old England?"

"A chance to ruin her bright young life? One is never too much in a hurry to save a precious human creature from drowning."

"As I understand it, then," said Ralph, "you wish me to push Mr. Goodwood overboard after her. Do you know," he added, "that I have never heard her mention his name?"

Henrietta Stackpole gave a brilliant smile. "I am delighted to hear that; it proves how much she thinks of him."

Ralph appeared to admit that there was a good deal in this, and he surrendered himself to meditation, while his companion watched him askance. "If I should invite Mr. Goodwood," he said, "it would be to quarrel with him."

"Don't do that; he would prove the better man."

"You certainly are doing your best to make me hate him! I really don't think I can ask him. I should be afraid of being rude to him."

"It's just as you please," said Henrietta. "I had no idea you were in love with her yourself."

"Do you really believe that?" the young man asked, with lifted eyebrows.

"That's the most natural speech I have ever heard you make! Of course I believe it," Miss Stackpole answered, ingeniously.

"Well," said Ralph, "to prove to you that you are wrong, I will invite him. It must be, of course, as a friend of yours."

"It will not be as a friend of mine that he will come; and it will not be to prove to me that I am wrong that you will ask him—but to prove it to yourself!"

These last words of Miss Stackpole's (on which the two presently separated) contained an amount of truth which Ralph Touchett was obliged to recognize; but it so far took the edge from too sharp a recognition that, in spite of his suspecting that it would be rather more indiscreet to keep his promise than it would be to break it, he wrote Mr. Goodwood a note of six lines, expressing the pleasure it would give Mr. Touchett the elder that he should join a little party at Gardencourt, of which Miss Stackpole was a valued member. Having sent his letter (to the care of a banker whom Henrietta suggested) he waited in some suspense. He had heard of Mr. Caspar Goodwood by name for the first time; for when his mother mentioned to him on her arrival that there was a story about the girl's having an "admirer" at home, the idea seemed deficient in reality, and Ralph took no pains to ask questions, the answers to which would suggest only the vague or the disagreeable. Now, however, the native admiration of which his cousin was the object had become more concrete; it took the form of a young man who had followed her to London; who was interested in a cotton-mill, and had manners in the American style. Ralph had two theories about this young man. Either his passion was a sentimental fiction of Miss Stackpole's (there was always a sort of tacit understanding among women, born of the solidarity of the sex, that they should discover or invent lovers for each other), in which case he was not to be feared, and would probably not accept the invitation; or else he would accept the invitation, and in this event would prove himself a creature too irrational to demand further consideration. The latter clause of Ralph's argument might have seemed incoherent; but it embodied his conviction, that if Mr. Goodwood were interested in Isabel in the serious manner described by Miss Stackpole, he would not care to present himself at Gardencourt on a summons from the latter lady. "On this supposition," said Ralph, "he must regard her as a thorn on the stem of his rose; as an intercessor he must find her wanting in tact."

Two days after he had sent his invitation he received a very short note from Caspar Goodwood, thanking him for it, regretting that other engagements made a visit to Gardencourt impossible, and presenting many compliments to Miss Stackpole. Ralph handed the note to Henrietta, who, when she had read it, exclaimed—

"Well, I never have heard of anything so stiff!"

"I am afraid he doesn't care so much about my cousin as you suppose," Ralph observed.

"No, it's not that; it's some deeper motive. His nature is very deep. But I am determined to fathom it, and I will write to him to know what he means."

His refusal of Ralph's overtures made this young man vaguely uncomfortable; from the moment he declined to come to Gardencourt Ralph began to think him of importance. He asked himself what it signified to him whether Isabel's admirers should be desperadoes or laggards; they were not rivals of his, and were perfectly welcome to act out their genius. Nevertheless he felt much curiosity as to the result of Miss Stackpole's promised inquiry into the causes of Mr. Goodwood's stiffness—a curiosity for the present ungratified, inasmuch as when he asked her three days later whether she had written to London, she was obliged to confess that she had written in vain. Mr. Goodwood had not answered her.

"I suppose he is thinking it over," she said; "he thinks everything over; he is not at all impulsive. But I am accustomed to having my letters answered the same day."

Whether it was to pursue her investigations, or whether it was in compliance with still larger interests, is a point which remains somewhat uncertain; at all events, she presently proposed to Isabel that they should make an excursion to London together.

"If I must tell the truth," she said, "I am not seeing much at this place, and I shouldn't think you were either. I have not even seen that aristocrat—what's his name?—Lord Washburton. He seems to let you severely alone."

"Lord Warburton is coming to-morrow, I happen to know," replied Isabel, who had received a note from the master of Lockleigh in answer to her own letter. "You will have every opportunity of examining him."

"Well, he may do for one letter, but what is one letter when you want to write fifty? I have described all the scenery in this vicinity, and raved about all the old women and donkeys. You may say what you please, scenery makes a thin letter. I must go back to London and get some impressions of real life. I was there but three days before I came away, and that is hardly time to get started."

As Isabel, on her journey from New York to Gardencourt, had seen even less of the metropolis than this, it appeared a happy suggestion of Henrietta's that the two should go thither on a visit of pleasure. The idea struck Isabel as charming; she had a great desire to see something of London, which had always been the city of her imagination. They turned over their scheme together and indulged in visions of æsthetic hours. They would stay at some picturesque old inn—one of the inns described by Dickens—and drive over the town in those delightful hansoms. Henrietta was a literary woman, and the great advantage of being a literary woman was that you could go everywhere and do everything. They would dine at a coffee-house, and go afterwards to the play; they would frequent the Abbey and the British Museum, and find out where Doctor Johnson had lived, and Goldsmith and Addison. Isabel grew eager, and presently mentioned these bright intentions to Ralph, who burst into a fit of laughter, which did not express the sympathy she had desired.

"It's a delightful plan," he said. "I advise you to go to the Tavistock Hotel in Covent Garden, an easy, informal, old-fashioned place, and I will have you put down at my club."

"Do you mean it's improper?" Isabel asked. "Dear me, isn't anything proper here? With Henrietta, surely I may go anywhere; she isn't hampered in that way. She has travelled over the whole American continent, and she can surely find her way about this simple little island."

"Ah, then," said Ralph, "let me take advantage of her protection to go up to town as well. I may never have a chance to travel so safely!"

XIV

M ISS STACKPOLE would have prepared to start for London immediately; but Isabel, as we have seen, had been notified that Lord Warburton would come again to Gardencourt, and she believed it to be her duty to remain there and see him. For four or five days he had made no answer to her letter; then he had written, very briefly, to say that he would come to lunch two days later. There was something in these delays and postponements that touched the girl, and renewed her sense of his desire to be considerate and patient, not to appear to urge her too grossly; a discretion the more striking that she was so sure he really liked her. Isabel told her uncle that she had written to him, and let Mr. Touchett know of Lord Warburton's intention of coming; and the old man, in consequence, left his room earlier than usual, and made his appearance at the lunch-table. This was by no means an act of vigilance on his part, but the fruit of a benevolent belief that his being of the company might help to cover the visitor's temporary absence, in case Isabel should find it needful to give Lord Warburton another hearing. This personage drove over from Lockleigh, and brought the elder of his sisters with him, a measure presumably dictated by considerations of the same order as Mr. Touchett's. The two visitors were introduced to Miss Stackpole, who, at luncheon, occupied a seat adjoining Lord Warburton's. Isabel, who was nervous, and had no relish of the prospect of again arguing the question he had so precipitately opened, could not help admiring his good-humoured self-possession, which quite disguised the symptoms of that admiration it was natural she should suppose him to feel. He neither looked at her nor spoke to her, and the only sign of his emotion was that he avoided meeting her eye. He had plenty of talk for the others, however, and he appeared to eat his luncheon with discrimination and appetite. Miss Molyneux, who had a smooth, nun-like forehead, and wore a large silver cross suspended from her neck, was evidently preoccupied with Henrietta Stackpole, upon whom her eyes constantly rested in a manner which seemed to denote a conflict between attention and alienation. Of the two ladies from Lockleigh, she was the one that Isabel had liked best; there was such a world of hereditary quiet in her. Isabel was sure, moreover, that her mild forehead and silver cross had a romantic meaning—that she was a member of a High Church sisterhood, had taken some picturesque vows. She wondered what Miss Molyneux would think of her if she knew Miss Archer had refused her brother; and then she felt sure that Miss Molyneux would never know—that Lord Warburton never told her such things. He was fond of her and kind to her, but on the whole he told her little. Such, at least, was Isabel's theory; when, at table, she was not occupied in conversation, she was usually occupied in forming theories about her neighbours. According to Isabel, if Miss Molyneux should ever learn what had passed between Miss Archer and Lord Warburton, she would probably be shocked at the young lady's indifference to such an opportunity; or no, rather (this was our heroine's last impression) she would impute to the young American a high sense of general fitness.

Whatever Isabel might have made of her opportunities, Henrietta Stackpole was by no means disposed to neglect those in which she now found herself immersed.

"Do you know you are the first lord I have ever seen?" she said, very promptly, to her neighbour. "I suppose you think I am awfully benighted."

"You have escaped seeing some very ugly men," Lord Warburton answered, looking vaguely about the table and laughing a little.

"Are they very ugly? They try to make us believe in America that they are all handsome and magnificent, and that they wear wonderful robes and crowns."

"Ah, the robes and crowns have gone out of fashion," said Lord Warburton, "like your tomahawks and revolvers."

"I am sorry for that; I think an aristocracy ought to be splendid," Henrietta declared. "If it is not that, what is it?"

"Oh, you know, it isn't much, at the best," Lord Warburton answered. "Won't you have a potato?"

"I don't care much for these European potatoes. I shouldn't know you from an ordinary American gentleman."

"Do talk to me as if I were one," said Lord Warburton. "I

don't see how you manage to get on without potatoes; you must find so few things to eat over here."

Henrietta was silent a moment; there was a chance that he was not sincere.

"I have had hardly any appetite since I have been here," she went on at last; "so it doesn't much matter. I don't approve of *you*, you know; I feel as if I ought to tell you that."

"Don't approve of me?"

"Yes, I don't suppose any one ever said such a thing to you before, did they? I don't approve of lords, as an institution. I think the world has got beyond that—far beyond."

"Oh, so do I. I don't approve of myself in the least. Sometimes it comes over me—how I should object to myself if I were not myself, don't you know? But that's rather good, by the way—not to be vain-glorious."

"Why don't you give it up, then?" Miss Stackpole inquired.

"Give up—a—?" asked Lord Warburton, meeting her harsh inflection with a very mellow one.

"Give up being a lord."

"Oh, I am so little of one! One would really forget all about it, if you wretched Americans were not constantly reminding one. However, I do think of giving up—the little there is left of it—one of these days."

"I should like to see you do it," Henrietta exclaimed, rather grimly.

"I will invite you to the ceremony; we will have a supper and a dance."

"Well," said Miss Stackpole, "I like to see all sides. I don't approve of a privileged class, but I like to hear what they have got to say for themselves."

"Mighty little, as you see!"

"I should like to draw you out a little more," Henrietta continued. "But you are always looking away. You are afraid of meeting my eye. I see you want to escape me."

"No, I am only looking for those despised potatoes."

"Please explain about that young lady—your sister—then. I don't understand about her. Is she a Lady?"

"She's a capital good girl."

"I don't like the way you say that—as if you wanted to change the subject. Is her position inferior to yours?"

"We neither of us have any position to speak of; but she is better off than I, because she has none of the bother."

"Yes, she doesn't look as if she had much bother. I wish I had as little bother as that. You do produce quiet people over here, whatever you may do."

"Ah, you see one takes life easily, on the whole," said Lord Warburton. "And then you know we are very dull. Ah, we can be dull when we try!"

"I should advise you to try something else. I shouldn't know what to talk to your sister about; she looks so different. Is that silver cross a badge?"

"A badge?"

"A sign of rank."

Lord Warburton's glance had wandered a good deal, but at this it met the gaze of his neighbour.

"Oh, yes," he answered, in a moment; "the women go in for those things. The silver cross is worn by the eldest daughters of Viscounts."

This was his harmless revenge for having occasionally had his credulity too easily engaged in America.

After lunch he proposed to Isabel to come into the gallery and look at the pictures; and though she knew that he had seen the pictures twenty times, she complied without criticising this pretext. Her conscience now was very easy; ever since she sent him her letter she had felt particularly light of spirit. He walked slowly to the end of the gallery, staring at the paintings and saying nothing; and then he suddenly broke out—

"I hoped you wouldn't write to me that way."

"It was the only way, Lord Warburton," said the girl. "Do try and believe that."

"If I could believe it, of course I should let you alone. But we can't believe by willing it; and I confess I don't understand. I could understand your disliking me; that I could understand well. But that you should admit what you do——"

"What have I admitted?" Isabel interrupted, blushing a little.

"That you think me a good fellow; isn't that it?" She said nothing, and he went on—"You don't seem to have any reason, and that gives me a sense of injustice."

"I have a reason, Lord Warburton," said the girl; and she said it in a tone that made his heart contract.

"I should like very much to know it."

"I will tell you some day when there is more to show for it."

"Excuse my saying that in the meantime I must doubt of it."

"You make me very unhappy," said Isabel.

"I am not sorry for that; it may help you to know how I feel. Will you kindly answer me a question?" Isabel made no audible assent, but he apparently saw something in her eyes which gave him courage to go on. "Do you prefer some one else?"

"That's a question I would rather not answer."

"Ah, you *do* then!" her suitor murmured with bitterness.

The bitterness touched her, and she cried out—

"You are mistaken! I don't."

He sat down on a bench, unceremoniously, doggedly, like a man in trouble; leaning his elbows on his knees and staring at the floor.

"I can't even be glad of that," he said at last, throwing himself back against the wall, "for that would be an excuse."

Isabel raised her eyebrows, with a certain eagerness.

"An excuse? Must I excuse myself?"

He paid, however, no answer to the question. Another idea had come into his head.

"Is it my political opinions? Do you think I go too far?"

"I can't object to your political opinions, Lord Warburton," said the girl, "because I don't understand them."

"You don't care what I think," he cried, getting up. "It's all the same to you."

Isabel walked away, to the other side of the gallery, and stood there, showing him her charming back, her light slim figure, the length of her white neck as she bent her head, and the density of her dark braids. She stopped in front of a small picture, as if for the purpose of examining it; and there was something young and flexible in her movement, which her companion noticed. Isabel's eyes, however, saw nothing; they had suddenly been suffused with tears. In a moment he followed her, and by this time she had brushed her tears away;

but when she turned round, her face was pale, and the expression of her eyes was strange.

"That reason that I wouldn't tell you," she said, "I will tell it you, after all. It is that I can't escape my fate."

"Your fate?"

"I should try to escape it if I should marry you."

"I don't understand. Why should not that be your fate, as well as anything else?"

"Because it is not," said Isabel, femininely. "I know it is not. It's not my fate to give up—I know it can't be."

Poor Lord Warburton stared, with an interrogative point in either eye.

"Do you call marrying me giving up?"

"Not in the usual sense. It is getting—getting—getting a great deal. But it is giving up other chances."

"Other chances?" Lord Warburton repeated, more and more puzzled.

"I don't mean chances to marry," said Isabel, her colour rapidly coming back to her. And then she stopped, looking down with a deep frown, as if it were hopeless to attempt to make her meaning clear.

"I don't think it is presumptuous in me to say that I think you will gain more than you will lose," Lord Warburton observed.

"I can't escape unhappiness," said Isabel. "In marrying you, I shall be trying to."

"I don't know whether you would try to, but you certainly would: that I must in candour admit!" Lord Warburton exclaimed, with an anxious laugh.

"I must not—I can't!" cried the girl.

"Well, if you are bent on being miserable, I don't see why you should make me so. Whatever charms unhappiness may have for you, it has none for me."

"I am not bent on being miserable," said Isabel. "I have always been intensely determined to be happy, and I have often believed I should be. I have told people that; you can ask them. But it comes over me every now and then that I can never be happy in any extraordinary way; not by turning away, by separating myself."

"By separating yourself from what?"

"From life. From the usual chances and dangers, from what most people know and suffer."

Lord Warburton broke into a smile that almost denoted hope.

"Why, my dear Miss Archer," he began to explain, with the most considerate eagerness, "I don't offer you any exoneration from life, or from any chances or dangers whatever. I wish I could; depend upon it I would! For what do you take me, pray? Heaven help me, I am not the Emperor of China! All I offer you is the chance of taking the common lot in a comfortable sort of way. The common lot? Why, I am devoted to the common lot! Strike an alliance with me, and I promise you that you shall have plenty of it. You shall separate from nothing whatever—not even from your friend Miss Stackpole."

"She would never approve of it," said Isabel, trying to smile and take advantage of this side-issue; despising herself too, not a little, for doing so.

"Are we speaking of Miss Stackpole?" Lord Warburton asked, impatiently. "I never saw a person judge things on such theoretic grounds."

"Now I suppose you are speaking of me," said Isabel, with humility; and she turned away again, for she saw Miss Molyneux enter the gallery, accompanied by Henrietta and by Ralph.

Lord Warburton's sister addressed him with a certain timidity, and reminded him that she ought to return home in time for tea, as she was expecting some company. He made no answer—apparently not having heard her; he was preoccupied—with good reason. Miss Molyneux looked lady-like and patient, and awaited his pleasure.

"Well, I never, Miss Molyneux!" said Henrietta Stackpole. "If I wanted to go, he would have to go. If I wanted my brother to do a thing, he would have to do it."

"Oh, Warburton does everything one wants," Miss Molyneux answered, with a quick, shy laugh. "How very many pictures you have!" she went on, turning to Ralph.

"They look a good many, because they are all put together," said Ralph. "But it's really a bad way."

"Oh, I think it's so nice. I wish we had a gallery at Lockleigh. I am so very fond of pictures," Miss Molyneux went on, persistently, to Ralph, as if she were afraid that Miss Stackpole would address her again. Henrietta appeared at once to fascinate and to frighten her.

"Oh yes, pictures are very indispensable," said Ralph, who appeared to know better what style of reflection was acceptable to her.

"They are so very pleasant when it rains," the young lady continued. "It rains so very often."

"I am sorry you are going away, Lord Warburton," said Henrietta. "I wanted to get a great deal more out of you."

"I am not going away," Lord Warburton answered.

"Your sister says you must. In America the gentlemen obey the ladies."

"I am afraid we have got some people to tea," said Miss Molyneux, looking at her brother.

"Very good, my dear. We'll go."

"I hoped you would resist!" Henrietta exclaimed. "I wanted to see what Miss Molyneux would do."

"I never do anything," said this young lady.

"I suppose in your position it's sufficient for you to exist!" Miss Stackpole rejoined. "I should like very much to see you at home."

"You must come to Lockleigh again," said Miss Molyneux, very sweetly, to Isabel, ignoring this remark of Isabel's friend.

Isabel looked into her quiet eyes a moment, and for that moment seemed to see in their grey depths the reflection of everything she had rejected in rejecting Lord Warburton—the peace, the kindness, the honour, the possessions, a deep security and a great exclusion. She kissed Miss Molyneux, and then she said—

"I am afraid I can never come again."

"Never again?"

"I am afraid I am going away."

"Oh, I am so very sorry," said Miss Molyneux. "I think that's so very wrong of you."

Lord Warburton watched this little passage; then he turned away and stared at a picture. Ralph, leaning against the rail before the picture, with his hands in his pockets, had for the moment been watching him.

"I should like to see you at home," said Henrietta, whom Lord Warburton found beside him. "I should like an hour's talk with you; there are a great many questions I wish to ask you."

"I shall be delighted to see you," the proprietor of Lockleigh answered; "but I am certain not to be able to answer many of your questions. When will you come?"

"Whenever Miss Archer will take me. We are thinking of going to London, but we will go and see you first. I am determined to get some satisfaction out of you."

"If it depends upon Miss Archer, I am afraid you won't get much. She will not come to Lockleigh; she doesn't like the place."

"She told me it was lovely!" said Henrietta.

Lord Warburton hesitated a moment.

"She won't come, all the same. You had better come alone," he added.

Henrietta straightened herself, and her large eyes expanded.

"Would you make that remark to an English lady?" she inquired, with soft asperity.

Lord Warburton stared.

"Yes, if I liked her enough."

"You would be careful not to like her enough. If Miss Archer won't visit your place again, it's because she doesn't want to take me. I know what she thinks of me, and I suppose you think the same—that I oughtn't to bring in individuals."

Lord Warburton was at a loss; he had not been made acquainted with Miss Stackpole's professional character, and did not catch her allusion.

"Miss Archer has been warning you!" she went on.

"Warning me?"

"Isn't that why she came off alone with you here—to put you on your guard?"

"Oh, dear no," said Lord Warburton, blushing; "our talk had no such solemn character as that."

"Well, you have been on your guard—intensely. I suppose it's natural to you; that's just what I wanted to observe. And so, too, Miss Molyneux—she wouldn't commit herself. *You* have been warned, anyway," Henrietta continued, addressing this young lady, "but for you it wasn't necessary."

"I hope not," said Miss Molyneux, vaguely.

"Miss Stackpole takes notes," Ralph explained, humorously. "She is a great satirist; she sees through us all, and she works us up."

"Well, I must say I never have had such a collection of bad material!" Henrietta declared, looking from Isabel to Lord Warburton, and from this nobleman to his sister and to Ralph. "There is something the matter with you all; you are as dismal as if you had got a bad telegram."

"You do see through us, Miss Stackpole," said Ralph in a low tone, giving her a little intelligent nod, as he led the party out of the gallery. "There is something the matter with us all."

Isabel came behind these two; Miss Molyneux, who decidedly liked her immensely, had taken her arm, to walk beside her over the polished floor. Lord Warburton strolled on the other side, with his hands behind him, and his eyes lowered. For some moments he said nothing; and then—

"Is it true that you are going to London?" he asked.

"I believe it has been arranged."

"And when shall you come back?"

"In a few days; but probably for a very short time. I am going to Paris with my aunt."

"When, then, shall I see you again?"

"Not for a good while," said Isabel; "but some day or other, I hope."

"Do you really hope it?"

"Very much."

He went a few steps in silence; then he stopped, and put out his hand.

"Good-bye."

"Good-bye," said Isabel.

Miss Molyneux kissed her again, and she let the two depart; after which, without rejoining Henrietta and Ralph, she retreated to her own room.

In this apartment, before dinner, she was found by Mrs. Touchett, who had stopped on her way to the drawing-room.

"I may as well tell you," said her aunt, "that your uncle has informed me of your relations with Lord Warburton."

Isabel hesitated an instant.

"Relations? They are hardly relations. That is the strange part of it; he has seen me but three or four times."

"Why did you tell your uncle rather than me?" Mrs. Touchett inquired, dryly, but dispassionately.

Again Isabel hesitated.

"Because he knows Lord Warburton better."

"Yes, but I know you better."

"I am not sure of that," said Isabel, smiling.

"Neither am I, after all; especially when you smile that way. One would think you had carried off a prize! I suppose that when you refuse an offer like Lord Warburton's it's because you expect to do something better."

"Ah, my uncle didn't say that!" cried Isabel, smiling still.

XV

IT HAD BEEN arranged that the two young ladies should proceed to London under Ralph's escort, though Mrs. Touchett looked with little favour upon the plan. It was just the sort of plan, she said, that Miss Stackpole would be sure to suggest, and she inquired if the correspondent of the *Interviewer* was to take the party to stay at a boarding-house.

"I don't care where she takes us to stay, so long as there is local colour," said Isabel. "That is what we are going to London for."

"I suppose that after a girl has refused an English lord she may do anything," her aunt rejoined. "After that one needn't stand on trifles."

"Should you have liked me to marry Lord Warburton?" Isabel inquired.

"Of course I should."

"I thought you disliked the English so much."

"So I do; but it's all the more reason for making use of them."

"Is that your idea of marriage?" And Isabel ventured to add that her aunt appeared to her to have made very little use of Mr. Touchett.

"Your uncle is not an English nobleman," said Mrs. Touchett, "though even if he had been, I should still probably have taken up my residence in Florence."

"Do you think Lord Warburton could make me any better than I am?" the girl asked, with some animation. "I don't mean that I am too good to improve. I mean—I mean that I don't love Lord Warburton enough to marry him."

"You did right to refuse him, then," said Mrs. Touchett, in her little spare voice. "Only, the next great offer you get, I hope you will manage to come up to your standard."

"We had better wait till the offer comes, before we talk about it. I hope very much that I may have no more offers for the present. They bother me fearfully."

"You probably won't be troubled with them if you adopt permanently the Bohemian manner of life. However, I have promised Ralph not to criticise the affair."

"I will do whatever Ralph says is right," Isabel said. "I have unbounded confidence in Ralph."

"His mother is much obliged to you!" cried this lady, with a laugh.

"It seems to me she ought to be," Isabel rejoined, smiling.

Ralph had assured her that there would be no violation of decency in their paying a visit—the little party of three—to the sights of the metropolis; but Mrs. Touchett took a different view. Like many ladies of her country who have lived a long time in Europe, she had completely lost her native tact on such points, and in her reaction, not in itself deplorable, against the liberty allowed to young persons beyond the seas, had fallen into gratuitous and exaggerated scruples. Ralph accompanied the two young ladies to town and established them at a quiet inn in a street that ran at right angles to Piccadilly. His first idea had been to take them to his father's house in Winchester Square, a large, dull mansion, which at this period of the year was shrouded in silence and brown holland; but he bethought himself that, the cook being at Gardencourt, there was no one in the house to get them their meals; and Pratt's Hotel accordingly became their resting-place. Ralph, on his side, found quarters in Winchester Square, having a "den" there of which he was very fond, and not being dependent on the local *cuisine*. He availed himself largely indeed of that of Pratt's Hotel, beginning his day with an early visit to his fellow-travellers, who had Mr. Pratt in person, in a large bulging white waistcoat, to remove their dish-covers. Ralph turned up, as he said, after breakfast, and the little party made out a scheme of entertainment for the day. As London does not wear in the month of September its most brilliant face, the young man, who occasionally took an apologetic tone, was obliged to remind his companion, to Miss Stackpole's high irritation, that there was not a creature in town.

"I suppose you mean that the aristocracy are absent," Henrietta answered; "but I don't think you could have a better proof that if they were absent altogether they would not be missed. It seems to me the place is about as full as it can be. There is no one here, of course, except three or four millions of people. What is it you call them—the lower-middle class?

They are only the population of London, and that is of no consequence."

Ralph declared that for him the aristocracy left no void that Miss Stackpole herself did not fill, and that a more contented man was nowhere at that moment to be found. In this he spoke the truth, for the stale September days, in the huge half-empty town, borrowed a charm from his circumstances. When he went home at night to the empty house in Winchester Square, after a day spent with his inquisitive countrywomen, he wandered into the big dusky dining-room, where the candle he took from the hall-table, after letting himself in, constituted the only illumination. The square was still, the house was still; when he raised one of the windows of the dining-room to let in the air, he heard the slow creak of the boots of a solitary policeman. His own step, in the empty room, seemed loud and sonorous; some of the carpets had been raised, and whenever he moved he roused a melancholy echo. He sat down in one of the arm-chairs; the big, dark, dining table twinkled here and there in the small candle-light; the pictures on the wall, all of them very brown, looked vague and incoherent. There was a ghostly presence in the room, as of dinners long since digested, of table-talk that had lost its actuality. This hint of the supernatural perhaps had something to do with the fact that Ralph's imagination took a flight, and that he remained in his chair a long time beyond the hour at which he should have been in bed; doing nothing, not even reading the evening paper. I say he did nothing, and I maintain the phrase in the face of the fact that he thought at these moments of Isabel. To think of Isabel could only be for Ralph an idle pursuit, leading to nothing and profiting little to any one. His cousin had not yet seemed to him so charming as during these days spent in sounding, tourist-fashion, the deeps and shallows of the metropolitan element. Isabel was constantly interested and often excited; if she had come in search of local colour she found it everywhere. She asked more questions than he could answer, and launched little theories that he was equally unable to accept or to refute. The party went more than once to the British Museum, and to that brighter palace of art which reclaims for antique variety so large an area of a monotonous suburb; they spent a morning in the Abbey and went on a penny-steamer to the Tower; they looked at pictures both in public and private collections, and sat on various occasions beneath the great trees in Kensington Gardens. Henrietta Stackpole proved to be an indefatigable sight-seer and a more good-natured critic than Ralph had ventured to hope. She had indeed many disappointments, and London at large suffered from her vivid remembrance of many of the cities of her native land; but she made the best of its dingy peculiarities and only heaved an occasional sigh, and uttered a desultory "Well!" which led no further and lost itself in retrospect. The truth was that, as she said herself, she was not in her element. "I have not a sympathy with inanimate objects," she remarked to Isabel at the National Gallery; and she continued to suffer from the meagreness of the glimpse that had as yet been vouchsafed to her of the inner life. Landscapes by Turner and Assyrian bulls were a poor substitute for the literary dinner-parties at which she had hoped to meet the genius and renown of Great Britain.

"Where are your public men, where are your men and women of intellect?" she inquired of Ralph, standing in the middle of Trafalgar Square, as if she had supposed this to be a place where she would naturally meet a few. "That's one of them on the top of the column, you say—Lord Nelson? Was he a lord too? Wasn't he high enough, that they had to stick him a hundred feet in the air? That's the past—I don't care about the past; I want to see some of the leading minds of the present. I won't say of the future, because I don't believe much in your future." Poor Ralph had few leading minds among his acquaintance, and rarely enjoyed the pleasure of button-holding a celebrity; a state of things which appeared to Miss Stackpole to indicate a deplorable want of enterprise. "If I were on the other side I should call," she said, "and tell the gentleman, whoever he might be, that I had heard a great deal about him and had come to see for myself. But I gather from what you say that this is not the custom here. You seem to have plenty of meaningless customs, and none of those that one really wants. We *are* in advance, certainly. I suppose I shall have to give up the social side altogether;" and Henrietta, though she went about with her guide-book and pencil, and wrote a letter to the *Interviewer* about the Tower (in which she described the execution of Lady Jane Grey), had a depressing sense of falling below her own standard.

The incident which had preceded Isabel's departure from Gardencourt left a painful trace in the girl's mind; she took no pleasure in recalling Lord Warburton's magnanimous disappointment. She could not have done less than what she did; this was certainly true. But her necessity, all the same, had been a distasteful one, and she felt no desire to take credit for her conduct. Nevertheless, mingled with this absence of an intellectual relish of it, was a feeling of freedom which in itself was sweet, and which, as she wandered through the great city with her ill-matched companions, occasionally throbbed into joyous excitement. When she walked in Kensington Gardens, she stopped the children (mainly of the poorer sort) whom she saw playing on the grass; she asked them their names and gave them sixpence, and when they were pretty she kissed them. Ralph noticed such incidents; he noticed everything that Isabel did.

One afternoon, by way of amusing his companions, he invited them to tea in Winchester Square, and he had the house set in order as much as possible, to do honour to their visit. There was another guest, also, to meet the ladies, an amiable bachelor, an old friend of Ralph's, who happened to be in town, and who got on uncommonly well with Miss Stackpole. Mr. Bantling, a stout, fair, smiling man of forty, who was extraordinarily well dressed, and whose contributions to the conversation were characterised by vivacity rather than continuity, laughed immoderately at everything Henrietta said, gave her several cups of tea, examined in her society the *bric-à-brac*, of which Ralph had a considerable collection, and afterwards, when the host proposed they should go out into the square and pretend it was a *fête-champêtre*, walked round the limited inclosure several times with her and listened with candid interest to her remarks upon the inner life.

"Oh, I see," said Mr. Bantling; "I dare say you found it very quiet at Gardencourt. Naturally there's not much going on there when there's such a lot of illness about. Touchett's very bad, you know; the doctors have forbid his being in England at all, and he has only come back to take care of his

father. The old man, I believe, has half-a-dozen things the
matter with him. They call it gout, but to my certain knowledge he is dropsical as well, though he doesn't look it. You
may depend upon it he has got a lot of water somewhere. Of
course that sort of thing makes it awfully slow for people in
the house; I wonder they have them under such circumstances. Then I believe Mr. Touchett is always squabbling
with his wife; she lives away from her husband, you know, in
that extraordinary American way of yours. If you want a
house where there is always something going on, I recommend you to go down and stay with my sister, Lady Pensil,
in Bedfordshire. I'll write to her to-morrow, and I am sure
she'll be delighted to ask you. I know just what you want—
you want a house where they go in for theatricals and picnics
and that sort of thing. My sister is just that sort of woman;
she is always getting up something or other, and she is always
glad to have the sort of people that help her. I am sure she'll
ask you down by return of post; she is tremendously fond of
distinguished people and writers. She writes herself, you
know; but I haven't read everything she has written. It's usually poetry, and I don't go in much for poetry—unless it's
Byron. I suppose you think a great deal of Byron in America," Mr. Bantling continued, expanding in the stimulating air
of Miss Stackpole's attention, bringing up his sequences
promptly, and at last changing his topic, with a natural eagerness to provide suitable conversation for so remarkable a
woman. He returned, however, ultimately to the idea of Henrietta's going to stay with Lady Pensil, in Bedfordshire. "I
understand what you want," he repeated; "you want to see
some genuine English sport. The Touchetts are not English
at all, you know; they live on a kind of foreign system; they
have got some awfully queer ideas. The old man thinks it's
wicked to hunt, I am told. You must get down to my sister's
in time for the theatricals, and I am sure she will be glad to
give you a part. I am sure you act well; I know you are very
clever. My sister is forty years old, and she has seven children;
but she is going to play the principal part. Of course you
needn't act if you don't want to."

In this manner Mr. Bantling delivered himself, while they
strolled over the grass in Winchester Square, which, although

it had been peppered by the London soot, invited the tread to linger. Henrietta thought her blooming, easy-voiced bachelor, with his impressibility to feminine merit and his suggestiveness of allusion, a very agreeable man, and she valued the opportunity he offered her.

"I don't know but I would go, if your sister should ask me," she said. "I think it would be my duty. What do you call her name?"

"Pensil. It's an odd name, but it isn't a bad one."

"I think one name is as good as another. But what is her rank?"

"Oh, she's a baron's wife; a convenient sort of rank. You are fine enough, and you are not too fine."

"I don't know but what she'd be too fine for me. What do you call the place she lives in—Bedfordshire?"

"She lives away in the northern corner of it. It's a tiresome country, but I daresay you won't mind it. I'll try and run down while you are there."

All this was very pleasant to Miss Stackpole, and she was sorry to be obliged to separate from Lady Pensil's obliging brother. But it happened that she had met the day before, in Piccadilly, some friends whom she had not seen for a year; the Miss Climbers, two ladies from Wilmington, Delaware, who had been travelling on the continent and were now preparing to re-embark. Henrietta had a long interview with them on the Piccadilly pavement, and though the three ladies all talked at once, they had not exhausted their accumulated topics. It had been agreed therefore that Henrietta should come and dine with them in their lodgings in Jermyn Street at six o'clock on the morrow, and she now bethought herself of this engagement. She prepared to start for Jermyn Street, taking leave first of Ralph Touchett and Isabel, who, seated on garden chairs in another part of the inclosure, were occupied—if the term may be used—with an exchange of amenities less pointed than the practical colloquy of Miss Stackpole and Mr. Bantling. When it had been settled between Isabel and her friend that they should be re-united at some reputable hour at Pratt's Hotel, Ralph remarked that the latter must have a cab. She could not walk all the way to Jermyn Street.

"I suppose you mean it's improper for me to walk alone!" Henrietta exclaimed. "Merciful powers, have I come to this?"

"There is not the slightest need of your walking alone," said Mr. Bantling, in an off-hand tone expressive of gallantry. "I should be greatly pleased to go with you."

"I simply meant that you would be late for dinner," Ralph answered. "Think of those poor ladies, in their impatience, waiting for you."

"You had better have a hansom, Henrietta," said Isabel.

"I will get you a hansom, if you will trust to me," Mr. Bantling went on. "We might walk a little till we met one."

"I don't see why I shouldn't trust to him, do you?" Henrietta inquired of Isabel.

"I don't see what Mr. Bantling could do to you," Isabel answered, smiling; "but if you like, we will walk with you till you find your cab."

"Never mind; we will go alone. Come on, Mr. Bantling, and take care you get me a good one."

Mr. Bantling promised to do his best, and the two took their departure, leaving Isabel and her cousin standing in the square, over which a clear September twilight had now begun to gather. It was perfectly still; the wide quadrangle of dusky houses showed lights in none of the windows, where the shutters and blinds were closed; the pavements were a vacant expanse, and putting aside two small children from a neighbouring slum, who, attracted by symptoms of abnormal animation in the interior, were squeezing their necks between the rusty railings of the inclosure, the most vivid object within sight was the big red pillar-post on the south-east corner.

"Henrietta will ask him to get into the cab and go with her to Jermyn Street," Ralph observed. He always spoke of Miss Stackpole as Henrietta.

"Very possibly," said his companion.

"Or rather, no, she won't," he went on. "But Bantling will ask leave to get in."

"Very likely again. I am very glad they are such good friends."

"She has made a conquest. He thinks her a brilliant woman. It may go far," said Ralph.

Isabel was silent a moment.

"I call Henrietta a very brilliant woman; but I don't think it will go far," she rejoined at last. "They would never really know each other. He has not the least idea what she really is, and she has no just comprehension of Mr. Bantling."

"There is no more usual basis of matrimony than a mutual misunderstanding. But it ought not to be so difficult to understand Bob Bantling," Ralph added. "He is a very simple fellow."

"Yes, but Henrietta is simpler still. And pray, what am I to do?" Isabel asked, looking about her through the fading light, in which the limited landscape-gardening of the square took on a large and effective appearance. "I don't imagine that you will propose that you and I, for our amusement, should drive about London in a hansom."

"There is no reason why we should not stay here—if you don't dislike it. It is very warm; there will be half-an-hour yet before dark; and if you permit it, I will light a cigarette."

"You may do what you please," said Isabel, "if you will amuse me till seven o'clock. I propose at that hour to go back and partake of a simple and solitary repast—two poached eggs and a muffin—at Pratt's Hotel."

"May I not dine with you?" Ralph asked.

"No, you will dine at your club."

They had wandered back to their chairs in the centre of the square again, and Ralph had lighted his cigarette. It would have given him extreme pleasure to be present in person at the modest little feast she had sketched; but in default of this he liked even being forbidden. For the moment, however, he liked immensely being alone with her, in the thickening dusk, in the centre of the multitudinous town; it made her seem to depend upon him and to be in his power. This power he could exert but vaguely; the best exercise of it was to accept her decisions submissively. There was almost an emotion in doing so.

"Why won't you let me dine with you?" he asked, after a pause.

"Because I don't care for it."

"I suppose you are tired of me."

"I shall be an hour hence. You see I have the gift of fore-knowledge."

"Oh, I shall be delightful meanwhile," said Ralph. But he said nothing more, and as Isabel made no rejoinder, they sat some time in silence which seemed to contradict his promise of entertainment. It seemed to him that she was preoccupied, and he wondered what she was thinking about; there were two or three very possible subjects. At last he spoke again. "Is your objection to my society this evening caused by your expectation of another visitor?"

She turned her head with a glance of her clear, fair eyes.

"Another visitor? What visitor should I have?"

He had none to suggest; which made his question seem to himself silly as well as brutal.

"You have a great many friends that I don't know," he said, laughing a little awkwardly. "You have a whole past from which I was perversely excluded."

"You were reserved for my future. You must remember that my past is over there across the water. There is none of it here in London."

"Very good, then, since your future is seated beside you. Capital thing to have your future so handy." And Ralph lighted another cigarette and reflected that Isabel probably meant that she had received news that Mr. Caspar Goodwood had crossed to Paris. After he had lighted his cigarette he puffed it a while, and then he went on. "I promised a while ago to be very amusing; but you see I don't come up to the mark, and the fact is there is a good deal of temerity in my undertaking to amuse a person like you. What do you care for my feeble attempts? You have grand ideas—you have a high standard in such matters. I ought at least to bring in a band of music or a company of mountebanks."

"One mountebank is enough, and you do very well. Pray go on, and in another ten minutes I shall begin to laugh."

"I assure you that I am very serious," said Ralph. "You do really ask a great deal."

"I don't know what you mean. I ask nothing!"

"You accept nothing," said Ralph. She coloured, and now suddenly it seemed to her that she guessed his meaning. But why should he speak to her of such things? He hesitated a little, and then he continued. "There is something I should like very much to say to you. It's a question I wish to ask. It seems to me I have a right to ask it, because I have a kind of interest in the answer."

"Ask what you will," Isabel answered gently, "and I will try and satisfy you."

"Well, then, I hope you won't mind my saying that Lord Warburton has told me of something that has passed between you."

Isabel started a little; she sat looking at her open fan. "Very good; I suppose it was natural he should tell you."

"I have his leave to let you know he has done so. He has some hope still," said Ralph.

"Still?"

"He had it a few days ago."

"I don't believe he has any now," said the girl.

"I am very sorry for him, then; he is such a fine fellow."

"Pray, did he ask you to talk to me?"

"No, not that. But he told me because he couldn't help it. We are old friends, and he was greatly disappointed. He sent me a line asking me to come and see him, and I rode over to Lockleigh the day before he and his sister lunched with us. He was very heavy-hearted; he had just got a letter from you."

"Did he show you the letter?" asked Isabel, with momentary loftiness.

"By no means. But he told me it was a neat refusal. I was very sorry for him," Ralph repeated.

For some moments Isabel said nothing; then at last, "Do you know how often he had seen me? Five or six times."

"That's to your glory."

"It's not for that I say it."

"What then do you say it for? Not to prove that poor Warburton's state of mind is superficial, because I am pretty sure you don't think that."

Isabel certainly was unable to say that she thought it; but presently she said something else. "If you have not been requested by Lord Warburton to argue with me, then you are doing it disinterestedly—or for the love of argument."

"I have no wish to argue with you at all. I only wish to

leave you alone. I am simply greatly interested in your own sentiments."

"I am greatly obliged to you!" cried Isabel, with a laugh.

"Of course you mean that I am meddling in what doesn't concern me. But why shouldn't I speak to you of this matter without annoying you or embarrassing myself? What's the use of being your cousin, if I can't have a few privileges? What is the use of adoring you without the hope of a reward, if I can't have a few compensations? What is the use of being ill and disabled, and restricted to mere spectatorship at the game of life, if I really can't see the show when I have paid so much for my ticket? Tell me this," Ralph went on, while Isabel listened to him with quickened attention: "What had you in your mind when you refused Lord Warburton?"

"What had I in my mind?"

"What was the logic—the view of your situation—that dictated so remarkable an act?"

"I didn't wish to marry him—if that is logic."

"No, that is not logic—and I knew that before. What was it you said to yourself? You certainly said more than that."

Isabel reflected a moment and then she answered this inquiry with a question of her own. "Why do you call it a remarkable act? That is what your mother thinks, too."

"Warburton is such a fine fellow; as a man I think he has hardly a fault. And then, he is what they call here a swell. He has immense possessions, and his wife would be thought a superior being. He unites the intrinsic and the extrinsic advantages."

Isabel watched her cousin while he spoke, as if to see how far he would go. "I refused him because he was too perfect then. I am not perfect myself, and he is too good for me. Besides, his perfection would irritate me."

"That is ingenious rather than candid," said Ralph. "As a fact, you think nothing in the world too perfect for you."

"Do you think I am so good?"

"No, but you are exacting, all the same, without the excuse of thinking yourself good. Nineteen women out of twenty, however, even of the most exacting sort, would have contented themselves with Warburton. Perhaps you don't know he has been run after."

"I don't wish to know. But it seems to me," said Isabel, "that you told me of several faults that he has, one day when I spoke of him to you."

Ralph looked grave. "I hope that what I said then had no weight with you; for they were not faults, the things I spoke of; they were simply peculiarities of his position. If I had known he wished to marry you, I would never have alluded to them. I think I said that as regards that position he was rather a sceptic. It would have been in your power to make him a believer."

"I think not. I don't understand the matter, and I am not conscious of any mission of that sort.—You are evidently disappointed," Isabel added, looking gently but earnestly at her cousin. "You would have liked me to marry Lord Warburton."

"Not in the least. I am absolutely without a wish on the subject. I don't pretend to advise you, and I content myself with watching you—with the deepest interest."

Isabel gave a rather conscious sigh. "I wish I could be as interesting to myself as I am to you!"

"There you are not candid again; you are extremely interesting to yourself. Do you know, however," said Ralph, "that if you have really given Lord Warburton his final answer, I am rather glad it has been what it was. I don't mean I am glad for you, and still less, of course, for him. I am glad for myself."

"Are you thinking of proposing to me?"

"By no means. From the point of view I speak of that would be fatal; I should kill the goose that supplies me with golden eggs. I use that animal as a symbol of my insane illusions. What I mean is, I shall have the entertainment of seeing what a young lady does who won't marry Lord Warburton."

"That is what your mother counts upon too," said Isabel.

"Ah, there will be plenty of spectators! We shall contemplate the rest of your career. I shall not see all of it, but I shall probably see the most interesting years. Of course, if you were to marry our friend, you would still have a career—a very honourable and brilliant one. But relatively speaking, it would be a little prosaic. It would be definitely marked out in advance; it would be wanting in the unexpected. You know I am extremely fond of the unexpected, and now that you have kept the game in your hands I depend on your giving us some magnificent example of it."

"I don't understand you very well," said Isabel, "but I do so well enough to be able to say that if you look for magnificent examples of anything I shall disappoint you."

"You will do so only by disappointing yourself—and that will go hard with you!"

To this Isabel made no direct reply; there was an amount of truth in it which would bear consideration. At last she said, abruptly—"I don't see what harm there is in my wishing not to tie myself. I don't want to begin life by marrying. There are other things a woman can do."

"There is nothing she can do so well. But you are many-sided."

"If one is two-sided, it is enough," said Isabel.

"You are the most charming of polygons!" Ralph broke out, with a laugh. At a glance from his companion, however, he became grave, and to prove it he went on—"You want to see life, as the young men say."

"I don't think I want to see it as the young men want to see it; but I do want to look about me."

"You want to drain the cup of experience."

"No, I don't wish to touch the cup of experience. It's a poisoned drink! I only want to see for myself."

"You want to see, but not to feel," said Ralph.

"I don't think that if one is a sentient being, one can make the distinction," Isabel returned. "I am a good deal like Henrietta. The other day, when I asked her if she wished to marry, she said—'Not till I have seen Europe!' I too don't wish to marry until I have seen Europe."

"You evidently expect that a crowned head will be struck with you."

"No, that would be worse than marrying Lord Warburton. But it is getting very dark," Isabel continued, "and I must go home." She rose from her place, but Ralph sat still a moment, looking at her. As he did not follow her, she stopped, and they remained a while exchanging a gaze, full on either side, but especially on Ralph's, of utterances too vague for words.

"You have answered my question," said Ralph at last. "You have told me what I wanted. I am greatly obliged to you."

"It seems to me I have told you very little."

"You have told me the great thing: that the world interests you and that you want to throw yourself into it."

Isabel's silvery eyes shone for a moment in the darkness. "I never said that."

"I think you meant it. Don't repudiate it; it's so fine!"

"I don't know what you are trying to fasten upon me, for I am not in the least an adventurous spirit. Women are not like men."

Ralph slowly rose from his seat, and they walked together to the gate of the square. "No," he said; " women rarely boast of their courage; men do so with a certain frequency."

"Men have it to boast of!"

"Women have it too; you have a great deal."

"Enough to go home in a cab to Pratt's Hotel; but not more."

Ralph unlocked the gate, and after they had passed out he fastened it.

"We will find your cab," he said; and as they turned towards a neighbouring street in which it seemed that this quest would be fruitful, he asked her again if he might not see her safely to the inn.

"By no means," she answered; "you are very tired; you must go home and go to bed."

The cab was found, and he helped her into it, standing a moment at the door.

"When people forget I am a sick man I am often annoyed," he said. "But it's worse when they remember it!"

XVI

ISABEL HAD had no hidden motive in wishing her cousin not to take her home; it simply seemed to her that for some days past she had consumed an inordinate quantity of his time, and the independent spirit of the American girl who ends by regarding perpetual assistance as a sort of derogation to her sanity, had made her decide that for these few hours she must suffice to herself. She had moreover a great fondness for intervals of solitude, and since her arrival in England it had been but scantily gratified. It was a luxury she could always command at home, and she had missed it. That evening, however, an incident occurred which—had there been a critic to note it—would have taken all colour from the theory that the love of solitude had caused her to dispense with Ralph's attendance. She was sitting, towards nine o'clock, in the dim illumination of Pratt's Hotel, trying with the aid of two tall candles to lose herself in a volume she had brought from Gardencourt, but succeeding only to the extent of reading other words on the page than those that were printed there—words that Ralph had spoken to her in the afternoon.

Suddenly the well-muffled knuckle of the waiter was applied to the door, which presently admitted him, bearing the card of a visitor. This card, duly considered, offered to Isabel's startled vision the name of Mr. Caspar Goodwood. She let the servant stand before her inquiringly for some instants, without signifying her wishes.

"Shall I show the gentleman up, ma'am?" he asked at last, with a slightly encouraging inflection.

Isabel hesitated still, and while she hesitated she glanced at the mirror.

"He may come in," she said at last; and waited for him with some emotion.

Caspar Goodwood came in and shook hands with her. He said nothing till the servant had left the room again, then he said—

"Why didn't you answer my letter?"

He spoke in a quick, full, slightly peremptory tone—the

tone of a man whose questions were usually pointed, and who was capable of much insistence.

Isabel answered him by a question.

"How did you know I was here?"

"Miss Stackpole let me know," said Caspar Goodwood. "She told me that you would probably be at home alone this evening, and would be willing to see me."

"Where did she see you—to tell you that?"

"She didn't see me; she wrote to me."

Isabel was silent; neither of them had seated themselves; they stood there with a certain air of defiance, or at least of contention.

"Henrietta never told me that she was writing to you," Isabel said at last. "This is not kind of her."

"Is it so disagreeable to you to see me?" asked the young man.

"I didn't expect it. I don't like such surprises."

"But you knew I was in town; it was natural we should meet."

"Do you call this meeting? I hoped I should not see you. In so large a place as London it seemed to me very possible."

"Apparently it was disagreeable to you even to write to me," said Mr. Goodwood.

Isabel made no answer to this; the sense of Henrietta Stackpole's treachery, as she momentarily qualified it, was strong within her.

"Henrietta is not delicate!" she exclaimed with a certain bitterness. "It was a great liberty to take."

"I suppose I am not delicate either. The fault is mine as much as hers."

As Isabel looked at him it seemed to her that his jaw had never been more square. This might have displeased her; nevertheless she rejoined inconsequently—

"No, it is not your fault so much as hers. What you have done is very natural."

"It is indeed!" cried Caspar Goodwood, with a voluntary laugh. "And now that I have come, at any rate, may I not stay?"

"You may sit down, certainly."

And Isabel went back to her chair again, while her visitor

took the first place that offered, in the manner of a man accustomed to pay little thought to the sort of chair he sat in.

"I have been hoping every day for an answer to my letter," he said. "You might have written me a few lines."

"It was not the trouble of writing that prevented me; I could as easily have written you four pages as one. But my silence was deliberate; I thought it best."

He sat with his eyes fixed on hers while she said this; then he lowered them and attached them to a spot in the carpet, as if he were making a strong effort to say nothing but what he ought to say. He was a strong man in the wrong, and he was acute enough to see that an uncompromising exhibition of his strength would only throw the falsity of his position into relief. Isabel was not incapable of finding it agreeable to have an advantage of position over a person of this quality, and though she was not a girl to flaunt her advantage in his face, she was woman enough to enjoy being able to say "You know you ought not to have written to me yourself!" and to say it with a certain air of triumph.

Caspar Goodwood raised his eyes to hers again; they wore an expression of ardent remonstrance. He had a strong sense of justice, and he was ready any day in the year—over and above this—to argue the question of his rights.

"You said you hoped never to hear from me again; I know that. But I never accepted the prohibition. I promised you that you should hear very soon."

"I did not say that I hoped never to hear from you," said Isabel.

"Not for five years, then; for ten years. It is the same thing."

"Do you find it so? It seems to me there is a great difference. I can imagine that at the end of ten years we might have a very pleasant correspondence. I shall have matured my epistolary style."

Isabel looked away while she spoke these words, for she knew they were of a much less earnest cast than the countenance of her listener. Her eyes, however, at last came back to him, just as he said, very irrelevantly—

"Are you enjoying your visit to your uncle?"

"Very much indeed." She hesitated, and then she broke out

with even greater irrelevance, "What good do you expect to get by insisting?"

"The good of not losing you."

"You have no right to talk about losing what is not yours. And even from your own point of view," Isabel added, "you ought to know when to let one alone."

"I displease you very much," said Caspar Goodwood gloomily; not as if to provoke her to compassion for a man conscious of this blighting fact, but as if to set it well before himself, so that he might endeavour to act with his eyes upon it.

"Yes, you displease me very much, and the worst is that it is needless."

Isabel knew that his was not a soft nature, from which pin-pricks would draw blood; and from the first of her acquaintance with him and of her having to defend herself against a certain air that he had of knowing better what was good for her than she knew herself, she had recognised the fact that perfect frankness was her best weapon. To attempt to spare his sensibility or to escape from him edgewise, as one might do from a man who had barred the way less sturdily—this, in dealing with Caspar Goodwood, who would take everything of every sort that one might give him, was wasted agility. It was not that he had not susceptibilities, but his passive surface, as well as his active, was large and firm, and he might always be trusted to dress his wounds himself. In measuring the effect of his suffering, one might always reflect that he had a sound constitution.

"I can't reconcile myself to that," he said.

There was a dangerous liberality about this; for Isabel felt that it was quite open to him to say that he had not always displeased her.

"I can't reconcile myself to it either, and it is not the state of things that ought to exist between us. If you would only try and banish me from your mind for a few months we should be on good terms again."

"I see. If I should cease to think of you for a few months I should find I could keep it up indefinitely."

"Indefinitely is more than I ask. It is more even than I should like."

"You know that what you ask is impossible," said the young man, taking his adjective for granted in a manner that Isabel found irritating.

"Are you not capable of making an effort?" she demanded. "You are strong for everything else; why shouldn't you be strong for that?"

"Because I am in love with you," said Caspar Goodwood simply. "If one is strong, one loves only the more strongly."

"There is a good deal in that;" and indeed our young lady felt the force of it. "Think of me or not, as you find most possible; only leave me alone."

"Until when?"

"Well, for a year or two."

"Which do you mean? Between one year and two there is a great difference."

"Call it two, then," said Isabel, wondering whether a little cynicism might not be effective.

"And what shall I gain by that?" Mr. Goodwood asked, giving no sign of wincing.

"You will have obliged me greatly."

"But what will be my reward?"

"Do you need a reward for an act of generosity?"

"Yes, when it involves a great sacrifice."

"There is no generosity without sacrifice. Men don't understand such things. If you make this sacrifice I shall admire you greatly."

"I don't care a straw for your admiration. Will you marry me? That is the question."

"Assuredly not, if I feel as I feel at present."

"Then I ask again, what I shall gain?"

"You will gain quite as much as by worrying me to death!"

Caspar Goodwood bent his eyes again and gazed for a while into the crown of his hat. A deep flush overspread his face, and Isabel could perceive that this dart at last had struck home. To see a strong man in pain had something terrible for her, and she immediately felt very sorry for her visitor.

"Why do you make me say such things to you?" she cried in a trembling voice. "I only want to be gentle—to be kind. It is not delightful to me to feel that people care for me, and yet to have to try and reason them out of it. I think others also ought to be considerate; we have each to judge for ourselves. I know you are considerate, as much as you can be; you have good reasons for what you do. But I don't want to marry. I shall probably never marry. I have a perfect right to feel that way, and it is no kindness to a woman to urge her—to persuade her against her will. If I give you pain I can only say I am very sorry. It is not my fault; I can't marry you simply to please you. I won't say that I shall always remain your friend, because when women say that, in these circumstances, it is supposed, I believe, to be a sort of mockery. But try me some day."

Caspar Goodwood, during this speech, had kept his eyes fixed upon the name of his hatter, and it was not until some time after she had ceased speaking that he raised them. When he did so, the sight of a certain rosy, lovely eagerness in Isabel's face threw some confusion into his attempt to analyse what she had said. "I will go home—I will go to-morrow—I will leave you alone," he murmured at last. "Only," he added in a louder tone—"I hate to lose sight of you!"

"Never fear. I will do no harm."

"You will marry some one else," said Caspar Goodwood.

"Do you think that is a generous charge?"

"Why not? Plenty of men will ask you."

"I told you just now that I don't wish to marry, and that I shall probably never do so."

"I know you did; but I don't believe it."

"Thank you very much. You appear to think I am attempting to deceive you; you say very delicate things."

"Why should I not say that? You have given me no promise that you will not marry."

"No, that is all that would be wanting!" cried Isabel, with a bitter laugh.

"You think you won't, but you will," her visitor went on, as if he were preparing himself for the worst.

"Very well, I will then. Have it as you please."

"I don't know, however," said Caspar Goodwood, "that my keeping you in sight would prevent it."

"Don't you indeed? I am, after all, very much afraid of you. Do you think I am so very easily pleased?" she asked suddenly, changing her tone.

"No, I don't; I shall try and console myself with that. But there are a certain number of very clever men in the world; if there were only one, it would be enough. You will be sure to take no one who is not."

"I don't need the aid of a clever man to teach me how to live," said Isabel. "I can find it out for myself."

"To live alone, do you mean? I wish that when you have found that out, you would teach me."

Isabel glanced at him a moment; then, with a quick smile— "Oh, *you* ought to marry!" she said.

Poor Caspar may be pardoned if for an instant this exclamation seemed to him to have the infernal note, and I cannot take upon myself to say that Isabel uttered it in obedience to an impulse strictly celestial. It was a fact, however, that it had always seemed to her that Caspar Goodwood, of all men, ought to enjoy the whole devotion of some tender woman. "God forgive you!" he murmured between his teeth, turning away.

Her exclamation had put her slightly in the wrong, and after a moment she felt the need to right herself. The easiest way to do it was to put her suitor in the wrong. "You do me great injustice—you say what you don't know!" she broke out. "I should not be an easy victim—I have proved it."

"Oh, to me, perfectly."

"I have proved it to others as well." And she paused a moment. "I refused a proposal of marriage last week—what they call a brilliant one."

"I am very glad to hear it," said the young man, gravely.

"It was a proposal that many girls would have accepted; it had everything to recommend it." Isabel had hesitated to tell this story, but now she had begun, the satisfaction of speaking it out and doing herself justice took possession of her. "I was offered a great position and a great fortune—by a person whom I like extremely."

Caspar gazed at her with great interest. "Is he an Englishman?"

"He is an English nobleman," said Isabel.

Mr. Goodwood received this announcement in silence; then, at last, he said—"I am glad he is disappointed."

"Well, then, as you have companions in misfortune, make the best of it."

"I don't call him a companion," said Caspar, grimly.

"Why not—since I declined his offer absolutely?"

"That doesn't make him my companion. Besides, he's an Englishman."

"And pray is not an Englishman a human being?" Isabel inquired.

"Oh, no; he's superhuman."

"You are angry," said the girl. "We have discussed this matter quite enough."

"Oh, yes, I am angry. I plead guilty to that!"

Isabel turned away from him, walked to the open window, and stood a moment looking into the dusky vacancy of the street, where a turbid gaslight alone represented social animation. For some time neither of these young persons spoke; Caspar lingered near the chimney-piece, with his eyes gloomily fixed upon our heroine. She had virtually requested him to withdraw—he knew that; but at the risk of making himself odious to her he kept his ground. She was far too dear to him to be easily forfeited, and he had sailed across the Atlantic to extract some pledge from her. Presently she left the window and stood before him again.

"You do me very little justice," she said—"after my telling you what I told you just now. I am sorry I told you—since it matters so little to you."

"Ah," cried the young man, "if you were thinking of *me* when you did it!" And then he paused, with the fear that she might contradict so happy a thought.

"I was thinking of you a little," said Isabel.

"A little? I don't understand. If the knowledge that I love you had any weight with you at all, it must have had a good deal."

Isabel shook her head impatiently, as if to carry off a blush. "I have refused a noble gentleman. Make the most of that."

"I thank you, then," said Caspar Goodwood, gravely. "I thank you immensely."

"And now you had better go home."

"May I not see you again?" he asked.

"I think it is better not. You will be sure to talk of this, and you see it leads to nothing."

"I promise you not to say a word that will annoy you."

Isabel reflected a little, and then she said—"I return in a day or two to my uncle's, and I can't propose to you to come there; it would be very inconsistent."

Caspar Goodwood, on his side, debated within himself. "You must do me justice too. I received an invitation to your uncle's more than a week ago, and I declined it."

"From whom was your invitation?" Isabel asked, surprised.

"From Mr. Ralph Touchett, whom I suppose to be your cousin. I declined it because I had not your authorisation to accept it. The suggestion that Mr. Touchett should invite me appeared to have come from Miss Stackpole."

"It certainly did not come from me. Henrietta certainly goes very far," Isabel added.

"Don't be too hard on her—that touches me."

"No; if you declined, that was very proper of you, and I thank you for it." And Isabel gave a little shudder of dismay at the thought that Lord Warburton and Mr. Goodwood might have met at Gardencourt: it would have been so awkward for Lord Warburton!

"When you leave your uncle, where are you going?" Caspar asked.

"I shall go abroad with my aunt—to Florence and other places."

The serenity of this announcement struck a chill to the young man's heart; he seemed to see her whirled away into circles from which he was inexorably excluded. Nevertheless he went on quickly with his questions. "And when shall you come back to America?"

"Perhaps not for a long time; I am very happy here."

"Do you mean to give up your country?"

"Don't be an infant."

"Well, you will be out of my sight indeed!" said Caspar Goodwood.

"I don't know," she answered, rather grandly. "The world strikes me as small."

"It is too large for me!" Caspar exclaimed, with a simplicity which our young lady might have found touching if her face had not been set against concessions.

This attitude was part of a system, a theory, that she had

lately embraced, and to be thorough she said after a moment—"Don't think me unkind if I say that it's just that—
being out of your sight—that I like. If you were in the same
place as I, I should feel as if you were watching me, and I
don't like that. I like my liberty too much. If there is a thing
in the world that I am fond of," Isabel went on, with a slight
recurrence of the grandeur that had shown itself a moment
before—"it is my personal independence."

But whatever there was of grandeur in this speech moved
Caspar Goodwood's admiration; there was nothing that displeased him in the sort of feeling it expressed. This feeling
not only did no violence to his way of looking at the girl he
wished to make his wife, but seemed a grace the more in so
ardent a spirit. To his mind she had always had wings, and
this was but the flutter of those stainless pinions. He was not
afraid of having a wife with a certain largeness of movement;
he was a man of long steps himself. Isabel's words, if they
had been meant to shock him, failed of the mark, and only
made him smile with the sense that here was common
ground. "Who would wish less to curtail your liberty than I?"
he asked. "What can give me greater pleasure than to see you
perfectly independent—doing whatever you like? It is to
make you independent that I want to marry you."

"That's a beautiful sophism," said the girl, with a smile
more beautiful still.

"An unmarried woman—a girl of your age—is not independent. There are all sorts of things she can't do. She is hampered at every step."

"That's as she looks at the question," Isabel answered, with
much spirit. "I am not in my first youth—I can do what I
choose—I belong quite to the independent class. I have neither father nor mother; I am poor; I am of a serious disposition, and not pretty. I therefore am not bound to be timid
and conventional; indeed I can't afford such luxuries. Besides,
I try to judge things for myself; to judge wrong, I think, is
more honourable than not to judge at all. I don't wish to be
a mere sheep in the flock; I wish to choose my fate and know
something of human affairs beyond what other people think
it compatible with propriety to tell me." She paused a moment, but not long enough for her companion to reply. He

was apparently on the point of doing so, when she went on—
"Let me say this to you, Mr. Goodwood. You are so kind as
to speak of being afraid of my marrying. If you should hear a
rumour that I am on the point of doing so—girls are liable
to have such things said about them—remember what I have
told you about my love of liberty, and venture to doubt it."

There was something almost passionately positive in the
tone in which Isabel gave him this advice, and he saw a shining candour in her eyes which helped him to believe her. On
the whole he felt reassured, and you might have perceived it
by the manner in which he said, quite eagerly—"You want
simply to travel for two years? I am quite willing to wait two
years, and you may do what you like in the interval. If that is
all you want, pray say so. I don't want you to be conventional; do I strike you as conventional myself? Do you want
to improve your mind? Your mind is quite good enough for
me; but if it interests you to wander about a while and see
different countries, I shall be delighted to help you, in any
way in my power."

"You are very generous; that is nothing new to me. The
best way to help me will be to put as many hundred miles of
sea between us as possible."

"One would think you were going to commit a crime!"
said Caspar Goodwood.

"Perhaps I am. I wish to be free even to do that, if the
fancy takes me."

"Well then," he said, slowly, "I will go home." And he put
out his hand, trying to look contented and confident.

Isabel's confidence in him, however, was greater than any
he could feel in her. Not that he thought her capable of committing a crime; but, turn it over as he would, there was
something ominous in the way she reserved her option. As
Isabel took his hand, she felt a great respect for him; she
knew how much he cared for her, and she thought him magnanimous. They stood so for a moment, looking at each
other, united by a handclasp which was not merely passive on
her side. "That's right," she said, very kindly, almost tenderly.
"You will lose nothing by being a reasonable man."

"But I will come back, wherever you are, two years hence,"
he returned, with characteristic grimness.

We have seen that our young lady was inconsequent, and at this she suddenly changed her note. "Ah, remember, I promise nothing—absolutely nothing!" Then more softly, as if to help him to leave her, she added—"And remember, too, that I shall not be an easy victim!"

"You will get very sick of your independence."

"Perhaps I shall; it is even very probable. When that day comes I shall be very glad to see you."

She had laid her hand on the knob of the door that led into her room, and she waited a moment to see whether her visitor would not take his departure. But he appeared unable to move; there was still an immense unwillingness in his attitude—a deep remonstrance in his eyes.

"I must leave you now," said Isabel; and she opened the door, and passed into the other room.

This apartment was dark, but the darkness was tempered by a vague radiance sent up through the window from the court of the hotel, and Isabel could make out the masses of the furniture, the dim shining of the mirror, and the looming of the big four-posted bed. She stood still a moment, listening, and at last she heard Caspar Goodwood walk out of the sitting-room and close the door behind him. She stood still a moment longer, and then, by an irresistible impulse, she dropped on her knees before her bed, and hid her face in her arms.

XVII

S HE WAS NOT praying; she was trembling—trembling all
over. She was an excitable creature, and now she was
much excited; but she wished to resist her excitement, and
the attitude of prayer, which she kept for some time, seemed
to help her to be still. She was extremely glad Caspar Goodwood was gone; there was something exhilarating in having
got rid of him. As Isabel became conscious of this feeling she
bowed her head a little lower; the feeling was there, throb-
bing in her heart; it was a part of her emotion; but it was a
thing to be ashamed of—it was profane and out of place. It
was not for some ten minutes that she rose from her knees,
and when she came back to the sitting-room she was still
trembling a little. Her agitation had two causes; part of it was
to be accounted for by her long discussion with Mr. Goodwood, but it might be feared that the rest was simply the
enjoyment she found in the exercise of her power. She sat
down in the same chair again, and took up her book, but
without going through the form of opening the volume. She
leaned back, with that low, soft, aspiring murmur with which
she often expressed her gladness in accidents of which the
brighter side was not superficially obvious, and gave herself
up to the satisfaction of having refused two ardent suitors
within a fortnight. That love of liberty of which she had given
Caspar Goodwood so bold a sketch was as yet almost exclusively theoretic; she had not been able to indulge it on a large
scale. But it seemed to her that she had done something; she
had tasted of the delight, if not of battle, at least of victory;
she had done what she preferred. In the midst of this agreeable sensation the image of Mr. Goodwood taking his sad
walk homeward through the dingy town presented itself with
a certain reproachful force; so that, as at the same moment
the door of the room was opened, she rose quickly with an
apprehension that he had come back. But it was only Henrietta Stackpole returning from her dinner.

Miss Stackpole immediately saw that something had happened to Isabel, and indeed the discovery demanded no great
penetration. Henrietta went straight up to her friend, who

received her without a greeting. Isabel's elation in having sent Caspar Goodwood back to America pre-supposed her being glad that he had come to see her; but at the same time she perfectly remembered that Henrietta had had no right to set a trap for her.

"Has he been here, dear?" Miss Stackpole inquired, softly.

Isabel turned away, and for some moments answered nothing.

"You acted very wrongly," she said at last.

"I acted for the best, dear. I only hope you acted as well."

"You are not the judge. I can't trust you," said Isabel.

This declaration was unflattering, but Henrietta was much too unselfish to heed the charge it conveyed; she cared only for what it intimated with regard to her friend.

"Isabel Archer," she declared, with equal abruptness and solemnity, "if you marry one of these people, I will never speak to you again!"

"Before making so terrible a threat, you had better wait till I am asked," Isabel replied. Never having said a word to Miss Stackpole about Lord Warburton's overtures, she had now no impulse whatever to justify herself to Henrietta by telling her that she had refused that nobleman.

"Oh, you'll be asked quick enough, once you get off on the continent. Annie Climber was asked three times in Italy—poor plain little Annie."

"Well, if Annie Climber was not captured, why should I be?"

"I don't believe Annie was pressed; but you'll be."

"That's a flattering conviction," said Isabel, with a laugh.

"I don't flatter you, Isabel, I tell you the truth!" cried her friend. "I hope you don't mean to tell me that you didn't give Mr. Goodwood some hope."

"I don't see why I should tell you anything; as I said to you just now, I can't trust you. But since you are so much interested in Mr. Goodwood, I won't conceal from you that he returns immediately to America."

"You don't mean to say you have sent him off?" Henrietta broke out in dismay.

"I asked him to leave me alone; and I ask you the same, Henrietta."

Miss Stackpole stood there with expanded eyes, and then she went to the mirror over the chimney-piece and took off her bonnet.

"I hope you have enjoyed your dinner," Isabel remarked, lightly, as she did so.

But Miss Stackpole was not to be diverted by frivolous propositions, nor bribed by the offer of autobiographic opportunities.

"Do you know where you are going, Isabel Archer?"

"Just now I am going to bed," said Isabel, with persistent frivolity.

"Do you know where you are drifting?" Henrietta went on, holding out her bonnet delicately.

"No, I haven't the least idea, and I find it very pleasant not to know. A swift carriage, of a dark night, rattling with four horses over roads that one can't see—that's my idea of happiness."

"Mr. Goodwood certainly didn't teach you to say such things as that—like the heroine of an immoral novel," said Miss Stackpole. "You are drifting to some great mistake."

Isabel was irritated by her friend's interference, but even in the midst of her irritation she tried to think what truth this declaration could represent. She could think of nothing that diverted her from saying—"You must be very fond of me, Henrietta, to be willing to be so disagreeable to me."

"I love you, Isabel," said Miss Stackpole, with feeling.

"Well, if you love me, let me alone. I asked that of Mr. Goodwood, and I must also ask it of you."

"Take care you are not let alone too much."

"That is what Mr. Goodwood said to me. I told him I must take the risks."

"You are a creature of risks—you make me shudder!" cried Henrietta. "When does Mr. Goodwood return to America?"

"I don't know—he didn't tell me."

"Perhaps you didn't inquire," said Henrietta, with the note of righteous irony.

"I gave him too little satisfaction to have the right to ask questions of him."

This assertion seemed to Miss Stackpole for a moment to bid defiance to comment; but at last she exclaimed—"Well,

Isabel, if I didn't know you, I might think you were heartless!"

"Take care," said Isabel; "you are spoiling me."

"I am afraid I have done that already. I hope, at least," Miss Stackpole added, "that he may cross with Annie Climber!"

Isabel learned from her the next morning that she had determined not to return to Gardencourt (where old Mr. Touchett had promised her a renewed welcome), but to await in London the arrival of the invitation that Mr. Bantling had promised her from his sister, Lady Pensil. Miss Stackpole related very freely her conversation with Ralph Touchett's sociable friend, and declared to Isabel that she really believed she had now got hold of something that would lead to something. On the receipt of Lady Pensil's letter—Mr. Bantling had virtually guaranteed the arrival of this document—she would immediately depart for Bedfordshire, and if Isabel cared to look out for her impressions in the *Interviewer*, she would certainly find them. Henrietta was evidently going to see something of the inner life this time.

"Do you know where you are drifting, Henrietta Stackpole?" Isabel asked, imitating the tone in which her friend had spoken the night before.

"I am drifting to a big position—that of queen of American journalism. If my next letter isn't copied all over the West, I'll swallow my pen-wiper!"

She had arranged with her friend Miss Annie Climber, the young lady of the continental offers, that they should go together to make those purchases which were to constitute Miss Climber's farewell to a hemisphere in which she at least had been appreciated; and she presently repaired to Jermyn Street to pick up her companion. Shortly after her departure Ralph Touchett was announced, and as soon as he came in Isabel saw that he had something on his mind. He very soon took his cousin into his confidence. He had received a telegram from his mother, telling him that his father had had a sharp attack of his old malady, that she was much alarmed, and that she begged Ralph would instantly return to Gardencourt. On this occasion, at least, Mrs. Touchett's devotion to the electric wire had nothing incongruous.

"I have judged it best to see the great doctor, Sir Matthew

Hope, first," Ralph said; "by great good luck he's in town. He is to see me at half-past twelve, and I shall make sure of his coming down to Gardencourt—which he will do the more readily as he has already seen my father several times, both there and in London. There is an express at two-forty-five, which I shall take, and you will come back with me, or remain here a few days longer, exactly as you prefer."

"I will go with you!" Isabel exclaimed. "I don't suppose I can be of any use to my uncle, but if he is ill I should like to be near him."

"I think you like him," said Ralph, with a certain shy pleasure in his eye. "You appreciate him, which all the world hasn't done. The quality is too fine."

"I think I love him," said Isabel, simply.

"That's very well. After his son, he is your greatest admirer."

Isabel welcomed this assurance, but she gave secretly a little sigh of relief at the thought that Mr. Touchett was one of those admirers who could not propose to marry her. This, however, was not what she said; she went on to inform Ralph that there were other reasons why she should not remain in London. She was tired of it and wished to leave it; and then Henrietta was going away—going to stay in Bedfordshire.

"In Bedfordshire?" Ralph exclaimed, with surprise.

"With Lady Pensil, the sister of Mr. Bantling, who has answered for an invitation."

Ralph was feeling anxious, but at this he broke into a laugh. Suddenly, however, he looked grave again. "Bantling is a man of courage. But if the invitation should get lost on the way?"

"I thought the British post-office was impeccable."

"The good Homer sometimes nods," said Ralph. "However," he went on, more brightly, "the good Bantling never does, and, whatever happens, he will take care of Henrietta."

Ralph went to keep his appointment with Sir Matthew Hope, and Isabel made her arrangements for quitting Pratt's Hotel. Her uncle's danger touched her nearly, and while she stood before her open trunk, looking about her vaguely for what she should put into it, the tears suddenly rushed into her eyes. It was perhaps for this reason that when Ralph came back at two o'clock to take her to the station she was not yet ready.

He found Miss Stackpole, however, in the sitting-room, where she had just risen from the lunch-table, and this lady immediately expressed her regret at his father's illness.

"He is a grand old man," she said; "he is faithful to the last. If it is really to be the last—excuse my alluding to it, but you must often have thought of the possibility—I am sorry that I shall not be at Gardencourt."

"You will amuse yourself much more in Bedfordshire."

"I shall be sorry to amuse myself at such a time," said Henrietta, with much propriety. But she immediately added—"I should like so to commemorate the closing scene."

"My father may live a long time," said Ralph, simply. Then, adverting to topics more cheerful, he interrogated Miss Stackpole as to her own future.

Now that Ralph was in trouble, she addressed him in a tone of larger allowance, and told him that she was much indebted to him for having made her acquainted with Mr. Bantling. "He has told me just the things I want to know," she said; "all the society-items and all about the royal family. I can't make out that what he tells me about the royal family is much to their credit; but he says that's only my peculiar way of looking at it. Well, all I want is that he should give me the facts; I can put them together quick enough, once I've got them." And she added that Mr. Bantling had been so good as to promise to come and take her out in the afternoon.

"To take you where?" Ralph ventured to inquire.

"To Buckingham Palace. He is going to show me over it, so that I may get some idea how they live."

"Ah," said Ralph, "we leave you in good hands. The first thing we shall hear is that you are invited to Windsor Castle."

"If they ask me, I shall certainly go. Once I get started I am not afraid. But for all that," Henrietta added in a moment, "I am not satisfied; I am not satisfied about Isabel."

"What is her last misdemeanour?"

"Well, I have told you before, and I suppose there is no harm in my going on. I always finish a subject that I take up. Mr. Goodwood was here last night."

Ralph opened his eyes; he even blushed a little—his blush being the sign of an emotion somewhat acute. He remembered that Isabel, in separating from him in Winchester Square, had repudiated his suggestion that her motive in doing so was the expectation of a visitor at Pratt's Hotel, and it was a novel sensation to him to have to suspect her of duplicity. On the other hand, he quickly said to himself, what concern was it of his that she should have made an appointment with a lover? Had it not been thought graceful in every age that young ladies should make a mystery of such appointments? Ralph made Miss Stackpole a diplomatic answer. "I should have thought that, with the views you expressed to me the other day, that would satisfy you perfectly."

"That he should come to see her? That was very well, as far as it went. It was a little plot of mine; I let him know that we were in London, and when it had been arranged that I should spend the evening out, I just sent him a word—a word to the wise. I hoped he would find her alone; I won't pretend I didn't hope that you would be out of the way. He came to see her; but he might as well have stayed away."

"Isabel was cruel?" Ralph inquired, smiling, and relieved at learning that his cousin had not deceived him.

"I don't exactly know what passed between them. But she gave him no satisfaction—she sent him back to America."

"Poor Mr. Goodwood!" Ralph exclaimed.

"Her only idea seems to be to get rid of him," Henrietta went on.

"Poor Mr. Goodwood!" repeated Ralph. The exclamation, it must be confessed, was somewhat mechanical. It failed exactly to express his thoughts, which were taking another line.

"You don't say that as if you felt it; I don't believe you care."

"Ah," said Ralph, "you must remember that I don't know this interesting young man—that I have never seen him."

"Well, I shall see him, and I shall tell him not to give up. If I didn't believe Isabel would come round," said Miss Stackpole—"well, I'd give her up myself!"

XVIII

IT HAD OCCURRED to Ralph that under the circumstances Isabel's parting with Miss Stackpole might be of a slightly embarrassed nature, and he went down to the door of the hotel in advance of his cousin, who after a slight delay followed, with the traces of an unaccepted remonstrance, as he thought, in her eye. The two made the journey to Gardencourt in almost unbroken silence, and the servant who met them at the station had no better news to give them of Mr. Touchett—a fact which caused Ralph to congratulate himself afresh on Sir Matthew Hope's having promised to come down in the five o'clock train and spend the night. Mrs. Touchett, he learned, on reaching home, had been constantly with the old man, and was with him at that moment; and this fact made Ralph say to himself that, after all, what his mother wanted was simply opportunity. The finest natures were those that shone on large occasions. Isabel went to her own room, noting, throughout the house, that perceptible hush which precedes a crisis. At the end of an hour, however, she came down-stairs in search of her aunt, whom she wished to ask about Mr. Touchett. She went into the library, but Mrs. Touchett was not there, and as the weather, which had been damp and chill, was now altogether spoiled, it was not probable that she had gone for her usual walk in the grounds. Isabel was on the point of ringing to send an inquiry to her room, when her attention was taken by an unexpected sound—the sound of low music proceeding apparently from the drawing-room. She knew that her aunt never touched the piano, and the musician was therefore probably Ralph, who played for his own amusement. That he should have resorted to this recreation at the present time, indicated apparently that his anxiety about his father had been relieved; so that Isabel took her way to the drawing-room with much alertness. The drawing-room at Gardencourt was an apartment of great distances, and as the piano was placed at the end of it furthest removed from the door at which Isabel entered, her arrival was not noticed by the person seated before the instrument. This person was neither Ralph nor his mother; it was a lady whom Isabel immediately saw to be a stranger to herself, although her back was presented to the door. This back—an ample and well-dressed one—Isabel contemplated for some moments in surprise. The lady was of course a visitor who had arrived during her absence, and who had not been mentioned by either of the servants—one of them her aunt's maid—of whom she had had speech since her return. Isabel had already learned, however, that the British domestic is not effusive, and she was particularly conscious of having been treated with dryness by her aunt's maid, whose offered assistance the young lady from Albany—versed, as young ladies are in Albany, in the very metaphysics of the toilet—had perhaps made too light of. The arrival of a visitor was far from disagreeable to Isabel; she had not yet divested herself of a youthful impression that each new acquaintance would exert some momentous influence upon her life. By the time she had made these reflections she became aware that the lady at the piano played remarkably well. She was playing something of Beethoven's—Isabel knew not what, but she recognised Beethoven—and she touched the piano softly and discreetly, but with evident skill. Her touch was that of an artist; Isabel sat down noiselessly on the nearest chair and waited till the end of the piece. When it was finished she felt a strong desire to thank the player, and rose from her seat to do so, while at the same time the lady at the piano turned quickly round, as if she had become aware of her presence.

"That is very beautiful, and your playing makes it more beautiful still," said Isabel, with all the young radiance with which she usually uttered a truthful rapture.

"You don't think I disturbed Mr. Touchett, then?" the musician answered, as sweetly as this compliment deserved. "The house is so large, and his room so far away, that I thought I might venture—especially as I played just—just *du bout des doigts*."

"She is a Frenchwoman," Isabel said to herself; "she says that as if she were French." And this supposition made the stranger more interesting to our speculative heroine. "I hope my uncle is doing well," Isabel added. "I should think that to hear such lovely music as that would really make him feel better."

The lady gave a discriminating smile.

"I am afraid there are moments in life when even Beethoven has nothing to say to us. We must admit, however, that they are our worst moments."

"I am not in that state now," said Isabel. "On the contrary, I should be so glad if you would play something more."

"If it will give you pleasure—most willingly." And this obliging person took her place again, and struck a few chords, while Isabel sat down nearer the instrument. Suddenly the stranger stopped, with her hands on the keys, half-turning and looking over her shoulder at the girl. She was forty years old, and she was not pretty; but she had a delightful expression. "Excuse me," she said; "but are you the niece—the young American?"

"I am my aunt's niece," said Isabel, with *naïveté*.

The lady at the piano sat still a moment longer, looking over her shoulder with her charming smile.

"That's very well," she said, " we are compatriots."

And then she began to play.

"Ah, then she is not French," Isabel murmured; and as the opposite supposition had made her interesting, it might have seemed that this revelation would have diminished her effectiveness. But such was not the fact; for Isabel, as she listened to the music, found much stimulus to conjecture in the fact that an American should so strongly resemble a foreign woman.

Her companion played in the same manner as before, softly and solemnly, and while she played the shadows deepened in the room. The autumn twilight gathered in, and from her place Isabel could see the rain, which had now begun in earnest, washing the cold-looking lawn, and the wind shaking the great trees. At last, when the music had ceased, the lady got up, and, coming to her auditor, smiling, before Isabel had time to thank her again, said—

"I am very glad you have come back; I have heard a great deal about you."

Isabel thought her a very attractive person; but she nevertheless said, with a certain abruptness, in answer to this speech—

"From whom have you heard about me?"

The stranger hesitated a single moment, and then—

"From your uncle," she answered. "I have been here three days, and the first day he let me come and pay him a visit in his room. Then he talked constantly of you."

"As you didn't know me, that must have bored you."

"It made me want to know you. All the more that since then—your aunt being so much with Mr. Touchett—I have been quite alone, and have got rather tired of my own society. I have not chosen a good moment for my visit."

A servant had come in with lamps, and was presently followed by another, bearing the tea-tray. On the appearance of this repast Mrs. Touchett had apparently been notified, for she now arrived and addressed herself to the tea-pot. Her greeting to her niece did not differ materially from her manner of raising the lid of this receptacle in order to glance at the contents: in neither act was it becoming to make a show of avidity. Questioned about her husband, she was unable to say that he was better; but the local doctor was with him, and much light was expected from this gentleman's consultation with Sir Matthew Hope.

"I suppose you two ladies have made acquaintance?" she said. "If you have not, I recommend you to do so; for so long as we continue—Ralph and I—to cluster about Mr. Touchett's bed, you are not likely to have much society but each other."

"I know nothing about you but that you are a great musician," Isabel said to the visitor.

"There is a good deal more than that to know," Mrs. Touchett affirmed, in her little dry tone.

"A very little of it, I am sure, will content Miss Archer!" the lady exclaimed, with a light laugh. "I am an old friend of your aunt's—I have lived much in Florence—I am Madame Merle."

She made this last announcement as if she were referring to a person of tolerably distinct identity.

For Isabel, however, it represented but little; she could only continue to feel that Madame Merle had a charming manner.

"She is not a foreigner, in spite of her name," said Mrs.

Touchett. "She was born—I always forget where you were born."

"It is hardly worth while I should tell you, then."

"On the contrary," said Mrs. Touchett, who rarely missed a logical point; "if I remembered, your telling me would be quite superfluous."

Madame Merle glanced at Isabel with a fine, frank smile.

"I was born under the shadow of the national banner."

"She is too fond of mystery," said Mrs. Touchett; "that is her great fault."

"Ah," exclaimed Madame Merle, "I have great faults, but I don't think that is one of them; it certainly is not the greatest. I came into the world in the Brooklyn navy-yard. My father was a high officer in the United States navy, and had a post— a post of responsibility—in that establishment at the time. I suppose I ought to love the sea, but I hate it. That's why I don't return to America. I love the land; the great thing is to love something."

Isabel, as a dispassionate witness, had not been struck with the force of Mrs. Touchett's characterisation of her visitor, who had an expressive, communicative, responsive face, by no means of the sort which, to Isabel's mind, suggested a secretive disposition. It was a face that told of a rich nature and of quick and liberal impulses, and though it had no regular beauty was in the highest degree agreeable to contemplate.

Madame Merle was a tall, fair, plump woman; everything in her person was round and replete, though without those accumulations which minister to indolence. Her features were thick, but there was a graceful harmony among them, and her complexion had a healthy clearness. She had a small grey eye, with a great deal of light in it—an eye incapable of dulness, and, according to some people, incapable of tears; and a wide, firm mouth, which, when she smiled, drew itself upward to the left side, in a manner that most people thought very odd, some very affected, and a few very graceful. Isabel inclined to range herself in the last category. Madame Merle had thick, fair hair, which was arranged with picturesque simplicity, and a large white hand, of a perfect shape—a shape so perfect that its owner, preferring to leave it unadorned, wore no rings. Isabel had taken her at first, as we have seen, for a

Frenchwoman; but extended observation led her to say to herself that Madame Merle might be a German—a German of rank, a countess, a princess. Isabel would never have supposed that she had been born in Brooklyn—though she could doubtless not have justified her assumption that the air of distinction, possessed by Madame Merle in so eminent a degree, was inconsistent with such a birth. It was true that the national banner had floated immediately over the spot of the lady's nativity, and the breezy freedom of the stars and stripes might have shed an influence upon the attitude which she then and there took towards life. And yet Madame Merle had evidently nothing of the fluttered, flapping quality of a morsel of bunting in the wind; her deportment expressed the repose and confidence which come from a large experience. Experience, however, had not quenched her youth; it had simply made her sympathetic and supple. She was in a word a woman of ardent impulses, kept in admirable order. What an ideal combination! thought Isabel.

She made these reflections while the three ladies sat at their tea; but this ceremony was interrupted before long by the arrival of the great doctor from London, who had been immediately ushered into the drawing-room. Mrs. Touchett took him off to the library, to confer with him in private; and then Madame Merle and Isabel parted, to meet again at dinner. The idea of seeing more of this interesting woman did much to mitigate Isabel's perception of the melancholy that now hung over Gardencourt.

When she came into the drawing-room before dinner she found the place empty; but in the course of a moment Ralph arrived. His anxiety about his father had been lightened; Sir Matthew Hope's view of his condition was less sombre than Ralph's had been. The doctor recommended that the nurse alone should remain with the old man for the next three or four hours; so that Ralph, his mother, and the great physician himself, were free to dine at table. Mrs. Touchett and Sir Matthew came in; Madame Merle was the last to appear.

Before she came, Isabel spoke of her to Ralph, who was standing before the fireplace.

"Pray who is Madame Merle?"

"The cleverest woman I know, not excepting yourself," said Ralph.

"I thought she seemed very pleasant."

"I was sure you would think her pleasant," said Ralph.

"Is that why you invited her?"

"I didn't invite her, and when we came back from London I didn't know she was here. No one invited her. She is a friend of my mother's, and just after you and I went to town, my mother got a note from her. She had arrived in England (she usually lives abroad, though she has first and last spent a good deal of time here), and she asked leave to come down for a few days. Madame Merle is a woman who can make such proposals with perfect confidence; she is so welcome wherever she goes. And with my mother there could be no question of hesitating; she is the one person in the world whom my mother very much admires. If she were not herself (which she after all much prefers), she would like to be Madame Merle. It would, indeed, be a great change."

"Well, she is very charming," said Isabel. "And she plays beautifully."

"She does everything beautifully. She is complete."

Isabel looked at her cousin a moment. "You don't like her."

"On the contrary, I was once in love with her."

"And she didn't care for you, and that's why you don't like her."

"How can we have discussed such things? M. Merle was then living."

"Is he dead now?"

"So she says."

"Don't you believe her?"

"Yes, because the statement agrees with the probabilities. The husband of Madame Merle would be likely to pass away."

Isabel gazed at her cousin again. "I don't know what you mean. You mean something—that you don't mean. What was M. Merle?"

"The husband of Madame."

"You are very odious. Has she any children?"

"Not the least little child—fortunately."

"Fortunately?"

"I mean fortunately for the child; she would be sure to spoil it."

Isabel was apparently on the point of assuring her cousin for the third time that he was odious; but the discussion was interrupted by the arrival of the lady who was the topic of it. She came rustling in quickly, apologising for being late, fastening a bracelet, dressed in dark blue satin, which exposed a white bosom that was ineffectually covered by a curious silver necklace. Ralph offered her his arm with the exaggerated alertness of a man who was no longer a lover.

Even if this had still been his condition, however, Ralph had other things to think about. The great doctor spent the night at Gardencourt, and returning to London on the morrow, after another consultation with Mr. Touchett's own medical adviser, concurred in Ralph's desire that he should see the patient again on the day following. On the day following Sir Matthew Hope reappeared at Gardencourt, and on this occasion took a less encouraging view of the old man, who had grown worse in the twenty-four hours. His feebleness was extreme, and to his son, who constantly sat by his bedside, it often seemed that his end was at hand. The local doctor, who was a very sagacious man, and in whom Ralph had secretly more confidence than in his distinguished colleague, was constantly in attendance, and Sir Matthew Hope returned several times to Gardencourt. Mr. Touchett was much of the time unconscious; he slept a great deal; he rarely spoke. Isabel had a great desire to be useful to him, and was allowed to watch with him several times when his other attendants (of whom Mrs. Touchett was not the least regular) went to take rest. He never seemed to know her, and she always said to herself—"Suppose he should die while I am sitting here;" an idea which excited her and kept her awake. Once he opened his eyes for a while and fixed them upon her intelligently, but when she went to him, hoping he would recognise her, he closed them and relapsed into unconsciousness. The day after this, however, he revived for a longer time; but on this occasion Ralph was with him alone. The old man began to talk, much to his son's satisfaction, who assured him that they should presently have him sitting up.

"No, my boy," said Mr. Touchett, "not unless you bury me

in a sitting posture, as some of the ancients—was it the ancients?—used to do."

"Ah, daddy, don't talk about that," Ralph murmured. "You must not deny that you are getting better."

"There will be no need of my denying it if you don't say so," the old man answered. "Why should we prevaricate, just at the last? We never prevaricated before. I have got to die some time, and it's better to die when one is sick than when one is well. I am very sick—as sick as I shall ever be. I hope you don't want to prove that I shall ever be worse than this? That would be too bad. You don't? Well then."

Having made this excellent point he became quiet, but the next time that Ralph was with him he again addressed himself to conversation. The nurse had gone to her supper and Ralph was alone with him, having just relieved Mrs. Touchett, who had been on guard since dinner. The room was lighted only by the flickering fire, which of late had become necessary, and Ralph's tall shadow was projected upon the wall and ceiling, with an outline constantly varying but always grotesque.

"Who is that with me—is it my son?" the old man asked.

"Yes, it's your son, daddy."

"And is there no one else?"

"No one else."

Mr. Touchett said nothing for a while; and then, "I want to talk a little," he went on.

"Won't it tire you?" Ralph inquired.

"It won't matter if it does. I shall have a long rest. I want to talk about you."

Ralph had drawn nearer to the bed; he sat leaning forward, with his hand on his father's. "You had better select a brighter topic," he said.

"You were always bright; I used to be proud of your brightness. I should like so much to think that you would do something."

"If you leave us," said Ralph, "I shall do nothing but miss you."

"That is just what I don't want; it's what I want to talk about. You must get a new interest."

"I don't want a new interest, daddy. I have more old ones than I know what to do with."

The old man lay there looking at his son; his face was the face of the dying, but his eyes were the eyes of Daniel Touchett. He seemed to be reckoning over Ralph's interests. "Of course you have got your mother," he said at last. "You will take care of her."

"My mother will always take care of herself," Ralph answered.

"Well," said his father, "perhaps as she grows older she will need a little help."

"I shall not see that. She will outlive me."

"Very likely she will; but that's no reason—" Mr. Touchett let his phrase die away in a helpless but not exactly querulous sigh, and remained silent again.

"Don't trouble yourself about us," said his son. "My mother and I get on very well together, you know."

"You get on by always being apart; that's not natural."

"If you leave us, we shall probably see more of each other."

"Well," the old man observed, with wandering irrelevance, "it cannot be said that my death will make much difference in your mother's life."

"It will probably make more than you think."

"Well, she'll have more money," said Mr. Touchett. "I have left her a good wife's portion, just as if she had been a good wife."

"She has been one, daddy, according to her own theory. She has never troubled you."

"Ah, some troubles are pleasant," Mr. Touchett murmured. "Those you have given me, for instance. But your mother has been less—less—what shall I call it? less out of the way since I have been ill. I presume she knows I have noticed it."

"I shall certainly tell her so; I am so glad you mention it."

"It won't make any difference to her; she doesn't do it to please me. She does it to please—to please—" And he lay a while, trying to think why she did it. "She does it to please herself. But that is not what I want to talk about," he added. "It's about you. You will be very well off."

"Yes," said Ralph, "I know that. But I hope you have not forgotten the talk we had a year ago—when I told you exactly what money I should need and begged you to make some good use of the rest."

"Yes, yes, I remember. I made a new will—in a few days. I suppose it was the first time such a thing had happened—a young man trying to get a will made against him."

"It is not against me," said Ralph. "It would be against me to have a large property to take care of. It is impossible for a man in my state of health to spend much money, and enough is as good as a feast."

"Well, you will have enough—and something over. There will be more than enough for one—there will be enough for two."

"That's too much," said Ralph.

"Ah, don't say that. The best thing you can do, when I am gone, will be to marry."

Ralph had foreseen what his father was coming to, and this suggestion was by no means novel. It had long been Mr. Touchett's most ingenious way of expressing the optimistic view of his son's health. Ralph had usually treated it humorously; but present circumstances made the humorous tone impossible. He simply fell back in his chair and returned his father's appealing gaze in silence.

"If I, with a wife who hasn't been very fond of me, have had a very happy life," said the old man, carrying his ingenuity further still, "what a life might you not have, if you should marry a person different from Mrs. Touchett. There are more different from her than there are like her."

Ralph still said nothing; and after a pause his father asked softly—"What do you think of your cousin?"

At this Ralph started, meeting the question with a rather fixed smile. "Do I understand you to propose that I should marry Isabel?"

"Well, that's what it comes to in the end. Don't you like her?"

"Yes, very much." And Ralph got up from his chair and wandered over to the fire. He stood before it an instant and then he stooped and stirred it, mechanically. "I like Isabel very much," he repeated.

"Well," said his father, "I know she likes you. She told me so."

"Did she remark that she would like to marry me?"

"No, but she can't have anything against you. And she is

the most charming young lady I have ever seen. And she would be good to you. I have thought a great deal about it."

"So have I," said Ralph, coming back to the bedside again. "I don't mind telling you that."

"You *are* in love with her, then? I should think you would be. It's as if she came over on purpose."

"No, I am not in love with her; but I should be if—if certain things were different."

"Ah, things are always different from what they might be," said the old man. "If you wait for them to change, you will never do anything. I don't know whether you know," he went on; "but I suppose there is no harm in my alluding to it in such an hour as this: there was some one wanted to marry Isabel the other day, and she wouldn't have him."

"I know she refused Lord Warburton; he told me himself."

"Well, that proves that there is a chance for somebody else."

"Somebody else took his chance the other day in London—and got nothing by it."

"Was it you?" Mr. Touchett asked, eagerly.

"No, it was an older friend; a poor gentleman who came over from America to see about it."

"Well, I am sorry for him. But it only proves what I say—that the way is open to you."

"If it is, dear father, it is all the greater pity that I am unable to tread it. I haven't many convictions; but I have three or four that I hold strongly. One is that people, on the whole, had better not marry their cousins. Another is, that people in an advanced stage of pulmonary weakness had better not marry at all."

The old man raised his feeble hand and moved it to and fro a little before his face. "What do you mean by that? You look at things in a way that would make everything wrong. What sort of a cousin is a cousin that you have never seen for more than twenty years of her life? We are all each other's cousins, and if we stopped at that the human race would die out. It is just the same with your weak lungs. You are a great deal better than you used to be. All you want is to lead a natural life. It is a great deal more natural to marry a pretty young lady that you are in love with than it is to remain single on false principles."

"I am not in love with Isabel," said Ralph.

"You said just now that you would be if you didn't think it was wrong. I want to prove to you that it isn't wrong."

"It will only tire you, dear daddy," said Ralph, who marvelled at his father's tenacity and at his finding strength to insist. "Then where shall we all be?"

"Where shall you be if I don't provide for you? You won't have anything to do with the bank, and you won't have me to take care of. You say you have got so many interests; but I can't make them out."

Ralph leaned back in his chair, with folded arms; his eyes were fixed for some time in meditation. At last, with the air of a man fairly mustering courage—"I take a great interest in my cousin," he said, "but not the sort of interest you desire. I shall not live many years; but I hope I shall live long enough to see what she does with herself. She is entirely independent of me; I can exercise very little influence upon her life. But I should like to do something for her."

"What should you like to do?"

"I should like to put a little wind in her sails."

"What do you mean by that?"

"I should like to put it into her power to do some of the things she wants. She wants to see the world, for instance. I should like to put money in her purse."

"Ah, I am glad you have thought of that," said the old man. "But I have thought of it too. I have left her a legacy—five thousand pounds."

"That is capital; it is very kind of you. But I should like to do a little more."

Something of that veiled acuteness with which it had been, on Daniel Touchett's part, the habit of a lifetime to listen to a financial proposition, still lingered in the face in which the invalid had not obliterated the man of business. "I shall be happy to consider it," he said, softly.

"Isabel is poor, then. My mother tells me that she has but a few hundred dollars a year. I should like to make her rich."

"What do you mean by rich?"

"I call people rich when they are able to gratify their imagination. Isabel has a great deal of imagination."

"So have you, my son," said Mr. Touchett, listening very attentively, but a little confusedly.

"You tell me I shall have money enough for two. What I want is that you should kindly relieve me of my superfluity and give it to Isabel. Divide my inheritance into two equal halves, and give the second half to her."

"To do what she likes with?"

"Absolutely what she likes."

"And without an equivalent?"

"What equivalent could there be?"

"The one I have already mentioned."

"Her marrying—some one or other? It's just to do away with anything of that sort that I make my suggestion. If she has an easy income she will never have to marry for a support. She wishes to be free, and your bequest will make her free."

"Well, you seem to have thought it out," said Mr. Touchett. "But I don't see why you appeal to me. The money will be yours, and you can easily give it to her yourself."

Ralph started a little. "Ah, dear father, *I* can't offer Isabel money!"

The old man gave a groan. "Don't tell me you are not in love with her! Do you want me to have the credit of it?"

"Entirely. I should like it simply to be a clause in your will, without the slightest reference to me."

"Do you want me to make a new will, then?"

"A few words will do it; you can attend to it the next time you feel a little lively."

"You must telegraph to Mr. Hilary, then. I will do nothing without my solicitor."

"You shall see Mr. Hilary to-morrow."

"He will think we have quarrelled, you and I," said the old man.

"Very probably; I shall like him to think it," said Ralph, smiling; "and to carry out the idea, I give you notice that I shall be very sharp with you."

The humour of this appeared to touch his father; he lay a little while taking it in.

"I will do anything you like," he said at last; "but I'm not sure it's right. You say you want to put wind in her sails; but aren't you afraid of putting too much?"

"I should like to see her going before the breeze!" Ralph answered.

"You speak as if it were for your entertainment."

"So it is, a good deal."

"Well, I don't think I understand," said Mr. Touchett, with a sigh. "Young men are very different from what I was. When I cared for a girl—when I was young—I wanted to do more than look at her. You have scruples that I shouldn't have had, and you have ideas that I shouldn't have had either. You say that Isabel wants to be free, and that her being rich will keep her from marrying for money. Do you think that she is a girl to do that?"

"By no means. But she has less money than she has ever had before; her father gave her everything, because he used to spend his capital. She has nothing but the crumbs of that feast to live on, and she doesn't really know how meagre they are—she has yet to learn it. My mother has told me all about it. Isabel will learn it when she is really thrown upon the world, and it would be very painful to me to think of her coming to the consciousness of a lot of wants that she should be unable to satisfy."

"I have left her five thousand pounds. She can satisfy a good many wants with that."

"She can indeed. But she would probably spend it in two or three years."

"You think she would be extravagant then?"

"Most certainly," said Ralph, smiling serenely.

Poor Mr. Touchett's acuteness was rapidly giving place to pure confusion. "It would merely be a question of time, then, her spending the larger sum?"

"No, at first I think she would plunge into that pretty freely; she would probably make over a part of it to each of her sisters. But after that she would come to her senses, remember that she had still a lifetime before her, and live within her means."

"Well, you *have* worked it out," said the old man, with a sigh. "You do take an interest in her, certainly."

"You can't consistently say I go too far. You wished me to go further."

"Well, I don't know," the old man answered. "I don't think I enter into your spirit. It seems to me immoral."

"Immoral, dear daddy?"

"Well, I don't know that it's right to make everything so easy for a person."

"It surely depends upon the person. When the person is good, your making things easy is all to the credit of virtue. To facilitate the execution of good impulses, what can be a nobler act?"

This was a little difficult to follow, and Mr. Touchett considered it for a while. At last he said—

"Isabel is a sweet young girl; but do you think she is as good as that?"

"She is as good as her best opportunities," said Ralph.

"Well," Mr. Touchett declared, "she ought to get a great many opportunities for sixty thousand pounds."

"I have no doubt she will."

"Of course I will do what you want," said the old man. "I only want to understand it a little."

"Well, dear daddy, don't you understand it now?" his son asked, caressingly. "If you don't, we won't take any more trouble about it; we will leave it alone."

Mr. Touchett lay silent a long time. Ralph supposed that he had given up the attempt to understand it. But at last he began again—

"Tell me this first. Doesn't it occur to you that a young lady with sixty thousand pounds may fall a victim to the fortune-hunters?"

"She will hardly fall a victim to more than one."

"Well, one is too many."

"Decidedly. That's a risk, and it has entered into my calculation. I think it's appreciable, but I think it's small, and I am prepared to take it."

Poor Mr. Touchett's acuteness had passed into perplexity, and his perplexity now passed into admiration.

"Well, you *have* gone into it!" he exclaimed. "But I don't see what good you are to get of it."

Ralph leaned over his father's pillows and gently smoothed

them; he was aware that their conversation had been pro-longed to a dangerous point. "I shall get just the good that I said just now I wished to put into Isabel's reach—that of having gratified my imagination. But it's scandalous, the way I have taken advantage of you!"

XIX

As MRS. TOUCHETT had foretold, Isabel and Madame Merle were thrown much together during the illness of their host, and if they had not become intimate it would have been almost a breach of good manners. Their manners were of the best; but in addition to this they happened to please each other. It is perhaps too much to say that they swore an eternal friendship; but tacitly, at least, they called the future to witness. Isabel did so with a perfectly good conscience, although she would have hesitated to admit that she was intimate with her new friend in the sense which she privately attached to this term. She often wondered, indeed, whether she ever had been, or ever could be, intimate with any one. She had an ideal of friendship, as well as of several other sentiments, and it did not seem to her in this case—it had not seemed to her in other cases—that the actual completely expressed it. But she often reminded herself that there were essential reasons why one's ideal could not become concrete. It was a thing to believe in, not to see—a matter of faith, not of experience. Experience, however, might supply us with very creditable imitations of it, and the part of wisdom was to make the best of these. Certainly, on the whole, Isabel had never encountered a more agreeable and interesting woman than Madame Merle; she had never met a woman who had less of that fault which is the principal obstacle to friendship—the air of reproducing the more tiresome parts of one's own personality. The gates of the girl's confidence were opened wider than they had ever been; she said things to Madame Merle that she had not yet said to any one. Sometimes she took alarm at her candour; it was as if she had given to a comparative stranger the key to her cabinet of jewels. These spiritual gems were the only ones of any magnitude that Isabel possessed; but that was all the greater reason why they should be carefully guarded. Afterwards, however, the girl always said to herself that one should never regret a generous error, and that if Madame Merle had not the merits she attributed to her, so much the worse for Madame Merle. There was no doubt she had great merits—she was a charming, sympathetic, intelligent, cultivated woman. More than this (for it had not been Isabel's ill-fortune to go through life without meeting several persons of her own sex, of whom no less could fairly be said), she was rare, she was superior, she was pre-eminent. There are a great many amiable people in the world, and Madame Merle was far from being vulgarly good-natured and restlessly witty. She knew how to think—an accomplishment rare in women; and she had thought to very good purpose. Of course, too, she knew how to feel; Isabel could not have spent a week with her without being sure of that. This was, indeed, Madame Merle's great talent, her most perfect gift. Life had told upon her; she had felt it strongly, and it was part of the satisfaction that Isabel found in her society that when the girl talked of what she was pleased to call serious matters, her companion understood her so easily and quickly. Emotion, it is true, had become with her rather historic; she made no secret of the fact that the fountain of sentiment, thanks to having been rather violently tapped at one period, did not flow quite so freely as of yore. Her pleasure was now to judge rather than to feel; she freely admitted that of old she had been rather foolish, and now she pretended to be wise.

"I judge more than I used to," she said to Isabel; "but it seems to me that I have earned the right. One can't judge till one is forty; before that we are too eager, too hard, too cruel, and in addition too ignorant. I am sorry for you; it will be a long time before you are forty. But every gain is a loss of some kind; I often think that after forty one can't really feel. The freshness, the quickness have certainly gone. You will keep them longer than most people; it will be a great satisfaction to me to see you some years hence. I want to see what life makes of you. One thing is certain—it can't spoil you. It may pull you about horribly; but I defy it to break you up."

Isabel received this assurance as a young soldier, still panting from a slight skirmish in which he has come off with honour, might receive a pat on the shoulder from his colonel. Like such a recognition of merit, it seemed to come with authority. How could the lightest word do less, of a person who was prepared to say, of almost everything Isabel told her— "Oh, I have been in that, my dear; it passes, like everything else." Upon many of her interlocutors, Madame Merle might have produced an irritating effect; it was so difficult to surprise her. But Isabel, though by no means incapable of desiring to be effective, had not at present this motive. She was too sincere, too interested in her judicious companion. And then, moreover, Madame Merle never said such things in the tone of triumph or of boastfulness; they dropped from her like grave confessions.

A period of bad weather had settled down upon Gardencourt; the days grew shorter, and there was an end to the pretty tea-parties on the lawn. But Isabel had long in-door conversations with her fellow-visitor, and in spite of the rain the two ladies often sallied forth for a walk, equipped with the defensive apparatus which the English climate and the English genius have between them brought to such perfection. Madame Merle was very appreciative; she liked almost everything, including the English rain. "There is always a little of it, and never too much at once," she said; "and it never wets you, and it always smells good." She declared that in England the pleasures of smell were great—that in this inimitable island there was a certain mixture of fog and beer and soot which, however odd it might sound, was the national aroma, and was most agreeable to the nostril; and she used to lift the sleeve of her British overcoat and bury her nose in it, to inhale the clear, fine odour of the wool. Poor Ralph Touchett, as soon as the autumn had begun to define itself, became almost a prisoner; in bad weather he was unable to step out of the house, and he used sometimes to stand at one of the windows, with his hands in his pockets, and, with a countenance half rueful, half critical, watch Isabel and Madame Merle as they walked down the avenue under a pair of umbrellas. The roads about Gardencourt were so firm, even in the worst weather, that the two ladies always came back with a healthy glow in their cheeks, looking at the soles of their neat, stout boots, and declaring that their walk had done them inexpressible good. Before lunch Madame Merle was always engaged; Isabel admired the inveteracy with which she occupied herself. Our heroine had always passed for a person of resources and had taken a certain pride in being one; but she envied the talents, the accomplishments, the aptitudes, of Madame Merle. She found herself desiring to emulate them, and in this and other ways Madame Merle presented herself as a model. "I should like to be like that!" Isabel secretly exclaimed, more than once, as one of her friend's numerous facets suddenly caught the light, and before long she knew that she had learned a lesson from this exemplary woman. It took no very long time, indeed, for Isabel to feel that she was, as the phrase is, under an influence. "What is the harm," she asked herself, "so long as it is a good one? The more one is under a good influence the better. The only thing is to see our steps as we take them—to understand them as we go. That I think I shall always do. I needn't be afraid of becoming too pliable; it is my fault that I am not pliable enough." It is said that imitation is the sincerest flattery; and if Isabel was tempted to reproduce in her deportment some of the most graceful features of that of her friend, it was not so much because she desired herself to shine as because she wished to hold up the lamp for Madame Merle. She liked her extremely; but she admired her even more than she liked her. She sometimes wondered what Henrietta Stackpole would say to her thinking so much of this brilliant fugitive from Brooklyn; and had a conviction that Henrietta would not approve of it. Henrietta would not like Madame Merle; for reasons that she could not have defined, this truth came home to Isabel. On the other hand she was equally sure that should the occasion offer, her new friend would accommodate herself perfectly to her old; Madame Merle was too humorous, too observant, not to do justice to Henrietta, and on becoming acquainted with her would probably give the measure of a tact which Miss Stackpole could not hope to emulate. She appeared to have, in her experience, a touchstone for everything, and somewhere in the capacious pocket of her genial memory she would find the key to Henrietta's virtues. "That is the great thing," Isabel reflected; "that is the supreme good fortune: to be in a better position for appreciating people than they are for appreciating you." And she added that this, when one considered it, was simply the essence of the aristocratic situation. In this light, if in none other, one should aim at the aristocratic situation.

I cannot enumerate all the links in the chain which led Isabel to think of Madame Merle's situation as aristocratic—a view of it never expressed in any reference made to it by that lady herself. She had known great things and great people, but she had never played a great part. She was one of the small ones of the earth; she had not been born to honours; she knew the world too well to be guilty of any fatuous illusions on the subject of her own place in it. She had known a good many of the fortunate few, and was perfectly aware of those points at which their fortune differed from hers. But if by her own measure she was nothing of a personage, she had yet, to Isabel's imagination, a sort of greatness. To be so graceful, so gracious, so wise, so good, and to make so light of it all—that was really to be a great lady; especially when one looked so much like one. If Madame Merle, however, made light of her advantages as regards the world, it was not because she had not, for her own entertainment, taken them, as I have intimated, as seriously as possible. Her natural talents, for instance; these she had zealously cultivated. After breakfast she wrote a succession of letters; her correspondence was a source of surprise to Isabel when they sometimes walked together to the village post-office, to deposit Madame Merle's contribution to the mail. She knew a multitude of people, and, as she told Isabel, something was always turning up to be written about. Of painting she was devotedly fond, and made no more of taking a sketch than of pulling off her gloves. At Gardencourt she was perpetually taking advantage of an hour's sunshine to go out with a camp-stool and a box of water-colours. That she was a brilliant musician we have already perceived, and it was evidence of the fact that when she seated herself at the piano, as she always did in the evening, her listeners resigned themselves without a murmur to losing the entertainment of her talk. Isabel, since she had known Madame Merle, felt ashamed of her own playing, which she now looked upon as meagre and artless; and indeed, though she had been thought to play very well, the loss to society when, in taking her place upon the music-stool, she turned her back to the room, was usually deemed greater than the gain. When Madame Merle was neither writing, nor painting, nor touching the piano, she was usually employed upon wonderful morsels of picturesque embroidery, cushions, curtains, decorations for the chimney-piece; a sort of work in which her bold, free invention was as remarkable as the agility of her needle. She was never idle, for when she was engaged in none of the ways I have mentioned, she was either reading (she appeared to Isabel to read everything important), or walking out, or playing patience with the cards, or talking with her fellow inmates. And with all this, she always had the social quality; she never was preoccupied, she never pressed too hard. She laid down her pastimes as easily as she took them up; she worked and talked at the same time, and she appeared to attach no importance to anything she did. She gave away her sketches and tapestries; she rose from the piano, or remained there, according to the convenience of her auditors, which she always unerringly divined. She was, in short, a most comfortable, profitable, agreeable person to live with. If for Isabel she had a fault, it was that she was not natural; by which the girl meant, not that she was affected or pretentious; for from these vulgar vices no woman could have been more exempt; but that her nature had been too much overlaid by custom and her angles too much smoothed. She had become too flexible, too supple; she was too finished, too civilised. She was, in a word, too perfectly the social animal that man and woman are supposed to have been intended to be; and she had rid herself of every remnant of that tonic wildness which we may assume to have belonged even to the most amiable persons in the ages before country-house life was the fashion. Isabel found it difficult to think of Madame Merle as an isolated figure; she existed only in her relations with her fellow-mortals. Isabel often wondered what her relations might be with her own soul. She always ended, however, by feeling that having a charming surface does not necessarily prove that one is superficial; this was an illusion in which, in her youth, she had only just sufficiently escaped being nourished. Madame Merle was not superficial—not she. She was deep; and her nature spoke none the less in her behaviour because it spoke a conventional language. "What is language at all but a convention?" said Isabel. "She has the good taste not to pretend, like some people I have met, to express herself by original signs."

"I am afraid you have suffered much," Isabel once found

occasion to say to her, in response to some allusion that she had dropped.

"What makes you think that?" Madame Merle asked, with a picturesque smile. "I hope I have not the pose of a martyr."

"No; but you sometimes say things that I think people who have always been happy would not have found out."

"I have not always been happy," said Madame Merle, smiling still, but with a mock gravity, as if she were telling a child a secret. "What a wonderful thing!"

"A great many people give me the impression of never having felt anything very much," Isabel answered.

"It's very true; there are more iron pots, I think, than porcelain ones. But you may depend upon it that every one has something; even the hardest iron pots have a little bruise, a little hole, somewhere. I flatter myself that I am rather stout porcelain; but if I must tell you the truth I have been chipped and cracked! I do very well for service yet, because I have been cleverly mended; and I try to remain in the cupboard—the quiet, dusky cupboard, where there is an odour of stale spices—as much as I can. But when I have to come out, and into a strong light, then, my dear, I am a horror!"

I know not whether it was on this occasion or some other, that when the conversation had taken the turn I have just indicated, she said to Isabel that some day she would relate her history. Isabel assured her that she should delight to listen to it, and reminded her more than once of this engagement. Madame Merle, however, appeared to desire a postponement, and at last frankly told the young girl that she must wait till they knew each other better. This would certainly happen; a long friendship lay before them. Isabel assented, but at the same time asked Madame Merle if she could not trust her—if she feared a betrayal of confidence.

"It is not that I am afraid of your repeating what I say," the elder lady answered; "I am afraid, on the contrary, of your taking it too much to yourself. You would judge me too harshly; you are of the cruel age." She preferred for the present to talk to Isabel about Isabel, and exhibited the greatest interest in our heroine's history, her sentiments, opinions, prospects. She made her chatter, and listened to her chatter with inexhaustible sympathy and good nature. In all this there was something flattering to the girl, who knew that Madame Merle knew a great many distinguished people, and had lived, as Mrs. Touchett said, in the best company in Europe. Isabel thought the better of herself for enjoying the favour of a person who had so large a field of comparison; and it was perhaps partly to gratify this sense of profiting by comparison that she often begged her friend to tell her about the people she knew. Madame Merle had been a dweller in many lands, and had social ties in a dozen different countries. "I don't pretend to be learned," she would say, "but I think I know my Europe;" and she spoke one day of going to Sweden to stay with an old friend, and another of going to Wallachia to follow up a new acquaintance. With England, where she had often stayed, she was thoroughly familiar; and for Isabel's benefit threw a great deal of light upon the customs of the country and the character of the people, who "after all," as she was fond of saying, were the finest people in the world.

"You must not think it strange, her staying in the house at such a time as this, when Mr. Touchett is passing away," Mrs. Touchett remarked to Isabel. "She is incapable of doing anything indiscreet; she is the best-bred woman I know. It's a favour to me that she stays; she is putting off a lot of visits at great houses," said Mrs. Touchett, who never forgot that when she herself was in England her social value sank two or three degrees in the scale. "She has her pick of places; she is not in want of a shelter. But I have asked her to stay because I wish you to know her. I think it will be a good thing for you. Serena Merle has no faults."

"If I didn't already like her very much that description might alarm me," Isabel said.

"She never does anything wrong. I have brought you out here, and I wish to do the best for you. Your sister Lily told me that she hoped I would give you plenty of opportunities. I give you one in securing Madame Merle. She is one of the most brilliant women in Europe."

"I like her better than I like your description of her," Isabel persisted in saying.

"Do you flatter yourself that you will find a fault in her? I hope you will let me know when you do."

"That will be cruel—to you," said Isabel.

"You needn't mind me. You never will find one."

"Perhaps not; but I think I shall not miss it."

"She is always up to the mark!" said Mrs. Touchett.

Isabel after this said to Madame Merle that she hoped she knew Mrs. Touchett believed she had not a fault.

"I am obliged to you, but I am afraid your aunt has no perception of spiritual things," Madame Merle answered.

"Do you mean by that that you have spiritual faults?"

"Ah no; I mean nothing so flat! I mean that having no faults, for your aunt, means that one is never late for dinner—that is, for *her* dinner. I was not late, by the way, the other day, when you came back from London; the clock was just at eight when I came into the drawing-room; it was the rest of you that were before the time. It means that one answers a letter the day one gets it, and that when one comes to stay with her one doesn't bring too much luggage, and is careful not to be taken ill. For Mrs. Touchett those things constitute virtue; it's a blessing to be able to reduce it to its elements."

Madame Merle's conversation, it will be perceived, was enriched with bold, free touches of criticism, which, even when they had a restrictive effect, never struck Isabel as ill-natured. It never occurred to the girl, for instance, that Mrs. Touchett's accomplished guest was abusing her; and this for very good reasons. In the first place Isabel agreed with her; in the second Madame Merle implied that there was a great deal more to say; and in the third, to speak to one without ceremony of one's near relations was an agreeable sign of intimacy. These signs of intimacy multiplied as the days elapsed, and there was none of which Isabel was more sensible than of her companion's preference for making Miss Archer herself a topic. Though she alluded frequently to the incidents of her own life, she never lingered upon them; she was as little of an egotist as she was of a gossip.

"I am old, and stale, and faded," she said more than once; "I am of no more interest than last week's newspaper. You are young and fresh, and of to-day; you have the great thing—you have actuality. I once had it—we all have it for an hour. You, however, will have it for longer. Let us talk about you, then; you can say nothing that I shall not care to hear. It is a sign that I am growing old—that I like to talk

with younger people. I think it's a very pretty compensation.
If we can't have youth within us we can have it outside of us,
and I really think we see it and feel it better that way. Of
course we must be in sympathy with it—that I shall always
be. I don't know that I shall ever be ill-natured with old people—I hope not; there are certainly some old people that I
adore. But I shall never be ill-natured with the young; they
touch me too much. I give you *carte blanche*, then; you can
even be impertinent if you like; I shall let it pass. I talk as if I
were a hundred years old, you say? Well, I am, if you please;
I was born before the French Revolution. Ah, my dear *je
viens de loin*; I belong to the old world. But it is not of that I
wish to talk; I wish to talk about the new. You must tell me
more about America; you never tell me enough. Here I have
been since I was brought here as a helpless child, and it is
ridiculous, or rather it's scandalous, how little I know about
the land of my birth. There are a great many of us like that,
over here; and I must say I think we are a wretched set of
people. You should live in your own country; whatever it may
be you have your natural place there. If we are not good
Americans we are certainly poor Europeans; we have no natural place here. We are mere parasites, crawling over the surface; we haven't our feet in the soil. At least one can know it,
and not have illusions. A woman, perhaps, can get on; a
woman, it seems to me, has no natural place anywhere;
wherever she finds herself she has to remain on the surface
and, more or less, to crawl. You protest, my dear? you are
horrified? you declare you will never crawl? It is very true that
I don't see you crawling; you stand more upright than a good
many poor creatures. Very good; on the whole, I don't think
you will crawl. But the men, the Americans; *je vous demande
un peu*, what do they make of it over here? I don't envy them,
trying to arrange themselves. Look at poor Ralph Touchett;
what sort of a figure do you call that? Fortunately he has got
a consumption; I say fortunately, because it gives him something to do. His consumption is his career; it's a kind of position. You can say, 'Oh, Mr. Touchett, he takes care of his
lungs, he knows a great deal about climates.' But without
that, who would he be, what would he represent? 'Mr. Ralph
Touchett, an American who lives in Europe.' That signifies

absolutely nothing—it's impossible that anything should signify less. 'He is very cultivated,' they say; 'he has got a very pretty collection of old snuff-boxes.' The collection is all that is wanted to make it pitiful. I am tired of the sound of the word; I think it's grotesque. With the poor old father it's different; he has his identity, and it is rather a massive one. He represents a great financial house, and that, in our day, is as good as anything else. For an American, at any rate, that will do very well. But I persist in thinking your cousin is very lucky to have a chronic malady; so long as he doesn't die of it. It's much better than the snuff-boxes. If he were not ill, you say, he would do something?—he would take his father's place in the house. My poor child, I doubt it; I don't think he is at all fond of the house. However, you know him better than I, though I used to know him rather well, and he may have the benefit of the doubt. The worst case, I think, is a friend of mine, a countryman of ours, who lives in Italy (where he also was brought before he knew better), and who is one of the most delightful men I know. Some day you must know him. I will bring you together, and then you will see what I mean. He is Gilbert Osmond—he lives in Italy; that is all one can say about him. He is exceedingly clever, a man made to be distinguished; but, as I say, you exhaust the description when you say that he is Mr. Osmond, who lives in Italy. No career, no name, no position, no fortune, no past, no future, no anything. Oh yes, he paints, if you please— paints in water-colours, like me, only better than I. His painting is pretty bad; on the whole I am rather glad of that. Fortunately he is very indolent, so indolent that it amounts to a sort of position. He can say, 'Oh, I do nothing; I am too deadly lazy. You can do nothing to-day unless you get up at five o'clock in the morning.' In that way he becomes a sort of exception; you feel that he might do something if he would only rise early. He never speaks of his painting—to people at large; he is too clever for that. But he has a little girl—a dear little girl; he does speak of her. He is devoted to her, and if it were a career to be an excellent father he would be very distinguished. But I am afraid that is no better than the snuff-boxes; perhaps not even so good. Tell me what they do in America," pursued Madame Merle, who, it must be observed, parenthetically, did not deliver herself all at once of these reflections, which are presented in a cluster for the convenience of the reader. She talked of Florence, where Mr. Osmond lived, and where Mrs. Touchett occupied a mediæval palace; she talked of Rome, where she herself had a little *pied-à-terre*, with some rather good old damask. She talked of places, of people, and even, as the phrase is, of "subjects"; and from time to time she talked of their kind old host and of the prospect of his recovery. From the first she had thought this prospect small, and Isabel had been struck with the positive, discriminating, competent way which she took of the measure of his remainder of life. One evening she announced definitely that he would not live.

"Sir Matthew Hope told me so, as plainly as was proper," she said; "standing there, near the fire, before dinner. He makes himself very agreeable, the great doctor. I don't mean that his saying that has anything to do with it. But he says such things with great tact. I had said to him that I felt ill at my ease, staying here at such a time; it seemed to me so indiscreet—it was not as if I could nurse. 'You must remain, you must remain,' he answered; 'your office will come later.' Was not that a very delicate way both of saying that poor Mr. Touchett would go, and that I might be of some use as a consoler? In fact, however, I shall not be of the slightest use. Your aunt will console herself; she, and she alone, knows just how much consolation she will require. It would be a very delicate matter for another person to undertake to administer the dose. With your cousin it will be different; he will miss his father sadly. But I should never presume to condole with Mr. Ralph; we are not on those terms."

Madame Merle had alluded more than once to some undefined incongruity in her relations with Ralph Touchett; so Isabel took this occasion of asking her if they were not good friends.

"Perfectly, but he doesn't like me."

"What have you done to him?"

"Nothing whatever. But one has no need of a reason for that."

"For not liking you? I think one has need of a very good reason."

"You are very kind. Be sure you have one ready for the day when you begin."

"Begin to dislike you? I shall never begin."

"I hope not; because if you do, you will never end. That is the way with your cousin; he doesn't get over it. It's an antipathy of nature—if I can call it that when it is all on his side. I have nothing whatever against him, and don't bear him the least little grudge for not doing me justice. Justice is all I want. However, one feels that he is a gentleman, and would never say anything underhand about one. *Cartes sur table*," Madame Merle subjoined in a moment, "I am not afraid of him."

"I hope not, indeed," said Isabel, who added something about his being the kindest fellow living. She remembered, however, that on her first asking him about Madame Merle he had answered her in a manner which this lady might have thought injurious without being explicit. There was something between them, Isabel said to herself, but she said nothing more than this. If it were something of importance, it should inspire respect; if it were not, it was not worth her curiosity. With all her love of knowledge, Isabel had a natural shrinking from raising curtains and looking into unlighted corners. The love of knowledge co-existed in her mind with a still tenderer love of ignorance.

But Madame Merle sometimes said things that startled her, made her raise her clear eyebrows at the time, and think of the words afterwards.

"I would give a great deal to be your age again," she broke out once, with a bitterness which, though diluted in her customary smile, was by no means disguised by it. "If I could only begin again—if I could have my life before me!"

"Your life is before you yet," Isabel answered gently, for she was vaguely awe-struck.

"No; the best part is gone, and gone for nothing."

"Surely, not for nothing," said Isabel.

"Why not—what have I got? Neither husband, nor child, nor fortune, nor position, nor the traces of a beauty which I never had."

"You have friends, dear lady."

"I am not so sure!" cried Madame Merle.

"Ah, you are wrong. You have memories, talents——"

Madame Merle interrupted her.

"What have my talents brought me? Nothing but the need of using them still, to get through the hours, the years, to cheat myself with some pretence of action. As for my memories, the less said about them the better. You will be my friend till you find a better use for your friendship."

"It will be for you to see that I don't then," said Isabel.

"Yes; I would make an effort to keep you," Madame Merle rejoined, looking at her gravely. "When I say I should like to be your age," she went on, "I mean with your qualities—frank, generous, sincere, like you. In that case I should have made something better of my life."

"What should you have liked to do that you have not done?"

Madame Merle took a sheet of music—she was seated at the piano, and had abruptly wheeled about on the stool when she first spoke—and mechanically turned the leaves. At last she said—

"I am very ambitious!"

"And your ambitions have not been satisfied? They must have been great."

"They were great. I should make myself ridiculous by talking of them."

Isabel wondered what they could have been—whether Madame Merle had aspired to wear a crown. "I don't know what your idea of success may be, but you seem to me to have been successful. To me, indeed, you are an image of success."

Madame Merle tossed away the music with a smile.

"What is *your* idea of success?"

"You evidently think it must be very tame," said Isabel. "It is to see some dream of one's youth come true."

"Ah," Madame Merle exclaimed, "that I have never seen! But my dreams were so great—so preposterous. Heaven forgive me, I am dreaming now." And she turned back to the piano and began to play with energy.

On the morrow she said to Isabel that her definition of success had been very pretty, but frightfully sad. Measured in that way, who had succeeded? The dreams of one's youth, why they were enchanting, they were divine! Who had ever seen such things come to pass?

"I myself—a few of them," Isabel ventured to answer.

"Already? They must have been dreams of yesterday."

"I began to dream very young," said Isabel, smiling.

"Ah, if you mean the aspirations of your childhood—that of having a pink sash and a doll that could close her eyes."

"No, I don't mean that."

"Or a young man with a moustache going down on his knees to you."

"No, nor that either," Isabel declared, blushing.

Madame Merle gave a glance at her blush which caused it to deepen.

"I suspect that is what you do mean. We have all had the young man with the moustache. He is the inevitable young man; he doesn't count."

Isabel was silent for a moment, and then, with extreme and characteristic inconsequence—

"Why shouldn't he count? There are young men and young men."

"And yours was a paragon—is that what you mean?" cried her friend with a laugh. "If you have had the identical young man you dreamed of, then that was success, and I congratulate you. Only, in that case, why didn't you fly with him to his castle in the Apennines?"

"He has no castle in the Apennines."

"What has he? An ugly brick house in Fortieth Street? Don't tell me that; I refuse to recognise that as an ideal."

"I don't care anything about his house," said Isabel.

"That is very crude of you. When you have lived as long as I, you will see that every human being has his shell, and that you must take the shell into account. By the shell I mean the whole envelope of circumstances. There is no such thing as an isolated man or woman; we are each of us made up of a cluster of appurtenances. What do you call one's self? Where does it begin? where does it end? It overflows into everything that belongs to us—and then it flows back again. I know that a large part of myself is in the dresses I choose to wear. I have a great respect for *things*! One's self—for other people—is one's expression of one's self; and one's house, one's clothes, the book one reads, the company one keeps—these things are all expressive."

This was very metaphysical; not more so, however, than several observations Madame Merle had already made. Isabel was fond of metaphysics, but she was unable to accompany her friend into this bold analysis of the human personality.

"I don't agree with you," she said. "I think just the other way. I don't know whether I succeed in expressing myself, but I know that nothing else expresses me. Nothing that belongs to me is any measure of me; on the contrary, it's a limit, a barrier, and a perfectly arbitrary one. Certainly, the clothes which, as you say, I choose to wear, don't express me; and heaven forbid they should!"

"You dress very well," interposed Madame Merle, skilfully.

"Possibly; but I don't care to be judged by that. My clothes may express the dressmaker, but they don't express me. To begin with, it's not my own choice that I wear them; they are imposed upon me by society."

"Should you prefer to go without them?" Madame Merle inquired, in a tone which virtually terminated the discussion.

I am bound to confess, though it may cast some discredit upon the sketch I have given of the youthful loyalty which our heroine practised towards this accomplished woman, that Isabel had said nothing whatever to her about Lord Warburton, and had been equally reticent on the subject of Caspar Goodwood. Isabel had not concealed from her, however, that she had had opportunities of marrying, and had even let her know that they were of a highly advantageous kind. Lord Warburton had left Lockleigh, and was gone to Scotland, taking his sisters with him; and though he had written to Ralph more than once, to ask about Mr. Touchett's health, the girl was not liable to the embarrassment of such inquiries as, had he still been in the neighbourhood, he would probably have felt bound to make in person. He had admirable self-control, but she felt sure that if he had come to Gardencourt he would have seen Madame Merle, and that if he had seen her he would have liked her, and betrayed to her that he was in love with her young friend.

It so happened that during Madame Merle's previous visits to Gardencourt—each of them much shorter than the present one—he had either not been at Lockleigh or had not called at Mr. Touchett's. Therefore, though she knew him by name as the great man of that county, she had no cause to suspect him of being a suitor of Mrs. Touchett's freshly-imported niece.

"You have plenty of time," she had said to Isabel, in return for the mutilated confidences which Isabel made her, and which did not pretend to be perfect, though we have seen that at moments the girl had compunctions at having said so much. "I am glad you have done nothing yet—that you have it still to do. It is a very good thing for a girl to have refused a few good offers—so long, of course, as they are not the best she is likely to have. Excuse me if my tone seems horribly worldly; one must take that view sometimes. Only don't keep on refusing for the sake of refusing. It's a pleasant exercise of power; but accepting is after all an exercise of power as well. There is always the danger of refusing once too often. It was not the one I fell into—I didn't refuse often enough. You are an exquisite creature, and I should like to see you married to a prime minister. But speaking strictly, you know you are not what is technically called a *parti*. You are extremely good-looking, and extremely clever; in yourself you are quite exceptional. You appear to have the vaguest ideas about your earthly possessions; but from what I can make out, you are not embarrassed with an income. I wish you had a little money."

"I wish I had!" said Isabel, simply, apparently forgetting for the moment that her poverty had been a venial fault for two gallant gentlemen.

In spite of Sir Matthew Hope's benevolent recommendation, Madame Merle did not remain to the end, as the issue of poor Mr. Touchett's malady had now come frankly to be designated. She was under pledges to other people which had at last to be redeemed, and she left Gardencourt with the understanding that she should in any event see Mrs. Touchett there again, or in town, before quitting England. Her parting with Isabel was even more like the beginning of a friendship than their meeting had been.

"I am going to six places in succession," she said, "but I shall see no one I like so well as you. They will all be old friends, however; one doesn't make new friends at my age. I have made a great exception for you. You must remember that, and you must think well of me. You must reward me by believing in me."

By way of answer, Isabel kissed her, and though some women kiss with facility, there are kisses and kisses, and this embrace was satisfactory to Madame Merle.

Isabel, after this, was much alone; she saw her aunt and cousin only at meals, and discovered that of the hours that Mrs. Touchett was invisible, only a minor portion was now devoted to nursing her husband. She spent the rest in her own apartments, to which access was not allowed even to her niece, in mysterious and inscrutable exercises. At table she was grave and silent; but her solemnity was not an attitude—Isabel could see that it was a conviction. She wondered whether her aunt repented of having taken her own way so much; but there was no visible evidence of this—no tears, no sighs, no exaggeration of a zeal which had always deemed itself sufficient. Mrs. Touchett seemed simply to feel the need of thinking things over and summing them up; she had a little moral account-book—with columns unerringly ruled, and a sharp steel clasp—which she kept with exemplary neatness.

"If I had foreseen this I would not have proposed your coming abroad now," she said to Isabel after Madame Merle had left the house. "I would have waited and sent for you next year."

Her remarks had usually a practical ring.

"So that perhaps I should never have known my uncle? It's a great happiness to me to have come now."

"That's very well. But it was not that you might know your uncle that I brought you to Europe." A perfectly veracious speech; but, as Isabel thought, not as perfectly timed.

She had leisure to think of this and other matters. She took a solitary walk every day, and spent much time in turning over the books in the library. Among the subjects that engaged her attention were the adventures of her friend Miss Stackpole, with whom she was in regular correspondence. Isabel liked her friend's private epistolary style better than her public; that is, she thought her public letters would have been excellent if they had not been printed. Henrietta's career, however, was not so successful as might have been wished even in the interest of her private felicity; that view of the inner life of Great Britain which she was so eager to take appeared to dance before her like an *ignis fatuus.* The invitation from Lady Pensil, for mysterious reasons, had never arrived; and poor Mr. Bantling himself, with all his friendly ingenuity, had been unable to explain so grave a dereliction on the part of a missive that had obviously been sent. Mr. Bantling, however, had evidently taken Henrietta's affairs much to heart, and believed that he owed her a set-off to this illusory visit to Bedfordshire. "He says he should think I would go to the Continent," Henrietta wrote; "and as he thinks of going there himself, I suppose his advice is sincere. He wants to know why I don't take a view of French life; and it is a fact that I want very much to see the new Republic. Mr. Bantling doesn't care much about the Republic, but he thinks of going over to Paris any way. I must say he is quite as attentive as I could wish, and at any rate I shall have seen one polite Englishman. I keep telling Mr. Bantling that he ought to have been an American; and you ought to see how it pleases him. Whenever I say so, he always breaks out with the same exclamation—'Ah, but really, come now!'" A few days later she wrote that she had decided to go to Paris at the end of the week, and that Mr. Bantling had promised to see her off—perhaps even he would go as far as Dover with her. She would wait in Paris till Isabel should arrive, Henrietta added; speaking quite as if Isabel were to start on her Continental journey alone, and making no allusion to Mrs. Touchett. Bearing in mind his interest in their late companion, our heroine communicated several passages from Miss Stackpole's letters to Ralph, who followed with an emotion akin to suspense the career of the correspondent of the *Interviewer.*

"It seems to me that she is doing very well," he said, "going over to Paris with an ex-guardsman! If she wants something to write about, she has only to describe that episode."

"It is not conventional, certainly," Isabel answered; "but if you mean that—as far as Henrietta is concerned—it is not perfectly innocent, you are very much mistaken. You will never understand Henrietta."

"Excuse me; I understand her perfectly. I didn't at all at first; but now I have got the point of view. I am afraid, however, that Bantling has not; he may have some surprises. Oh, I understand Henrietta as well as if I had made her!"

Isabel was by no means sure of this; but she abstained from expressing further doubt, for she was disposed in these days to extend a great charity to her cousin. One afternoon, less than a week after Madame Merle's departure, she was seated in the library with a volume to which her attention was not fastened. She had placed herself in a deep window-bench, from which she looked out into the dull, damp park; and as the library stood at right angles to the entrance-front of the house, she could see the doctor's dog-cart, which had been waiting for the last two hours before the door. She was struck with the doctor's remaining so long; but at last she saw him appear in the portico, stand a moment, slowly drawing on his gloves and looking at the knees of his horse, and then get into the vehicle and drive away. Isabel kept her place for half-an-hour; there was a great stillness in the house. It was so great that when she at last heard a soft, slow step on the deep carpet of the room, she was almost startled by the sound. She turned quickly away from the window, and saw Ralph Touchett standing there, with his hands still in his pockets, but with a face absolutely void of its usual latent smile. She got up, and her movement and glance were a question.

"It's all over," said Ralph.

"Do you mean that my uncle——?" And Isabel stopped.

"My father died an hour ago."

"Ah, my poor Ralph!" the girl murmured, putting out her hand to him.

XX

SOME FORTNIGHT after this incident Madame Merle drove up in a hansom cab to the house in Winchester Square. As she descended from her vehicle she observed, suspended between the dining-room windows, a large, neat, wooden tablet, on whose fresh black ground were inscribed in white paint the words—"This noble freehold mansion to be sold;" with the name of the agent to whom application should be made. "They certainly lose no time," said the visitor, as, after sounding the big brass knocker, she waited to be admitted; "it's a practical country!" And within the house, as she ascended to the drawing-room, she perceived numerous signs of abdication; pictures removed from the walls and placed upon sofas, windows undraped and floors laid bare. Mrs. Touchett presently received her, and intimated in a few words that condolences might be taken for granted.

"I know what you are going to say—he was a very good man. But I know it better than any one, because I gave him more chance to show it. In that I think I was a good wife." Mrs. Touchett added that at the end her husband apparently recognised this fact. "He has treated me liberally," she said; "I won't say more liberally than I expected, because I didn't expect. You know that as a general thing I don't expect. But he chose, I presume, to recognise the fact that though I lived much abroad, and mingled—you may say freely—in foreign life, I never exhibited the smallest preference for any one else."

"For any one but yourself," Madame Merle mentally observed; but the reflection was perfectly inaudible.

"I never sacrificed my husband to another," Mrs. Touchett continued, with her stout curtness.

"Oh no," thought Madame Merle; "you never did anything for another!"

There was a certain cynicism in these mute comments which demands an explanation; the more so as they are not in accord either with the view—somewhat superficial perhaps—that we have hitherto enjoyed of Madame Merle's character, or with the literal facts of Mrs. Touchett's history;

the more so, too, as Madame Merle had a well-founded conviction that her friend's last remark was not in the least to be construed as a side-thrust at herself. The truth is, that the moment she had crossed the threshold she received a subtle impression that Mr. Touchett's death had had consequences, and that these consequences had been profitable to a little circle of persons among whom she was not numbered. Of course it was an event which would naturally have consequences; her imagination had more than once rested upon this fact during her stay at Gardencourt. But it had been one thing to foresee it mentally, and it was another to behold it actually. The idea of a distribution of property—she would almost have said of spoils—just now pressed upon her senses and irritated her with a sense of exclusion. I am far from wishing to say that Madame Merle was one of the hungry ones of the world; but we have already perceived that she had desires which had never been satisfied. If she had been questioned, she would of course have admitted—with a most becoming smile—that she had not the faintest claim to a share in Mr. Touchett's relics. "There was never anything in the world between us," she would have said. "There was never that, poor man!"—with a fillip of her thumb and her third finger. I hasten to add, moreover, that if her private attitude at the present moment was somewhat incongruously invidious, she was very careful not to betray herself. She had, after all, as much sympathy for Mrs. Touchett's gains as for her losses.

"He has left me this house," the newly-made widow said; "but of course I shall not live in it; I have a much better house in Florence. The will was opened only three days since, but I have already offered the house for sale. I have also a share in the bank; but I don't yet understand whether I am obliged to leave it there. If not, I shall certainly take it out. Ralph, of course, has Gardencourt; but I am not sure that he will have means to keep up the place. He is of course left very well off, but his father has given away an immense deal of money; there are bequests to a string of third cousins in Vermont. Ralph, however, is very fond of Gardencourt, and would be quite capable of living there—in summer—with a maid-of-all-work and a gardener's boy. There is one remarkable clause in my husband's will," Mrs. Touchett added. "He has left my niece a fortune."

"A fortune!" Madame Merle repeated, softly.

"Isabel steps into something like seventy thousand pounds."

Madame Merle's hands were clasped in her lap; at this she raised them, still clasped, and held them a moment against her bosom, while her eyes, a little dilated, fixed themselves on those of her friend. "Ah," she cried, "the clever creature!"

Mrs. Touchett gave her a quick look. "What do you mean by that?"

For an instant Madame Merle's colour rose, and she dropped her eyes. "It certainly is clever to achieve such results—without an effort!"

"There certainly was no effort; don't call it an achievement."

Madame Merle was rarely guilty of the awkwardness of retracting what she had said; her wisdom was shown rather in maintaining it and placing it in a favourable light. "My dear friend, Isabel would certainly not have had seventy thousand pounds left her if she had not been the most charming girl in the world. Her charm includes great cleverness."

"She never dreamed, I am sure, of my husband's doing anything for her; and I never dreamed of it either, for he never spoke to me of his intention," Mrs. Touchett said. "She had no claim upon him whatever; it was no great recommendation to him that she was my niece. Whatever she achieved she achieved unconsciously."

"Ah," rejoined Madame Merle, "those are the greatest strokes!"

Mrs. Touchett gave a shrug. "The girl is fortunate; I don't deny that. But for the present she is simply stupefied."

"Do you mean that she doesn't know what to do with the money?"

"That, I think, she has hardly considered. She doesn't know what to think about the matter at all. It has been as if a big gun were suddenly fired off behind her; she is feeling herself, to see if she be hurt. It is but three days since she received a visit from the principal executor who came in person, very gallantly, to notify her. He told me afterwards that when he had made his little speech she suddenly burst into tears. The money is to remain in the bank, and she is to draw the interest."

Madame Merle shook her head, with a wise, and now quite benignant, smile. "After she has done that two or three times she will get used to it." Then after a silence—"What does your son think of it?" she abruptly asked.

"He left England just before it came out—used up by his fatigue and anxiety, and hurrying off to the south. He is on his way to the Riviera, and I have not yet heard from him. But it is not likely he will ever object to anything done by his father."

"Didn't you say his own share had been cut down?"

"Only at his wish. I know that he urged his father to do something for the people in America. He is not in the least addicted to looking after number one."

"It depends upon whom he regards as number one!" said Madame Merle. And she remained thoughtful a moment, with her eyes bent upon the floor. "Am I not to see your happy niece?" she asked at last, looking up.

"You may see her; but you will not be struck with her being happy. She has looked as solemn, these three days, as a Cimabue Madonna!" And Mrs. Touchett rang for a servant.

Isabel came in shortly after the footman had been sent to call her; and Madame Merle thought, as she appeared, that Mrs. Touchett's comparison had its force. The girl was pale and grave—an effect not mitigated by her deeper mourning; but the smile of her brightest moments came into her face as she saw Madame Merle, who went forward, laid her hand on our heroine's shoulder, and after looking at her a moment, kissed her as if she were returning the kiss that she had received from Isabel at Gardencourt. This was the only allusion that Madame Merle, in her great good taste, made for the present to her young friend's inheritance.

Mrs. Touchett did not remain in London until she had sold her house. After selecting from among its furniture those objects which she wished to transport to her Florentine residence, she left the rest of its contents to be disposed of by the auctioneer, and took her departure for the Continent. She was, of course, accompanied on this journey by her niece, who now had plenty of leisure to contemplate the windfall on which Madame Merle had covertly congratulated her. Isabel thought of it very often and looked at it in a dozen different lights; but we shall not at present attempt to enter into her meditations or to explain why it was that some of them were of a rather pessimistic cast. The pessimism of this young lady was transient; she ultimately made up her mind that to be rich was a virtue, because it was to be able to *do*, and to do was sweet. It was the contrary of weakness. To be weak was, for a young lady, rather graceful, but, after all, as Isabel said to herself, there was a larger grace than that. Just now, it is true, there was not much to do—once she had sent off a cheque to Lily and another to poor Edith; but she was thankful for the quiet months which her mourning robes and her aunt's fresh widowhood compelled the two ladies to spend. The acquisition of power made her serious; she scrutinised her power with a kind of tender ferocity, but she was not eager to exercise it. She began to do so indeed during a stay of some weeks which she presently made with her aunt in Paris, but in ways that will probably be thought rather vulgar. They were the ways that most naturally presented themselves in a city in which the shops are the admiration of the world, especially under the guidance of Mrs. Touchett, who took a rigidly practical view of the transformation of her niece from a poor girl to a rich one. "Now that you are a young woman of fortune you must know how to play the part—I mean to play it well," she said to Isabel, once for all; and she added that the girl's first duty was to have everything handsome. "You don't know how to take care of your things, but you must learn," she went on; this was Isabel's second duty. Isabel submitted, but for the present her imagination was not kindled; she longed for opportunities, but these were not the opportunities she meant.

Mrs. Touchett rarely changed her plans, and having intended before her husband's death to spend a part of the winter in Paris she saw no reason to deprive herself—still less to deprive her companion—of this advantage. Though they would live in great retirement, she might still present her niece, informally, to the little circle of her fellow-countrymen dwelling upon the skirts of the Champs Elysées. With many of these amiable colonists Mrs. Touchett was intimate; she shared their expatriation, their convictions, their pastimes, their ennui. Isabel saw them come with a good deal of assiduity to her aunt's hotel, and judged them with a trenchancy which is doubtless to be accounted for by the temporary exaltation of her sense of human duty. She made up her mind that their manner of life was superficial, and incurred some disfavour by expressing this view on bright Sunday afternoons, when the American absentees were engaged in calling upon each other. Though her listeners were the most good-natured people in the world, two or three of them thought her cleverness, which was generally admitted, only a dangerous variation of impertinence.

"You all live here this way, but what does it all lead to?" she was pleased to ask. "It doesn't seem to lead to anything, and I should think you would get very tired of it."

Mrs. Touchett thought the question worthy of Henrietta Stackpole. The two ladies had found Henrietta in Paris, and Isabel constantly saw her; so that Mrs. Touchett had some reason for saying to herself that if her niece were not clever enough to originate almost anything, she might be suspected of having borrowed that style of remark from her journalistic friend. The first occasion on which Isabel had spoken was that of a visit paid by the two ladies to Mrs. Luce, an old friend of Mrs. Touchett's, and the only person in Paris she now went to see. Mrs. Luce had been living in Paris since the days of Louis Philippe; she used to say jocosely that she was one of the generation of 1830—a joke of which the point was not always taken. When it failed Mrs. Luce used always to explain—"Oh yes, I am one of the romantics;" her French had never become very perfect. She was always at home on Sunday afternoons, and surrounded by sympathetic compatriots, usually the same. In fact she was at home at all times, and led in her well-cushioned little corner of the brilliant city as quiet and domestic a life as she might have led in her native Baltimore. The existence of Mr. Luce, her worthy husband, was somewhat more inscrutable. Superficially indeed, there was no mystery about it; the mystery lay deeper, and resided in the wonder of his supporting existence at all. He was the most unoccupied man in Europe, for he not only had no duties, but he had no pleasures. Habits certainly he had, but they were few in number, and had been worn threadbare by forty years of use. Mr. Luce was a tall, lean, grizzled, well-brushed gentleman, who wore a gold eye-glass and carried his hat a little too much on the back of his head. He went every day to the American banker's, where there was a post-office which was almost as sociable and colloquial an institution as that of an American country town. He passed an hour (in fine weather) in a chair in the Champs Elysées, and he dined uncommonly well at his own table, seated above a waxed floor, which it was Mrs. Luce's happiness to believe had a finer polish than any other in Paris. Occasionally he dined with a friend or two at the Café Anglais, where his talent for ordering a dinner was a source of felicity to his companions and an object of admiration even to the head-waiter of the establishment. These were his only known avocations, but they had beguiled his hours for upwards of half a century, and they doubtless justified his frequent declaration that there was no place like Paris. In no other place, on these terms, could Mr. Luce flatter himself that he was enjoying life. There was nothing like Paris, but it must be confessed that Mr. Luce thought less highly of the French capital than in earlier days. In the list of his occupations his political reveries should not be omitted, for they were doubtless the animating principle of many hours that superficially seemed vacant. Like many of his fellow colonists, Mr. Luce was a high—or rather a deep—conservative, and gave no countenance to the government recently established in France. He had no faith in its duration, and would assure you from year to year that its end was close at hand. "They want to be kept down, sir, to be kept down; nothing but the strong hand—the iron heel—will do for them," he would frequently say of the French people; and his ideal of a fine government was that of the lately-abolished Empire. "Paris is much less attractive than in the days of the Emperor; he knew how to make a city pleasant," Mr. Luce had often remarked to Mrs. Touchett, who was quite of his own way of thinking, and wished to know what one had crossed that odious Atlantic for but to get away from republics.

"Why, madam, sitting in the Champs Elysées, opposite to

the Palace of Industry, I have seen the court-carriages from the Tuileries pass up and down as many as seven times a day. I remember one occasion when they went as high as nine times. What do you see now? It's no use talking, the style's all gone. Napoleon knew what the French people want, and there'll be a cloud over Paris till they get the Empire back again."

Among Mrs. Luce's visitors on Sunday afternoons was a young man with whom Isabel had had a good deal of conversation, and whom she found full of valuable knowledge. Mr. Edward Rosier—Ned Rosier, as he was called—was a native of New York, and had been brought up in Paris, living there under the eye of his father, who, as it happened, had been an old and intimate friend of the late Mr. Archer. Edward Rosier remembered Isabel as a little girl; it had been his father who came to the rescue of the little Archers at the inn at Neufchâtel (he was travelling that way with the boy, and stopped at the hotel by chance), after their *bonne* had gone off with the Russian prince and when Mr. Archer's whereabouts remained for some days a mystery. Isabel remembered perfectly the neat little male child, whose hair smelt of a delicious cosmetic, and who had a *bonne* of his own, warranted to lose sight of him under no provocation. Isabel took a walk with the pair beside the lake, and thought little Edward as pretty as an angel—a comparison by no means conventional in her mind, for she had a very definite conception of a type of features which she supposed to be angelic, and which her new friend perfectly illustrated. A small pink face, surmounted by a blue velvet bonnet and set off by a stiff embroidered collar, became the countenance of her childish dreams; and she firmly believed for some time afterwards that the heavenly hosts conversed among themselves in a queer little dialect of French-English, expressing the properest sentiments, as when Edward told her that he was "defended" by his *bonne* to go near the edge of the lake, and that one must always obey to one's *bonne*. Ned Rosier's English had improved; at least it exhibited in a less degree the French variation. His father was dead and his *bonne* was dismissed, but the young man still conformed to the spirit of their teaching—he never went to the edge of the lake. There was still something agreeable to the nostril about him, and something not offensive to nobler organs. He was a very gentle and gracious youth, with what are called cultivated tastes—an acquaintance with old china, with good wine, with the bindings of books, with the *Almanach de Gotha*, with the best shops, the best hotels, the hours of railway-trains. He could order a dinner almost as well as Mr. Luce, and it was probable that as his experience accumulated he would be a worthy successor to that gentleman, whose rather grim politics he also advocated, in a soft and innocent voice. He had some charming rooms in Paris, decorated with old Spanish altar-lace, the envy of his female friends, who declared that his chimney-piece was better draped than many a duchess. He usually, however, spent a part of every winter at Pau, and had once passed a couple of months in the United States.

He took a great interest in Isabel, and remembered perfectly the walk at Neufchâtel, when she would persist in going so near the edge. He seemed to recognise this same tendency in the subversive inquiry that I quoted a moment ago, and set himself to answer our heroine's question with greater urbanity than it perhaps deserved. "What does it lead to, Miss Archer? Why Paris leads everywhere. You can't go anywhere unless you come here first. Every one that comes to Europe has got to pass through. You don't mean it in that sense so much? You mean what good it does you? Well, how can you penetrate futurity? How can you tell what lies ahead? If it's a pleasant road I don't care where it leads. I like the road, Miss Archer; I like the dear old asphalte. You can't get tired of it— you can't if you try. You think you would, but you wouldn't; there's always something new and fresh. Take the Hôtel Drouot, now; they sometimes have three and four sales a week. Where can you get such things as you can here? In spite of all they say, I maintain they are cheaper too, if you know the right places. I know plenty of places, but I keep them to myself. I'll tell you, if you like, as a particular favour; only you must not tell any one else. Don't you go anywhere without asking me first; I want you to promise me that. As a general thing avoid the Boulevards; there is very little to be done on the Boulevards. Speaking conscientiously—*sans blague*—I don't believe any one knows Paris better than I.

You and Mrs. Touchett must come and breakfast with me some day, and I'll show you my things; *je ne vous dis que ça!* There has been a great deal of talk about London of late; it's the fashion to cry up London. But there is nothing in it— you can't do anything in London. No Louis Quinze—nothing of the First Empire; nothing but their eternal Queen Anne. It's good for one's bed-room, Queen Anne—for one's washing-room; but it isn't proper for a *salon*. Do I spend my life at the auctioneer's?" Mr. Rosier pursued, in answer to another question of Isabel's. "Oh, no; I haven't the means. I wish I had. You think I'm a mere trifler; I can tell by the expression of your face—you have got a wonderfully expressive face. I hope you don't mind my saying that; I mean it as a kind of warning. You think I ought to do something, and so do I, so long as you leave it vague. But when you come to the point, you see you have to stop. I can't go home and be a shopkeeper. You think I am very well fitted? Ah, Miss Archer, you overrate me. I can buy very well, but I can't sell; you should see when I sometimes try to get rid of my things. It takes much more ability to make other people buy than to buy yourself. When I think how clever they must be, the people who make *me* buy! Ah, no; I couldn't be a shopkeeper. I can't be a doctor, it's a repulsive business. I can't be a clergyman, I haven't got convictions. And then I can't pronounce the names right in the Bible. They are very difficult, in the Old Testament particularly. I can't be a lawyer; I don't understand—how do you call it?—the American *procédure*. Is there anything else? There is nothing for a gentleman to do in America. I should like to be a diplomatist; but American diplomacy—that is not for gentlemen either. I am sure if you had seen the last min——"

Henrietta Stackpole, who was often with her friend when Mr. Rosier, coming to pay his compliments, late in the afternoon, expressed himself after the fashion I have sketched, usually interrupted the young man at this point and read him a lecture on the duties of the American citizen. She thought him most unnatural; he was worse than Mr. Ralph Touchett. Henrietta, however, was at this time more than ever addicted to fine criticism, for her conscience had been freshly alarmed as regards Isabel. She had not congratulated this young lady on her accession of fortune, and begged to be excused from doing so.

"If Mr. Touchett had consulted me about leaving you the money," she frankly said, "I would have said to him, 'Never!'"

"I see," Isabel had answered. "You think it will prove a curse in disguise. Perhaps it will."

"Leave it to some one you care less for—that's what I should have said."

"To yourself, for instance?" Isabel suggested, jocosely. And then—"Do you really believe it will ruin me?" she asked, in quite another tone.

"I hope it won't ruin you; but it will certainly confirm your dangerous tendencies."

"Do you mean the love of luxury—of extravagance?"

"No, no," said Henrietta; "I mean your moral tendencies. I approve of luxury; I think we ought to be as elegant as possible. Look at the luxury of our western cities; I have seen nothing over here to compare with it. I hope you will never become sensual; but I am not afraid of that. The peril for you is that you live too much in the world of your own dreams— you are not enough in contact with reality—with the toiling, striving, suffering, I may even say sinning, world that sur- rounds you. You are too fastidious; you have too many grace- ful illusions. Your newly-acquired thousands will shut you up more and more to the society of a few selfish and heartless people, who will be interested in keeping up those illusions."

Isabel's eyes expanded as she gazed upon this vivid but dusky picture of her future. "What are my illusions?" she asked. "I try so hard not to have any."

"Well," said Henrietta, "you think that you can lead a ro- mantic life, that you can live by pleasing yourself and pleasing others. You will find you are mistaken. Whatever life you lead, you must put your soul into it—to make any sort of success of it; and from the moment you do that it ceases to be ro- mance, I assure you; it becomes reality! And you can't always please yourself; you must sometimes please other people. That, I admit, you are very ready to do; but there is another thing that is still more important—you must often *dis*please others. You must always be ready for that—you must never shrink from it. That doesn't suit you at all—you are too fond of admiration, you like to be thought well of. You think we can escape disagreeable duties by taking romantic views— that is your great illusion, my dear. But we can't. You must be prepared on many occasions in life to please no one at all—not even yourself."

Isabel shook her head sadly; she looked troubled and frightened. "This, for you, Henrietta," she said, "must be one of those occasions!"

It was certainly true that Miss Stackpole, during her visit to Paris, which had been professionally more remunerative than her English sojourn, had not been living in the world of dreams. Mr. Bantling, who had now returned to England, was her companion for the first four weeks of her stay; and about Mr. Bantling there was nothing dreamy. Isabel learned from her friend that the two had led a life of great intimacy, and that this had been a peculiar advantage to Henrietta, owing to the gentleman's remarkable knowledge of Paris. He had explained everything, shown her everything, been her constant guide and interpreter. They had breakfasted together, dined together, gone to the theatre together, supped together, really in a manner quite lived together. He was a true friend, Henrietta more than once assured our heroine; and she had never supposed that she could like any Englishman so well. Isabel could not have told you why, but she found something that ministered to mirth in the alliance the correspondent of the *Interviewer* had struck with Lady Pensil's brother; and her amusement subsisted in the face of the fact that she thought it a credit to each of them. Isabel could not rid herself of a suspicion that they were playing, somehow, at cross-purposes—that the simplicity of each of them had been entrapped. But this simplicity was none the less honourable on either side; it was as graceful on Henrietta's part to believe that Mr. Bantling took an interest in the diffusion of lively journalism, and in consolidating the position of lady-corre-spondents, as it was on the part of her companion to suppose that the cause of the *Interviewer*—a periodical of which he never formed a very definite conception—was, if subtly ana-lysed (a task to which Mr. Bantling felt himself quite equal), but the cause of Miss Stackpole's coquetry. Each of these harmless confederates supplied at any rate a want of which the other was somewhat eagerly conscious. Mr. Bantling, who was of a rather slow and discursive habit, relished a prompt, keen, positive woman, who charmed him with the spectacle of a brilliant eye and a kind of bandbox neatness, and who kindled a perception of raciness in a mind to which the usual fare of life seemed unsalted. Henrietta, on the other hand, enjoyed the society of a fresh-looking, professionless gentleman, whose leisured state, though generally indefensible, was a decided advantage to Miss Stackpole, and who was furnished with an easy, traditional, though by no means exhaustive, answer to almost any social or practical question that could come up. She often found Mr. Bantling's answers very convenient, and in the press of catching the American post would make use of them in her correspondence. It was to be feared that she was indeed drifting toward those mysterious shallows as to which Isabel, wishing for a good-humoured retort, had warned her. There might be danger in store for Isabel; but it was scarcely to be hoped that Miss Stackpole, on her side, would find permanent safety in the adoption of second-hand views. Isabel continued to warn her, good-humouredly; Lady Pensil's obliging brother was sometimes, on our heroine's lips, an object of irreverent and facetious allusion. Nothing, however, could exceed Henrietta's amiability on this point; she used to abound in the sense of Isabel's irony, and to enumerate with elation the hours she had spent with the good Mr. Bantling. Then, a few moments later, she would forget that they had been talking jocosely, and would mention with impulsive earnestness some expedition she had made in the company of the gallant ex-guardsman. She would say—"Oh, I know all about Versailles; I went there with Mr. Bantling. I was bound to see it thoroughly—I warned him when we went out there that I was thorough; so we spent three days at the hotel and wandered all over the place. It was lovely weather—a kind of Indian summer, only not so good. We just lived in that park. Oh yes; you can't tell me anything about Versailles." Henrietta appeared to have made arrangements to meet Mr. Bantling in the spring, in Italy.

XXI

M RS. TOUCHETT, before arriving in Paris, had fixed the
day for her departure; and by the middle of February
she had begun to travel southward. She did not go directly
to Florence, but interrupted her journey to pay a visit to her
son, who at San Remo, on the Italian shore of the Mediterranean, had been spending a dull, bright winter, under a
white umbrella. Isabel went with her aunt, as a matter of
course, though Mrs. Touchett, with her usual homely logic,
had laid before her a pair of alternatives.

"Now, of course, you are completely your own mistress,"
she said. "Excuse me; I don't mean that you were not so before. But you are on a different footing—property erects a
kind of barrier. You can do a great many things if you are
rich, which would be severely criticised if you were poor. You
can go and come, you can travel alone, you can have your
own establishment: I mean of course if you will take a companion—some decayed gentlewoman with a darned cashmere
and dyed hair, who paints on velvet. You don't think you
would like that? Of course you can do as you please; I only
want you to understand that you are at liberty. You might
take Miss Stackpole as your *dame de compagnie*; she would
keep people off very well. I think, however, that it is a great
deal better you should remain with me, in spite of there being
no obligation. It's better for several reasons, quite apart from
your liking it. I shouldn't think you would like it, but I recommend you to make the sacrifice. Of course, whatever novelty there may have been at first in my society has quite passed
away, and you see me as I am—a dull, obstinate, narrow-
minded old woman."

"I don't think you are at all dull," Isabel had replied to this.

"But you do think I am obstinate and narrow-minded? I
told you so!" said Mrs. Touchett, with much elation at being
justified.

Isabel remained for the present with her aunt, because, in
spite of eccentric impulses, she had a great regard for what
was usually deemed decent, and a young gentlewoman without visible relations had always struck her as a flower without

foliage. It was true that Mrs. Touchett's conversation had never again appeared so brilliant as that first afternoon in Albany, when she sat in her damp waterproof and sketched the opportunities that Europe would offer to a young person of taste. This, however, was in a great measure the girl's own fault; she had got a glimpse of her aunt's experience, and her imagination constantly anticipated the judgments and emotions of a woman who had very little of the same faculty. Apart from this, Mrs. Touchett had a great merit; she was as honest as a pair of compasses. There was a comfort in her stiffness and firmness; you knew exactly where to find her, and were never liable to chance encounters with her. On her own ground she was always to be found; but she was never over-inquisitive as regards the territory of her neighbour. Isabel came at last to have a kind of undemonstrable pity for her; there seemed something so dreary in the condition of a person whose nature had, as it were, so little surface—offered so limited a face to the accretions of human contact. Nothing tender, nothing sympathetic, had ever had a chance to fasten upon it—no wind-sown blossom, no familiar moss. Her passive extent, in other words, was about that of a knife-edge. Isabel had reason to believe, however, that as she advanced in life she grew more disposed to confer those sentimental favours which she was still unable to accept—to sacrifice consistency to considerations of that inferior order for which the excuse must be found in the particular case. It was not to the credit of her absolute rectitude that she should have gone the longest way round to Florence, in order to spend a few weeks with her invalid son; for in former years it had been one of her most definite convictions that when Ralph wished to see her he was at liberty to remember that the Palazzo Crescentini contained a spacious apartment which was known as the room of the signorino.

"I want to ask you something," Isabel said to this young man, the day after her arrival at San Remo—"something that I have thought more than once of asking you by letter, but that I have hesitated on the whole to write about. Face to face, nevertheless, my question seems easy enough. Did you know that your father intended to leave me so much money?"

Ralph stretched his legs a little further than usual, and

gazed a little more fixedly at the Mediterranean. "What does it matter, my dear Isabel, whether I knew? My father was very obstinate."

"So," said the girl, "you did know."

"Yes; he told me. We even talked it over a little."

"What did he do it for?" asked Isabel, abruptly.

"Why, as a kind of souvenir."

"He liked me too much," said Isabel.

"That's a way we all have."

"If I believed that, I should be very unhappy. Fortunately I don't believe it. I want to be treated with justice; I want nothing but that."

"Very good. But you must remember that justice to a lovely being is after all a florid sort of sentiment."

"I am not a lovely being. How can you say that, at the very moment when I am asking such odious questions? I must seem to you delicate."

"You seem to me troubled," said Ralph.

"I am troubled."

"About what?"

For a moment she answered nothing; then she broke out—

"Do you think it good for me suddenly to be made so rich? Henrietta doesn't."

"Oh, hang Henrietta!" said Ralph, coarsely. "If you ask me, I am delighted at it."

"Is that why your father did it—for your amusement?"

"I differ with Miss Stackpole," Ralph said, more gravely. "I think it's very good for you to have means."

Isabel looked at him a moment with serious eyes. "I wonder whether you know what is good for me—or whether you care."

"If I know, depend upon it I care. Shall I tell you what it is? Not to torment yourself."

"Not to torment you, I suppose you mean."

"You can't do that; I am proof. Take things more easily. Don't ask yourself so much whether this or that is good for you. Don't question your conscience so much—it will get out of tune, like a strummed piano. Keep it for great occasions. Don't try so much to form your character—it's like trying to pull open a rosebud. Live as you like best, and your character will form itself. Most things are good for you; the exceptions are very rare, and a comfortable income is not one of them." Ralph paused, smiling; Isabel had listened quickly. "You have too much conscience," Ralph added. "It's out of all reason, the number of things you think wrong. Spread your wings; rise above the ground. It's never wrong to do that."

She had listened eagerly, as I say; and it was her nature to understand quickly.

"I wonder if you appreciate what you say. If you do, you take a great responsibility."

"You frighten me a little, but I think I am right," said Ralph, continuing to smile.

"All the same, what you say is very true," Isabel went on. "You could say nothing more true. I am absorbed in myself— I look at life too much as a doctor's prescription. Why, indeed, should we perpetually be thinking whether things are good for us, as if we were patients lying in a hospital? Why should I be so afraid of not doing right? As if it mattered to the world whether I do right or wrong!"

"You are a capital person to advise," said Ralph; "you take the wind out of *my* sails!"

She looked at him as if she had not heard him—though she was following out the train of reflection which he himself had kindled. "I try to care more about the world than about myself—but I always come back to myself. It's because I am afraid." She stopped; her voice had trembled a little. "Yes, I am afraid; I can't tell you. A large fortune means freedom, and I am afraid of that. It's such a fine thing, and one should make such a good use of it. If one shouldn't, one would be ashamed. And one must always be thinking—it's a constant effort. I am not sure that it's not a greater happiness to be powerless."

"For weak people I have no doubt it's a greater happiness. For weak people the effort not to be contemptible must be great."

"And how do you know I am not weak?" Isabel asked.

"Ah," Ralph answered, with a blush which the girl noticed, "if you are, I am awfully sold!"

The charm of the Mediterranean coast only deepened for

our heroine on acquaintance; for it was the threshold of Italy—the gate of admirations. Italy, as yet imperfectly seen and felt, stretched before her as a land of promise, a land in which a love of the beautiful might be comforted by endless knowledge. Whenever she strolled upon the shore with her cousin—and she was the companion of his daily walk—she looked a while across the sea, with longing eyes, to where she knew that Genoa lay. She was glad to pause, however, on the edge of this larger knowledge; the stillness of these soft weeks seemed good to her. They were a peaceful interlude in a career which she had little warrant as yet for regarding as agitated, but which nevertheless she was constantly picturing to herself by the light of her hopes, her fears, her fancies, her ambitions, her predilections, and which reflected these subjective accidents in a manner sufficiently dramatic. Madame Merle had predicted to Mrs. Touchett that after Isabel had put her hand into her pocket half-a-dozen times she would be reconciled to the idea that it had been filled by a munificent uncle; and the event justified, as it had so often justified before, Madame Merle's perspicacity. Ralph Touchett had praised his cousin for being morally inflammable; that is, for being quick to take a hint that was meant as good advice. His advice had perhaps helped the matter; at any rate before she left San Remo she had grown used to feeling rich. The consciousness found a place in rather a dense little group of ideas that she had about her herself, and often it was by no means the least agreeable. It was a perpetual implication of good intentions. She lost herself in a maze of visions; the fine things a rich, independent, generous girl, who took a large, human view of her opportunities and obligations, might do, were really innumerable. Her fortune therefore became to her mind a part of her better self; it gave her importance, gave her even, to her own imagination, a certain ideal beauty. What it did for her in the imagination of others is another affair, and on this point we must also touch in time. The visions I have just spoken of were intermingled with other reveries. Isabel liked better to think of the future than of the past; but at times, as she listened to the murmur of the Mediterranean waves, her glance took a backward flight. It rested upon two figures which, in spite of increasing distance, were

still sufficiently salient; they were recognisable without difficulty as those of Caspar Goodwood and Lord Warburton. It
was strange how quickly these gentlemen had fallen into the
background of our young lady's life. It was in her disposition
at all times to lose faith in the reality of absent things; she
could summon back her faith, in case of need, with an effort,
but the effort was often painful, even when the reality had
been pleasant. The past was apt to look dead, and its revival
to wear the supernatural aspect of a resurrection. Isabel moreover was not prone to take for granted that she herself lived
in the mind of others—she had not the fatuity to believe that
she left indelible traces. She was capable of being wounded
by the discovery that she had been forgotten; and yet, of all
liberties, the one she herself found sweetest was the liberty to
forget. She had not given her last shilling, sentimentally
speaking, either to Caspar Goodwood or to Lord Warburton,
and yet she did not regard them as appreciably in her debt.
She had, of course, reminded herself that she was to hear
from Mr. Goodwood again; but this was not to be for another year and a half, and in that time a great many things
might happen. Isabel did not say to herself that her American
suitor might find some other girl more comfortable to woo;
because, though it was certain that many other girls would
prove so, she had not the smallest belief that this merit would
attract him. But she reflected that she herself might change
her humour—might weary of those things that were not Caspar (and there were so many things that were not Caspar!),
and might find satisfaction in the very qualities which struck
her to-day as his limitations. It was conceivable that his limitations should some day prove a sort of blessing in disguise—
a clear and quiet harbour, inclosed by a fine granite break-
water. But that day could only come in its order, and she
could not wait for it with folded hands. That Lord Warburton
should continue to cherish her image seemed to her more
than modesty should not only expect, but even desire. She
had so definitely undertaken to forget him, as a lover, that a
corresponding effort on his own part would be eminently
proper. This was not, as it may seem, merely a theory tinged
with sarcasm. Isabel really believed that his lordship would,
in the usual phrase, get over it. He had been deeply smitten—

this she believed, and she was still capable of deriving pleasure from the belief; but it was absurd that a man so completely absolved from fidelity should stiffen himself in an attitude it would be more graceful to discontinue. Englishmen liked to be comfortable, said Isabel, and there could be little comfort for Lord Warburton, in the long run, in thinking of a self-sufficient American girl who had been but a casual acquaintance. Isabel flattered herself that should she hear, from one day to another, that he had married some young lady of his own country who had done more to deserve him, she should receive the news without an impulse of jealousy. It would have proved that he believed she was firm—which was what she wished to seem to him; and this was grateful to her pride.

XXII

O N ONE of the first days of May, some six months after
old Mr. Touchett's death, a picturesque little group was
gathered in one of the many rooms of an ancient villa which
stood on the summit of an olive-muffled hill, outside of the
Roman gate of Florence. The villa was a long, rather blank-
looking structure, with the far-projecting roof which Tuscany
loves, and which, on the hills that encircle Florence, when
looked at from a distance, makes so harmonious a rectangle
with the straight, dark, definite cypresses that usually rise, in
groups of three or four, beside it. The house had a front upon
a little grassy, empty, rural piazza which occupied a part of
the hill-top; and this front, pierced with a few windows in
irregular relations and furnished with a stone bench which
ran along the base of the structure and usually afforded a
lounging-place to one or two persons wearing more or less of
that air of under-valued merit which in Italy, for some reason
or other, always gracefully invests any one who confidently
assumes a perfectly passive attitude—this ancient, solid,
weather-worn, yet imposing front, had a somewhat incom-
municative character. It was the mask of the house; it was not
its face. It had heavy lids, but no eyes; the house in reality
looked another way—looked off behind, into splendid open-
ness and the range of the afternoon light. In that quarter the
villa overhung the slope of its hill and the long valley of the
Arno, hazy with Italian colour. It had a narrow garden, in the
manner of a terrace, productive chiefly of tangles of wild roses
and old stone benches, mossy and sun-warmed. The parapet
of the terrace was just the height to lean upon, and beneath
it the ground declined into the vagueness of olive-crops and
vineyards. It is not, however, with the outside of the place
that we are concerned; on this bright morning of ripened
spring its tenants had reason to prefer the shady side of the
wall. The windows of the ground-floor, as you saw them
from the piazza, were, in their noble proportions, extremely
architectural; but their function seemed to be less to offer
communication with the world than to defy the world to look
in. They were massively cross-barred and placed at such a

height that curiosity, even on tip-toe, expired before it reached them. In an apartment lighted by a row of three of these obstructive apertures—one of the several distinct apartments into which the villa was divided, and which were mainly occupied by foreigners of conflicting nationality long resident in Florence—a gentleman was seated, in company with a young girl and two good sisters from a religious house. The room was, however, much less gloomy than my indications may have represented, for it had a wide, high door, which now stood open into the tangled garden behind; and the tall iron lattices admitted on occasion more than enough of the Italian sunshine. The place, moreover, was almost luxuriously comfortable; it told of habitation being practised as a fine art. It contained a variety of those faded hangings of damask and tapestry, those chests and cabinets of carved and time-polished oak, those primitive specimens of pictorial art in frames pedantically rusty, those perverse-looking relics of mediæval brass and pottery, of which Italy has long been the not quite exhausted storehouse. These things were intermingled with articles of modern furniture, in which liberal concession had been made to cultivated sensibilities; it was to be noticed that all the chairs were deep and well padded, and that much space was occupied by a writing-table of which the ingenious perfection bore the stamp of London and the nineteenth century. There were books in profusion, and magazines and newspapers, and a few small modern pictures, chiefly in water-colour. One of these productions stood on a drawing-room easel, before which, at the moment when we begin to be concerned with her, the young girl I have mentioned had placed herself. She was looking at the picture in silence.

Silence—absolute silence—had not fallen upon her companions; but their conversation had an appearance of embarrassed continuity. The two good sisters had not settled themselves in their respective chairs; their attitude was noticeably provisional, and they evidently wished to emphasise the transitory character of their presence. They were plain, comfortable, mild-faced women, with a kind of business-like modesty, to which the impersonal aspect of their stiffened linen and inexpressive serge gave an advantage. One of them, a person of a certain age, in spectacles, with a fresh complexion and a full cheek, had a more discriminating manner than her colleague, and had evidently the responsibility of their errand, which apparently related to the young girl. This young lady wore her hat—a coiffure of extreme simplicity, which was not at variance with a plain muslin gown, too short for the wearer, though it must already have been "let out." The gentleman who might have been supposed to be entertaining the two nuns was perhaps conscious of the difficulties of his function; to entertain a nun is, in fact, a sufficiently delicate operation. At the same time he was plainly much interested in his youthful companion, and while she turned her back to him his eyes rested gravely upon her slim, small figure. He was a man of forty, with a well-shaped head, upon which the hair, still dense, but prematurely grizzled, had been cropped close. He had a thin, delicate, sharply-cut face, of which the only fault was that it looked too pointed; an appearance to which the shape of his beard contributed not a little. This beard, cut in the manner of the portraits of the sixteenth century and surmounted by a fair moustache, of which the ends had a picturesque upward flourish, gave its wearer a somewhat foreign, traditionary look, and suggested that he was a gentleman who studied effect. His luminous intelligent eye, an eye which expressed both softness and keenness—the nature of the observer as well as of the dreamer—would have assured you, however, that he studied it only within well-chosen limits, and that in so far as he sought it he found it. You would have been much at a loss to determine his nationality; he had none of the superficial signs that usually render the answer to this question an insipidly easy one. If he had English blood in his veins, it had probably received some French or Italian commixture; he was one of those persons who, in the matter of race, may, as the phrase is, pass for anything. He had a light, lean, lazy-looking figure, and was apparently neither tall nor short. He was dressed as a man dresses who takes little trouble about it.

"Well, my dear, what do you think of it?" he asked of the young girl. He used the Italian tongue, and used it with perfect ease; but this would not have convinced you that he was an Italian.

The girl turned her head a little to one side and the other.

"It is very pretty, papa. Did you make it yourself?"

"Yes, my child; I made it. Don't you think I am clever?"

"Yes, papa, very clever; I also have learned to make pictures." And she turned round and showed a small, fair face, of which the natural and usual expression seemed to be a smile of perfect sweetness.

"You should have brought me a specimen of your powers."

"I have brought a great many; they are in my trunk," said the child.

"She draws very—very carefully," the elder of the nuns remarked, speaking in French.

"I am glad to hear it. Is it you who have instructed her?"

"Happily, no," said the good sister, blushing a little. "*Ce n'est pas ma partie*. I teach nothing; I leave that to those who are wiser. We have an excellent drawing-master, Mr.—Mr.—what is his name?" she asked of her companion.

Her companion looked about at the carpet.

"It's a German name," she said in Italian, as if it needed to be translated.

"Yes," the other went on, "he is a German, and we have had him for many years."

The young girl, who was not heeding the conversation, had wandered away to the open door of the large room, and stood looking into the garden.

"And you, my sister, are French," said the gentleman.

"Yes, sir," the woman replied, gently. "I speak to the pupils in my own language. I know no other. But we have sisters of other countries—English, German, Irish. They all speak their own tongue."

The gentleman gave a smile.

"Has my daughter been under the care of one of the Irish ladies?" And then, as he saw that his visitors suspected a joke, but failed to understand it—"You are very complete," he said, instantly.

"Oh, yes, we are complete. We have everything, and everything is of the best."

"We have gymnastics," the Italian sister ventured to remark. "But not dangerous."

"I hope not. Is that your branch?" A question which provoked much candid hilarity on the part of the two ladies; on the subsidence of which their entertainer, glancing at his daughter, remarked that she had grown.

"Yes, but I think she has finished. She will remain little," said the French sister.

"I am not sorry. I like little women," the gentleman declared, frankly. "But I know no particular reason why my child should be short."

The nun gave a temperate shrug, as if to intimate that such things might be beyond our knowledge.

"She is in very good health; that is the best thing."

"Yes, she looks well." And the young girl's father watched her a moment. "What do you see in the garden?" he asked, in French.

"I see many flowers," she replied, in a sweet, small voice, and with a French accent as good as his own.

"Yes, but not many good ones. However, such as they are, go out and gather some for *ces dames*."

The child turned to him, with her smile brightened by pleasure. "May I, truly?" she asked.

"Ah, when I tell you," said her father.

The girl glanced at the elder of the nuns.

"May I, truly, *ma mère*?"

"Obey monsieur your father, my child," said the sister, blushing again.

The child, satisfied with this authorisation, descended from the threshold, and was presently lost to sight.

"You don't spoil them," said her father, smiling.

"For everything they must ask leave. That is our system. Leave is freely granted, but they must ask it."

"Oh, I don't quarrel with your system; I have no doubt it is a very good one. I sent you my daughter to see what you would make of her. I had faith."

"One must have faith," the sister blandly rejoined, gazing through her spectacles.

"Well, has my faith been rewarded? What have you made of her?"

The sister dropped her eyes a moment.

"A good Christian, monsieur."

Her host dropped his eyes as well; but it was probable that the movement had in each case a different spring.

"Yes," he said in a moment, "and what else?"

He watched the lady from the convent, probably thinking that she would say that a good Christian was everything.

But for all her simplicity, she was not so crude as that. "A charming young lady—a real little woman—a daughter in whom you will have nothing but contentment."

"She seems to me very nice," said the father. "She is very pretty."

"She is perfect. She has no faults."

"She never had any as a child, and I am glad you have given her none."

"We love her too much," said the spectacled sister, with dignity. "And as for faults, how can we give what we have not? *Le couvent n'est pas comme le monde, monsieur.* She is our child, as you may say. We have had her since she was so small."

"Of all those we shall lose this year she is the one we shall miss most," the younger woman murmured, deferentially.

"Ah, yes, we shall talk long of her," said the other. "We shall hold her up to the new ones."

And at this the good sister appeared to find her spectacles dim; while her companion, after fumbling a moment, presently drew forth a pocket-handkerchief of durable texture.

"It is not certain that you will lose her; nothing is settled yet," the host rejoined, quickly; not as if to anticipate their tears, but in the tone of a man saying what was most agreeable to himself.

"We should be very happy to believe that. Fifteen is very young to leave us."

"Oh," exclaimed the gentleman, with more vivacity than he had yet used, "it is not I who wish to take her away. I wish you could keep her always!"

"Ah, monsieur," said the elder sister, smiling and getting up, "good as she is, she is made for the world. *Le monde y gagnera.*"

"If all the good people were hidden away in convents, how would the world get on?" her companion softly inquired, rising also.

This was a question of a wider bearing than the good woman apparently supposed; and the lady in spectacles took a harmonising view by saying comfortably—

"Fortunately there are good people everywhere."

"If you are going there will be two less here," her host remarked, gallantly.

For this extravagant sally his simple visitors had no answer, and they simply looked at each other in decent deprecation; but their confusion was speedily covered by the return of the young girl, with two large bunches of roses—one of them all white, the other red.

"I give you your choice, mamman Catherine," said the child. "It is only the colour that is different, mamman Justine; there are just as many roses in one bunch as another."

The two sisters turned to each other, smiling and hesitating, with—"Which will you take?" and "No, it's for you to choose."

"I will take the red," said mother Catherine, in the spectacles. "I am so red myself. They will comfort us on our way back to Rome."

"Ah, they won't last," cried the young girl. "I wish I could give you something that would last!"

"You have given us a good memory of yourself, my daughter. That will last!"

"I wish nuns could wear pretty things. I would give you my blue beads," the child went on.

"And do you go back to Rome to-night?" her father asked.

"Yes, we take the train again. We have so much to do *là-bas*."

"Are you not tired?"

"We are never tired."

"Ah, my sister, sometimes," murmured the junior votaress.

"Not to-day, at any rate. We have rested too well here. *Que Dieu vous garde, ma fille*."

Their host, while they exchanged kisses with his daughter, went forward to open the door through which they were to pass; but as he did so he gave a slight exclamation, and stood looking beyond. The door opened into a vaulted ante-chamber, as high as a chapel, and paved with red tiles; and into this ante-chamber a lady had just been admitted by a servant, a lad in shabby livery, who was now ushering her toward the apartment in which our friends were grouped. The gentleman at the door, after dropping his exclamation, remained silent; in silence, too, the lady advanced. He gave her no further audible greeting, and offered her no hand, but stood aside to let her pass into the drawing-room. At the threshold she hesitated.

"Is there any one?" she asked.

"Some one you may see."

She went in, and found herself confronted with the two nuns and their pupil, who was coming forward between them, with a hand in the arm of each. At the sight of the new visitor they all paused, and the lady, who had stopped too, stood looking at them. The young girl gave a little soft cry—

"Ah, Madame Merle!"

The visitor had been slightly startled; but her manner the next instant was none the less gracious.

"Yes, it's Madame Merle, come to welcome you home."

And she held out two hands to the girl, who immediately came up to her, presenting her forehead to be kissed. Madame Merle saluted this portion of her charming little person, and then stood smiling at the two nuns. They acknowledged her smile with a decent obeisance, but permitted themselves no direct scrutiny of this imposing, brilliant woman, who seemed to bring in with her something of the radiance of the outer world.

"These ladies have brought my daughter home, and now they return to the convent," the gentleman explained.

"Ah, you go back to Rome? I have lately come from there. It is very lovely now," said Madame Merle.

The good sisters, standing with their hands folded into their sleeves, accepted this statement uncritically; and the master of the house asked Madame Merle how long it was since she had left Rome.

"She came to see me at the convent," said the young girl, before her father's visitors had time to reply.

"I have been more than once, Pansy," Madame Merle answered. "Am I not your great friend in Rome?"

"I remember the last time best," said Pansy, "because you told me I should leave the place."

"Did you tell her that?" the child's father asked.

"I hardly remember. I told her what I thought would please her. I have been in Florence a week. I hoped you would come and see me."

"I should have done so if I had known you were here. One doesn't know such things by inspiration—though I suppose one ought. You had better sit down."

These two speeches were made in a peculiar tone of voice—a tone half-lowered, and carefully quiet, but as from habit rather than from any definite need.

Madame Merle looked about her, choosing her seat.

"You are going to the door with these women? Let me of course not interrupt the ceremony. *Je vous salue, mesdames,*" she added, in French, to the nuns, as if to dismiss them.

"This lady is a great friend of ours; you will have seen her at the convent," said the host. "We have much faith in her judgment, and she will help me to decide whether my daughter shall return to you at the end of the holidays."

"I hope you will decide in our favour, madam," the sister in spectacles ventured to remark.

"That is Mr. Osmond's pleasantry; I decide nothing," said Madame Merle, smiling still. "I believe you have a very good school, but Miss Osmond's friends must remember that she is meant for the world."

"That is what I have told monsieur," sister Catherine answered. "It is precisely to fit her for the world," she murmured, glancing at Pansy, who stood at a little distance, looking at Madame Merle's elegant apparel.

"Do you hear that, Pansy? You are meant for the world," said Pansy's father.

The child gazed at him an instant with her pure young eyes.

"Am I not meant for you, papa?" she asked.

Papa gave a quick, light laugh.

"That doesn't prevent it! I am of the world, Pansy."

"Kindly permit us to retire," said sister Catherine. "Be good, in any case, my daughter."

"I shall certainly come back and see you," Pansy declared, recommencing her embraces, which were presently interrupted by Madame Merle.

"Stay with me, my child," she said, "while your father takes the good ladies to the door."

Pansy stared, disappointed, but not protesting. She was evidently impregnated with the idea of submission, which was due to any one who took the tone of authority; and she was a passive spectator of the operation of her fate.

"May I not see mamman Catherine get into the carriage?" she asked very gently.

"It would please me better if you would remain with me," said Madame Merle, while Mr. Osmond and his companions, who had bowed low again to the other visitor, passed into the ante-chamber.

"Oh yes, I will stay," Pansy answered; and she stood near Madame Merle, surrendering her little hand, which this lady took. She stared out of the window; her eyes had filled with tears.

"I am glad they have taught you to obey," said Madame Merle. "That is what little girls should do."

"Oh yes, I obey very well," said Pansy, with soft eagerness, almost with boastfulness, as if she had been speaking of her piano-playing. And then she gave a faint, just audible sigh.

Madame Merle, holding her hand, drew it across her own fine palm and looked at it. The gaze was critical, but it found nothing to deprecate; the child's small hand was delicate and fair.

"I hope they always see that you wear gloves," she said in a moment. "Little girls usually dislike them."

"I used to dislike them, but I like them now," the child answered.

"Very good, I will make you a present of a dozen."

"I thank you very much. What colours will they be?" Pansy demanded, with interest.

Madame Merle meditated a moment.

"Useful colours."

"But will they be pretty?"

"Are you fond of pretty things?"

"Yes; but—but not too fond," said Pansy, with a trace of asceticism.

"Well, they will not be too pretty," Madame Merle answered, with a laugh. She took the child's other hand, and drew her nearer; and then, looking at her a moment—"Shall you miss mother Catherine?"

"Yes—when I think of her."

"Try, then, not to think of her. Perhaps some day," added Madame Merle, "you will have another mother."

"I don't think that is necessary," Pansy said, repeating her little soft, conciliatory sigh. "I had more than thirty mothers at the convent."

Her father's step sounded again in the ante-chamber, and Madame Merle got up, releasing the child. Mr. Osmond came in and closed the door; then, without looking at Madame Merle, he pushed one or two chairs back into their places.

His visitor waited a moment for him to speak, watching him as he moved about. Then at last she said—"I hoped you would have come to Rome. I thought it possible you would have come to fetch Pansy away."

"That was a natural supposition; but I am afraid it is not the first time I have acted in defiance of your calculations."

"Yes," said Madame Merle, "I think you are very perverse."

Mr. Osmond busied himself for a moment in the room— there was plenty of space in it to move about—in the fashion of a man mechanically seeking pretexts for not giving an attention which may be embarrassing. Presently, however, he had exhausted his pretexts; there was nothing left for him— unless he took up a book—but to stand with his hands behind him, looking at Pansy. "Why didn't you come and see the last of mamman Catherine?" he asked of her abruptly, in French.

Pansy hesitated a moment, glancing at Madame Merle. "I asked her to stay with me," said this lady, who had seated herself again in another place.

"Ah, that was better," said Osmond. Then, at last, he dropped into a chair, and sat looking at Madame Merle; leaning forward a little, with his elbows on the edge of the arms and his hands interlocked.

"She is going to give me some gloves," said Pansy.

"You needn't tell that to every one, my dear," Madame Merle observed.

"You are very kind to her," said Osmond. "She is supposed to have everything she needs."

"I should think she had had enough of the nuns."

"If we are going to discuss that matter, she had better go out of the room."

"Let her stay," said Madame Merle. "We will talk of something else."

"If you like, I won't listen," Pansy suggested, with an appearance of candour which imposed conviction.

"You may listen, charming child, because you won't understand," her father replied. The child sat down deferentially, near the open door, within sight of the garden, into which she directed her innocent, wistful eyes; and Mr. Osmond went on, irrelevantly, addressing himself to his other companion. "You are looking particularly well."

"I think I always look the same," said Madame Merle.

"You always *are* the same. You don't vary. You are a wonderful woman."

"Yes, I think I am."

"You sometimes change your mind, however. You told me on your return from England that you would not leave Rome again for the present."

"I am pleased that you remember so well what I say. That was my intention. But I have come to Florence to meet some friends who have lately arrived, and as to whose movements I was at that time uncertain."

"That reason is characteristic. You are always doing something for your friends."

Madame Merle looked straight at her interlocutor, smiling. "It is less characteristic than your comment upon it—which is perfectly insincere. I don't, however, make a crime of that," she added, "because if you don't believe what you say there is no reason why you should. I don't ruin myself for my friends; I don't deserve your praise. I care greatly for myself."

"Exactly; but yourself includes so many other selves—so much of everything. I never knew a person whose life touched so many other lives."

"What do you call one's life?" asked Madame Merle. "One's appearance, one's movements, one's engagements, one's society?"

"I call your life—your ambitions," said Osmond.

Madame Merle looked a moment at Pansy. "I wonder whether she understands that," she murmured.

"You see she can't stay with us!" And Pansy's father gave a rather joyless smile. "Go into the garden, *ma bonne*, and pluck a flower or two for Madame Merle," he went on, in French.

"That's just what I wanted to do," Pansy exclaimed, rising with promptness and noiselessly departing. Her father followed her to the open door, stood a moment watching her, and then came back, but remained standing, or rather strolling to and fro, as if to cultivate a sense of freedom which in another attitude might be wanting.

"My ambitions are principally for you," said Madame Merle, looking up at him with a certain nobleness of expression.

"That comes back to what I say. I am part of your life—I and a thousand others. You are not selfish—I can't admit that. If you were selfish, what should I be? What epithet would properly describe me?"

"You are indolent. For me that is your worst fault."

"I am afraid it is really my best."

"You don't care," said Madame Merle, gravely.

"No; I don't think I care much. What sort of a fault do you call that? My indolence, at any rate, was one of the reasons I didn't go to Rome. But it was only one of them."

"It is not of importance—to me at least—that you didn't go; though I should have been glad to see you. I am glad that you are not in Rome now—which you might be, would probably be, if you had gone there a month ago. There is something I should like you to do at present in Florence."

"Please remember my indolence," said Osmond.

"I will remember it; but I beg you to forget it. In that way you will have both the virtue and the reward. This is not a great labour, and it may prove a great pleasure. How long is it since you made a new acquaintance?"

"I don't think I have made any since I made yours."

"It is time you should make another, then. There is a friend of mine I want you to know."

Mr. Osmond, in his walk, had gone back to the open door again, and was looking at his daughter, as she moved about in the intense sunshine. "What good will it do me?" he asked, with a sort of genial crudity.

Madame Merle reflected a moment. "It will amuse you." There was nothing crude in this rejoinder; it had been thoroughly well considered.

"If you say that, I believe it," said Osmond, coming toward her. "There are some points in which my confidence in you is complete. I am perfectly aware, for instance, that you know good society from bad."

"Society is all bad."

"Excuse me. That isn't a common sort of wisdom. You have gained it in the right way—experimentally; you have compared an immense number of people with each other."

"Well, I invite you to profit by my knowledge."

"To profit? Are you very sure that I shall?"

"It's what I hope. It will depend upon yourself. If I could only induce you to make an effort!"

"Ah, there you are! I knew something tiresome was coming. What in the world—that is likely to turn up here—is worth an effort?"

Madame Merle flushed a little, and her eye betrayed vexation. "Don't be foolish, Osmond. There is no one knows better than you that there are many things worth an effort."

"Many things, I admit. But they are none of them probable things."

"It is the effort that makes them probable," said Madame Merle.

"There's something in that. Who is your friend?"

"The person I came to Florence to see. She is a niece of Mrs. Touchett, whom you will not have forgotten."

"A niece? The word niece suggests youth. I see what you are coming to."

"Yes, she is young—twenty-two years old. She is a great friend of mine. I met her for the first time in England, several months ago, and we took a great fancy to each other. I like her immensely, and I do what I don't do every day—I admire her. You will do the same."

"Not if I can help it."

"Precisely. But you won't be able to help it."

"Is she beautiful, clever, rich, splendid, universally intelli-

gent and unprecedentedly virtuous? It is only on those conditions that I care to make her acquaintance. You know I
asked you some time ago never to speak to me of any one
who should not correspond to that description. I know plenty
of dingy people; I don't want to know any more."

"Miss Archer is not dingy; she's as bright as the morning.
She corresponds to your description; it is for that I wish you
to know her. She fills all your requirements."

"More or less, of course."

"No; quite literally. She is beautiful, accomplished, generous, and for an American, well-born. She is also very clever
and very amiable, and she has a handsome fortune."

Mr. Osmond listened to this in silence, appearing to turn
it over in his mind, with his eyes on his informant. "What do
you want to do with her?" he asked, at last.

"What you see. Put her in your way."

"Isn't she meant for something better than that?"

"I don't pretend to know what people are meant for," said
Madame Merle. "I only know what I can do with them."

"I am sorry for Miss Archer!" Osmond declared.

Madame Merle got up. "If that is a beginning of interest in
her, I take note of it."

The two stood there, face to face; she settled her mantilla,
looking down at it as she did so.

"You are looking very well," Osmond repeated, still more
irrelevantly than before. "You have got some idea. You are
never as well as when you have got an idea; they are always
becoming to you."

In the manner of these two persons, on first meeting on
any occasion, and especially when they met in the presence of
others, there was something indirect and circumspect, which
showed itself in glance and tone. They approached each other
obliquely, as it were, and they addressed each other by implication. The effect of each appeared to be to intensify to an
embarrassing degree the self-consciousness of the other. Madame Merle of course carried off such embarrassments better
than her friend; but even Madame Merle had not on this occasion the manner she would have liked to have—the perfect
self-possession she would have wished to exhibit to her host.
The point I wish to make is, however, that at a certain mo-

ment the obstruction, whatever it was, always levelled itself, and left them more closely face to face than either of them ever was with any one else. This was what had happened now. They stood there, knowing each other well, and each of them on the whole willing to accept the satisfaction of knowing, as a compensation for the inconvenience—whatever it might be—of being known.

"I wish very much you were not so heartless," said Madame Merle, quietly. "It has always been against you, and it will be against you now."

"I am not so heartless as you think. Every now and then something touches me—as for instance your saying just now that your ambitions are for me. I don't understand it; I don't see how or why they should be. But it touches me, all the same."

"You will probably understand it even less as time goes on. There are some things you will never understand. There is no particular need that you should."

"You, after all, are the most remarkable woman," said Osmond. "You have more in you than almost any one. I don't see why you think Mrs. Touchett's niece should matter very much to me, when—when——" and he paused a moment.

"When I myself have mattered so little?"

"That of course is not what I meant to say. When I have known and appreciated such a woman as you."

"Isabel Archer is better than I," said Madame Merle.

Her companion gave a laugh. "How little you must think of her to say that!"

"Do you suppose I am capable of jealousy? Please answer me that."

"With regard to me? No; on the whole I don't."

"Come and see me, then, two days hence. I am staying at Mrs. Touchett's—the Palazzo Crescentini—and the girl will be there."

"Why didn't you ask me that at first, simply, without speaking of the girl?" said Osmond. "You could have had her there at any rate."

Madame Merle looked at him in the manner of a woman whom no question that he could ask would find unprepared.

"Do you wish to know why? Because I have spoken of you to her."

Osmond frowned and turned away. "I would rather not know that." Then, in a moment, he pointed out the easel supporting the little water-colour drawing. "Have you seen that—my last?"

Madame Merle drew near and looked at it a moment. "Is it the Venetian Alps—one of your last year's sketches?"

"Yes—but how you guess everything!"

Madame Merle looked for a moment longer; then she turned away. "You know I don't care for your drawings."

"I know it, yet I am always surprised at it. They are really so much better than most people's."

"That may very well be. But as the only thing you do, it's so little. I should have liked you to do so many other things: those were my ambitions."

"Yes; you have told me many times—things that were impossible."

"Things that were impossible," said Madame Merle. And then, in quite a different tone—"In itself your little picture is very good." She looked about the room—at the old cabinets, the pictures, the tapestries, the surfaces of faded silk. "Your rooms, at least, are perfect," she went on. "I am struck with that afresh, whenever I come back; I know none better anywhere. You understand this sort of thing as no one else does."

"I am very sick of it," said Osmond.

"You must let Miss Archer come and see all this. I have told her about it."

"I don't object to showing my things—when people are not idiots."

"You do it delightfully. As a cicerone in your own museum you appear to particular advantage."

Mr. Osmond, in return for this compliment, simply turned upon his companion an eye expressive of perfect clairvoyance.

"Did you say she was rich?" he asked in a moment.

"She has seventy thousand pounds."

"En écus bien comptés?"

"There is no doubt whatever about her fortune. I have seen it, as I may say."

"Satisfactory woman!—I mean you. And if I go to see her, shall I see the mother?"

"The mother? She has none—nor father either."

"The aunt then; whom did you say?—Mrs. Touchett."

"I can easily keep her out of the way."

"I don't object to her," said Osmond; "I rather like Mrs. Touchett. She has a sort of old-fashioned character that is passing away—a vivid identity. But that long jackanapes, the son—is he about the place?"

"He is there, but he won't trouble you."

"He's an awful ass."

"I think you are mistaken. He is a very clever man. But he is not fond of being about when I am there, because he doesn't like me."

"What could be more asinine than that? Did you say that she was pretty?" Osmond went on.

"Yes; but I won't say it again, lest you should be disappointed. Come and make a beginning; that is all I ask of you."

"A beginning of what?"

Madame Merle was silent a moment. "I want you of course to marry her."

"The beginning of the end! Well, I will see for myself. Have you told her that?"

"For what do you take me? She is a very delicate piece of machinery."

"Really," said Osmond, after some meditation, "I don't understand your ambitions."

"I think you will understand this one after you have seen Miss Archer. Suspend your judgment till then." Madame Merle, as she spoke, had drawn near the open door of the garden, where she stood a moment, looking out. "Pansy has grown pretty," she presently added.

"So it seemed to me."

"But she has had enough of the convent."

"I don't know," said Osmond. "I like what they have made of her. It's very charming."

"That's not the convent. It's the child's nature."

"It's the combination, I think. She's as pure as a pearl."

"Why doesn't she come back with my flowers, then?" Madame Merle asked. "She is not in a hurry."

"We will go and get them," said her companion.

"She doesn't like me," murmured Madame Merle, as she raised her parasol, and they passed into the garden.

XXIII

MADAME MERLE, who had come to Florence on Mrs. Touchett's arrival at the invitation of this lady—Mrs. Touchett offering her for a month the hospitality of the Palazzo Crescentini—the judicious Madame Merle spoke to Isabel afresh about Gilbert Osmond, and expressed the wish that she should know him; but made no such point of the matter as we have seen her do in recommending the girl herself to Mr. Osmond's attention. The reason of this was perhaps that Isabel offered no resistance whatever to Madame Merle's proposal. In Italy, as in England, the lady had a multitude of friends, both among the natives of the country and its heterogeneous visitors. She had mentioned to Isabel most of the people the girl would find it well to know—of course, she said, Isabel could know whomever she would—and she had placed Mr. Osmond near the top of the list. He was an old friend of her own; she had known him these ten years; he was one of the cleverest and most agreeable men it was possible to meet. He was altogether above the respectable average; quite another affair. He was not perfect—far from it; the effect he produced depended a good deal on the state of his nerves and his spirits. If he were not in the right mood he could be very unsatisfactory—like most people, after all; but when he chose to exert himself no man could do it to better purpose. He had his peculiarities—which indeed Isabel would find to be the case with all the men really worth knowing—and he did not cause his light to shine equally for all persons. Madame Merle, however, thought she could undertake that for Isabel he would be brilliant. He was easily bored—too easily, and dull people always put him out; but a quick and cultivated girl like Isabel would give him a stimulus which was too absent from his life. At any rate, he was a person to know. One should not attempt to live in Italy without making a friend of Gilbert Osmond, who knew more about the country than any one except two or three German professors. And if they had more knowledge than he, he had infinitely more taste; he had a taste which was quite by itself. Isabel remembered that her friend had spoken of him during their multifarious colloquies at Gardencourt, and wondered a little what was the nature of the tie that united them. She was inclined to imagine that Madame Merle's ties were peculiar, and such a possibility was a part of the interest created by this suggestive woman. As regards her relations with Mr. Osmond, however, Madame Merle hinted at nothing but a long-established and tranquil friendship. Isabel said that she should be happy to know a person who had enjoyed her friend's confidence for so many years. "You ought to see a great many men," Madame Merle remarked; "you ought to see as many as possible, so as to get used to them."

"Used to them?" Isabel repeated, with that exceedingly serious gaze which sometimes seemed to proclaim that she was deficient in a sense of humour—an intimation which at other moments she effectively refuted. "I am not afraid of them!"

"Used to them, I mean, so as to despise them. That's what one comes to with most of them. You will pick out, for your society, the few whom you don't despise."

This remark had a bitterness which Madame Merle did not often allow herself to betray; but Isabel was not alarmed by it, for she had never supposed that, as one saw more of the world, the sentiment of respect became the most active of one's emotions. This sentiment was excited, however, by the beautiful city of Florence, which pleased her not less than Madame Merle had promised; and if her unassisted perception had not been able to gauge its charms, she had clever companions to call attention to latent merits. She was in no want, indeed, of æsthetic illumination, for Ralph found it a pleasure which renewed his own earlier sensations, to act as cicerone to his eager young kinswoman. Madame Merle remained at home; she had seen the treasures of Florence so often, and she had always something to do. But she talked of all things with remarkable vividness of memory—she remembered the right-hand angle in the large Perugino, and the position of the hands of the Saint Elizabeth in the picture next to it; and had her own opinions as to the character of many famous works of art, differing often from Ralph with great sharpness, and defending her interpretations with as much ingenuity as good-humour. Isabel listened to the discussions which took place between the two, with a sense that she might derive much benefit from them and that they were among the advantages which—for instance—she could not have enjoyed in Albany. In the clear May mornings, before the formal breakfast—this repast at Mrs. Touchett's was served at twelve o'clock—Isabel wandered about with her cousin through the narrow and sombre Florentine streets, resting a while in the thicker dusk of some historic church, or the vaulted chambers of some dispeopled convent. She went to the galleries and palaces; she looked at the pictures and statutes which had hitherto been great names to her, and exchanged for a knowledge which was sometimes a limitation a presentiment which proved usually to have been a blank. She performed all those acts of mental prostration in which, on a first visit to Italy, youth and enthusiasm so freely indulge; she felt her heart beat in the presence of immortal genius, and knew the sweetness of rising tears in eyes to which faded fresco and darkened marble grew dim. But the return, every day, was even pleasanter than the going forth; the return into the wide, monumental court of the great house in which Mrs. Touchett, many years before, had established herself, and into the high, cool rooms where carven rafters and pompous frescoes of the sixteenth century looked down upon the familiar commodities of the nineteenth. Mrs. Touchett inhabited an historic building in a narrow street whose very name recalled the strife of mediæval factions; and found compensation for the darkness of her frontage in the modicity of her rent and the brightness of a garden in which nature itself looked as archaic as the rugged architecture of the palace and which illumined the rooms that were in regular use. Isabel found that to live in such a place might be a source of happiness—almost of excitement. At first it had struck her as a sort of prison; but very soon its prison-like quality became a merit, for she discovered that it contained other prisoners than the members of her aunt's household. The spirit of the past was shut up there, like a refugee from the outer world; it lurked in lonely corners, and, at night, haunted even the rooms in which Mrs. Touchett diffused her matter-of-fact influence. Isabel used to hear vague echoes and strange reverberations; she had a sense of the hovering of unseen figures, of the flitting of ghosts.

Often she paused, listening, half-startled, half-disappointed, on the great cold stone staircase.

Gilbert Osmond came to see Madame Merle, who presented him to the young lady seated almost out of sight at the other end of the room. Isabel, on this occasion, took little share in the conversation; she scarcely even smiled when the others turned to her appealingly; but sat there as an impartial auditor of their brilliant discourse. Mrs. Touchett was not present, and these two had it their own way. They talked extremely well; it struck Isabel almost as a dramatic entertainment, rehearsed in advance. Madame Merle referred everything to her, but the girl answered nothing, though she knew this attitude would make Mr. Osmond think she was one of those dull people who bored him. It was the worse, too, that Madame Merle would have told him she was almost as much above the merely respectable average as he himself, and that she was putting her friend dreadfully in the wrong. But this was no matter, for once; even if more had depended on it, Isabel could not have made an attempt to shine. There was something in Mr. Osmond that arrested her and held her in suspense—made it seem more important that she should get an impression of him than that she should produce one herself. Besides, Isabel had little skill in producing an impression which she knew to be expected; nothing could be more charming, in general, than to seem dazzling; but she had a perverse unwillingness to perform by arrangement. Mr. Osmond, to do him justice, had a well-bred air of expecting nothing; he was a quiet gentleman, with a colourless manner, who said elaborate things with a great deal of simplicity. Isabel, however, privately perceived that if he did not expect he observed; she was very sure he was sensitive. His face, his head was sensitive; he was not handsome, but he was fine, as fine as one of the drawings in the long gallery above the bridge, at the Uffizi. Mr. Osmond was very delicate; the tone of his voice alone would have proved it. It was the visitor's delicacy that made her abstain from interference. His talk was like the tinkling of glass, and if she had put out her finger she might have changed the pitch and spoiled the concert. Before he went he made an appeal to her.

"Madame Merle says she will come up to my hill-top some day next week and drink tea in my garden. It would give me much pleasure if you would come with her. It's thought rather pretty—there's what they call a general view. My daughter, too, would be so glad—or rather, for she is too young to have strong emotions, I should be so glad—so very glad." And Mr. Osmond paused a moment, with a slight air of embarrassment, leaving his sentence unfinished. "I should be so happy if you could know my daughter," he went on, a moment afterwards.

Isabel answered that she should be delighted to see Miss Osmond, and that if Madame Merle would show her the way to the hill-top she should be very grateful. Upon this assurance the visitor took his leave; after which Isabel fully expected that her friend would scold her for having been so stupid. But to her surprise, Madame Merle, who indeed never fell into the matter-of-course, said to her in a few moments—

"You were charming, my dear; you were just as one would have wished you. You are never disappointing."

A rebuke might possibly have been irritating, though it is much more probable that Isabel would have taken it in good part; but, strange to say, the words that Madame Merle actually used caused her the first feeling of displeasure she had known this lady to excite. "That is more than I intended," she answered, coldly. "I am under no obligation that I know of to charm Mr. Osmond."

Madame Merle coloured a moment; but we know it was not her habit to retract. "My dear child, I didn't speak for him, poor man; I spoke for yourself. It is not of course a question as to his liking you; it matters little whether he likes you or not! But I thought you liked him."

"I did," said Isabel, honestly. "But I don't see what that matters, either."

"Everything that concerns you matters to me," Madame Merle returned, with a sort of noble gentleness, "especially when at the same time another old friend is concerned."

Whatever Isabel's obligations may have been to Mr. Osmond, it must be admitted that she found them sufficient to lead her to ask Ralph sundry questions about him. She thought Ralph's judgments cynical, but she flattered herself that she had learned to make allowance for that.

"Do I know him?" said her cousin. "Oh, yes, I know him; not well, but on the whole enough. I have never cultivated his society, and he apparently has never found mine indispensable to his happiness. Who is he—what is he? He is a mysterious American, who has been living these twenty years, or more, in Italy. Why do I call him mysterious? Only as a cover for my ignorance; I don't know his antecedents, his family, his origin. For all I know, he may be a prince in disguise; he rather looks like one, by the way—like a prince who has abdicated in a fit of magnanimity, and has been in a state of disgust ever since. He used to live in Rome; but of late years he has taken up his abode in Florence; I remember hearing him say once that Rome has grown vulgar. He has a great dread of vulgarity; that's his special line; he hasn't any other that I know of. He lives on his income, which I suspect of not being vulgarly large. He's a poor gentleman—that's what he calls himself. He married young and lost his wife, and I believe he has a daughter. He also has a sister, who is married to some little Count or other, of these parts; I remember meeting her of old. She is nicer than he, I should think, but rather wicked. I remember there used to be some stories about her. I don't think I recommend you to know her. But why don't you ask Madame Merle about these people? She knows them all much better than I."

"I ask you because I want your opinion as well as hers," said Isabel.

"A fig for my opinion! If you fall in love with Mr. Osmond, what will you care for that?"

"Not much, probably. But meanwhile it has a certain importance. The more information one has about a person the better."

"I don't agree to that. We know too much about people in these days; we hear too much. Our ears, our minds, our mouths, are stuffed with personalities. Don't mind anything that any one tells you about any one else. Judge every one and everything for yourself."

"That's what I try to do," said Isabel; "but when you do that people call you conceited."

"You are not to mind them—that's precisely my argument; not to mind what they say about yourself any more than what they say about your friend or your enemy."

Isabel was silent a moment. "I think you are right; but there are some things I can't help minding: for instance, when my friend is attacked, or when I myself am praised."

"Of course you are always at liberty to judge the critic. Judge people as critics, however," Ralph added, "and you will condemn them all!"

"I shall see Mr. Osmond for myself," said Isabel. "I have promised to pay him a visit."

"To pay him a visit?"

"To go and see his view, his pictures, his daughter—I don't know exactly what. Madame Merle is to take me; she tells me a great many ladies call upon him."

"Ah, with Madame Merle you may go anywhere, *de confiance*," said Ralph. "She knows none but the best people."

Isabel said no more about Mr. Osmond, but she presently remarked to her cousin that she was not satisfied with his tone about Madame Merle. "It seems to me that you insinuate things about her. I don't know what you mean, but if you have any grounds for disliking her, I think you should either mention them frankly or else say nothing at all."

Ralph, however, resented this charge with more apparent earnestness than he commonly used. "I speak of Madame Merle exactly as I speak to her: with an even exaggerated respect."

"Exaggerated, precisely. That is what I complain of."

"I do so because Madame Merle's merits are exaggerated."

"By whom, pray? By me? If so, I do her a poor service."

"No, no; by herself."

"Ah, I protest!" Isabel cried with fervour. "If ever there was a woman who made small claims——"

"You put your finger on it," Ralph interrupted. "Her modesty is exaggerated. She has no business with small claims—she has a perfect right to make large ones."

"Her merits are large, then. You contradict yourself."

"Her merits are immense," said Ralph. "She is perfect; she is the only woman I know who has but that one little fault."

Isabel turned away with impatience. "I don't understand you; you are too paradoxical for my plain mind."

"Let me explain. When I say she exaggerates, I don't mean it in the vulgar sense—that she boasts, overstates, gives too fine an account of herself. I mean literally that she pushes the search for perfection too far—that her merits are in themselves overstrained. She is too good, too kind, too clever, too learned, too accomplished, too everything. She is too complete, in a word. I confess to you that she acts a little on my nerves, and that I feel about her a good deal as that intensely human Athenian felt about Aristides the Just."

Isabel looked hard at her cousin; but the mocking spirit, if it lurked in his words, failed on this occasion to peep from his eye. "Do you wish Madame Merle to be banished?" she inquired.

"By no means. She is much too good company. I delight in Madame Merle," said Ralph Touchett, simply.

"You are very odious, sir!" Isabel exclaimed. And then she asked him if he knew anything that was not to the honour of her brilliant friend.

"Nothing whatever. Don't you see that is just what I mean? Upon the character of every one else you may find some little black speck; if I were to take half-an-hour to it, some day, I have no doubt I should be able to find one on yours. For my own, of course, I am spotted like a leopard. But on Madame Merle's nothing, nothing, nothing!"

"That is just what I think!" said Isabel, with a toss of her head. "That is why I like her so much."

"She is a capital person for you to know. Since you wish to see the world you couldn't have a better guide."

"I suppose you mean by that that she is worldly?"

"Worldly? No," said Ralph, "she is the world itself!"

It had certainly not, as Isabel for the moment took it into her head to believe, been a refinement of malice in him to say that he delighted in Madame Merle. Ralph Touchett took his entertainment wherever he could find it, and he would not have forgiven himself if he had not been able to find a great deal in the society of a woman in whom the social virtues existed in polished perfection. There are deep-lying sympathies and antipathies; and it may have been that in spite of the intellectual justice he rendered her, her absence from his mother's house would not have made life seem barren. But Ralph Touchett had learned to appreciate, and there could be no better field for such a talent than the table-talk of Madame Merle. He talked with her largely, treated her with conspicuous civility, occupied himself with her and let her alone, with an opportuneness which she herself could not have surpassed. There were moments when he felt almost sorry for her; and these, oddly enough, were the moments when his kindness was least demonstrative. He was sure that she had been richly ambitious, and that what she had visibly accomplished was far below her ambition. She had got herself into perfect training, but she had won none of the prizes. She was always plain Madame Merle, the widow of a Swiss *négociant*, with a small income and a large acquaintance, who stayed with people a great deal, and was universally liked. The contrast between this position and any one of some half-dozen others which he vividly imagined her to have had her eyes upon at various moments, had an element of the tragical. His mother thought he got on beautifully with their pliable guest; to Mrs. Touchett's sense two people who dealt so largely in factitious theories of conduct would have much in common. He had given a great deal of consideration to Isabel's intimacy with Madame Merle—having long since made up his mind that he could not, without opposition, keep his cousin to himself; and he regarded it on the whole with philosophic tolerance. He believed it would take care of itself; it would not last for ever. Neither of these two superior persons knew the other as well as she supposed, and when each of them had made certain discoveries, there would be, if not a rupture, at least a relaxation. Meanwhile he was quite willing to admit that the conversation of the elder lady was an advantage to the younger, who had a great deal to learn, and would doubtless learn it better from Madame Merle than from some other instructors of the young. It was not probable that Isabel would be injured.

XXIV

I T WOULD certainly have been hard to see what injury
could arise to her from the visit she presently paid to Mr.
Osmond's hill-top. Nothing could have been more charming
than this occasion—a soft afternoon in May, in the full maturity of the Italian spring. The two ladies drove out of the
Roman Gate, beneath the enormous blank superstructure
which crowns the fine clear arch of that portal and makes it
nakedly impressive, and wound between high-walled lanes,
into which the wealth of blossoming orchards overdrooped
and flung a perfume, until they reached the small superurban
piazza, of crooked shape, of which the long brown wall of the
villa occupied in part by Mr. Osmond, formed the principal,
or at least the most imposing, side. Isabel went with her
friend through a wide, high court, where a clear shadow
rested below, and a pair of light-arched galleries, facing each
other above, caught the upper sunshine upon their slim columns and the flowering plants in which they were dressed.
There was something rather severe about the place; it looked
somehow as if, once you were in, it would not be easy to get
out. For Isabel, however, there was of course as yet no
thought of getting out, but only of advancing. Mr. Osmond
met her in the cold ante-chamber—it was cold even in the
month of May—and ushered her, with her companion, into
the apartment to which we have already been introduced. Madame Merle was in front, and while Isabel lingered a little,
talking with Mr. Osmond, she went forward, familiarly, and
greeted two persons who were seated in the drawing-room.
One of these was little Pansy, on whom she bestowed a kiss;
the other was a lady whom Mr. Osmond presented to Isabel
as his sister, the Countess Gemini. "And that is my little girl,"
he said, " who has just come out of a convent."

Pansy had on a scanty white dress, and her fair hair was
neatly arranged in a net; she wore a pair of slippers, tied,
sandal-fashion, about her ankles. She made Isabel a little conventual curtsey, and then came to be kissed. The Countess
Gemini simply nodded, without getting up; Isabel could see
that she was a woman of fashion. She was thin and dark, and

not at all pretty, having features that suggested some tropical bird—a long beak-like nose, a small, quickly-moving eye, and a mouth and chin that receded extremely. Her face, however, thanks to a very human and feminine expression, was by no means disagreeable, and, as regards her appearance, it was evident that she understood herself and made the most of her points. The soft brilliancy of her toilet had the look of shimmering plumage, and her attitudes were light and sudden, like those of a creature that perched upon twigs. She had a great deal of manner; Isabel, who had never known any one with so much manner, immediately classified the Countess Gemini as the most affected of women. She remembered that Ralph had not recommended her as an acquaintance; but she was ready to acknowledge that on a casual view the Countess presented no appearance of wickedness. Nothing could have been kinder or more innocent than her greeting to Isabel.

"You will believe that I am glad to see you when I tell you that it is only because I knew you were to be here that I came myself. I don't come and see my brother—I make him come and see me. This hill of his is impossible—I don't see what possesses him. Really, Osmond, you will be the ruin of my horses some day; and if they receive an injury you will have to give me another pair. I heard them panting to-day; I assure you I did. It is very disagreeable to hear one's horses panting when one is sitting in the carriage; it sounds, too, as if they were not what they should be. But I have always had good horses; whatever else I may have lacked, I have always managed that. My husband doesn't know much, but I think he does know a horse. In general the Italians don't, but my husband goes in, according to his poor light, for everything English. My horses are English—so it is all the greater pity they should be ruined. I must tell you," she went on, directly addressing Isabel, "that Osmond doesn't often invite me; I don't think he likes to have me. It was quite my own idea, coming to-day. I like to see new people, and I am sure you are very new. But don't sit there; that chair is not what it looks. There are some very good seats here, but there are also some horrors."

These remarks were delivered with a variety of little jerks and glances, in a tone which, although it expressed a high degree of good-nature, was rather shrill than sweet.

"I don't like to have you, my dear?" said her brother. "I am sure you are invaluable."

"I don't see any horrors anywhere," Isabel declared, looking about her. "Everything here seems to me very beautiful."

"I have got a few good things," Mr. Osmond murmured; "indeed I have nothing very bad. But I have not what I should have liked."

He stood there a little awkwardly, smiling and glancing about; his manner was an odd mixture of the indifferent and the expressive. He seemed to intimate that nothing was of much consequence. Isabel made a rapid induction: perfect simplicity was not the badge of his family. Even the little girl from the convent, who, in her prim white dress, with her small submissive face and her hands locked before her, stood there as if she were about to partake of her first communion—even Mr. Osmond's diminutive daughter had a kind of finish which was not entirely artless.

"You would have liked a few things from the Uffizi and the Pitti—that's what you would have liked," said Madame Merle.

"Poor Osmond, with his old curtains and crucifixes!" the Countess Gemini exclaimed; she appeared to call her brother only by his family-name. Her ejaculation had no particular object; she smiled at Isabel as she made it, and looked at her from head to foot.

Her brother had not heard her; he seemed to be thinking what he could say to Isabel. "Won't you have some tea?— you must be very tired," he at last bethought himself of remarking.

"No, indeed, I am not tired; what have I done to tire me?" Isabel felt a certain need of being very direct, of pretending to nothing; there was something in the air, in her general impression of things—she could hardly have said what it was—that deprived her of all disposition to put herself forward. The place, the occasion, the combination of people, signified more than lay on the surface; she would try to understand—she would not simply utter graceful platitudes. Poor Isabel was perhaps not aware that many women would have uttered graceful platitudes to cover the working of their observation. It must be confessed that her pride was a trifle alarmed. A man whom she had heard spoken of in terms that excited interest, and who was evidently capable of distinguishing himself, had invited her, a young lady not lavish of her favours, to come to his house. Now that she had done so, the burden of the entertainment rested naturally upon himself. Isabel was not rendered less observant, and for the moment, I am afraid, she was not rendered more indulgent, by perceiving that Mr. Osmond carried his burden less complacently than might have been expected. "What a fool I was to have invited these women here!" she could fancy his exclaiming to himself.

"You will be tired when you go home, if he shows you all his *bibelots* and gives you a lecture on each," said the Countess Gemini.

"I am not afraid of that; but if I am tired, I shall at least have learned something."

"Very little, I suspect. But my sister is dreadfully afraid of learning anything," said Mr. Osmond.

"Oh, I confess to that; I don't want to know anything more—I know too much already. The more you know, the more unhappy you are."

"You should not undervalue knowledge before Pansy, who has not finished her education," Madame Merle interposed, with a smile.

"Pansy will never know any harm," said the child's father. "Pansy is a little convent-flower."

"Oh, the convents, the convents!" cried the Countess, with a sharp laugh. "Speak to me of the convents. You may learn anything there; I am a convent-flower myself. I don't pretend to be good, but the nuns do. Don't you see what I mean?" she went on, appealing to Isabel.

Isabel was not sure that she saw, and she answered that she was very bad at following arguments. The Countess then declared that she herself detested arguments, but that this was her brother's taste—he would always discuss. "For me," she said, "one should like a thing or one shouldn't; one can't like everything, of course. But one shouldn't attempt to reason it out—you never know where it may lead you. There are some very good feelings that may have bad reasons; don't you know? And then there are very bad feelings, sometimes, that have good reasons. Don't you see what I mean? I don't care anything about reasons, but I know what I like."

"Ah, that's the great thing," said Isabel, smiling, but suspecting that her acquaintance with this lightly-flitting personage would not lead to intellectual repose. If the Countess objected to argument, Isabel at this moment had as little taste for it, and she put out her hand to Pansy with a pleasant sense that such a gesture committed her to nothing that would admit of a divergence of views. Gilbert Osmond apparently took a rather hopeless view of his sister's tone, and he turned the conversation to another topic. He presently sat down on the other side of his daughter, who had taken Isabel's hand for a moment; but he ended by drawing her out of her chair, and making her stand between his knees, leaning against him while he passed his arm round her little waist. The child fixed her eyes on Isabel with a still, disinterested gaze, which seemed void of an intention, but conscious of an attraction. Mr. Osmond talked of many things; Madame Merle had said he could be agreeable when he chose, and to-day, after a little, he appeared not only to have chosen, but to have determined. Madame Merle and the Countess Gemini sat a little apart, conversing in the effortless manner of persons who knew each other well enough to take their ease; every now and then Isabel heard the Countess say something extravagant. Mr. Osmond talked of Florence, of Italy, of the pleasure of living in that country, and of the abatements to such pleasure. There were both satisfactions and drawbacks; the drawbacks were pretty numerous; strangers were too apt to see Italy in rose-colour. On the whole it was better than other countries, if one was content to lead a quiet life and take things as they came. It was very dull sometimes, but there were advantages in living in the country which contained the most beauty. There were certain impressions that one could get only in Italy. There were others that one never got there, and one got some that were very bad. But from time to time one got a delightful one, which made up for everything. He was inclined to think that Italy had spoiled a great many people; he was even fatuous enough to believe at times that he himself might have been a better man if he had spent less of his life there. It made people idle and dilettantish, and second-rate;

there was nothing tonic in an Italian life. One was out of the current; one was not *dans le mouvement*, as the French said; one was too far from Paris and London. "We are gloriously provincial, I assure you," said Mr. Osmond, "and I am perfectly aware that I myself am as rusty as a key that has no lock to fit it. It polishes me up a little to talk with you—not that I venture to pretend I can turn that very complicated lock I suspect your intellect of being! But you will be going away before I have seen you three times, and I shall perhaps never see you after that. That's what it is to live in a country that people come to. When they are disagreeable it is bad enough; when they are agreeable it is still worse. As soon as you find you like them they are off again! I have been deceived too often; I have ceased to form attachments; to permit myself to feel attractions. You mean to stay—to settle? That would be really comfortable. Ah yes, your aunt is a sort of guarantee; I believe she may be depended upon. Oh, she's an old Florentine; I mean literally an old one; not a modern outsider. She is a contemporary of the Medici; she must have been present at the burning of Savonarola, and I am not sure she didn't throw a handful of chips into the flame. Her face is very much like some faces in the early pictures; little, dry, definite faces, that must have had a good deal of expression, but almost always the same one. Indeed, I can show you her portrait in a fresco of Ghirlandaio's. I hope you don't object to my speaking that way of your aunt, eh? I have an idea you don't. Perhaps you think that's even worse. I assure you there is no want of respect in it, to either of you. You know I'm a particular admirer of Mrs. Touchett."

While Isabel's host exerted himself to entertain her in this somewhat confidential fashion, she looked occasionally at Madame Merle, who met her eyes with an inattentive smile in which, on this occasion, there was no infelicitous intimation that our heroine appeared to advantage. Madame Merle eventually proposed to the Countess Gemini that they should go into the garden, and the Countess, rising and shaking out her soft plumage, began to rustle toward the door.

"Poor Miss Archer!" she exclaimed, surveying the other group with expressive compassion. "She has been brought quite into the family."

"Miss Archer can certainly have nothing but sympathy for a family to which you belong," Mr. Osmond answered, with a laugh which, though it had something of a mocking ring, was not ill-natured.

"I don't know what you mean by that! I am sure she will see no harm in me but what you tell her. I am better than he says, Miss Archer," the Countess went on. "I am only rather light. Is that all he has said? Ah then, you keep him in good humour. Has he opened on one of his favourite subjects? I give you notice that there are two or three that he treats *à fond*. In that case you had better take off your bonnet."

"I don't think I know what Mr. Osmond's favourite subjects are," said Isabel, who had risen to her feet.

The Countess assumed, for an instant, an attitude of intense meditation; pressing one of her hands, with the fingertips gathered together, to her forehead.

"I'll tell you in a moment," she answered. "One is Machiavelli, the other is Vittoria Colonna, the next is Metastasio."

"Ah, with me," said Madame Merle, passing her arm into the Countess Gemini's, as if to guide her course to the garden, "Mr. Osmond is never so historical."

"Oh you," the Countess answered as they moved away, "you yourself are Machiavelli—you yourself are Vittoria Colonna!"

"We shall hear next that poor Madame Merle is Metastasio!" Gilbert Osmond murmured, with a little melancholy smile.

Isabel had got up, on the assumption that they too were to go into the garden; but Mr. Osmond stood there, with no apparent inclination to leave the room, with his hands in the pockets of his jacket, and his daughter, who had now locked her arm into one of his own, clinging to him and looking up, while her eyes moved from his own face to Isabel's. Isabel waited, with a certain unuttered contentedness, to have her movements directed; she liked Mr. Osmond's talk, his company; she felt that she was being entertained. Through the open doors of the great room she saw Madame Merle and the Countess stroll across the deep grass of the garden; then she turned, and her eyes wandered over the things that were scattered about her. The understanding had been that her host

should show her his treasures; his pictures and cabinets all
looked like treasures. Isabel, after a moment, went toward
one of the pictures to see it better; but just as she had done
so Mr. Osmond said to her abruptly—

"Miss Archer, what do you think of my sister?"

Isabel turned, with a good deal of surprise.

"Ah, don't ask me that—I have seen your sister too little."

"Yes, you have seen her very little; but you must have observed that there is not a great deal of her to see. What do
you think of our family tone?" Osmond went on, smiling. "I
should like to know how it strikes a fresh, unprejudiced mind.
I know what you are going to say—you have had too little
observation of it. Of course this is only a glimpse. But just
take notice, in future, if you have a chance. I sometimes think
we have got into a rather bad way, living off here among
things and people not our own, without responsibilities or
attachments, with nothing to hold us together or keep us up;
marrying foreigners, forming artificial tastes, playing tricks
with our natural mission. Let me add, though, that I say that
much more for myself than for my sister. She's a very good
woman—better than she seems. She is rather unhappy, and
as she is not of a very serious disposition, she doesn't tend to
show it tragically; she shows it comically instead. She has got
a nasty husband, though I am not sure she makes the best of
him. Of course, however, a nasty husband is an awkward
thing. Madame Merle gives her excellent advice, but it's a
good deal like giving a child a dictionary to learn a language
with. He can look out the words, but he can't put them together. My sister needs a grammar, but unfortunately she is
not grammatical. Excuse my troubling you with these details;
my sister was very right in saying that you have been taken
into the family. Let me take down that picture; you want
more light."

He took down the picture, carried it toward the window,
related some curious facts about it. She looked at the other
works of art, and he gave her such further information as
might appear to be most acceptable to a young lady making
a call on a summer afternoon. His pictures, his carvings and
tapestries were interesting; but after a while Isabel became
conscious that the owner was more interesting still. He re-

sembled no one she had ever seen; most of the people she knew might be divided into groups of half-a-dozen specimens. There were one or two exceptions to this; she could think, for instance, of no group that would contain her Aunt Lydia. There were other people who were, relatively speaking, original—original, as one might say, by courtesy—such as Mr. Goodwood, as her cousin Ralph, as Henrietta Stackpole, as Lord Warburton, as Madame Merle. But in essentials, when one came to look at them, these individuals belonged to types which were already present to her mind. Her mind contained no class which offered a natural place to Mr. Osmond—he was a specimen apart. Isabel did not say all these things to herself at the time; but she felt them, and afterwards they became distinct. For the moment she only said to herself that Mr. Osmond had the interest of rareness. It was not so much what he said and did, but rather what he withheld, that distinguished him; he indulged in no striking deflections from common usage; he was an original without being an eccentric. Isabel had never met a person of so fine a grain. The peculiarity was physical, to begin with, and it extended to his immaterial part. His dense, delicate hair, his overdrawn, retouched features, his clear complexion, ripe without being coarse, the very evenness of the growth of his beard, and that light, smooth, slenderness of structure which made the movement of a single one of his fingers produce the effect of an expressive gesture—these personal points struck our observant young lady as the signs of an unusual sensibility. He was certainly fastidious and critical; he was probably irritable. His sensibility had governed him—possibly governed him too much; it had made him impatient of vulgar troubles and had led him to live by himself, in a serene, impersonal way, thinking about art and beauty and history. He had consulted his taste in everything—his taste alone, perhaps; that was what made him so different from every one else. Ralph had something of this same quality, this appearance of thinking that life was a matter of connoisseurship; but in Ralph it was an anomaly, a kind of humorous excrescence, whereas in Mr. Osmond it was the key-note, and everything was in harmony with it. Isabel was certainly far from understanding him completely; his meaning was not at all times obvious. It was hard to see what he meant, for instance, by saying that he was gloriously provincial—which was so exactly the opposite of what she had supposed. Was it a harmless paradox, intended to puzzle her? or was it the last refinement of high culture? Isabel trusted that she should learn in time; it would be very interesting to learn. If Mr. Osmond were provincial, pray what were the characteristics of the capital? Isabel could ask herself this question, in spite of having perceived that her host was a shy personage; for such shyness as his—the shyness of ticklish nerves and fine perceptions—was perfectly consistent with the best breeding. Indeed, it was almost a proof of superior qualities. Mr. Osmond was not a man of easy assurance, who chatted and gossiped with the fluency of a superficial nature; he was critical of himself as well as of others, and exacting a good deal of others (to think them agreeable), he probably took a rather ironical view of what he himself offered: a proof, into the bargain, that he was not grossly conceited. If he had not been shy, he would not have made that gradual, subtle, successful effort to overcome his shyness, to which Isabel felt that she owed both what pleased and what puzzled her in his conversation to-day. He suddenly asked her what she thought of the Countess Gemini—that was doubtless a proof that he was interested in her feelings; it could scarcely be as a help to knowledge of his own sister. That he should be so interested showed an inquiring mind; but it was a little singular that he should sacrifice his fraternal feeling to his curiosity. This was the most eccentric thing he had done.

There were two other rooms, beyond the one in which she had been received, equally full of picturesque objects, and in these apartments Isabel spent a quarter of an hour. Every thing was very curious and valuable, and Mr. Osmond continued to be the kindest of ciceroni, as he led her from one fine piece to another, still holding his little girl by the hand. His kindness almost surprised our young lady, who wondered why he should take so much trouble for her; and she was oppressed at last with the accumulation of beauty and knowledge to which she found herself introduced. There was enough for the present; she had ceased to attend to what he said; she listened to him with attentive eyes, but she was not thinking of what he told her. He probably thought she was cleverer than she was; Madame Merle would have told him so; which was a pity, because in the end he would be sure to find out, and then perhaps even her real cleverness would not reconcile him to his mistake. A part of Isabel's fatigue came from the effort to appear as intelligent as she believed Madame Merle had described her, and from the fear (very unusual with her) of exposing—not her ignorance; for that she cared comparatively little—but her possible grossness of perception. It would have annoyed her to express a liking for something which her host, in his superior enlightenment, would think she ought not to like; or to pass by something at which the truly initiated mind would arrest itself. She was very careful, therefore, as to what she said, as to what she noticed or failed to notice—more careful than she had ever been before.

They came back into the first of the rooms, where the tea had been served; but as the two other ladies were still on the terrace, and as Isabel had not yet been made acquainted with the view, which constituted the paramount distinction of the place, Mr. Osmond directed her steps into the garden without more delay. Madame Merle and the Countess had had chairs brought out, and as the afternoon was lovely, the Countess proposed they should take their tea in the open air. Pansy, therefore, was sent to bid the servant bring out the tray. The sun had got low, the golden light took a deeper tone, and on the mountains and the plain that stretched beneath them, the masses of purple shadow seemed to glow as richly as the places that were still exposed. The scene had an extraordinary charm. The air was almost solemnly still, and the large expanse of the landscape, with its gardenlike culture and nobleness of outline, its teeming valley and delicately-fretted hills, its peculiarly human-looking touches of habitation, lay there in splendid harmony and classic grace.

"You seem so well pleased that I think you can be trusted to come back," Mr. Osmond said, as he led his companion to one of the angles of the terrace.

"I shall certainly come back," Isabel answered, "in spite of what you say about its being bad to live in Italy. What was that you said about one's natural mission? I wonder if I should forsake my natural mission if I were to settle in Florence."

"A woman's natural mission is to be where she is most appreciated."

"The point is to find out where that is."

"Very true—a woman often wastes a great deal of time in the inquiry. People ought to make it very plain to her."

"Such a matter would have to be made very plain to me," said Isabel, smiling.

"I am glad, at any rate, to hear you talk of settling. Madame Merle had given me an idea that you were of a rather roving disposition. I thought she spoke of your having some plan of going round the world."

"I am rather ashamed of my plans; I make a new one every day."

"I don't see why you should be ashamed; it's the greatest of pleasures."

"It seems frivolous, I think," said Isabel. "One ought to choose something very deliberately, and be faithful to that."

"By that rule, then, I have not been frivolous."

"Have you never made plans?"

"Yes, I made one years ago, and I am acting on it to-day."

"It must have been a very pleasant one," said Isabel.

"It was very simple. It was to be as quiet as possible."

"As quiet?" the girl repeated.

"Not to worry—not to strive nor struggle. To resign myself. To be content with a little." He uttered these sentences slowly, with little pauses between, and his intelligent eyes were fixed upon Isabel's with the conscious look of a man who has brought himself to confess something.

"Do you call that simple?" Isabel asked, with a gentle laugh.

"Yes, because it's negative."

"Has your life been negative?"

"Call it affirmative if you like. Only it has affirmed my indifference. Mind you, not my natural indifference—I had none. But my studied, my wilful renunciation."

Isabel scarcely understood him; it seemed a question whether he were joking or not. Why should a man who struck her as having a great fund of reserve suddenly bring himself to be so confidential? This was his affair, however, and his confidences were interesting. "I don't see why you should have renounced," she said in a moment.

"Because I could do nothing. I had no prospects, I was poor, and I was not a man of genius. I had no talents even; I took my measure early in life. I was simply the most fastidious young gentleman living. There were two or three people in the world I envied—the Emperor of Russia, for instance, and the Sultan of Turkey! There were even moments when I envied the Pope of Rome—for the consideration he enjoys. I should have been delighted to be considered to that extent; but since that couldn't be, I didn't care for anything less, and I made up my mind not to go in for honours. A gentleman can always consider himself, and fortunately, I was a gentleman. I could do nothing in Italy—I couldn't even be an Italian patriot. To do that, I should have had to go out of the country; and I was too fond of it to leave it. So I have passed a great many years here, on that quiet plan I spoke of. I have not been at all unhappy. I don't mean to say I have cared for nothing; but the things I have cared for have been definite—limited. The events of my life have been absolutely unperceived by any one save myself; getting an old silver crucifix at a bargain (I have never bought anything dear, of course), or discovering, as I once did, a sketch by Correggio on a panel daubed over by some inspired idiot!"

This would have been rather a dry account of Mr. Osmond's career if Isabel had fully believed it; but her imagination supplied the human element which she was sure had not been wanting. His life had been mingled with other lives more than he admitted; of course she could not expect him to enter into this. For the present she abstained from provoking further revelations; to intimate that he had not told her everything would be more familiar and less considerate than she now desired to be. He had certainly told her quite enough. It was her present inclination, however, to express considerable sympathy for the success with which he had preserved his independence. "That's a very pleasant life," she said, "to renounce everything but Correggio!"

"Oh, I have been very happy; don't imagine me to suggest

for a moment that I have not. It's one's own fault if one is not happy."

"Have you lived here always?"

"No, not always. I lived a long time at Naples, and many years in Rome. But I have been here a good while. Perhaps I shall have to change, however; to do something else. I have no longer myself to think of. My daughter is growing up, and it is very possible she may not care so much for the Correggios and crucifixes as I. I shall have to do what is best for her."

"Yes, do that," said Isabel. "She is such a dear little girl."

"Ah," cried Gilbert Osmond, with feeling, "she is a little saint of heaven! She is my great happiness!"

XXV

WHILE this sufficiently intimate colloquy (prolonged for some time after we cease to follow it) was going on, Madame Merle and her companion, breaking a silence of some duration, had begun to exchange remarks. They were sitting in an attitude of unexpressed expectancy; an attitude especially marked on the part of the Countess Gemini, who, being of a more nervous temperament than Madame Merle, practised with less success the art of disguising impatience. What these ladies were waiting for would not have been apparent, and was perhaps not very definite to their own minds. Madame Merle waited for Osmond to release their young friend from her *tête-à-tête*, and the Countess waited because Madame Merle did. The Countess, moreover, by waiting, found the time ripe for saying something discordant; a necessity of which she had been conscious for the last twenty minutes. Her brother wandered with Isabel to the end of the garden, and she followed the pair for a while with her eyes.

"My dear," she then observed to Madame Merle, "you will excuse me if I don't congratulate you!"

"Very willingly; for I don't in the least know why you should."

"Haven't you a little plan that you think rather well of?" And the Countess nodded towards the retreating couple.

Madame Merle's eyes took the same direction; then she looked serenely at her neighbour. "You know I never understand you very well," she answered, smiling.

"No one can understand better than you when you wish. I see that, just now, you don't wish to."

"You say things to me that no one else does," said Madame Merle, gravely, but without bitterness.

"You mean things you don't like? Doesn't Osmond sometimes say such things?"

"What your brother says has a point."

"Yes, a very sharp one sometimes. If you mean that I am not so clever as he, you must not think I shall suffer from your saying it. But it will be much better that you should understand me."

"Why so?" asked Madame Merle; "what difference will it make?"

"If I don't approve of your plan, you ought to know it in order to appreciate the danger of my interfering with it."

Madame Merle looked as if she were ready to admit that there might be something in this; but in a moment she said quietly—"You think me more calculating than I am."

"It's not your calculating that I think ill of; it's your calculating wrong. You have done so in this case."

"You must have made extensive calculations yourself to discover it."

"No, I have not had time for that. I have seen the girl but this once," said the Countess, "and the conviction has suddenly come to me. I like her very much."

"So do I," Madame Merle declared.

"You have a strange way of showing it."

"Surely—I have given her the advantage of making your acquaintance."

"That, indeed," cried the Countess, with a laugh, "is perhaps the best thing that could happen to her!"

Madame Merle said nothing for some time. The Countess's manner was impertinent, but she did not suffer this to discompose her; and with her eyes upon the violet slope of Monte Morello she gave herself up to reflection.

"My dear lady," she said at last, "I advise you not to agitate yourself. The matter you allude to concerns three persons much stronger of purpose than yourself."

"Three persons? You and Osmond, of course. But is Miss Archer also very strong of purpose?"

"Quite as much so as we."

"Ah then," said the Countess radiantly, "if I convince her it's her interest to resist you, she will do so successfully!"

"Resist us? Why do you express yourself so coarsely? She is not to be subjected to force."

"I am not sure of that. You are capable of anything, you and Osmond. I don't mean Osmond by himself, and I don't mean you by yourself. But together you are dangerous—like some chemical combination."

"You had better leave us alone, then," said Madame Merle, smiling.

"I don't mean to touch you—but I shall talk to that girl."

"My poor Amy," Madame Merle murmured, "I don't see what has got into your head."

"I take an interest in her—that is what has got into my head. I like her."

Madame Merle hesitated a moment. "I don't think she likes you."

The Countess's bright little eyes expanded, and her face was set in a grimace. "Ah, you *are* dangerous," she cried, "even by yourself!"

"If you want her to like you, don't abuse your brother to her," said Madame Merle.

"I don't suppose you pretend she has fallen in love with him—in two interviews."

Madame Merle looked a moment at Isabel and at the master of the house. He was leaning against the parapet, facing her, with his arms folded; and she, at present, though she had her face turned to the opposite prospect, was evidently not scrutinising it. As Madame Merle watched her she lowered her eyes; she was listening, possibly with a certain embarrassment, while she pressed the point of her parasol into the path. Madame Merle rose from her chair. "Yes, I think so!" she said.

The shabby footboy, summoned by Pansy, had come out with a small table, which he placed upon the grass, and then had gone back and fetched the tea-tray; after which he again disappeared, to return with a couple of chairs. Pansy had watched these proceedings with the deepest interest, standing with her small hands folded together upon the front of her scanty frock; but she had not presumed to offer assistance to the servant. When the tea-table had been arranged, however, she gently approached her aunt.

"Do you think papa would object to my making the tea?"

The Countess looked at her with a deliberately critical gaze, and without answering her question. "My poor niece," she said, "is that your best frock?"

"Ah no," Pansy answered, "it's just a little toilet for common occasions."

"Do you call it a common occasion when I come to see you?—to say nothing of Madame Merle and the pretty lady yonder."

Pansy reflected a moment, looking gravely from one of the persons mentioned to the other. Then her face broke into its perfect smile. "I have a pretty dress, but even that one is very simple. Why should I expose it beside your beautiful things?"

"Because it's the prettiest you have; for me you must always wear the prettiest. Please put it on the next time. It seems to me they don't dress you so well as they might."

The child stroked down her antiquated skirt, sparingly. "It's a good little dress to make tea—don't you think? Do you not believe papa would allow me?"

"Impossible for me to say, my child," said the Countess. "For me, your father's ideas are unfathomable. Madame Merle understands them better; ask her."

Madame Merle smiled with her usual geniality. "It's a weighty question—let me think. It seems to me it would please your father to see a careful little daughter making his tea. It's the proper duty of the daughter of the house—when she grows up."

"So it seems to me, Madame Merle!" Pansy cried. "You shall see how well I will make it. A spoonful for each." And she began to busy herself at the table.

"Two spoonfuls for me," said the Countess, who, with Madame Merle, remained for some moments watching her. "Listen to me, Pansy," the Countess resumed at last. "I should like to know what you think of your visitor."

"Ah, she is not mine—she is papa's," said Pansy.

"Miss Archer came to see you as well," Madame Merle remarked.

"I am very happy to hear that. She has been very polite to me."

"Do you like her, then?" the Countess asked.

"She is charming—charming," said Pansy, in her little neat, conversational tone. "She pleases me exceedingly."

"And you think she pleases your father?"

"Ah, really, Countess," murmured Madame Merle, dissuasively. "Go and call them to tea," she went on, to the child.

"You will see if they don't like it!" Pansy declared; and went off to summon the others, who were still lingering at the end of the terrace.

"If Miss Archer is to become her mother it is surely interesting to know whether the child likes her," said the Countess.

"If your brother marries again it won't be for Pansy's sake," Madame Merle replied. "She will soon be sixteen, and after that she will begin to need a husband rather than a step-mother."

"And will you provide the husband as well?"

"I shall certainly take an interest in her marrying well. I imagine you will do the same."

"Indeed I shan't!" cried the Countess. "Why should I, of all women, set such a price on a husband?"

"You didn't marry well; that's what I am speaking of. When I say a husband, I mean a good one."

"There are no good ones. Osmond won't be a good one."

Madame Merle closed her eyes a moment. "You are irritated just now; I don't know why," she said, presently. "I don't think you will really object either to your brother, or to your niece's, marrying, when the time comes for them to do so; and as regards Pansy, I am confident that we shall some day have the pleasure of looking for a husband for her together. Your large acquaintance will be a great help."

"Yes, I am irritated," the Countess answered. "You often irritate me. Your own coolness is fabulous; you are a strange woman."

"It is much better that we should always act together," Madame Merle went on.

"Do you mean that as a threat?" asked the Countess, rising.

Madame Merle shook her head, with a smile of sadness. "No indeed, you have not my coolness!"

Isabel and Mr. Osmond were now coming toward them, and Isabel had taken Pansy by the hand.

"Do you pretend to believe he would make her happy?" the Countess demanded.

"If he should marry Miss Archer I suppose he would behave like a gentleman."

The Countess jerked herself into a succession of attitudes. "Do you mean as most gentlemen behave? That would be much to be thankful for! Of course Osmond's a gentleman; his own sister needn't be reminded of that. But does he think he can marry any girl he happens to pick out? Osmond's a gentleman, of course; but I must say I have never, no never, seen any one of Osmond's pretensions! What they are all based upon is more than I can say. I am his own sister; I might be supposed to know. Who is he, if you please? What has he ever done? If there had been anything particularly grand in his origin—if he were made of some superior clay— I suppose I should have got some inkling of it. If there had been any great honours or splendours in the family, I should certainly have made the most of them; they would have been quite in my line. But there is nothing, nothing, nothing. One's parents were charming people of course; but so were yours, I have no doubt. Every one is a charming person, now-a-days. Even I am a charming person; don't laugh, it has literally been said. As for Osmond, he has always appeared to believe that he is descended from the gods."

"You may say what you please," said Madame Merle, who had listened to this quick outbreak none the less attentively, we may believe, because her eye wandered away from the speaker, and her hands busied themselves with adjusting the knots of ribbon on her dress. "You Osmonds are a fine race— your blood must flow from some very pure source. Your brother, like an intelligent man, has had the conviction of it, if he has not had the proofs. You are modest about it, but you yourself are extremely distinguished. What do you say about your niece? The child's a little duchess. Nevertheless," Madame Merle added, "it will not be an easy matter for Osmond to marry Miss Archer. But he can try."

"I hope she will refuse him. It will take him down a little."

"We must not forget that he is one of the cleverest of men."

"I have heard you say that before; but I haven't yet discovered what he has done."

"What he has done? He has done nothing that has had to be undone. And he has known how to wait."

"To wait for Miss Archer's money? How much of it is there?"

"That's not what I mean," said Madame Merle. "Miss Archer has seventy thousand pounds."

"Well, it is a pity she is so nice," the Countess declared. "To be sacrificed, any girl would do. She needn't be superior."

"If she were not superior, your brother would never look at her. He must have the best."

"Yes," rejoined the Countess, as they went forward a little to meet the others, "he is very hard to please. That makes me fear for her happiness!"

XXVI

G ILBERT OSMOND came to see Isabel again; that is, he came to the Palazzo Crescentini. He had other friends there as well; and to Mrs. Touchett and Madame Merle he was always impartially civil; but the former of these ladies noted the fact that in the course of a fortnight he called five times, and compared it with another fact that she found no difficulty in remembering. Two visits a year had hitherto constituted his regular tribute to Mrs. Touchett's charms, and she had never observed that he selected for such visits those moments, of almost periodical recurrence, when Madame Merle was under her roof. It was not for Madame Merle that he came; these two were old friends, and he never put himself out for her. He was not fond of Ralph—Ralph had told her so—and it was not supposable that Mr. Osmond had suddenly taken a fancy to her son. Ralph was imperturbable—Ralph had a kind of loose-fitting urbanity that wrapped him about like an ill-made overcoat, but of which he never divested himself; he thought Mr. Osmond very good company, and would have been willing at any time to take the hospitable view of his idiosyncracies. But he did not flatter himself that the desire to repair a past injustice was the motive of their visitor's calls; he read the situation more clearly. Isabel was the attraction, and in all conscience a sufficient one. Osmond was a critic, a student of the exquisite, and it was natural he should admire an admirable person. So when his mother said to him that it was very plain what Mr. Osmond was thinking of, Ralph replied that he was quite of her opinion. Mrs. Touchett had always liked Mr. Osmond; she thought him so much of a gentleman. As he had never been an importunate visitor he had had no chance to be offensive, and he was recommended to Mrs. Touchett by his appearance of being as well able to do without her as she was to do without him—a quality that always excited her esteem. It gave her no satisfaction, however, to think that he had taken it into his head to marry her niece. Such an alliance, on Isabel's part, would have an air of almost morbid perversity. Mrs. Touchett easily remembered that the girl had refused an

English peer; and that a young lady for whom Lord Warburton had not been up to the mark should content herself with an obscure American dilettante, a middle-aged widower with an overgrown daughter and an income of nothing—this answered to nothing in Mrs. Touchett's conception of success. She took, it will be observed, not the sentimental, but the political, view of matrimony—a view which has always had much to recommend it. "I trust she won't have the folly to listen to him," she said to her son; to which Ralph replied that Isabel's listening was one thing and her answering quite another. He knew that she had listened to others, but that she had made them listen to her in return; and he found much entertainment in the idea that, in these few months that he had known her, he should see a third suitor at her gate. She had wanted to see life, and fortune was serving her to her taste; a succession of gentlemen going down on their knees to her was by itself a respectable chapter of experience. Ralph looked forward to a fourth and a fifth *soupirant*; he had no conviction that she would stop at a third. She would keep the gate ajar and open a parley; she would certainly not allow number three to come in. He expressed this view, somewhat after this fashion, to his mother, who looked at him as if he had been dancing a jig. He had such a fanciful, pictorial way of saying things that he might as well address her in the deaf-mute's alphabet.

"I don't think I know what you mean," she said; "you use too many metaphors; I could never understand allegories. The two words in the language I most respect are Yes and No. If Isabel wants to marry Mr. Osmond, she will do so in spite of all your similes. Let her alone to find a favourable comparison for anything she undertakes. I know very little about the young man in America; I don't think she spends much of her time in thinking of him, and I suspect he has got tired of waiting for her. There is nothing in life to prevent her marrying Mr. Osmond, if she only looks at him in a certain way. That is all very well; no one approves more than I of one's pleasing one's self. But she takes her pleasure in such odd things; she is capable of marrying Mr. Osmond for his opinions. She wants to be disinterested: as if she were the only person who is in danger of not being so! Will he be so disinterested when he has the spending of her money? That was her idea before your father's death, and it has acquired new charms for her since. She ought to marry some one of whose disinterestedness she should be sure, herself; and there would be no such proof of that as his having a fortune of his own."

"My dear mother, I am not afraid," Ralph answered. "She is making fools of us all. She will please herself, of course; but she will do so by studying human nature and retaining her liberty. She has started on an exploring expedition, and I don't think she will change her course, at the outset, at a signal from Gilbert Osmond. She may have slackened speed for an hour, but before we know it she will be steaming away again. Excuse another metaphor."

Mrs. Touchett excused it perhaps, but she was not so much reassured as to withhold from Madame Merle the expression of her fears. "You who know everything," she said, "you must know this: whether that man is making love to my niece."

Madame Merle opened her expressive eyes, and with a brilliant smile—"Heaven help us," she exclaimed, "that's an idea!"

"Has it never occurred to you?"

"You make me feel like a fool—but I confess it hasn't. I wonder," added Madame Merle, "whether it has occurred to her."

"I think I will ask her," said Mrs. Touchett.

Madame Merle reflected a moment. "Don't put it into her head. The thing would be to ask Mr. Osmond."

"I can't do that," said Mrs. Touchett; "it's none of my business."

"I will ask him myself," Madame Merle declared, bravely.

"It's none of yours, either."

"That's precisely why I can afford to ask him; it is so much less my business than any one's else, that in me the question will not seem to him embarrassing."

"Pray let me know on the first day, then," said Mrs. Touchett. "If I can't speak to him, at least I can speak to her."

"Don't be too quick with her; don't inflame her imagination."

"I never did anything to any one's imagination. But I am always sure she will do something I don't like."

"You wouldn't like this," Madame Merle observed, without the point of interrogation.

"Why should I, pray? Mr. Osmond has nothing to offer."

Again Madame Merle was silent, while her thoughtful smile drew up her mouth more than usual toward the left corner. "Let us distinguish. Gilbert Osmond is certainly not the first comer. He is a man who under favourable circumstances might very well make an impression. He has made an impression, to my knowledge, more than once."

"Don't tell me about his love-affairs; they are nothing to me!" Mrs. Touchett cried. "What you say is precisely why I wish he would cease his visits. He has nothing in the world that I know of but a dozen or two of early masters and a grown-up daughter."

"The early masters are worth a good deal of money," said Madame Merle, "and the daughter is a very young and very harmless person."

"In other words, she is an insipid school-girl. Is that what you mean? Having no fortune, she can't hope to marry, as they marry here; so that Isabel will have to furnish her either with a maintenance or with a dowry."

"Isabel probably would not object to being kind to her. I think she likes the child."

"Another reason for Mr. Osmond stopping at home! Otherwise, a week hence, we shall have Isabel arriving at the conviction that her mission in life is to prove that a stepmother may sacrifice herself—and that, to prove it, she must first become one."

"She would make a charming stepmother," said Madame Merle, smiling; "but I quite agree with you that she had better not decide upon her mission too hastily. Changing one's mission is often awkward! I will investigate and report to you."

All this went on quite over Isabel's head; she had no suspicion that her relations with Mr. Osmond were being discussed. Madame Merle had said nothing to put her on her guard; she alluded no more pointedly to Mr. Osmond than to the other gentlemen of Florence, native and foreign, who

came in considerable numbers to pay their respects to Miss
Archer's aunt. Isabel thought him very pleasant; she liked to
think of him. She had carried away an image from her visit
to his hill-top which her subsequent knowledge of him did
nothing to efface and which happened to take her fancy particularly—the image of a quiet, clever, sensitive, distinguished man, strolling on a moss-grown terrace above the
sweet Val d'Arno, and holding by the hand a little girl whose
sympathetic docility gave a new aspect to childhood. The picture was not brilliant, but she liked its lowness of tone, and
the atmosphere of summer twilight that pervaded it. It
seemed to tell a story—a story of the sort that touched her
most easily; to speak of a serious choice, a choice between
things of a shallow, and things of a deep, interest; of a lonely,
studious life in a lovely land; of an old sorrow that sometimes
ached to-day; a feeling of pride that was perhaps exaggerated,
but that had an element of nobleness; a care for beauty and
perfection so natural and so cultivated together, that it had
been the main occupation of a lifetime of which the arid
places were watered with the sweet sense of a quaint, half-
anxious, half-helpless fatherhood. At the Palazzo Crescentini
Mr. Osmond's manner remained the same; shy at first, and
full of the effort (visible only to a sympathetic eye) to overcome this disadvantage; an effort which usually resulted in a
great deal of easy, lively, very positive, rather aggressive, and
always effective, talk. Mr. Osmond's talk was not injured by
the indication of an eagerness to shine; Isabel found no difficulty in believing that a person was sincere who had so many
of the signs of strong conviction—as, for instance, an explicit
and graceful appreciation of anything that might be said on
his own side, said perhaps by Miss Archer in particular. What
continued to please this young lady was his extraordinary subtlety. There was such a fine intellectual intention in what he
said, and the movement of his wit was like that of a quick-
flashing blade. One day he brought his little daughter with
him, and Isabel was delighted to renew acquaintance with the
child, who, as she presented her forehead to be kissed by
every member of the circle, reminded her vividly of an *in-
génue* in a French play. Isabel had never seen a young girl of
this pattern; American girls were very different—different

too were the daughters of England. This young lady was so neat, so complete in her manner; and yet in character, as one could see, so innocent and infantine. She sat on the sofa, by Isabel; she wore a small grenadine mantle and a pair of the useful gloves that Madame Merle had given her—little grey gloves, with a single button. She was like a sheet of blank paper—the ideal *jeune fille* of foreign fiction. Isabel hoped that so fair and smooth a page would be covered with an edifying text.

The Countess Gemini also came to call upon her, but the Countess was quite another affair. She was by no means a blank sheet; she had been written over in a variety of hands, and Mrs. Touchett, who felt by no means honoured by her visit, declared that a number of unmistakable blots were to be seen upon her surface. The Countess Gemini was indeed the occasion of a slight discussion between the mistress of the house and the visitor from Rome, in which Madame Merle (who was not such a fool as to irritate people by always agreeing with them) availed herself humorously of that large license of dissent which her hostess permitted as freely as she practised it. Mrs. Touchett had pronounced it a piece of audacity that the Countess Gemini should have presented herself at this time of day at the door of a house in which she was esteemed so little as she must long have known herself to be at the Palazzo Crescentini. Isabel had been made acquainted with the estimate which prevailed under this roof; it represented Mr. Osmond's sister as a kind of flighty reprobate. She had been married by her mother—a heartless featherhead like herself, with an appreciation of foreign titles which the daughter, to do her justice, had probably by this time thrown off—to an Italian nobleman who had perhaps given her some excuse for attempting to quench the consciousness of neglect. The Countess, however, had consoled herself too well, and it was notorious in Florence that she had consoled others also. Mrs. Touchett had never consented to receive her, though the Countess had made overtures of old. Florence was not an austere city; but, as Mrs. Touchett said, she had to draw the line somewhere.

Madame Merle defended the unhappy lady with a great deal of zeal and wit. She could not see why Mrs. Touchett should make a scapegoat of that poor Countess, who had really done no harm, who had only done good in the wrong way. One must certainly draw the line, but while one was about it one should draw it straight; it was a very crooked chalk-mark that would exclude the Countess Gemini. In that case Mrs. Touchett had better shut up her house; this perhaps would be the best course so long as she remained in Florence. One must be fair and not make arbitrary differences; the Countess had doubtless been imprudent; she had not been so clever as other women. She was a good creature, not clever at all; but since when had that been a ground of exclusion from the best society? It was a long time since one had heard anything about her, and there could be no better proof of her having renounced the error of her ways than her desire to become a member of Mrs. Touchett's circle. Isabel could contribute nothing to this interesting dispute, not even a patient attention; she contented herself with having given a friendly welcome to the Countess Gemini, who, whatever her defects, had at least the merit of being Mr. Osmond's sister. As she liked the brother, Isabel thought it proper to try and like the sister; in spite of the growing perplexity of things she was still perfectly capable of these rather primitive sequences of feeling. She had not received the happiest impression of the Countess on meeting her at the villa, but she was thankful for an opportunity to repair this accident. Had not Mr. Osmond declared that she was a good woman? To have proceeded from Gilbert Osmond, this was rather a rough statement; but Madame Merle bestowed upon it a certain improving polish. She told Isabel more about the poor Countess than Mr. Osmond had done, and related the history of her marriage and its consequences. The Count was a member of an ancient Tuscan family, but so poor that he had been glad to accept Amy Osmond, in spite of her being no beauty, with the modest dowry her mother was able to offer—a sum about equivalent to that which had already formed her brother's share of their patrimony. Count Gemini, since then, however, had inherited money, and now they were well enough off, as Italians went, though Amy was horribly extravagant. The Count was a low-lived brute; he had given his wife every excuse. She had no children; she had lost three within a year of their birth. Her mother, who had pretensions to "culture," wrote descriptive poems, and corresponded on Italian subjects with the English weekly journals—her mother had died three years after the Countess's marriage, the father having died long before. One could see this in Gilbert Osmond, Madame Merle thought—see that he had been brought up by a woman; though, to do him justice, one would suppose it had been by a more sensible woman than the American Corinne, as Mrs. Osmond liked to be called. She had brought her children to Italy after her husband's death, and Mrs. Touchett remembered her during the years that followed her arrival. She thought her a horrible snob; but this was an irregularity of judgment on Mrs. Touchett's part, for she, like Mrs. Osmond, approved of political marriages. The Countess was very good company, and not such a fool as she seemed; one got on with her perfectly if one observed a single simple condition—that of not believing a word she said. Madame Merle had always made the best of her for her brother's sake; he always appreciated any kindness shown to Amy, because (if it had to be confessed for him) he was rather ashamed of her. Naturally, he couldn't like her style, her loudness, her want of repose. She displeased him; she acted on his nerves; she was not *his* sort of woman. What was his sort of woman? Oh, the opposite of the Countess, a woman who should always speak the truth. Isabel was unable to estimate the number of fibs her visitor had told her; the Countess indeed had given her an impression of rather silly sincerity. She had talked almost exclusively about herself; how much she should like to know Miss Archer; how thankful she should be for a real friend; how nasty the people in Florence were; how tired she was of the place; how much she should like to live somewhere else—in Paris, or London, or St. Petersburg; how impossible it was to get anything nice to wear in Italy, except a little old lace; how dear the world was growing everywhere; what a life of suffering and privation she had led. Madame Merle listened with interest to Isabel's account of her conversation with this plaintive butterfly; but she had not needed it to feel exempt from anxiety. On the whole, she was not afraid of the Countess, and she could afford to do what was altogether best—not to appear so.

Isabel had another visitor, whom it was not, even behind her back, so easy a matter to patronise. Henrietta Stackpole, who had left Paris after Mrs. Touchett's departure for San Remo and had worked her way down, as she said, through the cities of North Italy, arrived in Florence about the middle of May. Madame Merle surveyed her with a single glance, comprehended her, and, after a moment's concentrated reflection, determined to like her. She determined, indeed, to delight in her. To like her was impossible; but the intenser sentiment might be managed. Madame Merle managed it beautifully, and Isabel felt that in foreseeing this event she had done justice to her friend's breadth of mind. Henrietta's arrival had been announced by Mr. Bantling, who, coming down from Nice while she was at Venice, and expecting to find her in Florence, which she had not yet reached, came to the Palazzo Crescentini to express his disappointment. Henrietta's own advent occurred two days later, and produced in Mr. Bantling an emotion amply accounted for by the fact that he had not seen her since the termination of the episode at Versailles. The humorous view of his situation was generally taken, but it was openly expressed only by Ralph Touchett, who, in the privacy of his own apartment, when Bantling smoked a cigar there, indulged in Heaven knows what genial pleasantries on the subject of the incisive Miss Stackpole and her British ally. This gentleman took the joke in perfectly good part, and artlessly confessed that he regarded the affair as an intellectual flirtation. He liked Miss Stackpole extremely; he thought she had a wonderful head on her shoulders, and found great comfort in the society of a woman who was not perpetually thinking about what would be said and how it would look. Miss Stackpole never cared how it looked, and if she didn't care, pray why should he? But his curiosity had been roused; he wanted awfully to see whether she ever would care. He was prepared to go as far as she—he did not see why he should stop first.

Henrietta showed no signs of stopping at all. Her prospects, as we know, had brightened upon her leaving England, and she was now in the full enjoyment of her copious resources. She had indeed been obliged to sacrifice her hopes with regard to the inner life; the social question, on the continent, bristled with difficulties even more numerous than those she had encountered in England. But on the continent there was the outer life, which was palpable and visible at every turn, and more easily convertible to literary uses than the customs of those opaque islanders. Out of doors, in foreign lands, as Miss Stackpole ingeniously remarked, one seemed to see the right side of the tapestry; out of doors, in England, one seemed to see the wrong side, which gave one no notion of the figure. It is mortifying to be obliged to confess it, but Henrietta, despairing of more occult things, was now paying much attention to the outer life. She had been studying it for two months at Venice, from which city she sent to the *Interviewer* a conscientious account of the gondolas, the Piazza, the Bridge of Sighs, the pigeons and the young boatman who chanted Tasso. The *Interviewer* was perhaps disappointed, but Henrietta was at least seeing Europe. Her present purpose was to get down to Rome before the malaria should come on—she apparently supposed that it began on a fixed day; and with this design she was to spend at present but few days in Florence. Mr. Bantling was to go with her to Rome, and she pointed out to Isabel that as he had been there before, as he was a military man, and as he had had a classical education—he was brought up at Eton, where they study nothing but Latin, said Miss Stackpole—he would be a most useful companion in the city of the Cæsars. At this juncture Ralph had the happy idea of proposing to Isabel that she also, under his own escort, should make a pilgrimage to Rome. She expected to pass a portion of the next winter there—that was very well; but meantime there was no harm in surveying the field. There were ten days left of the beautiful month of May—the most precious month of all to the true Rome-lover. Isabel would become a Rome-lover; that was a foregone conclusion. She was provided with a well-tested companion of her own sex, whose society, thanks to the fact that she had other calls upon her sympathy, would probably not be oppressive. Madame Merle would remain with Mrs. Touchett; she had left Rome for the summer and would not care to return. This lady professed herself delighted to be left at peace in Florence; she had locked up her apartment and sent her cook home to Palestrina. She urged

Isabel, however, to assent to Ralph's proposal, and assured
her that a good introduction to Rome was not a thing to be
despised. Isabel, in truth, needed no urging, and the party of
four arranged its little journey. Mrs. Touchett, on this occasion, had resigned herself to the absence of a duenna; we have
seen that she now inclined to the belief that her niece should
stand alone.

Isabel saw Gilbert Osmond before she started, and mentioned her intention to him.

"I should like to be in Rome with you," he said; "I should
like to see you there."

She hesitated a moment.

"You might come, then."

"But you'll have a lot of people with you."

"Ah," Isabel admitted, "of course I shall not be alone."

For a moment he said nothing more.

"You'll like it," he went on, at last. "They have spoiled it,
but you'll like it."

"Ought I to dislike it, because it's spoiled?" she asked.

"No, I think not. It has been spoiled so often. If I were to
go, what should I do with my little girl?"

"Can't you leave her at the villa?"

"I don't know that I like that—though there is a very good
old woman who looks after her. I can't afford a governess."

"Bring her with you, then," said Isabel, smiling.

Mr. Osmond looked grave.

"She has been in Rome all winter, at her convent; and she
is too young to make journeys of pleasure."

"You don't like bringing her forward?" Isabel suggested.

"No, I think young girls should be kept out of the world."

"I was brought up on a different system."

"You? Oh, with you it succeeded, because you—you were
exceptional."

"I don't see why," said Isabel, who, however, was not sure
there was not some truth in the speech.

Mr. Osmond did not explain; he simply went on. "If I
thought it would make her resemble you to join a social
group in Rome, I would take her there to-morrow."

"Don't make her resemble me," said Isabel; "keep her like
herself."

"I might send her to my sister," Mr. Osmond suggested. He had almost the air of asking advice; he seemed to like to talk over his domestic matters with Isabel.

"Yes," said the girl; "I think that would not do much towards making her resemble me!"

After she had left Florence, Gilbert Osmond met Madame Merle at the Countess Gemini's. There were other people present; the Countess's drawing-room was usually well filled, and the talk had been general; but after a while Osmond left his place and came and sat on an ottoman half-behind, half-beside, Madame Merle's chair.

"She wants me to go to Rome with her," he announced, in a low voice.

"To go with her?"

"To be there while she is there. She proposed it."

"I suppose you mean that you proposed it, and that she assented."

"Of course I gave her a chance. But she is encouraging—she is very encouraging."

"I am glad to hear it—but don't cry victory too soon. Of course you will go to Rome."

"Ah," said Osmond, "it makes one work, this idea of yours!"

"Don't pretend you don't enjoy it—you are very ungrateful. You have not been so well occupied these many years."

"The way you take it is beautiful," said Osmond. "I ought to be grateful for that."

"Not too much so, however," Madame Merle answered. She talked with her usual smile, leaning back in her chair, and looking round the room. "You have made a very good impression, and I have seen for myself that you have received one. You have not come to Mrs. Touchett's seven times to oblige me."

"The girl is not disagreeable," Osmond quietly remarked.

Madame Merle dropped her eye on him a moment, during which her lips closed with a certain firmness.

"Is that all you can find to say about that fine creature?"

"All? Isn't it enough? Of how many people have you heard me say more?"

She made no answer to this, but still presented her conversational smile to the room.

"You're unfathomable," she murmured at last. "I am frightened at the abyss into which I shall have dropped her!"

Osmond gave a laugh.

"You can't draw back—you have gone too far."

"Very good; but you must do the rest yourself."

"I shall do it," said Osmond.

Madame Merle remained silent, and he changed his place again; but when she rose to go he also took leave. Mrs. Touchett's victoria was awaiting her in the court, and after he had helped Madame Merle into it he stood there detaining her.

"You are very indiscreet," she said, rather wearily; "you should not have moved when I did."

He had taken off his hat; he passed his hand over his forehead.

"I always forget; I am out of the habit."

"You are quite unfathomable," she repeated, glancing up at the windows of the house; a modern structure in the new part of the town.

He paid no heed to this remark, but said to Madame Merle, with a considerable appearance of earnestness—

"She is really very charming; I have scarcely known any one more graceful."

"I like to hear you say that. The better you like her, the better for me."

"I like her very much. She is all you said, and into the bargain she is capable of great devotion. She has only one fault."

"What is that?"

"She has too many ideas."

"I warned you she was clever."

"Fortunately they are very bad ones," said Osmond.

"Why is that fortunate?"

"*Dame*, if they must be sacrificed!"

Madame Merle leaned back, looking straight before her; then she spoke to the coachman. But Osmond again detained her.

"If I go to Rome, what shall I do with Pansy?"

"I will go and see her," said Madame Merle.

XXVII

I SHALL NOT undertake to give an account of Isabel's
impressions of Rome, to analyse her feelings as she trod
the ancient pavement of the Forum, or to number her pulsations as she crossed the threshold of St. Peter's. It is enough
to say that her perception of the endless interest of the place
was such as might have been expected in a young woman of
her intelligence and culture. She had always been fond of history, and here was history in the stones of the street and the
atoms of the sunshine. She had an imagination that kindled
at the mention of great deeds, and wherever she turned some
great deed had been acted. These things excited her, but she
was quietly excited. It seemed to her companions that she
spoke less than usual, and Ralph Touchett, when he appeared
to be looking listlessly and awkwardly over her head, was
really dropping an eye of observation upon her. To her own
knowledge she was very happy; she would even have been
willing to believe that these were to be on the whole the happiest hours of her life. The sense of the mighty human past
was heavy upon her, but it was interfused in the strangest,
suddenest, most capricious way, with the fresh, cool breath
of the future. Her feelings were so mingled that she scarcely
knew whither any of them would lead her, and she went
about in a kind of repressed ecstasy of contemplation, seeing
often in the things she looked at a great deal more than was
there, and yet not seeing many of the items enumerated in
"Murray." Rome, as Ralph said, was in capital condition. The
herd of re-echoing tourists had departed, and most of the solemn places had relapsed into solemnity. The sky was a blaze
of blue, and the plash of the fountains, in their mossy niches,
had lost its chill and doubled its music. On the corners of the
warm, bright streets one stumbled upon bundles of flowers.

Our friends had gone one afternoon—it was the third of
their stay—to look at the latest excavations in the Forum;
these labours having been for some time previous largely extended. They had gone down from the modern street to the
level of the Sacred Way, along which they wandered with a
reverence of step which was not the same on the part of each.

Henrietta Stackpole was struck with the fact that ancient Rome had been paved a good deal like New York, and even found an analogy between the deep chariot-ruts which are traceable in the antique street, and the iron grooves which mark the course of the American horse-car. The sun had begun to sink, the air was filled with a golden haze, and the long shadows of broken column and formless pedestal were thrown across the field of ruin. Henrietta wandered away with Mr. Bantling, in whose Latin reminiscences she was apparently much engrossed, and Ralph addressed such elucidations as he was prepared to offer, to the attentive ear of our heroine. One of the humble archæologists who hover about the place had put himself at the disposal of the two, and repeated his lesson with a fluency which the decline of the season had done nothing to impair. A process of digging was going on in a remote corner of the Forum, and he presently remarked that if it should please the *signori* to go and watch it a little, they might see something interesting. The proposal commended itself more to Ralph than to Isabel, who was weary with much wandering; so that she charged her companion to satisfy his curiosity while she patiently awaited his return. The hour and the place were much to her taste, and she should enjoy being alone. Ralph accordingly went off with the cicerone, while Isabel sat down on a prostrate column, near the foundations of the Capitol. She desired a quarter of an hour's solitude, but she was not long to enjoy it. Keen as was her interest in the rugged relics of the Roman past that lay scattered around her, and in which the corrosion of centuries had still left so much of individual life, her thoughts, after resting a while on these things, had wandered, by a concatenation of stages it might require some subtlety to trace, to regions and objects more contemporaneous. From the Roman past to Isabel Archer's future was a long stride, but her imagination had taken it in a single flight, and now hovered in slow circles over the nearer and richer field. She was so absorbed in her thoughts, as she bent her eyes upon a row of cracked but not dislocated slabs covering the ground at her feet, that she had not heard the sound of approaching footsteps before a shadow was thrown across the line of her vision. She looked up and saw a gentleman—a gentleman who was not Ralph come back to say that the excavations were a bore. This personage was startled as she was startled; he stood there, smiling a little, blushing a good deal, and raising his hat.

"Lord Warburton!" Isabel exclaimed, getting up.

"I had no idea it was you," he said. "I turned that corner and came upon you."

Isabel looked about her.

"I am alone, but my companions have just left me. My cousin is gone to look at the digging over there."

"Ah yes; I see." And Lord Warburton's eyes wandered vaguely in the direction Isabel had indicated. He stood firmly before her; he had stopped smiling; he folded his arms with a kind of deliberation. "Don't let me disturb you," he went on, looking at her dejected pillar. "I am afraid you are tired."

"Yes, I am rather tired." She hesitated a moment, and then she sat down. "But don't let me interrupt you," she added.

"Oh dear, I am quite alone, I have nothing on earth to do. I had no idea you were in Rome. I have just come from the East. I am only passing through."

"You have been making a long journey," said Isabel, who had learned from Ralph that Lord Warburton was absent from England.

"Yes, I came abroad for six months—soon after I saw you last. I have been in Turkey and Asia Minor; I came the other day from Athens." He spoke with visible embarrassment; this unexpected meeting caused him an emotion he was unable to conceal. He looked at Isabel a moment, and then he said, abruptly—"Do you wish me to leave you, or will you let me stay a little?"

She looked up at him, gently. "I don't wish you to leave me, Lord Warburton; I am very glad to see you."

"Thank you for saying that. May I sit down?"

The fluted shaft on which Isabel had taken her seat would have afforded a resting-place to several persons, and there was plenty of room even for a highly-developed Englishman. This fine specimen of that great class seated himself near our young lady, and in the course of five minutes he had asked her several questions, taken rather at random, and of which, as he asked some of them twice over, he apparently did not always heed the answer; had given her, too, some information about himself which was not wasted upon her calmer feminine sense. Lord Warburton, though he tried hard to seem easy, was agitated; he repeated more than once that he had not expected to meet her, and it was evident that the encounter touched him in a way that would have made preparation advisable. He had abrupt alternations of gaiety and gravity; he appeared at one moment to seek his neighbour's eye and at the next to avoid it. He was splendidly sunburnt; even his multitudinous beard seemed to have been burnished by the fire of Asia. He was dressed in the loose-fitting, heterogeneous garments in which the English traveller in foreign lands is wont to consult his comfort and affirm his nationality; and with his clear grey eye, his bronzed complexion, fresh beneath its brownness, his manly figure, his modest manner, and his general air of being a gentleman and an explorer, he was such a representative of the British race as need not in any clime have been disavowed by those who have a kindness for it. Isabel noted these things, and was glad she had always liked Lord Warburton. He was evidently as likeable as before, and the tone of his voice, which she had formerly thought delightful, was as good as an assurance that he would never change for the worse. They talked about the matters that were naturally in order; her uncle's death, Ralph's state of health, the way she had passed her winter, her visit to Rome, her return to Florence, her plans for the summer, the hotel she was staying at; and then Lord Warburton's own adventures, movements, intentions, impressions and present domicile. At last there was a silence, and she knew what he was thinking of. His eyes were fixed on the ground; but at last he raised them and said gravely—"I have written to you several times."

"Written to me? I have never got your letters."

"I never sent them. I burned them up."

"Ah," said Isabel with a laugh, "it was better that you should do that than I!"

"I thought you wouldn't care about them," he went on, with a simplicity that might have touched her. "It seemed to me that after all I had no right to trouble you with letters."

"I should have been very glad to have news of you. You know that I hoped that—that—" Isabel stopped; it seemed to her there would be a certain flatness in the utterance of her thought.

"I know what you are going to say. You hoped we should always remain good friends." This formula, as Lord Warburton uttered it, was certainly flat enough; but then he was interested in making it appear so.

Isabel found herself reduced simply to saying—"Please don't talk of all that;" a speech which hardly seemed to her an improvement on the other.

"It's a small consolation to allow me!" Lord Warburton exclaimed, with force.

"I can't pretend to console you," said the girl, who, as she sat there, found it good to think that she had given him the answer that had satisfied him so little six months before. He was pleasant, he was powerful, he was gallant, there was no better man than he. But her answer remained.

"It's very well you don't try to console me; it would not be in your power," she heard him say, through the medium of her quickened reflections.

"I hoped we should meet again, because I had no fear you would attempt to make me feel I had wronged you. But when you do that—the pain is greater than the pleasure." And Isabel got up, looking for her companions.

"I don't want to make you feel that; of course I can't say that. I only just want you to know one or two things, in fairness to myself as it were. I won't return to the subject again. I felt very strongly what I expressed to you last year; I couldn't think of anything else. I tried to forget—energetically, systematically. I tried to take an interest in some one else. I tell you this because I want you to know I did my duty. I didn't succeed. It was for the same purpose I went abroad—as far away as possible. They say travelling distracts the mind; but it didn't distract mine. I have thought of you perpetually, ever since I last saw you. I am exactly the same. I love you just as much, and everything I said to you then is just as true. However, I don't mean to trouble you now; it's only for a moment. I may add that when I came upon you a moment since, without the smallest idea of seeing you, I was in the very act of wishing I knew where you were."

He had recovered his self-control, as I say, and while he

spoke it became complete. He spoke plainly and simply, in a low tone of voice, in a matter-of-fact way. There might have been something impressive, even to a woman of less imagination than the one he addressed, in hearing this brilliant, brave-looking gentleman express himself so modestly and reasonably.

"I have often thought of you, Lord Warburton," Isabel answered. "You may be sure I shall always do that." And then she added, with a smile—"There is no harm in that, on either side."

They walked along together, and she asked kindly about his sisters and requested him to let them know she had done so. He said nothing more about his own feelings, but returned to those more objective topics they had already touched upon. Presently he asked her when she was to leave Rome, and on her mentioning the limit of her stay, declared he was glad it was still so distant.

"Why do you say that, if you yourself are only passing through?" she inquired, with some anxiety.

"Ah, when I said I was passing through, I didn't mean that one would treat Rome as if it were Clapham Junction. To pass through Rome is to stop a week or two."

"Say frankly that you mean to stay as long as I do!"

Lord Warburton looked at her a moment, with an uncomfortable smile. "You won't like that. You are afraid you will see too much of me."

"It doesn't matter what I like. I certainly can't expect you to leave this delightful place on my account. But I confess I am afraid of you."

"Afraid I will begin again? I promise to be very careful."

They had gradually stopped, and they stood a moment face to face. "Poor Lord Warburton!" said Isabel, with a melancholy smile.

"Poor Lord Warburton, indeed! But I will be careful."

"You may be unhappy, but you shall not make me so. That I can't allow."

"If I believed I could make you unhappy, I think I should try it." At this she walked in advance, and he also proceeded. "I will never say a word to displease you," he promised, very gently.

"Very good. If you do, our friendship's at an end."

"Perhaps some day—after a while—you will give me leave," he suggested.

"Give you leave—to make me unhappy?"

He hesitated. "To tell you again—" But he checked himself. "I will be silent," he said; "silent always."

Ralph Touchett had been joined, in his visit to the excavation, by Miss Stackpole and her attendant, and these three now emerged from among the mounds of earth and stone collected round the aperture, and came into sight of Isabel and her companion. Ralph Touchett gave signs of greeting to Lord Warburton, and Henrietta exclaimed in a high voice, "Gracious, there's that lord!" Ralph and his friend met each other with undemonstrative cordiality, and Miss Stackpole rested her large intellectual gaze upon the sunburnt traveller.

"I don't suppose you remember me, sir," she soon remarked.

"Indeed I do remember you," said Lord Warburton. "I asked you to come and see me, and you never came."

"I don't go everywhere I am asked," Miss Stackpole answered, coldly.

"Ah, well, I won't ask you again," said the master of Lockleigh, good-humouredly.

"If you do I will go; so be sure!"

Lord Warburton, for all his good-humour, seemed sure enough. Mr. Bantling had stood by, without claiming a recognition, but he now took occasion to nod to his lordship, who answered him with a friendly "Oh, you here, Bantling?" and a hand-shake.

"Well," said Henrietta, "I didn't know you knew him!"

"I guess you don't know every one I know," Mr. Bantling rejoined, facetiously.

"I thought that when an Englishman knew a lord he always told you."

"Ah, I am afraid Bantling was ashamed of me," said Lord Warburton, laughing. Isabel was glad to hear him laugh; she gave a little sigh of relief as they took their way homeward.

The next day was Sunday; she spent her morning writing two long letters—one to her sister Lily, the other to Madame Merle; but in neither of these epistles did she mention the fact that a rejected suitor had threatened her with another appeal. Of a Sunday afternoon all good Romans (and the best Romans are often the northern barbarians) follow the custom of going to hear vespers at St. Peter's; and it had been agreed among our friends that they would drive together to the great church. After lunch, an hour before the carriage came, Lord Warburton presented himself at the Hôtel de Paris and paid a visit to the two ladies, Ralph Touchett and Mr. Bantling having gone out together. The visitor seemed to have wished to give Isabel an example of his intention to keep the promise he had made her the evening before; he was both discreet and frank; he made not even a tacit appeal, but left it for her to judge what a mere good friend he could be. He talked about his travels, about Persia, about Turkey, and when Miss Stackpole asked him whether it would "pay" for her to visit those countries, assured her that they offered a great field to female enterprise. Isabel did him justice, but she wondered what his purpose was, and what he expected to gain even by behaving heroically. If he expected to melt her by showing what a good fellow he was, he might spare himself the trouble. She knew already he was a good fellow, and nothing he could do would add to this conviction. Moreover, his being in Rome at all made her vaguely uneasy. Nevertheless, when on bringing his call to a close, he said that he too should be at St. Peter's and should look out for Isabel and her friends, she was obliged to reply that it would be a pleasure to see him again.

In the church, as she strolled over its tesselated acres, he was the first person she encountered. She had not been one of the superior tourists who are "disappointed" in St. Peter's and find it smaller than its fame; the first time she passed beneath the huge leathern curtain that strains and bangs at the entrance—the first time she found herself beneath the far-arching dome and saw the light drizzle down through the air thickened with incense and with the reflections of marble and gilt, of mosaic and bronze, her conception of greatness received an extension. After this it never lacked space to soar. She gazed and wondered, like a child or a peasant, and paid her silent tribute to visible grandeur. Lord Warburton walked beside her and talked of Saint Sophia of Constantinople; she was afraid that he would end by calling attention to his exemplary conduct. The service had not yet begun, but at St. Peter's there is much to observe, and as there is something almost profane in the vastness of the place, which seems meant as much for physical as for spiritual exercise, the different figures and groups, the mingled worshippers and spectators, may follow their various intentions without mutual scandal. In that splendid immensity individual indiscretion carries but a short distance. Isabel and her companions, however, were guilty of none; for though Henrietta was obliged to declare that Michael Angelo's dome suffered by comparison with that of the Capitol at Washington, she addressed her protest chiefly to Mr. Bantling's ear, and reserved it, in its more accentuated form, for the columns of the *Interviewer*. Isabel made the circuit of the church with Lord Warburton, and as they drew near the choir on the left of the entrance the voices of the Pope's singers were borne towards them over the heads of the large number of persons clustered outside the doors. They paused a while on the skirts of this crowd, composed in equal measure of Roman cockneys and inquisitive strangers, and while they stood there the sacred concert went forward. Ralph, with Henrietta and Mr. Bantling, was apparently within, where Isabel, above the heads of the dense group in front of her, saw the afternoon light, silvered by clouds of incense that seemed to mingle with the splendid chant, sloping through the embossed recesses of high windows. After a while the singing stopped, and then Lord Warburton seemed disposed to turn away again. Isabel for a moment did the same; whereupon she found herself confronted with Gilbert Osmond, who appeared to have been standing at a short distance behind her. He now approached, with a formal salutation.

"So you decided to come?" she said, putting out her hand.

"Yes, I came last night, and called this afternoon at your hotel. They told me you had come here, and I looked about for you."

"The others are inside," said Isabel.

"I didn't come for the others," Gilbert Osmond murmured, smiling.

She turned away; Lord Warburton was looking at them; perhaps he had heard this. Suddenly she remembered that it was just what he had said to her the morning he came to Gardencourt to ask her to marry him. Mr. Osmond's words had brought the colour to her cheek, and this reminiscence had not the effect of dispelling it. Isabel sought refuge from her slight agitation in mentioning to each gentleman the name of the other, and fortunately at this moment Mr. Bantling made his way out of the choir, cleaving the crowd with British valour, and followed by Miss Stackpole and Ralph Touchett. I say fortunately, but this is perhaps a superficial view of the matter; for on perceiving the gentleman from Florence, Ralph Touchett exhibited symptoms of surprise which might not perhaps have seemed flattering to Mr. Osmond. It must be added, however, that these manifestations were momentary, and Ralph was presently able to say to his cousin, with due jocularity, that she would soon have all her friends about her. His greeting to Mr. Osmond was apparently frank; that is, the two men shook hands and looked at each other. Miss Stackpole had met the new-comer in Florence, but she had already found occasion to say to Isabel that she liked him no better than her other admirers—than Mr. Touchett, Lord Warburton, and little Mr. Rosier in Paris. "I don't know what it is in you," she had been pleased to remark, "but for a nice girl you do attract the most unpleasant people. Mr. Goodwood is the only one I have any respect for, and he's just the one you don't appreciate."

"What's your opinion of St. Peter's?" Mr. Osmond asked of Isabel.

"It's very large and very bright," said the girl.

"It's too large; it makes one feel like an atom."

"Is not that the right way to feel—in a church?" Isabel asked, with a faint but interested smile.

"I suppose it's the right way to feel everywhere, when one *is* nobody. But I like it in a church as little as anywhere else."

"You ought indeed to be a Pope!" Isabel exclaimed, remembering something he had said to her in Florence.

"Ah, I should have enjoyed that!" said Gilbert Osmond.

Lord Warburton meanwhile had joined Ralph Touchett, and the two strolled away together.

"Who is the gentleman speaking to Miss Archer?" his lordship inquired.

"His name is Gilbert Osmond—he lives in Florence," Ralph said.

"What is he besides?"

"Nothing at all. Oh yes, he is an American; but one forgets that; he is so little of one."

"Has he known Miss Archer long?"

"No, about a fortnight."

"Does she like him?"

"Yes, I think she does."

"Is he a good fellow?"

Ralph hesitated a moment. "No, he's not," he said, at last.

"Why then does she like him?" pursued Lord Warburton, with noble *naïveté*.

"Because she's a woman."

Lord Warburton was silent a moment. "There are other men who *are* good fellows," he presently said, "and them—and them——"

"And them she likes also!" Ralph interrupted, smiling.

"Oh, if you mean she likes him in that way!" And Lord Warburton turned round again. As far as he was concerned, however, the party was broken up. Isabel remained in conversation with the gentleman from Florence till they left the church, and her English lover consoled himself by lending such attention as he might to the strains which continued to proceed from the choir.

XXVIII

O N THE MORROW, in the evening, Lord Warburton went
again to see his friends at their hotel, and at this establishment he learned that they had gone to the opera. He
drove to the opera, with the idea of paying them a visit in
their box, in accordance with the time-honoured Italian custom; and after he had obtained his admittance—it was one
of the secondary theatres—looked about the large, bare, ill-
lighted house. An act had just terminated, and he was at liberty to pursue his quest. After scanning two or three tiers of
boxes, he perceived in one of the largest of these receptacles
a lady whom he easily recognised. Miss Archer was seated
facing the stage, and partly screened by the curtain of the
box; and beside her, leaning back in his chair, was Mr. Gilbert Osmond. They appeared to have the place to themselves,
and Warburton supposed that their companions had taken advantage of the *entracte* to enjoy the relative coolness of the
lobby. He stood a while watching the interesting pair in the
box, and asking himself whether he should go up and interrupt their harmonious colloquy. At last it became apparent
that Isabel had seen him, and this accident determined him.
He took his way to the upper regions, and on the staircase he
met Ralph Touchett, slowly descending, with his hat in the
attitude of ennui and his hands where they usually were.

"I saw you below a moment since, and was going down to
you. I feel lonely and want company," Ralph remarked.

"You have some that is very good that you have deserted."

"Do you mean my cousin? Oh, she has got a visitor and
doesn't want me. Then Miss Stackpole and Bantling have
gone out to a café to eat an ice—Miss Stackpole delights in
an ice. I didn't think they wanted me either. The opera is very
bad; the women look like laundresses and sing like peacocks.
I feel very low."

"You had better go home," Lord Warburton said, without
affectation.

"And leave my young lady in this sad place? Ah no, I must
watch over her."

"She seems to have plenty of friends."

"Yes, that's why I must watch," said Ralph, with the same low-voiced mock-melancholy.

"If she doesn't want you, it's probable she doesn't want me."

"No, you are different. Go to the box and stay there while I walk about."

Lord Warburton went to the box, where he received a very gracious welcome from the more attractive of its occupants. He exchanged greetings with Mr. Osmond, to whom he had been introduced the day before, and who, after he came in, sat very quietly, scarcely mingling in the somewhat disjointed talk in which Lord Warburton engaged with Isabel. It seemed to the latter gentleman that Miss Archer looked very pretty; he even thought she looked excited; as she was, however, at all times a keenly-glancing, quickly-moving, completely animated young woman, he may have been mistaken on this point. Her talk with him betrayed little agitation; it expressed a kindness so ingenious and deliberate as to indicate that she was in undisturbed possession of her faculties. Poor Lord Warburton had moments of bewilderment. She had discouraged him, formally, as much as a woman could; what business had she then to have such soft, reassuring tones in her voice? The others came back; the bare, familiar, trivial opera began again. The box was large, and there was room for Lord Warburton to remain if he would sit a little behind, in the dark. He did so for half-an-hour, while Mr. Osmond sat in front, leaning forward, with his elbows on his knees, just behind Isabel. Lord Warburton heard nothing, and from his gloomy corner saw nothing but the clear profile of this young lady, defined against the dim illumination of the house. When there was another interval no one moved. Mr. Osmond talked to Isabel, and Lord Warburton remained in his corner. He did so but for a short time, however; after which he got up and bade good-night to the ladies. Isabel said nothing to detain him, and then he was puzzled again. Why had she so sweet a voice—such a friendly accent? He was angry with himself for being puzzled, and then angry for being angry. Verdi's music did little to comfort him, and he left the theatre and walked homeward, without knowing his way, through the tortuous, tragical streets of Rome, where heavier sorrows than his had been carried under the stars.

"What is the character of that gentleman?" Osmond asked of Isabel, after the visitor had gone.

"Irreproachable—don't you see it?"

"He owns about half England; that's his character," Henrietta remarked. "That's what they call a free country!"

"Ah, he is a great proprietor? Happy man!" said Gilbert Osmond.

"Do you call that happiness—the ownership of human beings?" cried Miss Stackpole. "He owns his tenants, and he has thousands of them. It is pleasant to own something, but inanimate objects are enough for me. I don't insist on flesh and blood, and minds and consciences."

"It seems to me you own a human being or two," Mr. Bantling suggested jocosely. "I wonder if Warburton orders his tenants about as you do me."

"Lord Warburton is a great radical," Isabel said. "He has very advanced opinions."

"He has very advanced stone walls. His park is inclosed by a gigantic iron fence, some thirty miles round," Henrietta announced, for the information of Mr. Osmond. "I should like him to converse with a few of our Boston radicals."

"Don't they approve of iron fences?" asked Mr. Bantling.

"Only to shut up wicked conservatives. I always feel as if I were talking to you over a fence!"

"Do you know him well, this unreformed reformer?" Osmond went on, questioning Isabel.

"Well enough."

"Do you like him?"

"Very much."

"Is he a man of ability?"

"Of excellent ability, and as good as he looks."

"As good as he is good-looking do you mean? He is very good-looking. How detestably fortunate! to be a great English magnate, to be clever and handsome into the bargain, and, by way of finishing off, to enjoy your favour! That's a man I could envy."

Isabel gave a serious smile.

"You seem to me to be always envying some one. Yesterday it was the Pope; to-day it's poor Lord Warburton."

"My envy is not dangerous; it is very platonic. Why do you call him poor?"

"Women usually pity men after they have hurt them; that is their great way of showing kindness," said Ralph, joining in the conversation for the first time, with a cynicism so transparently ingenious as to be virtually innocent.

"Pray, have I hurt Lord Warburton?" Isabel asked, raising her eyebrows, as if the idea were perfectly novel.

"It serves him right if you have," said Henrietta, while the curtain rose for the ballet.

Isabel saw no more of her attributive victim for the next twenty-four hours, but on the second day after the visit to the opera she encountered him in the gallery of the Capitol, where he was standing before the lion of the collection, the statue of the Dying Gladiator. She had come in with her companions, among whom, on this occasion again, Gilbert Osmond was numbered, and the party, having ascended the staircase, entered the first and finest of the rooms. Lord Warburton spoke to her with all his usual geniality, but said in a moment that he was leaving the gallery.

"And I am leaving Rome," he added. "I should bid you good-bye."

I shall not undertake to explain why, but Isabel was sorry to hear it. It was, perhaps, because she had ceased to be afraid of his renewing his suit; she was thinking of something else. She was on the point of saying she was sorry, but she checked herself and simply wished him a happy journey.

He looked at her with a somewhat heavy eye.

"I am afraid you think me rather inconsistent," he said. "I told you the other day that I wanted so much to stay a while."

"Oh no; you could easily change your mind."

"That's what I have done."

"*Bon voyage*, then."

"You're in a great hurry to get rid of me," said his lordship, rather dismally.

"Not in the least. But I hate partings."

"You don't care what I do," he went on pitifully.

Isabel looked at him for a moment.

"Ah," she said, "you are not keeping your promise!"

He coloured like a boy of fifteen.

"If I am not, then it's because I can't; and that's why I am going."

"Good-bye, then."

"Good-bye." He lingered still, however. "When shall I see you again?"

Isabel hesitated, and then, as if she had had a happy inspiration—"Some day after you are married."

"That will never be. It will be after you are."

"That will do as well," said Isabel, smiling.

"Yes, quite as well. Good-bye."

They shook hands, and he left her alone in the beautiful room, among the shining antique marbles. She sat down in the middle of the circle of statues, looking at them vaguely, resting her eyes on their beautiful blank faces; listening, as it were, to their eternal silence. It is impossible, in Rome at least, to look long at a great company of Greek sculptures without feeling the effect of their noble quietude. It soothes and moderates the spirit, it purifies the imagination. I say in Rome especially, because the Roman air is an exquisite medium for such impressions. The golden sunshine mingles with them, the great stillness of the past, so vivid yet, though it is nothing but a void full of names, seems to throw a solemn spell upon them. The blinds were partly closed in the windows of the Capitol, and a clear, warm shadow rested on the figures and made them more perfectly human. Isabel sat there a long time, under the charm of their motionless grace, seeing life between their gazing eyelids and purpose in their marble lips. The dark red walls of the room threw them into relief; the polished marble floor reflected their beauty. She had seen them all before, but her enjoyment repeated itself, and it was all the greater because she was glad, for the time, to be alone. At the last her thoughts wandered away from them, solicited by images of a vitality more complete. An occasional tourist came into the room, stopped and stared a moment at the Dying Gladiator, and then passed out of the other door, creaking over the smooth pavement. At the end of half-an-hour Gilbert Osmond reappeared, apparently in advance of his companions. He strolled towards her slowly, with his hands behind him, and with his usual bright, inquiring, yet not appealing smile.

"I am surprised to find you alone," he said. "I thought you had company."

"So I have—the best." And Isabel glanced at the circle of sculpture.

"Do you call this better company than an English peer?"

"Ah, my English peer left me some time ago," said Isabel, getting up. She spoke, with intention, a little dryly.

Mr. Osmond noted her dryness, but it did not prevent him from giving a laugh.

"I am afraid that what I heard the other evening is true; you are rather cruel to that nobleman."

Isabel looked a moment at the vanquished Gladiator.

"It is not true. I am scrupulously kind."

"That's exactly what I mean!" Gilbert Osmond exclaimed, so humorously that his joke needs to be explained.

We knew that he was fond of originals, of rarities, of the superior, the exquisite; and now that he had seen Lord Warburton, whom he thought a very fine example of his race and order, he perceived a new attraction in the idea of taking to himself a young lady who had qualified herself to figure in his collection of choice objects by rejecting the splendid offer of a British aristocrat. Gilbert Osmond had a high appreciation of the British aristocracy—he had never forgiven Providence for not making him an English duke—and could measure the unexpectedness of this conduct. It would be proper that the woman he should marry should have done something of that sort.

XXIX

RALPH TOUCHETT, for reasons best known to himself, had seen fit to say that Gilbert Osmond was not a good fellow; but this assertion was not borne out by the gentleman's conduct during the rest of the visit to Rome. He spent a portion of each day with Isabel and her companions, and gave every indication of being an easy man to live with. It was impossible not to feel that he had excellent points, and indeed this is perhaps why Ralph Touchett made his want of good fellowship a reproach to him. Even Ralph was obliged to admit that just now he was a delightful companion. His good humour was imperturbable, his knowledge universal, his manners were the gentlest in the world. His spirits were not visibly high; it was difficult to think of Gilbert Osmond as boisterous; he had a mortal dislike to loudness or eagerness. He thought Miss Archer sometimes too eager, too pronounced. It was a pity she had that fault; because if she had not had it she would really have had none; she would have been as bright and soft as an April cloud. If Osmond was not loud, however, he was deep, and during these closing days of the Roman May he had a gaiety that matched with slow irregular walks under the pines of the Villa Borghese, among the small sweet meadow-flowers and the mossy marbles. He was pleased with everything; he had never before been pleased with so many things at once. Old impressions, old enjoyments, renewed themselves; one evening, going home to his room at the inn, he wrote down a little sonnet to which he prefixed the title of "Rome Revisited." A day or two later he showed this piece of correct and ingenious verse to Isabel, explaining to her that it was an Italian fashion to commemorate the pleasant occasions of life by a tribute to the muse. In general Osmond took his pleasures singly; he was usually disgusted with something that seemed to him ugly or offensive; his mind was rarely visited with moods of comprehensive satisfaction. But at present he was happy—happier than he had perhaps ever been in his life; and the feeling had a large foundation. This was simply the sense of success—the most agreeable emotion of the human heart. Osmond had never had too much of it; in this respect he had never been spoiled; as he knew perfectly well and often reminded himself. "Ah no, I have not been spoiled; certainly I have not been spoiled," he used to repeat to himself. "If I do succeed before I die, I shall have earned it well." Absolutely void of success his career had not been; a very moderate amount of reflection would have assured him of this. But his triumphs were, some of them, now, too old; others had been too easy. The present one had been less difficult than might have been expected; but it had been easy—that is, it had been rapid—only because he had made an altogether exceptional effort, a greater effort than he had believed it was in him to make. The desire to succeed greatly—in something or other—had been the dream of his youth; but as the years went on, the conditions attached to success became so various and repulsive that the idea of making an effort gradually lost its charm. It was not dead, however; it only slept; it revived after he had made the acquaintance of Isabel Archer. Osmond had felt that any enterprise in which the chance of failure was at all considerable would never have an attraction for him; to fail would have been unspeakably odious, would have left an ineffaceable stain upon his life. Success was to seem in advance definitely certain—certain, that is, on this one condition, that the effort should be an agreeable one to make. That of exciting an interest on the part of Isabel Archer corresponded to this description, for the girl had pleased him from the first of his seeing her. We have seen that she thought him "fine"; and Gilbert Osmond returned the compliment. We have also seen (or heard) that he had a great dread of vulgarity, and on this score his mind was at rest with regard to our young lady. He was not afraid that she would disgust him or irritate him; he had no fear that she would even, in the more special sense of the word, displease him. If she was too eager, she could be taught to be less so; that was a fault which diminished with growing knowledge. She might defy him, she might anger him; this was another matter from displeasing him, and on the whole a less serious one. If a woman were ungraceful and common, her whole quality was vitiated, and one could take no precautions against that; one's own delicacy would avail little. If, however, she were only wilful and high-tempered, the defect might be managed with comparative ease; for had one not a will of one's own that one had been keeping for years in the best condition—as pure and keen as a sword protected by its sheath?

Though I have tried to speak with extreme discretion, the reader may have gathered a suspicion that Gilbert Osmond was not untainted by selfishness. This is rather a coarse imputation to put upon a man of his refinement; and it behoves us at all times to remember the familiar proverb about those who live in glass houses. If Mr. Osmond was more selfish than most of his fellows, the fact will still establish itself. Lest it should fail to do so, I must decline to commit myself to an accusation so gross; the more especially as several of the items of our story would seem to point the other way. It is well known that there are few indications of selfishness more conclusive (on the part of a gentleman at least) than the preference for a single life. Gilbert Osmond, after having tasted of matrimony, had spent a succession of years in the full enjoyment of recovered singleness. He was familiar with the simplicity of purpose, the lonely liberties, of bachelorhood. He had reached that period of life when it is supposed to be doubly difficult to renounce these liberties, endeared as they are by long association; and yet he was prepared to make the generous sacrifice. It would seem that this might fairly be set down to the credit of the noblest of our qualities—the faculty of self-devotion. Certain it is that Osmond's desire to marry had been deep and distinct. It had not been notorious; he had not gone about asking people whether they knew a nice girl with a little money. Money was an object; but this was not his manner of proceeding, and no one knew—or even greatly cared—whether he wished to marry or not. Madame Merle knew—that we have already perceived. It was not that he had told her; on the whole he would not have cared to tell her. But there were things of which she had no need to be told—things as to which she had a sort of creative intuition. She had recognised a truth that was none the less pertinent for being very subtle: the truth that there was something very imperfect in Osmond's situation as it stood. He was a failure, of course; that was an old story; to Madame Merle's perception he would always be a failure. But there were degrees of ineffectiveness, and there was no need of taking one of the highest. Success, for Gilbert Osmond, would be to make himself felt; that was the only success to which he could now pretend. It is not a kind of distinction that is officially recognised—unless indeed the operation be performed upon multitudes of men. Osmond's line would be to impress himself not largely but deeply; a distinction of the most private sort. A single character might offer the whole measure of it; the clear and sensitive nature of a generous girl would make space for the record. The record of course would be complete if the young lady should have a fortune, and Madame Merle would have taken no pains to make Mr. Osmond acquainted with Mrs. Touchett's niece if Isabel had been as scantily dowered as when first she met her. He had waited all these years because he wanted only the best, and a portionless bride naturally would not have been the best. He had waited so long in vain that he finally almost lost his interest in the subject—not having kept it up by venturesome experiments. It had become improbable that the best was now to be had, and if he wished to make himself felt, there was soft and supple little Pansy, who would evidently respond to the slightest pressure. When at last the best did present itself Osmond recognised it like a gentleman. There was therefore no incongruity in his wishing to marry—it was his own idea of success, as well as that which Madame Merle, with her old-time interest in his affairs, entertained for him. Let it not, however, be supposed that he was guilty of the error of believing that Isabel's character was of that passive sort which offers a free field for domination. He was sure that she would constantly act—act in the sense of enthusiastic concession.

Shortly before the time which had been fixed in advance for her return to Florence, this young lady received from Mrs. Touchett a telegram which ran as follows:—"Leave Florence 4th June, Bellaggio, and take you if you have not other views. But can't wait if you dawdle in Rome." The dawdling in Rome was very pleasant, but Isabel had no other views, and she wrote to her aunt that she would immediately join her. She told Gilbert Osmond that she had done so, and he replied that, spending many of his summers as well as his winters in Italy, he himself would loiter a little longer among the

Seven Hills. He should not return to Florence for ten days more, and in that time she would have started for Bellaggio. It might be long, in this case, before he should see her again. This conversation took place in the large decorated sitting-room which our friends occupied at the hotel; it was late in the evening, and Ralph Touchett was to take his cousin back to Florence on the morrow. Osmond had found the girl alone; Miss Stackpole had contracted a friendship with a delightful American family on the fourth floor, and had mounted the interminable staircase to pay them a visit. Miss Stackpole contracted friendships, in travelling, with great freedom, and had formed several in railway-carriages, which were among her most valued ties. Ralph was making arrangements for the morrow's journey, and Isabel sat alone in a wilderness of yellow upholstery. The chairs and sofas were orange; the walls and windows were draped in purple and gilt. The mirrors, the pictures, had great flamboyant frames; the ceiling was deeply vaulted and painted over with naked muses and cherubs. To Osmond the place was painfully ugly; the false colours, the sham splendour, made him suffer. Isabel had taken in hand a volume of Ampère, presented, on their arrival in Rome, by Ralph; but though she held it in her lap with her finger vaguely kept in the place, she was not impatient to go on with her reading. A lamp covered with a drooping veil of pink tissue-paper burned on the table beside her, and diffused a strange pale rosiness over the scene.

"You say you will come back; but who knows?" Gilbert Osmond said. "I think you are much more likely to start on your voyage round the world. You are under no obligation to come back; you can do exactly what you choose; you can roam through space."

"Well, Italy is a part of space," Isabel answered; "I can take it on the way."

"On the way round the world? No, don't do that. Don't put us into a parenthesis—give us a chapter to ourselves. I don't want to see you on your travels. I would rather see you when they are over. I should like to see you when you are tired and satiated," Osmond added, in a moment. "I shall prefer you in that state."

Isabel, with her eyes bent down, fingered the pages of M. Ampère a little.

"You turn things into ridicule without seeming to do it, though not, I think, without intending it," she said at last. "You have no respect for my travels—you think them ridiculous."

"Where do you find that?"

Isabel went on in the same tone, fretting the edge of her book with the paper-knife.

"You see my ignorance, my blunders, the way I wander about as if the world belonged to me, simply because—because it has been put into my power to do so. You don't think a woman ought to do that. You think it bold and ungraceful."

"I think it beautiful," said Osmond. "You know my opinions—I have treated you to enough of them. Don't you remember my telling you that one ought to make one's life a work of art? You looked rather shocked at first; but then I told you that it was exactly what you seemed to me to be trying to do with your own life."

Isabel looked up from her book.

"What you despise most in the world is bad art."

"Possibly. But yours seems to me very good."

"If I were to go to Japan next winter, you would laugh at me," Isabel continued.

Osmond gave a smile—a keen one, but not a laugh, for the tone of their conversation was not jocular. Isabel was almost tremulously serious; he had seen her so before.

"You have an imagination that startles one!"

"That is exactly what I say. You think such an idea absurd."

"I would give my little finger to go to Japan; it is one of the countries I want most to see. Can't you believe that, with my taste for old lacquer?"

"I haven't a taste for old lacquer to excuse me," said Isabel.

"You have a better excuse—the means of going. You are quite wrong in your theory that I laugh at you. I don't know what put it into your head."

"It wouldn't be remarkable if you did think it ridiculous that I should have the means to travel, when you have not; for you know everything, and I know nothing."

"The more reason why you should travel and learn," said Osmond, smiling. "Besides," he added, more gravely, "I don't know everything."

Isabel was not struck with the oddity of his saying this gravely; she was thinking that the pleasantest incident of her life—so it pleased her to qualify her little visit to Rome—was coming to an end. That most of the interest of this episode had been owing to Mr. Osmond—this reflection she was not just now at pains to make; she had already done the point abundant justice. But she said to herself that if there were a danger that they should not meet again, perhaps after all it would be as well. Happy things do not repeat themselves, and these few days had been interfused with the element of success. She might come back to Italy and find him different—this strange man who pleased her just as he was; and it would be better not to come than run the risk of that. But if she was not to come, the greater was the pity that this happy week was over; for a moment she felt her heart throb with a kind of delicious pain. The sensation kept her silent, and Gilbert Osmond was silent too; he was looking at her.

"Go everywhere," he said at last, in a low, kind voice; "do everything; get everything out of life. Be happy—be triumphant."

"What do you mean by being triumphant?"

"Doing what you like."

"To triumph, then, it seems to me, is to fail! Doing what we like is often very tiresome."

"Exactly," said Osmond, with his quick responsiveness.

"As I intimated just now, you will be tired some day." He paused a moment, and then he went on: "I don't know whether I had better not wait till then for something I wish to say to you."

"Ah, I can't advise you without knowing what it is. But I am horrid when I am tired," Isabel added, with due inconsequence.

"I don't believe that. You are angry, sometimes—that I can believe, though I have never seen it. But I am sure you are never disagreeable."

"Not even when I lose my temper?"

"You don't lose it—you find it, and that must be beautiful." Osmond spoke very simply—almost solemnly. "There must be something very noble about that."

"If I could only find it now!" the girl exclaimed, laughing, yet frowning.

"I am not afraid; I should fold my arms and admire you. I am speaking very seriously." He was leaning forward, with a hand on each knee; for some moments he bent his eyes on the floor. "What I wish to say to you," he went on at last, looking up, "is that I find I am in love with you."

Isabel instantly rose from her chair.

"Ah, keep that till I am tired!" she murmured.

"Tired of hearing it from others?" And Osmond sat there, looking up at her. "No, you may heed it now, or never, as you please. But, after all, I must say it now."

She had turned away, but in the movement she had stopped herself and dropped her gaze upon him. The two remained a moment in this situation, exchanging a long look—the large, conscious look of the critical hours of life. Then he got up and came near her, deeply respectful, as if he were afraid he had been too familiar.

"I am thoroughly in love with you."

He repeated the announcement in a tone of almost impersonal discretion; like a man who expected very little from it, but spoke for his own relief.

The tears came into Isabel's eyes—they were caused by an intenser throb of that pleasant pain I spoke of a moment ago. There was an immense sweetness in the words he had uttered; but, morally speaking, she retreated before them—facing him still—as she had retreated in two or three cases that we know of in which the same words had been spoken.

"Oh, don't say that, please," she answered at last, in a tone of entreaty which had nothing of conventional modesty, but which expressed the dread of having, in this case too, to choose and decide. What made her dread great was precisely the force which, as it would seem, ought to have banished all dread—the consciousness of what was in her own heart. It was terrible to have to surrender herself to that.

"I haven't the idea that it will matter much to you," said Osmond. "I have too little to offer you. What I have—it's enough for me; but it's not enough for you. I have neither fortune, nor fame, nor extrinsic advantages of any kind. So I offer nothing. I only tell you because I think it can't offend you, and some day or other it may give you pleasure. It gives me pleasure, I assure you," he went on, standing there before her, bending forward a little, turning his hat, which he had taken up, slowly round, with a movement which had all the decent tremor of awkwardness and none of its oddity, and presenting to her his keen, expressive, emphatic face. "It gives me no pain, because it is perfectly simple. For me you will always be the most important woman in the world."

Isabel looked at herself in this character—looked intently, and thought that she filled it with a certain grace. But what she said was not an expression of this complacency. "You don't offend me; but you ought to remember that, without being offended, one may be incommoded, troubled." "Incommoded": she heard herself saying that, and thought it a ridiculous word. But it was the word that came to her.

"I remember, perfectly. Of course you are surprised and startled. But if it is nothing but that, it will pass away. And it will perhaps leave something that I may not be ashamed of."

"I don't know what it may leave. You see at all events that I am not overwhelmed," said Isabel, with rather a pale smile. "I am not too troubled to think. And I think that I am glad we are separating—that I leave Rome to-morrow."

"Of course I don't agree with you there."

"I don't know you," said Isabel, abruptly; and then she coloured, as she heard herself saying what she had said almost a year before to Lord Warburton.

"If you were not going away you would know me better."

"I shall do that some other time."

"I hope so. I am very easy to know."

"No, no," said the girl, with a flash of bright eagerness; "there you are not sincere. You are not easy to know; no one could be less so."

"Well," Osmond answered, with a laugh, "I said that because I know myself. That may be a boast, but I do."

"Very likely; but you are very wise."

"So are you, Miss Archer!" Osmond exclaimed.

"I don't feel so just now. Still, I am wise enough to think you had better go. Good night."

"God bless you!" said Gilbert Osmond, taking the hand which she failed to surrender to him. And then in a moment he added, "If we meet again, you will find me as you leave me. If we don't, I shall be so, all the same."

"Thank you very much. Good-bye."

There was something quietly firm about Isabel's visitor; he might go of his own movement, but he would not be dismissed. "There is one thing more," he said. "I haven't asked anything of you—not even a thought in the future; you must do me that justice. But there is a little service I should like to ask. I shall not return home for several days; Rome is delightful, and it is a good place for a man in my state of mind. Oh, I know you are sorry to leave it; but you are right to do what your aunt wishes."

"She doesn't even wish it!" Isabel broke out, strangely.

Osmond for a moment was apparently on the point of saying something that would match these words. But he changed his mind, and rejoined, simply—"Ah well, it's proper you should go with her, all the same. Do everything that's proper; I go in for that. Excuse my being so patronising. You say you don't know me; but when you do you will discover what a worship I have for propriety."

"You are not conventional?" said Isabel, very gravely.

"I like the way you utter that word! No, I am not conventional: I am convention itself. You don't understand that?" And Osmond paused a moment, smiling. "I should like to explain it." Then, with a sudden, quick, bright naturalness—"Do come back again!" he cried. "There are so many things we might talk about."

Isabel stood there with lowered eyes. "What service did you speak of just now?"

"Go and see my little daughter before you leave Florence. She is alone at the villa; I decided not to send her to my sister, who hasn't my ideas. Tell her she must love her poor father very much," said Gilbert Osmond, gently.

"It will be a great pleasure to me to go," Isabel answered. "I will tell her what you say. Once more, good-bye."

On this he took a rapid, respectful leave. When he had gone, she stood a moment, looking about her, and then she seated herself, slowly, with an air of deliberation. She sat there till her companions came back, with folded hands, gazing at the ugly carpet. Her agitation—for it had not diminished—was very still, very deep. That which had happened was something that for a week past her imagination had been going forward to meet; but here, when it came, she stopped—her imagination halted. The working of this young lady's spirit was strange, and I can only give it to you as I see it, not hoping to make it seem altogether natural. Her imagination stopped, as I say; there was a last vague space it could not cross—a dusky, uncertain tract which looked ambiguous, and even slightly treacherous, like a moorland seen in the winter twilight. But she was to cross it yet.

XXX

UNDER HER cousin's escort Isabel returned on the morrow to Florence, and Ralph Touchett, though usually he was not fond of railway journeys, thought very well of the successive hours passed in the train which hurried his companion away from the city now distinguished by Gilbert Osmond's preference—hours that were to form the first stage in a still larger scheme of travel. Miss Stackpole had remained behind; she was planning a little trip to Naples, to be executed with Mr. Bantling's assistance. Isabel was to have but three days in Florence before the 4th of June, the date of Mrs. Touchett's departure, and she determined to devote the last of these to her promise to go and see Pansy Osmond. Her plan, however, seemed for a moment likely to modify itself, in deference to a plan of Madame Merle's. This lady was still at Casa Touchett; but she too was on the point of leaving Florence, her next station being an ancient castle in the mountains of Tuscany, the residence of a noble family of that country, whose acquaintance (she had known them, as she said, "for ever") seemed to Isabel, in the light of certain photographs of their immense crenellated dwelling which her friend was able to show her, a precious privilege.

She mentioned to Madame Merle that Mr. Osmond had asked her to call upon his daughter; she did not mention to her that he had also made her a declaration of love.

"*Ah, comme cela se trouve!*" the elder lady exclaimed. "I myself have been thinking it would be a kindness to take a look at the child before I go into the country."

"We can go together, then," said Isabel, reasonably. I say "reasonably," because the proposal was not uttered in the spirit of enthusiasm. She had prefigured her visit as made in solitude; she should like it better so. Nevertheless, to her great consideration for Madame Merle she was prepared to sacrifice this mystic sentiment.

Her friend meditated, with her usual suggestive smile. "After all," she presently said, " why should we both go; having, each of us, so much to do during these last hours?"

"Very good; I can easily go alone."

"I don't know about your going alone—to the house of a handsome bachelor. He has been married—but so long ago!"

Isabel stared. "When Mr. Osmond is away, what does it matter?"

"They don't know he is away, you see."

"They? Whom do you mean?"

"Every one. But perhaps it doesn't matter."

"If you were going, why shouldn't I?" Isabel asked.

"Because I am an old frump, and you are a beautiful young woman."

"Granting all that, you have not promised."

"How much you think of your promises!" said Madame Merle, with a smile of genial mockery.

"I think a great deal of my promises. Does that surprise you?"

"You are right," Madame Merle reflected audibly. "I really think you wish to be kind to the child."

"I wish very much to be kind to her."

"Go and see her, then; no one will be the wiser. And tell her I would have come if you had not.—Or rather," Madame Merle added—"don't tell her; she won't care."

As Isabel drove, in the publicity of an open vehicle, along the charming winding way which led to Mr. Osmond's hilltop, she wondered what Madame Merle had meant by no one being the wiser. Once in a while, at large intervals, this lady, in whose discretion, as a general thing, there was something almost brilliant, dropped a remark of ambiguous quality, struck a note that sounded false. What cared Isabel Archer for the vulgar judgments of obscure people? and did Madame Merle suppose that she was capable of doing a deed in secret? Of course not—she must have meant something else—something which in the press of the hours that preceded her departure she had not had time to explain. Isabel would return to this some day; there were certain things as to which she liked to be clear. She heard Pansy strumming at the piano in another apartment, as she herself was ushered into Mr. Osmond's drawing-room; the little girl was "practising," and Isabel was pleased to think that she performed this duty faithfully. Presently Pansy came in, smoothing down her frock, and did the honours of her father's house with the wide-eyed conscientiousness of a sensitive child. Isabel sat there for half-an-hour, and Pansy entertained her like a little lady—not chattering, but conversing, and showing the same courteous interest in Isabel's affairs that Isabel was so good as to take in hers. Isabel wondered at her; as I have said before, she had never seen a child like that. How well she had been taught, said our keen young lady, how prettily she had been directed and fashioned; and yet how simple, how natural, how inno-cent she has been kept! Isabel was fond of psychological problems, and it had pleased her, up to this time, to be in doubt as to whether Miss Pansy were not all-knowing. Was her infantine serenity but the perfection of self-consciousness? Was it put on to please her father's visitor, or was it the direct expression of a little neat, orderly character? The hour that Isabel spent in Mr. Osmond's beautiful empty, dusky rooms—the windows had been half-darkened, to keep out the heat, and here and there, through an easy crevice, the splendid summer day peeped in, lighting a gleam of faded colour or tarnished gilt in the rich-looking gloom—Isabel's interview with the daughter of the house, I say, effectually settled this question. Pansy was really a blank page, a pure white surface; she was not clever enough for precocious co-quetries. She was not clever; Isabel could see that; she only had nice feelings. There was something touching about her; Isabel had felt it before; she would be an easy victim of fate. She would have no will, no power to resist, no sense of her own importance; only an exquisite taste, and an appreciation, equally exquisite, of such affection as might be bestowed upon her. She would easily be mystified, easily crushed; her force would be solely in her power to cling. She moved about the place with Isabel, who had asked leave to walk through the other rooms again, where Pansy gave her judgment on several works of art. She talked about her prospects, her oc-cupations, her father's intentions; she was not egotistical, but she felt the propriety of giving Isabel the information that so observant a visitor would naturally expect.

"Please tell me," she said, "did papa, in Rome, go to see Madame Catherine? He told me he would if he had time. Perhaps he had not time. Papa likes a great deal of time. He wished to speak about my education; it isn't finished yet, you

know. I don't know what they can do with me more; but it
appears it is far from finished. Papa told me one day he
thought he would finish it himself; for the last year or two,
at the convent, the masters that teach the tall girls are so very
dear. Papa is not rich, and I should be very sorry if he were
to pay much money for me, because I don't think I am worth
it. I don't learn quickly enough, and I have got no memory.
For what I am told, yes—especially when it is pleasant; but
not for what I learn in a book. There was a young girl, who
was my best friend, and they took her away from the convent
when she was fourteen, to make—how do you say it in English?—to make a *dot*. You don't say it in English? I hope it
isn't wrong; I only mean they wished to keep the money, to
marry her. I don't know whether it is for that that papa
wishes to keep the money, to marry me. It costs so much to
marry!" Pansy went on, with a sigh; "I think papa might
make that economy. At any rate I am too young to think
about it yet, and I don't care for any gentleman; I mean for
any but him. If he were not my papa I should like to marry
him; I would rather be his daughter than the wife of—of
some strange person. I miss him very much, but not so much
as you might think, for I have been so much away from him.
Papa has always been principally for holidays. I miss Madame
Catherine almost more; but you must not tell him that. You
shall not see him again? I am very sorry for that. Of every one
who comes here I like you the best. That is not a great compliment, for there are not many people. It was very kind of
you to come to-day—so far from your house; for I am as yet
only a child. Oh, yes, I have only the occupations of a child.
When did you give them up, the occupations of a child? I
should like to know how old you are, but I don't know
whether it is right to ask. At the convent they told us that we
must never ask the age. I don't like to do anything that is not
expected; it looks as if one had not been properly taught. I
myself—I should never like to be taken by surprise. Papa left
directions for everything. I go to bed very early. When the
sun goes off that side I go into the garden. Papa left strict
orders that I was not to get scorched. I always enjoy the view;
the mountains are so graceful. In Rome, from the convent,
we saw nothing but roofs and bell-towers. I practise three

hours. I do not play very well. You play yourself? I wish very much that you would play something for me; papa wishes very much that I should hear good music. Madame Merle has played for me several times; that is what I like best about Madame Merle; she has great facility. I shall never have facility. And I have no voice—just a little thread."

Isabel gratified this respectful wish, drew off her gloves, and sat down to the piano, while Pansy, standing beside her, watched her white hands move quickly over the keys. When she stopped, she kissed the child good-bye, and held her a moment, looking at her.

"Be a good child," she said; "give pleasure to your father."

"I think that is what I live for," Pansy answered. "He has not much pleasure; he is rather a sad man."

Isabel listened to this assertion with an interest which she felt it to be almost a torment that she was obliged to conceal from the child. It was her pride that obliged her, and a certain sense of decency; there were still other things in her head which she felt a strong impulse, instantly checked, to say to Pansy about her father; there were things it would have given her pleasure to hear the child, to make the child, say. But she no sooner became conscious of these things than her imagination was hushed with horror at the idea of taking advantage of the little girl—it was of this she would have accused herself—and of leaving an audible trace of her emotion behind. She had come—she had come; but she had stayed only an hour! She rose quickly from the music-stool; even then, however, she lingered a moment, still holding her small companion, drawing the child's little tender person closer, and looking down at her. She was obliged to confess it to herself—she would have taken a passionate pleasure in talking about Gilbert Osmond to this innocent, diminutive creature who was near to him. But she said not another word; she only kissed Pansy once more. They went together through the vestibule, to the door which opened into the court; and there Pansy stopped, looking rather wistfully beyond.

"I may go no further," she said. "I have promised papa not to go out of this door."

"You are right to obey him; he will never ask you anything unreasonable."

"I shall always obey him. But when will you come again?"

"Not for a long time, I am afraid."

"As soon as you can, I hope. I am only a little girl," said Pansy, "but I shall always expect you."

And the small figure stood in the high, dark doorway, watching Isabel cross the clear, grey court, and disappear into the brightness beyond the big *portone*, which gave a wider gleam as it opened.

XXXI

ISABEL CAME BACK to Florence, but only after several
months; an interval sufficiently replete with incident. It is
not, however, during this interval that we are closely concerned with her; our attention is engaged again on a certain
day in the late spring-time, shortly after her return to the Palazzo Crescentini, and a year from the date of the incidents I
have just narrated. She was alone on this occasion, in one of
the smaller of the numerous rooms devoted by Mrs. Touchett
to social uses, and there was that in her expression and attitude
which would have suggested that she was expecting a visitor.
The tall window was open, and though its green shutters
were partly drawn, the bright air of the garden had come in
through a broad interstice and filled the room with warmth
and perfume. Our young lady stood for some time at the window, with her hands clasped behind her, gazing into the brilliant aperture in the manner of a person relapsing into reverie.
She was pre-occupied; she was too restless to sit down, to
work, to read. It was evidently not her design, however, to
catch a glimpse of her visitor before he should pass into the
house; for the entrance to the palace was not through the
garden, in which stillness and privacy always reigned. She
was endeavouring rather to anticipate his arrival by a process
of conjecture, and to judge by the expression of her face this
attempt gave her plenty to do. She was extremely grave; not
sad exactly, but deeply serious. The lapse of a year may
doubtless account for a considerable increase of gravity;
though this will depend a good deal upon the manner in
which the year has been spent. Isabel had spent hers in seeing
the world; she had moved about; she had travelled; she had
exerted herself with an almost passionate activity. She was
now, to her own sense, a very different person from the frivolous young woman from Albany who had begun to see Europe upon the lawn at Gardencourt a couple of years before.
She flattered herself that she had gathered a rich experience,
that she knew a great deal more of life than this light-minded
creature had even suspected. If her thoughts just now had
inclined themselves to retrospect, instead of fluttering their

wings nervously about the present, they would have evoked a multitude of interesting pictures. These pictures would have been both landscapes and figure-pieces; the latter, however, would have been the more numerous. With several of the figures concerned in these combinations we are already acquainted. There would be, for instance, the conciliatory Lily, our heroine's sister and Edmund Ludlow's wife, who came out from New York to spend five months with Isabel. She left her husband behind her, but she brought her children, to whom Isabel now played with equal munificence and tenderness the part of maiden-aunt. Mr. Ludlow, towards the last, had been able to snatch a few weeks from his forensic triumphs, and, crossing the ocean with extreme rapidity, spent a month with the two ladies in Paris, before taking his wife home. The little Ludlows had not yet, even from the American point of view, reached the proper tourist-age; so that while her sister was with her, Isabel confined her movements to a narrow circle. Lily and the babies had joined her in Switzerland in the month of July, and they had spent a summer of fine weather in an Alpine valley where the flowers were thick in the meadows, and the shade of great chestnuts made a resting-place in such upward wanderings as might be undertaken by ladies and children on warm afternoons. Afterwards they had come to Paris, a city beloved by Lily, but less appreciated by Isabel, who in those days was constantly thinking of Rome. Mrs. Ludlow enjoyed Paris, but she was nevertheless somewhat disappointed and puzzled; and after her husband had joined her she was in addition a good deal depressed at not being able to induce him to enter into these somewhat subtle and complex emotions. They all had Isabel for their object; but Edmund Ludlow, as he had always done before, declined to be surprised, or distressed, or mystified, or elated, at anything his sister-in-law might have done or have failed to do. Mrs. Ludlow's feelings were various. At one moment she thought it would be so natural for Isabel to come home and take a house in New York—the Rossiters', for instance, which had an elegant conservatory, and was just round the corner from her own; at another she could not conceal her surprise at the girl's not marrying some gentleman of rank in one of the foreign countries. On the whole, as I have said, she was rather disappointed. She had taken more satisfaction in Isabel's accession of fortune than if the money had been left to herself; it had seemed to her to offer just the proper setting for her sister's slender but eminent figure. Isabel had developed less, however, than Lily had thought likely—development, to Lily's understanding, being somehow mysteriously connected with morning-calls and evening-parties. Intellectually, doubtless, she had made immense strides; but she appeared to have achieved few of those social conquests of which Mrs. Ludlow had expected to admire the trophies. Lily's conception of such achievements was extremely vague; but this was exactly what she had expected of Isabel—to give it form and body. Isabel could have done as well as she had done in New York; and Mrs. Ludlow appealed to her husband to know whether there was any privilege that she enjoyed in Europe which the society of that city might not offer her. We know, ourselves, that Isabel had made conquests—whether inferior or not to those she might have effected in her native land, it would be a delicate matter to decide; and it is not altogether with a feeling of complacency that I again mention that she had not made these honourable victories public. She had not told her sister the history of Lord Warburton, nor had she given her a hint of Mr. Osmond's state of mind; and she had no better reason for her silence than that she didn't wish to speak. It entertained her more to say nothing, and she had no idea of asking poor Lily's advice. But Lily knew nothing of these rich mysteries, and it is no wonder, therefore, that she pronounced her sister's career in Europe rather dull—an impression confirmed by the fact that Isabel's silence about Mr. Osmond, for instance, was in direct proportion to the frequency with which he occupied her thoughts. As this happened very often, it sometimes appeared to Mrs. Ludlow that her sister was really losing her gaiety. So very strange a result of so exhilarating an incident as inheriting a fortune was of course perplexing to the cheerful Lily; it added to her general sense that Isabel was not at all like other people.

Isabel's gaiety, however—superficially speaking, at least—exhibited itself rather more after her sister had gone home. She could imagine something more poetic than spending the winter in Paris—Paris was like smart, neat prose—and her frequent correspondence with Madame Merle did much to stimulate such fancies. She had never had a keener sense of freedom, of the absolute boldness and wantonness of liberty, than when she turned away from the platform at the Euston station, on one of the latter days of November, after the departure of the train which was to convey poor Lily, her husband, and her children, to their ship at Liverpool. It had been good for her to have them with her; she was very conscious of that; she was very observant, as we know, of what was good for her, and her effort was constantly to find something that was good enough. To profit by the present advantage till the latest moment, she had made the journey from Paris with the unenvied travellers. She would have accompanied them to Liverpool as well, only Edmund Ludlow had asked her, as a favour, not to do so; it made Lily so fidgety, and she asked such impossible questions. Isabel watched the train move away; she kissed her hand to the elder of her small nephews, a demonstrative child who leaned dangerously far out of the window of the carriage and made separation an occasion of violent hilarity, and then she walked back into the foggy London street. The world lay before her—she could do whatever she chose. There was something exciting in the feeling, but for the present her choice was tolerably discreet; she chose simply to walk back from Euston Square to her hotel. The early dusk of a November afternoon had already closed in; the street lamps, in the thick, brown air, looked weak and red; our young lady was unattended, and Euston Square was a long way from Piccadilly. But Isabel performed the journey with a positive enjoyment of its dangers, and lost her way almost on purpose, in order to get more sensations, so that she was disappointed when an obliging policeman easily set her right again. She was so fond of the spectacle of human life that she enjoyed even the aspect of gathering dusk in the London streets—the moving crowds, the hurrying cabs, the lighted shops, the flaring stalls, the dark, shining dampness of everything. That evening, at her hotel, she wrote to Madame Merle that she should start in a day or two for Rome. She made her way down to Rome without touching at Florence—having gone first to Venice and then proceeded southward by Ancona. She accomplished this journey without other assistance than that of her servant, for her natural protectors were not now on the ground. Ralph Touchett was spending the winter at Corfu, and Miss Stackpole, in the September previous, had been recalled to America by a telegram from the *Interviewer*. This journal offered its brilliant correspondent a fresher field for her talents than the mouldering cities of Europe, and Henrietta was cheered on her way by a promise from Mr. Bantling that he would soon come over and see her. Isabel wrote to Mrs. Touchett to apologise for not coming just then to Florence, and her aunt replied characteristically enough. Apologies, Mrs. Touchett intimated, were of no more use than soap-bubbles, and she herself never dealt in such articles. One either did the thing or one didn't, and what one would have done belonged to the sphere of the irrelevant, like the idea of a future life or of the origin of things. Her letter was frank, but (a rare case with Mrs. Touchett) it was not so frank as it seemed. She easily forgave her niece for not stopping at Florence, because she thought it was a sign that there was nothing going on with Gilbert Osmond. She watched, of course, to see whether Mr. Osmond would now go to Rome, and took some comfort in learning that he was not guilty of an absence. Isabel, on her side, had not been a fortnight in Rome before she proposed to Madame Merle that they should make a little pilgrimage to the East. Madame Merle remarked that her friend was restless, but she added that she herself had always been consumed with the desire to visit Athens and Constantinople. The two ladies accordingly embarked on this expedition, and spent three months in Greece, in Turkey, in Egypt. Isabel found much to interest her in these countries, though Madame Merle continued to remark that even among the most classic sites, the scenes most calculated to suggest repose and reflection, her restlessness prevailed. Isabel travelled rapidly, eagerly, audaciously; she was like a thirsty person draining cup after cup. Madame Merle, for the present, was a most efficient duenna. It was on Isabel's invitation she had come, and she imparted all necessary dignity to the girl's uncountenanced condition. She played her part with the sagacity that might have been expected of her; she effaced herself, she accepted the position of a companion whose expenses were profusely paid. The situation, however, had no hardships, and people who met this graceful pair on their travels would not have been able to tell you which was the patroness and which the client. To say that Madame Merle improved on acquaintance would misrepresent the impression she made upon Isabel, who had thought her from the first a perfectly enlightened woman. At the end of an intimacy of three months Isabel felt that she knew her better; her character had revealed itself, and Madame Merle had also at last redeemed her promise of relating her history from her own point of view—a consummation the more desirable as Isabel had already heard it related from the point of view of others. This history was so sad a one (in so far as it concerned the late M. Merle, an adventurer of the lowest class, who had taken advantage, years before, of her youth, and of an inexperience in which doubtless those who knew her only now would find it difficult to believe); it abounded so in startling and lamentable incidents, that Isabel wondered the poor lady had kept so much of her freshness, her interest in life. Into this freshness of Madame Merle's she obtained a considerable insight; she saw that it was, after all, a tolerably artificial bloom. Isabel liked her as much as ever, but there was a certain corner of the curtain that never was lifted; it was as if Madame Merle had remained after all a foreigner. She had once said that she came from a distance, that she belonged to the old world, and Isabel never lost the impression that she was the product of a different clime from her own, that she had grown up under other stars. Isabel believed that at bottom she had a different morality. Of course the morality of civilised persons has always much in common; but Isabel suspected that her friend had esoteric views. She believed, with the presumption of youth, that a morality which differed from her own must be inferior to it; and this conviction was an aid to detecting an occasional flash of cruelty, an occasional lapse from candour, in the conversation of a woman who had raised delicate kindness to an art, and whose nature was too large for the narrow ways of deception. Her conception of human motives was different from Isabel's, and there were several in her list of which our heroine had not even heard. She had not heard of everything, that was very plain; and there were evidently things in the world of which it was not advantageous to hear. Once or twice Isabel had a sort of fright, but the reader will be amused at the cause of it. Madame Merle, as we know, comprehended, responded, sympathised, with wonderful readiness; yet it had nevertheless happened that her young friend mentally exclaimed— "Heaven forgive her, she doesn't understand me!" Absurd as it may seem, this discovery operated as a shock; it left Isabel with a vague horror, in which there was even an element of foreboding. The horror of course subsided, in the light of some sudden proof of Madame Merle's remarkable intelligence; but it left a sort of high-water-mark in the development of this delightful intimacy. Madame Merle had once said that, in her belief, when a friendship ceased to grow, it immediately began to decline—there was no point of equilibrium between liking a person more and liking him less. A stationary affection, in other words, was impossible—it must move one way or the other. Without estimating the value of this doctrine, I may say that if Isabel's imagination, which had hitherto been so actively engaged on her friend's behalf, began at last to languish, she enjoyed her society not a particle less than before. If their friendship had declined, it had declined to a very comfortable level. The truth is that in these days the girl had other uses for her imagination, which was better occupied than it had ever been. I do not allude to the impulse it received as she gazed at the Pyramids in the course of an excursion from Cairo, or as she stood among the broken columns of the Acropolis and fixed her eyes upon the point designated to her as the Strait of Salamis; deep and memorable as these emotions had been. She came back by the last of March from Egypt and Greece, and made another stay in Rome. A few days after her arrival Gilbert Osmond came down from Florence, and remained three weeks, during which the fact of her being with his old friend, Madame Merle, in whose house she had gone to lodge, made it virtually inevitable that he should see her every day. When the last of April came she wrote to Mrs. Touchett that she should now be very happy to accept an invitation given long before, and went to pay a visit at the Palazzo Crescentini, Madame Merle on this occasion remaining in Rome. Isabel found her aunt alone; her cousin was still at Corfu. Ralph, however, was expected in Florence from day to day, and Isabel, who had not seen him for upwards of a year, was prepared to give him the most affectionate welcome.

XXXII

IT WAS NOT of him, nevertheless, that she was thinking while she stood at the window, where we found her a while ago, and it was not of any of the matters that I have just rapidly sketched. She was not thinking of the past, but of the future; of the immediate, impending hour. She had reason to expect a scene, and she was not fond of scenes. She was not asking herself what she should say to her visitor; this question had already been answered. What he would say to her—that was the interesting speculation. It could be nothing agreeable; Isabel was convinced of this, and the conviction had something to do with her being rather paler than usual. For the rest, however, she wore her natural brightness of aspect; even deep grief, with this vivid young lady, would have had a certain soft effulgence. She had laid aside her mourning, but she was still very simply dressed, and as she felt a good deal older than she had done a year before, it is probable that to a certain extent she looked so. She was not left indefinitely to her apprehensions, for the servant at last came in and presented her a card.

"Let the gentleman come in," said Isabel, who continued to gaze out of the window after the footman had retired. It was only when she had heard the door close behind the person who presently entered that she looked round.

Caspar Goodwood stood there—stood and received a moment, from head to foot, the bright, dry gaze with which she rather withheld than offered a greeting. Whether on his side Mr. Goodwood felt himself older than on the first occasion of our meeting him, is a point which we shall perhaps presently ascertain; let me say meanwhile that to Isabel's critical glance he showed nothing of the injury of time. Straight, strong, and fresh, there was nothing in his appearance that spoke positively either of youth or of age; he looked too deliberate, too serious to be young, and too eager, too active to be old. Old he would never be, and this would serve as a compensation for his never having known the age of chubbiness. Isabel perceived that his jaw had quite the same voluntary look that it had worn in earlier days; but she was prepared to admit that such a moment as the present was not a time for relaxation. He had the air of a man who had travelled hard; he said nothing at first, as if he had been out of breath. This gave Isabel time to make a reflection. "Poor fellow," she mentally murmured, "what great things he is capable of, and what a pity that he should waste his splendid force! What a pity, too, that one can't satisfy everybody!" It gave her time to do more—to say at the end of a minute,

"I can't tell you how I hoped that you wouldn't come."

"I have no doubt of that." And Caspar Goodwood looked about him for a seat. Not only had he come, but he meant to stay a little.

"You must be very tired," said Isabel, seating herself, generously, as she thought, to give him his opportunity.

"No, I am not at all tired. Did you ever know me to be tired?"

"Never; I wish I had. When did you arrive here?"

"Last night, very late; in a kind of snail-train they call the express. These Italian trains go at about the rate of an American funeral."

"That is in keeping—you must have felt as if you were coming to a funeral," Isabel said, forcing a smile, in order to offer such encouragement as she might to an easy treatment of their situation. She had reasoned out the matter elaborately; she had made it perfectly clear that she broke no faith, that she falsified no contract; but for all this she was afraid of him. She was ashamed of her fear; but she was devoutly thankful there was nothing else to be ashamed of. He looked at her with his stiff persistency—a persistency in which there was almost a want of tact; especially as there was a dull dark beam in his eye which rested on her almost like a physical weight.

"No, I didn't feel that; because I couldn't think of you as dead. I wish I could!" said Caspar Goodwood, plainly.

"I thank you immensely."

"I would rather think of you as dead than as married to another man."

"That is very selfish of you!" Isabel cried, with the ardour of a real conviction. "If you are not happy yourself, others have a right to be."

"Very likely it is selfish; but I don't in the least mind your saying so. I don't mind anything you can say now—I don't feel it. The cruellest things you could think of would be mere pin-pricks. After what you have done I shall never feel anything. I mean anything but that. That I shall feel all my life."

Mr. Goodwood made these detached assertions with a sort of dry deliberateness, in his hard, slow American tone, which flung no atmospheric colour over propositions intrinsically crude. The tone made Isabel angry rather than touched her; but her anger perhaps was fortunate, inasmuch as it gave her a further reason for controlling herself. It was under the pressure of this control that she said, after a little, irrelevantly, by way of answer to Mr. Goodwood's speech—"When did you leave New York?"

He threw up his head a moment, as if he were calculating. "Seventeen days ago."

"You must have travelled fast in spite of your slow trains."

"I came as fast as I could. I would have come five days ago if I had been able."

"It wouldn't have made any difference, Mr. Goodwood," said Isabel, smiling.

"Not to you—no. But to me."

"You gain nothing that I see."

"That is for me to judge!"

"Of course. To me it seems that you only torment yourself." And then, to change the subject, Isabel asked him if he had seen Henrietta Stackpole.

He looked as if he had not come from Boston to Florence to talk about Henrietta Stackpole; but he answered distinctly enough, that this young lady had come to see him just before he left America.

"She came to see you?"

"Yes, she was in Boston, and she called at my office. It was the day I had got your letter."

"Did you tell her?" Isabel asked, with a certain anxiety.

"Oh no," said Caspar Goodwood, simply; "I didn't want to. She will hear it soon enough; she hears everything."

"I shall write to her; and then she will write to me and scold me," Isabel declared, trying to smile again.

Caspar, however, remained sternly grave. "I guess she'll come out," he said.

"On purpose to scold me?"

"I don't know. She seemed to think she had not seen Europe thoroughly."

"I am glad you tell me that," Isabel said. "I must prepare for her."

Mr. Goodwood fixed his eyes for a moment on the floor; then at last, raising them—"Does she know Mr. Osmond?" he asked.

"A little. And she doesn't like him. But of course I don't marry to please Henrietta," Isabel added.

It would have been better for poor Caspar if she had tried a little more to gratify Miss Stackpole; but he did not say so; he only asked, presently, when her marriage would take place.

"I don't know yet. I can only say it will be soon. I have told no one but yourself and one other person—an old friend of Mr. Osmond's."

"Is it a marriage your friends won't like?" Caspar Goodwood asked.

"I really haven't an idea. As I say, I don't marry for my friends."

He went on, making no exclamation, no comment, only asking questions.

"What is Mr. Osmond?"

"What is he? Nothing at all but a very good man. He is not in business," said Isabel. "He is not rich; he is not known for anything in particular."

She disliked Mr. Goodwood's questions, but she said to herself that she owed it to him to satisfy him as far as possible.

The satisfaction poor Caspar exhibited was certainly small; he sat very upright, gazing at her.

"Where does he come from?" he went on.

"From nowhere. He has spent most of his life in Italy."

"You said in your letter that he was an American. Hasn't he a native place?"

"Yes, but he has forgotten it. He left it as a small boy."

"Has he never gone back?"

"Why should he go back?" Isabel asked, flushing a little, and defensively. "He has no profession."

"He might have gone back for his pleasure. Doesn't he like the United States?"

"He doesn't know them. Then he is very simple—he contents himself with Italy."

"With Italy and with you," said Mr. Goodwood, with gloomy plainness, and no appearance of trying to make an epigram. "What has he ever done?" he added, abruptly.

"That I should marry him? Nothing at all," Isabel replied, with a smile that had gradually become a trifle defiant. "If he had done great things would you forgive me any better? Give me up, Mr. Goodwood; I am marrying a nonentity. Don't try to take an interest in him; you can't."

"I can't appreciate him; that's what you mean. And you don't mean in the least that he is a nonentity. You think he is a great man, though no one else thinks so."

Isabel's colour deepened; she thought this very clever of her companion, and it was certainly a proof of the clairvoyance of such a feeling as his.

"Why do you always come back to what others think? I can't discuss Mr. Osmond with you."

"Of course not," said Caspar, reasonably.

And he sat there with his air of stiff helplessness, as if not only this were true, but there were nothing else that they might discuss.

"You see how little you gain," Isabel broke out—"how little comfort or satisfaction I can give you."

"I didn't expect you to give me much."

"I don't understand, then, why you came."

"I came because I wanted to see you once more—as you are."

"I appreciate that; but if you had waited a while, sooner or later we should have been sure to meet, and our meeting would have been pleasanter for each of us than this."

"Waited till after you are married? That is just what I didn't want to do. You will be different then."

"Not very. I shall still be a great friend of yours. You will see."

"That will make it all the worse," said Mr. Goodwood, grimly.

"Ah, you are unaccommodating! I can't promise to dislike you, in order to help you to resign yourself."

"I shouldn't care if you did!"

Isabel got up, with a movement of repressed impatience, and walked to the window, where she remained a moment, looking out. When she turned round, her visitor was still motionless in his place. She came towards him again and stopped, resting her hand on the back of the chair she had just quitted.

"Do you mean you came simply to look at me? That's better for you, perhaps, than for me."

"I wished to hear the sound of your voice," said Caspar.

"You have heard it, and you see it says nothing very sweet."

"It gives me pleasure, all the same."

And with this he got up.

She had felt pain and displeasure when she received that morning the note in which he told her that he was in Florence, and, with her permission, would come within an hour to see her. She had been vexed and distressed, though she had sent back word by his messenger that he might come when he would. She had not been better pleased when she saw him; his being there at all was so full of implication. It implied things she could never assent to—rights, reproaches, remonstrance, rebuke, the expectation of making her change her purpose. These things, however, if implied, had not been expressed; and now our young lady, strangely enough, began to resent her visitor's remarkable self-control. There was a dumb misery about him which irritated her; there was a manly staying of his hand which made her heart beat faster. She felt her agitation rising, and she said to herself that she was as angry as a woman who had been in the wrong. She was not in the wrong; she had fortunately not that bitterness to swallow; but, all the same, she wished he would denounce her a little. She had wished his visit would be short; it had no purpose, no propriety; yet now that he seemed to be turning away, she felt a sudden horror of his leaving her without uttering a word that would give her an opportunity to defend herself more than she had done in writing to him a month before, in a few carefully chosen words, to announce her engagement. If she were not in the wrong, however, why should she desire to defend herself? It was an excess of generosity on Isabel's part to desire that Mr. Goodwood should be angry.

If he had not held himself hard it might have made him so to hear the tone in which she suddenly exclaimed, as if she were accusing him of having accused her,

"I have not deceived you! I was perfectly free!"

"Yes, I know that," said Caspar.

"I gave you full warning that I would do as I chose."

"You said you would probably never marry, and you said it so positively that I pretty well believed it."

Isabel was silent an instant.

"No one can be more surprised than myself at my present intention."

"You told me that if I heard you were engaged, I was not to believe it," Caspar went on. "I heard it twenty days ago from yourself, but I remembered what you had said. I thought there might be some mistake, and that is partly why I came."

"If you wish me to repeat it by word of mouth, that is soon done. There is no mistake at all."

"I saw that as soon as I came into the room."

"What good would it do you that I shouldn't marry?" Isabel asked, with a certain fierceness.

"I should like it better than this."

"You are very selfish, as I said before."

"I know that. I am selfish as iron."

"Even iron sometimes melts. If you will be reasonable I will see you again."

"Don't you call me reasonable now?"

"I don't know what to say to you," she answered, with sudden humility.

"I sha'n't trouble you for a long time," the young man went on. He made a step towards the door, but he stopped. "Another reason why I came was that I wanted to hear what you would say in explanation of your having changed your mind."

Isabel's humbleness as suddenly deserted her.

"In explanation? Do you think I am bound to explain?"

Caspar gave her one of his long dumb looks.

"You were very positive. I did believe it."

"So did I. Do you think I could explain if I would?"

"No, I suppose not. Well," he added, "I have done what I wished. I have seen you."

"How little you make of these terrible journeys," Isabel murmured.

"If you are afraid I am tired, you may be at your ease about that." He turned away, this time in earnest, and no handshake, no sign of parting, was exchanged between them. At the door he stopped, with his hand on the knob. "I shall leave Florence to-morrow," he said.

"I am delighted to hear it!" she answered, passionately. And he went out. Five minutes after he had gone she burst into tears.

XXXIII

HER FIT of weeping, however, was of brief duration, and the signs of it had vanished when, an hour later, she broke the news to her aunt. I use this expression because she had been sure Mrs. Touchett would not be pleased; Isabel had only waited to tell her till she had seen Mr. Goodwood. She had an odd impression that it would not be honourable to make the fact public before she should have heard what Mr. Goodwood would say about it. He had said rather less than she expected, and she now had a somewhat angry sense of having lost time. But she would lose no more; she waited till Mrs. Touchett came into the drawing-room before the mid-day breakfast, and then she said to her—

"Aunt Lydia, I have something to tell you."

Mrs. Touchett gave a little jump and looked at the girl almost fiercely.

"You needn't tell me; I know what it is."

"I don't know how you know."

"The same way that I know when the window is open—by feeling a draught. You are going to marry that man."

"What man do you mean?" Isabel inquired, with great dignity.

"Madame Merle's friend—Mr. Osmond."

"I don't know why you call him Madame Merle's friend. Is that the principal thing he is known by?"

"If he is not her friend he ought to be—after what she has done for him!" cried Mrs. Touchett. "I shouldn't have expected it of her; I am disappointed."

"If you mean that Madame Merle has had anything to do with my engagement you are greatly mistaken," Isabel declared, with a sort of ardent coldness.

"You mean that your attractions were sufficient, without the gentleman being urged? You are quite right. They are immense, your attractions, and he would never have presumed to think of you if she had not put him up to it. He has a very good opinion of himself, but he was not a man to take trouble. Madame Merle took the trouble for him."

"He has taken a great deal for himself!" cried Isabel, with a voluntary laugh.

Mrs. Touchett gave a sharp nod.

"I think he must, after all, to have made you like him."

"I thought you liked him yourself."

"I did, and that is why I am angry with him."

"Be angry with me, not with him," said the girl.

"Oh, I am always angry with you; that's no satisfaction! Was it for this that you refused Lord Warburton?"

"Please don't go back to that. Why shouldn't I like Mr. Osmond, since you did?"

"I never wanted to marry him; there is nothing of him."

"Then he can't hurt me," said Isabel.

"Do you think you are going to be happy? No one is happy."

"I shall set the fashion then. What does one marry for?"

"What you will marry for, heaven only knows. People usually marry as they go into partnership—to set up a house. But in your partnership you will bring everything."

"Is it that Mr. Osmond is not rich? Is that what you are talking about?" Isabel asked.

"He has no money; he has no name; he has no importance. I value such things and I have the courage to say it; I think they are very precious. Many other people think the same, and they show it. But they give some other reason!"

Isabel hesitated a little.

"I think I value everything that is valuable. I care very much for money, and that is why I wish Mr. Osmond to have some."

"Give it to him, then; but marry some one else."

"His name is good enough for me," the girl went on. "It's a very pretty name. Have I such a fine one myself?"

"All the more reason you should improve on it. There are only a dozen American names. Do you marry him out of charity?"

"It was my duty to tell you, Aunt Lydia, but I don't think it is my duty to explain to you. Even if it were, I shouldn't be able. So please don't remonstrate; in talking about it you have me at a disadvantage. I can't talk about it."

"I don't remonstrate, I simply answer you; I must give some sign of intelligence. I saw it coming, and I said nothing. I never meddle."

"You never do, and I am greatly obliged to you. You have been very considerate."

"It was not considerate—it was convenient," said Mrs. Touchett. "But I shall talk to Madame Merle."

"I don't see why you keep bringing her in. She has been a very good friend to me."

"Possibly; but she has been a poor one to me."

"What has she done to you?"

"She has deceived me. She had as good as promised me to prevent your engagement."

"She couldn't have prevented it."

"She can do anything; that is what I have always liked her for. I knew she could play any part; but I understood that she played them one by one. I didn't understand that she would play two at the same time."

"I don't know what part she may have played to you," Isabel said; "that is between yourselves. To me she has been honest, and kind, and devoted."

"Devoted, of course; she wished you to marry her candidate. She told me that she was watching you only in order to interpose."

"She said that to please you," the girl answered; conscious, however, of the inadequacy of the explanation.

"To please me by deceiving me? She knows me better. Am I pleased to-day?"

"I don't think you are ever much pleased," Isabel was obliged to reply. "If Madame Merle knew you would learn the truth, what had she to gain by insincerity?"

"She gained time, as you see. While I waited for her to interfere you were marching away, and she was really beating the drum."

"That is very well. But by your own admission you saw I was marching, and even if she had given the alarm you would not have tried to stop me."

"No, but some one else would."

"Whom do you mean?" Isabel asked, looking very hard at her aunt.

Mrs. Touchett's little bright eyes, active as they usually were, sustained her gaze rather than returned it.

"Would you have listened to Ralph?"

"Not if he had abused Mr. Osmond."

"Ralph doesn't abuse people; you know that perfectly. He cares very much for you."

"I know he does," said Isabel; "and I shall feel the value of it now, for he knows that whatever I do I do with reason."

"He never believed you would do this. I told him you were capable of it, and he argued the other way."

"He did it for the sake of argument," said Isabel, smiling. "You don't accuse him of having deceived you; why should you accuse Madame Merle?"

"He never pretended he would prevent it."

"I am glad of that!" cried the girl, gaily. "I wish very much," she presently added, "that when he comes you would tell him first of my engagement."

"Of course I will mention it," said Mrs. Touchett. "I will say nothing more to you about it, but I give you notice I will talk to others."

"That's as you please. I only meant that it is rather better the announcement should come from you than from me."

"I quite agree with you; it is much more proper!"

And on this the two ladies went to breakfast, where Mrs. Touchett was as good as her word, and made no allusion to Gilbert Osmond. After an interval of silence, however, she asked her companion from whom she had received a visit an hour before.

"From an old friend—an American gentleman," Isabel said, with a colour in her cheek.

"An American, of course. It is only an American that calls at ten o'clock in the morning."

"It was half-past ten; he was in a great hurry; he goes away this evening."

"Couldn't he have come yesterday, at the usual time?"

"He only arrived last night."

"He spends but twenty-four hours in Florence?" Mrs. Touchett cried. "He's an American truly."

"He is indeed," said Isabel, thinking with a perverse admiration of what Caspar Goodwood had done for her.

Two days afterward Ralph arrived; but though Isabel was sure that Mrs. Touchett had lost no time in telling him the news, he betrayed at first no knowledge of the great fact. Their first talk was naturally about his health; Isabel had many questions to ask about Corfu. She had been shocked by his appearance when he came into the room; she had forgotten how ill he looked. In spite of Corfu, he looked very ill today, and Isabel wondered whether he were really worse or whether she was simply disaccustomed to living with an invalid. Poor Ralph grew no handsomer as he advanced in life, and the now apparently complete loss of his health had done little to mitigate the natural oddity of his person. His face wore its pleasant perpetual smile, which perhaps suggested wit rather than achieved it; his thin whisker languished upon a lean cheek; the exorbitant curve of his nose defined itself more sharply. Lean he was altogether; lean and long and loose-jointed; an accidental cohesion of relaxed angles. His brown velvet jacket had become perennial; his hands had fixed themselves in his pockets; he shambled, and stumbled, and shuffled, in a manner that denoted great physical helplessness. It was perhaps this whimsical gait that helped to mark his character more than ever as that of the humorous invalid—the invalid for whom even his own disabilities are part of the general joke. They might well indeed with Ralph have been the chief cause of the want of seriousness with which he appeared to regard a world in which the reason for his own presence was past finding out. Isabel had grown fond of his ugliness; his awkwardness had become dear to her. These things were endeared by association; they struck her as the conditions of his being so charming. Ralph was so charming that her sense of his being ill had hitherto had a sort of comfort in it; the state of his health had seemed not a limitation, but a kind of intellectual advantage; it absolved him from all professional and official emotions and left him the luxury of being simply personal. This personality of Ralph's was delightful; it had none of the staleness of disease; it was always easy and fresh and genial. Such had been the girl's impression of her cousin; and when she had pitied him it was only on reflection. As she reflected a good deal she had given him a certain amount of compassion; but Isabel always had a dread of wasting compassion—a precious article, worth more to the giver than to any one else. Now, however, it took no great ingenuity to discover that poor Ralph's tenure of life was less elastic than it should be. He was a dear, bright, generous fellow; he had all the illumination of wisdom and none of its pedantry, and yet he was dying. Isabel said to herself that life was certainly hard for some people, and she felt a delicate glow of shame as she thought how easy it now promised to become for herself. She was prepared to learn that Ralph was not pleased with her engagement; but she was not prepared, in spite of her affection for her cousin, to let this fact spoil the situation. She was not even prepared—or so she thought—to resent his want of sympathy; for it would be his privilege—it would be indeed his natural line—to find fault with any step she might take toward marriage. One's cousin always pretended to hate one's husband; that was traditional, classical; it was a part of one's cousin's always pretending to adore one. Ralph was nothing if not critical; and though she would certainly, other things being equal, have been as glad to marry to please Ralph as to please any one, it would be absurd to think it important that her choice should square with his views. What were his views, after all? He had pretended to think she had better marry Lord Warburton; but this was only because she had refused that excellent man. If she had accepted him Ralph would certainly have taken another tone; he always took the opposite one. You could criticise any marriage; it was the essence of a marriage to be open to criticism. How well she herself, if she would only give her mind to it, might criticise this union of her own! She had other employment, however, and Ralph was welcome to relieve her of the care. Isabel was prepared to be wonderfully good-humoured.

He must have seen that, and this made it the more odd that he should say nothing. After three days had elapsed without his speaking, Isabel became impatient; dislike it as he would, he might at least go through the form. We who know more about poor Ralph than his cousin, may easily believe that during the hours that followed his arrival at the Palazzo Crescentini, he had privately gone through many forms. His mother had literally greeted him with the great news, which was even more sensibly chilling than Mrs. Touchett's maternal kiss. Ralph was shocked and humiliated; his calculations had been false, and his cousin was lost. He drifted about the house like a rudderless vessel in a rocky stream, or sat in the garden of the palace in a great cane chair, with his long legs extended, his head thrown back, and his hat pulled over his eyes. He felt cold about the heart; he had never liked anything less. What could he do, what could he say? If Isabel were irreclaimable, could he pretend to like it? To attempt to reclaim her was permissible only if the attempt should succeed. To try to persuade her that the man to whom she had pledged her faith was a humbug would be decently discreet only in the event of her being persuaded. Otherwise he should simply have damned himself. It cost him an equal effort to speak his thought and to dissemble; he could neither assent with sincerity nor protest with hope. Meanwhile he knew—or rather he supposed—that the affianced pair were daily renewing their mutual vows. Osmond, at this moment, showed himself little at the Palazzo Crescentini; but Isabel met him every day elsewhere, as she was free to do after their engagement had been made public. She had taken a carriage by the month, so as not to be indebted to her aunt for the means of pursuing a course of which Mrs. Touchett disapproved, and she drove in the morning to the Cascine. This suburban wilderness, during the early hours, was void of all intruders, and our young lady, joined by her lover in its quietest part, strolled with him a while in the grey Italian shade and listened to the nightingales.

XXXIV

ONE MORNING, on her return from her drive, some half-hour before luncheon, she quitted her vehicle in the court of the palace, and instead of ascending the great staircase, crossed the court, passed beneath another archway, and entered the garden. A sweeter spot, at this moment, could not have been imagined. The stillness of noontide hung over it; the warm shade was motionless, and the hot light made it pleasant. Ralph was sitting there in the clear gloom, at the base of a statue of Terpsichore—a dancing nymph with taper fingers and inflated draperies, in the manner of Bernini; the extreme relaxation of his attitude suggested at first to Isabel that he was asleep. Her light footstep on the grass had not roused him, and before turning away she stood for a moment looking at him. During this instant he opened his eyes; upon which she sat down on a rustic chair that matched with his own. Though in her irritation she had accused him of indifference, she was not blind to the fact that he was visibly preoccupied. But she had attributed his long reveries partly to the languor of his increased weakness, partly to his being troubled about certain arrangements he had made as to the property inherited from his father—arrangements of which Mrs. Touchett disapproved, and which, as she had told Isabel, now encountered opposition from the other partners in the bank. He ought to have gone to England, his mother said, instead of coming to Florence; he had not been there for months, and he took no more interest in the bank than in the state of Patagonia.

"I am sorry I waked you," Isabel said; "you look tired."

"I feel tired. But I was not asleep. I was thinking of you."

"Are you tired of that?"

"Very much so. It leads to nothing. The road is long and I never arrive."

"What do you wish to arrive at?" Isabel said, closing her parasol.

"At the point of expressing to myself properly what I think of your engagement."

"Don't think too much of it," said Isabel, lightly.

"Do you mean that it's none of my business?"

"Beyond a certain point, yes."

"That's the point I wish to fix. I had an idea that you have found me wanting in good manners; I have never congratulated you."

"Of course I have noticed that; I wondered why you were silent."

"There have been a good many reasons; I will tell you now," said Ralph.

He pulled off his hat and laid it on the ground; then he sat looking at her. He leaned back, with his head against the marble pedestal of Terpsichore, his arms dropped on either side of him, his hands laid upon the sides of his wide chair. He looked awkward, uncomfortable; he hesitated for a long time. Isabel said nothing; when people were embarrassed she was usually sorry for them; but she was determined not to help Ralph to utter a word that should not be to the honour of her ingenious purpose.

"I think I have hardly got over my surprise," he said at last. "You were the last person I expected to see caught."

"I don't know why you call it caught."

"Because you are going to be put into a cage."

"If I like my cage, that needn't trouble you," said Isabel.

"That's what I wonder at; that's what I have been thinking of."

"If you have been thinking, you may imagine how I have thought! I am satisfied that I am doing well."

"You must have changed immensely. A year ago you valued your liberty beyond everything. You wanted only to see life."

"I have seen it," said Isabel. "It doesn't seem to me so charming."

"I don't pretend it is; only I had an idea that you took a genial view of it and wanted to survey the whole field."

"I have seen that one can't do that. One must choose a corner and cultivate that."

"That's what I think. And one must choose a good corner. I had no idea, all winter, while I read your delightful letters, that you were choosing. You said nothing about it, and your silence put me off my guard."

"It was not a matter I was likely to write to you about.

Besides, I knew nothing of the future. It has all come lately. If you had been on your guard, however," Isabel asked, " what would you have done?"

"I should have said—'Wait a little longer.' "

"Wait for what?"

"Well, for a little more light," said Ralph, with a rather absurd smile, while his hands found their way into his pockets.

"Where should my light have come from? From you?"

"I might have struck a spark or two!"

Isabel had drawn off her gloves; she smoothed them out as they lay upon her knee. The gentleness of this movement was accidental, for her expression was not conciliatory.

"You are beating about the bush, Ralph. You wish to say that you don't like Mr. Osmond, and yet you are afraid."

"I am afraid of you, not of him. If you marry him it won't be a nice thing to have said."

"*If* I marry him! Have you had any expectation of dissuading me?"

"Of course that seems to you too fatuous."

"No," said Isabel, after a little; "it seems to me touching."

"That's the same thing. It makes me so ridiculous that you pity me."

Isabel stroked out her long gloves again.

"I know you have a great affection for me. I can't get rid of that."

"For heaven's sake don't try. Keep that well in sight. It will convince you how intensely I want you to do well."

"And how little you trust me!"

There was a moment's silence; the warm noon-tide seemed to listen.

"I trust you, but I don't trust him," said Ralph.

Isabel raised her eyes and gave him a wide, deep look.

"You have said it now; you will suffer for it."

"Not if you are just."

"I am very just," said Isabel. "What better proof of it can there be than that I am not angry with you? I don't know what is the matter with me, but I am not. I was when you began, but it has passed away. Perhaps I ought to be angry, but Mr. Osmond wouldn't think so. He wants me to know everything; that's what I like him for. You have nothing to gain, I know that. I have never been so nice to you, as a girl, that you should have much reason for wishing me to remain one. You give very good advice; you have often done so. No, I am very quiet; I have always believed in your wisdom," Isabel went on, boasting of her quietness, yet speaking with a kind of contained exaltation. It was her passionate desire to be just; it touched Ralph to the heart, affected him like a caress from a creature he had injured. He wished to interrupt, to reassure, her; for a moment he was absurdly inconsistent; he would have retracted what he had said. But she gave him no chance; she went on, having caught a glimpse, as she thought, of the heroic line, and desiring to advance in that direction. "I see you have got some idea; I should like very much to hear it. I am sure it's disinterested; I feel that. It seems a strange thing to argue about, and of course I ought to tell you definitely that if you expect to dissuade me you may give it up. You will not move me at all; it is too late. As you say, I am caught. Certainly it won't be pleasant for you to remember this, but your pain will be in your own thoughts. I shall never reproach you."

"I don't think you ever will," said Ralph. "It is not in the least the sort of marriage I thought you would make."

"What sort of marriage was that, pray?"

"Well, I can hardly say. I hadn't exactly a positive view of it, but I had a negative. I didn't think you would marry a man like Mr. Osmond."

"What do you know against him? You know him scarcely at all."

"Yes," Ralph said, "I know him very little, and I know nothing against him. But all the same I can't help feeling that you are running a risk."

"Marriage is always a risk, and his risk is as great as mine."

"That's his affair! If he is afraid, let him recede; I wish he would."

Isabel leaned back in her chair, folded her arms, and gazed a while at her cousin.

"I don't think I understand you," she said at last, coldly. "I don't know what you are talking about."

"I thought you would marry a man of more importance."

Cold, I say, her tone had been, but at this a colour like a flame leaped into her face.

"Of more importance to whom? It seems to me enough that one's husband should be important to one's self!"

Ralph blushed as well; his attitude embarrassed him. Physically speaking, he proceeded to change it; he straightened himself, then leaned forward, resting a hand on each knee. He fixed his eyes on the ground; he had an air of the most respectful deliberation.

"I will tell you in a moment what I mean," he presently said. He felt agitated, intensely eager; now that he had opened the discussion he wished to discharge his mind. But he wished also to be superlatively gentle.

Isabel waited a little, and then she went on, with majesty.

"In everything that makes one care for people, Mr. Osmond is pre-eminent. There may be nobler natures, but I have never had the pleasure of meeting one. Mr. Osmond is the best I know; he is important enough for me."

"I had a sort of vision of your future," Ralph said, without answering this; "I amused myself with planning out a kind of destiny for you. There was to be nothing of this sort in it. You were not to come down so easily, so soon."

"To come down? What strange expressions you use! Is that your description of my marriage?"

"It expresses my idea of it. You seemed to me to be soaring far up in the blue—to be sailing in the bright light, over the heads of men. Suddenly some one tosses up a faded rosebud—a missile that should never have reached you—and down you drop to the ground. It hurts me," said Ralph, audaciously, "as if I had fallen myself!"

The look of pain and bewilderment deepened in his companion's face.

"I don't understand you in the least," she repeated. "You say you amused yourself with planning out my future—I don't understand that. Don't amuse yourself too much, or I shall think you are doing it at my expense."

Ralph shook his head.

"I am not afraid of your not believing that I have had great ideas for you."

"What do you mean by my soaring and sailing?" the girl

asked. "I have never moved on a higher line than I am moving on now. There is nothing higher for a girl than to marry a—a person she likes," said poor Isabel, wandering into the didactic.

"It's your liking the person we speak of that I venture to criticise, my dear Isabel! I should have said that the man for you would have been a more active, larger, freer sort of nature." Ralph hesitated a moment, then he added, "I can't get over the belief that there's something small in Osmond."

He had uttered these last words with a tremor of the voice; he was afraid that she would flash out again. But to his surprise she was quiet; she had the air of considering.

"Something small?" she said reflectively.

"I think he's narrow, selfish. He takes himself so seriously!"

"He has a great respect for himself; I don't blame him for that," said Isabel. "It's the proper way to respect others."

Ralph for a moment felt almost reassured by her reasonable tone.

"Yes, but everything is relative; one ought to feel one's relations. I don't think Mr. Osmond does that."

"I have chiefly to do with the relation in which he stands to me. In that he is excellent."

"He is the incarnation of taste," Ralph went on, thinking hard how he could best express Gilbert Osmond's sinister attributes without putting himself in the wrong by seeming to describe him coarsely. He wished to describe him impersonally, scientifically. "He judges and measures, approves and condemns, altogether by that."

"It is a happy thing then that his tastes should be exquisite."

"It is exquisite, indeed, since it has led him to select you as his wife. But have you ever seen an exquisite taste ruffled?"

"I hope it may never be my fortune to fail to gratify my husband's."

At these words a sudden passion leaped to Ralph's lips. "Ah, that's wilful, that's unworthy of you!" he cried. "You were not meant to be measured in that way—you were meant for something better than to keep guard over the sensibilities of a sterile dilettante!"

Isabel rose quickly and Ralph did the same, so that they

stood for a moment looking at each other as if he had flung down a defiance or an insult.

"You go too far," she murmured.

"I have said what I had on my mind—and I have said it because I love you!"

Isabel turned pale: was he too on that tiresome list? She had a sudden wish to strike him off. "Ah then, you are not disinterested!"

"I love you, but I love without hope," said Ralph, quickly, forcing a smile, and feeling that in that last declaration he had expressed more than he intended.

Isabel moved away and stood looking into the sunny stillness of the garden; but after a little she turned back to him. "I am afraid your talk, then, is the wildness of despair. I don't understand it—but it doesn't matter. I am not arguing with you; it is impossible that I should; I have only tried to listen to you. I am much obliged to you for attempting to explain," she said gently, as if the anger with which she had just sprung up had already subsided. "It is very good of you to try to warn me, if you are really alarmed. But I won't promise to think of what you have said; I shall forget it as soon as possible. Try and forget it yourself; you have done your duty, and no man can do more. I can't explain to you what I feel, what I believe, and I wouldn't if I could." She paused a moment, and then she went on, with an inconsequence that Ralph observed even in the midst of his eagerness to discover some symptom of concession. "I can't enter into your idea of Mr. Osmond; I can't do it justice, because I see him in quite another way. He is not important—no, he is not important; he is a man to whom importance is supremely indifferent. If that is what you mean when you call him 'small,' then he is as small as you please. I call that large—it's the largest thing I know. I won't pretend to argue with you about a person I am going to marry," Isabel repeated. "I am not in the least concerned to defend Mr. Osmond; he is not so weak as to need my defence. I should think it would seem strange, even to yourself, that I should talk of him so quietly and coldly, as if he were any one else. I would not talk of him at all, to any one but you; and you, after what you have said—I may just answer you once for all. Pray, would you wish me to make a mercenary marriage—what they call a marriage of ambition? I have only one ambition—to be free to follow out a good feeling. I had others once; but they have passed away. Do you complain of Mr. Osmond because he is not rich? That is just what I like him for. I have fortunately money enough; I have never felt so thankful for it as to-day. There have been moments when I should like to go and kneel down by your father's grave; he did perhaps a better thing than he knew when he put it into my power to marry a poor man—a man who has borne his poverty with such dignity, with such indifference. Mr. Osmond has never scrambled nor struggled—he has cared for no worldly prize. If that is to be narrow, if that is to be selfish, then it's very well. I am not frightened by such words, I am not even displeased; I am only sorry that you should make a mistake. Others might have done so, but I am surprised that you should. You might know a gentleman when you see one—you might know a fine mind. Mr. Osmond makes no mistakes! He knows everything, he understands everything, he has the kindest, gentlest, highest spirit. You have got hold of some false idea; it's a pity, but I can't help it; it regards you more than me." Isabel paused a moment, looking at her cousin with an eye illuminated by a sentiment which contradicted the careful calmness of her manner—a mingled sentiment, to which the angry pain excited by his words and the wounded pride of having needed to justify a choice of which she felt only the nobleness and purity, equally contributed. Though she paused, Ralph said nothing; he saw she had more to say. She was superb, but she was eager; she was indifferent, but she was secretly trembling. "What sort of a person should you have liked me to marry?" she asked, suddenly. "You talk about one's soaring and sailing, but if one marries at all one touches the earth. One has human feelings and needs, one has a heart in one's bosom, and one must marry a particular individual. Your mother has never forgiven me for not having come to a better understanding with Lord Warburton, and she is horrified at my contenting myself with a person who has none of Lord Warburton's great advantages—no property, no title, no honours, no houses, nor lands, nor position, nor reputation, nor brilliant belongings of any sort. It is the total absence of all

these things that pleases me. Mr. Osmond is simply a man—
he is not a proprietor!"

Ralph had listened with great attention, as if everything she
said merited deep consideration; but in reality he was only
half thinking of the things she said, he was for the rest simply
accommodating himself to the weight of his total impression—the impression of her passionate good faith. She was
wrong, but she believed; she was deluded, but she was consistent. It was wonderfully characteristic of her that she had
invented a fine theory about Gilbert Osmond, and loved him,
not for what he really possessed, but for his very poverties
dressed out as honours. Ralph remembered what he had said
to his father about wishing to put it into Isabel's power to
gratify her imagination. He had done so, and the girl had
taken full advantage of the privilege. Poor Ralph felt sick; he
felt ashamed. Isabel had uttered her last words with a low
solemnity of conviction which virtually terminated the discussion, and she closed it formally by turning away and walking
back to the house. Ralph walked beside her, and they passed
into the court together and reached the big staircase. Here
Ralph stopped, and Isabel paused, turning on him a face full
of a deep elation at his opposition having made her own conception of her conduct more clear to her.

"Shall you not come up to breakfast?" she asked.

"No; I want no breakfast, I am not hungry."

"You ought to eat," said the girl; "you live on air."

"I do, very much, and I shall go back into the garden and
take another mouthful of it. I came thus far simply to say this.
I said to you last year that if you were to get into trouble I
should feel terribly sold. That's how I feel to-day."

"Do you think I am in trouble?"

"One is in trouble when one is in error."

"Very well," said Isabel; "I shall never complain of my trouble to you!" And she moved up the staircase.

Ralph, standing there with his hands in his pockets, followed her with his eyes; then the lurking chill of the high-
walled court struck him and made him shiver, so that he
returned to the garden, to breakfast on the Florentine sunshine.

XXXV

ISABEL, when she strolled in the Cascine with her lover, felt no impulse to tell him that he was not thought well of at the Palazzo Crescentini. The discreet opposition offered to her marriage by her aunt and her cousin made on the whole little impression upon her; the moral of it was simply that they disliked Gilbert Osmond. This dislike was not alarming to Isabel; she scarcely even regretted it; for it served mainly to throw into higher relief the fact, in every way so honourable, that she married to please herself. One did other things to please other people; one did this for a more personal satisfaction; and Isabel's satisfaction was confirmed by her lover's admirable good conduct. Gilbert Osmond was in love, and he had never deserved less than during these still, bright days, each of them numbered, which preceded the fulfilment of his hopes, the harsh criticism passed upon him by Ralph Touchett. The chief impression produced upon Isabel's mind by this criticism was that the passion of love separated its victim terribly from every one but the loved object. She felt herself disjoined from every one she had ever known before—from her two sisters, who wrote to express a dutiful hope that she would be happy, and a surprise, somewhat more vague, at her not having chosen a consort who was the hero of a richer accumulation of anecdote; from Henrietta, who, she was sure, would come out, too late, on purpose to remonstrate; from Lord Warburton, who would certainly console himself, and from Caspar Goodwood, who perhaps would not; from her aunt, who had cold, shallow ideas about marriage, for which she was not sorry to manifest her contempt; and from Ralph, whose talk about having great views for her was surely but a whimsical cover for a personal disappointment. Ralph apparently wished her not to marry at all—that was what it really meant—because he was amused with the spectacle of her adventures as a single woman. His disappointment made him say angry things about the man she had preferred even to him: Isabel flattered herself that she believed Ralph had been angry. It was the more easy for her to believe this, because, as I say, she thought on the whole but little

about it, and accepted as an incident of her lot the idea that
to prefer Gilbert Osmond as she preferred him was perforce
to break all other ties. She tasted of the sweets of this preference, and they made her feel that there was after all something very invidious in being in love; much as the sentiment
was theoretically approved of. It was the tragical side of happiness; one's right was always made of the wrong of some
one else. Gilbert Osmond was not demonstrative; the consciousness of success, which must now have flamed high
within him, emitted very little smoke for so brilliant a blaze.
Contentment, on his part, never took a vulgar form; excitement, in the most self-conscious of men, was a kind of ecstasy
of self-control. This disposition, however, made him an admirable lover; it gave him a constant view of the amorous character. He never forgot himself, as I say; and so he never
forgot to be graceful and tender, to wear the appearance of
devoted intention. He was immensely pleased with his young
lady; Madame Merle had made him a present of incalculable
value. What could be a finer thing to live with than a high
spirit attuned to softness? For would not the softness be all
for one's self, and the strenuousness for society, which admired the air of superiority? What could be a happier gift in
a companion than a quick, fanciful mind, which saved one
repetitions, and reflected one's thought upon a scintillating
surface? Osmond disliked to see his thought reproduced literally—that made it look stale and stupid; he preferred it to
be brightened in the reproduction. His egotism, if egotism it
was, had never taken the crude form of wishing for a dull
wife; this lady's intelligence was to be a silver plate, not an
earthen one—a plate that he might heap up with ripe fruits,
to which it would give a decorative value, so that conversation might become a sort of perpetual dessert. He found the
silvery quality in perfection in Isabel; he could tap her imagination with his knuckle and make it ring. He knew perfectly, though he had not been told, that the union found
little favour among the girl's relations; but he had always
treated her so completely as an independent person that it
hardly seemed necessary to express regret for the attitude of
her family. Nevertheless, one morning, he made an abrupt
allusion to it.

"It's the difference in our fortune they don't like," he said. "They think I am in love with your money."

"Are you speaking of my aunt—of my cousin?" Isabel asked. "How do you know what they think?"

"You have not told me that they are pleased, and when I wrote to Mrs. Touchett the other day she never answered my note. If they had been delighted I should have learnt it, and the fact of my being poor and you rich is the most obvious explanation of their want of delight. But, of course, when a poor man marries a rich girl he must be prepared for imputations. I don't mind them; I only care for one thing—your thinking it's all right. I don't care what others think. I have never cared much, and why should I begin to-day, when I have taken to myself a compensation for everything? I won't pretend that I am sorry you are rich; I am delighted. I delight in everything that is yours—whether it be money or virtue. Money is a great advantage. It seems to me, however, that I have sufficiently proved that I can get on without it; I never in my life tried to earn a penny, and I ought to be less subject to suspicion than most people. I suppose it is their business to suspect—that of your own family; it's proper on the whole they should. They will like me better some day; so will you, for that matter. Meanwhile my business is not to bother, but simply to be thankful for life and love. It has made me better, loving you," he said on another occasion; "it has made me wiser, and easier, and brighter. I used to want a great many things before, and to be angry that I didn't have them. Theoretically, I was satisfied, as I once told you. I flattered myself that I had limited my wants. But I was subject to irritation; I used to have morbid, sterile, hateful fits of hunger, of desire. Now I am really satisfied, because I can't think of anything better. It is just as when one has been trying to spell out a book in the twilight, and suddenly the lamp comes in. I had been putting out my eyes over the book of life, and finding nothing to reward me for my pains; but now that I can read it properly I see that it's a delightful story. My dear girl, I can't tell you how life seems to stretch there before us—what a long summer afternoon awaits us. It's the latter half of an Italian day—with a golden haze, and the shadows just lengthening, and that divine delicacy in the light, the air, the landscape, which I have loved all my life, and which you love to-day. Upon my word, I don't see why we shouldn't get on. We have got what we like—to say nothing of having each other. We have the faculty of admiration, and several excellent beliefs. We are not stupid, we are not heavy, we are not under bonds to any dull limitations. You are very fresh, and I am well-seasoned. We have got my poor child to amuse us; we will try and make up some little life for her. It is all soft and mellow—it has the Italian colouring."

They made a good many plans, but they left themselves also a good deal of latitude; it was a matter of course, however, that they should live for the present in Italy. It was in Italy that they had met, Italy had been a party to their first impressions of each other, and Italy should be a party to their happiness. Osmond had the attachment of old acquaintance, and Isabel the stimulus of new, which seemed to assure her a future of beautiful hours. The desire for unlimited expansion had been succeeded in her mind by the sense that life was vacant without some private duty which gathered one's energies to a point. She told Ralph that she had "seen life" in a year or two, and that she was already tired, not of life, but of observation. What had become of all her ardours, her aspirations, her theories, her high estimate of her independence, and her incipient conviction that she should never marry? These things had been absorbed in a more primitive sentiment—a sentiment which answered all questions, satisfied all needs, solved all difficulties. It simplified the future at a stroke, it came down from above, like the light of the stars, and it needed no explanation. There was explanation enough in the fact that he was her lover, her own, and that she was able to be of use to him. She could marry him with a kind of pride; she was not only taking, but giving.

He brought Pansy with him two or three times to the Cascine—Pansy who was very little taller than a year before, and not much older. That she would always be a child was the conviction expressed by her father, who held her by the hand when she was in her sixteenth year, and told her to go and play while he sat down a while with the pretty lady. Pansy wore a short dress and a long coat; her hat always seemed too big for her. She amused herself with walking off, with quick, short steps, to the end of the alley, and then walking back with a smile that seemed an appeal for approbation. Isabel gave her approbation in abundance, and it was of that demonstrated personal kind which the child's affectionate nature craved. She watched her development with a kind of amused suspense; Pansy had already become a little daughter. She was treated so completely as a child that Osmond had not yet explained to her the new relation in which he stood to the elegant Miss Archer. "She doesn't know," he said to Isabel; "she doesn't suspect; she thinks it perfectly natural that you and I should come and walk here together, simply as good friends. There seems to me something enchantingly innocent in that; it's the way I like her to be. No, I am not a failure, as I used to think; I have succeeded in two things. I am to marry the woman I adore, and I have brought up my child as I wished, in the old way."

He was very fond, in all things, of the "old way;" that had struck Isabel as an element in the refinement of his character.

"It seems to me you will not know whether you have succeeded until you have told her," she said. "You must see how she takes your news. She may be horrified—she may be jealous."

"I am not afraid of that; she is too fond of you on her own account. I should like to leave her in the dark a little longer— to see if it will come into her head that if we are not engaged we ought to be."

Isabel was impressed by Osmond's æsthetic relish of Pansy's innocence—her own appreciation of it being more moral. She was perhaps not the less pleased when he told her a few days later that he had broken the news to his daughter, who made such a pretty little speech. "Oh, then I shall have a sister!" She was neither surprised nor alarmed; she had not cried, as he expected.

"Perhaps she had guessed it," said Isabel.

"Don't say that; I should be disgusted if I believed that. I thought it would be just a little shock; but the way she took it proves that her good manners are paramount. That is also what I wished. You shall see for yourself; to-morrow she shall make you her congratulations in person."

The meeting, on the morrow, took place at the Countess

Gemini's, whither Pansy had been conducted by her father, who knew that Isabel was to come in the afternoon to return a visit made her by the Countess on learning that they were to become sisters-in-law. Calling at Casa Touchett, the visitor had not found Isabel at home; but after our young lady had been ushered into the Countess's drawing-room, Pansy came in to say that her aunt would presently appear. Pansy was spending the day with her aunt, who thought she was of an age when she should begin to learn how to carry herself in company. It was Isabel's view that the little girl might have given lessons in deportment to the elder lady, and nothing could have justified this conviction more than the manner in which Pansy acquitted herself while they waited together for the Countess. Her father's decision, the year before, had finally been to send her back to the convent to receive the last graces, and Madame Catherine had evidently carried out her theory that Pansy was to be fitted for the great world.

"Papa has told me that you have kindly consented to marry him," said the good woman's pupil. "It is very delightful; I think you will suit very well."

"You think I shall suit you?"

"You will suit me beautifully; but what I mean is that you and papa will suit each other. You are both so quiet and so serious. You are not so quiet as he—or even as Madame Merle; but you are more quiet than many others. He should not, for instance, have a wife like my aunt. She is always moving; to-day especially; you will see when she comes in. They told us at the convent it was wrong to judge our elders, but I suppose there is no harm if we judge them favourably. You will be a delightful companion for papa."

"For you too, I hope," Isabel said.

"I speak first of him on purpose. I have told you already what I myself think of you; I liked you from the first. I admire you so much that I think it will be a great good fortune to have you always before me. You will be my model; I shall try to imitate you—though I am afraid it will be very feeble. I am very glad for papa—he needed something more than me. Without you, I don't see how he could have got it. You will be my stepmother; but we must not use that word. You don't look at all like the word; it is somehow so ugly. They are always said to be cruel; but I think you will never be cruel. I am not afraid."

"My good little Pansy," said Isabel, gently, "I shall be very kind to you."

"Very well then; I have nothing to fear," the child declared, lightly.

Her description of her aunt had not been incorrect; the Countess Gemini was less than ever in a state of repose. She entered the room with a great deal of expression, and kissed Isabel, first on her lips, and then on each cheek, in the short, quick manner of a bird drinking. She made Isabel sit down on the sofa beside her, and looking at our heroine with a variety of turns of the head, delivered herself of a hundred remarks, from which I offer the reader but a brief selection.

"If you expect me to congratulate you, I must beg you to excuse me. I don't suppose you care whether I do or not; I believe you are very proud. But I care myself whether I tell fibs or not; I never tell them unless there is something to be gained. I don't see what there is to be gained with you—especially as you would not believe me. I don't make phrases—I never made a phrase in my life. My fibs are always very crude. I am very glad, for my own sake, that you are going to marry Osmond; but I won't pretend I am glad for yours. You are very remarkable—you know that's what people call you; you are an heiress, and very good-looking and clever, very original; so it's a good thing to have you in the family. Our family is very good, you know; Osmond will have told you that; and my mother was rather distinguished—she was called the American Corinne. But we are rather fallen, I think, and perhaps you will pick us up. I have great confidence in you; there are ever so many things I want to talk to you about. I never congratulate any girl on marrying; I think it's the worst thing she can do. I suppose Pansy oughtn't to hear all this; but that's what she has come to me for—to acquire the tone of society. There is no harm in her knowing that it isn't such a blessing to get married. When first I got an idea that my brother had designs upon you, I thought of writing to you, to recommend you, in the strongest terms, not to listen to him. Then I thought it would be disloyal, and I hate anything of that kind. Besides, as I say, I was enchanted, for myself; and after all, I am very selfish. By the way, you won't respect me, and we shall never be intimate. I should like it, but you won't. Some day, all the same, we shall be better friends than you will believe at first. My husband will come and see you, though, as you probably know, he is on no sort of terms with Osmond. He is very fond of going to see pretty women, but I am not afraid of you. In the first place, I don't care what he does. In the second, you won't care a straw for him; you will take his measure at a glance. Some day I will tell you all about him. Do you think my niece ought to go out of the room? Pansy, go and practise a little in my boudoir."

"Let her stay, please," said Isabel. "I would rather hear nothing that Pansy may not!"

XXXVI

O NE AFTERNOON, towards dusk, in the autumn of 1876, a young man of pleasing appearance rang at the door of a small apartment on the third floor of an old Roman house. On its being opened he inquired for Madame Merle, whereupon the servant, a neat, plain woman, with a French face and a lady's maid's manner, ushered him into a diminutive drawing-room and requested the favour of his name.

"Mr. Edward Rosier," said the young man, who sat down to wait till his hostess should appear.

The reader will perhaps not have forgotten that Mr. Rosier was an ornament of the American circle in Paris, but it may also be remembered that he sometimes vanished from its horizon. He had spent a portion of several winters at Pau, and as he was a gentleman of tolerably inveterate habits he might have continued for years to pay his annual visit to this charming resort. In the summer of 1876, however, an incident befell him which changed the current, not only of his thoughts, but of his proceedings. He passed a month in the Upper Engadine, and encountered at St. Moritz a charming young girl. For this young lady he conceived a peculiar admiration; she was exactly the household angel he had long been looking for. He was never precipitate; he was nothing if not discreet; so he forbore for the present to declare his passion; but it seemed to him when they parted—the young lady to go down into Italy, and her admirer to proceed to Geneva, where he was under bonds to join some friends—that he should be very unhappy if he were not to see her again. The simplest way to do so was to go in the autumn to Rome, where Miss Osmond was domiciled with her family. Rosier started on his pilgrimage to the Italian capital and reached it on the first of November. It was a pleasant thing to do; but for the young man there was a strain of the heroic in the enterprise. He was nervous about the fever, and November, after all, was rather early in the season. Fortune, however, favours the brave; and Mr. Rosier, who took three grains of quinine every day, had at the end of a month no cause to deplore his temerity. He had made to a certain extent good

use of his time; that is, he had perceived that Miss Pansy Osmond had not a flaw in her composition. She was admirably
finished—she was in excellent style. He thought of her in
amorous meditation a good deal as he might have thought of
a Dresden-china shepherdess. Miss Osmond, indeed, in the
bloom of her juvenility, had a touch of the rococo, which
Rosier, whose taste was predominantly for that manner,
could not fail to appreciate. That he esteemed the productions
of comparatively frivolous periods would have been apparent
from the attention he bestowed upon Madame Merle's drawing-room, which, although furnished with specimens of every
style, was especially rich in articles of the last two centuries.
He had immediately put a glass into one eye and looked
round; and then—"By Jove! she has some jolly good things!"
he had murmured to himself. The room was small, and
densely filled with furniture; it gave an impression of faded
silk and little statuettes which might totter if one moved. Rosier got up and wandered about with his careful tread, bending over the tables charged with knickknacks and the cushions
embossed with princely arms. When Madame Merle came in
she found him standing before the fireplace, with his nose
very close to the great lace flounce attached to the damask
cover of the mantel. He had lifted it delicately, as if he were
smelling it.

"It's old Venetian," she said; "it's rather good."

"It's too good for this; you ought to wear it."

"They tell me you have some better in Paris, in the same
situation."

"Ah, but I can't wear mine," said Rosier, smiling.

"I don't see why you shouldn't! I have better lace than that
to wear."

Rosier's eyes wandered, lingeringly, round the room
again.

"You have some very good things."

"Yes, but I hate them."

"Do you want to get rid of them?" the young man asked
quickly.

"No, it's good to have something to hate; one works it
off."

"I love my things," said Rosier, as he sat there smiling.

"But it's not about them—nor about yours, that I came to talk to you." He paused a moment, and then, with greater softness—"I care more for Miss Osmond than for all the *bibelots* in Europe!"

Madame Merle started a little.

"Did you come to tell me that?"

"I came to ask your advice."

She looked at him with a little frown, stroking her chin.

"A man in love, you know, doesn't ask advice."

"Why not, if he is in a difficult position? That's often the case with a man in love. I have been in love before, and I know. But never so much as this time—really, never so much. I should like particularly to know what you think of my prospects. I'm afraid Mr. Osmond doesn't think me a phœnix."

"Do you wish me to intercede?" Madame Merle asked, with her fine arms folded, and her mouth drawn up to the left.

"If you could say a good word for me, I should be greatly obliged. There will be no use in my troubling Miss Osmond unless I have good reason to believe her father will consent."

"You are very considerate; that's in your favour. But you assume, in rather an off-hand way, that I think you a prize."

"You have been very kind to me," said the young man. "That's why I came."

"I am always kind to people who have good *bibelots*; there is no telling what one may get by it."

And the left-hand corner of Madame Merle's mouth gave expression to the joke.

Edward Rosier stared and blushed; his correct features were suffused with disappointment.

"Ah, I thought you liked me for myself!"

"I like you very much; but, if you please, we won't analyse. Excuse me if I seem patronising; but I think you a perfect little gentleman. I must tell you, however, that I have not the marrying of Pansy Osmond."

"I didn't suppose that. But you have seemed to me intimate with her family, and I thought you might have influence."

Madame Merle was silent a moment.

"Whom do you call her family?"

"Why, her father; and—how do you say it in English?—her *belle-mère*."

"Mr. Osmond is her father, certainly; but his wife can scarcely be termed a member of her family. Mrs. Osmond has nothing to do with marrying her."

"I am sorry for that," said Rosier, with an amiable sigh. "I think Mrs. Osmond would favour me."

"Very likely—if her husband does not."

Edward Rosier raised his eyebrows.

"Does she take the opposite line from him?"

"In everything. They think very differently."

"Well," said Rosier, "I am sorry for that; but it's none of my business. She is very fond of Pansy."

"Yes, she is very fond of Pansy."

"And Pansy has a great affection for her. She has told me that she loves her as if she were her own mother."

"You must, after all, have had some very intimate talk with the poor child," said Madame Merle. "Have you declared your sentiments?"

"Never!" cried Rosier, lifting his neatly-gloved hand. "Never, until I have assured myself of those of the parents."

"You always wait for that? You have excellent principles; your conduct is most estimable."

"I think you are laughing at me," poor Rosier murmured, dropping back in his chair, and feeling his small moustache. "I didn't expect that of you, Madame Merle."

She shook her head calmly, like a person who saw things clearly.

"You don't do me justice. I think your conduct is in excellent taste and the best you could adopt. Yes, that's what I think."

"I wouldn't agitate her—only to agitate her; I love her too much for that," said Ned Rosier.

"I am glad, after all, that you have told me," Madame Merle went on. "Leave it to me a little; I think I can help you."

"I said you were the person to come to!" cried the young man, with an ingenuous radiance in his face.

"You were very clever," Madame Merle returned, more

drily. "When I say I can help you, I mean once assuming that your cause is good. Let us think a little whether it is."

"I'm a dear little fellow," said Rosier, earnestly. "I won't say I have no faults, but I will say I have no vices."

"All that is negative. What is the positive side? What have you got besides your Spanish lace and your Dresden tea-cups?"

"I have got a comfortable little fortune—about forty thousand francs a year. With the talent that I have for arranging, we can live beautifully on such an income."

"Beautifully, no. Sufficiently, yes. Even that depends on where you live."

"Well, in Paris. I would undertake it in Paris."

Madame Merle's mouth rose to the left.

"It wouldn't be splendid; you would have to make use of the tea-cups, and they would get broken."

"We don't want to be splendid. If Miss Osmond should have everything pretty, it would be enough. When one is as pretty as she, one can afford to be simple. She ought never to wear anything but muslin," said Rosier, reflectively.

"She would be much obliged to you for that theory."

"It's the correct one, I assure you; and I am sure she would enter into it. She understands all that; that's why I love her."

"She is a very good little girl, and extremely graceful. But her father, to the best of my belief, can give her nothing."

Rosier hesitated a moment.

"I don't in the least desire that he should. But I may remark, all the same, that he lives like a rich man."

"The money is his wife's; she brought him a fortune."

"Mrs. Osmond, then, is very fond of her step-daughter; she may do something."

"For a love-sick swain you have your eyes about you!" Madame Merle exclaimed, with a laugh.

"I esteem a *dot* very much. I can do without it, but I esteem it."

"Mrs. Osmond," Madame Merle went on, "will probably prefer to keep her money for her own children."

"Her own children? Surely she has none."

"She may have yet. She had a poor little boy, who died

two years ago, six months after his birth. Others, therefore, may come."

"I hope they will, if it will make her happy. She is a splendid woman."

Madame Merle was silent a moment.

"Ah, about her there is much to be said. Splendid as you like! We have not exactly made out that you are a *parti*. The absence of vices is hardly a source of income."

"Excuse me, I think it may be," said Rosier, with his persuasive smile.

"You'll be a touching couple, living on your innocence!"

"I think you underrate me."

"You are not so innocent as that? Seriously," said Madame Merle, "of course forty thousand francs a year and a nice character are a combination to be considered. I don't say it's to be jumped at; but there might be a worse offer. Mr. Osmond will probably incline to believe he can do better."

"He can do so, perhaps; but what can his daughter do? She can't do better than marry the man she loves. For she does, you know," Rosier added, eagerly.

"She does—I know it."

"Ah," cried the young man, "I said you were the person to come to."

"But I don't know how you know it, if you haven't asked her," Madame Merle went on.

"In such a case there is no need of asking and telling; as you say, we are an innocent couple. How did *you* know it?"

"I who am not innocent? By being very crafty. Leave it to me; I will find out for you."

Rosier got up, and stood smoothing his hat.

"You say that rather coldly. Don't simply find out how it is, but try to make it as it should be."

"I will do my best. I will try to make the most of your advantages."

"Thank you so very much. Meanwhile, I will say a word to Mrs. Osmond."

"*Gardez-vous en bien!*" And Madame Merle rose, rapidly. "Don't set her going, or you'll spoil everything."

Rosier gazed into his hat; he wondered whether his hostess had been after all the right person to come to.

"I don't think I understand you. I am an old friend of Mrs. Osmond, and I think she would like me to succeed."

"Be an old friend as much as you like; the more old friends she has the better, for she doesn't get on very well with some of her new. But don't for the present try to make her take up the cudgels for you. Her husband may have other views, and, as a person who wishes her well, I advise you not to multiply points of difference between them."

Poor Rosier's face assumed an expression of alarm; a suit for the hand of Pansy Osmond was even a more complicated business than his taste for proper transitions had allowed. But the extreme good sense which he concealed under a surface suggesting sprigged porcelain, came to his assistance.

"I don't see that I am bound to consider Mr. Osmond so much!" he exclaimed.

"No, but you should consider her. You say you are an old friend. Would you make her suffer?"

"Not for the world."

"Then be very careful, and let the matter alone until I have taken a few soundings."

"Let the matter alone, dear Madame Merle? Remember that I am in love."

"Oh, you won't burn up. Why did you come to me, if you are not to heed what I say?"

"You are very kind; I will be very good," the young man promised. "But I am afraid Mr. Osmond is rather difficult," he added, in his mild voice, as he went to the door.

Madame Merle gave a light laugh.

"It has been said before. But his wife is not easy either."

"Ah, she's a splendid woman!" Ned Rosier repeated, passing out.

He resolved that his conduct should be worthy of a young man who was already a model of discretion; but he saw nothing in any pledge he had given Madame Merle that made it improper he should keep himself in spirits by an occasional visit to Miss Osmond's home. He reflected constantly on what Madame Merle had said to him, and turned over in his mind the impression of her somewhat peculiar manner. He had gone to her *de confiance*, as they said in Paris; but it was possible that he had been precipitate. He found difficulty in thinking of himself as rash—he had incurred this reproach so rarely; but it certainly was true that he had known Madame Merle only for the last month, and that his thinking her a delightful woman was not, when one came to look into it, a reason for assuming that she would be eager to push Pansy Osmond into his arms—gracefully arranged as these members might be to receive her. Beyond this, Madame Merle had been very gracious to him, and she was a person of consideration among the girl's people, where she had a rather striking appearance (Rosier had more than once wondered how she managed it), of being intimate without being familiar. But possibly he had exaggerated these advantages. There was no particular reason why she should take trouble for him; a charming woman was charming to every one, and Rosier felt rather like a fool when he thought of his appealing to Madame Merle on the ground that she had distinguished him. Very likely—though she had appeared to say it in joke—she was really only thinking of his *bibelots*. Had it come into her head that he might offer her two or three of the gems of his collection? If she would only help him to marry Miss Osmond, he would present her with his whole museum. He could hardly say so to her outright; it would seem too gross a bribe. But he should like her to believe it.

It was with these thoughts that he went again to Mrs. Osmond's, Mrs. Osmond having an "evening"—she had taken the Thursday of each week—when his presence could be accounted for on general principles of civility. The object of Mr. Rosier's well-regulated affection dwelt in a high house in the very heart of Rome; a dark and massive structure, overlooking a sunny *piazzetta* in the neighbourhood of the Farnese Palace. In a palace, too, little Pansy lived—a palace in Roman parlance, but a dungeon to poor Rosier's apprehensive mind. It seemed to him of evil omen that the young lady he wished to marry, and whose fastidious father he doubted of his ability to conciliate, should be immured in a kind of domestic fortress, which bore a stern old Roman name, which smelt of historic deeds, of crime and craft and violence, which was mentioned in "Murray" and visited by tourists who looked disappointed and depressed, and which had frescoes by Caravaggio in the *piano nobile* and a row of mutilated statues and dusty urns in the wide, nobly-arched loggia overlooking the damp court where a fountain gushed out of a mossy niche. In a less preoccupied frame of mind he could have done justice to the Palazzo Roccanera; he could have entered into the sentiment of Mrs. Osmond, who had once told him that on settling themselves in Rome she and her husband chose this habitation for the love of local colour. It had local colour enough, and though he knew less about architecture than about Limoges enamel, he could see that the proportions of the windows, and even the details of the cornice, had quite the grand air. But Rosier was haunted by the conviction that at picturesque periods young girls had been shut up there to keep them from their true loves, and, under the threat of being thrown into convents, had been forced into unholy marriages. There was one point, however, to which he always did justice when once he found himself in Mrs. Osmond's warm, rich-looking reception-rooms, which were on the second floor. He acknowledged that these people were very strong in *bibelots*. It was a taste of Osmond's own—not at all of hers; this she had told him the first time he came to the house, when, after asking himself for a quarter of an hour whether they had better things than he, he was obliged to admit that they had, very much, and vanquished his envy, as a gentleman should, to the point of expressing to his hostess his pure admiration of her treasures. He learned from Mrs. Osmond that her husband had made a large collection before their marriage, and that, though he had obtained a number of fine pieces within the last three years, he had got his best things at a time when he had not the advantage of her advice. Rosier interpreted this information according to principles of his own. For "advice" read "money," he said to himself; and the fact that Gilbert Osmond had landed his great prizes during his impecunious season, confirmed his most cherished doctrine—the doctrine that a collector may freely be poor if he be only patient. In general, when Rosier presented himself on a Thursday evening, his first glance was bestowed upon the walls of the room; there were three or four objects that his eyes really yearned for. But after his talk with Madame Merle he felt the extreme seriousness of his position; and now, when he came in, he looked about for the daughter of

the house with such eagerness as might be permitted to a
gentleman who always crossed a threshold with an optimistic
smile.

XXXVII

P ANSY WAS NOT in the first of the rooms, a large apartment with a concave ceiling and walls covered with old red damask; it was here that Mrs. Osmond usually sat—though she was not in her usually customary place to-night—and that a circle of more especial intimates gathered about the fire. The room was warm, with a sort of subdued brightness; it contained the larger things, and—almost always—an odour of flowers. Pansy on this occasion was presumably in the chamber beyond, the resort of younger visitors, where tea was served. Osmond stood before the chimney, leaning back, with his hands behind him; he had one foot up and was warming the sole. Half-a-dozen people, scattered near him, were talking together; but he was not in the conversation; his eyes were fixed, abstractedly. Rosier, coming in unannounced, failed to attract his attention; but the young man, who was very punctilious, though he was even exceptionally conscious that it was the wife, not the husband, he had come to see, went up to shake hands with him. Osmond put out his left hand, without changing his attitude.

"How d'ye do? My wife's somewhere about."

"Never fear; I shall find her," said Rosier, cheerfully.

Osmond stood looking at him; he had never before felt the keenness of this gentleman's eyes. "Madame Merle has told him, and he doesn't like it," Rosier said to himself. He had hoped Madame Merle would be there; but she was not within sight; perhaps she was in one of the other rooms, or would come later. He had never especially delighted in Gilbert Osmond; he had a fancy that he gave himself airs. But Rosier was not quickly resentful, and where politeness was concerned he had an inveterate wish to be in the right. He looked round him, smiling, and then, in a moment, he said—

"I saw a jolly good piece of Capo di Monte to-day."

Osmond answered nothing at first; but presently, while he warmed his boot-sole, "I don't care a fig for Capo di Monte!" he returned.

"I hope you are not losing your interest?"

"In old pots and plates? Yes, I am losing my interest."

Rosier for a moment forgot the delicacy of his position.

"You are not thinking of parting with a—a piece or two?"

"No, I am not thinking of parting with anything at all, Mr. Rosier," said Osmond, with his eyes still on the eyes of his visitor.

"Ah, you want to keep, but not to add," Rosier remarked, brightly.

"Exactly. I have nothing that I wish to match."

Poor Rosier was aware that he had blushed, and he was distressed at his want of assurance. "Ah, well, I have!" was all that he could murmur; and he knew that his murmur was partly lost as he turned away. He took his course to the adjoining room, and met Mrs. Osmond coming out of the deep doorway. She was dressed in black velvet; she looked brilliant and noble. We know what Mr. Rosier thought of her, and the terms in which, to Madame Merle, he had expressed his admiration. Like his appreciation of her dear little stepdaughter, it was based partly on his fine sense of the plastic; but also on a relish for a more impalpable sort of merit—that merit of a bright spirit, which Rosier's devotion to brittle wares had not made him cease to regard as a quality. Mrs. Osmond, at present, might well have gratified such tastes. The years had touched her only to enrich her; the flower of her youth had not faded, it only hung more quietly on its stem. She had lost something of that quick eagerness to which her husband had privately taken exception—she had more the air of being able to wait. Now, at all events, framed in the gilded doorway, she struck our young man as the picture of a gracious lady.

"You see I am very regular," he said. "But who should be if I am not?"

"Yes, I have known you longer than any one here. But we must not indulge in tender reminiscences. I want to introduce you to a young lady."

"Ah, please, what young lady?" Rosier was immensely obliging; but this was not what he had come for.

"She sits there by the fire in pink, and has no one to speak to."

Rosier hesitated a moment.

"Can't Mr. Osmond speak to her? He is within six feet of her."

Mrs. Osmond also hesitated.

"She is not very lively, and he doesn't like dull people."

"But she is good enough for me? Ah now, that is hard."

"I only mean that you have ideas for two. And then you are so obliging."

"So is your husband."

"No, he is not—to me." And Mrs. Osmond smiled vaguely.

"That's a sign he should be doubly so to other women."

"So I tell him," said Mrs. Osmond, still smiling.

"You see I want some tea," Rosier went on, looking wistfully beyond.

"That's perfect. Go and give some to my young lady."

"Very good; but after that I will abandon her to her fate. The simple truth is that I am dying to have a little talk with Miss Osmond."

"Ah," said Isabel, turning away, "I can't help you there!"

Five minutes later, while he handed a tea-cup to the young lady in pink, whom he had conducted into the other room, he wondered whether, in making to Mrs. Osmond the profession I have just quoted, he had broken the spirit of his promise to Madame Merle. Such a question was capable of occupying this young man's mind for a considerable time. At last, however, he became—comparatively speaking—reckless, and cared little what promises he might break. The fate to which he had threatened to abandon the young lady in pink proved to be none so terrible; for Pansy Osmond, who had given him the tea for his companion—Pansy was as fond as ever of making tea—presently came and talked to her. Into this mild colloquy Edward Rosier entered little; he sat by moodily, watching his small sweetheart. If we look at her now through his eyes, we shall at first not see much to remind us of the obedient little girl who, at Florence, three years before, was sent to walk short distances in the Cascine while her father and Miss Archer talked together of matters sacred to elder people. But after a moment we shall perceive that if at nineteen Pansy has become a young lady, she does not really fill out the part; that if she has grown very pretty, she lacks in a deplorable degree the quality known and esteemed in the appearance of females as style; and that if she is dressed with great freshness, she wears her smart attire with an undisguised appearance of saving it—very much as if it were lent her for the occasion. Edward Rosier, it would seem, would have been just the man to note these defects; and in point of fact there was not a quality of this young lady, of any sort, that he had not noted. Only he called her qualities by names of his own—some of which indeed were happy enough. "No, she is unique—she is absolutely unique," he used to say to himself; and you may be sure that not for an instant would he have admitted to you that she was wanting in style. Style? Why, she had the style of a little princess; if you couldn't see it you had no eye. It was not modern, it was not conscious, it would produce no impression in Broadway; the small, serious damsel, in her stiff little dress, only looked like an Infanta of Velasquez. This was enough for Edward Rosier, who thought her delightfully old-fashioned. Her anxious eyes, her charming lips, her slip of a figure, were as touching as a childish prayer. He had now an acute desire to know just to what point she liked him—a desire which made him fidget as he sat in his chair. It made him feel hot, so that he had to pat his forehead with his handkerchief; he had never been so uncomfortable. She was such a perfect *jeune fille*; and one couldn't make of a *jeune fille* the inquiry necessary for throwing light on such a point. A *jeune fille* was what Rosier had always dreamed of—a *jeune fille* who should yet not be French, for he had felt that this nationality would complicate the question. He was sure that Pansy had never looked at a newspaper, and that, in the way of novels, if she had read Sir Walter Scott it was the very most. An American *jeune fille*; what would be better than that? She would be frank and gay, and yet would not have walked alone, nor have received letters from men, nor have been taken to the theatre to see the comedy of manners. Rosier could not deny that, as the matter stood, it would be a breach of hospitality to appeal directly to this unsophisticated creature; but he was now in imminent danger of asking himself whether hospitality were the most sacred thing in the world. Was not the sentiment that he entertained for Miss Osmond of infinitely greater importance? Of greater importance to him—yes; but not probably to the master of the house. There was one comfort; even if this gentleman had been placed on his guard by Madame Merle, he would not have extended the warning to Pansy; it would not have been part of his policy to let her know that a prepossessing young man was in love with her. But he *was* in love with her, the prepossessing young man; and all these restrictions of circumstance had ended by irritating him. What had Gilbert Osmond meant by giving him two fingers of his left hand? If Osmond was rude, surely he himself might be bold. He felt extremely bold after the dull girl in pink had responded to the call of her mother, who came in to say, with a significant simper at Rosier, that she must carry her off to other triumphs. The mother and daughter departed together, and now it depended only upon him that he should be virtually alone with Pansy. He had never been alone with her before; he had never been alone with a *jeune fille*. It was a great moment; poor Rosier began to pat his forehead again. There was another room, beyond the one in which they stood—a small room which had been thrown open and lighted, but, the company not being numerous, had remained empty all the evening. It was empty yet; it was upholstered in pale yellow; there were several lamps; through the open door it looked very pretty. Rosier stood a moment, gazing through this aperture; he was afraid that Pansy would run away, and felt almost capable of stretching out a hand to detain her. But she lingered where the young lady in pink had left them, making no motion to join a knot of visitors on the other side of the room. For a moment it occurred to him that she was frightened—too frightened perhaps to move; but a glance assured him that she was not, and then he reflected that she was too innocent, indeed, for that. After a moment's supreme hesitation he asked her whether he might go and look at the yellow room, which seemed so attractive yet so virginal. He had been there already with Osmond, to inspect the furniture, which was of the First French Empire, and especially to admire the clock (which he did not really admire), an immense classic structure of that period. He therefore felt that he had now begun to manœuvre.

"Certainly, you may go," said Pansy; "and if you like, I will show you." She was not in the least frightened.

"That's just what I hoped you would say; you are so very kind," Rosier murmured.

They went in together; Rosier really thought the room very ugly, and it seemed cold. The same idea appeared to have struck Pansy.

"It's not for winter evenings; it's more for summer," she said. "It's papa's taste; he has so much."

He had a good deal, Rosier thought; but some of it was bad. He looked about him; he hardly knew what to say in such a situation. "Doesn't Mrs. Osmond care how her rooms are done? Has she no taste?" he asked.

"Oh yes, a great deal; but it's more for literature," said Pansy—"and for conversation. But papa cares also for those things: I think he knows everything."

Rosier was silent a moment. "There is one thing I am sure he knows!" he broke out presently. "He knows that when I come here it is, with all respect to him, with all respect to Mrs. Osmond, who is so charming—it is really," said the young man, "to see you!"

"To see me?" asked Pansy, raising her vaguely-troubled eyes.

"To see you; that's what I come for," Rosier repeated, feeling the intoxication of a rupture with authority. Pansy stood looking at him, simply, intently, openly; a blush was not needed to make her face more modest.

"I thought it was for that," she said.

"And it was not disagreeable to you?"

"I couldn't tell; I didn't know. You never told me," said Pansy.

"I was afraid of offending you."

"You don't offend me," the young girl murmured, smiling as if an angel had kissed her.

"You like me then, Pansy?" Rosier asked, very gently, feeling very happy.

"Yes—I like you."

They had walked to the chimney-piece, where the big cold Empire clock was perched; they were well within the room, and beyond observation from without. The tone in which she

had said these four words seemed to him the very breath of
nature, and his only answer could be to take her hand and
hold it a moment. Then he raised it to his lips. She submitted,
still with her pure, trusting smile, in which there was something ineffably passive. She liked him—she had liked him all
the while; now anything might happen! She was ready—she
had been ready always, waiting for him to speak. If he had
not spoken she would have waited for ever; but when the
word came she dropped like the peach from the shaken tree.
Rosier felt that if he should draw her towards him and hold
her to his heart, she would submit without a murmur, she
would rest there without a question. It was true that this
would be a rash experiment in a yellow Empire *salottino*. She
had known it was for her he came; and yet like what a perfect
little lady she had carried it off!

"You are very dear to me," he murmured, trying to believe
that there was after all such a thing as hospitality.

She looked a moment at her hand, where he had kissed it.
"Did you say that papa knows?"

"You told me just now he knows everything."

"I think you must make sure," said Pansy.

"Ah, my dear, when once I am sure of you!" Rosier murmured in her ear, while she turned back to the other rooms
with a little air of consistency which seemed to imply that
their appeal should be immediate.

The other rooms meanwhile had become conscious of the
arrival of Madame Merle, who, wherever she went, produced
an impression when she entered. How she did it the most
attentive spectator could not have told you; for she neither
spoke loud, nor laughed profusely, nor moved rapidly, nor
dressed with splendour, nor appealed in any appreciable manner to the audience. Large, fair, smiling, serene, there was
something in her very tranquillity that diffused itself, and
when people looked round it was because of a sudden quiet.
On this occasion she had done the quietest thing she could
do; after embracing Mrs. Osmond, which was more striking,
she had sat down on a small sofa to commune with the master
of the house. There was a brief exchange of commonplaces
between these two—they always paid, in public, a certain formal tribute to the commonplace—and then Madame Merle,

whose eyes had been wandering, asked if little Mr. Rosier had come this evening.

"He came nearly an hour ago—but he has disappeared," Osmond said.

"And where is Pansy?"

"In the other room. There are several people there."

"He is probably among them," said Madame Merle.

"Do you wish to see him?" Osmond asked, in a provokingly pointless tone.

Madame Merle looked at him a moment; she knew his tones, to the eighth of a note. "Yes, I should like to say to him that I have told you what he wants, and that it interests you but feebly."

"Don't tell him that, he will try to interest me more—which is exactly what I don't want. Tell him I hate his proposal."

"But you don't hate it."

"It doesn't signify: I don't love it. I let him see that, myself, this evening; I was rude to him on purpose. That sort of thing is a great bore. There is no hurry."

"I will tell him that you will take time and think it over."

"No, don't do that. He will hang on."

"If I discourage him he will do the same."

"Yes, but in the one case he will try and talk and explain; which would be exceedingly tiresome. In the other he will probably hold his tongue and go in for some deeper game. That will leave me quiet. I hate talking with a donkey."

"Is that what you call poor Mr. Rosier?"

"Oh, he's enervating, with his eternal majolica."

Madame Merle dropped her eyes, with a faint smile. "He's a gentleman, he has a charming temper; and, after all, an income of forty thousand francs——"

"It's misery—genteel misery," Osmond broke in. "It's not what I have dreamed of for Pansy."

"Very good, then. He has promised me not to speak to her."

"Do you believe him?" Osmond asked, absent-mindedly.

"Perfectly. Pansy has thought a great deal about him; but I don't suppose you think that matters."

"I don't think it matters at all; but neither do I believe she has thought about him."

"That opinion is more convenient," said Madame Merle, quietly.

"Has she told you that she is in love with him?"

"For what do you take her? And for what do you take me?" Madame Merle added in a moment.

Osmond had raised his foot and was resting his slim ankle on the other knee; he clasped his ankle in his hand, familiarly, and gazed a while before him. "This kind of thing doesn't find me unprepared. It's what I educated her for. It was all for this—that when such a case should come up she should do what I prefer."

"I am not afraid that she will not do it."

"Well then, where is the hitch?"

"I don't see any. But all the same, I recommend you not to get rid of Mr. Rosier. Keep him on hand, he may be useful."

"I can't keep him. Do it yourself."

"Very good; I will put him into a corner and allow him so much a day." Madame Merle had, for the most part, while they talked, been glancing about her; it was her habit, in this situation, just as it was her habit to interpose a good many blank-looking pauses. A long pause followed the last words I have quoted; and before it was broken again, she saw Pansy come out of the adjoining room, followed by Edward Rosier. Pansy advanced a few steps and then stopped and stood looking at Madame Merle and at her father.

"He has spoken to her," Madame Merle said, simply, to Osmond.

Her companion never turned his head. "So much for your belief in his promises. He ought to be horsewhipped."

"He intends to confess, poor little man!"

Osmond got up; he had now taken a sharp look at his daughter. "It doesn't matter," he murmured, turning away.

Pansy after a moment came up to Madame Merle with her little manner of unfamiliar politeness. This lady's reception of her was not more intimate; she simply, as she rose from the sofa, gave her a friendly smile.

"You are very late," said the young girl, gently.

"My dear child, I am never later than I intend to be."

Madame Merle had not got up to be gracious to Pansy; she moved towards Edward Rosier. He came to meet her, and, very quickly, as if to get it off his mind—"I have spoken to her!" he whispered.

"I know it, Mr. Rosier."

"Did she tell you?"

"Yes, she told me. Behave properly for the rest of the evening, and come and see me to-morrow at a quarter past five."

She was severe, and in the manner in which she turned her back to him there was a degree of contempt which caused him to mutter a decent imprecation.

He had no intention of speaking to Osmond; it was neither the time nor the place. But he instinctively wandered towards Isabel, who sat talking with an old lady. He sat down on the other side of her; the old lady was an Italian, and Rosier took for granted that she understood no English.

"You said just now you wouldn't help me," he began, to Mrs. Osmond. "Perhaps you will feel differently when you know—when you know——"

He hesitated a little.

"When I know what?" Isabel asked, gently.

"That she is all right."

"What do you mean by that?"

"Well, that we have come to an understanding."

"She is all wrong," said Isabel. "It won't do."

Poor Rosier gazed at her half-pleadingly, half-angrily; a sudden flush testified to his sense of injury.

"I have never been treated so," he said. "What is there against me, after all? That is not the way I am usually considered. I could have married twenty times."

"It's a pity you didn't. I don't mean twenty times, but once, comfortably," Isabel added, smiling kindly. "You are not rich enough for Pansy."

"She doesn't care a straw for one's money."

"No, but her father does."

"Ah yes, he has proved that!" cried the young man.

Isabel got up, turning away from him, leaving her old lady, without saying anything; and he occupied himself for the next ten minutes in pretending to look at Gilbert Osmond's collection of miniatures, which were neatly arranged on a series of small velvet screens. But he looked without seeing; his cheek burned; he was too full of his sense of injury. It was certain that he had never been treated that way before; he was not used to being thought not good enough. He knew how good he was, and if such a fallacy had not been so pernicious, he could have laughed at it. He looked about again for Pansy, but she had disappeared, and his main desire was now to get out of the house. Before doing so he spoke to Isabel again; it was not agreeable to him to reflect that he had just said a rude thing to her—the only point that would now justify a low view of him.

"I spoke of Mr. Osmond as I shouldn't have done, a while ago," he said. "But you must remember my situation."

"I don't remember what you said," she answered, coldly.

"Ah, you are offended, and now you will never help me."

She was silent an instant, and then, with a change of tone—

"It's not that I won't; I simply can't!" Her manner was almost passionate.

"If you could—just a little," said Rosier, "I would never again speak of your husband save as an angel."

"The inducement is great," said Isabel gravely—inscrutably, as he afterwards, to himself, called it; and she gave him, straight in the eyes, a look which was also inscrutable. It made him remember, somehow, that he had known her as a child; and yet it was keener than he liked, and he took himself off.

XXXVIII

H<small>E WENT</small> to see Madame Merle on the morrow, and to his surprise she let him off rather easily. But she made him promise that he would stop there until something should have been decided. Mr. Osmond had had higher expectations; it was very true that as he had no intention of giving his daughter a portion, such expectations were open to criticism, or even, if one would, to ridicule. But she would advise Mr. Rosier not to take that tone; if he would possess his soul in patience he might arrive at his felicity. Mr. Osmond was not favourable to his suit, but it would not be a miracle if he should gradually come round. Pansy would never defy her father, he might depend upon that, so nothing was to be gained by precipitation. Mr. Osmond needed to accustom his mind to an offer of a sort that he had not hitherto entertained, and this result must come of itself—it was useless to try to force it. Rosier remarked that his own situation would be in the mean while the most uncomfortable in the world, and Madame Merle assured him that she felt for him. But, as she justly declared, one couldn't have everything one wanted; she had learned that lesson for herself. There would be no use in his writing to Gilbert Osmond, who had charged her to tell him as much. He wished the matter dropped for a few weeks, and would himself write when he should have anything to communicate which it would please Mr. Rosier to hear.

"He doesn't like your having spoken to Pansy. Ah, he doesn't like it at all," said Madame Merle.

"I am perfectly willing to give him a chance to tell me so!"

"If you do that he will tell you more than you care to hear. Go to the house, for the next month, as little as possible, and leave the rest to me."

"As little as possible? Who is to measure that?"

"Let me measure it. Go on Thursday evenings with the rest of the world; but don't go at all at odd times, and don't fret about Pansy. I will see that she understands everything. She's a calm little nature; she will take it quietly."

Edward Rosier fretted about Pansy a good deal, but he did

as he was advised, and waited for another Thursday evening before returning to the Palazzo Roccanera. There had been a party at dinner, so that although he went early the company was already tolerably numerous. Osmond, as usual, was in the first room, near the fire, staring straight at the door, so that, not to be distinctly uncivil, Rosier had to go and speak to him.

"I am glad that you can take a hint," Pansy's father said, slightly closing his keen, conscious eye.

"I take no hints. But I took a message, as I supposed it to be."

"You took it? Where did you take it?"

It seemed to poor Rosier that he was being insulted, and he waited a moment, asking himself how much a true lover ought to submit to.

"Madame Merle gave me, as I understood it, a message from you—to the effect that you declined to give me the opportunity I desire—the opportunity to explain my wishes to you."

Rosier flattered himself that he spoke rather sternly.

"I don't see what Madame Merle has to do with it. Why did you apply to Madame Merle?"

"I asked her for an opinion—for nothing more. I did so because she had seemed to me to know you very well."

"She doesn't know me so well as she thinks," said Osmond.

"I am sorry for that, because she has given me some little ground for hope."

Osmond stared into the fire for a moment.

"I set a great price on my daughter."

"You can't set a higher one than I do. Don't I prove it by wishing to marry her?"

"I wish to marry her very well," Osmond went on, with a dry impertinence which, in another mood, poor Rosier would have admired.

"Of course I pretend that she would marry well in marrying me. She couldn't marry a man who loves her more; or whom, I may venture to add, she loves more."

"I am not bound to accept your theories as to whom my daughter loves," Osmond said, looking up with a quick, cold smile.

"I am not theorising. Your daughter has spoken."

"Not to me," Osmond continued, bending forward a little and dropping his eyes to his boot-toes.

"I have her promise, sir!" cried Rosier, with the sharpness of exasperation.

As their voices had been pitched very low before, such a note attracted some attention from the company. Osmond waited till this little movement had subsided, then he said very quickly—

"I think she has no recollection of having given it."

They had been standing with their faces to the fire, and after he had uttered these last words Osmond turned round again to the room. Before Rosier had time to rejoin he perceived that a gentleman—a stranger—had just come in, unannounced, according to the Roman custom, and was about to present himself to the master of the house. The latter smiled blandly, but somewhat blankly; the visitor was a handsome man, with a large, fair beard—evidently an Englishman.

"You apparently don't recognise me," he said, with a smile that expressed more than Osmond's.

"Ah yes, now I do; I expected so little to see you."

Rosier departed, and went in direct pursuit of Pansy. He sought her, as usual, in the neighbouring room, but he again encountered Mrs. Osmond in his path. He gave this gracious lady no greeting—he was too righteously indignant; but said to her crudely—

"Your husband is awfully cold-blooded."

She gave the same mystical smile that he had noticed before.

"You can't expect every one to be as hot as yourself."

"I don't pretend to be cold, but I am cool. What has he been doing to his daughter?"

"I have no idea."

"Don't you take any interest?" Rosier demanded, feeling that she too was irritating.

For a moment she answered nothing. Then—

"No!" she said abruptly, and with a quickened light in her eye which directly contradicted the word.

"Excuse me if I don't believe that. Where is Miss Osmond?"

"In the corner, making tea. Please leave her there."

Rosier instantly discovered the young girl, who had been hidden by intervening groups. He watched her, but her own attention was entirely given to her occupation.

"What on earth has he done to her?" he asked again imploringly. "He declares to me that she has given me up."

"She has not given you up," Isabel said, in a low tone, without looking at him.

"Ah, thank you for that! Now I will leave her alone as long as you think proper!"

He had hardly spoken when he saw her change colour, and became aware that Osmond was coming towards her, accompanied by the gentleman who had just entered. He thought the latter, in spite of the advantage of good looks and evident social experience, was a little embarrassed.

"Isabel," said Osmond, "I bring you an old friend."

Mrs. Osmond's face, though it wore a smile, was, like her old friend's, not perfectly confident. "I am very happy to see Lord Warburton," she said. Rosier turned away, and now that his talk with her had been interrupted, felt absolved from the little pledge he had just taken. He had a quick impression that Mrs. Osmond would not notice what he did.

To do him justice, Isabel for some time quite ceased to observe him. She had been startled; she hardly knew whether she were glad or not. Lord Warburton, however, now that he was face to face with her, was plainly very well pleased; his frank grey eye expressed a deep, if still somewhat shy, satisfaction. He was larger, stouter than of yore, and he looked older; he stood there very solidly and sensibly.

"I suppose you didn't expect to see me," he said; "I have only just arrived. Literally, I only got here this evening. You see I have lost no time in coming to pay you my respects; I knew you were at home on Thursdays."

"You see the fame of your Thursdays has spread to England," Osmond remarked, smiling, to his wife.

"It is very kind of Lord Warburton to come so soon; we are greatly flattered," Isabel said.

"Ah well, it's better than stopping in one of those horrible inns," Osmond went on.

"The hotel seems very good; I think it is the same one

where I saw you four years ago. You know it was here in
Rome that we first met; it is a long time ago. Do you remember where I bade you good-bye? It was in the Capitol, in the
first room."

"I remember that myself," said Osmond; "I was there at
the time."

"Yes, I remember that you were there. I was very sorry to
leave Rome—so sorry that, somehow or other, it became a
melancholy sort of memory, and I have never cared to come
back till to-day. But I knew you were living here, and I assure
you I have often thought of you. It must be a charming place
to live in," said Lord Warburton, brightly, looking about
him.

"We should have been glad to see you at any time," Osmond remarked with propriety.

"Thank you very much. I haven't been out of England
since then. Till a month ago, I really supposed my travels
were over."

"I have heard of you from time to time," said Isabel, who
had now completely recovered her self-possession.

"I hope you have heard no harm. My life has been a blank."

"Like the good reigns in history," Osmond suggested. He
appeared to think his duties as a host had now terminated, he
had performed them very conscientiously. Nothing could
have been more adequate, more nicely measured, than his
courtesy to his wife's old friend. It was punctilious, it was
explicit, it was everything but natural—a deficiency which
Lord Warburton, who, himself, had on the whole a good deal
of nature, may be supposed to have perceived. "I will leave
you and Mrs. Osmond together," he added. "You have reminiscences into which I don't enter."

"I am afraid you lose a good deal!" said Lord Warburton,
in a tone which perhaps betrayed over-much his appreciation
of Osmond's generosity. He stood a moment, looking at Isabel with an eye that gradually became more serious. "I am
really very glad to see you."

"It is very pleasant. You are very kind."

"Do you know that you are changed—a little?"

Isabel hesitated a moment.

"Yes—a good deal."

"I don't mean for the worse, of course; and yet how can I say for the better?"

"I think I shall have no scruple in saying that to you," said Isabel, smiling.

"Ah well, for me—it's a long time. It would be a pity that there shouldn't be something to show for it."

They sat down, and Isabel asked him about his sisters, with other inquiries of a somewhat perfunctory kind. He answered her questions as if they interested him, and in a few moments she saw—or believed she saw—that he would prove a more comfortable companion than of yore. Time had breathed upon his heart, and without chilling this organ, had freely ventilated it. Isabel felt her usual esteem for Time rise at a bound. Lord Warburton's manner was certainly that of a contented man who would rather like one to know it.

"There is something I must tell you without more delay," he said. "I have brought Ralph Touchett with me."

"Brought him with you?" Isabel's surprise was great.

"He is at the hotel; he was too tired to come out, and has gone to bed."

"I will go and see him," said Isabel, quickly.

"That is exactly what I hoped you would do. I had an idea that you hadn't seen much of him since your marriage—that in fact your relations were a—a little more formal. That's why I hesitated—like an awkward Englishman."

"I am as fond of Ralph as ever," Isabel answered. "But why has he come to Rome?"

The declaration was very gentle; the question a little sharp.

"Because he is very far gone, Mrs. Osmond."

"Rome, then, is no place for him. I heard from him that he had determined to give up his custom of wintering abroad, and remain in England, indoors, in what he called an artificial climate."

"Poor fellow, he doesn't succeed with the artificial! I went to see him three weeks ago, at Gardencourt, and found him extremely ill. He has been getting worse every year, and now he has no strength left. He smokes no more cigarettes! He had got up an artificial climate indeed; the house was as hot as Calcutta. Nevertheless, he had suddenly taken it into his

head to start for Sicily. I didn't believe in it—neither did the
doctors, nor any of his friends. His mother, as I suppose you
know, is in America, so there was no one to prevent him. He
stuck to his idea that it would be the saving of him to spend
the winter at Catania. He said he could take servants and furniture, and make himself comfortable; but in point of fact he
hasn't brought anything. I wanted him at least to go by sea,
to save fatigue; but he said he hated the sea, and wished to
stop at Rome. After that, though I thought it all rubbish, I
made up my mind to come with him. I am acting as—what
do you call it in America?—as a kind of moderator. Poor
Touchett's very moderate now. We left England a fortnight
ago, and he has been very bad on the way. He can't keep
warm, and the further south we come the more he feels the
cold. He has got a rather good man, but I'm afraid he's beyond human help. If you don't mind my saying so, I think it
was a most extraordinary time for Mrs. Touchett to choose
for going to America."

Isabel had listened eagerly; her face was full of pain and
wonder.

"My aunt does that at fixed periods, and she lets nothing
turn her aside. When the date comes round she starts; I think
she would have started if Ralph had been dying."

"I sometimes think he is dying," Lord Warburton said.

Isabel started up.

"I will go to him now!"

He checked her; he was a little disconcerted at the quick
effect of his words.

"I don't mean that I thought so to-night. On the contrary,
to-day, in the train, he seemed particularly well; the idea of
our reaching Rome—he is very fond of Rome, you know—
gave him strength. An hour ago, when I bade him good-
night, he told me that he was very tired, but very happy. Go
to him in the morning; that's all I mean. I didn't tell him I
was coming here; I didn't think of it till after we separated.
Then I remembered that he had told me that you had an
evening, and that it was this very Thursday. It occurred to me
to come in and tell you that he was here, and let you know
that you had perhaps better not wait for him to call. I think
he said he had not written to you." There was no need of

Isabel's declaring that she would act upon Lord Warburton's information; she looked, as she sat there, like a winged creature held back. "Let alone that I wanted to see you for myself," her visitor added, gallantly.

"I don't understand Ralph's plan; it seems to me very wild," she said. "I was glad to think of him between those thick walls at Gardencourt."

"He was completely alone there; the thick walls were his only company."

"You went to see him; you have been extremely kind."

"Oh dear, I had nothing to do," said Lord Warburton.

"We hear, on the contrary, that you are doing great things. Every one speaks of you as a great statesman, and I am perpetually seeing your name in the *Times*, which, by the way, doesn't appear to hold it in reverence. You are apparently as bold a radical as ever."

"I don't feel nearly so bold; you know the world has come round to me. Touchett and I have kept up a sort of Parliamentary debate, all the way from London. I tell him he is the last of the Tories, and he calls me the head of the Communists. So you see there is life in him yet."

Isabel had many questions to ask about Ralph, but she abstained from asking them all. She would see for herself on the morrow. She perceived that after a little Lord Warburton would tire of that subject—that he had a consciousness of other possible topics. She was more and more able to say to herself that he had recovered, and, what is more to the point, she was able to say it without bitterness. He had been for her, of old, such an image of urgency, of insistence, of something to be resisted and reasoned with, that his reappearance at first menaced her with a new trouble. But she was now reassured; she could see that he only wished to live with her on good terms, that she was to understand that he had forgiven her and was incapable of the bad taste of making pointed allusions. This was not a form of revenge, of course; she had no suspicion that he wished to punish her by an exhibition of disillusionment; she did him the justice to believe that it had simply occurred to him that she would now take a good-natured interest in knowing that he was resigned. It was the resignation of a healthy, manly nature, in which sentimental wounds could never fester. British politics had cured him; she had known they would. She gave an envious thought to the happier lot of men, who are always free to plunge into the healing waters of action. Lord Warburton of course spoke of the past, but he spoke of it without implication; he even went so far as to allude to their former meeting in Rome as a very jolly time. And he told her that he had been immensely interested in hearing of her marriage—that it was a great pleasure to him to make Mr. Osmond's acquaintance—since he could hardly be said to have made it on the other occasion. He had not written to her when she married, but he did not apologise to her for that. The only thing he implied was that they were old friends, intimate friends. It was very much as an intimate friend that he said to her, suddenly, after a short pause which he had occupied in smiling, as he looked about him, like a man to whom everything suggested a cheerful interpretation—

"Well now, I suppose you are very happy, and all that sort of thing?"

Isabel answered with a quick laugh; the tone of his remark struck her almost as the accent of comedy.

"Do you suppose if I were not I would tell you?"

"Well, I don't know. I don't see why not."

"I do, then. Fortunately, however, I am very happy."

"You have got a very good house."

"Yes, it's very pleasant. But that's not my merit—it's my husband's."

"You mean that he has arranged it?"

"Yes, it was nothing when we came."

"He must be very clever."

"He has a genius for upholstery," said Isabel.

"There is a great rage for that sort of thing now. But you must have a taste of your own."

"I enjoy things when they are done; but I have no ideas. I can never propose anything."

"Do you mean that you accept what others propose?"

"Very willingly, for the most part."

"That's a good thing to know. I shall propose you something."

"It will be very kind. I must say, however, that I have in a few small ways a certain initiative. I should like, for instance, to introduce you to some of these people."

"Oh, please don't; I like sitting here. Unless it be to that young lady in the blue dress. She has a charming face."

"The one talking to the rosy young man? That's my husband's daughter."

"Lucky man, your husband. What a dear little maid!"

"You must make her acquaintance."

"In a moment, with pleasure. I like looking at her from here." He ceased to look at her, however, very soon; his eyes constantly reverted to Mrs. Osmond. "Do you know I was wrong just now in saying that you had changed?" he presently went on. "You seem to me, after all, very much the same."

"And yet I find it's a great change to be married," said Isabel, with gaiety.

"It affects most people more than it has affected you. You see I haven't gone in for that."

"It rather surprises me."

"You ought to understand it, Mrs. Osmond. But I want to marry," he added, more simply.

"It ought to be very easy," Isabel said, rising, and then blushing a little at the thought that she was hardly the person to say this. It was perhaps because Lord Warburton noticed her blush that he generously forbore to call her attention to the incongruity.

Edward Rosier meanwhile had seated himself on an ottoman beside Pansy's tea-table. He pretended at first to talk to her about trifles, and she asked him who was the new gentleman conversing with her stepmother.

"He's an English lord," said Rosier. "I don't know more."

"I wonder if he will have some tea. The English are so fond of tea."

"Never mind that; I have something particular to say to you."

"Don't speak so loud, or every one will hear us," said Pansy.

"They won't hear us if you continue to look that way: as if your only thought in life was the wish that the kettle would boil."

"It has just been filled; the servants never know!" the young girl exclaimed, with a little sigh.

"Do you know what your father said to me just now? That you didn't mean what you said a week ago."

"I don't mean everything I say. How can a young girl do that? But I mean what I say to you."

"He told me that you had forgotten me."

"Ah no, I don't forget," said Pansy, showing her pretty teeth in a fixed smile.

"Then everything is just the same?"

"Ah no, it's not just the same. Papa has been very severe."

"What has he done to you?"

"He asked me what *you* had done to me, and I told him everything. Then he forbade me to marry you."

"You needn't mind that."

"Oh yes, I must indeed. I can't disobey papa."

"Not for one who loves you as I do, and whom you pretend to love?"

Pansy raised the lid of the tea-pot, gazing into this vessel for a moment; then she dropped six words into its aromatic depths. "I love you just as much."

"What good will that do me?"

"Ah," said Pansy, raising her sweet, vague eyes, "I don't know that."

"You disappoint me," groaned poor Rosier.

Pansy was silent a moment; she handed a tea-cup to a servant.

"Please don't talk any more."

"Is this to be all my satisfaction?"

"Papa said I was not to talk with you."

"Do you sacrifice me like that? Ah, it's too much!"

"I wish you would wait a little," said the young girl, in a voice just distinct enough to betray a quaver.

"Of course I will wait if you will give me hope. But you take my life away."

"I will not give you up—oh, no!" Pansy went on.

"He will try and make you marry some one else."

"I will never do that."

"What then are we to wait for?"

She hesitated a moment.

"I will speak to Mrs. Osmond, and she will help us." It was in this manner that she for the most part designated her stepmother.

"She won't help as much. She is afraid."

"Afraid of what?"

"Of your father, I suppose."

Pansy shook her little head.

"She is not afraid of any one! We must have patience."

"Ah, that's an awful word," Rosier groaned; he was deeply disconcerted. Oblivious of the customs of good society, he dropped his head into his hands, and, supporting it with a melancholy grace, sat staring at the carpet. Presently he became aware of a good deal of movement about him, and when he looked up saw Pansy making a curtsey—it was still her little curtsey of the convent—to the English lord whom Mrs. Osmond had presented.

XXXIX

IT PROBABLY will not be surprising to the reflective reader
that Ralph Touchett should have seen less of his cousin
since her marriage than he had done before that event—an
event of which he took such a view as could hardly prove a
confirmation of intimacy. He had uttered his thought, as we
know, and after this he had held his peace, Isabel not having
invited him to resume a discussion which marked an era in
their relations. That discussion had made a difference—the
difference that he feared, rather than the one he hoped. It had
not chilled the girl's zeal in carrying out her engagement, but
it had come dangerously near to spoiling a friendship. No
reference was ever again made between them to Ralph's opinion of Gilbert Osmond; and by surrounding this topic with a
sacred silence, they managed to preserve a semblance of recip-
rocal frankness. But there was a difference, as Ralph often
said to himself—there was a difference. She had not forgiven
him, she never would forgive him; that was all he had gained.
She thought she had forgiven him; she believed she didn't
care; and as she was both very generous and very proud, these
convictions represented a certain reality. But whether or no
the event should justify him, he would virtually have done her
a wrong, and the wrong was of the sort that women remember best. As Osmond's wife, she could never again be his
friend. If in this character she should enjoy the felicity she
expected, she would have nothing but contempt for the man
who had attempted, in advance, to undermine a blessing so
dear; and if on the other hand his warning should be justified,
the vow she had taken that he should never know it, would
lay upon her spirit a burden that would make her hate him.
Such had been, during the year that followed his cousin's
marriage, Ralph's rather dismal prevision of the future; and if
his meditations appear morbid, we must remember that he
was not in the bloom of health. He consoled himself as he
might by behaving (as he deemed) beautifully, and was present at the ceremony by which Isabel was united to Mr. Osmond, and which was performed in Florence in the month of
June. He learned from his mother that Isabel at first had

thoughts of celebrating her nuptials in her native land, but that as simplicity was what she chiefly desired to secure, she had finally decided, in spite of Osmond's professed willingness to make a journey of any length, that this characteristic would best be preserved by their being married by the nearest clergyman in the shortest time. The thing was done, therefore, at the little American chapel, on a very hot day, in the presence only of Mrs. Touchett and her son, of Pansy Osmond and the Countess Gemini. That severity in the proceedings of which I just spoke, was in part the result of the absence of two persons who might have been looked for on the occasion, and who would have lent it a certain richness. Madame Merle had been invited, but Madame Merle, who was unable to leave Rome, sent a gracious letter of excuses. Henrietta Stackpole had not been invited, as her departure from America, announced to Isabel by Mr. Goodwood, was in fact frustrated by the duties of her profession; but she had sent a letter, less gracious than Madame Merle's, intimating that had she been able to cross the Atlantic, she would have been present not only as a witness but as a critic. Her return to Europe took place somewhat later, and she effected a meeting with Isabel in the autumn, in Paris, when she indulged—perhaps a trifle too freely—her critical genius. Poor Osmond, who was chiefly the subject of it, protested so sharply that Henrietta was obliged to declare to Isabel that she had taken a step which erected a barrier between them. "It isn't in the least that you have married—it is that you have married *him*," she deemed it her duty to remark; agreeing, it will be seen, much more with Ralph Touchett than she suspected, though she had few of his hesitations and compunctions. Henrietta's second visit to Europe, however, was not made in vain; for just at the moment when Osmond had declared to Isabel that he really must object to that newspaper-woman, and Isabel had answered that it seemed to her he took Henrietta too hard, the good Mr. Bantling appeared upon the scene and proposed that they should take a run down to Spain. Henrietta's letters from Spain proved to be the most picturesque she had yet published, and there was one in especial, dated from the Alhambra, and entitled 'Moors and Moonlight,' which generally passed for her masterpiece.

Isabel was secretly disappointed at her husband's not having been able to judge the poor girl more humorously. She even wondered whether his sense of humour were by chance defective. Of course she herself looked at the matter as a person whose present happiness had nothing to grudge to Henrietta's violated conscience. Osmond thought their alliance a kind of monstrosity; he couldn't imagine what they had in common. For him, Mr. Bantling's fellow-tourist was simply the most vulgar of women, and he also pronounced her the most abandoned. Against this latter clause of the verdict Isabel protested with an ardour which made him wonder afresh at the oddity of some of his wife's tastes. Isabel could explain it only by saying that she liked to know people who were as different as possible from herself. "Why then don't you make the acquaintance of your washerwoman?" Osmond had inquired; to which Isabel answered that she was afraid her washerwoman wouldn't care for her. Now Henrietta cared so much.

Ralph saw nothing of her for the greater part of the two years that followed her marriage; the winter that formed the beginning of her residence in Rome he spent again at San Remo, where he was joined in the spring by his mother, who afterwards went with him to England, to see what they were doing at the bank—an operation she could not induce him to perform. Ralph had taken a lease of his house at San Remo, a small villa, which he occupied still another winter; but late in the month of April of this second year he came down to Rome. It was the first time since her marriage that he had stood face to face with Isabel; his desire to see her again was of the keenest. She had written to him from time to time, but her letters told him nothing that he wanted to know. He had asked his mother what she was making of her life, and his mother had simply answered that she supposed she was making the best of it. Mrs. Touchett had not the imagination that communes with the unseen, and she now pretended to no intimacy with her niece, whom she rarely encountered. This young woman appeared to be living in a sufficiently honourable way, but Mrs. Touchett still remained of the opinion that her marriage was a shabby affair. It gave her no pleasure to think of Isabel's establishment, which she was sure was a very lame business. From time to time, in

Florence, she rubbed against the Countess Gemini, doing her best, always, to minimise the contact; and the Countess reminded her of Osmond, who made her think of Isabel. The Countess was less talked about in these days; but Mrs. Touchett augured no good of that; it only proved how she had been talked about before. There was a more direct suggestion of Isabel in the person of Madame Merle; but Madame Merle's relations with Mrs. Touchett had undergone a perceptible change. Isabel's aunt had told her, without circumlocution, that she had played too ingenious a part; and Madame Merle, who never quarrelled with any one, who appeared to think no one worth it, and who had performed the miracle of living, more or less, for several years with Mrs. Touchett, without a symptom of irritation—Madame Merle now took a very high tone, and declared that this was an accusation from which she could not stoop to defend herself. She added, however (without stooping), that her behaviour had been only too simple, that she had believed only what she saw, that she saw that Isabel was not eager to marry, and that Osmond was not eager to please (his repeated visits were nothing; he was boring himself to death on his hill-top, and he came merely for amusement). Isabel had kept her sentiments to herself, and her journey to Greece and Egypt had effectually thrown dust in her companion's eyes. Madame Merle accepted the event—she was unprepared to think of it as a scandal; but that she had played any part in it, double or single, was an imputation against which she proudly protested. It was doubtless in consequence of Mrs. Touchett's attitude and of the injury it offered to habits consecrated by many charming seasons, that Madame Merle, after this, chose to pass many months in England, where her credit was quite unimpaired. Mrs. Touchett had done her a wrong; there are some things that can't be forgiven. But Madame Merle suffered in silence; there was always something exquisite in her dignity.

Ralph, as I say, had wished to see for himself; but while he was engaged in this pursuit he felt afresh what a fool he had been to put the girl on her guard. He had played the wrong card, and now he had lost the game. He should see nothing, he should learn nothing; for him she would always wear a mask. His true line would have been to profess delight in her marriage, so that later, when, as Ralph phrased it, the bottom should fall out of it, she might have the pleasure of saying to him that he had been a goose. He would gladly have consented to pass for a goose in order to know Isabel's real situation. But now she neither taunted him with his fallacies nor pretended that her own confidence was justified; if she wore a mask, it completely covered her face. There was something fixed and mechanical in the serenity painted upon it; this was not an expression, Ralph said—it was a representation. She had lost her child; that was a sorrow, but it was a sorrow she scarcely spoke of; there was more to say about it than she could say to Ralph. It belonged to the past, moreover; it had occurred six months before, and she had already laid aside the tokens of mourning. She seemed to be leading the life of the world; Ralph heard her spoken of as having a "charming position." He observed that she produced the impression of being peculiarly enviable, that it was supposed, among many people, to be a privilege even to know her. Her house was not open to every one, and she had an evening in the week, to which people were not invited as a matter of course. She lived with a certain magnificence, but you needed to be a member of her circle to perceive it; for there was nothing to gape at, nothing to criticise, nothing even to admire, in the daily proceedings of Mr. and Mrs. Osmond. Ralph, in all this, recognised the hand of the master; for he knew that Isabel had no faculty for producing calculated impressions. She struck him as having a great love of movement, of gaiety, of late hours, of long drives, of fatigue; an eagerness to be entertained, to be interested, even to be bored, to make acquaintances, to see people that were talked about, to explore the neighbourhood of Rome, to enter into relation with certain of the mustiest relics of its old society. In all this there was much less discrimination than in that desire for comprehensiveness of development on which he used to exercise his wit. There was a kind of violence in some of her impulses, of crudity in some of her experiments, which took him by surprise; it seemed to him that she even spoke faster, moved faster, than before her marriage. Certainly she had fallen into exaggerations—she who used to care so much for the pure truth; and whereas of old she had a great delight in good-humoured argument, in intellectual play (she never looked so charming as when in the genial heat of discussion she received a crushing blow full in the face and brushed it away as a feather), she appeared now to think there was nothing worth people's either differing about or agreeing upon. Of old she had been curious, and now she was indifferent, and yet in spite of her indifference her activity was greater than ever. Slender still, but lovelier than before, she had gained no great maturity of aspect; but there was a kind of amplitude and brilliancy in her personal arrangements which gave a touch of insolence to her beauty. Poor human-hearted Isabel, what perversity had bitten her? Her light step drew a mass of drapery behind it; her intelligent head sustained a majesty of ornament. The free, keen girl had become quite another person; what he saw was the fine lady who was supposed to represent something. "What did Isabel represent?" Ralph asked himself; and he could only answer by saying that she represented Gilbert Osmond. "Good heavens, what a function!" he exclaimed. He was lost in wonder at the mystery of things. He recognised Osmond, as I say; he recognised him at every turn. He saw how he kept all things within limits; how he adjusted, regulated, animated their manner of life. Osmond was in his element; at last he had material to work with. He always had an eye to effect; and his effects were elaborately studied. They were produced by no vulgar means, but the motive was as vulgar as the art was great. To surround his interior with a sort of invidious sanctity, to tantalise society with a sense of exclusion, to make people believe his house was different from every other, to impart to the face that he presented to the world a cold originality—this was the ingenious effort of the personage to whom Isabel had attributed a superior morality. "He works with superior material," Ralph said to himself; "but it's rich abundance compared with his former resources." Ralph was a clever man; but Ralph had never—to his own sense—been so clever as when he observed, *in petto*, that under the guise of caring only for intrinsic values, Osmond lived exclusively for the world. Far from being its master, as he pretended to be, he was its very humble servant, and the degree of its attention was his only measure of success. He lived with his eye on it, from morning till night, and the world was so stupid it never suspected the trick. Everything he did was *pose—pose* so deeply calculated that if one were not on the lookout one mistook it for impulse. Ralph had never met a man who lived so much in the land of calculation. His tastes, his studies, his accomplishments, his collections, were all for a purpose. His life on his hill-top at Florence had been a *pose* of years. His solitude, his ennui, his love for his daughter, his good manners, his bad manners, were so many features of a mental image constantly present to him as a model of impertinence and mystification. His ambition was not to please the world, but to please himself by exciting the world's curiosity and then declining to satisfy it. It made him feel great to play the world a trick. The thing he had done in his life most directly to please himself was his marrying Isabel Archer; though in this case indeed the gullible world was in a manner embodied in poor Isabel, who had been mystified to the top of her bent. Ralph of course found a fitness in being consistent; he had embraced a creed, and as he had suffered for it he could not in honour forsake it. I give this little sketch of its articles for what they are worth. It was certain that he was very skilful in fitting the facts to his theory—even the fact that during the month he spent in Rome at this period Gilbert Osmond appeared to regard him not in the least as an enemy. For Mr. Osmond Ralph had not now that importance. It was not that he had the importance of a friend; it was rather that he had none at all. He was Isabel's cousin, and he was rather unpleasantly ill—it was on this basis that Osmond treated with him. He made the proper inquiries, asked about his health, about Mrs. Touchett, about his opinion of winter climates, whether he was comfortable at his hotel. He addressed him, on the few occasions of their meeting, not a word that was not necessary; but his manner had always the urbanity proper to conscious success in the presence of conscious failure. For all this, Ralph had, towards the end, an inward conviction that Osmond had made it uncomfortable for his wife that she should continue to receive her cousin. He was not jealous—he had not that excuse; no one could be jealous of Ralph. But he made Isabel pay for her old-time kindness, of which so much was still left; and as Ralph had no idea of her paying too much, when his suspicion had become sharp, he took himself off. In doing so he deprived Isabel of a very interesting occupation: she had been constantly wondering what fine principle kept him alive. She decided that it was his love of conversation; his conversation was better than ever. He had given up walking; he was no longer a humorous stroller. He sat all day in a chair—almost any chair would do, and was so dependent on what you would do for him that, had not his talk been highly contemplative, you might have thought he was blind. The reader already knows more about him than Isabel was ever to know, and the reader may therefore be given the key to the mystery. What kept Ralph alive was simply the fact that he had not yet seen enough of his cousin; he was not yet satisfied. There was more to come; he couldn't make up his mind to lose that. He wished to see what she would make of her husband—or what he would make of her. This was only the first act of the drama, and he was determined to sit out the performance. His determination held good; it kept him going some eighteen months more, till the time of his return to Rome with Lord Warburton. It gave him indeed such an air of intending to live indefinitely that Mrs. Touchett, though more accessible to confusions of thought in the matter of this strange, unremunerative—and unremunerated—son of hers than she had ever been before, had, as we have learned, not scrupled to embark for a distant land. If Ralph had been kept alive by suspense, it was with a good deal of the same emotion—the excitement of wondering in what state she should find him—that Isabel ascended to his apartment the day after Lord Warburton had notified her of his arrival in Rome.

She spent an hour with him; it was the first of several visits. Gilbert Osmond called on him punctually, and on Isabel sending a carriage for him Ralph came more than once to the Palazzo Roccanera. A fortnight elapsed, at the end of which Ralph announced to Lord Warburton that he thought after all he wouldn't go to Sicily. The two men had been dining together after a day spent by the latter in ranging about the Campagna. They had left the table, and Warburton, before the chimney, was lighting a cigar, which he instantly removed from his lips.

"Won't go to Sicily? Where then will you go?"

"Well, I guess I won't go anywhere," said Ralph, from the sofa, in a tone of jocosity.

"Do you mean that you will return to England?"

"Oh dear no; I will stay in Rome."

"Rome won't do for you; it's not warm enough."

"It will have to do; I will make it do. See how well I have been."

Lord Warburton looked at him a while, puffing his cigar, as if he were trying to see it.

"You have been better than you were on the journey, certainly. I wonder how you lived through that. But I don't understand your condition. I recommend you to try Sicily."

"I can't try," said poor Ralph; "I can't move further. I can't face that journey. Fancy me between Scylla and Charybdis! I don't want to die on the Sicilian plains—to be snatched away, like Proserpine in the same locality, to the Plutonian shades."

"What the deuce then did you come for?" his lordship inquired.

"Because the idea took me. I see it won't do. It really doesn't matter where I am now. I've exhausted all remedies, I've swallowed all climates. As I'm here I'll stay; I haven't got any cousins in Sicily."

"Your cousin is certainly an inducement. But what does the doctor say?"

"I haven't asked him, and I don't care a fig. If I die here Mrs. Osmond will bury me. But I shall not die here."

"I hope not." Lord Warburton continued to smoke reflectively. "Well, I must say," he resumed, "for myself I am very glad you don't go to Sicily. I had a horror of that journey."

"Ah, but for you it needn't have mattered. I had no idea of dragging you in my train."

"I certainly didn't mean to let you go alone."

"My dear Warburton, I never expected you to come further than this," Ralph cried.

"I should have gone with you and seen you settled," said Lord Warburton.

"You are a very good fellow. You are very kind."

"Then I should have come back here."

"And then you would have gone to England."

"No, no; I should have stayed."

"Well," said Ralph, "if that's what we are both up to, I don't see where Sicily comes in!"

His companion was silent; he sat staring at the fire. At last, looking up—

"I say, tell me this," he broke out; "did you really mean to go to Sicily when we started?"

"Ah, *vous m'en demandez trop*! Let me put a question first. Did you come with me quite—platonically?"

"I don't know what you mean by that. I wanted to come abroad."

"I suspect we have each been playing our little game."

"Speak for yourself. I made no secret whatever of my wanting to be here a while."

"Yes, I remember you said you wished to see the Minister of Foreign Affairs."

"I have seen him three times; he is very amusing."

"I think you have forgotten what you came for," said Ralph.

"Perhaps I have," his companion answered, rather gravely.

These two gentlemen were children of a race which is not distinguished by the absence of reserve, and they had travelled together from London to Rome without an allusion to matters that were uppermost in the mind of each. There was an old subject that they had once discussed, but it had lost its recognised place in their attention, and even after their arrival in Rome, where many things led back to it, they had kept the same half-diffident, half-confident silence.

"I recommend you to get the doctor's consent, all the same," Lord Warburton went on, abruptly, after an interval.

"The doctor's consent will spoil it; I never have it when I can help it!"

"What does Mrs. Osmond think?"

"I have not told her. She will probably say that Rome is too cold, and even offer to go with me to Catania. She is capable of that."

"In your place I should like it."

"Her husband won't like it."

"Ah well, I can fancy that; though it seems to me you are not bound to mind it. It's his affair."

"I don't want to make any more trouble between them," said Ralph.

"Is there so much already?"

"There's complete preparation for it. Her going off with me would make the explosion. Osmond isn't fond of his wife's cousin."

"Then of course he would make a row. But won't he make a row if you stop here?"

"That's what I want to see. He made one the last time I was in Rome, and then I thought it my duty to go away. Now I think it's my duty to stop and defend her."

"My dear Touchett, your defensive powers—" Lord Warburton began, with a smile. But he saw something in his companion's face that checked him. "Your duty, in these premises, seems to me rather a nice question," he said.

Ralph for a short time answered nothing.

"It is true that my defensive powers are small," he remarked at last; "but as my aggressive ones are still smaller, Osmond may, after all, not think me worth his gunpowder. At any rate," he added, "there are things I am curious to see."

"You are sacrificing your health to your curiosity then?"

"I am not much interested in my health, and I am deeply interested in Mrs. Osmond."

"So am I. But not as I once was," Lord Warburton added quickly. This was one of the allusions he had not hitherto found occasion to make.

"Does she strike you as very happy?" Ralph inquired, emboldened by this confidence.

"Well, I don't know; I have hardly thought. She told me the other night that she was happy."

"Ah, she told *you*, of course," Ralph exclaimed, smiling.

"I don't know that. It seems to me I was rather the sort of person she might have complained to."

"Complain? She will never complain. She has done it, and she knows it. She will complain to you least of all. She is very careful."

"She needn't be. I don't mean to make love to her again."

"I am delighted to hear it; there can be no doubt at least of *your* duty."

"Ah no," said Lord Warburton, gravely; "none!"

"Permit me to ask," Ralph went on, " whether it is to bring out the fact that you don't mean to make love to her that you are so very civil to the little girl?"

Lord Warburton gave a slight start; he got up and stood before the fire, blushing a little.

"Does that strike you as very ridiculous?"

"Ridiculous? Not in the least, if you really like her."

"I think her a delightful little person. I don't know when a girl of that age has pleased me more."

"She's a charming creature. Ah, she at least is genuine."

"Of course there's the difference in our ages—more than twenty years."

"My dear Warburton," said Ralph, "are you serious?"

"Perfectly serious—as far as I've got."

"I am very glad. And, heaven help us," cried Ralph, "how tickled Gilbert Osmond will be!"

His companion frowned.

"I say, don't spoil it. I shan't marry his daughter to please him."

"He will have the perversity to be pleased all the same."

"He's not so fond of me as that," said his lordship.

"As that? My dear Warburton, the drawback of your position is that people needn't be fond of you at all to wish to be connected with you. Now, with me in such a case, I should have the happy confidence that they loved me."

Lord Warburton seemed scarcely to be in the mood for doing justice to general axioms; he was thinking of a special case.

"Do you think she'll be pleased?"

"The girl herself? Delighted, surely."

"No, no; I mean Mrs. Osmond."

Ralph looked at him a moment.

"My dear fellow, what has she to do with it?"

"Whatever she chooses. She is very fond of the girl."

"Very true—very true." And Ralph slowly got up. "It's an interesting question—how far her fondness for the girl will carry her." He stood there a moment with his hands in his pockets, with a rather sombre eye. "I hope, you know, that you are very—very sure— The deuce!" he broke off, "I don't know how to say it."

"Yes, you do; you know how to say everything."

"Well, it's awkward. I hope you are sure that among Miss Osmond's merits her being a—so near her stepmother isn't a leading one?"

"Good heavens, Touchett!" cried Lord Warburton, angrily, "for what do you take me?"

XL

ISABEL HAD NOT seen much of Madame Merle since her marriage, this lady having indulged in frequent absences from Rome. At one time she had spent six months in England; at another she had passed a portion of a winter in Paris. She had made numerous visits to distant friends, and gave countenance to the idea that for the future she should be a less inveterate Roman than in the past. As she had been inveterate in the past only in the sense of constantly having an apartment in one of the sunniest niches of the Pincian—an apartment which often stood empty—this suggested a prospect of almost constant absence; a danger which Isabel at one period had been much inclined to deplore. Familiarity had modified in some degree her first impression of Madame Merle, but it had not essentially altered it; there was still a kind of wonder of admiration in it. Madame Merle was armed at all points; it was a pleasure to see a person so completely equipped for the social battle. She carried her flag discreetly, but her weapons were polished steel, and she used them with a skill which struck Isabel as more and more that of a veteran. She was never weary, never overcome with disgust; she never appeared to need rest or consolation. She had her own ideas; she had of old exposed a great many of them to Isabel, who knew also that under an appearance of extreme self-control her highly-cultivated friend concealed a rich sensibility. But her will was mistress of her life; there was something brilliant in the way she kept going. It was as if she had learned the secret of it—as if the art of life were some clever trick that she had guessed. Isabel, as she herself grew older, became acquainted with revulsions, with disgust; there were days when the world looked black, and she asked herself with some peremptoriness what it was that she was pretending to live for. Her old habit had been to live by enthusiasm, to fall in love with suddenly-perceived possibilities, with the idea of a new attempt. As a young girl, she used to proceed from one little exaltation to the other; there were scarcely any dull places between. But Madame Merle had suppressed enthusiasm; she fell in love now-a-days with nothing; she lived entirely by reason, by wisdom. There were hours when Isabel would have given anything for lessons in this art; if Madame Merle had been near, she would have made an appeal to her. She had become aware more than before of the advantage of being like that—of having made one's self a firm surface, a sort of corselet of silver. But, as I say, it was not till the winter, during which we lately renewed acquaintance with our heroine, that Madame Merle made a continuous stay in Rome. Isabel now saw more of her than she had done since her marriage; but by this time Isabel's needs and inclinations had considerably changed. It was not at present to Madame Merle that she would have applied for instruction; she had lost the desire to know this lady's clever trick. If she had troubles she must keep them to herself, and if life was difficult it would not make it easier to confess herself beaten. Madame Merle was doubtless of great use to herself, and an ornament to any circle; but was she—would she be—of use to others in periods of refined embarrassment? The best way to profit by Madame Merle—this indeed Isabel had always thought—was to imitate her; to be as firm and bright as she. She recognised no embarrassments, and Isabel, considering this fact, determined, for the fiftieth time, to brush aside her own. It seemed to her, too, on the renewal of an intercourse which had virtually been interrupted, that Madame Merle was changed—that she pushed to the extreme a certain rather artificial fear of being indiscreet. Ralph Touchett, we know, had been of the opinion that she was prone to exaggeration, to forcing the note—was apt, in the vulgar phrase, to overdo it. Isabel had never admitted this charge—had never, indeed, quite understood it; Madame Merle's conduct, to her perception, always bore the stamp of good taste, was always "quiet." But in this matter of not wishing to intrude upon the inner life of the Osmond family, it at last occurred to our heroine that she overdid it a little. That, of course, was not the best taste; that was rather violent. She remembered too much that Isabel was married; that she had now other interests; that though she, Madame Merle, had known Gilbert Osmond and his little Pansy very well, better almost than any one, she was after all not one of them. She was on her guard; she never spoke of their affairs till she was asked, even pressed—as when her opinion was wanted; she had a dread of seeming to meddle. Madame Merle was as candid as we know, and one day she candidly expressed this dread to Isabel.

"I must be on my guard," she said; "I might so easily, without suspecting it, offend you. You would be right to be offended, even if my intention should have been of the purest. I must not forget that I knew your husband long before you did; I must not let that betray me. If you were a silly woman you might be jealous. You are not a silly woman; I know that perfectly. But neither am I; therefore I am determined not to get into trouble. A little harm is very soon done; a mistake is made before one knows it. Of course, if I had wished to make love to your husband, I had ten years to do it in, and nothing to prevent; so it isn't likely I shall begin to-day, when I am so much less attractive than I was. But if I were to annoy you by seeming to take a place that doesn't belong to me, you wouldn't make that reflection; you would simply say that I was forgetting certain differences. I am determined not to forget them. Of course a good friend isn't always thinking of that; one doesn't suspect one's friends of injustice. I don't suspect you, my dear, in the least; but I suspect human nature. Don't think I make myself uncomfortable; I am not always watching myself. I think I sufficiently prove it in talking to you as I do now. All I wish to say is, however, that if you were to be jealous—that is the form it would take—I should be sure to think it was a little my fault. It certainly wouldn't be your husband's."

Isabel had had three years to think over Mrs. Touchett's theory that Madame Merle had made Gilbert Osmond's marriage. We know how she had at first received it. Madame Merle might have made Gilbert Osmond's marriage, but she certainly had not made Isabel Archer's. That was the work of—Isabel scarcely knew what: of nature, of providence, of fortune, of the eternal mystery of things. It was true that her aunt's complaint had been not so much of Madame Merle's activity as of her duplicity; she had brought about the marriage and then she had denied her guilt. Such guilt would not have been great, to Isabel's mind; she couldn't make a crime of Madame Merle's having been the cause of the most fertile friendship she had ever formed. That occurred to her just

before her marriage, after her little discussion with her aunt.
If Madame Merle had desired the event, she could only say it
had been a very happy thought. With her, moreover, she had
been perfectly straightforward; she had never concealed her
high opinion of Gilbert Osmond. After her marriage Isabel
discovered that her husband took a less comfortable view of
the matter; he seldom spoke of Madame Merle, and when his
wife alluded to her he usually let the allusion drop.

"Don't you like her?" Isabel had once said to him. "She
thinks a great deal of you."

"I will tell you once for all," Osmond had answered. "I
liked her once better than I do to-day. I am tired of her, and
I am rather ashamed of it. She is so good! I am glad she is
not in Italy; it's a sort of rest. Don't talk of her too much; it
seems to bring her back. She will come back in plenty of
time."

Madame Merle, in fact, had come back before it was too
late—too late, I mean, to recover whatever advantage she
might have lost. But meantime, if, as I have said, she was
somewhat changed, Isabel's feelings were also altered. Her
consciousness of the situation was as acute as of old, but it
was much less satisfying. A dissatisfied mind, whatever else it
lack, is rarely in want of reasons; they bloom as thick as but-
tercups in June. The fact of Madame Merle having had a hand
in Gilbert Osmond's marriage ceased to be one of her titles
to consideration; it seemed, after all, that there was not so
much to thank her for. As time went on there was less and
less; and Isabel once said to herself that perhaps without her
these things would not have been. This reflection, however,
was instantly stifled; Isabel felt a sort of horror at having
made it. "Whatever happens to me, let me not be unjust," she
said; "let me bear my burdens myself, and not shift them
upon others!" This disposition was tested, eventually, by that
ingenious apology for her present conduct which Madame
Merle saw fit to make, and of which I have given a sketch;
for there was something irritating—there was almost an air
of mockery—in her neat discriminations and clear convictions. In Isabel's mind to-day there was nothing clear; there
was a confusion of regrets, a complication of fears. She felt
helpless as she turned away from her brilliant friend, who had

just made the statements I have quoted; Madame Merle knew so little what she was thinking of! Moreover, she herself was so unable to explain. Jealous of her—jealous of her with Gilbert? The idea just then suggested no near reality. She almost wished that jealousy had been possible; it would be a kind of refreshment. Jealousy, after all, was in a sense one of the symptoms of happiness. Madame Merle, however, was wise; it would seem that she knew Isabel better than Isabel knew herself. This young woman had always been fertile in resolutions—many of them of an elevated character; but at no period had they flourished (in the privacy of her heart) more richly than to-day. It is true that they all had a family likeness; they might have been summed up in the determination that if she was to be unhappy it should not be by a fault of her own. The poor girl had always had a great desire to do her best, and she had not as yet been seriously discouraged. She wished, therefore, to hold fast to justice—not to pay herself by petty revenges. To associate Madame Merle with her disappointment would be a petty revenge—especially as the pleasure she might derive from it would be perfectly insincere. It might feed her sense of bitterness, but it would not loosen her bonds. It was impossible to pretend that she had not acted with her eyes open; if ever a girl was a free agent, she had been. A girl in love was doubtless not a free agent; but the sole source of her mistake had been within herself. There had been no plot, no snare; she had looked, and considered, and chosen. When a woman had made such a mistake, there was only one way to repair it—to accept it. One folly was enough, especially when it was to last for ever; a second one would not much set it off. In this vow of reticence there was a certain nobleness which kept Isabel going; but Madame Merle had been right, for all that, in taking her precautions.

One day, about a month after Ralph Touchett's arrival in Rome, Isabel came back from a walk with Pansy. It was not only a part of her general determination to be just that she was at present very thankful for Pansy. It was a part of her tenderness for things that were pure and weak. Pansy was dear to her, and there was nothing in her life so much as it should be as the young girl's attachment and the pleasantness of feeling it. It was like a soft presence—like a small hand in her own; on Pansy's part it was more than an affection—it was a kind of faith. On her own side her sense of Pansy's dependence was more than a pleasure; it operated as a command, as a definite reason when motives threatened to fail her. She had said to herself that we must take our duty where we find it, and that we must look for it as much as possible. Pansy's sympathy was a kind of admonition; it seemed to say that here was an opportunity. An opportunity for what, Isabel could hardly have said; in general, to be more for the child than the child was able to be for herself. Isabel could have smiled, in these days, to remember that her little companion had once been ambiguous; for she now perceived that Pansy's ambiguities were simply her own grossness of vision. She had been unable to believe that any one could care so much—so extraordinarily much—to please. But since then she had seen this delicate faculty in operation, and she knew what to think of it. It was the whole creature—it was a sort of genius. Pansy had no pride to interfere with it, and though she was constantly extending her conquests she took no credit for them. The two were constantly together; Mrs. Osmond was rarely seen without her step-daughter. Isabel liked her company; it had the effect of one's carrying a nosegay composed all of the same flower. And then not to neglect Pansy—not under any provocation to neglect her; this she had made an article of religion. The young girl had every appearance of being happier in Isabel's society than in that of any one save her father, whom she admired with an intensity justified by the fact that, as paternity was an exquisite pleasure to Gilbert Osmond, he had always been elaborately soft. Isabel knew that Pansy liked immensely to be with her and studied the means of pleasing her. She had decided that the best way of pleasing her was negative, and consisted in not giving her trouble—a conviction which certainly could not have had any reference to trouble already existing. She was therefore ingeniously passive and almost imaginatively docile; she was careful even to moderate the eagerness with which she assented to Isabel's propositions, and which might have implied that she thought otherwise. She never interrupted, never asked social questions, and though she delighted in approbation, to the point of turning pale when it came to her, never held out her hand for it. She only looked toward it wistfully—an attitude which, as she grew older, made her eyes the prettiest in the world. When during the second winter at the Palazzo Roccanera, she began to go to parties, to dances, she always, at a reasonable hour, lest Mrs. Osmond should be tired, was the first to propose departure. Isabel appreciated the sacrifice of the late dances, for she knew that Pansy had a passionate pleasure in this exercise, taking her steps to the music like a conscientious fairy. Society, moreover, had no drawbacks for her; she liked even the tiresome parts—the heat of ball-rooms, the dulness of dinners, the crush at the door, the awkward waiting for the carriage. During the day, in this vehicle, beside Isabel, she sat in a little fixed appreciative posture, bending forward and faintly smiling, as if she had been taken to drive for the first time.

On the day I speak of they had been driven out of one of the gates of the city, and at the end of half-an-hour had left the carriage to await them by the roadside, while they walked away over the short grass of the Campagna, which even in the winter months is sprinkled with delicate flowers. This was almost a daily habit with Isabel, who was fond of a walk, and stepped quickly, though not so quickly as when she first came to Europe. It was not the form of exercise that Pansy loved best, but she liked it, because she liked everything; and she moved with a shorter undulation beside her stepmother, who afterwards, on their return to Rome, paid a tribute to Pansy's preferences by making the circuit of the Pincian or the Villa Borghese. Pansy had gathered a handful of flowers in a sunny hollow, far from the walls of Rome, and on reaching the Palazzo Roccanera she went straight to her room, to put them into water. Isabel passed into the drawing-room, the one she herself usually occupied, the second in order from the large ante-chamber which was entered from the staircase, and in which even Gilbert Osmond's rich devices had not been able to correct a look of rather grand nudity. Just beyond the threshold of the drawing-room she stopped short, the reason for her doing so being that she had received an impression. The impression had, in strictness, nothing unprecedented; but she felt it as something new, and the soundlessness of her step gave her time to take in the scene before she interrupted it. Madame Merle sat there in her bonnet, and Gilbert Osmond was talking to her; for a minute they were unaware that she had come in. Isabel had often seen that before, certainly; but what she had not seen, or at least had not noticed—was that their dialogue had for the moment converted itself into a sort of familiar silence, from which she instantly perceived that her entrance would startle them. Madame Merle was standing on the rug, a little way from the fire; Osmond was in a deep chair, leaning back and looking at her. Her head was erect, as usual, but her eyes were bent upon his. What struck Isabel first was that he was sitting while Madame Merle stood; there was an anomaly in this that arrested her. Then she perceived that they had arrived at a desultory pause in their exchange of ideas, and were musing, face to face, with the freedom of old friends who sometimes exchange ideas without uttering them. There was nothing shocking in this; they were old friends in fact. But the thing made an image, lasting only a moment, like a sudden flicker of light. Their relative position, their absorbed mutual gaze, struck her as something detected. But it was all over by the time she had fairly seen it. Madame Merle had seen her, and had welcomed her without moving; Gilbert Osmond, on the other hand, had instantly jumped up. He presently murmured something about wanting a walk, and after having asked Madame Merle to excuse him, he left the room.

"I came to see you, thinking you would have come in; and as you had not, I waited for you," Madame Merle said.

"Didn't he ask you to sit down?" asked Isabel, smiling.

Madame Merle looked about her.

"Ah, it's very true; I was going away."

"You must stay now."

"Certainly. I came for a reason; I have something on my mind."

"I have told you that before," Isabel said—"that it takes something extraordinary to bring you to this house."

"And you know what I have told you; that whether I come or whether I stay away, I have always the same motive—the affection I bear you."

"Yes, you have told me that."

"You look just now as if you didn't believe me," said Madame Merle.

"Ah," Isabel answered, "the profundity of your motives, that is the last thing I doubt!"

"You doubt sooner of the sincerity of my words."

Isabel shook her head gravely. "I know you have always been kind to me."

"As often as you would let me. You don't always take it; then one has to let you alone. It's not to do you a kindness, however, that I have come to-day; it's quite another affair. I have come to get rid of a trouble of my own—to make it over to you. I have been talking to your husband about it."

"I am surprised at that; he doesn't like troubles."

"Especially other people's; I know that. But neither do you, I suppose. At any rate, whether you do or not, you must help me. It's about poor Mr. Rosier."

"Ah," said Isabel, reflectively, "it's his trouble, then, not yours."

"He has succeeded in saddling me with it. He comes to see me ten times a week, to talk about Pansy."

"Yes, he wants to marry her. I know all about it."

Madame Merle hesitated a moment. "I gathered from your husband that perhaps you didn't."

"How should he know what I know? He has never spoken to me of the matter."

"It is probably because he doesn't know how to speak of it."

"It's nevertheless a sort of question in which he is rarely at fault."

"Yes, because as a general thing he knows perfectly well what to think. To-day he doesn't."

"Haven't you been telling him?" Isabel asked.

Madame Merle gave a bright, voluntary smile. "Do you know you're a little dry?"

"Yes; I can't help it. Mr. Rosier has also talked to me."

"In that there is some reason. You are so near the child."

"Ah," said Isabel, "for all the comfort I have given him! If you think me dry, I wonder what he thinks."

"I believe he thinks you can do more than you have done."

"I can do nothing."

"You can do more at least than I. I don't know what mysterious connection he may have discovered between me and Pansy; but he came to me from the first, as if I held his fortune in my hand. Now he keeps coming back, to spur me up, to know what hope there is, to pour out his feelings."

"He is very much in love," said Isabel.

"Very much—for him."

"Very much for Pansy, you might say as well."

Madame Merle dropped her eyes a moment. "Don't you think she's attractive?"

"She is the dearest little person possible; but she is very limited."

"She ought to be all the easier for Mr. Rosier to love. Mr. Rosier is not unlimited."

"No," said Isabel, "he has about the extent of one's pocket-handkerchief—the small ones, with lace." Her humour had lately turned a good deal to sarcasm, but in a moment she was ashamed of exercising it on so innocent an object as Pansy's suitor. "He is very kind, very honest," she presently added; "and he is not such a fool as he seems."

"He assures me that she delights in him," said Madame Merle.

"I don't know; I have not asked her."

"You have never sounded her a little?"

"It's not my place; it's her father's."

"Ah, you are too literal!" said Madame Merle.

"I must judge for myself."

Madame Merle gave her smile again. "It isn't easy to help you."

"To help me?" said Isabel, very seriously. "What do you mean?"

"It's easy to displease you. Don't you see how wise I am to be careful? I notify you, at any rate, as I notified Osmond, that I wash my hands of the love-affairs of Miss Pansy and Mr. Edward Rosier. *Je n'y peux rien, moi!* I can't talk to Pansy about him. Especially," added Madame Merle, "as I don't think him a paragon of husbands."

Isabel reflected a little; after which, with a smile—"You don't wash your hands, then!" she said. Then she added, in another tone—"You can't—you are too much interested."

Madame Merle slowly rose; she had given Isabel a look as rapid as the intimation that had gleamed before our heroine a few moments before. Only, this time Isabel saw nothing. "Ask him the next time, and you will see."

"I can't ask him; he has ceased to come to the house. Gilbert has let him know that he is not welcome."

"Ah yes," said Madame Merle, "I forgot that, though it's the burden of his lamentation. He says Osmond has insulted him. All the same," she went on, "Osmond doesn't dislike him as much as he thinks." She had got up, as if to close the conversation, but she lingered, looking about her, and had evidently more to say. Isabel perceived this, and even saw the point she had in view; but Isabel also had her own reasons for not opening the way.

"That must have pleased him, if you have told him," she answered, smiling.

"Certainly I have told him; as far as that goes, I have encouraged him. I have preached patience, have said that his case is not desperate, if he will only hold his tongue and be quiet. Unfortunately he has taken it into his head to be jealous."

"Jealous?"

"Jealous of Lord Warburton, who, he says, is always here."

Isabel, who was tired, had remained sitting; but at this she also rose. "Ah!" she exclaimed simply, moving slowly to the fireplace. Madame Merle observed her as she passed and as she stood a moment before the mantel-glass, pushing into its place a wandering tress of hair.

"Poor Mr. Rosier keeps saying that there is nothing impossible in Lord Warburton falling in love with Pansy," Madame Merle went on.

Isabel was silent a little; she turned away from the glass. "It is true—there is nothing impossible," she rejoined at last, gravely and more gently.

"So I have had to admit to Mr. Rosier. So, too, your husband thinks."

"That I don't know."

"Ask him, and you will see."

"I shall not ask him," said Isabel.

"Excuse me; I forgot that you had pointed that out. Of

course," Madame Merle added, "you have had infinitely more observation of Lord Warburton's behaviour than I."

"I see no reason why I shouldn't tell you that he likes my step-daughter very much."

Madame Merle gave one of her quick looks again. "Likes her, you mean—as Mr. Rosier means?"

"I don't know how Mr. Rosier means; but Lord Warburton has let me know that he is charmed with Pansy."

"And you have never told Osmond?" This observation was immediate, precipitate; it almost burst from Madame Merle's lips.

Isabel smiled a little. "I suppose he will know in time; Lord Warburton has a tongue, and knows how to express himself."

Madame Merle instantly became conscious that she had spoken more quickly than usual, and the reflection brought the colour to her cheek. She gave the treacherous impulse time to subside, and then she said, as if she had been thinking it over a little: "That would be better than marrying poor Mr. Rosier."

"Much better, I think."

"It would be very delightful; it would be a great marriage. It is really very kind of him."

"Very kind of him?"

"To drop his eyes on a simple little girl."

"I don't see that."

"It's very good of you. But after all, Pansy Osmond——"

"After all, Pansy Osmond is the most attractive person he has ever known!" Isabel exclaimed.

Madame Merle stared, and indeed she was justly bewildered. "Ah, a moment ago, I thought you seemed rather to disparage her."

"I said she was limited. And so she is. And so is Lord Warburton."

"So are we all, if you come to that. If it's no more than Pansy deserves, all the better. But if she fixes her affections on Mr. Rosier, I won't admit that she deserves it. That will be too perverse."

"Mr. Rosier's a nuisance!" cried Isabel, abruptly.

"I quite agree with you, and I am delighted to know that I am not expected to feed his flame. For the future, when he calls on me, my door shall be closed to him." And gathering her mantle together, Madame Merle prepared to depart. She was checked, however, on her progress to the door, by an inconsequent request from Isabel.

"All the same, you know, be kind to him."

She lifted her shoulders and eyebrows, and stood looking at her friend. "I don't understand your contradictions! Decidedly, I shall not be kind to him, for it will be a false kindness. I wish to see her married to Lord Warburton."

"You had better wait till he asks her."

"If what you say is true, he will ask her. Especially," said Madame Merle in a moment, "if you make him."

"If I make him?"

"It's quite in your power. You have great influence with him."

Isabel frowned a little. "Where did you learn that?"

"Mrs. Touchett told me. Not you—never!" said Madame Merle, smiling.

"I certainly never told you that."

"You might have done so when we were by way of being confidential with each other. But you really told me very little; I have often thought so since."

Isabel had thought so too, sometimes with a certain satisfaction. But she did not admit it now—perhaps because she did not wish to appear to exult in it. "You seem to have had an excellent informant in my aunt," she simply said.

"She let me know that you had declined an offer of marriage from Lord Warburton, because she was greatly vexed, and was full of the subject. Of course I think you have done better in doing as you did. But if you wouldn't marry Lord Warburton yourself, make him the reparation of helping him to marry some one else."

Isabel listened to this with a face which persisted in not reflecting the bright expressiveness of Madame Merle's. But in a moment she said, reasonably and gently enough, "I should be very glad indeed if, as regards Pansy, it could be arranged." Upon which her companion, who seemed to regard this as a speech of good omen, embraced her more tenderly than might have been expected, and took her departure.

XLI

OSMOND TOUCHED on this matter that evening for the first time; coming very late into the drawing-room, where she was sitting alone. They had spent the evening at home, and Pansy had gone to bed; he himself had been sitting since dinner in a small apartment in which he had arranged his books and which he called his study. At ten o'clock Lord Warburton had come in, as he always did when he knew from Isabel that she was to be at home; he was going somewhere else, and he sat for half-an-hour. Isabel, after asking him for news of Ralph, said very little to him, on purpose; she wished him to talk with the young girl. She pretended to read; she even went after a little to the piano; she asked herself whether she might not leave the room. She had come little by little to think well of the idea of Pansy's becoming the wife of the master of beautiful Lockleigh, though at first it had not presented itself in a manner to excite her enthusiasm. Madame Merle, that afternoon, had applied the match to an accumulation of inflammable material. When Isabel was unhappy, she always looked about her—partly from impulse and partly by theory—for some form of exertion. She could never rid herself of the conviction that unhappiness was a state of disease; it was suffering as opposed to action. To act, to do something—it hardly mattered what—would therefore be an escape, perhaps in some degree a remedy. Besides, she wished to convince herself that she had done everything possible to content her husband; she was determined not to be haunted by images of a flat want of zeal. It would please him greatly to see Pansy married to an English nobleman, and justly please him, since this nobleman was such a fine fellow. It seemed to Isabel that if she could make it her duty to bring about such an event, she should play the part of a good wife. She wanted to be that; she wanted to be able to believe, sincerely, that she had been that. Then, such an undertaking had other recommendations. It would occupy her, and she desired occupation. It would even amuse her, and if she could really amuse herself she perhaps might be saved. Lastly, it would be a service to Lord Warburton, who evidently pleased himself

greatly with the young girl. It was a little odd that he
should—being what he was; but there was no accounting for
such impressions. Pansy might captivate any one—any one,
at least, but Lord Warburton. Isabel would have thought her
too small, too slight, perhaps even too artificial for that.
There was always a little of the doll about her, and that was
not what Lord Warburton had been looking for. Still, who
could say what men looked for? They looked for what they
found; they knew what pleased them only when they saw it.
No theory was valid in such matters, and nothing was more
unaccountable or more natural than anything else. If he had
cared for *her* it might seem odd that he cared for Pansy, who
was so different; but he had not cared for her so much as he
supposed. Or if he had, he had completely got over it, and it
was natural that as that affair had failed, he should think that
something of quite another sort might succeed. Enthusiasm,
as I say, had not come at first to Isabel, but it came to-day
and made her feel almost happy. It was astonishing what happiness she could still find in the idea of procuring a pleasure
for her husband. It was a pity, however, that Edward Rosier
had crossed their path!

At this reflection the light that had suddenly gleamed upon
that path lost something of its brightness. Isabel was unfortunately as sure that Pansy thought Mr. Rosier the nicest of
all the young men—as sure as if she had held an interview
with her on the subject. It was very tiresome that she should
be so sure, when she had carefully abstained from informing
herself; almost as tiresome as that poor Mr. Rosier should
have taken it into his own head. He was certainly very inferior
to Lord Warburton. It was not the difference in fortune so
much as the difference in the men; the young American was
really so very flimsy. He was much more of the type of the
useless fine gentleman than the English nobleman. It was true
that there was no particular reason why Pansy should marry a
statesman; still, if a statesman admired her, that was his affair,
and she would make a very picturesque little peeress.

It may seem to the reader that Isabel had suddenly grown
strangely cynical; for she ended by saying to herself that this
difficulty could probably be arranged. Somehow, an impediment that was embodied in poor Rosier could not present

itself as a dangerous one; there were always means of levelling secondary obstacles. Isabel was perfectly aware that she had not taken the measure of Pansy's tenacity, which might prove to be inconveniently great; but she inclined to think the young girl would not be tenacious, for she had the faculty of assent developed in a very much higher degree than that of resistance. She would cling, yes, she would cling; but it really mattered to her very little what she clung to. Lord Warburton would do as well as Mr. Rosier—especially as she seemed quite to like him. She had expressed this sentiment to Isabel without a single reservation; she said she thought his conversation most interesting—he had told her all about India. His manner to Pansy had been of the happiest; Isabel noticed that for herself, as she also observed that he talked to her not in the least in a patronising way, reminding himself of her youth and simplicity, but quite as if she could understand everything. He was careful only to be kind—he was as kind as he had been to Isabel herself at Gardencourt. A girl might well be touched by that; she remembered how she herself had been touched, and said to herself that if she had been as simple as Pansy, the impression would have been deeper still. She had not been simple when she refused him; that operation had been as complicated, as, later, her acceptance of Osmond. Pansy, however, in spite of *her* simplicity, really did understand, and was glad that Lord Warburton should talk to her, not about her partners and bouquets, but about the state of Italy, the condition of the peasantry, the famous grist-tax, the *pellagra*, his impressions of Roman society. She looked at him as she drew her needle through her tapestry, with sweet, attentive eyes, and when she lowered them she gave little quiet oblique glances at his person, his hands, his feet, his clothes, as if she were considering him. Even his person, Isabel might have reminded her, was better than Mr. Rosier's. But Isabel contented herself at such moments with wondering where this gentleman was; he came no more at all to the Palazzo Roccanera. It was surprising, as I say, the hold it had taken of her—the idea of assisting her husband to be pleased.

It was surprising for a variety of reasons, which I shall presently touch upon. On the evening I speak of, while Lord Warburton sat there, she had been on the point of taking the great step of going out of the room and leaving her companions alone. I say the great step, because it was in this light that Gilbert Osmond would have regarded it, and Isabel was trying as much as possible to take her husband's view. She succeeded after a fashion, but she did not succeed in coming to the point I mention. After all, she couldn't; something held her and made it impossible. It was not exactly that it would be base, insidious; for women as a general thing practise such manœuvres with a perfectly good conscience, and Isabel had all the qualities of her sex. It was a vague doubt that interposed—a sense that she was not quite sure. So she remained in the drawing-room, and after a while Lord Warburton went off to his party, of which he promised to give Pansy a full account on the morrow. After he had gone, Isabel asked herself whether she had prevented something which would have happened if she had absented herself for a quarter of an hour; and then she exclaimed—always mentally—that when Lord Warburton wished her to go away he would easily find means to let her know it. Pansy said nothing whatever about him after he had gone, and Isabel said nothing, as she had taken a vow of reserve until after he should have declared himself. He was a little longer in coming to this than might seem to accord with the description he had given Isabel of his feelings. Pansy went to bed, and Isabel had to admit that she could not now guess what her step-daughter was thinking of. Her transparent little companion was for the moment rather opaque.

Isabel remained alone, looking at the fire, until, at the end of half-an-hour, her husband came in. He moved about a while in silence, and then sat down, looking at the fire like herself. But Isabel now had transferred her eyes from the flickering flame in the chimney to Osmond's face, and she watched him while he sat silent. Covert observation had become a habit with her; an instinct, of which it is not an exaggeration to say that it was allied to that of self-defence, had made it habitual. She wished as much as possible to know his thoughts, to know what he would say, beforehand, so that she might prepare her answer. Preparing answers had not been her strong point of old; she had rarely in this respect got further than thinking afterwards of clever things she might have said. But she had learned caution—learned it in a measure from her husband's very countenance. It was the same face she had looked into with eyes equally earnest perhaps, but less penetrating, on the terrace of a Florentine villa; except that Osmond had grown a little stouter since his marriage. He still, however, looked very distinguished.

"Has Lord Warburton been here?" he presently asked.

"Yes, he stayed for half-an-hour."

"Did he see Pansy?"

"Yes; he sat on the sofa beside her."

"Did he talk with her much?"

"He talked almost only to her."

"It seems to me he's attentive. Isn't that what you call it?"

"I don't call it anything," said Isabel; "I have waited for you to give it a name."

"That's a consideration you don't always show," Osmond answered, after a moment.

"I have determined, this time, to try and act as you would like. I have so often failed in that."

Osmond turned his head, slowly, looking at her.

"Are you trying to quarrel with me?"

"No, I am trying to live at peace."

"Nothing is more easy; you know I don't quarrel myself."

"What do you call it when you try to make me angry?" Isabel asked.

"I don't try; if I have done so, it has been the most natural thing in the world. Moreover, I am not in the least trying now."

Isabel smiled. "It doesn't matter. I have determined never to be angry again."

"That's an excellent resolve. Your temper isn't good."

"No—it's not good." She pushed away the book she had been reading, and took up the band of tapestry that Pansy had left on the table.

"That's partly why I have not spoken to you about this business of my daughter's," Osmond said, designating Pansy in the manner that was most frequent with him. "I was afraid I should encounter opposition—that you too would have views on the subject. I have sent little Rosier about his business."

"You were afraid that I would plead for Mr. Rosier? Haven't you noticed that I have never spoken to you of him?"

"I have never given you a chance. We have so little conversation in these days. I know he was an old friend of yours."

"Yes; he's an old friend of mine." Isabel cared little more for him than for the tapestry that she held in her hand; but it was true that he was an old friend, and with her husband she felt a desire not to extenuate such ties. He had a way of expressing contempt for them which fortified her loyalty to them, even when, as in the present case, they were in themselves insignificant. She sometimes felt a sort of passion of tenderness for memories which had no other merit than that they belonged to her unmarried life. "But as regards Pansy," she added in a moment, "I have given him no encouragement."

"That's fortunate," Osmond observed.

"Fortunate for me, I suppose you mean. For him it matters little."

"There is no use talking of him," Osmond said. "As I tell you, I have turned him out."

"Yes; but a lover outside is always a lover. He is sometimes even more of one. Mr. Rosier still has hope."

"He's welcome to the comfort of it! My daughter has only to sit still, to become Lady Warburton."

"Should you like that?" Isabel asked, with a simplicity which was not so affected as it may appear. She was resolved to assume nothing, for Osmond had a way of unexpectedly turning her assumptions against her. The intensity with which he would like his daughter to become Lady Warburton had been the very basis of her own recent reflections. But that was for herself; she would recognise nothing until Osmond should have put it into words; she would not take for granted with him that he thought Lord Warburton a prize worth an amount of effort that was unusual among the Osmonds. It was Gilbert's constant intimation that, for him, nothing was a prize; that he treated as from equal to equal with the most distinguished people in the world, and that his daughter had only to look about her to pick out a prince. It cost him therefore a lapse from consistency to say explicitly that he yearned for Lord Warburton, that if this nobleman should escape, his equivalent might not be found; and it was another of his customary implications that he was never inconsistent. He would have liked his wife to glide over the point. But strangely enough, now that she was face to face with him, though an hour before she had almost invented a scheme for pleasing him, Isabel was not accommodating, would not glide. And yet she knew exactly the effect on his mind of her question: it would operate as a humiliation. Never mind; he was terribly capable of humiliating her—all the more so that he was also capable of waiting for great opportunities and of showing, sometimes, an almost unaccountable indifference to small ones. Isabel perhaps took a small opportunity because she would not have availed herself of a great one.

Osmond at present acquitted himself very honourably. "I should like it extremely; it would be a great marriage. And then Lord Warburton has another advantage; he is an old friend of yours. It would be pleasant for him to come into the family. It is very singular that Pansy's admirers should all be your old friends."

"It is natural that they should come to see me. In coming to see me, they see Pansy. Seeing her, it is natural that they should fall in love with her."

"So I think. But you are not bound to do so."

"If she should marry Lord Warburton, I should be very glad," Isabel went on, frankly. "He's an excellent man. You say, however, that she has only to sit still. Perhaps she won't sit still; if she loses Mr. Rosier she may jump up!"

Osmond appeared to give no heed to this; he sat gazing at the fire. "Pansy would like to be a great lady," he remarked in a moment, with a certain tenderness of tone. "She wishes, above all, to please," he added.

"To please Mr. Rosier, perhaps."

"No, to please me."

"Me too a little, I think," said Isabel.

"Yes, she has a great opinion of you. But she will do what I like."

"If you are sure of that, it's very well," Isabel said.

"Meantime," said Osmond, "I should like our distinguished visitor to speak."

"He has spoken—to me. He has told me that it would be a great pleasure to him to believe she could care for him."

Osmond turned his head quickly; but at first he said nothing. Then—"Why didn't you tell me that?" he asked, quickly.

"There was no opportunity. You know how we live. I have taken the first chance that has offered."

"Did you speak to him of Rosier?"

"Oh yes, a little."

"That was hardly necessary."

"I thought it best he should know, so that, so that——" And Isabel paused.

"So that what?"

"So that he should act accordingly."

"So that he should back out, do you mean?"

"No, so that he should advance while there is yet time."

"That is not the effect it seems to have had."

"You should have patience," said Isabel. "You know Englishmen are shy."

"This one is not. He was not when he made love to you."

She had been afraid Osmond would speak of that; it was disagreeable to her. "I beg your pardon; he was extremely so," she said simply.

He answered nothing for some time; he took up a book and turned over the pages, while Isabel sat silent, occupying herself with Pansy's tapestry. "You must have a great deal of influence with him," Osmond went on at last. "The moment you really wish it, you can bring him to the point."

This was more disagreeable still; but Isabel felt it to be natural that her husband should say it, and it was after all something very much of the same sort that she had said to herself. "Why should I have influence?" she asked. "What have I ever done to put him under an obligation to me?"

"You refused to marry him," said Osmond, with his eyes on his book.

"I must not presume too much on that," Isabel answered, gently.

He threw down the book presently, and got up, standing before the fire with his hands behind him. "Well," he said, "I hold that it lies in your hands. I shall leave it there. With a little good-will you may manage it. Think that over and remember that I count upon you."

He waited a little, to give her time to answer; but she answered nothing, and he presently strolled out of the room.

XLII

SHE ANSWERED nothing, because his words had put the situation before her, and she was absorbed in looking at it. There was something in them that suddenly opened the door to agitation, so that she was afraid to trust herself to speak. After Osmond had gone, she leaned back in her chair and closed her eyes; and for a long time, far into the night, and still further, she sat in the silent drawing-room, given up to her meditation. A servant came in to attend to the fire, and she bade him bring fresh candles and then go to bed. Osmond had told her to think of what he had said; and she did so indeed, and of many other things. The suggestion, from another, that she had a peculiar influence on Lord Warburton, had given her the start that accompanies unexpected recognition. Was it true that there was something still between them that might be a handle to make him declare himself to Pansy—a susceptibility, on his part, to approval, a desire to do what would please her? Isabel had hitherto not asked herself the question, because she had not been forced; but now that it was directly presented to her, she saw the answer, and the answer frightened her. Yes, there was something—something on Lord Warburton's part. When he first came to Rome she believed that the link which united them had completely snapped; but little by little she had been reminded that it still had a palpable existence. It was as thin as a hair, but there were moments when she seemed to hear it vibrate. For herself, nothing was changed; what she once thought of Lord Warburton she still thought; it was needless that feeling should change; on the contrary, it seemed to her a better feeling than ever. But he? had he still the idea that she might be more to him than other women? Had he the wish to profit by the memory of the few moments of intimacy through which they had once passed? Isabel knew that she had read some of the signs of such a disposition. But what were his hopes, his pretensions, and in what strange way were they mingled with his evidently very sincere appreciation of poor Pansy? Was he in love with Gilbert Osmond's wife, and if so, what comfort did he expect to derive from it? If he was in

love with Pansy, he was not in love with her stepmother; and
if he was in love with her stepmother, he was not in love with
Pansy. Was she to cultivate the advantage she possessed, in
order to make him commit himself to Pansy, knowing that he
would do so for her sake, and not for the young girl's—was
this the service her husband had asked of her? This at any rate
was the duty with which Isabel found herself confronted from
the moment that she admitted to herself that Lord Warburton
had still an uneradicated predilection for her society. It was
not an agreeable task; it was, in fact, a repulsive one. She
asked herself with dismay whether Lord Warburton were pretending to be in love with Pansy in order to cultivate another
satisfaction. Of this refinement of duplicity she presently acquitted him; she preferred to believe that he was in good
faith. But if his admiration for Pansy was a delusion, this was
scarcely better than its being an affectation. Isabel wandered
among these ugly possibilities until she completely lost her
way; some of them, as she suddenly encountered them,
seemed ugly enough. Then she broke out of the labyrinth,
rubbing her eyes, and declared that her imagination surely did
her little honour, and that her husband's did him even less.
Lord Warburton was as disinterested as he need be, and she
was no more to him than she need wish. She would rest upon
this until the contrary should be proved; proved more effectually than by a cynical intimation of Osmond's.

Such a resolution, however, brought her this evening but
little peace, for her soul was haunted with terrors which
crowded to the foreground of thought as quickly as a place
was made for them. What had suddenly set them into livelier
motion she hardly knew, unless it were the strange impression
she had received in the afternoon of her husband and Madame Merle being in more direct communication than she
suspected. This impression came back to her from time to
time, and now she wondered that it had never come before.
Besides this, her short interview with Osmond, half-an-hour
before, was a striking example of his faculty for making everything wither that he touched, spoiling everything for her that
he looked at. It was very well to undertake to give him a
proof of loyalty; the real fact was that the knowledge of his
expecting a thing raised a presumption against it. It was as if

he had had the evil eye; as if his presence were a blight and his favour a misfortune. Was the fault in himself, or only in the deep mistrust she had conceived for him? This mistrust was the clearest result of their short married life; a gulf had opened between them over which they looked at each other with eyes that were on either side a declaration of the deception suffered. It was a strange opposition, of the like of which she had never dreamed—an opposition in which the vital principle of the one was a thing of contempt to the other. It was not her fault—she had practised no deception; she had only admired and believed. She had taken all the first steps in the purest confidence, and then she had suddenly found the infinite vista of a multiplied life to be a dark, narrow alley, with a dead wall at the end. Instead of leading to the high places of happiness, from which the world would seem to lie below one, so that one could look down with a sense of exaltation and advantage, and judge and choose and pity, it led rather downward and earthward, into realms of restriction and depression, where the sound of other lives, easier and freer, was heard as from above, and served to deepen the feeling of failure. It was her deep distrust of her husband—this was what darkened the world. That is a sentiment easily indicated, but not so easily explained, and so composite in its character that much time and still more suffering had been needed to bring it to its actual perfection. Suffering, with Isabel, was an active condition; it was not a chill, a stupor, a despair; it was a passion of thought, of speculation, of response to every pressure. She flattered herself, however, that she had kept her failing faith to herself—that no one suspected it but Osmond. Oh, he knew it, and there were times when she thought that he enjoyed it. It had come gradually—it was not till the first year of her marriage had closed that she took the alarm. Then the shadows began to gather; it was as if Osmond deliberately, almost malignantly, had put the lights out one by one. The dusk at first was vague and thin, and she could still see her way in it. But it steadily increased, and if here and there it had occasionally lifted, there were certain corners of her life that were impenetrably black. These shadows were not an emanation from her own mind; she was very sure of that; she had done her best to be just and temperate, to see only the truth. They were a part of her husband's very presence. They were not his misdeeds, his turpitudes; she accused him of nothing—that is, of but one thing, which was not a crime. She knew of no wrong that he had done; he was not violent, he was not cruel; she simply believed that he hated her. That was all she accused him of, and the miserable part of it was precisely that it was not a crime, for against a crime she might have found redress. He had discovered that she was so different, that she was not what he had believed she would prove to be. He had thought at first he could change her, and she had done her best to be what he would like. But she was, after all, herself—she couldn't help that; and now there was no use pretending, playing a part, for he knew her and he had made up his mind. She was not afraid of him; she had no apprehension that he would hurt her; for the ill-will he bore her was not of that sort. He would, if possible, never give her a pretext, never put himself in the wrong. Isabel, scanning the future with dry, fixed eyes, saw that he would have the better of her there. She would give him many pretexts, she would often put her-self in the wrong. There were times when she almost pitied him; for if she had not deceived him in intention she under-stood how completely she must have done so in fact. She had effaced herself, when he first knew her; she had made herself small, pretending there was less of her than there really was. It was because she had been under the extraordinary charm that he, on his side, had taken pains to put forth. He was not changed; he had not disguised himself, during the year of his courtship, any more than she. But she had seen only half his nature then, as one saw the disk of the moon when it was partly masked by the shadow of the earth. She saw the full moon now—she saw the whole man. She had kept still, as it were, so that he should have a free field, and yet in spite of this she had mistaken a part for the whole.

Ah, she had him immensely under the charm! It had not passed away; it was there still; she still knew perfectly what it was that made Osmond delightful when he chose to be. He had wished to be when he made love to her, and as she had wished to be charmed it was not wonderful that he suc-ceeded. He succeeded because he was sincere; it never oc-

curred to her to deny him that. He admired her—he had told
her why; because she was the most imaginative woman he
had known. It might very well have been true; for during
those months she had imagined a world of things that had no
substance. She had a vision of him—she had not read him
right. A certain combination of features had touched her, and
in them she had seen the most striking of portraits. That he
was poor and lonely, and yet that somehow he was noble—
that was what interested her and seemed to give her her opportunity. There was an indefinable beauty about him—in his
situation, in his mind, in his face. She had felt at the same
time that he was helpless and ineffectual, but the feeling had
taken the form of a tenderness which was the very flower of
respect. He was like a sceptical voyager, strolling on the beach
while he waited for the tide, looking seaward yet not putting
to sea. It was in all this that she found her occasion. She
would launch his boat for him; she would be his providence;
it would be a good thing to love him. And she loved him—
a good deal for what she found in him, but a good deal also
for what she brought him. As she looked back at the passion
of those weeks she perceived in it a kind of maternal strain—
the happiness of a woman who felt that she was a contributor, that she came with full hands. But for her money, as she
saw to-day, she wouldn't have done it. And then her mind
wandered off to poor Mr. Touchett, sleeping under English
turf, the beneficent author of infinite woe! For this was a fact.
At bottom her money had been a burden, had been on her
mind, which was filled with the desire to transfer the weight
of it to some other conscience. What would lighten her own
conscience more effectually than to make it over to the man
who had the best taste in the world? Unless she should give
it to a hospital, there was nothing better she could do with
it; and there was no charitable institution in which she was as
much interested as in Gilbert Osmond. He would use her
fortune in a way that would make her think better of it, and
rub off a certain grossness which attached to the good luck of
an unexpected inheritance. There had been nothing very delicate in inheriting seventy thousand pounds; the delicacy had
been all in Mr. Touchett's leaving them to her. But to marry
Gilbert Osmond and bring him such a portion—in that there

would be delicacy for her as well. There would be less for him—that was true; but that was his affair, and if he loved her he would not object to her being rich. Had he not had the courage to say he was glad she was rich?

Isabel's cheek tingled when she asked herself if she had really married on a factitious theory, in order to do something finely appreciable with her money. But she was able to answer quickly enough that this was only half the story. It was because a certain feeling took possession of her—a sense of the earnestness of his affection and a delight in his personal qualities. He was better than any one else. This supreme conviction had filled her life for months, and enough of it still remained to prove to her that she could not have done otherwise. The finest individual she had ever known was hers; the simple knowledge was a sort of act of devotion. She had not been mistaken about the beauty of his mind; she knew that organ perfectly now. She had lived with it, she had lived in it almost—it appeared to have become her habitation. If she had been captured, it had taken a firm hand to do it; that reflection perhaps had some worth. A mind more ingenious, more subtle, more cultivated, more trained to admirable exercises, she had not encountered; and it was this exquisite instrument that she had now to reckon with. She lost herself in infinite dismay when she thought of the magnitude of *his* deception. It was a wonder, perhaps, in view of this, that he didn't hate her more. She remembered perfectly the first sign he had given of it—it had been like the bell that was to ring up the curtain upon the real drama of their life. He said to her one day that she had too many ideas, and that she must get rid of them. He had told her that already, before their marriage; but then she had not noticed it; it came back to her only afterwards. This time she might well notice it, because he had really meant it. The words were nothing, superficially; but when in the light of deepening experience she looked into them, they appeared portentous. He really meant it—he would have liked her to have nothing of her own but her pretty appearance. She knew she had too many ideas; she had more even than he supposed, many more than she had expressed to him when he asked her to marry him. Yes, she *had* been hypocritical; she liked him so much. She had too many ideas for herself; but that was just what one married for, to share them with some one else. One couldn't pluck them up by the roots, though of course one might suppress them, be careful not to utter them. It was not that, however, his objecting to her opinions; that was nothing. She had no opinions—none that she would not have been eager to sacrifice in the satisfaction of feeling herself loved for it. What he meant was the whole thing—her character, the way she felt, the way she judged. This was what she had kept in reserve; this was what he had not known until he found himself—with the door closed behind, as it were—set down face to face with it. She had a certain way of looking at life which he took as a personal offence. Heaven knew that, now at least, it was a very humble, accommodating way! The strange thing was that she should not have suspected from the first that his own was so different. She had thought it so large, so enlightened, so perfectly that of an honest man and a gentleman. Had not he assured her that he had no superstitions, no dull limitations, no prejudices that had lost their freshness? Hadn't he all the appearance of a man living in the open air of the world, indifferent to small considerations, caring only for truth and knowledge, and believing that two intelligent people ought to look for them together, and whether they found them or not, to find at least some happiness in the search? He had told her that he loved the conventional; but there was a sense in which this seemed a noble declaration. In that sense, the love of harmony, and order, and decency, and all the stately offices of life, she went with him freely, and his warning had contained nothing ominous. But when, as the months elapsed, she followed him further and he led her into the mansion of his own habitation, then, then she had seen where she really was. She could live it over again, the incredulous terror with which she had taken the measure of her dwelling. Between those four walls she had lived ever since; they were to surround her for the rest of her life. It was the house of darkness, the house of dumbness, the house of suffocation. Osmond's beautiful mind gave it neither light nor air; Osmond's beautiful mind, indeed, seemed to peep down from a small high window and mock at her. Of course it was not physical suffering; for physical suffering there might have been a remedy. She could come and go; she had her liberty; her husband was perfectly polite. He took himself so seriously; it was something appalling. Under all his culture, his cleverness, his amenity, under his good-nature, his facility, his knowledge of life, his egotism lay hidden like a serpent in a bank of flowers. She had taken him seriously, but she had not taken him so seriously as that. How could she—especially when she knew him better? She was to think of him as he thought of himself—as the first gentleman in Europe. So it was that she had thought of him at first, and that indeed was the reason she had married him. But when she began to see what it implied, she drew back; there was more in the bond than she had meant to put her name to. It implied a sovereign contempt for every one but some three or four very exalted people whom he envied, and for everything in the world but half-a-dozen ideas of his own. That was very well; she would have gone with him even there, a long distance; for he pointed out to her so much of the baseness and shabbiness of life, opened her eyes so wide to the stupidity, the depravity, the ignorance of mankind, that she had been properly impressed with the infinite vulgarity of things, and of the virtue of keeping one's self unspotted by it. But this base, ignoble world, it appeared, was after all what one was to live for; one was to keep it for ever in one's eye, in order, not to enlighten, or convert, or redeem it, but to extract from it some recognition of one's own superiority. On the one hand it was despicable, but on the other it afforded a standard. Osmond had talked to Isabel about his renunciation, his indifference, the ease with which he dispensed with the usual aids to success; and all this had seemed to her admirable. She had thought it a noble indifference, an exquisite independence. But indifference was really the last of his qualities; she had never seen any one who thought so much of others. For herself, the world had always interested her, and the study of her fellow-creatures was her constant passion. She would have been willing, however, to renounce all her curiosities and sympathies for the sake of a personal life, if the person concerned had only been able to make her believe it was a gain! This, at least, was her present conviction; and the thing certainly would have been easier than to care for society as Osmond cared for it.

He was unable to live without it, and she saw that he had never really done so; he had looked at it out of his window even when he appeared to be most detached from it. He had his ideal, just as she had tried to have hers; only it was strange that people should seek for justice in such different quarters. His ideal was a conception of high prosperity and propriety, of the aristocratic life, which she now saw that Osmond deemed himself always, in essence at least, to have led. He had never lapsed from it for an hour; he would never have recovered from the shame of doing so. That again was very well; here too she would have agreed; but they attached such different ideas, such different associations and desires, to the same formulas. Her notion of the aristocratic life was simply the union of great knowledge with great liberty; the knowledge would give one a sense of duty, and the liberty a sense of enjoyment. But for Osmond it was altogether a thing of forms, a conscious, calculated attitude. He was fond of the old, the consecrated, and transmitted; so was she, but she pretended to do what she chose with it. He had an immense esteem for tradition; he had told her once that the best thing in the world was to have it, but that if one was so unfortunate as not to have it, one must immediately proceed to make it. She knew that he meant by this that she hadn't it, but that he was better off; though where he had got his traditions she never learned. He had a very large collection of them, however; that was very certain; after a little she began to see. The great thing was to act in accordance with them; the great thing not only for him but for her. Isabel had an undefined conviction that, to serve for another person than their proprietor, traditions must be of a thoroughly superior kind; but she nevertheless assented to this intimation that she too must march to the stately music that floated down from unknown periods in her husband's past; she who of old had been so free of step, so desultory, so devious, so much the reverse of processional. There were certain things they must do, a certain posture they must take, certain people they must know and not know. When Isabel saw this rigid system closing about her, draped though it was in pictured tapestries, that sense of darkness and suffocation of which I have spoken took possession of her; she seemed to be shut up with an odour of mould and decay. She had resisted, of course; at first very humorously, ironically, tenderly; then as the situation grew more serious, eagerly, passionately, pleadingly. She had pleaded the cause of freedom, of doing as they chose, of not caring for the aspect and denomination of their life—the cause of other instincts and longings, of quite another ideal. Then it was that her husband's personality, touched as it never had been, stepped forth and stood erect. The things that she had said were answered only by his scorn, and she could see that he was ineffably ashamed of her. What did he think of her—that she was base, vulgar, ignoble? He at least knew now that she had no traditions! It had not been in his prevision of things that she should reveal such flatness; her sentiments were worthy of a radical newspaper or of a Unitarian preacher. The real offence, as she ultimately perceived, was her having a mind of her own at all. Her mind was to be his—attached to his own like a small garden-plot to a deer-park. He would rake the soil gently and water the flowers; he would weed the beds and gather an occasional nosegay. It would be a pretty piece of property for a proprietor already far-reaching. He didn't wish her to be stupid. On the contrary, it was because she was clever that she had pleased him. But he expected her intelligence to operate altogether in his favour, and so far from desiring her mind to be a blank, he had flattered himself that it would be richly receptive. He had expected his wife to feel with him and for him, to enter into his opinions, his ambitions, his preferences; and Isabel was obliged to confess that this was no very unwarrantable demand on the part of a husband. But there were certain things she could never take in. To begin with, they were hideously unclean. She was not a daughter of the Puritans, but for all that she believed in such a thing as purity. It would appear that Osmond didn't; some of his traditions made her push back her skirts. Did all women have lovers? Did they all lie, and even the best have their price? Were there only three or four that didn't deceive their husbands? When Isabel heard such things she felt a greater scorn for them than for the gossip of a village-parlour—a scorn that kept its freshness in a very tainted air. There was the taint of her sister-in-law; did her husband judge only by the Countess Gemini? This lady very often lied, and she had practised deceptions which were not simply verbal. It was enough to find these facts assumed among Osmond's traditions, without giving them such a general extension. It was her scorn of his assumptions—it was that that made him draw himself up. He had plenty of contempt, and it was proper that his wife should be as well furnished; but that she should turn the hot light of her disdain upon his own conception of things—this was a danger he had not allowed for. He believed he should have regulated her emotions before she came to that; and Isabel could easily imagine how his ears scorched when he discovered that he had been too confident. When one had a wife who gave one that sensation there was nothing left but to hate her!

She was morally certain now that this feeling of hatred, which at first had been a refuge and a refreshment, had become the occupation and comfort of Osmond's life. The feeling was deep, because it was sincere; he had had a revelation that, after all, she could dispense with him. If to herself the idea was startling, if it presented itself at first as a kind of infidelity, a capacity for pollution, what infinite effect might it not be expected to have had upon him? It was very simple; he despised her; she had no traditions, and the moral horizon of a Unitarian minister. Poor Isabel, who had never been able to understand Unitarianism! This was the conviction that she had been living with now for a time that she had ceased to measure. What was coming—what was before them? That was her constant question. What would he do—what ought she to do? When a man hated his wife, what did it lead to? She didn't hate him, that she was sure of, for every little while she felt a passionate wish to give him a pleasant surprise. Very often, however, she felt afraid, and it used to come over her, as I have intimated, that she had deceived him at the very first. They were strangely married, at all events, and it was an awful life. Until that morning he had scarcely spoken to her for a week; his manner was as dry as a burned-out fire. She knew there was a special reason; he was displeased at Ralph Touchett's staying on in Rome. He thought she saw too much of her cousin—he had told her a week before that it was indecent she should go to him at his hotel. He would have said more than this if Ralph's invalid state had not appeared to make it brutal to denounce him; but having to contain himself only deepened Osmond's disgust. Isabel read all this as she would have read the hour on the clock-face; she was as perfectly aware that the sight of her interest in her cousin stirred her husband's rage, as if Osmond had locked her into her bedroom—which she was sure he wanted to do. It was her honest belief that on the whole she was not defiant; but she certainly could not pretend to be indifferent to Ralph. She believed he was dying, at last, and that she should never see him again, and this gave her a tenderness for him that she had never known before. Nothing was a pleasure to her now; how could anything be a pleasure to a woman who knew that she had thrown away her life? There was an everlasting weight upon her heart—there was a livid light upon everything. But Ralph's little visit was a lamp in the darkness; for the hour that she sat with him her spirit rose. She felt to-day as if he had been her brother. She had never had a brother, but if she had, and she were in trouble, and he were dying, he would be dear to her as Ralph was. Ah yes, if Gilbert was jealous of her there was perhaps some reason; it didn't make Gilbert look better to sit for half-an-hour with Ralph. It was not that they talked of him—it was not that she complained. His name was never uttered between them. It was simply that Ralph was generous and that her husband was not. There was something in Ralph's talk, in his smile, in the mere fact of his being in Rome, that made the blasted circle round which she walked more spacious. He made her feel the good of the world; he made her feel what might have been. He was, after all, as intelligent as Osmond—quite apart from his being better. And thus it seemed to her an act of devotion to conceal her misery from him. She concealed it elaborately; in their talk she was perpetually hanging out curtains and arranging screens. It lived before her again—it had never had time to die—that morning in the garden at Florence, when he warned her against Osmond. She had only to close her eyes to see the place, to hear his voice, to feel the warm, sweet air. How could he have known? What a mystery! what a wonder of wisdom! As intelligent as Gilbert? He was much more intelligent, to arrive at such a judgment as that. Gilbert had never been so deep, so just. She had told him then that from her at least he should never know if he was right; and this was what she was taking care of now. It gave her plenty to do; there was passion, exaltation, religion in it. Women find their religion sometimes in strange exercises, and Isabel, at present, in playing a part before her cousin, had an idea that she was doing him a kindness. It would have been a kindness, perhaps, if he had been for a single instant a dupe. As it was, the kindness consisted mainly in trying to make him believe that he had once wounded her greatly and that the event had put him to shame, but that as she was very generous and he was so ill, she bore him no grudge and even considerately forbore to flaunt her happiness in his face. Ralph smiled to himself, as he lay on his sofa, at this extraordinary form of consideration; but he forgave her for having forgiven him. She didn't wish him to have the pain of knowing she was unhappy; that was the great thing, and it didn't matter that such knowledge would rather have righted him.

For herself, she lingered in the soundless drawing-room long after the fire had gone out. There was no danger of her feeling the cold; she was in a fever. She heard the small hours strike, and then the great ones, but her vigil took no heed of time. Her mind, assailed by visions, was in a state of extraordinary activity, and her visions might as well come to her there, where she sat up to meet them, as on her pillow, to make a mockery of rest. As I have said, she believed she was not defiant, and what could be a better proof of it than that she should linger there half the night, trying to persuade herself that there was no reason why Pansy shouldn't be married as you would put a letter in the post-office? When the clock struck four she got up; she was going to bed at last, for the lamp had long since gone out and the candles had burned down to their sockets. But even then she stopped again in the middle of the room, and stood there gazing at a remembered vision—that of her husband and Madame Merle, grouped unconsciously and familiarly.

XLIII

THREE NIGHTS after this she took Pansy to a great party,
to which Osmond, who never went to dances, did not
accompany them. Pansy was as ready for a dance as ever; she
was not of a generalising turn, and she had not extended to
other pleasures the interdict that she had seen placed on those
of love. If she was biding her time or hoping to circumvent
her father, she must have had a prevision of success. Isabel
thought that this was not likely; it was much more likely that
Pansy had simply determined to be a good girl. She had never
had such a chance, and she had a proper esteem for chances.
She carried herself no less attentively than usual, and kept no
less anxious an eye upon her vaporous skirts; she held her
bouquet very tight, and counted over the flowers for the
twentieth time. She made Isabel feel old; it seemed so long
since she had been in a flutter about a ball. Pansy, who was
greatly admired, was never in want of partners, and very soon
after their arrival she gave Isabel, who was not dancing, her
bouquet to hold. Isabel had rendered this service for some
minutes when she became aware that Edward Rosier was
standing before her. He had lost his affable smile, and wore a
look of almost military resolution; the change in his appearance would have made Isabel smile if she had not felt that at
bottom his case was a hard one; he had always smelt so much
more of heliotrope than of gunpowder. He looked at her a
moment somewhat fiercely, as if to notify her that he was
dangerous, and then he dropped his eyes on her bouquet.
After he had inspected it his glance softened, and he said
quickly,

"It's all pansies; it must be hers!"

Isabel smiled kindly.

"Yes, it's hers; she gave it to me to hold."

"May I hold it a little, Mrs. Osmond?" the poor young man
asked.

"No, I can't trust you; I am afraid you wouldn't give it
back."

"I am not sure that I should; I should leave the house with
it instantly. But may I not at least have a single flower?"

Isabel hesitated a moment, and then, smiling still, held out the bouquet.

"Choose one yourself. It's frightful what I am doing for you."

"Ah, if you do no more than this, Mrs. Osmond!" Rosier exclaimed, with his glass in one eye, carefully choosing his flower.

"Don't put it into your button-hole," she said. "Don't for the world!"

"I should like her to see it. She has refused to dance with me, but I wish to show her that I believe in her still."

"It's very well to show it to her, but it's out of place to show it to others. Her father has told her not to dance with you."

"And is that all *you* can do for me? I expected more from you, Mrs. Osmond," said the young man, in a tone of fine general reference. "You know that our acquaintance goes back very far—quite into the days of our innocent childhood."

"Don't make me out too old," Isabel answered, smiling. "You come back to that very often, and I have never denied it. But I must tell you that, old friends as we are, if you had done me the honour to ask me to marry you I should have refused you."

"Ah, you don't esteem me, then. Say at once that you think I'm a trifler!"

"I esteem you very much, but I'm not in love with you. What I mean by that, of course, is that I am not in love with you for Pansy."

"Very good; I see; you pity me, that's all."

And Edward Rosier looked all round, inconsequently, with his single glass. It was a revelation to him that people shouldn't be more pleased; but he was at least too proud to show that the movement struck him as general.

Isabel for a moment said nothing. His manner and appearance had not the dignity of the deepest tragedy; his little glass, among other things, was against that. But she suddenly felt touched; her own unhappiness, after all, had something in common with his, and it came over her, more than before, that here, in recognisable, if not in romantic form, was the most affecting thing in the world—young love struggling with adversity.

"Would you really be very kind to her?" she said, in a low tone.

He dropped his eyes, devoutly, and raised the little flower which he held in his fingers to his lips. Then he looked at her. "You pity me; but don't you pity her a little?"

"I don't know; I am not sure. She will always enjoy life."

"It will depend on what you call life!" Rosier exclaimed. "She won't enjoy being tortured."

"There will be nothing of that."

"I am glad to hear it. She knows what she is about. You will see."

"I think she does, and she will never disobey her father. But she is coming back to me," Isabel added, "and I must beg you to go away."

Rosier lingered a moment, till Pansy came in sight, on the arm of her cavalier; he stood just long enough to look her in the face. Then he walked away, holding up his head; and the manner in which he achieved this sacrifice to expediency convinced Isabel that he was very much in love.

Pansy, who seldom got disarranged in dancing, and looked perfectly fresh and cool after this exercise, waited a moment and then took back her bouquet. Isabel watched her and saw that she was counting the flowers; whereupon she said to herself that, decidedly, there were deeper forces at play than she had recognised. Pansy had seen Rosier turn away, but she said nothing to Isabel about him; she talked only of her partner, after he had made his bow and retired; of the music, the floor, the rare misfortune of having already torn her dress. Isabel was sure, however, that she perceived that her lover had abstracted a flower; though this knowledge was not needed to account for the dutiful grace with which she responded to the appeal of her next partner. That perfect amenity under acute constraint was part of a larger system. She was again led forth by a flushed young man, this time carrying her bouquet; and she had not been absent many minutes when Isabel saw Lord Warburton advancing through the crowd. He presently drew near and bade her good evening; she had not seen him since the day before. He looked about him, and then—"Where is the little maid?" he asked. It was in this manner that he formed the harmless habit of alluding to Miss Osmond.

"She is dancing," said Isabel; "you will see her somewhere."

He looked among the dancers, and at last caught Pansy's eye. "She sees me, but she won't notice me," he then remarked. "Are you not dancing?"

"As you see, I'm a wall-flower."

"Won't you dance with me?"

"Thank you; I would rather you should dance with my little maid."

"One needn't prevent the other; especially as she is engaged."

"She is not engaged for everything, and you can reserve yourself. She dances very hard, and you will be the fresher."

"She dances beautifully," said Lord Warburton, following her with his eyes. "Ah, at last," he added, "she has given me a smile." He stood there with his handsome, easy, important physiognomy; and as Isabel observed him it came over her, as it had done before, that it was strange a man of his importance should take an interest in a little maid. It struck her as a great incongruity; neither Pansy's small fascinations, nor his own kindness, his good-nature, not even his need for amusement, which was extreme and constant, were sufficient to account for it. "I shall like to dance with you," he went on in a moment, turning back to Isabel; "but I think I like even better to talk with you."

"Yes, it's better, and it's more worthy of your dignity. Great statesmen oughtn't to waltz."

"Don't be cruel. Why did you recommend me then to dance with Miss Osmond?"

"Ah, that's different. If you dance with her, it would look simply like a piece of kindness—as if you were doing it for her amusement. If you dance with me you will look as if you were doing it for your own."

"And pray haven't I a right to amuse myself?"

"No, not with the affairs of the British Empire on your hands."

"The British Empire be hanged! You are always laughing at it."

"Amuse yourself with talking to me," said Isabel.

"I am not sure that is a recreation. You are too pointed; I have always to be defending myself. And you strike me as more than usually dangerous to-night. Won't you really dance?"

"I can't leave my place. Pansy must find me here."

He was silent a moment. "You are wonderfully good to her," he said, suddenly.

Isabel stared a little, and smiled. "Can you imagine one's not being?"

"No, indeed. I know how one cares for her. But you must have done a great deal for her."

"I have taken her out with me," said Isabel, smiling still. "And I have seen that she has proper clothes."

"Your society must have been a great benefit to her. You have talked to her, advised her, helped her to develop."

"Ah, yes, if she isn't the rose, she has lived near it."

Isabel laughed, and her companion smiled; but there was a certain visible preoccupation in his face which interfered with complete hilarity. "We all try to live as near it as we can," he said, after a moment's hesitation.

Isabel turned away; Pansy was about to be restored to her, and she welcomed the diversion. We know how much she liked Lord Warburton; she thought him delightful; there was something in his friendship which appeared a kind of resource in case of indefinite need; it was like having a large balance at the bank. She felt happier when he was in the room; there was something reassuring in his approach; the sound of his voice reminded her of the beneficence of nature. Yet for all that it did not please her that he should be too near to her, that he should take too much of her good-will for granted. She was afraid of that; she averted herself from it; she wished he wouldn't. She felt that if he should come too near, as it were, it was in her to flash out and bid him keep his distance. Pansy came back to Isabel with another rent in her skirt, which was the inevitable consequence of the first, and which she displayed to Isabel with serious eyes. There were too many gentlemen in uniform; they wore those dreadful spurs, which were fatal to the dresses of young girls. It hereupon became apparent that the resources of women are innumerable. Isabel devoted herself to Pansy's desecrated drapery; she fumbled for a pin and repaired the injury; she smiled and listened to her account of her adventures. Her attention, her sympathy, were most active; and they were in direct proportion to a sentiment with which they were in no way connected—a lively conjecture as to whether Lord Warburton was trying to make love to her. It was not simply his words just then; it was others as well; it was the reference and the continuity. This was what she thought about while she pinned up Pansy's dress. If it were so, as she feared, he was of course unconscious; he himself had not taken account of his intention. But this made it none the more auspicious, made the situation none the less unacceptable. The sooner Lord Warburton should come to self-consciousness the better. He immediately began to talk to Pansy—on whom it was certainly mystifying to see that he dropped a smile of chastened devotion. Pansy replied as usual, with a little air of conscientious aspiration; he had to bend toward her a good deal in conversation, and her eyes, as usual, wandered up and down his robust person, as if he had offered it to her for exhibition. She always seemed a little frightened; yet her fright was not of the painful character that suggests dislike; on the contrary, she looked as if she knew that he knew that she liked him. Isabel left them together a little, and wandered toward a friend whom she saw near, and with whom she talked till the music of the following dance began, for which she knew that Pansy was also engaged. The young girl joined her presently, with a little fluttered look, and Isabel, who scrupulously took Osmond's view of his daughter's complete dependence, consigned her, as a precious and momentary loan, to her appointed partner. About all this matter she had her own imaginations, her own reserves; there were moments when Pansy's extreme adhesiveness made each of them, to her sense, look foolish. But Osmond had given her a sort of tableau of her position as his daughter's duenna, which consisted of gracious alternation of concession and contraction; and there were directions of his which she liked to think that she obeyed to the letter. Perhaps, as regards some of them, it was because her doing so appeared to reduce them to the absurd.

After Pansy had been led away, Isabel found Lord Warburton drawing near her again. She rested her eyes on him, steadily; she wished she could sound his thoughts. But he had no appearance of confusion.

"She has promised to dance with me later," he said.

"I am glad of that. I suppose you have engaged her for the cotillion."

At this he looked a little awkward. "No, I didn't ask her for that. It's a quadrille."

"Ah, you are not clever!" said Isabel, almost angrily. "I told her to keep the cotillion, in case you should ask for it."

"Poor little maid, fancy that!" And Lord Warburton laughed frankly. "Of course I will if you like."

"If I like? Oh, if you dance with her only because I like it!"

"I am afraid I bore her. She seems to have a lot of young fellows on her book."

Isabel dropped her eyes, reflecting rapidly; Lord Warburton stood there looking at her and she felt his eyes on her face. She felt much inclined to ask him to remove them. She did not do so, however; she only said to him, after a minute, looking up—"Please to let me understand."

"Understand what?"

"You told me ten days ago that you should like to marry my step-daughter. You have not forgotten it!"

"Forgotten it? I wrote to Mr. Osmond about it this morning."

"Ah," said Isabel, "he didn't mention to me that he had heard from you."

Lord Warburton stammered a little. "I—I didn't send my letter."

"Perhaps you forgot that."

"No, I wasn't satisfied with it. It's an awkward sort of letter to write, you know. But I shall send it to-night."

"At three o'clock in the morning?"

"I mean later, in the course of the day."

"Very good. You still wish, then, to marry her?"

"Very much indeed."

"Aren't you afraid that you will bore her?" And as her companion stared at this inquiry, Isabel added—"If she can't dance with you for half-an-hour, how will she be able to dance with you for life?"

"Ah," said Lord Warburton, readily, "I will let her dance with other people! About the cotillion, the fact is I thought that you—that you—"

"That I would dance with you? I told you I would dance nothing."

"Exactly; so that while it is going on I might find some quiet corner where we might sit down and talk."

"Oh," said Isabel gravely, "you are much too considerate of me."

When the cotillion came, Pansy was found to have engaged herself, thinking, in perfect humility, that Lord Warburton had no intentions. Isabel recommended him to seek another partner, but he assured her that he would dance with no one but herself. As, however, she had, in spite of the remonstrances of her hostess, declined other invitations on the ground that she was not dancing at all, it was not possible for her to make an exception in Lord Warburton's favour.

"After all, I don't care to dance," he said, "it's a barbarous amusement; I would much rather talk." And he intimated that he had discovered exactly the corner he had been looking for—a quiet nook in one of the smaller rooms, where the music would come to them faintly and not interfere with conversation. Isabel had decided to let him carry out his idea; she wished to be satisfied. She wandered away from the ball-room with him, though she knew that her husband desired she should not lose sight of his daughter. It was with his daughter's *prétendant*, however; that would make it right for Osmond. On her way out of the ball-room she came upon Edward Rosier, who was standing in a doorway, with folded arms, looking at the dance, in the attitude of a young man without illusions. She stopped a moment and asked him if he were not dancing.

"Certainly not, if I can't dance with her!" he answered.

"You had better go away, then," said Isabel, with the manner of good counsel.

"I shall not go till she does!" And he let Lord Warburton pass, without giving him a look.

This nobleman, however, had noticed the melancholy youth, and he asked Isabel who her dismal friend was, remarking that he had seen him somewhere before.

"It's the young man I have told you about, who is in love with Pansy," said Isabel.

"Ah yes, I remember. He looks rather bad."

"He has reason. My husband won't listen to him."

"What's the matter with him?" Lord Warburton inquired. "He seems very harmless."

"He hasn't money enough, and he isn't very clever."

Lord Warburton listened with interest; he seemed struck with this account of Edward Rosier. "Dear me; he looked a well-set-up young fellow."

"So he is, but my husband is very particular."

"Oh, I see." And Lord Warburton paused a moment. "How much money has he got?" he then ventured to ask.

"Some forty thousand francs a year."

"Sixteen hundred pounds? Ah, but that's very good, you know."

"So I think. But my husband has larger ideas."

"Yes; I have noticed that your husband has very large ideas. Is he really an idiot, the young man?"

"An idiot? Not in the least; he's charming. When he was twelve years old I myself was in love with him."

"He doesn't look much more than twelve to-day," Lord Warburton rejoined, vaguely, looking about him. Then, with more point—"Don't you think we might sit here?" he asked.

"Wherever you please." The room was a sort of boudoir, pervaded by a subdued, rose-coloured light; a lady and gentleman moved out of it as our friends came in. "It's very kind of you to take such an interest in Mr. Rosier," Isabel said.

"He seems to me rather ill-treated. He had a face a yard long; I wondered what ailed him."

"You are a just man," said Isabel. "You have a kind thought even for a rival."

Lord Warburton turned, suddenly, with a stare. "A rival! Do you call him my rival?"

"Surely—if you both wish to marry the same person."

"Yes—but since he has no chance!"

"All the same, I like you for putting yourself in his place. It shows imagination."

"You like me for it?" And Lord Warburton looked at her with an uncertain eye. "I think you mean that you are laughing at me for it."

"Yes, I am laughing at you, a little. But I like you, too."

"Ah well, then, let me enter into his situation a little more. What do you suppose one could do for him?"

"Since I have been praising your imagination, I will leave you to imagine that yourself," Isabel said. "Pansy, too, would like you for that."

"Miss Osmond? Ah, she, I flatter myself, likes me already."

"Very much, I think."

He hesitated a little; he was still questioning her face. "Well, then, I don't understand you. You don't mean that she cares for him?"

"Surely, I have told you that I thought she did."

A sudden blush sprung to his face. "You told me that she would have no wish apart from her father's, and as I have gathered that he would favour me—" He paused a little, and then he added—"Don't you see?" suggestively, through his blush.

"Yes, I told you that she had an immense wish to please her father, and that it would probably take her very far."

"That seems to me a very proper feeling," said Lord Warburton.

"Certainly; it's a very proper feeling." Isabel remained silent for some moments; the room continued to be empty; the sound of the music reached them with its richness softened by the interposing apartments. Then at last she said—"But it hardly strikes me as the sort of feeling to which a man would wish to be indebted for a wife."

"I don't know; if the wife is a good one, and he thinks she does well!"

"Yes, of course you must think that."

"I do; I can't help it. You call that very British, of course."

"No, I don't. I think Pansy would do wonderfully well to marry you, and I don't know who should know it better than you. But you are not in love."

"Ah, yes I am, Mrs. Osmond!"

Isabel shook her head. "You like to think you are, while you sit here with me. But that's not how you strike me."

"I'm not like the young man in the doorway. I admit that. But what makes it so unnatural? Could anything in the world be more charming than Miss Osmond?"

"Nothing, possibly. But love has nothing to do with good reasons."

"I don't agree with you. I am delighted to have good reasons."

"Of course you are. If you were really in love you wouldn't care a straw for them."

"Ah, really in love—really in love!" Lord Warburton exclaimed, folding his arms, leaning back his head, and stretching himself a little. "You must remember that I am forty years old. I won't pretend that I am as I once was."

"Well, if you are sure," said Isabel, "it's all right."

He answered nothing; he sat there, with his head back, looking before him. Abruptly, however, he changed his position; he turned quickly to his companion. "Why, are you so unwilling, so sceptical?"

She met his eye, and for a moment they looked straight at each other. If she wished to be satisfied, she saw something that satisfied her; she saw in his eye the gleam of an idea that she was uneasy on her own account—that she was perhaps even frightened. It expressed a suspicion, not a hope, but such as it was it told her what she wished to know. Not for an instant should he suspect that she detected in his wish to marry her step-daughter an implication of increased nearness to herself, or that if she did detect it she thought it alarming or compromising. In that brief, extremely personal gaze, however, deeper meanings passed between them than they were conscious of at the moment.

"My dear Lord Warburton," she said, smiling, "you may do, as far as I am concerned, whatever comes into your head."

And with this she got up, and wandered into the adjoining room, where she encountered several acquaintances. While she talked with them she found herself regretting that she had moved; it looked a little like running away—all the more as Lord Warburton didn't follow her. She was glad of this, however, and, at any rate, she was satisfied. She was so well satisfied that when, in passing back into the ball-room, she found Edward Rosier still planted in the doorway, she stopped and spoke to him again.

"You did right not to go away. I have got some comfort for you."

"I need it," the young man murmured, "when I see you so awfully thick with *him*!"

"Don't speak of him, I will do what I can for you. I am afraid it won't be much, but what I can I will do."

He looked at her with gloomy obliqueness. "What has suddenly brought you round?"

"The sense that you are an inconvenience in the doorways!" she answered, smiling, as she passed him. Half-an-hour later she took leave, with Pansy, and at the foot of the staircase the two ladies, with many other departing guests, waited a while for their carriage. Just as it approached, Lord Warburton came out of the house, and assisted them to reach their vehicle. He stood a moment at the door, asking Pansy if she had amused herself; and she, having answered him, fell back with a little air of fatigue. Then Isabel, at the window, detaining him by a movement of her finger, murmured gently—"Don't forget to send your letter to her father!"

XLIV

THE COUNTESS GEMINI was often extremely bored—bored, in her own phrase, to extinction. She had not been extinguished, however, and she struggled bravely enough with her destiny, which had been to marry an unaccommodating Florentine who insisted upon living in his native town, where he enjoyed such consideration as might attach to a gentleman whose talent for losing at cards had not the merit of being incidental to an obliging disposition. The Count Gemini was not liked even by those who won from him; and he bore a name which, having a measurable value in Florence, was, like the local coin of the old Italian states, without currency in other parts of the peninsula. In Rome he was simply a very dull Florentine, and it is not remarkable that he should not have cared to pay frequent visits to a city where, to carry it off, his dulness needed more explanation than was convenient. The Countess lived with her eyes upon Rome, and it was the constant grievance of her life that she had not a habitation there. She was ashamed to say how seldom she had been allowed to go there; it scarcely made the matter better that there were other members of the Florentine nobility who never had been there at all. She went whenever she could; that was all she could say. Or rather, not all; but all she said she could say. In fact, she had much more to say about it, and had often set forth the reasons why she hated Florence and wished to end her days in the shadow of St. Peter's. They are reasons, however, which do not closely concern us, and were usually summed up in the declaration that Rome, in short, was the Eternal City, and that Florence was simply a pretty little place like any other. The Countess apparently needed to connect the idea of eternity with her amusements. She was convinced that society was infinitely more interesting in Rome, where you met celebrities all winter at evening parties. At Florence there were no celebrities; none at least one had heard of. Since her brother's marriage her impatience had greatly increased; she was so sure that his wife had a more brilliant life than herself. She was not so intellectual as Isabel, but she was intellectual enough to do justice to Rome—not to the ruins and the catacombs, not even perhaps to the church-ceremonies and the scenery; but certainly to all the rest. She heard a great deal about her sister-in-law, and knew perfectly that Isabel was having a beautiful time. She had indeed seen it for herself on the only occasion on which she had enjoyed the hospitality of the Palazzo Roccanera. She had spent a week there during the first winter of her brother's marriage; but she had not been encouraged to renew this satisfaction. Osmond didn't want her—that she was perfectly aware of; but she would have gone all the same, for after all she didn't care two straws about Osmond. But her husband wouldn't let her, and the money-question was always a trouble. Isabel had been very nice; the Countess, who had liked her sister-in-law from the first, had not been blinded by envy to Isabel's personal merits. She had always observed that she got on better with clever women than with silly ones, like herself; the silly ones could never understand her wisdom, whereas the clever ones—the really clever ones—always understood her silliness. It appeared to her that, different as they were in appearance and general style, Isabel and she had a patch of common ground somewhere, which they would set their feet upon at last. It was not very large, but it was firm, and they would both know it when once they touched it. And then she lived, with Mrs. Osmond, under the influence of a pleasant surprise; she was constantly expecting that Isabel would "look down" upon her, and she as constantly saw this operation postponed. She asked herself when it would begin; not that she cared much; but she wondered what kept it in abeyance. Her sister-in-law regarded her with none but level glances, and expressed for the poor Countess as little contempt as admiration. In reality, Isabel would as soon have thought of despising her as of passing a moral judgment on a grasshopper. She was not indifferent to her husband's sister, however; she was rather a little afraid of her. She wondered at her; she thought her very extraordinary. The Countess seemed to her to have no soul; she was like a bright shell, with a polished surface, in which something would rattle when you shook it. This rattle was apparently the Countess's spiritual principle; a little loose nut that tumbled about inside of her. She was too odd for disdain, too anomalous for comparisons. Isabel would have invited her again (there was no question of inviting the Count); but Osmond, after his marriage, had not scrupled to say frankly that Amy was a fool of the worst species—a fool whose folly had the irrepressibility of genius. He said at another time that she had no heart; and he added in a moment that she had given it all away—in small pieces, like a wedding-cake. The fact of not having been asked was of course another obstacle to the Countess's going again to Rome; but at the period with which this history has now to deal, she was in receipt of an invitation to spend several weeks at the Palazzo Roccanera. The proposal had come from Osmond himself, who wrote to his sister that she must be prepared to be very quiet. Whether or no she found in this phrase all the meaning he had put into it, I am unable to say; but she accepted the invitation on any terms. She was curious, moreover; for one of the impressions of her former visit had been that her brother had found his match. Before the marriage she had been sorry for Isabel, so sorry as to have had serious thoughts—if any of the Countess's thoughts were serious—of putting her on her guard. But she had let that pass, and after a little she was reassured. Osmond was as lofty as ever, but his wife would not be an easy victim. The Countess was not very exact at measurements; but it seemed to her that if Isabel should draw herself up she would be the taller spirit of the two. What she wanted to learn now was whether Isabel had drawn herself up; it would give her immense pleasure to see Osmond overtopped.

Several days before she was to start for Rome a servant brought her the card of a visitor—a card with the simple superscription, "Henrietta C. Stackpole." The Countess pressed her finger-tips to her forehead; she did not remember to have known any such Henrietta as that. The servant then remarked that the lady had requested him to say that if the Countess should not recognise her name, she would know her well enough on seeing her. By the time she appeared before her visitor she had in fact reminded herself that there was once a literary lady at Mrs. Touchett's; the only woman of letters she had ever encountered. That is, the only modern one, since she was the daughter of a defunct poetess. She recognised Miss Stackpole immediately; the more so that Miss Stackpole seemed perfectly unchanged; and the Countess, who was thoroughly good-natured, thought it rather fine to be called on by a person of that sort of distinction. She wondered whether Miss Stackpole had come on account of her mother—whether she had heard of the American Corinne. Her mother was not at all like Isabel's friend; the Countess could see at a glance that this lady was much more modern; and she received an impression of the improvements that were taking place—chiefly in distant countries—in the character (the professional character) of literary ladies. Her mother used to wear a Roman scarf thrown over a pair of bare shoulders, and a gold laurel-wreath set upon a multitude of glossy ringlets. She spoke softly and vaguely, with a kind of Southern accent; she sighed a great deal, and was not at all enterprising. But Henrietta, the Countess could see, was always closely buttoned and compactly braided; there was something brisk and business-like in her appearance, and her manner was almost conscientiously familiar. The Countess could not but feel that the correspondent of the *Interviewer* was much more efficient than the American Corinne.

Henrietta explained that she had come to see the Countess because she was the only person she knew in Florence, and that when she visited a foreign city she liked to see something more than superficial travellers. She knew Mrs. Touchett, but Mrs. Touchett was in America, and even if she had been in Florence Henrietta would not have gone to see her, for Mrs. Touchett was not one of her admirations.

"Do you mean by that that I am?" the Countess asked, smiling graciously.

"Well, I like you better than I do her," said Miss Stackpole. "I seem to remember that when I saw you before you were very interesting. I don't know whether it was an accident, or whether it is your usual style. At any rate, I was a good deal struck with what you said. I made use of it afterwards in print."

"Dear me!" cried the Countess, staring and half-alarmed; "I

had no idea I ever said anything remarkable! I wish I had known it."

"It was about the position of woman in this city," Miss Stackpole remarked. "You threw a good deal of light upon it."

"The position of woman is very uncomfortable. Is that what you mean? And you wrote it down and published it?" the Countess went on. "Ah, do let me see it!"

"I will write to them to send you the paper if you like," Henrietta said. "I didn't mention your name; I only said a lady of high rank. And then I quoted your views."

The Countess threw herself hastily backward, tossing up her clasped hands.

"Do you know I am rather sorry you didn't mention my name? I should have rather liked to see my name in the papers. I forget what my views were; I have so many! But I am not ashamed of them. I am not at all like my brother—I suppose you know my brother? He thinks it a kind of disgrace to be put into the papers; if you were to quote him he would never forgive you."

"He needn't be afraid; I shall never refer to him," said Miss Stackpole, with soft dryness. "That's another reason," she added, "why I wanted to come and see you. You know Mr. Osmond married my dearest friend."

"Ah, yes; you were a friend of Isabel's. I was trying to think what I knew about you."

"I am quite willing to be known by that," Henrietta declared. "But that isn't what your brother likes to know me by. He has tried to break up my relations with Isabel."

"Don't permit it," said the Countess.

"That's what I want to talk about. I am going to Rome."

"So am I!" the Countess cried. "We will go together."

"With great pleasure. And when I write about my journey I will mention you by name, as my companion."

The Countess sprang from her chair and came and sat on the sofa beside her visitor.

"Ah, you must send me the paper! My husband won't like it; but he need never see it. Besides, he doesn't know how to read."

Henrietta's large eyes became immense.

"Doesn't know how to read? May I put that into my letter?"

"Into your letter?"

"In the *Interviewer*. That's my paper."

"Oh yes, if you like; with his name. Are you going to stay with Isabel?"

Henrietta held up her head, gazing a little in silence at her hostess.

"She has not asked me. I wrote to her I was coming, and she answered that she would engage a room for me at a *pension*."

The Countess listened with extreme interest.

"That's Osmond," she remarked, pregnantly.

"Isabel ought to resist," said Miss Stackpole. "I am afraid she has changed a great deal. I told her she would."

"I am sorry to hear it; I hoped she would have her own way. Why doesn't my brother like you?" the Countess added, ingenuously.

"I don't know, and I don't care. He is perfectly welcome not to like me; I don't want every one to like me; I should think less of myself if some people did. A journalist can't hope to do much good unless he gets a good deal hated; that's the way he knows how his work goes on. And it's just the same for a lady. But I didn't expect it of Isabel."

"Do you mean that she hates you?" the Countess inquired.

"I don't know; I want to see. That's what I am going to Rome for."

"Dear me, what a tiresome errand!" the Countess exclaimed.

"She doesn't write to me in the same way; it's easy to see there's a difference. If you know anything," Miss Stackpole went on, "I should like to hear it beforehand, so as to decide on the line I shall take."

The Countess thrust out her under lip and gave a gradual shrug.

"I know very little; I see and hear very little of Osmond. He doesn't like me any better than he appears to like you."

"Yet you are not a lady-correspondent," said Henrietta, pensively.

"Oh, he has plenty of reasons. Nevertheless they have invited me—I am to stay in the house!" And the Countess smiled almost fiercely; her exultation, for the moment, took little account of Miss Stackpole's disappointment.

This lady, however, regarded it very placidly.

"I should not have gone if she had asked me. That is, I think I should not; and I am glad I hadn't to make up my mind. It would have been a very difficult question. I should not have liked to turn away from her, and yet I should not have been happy under her roof. A *pension* will suit me very well. But that is not all."

"Rome is very good just now," said the Countess; "there are all sorts of smart people. Did you ever hear of Lord Warburton?"

"Hear of him? I know him very well. Do you consider him very smart?" Henrietta inquired.

"I don't know him, but I am told he is extremely *grand seigneur*. He is making love to Isabel."

"Making love to her?"

"So I'm told; I don't know the details," said the Countess lightly. "But Isabel is pretty safe."

Henrietta gazed earnestly at her companion; for a moment she said nothing.

"When do you go to Rome?" she inquired, abruptly.

"Not for a week, I am afraid."

"I shall go to-morrow," Henrietta said. "I think I had better not wait."

"Dear me, I am sorry; I am having some dresses made. I am told Isabel receives immensely. But I shall see you there; I shall call on you at your *pension*." Henrietta sat still—she was lost in thought; and suddenly the Countess cried, "Ah, but if you don't go with me you can't describe our journey!"

Miss Stackpole seemed unmoved by this consideration; she was thinking of something else, and she presently expressed it.

"I am not sure that I understand you about Lord Warburton."

"Understand me? I mean he's very nice, that's all."

"Do you consider it nice to make love to married women?" Henrietta inquired, softly.

The Countess stared, and then, with a little violent laugh—

"It's certain that all the nice men do it. Get married and you'll see!" she added.

"That idea would be enough to prevent me," said Miss Stackpole. "I should want my own husband; I shouldn't want any one else's. Do you mean that Isabel is guilty—is guilty—" and she paused a little, choosing her expression.

"Do I mean she's guilty? Oh dear no, not yet, I hope. I only mean that Osmond is very tiresome, and that Lord Warburton is, as I hear, a great deal at the house. I'm afraid you are scandalised."

"No, I am very anxious," Henrietta said.

"Ah, you are not very complimentary to Isabel! You should have more confidence. I tell you," the Countess added quickly, "if it will be a comfort to you I will engage to draw him off."

Miss Stackpole answered at first only with the deeper solemnity of her eyes.

"You don't understand me," she said after a while. "I haven't the idea that you seem to suppose. I am not afraid for Isabel—in that way. I am only afraid she is unhappy—that's what I want to get at."

The Countess gave a dozen turns of the head; she looked impatient and sarcastic.

"That may very well be; for my part I should like to know whether Osmond is."

Miss Stackpole had begun to bore her a little.

"If she is really changed that must be at the bottom of it," Henrietta went on.

"You will see; she will tell you," said the Countess.

"Ah, she may not tell me—that's what I am afraid of!"

"Well, if Osmond isn't enjoying himself I flatter myself I shall discover it," the Countess rejoined.

"I don't care for that," said Henrietta.

"I do immensely! If Isabel is unhappy I am very sorry for her, but I can't help it. I might tell her something that would make her worse, but I can't tell her anything that would console her. What did she go and marry him for? If she had listened to me she would have got rid of him. I will forgive her, however, if I find she has made things hot for him! If she has simply allowed him to trample upon her I don't know that I shall even pity her. But I don't think that's very likely. I count upon finding that if she is miserable she has at least made him so."

Henrietta got up; these seemed to her, naturally, very dreadful expectations. She honestly believed that she had no desire to see Mr. Osmond unhappy; and indeed he could not be for her the subject of a flight of fancy. She was on the whole rather disappointed in the Countess, whose mind moved in a narrower circle than she had imagined.

"It will be better if they love each other," she said, gravely.

"They can't. He can't love any one."

"I presumed that was the case. But it only increases my fear for Isabel. I shall positively start to-morrow."

"Isabel certainly has devotees," said the Countess, smiling very vividly. "I declare I don't pity her."

"It may be that I can't assist her," said Miss Stackpole, as if it were well not to have illusions.

"You can have wanted to, at any rate; that's something. I believe that's what you came from America for," the Countess suddenly added.

"Yes, I wanted to look after her," Henrietta said, serenely.

Her hostess stood there smiling at her, with her small bright eyes and her eager-looking nose; a flush had come into each of her cheeks.

"Ah, that's very pretty—*c'est bien gentil!*" she said. "Isn't that what they call friendship?"

"I don't know what they call it. I thought I had better come."

"She is very happy—she is very fortunate," the Countess went on. "She has others besides." And then she broke out, passionately. "She is more fortunate than I! I am as unhappy as she—I have a very bad husband; he is a great deal worse than Osmond. And I have no friends. I thought I had, but they are gone. No one would do for me what you have done for her."

Henrietta was touched; there was nature in this bitter effusion. She gazed at her companion a moment, and then—

"Look here, Countess, I will do anything for you that you like. I will wait over and travel with you."

"Never mind," the Countess answered, with a quick change of tone; "only describe me in the newspaper!"

Henrietta, before leaving her, however, was obliged to make her understand that she could not give a fictitious representation of her journey to Rome. Miss Stackpole was a strictly veracious reporter.

On quitting the Countess she took her way to the Lung' Arno, the sunny quay beside the yellow river, where the bright-faced hotels familiar to tourists stand all in a row. She had learned her way before this through the streets of Florence (she was very quick in such matters), and was therefore able to turn with great decision of step out of the little square which forms the approach to the bridge of the Holy Trinity. She proceeded to the left, towards the Ponte Vecchio, and stopped in front of one of the hotels which overlook that delightful structure. Here she drew forth a small pocket-book, took from it a card and a pencil, and, after meditating a moment, wrote a few words. It is our privilege to look over her shoulder, and if we exercise it we may read the brief query— "Could I see you this evening for a few moments on a very important matter?" Henrietta added that she should start on the morrow for Rome. Armed with this little document she approached the porter, who now had taken up his station in the doorway, and asked if Mr. Goodwood were at home. The porter replied, as porters always reply, that he had gone out about twenty minutes before; whereupon Henrietta presented her card and begged it might be handed to him on his return. She left the inn and took her course along the quay to the severe portico of the Uffizi, through which she presently reached the entrance of the famous gallery of paintings. Making her way in, she ascended the high staircase which leads to the upper chambers. The long corridor, glazed on one side and decorated with antique busts, which gives admission to these apartments, presented an empty vista, in which the bright winter light twinkled upon the marble floor. The gallery is very cold, and during the midwinter weeks is but scantily visited. Miss Stackpole may appear more ardent in her quest of artistic beauty than she has hitherto struck us as being, but she had after all her preferences and admirations. One of the latter was the little Correggio of the Tribune—

the Virgin kneeling down before the sacred infant, who lies
in a litter of straw, and clapping her hands to him while he
delightedly laughs and crows. Henrietta had taken a great
fancy to this intimate scene—she thought it the most beautiful picture in the world. On her way, at present, from New
York to Rome, she was spending but three days in Florence,
but she had reminded herself that they must not elapse without her paying another visit to her favourite work of art. She
had a great sense of beauty in all ways, and it involved a good
many intellectual obligations. She was about to turn into the
Tribune when a gentleman came out of it; whereupon she
gave a little exclamation and stood before Caspar Goodwood.

"I have just been at your hotel," she said. "I left a card for
you."

"I am very much honoured," Caspar Goodwood answered,
as if he really meant it.

"It was not to honour you I did it; I have called on you
before, and I know you don't like it. It was to talk to you a
little about something."

He looked for a moment at the buckle in her hat. "I shall
be very glad to hear what you wish to say."

"You don't like to talk with me," said Henrietta. "But I
don't care for that; I don't talk for your amusement. I wrote
a word to ask you to come and see me; but since I have met
you here this will do as well."

"I was just going away," Goodwood said; "but of course I
will stop." He was civil, but he was not enthusiastic.

Henrietta, however, never looked for great professions, and
she was so much in earnest that she was thankful he would
listen to her on any terms. She asked him first, however, if he
had seen all the pictures.

"All I want to. I have been here an hour."

"I wonder if you have seen my Correggio," said Henrietta.
"I came up on purpose to have a look at it." She went into
the Tribune, and he slowly accompanied her.

"I suppose I have seen it, but I didn't know it was yours. I
don't remember pictures—especially that sort." She had
pointed out her favourite work; and he asked her if it was
about Correggio that she wished to talk with him.

"No," said Henrietta, "it's about something less harmonious!" They had the small, brilliant room, a splendid cabinet of treasures, to themselves; there was only a custode hovering about the Medicean Venus. "I want you to do me a favour," Miss Stackpole went on.

Caspar Goodwood frowned a little, but he expressed no embarrassment at the sense of not looking eager. His face was that of a much older man than our earlier friend. "I'm sure it's something I shan't like," he said, rather loud.

"No, I don't think you will like it. If you did, it would be no favour."

"Well, let us hear it," he said, in the tone of a man quite conscious of his own reasonableness.

"You may say there is no particular reason why you should do me a favour. Indeed, I only know of one: the fact that if you would let me I would gladly do you one." Her soft, exact tone, in which there was no attempt at effect, had an extreme sincerity; and her companion, though he presented rather a hard surface, could not help being touched by it. When he was touched he rarely showed it, however, by the usual signs; he neither blushed, nor looked away, nor looked conscious. He only fixed his attention more directly; he seemed to consider with added firmness. Henrietta went on therefore disinterestedly, without the sense of an advantage. "I may say now, indeed—it seems a good time—that if I have ever annoyed you (and I think sometimes that I have), it is because I knew that I was willing to suffer annoyance for you. I have troubled you—doubtless. But I would take trouble for you."

Goodwood hesitated. "You are taking trouble now."

"Yes, I am, some. I want you to consider whether it is better on the whole that you should go to Rome."

"I thought you were going to say that!" Goodwood exclaimed, rather artlessly.

"You *have* considered it, then?"

"Of course I have, very carefully. I have looked all round it. Otherwise I shouldn't have come as far as this. That's what I stayed in Paris two months for; I was thinking it over."

"I am afraid you decided as you liked. You decided it was best, because you were so much attracted."

"Best for whom, do you mean?" Goodwood inquired.

"Well, for yourself first. For Mrs. Osmond next."

"Oh, it won't do her any good! I don't flatter myself that."

"Won't it do her harm?—that's the question."

"I don't see what it will matter to her. I am nothing to Mrs. Osmond. But if you want to know, I do want to see her myself."

"Yes, and that's why you go."

"Of course it is. Could there be a better reason?"

"How will it help you? that's what I want to know," said Miss Stackpole.

"That's just what I can't tell you; it's just what I was thinking about in Paris."

"It will make you more discontented."

"Why do you say more so?" Goodwood asked, rather sternly. "How do you know I am discontented?"

"Well," said Henrietta, hesitating a little—"you seem never to have cared for another."

"How do you know what I care for?" he cried, with a big blush. "Just now I care to go to Rome."

Henrietta looked at him in silence, with a sad yet luminous expression. "Well," she observed, at last, "I only wanted to tell you what I think; I had it on my mind. Of course you think it's none of my business. But nothing is any one's business, on that principle."

"It's very kind of you; I am greatly obliged to you for your interest," said Caspar Goodwood. "I shall go to Rome, and I shan't hurt Mrs. Osmond."

"You won't hurt her, perhaps. But will you help her?—that is the question."

"Is she in need of help?" he asked, slowly, with a penetrating look.

"Most women always are," said Henrietta, with conscientious evasiveness, and generalising less hopefully than usual. "If you go to Rome," she added, "I hope you will be a true friend—not a selfish one!" And she turned away and began to look at the pictures.

Caspar Goodwood let her go, and stood watching her while she wandered round the room; then, after a moment, he rejoined her. "You have heard something about her here," he said in a moment. "I should like to know what you have heard."

Henrietta had never prevaricated in her life, and though on this occasion there might have been a fitness in doing so, she decided, after a moment's hesitation, to make no superficial exception. "Yes, I have heard," she answered; "but as I don't want you to go to Rome I won't tell you."

"Just as you please. I shall see for myself," said Goodwood. Then, inconsistently—for him, "You have heard she is unhappy!" he added.

"Oh, you won't see that!" Henrietta exclaimed.

"I hope not. When do you start?"

"To-morrow, by the evening train. And you?"

Goodwood hesitated; he had no desire to make his journey to Rome in Miss Stackpole's company. His indifference to this advantage was not of the same character as Gilbert Osmond's, but it had at this moment an equal distinctness. It was rather a tribute to Miss Stackpole's virtues than a reference to her faults. He thought her very remarkable, very brilliant, and he had, in theory, no objection to the class to which she belonged. Lady correspondents appeared to him a part of the natural scheme of things in a progressive country, and though he never read their letters he supposed that they ministered somehow to social progress. But it was this very eminence of their position that made him wish that Miss Stackpole did not take so much for granted. She took for granted that he was always ready for some allusion to Mrs. Osmond; she had done so when they met in Paris, six weeks after his arrival in Europe, and she had repeated the assumption with every successive opportunity. He had no wish whatever to allude to Mrs. Osmond; he was *not* always thinking of her; he was perfectly sure of that. He was the most reserved, the least colloquial of men, and this inquiring authoress was constantly flashing her lantern into the quiet darkness of his soul. He wished she didn't care so much; he even wished, though it might seem rather brutal of him, that she would leave him alone. In spite of this, however, he just now made other reflections—which show how widely different, in effect, his ill-humour was from Gilbert Osmond's. He wished to go immediately to Rome; he would have liked to go alone, in the night-train. He hated the European railway-carriages, in which one sat for hours in a vice, knee to knee and nose to nose with a foreigner to whom one presently found one's self objecting with all the added vehemence of one's wish to have the window open; and if they were worse at night even than by day, at least at night one could sleep and dream of an American saloon-car. But he could not take a night-train when Miss Stackpole was starting in the morning; it seemed to him that this would be an insult to an unprotected woman. Nor could he wait until after she had gone, unless he should wait longer than he had patience for. It would not do to start the next day. She worried him; she oppressed him; the idea of spending the day in a European railway-carriage with her offered a complication of irritations. Still, she was a lady travelling alone; it was his duty to put himself out for her. There could be no two questions about that; it was a perfectly clear necessity. He looked extremely grave for some moments, and then he said, without any of the richness of gallantry, but in a tone of extreme distinctness—"Of course, if you are going to-morrow, I will go too, as I may be of assistance to you."

"Well, Mr. Goodwood, I should hope so!" Henrietta remarked, serenely.

XLV

I HAVE already had reason to say that Isabel knew that her husband was displeased by the continuance of Ralph's visit to Rome. This knowledge was very present to her as she went to her cousin's hotel the day after she had invited Lord Warburton to give a tangible proof of his sincerity; and at this moment, as at others, she had a sufficient perception of the sources of Osmond's displeasure. He wished her to have no freedom of mind, and he knew perfectly well that Ralph was an apostle of freedom. It was just because he was this, Isabel said to herself, that it was a refreshment to go and see him. It will be perceived that she partook of this refreshment in spite of her husband's disapproval; that is, she partook of it, as she flattered herself, discreetly. She had not as yet undertaken to act in direct opposition to Osmond's wishes; he was her master; she gazed at moments with a sort of incredulous blankness at this fact. It weighed upon her imagination, however; constantly present to her mind were all the traditionary decencies and sanctities of marriage. The idea of violating them filled her with shame as well as with dread, for when she gave herself away she had lost sight of this contingency in the perfect belief that her husband's intentions were as generous as her own. She seemed to see, however, the rapid approach of the day when she should have to take back something that she had solemnly given. Such a ceremony would be odious and monstrous; she tried to shut her eyes to it meanwhile. Osmond would do nothing to help it by beginning first; he would put that burden upon her. He had not yet formally forbidden her to go and see Ralph; but she felt sure that unless Ralph should very soon depart this prohibition would come. How could poor Ralph depart? The weather as yet made it impossible. She could perfectly understand her husband's wish for the event; to be just, she didn't see how he could like her to be with her cousin. Ralph never said a word against him; but Osmond's objections were none the less founded. If Osmond should positively interpose, then she should have to decide, and that would not be easy. The prospect made her heart beat and her cheeks burn, as I say, in advance; there were moments when, in her wish to avoid an open rupture with her husband, she found herself wishing that Ralph would start even at a risk. And it was of no use that when catching herself in this state of mind, she called herself a feeble spirit, a coward. It was not that she loved Ralph less, but that almost anything seemed preferable to repudiating the most serious act—the single sacred act—of her life. That appeared to make the whole future hideous. To break with Osmond once would be to break for ever; any open acknowledgment of irreconcilable needs would be an admission that their whole attempt had proved a failure. For them there could be no condonement, no compromise, no easy forgetfulness, no formal readjustment. They had attempted only one thing, but that one thing was to have been exquisite. Once they missed it, nothing else would do; there is no substitute for that success. For the moment, Isabel went to the Hôtel de Paris as often as she thought well; the measure of expediency resided in her moral consciousness. It had been very liberal to-day, for in addition to the general truth that she couldn't leave Ralph to die alone, she had something important to ask of him. This indeed was Gilbert's business as well as her own.

She came very soon to what she wished to speak of.

"I want you to answer me a question," she said. "It's about Lord Warburton."

"I think I know it," Ralph answered from his arm-chair, out of which his thin legs protruded at greater length than ever.

"It's very possible," said Isabel. "Please then answer it."

"Oh, I don't say I can do that."

"You are intimate with him," said Isabel; "you have a great deal of observation of him."

"Very true. But think how he must dissimulate!"

"Why should he dissimulate? That's not his nature."

"Ah, you must remember that the circumstances are peculiar," said Ralph, with an air of private amusement.

"To a certain extent—yes. But is he really in love?"

"Very much, I think. I can make that out."

"Ah!" said Isabel, with a certain dryness.

Ralph looked at her a moment; a shade of perplexity mingled with his mild hilarity.

"You said that as if you were disappointed."

Isabel got up, slowly, smoothing her gloves, and eyeing them thoughtfully.

"It's after all no business of mine."

"You are very philosophic," said her cousin. And then in a moment—"May I inquire what you are talking about?"

Isabel stared a little. "I thought you knew. Lord Warburton tells me he desires to marry Pansy. I have told you that before, without eliciting a comment from you. You might risk one this morning, I think. Is it your belief that he really cares for her?"

"Ah, for Pansy, no!" cried Ralph, very positively.

"But you said just now that he did."

Ralph hesitated a moment. "That he cared for you, Mrs. Osmond."

Isabel shook her head, gravely. "That's nonsense, you know."

"Of course it is. But the nonsense is Warburton's, not mine."

"That would be very tiresome," Isabel said, speaking, as she flattered herself, with much subtlety.

"I ought to tell you indeed," Ralph went on, "that to me he has denied it."

"It's very good of you to talk about it together! Has he also told you that he is in love with Pansy?"

"He has spoken very well of her—very properly. He has let me know, of course, that he thinks she would do very well at Lockleigh."

"Does he really think it?"

"Ah, what Warburton really thinks——!" said Ralph.

Isabel fell to smoothing her gloves again; they were long, loose gloves upon which she could freely expend herself. Soon, however, she looked up, and then—

"Ah, Ralph, you give me no help!" she cried, abruptly, passionately.

It was the first time she had alluded to the need for help, and the words shook her cousin with their violence. He gave a long murmur of relief, of pity, of tenderness; it seemed to him that at last the gulf between them had been bridged. It was this that made him exclaim in a moment—

"How unhappy you must be!"

He had no sooner spoken than she recovered her self-possession, and the first use she made of it was to pretend she had not heard him.

"When I talk of your helping me, I talk great nonsense," she said, with a quick smile. "The idea of my troubling you with my domestic embarrassments! The matter is very simple; Lord Warburton must get on by himself. I can't undertake to help him."

"He ought to succeed easily," said Ralph.

Isabel hesitated a moment. "Yes—but he has not always succeeded."

"Very true. You know, however, how that always surprised me. Is Miss Osmond capable of giving us a surprise?"

"It will come from him, rather. I suspect that after all he will let the matter drop."

"He will do nothing dishonourable," said Ralph.

"I am very sure of that. Nothing can be more honourable than for him to leave the poor child alone. She cares for some one else, and it is cruel to attempt to bribe her by magnificent offers to give him up."

"Cruel to the other person perhaps—the one she cares for. But Warburton isn't obliged to mind that."

"No, cruel to her," said Isabel. "She would be very unhappy if she were to allow herself to be persuaded to desert poor Mr. Rosier. That idea seems to amuse you; of course you are not in love with him. He has the merit of being in love with her. She can see at a glance that Lord Warburton is not."

"He would be very good to her," said Ralph.

"He has been good to her already. Fortunately, however, he has not said a word to disturb her. He could come and bid her good-bye to-morrow with perfect propriety."

"How would your husband like that?"

"Not at all; and he may be right in not liking it. Only he must obtain satisfaction himself."

"Has he commissioned you to obtain it?" Ralph ventured to ask.

"It was natural that as an old friend of Lord Warburton's—an older friend, that is, than Osmond—I should take an interest in his intentions."

"Take an interest in his renouncing them, you mean."

Isabel hesitated, frowning a little. "Let me understand. Are you pleading his cause?"

"Not in the least. I am very glad he should not become your step-daughter's husband. It makes such a very queer relation to you!" said Ralph, smiling. "But I'm rather nervous lest your husband should think you haven't pushed him enough."

Isabel found herself able to smile as well as he.

"He knows me well enough not to have expected me to push. He himself has no intention of pushing, I presume. I am not afraid I shall not be able to justify myself!" she said, lightly.

Her mask had dropped for an instant, but she had put it on again, to Ralph's infinite disappointment. He had caught a glimpse of her natural face, and he wished immensely to look into it. He had an almost savage desire to hear her complain of her husband—hear her say that she should be held accountable for Lord Warburton's defection. Ralph was certain that this was her situation; he knew by instinct, in advance, the form that in such an event Osmond's displeasure would take. It could only take the meanest and cruellest. He would have liked to warn Isabel of it—to let her see at least that he knew it. It little mattered that Isabel would know it much better; it was for his own satisfaction more than for hers that he longed to show her that he was not deceived. He tried and tried again to make her betray Osmond; he felt cold-blooded, cruel, dishonourable almost, in doing so. But it scarcely mattered, for he only failed. What had she come for then, and why did she seem almost to offer him a chance to violate their tacit convention? Why did she ask him his advice, if she gave him no liberty to answer her? How could they talk of her domestic embarrassments, as it pleased her humourously to designate them, if the principal factor was not to be mentioned? These contradictions were themselves but an indication of her trouble, and her cry for help, just before, was the only thing he was bound to consider.

"You will be decidedly at variance, all the same," he said, in a moment. And as she answered nothing, looking as if she scarcely understood—"You will find yourselves thinking very differently," he continued.

"That may easily happen, among the most united couples!" She took up her parasol; he saw that she was nervous, afraid of what he might say. "It's a matter we can hardly quarrel about, however," she added; "for almost all the interest is on his side. That is very natural. Pansy is after all his daughter—not mine." And she put out her hand to wish him good-bye.

Ralph took an inward resolution that she should not leave him without his letting her know that he knew everything; it seemed too great an opportunity to lose. "Do you know what his interest will make him say?" he asked, as he took her hand. She shook her head, rather dryly—not discouragingly—and he went on, "It will make him say that your want of zeal is owing to jealousy." He stopped a moment; her face made him afraid.

"To jealousy?"

"To jealousy of his daughter."

She blushed red and threw back her head.

"You are not kind," she said, in a voice that he had never heard on her lips.

"Be frank with me, and you'll see," said Ralph.

But she made no answer; she only shook her hand out of his own, which he tried still to hold, and rapidly went out of the room. She made up her mind to speak to Pansy, and she took an occasion on the same day, going to the young girl's room before dinner. Pansy was already dressed; she was always in advance of the time; it seemed to illustrate her pretty patience and the graceful stillness with which she could sit and wait. At present she was seated in her fresh array, before the bed-room fire; she had blown out her candles on the completion of her toilet, in accordance with the economical habits in which she had been brought up and which she was now more careful than ever to observe; so that the room was lighted only by a couple of logs. The rooms in the Palazzo Roccanera were as spacious as they were numerous, and Pansy's virginal bower was an immense chamber with a dark, heavily-timbered ceiling. Its diminutive mistress, in the midst of it, appeared but a speck of humanity, and as she got up, with quick deference, to welcome Isabel, the latter was more than ever struck with her shy sincerity. Isabel had a difficult task—the only thing was to perform it as simply as possible. She felt bitter and angry, but she warned herself against betraying it to Pansy. She was afraid even of looking too grave, or at least too stern; she was afraid of frightening her. But Pansy seemed to have guessed that she had come a little as a confessor; for after she had moved the chair in which she had been sitting a little nearer to the fire, and Isabel had taken her place in it, she kneeled down on a cushion in front of her, looking up and resting her clasped hands on her stepmother's knees. What Isabel wished to do was to hear from her own lips that her mind was not occupied with Lord Warburton; but if she desired the assurance, she felt herself by no means at liberty to provoke it. The girl's father would have qualified this as rank treachery; and indeed Isabel knew that if Pansy should display the smallest germ of a disposition to encourage Lord Warburton, her own duty was to hold her tongue. It was difficult to interrogate without appearing to suggest; Pansy's supreme simplicity, an innocence even more complete than Isabel had yet judged it, gave to the most tentative inquiry something of the effect of an admonition. As she knelt there in the vague firelight, with her pretty dress vaguely shining, her hands folded half in appeal and half in submission, her soft eyes, raised and fixed, full of the seriousness of the situation, she looked to Isabel like a childish martyr decked out for sacrifice and scarcely presuming even to hope to avert it. When Isabel said to her that she had never yet spoken to her of what might have been going on in relation to her getting married, but that her silence had not been indifference or ignorance, had only been the desire to leave her at liberty, Pansy bent forward, raised her face nearer and nearer to Isabel's, and with a little murmur which evidently expressed a deep longing, answered that she had greatly wished her to speak, and that she begged her to advise her now.

"It's difficult for me to advise you," Isabel rejoined. "I don't know how I can undertake that. That's for your father; you must get his advice, and, above all, you must act upon it."

At this Pansy dropped her eyes; for a moment she said nothing.

"I think I should like your advice better than papa's," she presently remarked.

"That's not as it should be," said Isabel, coldly. "I love you very much, but your father loves you better."

"It isn't because you love me—it's because you're a lady," Pansy answered, with the air of saying something very reasonable. "A lady can advise a young girl better than a man."

"I advise you, then, to pay the greatest respect to your father's wishes."

"Ah, yes," said Pansy, eagerly, "I must do that."

"But if I speak to you now about your getting married, it's not for your own sake, it's for mine," Isabel went on. "If I try to learn from you what you expect, what you desire, it is only that I may act accordingly."

Pansy stared, and then, very quickly—

"Will you do everything I desire?" she asked.

"Before I say yes, I must know what such things are."

Pansy presently told her that the only thing she wished in life was to marry Mr. Rosier. He had asked her, and she had told him that she would do so if her papa would allow it. Now her papa wouldn't allow it.

"Very well, then, it's impossible," said Isabel.

"Yes, it's impossible," said Pansy, without a sigh, and with the same extreme attention in her clear little face.

"You must think of something else, then," Isabel went on; but Pansy, sighing then, told her that she had attempted this feat without the least success.

"You think of those that think of you," she said, with a faint smile. "I know that Mr. Rosier thinks of me."

"He ought not to," said Isabel, loftily. "Your father has expressly requested he shouldn't."

"He can't help it, because he knows that I think of him."

"You shouldn't think of him. There is some excuse for him, perhaps; but there is none for you!"

"I wish you would try to find one," the girl exclaimed, as if she were praying to the Madonna.

"I should be very sorry to attempt it," said the Madonna,

with unusual frigidity. "If you knew some one else was thinking of you, would you think of him?"

"No one can think of me as Mr. Rosier does; no one has the right."

"Ah, but I don't admit Mr. Rosier's right," Isabel cried, hypocritically.

Pansy only gazed at her; she was evidently deeply puzzled; and Isabel, taking advantage of it, began to represent to her the miserable consequences of disobeying her father. At this Pansy stopped her, with the assurance that she would never disobey him, would never marry without his consent. And she announced, in the serenest, simplest tone, that though she might never marry Mr. Rosier, she would never cease to think of him. She appeared to have accepted the idea of eternal singleness; but Isabel of course was free to reflect that she had no conception of its meaning. She was perfectly sincere; she was prepared to give up her lover. This might seem an important step toward taking another, but for Pansy, evidently, it did not lead in that direction. She felt no bitterness towards her father; there was no bitterness in her heart; there was only the sweetness of fidelity to Edward Rosier, and a strange, exquisite intimation that she could prove it better by remaining single than even by marrying him.

"Your father would like you to make a better marriage," said Isabel. "Mr. Rosier's fortune is not very large."

"How do you mean better—if that would be good enough? And I have very little money; why should I look for a fortune?"

"Your having so little is a reason for looking for more." Isabel was grateful for the dimness of the room; she felt as if her face were hideously insincere. She was doing this for Osmond; this was what one had to do for Osmond! Pansy's solemn eyes, fixed on her own, almost embarrassed her; she was ashamed to think that she had made so light of the girl's preference.

"What should you like me to do?" said Pansy, softly.

The question was a terrible one, and Isabel pusillanimously took refuge in a generalisation.

"To remember all the pleasure it is in your power to give your father."

"To marry some one else, you mean—if he should ask me?"

For a moment Isabel's answer caused itself to be waited for; then she heard herself utter it, in the stillness that Pansy's attention seemed to make.

"Yes—to marry some one else."

Pansy's eyes grew more penetrating; Isabel believed that she was doubting her sincerity, and the impression took force from her slowly getting up from her cushion. She stood there a moment, with her small hands unclasped, and then she said, with a timorous sigh—

"Well, I hope no one will ask me!"

"There has been a question of that. Some one else would have been ready to ask you."

"I don't think he can have been ready," said Pansy.

"It would appear so—if he had been sure that he would succeed."

"If he had been sure? Then he was not ready!"

Isabel thought this rather sharp; she also got up, and stood a moment, looking into the fire. "Lord Warburton has shown you great attention," she said; "of course you know it's of him I speak." She found herself, against her expectation, almost placed in the position of justifying herself; which led her to introduce this nobleman more crudely than she had intended.

"He has been very kind to me, and I like him very much. But if you mean that he will ask me to marry him, I think you are mistaken."

"Perhaps I am. But your father would like it extremely."

Pansy shook her head, with a little wise smile. "Lord Warburton won't ask me simply to please papa."

"Your father would like you to encourage him," Isabel went on, mechanically.

"How can I encourage him?"

"I don't know. Your father must tell you that."

Pansy said nothing for a moment; she only continued to smile as if she were in possession of a bright assurance. "There is no danger—no danger!" she declared at last.

There was a conviction in the way she said this, and a felicity in her believing it, which made Isabel feel very awkward.

She felt accused of dishonesty, and the idea was disgusting. To repair her self-respect, she was on the point of saying that Lord Warburton had let her know that there *was* a danger. But she did not; she only said—in her embarrassment rather wide of the mark—that he surely had been most kind, most friendly.

"Yes, he has been very kind," Pansy answered. "That's what I like him for."

"Why then is the difficulty so great?"

"I have always felt sure that he knows that I don't want—what did you say I should do?—to encourage him. He knows I don't want to marry, and he wants me to know that he therefore won't trouble me. That's the meaning of his kindness. It's as if he said to me, 'I like you very much, but if it doesn't please you I will never say it again.' I think that is very kind, very noble," Pansy went on, with deepening positiveness. "That is all we have said to each other. And he doesn't care for me, either. Ah no, there is no danger!"

Isabel was touched with wonder at the depths of perception of which this submissive little person was capable; she felt afraid of Pansy's wisdom—began almost to retreat before it. "You must tell your father that," she remarked, reservedly.

"I think I would rather not," Pansy answered.

"You ought not to let him have false hopes."

"Perhaps not; but it will be good for me that he should. So long as he believes that Lord Warburton intends anything of the kind you say, papa won't propose any one else. And that will be an advantage for me," said Pansy, very lucidly.

There was something brilliant in her lucidity, and it made Isabel draw a long breath. It relieved her of a heavy responsibility. Pansy had a sufficient illumination of her own, and Isabel felt that she herself just now had no light to spare from her small stock. Nevertheless it still clung to her that she must be loyal to Osmond, that she was on her honour in dealing with his daughter. Under the influence of this sentiment she threw out another suggestion before she retired—a suggestion with which it seemed to her that she should have done her utmost. "Your father takes for granted at least that you would like to marry a nobleman."

Pansy stood in the open doorway; she had drawn back the curtain for Isabel to pass. "I think Mr. Rosier looks like one!" she remarked, very gravely.

XLVI

LORD WARBURTON was not seen in Mrs. Osmond's drawing-room for several days, and Isabel could not fail to observe that her husband said nothing to her about having received a letter from him. She could not fail to observe, either, that Osmond was in a state of expectancy, and that though it was not agreeable to him to betray it, he thought their distinguished friend kept him waiting quite too long. At the end of four days he alluded to his absence.

"What has become of Warburton? What does he mean by treating one like a tradesman with a bill?"

"I know nothing about him," Isabel said. "I saw him last Friday, at the German ball. He told me then that he meant to write to you."

"He has never written to me."

"So I supposed, from your not having told me."

"He's an odd fish," said Osmond, comprehensively. And on Isabel's making no rejoinder, he went on to inquire whether it took his lordship five days to indite a letter. "Does he form his words with such difficulty?"

"I don't know," said Isabel. "I have never had a letter from him."

"Never had a letter? I had an idea that you were at one time in intimate correspondence."

Isabel answered that this had not been the case, and let the conversation drop. On the morrow, however, coming into the drawing-room late in the afternoon, her husband took it up again.

"When Lord Warburton told you of his intention of writing, what did you say to him?" he asked.

Isabel hesitated a moment. "I think I told him not to forget it."

"Did you believe there was a danger of that?"

"As you say, he's an odd fish."

"Apparently he has forgotten it," said Osmond. "Be so good as to remind him."

"Should you like me to write to him?" Isabel asked.

"I have no objection whatever."

"You expect too much of me."

"Ah yes, I expect a great deal of you."

"I am afraid I shall disappoint you," said Isabel.

"My expectations have survived a good deal of disappointment."

"Of course I know that. Think how I must have disappointed myself! If you really wish to capture Lord Warburton, you must do it yourself."

For a couple of minutes Osmond answered nothing; then he said—"That won't be easy, with you working against me."

Isabel started; she felt herself beginning to tremble. He had a way of looking at her through half-closed eyelids, as if he were thinking of her but scarcely saw her, which seemed to her to have a wonderfully cruel intention. It appeared to recognise her as a disagreeable necessity of thought, but to ignore her, for the time, as a presence. That was the expression of his eyes now. "I think you accuse me of something very base," she said.

"I accuse you of not being trustworthy. If he doesn't come up to the mark it will be because you have kept him off. I don't know that it's base; it is the kind of thing a woman always thinks she may do. I have no doubt you have the finest ideas about it."

"I told you I would do what I could," said Isabel.

"Yes, that gained you time."

It came over Isabel, after he had said this, that she had once thought him beautiful. "How much you must wish to capture him!" she exclaimed, in a moment.

She had no sooner spoken than she perceived the full reach of her words, of which she had not been conscious in uttering them. They made a comparison between Osmond and herself, recalled the fact that she had once held this coveted treasure in her hand and felt herself rich enough to let it fall. A momentary exultation took possession of her—a horrible delight in having wounded him; for his face instantly told her that none of the force of her exclamation was lost. Osmond expressed nothing otherwise, however; he only said, quickly, "Yes, I wish it very much."

At this moment a servant came in, as if to usher a visitor, and he was followed the next by Lord Warburton, who received a visible check on seeing Osmond. He looked rapidly from the master of the house to the mistress; a movement that seemed to denote a reluctance to interrupt or even a perception of ominous conditions. Then he advanced, with his English address, in which a vague shyness seemed to offer itself as an element of good-breeding; in which the only defect was a difficulty in achieving transitions.

Osmond was embarrassed; he found nothing to say; but Isabel remarked, promptly enough, that they had been in the act of talking about their visitor. Upon this her husband added that they hadn't known what was become of him—they had been afraid he had gone away.

"No," said Lord Warburton, smiling and looking at Osmond; "I am only on the point of going." And then he explained that he found himself suddenly recalled to England; he should start on the morrow or next day. "I am awfully sorry to leave poor Touchett!" he ended by exclaiming.

For a moment neither of his companions spoke; Osmond only leaned back in his chair, listening. Isabel didn't look at him; she could only fancy how he looked. Her eyes were upon Lord Warburton's face, where they were the more free to rest that those of his lordship carefully avoided them. Yet Isabel was sure that had she met her visitor's glance, she should have found it expressive. "You had better take poor Touchett with you," she heard her husband say, lightly enough, in a moment.

"He had better wait for warmer weather," Lord Warburton answered. "I shouldn't advise him to travel just now."

He sat there for a quarter of an hour, talking as if he might not soon see them again—unless indeed they should come to England, a course which he strongly recommended. Why shouldn't they come to England in the autumn? that struck him as a very happy thought. It would give him such pleasure to do what he could for them—to have them come and spend a month with him. Osmond, by his own admission, had been to England but once; which was an absurd state of things. It was just the country for him—he would be sure to get on well there. Then Lord Warburton asked Isabel if she remembered what a good time she had there, and if she didn't want to try it again. Didn't she want to see Gardencourt once more? Gardencourt was really very good. Touchett didn't take proper care of it, but it was the sort of place you could hardly spoil by letting it alone. Why didn't they come and pay Touchett a visit? He surely must have asked them. Hadn't asked them? What an ill-mannered wretch! and Lord Warburton promised to give the master of Gardencourt a piece of his mind. Of course it was a mere accident; he would be delighted to have them. Spending a month with Touchett and a month with himself, and seeing all the rest of the people they must know there, they really wouldn't find it half bad. Lord Warburton added that it would amuse Miss Osmond as well, who had told him that she had never been to England and whom he had assured it was a country she deserved to see. Of course she didn't need to go to England to be admired— that was her fate everywhere; but she would be immensely liked in England, Miss Osmond would, if that was any inducement. He asked if she were not at home: couldn't he say good-bye? Not that he liked good-byes—he always funked them. When he left England the other day he had not said good-bye to any one. He had had half a mind to leave Rome without troubling Mrs. Osmond for a final interview. What could be more dreary than a final interview? One never said the things one wanted to—one remembered them all an hour afterwards. On the other hand, one usually said a lot of things one shouldn't, simply from a sense that one had to say something. Such a sense was bewildering; it made one nervous. He had it at present, and that was the effect it produced on him. If Mrs. Osmond didn't think he spoke as he ought, she must set it down to agitation; it was no light thing to part with Mrs. Osmond. He was really very sorry to be going. He had thought of writing to her, instead of calling—but he would write to her at any rate, to tell her a lot of things that would be sure to occur to him as soon as he had left the house. They must think seriously about coming to Lockleigh.

If there was anything awkward in the circumstances of his visit or in the announcement of his departure, it failed to come to the surface. Lord Warburton talked about his agitation; but he showed it in no other manner, and Isabel saw that since he had determined on a retreat he was capable of executing it gallantly. She was very glad for him; she liked him quite well enough to wish him to appear to carry a thing off. He would do that on any occasion; not from impudence, but simply from the habit of success; and Isabel perceived that it was not in her husband's power to frustrate this faculty. A double operation, as she sat there, went on in her mind. On one side she listened to Lord Warburton; said what was proper to him; read, more or less, between the lines of what he said himself; and wondered how he would have spoken if he had found her alone. On the other she had a perfect consciousness of Osmond's emotion. She felt almost sorry for him; he was condemned to the sharp pain of loss without the relief of cursing. He had had a great hope, and now, as he saw it vanish into smoke, he was obliged to sit and smile and twirl his thumbs. Not that he troubled himself to smile very brightly; he treated Lord Warburton, on the whole, to as vacant a countenance as so clever a man could very well wear. It was indeed a part of Osmond's cleverness that he could look consummately uncompromised. His present appearance, however, was not a confession of disappointment; it was simply a part of Osmond's habitual system, which was to be inexpressive exactly in proportion as he was really intent. He had been intent upon Lord Warburton from the first; but he had never allowed his eagerness to irradiate his refined face. He had treated his possible son-in-law as he treated every one— with an air of being interested in him only for his own advantage, not for Gilbert Osmond's. He would give no sign now of an inward rage which was the result of a vanished prospect of gain—not the faintest nor subtlest. Isabel could be sure of that, if it was any satisfaction to her. Strangely, very strangely, it was a satisfaction; she wished Lord Warburton to triumph before her husband, and at the same time she wished her husband to be very superior before Lord Warburton. Osmond, in his way, was admirable; he had, like their visitor, the advantage of an acquired habit. It was not that of succeeding, but it was something almost as good—that of not attempting. As he leaned back in his place, listening but vaguely to Lord Warburton's friendly offers and suppressed explanations—as if it were only proper to assume that they were addressed essentially to his wife—he had at least (since so little else was left him) the comfort of thinking how well he personally had kept out of it, and how the air of indifference, which he was now able to wear, had the added beauty of consistency. It was something to be able to look as if their visitor's movements had no relation to his own mind. Their visitor did well, certainly; but Osmond's performance was in its very nature more finished. Lord Warburton's position was after all an easy one; there was no reason in the world why he should not leave Rome. He had beneficent inclinations; but they had stopped short of fruition; he had never committed himself, and his honour was safe. Osmond appeared to take but a moderate interest in the proposal that they should go and stay with him, and in his allusion to the success Pansy might extract from their visit. He murmured a recognition, but left Isabel to say that it was a matter requiring grave consideration. Isabel, even while she made this remark, could see the great vista which had suddenly opened out in her husband's mind, with Pansy's little figure marching up the middle of it.

Lord Warburton had asked leave to bid good-bye to Pansy, but neither Isabel nor Osmond had made any motion to send for her. He had the air of giving out that his visit must be short; he sat on a small chair, as if it were only for a moment, keeping his hat in his hand. But he stayed and stayed; Isabel wondered what he was waiting for. She believed it was not to see Pansy; she had an impression that on the whole he would rather not see Pansy. It was of course to see herself alone—he had something to say to her. Isabel had no great wish to hear it, for she was afraid it would be an explanation, and she could perfectly dispense with explanations. Osmond, however, presently got up, like a man of good taste to whom it had occurred that so inveterate a visitor might wish to say just the last word of all to the ladies.

"I have a letter to write before dinner," he said; "you must excuse me. I will see if my daughter is disengaged, and if she is she shall know you are here. Of course when you come to Rome you will always look us up. Isabel will talk to you about the English expedition; she decides all those things."

The nod with which, instead of a hand-shake, he terminated this little speech, was perhaps a rather meagre form of salutation; but on the whole it was all the occasion de-

manded. Isabel reflected that after he left the room Lord Warburton would have no pretext for saying—"Your husband is
very angry;" which would have been extremely disagreeable
to her. Nevertheless, if he had done so, she would have
said—"Oh, don't be anxious. He doesn't hate *you*: it's me
that he hates!"

It was only when they had been left alone together that
Lord Warburton showed a certain vague awkwardness—sitting down in another chair, handling two or three of the objects that were near him. "I hope he will make Miss Osmond
come," he presently remarked. "I want very much to see her."

"I'm glad it's the last time," said Isabel.

"So am I. She doesn't care for me."

"No, she doesn't care for you."

"I don't wonder at it," said Lord Warburton. Then he
added, with inconsequence—"You will come to England,
won't you?"

"I think we had better not."

"Ah, you owe me a visit. Don't you remember that you
were to have come to Lockleigh once, and you never did?"

"Everything is changed since then," said Isabel.

"Not changed for the worse, surely—as far as we are concerned. To see you under my roof"—and he hesitated a
moment—"would be a great satisfaction."

She had feared an explanation; but that was the only one
that occurred. They talked a little of Ralph, and in another
moment Pansy came in, already dressed for dinner and with a
little red spot in either cheek. She shook hands with Lord
Warburton and stood looking up into his face with a fixed
smile—a smile that Isabel knew, though his lordship probably never suspected it, to be near akin to a burst of tears.

"I am going away," he said. "I want to bid you good-
bye."

"Good-bye, Lord Warburton." The young girl's voice trembled a little.

"And I want to tell you how much I wish you may be very
happy."

"Thank you, Lord Warburton," Pansy answered.

He lingered a moment, and gave a glance at Isabel. "You
ought to be very happy—you have got a guardian angel."

"I am sure I shall be happy," said Pansy, in the tone of a person whose certainties were always cheerful.

"Such a conviction as that will take you a great way. But if it should ever fail you, remember—remember—" and Lord Warburton stammered a little. "Think of me sometimes, you know," he said with a vague laugh. Then he shook hands with Isabel, in silence, and presently he was gone.

When he had left the room Isabel expected an effusion of tears from her step-daughter; but Pansy in fact treated her to something very different.

"I think you *are* my guardian angel!" she exclaimed, very sweetly.

Isabel shook her head. "I am not an angel of any kind. I am at the most your good friend."

"You are a very good friend then—to have asked papa to be gentle with me."

"I have asked your father nothing," said Isabel, wondering.

"He told me just now to come to the drawing-room, and then he gave me a very kind kiss."

"Ah," said Isabel, "that was quite his own idea!"

She recognised the idea perfectly; it was very characteristic, and she was to see a great deal more of it. Even with Pansy, Osmond could not put himself the least in the wrong. They were dining out that day, and after their dinner they went to another entertainment; so that it was not till late in the evening that Isabel saw him alone. When Pansy kissed him, before going to bed, he returned her embrace with even more than his usual munificence, and Isabel wondered whether he meant it as a hint that his daughter had been injured by the machinations of her stepmother. It was a partial expression, at any rate, of what he continued to expect of his wife. Isabel was about to follow Pansy, but he remarked that he wished she would remain; he had something to say to her. Then he walked about the drawing-room a little, while she stood waiting, in her cloak.

"I don't understand what you wish to do," he said in a moment. "I should like to know—so that I may know how to act."

"Just now I wish to go to bed. I am very tired."

"Sit down and rest; I shall not keep you long. Not there—

take a comfortable place." And he arranged a multitude of cushions that were scattered in picturesque disorder upon a vast divan. This was not, however, where she seated herself; she dropped into the nearest chair. The fire had gone out; the lights in the great room were few. She drew her cloak about her; she felt mortally cold. "I think you are trying to humiliate me," Osmond went on. "It's a most absurd undertaking."

"I haven't the least idea what you mean," said Isabel.

"You have played a very deep game; you have managed it beautifully."

"What is it that I have managed?"

"You have not quite settled it, however; we shall see him again." And he stopped in front of her, with his hands in his pockets, looking down at her thoughtfully, in his usual way, which seemed meant to let her know that she was not an object, but only a rather disagreeable incident, of thought.

"If you mean that Lord Warburton is under an obligation to come back, you are wrong," Isabel said. "He is under none whatever."

"That's just what I complain of. But when I say he will come back, I don't mean that he will come from a sense of duty."

"There is nothing else to make him. I think he has quite exhausted Rome."

"Ah no, that's a shallow judgment. Rome is inexhaustible." And Osmond began to walk about again. "However, about that, perhaps, there is no hurry," he added. "It's rather a good idea of his that we should go to England. If it were not for the fear of finding your cousin there, I think I should try to persuade you."

"It may be that you will not find my cousin," said Isabel.

"I should like to be sure of it. However, I shall be as sure as possible. At the same time I should like to see his house, that you told me so much about at one time: what do you call it?—Gardencourt. It must be a charming thing. And then, you know, I have a devotion to the memory of your uncle; you made me take a great fancy to him. I should like to see where he lived and died. That, however, is a detail. Your friend was right; Pansy ought to see England."

"I have no doubt she would enjoy it," said Isabel.

"But that's a long time hence; next autumn is far off," Osmond continued; "and meantime there are things that more nearly interest us. Do you think me so very proud?" he asked, suddenly.

"I think you very strange."

"You don't understand me."

"No, not even when you insult me."

"I don't insult you; I am incapable of it. I merely speak of certain facts, and if the allusion is an injury to you the fault is not mine. It is surely a fact that you have kept all this matter quite in your own hands."

"Are you going back to Lord Warburton?" Isabel asked. "I am very tired of his name."

"You shall hear it again before we have done with it."

She had spoken of his insulting her, but it suddenly seemed to her that this ceased to be a pain. He was going down—down; the vision of such a fall made her almost giddy; that was the only pain. He was too strange, too different; he didn't touch her. Still, the working of his morbid passion was extraordinary, and she felt a rising curiosity to know in what light he saw himself justified. "I might say to you that I judge you have nothing to say to me that is worth hearing," she rejoined in a moment. "But I should perhaps be wrong. There is a thing that would be worth my hearing—to know in the plainest words of what it is you accuse me."

"Of preventing Pansy's marriage to Warburton. Are those words plain enough?"

"On the contrary, I took a great interest in it. I told you so; and when you told me that you counted on me—that I think was what you said—I accepted the obligation. I was a fool to do so, but I did it."

"You pretended to do it, and you even pretended reluctance, to make me more willing to trust you. Then you began to use your ingenuity to get him out of the way."

"I think I see what you mean," said Isabel.

"Where is the letter that you told me he had written me?" her husband asked.

"I haven't the least idea; I haven't asked him."

"You stopped it on the way," said Osmond.

Isabel slowly got up; standing there, in her white cloak,

which covered her to her feet, she might have represented the angel of disdain, first cousin to that of pity. "Oh, Osmond, for a man who was so fine!" she exclaimed, in a long murmur.

"I was never so fine as you! You have done everything you wanted. You have got him out of the way without appearing to do so, and you have placed me in the position in which you wished to see me—that of a man who tried to marry his daughter to a lord, but didn't succeed."

"Pansy doesn't care for him; she is very glad he is gone," said Isabel.

"That has nothing to do with the matter."

"And he doesn't care for Pansy."

"That won't do; you told me he did. I don't know why you wanted this particular satisfaction," Osmond continued; "you might have taken some other. It doesn't seem to me that I have been presumptuous—that I have taken too much for granted. I have been very modest about it, very quiet. The idea didn't originate with me. He began to show that he liked her before I ever thought of it. I left it all to you."

"Yes, you were very glad to leave it to me. After this you must attend to such things yourself."

He looked at her a moment, and then he turned away. "I thought you were very fond of my daughter."

"I have never been more so than to-day."

"Your affection is attended with immense limitations. However, that perhaps is natural."

"Is this all you wished to say to me?" Isabel asked, taking a candle that stood on one of the tables.

"Are you satisfied? Am I sufficiently disappointed?"

"I don't think that on the whole you are disappointed. You have had another opportunity to try to bewilder me."

"It's not that. It's proved that Pansy can aim high."

"Poor little Pansy!" said Isabel, turning away with her candle.

XLVII

IT WAS from Henrietta Stackpole that she learned that Caspar Goodwood had come to Rome; an event that took place three days after Lord Warburton's departure. This latter event had been preceded by an incident of some importance to Isabel—the temporary absence, once again, of Madame Merle, who had gone to Naples to stay with a friend, the happy possessor of a villa at Posilippo. Madame Merle had ceased to minister to Isabel's happiness, who found herself wondering whether the most discreet of women might not also by chance be the most dangerous. Sometimes, at night, she had strange visions; she seemed to see her husband and Madame Merle in dim, indistinguishable combination. It seemed to her that she had not done with her; this lady had something in reserve. Isabel's imagination applied itself actively to this elusive point, but every now and then it was checked by a nameless dread, so that when her brilliant friend was away from Rome she had almost a consciousness of respite. She had already learned from Miss Stackpole that Caspar Goodwood was in Europe, Henrietta having written to inform her of this fact immediately after meeting him in Paris. He himself never wrote to Isabel, and though he was in Europe she thought it very possible he might not desire to see her. Their last interview, before her marriage, had had quite the character of a complete rupture; if she remembered rightly he had said he wished to take his last look at her. Since then he had been the most inharmonious survival of her earlier time—the only one, in fact, with which a permanent pain was associated. He left her, that morning, with the sense of an unnecessary shock; it was like a collision between vessels in broad daylight. There had been no mist, no hidden current to excuse it, and she herself had only wished to steer skilfully. He had bumped against her prow, however, while her hand was on the tiller, and—to complete the metaphor—had given the lighter vessel a strain which still occasionally betrayed itself in a faint creaking. It had been painful to see him, because he represented the only serious harm that (to her belief) she had ever done in the world; he was the only person

with an unsatisfied claim upon her. She had made him unhappy; she couldn't help it; and his unhappiness was a great
reality. She cried with rage, after he had left her, at—she
hardly knew what: she tried to think it was at his want of
consideration. He had come to her with his unhappiness
when her own bliss was so perfect; he had done his best to
darken the brightness of these pure rays. He had not been
violent, and yet there was a violence in that. There was a violence at any rate in something, somewhere; perhaps it was
only in her own fit of weeping and that after-sense of it which
lasted for three or four days. The effect of Caspar Goodwood's visit faded away, and during the first year of Isabel's
marriage he dropped out of her books. He was a thankless
subject of reference; it was disagreeable to have to think of a
person who was unhappy on your account and whom you
could do nothing to relieve. It would have been different if
she had been able to doubt, even a little, of his unhappiness,
as she doubted of Lord Warburton's; unfortunately it was beyond question, and this aggressive, uncompromising look of
it was just what made it unattractive. She could never say to
herself that Caspar Goodwood had great compensations, as
she was able to say in the case of her English suitor. She had
no faith in his compensations, and no esteem for them. A
cotton-factory was not a compensation for anything—least of
all for having failed to marry Isabel Archer. And yet, beyond
that, she hardly knew what he had—save of course his intrinsic qualities. Oh, he was intrinsic enough; she never thought
of his even looking for artificial aids. If he extended his business—that, to the best of her belief, was the only form exertion could take with him—it would be because it was an
enterprising thing, or good for the business; not in the least
because he might hope it would overlay the past. This gave
his figure a kind of bareness and bleakness which made the
accident of meeting it in one's meditations always a sort of
shock; it was deficient in the social drapery which muffles the
sharpness of human contact. His perfect silence, moreover,
the fact that she never heard from him and very seldom heard
any mention of him, deepened this impression of his loneliness. She asked Lily for news of him, from time to time; but
Lily knew nothing about Boston; her imagination was con-

fined within the limits of Manhattan. As time went on Isabel
thought of him oftener, and with fewer restrictions; she had
more than once the idea of writing to him. She had never
told her husband about him—never let Osmond know of his
visits to her in Florence; a reserve not dictated in the early
period by a want of confidence in Osmond, but simply by the
consideration that Caspar Goodwood's disappointment was
not her secret but his own. It would be wrong of her, she
believed, to convey it to another, and Mr. Goodwood's affairs
could have, after all, but little interest for Gilbert. When it
came to the point she never wrote to him; it seemed to her
that, considering his grievance, the least she could do was to
let him alone. Nevertheless she would have been glad to be
in some way nearer to him. It was not that it ever occurred
to her that she might have married him; even after the consequences of her marriage became vivid to her, that particular
reflection, though she indulged in so many, had not the assurance to present itself. But when she found herself in trouble he became a member of that circle of things with which
she wished to set herself right. I have related how passionately
she desired to feel that her unhappiness should not have come
to her through her own fault. She had no near prospect of
dying, and yet she wished to make her peace with the
world—to put her spiritual affairs in order. It came back to
her from time to time that there was an account still to be
settled with Caspar Goodwood; it seemed to her that she
would settle it to-day on terms easy for him. Still, when she
learned that he was coming to Rome she felt afraid; it would
be more disagreeable for him than for any one else to learn
that she was unhappy. Deep in her breast she believed that he
had invested all his in her happiness, while the others had
invested only a part. He was one more person from whom
she should have to conceal her misery. She was reassured,
however, after he arrived in Rome, for he spent several days
without coming to see her.

Henrietta Stackpole, it may well be imagined, was much
more punctual, and Isabel was largely favoured with the society of her friend. She threw herself into it, for now that she
had made such a point of keeping her conscience clear, that
was one way of proving that she had not been superficial—

the more so that the years, in their flight, had rather enriched than blighted those peculiarities which had been humorously criticised by persons less interested than Isabel and were striking enough to give friendship a spice of heroism. Henrietta was as keen and quick and fresh as ever, and as neat and bright and fair. Her eye had lost none of its serenity, her toilet none of its crispness, her opinions none of their national flavour. She was by no means quite unchanged, however; it seemed to Isabel that she had grown restless. Of old she had never been restless; though she was perpetually in motion it was impossible to be more deliberate. She had a reason for everything she did; she fairly bristled with motives. Formerly, when she came to Europe it was because she wished to see it, but now, having already seen it, she had no such excuse. She did not for a moment pretend that the desire to examine decaying civilizations had anything to do with her present enterprise; her journey was rather an expression of her independence of the old world than of a sense of further obligations to it. "It's nothing to come to Europe," she said to Isabel; "it doesn't seem to me one needs so many reasons for that. It is something to stay at home; this is much more important." It was not therefore with a sense of doing anything very important that she treated herself to another pilgrimage to Rome; she had seen the place before and carefully inspected it; the actual episode was simply a sign of familiarity, of one's knowing all about it, of one's having as good a right as any one else to be there. This was all very well, and Henrietta was restless; she had a perfect right to be restless, too, if one came to that. But she had after all a better reason for coming to Rome than that she cared for it so little. Isabel easily recognised it, and with it the worth of her friend's fidelity. She had crossed the stormy ocean in midwinter because she guessed that Isabel was sad. Henrietta guessed a great deal, but she had never guessed so happily as that. Isabel's satisfactions just now were few, but even if they had been more numerous, there would still have been something of individual joy in her sense of being justified in having always thought highly of Henrietta. She had made large concessions with regard to her, but she had insisted that, with all abatements, she was very valuable. It was not her own triumph, however, that Isabel found good; it was simply the relief of confessing to Henrietta, the first person to whom she had owned it, that she was not contented. Henrietta had herself approached this point with the smallest possible delay, and had accused her to her face of being miserable. She was a woman, she was a sister; she was not Ralph, nor Lord Warburton, nor Caspar Goodwood, and Isabel could speak.

"Yes, I am miserable," she said, very gently. She hated to hear herself say it; she tried to say it as judicially as possible.

"What does he do to you?" Henrietta asked, frowning as if she were inquiring into the operations of a quack doctor.

"He does nothing. But he doesn't like me."

"He's very difficult!" cried Miss Stackpole. "Why don't you leave him?"

"I can't change, that way," Isabel said.

"Why not, I should like to know? You won't confess that you have made a mistake. You are too proud."

"I don't know whether I am too proud. But I can't publish my mistake. I don't think that's decent. I would much rather die."

"You won't think so always," said Henrietta.

"I don't know what great unhappiness might bring me to; but it seems to me I shall always be ashamed. One must accept one's deeds. I married him before all the world; I was perfectly free; it was impossible to do anything more deliberate. One can't change, that way," Isabel repeated.

"You have changed, in spite of the impossibility. I hope you don't mean to say that you like him."

Isabel hesitated a moment. "No, I don't like him. I can tell you, because I am weary of my secret. But that's enough; I can't tell all the world."

Henrietta gave a rich laugh. "Don't you think you are rather too considerate?"

"It's not of him that I am considerate—it's of myself!" Isabel answered.

It was not surprising that Gilbert Osmond should not have taken comfort in Miss Stackpole; his instinct had naturally set him in opposition to a young lady capable of advising his wife to withdraw from the conjugal mansion. When she arrived in Rome he said to Isabel that he hoped she would leave her friend the interviewer, alone; and Isabel answered that he at least had nothing to fear from her. She said to Henrietta that as Osmond didn't like her she could not invite her to dine; but they could easily see each other in other ways. Isabel received Miss Stackpole freely in her own sitting-room, and took her repeatedly to drive, face to face with Pansy, who, bending a little forward, on the opposite seat of the carriage, gazed at the celebrated authoress with a respectful attention which Henrietta occasionally found irritating. She complained to Isabel that Miss Osmond had a little look as if she should remember everything one said. "I don't want to be remembered that way," Miss Stackpole declared; "I consider that my conversation refers only to the moment, like the morning papers. Your step-daughter, as she sits there, looks as if she kept all the back numbers and would bring them out some day against me." She could not bring herself to think favourably of Pansy, whose absence of initiative, of conversation, of personal claims, seemed to her, in a girl of twenty, unnatural and even sinister. Isabel presently saw that Osmond would have liked her to urge a little the cause of her friend, insist a little upon his receiving her, so that he might appear to suffer for good manners' sake. Her immediate acceptance of his objections put him too much in the wrong—it being in effect one of the disadvantages of expressing contempt, that you cannot enjoy at the same time the credit of expressing sympathy. Osmond held to his credit, and yet he held to his objections—all of which were elements difficult to reconcile. The right thing would have been that Miss Stackpole should come to dine at the Palazzo Roccanera once or twice, so that (in spite of his superficial civility, always so great) she might judge for herself how little pleasure it gave him. From the moment, however, that both the ladies were so unaccommodating, there was nothing for Osmond but to wish that Henrietta would take herself off. It was surprising how little satisfaction he got from his wife's friends; he took occasion to call Isabel's attention to it.

"You are certainly not fortunate in your intimates; I wish you might make a new collection," he said to her one morning, in reference to nothing visible at the moment, but in a tone of ripe reflection which deprived the remark of all brutal abruptness. "It's as if you had taken the trouble to pick out the people in the world that I have least in common with. Your cousin I have always thought a conceited ass—besides his being the most ill-favoured animal I know. Then it's insufferably tiresome that one can't tell him so; one must spare him on account of his health. His health seems to me the best part of him; it gives him privileges enjoyed by no one else. If he is so desperately ill there is only one way to prove it; but he seems to have no mind for that. I can't say much more for the great Warburton. When one really thinks of it, the cool insolence of that performance was something rare! He comes and looks at one's daughter as if she were a suite of apartments; he tries the door-handles and looks out of the windows, raps on the walls and almost thinks he will take the place. Will you be so good as to draw up a lease? Then, on the whole, he decides that the rooms are too small; he doesn't think he could live on a third floor; he must look out for a *piano nobile*. And he goes away, after having got a month's lodging in the poor little apartment for nothing. Miss Stackpole, however, is your most wonderful invention. She strikes me as a kind of monster. One hasn't a nerve in one's body that she doesn't set quivering. You know I never have admitted that she is a woman. Do you know what she reminds me of? Of a new steel pen—the most odious thing in nature. She talks as a steel pen writes; aren't her letters, by the way, on ruled paper? She thinks and moves, and walks and looks, exactly as she talks. You may say that she doesn't hurt me, inasmuch as I don't see her. I don't see her, but I hear her; I hear her all day long. Her voice is in my ears; I can't get rid of it. I know exactly what she says, and every inflection of the tone in which she says it. She says charming things about me, and they give you great comfort. I don't like at all to think she talks about me—I feel as I should feel if I knew the footman were wearing my hat!"

Henrietta talked about Gilbert Osmond, as his wife assured him, rather less than he suspected. She had plenty of other subjects, in two of which the reader may be supposed to be especially interested. She let Isabel know that Caspar Goodwood had discovered for himself that she was unhappy, though indeed her ingenuity was unable to suggest what

comfort he hoped to give her by coming to Rome and yet
not calling on her. They met him twice in the street, but he
had no appearance of seeing them; they were driving, and he
had a habit of looking straight in front of him, as if he proposed to contemplate but one object at a time. Isabel could
have fancied she had seen him the day before; it must have
been with just that face and step that he walked out of Mrs.
Touchett's door at the close of their last interview. He was
dressed just as he had been dressed on that day; Isabel remembered the colour of his cravat; and yet in spite of this
familiar look there was a strangeness in his figure too; something that made her feel afresh that it was rather terrible he
should have come to Rome. He looked bigger and more
over-topping than of old, and in those days he certainly was
lofty enough. She noticed that the people whom he passed
looked back after him; but he went straight forward, lifting
above them a face like a February sky.

Miss Stackpole's other topic was very different; she gave
Isabel the latest news about Mr. Bantling. He had been out
in the United States the year before, and she was happy to
say she had been able to show him considerable attention.
She didn't know how much he had enjoyed it, but she would
undertake to say it had done him good; he wasn't the same
man when he left that he was when he came. It had opened
his eyes and shown him that England was not everything. He
was very much liked over there, and thought extremely simple—more simple than the English were commonly supposed
to be. There were some people thought him affected; she
didn't know whether they meant that his simplicity was an
affectation. Some of his questions were too discouraging; he
thought all the chamber-maids were farmers' daughters—or
all the farmers' daughters were chamber-maids—she couldn't
exactly remember which. He hadn't seemed able to grasp the
school-system; it seemed really too much for him. On the
whole he had appeared as if there were too much—as if he
could only take a small part. The part he had chosen was the
hotel-system, and the river-navigation. He seemed really fascinated with the hotels; he had a photograph of every one he
had visited. But the river-steamers were his principal interest;
he wanted to do nothing but sail on the big boats. They had

travelled together from New York to Milwaukee, stopping at the most interesting cities on the route; and whenever they started afresh he had wanted to know if they could go by the steamer. He seemed to have no idea of geography—had an impression that Baltimore was a western city, and was perpetually expecting to arrive at the Mississippi. He appeared never to have heard of any river in America but the Mississippi, and was unprepared to recognise the existence of the Hudson, though he was obliged to confess at last that it was fully equal to the Rhine. They had spent some pleasant hours in the palace-cars; he was always ordering ice-cream from the coloured man. He could never get used to that idea—that you could get ice-cream in the cars. Of course you couldn't, nor fans, nor candy, nor anything in the English cars! He found the heat quite overwhelming, and she had told him that she expected it was the greatest he had ever experienced. He was now in England, hunting—"hunting round," Henrietta called it. These amusements were those of the American red men; we had left that behind long ago, the pleasures of the chase. It seemed to be generally believed in England that we wore tomahawks and feathers; but such a costume was more in keeping with English habits. Mr. Bantling would not have time to join her in Italy, but when she should go to Paris again he expected to come over. He wanted very much to see Versailles again; he was very fond of the ancient *régime*. They didn't agree about that, but that was what she liked Versailles for, that you could see the ancient *régime* had been swept away. There were no dukes and marquises there now; on the contrary, she remembered one day when there were five American families, all walking round. Mr. Bantling was very anxious that she should take up the subject of England again, and he thought she might get on better with it now; England had changed a good deal within two or three years. He was determined that if she went there he should go to see his sister, Lady Pensil, and that this time the invitation should come to her straight. The mystery of that other one had never been explained.

Caspar Goodwood came at last to the Palazzo Roccanera; he had written Isabel a note beforehand, to ask leave. This was promptly granted; she would be at home at six o'clock that afternoon. She spent the day wondering what he was coming for—what good he expected to get of it. He had presented himself hitherto as a person destitute of the faculty of compromise, who would take what he had asked for or nothing. Isabel's hospitality, however, asked no questions, and she found no great difficulty in appearing happy enough to deceive him. It was her conviction, at least, that she deceived him, and made him say to himself that he had been misinformed. But she also saw, so she believed, that he was not disappointed, as some other men, she was sure, would have been; he had not come to Rome to look for an opportunity. She never found out what he had come for; he offered her no explanation; there could be none but the very simple one that he wanted to see her. In other words, he had come for his amusement. Isabel followed up this induction with a good deal of eagerness, and was delighted to have found a formula that would lay the ghost of this gentleman's ancient grievance. If he had come to Rome for his amusement this was exactly what she wanted; for if he cared for amusement he had got over his heartache. If he had got over his heartache everything was as it should be, and her responsibilities were at an end. It was true that he took his recreation a little stiffly, but he had never been demonstrative, and Isabel had every reason to believe that he was satisfied with what he saw. Henrietta was not in his confidence, though he was in hers, and Isabel consequently received no side-light upon his state of mind. He had little conversation upon general topics; it came back to her that she had said of him once, years before—"Mr. Goodwood speaks a good deal, but he doesn't talk." He spoke a good deal in Rome, but he talked, perhaps, as little as ever; considering, that is, how much there was to talk about. His arrival was not calculated to simplify her relations with her husband, for if Mr. Osmond didn't like her friends, Mr. Goodwood had no claim upon his attention save having been one of the first of them. There was nothing for her to say of him but that he was an old friend; this rather meagre synthesis exhausted the facts. She had been obliged to introduce him to Osmond; it was impossible she should not ask him to dinner, to her Thursday evenings, of which she had grown very weary, but to which her husband still held for the sake not so much of inviting people as of not inviting them. To the Thursdays Mr. Goodwood came regularly, solemnly, rather early; he appeared to regard them with a good deal of gravity. Isabel every now and then had a moment of anger; there was something so literal about him; she thought he might know that she didn't know what to do with him. But she couldn't call him stupid; he was not that in the least; he was only extraordinarily honest. To be as honest as that made a man very different from most people; one had to be almost equally honest with him. Isabel made this latter reflection at the very time she was flattering herself that she had persuaded him that she was the most light-hearted of women. He never threw any doubt on this point, never asked her any personal questions. He got on much better with Osmond than had seemed probable. Osmond had a great dislike to being counted upon; in such a case he had an irresistible need of disappointing you. It was in virtue of this principle that he gave himself the entertainment of taking a fancy to a perpendicular Bostonian whom he had been depended upon to treat with coldness. He asked Isabel if Mr. Goodwood also had wanted to marry her, and expressed surprise at her not having accepted him. It would have been an excellent thing, like living under a tall belfry which would strike all the hours and make a queer vibration in the upper air. He declared he liked to talk with the great Goodwood; it wasn't easy at first, you had to climb up an interminable steep staircase up to the top of the tower; but when you got there you had a big view and felt a little fresh breeze. Osmond, as we know, had delightful qualities, and he gave Caspar Goodwood the benefit of them all. Isabel could see that Mr. Goodwood thought better of her husband than he had ever wished to; he had given her the impression that morning in Florence of being inaccessible to a good impression. Osmond asked him repeatedly to dinner, and Goodwood smoked a cigar with him afterwards, and even desired to be shown his collections. Osmond said to Isabel that he was very original; he was as strong as an English portmanteau. Caspar Goodwood took to riding on the Campagna, and devoted much time to this exercise; it was therefore mainly in the evening that Isabel saw him. She bethought herself of saying to him one day that if he were willing he could render her a service. And then she added smiling—

"I don't know, however, what right I have to ask a service of you."

"You are the person in the world who has most right," he answered. "I have given you assurances that I have never given any one else."

The service was that he should go and see her cousin Ralph, who was ill at the Hôtel de Paris, alone, and be as kind to him as possible. Mr. Goodwood had never seen him, but he would know who the poor fellow was; if she was not mistaken, Ralph had once invited him to Gardencourt. Caspar remembered the invitation perfectly, and, though he was not supposed to be a man of imagination, had enough to put himself in the place of a poor gentleman who lay dying at a Roman inn. He called at the Hôtel de Paris, and on being shown into the presence of the master of Gardencourt, found Miss Stackpole sitting beside his sofa. A singular change had, in fact, occurred in this lady's relations with Ralph Touchett. She had not been asked by Isabel to go and see him, but on hearing that he was too ill to come out had immediately gone of her own motion. After this she had paid him a daily visit—always under the conviction that they were great enemies. "Oh yes, we are intimate enemies," Ralph used to say; and he accused her freely—as freely as the humour of it would allow—of coming to worry him to death. In reality they became excellent friends, and Henrietta wondered that she should never have liked him before. Ralph liked her exactly as much as he had always done; he had never doubted for a moment that she was an excellent fellow. They talked about everything, and always differed; about everything, that is, but Isabel—a topic as to which Ralph always had a thin forefinger on his lips. On the other hand, Mr. Bantling was a great resource; Ralph was capable of discussing Mr. Bantling with Henrietta for hours. Discussion was stimulated of course by their inevitable difference of view—Ralph having amused himself with taking the ground that the genial ex-guardsman was a regular Machiavelli. Caspar Goodwood could contribute nothing to such a debate; but after he had been left alone with Touchett, he found there were various other matters they could talk about. It must be admitted that the lady who had just gone out was not one of these; Caspar granted all Miss Stackpole's merits in advance, but had no further remark to make about her. Neither, after the first allusions, did the two men expatiate upon Mrs. Osmond—a theme in which Goodwood perceived as many dangers as his host. He felt very sorry for Ralph; he couldn't bear to see a pleasant man so helpless. There was help in Goodwood, when once the fountain had been tapped; and he repeated several times his visit to the Hôtel de Paris. It seemed to Isabel that she had been very clever; she had disposed of the superfluous Caspar. She had given him an occupation; she had converted him into a care-taker of Ralph. She had a plan of making him travel northward with her cousin as soon as the first mild weather should allow it. Lord Warburton had brought Ralph to Rome, and Mr. Goodwood should take him away. There seemed a happy symmetry in this, and she was now intensely eager that Ralph should leave Rome. She had a constant fear that he would die there, and a horror of this event occurring at an inn, at her door, which he had so rarely entered. Ralph must sink to his last rest in his own dear house, in one of those deep, dim chambers of Gardencourt, where the dark ivy would cluster round the edges of the glimmering window. There seemed to Isabel in these days something sacred about Gardencourt; no chapter of the past was more perfectly irrecoverable. When she thought of the months she had spent there the tears rose to her eyes. She flattered herself, as I say, upon her ingenuity, but she had need of all she could muster; for several events occurred which seemed to confront and defy her. The Countess Gemini arrived from Florence—arrived with her trunks, her dresses, her chatter, her little fibs, her frivolity, the strange memory of her lovers. Edward Rosier, who had been away somewhere—no one, not even Pansy, knew where—reappeared in Rome and began to write her long letters, which she never answered. Madame Merle returned from Naples and said to her with a strange smile— "What on earth did you do with Lord Warburton?" As if it were any business of hers!

XLVIII

O NE DAY, toward the end of February, Ralph Touchett made up his mind to return to England. He had his own reasons for this decision, which he was not bound to communicate; but Henrietta Stackpole, to whom he mentioned his intention, flattered herself that she guessed them. She forbore to express them, however; she only said, after a moment, as she sat by his sofa—

"I suppose you know that you can't go alone?"

"I have no idea of doing that," Ralph answered. "I shall have people with me."

"What do you mean by 'people'? Servants, whom you pay?"

"Ah," said Ralph, jocosely, "after all, they are human beings."

"Are there any women among them?" Miss Stackpole inquired, calmly.

"You speak as if I had a dozen! No, I confess I haven't a soubrette in my employment."

"Well," said Henrietta, tranquilly, "you can't go to England that way. You must have a woman's care."

"I have had so much of yours for the past fortnight that it will last me a good while."

"You have not had enough of it yet. I guess I will go with you," said Henrietta.

"Go with me?" Ralph slowly raised himself from his sofa.

"Yes, I know you don't like me, but I will go with you all the same. It would be better for your health to lie down again."

Ralph looked at her a little; then he slowly resumed his former posture.

"I like you very much," he said in a moment.

Miss Stackpole gave one of her infrequent laughs.

"You needn't think that by saying that you can buy me off. I will go with you, and what is more I will take care of you."

"You are a very good woman," said Ralph.

"Wait till I get you safely home before you say that. It won't be easy. But you had better go, all the same."

Before she left him, Ralph said to her—

"Do you really mean to take care of me?"

"Well, I mean to try."

"I notify you, then, that I submit. Oh, I submit!" And it was perhaps a sign of submission that a few minutes after she had left him alone he burst into a loud fit of laughter. It seemed to him so inconsequent, such a conclusive proof of his having abdicated all functions and renounced all exercise, that he should start on a journey across Europe under the supervision of Miss Stackpole. And the great oddity was that the prospect pleased him; he was gratefully, luxuriously passive. He felt even impatient to start; and indeed he had an immense longing to see his own house again. The end of everything was at hand; it seemed to him that he could stretch out his arm and touch the goal. But he wished to die at home; it was the only wish he had left—to extend himself in the large quiet room where he had last seen his father lie, and close his eyes upon the summer dawn.

That same day Caspar Goodwood came to see him, and he informed his visitor that Miss Stackpole had taken him up and was to conduct him back to England.

"Ah then," said Caspar, "I am afraid I shall be a fifth wheel to the coach. Mrs. Osmond has made *me* promise to go with you."

"Good heavens—it's the golden age! You are all too kind."

"The kindness on my part is to her; it's hardly to you."

"Granting that, *she* is kind," said Ralph, smiling.

"To get people to go with you? Yes, that's a sort of kindness," Goodwood answered, without lending himself to the joke. "For myself, however," he added, "I will go so far as to say that I would much rather travel with you and Miss Stackpole than with Miss Stackpole alone."

"And you would rather stay here than do either," said Ralph. "There is really no need of your coming. Henrietta is extraordinarily efficient."

"I am sure of that. But I have promised Mrs. Osmond."

"You can easily get her to let you off."

"She wouldn't let me off for the world. She wants me to look after you, but that isn't the principal thing. The principal thing is that she wants me to leave Rome."

"Ah, you see too much in it," Ralph suggested.

"I bore her," Goodwood went on; "she has nothing to say to me, so she invented that."

"Oh then, if it's a convenience to her, I certainly will take you with me. Though I don't see why it should be a convenience," Ralph added in a moment.

"Well," said Caspar Goodwood, simply, "she thinks I am watching her."

"Watching her?"

"Trying to see whether she's happy."

"That's easy to see," said Ralph. "She's the most visibly happy woman I know."

"Exactly so; I am satisfied," Goodwood answered, dryly. For all his dryness, however, he had more to say. "I have been watching her; I was an old friend, and it seemed to me I had the right. She pretends to be happy; that was what she undertook to be; and I thought I should like to see for myself what it amounts to. I have seen," he continued, in a strange voice, "and I don't want to see any more. I am now quite ready to go."

"Do you know it strikes me as about time you should?" Ralph rejoined. And this was the only conversation these gentlemen had about Isabel Osmond.

Henrietta made her preparations for departure, and among them she found it proper to say a few words to the Countess Gemini, who returned at Miss Stackpole's *pension* the visit which this lady had paid her in Florence.

"You were very wrong about Lord Warburton," she remarked, to the Countess. "I think it is right you should know that."

"About his making love to Isabel? My poor lady, he was at her house three times a day. He has left traces of his passage!" the Countess cried.

"He wished to marry your niece; that's why he came to the house."

The Countess stared, and then gave an inconsiderate laugh.

"Is that the story that Isabel tells? It isn't bad, as such things go. If he wishes to marry my niece, pray why doesn't he do it? Perhaps he has gone to buy the wedding-ring, and will come back with it next month, after I am gone."

"No, he will not come back. Miss Osmond doesn't wish to marry him."

"She is very accommodating! I knew she was fond of Isabel, but I didn't know she carried it so far."

"I don't understand you," said Henrietta, coldly, and reflecting that the Countess was unpleasantly perverse. "I really must stick to my point—that Isabel never encouraged the attentions of Lord Warburton."

"My dear friend, what do you and I know about it? All we know is that my brother is capable of everything."

"I don't know what he is capable of," said Henrietta, with dignity.

"It's not her encouraging Lord Warburton that I complain of; it's her sending him away. I want particularly to see him. Do you suppose she thought I would make him faithless?" the Countess continued, with audacious insistence. "However, she is only keeping him, one can feel that. The house is full of him there; he is quite in the air. Oh yes, he has left traces; I am sure I shall see him yet."

"Well," said Henrietta, after a little, with one of those inspirations which had made the fortune of her letters to the *Interviewer*, "perhaps he will be more successful with you than with Isabel!"

When she told her friend of the offer she had made to Ralph, Isabel replied that she could have done nothing that would have pleased her more. It had always been her faith that, at bottom, Ralph and Henrietta were made to understand each other.

"I don't care whether he understands me or not," said Henrietta. "The great thing is that he shouldn't die in the cars."

"He won't do that," Isabel said, shaking her head, with an extension of faith.

"He won't if I can help it. I see you want us all to go. I don't know what you want to do."

"I want to be alone," said Isabel.

"You won't be that so long as you have got so much company at home."

"Ah, they are part of the comedy. You others are spectators."

"Do you call it a comedy, Isabel Archer?" Henrietta inquired, severely.

"The tragedy, then, if you like. You are all looking at me; it makes me uncomfortable."

Henrietta contemplated her a while.

"You are like the stricken deer, seeking the innermost shade. Oh, you do give me such a sense of helplessness!" she broke out.

"I am not at all helpless. There are many things I mean to do."

"It's not you I am speaking of; it's myself. It's too much, having come on purpose, to leave you just as I find you."

"You don't do that; you leave me much refreshed," Isabel said.

"Very mild refreshment—sour lemonade! I want you to promise me something."

"I can't do that. I shall never make another promise. I made such a solemn one four years ago, and I have succeeded so ill in keeping it."

"You have had no encouragement. In this case I should give you the greatest. Leave your husband before the worst comes; that's what I want you to promise."

"The worst? What do you call the worst?"

"Before your character gets spoiled."

"Do you mean my disposition? It won't get spoiled," Isabel answered, smiling. "I am taking very good care of it. I am extremely struck," she added, turning away, "with the offhand way in which you speak of a woman leaving her husband. It's easy to see you have never had one!"

"Well," said Henrietta, as if she were beginning an argument, "nothing is more common in our western cities, and it is to them, after all, that we must look in the future." Her argument, however, does not concern this history, which has too many other threads to unwind. She announced to Ralph Touchett that she was ready to leave Rome by any train that he might designate, and Ralph immediately pulled himself together for departure. Isabel went to see him at the last, and he made the same remark that Henrietta had made. It struck him that Isabel was uncommonly glad to get rid of them all.

For all answer to this she gently laid her hand on his, and said in a low tone, with a quick smile—

"My dear Ralph!"

It was answer enough, and he was quite contented. But he went on, in the same way, jocosely, ingenuously—"I've seen less of you than I might, but it's better than nothing. And then I have heard a great deal about you."

"I don't know from whom, leading the life you have done."

"From the voices of the air! Oh, from no one else; I never let other people speak of you. They always say you are 'charming,' and that's so flat."

"I might have seen more of you, certainly," Isabel said. "But when one is married one has so much occupation."

"Fortunately I am not married. When you come to see me in England, I shall be able to entertain you with all the freedom of a bachelor." He continued to talk as if they should certainly meet again, and succeeded in making the assumption appear almost just. He made no allusion to his term being near, to the probability that he should not outlast the summer. If he preferred it so, Isabel was willing enough; the reality was sufficiently distinct, without their erecting finger-posts in conversation. That had been well enough for the earlier time, though about this as about his other affairs Ralph had never been egotistic. Isabel spoke of his journey, of the stages into which he should divide it, of the precautions he should take.

"Henrietta is my greatest precaution," Ralph said. "The conscience of that woman is sublime."

"Certainly, she will be very conscientious."

"Will be? She has been! It's only because she thinks it's her duty that she goes with me. There's a conception of duty for you."

"Yes, it's a generous one," said Isabel, "and it makes me deeply ashamed. I ought to go with you, you know."

"Your husband wouldn't like that."

"No, he wouldn't like it. But I might go, all the same."

"I am startled by the boldness of your imagination. Fancy my being a cause of disagreement between a lady and her husband!"

"That's why I don't go," said Isabel, simply, but not very lucidly.

Ralph understood well enough, however. "I should think so, with all those occupations you speak of."

"It isn't that. I am afraid," said Isabel. After a pause she repeated, as if to make herself, rather than him, hear the words—"I am afraid."

Ralph could hardly tell what her tone meant; it was so strangely deliberate—apparently so void of emotion. Did she wish to do public penance for a fault of which she had not been convicted? or were her words simply an attempt at enlightened self-analysis? However this might be, Ralph could not resist so easy an opportunity. "Afraid of your husband?" he said, jocosely.

"Afraid of myself!" said Isabel, getting up. She stood there a moment, and then she added—"If I were afraid of my husband, that would be simply my duty. That is what women are expected to be."

"Ah, yes," said Ralph, laughing; "but to make up for it there is always some man awfully afraid of some woman!"

She gave no heed to this pleasantry, but suddenly took a different turn. "With Henrietta at the head of your little band," she exclaimed abruptly, "there will be nothing left for Mr. Goodwood!"

"Ah, my dear Isabel," Ralph answered, "he's used to that. There *is* nothing left for Mr. Goodwood!"

Isabel coloured, and then she declared, quickly, that she must leave him. They stood together a moment; both her hands were in both of his. "You have been my best friend," she said.

"It was for you that I wanted—that I wanted to live. But I am of no use to you."

Then it came over her more poignantly that she should not see him again. She could not accept that; she could not part with him that way. "If you should send for me I would come," she said at last.

"Your husband won't consent to that."

"Oh yes, I can arrange it."

"I shall keep that for my last pleasure!" said Ralph.

In answer to which she simply kissed him.

It was a Thursday, and that evening Caspar Goodwood came to the Palazzo Roccanera. He was among the first to arrive, and he spent some time in conversation with Gilbert Osmond, who almost always was present when his wife received. They sat down together, and Osmond, talkative, communicative, expansive, seemed possessed with a kind of intellectual gaiety. He leaned back with his legs crossed, lounging and chatting, while Goodwood, more restless, but not at all lively, shifted his position, played with his hat, made the little sofa creak beneath him. Osmond's face wore a sharp, aggressive smile; he was like a man whose perceptions had been quickened by good news. He remarked to Goodwood that he was very sorry they were to lose him; he himself should particularly miss him. He saw so few intelligent men—they were surprisingly scarce in Rome. He must be sure to come back; there was something very refreshing, to an inveterate Italian like himself, in talking with a genuine outsider.

"I am very fond of Rome, you know," Osmond said; "but there is nothing I like better than to meet people who haven't that superstition. The modern world is after all very fine. Now you are thoroughly modern, and yet you are not at all flimsy. So many of the moderns we see are such very poor stuff. If they are the children of the future we are willing to die young. Of course the ancients too are often very tiresome. My wife and I like everything that is really new—not the mere pretence of it. There is nothing new, unfortunately, in ignorance and stupidity. We see plenty of that in forms that offer themselves as a revelation of progress, of light. A revelation of vulgarity! There is a certain kind of vulgarity which I believe is really new; I don't think there ever was anything like it before. Indeed I don't find vulgarity, at all, before the present century. You see a faint menace of it here and there in the last, but to-day the air has grown so dense that delicate things are literally not recognised. Now, we have liked you——" And Osmond hesitated a moment, laying his hand gently on Goodwood's knee and smiling with a mixture of assurance and embarrassment. "I am going to say something extremely offensive and patronising, but you must let me have the satisfaction of it. We have liked you because—because you have reconciled us a little to the future. If there are to be a certain number of people like you—*à la bonne heure!* I am talking for my wife as well as for myself, you see. She speaks for me; why shouldn't I speak for her? We are as united, you know, as the candlestick and the snuffers. Am I assuming too much when I say that I think I have understood from you that your occupations have been—a—commercial? There is a danger in that, you know; but it's the way you have escaped that strikes us. Excuse me if my little compliment seems in execrable taste; fortunately my wife doesn't hear me. What I mean is that you *might have been*—a—what I was mentioning just now. The whole American world was in a conspiracy to make you so. But you resisted, you have something that saved you. And yet you are so modern, so modern; the most modern man we know! We shall always be delighted to see you again."

I have said that Osmond was in good-humour, and these remarks will give ample evidence of the fact. They were infinitely more personal than he usually cared to be, and if Caspar Goodwood had attended to them more closely he might have thought that the defence of delicacy was in rather odd hands. We may believe, however, that Osmond knew very well what he was about, and that if he chose for once to be a little vulgar, he had an excellent reason for the escapade. Goodwood had only a vague sense that he was laying it on, somehow; he scarcely knew where the mixture was applied. Indeed he scarcely knew what Osmond was talking about; he wanted to be alone with Isabel, and that idea spoke louder to him than her husband's perfectly modulated voice. He watched her talking with other people, and wondered when she would be at liberty, and whether he might ask her to go into one of the other rooms. His humour was not, like Osmond's, of the best; there was an element of dull rage in his consciousness of things. Up to this time he had not disliked Osmond personally; he had only thought him very well-informed and obliging, and more than he had supposed like the person whom Isabel Archer would naturally marry. Osmond had won in the open field a great advantage over him, and Goodwood had too strong a sense of fair play to have been moved to underrate him on that account. He had not tried positively to like him; this was a flight of sentimental benevolence of which, even in the days when he came nearest to reconciling himself to what had happened, Goodwood was quite incapable. He accepted him as a rather brilliant personage of the amateurish kind, afflicted with a redundancy of leisure which it amused him to work off in little refinements of conversation. But he only half trusted him; he could never make out why the deuce Osmond should lavish refinements of any sort upon *him*. It made him suspect that he found some private entertainment in it, and it ministered to a general impression that his successful rival had a fantastic streak in his composition. He knew indeed that Osmond could have no reason to wish him evil; he had nothing to fear from him. He had carried off a supreme advantage, and he could afford to be kind to a man who had lost everything. It was true that Goodwood at times had wished Osmond were dead, and would have liked to kill him; but Osmond had no means of knowing this, for practice had made Goodwood quite perfect in the art of appearing inaccessible to-day to any violent emotion. He cultivated this art in order to deceive himself, but it was others that he deceived first. He cultivated it, moreover, with very limited success; of which there could be no better proof than the deep, dumb irritation that reigned in his soul when he heard Osmond speak of his wife's feelings as if he were commissioned to answer for them. That was all he had an ear for in what his host said to him this evening; he was conscious that Osmond made more of a point even than usual of referring to the conjugal harmony which prevailed at the Palazzo Roccanera. He was more careful than ever to speak as if he and his wife had all things in sweet community, and it were as natural to each of them to say " we" as to say "I." In all this there was an air of intention which puzzled and angered our poor Bostonian, who could only reflect for his comfort that Mrs. Osmond's relations with her husband were none of his business. He had no proof whatever that her husband misrepresented her, and if he judged her by the surface of things was bound to believe that she liked her life. She had never given him the faintest sign of discontent. Miss Stackpole had told him that she had lost her illusions, but writing for the papers had made Miss Stackpole sensational. She was too fond of early news. Moreover, since her arrival in Rome she had been much on her guard; she had ceased to flash her lantern at him. This, indeed, it may be said for her, would have been quite against her conscience. She had now seen the reality of Isabel's situation, and it had inspired her with a just reserve. Whatever could be done to improve it, the most useful form of assistance would not be to inflame her former lovers with a sense of her wrongs. Miss Stackpole continued to take a deep interest in the state of Mr. Goodwood's feelings, but she showed it at present only by sending him choice extracts, humorous and other, from the American journals, of which she received several by every post and which she always perused with a pair of scissors in her hand. The articles she cut out she placed in an envelope addressed to Mr. Goodwood, which she left with her own hand at his hotel. He never asked her a question about Isabel; hadn't he come five thousand miles to see for himself? He was thus not in the least authorised to think Mrs. Osmond unhappy; but the very absence of authorisation operated as an irritant, ministered to the angry pain with which, in spite of his theory that he had ceased to care, he now recognised that, as far as she was concerned, the future had nothing more for him. He had not even the satisfaction of knowing the truth; apparently he could not even be trusted to respect her if she *were* unhappy. He was hopeless, he was helpless, he was superfluous. To this last fact she had called his attention by her ingenious plan for making him leave Rome. He had no objection whatever to doing what he could for her cousin, but it made him grind his teeth to think that of all the services she might have asked of him this was the one she had been eager to select. There had been no danger of her choosing one that would have kept him in Rome!

To-night what he was chiefly thinking of was that he was to leave her to-morrow, and that he had gained nothing by coming but the knowledge that he was as superfluous as ever. About herself he had gained no knowledge; she was imperturbable, impenetrable. He felt the old bitterness, which he had tried so hard to swallow, rise again in his throat, and he knew that there are disappointments which last as long as life. Osmond went on talking; Goodwood was vaguely aware that he was touching again upon his perfect intimacy with his wife. It seemed to him for a moment that Osmond had a kind of demoniac imagination; it was impossible that without malice he should have selected so unusual a topic. But what did it matter, after all, whether he were demoniac or not, and whether she loved him or hated him? She might hate him to the death without Goodwood's gaining by it.

"You travel, by the by, with Touchett," Osmond said. "I suppose that means that you will move slowly?"

"I don't know; I shall do just as he likes."

"You are very accommodating. We are immensely obliged to you; you must really let me say it. My wife has probably expressed to you what we feel. Touchett has been on our minds all winter; it has looked more than once as if he would never leave Rome. He ought never to have come; it's worse than an imprudence for people in that state to travel; it's a kind of indelicacy. I wouldn't for the world be under such an obligation to Touchett as he has been to—to my wife and me. Other people inevitably have to look after him, and every one isn't so generous as you."

"I have nothing else to do," said Caspar, dryly.

Osmond looked at him a moment, askance. "You ought to marry, and then you would have plenty to do! It is true that in that case you wouldn't be quite so available for deeds of mercy."

"Do you find that as a married man you are so much occupied?"

"Ah, you see, being married is in itself an occupation. It isn't always active; it's often passive; but that takes even more attention. Then my wife and I do so many things together. We read, we study, we make music, we walk, we drive—we talk even, as when we first knew each other. I delight, to this hour, in my wife's conversation. If you are ever bored, get married. Your wife indeed may bore you, in that case; but you will never bore yourself. You will always have something to say to yourself—always have a subject of reflection."

"I am not bored," said Goodwood. "I have plenty to think about and to say to myself."

"More than to say to others!" Osmond exclaimed, with a light laugh. "Where shall you go next? I mean after you have consigned Touchett to his natural care-takers—I believe his mother is at last coming back to look after him. That little lady is superb; she neglects her duties with a finish! Perhaps you will spend the summer in England?"

"I don't know; I have no plans."

"Happy man! That's a little nude, but it's very free."

"Oh yes, I am very free."

"Free to come back to Rome, I hope," said Osmond, as he saw a group of new visitors enter the room. "Remember that when you do come we count upon you!"

Goodwood had meant to go away early, but the evening elapsed without his having a chance to speak to Isabel otherwise than as one of several associated interlocutors. There was something perverse in the inveteracy with which she avoided him; Goodwood's unquenchable rancour discovered an intention where there was certainly no appearance of one. There was absolutely no appearance of one. She met his eye with her sweet hospitable smile, which seemed almost to ask that he would come and help her to entertain some of her visitors. To such suggestions, however, he only opposed a stiff impatience. He wandered about and waited; he talked to the few people he knew, who found him for the first time rather self-contradictory. This was indeed rare with Caspar Goodwood, though he often contradicted others. There was often music at the Palazzo Roccanera, and it was usually very good. Under cover of the music he managed to contain himself; but toward the end, when he saw the people beginning to go, he drew near to Isabel and asked her in a low tone if he might not speak to her in one of the other rooms, which he had just assured himself was empty.

She smiled as if she wished to oblige him, but found herself absolutely prevented. "I'm afraid it's impossible. People are saying good-night, and I must be where they can see me."

"I shall wait till they are all gone, then!"

She hesitated a moment. "Ah, that will be delightful!" she exclaimed.

And he waited, though it took a long time yet. There were several people, at the end, who seemed tethered to the carpet. The Countess Gemini, who was never herself till midnight, as she said, displayed no consciousness that the entertainment was over; she had still a little circle of gentlemen in front of the fire, who every now and then broke into a united laugh.

Osmond had disappeared—he never bade good-bye to people; and as the Countess was extending her range, according to her custom at this period of the evening, Isabel had sent Pansy to bed. Isabel sat a little apart; she too appeared to wish that her sister-in-law would sound a lower note and let the last loiterers depart in peace.

"May I not say a word to you now?" Goodwood presently asked her.

She got up immediately, smiling. "Certainly, we will go somewhere else, if you like."

They went together, leaving the Countess with her little circle, and for a moment after they had crossed the threshold neither of them spoke. Isabel would not sit down; she stood in the middle of the room slowly fanning herself, with the same familiar grace. She seemed to be waiting for him to speak. Now that he was alone with her, all the passion that he had never stifled surged into his senses; it hummed in his eyes and made things swim around him. The bright, empty room grew dim and blurred, and through the rustling tissue he saw Isabel hover before him with gleaming eyes and parted lips. If he had seen more distinctly he would have perceived that her smile was fixed and a trifle forced—that she was frightened at what she saw in his own face.

"I suppose you wish to bid me good-bye?" she said.

"Yes—but I don't like it. I don't want to leave Rome," he answered, with almost plaintive honesty.

"I can well imagine. It is wonderfully good of you. I can't tell you how kind I think you."

For a moment more he said nothing. "With a few words like that you make me go."

"You must come back some day," Isabel rejoined, brightly.

"Some day? You mean as long a time hence as possible."

"Oh no; I don't mean all that."

"What *do* you mean? I don't understand! But I said I would go, and I will go," Goodwood added.

"Come back whenever you like," said Isabel, with attempted lightness.

"I don't care a straw for your cousin!" Caspar broke out.

"Is that what you wished to tell me?"

"No, no; I didn't want to tell you anything; I wanted to

ask you—" he paused a moment, and then—" what have you really made of your life?" he said, in a low, quick tone. He paused again, as if for an answer; but she said nothing, and he went on—"I can't understand, I can't penetrate you! What am I to believe—what do you want me to think?" Still she said nothing; she only stood looking at him, now quite without pretending to smile. "I am told you are unhappy, and if you are I should like to know it. That would be something for me. But you yourself say you are happy, and you are somehow so still, so smooth. You are completely changed. You conceal everything; I haven't really come near you."

"You come very near," Isabel said, gently, but in a tone of warning.

"And yet I don't touch you! I want to know the truth. Have you done well?"

"You ask a great deal."

"Yes—I have always asked a great deal. Of course you won't tell me. I shall never know, if you can help it. And then it's none of my business." He had spoken with a visible effort to control himself, to give a considerate form to an inconsiderate state of mind. But the sense that it was his last chance, that he loved her and had lost her, that she would think him a fool whatever he should say, suddenly gave him a lash and added a deep vibration to his low voice. "You are perfectly inscrutable, and that's what makes me think you have something to hide. I say that I don't care a straw for your cousin, but I don't mean that I don't like him. I mean that it isn't because I like him that I go away with him. I would go if he were an idiot, and you should have asked me. If you should ask me, I would go to Siberia to-morrow. Why do you want me to leave the place? You must have some reason for that; if you were as contented as you pretend you are, you wouldn't care. I would rather know the truth about you, even if it's damnable, than have come here for nothing. That isn't what I came for. I thought I shouldn't care. I came because I wanted to assure myself that I needn't think of you any more. I haven't thought of anything else, and you are quite right to wish me to go away. But if I must go, there is no harm in my letting myself out for a single moment, is there? If you are really hurt—if *he* hurts you—nothing *I* say will hurt you.

When I tell you I love you, it's simply what I came for. I thought it was for something else; but it was for that. I shouldn't say it if I didn't believe I should never see you again. It's the last time—let me pluck a single flower! I have no right to say that, I know; and you have no right to listen. But you don't listen; you never listen, you are always thinking of something else. After this I must go, of course; so I shall at least have a reason. Your asking me is no reason, not a real one. I can't judge by your husband," he went on, irrelevantly, almost incoherently, "I don't understand him; he tells me you adore each other. Why does he tell me that? What business is it of mine? When I say that to you, you look strange. But you always look strange. Yes, you have something to hide. It's none of my business—very true. But I love you," said Caspar Goodwood.

As he said, she looked strange. She turned her eyes to the door by which they had entered, and raised her fan as if in warning.

"You have behaved so well; don't spoil it," she said, softly.

"No one hears me. It's wonderful what you tried to put me off with. I love you as I have never loved you."

"I know it. I knew it as soon as you consented to go."

"You can't help it—of course not. You would if you could, but you can't, unfortunately. Unfortunately for me, I mean. I ask nothing—nothing, that is, that I shouldn't. But I do ask one sole satisfaction—that you tell me—that you tell me——"

"That I tell you what?"

"Whether I may pity you."

"Should you like that?" Isabel asked, trying to smile again.

"To pity you? Most assuredly! That at least would be doing something. I would give my life to it."

She raised her fan to her face, which it covered, all except her eyes. They rested a moment on his.

"Don't give your life to it; but give a thought to it every now and then."

And with that Isabel went back to the Countess Gemini.

XLIX

Madame Merle had not made her appearance at the Palazzo Roccanera on the evening of that Thursday of which I have narrated some of the incidents, and Isabel, though she observed her absence, was not surprised by it. Things had passed between them which added no stimulus to sociability, and to appreciate which we must glance a little backward. It has been mentioned that Madame Merle returned from Naples shortly after Lord Warburton had left Rome, and that on her first meeting with Isabel (whom, to do her justice, she came immediately to see) her first utterance was an inquiry as to the whereabouts of this nobleman, for whom she appeared to hold her dear friend accountable.

"Please don't talk of him," said Isabel, for answer; "we have heard so much of him of late."

Madame Merle bent her head on one side a little, protestingly, and smiled in the left corner of her mouth.

"You have heard, yes. But you must remember that I have not, in Naples. I hoped to find him here, and to be able to congratulate Pansy."

"You may congratulate Pansy still; but not on marrying Lord Warburton."

"How you say that! Don't you know I had set my heart on it?" Madame Merle asked, with a great deal of spirit, but still with the intonation of good-humour.

Isabel was discomposed, but she was determined to be good-humoured too.

"You shouldn't have gone to Naples, then. You should have stayed here to watch the affair."

"I had too much confidence in you. But do you think it is too late?"

"You had better ask Pansy," said Isabel.

"I shall ask her what you have said to her."

These words seemed to justify the impulse of self-defence aroused on Isabel's part by her perceiving that her visitor's attitude was a critical one. Madame Merle, as we know, had been very discreet hitherto; she had never criticised; she had been excessively afraid of intermeddling. But apparently she had only reserved herself for this occasion; for she had a dangerous quickness in her eye, and an air of irritation which even her admirable smile was not able to transmute. She had suffered a disappointment which excited Isabel's surprise— our heroine having no knowledge of her zealous interest in Pansy's marriage; and she betrayed it in a manner which quickened Mrs. Osmond's alarm. More clearly than ever before, Isabel heard a cold, mocking voice proceed from she knew not where, in the dim void that surrounded her, and declare that this bright, strong, definite, worldly woman, this incarnation of the practical, the personal, the immediate, was a powerful agent in her destiny. She was nearer to her than Isabel had yet discovered, and her nearness was not the charming accident that she had so long thought. The sense of accident indeed had died within her that day when she happened to be struck with the manner in which Madame Merle and her own husband sat together in private. No definite suspicion had as yet taken its place; but it was enough to make her look at this lady with a different eye, to have been led to reflect that there was more intention in her past behaviour than she had allowed for at the time. Ah, yes, there had been intention, there had been intention, Isabel said to herself; and she seemed to wake from a long, pernicious dream. What was it that brought it home to her that Madame Merle's intention had not been good? Nothing but the mistrust which had lately taken body, and which married itself now to the fruitful wonder produced by her visitor's challenge on behalf of poor Pansy. There was something in this challenge which at the very outset excited an answering defiance; a nameless vitality which Isabel now saw to have been absent from her friend's professions of delicacy and caution. Madame Merle had been unwilling to interfere, certainly, but only so long as there was nothing to interfere with. It will perhaps seem to the reader that Isabel went fast in casting doubt, on mere suspicion, on a sincerity proved by several years of good offices. She moved quickly, indeed, and with reason, for a strange truth was filtering into her soul. Madame Merle's interest was identical with Osmond's; that was enough.

"I think Pansy will tell you nothing that will make you

more angry," she said, in answer to her companion's last remark.

"I am not in the least angry. I have only a great desire to retrieve the situation. Do you think his lordship has left us for ever?"

"I can't tell you; I don't understand you. It's all over; please let it rest. Osmond has talked to me a great deal about it, and I have nothing more to say or to hear. I have no doubt," Isabel added, "that he will be very happy to discuss the subject with you."

"I know what he thinks; he came to see me last evening."

"As soon as you had arrived? Then you know all about it, and you needn't apply to me for information."

"It isn't information I want. At bottom, it's sympathy. I had set my heart on that marriage; the idea did what so few things do—it satisfied the imagination."

"Your imagination, yes. But not that of the persons concerned."

"You mean by that of course that I am not concerned. Of course not directly. But when one is such an old friend, one can't help having something at stake. You forget how long I have known Pansy. You mean, of course," Madame Merle added, "that *you* are one of the persons concerned."

"No; that's the last thing I mean. I am very weary of it all."

Madame Merle hesitated a little. "Ah yes, your work's done."

"Take care what you say," said Isabel, very gravely.

"Oh, I take care; never perhaps more than when it appears least. Your husband judges you severely."

Isabel made for a moment no answer to this; she felt choked with bitterness. It was not the insolence of Madame Merle's informing her that Osmond had been taking her into his confidence as against his wife that struck her most: for she was not quick to believe that this was meant for insolence. Madame Merle was very rarely insolent, and only when it was exactly right. It was not right now, or at least it was not right yet. What touched Isabel like a drop of corrosive acid upon an open wound, was the knowledge that Osmond dishonoured her in his words as well as in his thoughts.

"Should you like to know how I judge him?" she asked at last.

"No, because you would never tell me. And it would be painful for me to know."

There was a pause, and for the first time since she had known her, Isabel thought Madame Merle disagreeable. She wished she would leave her.

"Remember how attractive Pansy is, and don't despair," she said abruptly, with a desire that this should close their interview.

But Madame Merle's expansive presence underwent no contraction. She only gathered her mantle about her, and, with the movement, scattered upon the air a faint, agreeable fragrance.

"I don't despair," she answered; "I feel encouraged. And I didn't come to scold you; I came if possible to learn the truth. I know you will tell it if I ask you. It's an immense blessing with you, that one can count upon that. No, you won't believe what a comfort I take in it."

"What truth do you speak of?" Isabel asked, wondering.

"Just this: whether Lord Warburton changed his mind quite of his own movement, or because you recommended it. To please himself, I mean; or to please you. Think of the confidence I must still have in you, in spite of having lost a little of it," Madame Merle continued with a smile, "to ask such a question as that!" She sat looking at Isabel a moment, to judge of the effect of her words, and then she went on—"Now don't be heroic, don't be unreasonable, don't take offence. It seems to me I do you an honour in speaking so. I don't know another woman to whom I would do it. I haven't the least idea that any other woman would tell me the truth. And don't you see how well it is that your husband should know it? It is true that he doesn't appear to have had any tact whatever in trying to extract it; he has indulged in gratuitous suppositions. But that doesn't alter the fact that it would make a difference in his view of his daughter's prospects to know distinctly what really occurred. If Lord Warburton simply got tired of the poor child, that's one thing; it's a pity. If he gave her up to please you, it's another. That's a pity, too; but in a different way. Then, in the latter case, you would perhaps resign yourself to not being pleased—to simply seeing your step-daughter married. Let him off—let us have him!"

Madame Merle had proceeded very deliberately, watching her companion and apparently thinking she could proceed safely. As she went on, Isabel grew pale; she clasped her hands more tightly in her lap. It was not that Madame Merle had at last thought it the right time to be insolent; for this was not what was most apparent. It was a worse horror than that. "Who are you—what are you?" Isabel murmured. "What have you to do with my husband?" It was strange that, for the moment, she drew as near to him as if she had loved him.

"Ah, then you take it heroically! I am very sorry. Don't think, however, that I shall do so."

"What have you to do with me?" Isabel went on.

Madame Merle slowly got up, stroking her muff, but not removing her eyes from Isabel's face.

"Everything!" she answered.

Isabel sat there looking up at her, without rising; her face was almost a prayer to be enlightened. But the light of her visitor's eyes seemed only a darkness.

"Oh, misery!" she murmured at last; and she fell back, covering her face with her hands. It had come over her like a high-surging wave that Mrs. Touchett was right. Madame Merle had married her! Before she uncovered her face again, this lady had left the room.

Isabel took a drive, alone, that afternoon; she wished to be far away, under the sky, where she could descend from her carriage and tread upon the daisies. She had long before this taken old Rome into her confidence, for in a world of ruins the ruin of her happiness seemed a less unnatural catastrophe. She rested her weariness upon things that had crumbled for centuries and yet still were upright; she dropped her secret sadness into the silence of lonely places, where its very modern quality detached itself and grew objective, so that as she sat in a sun-warmed angle on a winter's day, or stood in a mouldy church to which no one came, she could almost smile at it and think of its smallness. Small it was, in the large Roman record, and her haunting sense of the continuity of the human lot easily carried her from the less to the greater. She had become deeply, tenderly acquainted with Rome; it interfused and moderated her passion. But she had grown to think of it chiefly as the place where people had suffered. This was what came to her in the starved churches, where the marble columns, transferred from pagan ruins, seemed to offer her a companionship in endurance, and the musty incense to be a compound of long-unanswered prayers. There was no gentler nor less consistent heretic than Isabel; the firmest of worshippers, gazing at dark altar-pictures or clustered candles, could not have felt more intimately the suggestiveness of these objects nor have been more liable at such moments to a spiritual visitation. Pansy, as we know, was almost always her companion, and of late the Countess Gemini, balancing a pink parasol, had lent brilliancy to their equipage; but she still occasionally found herself alone when it suited her mood, and where it suited the place. On such occasions she had several resorts; the most accessible of which perhaps was a seat on the low parapet which edges the wide grassy space lying before the high, cold front of St. John Lateran; where you look across the Campagna at the far-trailing outline of the Alban Mount, and at that mighty plain between, which is still so full of all that has vanished from it. After the departure of her cousin and his companions she wandered about more than usual; she carried her sombre spirit from one familiar shrine to the other. Even when Pansy and the Countess were with her, she felt the touch of a vanished world. The carriage, passing out of the walls of Rome, rolled through narrow lanes, where the wild honeysuckle had begun to tangle itself in the hedges, or waited for her in quiet places where the fields lay near, while she strolled further and further over the flower-freckled turf, or sat on a stone that had once had a use, and gazed through the veil of her personal sadness at the splendid sadness of the scene—at the dense, warm light, the far gradations and soft confusions of colour, the motionless shepherds in lonely attitudes, the hills where the cloud-shadows had the lightness of a blush.

On the afternoon I began with speaking of, she had taken a resolution not to think of Madame Merle; but the resolution proved vain, and this lady's image hovered constantly before her. She asked herself, with an almost childlike horror of the supposition, whether to this intimate friend of several years the great historical epithet of *wicked* were to be applied. She knew the idea only by the Bible and other literary works; to the best of her belief she had no personal acquaintance with wickedness. She had desired a large acquaintance with human life, and in spite of her having flattered herself that she cultivated it with some success, this elementary privilege had been denied her. Perhaps it was not wicked—in the historic sense—to be false; for that was what Madame Merle had been. Isabel's Aunt Lydia had made this discovery long before, and had mentioned it to her niece; but Isabel had flattered herself at this time that she had a much richer view of things, especially of the spontaneity of her own career and the nobleness of her own interpretations, than poor stiffly-reasoning Mrs. Touchett. Madame Merle had done what she wanted; she had brought about the union of her two friends; a reflection which could not fail to make it a matter of wonder that she should have desired such an event. There were people who had the match-making passion, like the votaries of art for art; but Madame Merle, great artist as she was, was scarcely one of these. She thought too ill of marriage, too ill even of life; she had desired that marriage, but she had not desired others. She therefore had had an idea of gain, and Isabel asked herself where she had found her profit. It took her, naturally, a long time to discover, and even then her discovery was very incomplete. It came back to her that Madame Merle, though she had seemed to like her from their first meeting at Gardencourt, had been doubly affectionate after Mr. Touchett's death, and after learning that her young friend was a victim of the good old man's benevolence. She had found her profit not in the gross device of borrowing money from Isabel, but in the more refined idea of introducing one of her intimates to the young girl's fortune. She had naturally chosen her closest intimate, and it was already vivid enough to Isabel that Gilbert Osmond occupied this position. She found herself confronted in this manner with the conviction that the man in the world whom she had supposed to be the least sordid, had married her for her money. Strange to say, it had never before occurred to her; if she had thought a good deal of harm of Osmond, she had not done him this particular injury. This was the worst she could think of, and she had been saying to herself that the worst was still to come. A man might marry a woman for her money, very well; the thing was often done. But at least he should let her know! She wondered whether, if he wanted her money, her money to-day would satisfy him. Would he take her money and let her go? Ah, if Mr. Touchett's great charity would help her to-day, it would be blessed indeed! It was not slow to occur to her that if Madame Merle had wished to do Osmond a service, his recognition of the fact must have lost its warmth. What must be his feelings to-day in regard to his too zealous benefactress, and what expression must they have found on the part of such a master of irony? It is a singular, but a characteristic, fact that before Isabel returned from her silent drive she had broken its silence by the soft exclamation—

"Poor Madame Merle!"

Her exclamation would perhaps have been justified if on this same afternoon she had been concealed behind one of the valuable curtains of time-softened damask which dressed the interesting little *salon* of the lady to whom it referred; the carefully-arranged apartment to which we once paid a visit in company with the discreet Mr. Rosier. In that apartment, towards six o'clock, Gilbert Osmond was seated, and his hostess stood before him as Isabel had seen her stand on an occasion commemorated in this history with an emphasis appropriate not so much to its apparent as to its real importance.

"I don't believe you are unhappy; I believe you like it," said Madame Merle.

"Did I say I was unhappy?" Osmond asked, with a face grave enough to suggest that he might have been so.

"No, but you don't say the contrary, as you ought in common gratitude."

"Don't talk about gratitude," Osmond returned, dryly. "And don't aggravate me," he added in a moment.

Madame Merle slowly seated herself, with her arms folded and her white hands arranged as a support to one of them and an ornament, as it were, to the other. She looked exquisitely calm, but impressively sad.

"On your side, don't try to frighten me," she said. "I wonder whether you know some of my thoughts."

"No more than I can help. I have quite enough of my own."

"That's because they are so delightful."

Osmond rested his head against the back of his chair and looked at his companion for a long time, with a kind of cynical directness which seemed also partly an expression of fatigue. "You do aggravate me," he remarked in a moment. "I am very tired."

"Eh moi, donc!" cried Madame Merle.

"With you, it's because you fatigue yourself. With me, it's not my own fault."

"When I fatigue myself it's for you. I have given you an interest; that's a great gift."

"Do you call it an interest?" Osmond inquired, languidly.

"Certainly, since it helps you to pass your time."

"The time has never seemed longer to me than this winter."

"You have never looked better; you have never been so agreeable, so brilliant."

"Damn my brilliancy!" Osmond murmured, thoughtfully. "How little, after all, you know me!"

"If I don't know you, I know nothing," said Madame Merle, smiling. "You have the feeling of complete success."

"No, I shall not have that till I have made you stop judging me."

"I did that long ago. I speak from old knowledge. But you express yourself more, too."

Osmond hesitated a moment. "I wish you would express yourself less!"

"You wish to condemn me to silence? Remember that I have never been a chatterbox. At any rate, there are three or four things that I should like to say to you first.—Your wife doesn't know what to do with herself," she went on, with a change of tone.

"Excuse me; she knows perfectly. She has a line sharply marked out. She means to carry out her ideas."

"Her ideas, to-day, must be remarkable."

"Certainly they are. She has more of them than ever."

"She was unable to show me any this morning," said

Madame Merle. "She seemed in a very simple, almost in a stupid, state of mind. She was completely bewildered."

"You had better say at once that she was pathetic."

"Ah no, I don't want to encourage you too much."

Osmond still had his head against the cushion behind him; the ankle of one foot rested on the other knee. So he sat for a while. "I should like to know what is the matter with you," he said, at last.

"The matter—the matter—" And here Madame Merle stopped. Then she went on, with a sudden outbreak of passion, a burst of summer thunder in a clear sky—"The matter is that I would give my right hand to be able to weep, and that I can't!"

"What good would it do you to weep?"

"It would make me feel as I felt before I knew you."

"If I have dried your tears, that's something. But I have seen you shed them."

"Oh, I believe you will make me cry still. I have a great hope of that. I was vile this morning; I was horrid," said Madame Merle.

"If Isabel was in the stupid state of mind you mention, she probably didn't perceive it," Osmond answered.

"It was precisely my devilry that stupefied her. I couldn't help it; I was full of something bad. Perhaps it was something good; I don't know. You have not only dried up my tears; you have dried up my soul."

"It is not I then that am responsible for my wife's condition," Osmond said. "It is pleasant to think that I shall get the benefit of your influence upon her. Don't you know the soul is an immortal principle? How can it suffer alteration?"

"I don't believe at all that it's an immortal principle. I believe it can perfectly be destroyed. That's what has happened to mine, which was a very good one to start with; and it's you I have to thank for it.—You are very bad," Madame Merle added, gravely.

"Is this the way we are to end?" Osmond asked, with the same studied coldness.

"I don't know how we are to end. I wish I did! How do bad people end? You have made me bad."

"I don't understand you. You seem to me quite good

enough," said Osmond, his conscious indifference giving an extreme effect to the words.

Madame Merle's self-possession tended on the contrary to diminish, and she was nearer losing it than on any occasion on which we have had the pleasure of meeting her. Her eye brightened, even flashed; her smile betrayed a painful effort. "Good enough for anything that I have done with myself? I suppose that's what you mean."

"Good enough to be always charming!" Osmond exclaimed, smiling too.

"Oh God!" his companion murmured; and, sitting there in her ripe freshness, she had recourse to the same gesture that she had provoked on Isabel's part in the morning; she bent her face and covered it with her hands.

"Are you going to weep, after all?" Osmond asked; and on her remaining motionless he went on—"Have I ever complained to you?"

She dropped her hands quickly. "No, you have taken your revenge otherwise—you have taken it on *her*."

Osmond threw back his head further; he looked a while at the ceiling, and might have been supposed to be appealing, in an informal way, to the heavenly powers. "Oh, the imagination of women! It's always vulgar, at bottom. You talk of revenge like a third-rate novelist."

"Of course you haven't complained. You have enjoyed your triumph too much."

"I am rather curious to know what you call my triumph."

"You have made your wife afraid of you."

Osmond changed his position; he leaned forward, resting his elbows on his knees and looking a while at a beautiful old Persian rug, at his feet. He had an air of refusing to accept any one's valuation of anything, even of time, and of preferring to abide by his own; a peculiarity which made him at moments an irritating person to converse with. "Isabel is not afraid of me, and it's not what I wish," he said at last. "To what do you wish to provoke me when you say such things as that?"

"I have thought over all the harm you can do me," Madame Merle answered. "Your wife was afraid of me this morning, but in me it was really you she feared."

"You may have said things that were in very bad taste; I am not responsible for that. I didn't see the use of your going to see her at all; you are capable of acting without her. I have not made you afraid of me, that I can see," Osmond went on; "how then should I have made her? You are at least as brave. I can't think where you have picked up such rubbish; one might suppose you knew me by this time." He got up, as he spoke, and walked to the chimney, where he stood a moment bending his eye, as if he had seen them for the first time, on the delicate specimens of rare porcelain with which it was covered. He took up a small cup and held it in his hand; then, still holding it and leaning his arm on the mantel, he continued: "You always see too much in everything; you overdo it; you lose sight of the real. I am much simpler than you think."

"I think you are very simple." And Madame Merle kept her eye upon her cup. "I have come to that with time. I judged you, as I say, of old; but it is only since your marriage that I have understood you. I have seen better what you have been to your wife than I ever saw what you were for me. Please be very careful of that precious object."

"It already has a small crack," said Osmond, dryly, as he put it down. "If you didn't understand me before I married, it was cruelly rash of you to put me into such a box. However, I took a fancy to my box myself; I thought it would be a comfortable fit. I asked very little; I only asked that she should like me."

"That she should like you so much!"

"So much, of course; in such a case one asks the maximum. That she should adore me, if you will. Oh yes, I wanted that."

"I never adored you," said Madame Merle.

"Ah, but you pretended to!"

"It is true that you never accused me of being a comfortable fit," Madame Merle went on.

"My wife has declined—declined to do anything of the sort," said Osmond. "If you are determined to make a tragedy of that, the tragedy is hardly for her."

"The tragedy is for me!" Madame Merle exclaimed, rising, with a long low sigh, but giving a glance at the same time at the contents of her mantel-shelf. "It appears that I am to be severely taught the disadvantages of a false position."

"You express yourself like a sentence in a copy-book. We must look for our comfort where we can find it. If my wife doesn't like me, at least my child does. I shall look for compensations in Pansy. Fortunately I haven't a fault to find with her."

"Ah," said Madame Merle, softly, "if I had a child—"

Osmond hesitated a moment; and then, with a little formal air—"The children of others may be a great interest!" he announced.

"You are more like a copy-book than I. There is something, after all, that holds us together."

"Is it the idea of the harm I may do you?" Osmond asked.

"No; it's the idea of the good I may do for you. It is that," said Madame Merle, "that made me so jealous of Isabel. I want it to be *my* work," she added, with her face, which had grown hard and bitter, relaxing into its usual social expression.

Osmond took up his hat and his umbrella, and after giving the former article two or three strokes with his coat-cuff— "On the whole, I think," he said, "you had better leave it to me."

After he had left her, Madame Merle went and lifted from the mantel-shelf the attenuated coffee-cup in which he had mentioned the existence of a crack; but she looked at it rather abstractedly. "Have I been so vile all for nothing?" she murmured to herself.

L

As THE COUNTESS GEMINI was not acquainted with the ancient monuments, Isabel occasionally offered to introduce her to these interesting relics and to give their afternoon drive an antiquarian aim. The Countess, who professed to think her sister-in-law a prodigy of learning, never made an objection, and gazed at masses of Roman brickwork as patiently as if they had been mounds of modern drapery. She was not an antiquarian; but she was so delighted to be in Rome that she only desired to float with the current. She would gladly have passed an hour every day in the damp darkness of the Baths of Titus, if it had been a condition of her remaining at the Palazzo Roccanera. Isabel, however, was not a severe cicerone; she used to visit the ruins chiefly because they offered an excuse for talking about other matters than the love-affairs of the ladies of Florence, as to which her companion was never weary of offering information. It must be added that during these visits the Countess was not very active; her preference was to sit in the carriage and exclaim that everything was most interesting. It was in this manner that she had hitherto examined the Coliseum, to the infinite regret of her niece, who—with all the respect that she owed her—could not see why she should not descend from the vehicle and enter the building. Pansy had so little chance to ramble that her view of the case was not wholly disinterested; it may be divined that she had a secret hope that, once inside, her aunt might be induced to climb to the upper tiers. There came a day when the Countess announced her willingness to undertake this feat—a mild afternoon in March, when the windy month expressed itself in occasional puffs of spring. The three ladies went into the Coliseum together, but Isabel left her companions to wander over the place. She had often ascended to those desolate ledges from which the Roman crowd used to bellow applause, and where now the wild flowers (when they are allowed), bloom in the deep crevices; and to-day she felt weary, and preferred to sit in the despoiled arena. It made an intermission, too, for the Countess often asked more from one's attention than she gave in return; and

Isabel believed that when she was alone with her niece she let the dust gather for a moment upon the ancient scandals of Florence. She remained below, therefore, while Pansy guided her undiscriminating aunt to the steep brick staircase at the foot of which the custodian unlocks the tall wooden gate. The great inclosure was half in shadow; the western sun brought out the pale red tone of the great blocks of travertine—the latent colour which is the only living element in the immense ruin. Here and there wandered a peasant or a tourist, looking up at the far sky-line where in the clear stillness a multitude of swallows kept circling and plunging. Isabel presently became aware that one of the other visitors, planted in the middle of the arena, had turned his attention to her own person, and was looking at her with a certain little poise of the head, which she had some weeks before perceived to be characteristic of baffled but indestructible purpose. Such an attitude, to-day, could belong only to Mr. Edward Rosier; and this gentleman proved in fact to have been considering the question of speaking to her. When he had assured himself that she was unaccompanied he drew near, remarking that though she would not answer his letters she would perhaps not wholly close her ears to his spoken eloquence. She replied that her step-daughter was close at hand and she could only give him five minutes; whereupon he took out his watch and sat down upon a broken block.

"It's very soon told," said Edward Rosier. "I have sold all my bibelots!"

Isabel gave, instinctively, an exclamation of horror; it was as if he had told her he had had all his teeth drawn.

"I have sold them by auction at the Hôtel Drouot," he went on. "The sale took place three days ago, and they have telegraphed me the result. It's magnificent."

"I am glad to hear it; but I wish you had kept your pretty things."

"I have the money instead—forty thousand dollars. Will Mr. Osmond think me rich enough now?"

"Is it for that you did it?" Isabel asked, gently.

"For what else in the world could it be? That is the only thing I think of. I went to Paris and made my arrangements. I couldn't stop for the sale; I couldn't have seen them going off; I think it would have killed me. But I put them into good hands, and they brought high prices. I should tell you I have kept my enamels. Now I have got the money in my pocket, and he can't say I'm poor!" the young man exclaimed, defiantly.

"He will say now that you are not wise," said Isabel, as if Gilbert Osmond had never said this before.

Rosier gave her a sharp look.

"Do you mean that without my bibelots I am nothing? Do you mean that they were the best thing about me? That's what they told me in Paris; oh, they were very frank about it. But they hadn't seen *her*!"

"My dear friend, you deserve to succeed," said Isabel, very kindly.

"You say that so sadly that it's the same as if you said I shouldn't." And he questioned her eye with the clear trepidation of his own. He had the air of a man who knows he has been the talk of Paris for a week and is full half a head taller in consequence; but who also has a painful suspicion that in spite of this increase of stature one or two persons still have the perversity to think him diminutive. "I know what happened here while I was away," he went on. "What does Mr. Osmond expect, after she has refused Lord Warburton?"

Isabel hesitated a moment.

"That she will marry another nobleman."

"What other nobleman?"

"One that he will pick out."

Rosier slowly got up, putting his watch into his waistcoat-pocket.

"You are laughing at some one; but this time I don't think it's at me."

"I didn't mean to laugh," said Isabel. "I laugh very seldom. Now you had better go away."

"I feel very safe!" Rosier declared, without moving. This might be; but it evidently made him feel more so to make the announcement in rather a loud voice, balancing himself a little complacently, on his toes, and looking all around the Coliseum, as if it were filled with an audience. Suddenly Isabel saw him change colour; there was more of an audience than he had suspected. She turned, and perceived that her two companions had returned from their excursion.

"You must really go away," she said, quickly.

"Ah, my dear lady, pity me!" Edward Rosier murmured, in a voice strangely at variance with the announcement I have just quoted. And then he added, eagerly, like a man who in the midst of his misery is seized by a happy thought—"Is that lady the Countess Gemini? I have a great desire to be presented to her."

Isabel looked at him a moment.

"She has no influence with her brother."

"Ah, what a monster you make him out!" Rosier exclaimed, glancing at the Countess, who advanced, in front of Pansy, with an animation partly due perhaps to the fact that she perceived her sister-in-law to be engaged in conversation with a very pretty young man.

"I am glad you have kept your enamels!" Isabel exclaimed, leaving him. She went straight to Pansy, who, on seeing Edward Rosier, had stopped short, with lowered eyes. "We will go back to the carriage," said Isabel gently.

"Yes, it is getting late," Pansy answered, more gently still. And she went on without a murmur, without faltering or glancing back.

Isabel, however, allowed herself this last liberty, and saw that a meeting had immediately taken place between the Countess and Mr. Rosier. He had removed his hat, and was bowing and smiling; he had evidently introduced himself; while the Countess's expressive back displayed to Isabel's eye a gracious inclination. These facts, however, were presently lost to sight, for Isabel and Pansy took their places again in the carriage. Pansy, who faced her stepmother, at first kept her eyes fixed on her lap; then she raised them and rested them on Isabel's. There shone out of each of them a little melancholy ray—a spark of timid passion which touched Isabel to the heart. At the same time a wave of envy passed over her soul, as she compared the tremulous longing, the definite ideal, of the young girl with her own dry despair.

"Poor little Pansy!" she said, affectionately.

"Oh, never mind!" Pansy answered, in the tone of eager apology.

And then there was a silence; the Countess was a long time coming.

"Did you show your aunt everything, and did she enjoy it?" Isabel asked at last.

"Yes, I showed her everything. I think she was very much pleased."

"And you are not tired, I hope."

"Oh no, thank you, I am not tired."

The Countess still remained behind, so that Isabel requested the footman to go into the Coliseum and tell her that they were waiting. He presently returned with the announcement that the Signora Contessa begged them not to wait—she would come home in a cab!

About a week after this lady's quick sympathies had enlisted themselves with Mr. Rosier, Isabel, going rather late to dress for dinner, found Pansy sitting in her room. The girl seemed to have been waiting for her; she got up from her low chair.

"Excuse my taking the liberty," she said, in a small voice. "It will be the last—for some time."

Her voice was strange, and her eyes, widely opened, had an excited, frightened look.

"You are not going away!" Isabel exclaimed.

"I am going to the convent."

"To the convent?"

Pansy drew nearer, till she was near enough to put her arms round Isabel and rest her head on her shoulder. She stood this way a moment, perfectly still; but Isabel could feel her trembling. The tremor of her little body expressed everything that she was unable to say.

Nevertheless, Isabel went on in a moment—

"Why are you going to the convent?"

"Because papa thinks it best. He says a young girl is better, every now and then, for making a little retreat. He says the world, always the world, is very bad for a young girl. This is just a chance for a little seclusion—a little reflection." Pansy spoke in short detached sentences, as if she could not trust herself. And then she added, with a triumph of self-control—"I think papa is right; I have been so much in the world this winter."

Her announcement had a strange effect upon Isabel; it seemed to carry a larger meaning than the girl herself knew.

"When was this decided?" she asked. "I have heard nothing of it."

"Papa told me half-an-hour ago; he thought it better it shouldn't be too much talked about in advance. Madame Catherine is to come for me at a quarter past seven, and I am only to take two dresses. It is only for a few weeks; I am sure it will be very good. I shall find all those ladies who used to be so kind to me, and I shall see the little girls who are being educated. I am very fond of little girls," said Pansy, with a sort of diminutive grandeur. "And I am also very fond of Mother Catherine. I shall be very quiet, and think a great deal."

Isabel listened to her, holding her breath; she was almost awe-struck.

"Think of *me*, sometimes," she said.

"Ah, come and see me soon!" cried Pansy; and the cry was very different from the heroic remarks of which she had just delivered herself.

Isabel could say nothing more; she understood nothing; she only felt that she did not know her husband yet. Her answer to Pansy was a long tender kiss.

Half-an-hour later she learned from her maid that Madame Catherine had arrived in a cab, and had departed again with the Signorina. On going to the drawing-room before dinner she found the Countess Gemini alone, and this lady characterised the incident by exclaiming, with a wonderful toss of the head—*"En voilà, ma chère, une pose!"* But if it was an affectation, she was at a loss to see what her husband affected. She could only dimly perceive that he had more traditions than she supposed. It had become her habit to be so careful as to what she said to him that, strange as it may appear, she hesitated, for several minutes after he had come in, to allude to his daughter's sudden departure; she spoke of it only after they were seated at table. But she had forbidden herself ever to ask Osmond a question. All she could do was to make a declaration, and there was one that came very naturally.

"I shall miss Pansy very much."

Osmond looked a while, with his head inclined a little, at the basket of flowers in the middle of the table.

"Ah, yes," he said at last, "I had thought of that. You must go and see her, you know; but not too often. I dare say you wonder why I sent her to the good sisters; but I doubt whether I can make you understand. It doesn't matter; don't trouble yourself about it. That's why I had not spoken of it. I didn't believe you would enter into it. But I have always had the idea; I have always thought it a part of the education of a young girl. A young girl should be fresh and fair; she should be innocent and gentle. With the manners of the present time she is liable to become so dusty and crumpled! Pansy is a little dusty, a little dishevelled; she has knocked about too much. This bustling, pushing rabble, that calls itself society—one should take her out of it occasionally. Convents are very quiet, very convenient, very salutary. I like to think of her there, in the old garden, under the arcade, among those tranquil, virtuous women. Many of them are gentlewomen born; several of them are noble. She will have her books and her drawing; she will have her piano. I have made the most liberal arrangements. There is to be nothing ascetic; there is just to be a certain little feeling. She will have time to think, and there is something I want her to think about." Osmond spoke deliberately, reasonably, still with his head on one side, as if he were looking at the basket of flowers. His tone, however, was that of a man not so much offering an explanation as putting a thing into words—almost into pictures—to see, himself, how it would look. He contemplated a while the picture he had evoked, and seemed greatly pleased with it. And then he went on—"The Catholics are very wise, after all. The convent is a great institution; we can't do without it; it corresponds to an essential need in families, in society. It's a school of good manners; it's a school of repose. Oh, I don't want to detach my daughter from the world," he added; "I don't want to make her fix her thoughts on the other one. This one is very well, after all, and she may think of it as much as she chooses. Only she must think of it in the right way."

Isabel gave an extreme attention to this little sketch; she found it indeed intensely interesting. It seemed to show her how far her husband's desire to be effective was capable of going—to the point of playing picturesque tricks upon the delicate organism of his daughter. She could not understand his purpose, no—not wholly; but she understood it better than he supposed or desired, inasmuch as she was convinced that the whole proceeding was an elaborate mystification, addressed to herself and destined to act upon her imagination. He wished to do something sudden and arbitrary, something unexpected and refined; to mark the difference between his sympathies and her own, and to show that if he regarded his daughter as a precious work of art, it was natural he should be more and more careful about the finishing touches. If he wished to be effective he had succeeded; the incident struck a chill into Isabel's heart. Pansy had known the convent in her childhood and had found a happy home there; she was fond of the good sisters, who were very fond of her, and there was therefore, for the moment, no definite hardship in her lot. But all the same, the girl had taken fright; the impression her father wanted to make would evidently be sharp enough. The old Protestant tradition had never faded from Isabel's imagination, and as her thoughts attached themselves to this striking example of her husband's genius—she sat looking, like him, at the basket of flowers— poor little Pansy became the heroine of a tragedy. Osmond wished it to be known that he shrank from nothing, and Isabel found it hard to pretend to eat her dinner. There was a certain relief, presently, in hearing the high, bright voice of her sister-in-law. The Countess, too, apparently, had been thinking the thing out; but she had arrived at a different conclusion from Isabel.

"It is very absurd, my dear Osmond," she said, "to invent so many pretty reasons for poor Pansy's banishment. Why don't you say at once that you want to get her out of my way? Haven't you discovered that I think very well of Mr. Rosier? I do indeed; he seems to me a delightful young man. He has made me believe in true love; I never did before! Of course you have made up your mind that with those convictions I am dreadful company for Pansy."

Osmond took a sip of a glass of wine; he looked perfectly good-humoured.

"My dear Amy," he answered, smiling as if he were uttering a piece of gallantry, "I don't know anything about your convictions, but if I suspected that they interfere with mine it would be much simpler to banish you."

LI

THE COUNTESS was not banished, but she felt the insecurity of her tenure of her brother's hospitality. A week after this incident Isabel received a telegram from England, dated from Gardencourt, and bearing the stamp of Mrs. Touchett's authorship. "Ralph cannot last many days," it ran, "and if convenient would like to see you. Wishes me to say that you must come only if you have not other duties. Say, for myself, that you used to talk a good deal about your duty and to wonder what it was; shall be curious to see whether you have found it out. Ralph is dying, and there is no other company." Isabel was prepared for this news, having received from Henrietta Stackpole a detailed account of her journey to England with her appreciative patient. Ralph had arrived more dead than alive, but she had managed to convey him to Gardencourt, where he had taken to his bed, which, as Miss Stackpole wrote, he evidently would never leave again. "I like him much better sick than when he used to be well," said Henrietta, who, it will be remembered, had taken a few years before a sceptical view of Ralph's disabilities. She added that she had really had two patients on her hands instead of one, for that Mr. Goodwood, who had been of no earthly use, was quite as sick, in a different way, as Mr. Touchett. Afterwards she wrote that she had been obliged to surrender the field to Mrs. Touchett, who had just returned from America, and had promptly given her to understand that she didn't wish any interviewing at Gardencourt. Isabel had written to her aunt shortly after Ralph came to Rome, letting her know of his critical condition, and suggesting that she should lose no time in returning to Europe. Mrs. Touchett had telegraphed an acknowledgment of this admonition, and the only further news Isabel received from her was the second telegram which I have just quoted.

Isabel stood a moment looking at the latter missive, then, thrusting it into her pocket, she went straight to the door of her husband's study. Here she again paused an instant, after which she opened the door and went in. Osmond was seated at the table near the window with a folio volume before him, propped against a pile of books. This volume was open at a page of small coloured plates, and Isabel presently saw that he had been copying from it the drawing of an antique coin. A box of water-colours and fine brushes lay before him, and he had already transferred to a sheet of immaculate paper the delicate, finely-tinted disk. His back was turned toward the door, but without looking round he recognised his wife.

"Excuse me for disturbing you," she said.

"When I come to your room I always knock," he answered, going on with his work.

"I forgot; I had something else to think of. My cousin is dying."

"Ah, I don't believe that," said Osmond, looking at his drawing through a magnifying glass. "He was dying when we married; he will outlive us all."

Isabel gave herself no time, no thought, to appreciate the careful cynicism of this declaration; she simply went on quickly, full of her own intention—

"My aunt has telegraphed for me; I must go to Gardencourt."

"Why must you go to Gardencourt?" Osmond asked, in the tone of impartial curiosity.

"To see Ralph before he dies."

To this, for some time, Osmond made no rejoinder; he continued to give his chief attention to his work, which was of a sort that would brook no negligence.

"I don't see the need of it," he said at last. "He came to see you here. I didn't like that; I thought his being in Rome a great mistake. But I tolerated it, because it was to be the last time you should see him. Now you tell me it is not to have been the last. Ah, you are not grateful!"

"What am I to be grateful for?"

Gilbert Osmond laid down his little implements, blew a speck of dust from his drawing, slowly got up, and for the first time looked at his wife.

"For my not having interfered while he was here."

"Oh yes, I am. I remember perfectly how distinctly you let me know you didn't like it. I was very glad when he went away."

"Leave him alone then. Don't run after him."

Isabel turned her eyes away from him; they rested upon his little drawing.

"I must go to England," she said, with a full consciousness that her tone might strike an irritable man of taste as stupidly obstinate.

"I shall not like it if you do," Osmond remarked.

"Why should I mind that? You won't like it if I don't. You like nothing I do or don't do. You pretend to think I lie."

Osmond turned slightly pale; he gave a cold smile.

"That's why you must go then? Not to see your cousin, but to take a revenge on me."

"I know nothing about revenge."

"I do," said Osmond. "Don't give me an occasion."

"You are only too eager to take one. You wish immensely that I would commit some folly."

"I shall be gratified then if you disobey me."

"If I disobey you?" said Isabel, in a low tone, which had the effect of gentleness.

"Let it be clear. If you leave Rome to-day it will be a piece of the most deliberate, the most calculated, opposition."

"How can you call it calculated? I received my aunt's telegram but three minutes ago."

"You calculate rapidly; it's a great accomplishment. I don't see why we should prolong our discussion; you know my wish." And he stood there as if he expected to see her withdraw.

But she never moved; she couldn't move, strange as it may seem; she still wished to justify herself; he had the power, in an extraordinary degree, of making her feel this need. There was something in her imagination that he could always appeal to against her judgment.

"You have no reason for such a wish," said Isabel, "and I have every reason for going. I can't tell you how unjust you seem to me. But I think you know. It is your own opposition that is calculated. It is malignant."

She had never uttered her worst thought to her husband before, and the sensation of hearing it was evidently new to Osmond. But he showed no surprise, and his coolness was apparently a proof that he had believed his wife would in fact be unable to resist for ever his ingenious endeavour to draw her out.

"It is all the more intense, then," he answered. And he added, almost as if he were giving her a friendly counsel— "This is a very important matter." She recognised this; she was fully conscious of the weight of the occasion; she knew that between them they had arrived at a crisis. Its gravity made her careful; she said nothing, and he went on. "You say I have no reason? I have the very best. I dislike, from the bottom of my soul, what you intend to do. It's dishonourable; it's indelicate; it's indecent. Your cousin is nothing whatever to me, and I am under no obligation to make concessions to him. I have already made the very handsomest. Your relations with him, while he was here, kept me on pins and needles; but I let that pass, because from week to week I expected him to go. I have never liked him and he has never liked me. That's why you like him—because he hates me," said Osmond, with a quick, barely audible tremor in his voice. "I have an ideal of what my wife should do and should not do. She should not travel across Europe alone, in defiance of my deepest desire, to sit at the bedside of other men. Your cousin is nothing to you; he is nothing to us. You smile most expressively when I talk about *us*; but I assure you that *we*, *we*, is all that I know. I take our marriage seriously; you appear to have found a way of not doing so. I am not aware that we are divorced or separated; for me we are indissolubly united. You are nearer to me than any human creature, and I am nearer to you. It may be a disagreeable proximity; it's one, at any rate, of our own deliberate making. You don't like to be reminded of that, I know; but I am perfectly willing, because—because—" And Osmond paused a moment, looking as if he had something to say which would be very much to the point. "Because I think we should accept the consequences of our actions, and what I value most in life is the honour of a thing!"

He spoke gravely and almost gently; the accent of sarcasm had dropped out of his tone. It had a gravity which checked his wife's quick emotion; the resolution with which she had entered the room found itself caught in a mesh of fine threads. His last words were not a command, they constituted a kind of appeal; and though she felt that any expression of respect on Osmond's part could only be a refinement of egotism, they represented something transcendent and absolute, like the sign of the cross or the flag of one's country. He spoke in the name of something sacred and precious—the observance of a magnificent form. They were as perfectly apart in feeling as two disillusioned lovers had ever been; but they had never yet separated in act. Isabel had not changed; her old passion for justice still abode within her; and now, in the very thick of her sense of her husband's blasphemous sophistry, it began to throb to a tune which for a moment promised him the victory. It came over her that in his wish to preserve appearances he was after all sincere, and that this, as far as it went, was a merit. Ten minutes before, she had felt all the joy of irreflective action—a joy to which she had so long been a stranger; but action had been suddenly changed to slow renunciation, transformed by the blight of her husband's touch. If she must renounce, however, she would let him know that she was a victim rather than a dupe. "I know you are a master of the art of mockery," she said. "How can you speak of an indissoluble union—how can you speak of your being contented? Where is our union when you accuse me of falsity? Where is your contentment when you have nothing but hideous suspicion in your heart?"

"It is in our living decently together, in spite of such drawbacks."

"We don't live decently together!" Isabel cried.

"Indeed we don't, if you go to England."

"That's very little; that's nothing. I might do much more."

Osmond raised his eyebrows and even his shoulders a little; he had lived long enough in Italy to catch this trick. "Ah, if you have come to threaten me, I prefer my drawing," he said, walking back to his table, where he took up the sheet of paper on which he had been working and stood a moment examining his work.

"I suppose that if I go you will not expect me to come back," said Isabel.

He turned quickly round, and she could see that this move-ment at least was not studied. He looked at her a little, and then—"Are you out of your mind?" he inquired.

"How can it be anything but a rupture?" she went on; "es-pecially if all you say is true?" She was unable to see how it could be anything but a rupture; she sincerely wished to know what else it might be.

Osmond sat down before his table. "I really can't argue with you on the hypothesis of your defying me," he said. And he took up one of his little brushes again.

Isabel lingered but a moment longer; long enough to em-brace with her eye his whole deliberately indifferent, yet most expressive, figure; after which she quickly left the room. Her faculties, her energy, her passion, were all dispersed again; she felt as if a cold, dark mist had suddenly encompassed her. Osmond possessed in a supreme degree the art of eliciting one's weakness.

On her way back to her room she found the Countess Gemini standing in the open doorway of a little parlour in which a small collection of heterogeneous books had been arranged. The Countess had an open volume in her hand; she appeared to have been glancing down a page which failed to strike her as interesting. At the sound of Isabel's step she raised her head.

"Ah my dear," she said, "you, who are so literary, do tell me some amusing book to read! Everything here is so fear-fully edifying. Do you think this would do me any good?"

Isabel glanced at the title of the volume she held out, but without reading or understanding it. "I am afraid I can't ad-vise you. I have had bad news. My cousin, Ralph Touchett, is dying."

The Countess threw down her book. "Ah, he was so nice! I am sorry for you," she said.

"You would be sorrier still if you knew."

"What is there to know? You look very badly," the Count-ess added. "You must have been with Osmond."

Half-an-hour before, Isabel would have listened very coldly to an intimation that she should ever feel a desire for the sympathy of her sister-in-law, and there can be no better proof of her present embarrassment than the fact that she almost clutched at this lady's fluttering attention. "I have been with Osmond," she said, while the Countess's bright eyes glittered at her.

"I am sure he has been odious!" the Countess cried. "Did he say he was glad poor Mr. Touchett is dying?"

"He said it is impossible I should go to England."

The Countess's mind, when her interests were concerned, was agile; she already foresaw the extinction of any further brightness in her visit to Rome. Ralph Touchett would die, Isabel would go into mourning, and then there would be no more dinner-parties. Such a prospect produced for a moment in her countenance an expressive grimace; but this rapid, picturesque play of feature was her only tribute to disappointment. After all, she reflected, the game was almost played out; she had already overstayed her invitation. And then she cared enough for Isabel's trouble to forget her own, and she saw that Isabel's trouble was deep. It seemed deeper than the mere death of a cousin, and the Countess had no hesitation in connecting her exasperating brother with the expression of her sister-in-law's eyes. Her heart beat with an almost joyous expectation; for if she had wished to see Osmond overtopped, the conditions looked favourable now. Of course, if Isabel should go to England, she herself would immediately leave the Palazzo Roccanera; nothing would induce her to remain there with Osmond. Nevertheless she felt an immense desire to hear that Isabel would go to England. "Nothing is impossible for you, my dear," she said, caressingly. "Why else are you rich and clever and good?"

"Why indeed? I feel stupidly weak."

"Why does Osmond say it's impossible?" the Countess asked, in a tone which sufficiently declared that she couldn't imagine.

From the moment that she began to question her, however, Isabel drew back; she disengaged her hand, which the Countess had affectionately taken. But she answered this inquiry with frank bitterness. "Because we are so happy together that we cannot separate even for a fortnight."

"Ah," cried the Countess, while Isabel turned away; "when I want to make a journey my husband simply tells me I can have no money!"

Isabel went to her room, where she walked up and down for an hour. It may seem to some readers that she took things very hard, and it is certain that for a woman of a high spirit she had allowed herself easily to be arrested. It seemed to her that only now she fully measured the great undertaking of matrimony. Marriage meant that in such a case as this, when one had to choose, one chose as a matter of course for one's husband. "I am afraid—yes, I am afraid," she said to herself more than once, stopping short in her walk. But what she was afraid of was not her husband—his displeasure, his hatred, his revenge; it was not even her own later judgment of her conduct—a consideration which had often held her in check; it was simply the violence there would be in going when Osmond wished her to remain. A gulf of difference had opened between them, but nevertheless it was his desire that she should stay, it was a horror to him that she should go. She knew the nervous fineness with which he could feel an objection. What he thought of her she knew; what he was capable of saying to her she had felt; yet they were married, for all that, and marriage meant that a woman should abide with her husband. She sank down on her sofa at last, and buried her head in a pile of cushions.

When she raised her head again, the Countess Gemini stood before her. She had come in noiselessly, unperceived; she had a strange smile on her thin lips, and a still stranger glitter in her small dark eye.

"I knocked," she said, "but you didn't answer me. So I ventured in. I have been looking at you for the last five minutes. You are very unhappy."

"Yes; but I don't think you can comfort me."

"Will you give me leave to try?" And the Countess sat down on the sofa beside her. She continued to smile, and there was something communicative and exultant in her expression. She appeared to have something to say, and it occurred to Isabel for the first time that her sister-in-law might say something important. She fixed her brilliant eyes upon Isabel, who found at last a disagreeable fascination in her gaze. "After all," the Countess went on, "I must tell you, to begin with, that I don't understand your state of mind.

You seem to have so many scruples, so many reasons, so many ties. When I discovered, ten years ago, that my husband's dearest wish was to make me miserable—of late he has simply let me alone—ah, it was a wonderful simplification! My poor Isabel, you are not simple enough."

"No, I am not simple enough," said Isabel.

"There is something I want you to know," the Countess declared—"because I think you ought to know it. Perhaps you do; perhaps you have guessed it. But if you have, all I can say is that I understand still less why you shouldn't do as you like."

"What do you wish me to know?" Isabel felt a foreboding which made her heart beat. The Countess was about to justify herself, and this alone was portentous.

But the Countess seemed disposed to play a little with her subject. "In your place I should have guessed it ages ago. Have you never really suspected?"

"I have guessed nothing. What should I have suspected? I don't know what you mean."

"That's because you have got such a pure mind. I never saw a woman with such a pure mind!" cried the Countess.

Isabel slowly got up. "You are going to tell me something horrible."

"You can call it by whatever name you will!" And the Countess rose also, while the sharp animation of her bright, capricious face emitted a kind of flash. She stood a moment looking at Isabel, and then she said—"My first sister-in-law had no children!"

Isabel stared back at her; the announcement was an anti-climax. "Your first sister-in-law?" she murmured.

"I suppose you know that Osmond has been married before? I have never spoken to you of his wife; I didn't suppose it was proper. But others, less particular, must have done so. The poor little woman lived but two years and died childless. It was after her death that Pansy made her appearance."

Isabel's brow had gathered itself into a frown; her lips were parted in pale, vague wonder. She was trying to follow; there seemed to be more to follow than she could see. "Pansy is not my husband's child, then?"

"Your husband's—in perfection! But no one else's husband's. Some one else's wife's. Ah, my good Isabel," cried the Countess, " with you one must dot one's *i* 's!"

"I don't understand; whose wife's?" said Isabel.

"The wife of a horrid little Swiss, who died twelve years ago. He never recognised Miss Pansy, and there was no reason he should. Osmond did, and that was better."

Isabel stayed the name which rose in a sudden question to her lips; she sank down on her seat again, hanging her head. "Why have you told me this?" she asked, in a voice which the Countess hardly recognised.

"Because I was so tired of your not knowing! I was tired of not having told you. It seemed to me so dull. It's not a lie, you know; it's exactly as I say."

"I never knew," said Isabel, looking up at her, simply.

"So I believed—though it was hard to believe. Has it never occurred to you that he has been her lover?"

"I don't know. Something has occurred to me. Perhaps it was that."

"She has been wonderfully clever about Pansy!" cried the Countess.

"That thing has never occurred to me," said Isabel. "And as it is—I don't understand."

She spoke in a low, thoughtful tone, and the poor Countess was equally surprised and disappointed at the effect of her revelation. She had expected to kindle a conflagration, and as yet she had barely extracted a spark. Isabel seemed more awe-stricken than anything else.

"Don't you perceive that the child could never pass for her husband's?" the Countess asked. "They had been separated too long for that, and M. Merle had gone to some far country; I think to South America. If she had ever had children— which I am not sure of—she had lost them. On the other hand, circumstances made it convenient enough for Osmond to acknowledge the little girl. His wife was dead—very true; but she had only been dead a year, and what was more natural than that she should have left behind a pledge of their affection? With the aid of a change of residence—he had been living at Naples, and he left it for ever—the little fable was easily set going. My poor sister-in-law, who was in her grave, couldn't help herself, and the real mother, to save her reputation, renounced all visible property in the child."

"Ah, poor creature!" cried Isabel, bursting into tears. It was a long time since she had shed any; she had suffered a reaction from weeping. But now they gushed with an abundance in which the Countess Gemini found only another discomfiture.

"It's very kind of you to pity her!" she cried, with a discordant laugh. "Yes, indeed, you have a pure mind!"

"He must have been false to his wife," said Isabel, suddenly controlling herself.

"That's all that's wanting—that you should take up *her* cause!" the Countess went on.

"But to me—to me—" And Isabel hesitated, though there was a question in her eyes.

"To you he has been faithful? It depends upon what you call faithful. When he married you, he was no longer the lover of another woman. That state of things had passed away; the lady had repented; and she had a worship of appearances so intense that even Osmond himself got tired of it. You may therefore imagine what it was! But the whole past was between them."

"Yes," said Isabel, "the whole past is between them."

"Ah, this later past is nothing. But for five years they were very intimate."

"Why then did she want him to marry me?"

"Ah, my dear, that's her superiority! Because you had money; and because she thought you would be good to Pansy."

"Poor woman—and Pansy who doesn't like her!" cried Isabel.

"That's the reason she wanted some one whom Pansy would like. She knows it; she knows everything."

"Will she know that you have told me this?"

"That will depend upon whether you tell her. She is prepared for it, and do you know what she counts upon for her defence? On your thinking that I lie. Perhaps you do; don't make yourself uncomfortable to hide it. Only, as it happens this time, I don't. I have told little fibs; but they have never hurt any one but myself."

Isabel sat staring at her companion's story as at a bale of fantastic wares that some strolling gipsy might have unpacked on the carpet at her feet. "Why did Osmond never marry her?" she asked, at last.

"Because she had no money." The Countess had an answer for everything, and if she lied she lied well. "No one knows, no one has ever known, what she lives on, or how she has got all those beautiful things. I don't believe Osmond himself knows. Besides, she wouldn't have married him."

"How can she have loved him then?"

"She doesn't love him, in that way. She did at first, and then, I suppose, she would have married him; but at that time her husband was living. By the time M. Merle had rejoined— I won't say his ancestors, because he never had any—her relations with Osmond had changed, and she had grown more ambitious. She hoped she might marry a great man; that has always been her idea. She has waited and watched and plotted and prayed; but she has never succeeded. I don't call Madame Merle a success, you know. I don't know what she may accomplish yet, but at present she has very little to show. The only tangible result she has ever achieved—except, of course, getting to know every one and staying with them free of expense—has been her bringing you and Osmond together. Oh, she did that, my dear; you needn't look as if you doubted it. I have watched them for years; I know everything—everything. I am thought a great scatterbrain, but I have had enough application of mind to follow up those two. She hates me, and her way of showing it is to pretend to be for ever defending me. When people say I have had fifteen lovers, she looks horrified, and declares that quite half of them were never proved. She has been afraid of me for years, and she has taken great comfort in the vile, false things that people have said about me. She has been afraid I would expose her, and she threatened me one day, when Osmond began to pay his court to you. It was at his house in Florence; do you remember that afternoon when she brought you there and we had tea in the garden? She let me know then that if I should tell tales, two could play at that game. She pretends there is a good deal more to tell about me than about her. It would be an interesting comparison! I don't care a fig what she may say, simply because I know you don't care a fig. You can't trouble your head about me less than you do already. So she may take her revenge as she chooses; I don't think she will frighten you very much. Her great idea has been to be tremendously irreproachable—a kind of full-blown lily—the incarnation of propriety. She has always worshipped that god. There should be no scandal about Cæsar's wife, you know; and, as I say, she has always hoped to marry Cæsar. That was one reason she wouldn't marry Osmond; the fear that on seeing her with Pansy people would put things together—would even see a resemblance. She has had a terror lest the mother should betray herself. She has been awfully careful; the mother has never done so."

"Yes, yes, the mother has done so," said Isabel, who had listened to all this with a face of deepening dreariness. "She betrayed herself to me the other day, though I didn't recognise her. There appeared to have been a chance of Pansy's making a great marriage, and in her disappointment at its not coming off she almost dropped the mask."

"Ah, that's where she would stumble!" cried the Countess. "She has failed so dreadfully herself that she is determined her daughter shall make it up."

Isabel started at the words "her daughter," which the Countess threw off so familiarly. "It seems very wonderful," she murmured; and in this bewildering impression she had almost lost her sense of being personally touched by the story.

"Now don't go and turn against the poor innocent child!" the Countess went on. "She is very nice, in spite of her lamentable parentage. I have liked Pansy, not because she was hers—but because she had become yours."

"Yes, she has become mine. And how the poor woman must have suffered at seeing me——!" Isabel exclaimed, flushing quickly at the thought.

"I don't believe she has suffered; on the contrary, she has enjoyed. Osmond's marriage has given Pansy a great lift. Before that she lived in a hole. And do you know what the mother thought? That you might take such a fancy to the child that you would do something for her. Osmond, of course, could never give her a portion. Osmond was really extremely poor; but of course you know all about that.—Ah, my dear," cried the Countess, "why did you ever inherit money?" She stopped a moment, as if she saw something singular in Isabel's face. "Don't tell me now that you will give her a dowry. You are capable of that, but I shouldn't believe it. Don't try to be too good. Be a little wicked, feel a little wicked, for once in your life!"

"It's very strange. I suppose I ought to know, but I am sorry," Isabel said. "I am much obliged to you."

"Yes, you seem to be!" cried the Countess, with a mocking laugh. "Perhaps you are—perhaps you are not. You don't take it as I should have thought."

"How should I take it?" Isabel asked.

"Well, I should say as a woman who has been made use of." Isabel made no answer to this; she only listened, and the Countess went on. "They have always been bound to each other; they remained so even after she became proper. But he has always been more for her than she has been for him. When their little carnival was over they made a bargain that each should give the other complete liberty, but that each should also do everything possible to help the other on. You may ask me how I know such a thing as that. I know it by the way they have behaved. Now see how much better women are than men! She has found a wife for Osmond, but Osmond has never lifted a little finger for her. She has worked for him, plotted for him, suffered for him; she has even more than once found money for him; and the end of it is that he is tired of her. She is an old habit; there are moments when he needs her; but on the whole he wouldn't miss her if she were removed. And, what's more, to-day she knows it. So you needn't be jealous!" the Countess added, humorously.

Isabel rose from her sofa again; she felt bruised and short of breath; her head was humming with new knowledge. "I am much obliged to you," she repeated. And then she added, abruptly, in quite a different tone—"How do you know all this?"

This inquiry appeared to ruffle the Countess more than Isabel's expression of gratitude pleased her. She gave her companion a bold stare, with which—"Let us assume that I have invented it!" she cried. She too, however, suddenly changed her tone, and, laying her hand on Isabel's arm, said softly, with her sharp, bright smile—"Now will you give up your journey?"

Isabel started a little; she turned away. But she felt weak and in a moment had to lay her arm upon the mantel-shelf for support. She stood a minute so, and then upon her arm she dropped her dizzy head, with closed eyes and pale lips.

"I have done wrong to speak—I have made you ill!" the Countess cried.

"Ah, I must see Ralph!" Isabel murmured; not in resentment, not in the quick passion her companion had looked for; but in a tone of exquisite far-reaching sadness.

LII

THERE WAS a train for Turin and Paris that evening; and after the Countess had left her, Isabel had a rapid and decisive conference with her maid, who was discreet, devoted, and active. After this, she thought (except of her journey) of only one thing. She must go and see Pansy; from her she could not turn away. She had not seen her yet, as Osmond had given her to understand that it was too soon to begin. She drove at five o'clock to a high door in a narrow street in the quarter of the Piazza Navona, and was admitted by the portress of the convent, a genial and obsequious person. Isabel had been at this institution before; she had come with Pansy to see the sisters. She knew they were good women, and she saw that the large rooms were clean and cheerful, and that the well-used garden had sun for winter and shade for spring. But she disliked the place, and it made her horribly sad; not for the world would she have spent a night there. It produced to-day more than before the impression of a well-appointed prison; for it was not possible to pretend that Pansy was free to leave it. This innocent creature had been presented to her in a new and violent light, but the secondary effect of the revelation was to make Isabel reach out her hand to her.

The portress left her to wait in the parlour of the convent, while she went to make it known that there was a visitor for the dear young lady. The parlour was a vast, cold apartment, with new-looking furniture; a large clean stove of white porcelain, unlighted; a collection of wax-flowers, under glass; and a series of engravings from religious pictures on the walls. On the other occasion Isabel had thought it less like Rome than like Philadelphia; but to-day she made no reflections; the apartment only seemed to her very empty and very soundless. The portress returned at the end of some five minutes, ushering in another person. Isabel got up, expecting to see one of the ladies of the sisterhood; but to her extreme surprise she found herself confronted with Madame Merle. The effect was strange, for Madame Merle was already so present to her vision that her appearance in the flesh was a sort of redup-

lication. Isabel had been thinking all day of her falsity, her
audacity, her ability, her probable suffering; and these dark
things seemed to flash with a sudden light as she entered the
room. Her being there at all was a kind of vivid proof. It
made Isabel feel faint; if it had been necessary to speak on the
spot, she would have been quite unable. But no such necessity
was distinct to her; it seemed to her indeed that she had absolutely nothing to say to Madame Merle. In one's relations
with this lady, however, there were never any absolute ne-
cessities; she had a manner which carried off not only her
own deficiencies, but those of other people. But she was different from usual; she came in slowly, behind the portress,
and Isabel instantly perceived that she was not likely to depend upon her habitual resources. For her, too, the occasion
was exceptional, and she had undertaken to treat it by the
light of the moment. This gave her a peculiar gravity; she did
not even pretend to smile, and though Isabel saw that she
was more than ever playing a part, it seemed to her that on
the whole the wonderful woman had never been so natural.
She looked at Isabel from head to foot, but not harshly nor
defiantly; with a cold gentleness rather, and an absence of
any air of allusion to their last meeting. It was as if she
had wished to mark a difference; she had been irritated then—
she was reconciled now.

"You can leave us alone," she said to the portress; "in five
minutes this lady will ring for you." And then she turned to
Isabel, who, after noting what has just been mentioned, had
ceased to look at her, and had let her eyes wander as far as
the limits of the room would allow. She wished never to look
at Madame Merle again. "You are surprised to find me here,
and I am afraid you are not pleased," this lady went on. "You
don't see why I should have come; it's as if I had anticipated
you. I confess I have been rather indiscreet—I ought to have
asked your permission." There was none of the oblique movement of irony in this; it was said simply and softly; but Isabel,
far afloat on a sea of wonder and pain, could not have told
herself with what intention it was uttered. "But I have not
been sitting long," Madame Merle continued; "that is, I have
not been long with Pansy. I came to see her because it occurred to me this afternoon that she must be rather lonely,

and perhaps even a little miserable. It may be good for a young girl; I know so little about young girls, I can't tell. At any rate it's a little dismal. Therefore I came—on the chance. I knew of course that you would come, and her father as well; still, I had not been told that other visitors were forbidden. The good woman—what's her name? Madame Catherine— made no objection whatever. I stayed twenty minutes with Pansy; she has a charming little room, not in the least conventual, with a piano and flowers. She has arranged it delightfully; she has so much taste. Of course it's all none of my business, but I feel happier since I have seen her. She may even have a maid if she likes; but of course she has no occasion to dress. She wears a little black dress; she looks so charming. I went afterwards to see Mother Catherine, who has a very good room too; I assure you I don't find the poor sisters at all monastic. Mother Catherine has a most coquettish little toilet-table, with something that looked uncommonly like a bottle of eau-de-Cologne. She speaks delightfully of Pansy; says it's a great happiness for them to have her. She is a little saint of heaven, and a model to the oldest of them. Just as I was leaving Madame Catherine, the portress came to say to her that there was a lady for the Signorina. Of course I knew it must be you, and I asked her to let me go and receive you in her place. She demurred greatly—I must tell you that—and said it was her duty to notify the Superior; it was of such high importance that you should be treated with respect. I requested her to let the poor Superior alone, and asked her how she supposed I would treat you!"

So Madame Merle went on, with much of the brilliancy of a woman who had long been a mistress of the art of conversation. But there were phases and gradations in her speech, not one of which was lost upon Isabel's ear, though her eyes were absent from her companion's face. She had not proceeded far before Isabel noted a sudden rupture in her voice, which was in itself a complete drama. This subtle modulation marked a momentous discovery—the perception of an entirely new attitude on the part of her listener. Madame Merle had guessed in the space of an instant that everything was at end between them, and in the space of another instant she had guessed the reason why. The person who stood there was not the same one she had seen hitherto; it was a very different person—a person who knew her secret. This discovery was tremendous, and for the moment she made it the most accomplished of women faltered and lost her courage. But only for that moment. Then the conscious stream of her perfect manner gathered itself again and flowed on as smoothly as might be to the end. But it was only because she had the end in view that she was able to go on. She had been touched with a point that made her quiver, and she needed all the alertness of her will to repress her agitation. Her only safety was in not betraying herself. She did not betray herself; but the startled quality of her voice refused to improve—she couldn't help it—while she heard herself say she hardly knew what. The tide of her confidence ebbed, and she was able only just to glide into port, faintly grazing the bottom.

Isabel saw all this as distinctly as if it had been a picture on the wall. It might have been a great moment for her, for it might have been a moment of triumph. That Madame Merle had lost her pluck and saw before her the phantom of exposure—this in itself was a revenge, this in itself was almost a symptom of a brighter day. And for a moment while she stood apparently looking out of the window, with her back half turned, Isabel enjoyed her knowledge. On the other side of the window lay the garden of the convent; but this is not what Isabel saw; she saw nothing of the budding plants and the glowing afternoon. She saw, in the crude light of that revelation which had already become a part of experience and to which the very frailty of the vessel in which it had been offered her only gave an intrinsic price, the dry, staring fact that she had been a dull un-reverenced tool. All the bitterness of this knowledge surged into her soul again; it was as if she felt on her lips the taste of dishonour. There was a moment during which, if she had turned and spoken, she would have said something that would hiss like a lash. But she closed her eyes, and then the hideous vision died away. What remained was the cleverest woman in the world, standing there within a few feet of her and knowing as little what to think as the meanest. Isabel's only revenge was to be silent still—to leave Madame Merle in this unprecedented situation. She left her there for a period which must have seemed long to this lady, who at last seated herself with a movement which was in itself a confession of helplessness. Then Isabel turned her eyes and looked down at her. Madame Merle was very pale; her own eyes covered Isabel's face. She might see what she would, but her danger was over. Isabel would never accuse her, never reproach her; perhaps because she never would give her the opportunity to defend herself.

"I am come to bid Pansy good-bye," Isabel said at last. "I am going to England to-night."

"Going to England to-night!" Madame Merle repeated, sitting there and looking up at her.

"I am going to Gardencourt. Ralph Touchett is dying."

"Ah, you will feel that." Madame Merle recovered herself; she had a chance to express sympathy. "Do you go alone?" she asked.

"Yes; without my husband."

Madame Merle gave a low, vague murmur; a sort of recognition of the general sadness of things.

"Mr. Touchett never liked me; but I am sorry he is dying. Shall you see his mother?"

"Yes; she has returned from America."

"She used to be very kind to me; but she has changed. Others, too, have changed," said Madame Merle, with a quiet, noble pathos. She paused a moment, and then she said, "And you will see dear old Gardencourt again!"

"I shall not enjoy it much," Isabel answered.

"Naturally—in your grief. But it is on the whole, of all the houses I know, and I know many, the one I should have liked best to live in. I don't venture to send a message to the people," Madame Merle added; "but I should like to give my love to the place."

Isabel turned away.

"I had better go to Pansy," she said. "I have not much time."

And while she looked about her for the proper egress, the door opened and admitted one of the ladies of the house, who advanced with a discreet smile, gently rubbing, under her long loose sleeves, a pair of plump white hands. Isabel recognised her as Madame Catherine, whose acquaintance she had already made, and begged that she would immediately let her see Miss Osmond. Madame Catherine looked doubly discreet, but smiled very blandly and said—

"It will be good for her to see you. I will take you to her myself." Then she directed her pleasant, cautious little eye towards Madame Merle.

"Will you let me remain a little?" this lady asked. "It is so good to be here."

"You may remain always, if you like!" And the good sister gave a knowing laugh.

She led Isabel out of the room, through several corridors, and up a long staircase. All these departments were solid and bare, light and clean; so, thought Isabel, are the great penal establishments. Madame Catherine gently pushed open the door of Pansy's room and ushered in the visitor; then stood smiling, with folded hands, while the two others met and embraced.

"She is glad to see you," she repeated; "it will do her good." And she placed the best chair carefully for Isabel. But she made no movement to seat herself; she seemed ready to retire. "How does this dear child look?" she asked of Isabel, lingering a moment.

"She looks pale," Isabel answered.

"That is the pleasure of seeing you. She is very happy. *Elle éclaire la maison*," said the good sister.

Pansy wore, as Madame Merle had said, a little black dress; it was perhaps this that made her look pale.

"They are very good to me—they think of everything!" she exclaimed, with all her customary eagerness to say something agreeable.

"We think of you always—you are a precious charge," Madame Catherine remarked, in the tone of a woman with whom benevolence was a habit, and whose conception of duty was the acceptance of every care. It fell with a leaden weight upon Isabel's ears; it seemed to represent the surrender of a personality, the authority of the Church.

When Madame Catherine had left them together, Pansy kneeled down before Isabel and hid her head in her stepmother's lap. So she remained some moments, while Isabel gently stroked her hair. Then she got up, averting her face and looking about the room.

"Don't you think I have arranged it well? I have everything I have at home."

"It is very pretty; you are very comfortable." Isabel scarcely knew what she could say to her. On the one hand she could not let her think she had come to pity her, and on the other it would be a dull mockery to pretend to rejoice with her. So she simply added, after a moment, "I have come to bid you good-bye. I am going to England."

Pansy's white little face turned red.

"To England! Not to come back?"

"I don't know when I shall come back."

"Ah; I'm sorry," said Pansy, faintly. She spoke as if she had no right to criticise; but her tone expressed a depth of disappointment.

"My cousin, Mr. Touchett, is very ill; he will probably die. I wish to see him," Isabel said.

"Ah, yes; you told me he would die. Of course you must go. And will papa go?"

"No; I shall go alone."

For a moment, Pansy said nothing. Isabel had often wondered what she thought of the apparent relations of her father with his wife; but never by a glance, by an intimation, had she let it be seen that she deemed them deficient in the quality of intimacy. She made her reflections, Isabel was sure; and she must have had a conviction that there were husbands and wives who were more intimate than that. But Pansy was not indiscreet even in thought; she would as little have ventured to judge her gentle stepmother as to criticise her magnificent father. Her heart may almost have stood still, as it would have done if she had seen two of the saints in the great picture in the convent-chapel turn their painted heads and shake them at each other; but as in this latter case she would (for very solemnity's sake), never have mentioned the awful phenomenon, so she put away all knowledge of the secrets of larger lives than her own.

"You will be very far away," she said presently.

"Yes; I shall be far away. But it will scarcely matter," Isabel answered; "for so long as you are here I am very far away from you."

"Yes; but you can come and see me; though you have not come very often."

"I have not come because your father forbade it. To-day I bring nothing with me. I can't amuse you."

"I am not to be amused. That's not what papa wishes."

"Then it hardly matters whether I am in Rome or in England."

"You are not happy, Mrs. Osmond," said Pansy.

"Not very. But it doesn't matter."

"That's what I say to myself. What does it matter? But I should like to come out."

"I wish indeed you might."

"Don't leave me here," Pansy went on, gently.

Isabel was silent a moment; her heart beat fast.

"Will you come away with me now?" she asked.

Pansy looked at her pleadingly.

"Did papa tell you to bring me?"

"No; it's my own proposal."

"I think I had better wait, then. Did papa send me no message?"

"I don't think he knew I was coming."

"He thinks I have not had enough," said Pansy. "But I have. The ladies are very kind to me, and the little girls come to see me. There are some very little ones—such charming children. Then my room—you can see for yourself. All that is very delightful. But I have had enough. Papa wished me to think a little—and I have thought a great deal."

"What have you thought?"

"Well, that I must never displease papa."

"You knew that before."

"Yes; but I know it better. I will do anything—I will do anything," said Pansy. Then, as she heard her own words, a deep, pure blush came into her face. Isabel read the meaning of it; she saw that the poor girl had been vanquished. It was well that Mr. Edward Rosier had kept his enamels! Isabel looked into her eyes and saw there mainly a prayer to be treated easily. She laid her hand on Pansy's, as if to let her know that her look conveyed no diminution of esteem; for the collapse of the girl's momentary resistance (mute and modest though it had been), seemed only her tribute to the truth of things. She didn't presume to judge others, but she had judged herself; she had seen the reality. She had no vocation for struggling with combinations; in the solemnity of sequestration there was something that overwhelmed her. She bowed her pretty head to authority, and only asked of authority to be merciful. Yes; it was very well that Edward Rosier had reserved a few articles!

Isabel got up; her time was rapidly shortening.

"Good-bye, then," she said; "I leave Rome to-night."

Pansy took hold of her dress; there was a sudden change in the girl's face.

"You look strange; you frighten me."

"Oh, I am very harmless," said Isabel.

"Perhaps you won't come back?"

"Perhaps not. I can't tell."

"Ah, Mrs. Osmond, you won't leave me!"

Isabel now saw that she had guessed everything.

"My dear child, what can I do for you?" she asked.

"I don't know—but I am happier when I think of you."

"You can always think of me."

"Not when you are so far. I am a little afraid," said Pansy.

"What are you afraid of?"

"Of papa—a little. And of Madame Merle. She has just been to see me."

"You must not say that," Isabel observed.

"Oh, I will do everything they want. Only if you are here I shall do it more easily."

Isabel reflected a little.

"I won't desert you," she said at last. "Good-bye, my child."

Then they held each other a moment in a silent embrace, like two sisters; and afterwards Pansy walked along the corridor with her visitor to the top of the staircase.

"Madame Merle has been here," Pansy remarked as they went; and as Isabel answered nothing she added, abruptly, "I don't like Madame Merle!"

Isabel hesitated a moment; then she stopped.

"You must never say that—that you don't like Madame Merle."

Pansy looked at her in wonder; but wonder with Pansy had never been a reason for non-compliance.

"I never will again," she said, with exquisite gentleness.

At the top of the staircase they had to separate, as it appeared to be part of the mild but very definite discipline under which Pansy lived that she should not go down. Isabel descended, and when she reached the bottom the girl was standing above.

"You will come back?" she called out in a voice that Isabel remembered afterwards.

"Yes—I will come back."

Madame Catherine met Isabel below, and conducted her to the door of the parlour, outside of which the two stood talking a minute.

"I won't go in," said the good sister. "Madame Merle is waiting for you."

At this announcement Isabel gave a start, and she was on the point of asking if there were no other egress from the convent. But a moment's reflection assured her that she would do well not to betray to the worthy nun her desire to avoid Pansy's other visitor. Her companion laid her hand very gently on her arm, and fixing her a moment with a wise, benevolent eye, said to her, speaking French, almost familiarly—

"*Eh bien, chère Madame, qu'en pensez-vous?*"

"About my step-daughter? Oh, it would take long to tell you."

"We think it's enough," said Madame Catherine, significantly. And she pushed open the door of the parlour.

Madame Merle was sitting just as Isabel had left her, like a woman so absorbed in thought that she had not moved a little-finger. As Madame Catherine closed the door behind Isabel, she got up, and Isabel saw that she had been thinking to some purpose. She had recovered her balance; she was in full possession of her resources.

"I found that I wished to wait for you," she said, urbanely. "But it's not to talk about Pansy."

Isabel wondered what it could be to talk about, and in spite of Madame Merle's declaration she answered after a moment—

"Madame Catherine says it's enough."

"Yes; it also seems to me enough. I wanted to ask you another word about poor Mr. Touchett," Madame Merle added. "Have you reason to believe that he is really at his last?"

"I have no information but a telegram. Unfortunately it only confirms a probability."

"I am going to ask you a strange question," said Madame Merle. "Are you very fond of your cousin?" And she gave a smile as strange as her question.

"Yes, I am very fond of him. But I don't understand you."

Madame Merle hesitated a moment.

"It is difficult to explain. Something has occurred to me which may not have occurred to you, and I give you the benefit of my idea. Your cousin did you once a great service. Have you never guessed it?"

"He has done me many services."

"Yes; but one was much above the rest. He made you a rich woman."

"*He* made me——?"

Madame Merle appeared to see herself successful, and she went on, more triumphantly—

"He imparted to you that extra lustre which was required to make you a brilliant match. At bottom, it is him that you have to thank." She stopped; there was something in Isabel's eyes.

"I don't understand you. It was my uncle's money."

"Yes; it was your uncle's money; but it was your cousin's idea. He brought his father over to it. Ah, my dear, the sum was large!"

Isabel stood staring; she seemed to-day to be living in a world illumined by lurid flashes.

"I don't know why you say such things! I don't know what you know."

"I know nothing but what I have guessed. But I have guessed that."

Isabel went to the door, and when she had opened it stood a moment with her hand on the latch. Then she said—it was her only revenge—

"I believed it was you I had to thank!"

Madame Merle dropped her eyes; she stood there in a kind of proud penance.

"You are very unhappy, I know. But I am more so."

"Yes; I can believe that. I think I should like never to see you again."

Madame Merle raised her eyes.

"I shall go to America," she announced, while Isabel passed out.

LIII

IT WAS NOT with surprise, it was with a feeling which in other circumstances would have had much of the effect of joy, that as Isabel descended from the Paris mail at Charing Cross, she stepped into the arms, as it were—or at any rate into the hands—of Henrietta Stackpole. She had telegraphed to her friend from Turin, and though she had not definitely said to herself that Henrietta would meet her, she had felt that her telegram would produce some helpful result. On her long journey from Rome her mind had been given up to vagueness; she was unable to question the future. She performed this journey with sightless eyes, and took little pleasure in the countries she traversed, decked out though they were in the richest freshness of spring. Her thoughts followed their course through other countries—strange-looking, dimly-lighted, pathless lands, in which there was no change of seasons, but only, as it seemed, a perpetual dreariness of winter. She had plenty to think about; but it was not reflection, nor conscious purpose, that filled her mind. Disconnected visions passed through it, and sudden dull gleams of memory, of expectation. The past and the future alternated at their will, but she saw them only in fitful images, which came and went by a logic of their own. It was extraordinary the things she remembered. Now that she was in the secret, now that she knew something that so much concerned her, and the eclipse of which had made life resemble an attempt to play whist with an imperfect pack of cards, the truth of things, their mutual relations, their meaning, and for the most part their horror, rose before her with a kind of architectural vastness. She remembered a thousand trifles; they started to life with the spontaneity of a shiver. That is, she had thought them trifles at the time; now she saw that they were leaden-weighted. Yet even now they were trifles, after all; for of what use was it to her to understand them? Nothing seemed of use to her to-day. All purpose, all intention, was suspended; all desire, too, save the single desire to reach her richly-constituted refuge. Gardencourt had been her starting-point, and to those muffled chambers it was at least a temporary solution to return. She had gone forth in her strength; she would come back in her weakness; and if the place had been a rest to her before, it would be a positive sanctuary now. She envied Ralph his dying; for if one were thinking of rest, that was the most perfect of all. To cease utterly, to give it all up and not know anything more—this idea was as sweet as the vision of a cool bath in a marble tank, in a darkened chamber, in a hot land. She had moments, indeed, in her journey from Rome, which were almost as good as being dead. She sat in her corner, so motionless, so passive, simply with the sense of being carried, so detached from hope and regret, that if her spirit was haunted with sudden pictures, it might have been the spirit disembarrassed of the flesh. There was nothing to regret now—that was all over. Not only the time of her folly, but the time of her repentance seemed far away. The only thing to regret was that Madame Merle had been so—so strange. Just here Isabel's imagination paused, from literal inability to say what it was that Madame Merle had been. Whatever it was, it was for Madame Merle herself to regret it; and doubtless she would do so in America, where she was going. It concerned Isabel no more; she only had an impression that she should never again see Madame Merle. This impression carried her into the future, of which from time to time she had a mutilated glimpse. She saw herself, in the distant years, still in the attitude of a woman who had her life to live, and these intimations contradicted the spirit of the present hour. It might be desirable to die; but this privilege was evidently to be denied her. Deep in her soul—deeper than any appetite for renunciation—was the sense that life would be her business for a long time to come. And at moments there was something inspiring, almost exhilarating, in the conviction. It was a proof of strength—it was a proof that she should some day be happy again. It couldn't be that she was to live only to suffer; she was still young, after all, and a great many things might happen to her yet. To live only to suffer—only to feel the injury of life repeated and enlarged—it seemed to her that she was too valuable, too capable, for that. Then she wondered whether it were vain and stupid to think so well of herself. When had it ever been a guarantee to be valuable? Was not all history full of the destruction of precious things? Was it not much more probable that if one were delicate one would suffer? It involved then, perhaps, an admission that one had a certain grossness; but Isabel recognised, as it passed before her eyes, the quick, vague shadow of a long future. She should not escape; she should last. Then the middle years wrapped her about again, and the grey curtain of her indifference closed her in.

Henrietta kissed her, as Henrietta usually kissed, as if she were afraid she should be caught doing it; and then Isabel stood there in the crowd, looking about her, looking for her servant. She asked nothing; she wished to wait. She had a sudden perception that she should be helped. She was so glad Henrietta was there; there was something terrible in an arrival in London. The dusky, smoky, far-arching vault of the station, the strange, livid light, the dense, dark, pushing crowd, filled her with a nervous fear and made her put her arm into her friend's. She remembered that she had once liked these things; they seemed part of a mighty spectacle, in which there was something that touched her. She remembered how she walked away from Euston, in the winter dusk, in the crowded streets, five years before. She could not have done that to-day, and the incident came before her as the deed of another person.

"It's too beautiful that you should have come," said Henrietta, looking at her as if she thought Isabel might be prepared to challenge the proposition. "If you hadn't—if you hadn't; well, I don't know," remarked Miss Stackpole, hinting ominously at her powers of disapproval.

Isabel looked about, without seeing her maid. Her eyes rested on another figure, however, which she felt that she had seen before; and in a moment she recognised the genial countenance of Mr. Bantling. He stood a little apart, and it was not in the power of the multitude that pressed about him to make him yield an inch of the ground he had taken—that of abstracting himself, discreetly, while the two ladies performed their embraces.

"There's Mr. Bantling," said Isabel, gently, irrelevantly, scarcely caring much now whether she should find her maid or not.

"Oh yes, he goes everywhere with me. Come here, Mr.

Bantling!" Henrietta exclaimed. Whereupon the gallant bachelor advanced with a smile—a smile tempered, however, by the gravity of the occasion. "Isn't it lovely that she has come?" Henrietta asked. "He knows all about it," she added; "we had quite a discussion; he said you wouldn't; I said you would."

"I thought you always agreed," Isabel answered, smiling. She found she could smile now; she had seen in an instant, in Mr. Bantling's excellent eye, that he had good news for her. It seemed to say that he wished her to remember that he was an old friend of her cousin—that he understood—that it was all right. Isabel gave him her hand; she thought him so kind.

"Oh, I always agree," said Mr. Bantling. "But she doesn't, you know."

"Didn't I tell you that a maid was a nuisance?" Henrietta inquired. "Your young lady has probably remained at Calais."

"I don't care," said Isabel, looking at Mr. Bantling, whom she had never thought so interesting.

"Stay with her while I go and see," Henrietta commanded, leaving the two for a moment together.

They stood there at first in silence, and then Mr. Bantling asked Isabel how it had been on the Channel.

"Very fine. No, I think it was rather rough," said Isabel, to her companion's obvious surprise. After which she added, "You have been to Gardencourt, I know."

"Now how do you know that?"

"I can't tell you—except that you look like a person who has been there."

"Do you think I look sad? It's very sad there, you know."

"I don't believe you ever look sad. You look kind," said Isabel, with a frankness that cost her no effort. It seemed to her that she should never again feel a superficial embarrassment.

Poor Mr. Bantling, however, was still in this inferior stage. He blushed a good deal, and laughed, and assured her that he was often very blue, and that when he was blue he was awfully fierce.

"You can ask Miss Stackpole, you know," he said. "I was at Gardencourt two days ago."

"Did you see my cousin?"

"Only for a little. But he had been seeing people; Warburton was there the day before. Touchett was just the same as usual, except that he was in bed, and that he looks tremendously ill, and that he can't speak," Mr. Bantling pursued. "He was immensely friendly all the same. He was just as clever as ever. It's awfully sad."

Even in the crowded, noisy station this simple picture was vivid. "Was that late in the day?"

"Yes; I went on purpose; we thought you would like to know."

"I am very much obliged to you. Can I go down to-night?"

"Ah, I don't think *she*'ll let you go," said Mr. Bantling. "She wants you to stop with her. I made Touchett's man promise to telegraph me to-day, and I found the telegram an hour ago at my club. 'Quiet and easy,' that's what it says, and it's dated two o'clock. So you see you can wait till to-morrow. You must be very tired."

"Yes, I am very tired. And I thank you again."

"Oh," said Mr. Bantling, " we were certain you would like the last news." While Isabel vaguely noted that after all he and Henrietta seemed to agree.

Miss Stackpole came back with Isabel's maid, whom she had caught in the act of proving her utility. This excellent person, instead of losing herself in the crowd, had simply attended to her mistress's luggage, so that now Isabel was at liberty to leave the station.

"You know you are not to think of going to the country to-night," Henrietta remarked to her. "It doesn't matter whether there is a train or not. You are to come straight to me, in Wimpole Street. There isn't a corner to be had in London, but I have got you one all the same. It isn't a Roman palace, but it will do for a night."

"I will do whatever you wish," Isabel said.

"You will come and answer a few questions; that's what I wish."

"She doesn't say anything about dinner, does she, Mrs. Osmond?" Mr. Bantling inquired jocosely.

Henrietta fixed him a moment with her speculative gaze. "I

see you are in a great hurry to get to your own. You will be at the Paddington station to-morrow morning at ten."

"Don't come for my sake, Mr. Bantling," said Isabel.

"He will come for mine," Henrietta declared, as she ushered Isabel into a cab.

Later, in a large, dusky parlour in Wimpole Street—to do her justice, there had been dinner enough—she asked Isabel those questions to which she had alluded at the station.

"Did your husband make a scene about your coming?" That was Miss Stackpole's first inquiry.

"No; I can't say he made a scene."

"He didn't object then?"

"Yes; he objected very much. But it was not what you would call a scene."

"What was it then?"

"It was a very quiet conversation."

Henrietta for a moment contemplated her friend.

"It must have been awful," she then remarked. And Isabel did not deny that it had been awful. But she confined herself to answering Henrietta's questions, which was easy, as they were tolerably definite. For the present she offered her no new information. "Well," said Miss Stackpole at last, "I have only one criticism to make. I don't see why you promised little Miss Osmond to go back."

"I am not sure that I see myself, now," Isabel replied. "But I did then."

"If you have forgotten your reason perhaps you won't return."

Isabel for a moment said nothing, then—

"Perhaps I shall find another," she rejoined.

"You will certainly never find a good one."

"In default of a better, my having promised will do," Isabel suggested.

"Yes; that's why I hate it."

"Don't speak of it now. I have a little time. Coming away was hard; but going back will be harder still."

"You must remember, after all, that he won't make a scene!" said Henrietta, with much intention.

"He will, though," Isabel answered gravely. "It will not be the scene of a moment; it will be a scene that will last always."

For some minutes the two women sat gazing at this prospect; and then Miss Stackpole, to change the subject, as Isabel had requested, announced abruptly—

"I have been to stay with Lady Pensil!"

"Ah, the letter came at last!"

"Yes; it took five years. But this time she wanted to see me."

"Naturally enough."

"It was more natural than I think you know," said Henrietta, fixing her eyes on a distant point. And then she added, turning suddenly: "Isabel Archer, I beg your pardon. You don't know why? Because I criticised you, and yet I have gone further than you. Mr. Osmond, at least, was born on the other side!"

It was a moment before Isabel perceived her meaning; it was so modestly, or at least so ingeniously, veiled. Isabel's mind was not possessed at present with the comicality of things; but she greeted with a quick laugh the image that her companion had raised. She immediately recovered herself, however, and with a gravity too pathetic to be real—

"Henrietta Stackpole," she asked, "are you going to give up your country?"

"Yes, my poor Isabel, I am. I won't pretend to deny it; I look the fact in the face. I am going to marry Mr. Bantling, and I am going to reside in London."

"It seems very strange," said Isabel, smiling now.

"Well yes, I suppose it does. I have come to it little by little. I think I know what I am doing; but I don't know that I can explain."

"One can't explain one's marriage," Isabel answered. "And yours doesn't need to be explained. Mr. Bantling is very good."

Henrietta said nothing; she seemed lost in reflection.

"He has a beautiful nature," she remarked at last. "I have studied him for many years, and I see right through him. He's as clear as glass—there's no mystery about him. He is not intellectual, but he appreciates intellect. On the other hand, he doesn't exaggerate its claims. I sometimes think we do in the United States."

"Ah," said Isabel, "you are changed indeed! It's the first

time I have ever heard you say anything against your native land."

"I only say that we are too intellectual; that, after all, is a glorious fault. But I *am* changed; a woman has to change a good deal to marry."

"I hope you will be very happy. You will at last—over here—see something of the inner life."

Henrietta gave a little significant sigh. "That's the key to the mystery, I believe. I couldn't endure to be kept off. Now I have as good a right as any one!" she added, with artless elation.

Isabel was deeply diverted, but there was a certain melancholy in her view. Henrietta, after all, was human and feminine, Henrietta whom she had hitherto regarded as a light keen flame, a disembodied voice. It was rather a disappointment to find that she had personal susceptibilities, that she was subject to common passions, and that her intimacy with Mr. Bantling had not been completely original. There was a want of originality in her marrying him—there was even a kind of stupidity; and for a moment, to Isabel's sense, the dreariness of the world took on a deeper tinge. A little later, indeed, she reflected that Mr. Bantling, after all, was original. But she didn't see how Henrietta could give up her country. She herself had relaxed her hold of it, but it had never been her country as it had been Henrietta's. She presently asked her if she had enjoyed her visit to Lady Pensil.

"Oh, yes," said Henrietta, "she didn't know what to make of me."

"And was that very enjoyable?"

"Very much so, because she is supposed to be very talented. She thinks she knows everything; but she doesn't understand a lady-correspondent! It would be so much easier for her if I were only a little better or a little worse. She's so puzzled; I believe she thinks it's my duty to go and do something immoral. She thinks it's immoral that I should marry her brother; but, after all, that isn't immoral enough. And she will never understand—never!"

"She is not so intelligent as her brother, then," said Isabel. "He appears to have understood."

"Oh no, he hasn't!" cried Miss Stackpole, with decision. "I

really believe that's what he wants to marry me for—just to find out. It's a fixed idea—a kind of fascination."

"It's very good in you to humour it."

"Oh well," said Henrietta, "I have something to find out too!" And Isabel saw that she had not renounced an allegiance, but planned an attack. She was at last about to grapple in earnest with England.

Isabel also perceived, however, on the morrow, at the Paddington station, where she found herself, at ten o'clock, in the company both of Miss Stackpole and Mr. Bantling, that the gentleman bore his perplexities lightly. If he had not found out everything, he had found out at least the great point—that Miss Stackpole would not be wanting in initiative. It was evident that in the selection of a wife he had been on his guard against this deficiency.

"Henrietta has told me, and I am very glad," Isabel said, as she gave him her hand.

"I dare say you think it's very odd," Mr. Bantling replied, resting on his neat umbrella.

"Yes, I think it's very odd."

"You can't think it's so odd as I do. But I have always rather liked striking out a line," said Mr. Bantling, serenely.

LIV

ISABEL'S ARRIVAL at Gardencourt on this second occasion was even quieter than it had been on the first. Ralph Touchett kept but a small household, and to the new servants Mrs. Osmond was a stranger; so that Isabel, instead of being conducted to her own apartment, was coldly shown into the drawing-room, and left to wait while her name was carried up to her aunt. She waited a long time; Mrs. Touchett appeared to be in no hurry to come to her. She grew impatient at last; she grew nervous and even frightened. The day was dark and cold; the dusk was thick in the corners of the wide brown rooms. The house was perfectly still—a stillness that Isabel remembered; it had filled all the place for days before the death of her uncle. She left the drawing-room and wandered about—strolled into the library and along the gallery of pictures, where, in the deep silence, her footstep made an echo. Nothing was changed; she recognised everything that she had seen years before; it might have been only yesterday that she stood there. She reflected that things change but little, while people change so much, and she became aware that she was walking about as her aunt had done on the day that she came to see her in Albany. She was changed enough since then—that had been the beginning. It suddenly struck her that if her Aunt Lydia had not come that day in just that way and found her alone, everything might have been different. She might have had another life, and to-day she might have been a happier woman. She stopped in the gallery in front of a small picture—a beautiful and valuable Bonington—upon which her eyes rested for a long time. But she was not looking at the picture; she was wondering whether if her aunt had not come that day in Albany she would have married Caspar Goodwood.

Mrs. Touchett appeared at last, just after Isabel had returned to the big uninhabited drawing-room. She looked a good deal older, but her eye was as bright as ever and her head as erect; her thin lips seemed a repository of latent meanings. She wore a little grey dress, of the most undecorated fashion, and Isabel wondered, as she had wondered the first time, whether her remarkable kinswoman resembled more a queen-regent or the matron of a gaol. Her lips felt very thin indeed as Isabel kissed her.

"I have kept you waiting because I have been sitting with Ralph," Mrs. Touchett said. "The nurse had gone to her lunch and I had taken her place. He has a man who is supposed to look after him, but the man is good for nothing; he is always looking out of the window—as if there were anything to see! I didn't wish to move, because Ralph seemed to be sleeping, and I was afraid the sound would disturb him. I waited till the nurse came back; I remembered that you knew the house."

"I find I know it better even than I thought; I have been walking," Isabel answered. And then she asked whether Ralph slept much.

"He lies with his eyes closed; he doesn't move. But I am not sure that it's always sleep."

"Will he see me? Can he speak to me?"

Mrs. Touchett hesitated a moment. "You can try him," she said. And then she offered to conduct Isabel to her room. "I thought they had taken you there; but it's not my house, it's Ralph's; and I don't know what they do. They must at least have taken your luggage; I don't suppose you have brought much. Not that I care, however. I believe they have given you the same room you had before; when Ralph heard you were coming he said you must have that one."

"Did he say anything else?"

"Ah, my dear, he doesn't chatter as he used!" cried Mrs. Touchett, as she preceded her niece up the staircase.

It was the same room, and something told Isabel that it had not been slept in since she occupied it. Her luggage was there, and it was not voluminous; Mrs. Touchett sat down a moment, with her eyes upon it.

"Is there really no hope?" Isabel asked, standing before her aunt.

"None whatever. There never has been. It has not been a successful life."

"No—it has only been a beautiful one." Isabel found herself already contradicting her aunt; she was irritated by her dryness.

"I don't know what you mean by that; there is no beauty without health. That is a very odd dress to travel in."

Isabel glanced at her garment. "I left Rome at an hour's notice; I took the first that came."

"Your sisters, in America, wished to know how you dress. That seemed to be their principal interest. I wasn't able to tell them—but they seemed to have the right idea: that you never wear anything less than black brocade."

"They think I am more brilliant than I am; I am afraid to tell them the truth," said Isabel. "Lily wrote me that you had dined with her."

"She invited me four times, and I went once. After the second time she should have let me alone. The dinner was very good; it must have been expensive. Her husband has a very bad manner. Did I enjoy my visit to America? Why should I have enjoyed it? I didn't go for my pleasure."

These were interesting items, but Mrs. Touchett soon left her niece, whom she was to meet in half-an-hour at the midday meal. At this repast the two ladies faced each other at an abbreviated table in the melancholy dining-room. Here, after a little, Isabel saw that her aunt was not so dry as she appeared, and her old pity for the poor woman's inexpressiveness, her want of regret, of disappointment, came back to her. It seemed to her she would find it a blessing to-day to be able to indulge a regret. She wondered whether Mrs. Touchett were not trying, whether she had not a desire for the recreation of grief. On the other hand, perhaps, she was afraid; if she began to regret, it might take her too far. Isabel could perceive, however, that it had come over her that she had missed something, that she saw herself in the future as an old woman without memories. Her little sharp face looked tragical. She told her niece that Ralph as yet had not moved, but that he probably would be able to see her before dinner. And then in a moment she added that he had seen Lord Warburton the day before; an announcement which startled Isabel a little, as it seemed an intimation that this personage was in the neighbourhood and that an accident might bring them together. Such an accident would not be happy; she had not come to England to converse with Lord Warburton. She presently said to her aunt that he had been very kind to Ralph; she had seen something of that in Rome.

"He has something else to think of now," Mrs. Touchett rejoined. And she paused, with a gaze like a gimlet.

Isabel saw that she meant something, and instantly guessed what she meant. But her reply concealed her guess; her heart beat faster, and she wished to gain a moment. "Ah yes—the House of Lords, and all that."

"He is not thinking of the Lords; he is thinking of the ladies. At least he is thinking of one of them; he told Ralph he was engaged to be married."

"Ah, to be married!" Isabel gently exclaimed.

"Unless he breaks it off. He seemed to think Ralph would like to know. Poor Ralph can't go to the wedding, though I believe it is to take place very soon."

"And who is the young lady?"

"A member of the aristocracy; Lady Flora, Lady Felicia—something of that sort."

"I am very glad," Isabel said. "It must be a sudden decision."

"Sudden enough, I believe; a courtship of three weeks. It has only just been made public."

"I am very glad," Isabel repeated, with a larger emphasis. She knew her aunt was watching her—looking for the signs of some curious emotion, and the desire to prevent her companion from seeing anything of this kind enabled her to speak in the tone of quick satisfaction—the tone, almost, of relief. Mrs. Touchett of course followed the tradition that ladies, even married ones, regard the marriage of their old lovers as an offence to themselves. Isabel's first care therefore was to show that however that might be in general, she was not offended now. But meanwhile, as I say, her heart beat faster; and if she sat for some moments thoughtful—she presently forgot Mrs. Touchett's observation—it was not because she had lost an admirer. Her imagination had traversed half Europe; it halted, panting, and even trembling a little, in the city of Rome. She figured herself announcing to her husband that Lord Warburton was to lead a bride to the altar, and she was of course not aware how extremely sad she looked while she made this intellectual effort. But at last she collected herself, and said to her aunt—"He was sure to do it some time or other."

Mrs. Touchett was silent; then she gave a sharp little shake of the head. "Ah, my dear, you're beyond me!" she cried, suddenly. They went on with their luncheon in silence; Isabel felt as if she had heard of Lord Warburton's death. She had known him only as a suitor, and now that was all over. He was dead for poor Pansy; by Pansy he might have lived. A servant had been hovering about; at last Mrs. Touchett requested him to leave them alone. She had finished her lunch; she sat with her hands folded on the edge of the table. "I should like to ask you three questions," she said to Isabel, when the servant had gone.

"Three are a great many."

"I can't do with less; I have been thinking. They are all very good ones."

"That's what I am afraid of. The best questions are the worst," Isabel answered. Mrs. Touchett had pushed back her chair, and Isabel left the table and walked, rather consciously, to one of the deep windows, while her aunt followed her with her eyes.

"Have you ever been sorry you didn't marry Lord Warburton?" Mrs. Touchett inquired.

Isabel shook her head slowly, smiling. "No, dear aunt."

"Good. I ought to tell you that I propose to believe what you say."

"Your believing me is an immense temptation," Isabel replied, smiling still.

"A temptation to lie? I don't recommend you to do that, for when I'm misinformed I'm as dangerous as a poisoned rat. I don't mean to crow over you."

"It is my husband that doesn't get on with me," said Isabel.

"I could have told him that. I don't call that crowing over *you*," Mrs. Touchett added. "Do you still like Serena Merle?" she went on.

"Not as I once did. But it doesn't matter, for she is going to America."

"To America? She must have done something very bad."

"Yes—very bad."

"May I ask what it is?"

"She made a convenience of me."

"Ah," cried Mrs. Touchett, "so she did of me! She does of every one."

"She will make a convenience of America," said Isabel, smiling again, and glad that her aunt's questions were over.

It was not till the evening that she was able to see Ralph. He had been dozing all day; at least he had been lying unconscious. The doctor was there, but after a while he went away; the local doctor, who had attended his father, and whom Ralph liked. He came three or four times a day; he was deeply interested in his patient. Ralph had had Sir Matthew Hope, but he had got tired of this celebrated man, to whom he had asked his mother to send word that he was now dead, and was therefore without further need of medical advice. Mrs. Touchett had simply written to Sir Matthew that her son disliked him. On the day of Isabel's arrival Ralph gave no sign, as I have related, for many hours; but towards evening he raised himself and said he knew that she had come. How he knew it was not apparent; inasmuch as, for fear of exciting him, no one had offered the information. Isabel came in and sat by his bed in the dim light; there was only a shaded candle in a corner of the room. She told the nurse that she might go—that she herself would sit with him for the rest of the evening. He had opened his eyes and recognised her, and had moved his hand, which lay very helpless beside him, so that she might take it. But he was unable to speak; he closed his eyes again and remained perfectly still, only keeping her hand in his own. She sat with him a long time—till the nurse came back; but he gave no further sign. He might have passed away while she looked at him; he was already the figure and pattern of death. She had thought him far gone in Rome, but this was worse; there was only one change possible now. There was a strange tranquillity in his face; it was as still as the lid of a box. With this, he was a mere lattice of bones; when he opened his eyes to greet her, it was as if she were looking into immeasurable space. It was not till midnight that the nurse came back; but the hours, to Isabel, had not seemed long; it was exactly what she had come for. If she had come simply to wait, she found ample occasion, for he lay for three days in a kind of grateful silence. He recognised her, and at moments he seemed to wish to speak; but he found no voice. Then he closed his eyes again, as if he too were waiting for something—for something that certainly would come. He was so absolutely quiet that it seemed to her what was coming had already arrived; and yet she never lost the sense that they were still together. But they were not always together; there were other hours that she passed in wandering through the empty house and listening for a voice that was not poor Ralph's. She had a constant fear; she thought it possible her husband would write to her. But he remained silent, and she only got a letter from Florence from the Countess Gemini. Ralph, however, spoke at last, on the evening of the third day.

"I feel better to-night," he murmured, abruptly, in the soundless dimness of her vigil; "I think I can say something."

She sank upon her knees beside his pillow; took his thin hand in her own; begged him not to make an effort—not to tire himself.

His face was of necessity serious—it was incapable of the muscular play of a smile; but its owner apparently had not lost a perception of incongruities. "What does it matter if I am tired, when I have all eternity to rest?" he asked. "There is no harm in making an effort when it is the very last. Don't people always feel better just before the end? I have often heard of that; it's what I was waiting for. Ever since you have been here; I thought it would come. I tried two or three times; I was afraid you would get tired of sitting there." He spoke slowly, with painful breaks and long pauses; his voice seemed to come from a distance. When he ceased, he lay with his face turned to Isabel, and his large unwinking eyes open into her own. "It was very good of you to come," he went on. "I thought you would; but I wasn't sure."

"I was not sure either, till I came," said Isabel.

"You have been like an angel beside my bed. You know they talk about the angel of death. It's the most beautiful of all. You have been like that; as if you were waiting for me."

"I was not waiting for your death; I was waiting for—for this. This is not death, dear Ralph."

"Not for you—no. There is nothing makes us feel so much alive as to see others die. That's the sensation of life—the sense that we remain. I have had it—even I. But now I am of no use but to give it to others. With me it's all over." And then he paused. Isabel bowed her head further, till it rested on the two hands that were clasped upon his own. She could not see him now; but his far-away voice was close to her ear. "Isabel," he went on, suddenly, "I wish it were over for you." She answered nothing; she had burst into sobs; she remained so, with her buried face. He lay silent, listening to her sobs; at last he gave a long groan. "Ah, what is it you have done for me?"

"What is it you did for me?" she cried, her now extreme agitation half smothered by her attitude. She had lost all her shame, all wish to hide things. Now he might know; she wished him to know, for it brought them supremely together, and he was beyond the reach of pain. "You did something once—you know it. Oh Ralph, you have been everything! What have I done for you—what can I do to-day? I would die if you could live. But I don't wish you to live; I would die myself, not to lose you." Her voice was as broken as his own, and full of tears and anguish.

"You won't lose me—you will keep me. Keep me in your heart; I shall be nearer to you than I have ever been. Dear Isabel, life is better; for in life there is love. Death is good—but there is no love."

"I never thanked you—I never spoke—I never was what I should be!" Isabel went on. She felt a passionate need to cry out and accuse herself, to let her sorrow possess her. All her troubles, for the moment, became single and melted together into this present pain. "What must you have thought of me? Yet how could I know? I never knew, and I only know to-day because there are people less stupid than I."

"Don't mind people," said Ralph. "I think I am glad to leave people."

She raised her head and her clasped hands; she seemed for a moment to pray to him.

"Is it true—is it true?" she asked.

"True that you have been stupid? Oh no," said Ralph, with a sensible intention of wit.

"That you made me rich—that all I have is yours?"

He turned away his head, and for some time said nothing. Then at last—

"Ah, don't speak of that—that was not happy." Slowly he moved his face toward her again, and they once more saw each other. "But for that—but for that—" And he paused. "I believe I ruined you," he added softly.

She was full of the sense that he was beyond the reach of pain; he seemed already so little of this world. But even if she had not had it she would still have spoken, for nothing mattered now but the only knowledge that was not pure anguish—the knowledge that they were looking at the truth together.

"He married me for my money," she said.

She wished to say everything; she was afraid he might die before she had done so.

He gazed at her a little, and for the first time his fixed eyes lowered their lids. But he raised them in a moment, and then—

"He was greatly in love with you," he answered.

"Yes, he was in love with me. But he would not have married me if I had been poor. I don't hurt you in saying that. How can I? I only want you to understand. I always tried to keep you from understanding; but that's all over."

"I always understood," said Ralph.

"I thought you did, and I didn't like it. But now I like it."

"You don't hurt me—you make me very happy." And as Ralph said this there was an extraordinary gladness in his voice. She bent her head again, and pressed her lips to the back of his hand. "I always understood," he continued, "though it was so strange—so pitiful. You wanted to look at life for yourself—but you were not allowed; you were punished for your wish. You were ground in the very mill of the conventional!"

"Oh yes, I have been punished," Isabel sobbed.

He listened to her a little, and then continued—

"Was he very bad about your coming?"

"He made it very hard for me. But I don't care."

"It is all over, then, between you?"

"Oh no; I don't think anything is over."

"Are you going back to him?" Ralph stammered.

"I don't know—I can't tell. I shall stay here as long as I may. I don't want to think—I needn't think. I don't care for anything but you, and that is enough for the present. It will last a little yet. Here on my knees, with you dying in my arms, I am happier than I have been for a long time. And I want you to be happy—not to think of anything sad; only to feel that I am near you and I love you. Why should there be pain? In such hours as this what have we to do with pain? That is not the deepest thing; there is something deeper."

Ralph evidently found, from moment to moment, greater difficulty in speaking; he had to wait longer to collect himself. At first he appeared to make no response to these last words; he let a long time elapse. Then he murmured simply—

"You must stay here."

"I should like to stay, as long as seems right."

"As seems right—as seems right?" He repeated her words. "Yes, you think a great deal about that."

"Of course one must. You are very tired," said Isabel.

"I am very tired. You said just now that pain is not the deepest thing. No—no. But it is very deep. If I could stay——"

"For me you will always be here," she softly interrupted. It was easy to interrupt him.

But he went on, after a moment—

"It passes, after all; it's passing now. But love remains. I don't know why we should suffer so much. Perhaps I shall find out. There are many things in life; you are very young."

"I feel very old," said Isabel.

"You will grow young again. That's how I see you. I don't believe—I don't believe——" And he stopped again; his strength failed him.

She begged him to be quiet now. "We needn't speak to understand each other," she said.

"I don't believe that such a generous mistake as yours—can hurt you for more than a little."

"Oh, Ralph, I am very happy now," she cried, through her tears.

"And remember this," he continued, "that if you have been hated, you have also been loved."

"Ah, my brother!" she cried, with a movement of still deeper prostration.

LV

HE HAD TOLD her, the first evening she ever spent at Gardencourt, that if she should live to suffer enough she might some day see the ghost with which the old house was duly provided. She apparently had fulfilled the necessary condition; for the next morning, in the cold, faint dawn, she knew that a spirit was standing by her bed. She had lain down without undressing, for it was her belief that Ralph would not outlast the night. She had no inclination to sleep; she was waiting, and such waiting was wakeful. But she closed her eyes; she believed that as the night wore on she should hear a knock at her door. She heard no knock, but at the time the darkness began vaguely to grow grey, she started up from her pillow as abruptly as if she had received a summons. It seemed to her for an instant that Ralph was standing there—a dim, hovering figure in the dimness of the room. She stared a moment; she saw his white face—his kind eyes; then she saw there was nothing. She was not afraid; she was only sure. She went out of her room, and in her certainty passed through dark corridors and down a flight of oaken steps that shone in the vague light of a hall-window. Outside of Ralph's door she stopped a moment, listening; but she seemed to hear only the hush that filled it. She opened the door with a hand as gentle as if she were lifting a veil from the face of the dead, and saw Mrs. Touchett sitting motionless and upright beside the couch of her son, with one of his hands in her own. The doctor was on the other side, with poor Ralph's further wrist resting in his professional fingers. The nurse was at the foot, between them. Mrs. Touchett took no notice of Isabel, but the doctor looked at her very hard; then he gently placed Ralph's hand in a proper position, close beside him. The nurse looked at her very hard too, and no one said a word; but Isabel only looked at what she had come to see. It was fairer than Ralph had ever been in life, and there was a strange resemblance to the face of his father, which, six years before, she had seen lying on the same pillow. She went to her aunt and put her arm round her; and Mrs. Touchett, who as a general thing neither invited nor enjoyed caresses, submitted for a moment to this one, rising, as it were, to take it. But she was stiff and dry-eyed; her acute white face was terrible.

"Poor Aunt Lydia," Isabel murmured.

"Go and thank God you have no child," said Mrs. Touchett, disengaging herself.

Three days after this a considerable number of people found time, in the height of the London "season," to take a morning train down to a quiet station in Berkshire and spend half-an-hour in a small grey church, which stood within an easy walk. It was in the green burial-place of this edifice that Mrs. Touchett consigned her son to earth. She stood herself at the edge of the grave, and Isabel stood beside her; the sexton himself had not a more practical interest in the scene than Mrs. Touchett. It was a solemn occasion, but it was not a disagreeable one; there was a certain geniality in the appearance of things. The weather had changed to fair; the day, one of the last of the treacherous May-time, was warm and windless, and the air had the brightness of the hawthorn and the blackbird. If it was sad to think of poor Touchett, it was not too sad, since death, for him, had had no violence. He had been dying so long; he was so ready; everything had been so expected and prepared. There were tears in Isabel's eyes, but they were not tears that blinded. She looked through them at the beauty of the day, the splendour of nature, the sweetness of the old English churchyard, the bowed heads of good friends. Lord Warburton was there, and a group of gentlemen unknown to Isabel, several of whom, as she afterwards learned, were connected with the bank; and there were others whom she knew. Miss Stackpole was among the first, with honest Mr. Bantling beside her; and Caspar Goodwood, lifting his head higher than the rest—bowing it rather less. During much of the time Isabel was conscious of Mr. Goodwood's gaze; he looked at her somewhat harder than he usually looked in public, while the others had fixed their eyes upon the churchyard turf. But she never let him see that she saw him; she thought of him only to wonder that he was still in England. She found that she had taken for granted that after accompanying Ralph to Gardencourt he had gone away; she remembered that it was not a country that pleased him.

He was there, however, very distinctly there; and something in his attitude seemed to say that he was there with a complex intention. She would not meet his eyes, though there was doubtless sympathy in them; he made her rather uneasy. With the dispersal of the little group he disappeared, and the only person who came to speak to her—though several spoke to Mrs. Touchett—was Henrietta Stackpole. Henrietta had been crying.

Ralph had said to Isabel that he hoped she would remain at Gardencourt, and she made no immediate motion to leave the place. She said to herself that it was but common charity to stay a little with her aunt. It was fortunate she had so good a formula; otherwise she might have been greatly in want of one. Her errand was over; she had done what she left her husband for. She had a husband in a foreign city, counting the hours of her absence; in such a case one needed an excellent motive. He was not one of the best husbands; but that didn't alter the case. Certain obligations were involved in the very fact of marriage, and were quite independent of the quantity of enjoyment extracted from it. Isabel thought of her husband as little as might be; but now that she was at a distance, beyond its spell, she thought with a kind of spiritual shudder of Rome. There was a deadly sadness in the thought, and she drew back into the deepest shade of Gardencourt. She lived from day to day, postponing, closing her eyes, trying not to think. She knew she must decide, but she decided nothing; her coming itself had not been a decision. On that occasion she had simply started. Osmond gave no sound, and now evidently he would give none; he would leave it all to her. From Pansy she heard nothing, but that was very simple; her father had told her not to write.

Mrs. Touchett accepted Isabel's company, but offered her no assistance; she appeared to be absorbed in considering, without enthusiasm, but with perfect lucidity, the new conveniences of her own situation. Mrs. Touchett was not an optimist, but even from painful occurrences she managed to extract a certain satisfaction. This consisted in the reflection that, after all, such things happened to other people and not to herself. Death was disagreeable, but in this case it was her

son's death, not her own; she had never flattered herself that
her own would be disagreeable to any one but Mrs. Touchett.
She was better off than poor Ralph, who had left all the commodities of life behind him, and indeed all the security; for
the worst of dying was, to Mrs. Touchett's mind, that it exposed one to be taken advantage of. For herself, she was on
the spot; there was nothing so good as that. She made known
to Isabel very punctually—it was the evening her son was
buried—several of Ralph's testamentary arrangements. He
had told her everything, had consulted her about everything.
He left her no money; of course she had no need of money.
He left her the furniture of Gardencourt, exclusive of the pictures and books, and the use of the place for a year; after
which it was to be sold. The money produced by the sale was
to constitute an endowment for a hospital for poor persons
suffering from the malady of which he died; and of this portion of the will Lord Warburton was appointed executor. The
rest of his property, which was to be withdrawn from the
bank, was disposed of in various bequests, several of them
to those cousins in Vermont to whom his father had already been so bountiful. Then there were a number of small
legacies.

"Some of them are extremely peculiar," said Mrs. Touchett;
"He has left considerable sums to persons I never heard of.
He gave me a list, and I asked then who some of them were,
and he told me they were people who at various times had
seemed to like him. Apparently he thought you didn't like
him, for he has not left you a penny. It was his opinion that
you were handsomely treated by his father, which I am bound
to say I think you were—though I don't mean that I ever
heard him complain of it. The pictures are to be dispersed;
he has distributed them about, one by one, as little keepsakes.
The most valuable of the collection goes to Lord Warburton.
And what do you think he has done with his library? It
sounds like a practical joke. He has left it to your friend Miss
Stackpole—'in recognition of her services to literature.' Does
he mean her following him up from Rome? Was that a service
to literature? It contains a great many rare and valuable
books, and as she can't carry it about the world in her trunk,
he recommends her to sell it at auction. She will sell it of

course at Christie's, and with the proceeds she will set up a newspaper. Will that be a service to literature?"

This question Isabel forbore to answer, as it exceeded the little interrogatory to which she had deemed it necessary to submit on her arrival. Besides, she had never been less interested in literature than to-day, as she found when she occasionally took down from the shelf one of the rare and valuable volumes of which Mrs. Touchett had spoken. She was quite unable to read; her attention had never been so little at her command. One afternoon, in the library, about a week after the ceremony in the churchyard, she was trying to fix it a little; but her eyes often wandered from the book in her hand to the open window, which looked down the long avenue. It was in this way that she saw a modest vehicle approach the door, and perceived Lord Warburton sitting, in rather an uncomfortable attitude, in a corner of it. He had always had a high standard of courtesy, and it was therefore not remarkable, under the circumstances, that he should have taken the trouble to come down from London to call upon Mrs. Touchett. It was of course Mrs. Touchett that he had come to see, and not Mrs. Osmond; and to prove to herself the validity of this theory, Isabel presently stepped out of the house and wandered away into the park. Since her arrival at Gardencourt she had been but little out of doors, the weather being unfavourable for visiting the grounds. This evening, however, was fine, and at first it struck her as a happy thought to have come out. The theory I have just mentioned was plausible enough, but it brought her little rest, and if you had seen her pacing about, you would have said she had a bad conscience. She was not pacified when at the end of a quarter of an hour, finding herself in view of the house, she saw Mrs. Touchett emerge from the portico, accompanied by her visitor. Her aunt had evidently proposed to Lord Warburton that they should come in search of her. She was in no humour for visitors, and if she had had time she would have drawn back, behind one of the great trees. But she saw that she had been seen and that nothing was left her but to advance. As the lawn at Gardencourt was a vast expanse, this took some time; during which she observed that, as he walked beside his hostess, Lord Warburton kept his hands rather stiffly behind him and his eyes upon the ground. Both persons apparently were silent; but Mrs. Touchett's thin little glance, as she directed it toward Isabel, had even at a distance an expression. It seemed to say, with cutting sharpness, "Here is the eminently amenable nobleman whom you might have married!" When Lord Warburton lifted his own eyes, however, that was not what they said. They only said, "This is rather awkward, you know, and I depend upon you to help me." He was very grave, very proper, and for the first time since Isabel had known him, he greeted her without a smile. Even in his days of distress he had always begun with a smile. He looked extremely self-conscious.

"Lord Warburton has been so good as to come out to see me," said Mrs. Touchett. "He tells me he didn't know you were still here. I know he's an old friend of yours, and as I was told you were not in the house, I brought him out to see for himself."

"Oh, I saw there was a good train at 6.40, that would get me back in time for dinner," Mrs. Touchett's companion explained, rather irrelevantly. "I am so glad to find you have not gone."

"I am not here for long, you know," Isabel said, with a certain eagerness.

"I suppose not; but I hope it's for some weeks. You came to England sooner than—a—than you thought?"

"Yes, I came very suddenly."

Mrs. Touchett turned away, as if she were looking at the condition of the grounds, which indeed was not what it should be; while Lord Warburton hesitated a little. Isabel fancied he had been on the point of asking about her husband—rather confusedly—and then had checked himself. He continued immitigably grave, either because he thought it becoming in a place over which death had just passed, or for more personal reasons. If he was conscious of personal reasons, it was very fortunate that he had the cover of the former motive; he could make the most of that. Isabel thought of all this. It was not that his face was sad, for that was another matter; but it was strangely inexpressive.

"My sisters would have been so glad to come if they had known you were still here—if they had thought you would see them," Lord Warburton went on. "Do kindly let them see you before you leave England."

"It would give me great pleasure; I have such a friendly recollection of them."

"I don't know whether you would come to Lockleigh for a day or two? You know there is always that old promise." And his lordship blushed a little as he made this suggestion, which gave his face a somewhat more familiar air. "Perhaps I'm not right in saying that just now; of course you are not thinking of visiting. But I meant what would hardly be a visit. My sisters are to be at Lockleigh at Whitsuntide for three days; and if you could come then—as you say you are not to be very long in England—I would see that there should be literally no one else."

Isabel wondered whether not even the young lady he was to marry would be there with her mamma; but she did not express this idea. "Thank you extremely," she contented herself with saying; "I'm afraid I hardly know about Whitsuntide."

"But I have your promise—haven't I?—for some other time."

There was an interrogation in this; but Isabel let it pass. She looked at her interlocutor a moment, and the result of her observation was that—as had happened before—she felt sorry for him. "Take care you don't miss your train," she said. And then she added, "I wish you every happiness."

He blushed again, more than before, and he looked at his watch.

"Ah yes, 6.40; I haven't much time, but I have a fly at the door. Thank you very much." It was not apparent whether the thanks applied to her having reminded him of his train, or to the more sentimental remark. "Good-bye, Mrs. Osmond; good-bye." He shook hands with her, without meeting her eye, and then he turned to Mrs. Touchett, who had wandered back to them. With her his parting was equally brief; and in a moment the two ladies saw him move with long steps across the lawn.

"Are you very sure he is to be married?" Isabel asked of her aunt.

"I can't be surer than he; but he seems sure. I congratulated him, and he accepted it."

"Ah," said Isabel, "I give it up!"—while her aunt returned to the house and to those avocations which the visitor had interrupted.

She gave it up, but she still thought of it—thought of it while she strolled again under the great oaks whose shadows were long upon the acres of turf. At the end of a few minutes she found herself near a rustic bench, which, a moment after she had looked at it, struck her as an object recognised. It was not simply that she had seen it before, nor even that she had sat upon it; it was that in this spot something important had happened to her—that the place had an air of association. Then she remembered that she had been sitting there six years before, when a servant brought her from the house the letter in which Caspar Goodwood informed her that he had followed her to Europe; and that when she had read that letter she looked up to hear Lord Warburton announcing that he should like to marry her. It was indeed an historical, an interesting, bench; she stood and looked at it as if it might have something to say to her. She would not sit down on it now— she felt rather afraid of it. She only stood before it, and while she stood, the past came back to her in one of those rushing waves of emotion by which people of sensibility are visited at odd hours. The effect of this agitation was a sudden sense of being very tired, under the influence of which she overcame her scruples and sank into the rustic seat. I have said that she was restless and unable to occupy herself; and whether or no, if you had seen her there, you would have admitted the justice of the former epithet, you would at least have allowed that at this moment she was the image of a victim of idleness. Her attitude had a singular absence of purpose; her hands, hanging at her sides, lost themselves in the folds of her black dress; her eyes gazed vaguely before her. There was nothing to recall her to the house, the two ladies, in their seclusion, dined early and had tea at an indefinite hour. How long she had sat in this position she could not have told you; but the twilight had grown thick when she became aware that she was not alone. She quickly straightened herself, glancing about, and then saw what had become of her solitude. She was sharing it with Caspar Goodwood, who stood looking at her, a few feet off, and whose footfall, on the unresonant turf, as he came near, she had not heard. It occurred to her, in the midst of this, that it was just so Lord Warburton had surprised her of old.

She instantly rose, and as soon as Goodwood saw that he was seen he started forward. She had had time only to rise, when with a motion that looked like violence, but felt like—she knew not what—he grasped her by the wrist and made her sink again into the seat. She closed her eyes; he had not hurt her, it was only a touch that she had obeyed. But there was something in his face that she wished not to see. That was the way he had looked at her the other day in the church-yard; only to-day it was worse. He said nothing at first; she only felt him close to her. It almost seemed to her that no one had ever been so close to her as that. All this, however, took but a moment, at the end of which she had disengaged her wrist, turning her eyes upon her visitant.

"You have frightened me," she said.

"I didn't mean to," he answered, "but if I did a little, no matter. I came from London a while ago by the train, but I couldn't come here directly. There was a man at the station who got ahead of me. He took a fly that was there, and I heard him give the order to drive here. I don't know who he was, but I didn't want to come with him; I wanted to see you alone. So I have been waiting and walking about. I have walked all over, and I was just coming to the house when I saw you here. There was a keeper, or some one, who met me; but that was all right, because I had made his acquaintance when I came here with your cousin. Is that gentleman gone? are you really alone? I want to speak to you." Goodwood spoke very fast; he was as excited as when they parted in Rome. Isabel had hoped that condition would subside; and she shrank into herself as she perceived that, on the contrary, he had only let out sail. She had a new sensation; he had never produced it before; it was a feeling of danger. There was indeed something awful in his persistency. Isabel gazed straight before her; he with a hand on each knee, leaned forward, looking deeply into her face. The twilight seemed to darken around them. "I want to speak to you," he repeated; "I have something particular to say. I don't want to trouble you—as I did the other day, in Rome. That was no use; it only distressed you. I couldn't help it; I knew I was wrong. But I am not wrong now; please don't think I am," he went on, with his hard, deep voice melting a moment into entreaty. "I came here to-day for a purpose! it's very different. It was no use for me to speak to you then; but now I can help you."

She could not have told you whether it was because she was afraid, or because such a voice in the darkness seemed of necessity a boon; but she listened to him as she had never listened before; his words dropped deep into her soul. They produced a sort of stillness in all her being; and it was with an effort, in a moment, that she answered him.

"How can you help me?" she asked, in a low tone; as if she were taking what he had said seriously enough to make the inquiry in confidence.

"By inducing you to trust me. Now I know—to-day I know.—Do you remember what I asked you in Rome? Then I was quite in the dark. But to-day I know on good authority; everything is clear to me to-day. It was a good thing, when you made me come away with your cousin. He was a good fellow—he was a noble fellow—he told me how the case stands. He explained everything; he guessed what I thought of you. He was a member of your family, and he left you—so long as you should be in England—to my care," said Goodwood, as if he were making a great point. "Do you know what he said to me the last time I saw him—as he lay there where he died? He said—'Do everything you can for her; do everything she will let you.'"

Isabel suddenly got up. "You had no business to talk about me!"

"Why not—why not, when we talked in that way?" he demanded, following her fast. "And he was dying—when a man's dying it's different." She checked the movement she had made to leave him; she was listening more than ever; it was true that he was not the same as that last time. That had been aimless, fruitless passion; but at present he had an idea. Isabel scented his idea in all her being. "But it doesn't matter!" he exclaimed, pressing her close, though now without touching a hem of her garment. "If Touchett had never opened his mouth, I should have known all the same. I had only to look at you at your cousin's funeral to see what's the matter with you. You can't deceive me any more; for God's sake be honest with a man who is so honest with you. You are the most unhappy of women, and your husband's a devil!"

She turned on him as if he had struck her. "Are you mad?" she cried.

"I have never been so sane; I see the whole thing. Don't think it's necessary to defend him. But I won't say another word against him; I will speak only of you," Goodwood added, quickly. "How can you pretend you are not heart-broken? You don't know what to do—you don't know where to turn. It's too late to play a part; didn't you leave all that behind you in Rome? Touchett knew all about it—and I knew it too—what it would cost you to come here. It will cost you your life! When I know that, how can I keep myself from wishing to save you? What would you think of me if I should stand still and see you go back to your reward? 'It's awful, what she'll have to pay for it!'—that's what Touchett said to me. I may tell you that, mayn't I? He was such a near relation!" cried Goodwood, making his point again. "I would sooner have been shot than let another man say those things to me; but he was different; he seemed to me to have the right. It was after he got home—when he saw he was dying, and when I saw it too. I understand all about it: you are afraid to go back. You are perfectly alone; you don't know where to turn. Now it is that I want you to think of me."

"To think of you?" Isabel said, standing before him in the dusk. The idea of which she had caught a glimpse a few moments before now loomed large. She threw back her head a little; she stared at it as if it had been a comet in the sky.

"You don't know where to turn; turn to me! I want to persuade you to trust me," Goodwood repeated. And then he paused a moment, with his shining eyes. "Why should you go back—why should you go through that ghastly form?"

"To get away from you!" she answered. But this expressed only a little of what she felt. The rest was that she had never been loved before. It wrapped her about; it lifted her off her feet.

At first, in rejoinder to what she had said, it seemed to her that he would break out into greater violence. But after an instant he was perfectly quiet; he wished to prove that he was sane, that he had reasoned it all out. "I wish to prevent that, and I think I may, if you will only listen to me. It's too monstrous to think of sinking back into that misery. It's you that are out of your mind. Trust me as if I had the care of you. Why shouldn't we be happy—when it's here before us, when it's so easy? I am yours for ever—for ever and ever. Here I stand; I'm as firm as a rock. What have you to care about? You have no children; that perhaps would be an obstacle. As it is, you have nothing to consider. You must save what you can of your life; you mustn't lose it all simply because you have lost a part. It would be an insult to you to assume that you care for the look of the thing—for what people will say—for the bottomless idiocy of the world! We have nothing to do with all that; we are quite out of it; we look at things as they are. You took the great step in coming away; the next is nothing; it's the natural one. I swear, as I stand here, that a woman deliberately made to suffer is justified in anything in life—in going down into the streets, if that will help her! I know how you suffer, and that's why I am here. We can do absolutely as we please; to whom under the sun do we owe anything? What is it that holds us—what is it that has the smallest right to interfere in such a question as this? Such a question is between ourselves—and to say that is to settle it! Were we born to rot in our misery—were we born to be afraid? I never knew *you* afraid! If you only trust me, how little you will be disappointed! The world is all before us—and the world is very large. I know something about that."

Isabel gave a long murmur, like a creature in pain; it was as if he were pressing something that hurt her. "The world is very small," she said, at random; she had an immense desire to appear to resist. She said it at random, to hear herself say something; but it was not what she meant. The world, in truth, had never seemed so large; it seemed to open out, all round her, to take the form of a mighty sea, where she floated in fathomless waters. She had wanted help, and here was help; it had come in a rushing torrent. I know not whether she believed everything that he said; but she believed that to let him take her in his arms would be the next best thing to dying. This belief, for a moment, was a kind of rapture, in which she felt herself sinking and sinking. In the movement she seemed to beat with her feet, in order to catch herself, to feel something to rest on.

"Ah, be mine as I am yours!" she heard her companion cry. He had suddenly given up argument, and his voice seemed to come through a confusion of sound.

This however, of course, was but a subjective fact, as the metaphysicians say; the confusion, the noise of waters, and all the rest of it, were in her own head. In an instant she became aware of this. "Do me the greatest kindness of all," she said. "I beseech you to go away!"

"Ah, don't say that. Don't kill me!" he cried.

She clasped her hands; her eyes were streaming with tears.

"As you love me, as you pity me, leave me alone!"

He glared at her a moment through the dusk, and the next instant she felt his arms about her, and his lips on her own lips. His kiss was like a flash of lightning; when it was dark again she was free. She never looked about her; she only darted away from the spot. There were lights in the windows of the house; they shone far across the lawn. In an extraordinarily short time—for the distance was considerable—she had moved through the darkness (for she saw nothing) and reached the door. Here only she paused. She looked all about her; she listened a little; then she put her hand on the latch. She had not known where to turn; but she knew now. There was a very straight path.

Two days afterwards, Caspar Goodwood knocked at the door of the house in Wimpole Street in which Henrietta Stackpole occupied furnished lodgings. He had hardly removed his hand from the knocker when the door was opened, and Miss Stackpole herself stood before him. She had on her bonnet and jacket; she was on the point of going out.

"Oh, good morning," he said, "I was in hope I should find Mrs. Osmond."

Henrietta kept him waiting a moment for her reply; but there was a good deal of expression about Miss Stackpole even when she was silent.

"Pray what led you to suppose she was here?"

"I went down to Gardencourt this morning, and the

servant told me she had come to London. He believed she was to come to you."

Again Miss Stackpole held him—with an intention of perfect kindness—in suspense.

"She came here yesterday, and spent the night. But this morning she started for Rome."

Caspar Goodwood was not looking at her; his eyes were fastened on the doorstep.

"Oh, she started—" he stammered. And without finishing his phrase, or looking up, he turned away.

Henrietta had come out, closing the door behind her, and now she put out her hand and grasped his arm.

"Look here, Mr. Goodwood," she said; "just you wait!"

On which he looked up at her.

THE END.

THE BOSTONIANS

I

OLIVE WILL come down in about ten minutes; she told me to tell you that. About ten; that is exactly like Olive. Neither five nor fifteen, and yet not ten exactly, but either nine or eleven. She didn't tell me to say she was glad to see you, because she doesn't know whether she is or not, and she wouldn't for the world expose herself to telling a fib. She is very honest, is Olive Chancellor; she is full of rectitude. Nobody tells fibs in Boston; I don't know what to make of them all. Well, I am very glad to see you, at any rate.'

These words were spoken with much volubility by a fair, plump, smiling woman who entered a narrow drawing-room in which a visitor, kept waiting for a few moments, was already absorbed in a book. The gentleman had not even needed to sit down to become interested: apparently he had taken up the volume from a table as soon as he came in, and, standing there, after a single glance round the apartment, had lost himself in its pages. He threw it down at the approach of Mrs. Luna, laughed, shook hands with her, and said in answer to her last remark, 'You imply that you do tell fibs. Perhaps that is one.'

'Oh no; there is nothing wonderful in my being glad to see you,' Mrs. Luna rejoined, 'when I tell you that I have been three long weeks in this unprevaricating city.'

'That has an unflattering sound for me,' said the young man. 'I pretend not to prevaricate.'

'Dear me, what's the good of being a Southerner?' the lady asked. 'Olive told me to tell you she hoped you will stay to dinner. And if she said it, she does really hope it. She is willing to risk that.'

'Just as I am?' the visitor inquired, presenting himself with rather a work-a-day aspect.

Mrs. Luna glanced at him from head to foot, and gave a little smiling sigh, as if he had been a long sum in addition. And, indeed, he was very long, Basil Ransom, and he even looked a little hard and discouraging, like a column of figures, in spite of the friendly face which he bent upon his hostess's deputy, and which, in its thinness, had a deep dry line, a sort of premature wrinkle, on either side of the mouth. He was tall and lean, and dressed throughout in black; his shirt-collar was low and wide, and the triangle of linen, a little crumpled, exhibited by the opening of his waistcoat, was adorned by a pin containing a small red stone. In spite of this decoration the young man looked poor—as poor as a young man could look who had such a fine head and such magnificent eyes. Those of Basil Ransom were dark, deep, and glowing; his head had a character of elevation which fairly added to his stature; it was a head to be seen above the level of a crowd, on some judicial bench or political platform, or even on a bronze medal. His forehead was high and broad, and his thick black hair, perfectly straight and glossy, and without any division, rolled back from it in a leonine manner. These things, the eyes especially, with their smouldering fire, might have indicated that he was to be a great American statesman; or, on the other hand, they might simply have proved that he came from Carolina or Alabama. He came, in fact, from Mississippi, and he spoke very perceptibly with the accent of that country. It is not in my power to reproduce by any combination of characters this charming dialect; but the initiated reader will have no difficulty in evoking the sound, which is to be associated in the present instance with nothing vulgar or vain. This lean, pale, sallow, shabby, striking young man, with his superior head, his sedentary shoulders, his expression of bright grimness and hard enthusiasm, his provincial, distinguished appearance, is, as a representative of his sex, the most important personage in my narrative; he played a very active part in the events I have undertaken in some degree to set forth. And yet the reader who likes a complete image, who desires to read with the senses as well as with the reason, is entreated not to forget that he prolonged his consonants and swallowed his vowels, that he was guilty of elisions and interpolations which were equally unexpected, and that his discourse was pervaded by something sultry and vast, something almost African in its rich, basking tone, something that suggested the teeming expanse of the cotton-field. Mrs. Luna looked up at all this, but saw only a part of it; otherwise she would not have replied in a bantering manner, in answer to his inquiry: 'Are you ever different from this?' Mrs. Luna was familiar—intolerably familiar.

Basil Ransom coloured a little. Then he said: 'Oh yes; when I dine out I usually carry a six-shooter and a bowie-knife.' And he took up his hat vaguely—a soft black hat with a low crown and an immense straight brim. Mrs. Luna wanted to know what he was doing. She made him sit down; she assured him that her sister quite expected him, would feel as sorry as she could ever feel for anything—for she was a kind of fatalist, anyhow—if he didn't stay to dinner. It was an immense pity—she herself was going out; in Boston you must jump at invitations. Olive, too, was going somewhere after dinner, but he mustn't mind that; perhaps he would like to go with her. It wasn't a party—Olive didn't go to parties; it was one of those weird meetings she was so fond of.

'What kind of meetings do you refer to? You speak as if it were a rendezvous of witches on the Brocken.'

'Well, so it is; they are all witches and wizards, mediums, and spirit-rappers, and roaring radicals.'

Basil Ransom stared; the yellow light in his brown eyes deepened. 'Do you mean to say your sister's a roaring radical?'

'A radical? She's a female Jacobin—she's a nihilist. Whatever is, is wrong, and all that sort of thing. If you are going to dine with her, you had better know it.'

'Oh, murder!' murmured the young man vaguely, sinking back in his chair with his arms folded. He looked at Mrs. Luna with intelligent incredulity. She was sufficiently pretty; her hair was in clusters of curls, like bunches of grapes; her tight bodice seemed to crack with her vivacity; and from beneath the stiff little plaits of her petticoat a small fat foot protruded, resting upon a stilted heel. She was attractive and impertinent, especially the latter. He seemed to think it was a great pity, what she had told him; but he lost himself in this consideration, or, at any rate, said nothing for some time, while his eyes wandered over Mrs. Luna, and he probably wondered what body of doctrine *she* represented, little as she might partake of the nature of her sister. Many things were strange to Basil Ransom; Boston especially was strewn with surprises, and he was a man who liked to understand. Mrs.

Luna was drawing on her gloves; Ransom had never seen any that were so long; they reminded him of stockings, and he wondered how she managed without garters above the elbow. 'Well, I suppose I might have known that,' he continued, at last.

'You might have known what?'

'Well, that Miss Chancellor would be all that you say. She was brought up in the city of reform.'

'Oh, it isn't the city; it's just Olive Chancellor. She would reform the solar system if she could get hold of it. She'll reform you, if you don't look out. That's the way I found her when I returned from Europe.'

'Have you been in Europe?' Ransom asked.

'Mercy, yes! Haven't you?'

'No, I haven't been anywhere. Has your sister?'

'Yes; but she stayed only an hour or two. She hates it; she would like to abolish it. Didn't you know I had been to Europe?' Mrs. Luna went on, in the slightly aggrieved tone of a woman who discovers the limits of her reputation.

Ransom reflected he might answer her that until five minutes ago he didn't know she existed; but he remembered that this was not the way in which a Southern gentleman spoke to ladies, and he contented himself with saying that she must condone his Bœotian ignorance (he was fond of an elegant phrase); that he lived in a part of the country where they didn't think much about Europe, and that he had always supposed she was domiciled in New York. This last remark he made at a venture, for he had, naturally, not devoted any supposition whatever to Mrs. Luna. His dishonesty, however, only exposed him the more.

'If you thought I lived in New York, why in the world didn't you come and see me?' the lady inquired.

'Well, you see, I don't go out much, except to the courts.'

'Do you mean the law-courts? Every one has got some profession over here! Are you very ambitious? You look as if you were.'

'Yes, very,' Basil Ransom replied, with a smile, and the curious feminine softness with which Southern gentlemen enunciate that adverb.

Mrs. Luna explained that she had been living in Europe for

several years—ever since her husband died—but had come home a month before, come home with her little boy, the only thing she had in the world, and was paying a visit to her sister, who, of course, was the nearest thing after the child. 'But it isn't the same,' she said. 'Olive and I disagree so much.'

'While you and your little boy don't,' the young man remarked.

'Oh no, I never differ from Newton!' And Mrs. Luna added that now she was back she didn't know what she should do. That was the worst of coming back; it was like being born again, at one's age—one had to begin life afresh. One didn't even know what one had come back for. There were people who wanted one to spend the winter in Boston; but she couldn't stand that—she knew, at least, what she had not come back for. Perhaps she should take a house in Washington; did he ever hear of that little place? They had invented it while she was away. Besides, Olive didn't want her in Boston, and didn't go through the form of saying so. That was one comfort with Olive; she never went through any forms.

Basil Ransom had got up just as Mrs. Luna made this last declaration; for a young lady had glided into the room, who stopped short as it fell upon her ears. She stood there looking, consciously and rather seriously, at Mr. Ransom; a smile of exceeding faintness played about her lips—it was just perceptible enough to light up the native gravity of her face. It might have been likened to a thin ray of moonlight resting upon the wall of a prison.

'If that were true,' she said, 'I shouldn't tell you that I am very sorry to have kept you waiting.'

Her voice was low and agreeable—a cultivated voice—and she extended a slender white hand to her visitor, who remarked with some solemnity (he felt a certain guilt of participation in Mrs. Luna's indiscretion) that he was intensely happy to make her acquaintance. He observed that Miss Chancellor's hand was at once cold and limp; she merely placed it in his, without exerting the smallest pressure. Mrs. Luna explained to her sister that her freedom of speech was caused by his being a relation—though, indeed, he didn't seem to know much about them. She didn't believe he had ever heard of her, Mrs. Luna, though he pretended, with his Southern chivalry, that he had. She must be off to her dinner now, she saw the carriage was there, and in her absence Olive might give any version of her she chose.

'I have told him you are a radical, and you may tell him, if you like, that I am a painted Jezebel. Try to reform him; a person from Mississippi is sure to be all wrong. I shall be back very late; we are going to a theatre-party; that's why we dine so early. Good-bye, Mr. Ransom,' Mrs. Luna continued, gathering up the feathery white shawl which added to the volume of her fairness. 'I hope you are going to stay a little, so that you may judge us for yourself. I should like you to see Newton, too; he is a noble little nature, and I want some advice about him. You only stay to-morrow? Why, what's the use of that? Well, mind you come and see me in New York; I shall be sure to be part of the winter there. I shall send you a card; I won't let you off. Don't come out; my sister has the first claim. Olive, why don't you take him to your female convention?' Mrs. Luna's familiarity extended even to her sister; she remarked to Miss Chancellor that she looked as if she were got up for a sea-voyage. 'I am glad I haven't opinions that prevent my dressing in the evening!' she declared from the doorway. 'The amount of thought they give to their clothing, the people who are afraid of looking frivolous!'

II

WHETHER MUCH or little consideration had been directed to the result, Miss Chancellor certainly would not have incurred this reproach. She was habited in a plain dark dress, without any ornaments, and her smooth, colourless hair was confined as carefully as that of her sister was encouraged to stray. She had instantly seated herself, and while Mrs. Luna talked she kept her eyes on the ground, glancing even less toward Basil Ransom than toward that woman of many words. The young man was therefore free to look at her; a contemplation which showed him that she was agitated and trying to conceal it. He wondered why she was agitated, not foreseeing that he was destined to discover, later, that her nature was like a skiff in a stormy sea. Even after her sister had passed out of the room she sat there with her eyes turned away, as if there had been a spell upon her which forbade her to raise them. Miss Olive Chancellor, it may be confided to the reader, to whom in the course of our history I shall be under the necessity of imparting much occult information, was subject to fits of tragic shyness, during which she was unable to meet even her own eyes in the mirror. One of these fits had suddenly seized her now, without any obvious cause, though, indeed, Mrs. Luna had made it worse by becoming instantly so personal. There was nothing in the world so personal as Mrs. Luna; her sister could have hated her for it if she had not forbidden herself this emotion as directed to individuals. Basil Ransom was a young man of first-rate intelligence, but conscious of the narrow range, as yet, of his experience. He was on his guard against generalisations which might be hasty; but he had arrived at two or three that were of value to a gentleman lately admitted to the New York bar and looking out for clients. One of them was to the effect that the simplest division it is possible to make of the human race is into the people who take things hard and the people who take them easy. He perceived very quickly that Miss Chancellor belonged to the former class. This was written so intensely in her delicate face that he felt an unformulated pity for her before they had exchanged twenty words. He himself, by nature, took things easy; if he had put on the screw of late, it was after reflection, and because circumstances pressed him close. But this pale girl, with her light-green eyes, her pointed features and nervous manner, was visibly morbid; it was as plain as day that she was morbid. Poor Ransom announced this fact to himself as if he had made a great discovery; but in reality he had never been so 'Bœotian' as at that moment. It proved nothing of any importance, with regard to Miss Chancellor, to say that she was morbid; any sufficient account of her would lie very much to the rear of that. Why was she morbid, and why was her morbidness typical? Ransom might have exulted if he had gone back far enough to explain that mystery. The women he had hitherto known had been mainly of his own soft clime, and it was not often they exhibited the tendency he detected (and cursorily deplored) in Mrs. Luna's sister. That was the way he liked them—not to think too much, not to feel any responsibility for the government of the world, such as he was sure Miss Chancellor felt. If they would only be private and passive, and have no feeling but for that, and leave publicity to the sex of tougher hide! Ransom was pleased with the vision of that remedy; it must be repeated that he was very provincial.

These considerations were not present to him as definitely as I have written them here; they were summed up in the vague compassion which his cousin's figure excited in his mind, and which was yet accompanied with a sensible reluctance to know her better, obvious as it was that with such a face as that she must be remarkable. He was sorry for her, but he saw in a flash that no one could help her: that was what made her tragic. He had not, seeking his fortune, come away from the blighted South, which weighed upon his heart, to look out for tragedies; at least he didn't want them outside of his office in Pine Street. He broke the silence ensuing upon Mrs. Luna's departure by one of the courteous speeches to which blighted regions may still encourage a tendency, and presently found himself talking comfortably enough with his hostess. Though he had said to himself that no one could help her, the effect of his tone was to dispel her shyness; it was her great advantage (for the career she had proposed to herself) that in certain conditions she was liable suddenly to become bold. She was reassured at finding that her visitor was peculiar; the way he spoke told her that it was no wonder he had fought on the Southern side. She had never yet encountered a personage so exotic, and she always felt more at her ease in the presence of anything strange. It was the usual things of life that filled her with silent rage; which was natural enough, inasmuch as, to her vision, almost everything that was usual was iniquitous. She had no difficulty in asking him now whether he would not stay to dinner—she hoped Adeline had given him her message. It had been when she was upstairs with Adeline, as his card was brought up, a sudden and very abnormal inspiration to offer him this (for her) really ultimate favour; nothing could be further from her common habit than to entertain alone, at any repast, a gentleman she had never seen.

It was the same sort of impulse that had moved her to write to Basil Ransom, in the spring, after hearing accidentally that he had come to the North and intended, in New York, to practise his profession. It was her nature to look out for duties, to appeal to her conscience for tasks. This attentive organ, earnestly consulted, had represented to her that he was an offshoot of the old slave-holding oligarchy which, within her own vivid remembrance, had plunged the country into blood and tears, and that, as associated with such abominations, he was not a worthy object of patronage for a person whose two brothers—her only ones—had given up life for the Northern cause. It reminded her, however, on the other hand, that he too had been much bereaved, and, moreover, that he had fought and offered his own life, even if it had not been taken. She could not defend herself against a rich admiration—a kind of tenderness of envy—of any one who had been so happy as to have that opportunity. The most secret, the most sacred hope of her nature was that she might some day have such a chance, that she might be a martyr and die for something. Basil Ransom had lived, but she knew he had lived to see bitter hours. His family was ruined; they had lost their slaves, their property, their friends and relations, their home; had tasted of all the cruelty of defeat. He had tried for a while to carry on the plantation himself, but he had a mill-

stone of debt round his neck, and he longed for some work
which would transport him to the haunts of men. The State
of Mississippi seemed to him the state of despair; so he surrendered the remnants of his patrimony to his mother and
sisters, and, at nearly thirty years of age, alighted for the first
time in New York, in the costume of his province, with fifty
dollars in his pocket and a gnawing hunger in his heart.

That this incident had revealed to the young man his ignorance of many things—only, however, to make him say to
himself, after the first angry blush, that here he would enter
the game and here he would win it—so much Olive Chancellor could not know; what was sufficient for her was that
he had rallied, as the French say, had accepted the accomplished fact, had admitted that North and South were a single, indivisible political organism. Their cousinship—that of
Chancellors and Ransoms—was not very close; it was the
kind of thing that one might take up or leave alone, as one
pleased. It was 'in the female line,' as Basil Ransom had written, in answering her letter with a good deal of form and
flourish; he spoke as if they had been royal houses. Her
mother had wished to take it up; it was only the fear of seeming patronising to people in misfortune that had prevented
her from writing to Mississippi. If it had been possible to
send Mrs. Ransom money, or even clothes, she would have
liked that; but she had no means of ascertaining how such an
offering would be taken. By the time Basil came to the
North—making advances, as it were—Mrs. Chancellor had
passed away; so it was for Olive, left alone in the little house
in Charles Street (Adeline being in Europe), to decide.

She knew what her mother would have done, and that
helped her decision; for her mother always chose the positive
course. Olive had a fear of everything, but her greatest fear
was of being afraid. She wished immensely to be generous,
and how could one be generous unless one ran a risk? She
had erected it into a sort of rule of conduct that whenever she
saw a risk she was to take it; and she had frequent humilia-
tions at finding herself safe after all. She was perfectly safe
after writing to Basil Ransom; and, indeed, it was difficult to
see what he could have done to her except thank her (he was
only exceptionally superlative) for her letter, and assure her

that he would come and see her the first time his business (he was beginning to get a little) should take him to Boston. He had now come, in redemption of his grateful vow, and even this did not make Miss Chancellor feel that she had courted danger. She saw (when once she had looked at him) that he would not put those worldly interpretations on things which, with her, it was both an impulse and a principle to defy. He was too simple—too Mississippian—for that; she was almost disappointed. She certainly had not hoped that she might have struck him as making unwomanly overtures (Miss Chancellor hated this epithet almost as much as she hated its opposite); but she had a presentiment that he would be too good-natured, primitive to that degree. Of all things in the world contention was most sweet to her (though why it is hard to imagine, for it always cost her tears, headaches, a day or two in bed, acute emotion), and it was very possible Basil Ransom would not care to contend. Nothing could be more displeasing than this indifference when people didn't agree with you. That he should agree she did not in the least expect of him; how could a Mississippian agree? If she had supposed he would agree, she would not have written to him.

III

WHEN HE had told her that if she would take him as he was he should be very happy to dine with her, she excused herself a moment and went to give an order in the dining-room. The young man, left alone, looked about the parlour—the two parlours which, in their prolonged, adjacent narrowness, formed evidently one apartment—and wandered to the windows at the back, where there was a view of the water; Miss Chancellor having the good fortune to dwell on that side of Charles Street toward which, in the rear, the afternoon sun slants redly, from an horizon indented at empty intervals with wooden spires, the masts of lonely boats, the chimneys of dirty 'works,' over a brackish expanse of anomalous character, which is too big for a river and too small for a bay. The view seemed to him very picturesque, though in the gathered dusk little was left of it save a cold yellow streak in the west, a gleam of brown water, and the reflection of the lights that had begun to show themselves in a row of houses, impressive to Ransom in their extreme modernness, which overlooked the same lagoon from a long embankment on the left, constructed of stones roughly piled. He thought this prospect, from a city-house, almost romantic; and he turned from it back to the interior (illuminated now by a lamp which the parlour-maid had placed on a table while he stood at the window) as to something still more genial and interesting. The artistic sense in Basil Ransom had not been highly cultivated; neither (though he had passed his early years as the son of a rich man) was his conception of material comfort very definite; it consisted mainly of the vision of plenty of cigars and brandy and water and newspapers, and a cane-bottomed arm-chair of the right inclination, from which he could stretch his legs. Nevertheless it seemed to him he had never seen an interior that was so much an interior as this queer corridor-shaped drawing-room of his new-found kinswoman; he had never felt himself in the presence of so much organised privacy or of so many objects that spoke of habits and tastes. Most of the people he had hitherto known had no tastes; they had a few habits, but these were not of a sort that required much upholstery. He had not as yet been in many houses in New York, and he had never before seen so many accessories. The general character of the place struck him as Bostonian; this was, in fact, very much what he had supposed Boston to be. He had always heard Boston was a city of culture, and now there was culture in Miss Chancellor's tables and sofas, in the books that were everywhere, on little shelves like brackets (as if a book were a statuette), in the photographs and water-colours that covered the walls, in the curtains that were festooned rather stiffly in the doorways. He looked at some of the books and saw that his cousin read German; and his impression of the importance of this (as a symptom of superiority) was not diminished by the fact that he himself had mastered the tongue (knowing it contained a large literature of jurisprudence) during a long, empty, deadly summer on the plantation. It is a curious proof of a certain crude modesty inherent in Basil Ransom that the main effect of his observing his cousin's German books was to give him an idea of the natural energy of Northerners. He had noticed it often before; he had already told himself that he must count with it. It was only after much experience he made the discovery that few Northerners were, in their secret soul, so energetic as he. Many other persons had made it before that. He knew very little about Miss Chancellor; he had come to see her only because she wrote to him; he would never have thought of looking her up, and since then there had been no one in New York he might ask about her. Therefore he could only guess that she was a rich young woman; such a house, inhabited in such a way by a quiet spinster, implied a considerable income. How much? he asked himself; five thousand, ten thousand, fifteen thousand a year? There was richness to our panting young man in the smallest of these figures. He was not of a mercenary spirit, but he had an immense desire for success, and he had more than once reflected that a moderate capital was an aid to achievement. He had seen in his younger years one of the biggest failures that history commemorates, an immense national *fiasco*, and it had implanted in his mind a deep aversion to the ineffectual. It came over him, while he waited for his hostess to reappear, that she was unmarried as well as rich, that she was sociable (her letter answered for that) as well as single; and he had for a moment a whimsical vision of becoming a partner in so flourishing a firm. He ground his teeth a little as he thought of the contrasts of the human lot; this cushioned feminine nest made him feel unhoused and underfed. Such a mood, however, could only be momentary, for he was conscious at bottom of a bigger stomach than all the culture of Charles Street could fill.

Afterwards, when his cousin had come back and they had gone down to dinner together, where he sat facing her at a little table decorated in the middle with flowers, a position from which he had another view, through a window where the curtain remained undrawn by her direction (she called his attention to this—it was for his benefit), of the dusky, empty river, spotted with points of light—at this period, I say, it was very easy for him to remark to himself that nothing would induce him to make love to such a type as that. Several months later, in New York, in conversation with Mrs. Luna, of whom he was destined to see a good deal, he alluded by chance to this repast, to the way her sister had placed him at table, and to the remark with which she had pointed out the advantage of his seat.

'That's what they call in Boston being very "thoughtful," ' Mrs. Luna said, 'giving you the Back Bay (don't you hate the name?) to look at, and then taking credit for it.'

This, however, was in the future; what Basil Ransom actually perceived was that Miss Chancellor was a signal old maid. That was her quality, her destiny; nothing could be more distinctly written. There are women who are unmarried by accident, and others who are unmarried by option; but Olive Chancellor was unmarried by every implication of her being. She was a spinster as Shelley was a lyric poet, or as the month of August is sultry. She was so essentially a celibate that Ransom found himself thinking of her as old, though when he came to look at her (as he said to himself) it was apparent that her years were fewer than his own. He did not dislike her, she had been so friendly; but, little by little, she gave him an uneasy feeling—the sense that you could never be safe with a person who took things so hard. It came over him that it was because she took things hard she had sought his acquaintance; it had been because she was strenuous, not because she was genial; she had had in her eye—and what an extraordinary eye it was!—not a pleasure, but a duty. She would expect him to be strenuous in return; but he couldn't—in private life, he couldn't; privacy for Basil Ransom consisted entirely in what he called 'laying off.' She was not so plain on further acquaintance as she had seemed to him at first; even the young Mississippian had culture enough to see that she was refined. Her white skin had a singular look of being drawn tightly across her face; but her features, though sharp and irregular, were delicate in a fashion that suggested good breeding. Their line was perverse, but it was not poor. The curious tint of her eyes was a living colour; when she turned it upon you, you thought vaguely of the glitter of green ice. She had absolutely no figure, and presented a certain appearance of feeling cold. With all this, there was something very modern and highly developed in her aspect; she had the advantages as well as the drawbacks of a nervous organisation. She smiled constantly at her guest, but from the beginning to the end of dinner, though he made several remarks that he thought might prove amusing, she never once laughed. Later, he saw that she was a woman without laughter; exhilaration, if it ever visited her, was dumb. Once only, in the course of his subsequent acquaintance with her, did it find a voice; and then the sound remained in Ransom's ear as one of the strangest he had heard.

She asked him a great many questions, and made no comment on his answers, which only served to suggest to her fresh inquiries. Her shyness had quite left her, it did not come back; she had confidence enough to wish him to see that she took a great interest in him. Why should she? he wondered. He couldn't believe he was one of *her* kind; he was conscious of much Bohemianism—he drank beer, in New York, in cellars, knew no ladies, and was familiar with a 'variety' actress. Certainly, as she knew him better, she would disapprove of him, though, of course, he would never mention the actress, nor even, if necessary, the beer. Ransom's conception of vice was purely as a series of special cases, of explicable accidents. Not that he cared; if it were a part of the Boston character to be inquiring, he would be to the last a courteous Mississippian. He would tell her about Mississippi as much as she liked; he didn't care how much he told her that the old ideas in the South were played out. She would not understand him any the better for that; she would not know how little his own views could be gathered from such a limited admission. What her sister imparted to him about her mania for 'reform' had left in his mouth a kind of unpleasant after-taste; he felt, at any rate, that if she had the religion of humanity—Basil Ransom had read Comte, he had read everything—she would never understand him. He, too, had a private vision of reform, but the first principle of it was to reform the reformers. As they drew to the close of a meal which, in spite of all latent incompatibilities, had gone off brilliantly, she said to him that she should have to leave him after dinner, unless perhaps he should be inclined to accompany her. She was going to a small gathering at the house of a friend who had asked a few people, 'interested in new ideas,' to meet Mrs. Farrinder.

'Oh, thank you,' said Basil Ransom. 'Is it a party? I haven't been to a party since Mississippi seceded.'

'No; Miss Birdseye doesn't give parties. She's an ascetic.'

'Oh, well, we have had our dinner,' Ransom rejoined, laughing.

His hostess sat silent a moment, with her eyes on the ground; she looked at such times as if she were hesitating greatly between several things she might say, all so important that it was difficult to choose.

'I think it might interest you,' she remarked presently. 'You will hear some discussion, if you are fond of that. Perhaps you wouldn't agree,' she added, resting her strange eyes on him.

'Perhaps I shouldn't—I don't agree with everything,' he said, smiling and stroking his leg.

'Don't you care for human progress?' Miss Chancellor went on.

'I don't know—I never saw any. Are you going to show me some?'

'I can show you an earnest effort towards it. That's the most one can be sure of. But I am not sure you are worthy.'

'Is it something very Bostonian? I should like to see that,' said Basil Ransom.

'There are movements in other cities. Mrs. Farrinder goes everywhere; she may speak to-night.'

'Mrs. Farrinder, the celebrated——?'

'Yes, the celebrated; the great apostle of the emancipation of women. She is a great friend of Miss Birdseye.'

'And who is Miss Birdseye?'

'She is one of our celebrities. She is the woman in the world, I suppose, who has laboured most for every wise reform. I think I ought to tell you,' Miss Chancellor went on in a moment, 'she was one of the earliest, one of the most passionate, of the old Abolitionists.'

She had thought, indeed, she ought to tell him that, and it threw her into a little tremor of excitement to do so. Yet, if she had been afraid he would show some irritation at this news, she was disappointed at the geniality with which he exclaimed:

'Why, poor old lady—she must be quite mature!'

It was therefore with some severity that she rejoined:

'She will never be old. She is the youngest spirit I know. But if you are not in sympathy, perhaps you had better not come,' she went on.

'In sympathy with what, dear madam?' Basil Ransom asked, failing still, to her perception, to catch the tone of real seriousness. 'If, as you say, there is to be a discussion, there will be different sides, and of course one can't sympathise with both.'

'Yes, but every one will, in his way—or in her way—plead the cause of the new truths. If you don't care for them, you won't go with us.'

'I tell you I haven't the least idea what they are! I have never yet encountered in the world any but old truths—as old as the sun and moon. How can I know? But *do* take me; it's such a chance to see Boston.'

'It isn't Boston—it's humanity!' Miss Chancellor, as she made this remark, rose from her chair, and her movement seemed to say that she consented. But before she quitted her kinsman to get ready, she observed to him that she was sure he knew what she meant; he was only pretending he didn't.

'Well, perhaps, after all, I have a general idea,' he confessed;

'but don't you see how this little reunion will give me a chance to fix it?'

She lingered an instant, with her anxious face. 'Mrs. Farrinder will fix it!' she said; and she went to prepare herself.

It was in this poor young lady's nature to be anxious, to have scruple within scruple and to forecast the consequences of things. She returned in ten minutes, in her bonnet, which she had apparently assumed in recognition of Miss Birdseye's asceticism. As she stood there drawing on her gloves—her visitor had fortified himself against Mrs. Farrinder by another glass of wine—she declared to him that she quite repented of having proposed to him to go; something told her that he would be an unfavourable element.

'Why, is it going to be a spiritual *séance*?' Basil Ransom asked.

'Well, I have heard at Miss Birdseye's some inspirational speaking.' Olive Chancellor was determined to look him straight in the face as she said this; her sense of the way it might strike him operated as a cogent, not as a deterrent, reason.

'Why, Miss Olive, it's just got up on purpose for me!' cried the young Mississippian, radiant, and clasping his hands. She thought him very handsome as he said this, but reflected that unfortunately men didn't care for the truth, especially the new kinds, in proportion as they were good-looking. She had, however, a moral resource that she could always fall back upon; it had already been a comfort to her, on occasions of acute feeling, that she hated men, as a class, anyway. 'And I want so much to see an old Abolitionist; I have never laid eyes on one,' Basil Ransom added.

'Of course you couldn't see one in the South; you were too afraid of them to let them come there!' She was now trying to think of something she might say that would be sufficiently disagreeable to make him cease to insist on accompanying her; for, strange to record—if anything, in a person of that intense sensibility, be stranger than any other—her second thought with regard to having asked him had deepened with the elapsing moments into an unreasoned terror of the effect of his presence. 'Perhaps Miss Birdseye won't like you,' she went on, as they waited for the carriage.

'I don't know; I reckon she will,' said Basil Ransom good-humouredly. He evidently had no intention of giving up his opportunity.

From the window of the dining-room, at that moment, they heard the carriage drive up. Miss Birdseye lived at the South End; the distance was considerable, and Miss Chancellor had ordered a hackney-coach, it being one of the advantages of living in Charles Street that stables were ·near. The logic of her conduct was none of the clearest; for if she had been alone she would have proceeded to her destination by the aid of the street-car; not from economy (for she had the good fortune not to be obliged to consult it to that degree), and not from any love of wandering about Boston at night (a kind of exposure she greatly disliked), but by reason of a theory she devotedly nursed, a theory which bade her put off invidious differences and mingle in the common life. She would have gone on foot to Boylston Street, and there she would have taken the public convey-ance (in her heart she loathed it) to the South End. Boston was full of poor girls who had to walk about at night and to squeeze into horse-cars in which every sense was dis-pleased; and why should she hold herself superior to these? Olive Chancellor regulated her conduct on lofty principles, and this is why, having to-night the advantage of a gentle-man's protection, she sent for a carriage to obliterate that patronage. If they had gone together in the common way she would have seemed to owe it to him that she should be so daring, and he belonged to a sex to which she wished to be under no obligations. Months before, when she wrote to him, it had been with the sense, rather, of putting *him* in debt. As they rolled toward the South End, side by side, in a good deal of silence, bouncing and bumping over the rail-way-tracks very little less, after all, than if their wheels had been fitted to them, and looking out on either side at rows of red houses, dusky in the lamp-light, with protuberant fronts, approached by ladders of stone; as they proceeded, with these contemplative undulations, Miss Chancellor said to her companion, with a concentrated desire to defy him, as a punishment for having thrown her (she couldn't tell why) into such a tremor:

'Don't you believe, then, in the coming of a better day—in its being possible to do something for the human race?'

Poor Ransom perceived the defiance, and he felt rather bewildered; he wondered what type, after all, he *had* got hold of, and what game was being played with him. Why had she made advances, if she wanted to pinch him this way? However, he was good for any game—that one as well as another—and he saw that he was 'in' for something of which he had long desired to have a nearer view. 'Well, Miss Olive,' he answered, putting on again his big hat, which he had been holding in his lap, ' what strikes me most is that the human race has got to bear its troubles.'

'That's what men say to women to make them patient in the position they have made for them.'

'Oh, the position of women!' Basil Ransom exclaimed. 'The position of women, is to make fools of men. I would change my position for yours any day,' he went on. 'That's what I said to myself as I sat there in your elegant home.'

He could not see, in the dimness of the carriage, that she had flushed quickly, and he did not know that she disliked to be reminded of certain things which, for her, were mitigations of the hard feminine lot. But the passionate quaver with which, a moment later, she answered him sufficiently assured him that he had touched her at a tender point.

'Do you make it a reproach to me that I happen to have a little money? The dearest wish of my heart is to do something with it for others—for the miserable.'

Basil Ransom might have greeted this last declaration with the sympathy it deserved, might have commended the noble aspirations of his kinswoman. But what struck him, rather, was the oddity of so sudden a sharpness of pitch in an intercourse which, an hour or two before, had begun in perfect amity, and he burst once more into an irrepressible laugh. This made his companion feel, with intensity, how little she was joking. 'I don't know why I should care what you think,' she said.

'Don't care—don't care. What does it matter? It is not of the slightest importance.'

He might say that, but it was not true; she felt that there were reasons why she should care. She had brought him into her life, and she should have to pay for it. But she wished to know the worst at once. 'Are you against our emancipation?' she asked, turning a white face on him in the momentary radiance of a street-lamp.

'Do you mean your voting and preaching and all that sort of thing?' He made this inquiry, but seeing how seriously she would take his answer, he was almost frightened, and hung fire. 'I will tell you when I have heard Mrs. Farrinder.'

They had arrived at the address given by Miss Chancellor to the coachman, and their vehicle stopped with a lurch. Basil Ransom got out; he stood at the door with an extended hand, to assist the young lady. But she seemed to hesitate; she sat there with her spectral face. 'You hate it!' she exclaimed, in a low tone.

'Miss Birdseye will convert me,' said Ransom, with intention; for he had grown very curious, and he was afraid that now, at the last, Miss Chancellor would prevent his entering the house. She alighted without his help, and behind her he ascended the high steps of Miss Birdseye's residence. He had grown very curious, and among the things he wanted to know was why in the world this ticklish spinster had written to him.

IV

S HE HAD TOLD him before they started that they should
be early; she wished to see Miss Birdseye alone, before
the arrival of any one else. This was just for the pleasure of
seeing her—it was an opportunity; she was always so taken
up with others. She received Miss Chancellor in the hall of
the mansion, which had a salient front, an enormous and very
high number—756—painted in gilt on the glass light above
the door, a tin sign bearing the name of a doctress (Mary J.
Prance) suspended from one of the windows of the basement,
and a peculiar look of being both new and faded—a kind of
modern fatigue—like certain articles of commerce which are
sold at a reduction as shop-worn. The hall was very narrow;
a considerable part of it was occupied by a large hat-tree, from
which several coats and shawls already depended; the rest offered space for certain lateral demonstrations on Miss Birdseye's part. She sidled about her visitors, and at last went
round to open for them a door of further admission, which
happened to be locked inside. She was a little old lady, with
an enormous head; that was the first thing Ransom noticed—
the vast, fair, protuberant, candid, ungarnished brow, sur-
mounting a pair of weak, kind, tired-looking eyes, and ineffectually balanced in the rear by a cap which had the air of
falling backward, and which Miss Birdseye suddenly felt for
while she talked, with unsuccessful irrelevant movements. She
had a sad, soft, pale face, which (and it was the effect of her
whole head) looked as if it had been soaked, blurred, and
made vague by exposure to some slow dissolvent. The long
practice of philanthropy had not given accent to her features;
it had rubbed out their transitions, their meanings. The waves
of sympathy, of enthusiasm, had wrought upon them in the
same way in which the waves of time finally modify the surface of old marble busts, gradually washing away their sharpness, their details. In her large countenance her dim little
smile scarcely showed. It was a mere sketch of a smile, a kind
of instalment, or payment on account; it seemed to say that
she would smile more if she had time, but that you could see,
without this, that she was gentle and easy to beguile.

She always dressed in the same way: she wore a loose black jacket, with deep pockets, which were stuffed with papers, memoranda of a voluminous correspondence; and from beneath her jacket depended a short stuff dress. The brevity of this simple garment was the one device by which Miss Birdseye managed to suggest that she was a woman of business, that she wished to be free for action. She belonged to the Short-Skirts League, as a matter of course; for she belonged to any and every league that had been founded for almost any purpose whatever. This did not prevent her being a confused, entangled, inconsequent, discursive old woman, whose charity began at home and ended nowhere, whose credulity kept pace with it, and who knew less about her fellow-creatures, if possible, after fifty years of humanitary zeal, than on the day she had gone into the field to testify against the iniquity of most arrangements. Basil Ransom knew very little about such a life as hers, but she seemed to him a revelation of a class, and a multitude of socialistic figures, of names and episodes that he had heard of, grouped themselves behind her. She looked as if she had spent her life on platforms, in audiences, in conventions, in phalansteries, in *séances*; in her faded face there was a kind of reflection of ugly lecture-lamps; with its habit of an upward angle, it seemed turned toward a public speaker, with an effort of respiration in the thick air in which social reforms are usually discussed. She talked continually, in a voice of which the spring seemed broken, like that of an over-worked bell-wire; and when Miss Chancellor explained that she had brought Mr. Ransom because he was so anxious to meet Mrs. Farrinder, she gave the young man a delicate, dirty, democratic little hand, looking at him kindly, as she could not help doing, but without the smallest discrimination as against others who might not have the good fortune (which involved, possibly, an injustice) to be present on such an interesting occasion. She struck him as very poor, but it was only afterward that he learned she had never had a penny in her life. No one had an idea how she lived; whenever money was given her she gave it away to a negro or a refugee. No woman could be less invidious, but on the whole she preferred these two classes of the human race. Since the Civil War much of her occupation was gone; for before that her best hours had been spent in fancying that she was helping some Southern slave to escape. It would have been a nice question whether, in her heart of hearts, for the sake of this excitement, she did not sometimes wish the blacks back in bondage. She had suffered in the same way by the relaxation of many European despotisms, for in former years much of the romance of her life had been in smoothing the pillow of exile for banished conspirators. Her refugees had been very precious to her; she was always trying to raise money for some cadaverous Pole, to obtain lessons for some shirtless Italian. There was a legend that an Hungarian had once possessed himself of her affections, and had disappeared after robbing her of everything she possessed. This, however, was very apocryphal, for she had never possessed anything, and it was open to grave doubt that she could have entertained a sentiment so personal. She was in love, even in those days, only with causes, and she languished only for emancipations. But they had been the happiest days, for when causes were embodied in foreigners (what else were the Africans?), they were certainly more appealing.

She had just come down to see Doctor Prance—to see whether she wouldn't like to come up. But she wasn't in her room, and Miss Birdseye guessed she had gone out to her supper; she got her supper at a boarding-table about two blocks off. Miss Birdseye expressed the hope that Miss Chancellor had had hers; she would have had plenty of time to take it, for no one had come in yet; she didn't know what made them all so late. Ransom perceived that the garments suspended to the hat-rack were not a sign that Miss Birdseye's friends had assembled; if he had gone a little further still he would have recognised the house as one of those in which mysterious articles of clothing are always hooked to something in the hall. Miss Birdseye's visitors, those of Doctor Prance, and of other tenants—for Number 756 was the common residence of several persons, among whom there prevailed much vagueness of boundary—used to leave things to be called for; many of them went about with satchels and reticules, for which they were always looking for places of deposit. What completed the character of this interior was Miss Birdseye's own apartment, into which her guests presently made their way, and where they were joined by various other members of the good lady's circle. Indeed, it completed Miss Birdseye herself, if anything could be said to render that office to this essentially formless old woman, who had no more outline than a bundle of hay. But the bareness of her long, loose, empty parlour (it was shaped exactly like Miss Chancellor's) told that she had never had any needs but moral needs, and that all her history had been that of her sympathies. The place was lighted by a small hot glare of gas, which made it look white and featureless. It struck even Basil Ransom with its flatness, and he said to himself that his cousin must have a very big bee in her bonnet to make her like such a house. He did not know then, and he never knew, that she mortally disliked it, and that in a career in which she was constantly exposing herself to offence and laceration, her most poignant suffering came from the injury of her taste. She had tried to kill that nerve, to persuade herself that taste was only frivolity in the disguise of knowledge; but her susceptibility was constantly blooming afresh and making her wonder whether an absence of nice arrangements were a necessary part of the enthusiasm of humanity. Miss Birdseye was always trying to obtain employment, lessons in drawing, orders for portraits, for poor foreign artists, as to the greatness of whose talent she pledged herself without reserve; but in point of fact she had not the faintest sense of the scenic or plastic side of life.

Toward nine o'clock the light of her hissing burners smote the majestic person of Mrs. Farrinder, who might have contributed to answer that question of Miss Chancellor's in the negative. She was a copious, handsome woman, in whom angularity had been corrected by the air of success; she had a rustling dress (it was evident what *she* thought about taste), abundant hair of a glossy blackness, a pair of folded arms, the expression of which seemed to say that rest, in such a career as hers, was as sweet as it was brief, and a terrible regularity of feature. I apply that adjective to her fine placid mask because she seemed to face you with a question of which the answer was preordained, to ask you how a countenance could fail to be noble of which the measurements were so correct. You could contest neither the measurements nor the nobleness, and had to feel that Mrs. Farrinder imposed herself. There was a lithographic smoothness about her, and a mixture of the American matron and the public character. There was something public in her eye, which was large, cold, and quiet; it had acquired a sort of exposed reticence from the habit of looking down from a lecture-desk, over a sea of heads, while its distinguished owner was eulogised by a leading citizen. Mrs. Farrinder, at almost any time, had the air of being introduced by a few remarks. She talked with great slowness and distinctness, and evidently a high sense of responsibility; she pronounced every syllable of every word and insisted on being explicit. If, in conversation with her, you attempted to take anything for granted, or to jump two or three steps at a time, she paused, looking at you with a cold patience, as if she knew that trick, and then went on at her own measured pace. She lectured on temperance and the rights of women; the ends she laboured for were to give the ballot to every woman in the country and to take the flowing bowl from every man. She was held to have a very fine manner, and to embody the domestic virtues and the graces of the drawing-room; to be a shining proof, in short, that the forum, for ladies, is not necessarily hostile to the fireside. She had a husband, and his name was Amariah.

Doctor Prance had come back from supper and made her appearance in response to an invitation that Miss Birdseye's relaxed voice had tinkled down to her from the hall over the banisters, with much repetition, to secure attention. She was a plain, spare young woman, with short hair and an eye-glass; she looked about her with a kind of near-sighted deprecation, and seemed to hope that she should not be expected to generalise in any way, or supposed to have come up for any purpose more social than to see what Miss Birdseye wanted this time. By nine o'clock twenty other persons had arrived, and had placed themselves in the chairs that were ranged along the sides of the long, bald room, in which they ended by producing the similitude of an enormous street-car. The apartment contained little else but these chairs, many of which had a borrowed aspect, an implication of bare bedrooms in the upper regions; a table or two with a discoloured marble top, a few books, and a collection of newspapers piled

up in corners. Ransom could see for himself that the occasion
was not crudely festive; there was a want of convivial movement, and, among most of the visitors, even of mutual
recognition. They sat there as if they were waiting for
something; they looked obliquely and silently at Mrs. Farrinder, and were plainly under the impression that, fortunately,
they were not there to amuse themselves. The ladies, who
were much the more numerous, wore their bonnets, like Miss
Chancellor; the men were in the garb of toil, many of them
in weary-looking overcoats. Two or three had retained their
overshoes, and as you approached them the odour of the
india-rubber was perceptible. It was not, however, that Miss
Birdseye ever noticed anything of that sort; she neither knew
what she smelled nor tasted what she ate. Most of her friends
had an anxious, haggard look, though there were sundry exceptions—half a dozen placid, florid faces. Basil Ransom
wondered who they all were; he had a general idea they were
mediums, communists, vegetarians. It was not, either, that
Miss Birdseye failed to wander about among them with repetitions of inquiry and friendly absences of attention; she sat
down near most of them in turn, saying 'Yes, yes,' vaguely
and kindly, to remarks they made to her, feeling for the papers in the pockets of her loosened bodice, recovering her cap
and sacrificing her spectacles, wondering most of all what had
been her idea in convoking these people. Then she remembered that it had been connected in some way with Mrs. Farrinder; that this eloquent woman had promised to favour the
company with a few reminiscences of her last campaign; to
sketch even, perhaps, the lines on which she intended to operate during the coming winter. This was what Olive Chancellor had come to hear; this would be the attraction for the
dark-eyed young man (he looked like a genius) she had
brought with her. Miss Birdseye made her way back to the
great lecturess, who was bending an indulgent attention on
Miss Chancellor; the latter compressed into a small space, to
be near her, and sitting with clasped hands and a concentration of inquiry which by contrast made Mrs. Farrinder's manner seem large and free. In her transit, however, the hostess
was checked by the arrival of fresh pilgrims; she had no idea
she had mentioned the occasion to so many people—she only

remembered, as it were, those she had forgotten—and it was certainly a proof of the interest felt in Mrs. Farrinder's work. The people who had just come in were Doctor and Mrs. Tarrant and their daughter Verena; he was a mesmeric healer and she was of old Abolitionist stock. Miss Birdseye rested her dim, dry smile upon the daughter, who was new to her, and it floated before her that she would probably be remarkable as a genius; her parentage was an implication of that. There was a genius for Miss Birdseye in every bush. Selah Tarrant had effected wonderful cures; she knew so many people—if they would only try him. His wife was a daughter of Abraham Greenstreet; she had kept a runaway slave in her house for thirty days. That was years before, when this girl must have been a child; but hadn't it thrown a kind of rainbow over her cradle, and wouldn't she naturally have some gift? The girl was very pretty, though she had red hair.

V

MRS. FARRINDER, meanwhile, was not eager to address the assembly. She confessed as much to Olive Chancellor, with a smile which asked that a temporary lapse of promptness might not be too harshly judged. She had addressed so many assemblies, and she wanted to hear what other people had to say. Miss Chancellor herself had thought so much on the vital subject; would not she make a few remarks and give them some of her experiences? How did the ladies on Beacon Street feel about the ballot? Perhaps she could speak for *them* more than for some others. That was a branch of the question on which, it might be, the leaders had not information enough; but they wanted to take in everything, and why shouldn't Miss Chancellor just make that field her own? Mrs. Farrinder spoke in the tone of one who took views so wide that they might easily, at first, before you could see how she worked round, look almost meretricious; she was conscious of a scope that exceeded the first flight of your imagination. She urged upon her companion the idea of labouring in the world of fashion, appeared to attribute to her familiar relations with that mysterious realm, and wanted to know why she shouldn't stir up some of her friends down there on the Mill-dam?

Olive Chancellor received this appeal with peculiar feelings. With her immense sympathy for reform, she found herself so often wishing that reformers were a little different. There was something grand about Mrs. Farrinder; it lifted one up to be with her: but there was a false note when she spoke to her young friend about the ladies in Beacon Street. Olive hated to hear that fine avenue talked about as if it were such a remarkable place, and to live there were a proof of worldly glory. All sorts of inferior people lived there, and so brilliant a woman as Mrs. Farrinder, who lived at Roxbury, ought not to mix things up. It was, of course, very wretched to be irritated by such mistakes; but this was not the first time Miss Chancellor had observed that the possession of nerves was not by itself a reason for embracing the new truths. She knew her place in the Boston hierarchy, and it was not what Mrs.

Farrinder supposed; so that there was a want of perspective in talking to her as if she had been a representative of the aristocracy. Nothing could be weaker, she knew very well, than (in the United States) to apply that term too literally; nevertheless, it would represent a reality if one were to say that, by distinction, the Chancellors belonged to the *bourgeoisie*—the oldest and best. They might care for such a position or not (as it happened, they were very proud of it), but there they were, and it made Mrs. Farrinder seem provincial (there was something provincial, after all, in the way she did her hair too) not to understand. When Miss Birdseye spoke as if one were a 'leader of society,' Olive could forgive her even that odious expression, because, of course, one never pretended that she, poor dear, had the smallest sense of the real. She was heroic, she was sublime, the whole moral history of Boston was reflected in her displaced spectacles; but it was a part of her originality, as it were, that she was deliciously provincial. Olive Chancellor seemed to herself to have privileges enough without being affiliated to the exclusive set and having invitations to the smaller parties, which were the real test; it was a mercy for her that she had not that added immorality on her conscience. The ladies Mrs. Farrinder meant (it was to be supposed she meant some particular ones) might speak for themselves. She wished to work in another field; she had long been preoccupied with the romance of the people. She had an immense desire to know intimately some *very* poor girl. This might seem one of the most accessible of pleasures; but, in point of fact, she had not found it so. There were two or three pale shop-maidens whose acquaintance she had sought; but they had seemed afraid of her, and the attempt had come to nothing. She took them more tragically than they took themselves; they couldn't make out what she wanted them to do, and they always ended by being odiously mixed up with Charlie. Charlie was a young man in a white overcoat and a paper collar; it was for him, in the last analysis, that they cared much the most. They cared far more about Charlie than about the ballot. Olive Chancellor wondered how Mrs. Farrinder would treat that branch of the question. In her researches among her young townswomen she had always found this obtrusive swain planted in her path, and she grew at last to dislike him extremely. It filled her with exasperation to think that he should be necessary to the happiness of his victims (she had learned that whatever they might talk about with her, it was of him and him only that they discoursed among themselves), and one of the main recommendations of the evening club for her fatigued, underpaid sisters, which it had long been her dream to establish, was that it would in some degree undermine his position—distinct as her prevision might be that he would be in waiting at the door. She hardly knew what to say to Mrs. Farrinder when this momentarily misdirected woman, still preoccupied with the Milldam, returned to the charge.

'We want labourers in that field, though I know two or three lovely women—sweet *home-women*—moving in circles that are for the most part closed to every new voice, who are doing their best to help on the fight. I have several names that might surprise you, names well known on State Street. But we can't have too many recruits, especially among those whose refinement is generally acknowledged. If it be necessary, we are prepared to take certain steps to conciliate the shrinking. Our movement is for all—it appeals to the most delicate ladies. Raise the standard among them, and bring me a thousand names. I know several that I should like to have. I look after the details as well as the big currents,' Mrs. Farrinder added, in a tone as explanatory as could be expected of such a woman, and with a smile of which the sweetness was thrilling to her listener.

'I can't talk to those people, I can't!' said Olive Chancellor, with a face which seemed to plead for a remission of responsibility. 'I want to give myself up to others; I want to know everything that lies beneath and out of sight, don't you know? I want to enter into the lives of women who are lonely, who are piteous. I want to be near to them—to help them. I want to do something—oh, I should like so to speak!'

'We should be glad to have you make a few remarks at present,' Mrs. Farrinder declared, with a punctuality which revealed the faculty of presiding.

'Oh dear, no, I can't speak; I have none of that sort of talent. I have no self-possession, no eloquence; I can't put three words together. But I do want to contribute.'

'What *have* you got?' Mrs. Farrinder inquired, looking at her interlocutress, up and down, with the eye of business, in which there was a certain chill. 'Have you got money?'

Olive was so agitated for the moment with the hope that this great woman would approve of her on the financial side that she took no time to reflect that some other quality might, in courtesy, have been suggested. But she confessed to possessing a certain capital, and the tone seemed rich and deep in which Mrs. Farrinder said to her, 'Then contribute that!' She was so good as to develop this idea, and her picture of the part Miss Chancellor might play by making liberal donations to a fund for the diffusion among the women of America of a more adequate conception of their public and private rights—a fund her adviser had herself lately inaugurated—this bold, rapid sketch had the vividness which characterised the speaker's most successful public efforts. It placed Olive under the spell; it made her feel almost inspired. If her life struck others in that way—especially a woman like Mrs. Farrinder, whose horizon was so full—then there must be something for her to do. It was one thing to choose for herself, but now the great representative of the enfranchisement of their sex (from every form of bondage) had chosen for her.

The barren, gas-lighted room grew richer and richer to her earnest eyes; it seemed to expand, to open itself to the great life of humanity. The serious, tired people, in their bonnets and overcoats, began to glow like a company of heroes. Yes, she would do something, Olive Chancellor said to herself; she would do something to brighten the darkness of that dreadful image that was always before her, and against which it seemed to her at times that she had been born to lead a crusade—the image of the unhappiness of women. The unhappiness of women! The voice of their silent suffering was always in her ears, the ocean of tears that they had shed from the beginning of time seemed to pour through her own eyes. Ages of oppression had rolled over them; uncounted millions had lived only to be tortured, to be crucified. They were her sisters, they were her own, and the day of their delivery had dawned. This was the only sacred cause; this was the great, the just revolution. It must triumph, it must sweep everything before it; it must exact from the other, the brutal, blood-stained, ravening race, the last particle of expiation! It would be the greatest change the world had seen; it would be a new era for the human family, and the names of those who had helped to show the way and lead the squadrons would be the brightest in the tables of fame. They would be names of women weak, insulted, persecuted, but devoted in every pulse of their being to the cause, and asking no better fate than to die for it. It was not clear to this interesting girl in what manner such a sacrifice (as this last) would be required of her, but she saw the matter through a kind of sunrise-mist of emotion which made danger as rosy as success. When Miss Birdseye approached, it transfigured her familiar, her comical shape, and made the poor little humanitary hack seem already a martyr. Olive Chancellor looked at her with love, remembered that she had never, in her long, unrewarded, weary life, had a thought or an impulse for herself. She had been consumed by the passion of sympathy; it had crumpled her into as many creases as an old glazed, distended glove. She had been laughed at, but she never knew it; she was treated as a bore, but she never cared. She had nothing in the world but the clothes on her back, and when she should go down into the grave she would leave nothing behind her but her grotesque, undistinguished, pathetic little name. And yet people said that women were vain, that they were personal, that they were interested! While Miss Birdseye stood there, asking Mrs. Farrinder if she wouldn't say something, Olive Chancellor tenderly fastened a small battered brooch which confined her collar and which had half detached itself.

VI

‘OH, THANK YOU,’ said Miss Birdseye, ‘I shouldn’t like to lose it; it was given me by Mirandola!’ He had been one of her refugees in the old time, when two or three of her friends, acquainted with the limits of his resources, wondered how he had come into possession of the trinket. She had been diverted again, after her greeting with Doctor and Mrs. Tarrant, by stopping to introduce the tall, dark young man whom Miss Chancellor had brought with her to Doctor Prance. She had become conscious of his somewhat sombre figure, uplifted against the wall, near the door; he was leaning there in solitude, unacquainted with opportunities which Miss Birdseye felt to be, collectively, of value, and which were really, of course, what strangers came to Boston for. It did not occur to her to ask herself why Miss Chancellor didn’t talk to him, since she had brought him; Miss Birdseye was incapable of a speculation of this kind. Olive, in fact, had remained vividly conscious of her kinsman’s isolation until the moment when Mrs. Farrinder lifted her, with a word, to a higher plane. She watched him across the room; she saw that he might be bored. But she proposed to herself not to mind that; she had asked him, after all, not to come. Then he was no worse off than others; he was only waiting, like the rest; and before they left she would introduce him to Mrs. Farrinder. She might tell that lady who he was first; it was not every one that would care to know a person who had borne such a part in the Southern disloyalty. It came over our young lady that when she sought the acquaintance of her distant kinsman she had indeed done a more complicated thing than she suspected. The sudden uneasiness that he flung over her in the carriage had not left her, though she felt it less now she was with others, and especially that she was close to Mrs. Farrinder, who was such a fountain of strength. At any rate, if he was bored, he could speak to some one; there were excellent people near him, even if they *were* ardent reformers. He could speak to that pretty girl who had just come in—the one with red hair—if he liked; Southerners were supposed to be so chivalrous!

Miss Birdseye reasoned much less, and did not offer to introduce him to Verena Tarrant, who was apparently being presented by her parents to a group of friends at the other end of the room. It came back to Miss Birdseye, in this connection, that, sure enough, Verena had been away for a long time—for nearly a year; had been on a visit to friends in the West, and would therefore naturally be a stranger to most of the Boston circle. Doctor Prance was looking at her—at Miss Birdseye—with little, sharp, fixed pupils; and the good lady wondered whether she were angry at having been induced to come up. She had a general impression that when genius was original its temper was high, and all this would be the case with Doctor Prance. She wanted to say to her that she could go down again if she liked; but even to Miss Birdseye's unsophisticated mind this scarcely appeared, as regards a guest, an adequate formula of dismissal. She tried to bring the young Southerner out; she said to him that she presumed they would have some entertainment soon—Mrs. Farrinder could be interesting when she tried! And then she bethought herself to introduce him to Doctor Prance; it might serve as a reason for having brought her up. Moreover, it would do her good to break up her work now and then; she pursued her medical studies far into the night, and Miss Birdseye, who was nothing of a sleeper (Mary Prance, precisely, had wanted to treat her for it), had heard her, in the stillness of the small hours, with her open windows (she had fresh air on the brain), sharpening instruments (it was Miss Birdseye's mild belief that she dissected), in a little physiological laboratory which she had set up in her back room, the room which, if she hadn't been a doctor, might have been her 'chamber,' and perhaps was, even with the dissecting, Miss Birdseye didn't know! She explained her young friends to each other, a trifle incoherently, perhaps, and then went to stir up Mrs. Farrinder.

Basil Ransom had already noticed Doctor Prance; he had not been at all bored, and had observed every one in the room, arriving at all sorts of ingenious inductions. The little medical lady struck him as a perfect example of the 'Yankee female'—the figure which, in the unregenerate imagination of the children of the cotton-States, was produced by the New

England school-system, the Puritan code, the ungenial climate, the absence of chivalry. Spare, dry, hard, without a curve, an inflection or a grace, she seemed to ask no odds in the battle of life and to be prepared to give none. But Ransom could see that she was not an enthusiast, and after his contact with his cousin's enthusiasm this was rather a relief to him. She looked like a boy, and not even like a good boy. It was evident that if she had been a boy, she would have 'cut' school, to try private experiments in mechanics or to make researches in natural history. It was true that if she had been a boy she would have borne some relation to a girl, whereas Doctor Prance appeared to bear none whatever. Except her intelligent eye, she had no features to speak of. Ransom asked her if she were acquainted with the lioness, and on her staring at him, without response, explained that he meant the renowned Mrs. Farrinder.

'Well, I don't know as I ought to say that I'm acquainted with her; but I've heard her on the platform. I have paid my half-dollar,' the doctor added, with a certain grimness.

'Well, did she convince you?' Ransom inquired.

'Convince me of what, sir?'

'That women are so superior to men.'

'Oh, deary me!' said Doctor Prance, with a little impatient sigh; 'I guess I know more about women than she does.'

'And that isn't your opinion, I hope,' said Ransom, laughing.

'Men and women are all the same to me,' Doctor Prance remarked. 'I don't see any difference. There is room for improvement in both sexes. Neither of them is up to the standard.' And on Ransom's asking her what the standard appeared to her to be, she said, 'Well, they ought to live better; that's what they ought to do.' And she went on to declare, further, that she thought they all talked too much. This had so long been Ransom's conviction that his heart quite warmed to Doctor Prance, and he paid homage to her wisdom in the manner of Mississippi—with a richness of compliment that made her turn her acute, suspicious eye upon him. This checked him; she was capable of thinking that *he* talked too much—she herself having, apparently, no general conversation. It was german to the matter, at any rate, for him to observe that he believed they were to have a lecture from Mrs. Farrinder—he didn't know why she didn't begin. 'Yes,' said Doctor Prance, rather drily, 'I suppose that's what Miss Birdseye called me up for. She seemed to think I wouldn't want to miss that.'

'Whereas, I infer, you could console yourself for the loss of the oration,' Ransom suggested.

'Well, I've got some work. I don't want any one to teach me what a woman can do!' Doctor Prance declared. 'She can find out some things, if she tries. Besides, I am familiar with Mrs. Farrinder's system; I know all she has got to say.'

'Well, what is it, then, since she continues to remain silent?'

'Well, what it amounts to is just that women want to have a better time. That's what it comes to in the end. I am aware of that, without her telling me.'

'And don't you sympathise with such an aspiration?'

'Well, I don't know as I cultivate the sentimental side,' said Doctor Prance. 'There's plenty of sympathy without mine. If they want to have a better time, I suppose it's natural; so do men too, I suppose. But I don't know as it appeals to me— to make sacrifices for it; it ain't such a wonderful time—the best you *can* have!'

This little lady was tough and technical; she evidently didn't care for great movements; she became more and more interesting to Basil Ransom, who, it is to be feared, had a fund of cynicism. He asked her if she knew his cousin, Miss Chancellor, whom he indicated, beside Mrs. Farrinder; *she* believed, on the contrary, in wonderful times (she thought they were coming); she had plenty of sympathy, and he was sure she was willing to make sacrifices.

Doctor Prance looked at her across the room for a moment; then she said she didn't know her, but she guessed she knew others like her—she went to see them when they were sick. 'She's having a private lecture to herself,' Ransom remarked; whereupon Doctor Prance rejoined, 'Well, I guess she'll have to pay for it!' She appeared to regret her own half-dollar, and to be vaguely impatient of the behaviour of her sex. Ransom became so sensible of this that he felt it was indelicate to allude further to the cause of woman, and, for a change, endeavoured to elicit from his companion some information about the gentlemen present. He had given her a chance, vainly, to start some topic herself; but he could see that she had no interests beyond the researches from which, this evening, she had been torn, and was incapable of asking him a personal question. She knew two or three of the gentlemen; she had seen them before at Miss Birdseye's. Of course she knew principally ladies; the time hadn't come when a lady-doctor was sent for by a gentleman, and she hoped it never would, though some people seemed to think that this was what lady-doctors were working for. She knew Mr. Pardon; that was the young man with the 'side-whiskers' and the white hair; he was a kind of editor, and he wrote, too, 'over his signature'—perhaps Basil had read some of his works; he was under thirty, in spite of his white hair. He was a great deal thought of in magazine circles. She believed he was very bright—but she hadn't read anything. She didn't read much—not for amusement; only the 'Transcript.' She believed Mr. Pardon sometimes wrote in the 'Transcript'; well, she supposed he *was* very bright. The other that she knew—only she didn't know him (she supposed Basil would think that queer)—was the tall, pale gentleman, with the black moustache and the eye-glass. She knew him because she had met him in society; but she didn't know him—well, because she didn't want to. If he should come and speak to her—and he looked as if he were going to work round that way—she should just say to him, 'Yes, sir,' or 'No, sir,' very coldly. She couldn't help it if he did think her dry; if *he* were a little more dry, it might be better for him. What was the matter with him? Oh, she thought she had mentioned that; he was a mesmeric healer, he made miraculous cures. She didn't believe in his system or disbelieve in it, one way or the other; she only knew that she had been called to see ladies he had worked on, and she found that he had made them lose a lot of valuable time. He talked to them—well, as if he didn't know what he was saying. She guessed he was quite ignorant of physiology, and she didn't think he ought to go round taking responsibilities. She didn't want to be narrow, but she thought a person ought to know something. She supposed Basil would think her very uplifted; but he had put the question to her, as she might say. All she could say was she didn't

want him to be laying his hands on any of *her* folks; it was
all done with the hands—what wasn't done with the tongue!
Basil could see that Doctor Prance was irritated; that this extreme candour of allusion to her neighbour was probably not
habitual to her, as a member of a society in which the casual
expression of strong opinion generally produced waves of silence. But he blessed her irritation, for him it was so illuminating; and to draw further profit from it he asked her who
the young lady was with the red hair—the pretty one, whom
he had only noticed during the last ten minutes. She was Miss
Tarrant, the daughter of the healer; hadn't she mentioned his
name? Selah Tarrant; if he wanted to send for him. Doctor
Prance wasn't acquainted with her, beyond knowing that she
was the mesmerist's only child, and having heard something
about her having some gift—she couldn't remember which it
was. Oh, if she was his child, she would be sure to have some
gift—if it was only the gift of the g—— well, she didn't
mean to say that; but a talent for conversation. Perhaps she
could die and come to life again; perhaps she would show
them her gift, as no one seemed inclined to do anything. Yes,
she was pretty-appearing, but there was a certain indication
of anæmia, and Doctor Prance would be surprised if she
didn't eat too much candy. Basil thought she had an engaging
exterior; it was his private reflection, coloured doubtless by
'sectional' prejudice, that she was the first pretty girl he had
seen in Boston. She was talking with some ladies at the other
end of the room; and she had a large red fan, which she kept
constantly in movement. She was not a quiet girl; she fid-
geted, was restless, while she talked, and had the air of a person who, whatever she might be doing, would wish to be
doing something else. If people watched her a good deal, she
also returned their contemplation, and her charming eyes had
several times encountered those of Basil Ransom. But they
wandered mainly in the direction of Mrs. Farrinder—they
lingered upon the serene solidity of the great oratress. It was
easy to see that the girl admired this beneficent woman, and
felt it a privilege to be near her. It was apparent, indeed, that
she was excited by the company in which she found herself;
a fact to be explained by a reference to that recent period of
exile in the West, of which we have had a hint, and in conse-

quence of which the present occasion may have seemed to her a return to intellectual life. Ransom secretly wished that his cousin—since fate was to reserve for him a cousin in Boston—had been more like that.

By this time a certain agitation was perceptible; several ladies, impatient of vain delay, had left their places, to appeal personally to Mrs. Farrinder, who was presently surrounded with sympathetic remonstrants. Miss Birdseye had given her up; it had been enough for Miss Birdseye that she should have said, when pressed (so far as her hostess, muffled in laxity, could press) on the subject of the general expectation, that she could only deliver her message to an audience which she felt to be partially hostile. There was no hostility there; they were all only too much in sympathy. 'I don't require sympathy,' she said, with a tranquil smile, to Olive Chancellor; 'I am only myself, I only rise to the occasion, when I see prejudice, when I see bigotry, when I see injustice, when I see conservatism, massed before me like an army. Then I feel—I feel as I imagine Napoleon Bonaparte to have felt on the eve of one of his great victories. I *must* have unfriendly elements—I like to win them over.'

Olive thought of Basil Ransom, and wondered whether he would do for an unfriendly element. She mentioned him to Mrs. Farrinder, who expressed an earnest hope that if he were opposed to the principles which were so dear to the rest of them, he might be induced to take the floor and testify on his own account. 'I should be so happy to answer him,' said Mrs. Farrinder, with supreme softness. 'I should be so glad, at any rate, to exchange ideas with him.' Olive felt a deep alarm at the idea of a public dispute between these two vigorous people (she had a perception that Ransom would be vigorous), not because she doubted of the happy issue, but because she herself would be in a false position, as having brought the offensive young man, and she had a horror of false positions. Miss Birdseye was incapable of resentment; she had invited forty people to hear Mrs. Farrinder speak, and now Mrs. Farrinder wouldn't speak. But she had such a beautiful reason for it! There was something martial and heroic in her pretext, and, besides, it was so characteristic, so free, that Miss Birdseye was quite consoled, and wandered away, looking at her other guests vaguely, as if she didn't know them from each other, while she mentioned to them, at a venture, the excuse for their disappointment, confident, evidently, that they would agree with her it was very fine. 'But we can't pretend to be on the other side, just to start her up, can we?' she asked of Mr. Tarrant, who sat there beside his wife with a rather conscious but by no means complacent air of isolation from the rest of the company.

'Well, I don't know—I guess we are all solid here,' this gentleman replied, looking round him with a slow, deliberate smile, which made his mouth enormous, developed two wrinkles, as long as the wings of a bat, on either side of it, and showed a set of big, even, carnivorous teeth.

'Selah,' said his wife, laying her hand on the sleeve of his waterproof, 'I wonder whether Miss Birdseye would be interested to hear Verena.'

'Well, if you mean she sings, it's a shame I haven't got a piano,' Miss Birdseye took upon herself to respond. It came back to her that the girl had a gift.

'She doesn't want a piano—she doesn't want anything,' Selah remarked, giving no apparent attention to his wife. It was a part of his attitude in life never to appear to be indebted to another person for a suggestion, never to be surprised or unprepared.

'Well, I don't know that the interest in singing is so general,' said Miss Birdseye, quite unconscious of any slackness in preparing a substitute for the entertainment that had failed her.

'It isn't singing, you'll see,' Mrs. Tarrant declared.

'What is it, then?'

Mr. Tarrant unfurled his wrinkles, showed his back teeth. 'It's inspirational.'

Miss Birdseye gave a small, vague, unsceptical laugh. 'Well, if you can guarantee that——'

'I think it would be acceptable,' said Mrs. Tarrant; and putting up a half-gloved, familiar hand, she drew Miss Birdseye down to her, and the pair explained in alternation what it was their child could do.

Meanwhile, Basil Ransom confessed to Doctor Prance that he was, after all, rather disappointed. He had expected more of a programme; he wanted to hear some of the new truths. Mrs. Farrinder, as he said, remained within her tent, and he had hoped not only to see these distinguished people but also to listen to them.

'Well, *I* ain't disappointed,' the sturdy little doctress replied. 'If any question had been opened, I suppose I should have had to stay.'

'But I presume you don't propose to retire.'

'Well, I've got to pursue my studies some time. I don't want the gentlemen-doctors to get ahead of me.'

'Oh, no one will ever get ahead of you, I'm very sure. And there is that pretty young lady going over to speak to Mrs. Farrinder. She's going to beg her for a speech—Mrs. Farrinder can't resist that.'

'Well, then, I'll just trickle out before she begins. Goodnight, sir,' said Doctor Prance, who by this time had begun to appear to Ransom more susceptible of domestication, as if she had been a small forest-creature, a catamount or a ruffled doe, that had learned to stand still while you stroked it, or even to extend a paw. She ministered to health, and she was healthy herself; if his cousin could have been even of this type Basil would have felt himself more fortunate.

'Good-night, Doctor,' he replied. 'You haven't told me, after all, your opinion of the capacity of the ladies.'

'Capacity for what?' said Doctor Prance. 'They've got a capacity for making people waste time. All I know is that I don't want any one to tell *me* what a lady can do!' And she edged away from him softly, as if she had been traversing a hospital-ward, and presently he saw her reach the door, which, with the arrival of the later comers, had remained open. She stood there an instant, turning over the whole assembly a glance like the flash of a watchman's bull's-eye, and then quickly passed out. Ransom could see that she was impatient of the general question and bored with being reminded, even for the sake of her rights, that she was a woman—a detail that she was in the habit of forgetting, having as many rights as she had time for. It was certain that whatever might become of the movement at large, Doctor Prance's own little revolution was a success.

VII

S HE HAD no sooner left him than Olive Chancellor came
towards him with eyes that seemed to say, 'I don't care
whether you are here now or not—I'm all right!' But what
her lips said was much more gracious; she asked him if she
mightn't have the pleasure of introducing him to Mrs. Farrinder. Ransom consented, with a little of his Southern flourish,
and in a moment the lady got up to receive him from the
midst of the circle that now surrounded her. It was an occasion for her to justify her reputation of an elegant manner,
and it must be impartially related that she struck Ransom as
having a dignity in conversation and a command of the noble
style which could not have been surpassed by a daughter—
one of the most accomplished, most far-descended daughters—of his own latitude. It was as if she had known that he
was not eager for the changes she advocated, and wished to
show him that, especially to a Southerner who had bitten the
dust, her sex could be magnanimous. This knowledge of his
secret heresy seemed to him to be also in the faces of the
other ladies, whose circumspect glances, however (for he had
not been introduced), treated it as a pity rather than as a
shame. He was conscious of all these middle-aged feminine
eyes, conscious of curls, rather limp, that depended from
dusky bonnets, of heads poked forward, as if with a waiting,
listening, familiar habit, of no one being very bright or gay—
no one, at least, but that girl he had noticed before, who
had a brilliant head, and who now hovered on the edge of
the conclave. He met her eye again; she was watching him
too. It had been in his thought that Mrs. Farrinder, to
whom his cousin might have betrayed or misrepresented
him, would perhaps defy him to combat, and he wondered
whether he could pull himself together (he was extremely
embarrassed) sufficiently to do honour to such a challenge.
If she would fling down the glove on the temperance question, it seemed to him that it would be in him to pick it up;
for the idea of a meddling legislation on this subject filled
him with rage; the taste of liquor being good to him, and
his conviction strong that civilisation itself would be in

danger if it should fall into the power of a herd of vocifer-
ating women (I am but the reporter of his angry *formulæ*) to
prevent a gentleman from taking his glass. Mrs. Farrinder
proved to him that she had not the eagerness of insecurity;
she asked him if he wouldn't like to give the company some
account of the social and political condition of the South.
He begged to be excused, expressing at the same time a high
sense of the honour done him by such a request, while he
smiled to himself at the idea of his extemporising a lecture.
He smiled even while he suspected the meaning of the look
Miss Chancellor gave him: 'Well, you are not of much account after all!' To talk to those people about the South—if
they could have guessed how little he cared to do it! He had
a passionate tenderness for his own country, and a sense of
intimate connection with it which would have made it as impossible for him to take a roomful of Northern fanatics into
his confidence as to read aloud his mother's or his mistress's
letters. To be quiet about the Southern land, not to touch
her with vulgar hands, to leave her alone with her wounds
and her memories, not prating in the market-place either of
her troubles or her hopes, but waiting as a man should wait,
for the slow process, the sensible beneficence, of time—this
was the desire of Ransom's heart, and he was aware of how
little it could minister to the entertainment of Miss Birdseye's guests.

'We know so little about the women of the South; they are
very voiceless,' Mrs. Farrinder remarked. 'How much can we
count upon them? in what numbers would they flock to our
standard? I have been recommended not to lecture in the
Southern cities.'

'Ah, madam, that was very cruel advice—for us!' Basil
Ransom exclaimed, with gallantry.

'*I* had a magnificent audience last spring in St. Louis,' a
fresh young voice announced, over the heads of the gathered
group—a voice which, on Basil's turning, like every one else,
for an explanation, appeared to have proceeded from the
pretty girl with red hair. She had coloured a little with the
effort of making this declaration, and she stood there smiling
at her listeners.

Mrs. Farrinder bent a benignant brow upon her, in spite of

her being, evidently, rather a surprise. 'Oh, indeed; and your subject, my dear young lady?'

'The past history, the present condition, and the future prospects of our sex.'

'Oh, well, St. Louis—that's scarcely the South,' said one of the ladies.

'I'm sure the young lady would have had equal success at Charleston or New Orleans,' Basil Ransom interposed.

'Well, I wanted to go farther,' the girl continued, 'but I had no friends. I have friends in St. Louis.'

'You oughtn't to want for them anywhere,' said Mrs. Farrinder, in a manner which, by this time, had quite explained her reputation. 'I am acquainted with the loyalty of St. Louis.'

'Well, after that, you must let me introduce Miss Tarrant; she's perfectly dying to know you, Mrs. Farrinder.' These words emanated from one of the gentlemen, the young man with white hair, who had been mentioned to Ransom by Doctor Prance as a celebrated magazinist. He, too, up to this moment, had hovered in the background, but he now gently clove the assembly (several of the ladies made way for him), leading in the daughter of the mesmerist.

She laughed and continued to blush—her blush was the faintest pink; she looked very young and slim and fair as Mrs. Farrinder made way for her on the sofa which Olive Chancellor had quitted. 'I *have* wanted to know you; I admire you so much; I hoped so you would speak to-night. It's too lovely to see you, Mrs. Farrinder.' So she expressed herself, while the company watched the encounter with a look of refreshed inanition. 'You don't know who I am, of course; I'm just a girl who wants to thank you for all you have done for us. For you have spoken for us girls, just as much as—just as much as——' She hesitated now, looking about with enthusiastic eyes at the rest of the group, and meeting once more the gaze of Basil Ransom.

'Just as much as for the old women,' said Mrs. Farrinder, genially. 'You seem very well able to speak for yourself.'

'She speaks so beautifully—if she would only make a little address,' the young man who had introduced her remarked. 'It's a new style, quite original,' he added. He stood there with folded arms, looking down at his work, the conjunction of the two ladies, with a smile; and Basil Ransom, remembering what Miss Prance had told him, and enlightened by his observation in New York of some of the sources from which newspapers are fed, was immediately touched by the conviction that he perceived in it the material of a paragraph.

'My dear child, if you'll take the floor, I'll call the meeting to order,' said Mrs. Farrinder.

The girl looked at her with extraordinary candour and confidence. 'If I could only hear you first—just to give me an atmosphere.'

'I've got no atmosphere; there's very little of the Indian summer about *me*! I deal with facts—hard facts,' Mrs. Farrinder replied. 'Have you ever heard me? If so, you know how crisp I am.'

'Heard you? I've lived on you! It's so much to me to see you. Ask mother if it ain't!' She had expressed herself, from the first word she uttered, with a promptness and assurance which gave almost the impression of a lesson rehearsed in advance. And yet there was a strange spontaneity in her manner, and an air of artless enthusiasm, of personal purity. If she was theatrical, she was naturally theatrical. She looked up at Mrs. Farrinder with all her emotion in her smiling eyes. This lady had been the object of many ovations; it was familiar to her that the collective heart of her sex had gone forth to her; but, visibly, she was puzzled by this unforeseen embodiment of gratitude and fluency, and her eyes wandered over the girl with a certain reserve, while, within the depth of her eminently public manner, she asked herself whether Miss Tarrant were a remarkable young woman or only a forward minx. She found a response which committed her to neither view; she only said, 'We want the young—of course we want the young!'

'Who is that charming creature?' Basil Ransom heard his cousin ask, in a grave, lowered tone, of Matthias Pardon, the young man who had brought Miss Tarrant forward. He didn't know whether Miss Chancellor knew him, or whether her curiosity had pushed her to boldness. Ransom was near the pair, and had the benefit of Mr. Pardon's answer.

'The daughter of Doctor Tarrant, the mesmeric healer—Miss Verena. She's a high-class speaker.'

'What do you mean?' Olive asked. 'Does she give public addresses?'

'Oh yes, she has had quite a career in the West. I heard her last spring at Topeka. They call it inspirational. I don't know what it is—only it's exquisite; so fresh and poetical. She has to have her father to start her up. It seems to pass into her.' And Mr. Pardon indulged in a gesture intended to signify the passage.

Olive Chancellor made no rejoinder save a low, impatient sigh; she transferred her attention to the girl, who now held Mrs. Farrinder's hand in both her own, and was pleading with her just to prelude a little. 'I want a starting-point—I want to know where I am,' she said. 'Just two or three of your grand old thoughts.'

Basil stepped nearer to his cousin; he remarked to her that Miss Verena was very pretty. She turned an instant, glanced at him, and then said, 'Do you think so?' An instant later she added, 'How you must hate this place!'

'Oh, not now, we are going to have some fun,' Ransom replied good-humouredly, if a trifle coarsely; and the declaration had a point, for Miss Birdseye at this moment reappeared, followed by the mesmeric healer and his wife.

'Ah, well, I see you are drawing her out,' said Miss Birdseye to Mrs. Farrinder; and at the idea that this process had been necessary Basil Ransom broke into a smothered hilarity, a spasm which indicated that, for him, the fun had already begun, and procured him another grave glance from Miss Chancellor. Miss Verena seemed to him as far 'out' as a young woman could be. 'Here's her father, Doctor Tarrant—he has a wonderful gift—and her mother—she was a daughter of Abraham Greenstreet.' Miss Birdseye presented her companion; she was sure Mrs. Farrinder would be interested; she wouldn't want to lose an opportunity, even if for herself the conditions were not favourable. And then Miss Birdseye addressed herself to the company more at large, widening the circle so as to take in the most scattered guests, and evidently feeling that after all it was a relief that one happened to have an obscurely inspired maiden on the premises when greater celebrities had betrayed the whimsicality of genius. It was a part of this whimsicality that Mrs. Farrinder—the reader may find it difficult to keep pace with her variations—appeared now to have decided to utter a few of her thoughts, so that her hostess could elicit a general response to the remark that it would be delightful to have both the old school and the new.

'Well, perhaps you'll be disappointed in Verena,' said Mrs. Tarrant, with an air of dolorous resignation to any event, and seating herself, with her gathered mantle, on the edge of a chair, as if she, at least, were ready, whoever else might keep on talking.

'It isn't *me*, mother,' Verena rejoined, with soft gravity, rather detached now from Mrs. Farrinder, and sitting with her eyes fixed thoughtfully on the ground. With deference to Mrs. Tarrant, a little more talk was necessary, for the young lady had as yet been insufficiently explained. Miss Birdseye felt this, but she was rather helpless about it, and delivered herself, with her universal familiarity, which embraced every one and everything, of a wandering, amiable tale, in which Abraham Greenstreet kept reappearing, in which Doctor Tarrant's miraculous cures were specified, with all the facts wanting, and in which Verena's successes in the West were related, not with emphasis or hyperbole, in which Miss Birdseye never indulged, but as accepted and recognised wonders, natural in an age of new revelations. She had heard of these things in detail only ten minutes before, from the girl's parents, but her hospitable soul had needed but a moment to swallow and assimilate them. If her account of them was not very lucid, it should be said in excuse for her that it was impossible to have any idea of Verena Tarrant unless one had heard her, and therefore still more impossible to give an idea to others. Mrs. Farrinder was perceptibly irritated; she appeared to have made up her mind, after her first hesitation, that the Tarrant family were fantastical and compromising. She had bent an eye of coldness on Selah and his wife—she might have regarded them all as a company of mountebanks.

'Stand up and tell us what you have to say,' she remarked, with some sternness, to Verena, who only raised her eyes to her, silently now, with the same sweetness, and then rested them on her father. This gentleman seemed to respond to an irresistible appeal; he looked round at the company with all his teeth, and said that these flattering allusions were not so embarrassing as they might otherwise be, inasmuch as any success that he and his daughter might have had was so thoroughly impersonal: he insisted on that word. They had just heard her say, 'It is not *me*, mother,' and he and Mrs. Tarrant and the girl herself were all equally aware it was not she. It was some power outside—it seemed to flow through her; he couldn't pretend to say why his daughter should be called, more than any one else. But it seemed as if she *was* called. When he just calmed her down by laying his hand on her a few moments, it seemed to come. It so happened that in the West it had taken the form of a considerable eloquence. She had certainly spoken with great facility to cultivated and high-minded audiences. She had long followed with sympathy the movement for the liberation of her sex from every sort of bondage; it had been her principal interest even as a child (he might mention that at the age of nine she had christened her favourite doll Eliza P. Moseley, in memory of a great precursor whom they all reverenced), and now the inspiration, if he might call it so, seemed just to flow in that channel. The voice that spoke from her lips seemed to want to take that form. It didn't seem as if it *could* take any other. She let it come out just as it would—she didn't pretend to have any control. They could judge for themselves whether the whole thing was not quite unique. That was why he was willing to talk about his own child that way, before a gathering of ladies and gentlemen; it was because they took no credit—they felt it was a power outside. If Verena felt she was going to be stimulated that evening, he was pretty sure they would be interested. Only he should have to request a few moments' silence, while she listened for the voice.

Several of the ladies declared that they should be delighted—they hoped that Miss Tarrant was in good trim; whereupon they were corrected by others, who reminded them that it wasn't *her*—she had nothing to do with it—so her trim didn't matter; and a gentleman added that he guessed there were many present who had conversed with Eliza P. Moseley. Meanwhile Verena, more and more withdrawn into herself, but perfectly undisturbed by the public discussion of her mystic faculty, turned yet again, very prettily,

to Mrs. Farrinder, and asked her if she wouldn't strike out
—just to give her courage. By this time Mrs. Farrinder was
in a condition of overhanging gloom; she greeted the charming suppliant with the frown of Juno. She disapproved completely of Doctor Tarrant's little speech, and she had less and
less disposition to be associated with a miracle-monger. Abraham Greenstreet was very well, but Abraham Greenstreet was
in his grave; and Eliza P. Moseley, after all, had been very
tepid. Basil Ransom wondered whether it were effrontery or
innocence that enabled Miss Tarrant to meet with such complacency the aloofness of the elder lady. At this moment he
heard Olive Chancellor, at his elbow, with the tremor of excitement in her tone, suddenly exclaim: 'Please begin, please
begin! A voice, a human voice, is what we want.'

'I'll speak after you, and if you're a humbug, I'll expose
you!' Mrs. Farrinder said. She was more majestic than facetious.

'I'm sure we are all solid, as Doctor Tarrant says. I suppose
we want to be quiet,' Miss Birdseye remarked.

VIII

VERENA TARRANT got up and went to her father in the middle of the room; Olive Chancellor crossed and resumed her place beside Mrs. Farrinder on the sofa the girl had quitted; and Miss Birdseye's visitors, for the rest, settled themselves attentively in chairs or leaned against the bare sides of the parlour. Verena took her father's hands, held them for a moment, while she stood before him, not looking at him, with her eyes towards the company; then, after an instant, her mother, rising, pushed forward, with an interesting sigh, the chair on which she had been sitting. Mrs. Tarrant was provided with another seat, and Verena, relinquishing her father's grasp, placed herself in the chair, which Tarrant put in position for her. She sat there with closed eyes, and her father now rested his long, lean hands upon her head. Basil Ransom watched these proceedings with much interest, for the girl amused and pleased him. She had far more colour than any one there, for whatever brightness was to be found in Miss Birdseye's rather faded and dingy human collection had gathered itself into this attractive but ambiguous young person. There was nothing ambiguous, by the way, about her confederate; Ransom simply loathed him, from the moment he opened his mouth; he was intensely familiar—that is, his type was; he was simply the detested carpet-bagger. He was false, cunning, vulgar, ignoble; the cheapest kind of human product. That he should be the father of a delicate, pretty girl, who was apparently clever too, whether she had a gift or no, this was an annoying, disconcerting fact. The white, puffy mother, with the high forehead, in the corner there, looked more like a lady; but if she were one, it was all the more shame to her to have mated with such a varlet, Ransom said to himself, making use, as he did generally, of terms of opprobrium extracted from the older English literature. He had seen Tarrant, or his equivalent, often before; he had 'whipped' him, as he believed, controversially, again and again, at political meetings in blighted Southern towns, during the horrible period of reconstruction. If Mrs. Farrinder had looked at Verena Tarrant as if she were a mountebank, there was some excuse for it, inasmuch as the girl made much the same impression on Basil Ransom. He had never seen such an odd mixture of elements; she had the sweetest, most unworldly face, and yet, with it, an air of being on exhibition, of belonging to a troupe, of living in the gaslight, which pervaded even the details of her dress, fashioned evidently with an attempt at the histrionic. If she had produced a pair of castanets or a tambourine, he felt that such accessories would have been quite in keeping.

Little Doctor Prance, with her hard good sense, had noted that she was anæmic, and had intimated that she was a deceiver. The value of her performance was yet to be proved, but she was certainly very pale, white as women are who have that shade of red hair; they look as if their blood had gone into it. There was, however, something rich in the fairness of this young lady; she was strong and supple, there was colour in her lips and eyes, and her tresses, gathered into a complicated coil, seemed to glow with the brightness of her nature. She had curious, radiant, liquid eyes (their smile was a sort of reflection, like the glisten of a gem), and though she was not tall, she appeared to spring up, and carried her head as if it reached rather high. Ransom would have thought she looked like an Oriental, if it were not that Orientals are dark; and if she had only had a goat she would have resembled Esmeralda, though he had but a vague recollection of who Esmeralda had been. She wore a light-brown dress, of a shape that struck him as fantastic, a yellow petticoat, and a large crimson sash fastened at the side; while round her neck, and falling low upon her flat young chest, she had a double chain of amber beads. It must be added that, in spite of her melodramatic appearance, there was no symptom that her performance, whatever it was, would be of a melodramatic character. She was very quiet now, at least (she had folded her big fan), and her father continued the mysterious process of calming her down. Ransom wondered whether he wouldn't put her to sleep; for some minutes her eyes had remained closed; he heard a lady near him, apparently familiar with phenomena of this class, remark that she was going off. As yet the exhibition was not exciting, though it was certainly pleasant to have such a pretty girl placed there before one, like a moving statue.

Doctor Tarrant looked at no one as he stroked and soothed his daughter; his eyes wandered round the cornice of the room, and he grinned upward, as if at an imaginary gallery. 'Quietly—quietly,' he murmured, from time to time. 'It will come, my good child, it will come. Just let it work—just let it gather. The spirit, you know; you've got to let the spirit come out when it will.' He threw up his arms at moments, to rid himself of the wings of his long waterproof, which fell forward over his hands. Basil Ransom noticed all these things, and noticed also, opposite, the waiting face of his cousin, fixed, from her sofa, upon the closed eyes of the young prophetess. He grew more impatient at last, not of the delay of the edifying voice (though some time had elapsed), but of Tarrant's grotesque manipulations, which he resented as much as if he himself had felt their touch, and which seemed a dishonour to the passive maiden. They made him nervous, they made him angry, and it was only afterwards that he asked himself wherein they concerned him, and whether even a carpet-bagger hadn't a right to do what he pleased with his daughter. It was a relief to him when Verena got up from her chair, with a movement which made Tarrant drop into the background as if his part were now over. She stood there with a quiet face, serious and sightless; then, after a short further delay, she began to speak.

She began incoherently, almost inaudibly, as if she were talking in a dream. Ransom could not understand her; he thought it very queer, and wondered what Doctor Prance would have said. 'She's just arranging her ideas, and trying to get in report; she'll come out all right.' This remark he heard dropped in a low tone by the mesmeric healer; 'in report' was apparently Tarrant's version of *en rapport*. His prophecy was verified, and Verena did come out, after a little; she came out with a great deal of sweetness—with a very quaint and peculiar effect. She proceeded slowly, cautiously, as if she were listening for the prompter, catching, one by one, certain phrases that were whispered to her a great distance off, behind the scenes of the world. Then memory, or inspiration, returned to her, and presently she was in possession of her part. She played it with extraordinary simplicity and grace; at the end of ten minutes Ransom became aware that the whole audience—Mrs. Farrinder, Miss Chancellor, and the tough subject from Mississippi—were under the charm. I speak of ten minutes, but to tell the truth the young man lost all sense of time. He wondered afterwards how long she had spoken; then he counted that her strange, sweet, crude, absurd, enchanting improvisation must have lasted half an hour. It was not what she said; he didn't care for that, he scarcely understood it; he could only see that it was all about the gentleness and goodness of women, and how, during the long ages of history, they had been trampled under the iron heel of man. It was about their equality—perhaps even (he was not definitely conscious) about their superiority. It was about their day having come at last, about the universal sisterhood, about their duty to themselves and to each other. It was about such matters as these, and Basil Ransom was delighted to observe that such matters as these didn't spoil it. The effect was not in what she said, though she said some such pretty things, but in the picture and figure of the half-bedizened damsel (playing, now again, with her red fan), the visible freshness and purity of the little effort. When she had gained confidence she opened her eyes, and their shining softness was half the effect of her discourse. It was full of school-girl phrases, of patches of remembered eloquence, of childish lapses of logic, of flights of fancy which might indeed have had success at Topeka; but Ransom thought that if it had been much worse it would have been quite as good, for the argument, the doctrine, had absolutely nothing to do with it. It was simply an intensely personal exhibition, and the person making it happened to be fascinating. She might have offended the taste of certain people—Ransom could imagine that there were other Boston circles in which she would be thought pert; but for himself all he could feel was that to *his* starved senses she irresistibly appealed. He was the stiffest of conservatives, and his mind was steeled against the inanities she uttered—the rights and wrongs of women, the equality of the sexes, the hysterics of conventions, the further stultification of the suffrage, the prospect of conscript mothers in the national Senate. It made no difference; she didn't mean it, she didn't know what she meant, she had been stuffed with this trash by her father, and she was neither more nor less willing to say it than to say anything else; for the necessity of her nature was not to make converts to a ridiculous cause, but to emit those charming notes of her voice, to stand in those free young attitudes, to shake her braided locks like a naiad rising from the waves, to please every one who came near her, and to be happy that she pleased. I know not whether Ransom was aware of the bearings of this interpretation, which attributed to Miss Tarrant a singular hollowness of character; he contented himself with believing that she was as innocent as she was lovely, and with regarding her as a vocalist of exquisite faculty, condemned to sing bad music. How prettily, indeed, she made some of it sound!

'Of course I only speak to women—to my own dear sisters; I don't speak to men, for I don't expect them to like what I say. They pretend to admire us very much, but I should like them to admire us a little less and to trust us a little more. I don't know what we have ever done to them that they should keep us out of everything. We have trusted *them* too much, and I think the time has come now for us to judge them, and say that by keeping us out we don't think they have done so well. When I look around me at the world, and at the state that men have brought it to, I confess I say to myself, "Well, if women had fixed it this way I should like to know what they would think of it!" When I see the dreadful misery of mankind and think of the suffering of which at any hour, at any moment, the world is full, I say that if this is the best they can do by themselves, they had better let us come in a little and see what *we* can do. We couldn't possibly make it worse, could we? If we had done only this, we shouldn't boast of it. Poverty, and ignorance, and crime; disease, and wickedness, and wars! Wars, always more wars, and always more and more. Blood, blood—the world is drenched with blood! To kill each other, with all sorts of expensive and perfected instruments, that is the most brilliant thing they have been able to invent. It seems to me that we might stop it, we might invent something better. The cruelty—the cruelty; there is so much, so much! Why shouldn't tenderness come in? Why should our woman's hearts be so full of it, and all so wasted and withered, while armies and prisons and helpless miseries grow greater all the while? I am only a girl, a simple American girl, and of course I haven't seen much, and there is a great deal of life that I don't know anything about. But there are some things I feel—it seems to me as if I had been born to feel them; they are in my ears in the still-ness of the night and before my face in the visions of the darkness. It is what the great sisterhood of women might do if they should all join hands, and lift up their voices above the brutal uproar of the world, in which it is so hard for the plea of mercy or of justice, the moan of weakness and suffering, to be heard. We should quench it, we should make it still, and the sound of our lips would become the voice of universal peace! For this we must trust one another, we must be true and gentle and kind. We must remember that the world is ours too, ours—little as we have ever had to say about any-thing!—and that the question is *not* yet definitely settled whether it shall be a place of injustice or a place of love!'

It was with this that the young lady finished her harangue, which was not followed by her sinking exhausted into her chair or by any of the traces of a laboured climax. She only turned away slowly towards her mother, smiling over her shoulder at the whole room, as if it had been a single person, without a flush in her whiteness, or the need of drawing a longer breath. The performance had evidently been very easy to her, and there might have been a kind of impertinence in her air of not having suffered from an exertion which had wrought so powerfully on every one else. Ransom broke into a genial laugh, which he instantly swallowed again, at the sweet grotesqueness of this virginal creature's standing be-fore a company of middle-aged people to talk to them about 'love,' the note on which she had closed her harangue. It was the most charming touch in the whole thing, and the most vivid proof of her innocence. She had had immense success, and Mrs. Tarrant, as she took her into her arms and kissed her, was certainly able to feel that the audience was not dis-appointed. They were exceedingly affected; they broke into exclamations and murmurs. Selah Tarrant went on conversing ostentatiously with his neighbours, slowly twirling his long thumbs and looking up at the cornice again, as if there could be nothing in the brilliant manner in which his daughter had acquitted herself to surprise *him*, who had heard her when she was still more remarkable, and who, moreover, remembered that the affair was so impersonal. Miss Birdseye looked round at the company with dim exultation; her large mild cheeks were shining with unwiped tears. Young Mr. Pardon remarked, in Ransom's hearing, that he knew parties who, if they had been present, would want to engage Miss Verena at a high figure for the winter campaign. And Ransom heard him add in a lower tone: 'There's money for some one in that girl; you see if she don't have quite a run!' As for our Mississippian he kept his agreeable sensation for himself, only wondering whether he might not ask Miss Birdseye to present him to the heroine of the evening. Not immediately, of course, for the young man mingled with his Southern pride a shyness which often served all the purpose of humility. He was aware how much he was an outsider in such a house as that, and he was ready to wait for his coveted satisfaction till the others, who all hung together, should have given her the assurance of an approval which she would value, naturally, more than anything he could say to her. This episode had imparted animation to the assembly; a certain gaiety, even, expressed in a higher pitch of conversation, seemed to float in the heated air. People circulated more freely, and Verena Tarrant was presently hidden from Ransom's sight by the close-pressed ranks of the new friends she had made. 'Well, I never heard it put *that* way!' Ransom heard one of the ladies exclaim; to which another replied that she wondered one of their bright women hadn't thought of it before. 'Well, it *is* a gift, and no mistake,' and 'Well, they may call it what they please, it's a pleasure to listen to it'—these genial tributes fell from the lips of a pair of ruminating gentlemen. It was affirmed within Ransom's hearing that if they had a few more like that the matter would soon be fixed; and it was rejoined that they couldn't expect to have a great many—the style was so peculiar. It was generally admitted that the style was peculiar, but Miss Tarrant's peculiarity was the explanation of her success.

IX

Ransom approached Mrs. Farrinder again, who had remained on her sofa with Olive Chancellor; and as she
turned her face to him he saw that she had felt the universal
contagion. Her keen eye sparkled, there was a flush on her
matronly cheek, and she had evidently made up her mind
what line to take. Olive Chancellor sat motionless; her eyes
were fixed on the floor with the rigid, alarmed expression of
her moments of nervous diffidence; she gave no sign of observing her kinsman's approach. He said something to Mrs.
Farrinder, something that imperfectly represented his admiration of Verena; and this lady replied with dignity that it was
no wonder the girl spoke so well—she spoke in such a good
cause. 'She is very graceful, has a fine command of language;
her father says it's a natural gift.' Ransom saw that he should
not in the least discover Mrs. Farrinder's real opinion, and
her dissimulation added to his impression that she was a
woman with a policy. It was none of his business whether in
her heart she thought Verena a parrot or a genius; it was
perceptible to him that she saw she would be effective, would
help the cause. He stood almost appalled for a moment, as he
said to himself that she would take her up and the girl would
be ruined, would force her note and become a screamer. But
he quickly dodged this vision, taking refuge in a mechanical
appeal to his cousin, of whom he inquired how she liked Miss
Verena. Olive made no answer; her head remained averted,
she bored the carpet with her conscious eyes. Mrs. Farrinder
glanced at her askance, and then said to Ransom serenely:

'You praise the grace of your Southern ladies, but you have
had to come North to see a human gazelle. Miss Tarrant is of
the best New England stock—what *I* call the best!'

'I'm sure from what I have seen of the Boston ladies, no
manifestation of grace can excite my surprise,' Ransom rejoined, looking, with his smile, at his cousin.

'She has been powerfully affected,' Mrs. Farrinder explained, very slightly dropping her voice, as Olive, apparently,
still remained deaf.

Miss Birdseye drew near at this moment; she wanted to

know if Mrs. Farrinder didn't want to express some acknowledgment, on the part of the company at large, for the real
stimulus Miss Tarrant had given them. Mrs. Farrinder said:
Oh yes, she would speak now with pleasure; only she must
have a glass of water first. Miss Birdseye replied that there
was some coming in a moment; one of the ladies had asked
for it, and Mr. Pardon had just stepped down to draw some.
Basil took advantage of this intermission to ask Miss Birdseye
if she would give him the great privilege of an introduction
to Miss Verena. 'Mrs. Farrinder will thank her for the company,' he said, laughing, 'but she won't thank her for me.'

Miss Birdseye manifested the greatest disposition to oblige
him; she was so glad he had been impressed. She was proceeding to lead him toward Miss Tarrant when Olive Chancellor rose abruptly from her chair and laid her hand, with an
arresting movement, on the arm of her hostess. She explained
to her that she must go, that she was not very well, that her
carriage was there; also that she hoped Miss Birdseye, if it
was not asking too much, would accompany her to the door.

'Well, you are impressed too,' said Miss Birdseye, looking
at her philosophically. 'It seems as if no one had escaped.'

Ransom was disappointed; he saw he was going to be
taken away, and, before he could suppress it, an exclamation
burst from his lips—the first exclamation he could think of
that would perhaps check his cousin's retreat: 'Ah, Miss
Olive, are you going to give up Mrs. Farrinder?'

At this Miss Olive looked at him, showed him an extraordinary face, a face he scarcely understood or even recognised.
It was portentously grave, the eyes were enlarged, there was
a red spot in each of the cheeks, and as directed to him, a
quick, piercing question, a kind of leaping challenge, in the
whole expression. He could only answer this sudden gleam
with a stare, and wonder afresh what trick his Northern kinswoman was destined to play him. Impressed too? He should
think he had been! Mrs. Farrinder, who was decidedly a
woman of the world, came to his assistance, or to Miss Chancellor's, and said she hoped very much Olive wouldn't stay—
she felt these things too much. 'If you stay, I won't speak,'
she added; 'I should upset you altogether.' And then she continued, tenderly, for so preponderantly intellectual a nature:

'When women feel as you do, how can I doubt that we shall come out all right?'

'Oh, we shall come out all right, I guess,' murmured Miss Birdseye.

'But you must remember Beacon Street,' Mrs. Farrinder subjoined. 'You must take advantage of your position—you must wake up the Back Bay!'

'I'm sick of the Back Bay!' said Olive fiercely; and she passed to the door with Miss Birdseye, bidding good-bye to no one. She was so agitated that, evidently, she could not trust herself, and there was nothing for Ransom but to follow. At the door of the room, however, he was checked by a sudden pause on the part of the two ladies: Olive stopped and stood there hesitating. She looked round the room and spied out Verena, where she sat with her mother, the centre of a gratified group; then, throwing back her head with an air of decision, she crossed over to her. Ransom said to himself that now, perhaps, was his chance, and he quickly accompanied Miss Chancellor. The little knot of reformers watched her as she arrived; their faces expressed a suspicion of her social importance, mingled with conscientious scruples as to whether it were right to recognise it. Verena Tarrant saw that she was the object of this manifestation, and she got up to meet the lady whose approach was so full of point. Ransom perceived, however, or thought he perceived, that she recognised nothing; she had no suspicions of social importance. Yet she smiled with all her radiance, as she looked from Miss Chancellor to him; smiled because she liked to smile, to please, to feel her success—or was it because she was a perfect little actress, and this was part of her training? She took the hand that Olive put out to her; the others, rather solemnly, sat looking up from their chairs.

'You don't know me, but I want to know you,' Olive said. 'I can't thank you now. Will you come and see me?'

'Oh yes; where do you live?' Verena answered, in the tone of a girl for whom an invitation (she hadn't so many) was always an invitation.

Miss Chancellor syllabled her address, and Mrs. Tarrant came forward, smiling. 'I know about you, Miss Chancellor. I guess your father knew my father—Mr. Greenstreet. Verena will be very glad to visit you. We shall be very happy to see you in *our* home.'

Basil Ransom, while the mother spoke, wanted to say something to the daughter, who stood there so near him, but he could think of nothing that would do; certain words that came to him, his Mississippi phrases, seemed patronising and ponderous. Besides, he didn't wish to assent to what she had said; he wished simply to tell her she was delightful, and it was difficult to mark that difference. So he only smiled at her in silence, and she smiled back at him—a smile that seemed to him quite for himself.

'Where do you live?' Olive asked; and Mrs. Tarrant replied that they lived at Cambridge, and that the horse-cars passed just near their door. Whereupon Olive insisted 'Will you come very soon?' and Verena said, Oh yes, she would come very soon, and repeated the number in Charles Street, to show that she had taken heed of it. This was done with child-like good faith. Ransom saw that she would come and see any one who would ask her like that, and he regretted for a minute that he was not a Boston lady, so that he might extend to her such an invitation. Olive Chancellor held her hand a moment longer, looked at her in farewell, and then, saying, 'Come, Mr. Ransom,' drew him out of the room. In the hall they met Mr. Pardon, coming up from the lower regions with a jug of water and a tumbler. Miss Chancellor's hackney-coach was there, and when Basil had put her into it she said to him that she wouldn't trouble him to drive with her—his hotel was not near Charles Street. He had so little desire to sit by her side—he wanted to smoke—that it was only after the vehicle had rolled off that he reflected upon her coolness, and asked himself why the deuce she had brought him away. She *was* a very odd cousin, was this Boston cousin of his. He stood there a moment, looking at the light in Miss Birdseye's windows and greatly minded to re-enter the house, now he might speak to the girl. But he contented himself with the memory of her smile, and turned away with a sense of relief, after all, at having got out of such wild company, as well as with (in a different order) a vulgar consciousness of being very thirsty.

X

VERENA TARRANT came in the very next day from Cambridge to Charles Street; that quarter of Boston is in direct communication with the academic suburb. It hardly seemed direct to poor Verena, perhaps, who, in the crowded street-car which deposited her finally at Miss Chancellor's door, had to stand up all the way, half suspended by a leathern strap from the glazed roof of the stifling vehicle, like some blooming cluster dangling in a hothouse. She was used, however, to these perpendicular journeys, and though, as we have seen, she was not inclined to accept without question the social arrangements of her time, it never would have occurred to her to criticise the railways of her native land. The promptness of her visit to Olive Chancellor had been an idea of her mother's, and Verena listened open-eyed while this lady, in the seclusion of the little house in Cambridge, while Selah Tarrant was 'off,' as they said, with his patients, sketched out a line of conduct for her. The girl was both submissive and unworldly, and she listened to her mother's enumeration of the possible advantages of an intimacy with Miss Chancellor as she would have listened to any other fairy-tale. It was still a part of the fairy-tale when this zealous parent put on with her own hands Verena's smart hat and feather, buttoned her little jacket (the buttons were immense and gilt), and presented her with twenty cents to pay her car-fare.

There was never any knowing in advance how Mrs. Tarrant would take a thing, and even Verena, who, filially, was much less argumentative than in her civic and, as it were, public capacity, had a perception that her mother was queer. She was queer, indeed—a flaccid, relaxed, unhealthy, whimsical woman, who still had a capacity to cling. What she clung to was 'society,' and a position in the world which a secret whisper told her she had never had and a voice more audible reminded her she was in danger of losing. To keep it, to recover it, to reconsecrate it, was the ambition of her heart; this was one of the many reasons why Providence had judged her worthy of having so wonderful a child. Verena was born not only to lead their common sex out of bondage, but to remodel a visiting-list which bulged and contracted in the wrong places, like a country-made garment. As the daughter of Abraham Greenstreet, Mrs. Tarrant had passed her youth in the first Abolitionist circles, and she was aware how much such a prospect was clouded by her union with a young man who had begun life as an itinerant vendor of lead-pencils (he had called at Mr. Greenstreet's door in the exercise of this function), had afterwards been for a while a member of the celebrated Cayuga community, where there were no wives, or no husbands, or something of that sort (Mrs. Tarrant could never remember), and had still later (though before the development of the healing faculty) achieved distinction in the spiritualistic world. (He was an extraordinarily favoured medium, only he had had to stop for reasons of which Mrs. Tarrant possessed her version.) Even in a society much occupied with the effacement of prejudice there had been certain dim presumptions against this versatile being, who naturally had not wanted arts to ingratiate himself with Miss Greenstreet, her eyes, like his own, being fixed exclusively on the future. The young couple (he was considerably her elder) had gazed on the future together until they found that the past had completely forsaken them and that the present offered but a slender foothold. Mrs. Tarrant, in other words, incurred the displeasure of her family, who gave her husband to understand that, much as they desired to remove the shackles from the slave, there were kinds of behaviour which struck them as too unfettered. These had prevailed, to their thinking, at Cayuga, and they naturally felt it was no use for him to say that his residence there had been (for him—the community still existed) but a momentary episode, inasmuch as there was little more to be urged for the spiritual picnics and vegetarian camp-meetings in which the discountenanced pair now sought consolation.

Such were the narrow views of people hitherto supposed capable of opening their hearts to all salutary novelties, but now put to a genuine test, as Mrs. Tarrant felt. Her husband's tastes rubbed off on her soft, moist moral surface, and the couple lived in an atmosphere of novelty, in which, occasionally, the accommodating wife encountered the fresh sensation of being in want of her dinner. Her father died, leaving, after all, very little money; he had spent his modest fortune upon the blacks. Selah Tarrant and his companion had strange adventures; she found herself completely enrolled in the great irregular army of nostrum-mongers, domiciled in humanitary Bohemia. It absorbed her like a social swamp; she sank into it a little more every day, without measuring the inches of her descent. Now she stood there up to her chin; it may probably be said of her that she had touched bottom. When she went to Miss Birdseye's it seemed to her that she re-entered society. The door that admitted her was not the door that admitted some of the others (she should never forget the tipped-up nose of Mrs. Farrinder), and the superior portal remained ajar, disclosing possible vistas. She had lived with long-haired men and short-haired women, she had contributed a flexible faith and an irremediable want of funds to a dozen social experiments, she had partaken of the comfort of a hundred religions, had followed innumerable dietary reforms, chiefly of the negative order, and had gone of an evening to a *séance* or a lecture as regularly as she had eaten her supper. Her husband always had tickets for lectures; in moments of irritation at the want of a certain sequence in their career, she had remarked to him that it was the only thing he did have. The memory of all the winter nights they had tramped through the slush (the tickets, alas! were not car-tickets) to hear Mrs. Ada T. P. Foat discourse on the 'Summer-land,' came back to her with bitterness. Selah was quite enthusiastic at one time about Mrs. Foat, and it was his wife's belief that he had been 'associated' with her (that was Selah's expression in referring to such episodes) at Cayuga. The poor woman, matrimonially, had a great deal to put up with; it took, at moments, all her belief in his genius to sustain her. She knew that he was very magnetic (that, in fact, was his genius), and she felt that it was his magnetism that held her to him. He had carried her through things where she really didn't know what to think; there were moments when she suspected that she had lost the strong moral sense for which the Greenstreets were always so celebrated.

Of course a woman who had had the bad taste to marry Selah Tarrant would not have been likely under any circumstances to possess a very straight judgment; but there is no doubt that this poor lady had grown dreadfully limp. She had blinked and compromised and shuffled; she asked herself whether, after all, it was any more than natural that she should have wanted to help her husband, in those exciting days of his mediumship, when the table, sometimes, wouldn't rise from the ground, the sofa wouldn't float through the air, and the soft hand of a lost loved one was not so alert as it might have been to visit the circle. Mrs. Tarrant's hand was soft enough for the most supernatural effect, and she consoled her conscience on such occasions by reflecting that she ministered to a belief in immortality. She was glad, somehow, for Verena's sake, that they had emerged from the phase of spirit-intercourse; her ambition for her daughter took another form than desiring that she, too, should minister to a belief in immortality. Yet among Mrs. Tarrant's multifarious memories these reminiscences of the darkened room, the waiting circle, the little taps on table and wall, the little touches on cheek and foot, the music in the air, the rain of flowers, the sense of something mysteriously flitting, were most tenderly cherished. She hated her husband for having magnetised her so that she consented to certain things, and even did them, the thought of which to-day would suddenly make her face burn; hated him for the manner in which, somehow, as she felt, he had lowered her social tone; yet at the same time she admired him for an impudence so consummate that it had ended (in the face of mortifications, exposures, failures, all the misery of a hand-to-mouth existence) by imposing itself on her as a kind of infallibility. She knew he was an awful humbug, and yet her knowledge had this imperfection, that he had never confessed it—a fact that was really grand when one thought of his opportunities for doing so. He had never allowed that he wasn't straight; the pair had so often been in the position of the two augurs behind the altar, and yet he had never given her a glance that the whole circle mightn't have observed. Even in the privacy of domestic intercourse he had phrases, excuses, explanations, ways of putting things, which, as she felt, were too sublime for just herself; they were pitched, as Selah's nature was pitched, altogether in the key of public life.

So it had come to pass, in her distended and demoralised

conscience, that with all the things she despised in her life and all the things she rather liked, between being worn out with her husband's inability to earn a living and a kind of terror of his consistency (he had a theory that they lived delightfully), it happened, I say, that the only very definite criticism she made of him to-day was that he didn't know how to speak. That was where the shoe pinched—that was where Selah was slim. He couldn't hold the attention of an audience, he was not acceptable as a lecturer. He had plenty of thoughts, but it seemed as if he couldn't fit them into each other. Public speaking had been a Greenstreet tradition, and if Mrs. Tarrant had been asked whether in her younger years she had ever supposed she should marry a mesmeric healer, she would have replied: 'Well, I never thought I should marry a gentleman who would be silent on the platform!' This was her most general humiliation; it included and exceeded every other, and it was a poor consolation that Selah possessed as a substitute—his career as a healer, to speak of none other, was there to prove it—the eloquence of the hand. The Greenstreets had never set much store on manual activity; they believed in the influence of the lips. It may be imagined, therefore, with what exultation, as time went on, Mrs. Tarrant found herself the mother of an inspired maiden, a young lady from whose lips eloquence flowed in streams. The Greenstreet tradition would not perish, and the dry places of her life would, perhaps, be plentifully watered. It must be added that, of late, this sandy surface had been irrigated, in moderation, from another source. Since Selah had addicted himself to the mesmeric mystery, their home had been a little more what the home of a Greenstreet should be. He had 'considerable many' patients, he got about two dollars a sitting, and he had effected some most gratifying cures. A lady in Cambridge had been so much indebted to him that she had recently persuaded them to take a house near her, in order that Doctor Tarrant might drop in at any time. He availed himself of this convenience—they had taken so many houses that another, more or less, didn't matter—and Mrs. Tarrant began to feel as if they really had 'struck' something.

Even to Verena, as we know, she was confused and confusing; the girl had not yet had an opportunity to ascertain the

principles on which her mother's limpness was liable suddenly to become rigid. This phenomenon occurred when the
vapours of social ambition mounted to her brain, when she
extended an arm from which a crumpled dressing-gown fluttered back to seize the passing occasion. Then she surprised
her daughter by a volubility of exhortation as to the duty of
making acquaintances, and by the apparent wealth of her
knowledge of the mysteries of good society. She had, in particular, a way of explaining confidentially—and in her desire
to be graphic she often made up the oddest faces—the interpretation that you must sometimes give to the manners of the
best people, and the delicate dignity with which you should
meet them, which made Verena wonder what secret sources
of information she possessed. Verena took life, as yet, very
simply; she was not conscious of so many differences of social
complexion. She knew that some people were rich and others
poor, and that her father's house had never been visited by
such abundance as might make one ask one's self whether it
were right, in a world so full of the disinherited, to roll in
luxury. But except when her mother made her slightly dizzy
by a resentment of some slight that she herself had never perceived, or a flutter over some opportunity that appeared already to have passed (while Mrs. Tarrant was looking for
something to 'put on'), Verena had no vivid sense that she
was not as good as any one else, for no authority appealing
really to her imagination had fixed the place of mesmeric healers in the scale of fashion. It was impossible to know in advance how Mrs. Tarrant would take things. Sometimes she
was abjectly indifferent; at others she thought that every one
who looked at her wished to insult her. At moments she was
full of suspicion of the ladies (they were mainly ladies) whom
Selah mesmerised; then again she appeared to have given up
everything but her slippers and the evening-paper (from this
publication she derived inscrutable solace), so that if Mrs.
Foat in person had returned from the summer-land (to which
she had some time since taken her flight), she would not have
disturbed Mrs. Tarrant's almost cynical equanimity.

It was, however, in her social subtleties that she was most
beyond her daughter; it was when she discovered extraordinary though latent longings on the part of people they met

to make their acquaintance, that the girl became conscious of how much she herself had still to learn. All her desire was to learn, and it must be added that she regarded her mother, in perfect good faith, as a wonderful teacher. She was perplexed sometimes by her worldliness; that, somehow, was not a part of the higher life which every one in such a house as theirs must wish above all things to lead; and it was not involved in the reign of justice, which they were all trying to bring about, that such a strict account should be kept of every little snub. Her father seemed to Verena to move more consecutively on the high plane; though his indifference to old-fashioned standards, his perpetual invocation of the brighter day, had not yet led her to ask herself whether, after all, men are more disinterested than women. Was it interest that prompted her mother to respond so warmly to Miss Chancellor, to say to Verena, with an air of knowingness, that the thing to do was to go in and see her *immediately*? No italics can represent the earnestness of Mrs. Tarrant's emphasis. Why hadn't she said, as she had done in former cases, that if people wanted to see them they could come out to their home; that she was not so low down in the world as not to know there was such a ceremony as leaving cards? When Mrs. Tarrant began on the question of ceremonies she was apt to go far; but she had waived it in this case; it suited her more to hold that Miss Chancellor had been very gracious, that she was a most desirable friend, that she had been more affected than any one by Verena's beautiful outpouring; that she would open to her the best saloons in Boston; that when she said 'Come soon' she meant the very next day, that this was the way to take it, anyhow (one must know when to go forward gracefully); and that in short she, Mrs. Tarrant, knew what she was talking about.

Verena accepted all this, for she was young enough to enjoy any journey in a horse-car, and she was ever-curious about the world; she only wondered a little how her mother knew so much about Miss Chancellor just from looking at her once. What Verena had mainly observed in the young lady who came up to her that way the night before was that she was rather dolefully dressed, that she looked as if she had been crying (Verena recognised that look quickly, she had seen it so much), and that she was in a hurry to get away. However, if she was as remarkable as her mother said, one would very soon see it; and meanwhile there was nothing in the girl's feeling about herself, in her sense of her importance, to make it a painful effort for her to run the risk of a mistake. She had no particular feeling about herself; she only cared, as yet, for outside things. Even the development of her 'gift' had not made her think herself too precious for mere experiments; she had neither a particle of diffidence nor a particle of vanity. Though it would have seemed to you eminently natural that a daughter of Selah Tarrant and his wife should be an inspirational speaker, yet, as you knew Verena better, you would have wondered immensely how she came to issue from such a pair. Her ideas of enjoyment were very simple; she enjoyed putting on her new hat, with its redundancy of feather, and twenty cents appeared to her a very large sum.

XI

I WAS CERTAIN you would come—I have felt it all day—
something told me!' It was with these words that Olive
Chancellor greeted her young visitor, coming to her quickly
from the window, where she might have been waiting for her
arrival. Some weeks later she explained to Verena how definite
this prevision had been, how it had filled her all day with a
nervous agitation so violent as to be painful. She told her that
such forebodings were a peculiarity of her organisation, that
she didn't know what to make of them, that she had to accept
them; and she mentioned, as another example, the sudden
dread that had come to her the evening before in the carriage,
after proposing to Mr. Ransom to go with her to Miss Birdseye's. This had been as strange as it had been instinctive, and
the strangeness, of course, was what must have struck Mr.
Ransom; for the idea that he might come had been hers, and
yet she suddenly veered round. She couldn't help it; her heart
had begun to throb with the conviction that if he crossed that
threshold some harm would come of it for her. She hadn't
prevented him, and now she didn't care, for now, as she intimated, she had the interest of Verena, and that made her
indifferent to every danger, to every ordinary pleasure. By this
time Verena had learned how peculiarly her friend was constituted, how nervous and serious she was, how personal,
how exclusive, what a force of will she had, what a concentration of purpose. Olive had taken her up, in the literal sense
of the phrase, like a bird of the air, had spread an extraordinary pair of wings, and carried her through the dizzying void
of space. Verena liked it, for the most part; liked to shoot
upward without an effort of her own and look down upon
all creation, upon all history, from such a height. From this
first interview she felt that she was seized, and she gave herself
up, only shutting her eyes a little, as we do whenever a person
in whom we have perfect confidence proposes, with our assent, to subject us to some sensation.

'I want to know you,' Olive said, on this occasion; 'I felt
that I must last night, as soon as I heard you speak. You
seem to me very wonderful. I don't know what to make of

you. I think we ought to be friends; so I just asked you to
come to me straight off, without preliminaries, and I believed you would come. It is so *right* that you have come,
and it proves how right I was.' These remarks fell from
Miss Chancellor's lips one by one, as she caught her breath,
with the tremor that was always in her voice, even when
she was the least excited, while she made Verena sit down
near her on the sofa, and looked at her all over in a manner
that caused the girl to rejoice at having put on the jacket
with the gilt buttons. It was this glance that was the beginning; it was with this quick survey, omitting nothing, that
Olive took possession of her. 'You are very remarkable; I
wonder if you know how remarkable!' she went on, murmuring the words as if she were losing herself, becoming
inadvertent in admiration.

Verena sat there smiling, without a blush, but with a pure,
bright look which, for her, would always make protests unnecessary. 'Oh, it isn't me, you know; it's something outside!'
She tossed this off lightly, as if she were in the habit of saying
it, and Olive wondered whether it were a sincere disclaimer
or only a phrase of the lips. The question was not a criticism,
for she might have been satisfied that the girl was a mass of
fluent catch-words and yet scarcely have liked her the less. It
was just as she was that she liked her; she was so strange, so
different from the girls one usually met, seemed to belong to
some queer gipsy-land or transcendental Bohemia. With her
bright, vulgar clothes, her salient appearance, she might have
been a rope-dancer or a fortune-teller; and this had the immense merit, for Olive, that it appeared to make her belong
to the 'people,' threw her into the social dusk of that mysterious democracy which Miss Chancellor held that the fortunate classes know so little about, and with which (in a future
possibly very near) they will have to count. Moreover, the girl
had moved her as she had never been moved, and the power
to do that, from whatever source it came, was a force that
one must admire. Her emotion was still acute, however much
she might speak to her visitor as if everything that had happened seemed to her natural; and what kept it, above all,
from subsiding was her sense that she found here what she
had been looking for so long—a friend of her own sex with

whom she might have a union of soul. It took a double consent to make a friendship, but it was not possible that this
intensely sympathetic girl would refuse. Olive had the penetration to discover in a moment that she was a creature of
unlimited generosity. I know not what may have been the
reality of Miss Chancellor's other premonitions, but there is
no doubt that in this respect she took Verena's measure on
the spot. This was what she wanted; after that the rest didn't
matter; Miss Tarrant might wear gilt buttons from head to
foot, her soul could not be vulgar.

'Mother told me I had better come right in,' said Verena,
looking now about the room, very glad to find herself in so
pleasant a place, and noticing a great many things that she
should like to see in detail.

'Your mother saw that I meant what I said; it isn't everybody that does me the honour to perceive that. She saw that
I was shaken from head to foot. I could only say three
words—I couldn't have spoken more! What a power—what
a power, Miss Tarrant!'

'Yes, I suppose it is a power. If it wasn't a power, it
couldn't do much with me!'

'You are so simple—so much like a child,' Olive Chancellor
said. That was the truth, and she wanted to say it because,
quickly, without forms or circumlocutions, it made them familiar. She wished to arrive at this; her impatience was such
that before the girl had been five minutes in the room she
jumped to her point—inquired of her, interrupting herself,
interrupting everything: 'Will you be my friend, my friend of
friends, beyond every one, everything, forever and forever?'
Her face was full of eagerness and tenderness.

Verena gave a laugh of clear amusement, without a shade
of embarrassment or confusion. 'Perhaps you like me too
much.'

'Of course I like you too much! When I like, I like too
much. But of course it's another thing, your liking me,' Olive
Chancellor added. 'We must wait—we must wait. When I
care for anything, I can be patient.' She put out her hand to
Verena, and the movement was at once so appealing and so
confident that the girl instinctively placed her own in it. So,
hand in hand, for some moments, these two young women

sat looking at each other. 'There is so much I want to ask you,' said Olive.

'Well, I can't say much except when father has worked on me,' Verena answered, with an ingenuousness beside which humility would have seemed pretentious.

'I don't care anything about your father,' Olive Chancellor rejoined very gravely, with a great air of security.

'He is very good,' Verena said simply. 'And he's wonderfully magnetic.'

'It isn't your father, and it isn't your mother; I don't think of them, and it's not them I want. It's only you—just as you are.'

Verena dropped her eyes over the front of her dress. 'Just as she was' seemed to her indeed very well.

'Do you want me to give up——?' she demanded, smiling.

Olive Chancellor drew in her breath for an instant, like a creature in pain; then, with her quavering voice, touched with a vibration of anguish, she said: 'Oh, how can I ask you to give up? *I* will give up—I will give up everything!'

Filled with the impression of her hostess's agreeable interior, and of what her mother had told her about Miss Chancellor's wealth, her position in Boston society, Verena, in her fresh, diverted scrutiny of the surrounding objects, wondered what could be the need of this scheme of renunciation. Oh no, indeed, she hoped she wouldn't give up—at least not before she, Verena, had had a chance to see. She felt, however, that for the present there would be no answer for her save in the mere pressure of Miss Chancellor's eager nature, that intensity of emotion which made her suddenly exclaim, as if in a nervous ecstasy of anticipation, 'But we must wait! Why do we talk of this? We must wait! All will be right,' she added more calmly, with great sweetness.

Verena wondered afterward why she had not been more afraid of her—why, indeed, she had not turned and saved herself by darting out of the room. But it was not in this young woman's nature to be either timid or cautious; she had as yet to make acquaintance with the sentiment of fear. She knew too little of the world to have learned to mistrust sudden enthusiasms, and if she had had a suspicion it would have been (in accordance with common worldly knowledge) the wrong one—the suspicion that such a whimsical liking would burn itself out. She could not have that one, for there was a light in Miss Chancellor's magnified face which seemed to say that a sentiment, with her, might consume its object, might consume Miss Chancellor, but would never consume itself. Verena, as yet, had no sense of being scorched; she was only agreeably warmed. She also had dreamed of a friendship, though it was not what she had dreamed of most, and it came over her that this was the one which fortune might have been keeping. She never held back.

'Do you live here all alone?' she asked of Olive.

'I shouldn't if you would come and live with me!'

Even this really passionate rejoinder failed to make Verena shrink; she thought it so possible that in the wealthy class people made each other such easy proposals. It was a part of the romance, the luxury, of wealth; it belonged to the world of invitations, in which she had had so little share. But it seemed almost a mockery when she thought of the little house in Cambridge, where the boards were loose in the steps of the porch.

'I must stay with my father and mother,' she said. 'And then I have my work, you know. That's the way I must live now.'

'Your work?' Olive repeated, not quite understanding.

'My gift,' said Verena, smiling.

'Oh yes, you must use it. That's what I mean; you must move the world with it; it's divine.'

It was so much what she meant that she had lain awake all night thinking of it, and the substance of her thought was that if she could only rescue the girl from the danger of vulgar exploitation, could only constitute herself her protectress and devotee, the two, between them, might achieve the great result. Verena's genius was a mystery, and it might remain a mystery; it was impossible to see how this charming, blooming, simple creature, all youth and grace and innocence, got her extraordinary powers of reflection. When her gift was not in exercise she appeared anything but reflective, and as she sat there now, for instance, you would never have dreamed that she had had a vivid revelation. Olive had to content herself, provisionally, with saying that her precious faculty had come to her just as her beauty and distinction (to Olive she was full of that quality) had come; it had dropped straight from heaven, without filtering through her parents, whom Miss Chancellor decidedly did not fancy. Even among reformers she discriminated; she thought all wise people wanted great changes, but the votaries of change were not necessarily wise. She remained silent a little, after her last remark, and then she repeated again, as if it were the solution of everything, as if it represented with absolute certainty some immense happiness in the future—'We must wait, we must wait!' Verena was perfectly willing to wait, though she did not exactly know what they were to wait for, and the aspiring frankness of her assent shone out of her face, and seemed to pacify their mutual gaze. Olive asked her innumerable questions; she wanted to enter into her life. It was one of those talks which people remember afterwards, in which every word has been given and taken, and in which they see the signs of a beginning that was to be justified. The more Olive learnt of her visitor's life the more she wanted to enter into it, the more it took her out of herself. Such strange lives are led in America, she always knew that; but this was queerer than anything she had dreamed of, and the queerest part was that the girl herself didn't appear to think it queer. She had been nursed in darkened rooms, and suckled in the midst of manifestations; she had begun to 'attend lectures,' as she said, when she was quite an infant, because her mother had no one to leave her with at home. She had sat on the knees of somnambulists, and had been passed from hand to hand by trance-speakers; she was familiar with every kind of 'cure,' and had grown up among lady-editors of newspapers advocating new religions, and people who disapproved of the marriage-tie. Verena talked of the marriage-tie as she would have talked of the last novel— as if she had heard it as frequently discussed; and at certain times, listening to the answers she made to her questions, Olive Chancellor closed her eyes in the manner of a person waiting till giddiness passed. Her young friend's revelations actually gave her a vertigo; they made her perceive everything from which she should have rescued her. Verena was perfectly uncontaminated, and she would never be touched by evil; but though Olive had no views about the marriage-tie except that she should hate it for herself—that particular reform she did not propose to consider—she didn't like the 'atmosphere' of circles in which such institutions were called into question. She had no wish now to enter into an examination of that particular one; nevertheless, to make sure, she would just ask Verena whether she disapproved of it.

'Well, I must say,' said Miss Tarrant, 'I prefer free unions.'

Olive held her breath an instant; such an idea was so disagreeable to her. Then, for all answer, she murmured, irresolutely, 'I wish you would let me help you!' Yet it seemed, at the same time, that Verena needed little help, for it was more and more clear that her eloquence, when she stood up that way before a roomful of people, was literally inspiration. She answered all her friend's questions with a good-nature which evidently took no pains to make things plausible, an effort to oblige, not to please; but, after all, she could give very little account of herself. This was very visible when Olive asked her where she had got her 'intense realisation' of the suffering of women; for her address at Miss Birdseye's showed that she, too (like Olive herself), had had that vision in the watches of the night. Verena thought a moment, as if to understand what her companion referred to, and then she inquired, always smiling, where Joan of Arc had got her idea of the suffering of France. This was so prettily said that Olive could scarcely keep from kissing her; she looked at the moment as if, like Joan, she might have had visits from the saints. Olive, of course, remembered afterwards that it had not literally answered the question; and she also reflected on something that made an answer seem more difficult—the fact that the girl had grown up among lady-doctors, lady-mediums, lady-editors, lady-preachers, lady-healers, women who, having rescued themselves from a passive existence, could illustrate only partially the misery of the sex at large. It was true that they might have illustrated it by their talk, by all they had 'been through' and all they could tell a younger sister; but Olive was sure that Verena's prophetic impulse had not been stirred by the chatter of women (Miss Chancellor knew that sound as well as any one); it had proceeded rather out of their silence. She said to her visitor that whether or no the angels came down to her in glittering armour, she struck her as the only person she had yet encountered who had exactly the same tenderness, the same pity, for women that she herself had. Miss Birdseye had something of it, but Miss Birdseye wanted passion, wanted keenness, was capable of the weakest concessions. Mrs. Farrinder was not weak, of course, and she brought a great intellect to the matter; but she was not personal enough—she was too abstract. Verena was not abstract; she seemed to have lived in imagination through all the ages. Verena said she *did* think she had a certain amount of imagination; she supposed she couldn't be so effective on the platform if she hadn't a rich fancy. Then Olive said to her, taking her hand again, that she wanted her to assure her of this— that it was the only thing in all the world she cared for, the redemption of women, the thing she hoped under Providence to give her life to. Verena flushed a little at this appeal, and the deeper glow of her eyes was the first sign of exaltation she had offered. 'Oh yes—I want to give my life!' she exclaimed, with a vibrating voice; and then she added gravely, 'I want to do something great!'

'You will, you will, we both will!' Olive Chancellor cried, in rapture. But after a little she went on: 'I wonder if you know what it means, young and lovely as you are—giving your life!'

Verena looked down for a moment in meditation.

'Well,' she replied, 'I guess I have thought more than I appear.'

'Do you understand German? Do you know "Faust"?' said Olive. ' "*Entsagen sollst du, sollst entsagen!*" '

'I don't know German; I should like so to study it; I want to know everything.'

'We will work at it together—we will study everything,' Olive almost panted; and while she spoke the peaceful picture hung before her of still winter evenings under the lamp, with falling snow outside, and tea on a little table, and successful renderings, with a chosen companion, of Goethe, almost the only foreign author she cared about; for she hated the writing of the French, in spite of the importance they have given to women. Such a vision as this was the highest indulgence she could offer herself; she had it only at considerable intervals. It seemed as if Verena caught a glimpse of it too, for her face kindled still more, and she said she should like that ever so much. At the same time she asked the meaning of the German words.

' "Thou shalt renounce, refrain, abstain!" That's the way Bayard Taylor has translated them,' Olive answered.

'Oh, well, I guess I can abstain!' Verena exclaimed, with a laugh. And she got up rather quickly, as if by taking leave she might give a proof of what she meant. Olive put out her hands to hold her, and at this moment one of the *portières* of the room was pushed aside, while a gentleman was ushered in by Miss Chancellor's little parlour-maid.

XII

VERENA recognised him; she had seen him the night before at Miss Birdseye's, and she said to her hostess, 'Now I must go—you have got another caller!' It was Verena's belief that in the fashionable world (like Mrs. Farrinder, she thought Miss Chancellor belonged to it—thought that, in standing there, she herself was in it)—in the highest social walks it was the custom of a prior guest to depart when another friend arrived. She had been told at people's doors that she could not be received because the lady of the house had a visitor, and she had retired on these occasions with a feeling of awe much more than a sense of injury. They had not been the portals of fashion, but in this respect, she deemed, they had emulated such bulwarks. Olive Chancellor offered Basil Ransom a greeting which she believed to be consummately lady-like, and which the young man, narrating the scene several months later to Mrs. Luna, whose susceptibilities he did not feel himself obliged to consider (she considered his so little), described by saying that she glared at him. Olive had thought it very possible he would come that day if he was to leave Boston; though she was perfectly mindful that she had given him no encouragement at the moment they separated. If he should not come she should be annoyed, and if he should come she should be furious; she was also sufficiently mindful of that. But she had a foreboding that, of the two grievances, fortune would confer upon her only the less; the only one she had as yet was that he had responded to her letter—a complaint rather wanting in richness. If he came, at any rate, he would be likely to come shortly before dinner, at the same hour as yesterday. He had now anticipated this period considerably, and it seemed to Miss Chancellor that he had taken a base advantage of her, stolen a march upon her privacy. She was startled, disconcerted, but as I have said, she was rigorously lady-like. She was determined not again to be fantastic, as she had been about his coming to Miss Birdseye's. The strange dread associating itself with that was something which, she devoutly trusted, she had felt once for all. She didn't know what he could do to her; he hadn't prevented, on the spot though he was, one of the happiest things that had befallen her for so long—this quick, confident visit of Verena Tarrant. It was only just at the last that he had come in, and Verena must go now; Olive's detaining hand immediately relaxed itself.

It is to be feared there was no disguise of Ransom's satisfaction at finding himself once more face to face with the charming creature with whom he had exchanged that final speechless smile the evening before. He was more glad to see her than if she had been an old friend, for it seemed to him that she had suddenly become a new one. 'The delightful girl,' he said to himself; 'she smiles at me as if she liked me!' He could not know that this was fatuous, that she smiled so at every one; the first time she saw people she treated them as if she recognised them. Moreover, she did not seat herself again in his honour; she let it be seen that she was still going. The three stood there together in the middle of the long, characteristic room, and, for the first time in her life, Olive Chancellor chose not to introduce two persons who met under her roof. She hated Europe, but she could be European if it were necessary. Neither of her companions had an idea that in leaving them simply planted face to face (the terror of the American heart) she had so high a warrant; and presently Basil Ransom felt that he didn't care whether he were introduced or not, for the greatness of an evil didn't matter if the remedy were equally great.

'Miss Tarrant won't be surprised if I recognise her—if I take the liberty to speak to her. She is a public character; she must pay the penalty of her distinction.' These words he boldly addressed to the girl, with his most gallant Southern manner, saying to himself meanwhile that she was prettier still by daylight.

'Oh, a great many gentlemen have spoken to me,' Verena said. 'There were quite a number at Topeka—' And her phrase lost itself in her look at Olive, as if she were wondering what was the matter with her.

'Now, I am afraid you are going the very moment I appear,' Ransom went on. 'Do you know that's very cruel to me? I know what your ideas are—you expressed them last night in such beautiful language; of course you convinced me.

I am ashamed of being a man; but I am, and I can't help it, and I'll do penance any way you may prescribe. *Must* she go, Miss Olive?' he asked of his cousin. 'Do you flee before the individual male?' And he turned again to Verena.

This young lady gave a laugh that resembled speech in liquid fusion. 'Oh no; I like the individual!'

As an incarnation of a 'movement,' Ransom thought her more and more singular, and he wondered how she came to be closeted so soon with his kinswoman, to whom, only a few hours before, she had been a complete stranger. These, however, were doubtless the normal proceedings of women. He begged her to sit down again; he was sure Miss Chancellor would be sorry to part with her. Verena, looking at her friend, not for permission, but for sympathy, dropped again into a chair, and Ransom waited to see Miss Chancellor do the same. She gratified him after a moment, because she could not refuse without appearing to put a hurt upon Verena; but it went hard with her, and she was altogether discomposed. She had never seen any one so free in her own drawing-room as this loud Southerner, to whom she had so rashly offered a footing; he extended invitations to her guests under her nose. That Verena should do as he asked her was a signal sign of the absence of that 'home-culture' (it was so that Miss Chancellor expressed the missing quality) which she never supposed the girl possessed: fortunately, as it would be supplied to her in abundance in Charles Street. (Olive of course held that home-culture was perfectly compatible with the widest emancipation.) It was with a perfectly good conscience that Verena complied with Basil Ransom's request; but it took her quick sensibility only a moment to discover that her friend was not pleased. She scarcely knew what had ruffled her, but at the same instant there passed before her the vision of the anxieties (of this sudden, unexplained sort, for instance, and much worse) which intimate relations with Miss Chancellor might entail.

'Now, I want you to tell me this,' Basil Ransom said, leaning forward towards Verena, with his hands on his knees, and completely oblivious to his hostess. 'Do you really believe all that pretty moonshine you talked last night? I could have listened to you for another hour; but I never heard such monstrous sentiments. I must protest—I must, as a calumniated, misrepresented man. Confess you meant it as a kind of *reductio ad absurdum*—a satire on Mrs. Farrinder?' He spoke in a tone of the freest pleasantry, with his familiar, friendly Southern cadence.

Verena looked at him with eyes that grew large. 'Why, you don't mean to say you don't believe in our cause?'

'Oh, it won't do—it won't do!' Ransom went on, laughing. 'You are on the wrong tack altogether. Do you really take the ground that your sex has been without influence? Influence? Why, you have led us all by the nose to where we are now! Wherever we are, it's all you. You are at the bottom of everything.'

'Oh yes, and we want to be at the top,' said Verena.

'Ah, the bottom is a better place, depend on it, when from there you move the whole mass! Besides, you are on the top as well; you are everywhere, you are everything. I am of the opinion of that historical character—wasn't he some king?— who thought there was a lady behind everything. Whatever it was, he held, you have only to look for her; she is the explanation. Well, I always look for her, and I always find her; of course, I am always delighted to do so; but it proves she is the universal cause. Now, you don't mean to deny that power, the power of setting men in motion. You are at the bottom of all the wars.'

'Well, I am like Mrs. Farrinder; I like opposition,' Verena exclaimed, with a happy smile.

'That proves, as I say, how in spite of your expressions of horror you delight in the shock of battle. What do you say to Helen of Troy and the fearful carnage she excited? It is well known that the Empress of France was at the bottom of the last war in that country. And as for our four fearful years of slaughter, of course you won't deny that there the ladies were the great motive power. The Abolitionists brought it on, and were not the Abolitionists principally females? Who was that celebrity that was mentioned last night?—Eliza P. Moseley. I regard Eliza as the cause of the biggest war of which history preserves the record.'

Basil Ransom enjoyed his humour the more because Verena appeared to enjoy it; and the look with which she replied to him, at the end of this little tirade, 'Why, sir, you ought to take the platform too; we might go round together as poison and antidote!'—this made him feel that he had convinced her, for the moment, quite as much as it was important he should. In Verena's face, however, it lasted but an instant—an instant after she had glanced at Olive Chancellor, who, with her eyes fixed intently on the ground (a look she was to learn to know so well), had a strange expression. The girl slowly got up; she felt that she must go. She guessed Miss Chancellor didn't like this handsome joker (it was so that Basil Ransom struck her); and it was impressed upon her ('in time,' as she thought) that her new friend would be more serious even than she about the woman-question, serious as she had hitherto believed herself to be.

'I should like so much to have the pleasure of seeing you again,' Ransom continued. 'I think I should be able to interpret history for you by a new light.'

'Well, I should be very happy to see you in my home.' These words had barely fallen from Verena's lips (her mother told her they were, in general, the proper thing to say when people expressed such a desire as that; she must not let it be assumed that she would come first to them)—she had hardly uttered this hospitable speech when she felt the hand of her hostess upon her arm and became aware that a passionate appeal sat in Olive's eyes.

'You will just catch the Charles Street car,' that young woman murmured, with muffled sweetness.

Verena did not understand further than to see that she ought already to have departed; and the simplest response was to kiss Miss Chancellor, an act which she briefly performed. Basil Ransom understood still less, and it was a melancholy commentary on his contention that men are not inferior, that this meeting could not come, however rapidly, to a close without his plunging into a blunder which necessarily aggravated those he had already made. He had been invited by the little prophetess, and yet he had not been invited; but he did not take that up, because he must absolutely leave Boston on the morrow, and, besides, Miss Chancellor appeared to have something to say to it. But he put out his hand to Verena and said, 'Good-bye, Miss Tarrant; are we not to have the pleasure of hearing you in New York? I am afraid we are sadly sunk.'

'Certainly, I should like to raise my voice in the biggest city,' the girl replied.

'Well, try to come on. I won't refute you. It would be a very stupid world, after all, if we always knew what women were going to say.'

Verena was conscious of the approach of the Charles Street car, as well as of the fact that Miss Chancellor was in pain; but she lingered long enough to remark that she could see he had the old-fashioned ideas—he regarded woman as the toy of man.

'Don't say the toy—say the joy!' Ransom exclaimed. 'There is one statement I will venture to advance; I am quite as fond of you as you are of each other!'

'Much he knows about that!' said Verena, with a sidelong smile at Olive Chancellor.

For Olive, it made her more beautiful than ever; still, there was no trace of this mere personal elation in the splendid sententiousness with which, turning to Mr. Ransom, she remarked: 'What women may be, or may not be, to each other, I won't attempt just now to say; but what *the truth* may be to a human soul, I think perhaps even a woman may faintly suspect!'

'The truth? My dear cousin, your truth is a most vain thing!'

'Gracious me!' cried Verena Tarrant; and the gay vibration of her voice as she uttered this simple ejaculation was the last that Ransom heard of her. Miss Chancellor swept her out of the room, leaving the young man to extract a relish from the ineffable irony with which she uttered the words 'even a woman.' It was to be supposed, on general grounds, that she would reappear, but there was nothing in the glance she gave him, as she turned her back, that was an earnest of this. He stood there a moment, wondering; then his wonder spent itself on the page of a book which, according to his habit at such times, he had mechanically taken up, and in which he speedily became interested. He read it for five minutes in an uncomfortable-looking attitude, and quite forgot that he had been forsaken. He was recalled to this fact by the entrance of

Mrs. Luna, arrayed as if for the street, and putting on her
gloves again—she seemed always to be putting on her gloves.
She wanted to know what in the world he was doing there
alone—whether her sister had not been notified.

'Oh yes,' said Ransom, 'she has just been with me, but she
has gone downstairs with Miss Tarrant.'

'And who in the world is Miss Tarrant?'

Ransom was surprised that Mrs. Luna should not know of
the intimacy of the two young ladies, in spite of the brevity
of their acquaintance, being already so great. But, apparently,
Miss Olive had not mentioned her new friend. 'Well, she is
an inspirational speaker—the most charming creature in the
world!'

Mrs. Luna paused in her manipulations, gave an amazed,
amused stare, then caused the room to ring with her laughter.
'You don't mean to say you are converted—already?'

'Converted to Miss Tarrant, decidedly.'

'You are not to belong to any Miss Tarrant; you are to
belong to me,' Mrs. Luna said, having thought over her
Southern kinsman during the twenty-four hours, and made
up her mind that he would be a good man for a lone woman
to know. Then she added: 'Did you come here to meet her—
the inspirational speaker?'

'No; I came to bid your sister good-bye.'

'Are you really going? I haven't made you promise half the
things I want yet. But we will settle that in New York. How
do you get on with Olive Chancellor?' Mrs. Luna continued,
making her points, as she always did, with eagerness, though
her roundness and her dimples had hitherto prevented her
from being accused of that vice. It was her practice to speak
of her sister by her whole name, and you would have supposed, from her usual manner of alluding to her, that Olive
was much the older, instead of having been born ten years
later than Adeline. She had as many ways as possible of marking the gulf that divided them; but she bridged it over lightly
now by saying to Basil Ransom: 'Isn't she a dear old thing?'

This bridge, he saw, would not bear his weight, and her
question seemed to him to have more audacity than sense.
Why should she be so insincere? She might know that a man
couldn't recognise Miss Chancellor in such a description as

that. She was not old—she was sharply young; and it was inconceivable to him, though he had just seen the little prophetess kiss her, that she should ever become any one's 'dear.' Least of all was she a 'thing'; she was intensely, fearfully, a person. He hesitated a moment, and then he replied: 'She's a very remarkable woman.'

'Take care—don't be reckless!' cried Mrs. Luna. 'Do you think she is very dreadful?'

'Don't say anything against my cousin,' Basil answered; and at that moment Miss Chancellor re-entered the room. She murmured some request that he would excuse her absence, but her sister interrupted her with an inquiry about Miss Tarrant.

'Mr. Ransom thinks her wonderfully charming. Why didn't you show her to me? Do you want to keep her all to yourself?'

Olive rested her eyes for some moments upon Mrs. Luna, without speaking. Then she said: 'Your veil is not put on straight, Adeline.'

'I look like a monster—that, evidently, is what you mean!' Adeline exclaimed, going to the mirror to rearrange the peccant tissue.

Miss Chancellor did not again ask Ransom to be seated; she appeared to take it for granted that he would leave her now. But instead of this he returned to the subject of Verena; he asked her whether she supposed the girl would come out in public—would go about like Mrs. Farrinder?

'Come out in public!' Olive repeated; 'in public? Why, you don't imagine that pure voice is to be hushed?'

'Oh, hushed, no! it's too sweet for that. But not raised to a scream; not forced and cracked and ruined. She oughtn't to become like the others. She ought to remain apart.'

'Apart—*apart?*' said Miss Chancellor; 'when we shall all be looking to her, gathering about her, praying for her!' There was an exceeding scorn in her voice. 'If *I* can help her, she shall be an immense power for good.'

'An immense power for quackery, my dear Miss Olive!' This broke from Basil Ransom's lips in spite of a vow he had just taken not to say anything that should 'aggravate' his hostess, who was in a state of tension it was not difficult to detect.

But he had lowered his tone to friendly pleading, and the offensive word was mitigated by his smile.

She moved away from him, backwards, as if he had given her a push. 'Ah, well, now you are reckless,' Mrs. Luna remarked, drawing out her ribbons before the mirror.

'I don't think you would interfere if you knew how little you understand us,' Miss Chancellor said to Ransom.

'Whom do you mean by "us"—your whole delightful sex? I don't understand *you*, Miss Olive.'

'Come away with me, and I'll explain her as we go,' Mrs. Luna went on, having finished her toilet.

Ransom offered his hand in farewell to his hostess; but Olive found it impossible to do anything but ignore the gesture. She could not have let him touch her. 'Well, then, if you must exhibit her to the multitude, bring her on to New York,' he said, with the same attempt at a light treatment.

'You'll have *me* in New York—you don't want any one else!' Mrs. Luna ejaculated, coquettishly. 'I have made up my mind to winter there now.'

Olive Chancellor looked from one to the other of her two relatives, one near and the other distant, but each so little in sympathy with her, and it came over her that there might be a kind of protection for her in binding them together, entangling them with each other. She had never had an idea of that kind in her life before, and that this sudden subtlety should have gleamed upon her as a momentary talisman gives the measure of her present nervousness.

'If I could take her to New York, I would take her farther,' she remarked, hoping she was enigmatical.

'You talk about "taking" her, as if you were a lecture-agent. Are you going into that business?' Mrs. Luna asked.

Ransom could not help noticing that Miss Chancellor would not shake hands with him, and he felt, on the whole, rather injured. He paused a moment before leaving the room—standing there with his hand on the knob of the door. 'Look here, Miss Olive, what did you write to me to come and see you for?' He made this inquiry with a countenance not destitute of gaiety, but his eyes showed something of that yellow light—just momentarily lurid—of which mention has been made. Mrs. Luna was on her way downstairs, and her companions remained face to face.

'Ask my sister—I think she will tell you,' said Olive, turning away from him and going to the window. She remained there, looking out; she heard the door of the house close, and saw the two cross the street together. As they passed out of sight her fingers played, softly, a little air upon the pane; it seemed to her that she had had an inspiration.

Basil Ransom, meanwhile, put the question to Mrs. Luna. 'If she was not going to like me, why in the world did she write to me?'

'Because she wanted you to know me—she thought *I* would like you!' And apparently she had not been wrong; for Mrs. Luna, when they reached Beacon Street, would not hear of his leaving her to go her way alone, would not in the least admit his plea that he had only an hour or two more in Boston (he was to travel, economically, by the boat) and must devote the time to his business. She appealed to his Southern chivalry, and not in vain; practically, at least, he admitted the rights of women.

XIII

M RS. TARRANT was delighted, as may be imagined, with
her daughter's account of Miss Chancellor's interior,
and the reception the girl had found there; and Verena, for
the next month, took her way very often to Charles Street.
'Just you be as nice to her as you know how,' Mrs. Tarrant
had said to her; and she reflected with some complacency that
her daughter did know—she knew how to do everything of
that sort. It was not that Verena had been taught; that branch
of the education of young ladies which is known as 'manners
and deportment' had not figured, as a definite head, in Miss
Tarrant's curriculum. She had been told, indeed, that she
must not lie nor steal; but she had been told very little else
about behaviour; her only great advantage, in short, had
been the parental example. But her mother liked to think
that she was quick and graceful, and she questioned her exhaustively as to the progress of this interesting episode; she
didn't see why, as she said, it shouldn't be a permanent
'stand-by' for Verena. In Mrs. Tarrant's meditations upon
the girl's future she had never thought of a fine marriage as
a reward of effort; she would have deemed herself very immoral if she had endeavoured to capture for her child a rich
husband. She had not, in fact, a very vivid sense of the existence of such agents of fate; all the rich men she had seen
already had wives, and the unmarried men, who were
generally very young, were distinguished from each other
not so much by the figure of their income, which came little
into question, as by the degree of their interest in regener-
ating ideas. She supposed Verena would marry some one,
some day, and she hoped the personage would be connected
with public life—which meant, for Mrs. Tarrant, that his
name would be visible, in the lamplight, on a coloured
poster, in the doorway of Tremont Temple. But she was not
eager about this vision, for the implications of matrimony
were for the most part wanting in brightness—consisted of
a tired woman holding a baby over a furnace-register that
emitted lukewarm air. A real lovely friendship with a young
woman who had, as Mrs. Tarrant expressed it, 'prop'ty,'

would occupy agreeably such an interval as might occur before Verena should meet her sterner fate; it would be a great thing for her to have a place to run into when she wanted a change, and there was no knowing but what it might end in her having two homes. For the idea of the home, like most American women of her quality, Mrs. Tarrant had an extreme reverence; and it was her candid faith that in all the vicissitudes of the past twenty years she had preserved the spirit of this institution. If it should exist in duplicate for Verena, the girl would be favoured indeed.

All this was as nothing, however, compared with the fact that Miss Chancellor seemed to think her young friend's gift *was* inspirational, or at any rate, as Selah had so often said, quite unique. She couldn't make out very exactly, by Verena, what she thought; but if the way Miss Chancellor had taken hold of her didn't show that she believed she could rouse the people, Mrs. Tarrant didn't know what it showed. It was a satisfaction to her that Verena evidently responded freely; she didn't think anything of what she spent in car-tickets, and indeed she had told her that Miss Chancellor wanted to stuff her pockets with them. At first she went in because her mother liked to have her; but now, evidently, she went because she was so much drawn. She expressed the highest admiration of her new friend; she said it took her a little while to see into her, but now that she did, well, she was perfectly splendid. When Verena wanted to admire she went ahead of every one, and it was delightful to see how she was stimulated by the young lady in Charles Street. They thought everything of each other—that was very plain; you could scarcely tell which thought most. Each thought the other so noble, and Mrs. Tarrant had a faith that between them they *would* rouse the people. What Verena wanted was some one who would know how to handle her (her father hadn't handled anything except the healing, up to this time, with real success), and perhaps Miss Chancellor would take hold better than some that made more of a profession.

'It's beautiful, the way she draws you out,' Verena had said to her mother; 'there's something so searching that the first time I visited her it quite realised my idea of the Day of Judgment. But she seems to show all that's in herself at the same time, and then you see how lovely it is. She's just as pure as she can live; you see if she is not, when you know her. She's so noble herself that she makes you feel as if you wouldn't want to be less so. She doesn't care for anything but the elevation of our sex; if she can work a little toward that, it's all she asks. I can tell you, she kindles me; she does, mother, really. She doesn't care a speck what she wears—only to have an elegant parlour. Well, she *has* got that; it's a regular dream-like place to sit. She's going to have a tree in, next week; she says she wants to see me sitting under a tree. I believe it's some oriental idea; it has lately been introduced in Paris. She doesn't like French ideas as a general thing; but she says this has more nature than most. She has got so many of her own that I shouldn't think she would require to borrow any. I'd sit in a forest to hear her bring some of them out,' Verena went on, with characteristic raciness. 'She just quivers when she describes what our sex has been through. It's so interesting to me to hear what I have always felt. If she wasn't afraid of facing the public, she would go far ahead of me. But she doesn't want to speak herself; she only wants to call me out. Mother, if she doesn't attract attention to me there isn't any attention to be attracted. She says I have got the gift of expression—it doesn't matter where it comes from. She says it's a great advantage to a movement to be personified in a bright young figure. Well, of course I'm young, and I feel bright enough when once I get started. She says my serenity while exposed to the gaze of hundreds is in itself a qualification; in fact, she seems to think my serenity is quite God-given. She hasn't got much of it herself; she's the most emotional woman I have met, up to now. She wants to know how I can speak the way I do unless I feel; and of course I tell her I do feel, so far as I realise. She seems to be realising all the time; I never saw any one that took so little rest. She says I ought to do something great, and she makes me feel as if I should. She says I ought to have a wide influence, if I can obtain the ear of the public; and I say to her that if I do it will be all her influence.'

Selah Tarrant looked at all this from a higher stand-point than his wife; at least such an altitude on his part was to be inferred from his increased solemnity. He committed himself

to no precipitate elation at the idea of his daughter's being
taken up by a patroness of movements who happened to have
money; he looked at his child only from the point of view of
the service she might render to humanity. To keep her ideal
pointing in the right direction, to guide and animate her
moral life—this was a duty more imperative for a parent so
closely identified with revelations and panaceas than seeing
that she formed profitable worldly connections. He was 'off,'
moreover, so much of the time that he could keep little account of her comings and goings, and he had an air of being
but vaguely aware of whom Miss Chancellor, the object now
of his wife's perpetual reference, might be. Verena's initial appearance in Boston, as he called her performance at Miss
Birdseye's, had been a great success; and this reflection added,
as I say, to his habitually sacerdotal expression. He looked like
the priest of a religion that was passing through the stage of
miracles; he carried his responsibility in the general elonga-
tion of his person, of his gestures (his hands were now always
in the air, as if he were being photographed in postures), of
his words and sentences, as well as in his smile, as noiseless as
a patent hinge, and in the folds of his eternal waterproof. He
was incapable of giving an off-hand answer or opinion on the
simplest occasion, and his tone of high deliberation increased
in proportion as the subject was trivial or domestic. If his wife
asked him at dinner if the potatoes were good, he replied that
they were strikingly fine (he used to speak of the newspaper
as 'fine'—he applied this term to objects the most dissimilar),
and embarked on a parallel worthy of Plutarch, in which he
compared them with other specimens of the same vegetable.
He produced, or would have liked to produce, the impression
of looking above and beyond everything, of not caring for
the immediate, of reckoning only with the long run. In reality
he had one all-absorbing solicitude—the desire to get paragraphs put into the newspapers, paragraphs of which he had
hitherto been the subject, but of which he was now to divide
the glory with his daughter. The newspapers were his world,
the richest expression, in his eyes, of human life; and, for him,
if a diviner day was to come upon earth, it would be brought
about by copious advertisement in the daily prints. He looked
with longing for the moment when Verena should be adver-

tised among the 'personals,' and to his mind the supremely happy people were those (and there were a good many of them) of whom there was some journalistic mention every day in the year. Nothing less than this would really have satisfied Selah Tarrant; his ideal of bliss was to be as regularly and indispensably a component part of the newspaper as the title and date, or the list of fires, or the column of Western jokes. The vision of that publicity haunted his dreams, and he would gladly have sacrificed to it the innermost sanctities of home. Human existence to him, indeed, was a huge publicity, in which the only fault was that it was sometimes not sufficiently effective. There had been a Spiritualist paper of old which he used to pervade; but he could not persuade himself that through this medium his personality had attracted general attention; and, moreover, the sheet, as he said, was played out anyway. Success was not success so long as his daughter's *physique*, the rumour of her engagement, were not included in the 'Jottings,' with the certainty of being extensively copied.

The account of her exploits in the West had not made their way to the seaboard with the promptitude that he had looked for; the reason of this being, he supposed, that the few addresses she had made had not been lectures, announced in advance, to which tickets had been sold, but incidents, of abrupt occurrence, of certain multitudinous meetings, where there had been other performers better known to fame. They had brought in no money; they had been delivered only for the good of the cause. If it could only be known that she spoke for nothing, that might deepen the reverberation; the only trouble was that her speaking for nothing was not the way to remind him that he had a remunerative daughter. It was not the way to stand out so very much either, Selah Tarrant felt; for there were plenty of others that knew how to make as little money as she would. To speak—that was the one thing that most people were willing to do for nothing; it was not a line in which it was easy to appear conspicuously disinterested. Disinterestedness, too, was incompatible with receipts; and receipts were what Selah Tarrant was, in his own parlance, after. He wished to bring about the day when they would flow in freely; the reader perhaps sees the gesture with

which, in his colloquies with himself, he accompanied this
mental image.

It seemed to him at present that the fruitful time was not
far off; it had been brought appreciably nearer by that fortunate evening at Miss Birdseye's. If Mrs. Farrinder could be
induced to write an 'open letter' about Verena, that would do
more than anything else. Selah was not remarkable for delicacy of perception, but he knew the world he lived in well
enough to be aware that Mrs. Farrinder was liable to rear up,
as they used to say down in Pennsylvania, where he lived before he began to peddle lead-pencils. She wouldn't always
take things as you might expect, and if it didn't meet her
views to pay a public tribute to Verena, there wasn't any way
known to Tarrant's ingenious mind of getting round her. If
it was a question of a favour from Mrs. Farrinder, you just
had to wait for it, as you would for a rise in the thermometer.
He had told Miss Birdseye what he would like, and she
seemed to think, from the way their celebrated friend had
been affected, that the idea might take her some day of just
letting the public know all she had felt. She was off somewhere now (since that evening), but Miss Birdseye had an
idea that when she was back in Roxbury she would send for
Verena and give her a few points. Meanwhile, at any rate,
Selah was sure he had a card; he felt there was money in the
air. It might already be said there were receipts from Charles
Street; that rich, peculiar young woman seemed to want to
lavish herself. He pretended, as I have intimated, not to notice this; but he never saw so much as when he had his eyes
fixed on the cornice. He had no doubt that if he should make
up his mind to take a hall some night, she would tell him
where the bill might be sent. That was what he was thinking
of now, whether he had better take a hall right away, so that
Verena might leap at a bound into renown, or wait till she
had made a few more appearances in private, so that curiosity
might be worked up.

These meditations accompanied him in his multifarious
wanderings through the streets and the suburbs of the New
England capital. As I have also mentioned, he was absent for
hours—long periods during which Mrs. Tarrant, sustaining
nature with a hard-boiled egg and a doughnut, wondered

how in the world he stayed his stomach. He never wanted anything but a piece of pie when he came in; the only thing about which he was particular was that it should be served up hot. She had a private conviction that he partook, at the houses of his lady patients, of little lunches; she applied this term to any episodical repast, at any hour of the twenty-four. It is but fair to add that once, when she betrayed her suspicion, Selah remarked that the only refreshment *he* ever wanted was the sense that he was doing some good. This effort with him had many forms; it involved, among other things, a perpetual perambulation of the streets, a haunting of horse-cars, railway-stations, shops that were 'selling off.' But the places that knew him best were the offices of the newspapers and the vestibules of the hotels—the big marble-paved chambers of informal reunion which offer to the streets, through high glass plates, the sight of the American citizen suspended by his heels. Here, amid the piled-up luggage, the convenient spittoons, the elbowing loungers, the disconsolate 'guests,' the truculent Irish porters, the rows of shaggy-backed men in strange hats, writing letters at a table inlaid with advertisements, Selah Tarrant made innumerable contemplative stations. He could not have told you, at any particular moment, what he was doing; he only had a general sense that such places were national nerve-centres, and that the more one looked in, the more one was 'on the spot.' The *penetralia* of the daily press were, however, still more fascinating, and the fact that they were less accessible, that here he found barriers in his path, only added to the zest of forcing an entrance. He abounded in pretexts; he even sometimes brought contributions; he was persistent and penetrating, he was known as the irrepressible Tarrant. He hung about, sat too long, took up the time of busy people, edged into the printing-rooms when he had been eliminated from the office, talked with the compositors till they set up his remarks by mistake, and to the newsboys when the compositors had turned their backs. He was always trying to find out what was 'going in'; he would have liked to go in himself, bodily, and, failing in this, he hoped to get advertisements inserted gratis. The wish of his soul was that he might be interviewed; that made him hover at the editorial elbow. Once he thought he had been, and the headings, five or six deep, danced for days before his eyes; but the report never appeared. He expected his revenge for this the day after Verena should have burst forth; he saw the attitude in which he should receive the emissaries who would come after his daughter.

XIV

W E OUGHT to have some one to meet her,' Mrs. Tarrant said; 'I presume she wouldn't care to come out just to see us.' 'She,' between the mother and the daughter, at this period, could refer only to Olive Chancellor, who was discussed in the little house at Cambridge at all hours and from every possible point of view. It was never Verena now who began, for she had grown rather weary of the topic; she had her own ways of thinking of it, which were not her mother's, and if she lent herself to this lady's extensive considerations it was because that was the best way of keeping her thoughts to herself.

Mrs. Tarrant had an idea that she (Mrs. Tarrant) liked to study people, and that she was now engaged in an analysis of Miss Chancellor. It carried her far, and she came out at unexpected times with her results. It was still her purpose to interpret the world to the ingenuous mind of her daughter, and she translated Miss Chancellor with a confidence which made little account of the fact that she had seen her but once, while Verena had this advantage nearly every day. Verena felt that by this time she knew Olive very well, and her mother's most complicated versions of motive and temperament (Mrs. Tarrant, with the most imperfect idea of the meaning of the term, was always talking about people's temperament), rendered small justice to the phenomena it was now her privilege to observe in Charles Street. Olive was much more remarkable than Mrs. Tarrant suspected, remarkable as Mrs. Tarrant believed her to be. She had opened Verena's eyes to extraordinary pictures, made the girl believe that she had a heavenly mission, given her, as we have seen, quite a new measure of the interest of life. These were larger consequences than the possibility of meeting the leaders of society at Olive's house. She had met no one, as yet, but Mrs. Luna; her new friend seemed to wish to keep her quite for herself. This was the only reproach that Mrs. Tarrant directed to the new friend as yet; she was disappointed that Verena had not obtained more insight into the world of fashion. It was one of the prime articles of her faith that the world of fashion was wicked and hollow, and, moreover, Verena told her that Miss Chancellor loathed and despised it. She could not have informed you wherein it would profit her daughter (for the way those ladies shrank from any new gospel was notorious); nevertheless she was vexed that Verena shouldn't come back to her with a little more of the fragrance of Beacon Street. The girl herself would have been the most interested person in the world if she had not been the most resigned; she took all that was given her and was grateful, and missed nothing that was withheld; she was the most extraordinary mixture of eagerness and docility. Mrs. Tarrant theorised about temperaments and she loved her daughter; but she was only vaguely aware of the fact that she had at her side the sweetest flower of character (as one might say) that had ever bloomed on earth. She was proud of Verena's brightness, and of her special talent; but the commonness of her own surface was a non-conductor of the girl's quality. Therefore she thought that it would add to her success in life to know a few high-flyers, if only to put them to shame; as if anything could add to Verena's success, as if it were not supreme success simply to have been made as she was made.

Mrs. Tarrant had gone into town to call upon Miss Chancellor; she carried out this resolve, on which she had bestowed infinite consideration, independently of Verena. She had decided that she had a pretext; her dignity required one, for she felt that at present the antique pride of the Greenstreets was terribly at the mercy of her curiosity. She wished to see Miss Chancellor again, and to see her among her charming appurtenances, which Verena had described to her with great minuteness. The pretext that she would have valued most was wanting—that of Olive's having come out to Cambridge to pay the visit that had been solicited from the first; so she had to take the next best—she had to say to herself that it was her duty to see what she should think of a place where her daughter spent so much time. To Miss Chancellor she would appear to have come to thank her for her hospitality; she knew, in advance, just the air she should take (or she fancied she knew it—Mrs. Tarrant's airs were not always what she supposed), just the *nuance* (she had also an impression she knew a little French) of her tone. Olive, after the lapse of weeks, still showed no symptoms of presenting herself, and Mrs. Tarrant rebuked Verena with some sternness for not having made her feel that this attention was due to the mother of her friend. Verena could scarcely say to her she guessed Miss Chancellor didn't think much of that personage, true as it was that the girl had discerned this angular fact, which she attributed to Olive's extraordinary comprehensiveness of view. Verena herself did not suppose that her mother occupied a very important place in the universe; and Miss Chancellor never looked at anything smaller than that. Nor was she free to report (she was certainly now less frank at home, and, moreover, the suspicion was only just becoming distinct to her) that Olive would like to detach her from her parents altogether, and was therefore not interested in appearing to cultivate relations with them. Mrs. Tarrant, I may mention, had a further motive: she was consumed with the desire to behold Mrs. Luna. This circumstance may operate as a proof that the aridity of her life was great, and if it should have that effect I shall not be able to gainsay it. She had seen all the people who went to lectures, but there were hours when she desired, for a change, to see some who didn't go; and Mrs. Luna, from Verena's description of her, summed up the characteristics of this eccentric class.

Verena had given great attention to Olive's brilliant sister; she had told her friend everything now—everything but one little secret, namely, that if she could have chosen at the beginning she would have liked to resemble Mrs. Luna. This lady fascinated her, carried off her imagination to strange lands; she should enjoy so much a long evening with her alone, when she might ask her ten thousand questions. But she never saw her alone, never saw her at all but in glimpses. Adeline flitted in and out, dressed for dinners and concerts, always saying something worldly to the young woman from Cambridge, and something to Olive that had a freedom which she herself would probably never arrive at (a failure of foresight on Verena's part). But Miss Chancellor never detained her, never gave Verena a chance to see her, never appeared to imagine that she could have the least interest in such a person; only took up the subject again after Adeline had left them—the subject, of course, which was always the same, the subject of what they should do together for their suffering sex. It was not that Verena was not interested in that—gracious, no; it opened up before her, in those wonderful colloquies with Olive, in the most inspiring way; but her fancy would make a dart to right or left when other game crossed their path, and her companion led her, intellectually, a dance in which her feet—that is, her head—failed her at times for weariness. Mrs. Tarrant found Miss Chancellor at home, but she was not gratified by even the most transient glimpse of Mrs. Luna; a fact which, in her heart, Verena regarded as fortunate, inasmuch as (she said to herself) if her mother, returning from Charles Street, began to explain Miss Chancellor to her with fresh energy, and as if she (Verena) had never seen her, and up to this time they had had nothing to say about her, to what developments (of the same sort) would not an encounter with Adeline have given rise?

When Verena at last said to her friend that she thought she ought to come out to Cambridge—she didn't understand why she didn't—Olive expressed her reasons very frankly, admitted that she was jealous, that she didn't wish to think of the girl's belonging to any one but herself. Mr. and Mrs. Tarrant would have authority, opposed claims, and she didn't wish to see them, to remember that they existed. This was true, so far as it went; but Olive could not tell Verena everything—could not tell her that she hated that dreadful pair at Cambridge. As we know, she had forbidden herself this emotion as regards individuals; and she flattered herself that she considered the Tarrants as a type, a deplorable one, a class that, with the public at large, discredited the cause of the new truths. She had talked them over with Miss Birdseye (Olive was always looking after her now and giving her things—the good lady appeared at this period in wonderful caps and shawls—for she felt she couldn't thank her enough), and even Doctor Prance's fellow-lodger, whose animosity to flourishing evils lived in the happiest (though the most illicit) union with the mania for finding excuses, even Miss Birdseye was obliged to confess that if you came to examine his record, poor Selah didn't amount to so very much. How little he amounted to Olive perceived after she had made Verena talk, as the girl did immensely, about her father and mother—

quite unconscious, meanwhile, of the conclusions she suggested to Miss Chancellor. Tarrant was a moralist without
moral sense—that was very clear to Olive as she listened to
the history of his daughter's childhood and youth, which Verena related with an extraordinary artless vividness. This narrative, tremendously fascinating to Miss Chancellor, made her
feel in all sorts of ways—prompted her to ask herself whether
the girl was also destitute of the perception of right and
wrong. No, she was only supremely innocent; she didn't understand, she didn't interpret nor see the *portée* of what she
described; she had no idea whatever of judging her parents.
Olive had wished to 'realise' the conditions in which her wonderful young friend (she thought her more wonderful every
day) had developed, and to this end, as I have related, she
prompted her to infinite discourse. But now she was satisfied,
the realisation was complete, and what she would have liked
to impose on the girl was an effectual rupture with her past.
That past she by no means absolutely deplored, for it had the
merit of having initiated Verena (and her patroness, through
her agency) into the miseries and mysteries of the People. It
was her theory that Verena (in spite of the blood of the
Greenstreets, and, after all, who were they?) was a flower of
the great Democracy, and that it was impossible to have had
an origin less distinguished than Tarrant himself. His birth, in
some unheard-of place in Pennsylvania, was quite inexpressibly low, and Olive would have been much disappointed if it
had been wanting in this defect. She liked to think that Verena, in her childhood, had known almost the extremity of
poverty, and there was a kind of ferocity in the joy with
which she reflected that there had been moments when this
delicate creature came near (if the pinch had only lasted a
little longer) to literally going without food. These things
added to her value for Olive; they made that young lady feel
that their common undertaking would, in consequence, be so
much more serious. It is always supposed that revolutionists
have been goaded, and the goading would have been rather
deficient here were it not for such happy accidents in Verena's
past. When she conveyed from her mother a summons to
Cambridge for a particular occasion, Olive perceived that the
great effort must now be made. Great efforts were nothing

new to her—it was a great effort to live at all—but this one
appeared to her exceptionally cruel. She determined, however,
to make it, promising herself that her first visit to Mrs. Tarrant should also be her last. Her only consolation was that
she expected to suffer intensely; for the prospect of suffering
was always, spiritually speaking, so much cash in her pocket.
It was arranged that Olive should come to tea (the repast that
Selah designated as his supper), when Mrs. Tarrant, as we
have seen, desired to do her honour by inviting another
guest. This guest, after much deliberation between that lady
and Verena, was selected, and the first person Olive saw on
entering the little parlour in Cambridge was a young man
with hair prematurely, or, as one felt that one should say,
precociously white, whom she had a vague impression she
had encountered before, and who was introduced to her as
Mr. Matthias Pardon.

She suffered less than she had hoped—she was so taken up
with the consideration of Verena's interior. It was as bad as
she could have desired; desired in order to feel that (to take
her out of such a *milieu* as that) she should have a right to
draw her altogether to herself. Olive wished more and more
to extract some definite pledge from her; she could hardly say
what it had best be as yet; she only felt that it must be something that would have an absolute sanctity for Verena and
would bind them together for life. On this occasion it seemed
to shape itself in her mind; she began to see what it ought to
be, though she also saw that she would perhaps have to wait
awhile. Mrs. Tarrant, too, in her own house, became now a
complete figure; there was no manner of doubt left as to her
being vulgar. Olive Chancellor despised vulgarity, had a scent
for it which she followed up in her own family, so that often,
with a rising flush, she detected the taint even in Adeline.
There were times, indeed, when every one seemed to have it,
every one but Miss Birdseye (who had nothing to do with
it—she was an antique) and the poorest, humblest people.
The toilers and spinners, the very obscure, these were the
only persons who were safe from it. Miss Chancellor would
have been much happier if the movements she was interested
in could have been carried on only by the people she liked,
and if revolutions, somehow, didn't always have to begin

with one's self—with internal convulsions, sacrifices, executions. A common end, unfortunately, however fine as regards a special result, does not make community impersonal.

Mrs. Tarrant, with her soft corpulence, looked to her guest very bleached and tumid; her complexion had a kind of withered glaze; her hair, very scanty, was drawn off her forehead *à la Chinoise*; she had no eyebrows, and her eyes seemed to stare, like those of a figure of wax. When she talked and wished to insist, and she was always insisting, she puckered and distorted her face, with an effort to express the inexpressible, which turned out, after all, to be nothing. She had a kind of doleful elegance, tried to be confidential, lowered her voice and looked as if she wished to establish a secret understanding, in order to ask her visitor if she would venture on an apple-fritter. She wore a flowing mantle, which resembled her husband's waterproof—a garment which, when she turned to her daughter or talked about her, might have passed for the robe of a sort of priestess of maternity. She endeavoured to keep the conversation in a channel which would enable her to ask sudden incoherent questions of Olive, mainly as to whether she knew the principal ladies (the expression was Mrs. Tarrant's), not only in Boston, but in the other cities which, in her nomadic course, she herself had visited. Olive knew some of them, and of some of them had never heard; but she was irritated, and pretended a universal ignorance (she was conscious that she had never told so many fibs), by which her hostess was much disconcerted, although her questions had apparently been questions pure and simple, leading nowhither and without bearings on any new truth.

XV

TARRANT, HOWEVER, kept an eye in that direction; he was solemnly civil to Miss Chancellor, handed her the dishes at table over and over again, and ventured to intimate that the apple-fritters were very fine; but, save for this, alluded to nothing more trivial than the regeneration of humanity and the strong hope he felt that Miss Birdseye would again have one of her delightful gatherings. With regard to this latter point he explained that it was not in order that he might again present his daughter to the company, but simply because on such occasions there was a valuable interchange of hopeful thought, a contact of mind with mind. If Verena had anything suggestive to contribute to the social problem, the opportunity would come—that was part of their faith. They couldn't reach out for it and try and push their way; if they were wanted, their hour would strike; if they were not, they would just keep still and let others press forward who seemed to be called. If they were called, they would know it; and if they weren't, they could just hold on to each other as they had always done. Tarrant was very fond of alternatives, and he mentioned several others; it was never his fault if his listeners failed to think him impartial. They hadn't much, as Miss Chancellor could see; she could tell by their manner of life that they hadn't raked in the dollars; but they had faith that, whether one raised one's voice or simply worked on in silence, the principal difficulties would straighten themselves out; and they had also a considerable experience of great questions. Tarrant spoke as if, as a family, they were prepared to take charge of them on moderate terms. He always said 'ma'am' in speaking to Olive, to whom, moreover, the air had never been so filled with the sound of her own name. It was always in her ear, save when Mrs. Tarrant and Verena conversed in prolonged and ingenuous asides; this was still for her benefit, but the pronoun sufficed them. She had wished to judge Doctor Tarrant (not that she believed he had come honestly by his title), to make up her mind. She had done these things now, and she expressed to herself the kind of man she believed him to be in reflecting that if she should offer him ten thousand dollars to renounce all claim to Verena, keeping—he and his wife—clear of her for the rest of time, he would probably say, with his fearful smile, 'Make it twenty, money down, and I'll do it.' Some image of this transaction, as one of the possibilities of the future, outlined itself for Olive among the moral incisions of that evening. It seemed implied in the very place, the bald bareness of Tarrant's temporary lair, a wooden cottage, with a rough front yard, a little naked piazza, which seemed rather to expose than to protect, facing upon an unpaved road, in which the footway was overlaid with a strip of planks. These planks were embedded in ice or in liquid thaw, according to the momentary mood of the weather, and the advancing pedestrian traversed them in the attitude, and with a good deal of the suspense, of a rope-dancer. There was nothing in the house to speak of; nothing, to Olive's sense, but a smell of kerosene; though she had a consciousness of sitting down somewhere— the object creaked and rocked beneath her—and of the table at tea being covered with a cloth stamped in bright colours.

As regards the pecuniary transaction with Selah, it was strange how she should have seen it through the conviction that Verena would never give up her parents. Olive was sure that she would never turn her back upon them, would always share with them. She would have despised her had she thought her capable of another course; yet it baffled her to understand why, when parents were so trashy, this natural law should not be suspended. Such a question brought her back, however, to her perpetual enigma, the mystery she had already turned over in her mind for hours together—the wonder of such people being Verena's progenitors at all. She had explained it, as we explain all exceptional things, by making the part, as the French say, of the miraculous. She had come to consider the girl as a wonder of wonders, to hold that no human origin, however congruous it might superficially appear, would sufficiently account for her; that her springing up between Selah and his wife was an exquisite whim of the creative force; and that in such a case a few shades more or less of the inexplicable didn't matter. It was notorious that great beauties, great geniuses, great characters, take their own times and places for coming into the world, leaving the gaping spectators to make them 'fit in,' and holding from far-off ancestors, or even, perhaps, straight from the divine generosity, much more than from their ugly or stupid progenitors. They were incalculable phenomena, anyway, as Selah would have said. Verena, for Olive, was the very type and model of the 'gifted being;' her qualities had not been bought and paid for; they were like some brilliant birthday-present, left at the door by an unknown messenger, to be delightful for ever as an inexhaustible legacy, and amusing for ever from the obscurity of its source. They were superabundantly crude as yet—happily for Olive, who promised herself, as we know, to train and polish them—but they were as genuine as fruit and flowers, as the glow of the fire or the plash of water. For her scrutinising friend Verena had the disposition of the artist, the spirit to which all charming forms come easily and naturally. It required an effort at first to imagine an artist so untaught, so mistaught, so poor in experience; but then it required an effort also to imagine people like the old Tarrants, or a life so full as her life had been of ugly things. Only an exquisite creature could have resisted such associations, only a girl who had some natural light, some divine spark of taste. There were people like that, fresh from the hand of Omnipotence; they were far from common, but their existence was as incontestable as it was beneficent.

Tarrant's talk about his daughter, her prospects, her enthusiasm, was terribly painful to Olive; it brought back to her what she had suffered already from the idea that he laid his hands upon her to make her speak. That he should be mixed up in any way with this exercise of her genius was a great injury to the cause, and Olive had already determined that in future Verena should dispense with his co-operation. The girl had virtually confessed that she lent herself to it only because it gave him pleasure, and that anything else would do as well, anything that would make her quiet a little before she began to 'give out.' Olive took upon herself to believe that *she* could make her quiet, though, certainly, she had never had that effect upon any one; she would mount the platform with Verena if necessary, and lay her hands upon her head. Why in the world had a perverse fate decreed that Tarrant should take an interest in the affairs of Woman—as if she wanted *his* aid

to arrive at her goal; a charlatan of the poor, lean, shabby
sort, without the humour, brilliancy, prestige, which sometimes throw a drapery over shallowness? Mr. Pardon evidently
took an interest as well, and there was something in his appearance that seemed to say that his sympathy would not be
dangerous. He was much at his ease, plainly, beneath the roof
of the Tarrants, and Olive reflected that though Verena had
told her much about him, she had not given her the idea that
he was as intimate as that. What she had mainly said was that
he sometimes took her to the theatre. Olive could enter, to a
certain extent, into that; she herself had had a phase (some
time after her father's death—her mother's had preceded
his—when she bought the little house in Charles Street and
began to live alone), during which she accompanied gentlemen to respectable places of amusement. She was accordingly
not shocked at the idea of such adventures on Verena's part;
than which, indeed, judging from her own experience, nothing could well have been less adventurous. Her recollections
of these expeditions were as of something solemn and edifying—of the earnest interest in her welfare exhibited by her
companion (there were few occasions on which the young
Bostonian appeared to more advantage), of the comfort of
other friends sitting near, who were sure to know whom she
was with, of serious discussion between the acts in regard to
the behaviour of the characters in the piece, and of the speech
at the end with which, as the young man quitted her at her
door, she rewarded his civility—'I must thank you for a very
pleasant evening.' She always felt that she made that too
prim; her lips stiffened themselves as she spoke. But the
whole affair had always a primness; this was discernible even
to Olive's very limited sense of humour. It was not so religious as going to evening-service at King's Chapel; but it was
the next thing to it. Of course all girls didn't do it; there were
families that viewed such a custom with disfavour. But this
was where the girls were of the romping sort; there had to be
some things they were known not to do. As a general thing,
moreover, the practice was confined to the decorous; it was a
sign of culture and quiet tastes. All this made it innocent for
Verena, whose life had exposed her to much worse dangers;
but the thing referred itself in Olive's mind to a danger which

cast a perpetual shadow there—the possibility of the girl's
embarking with some ingenuous youth on an expedition that
would last much longer than an evening. She was haunted, in
a word, with the fear that Verena would marry, a fate to
which she was altogether unprepared to surrender her; and
this made her look with suspicion upon all male acquaintance.

Mr. Pardon was not the only one she knew; she had an
example of the rest in the persons of two young Harvard law-
students, who presented themselves after tea on this same occasion. As they sat there Olive wondered whether Verena had
kept something from her, whether she were, after all (like so
many other girls in Cambridge), a college-'belle,' an object of
frequentation to undergraduates. It was natural that at the
seat of a big university there should be girls like that, with
students dangling after them, but she didn't want Verena to
be one of them. There were some that received the Seniors
and Juniors; others that were accessible to Sophomores and
Freshmen. Certain young ladies distinguished the professional
students; there was a group, even, that was on the best terms
with the young men who were studying for the Unitarian
ministry in that queer little barrack at the end of Divinity
Avenue. The advent of the new visitors made Mrs. Tarrant
bustle immensely; but after she had caused every one to
change places two or three times with every one else the company subsided into a circle which was occasionally broken by
wandering movements on the part of her husband, who, in
the absence of anything to say on any subject whatever,
placed himself at different points in listening attitudes, shaking his head slowly up and down, and gazing at the carpet
with an air of supernatural attention. Mrs. Tarrant asked the
young men from the Law School about their studies, and
whether they meant to follow them up seriously; said she
thought some of the laws were very unjust, and she hoped
they meant to try and improve them. She had suffered by the
laws herself, at the time her father died; she hadn't got half
the prop'ty she should have got if they had been different.
She thought they should be for public matters, not for people's private affairs; the idea always seemed to her to keep you
down if you *were* down, and to hedge you in with difficulties.
Sometimes she thought it was a wonder how she had de-

veloped in the face of so many; but it was a proof that freedom was everywhere, if you only knew how to look for it.

The two young men were in the best humour; they greeted
these sallies with a merriment of which, though it was courteous in form, Olive was by no means unable to define the
spirit. They talked naturally more with Verena than with her
mother; and while they were so engaged Mrs. Tarrant explained to her who they were, and how one of them, the
smaller, who was not quite so spruce, had brought the other,
his particular friend, to introduce him. This friend, Mr. Burrage, was from New York; he was very fashionable, he went
out a great deal in Boston ('I have no doubt you know some
of the places,' said Mrs. Tarrant); his 'fam'ly' was very rich.

'Well, he knows plenty of that sort,' Mrs. Tarrant went on,
'but he felt unsatisfied; he didn't know any one like *us*. He
told Mr. Gracie (that's the little one) that he felt as if he
must; it seemed as if he couldn't hold out. So we told Mr.
Gracie, of course, to bring him right round. Well, I hope he'll
get something from us, I'm sure. He has been reported to be
engaged to Miss Winkworth; I have no doubt you know who
I mean. But Mr. Gracie says he hasn't looked at her more
than twice. That's the way rumours fly round in that set, I
presume. Well, I am glad we are not in it, wherever we are!
Mr. Gracie is very different; he is intensely plain, but I believe
he is very learned. You don't think him plain? Oh, you don't
know? Well, I suppose you don't care, you must see so many.
But I must say, when a young man looks like that, I call him
painfully plain. I heard Doctor Tarrant make the remark the
last time he was here. I don't say but what the plainest are
the best. Well, I had no idea we were going to have a party
when I asked you. I wonder whether Verena hadn't better
hand the cake; we generally find the students enjoy it so
much.'

This office was ultimately delegated to Selah, who, after a
considerable absence, reappeared with a dish of dainties,
which he presented successively to each member of the company. Olive saw Verena lavish her smiles on Mr. Gracie and
Mr. Burrage; the liveliest relation had established itself, and
the latter gentleman in especial abounded in appreciative
laughter. It might have been fancied, just from looking at the

group, that Verena's vocation was to smile and talk with
young men who bent towards her; might have been fancied,
that is, by a person less sure of the contrary than Olive, who
had reason to know that a 'gifted being' is sent into the world
for a very different purpose, and that making the time pass
pleasantly for conceited young men is the last duty you are
bound to think of if you happen to have a talent for embody-
ing a cause. Olive tried to be glad that her friend had the
richness of nature that makes a woman gracious without
latent purposes; she reflected that Verena was not in the
smallest degree a flirt, that she was only enchantingly and
universally genial, that nature had given her a beautiful smile,
which fell impartially on every one, man and woman, alike.
Olive may have been right, but it shall be confided to the
reader that in reality she never knew, by any sense of her own,
whether Verena were a flirt or not. This young lady could not
possibly have told her (even if she herself knew, which she
didn't), and Olive, destitute of the quality, had no means of
taking the measure in another of the subtle feminine desire to
please. She could see the difference between Mr. Gracie and
Mr. Burrage; her being bored by Mrs. Tarrant's attempting
to point it out is perhaps a proof of that. It was a curious
incident of her zeal for the regeneration of her sex that manly
things were, perhaps on the whole, what she understood best.
Mr. Burrage was rather a handsome youth, with a laughing,
clever face, a certain sumptuosity of apparel, an air of belonging to the 'fast set'—a precocious, good-natured man of the
world, curious of new sensations and containing, perhaps, the
making of a *dilettante*. Being, doubtless, a little ambitious,
and liking to flatter himself that he appreciated worth in
lowly forms, he had associated himself with the ruder but at
the same time acuter personality of a genuine son of New
England, who had a harder head than his own and a humour
in reality more cynical, and who, having earlier knowledge of
the Tarrants, had undertaken to show him something indige-
nous and curious, possibly even fascinating. Mr. Gracie was
short, with a big head; he wore eye-glasses, looked unkempt,
almost rustic, and said good things with his ugly lips. Verena
had replies for a good many of them, and a pretty colour
came into her face as she talked. Olive could see that she pro-

duced herself quite as well as one of these gentlemen had foretold the other that she would. Miss Chancellor knew what had passed between them as well as if she had heard it; Mr. Gracie had promised that he would lead her on, that she should justify his description and prove the raciest of her class. They would laugh about her as they went away, lighting their cigars, and for many days afterwards their discourse would be enlivened with quotations from the ' women's rights girl.'

It was amazing how many ways men had of being antipathetic; these two were very different from Basil Ransom, and different from each other, and yet the manner of each conveyed an insult to one's womanhood. The worst of the case was that Verena would be sure not to perceive this outrage— not to dislike them in consequence. There were so many things that she hadn't yet learned to dislike, in spite of her friend's earnest efforts to teach her. She had the idea vividly (that was the marvel) of the cruelty of man, of his immemorial injustice; but it remained abstract, platonic; she didn't detest him in consequence. What was the use of her having that sharp, inspired vision of the history of the sex (it was, as she had said herself, exactly like Joan of Arc's absolutely supernatural apprehension of the state of France), if she wasn't going to carry it out, if she was going to behave as the ordinary pusillanimous, conventional young lady? It was all very well for her to have said that first day that she would renounce: did she look, at such a moment as this, like a young woman who had renounced? Suppose this glittering, laughing Burrage youth, with his chains and rings and shining shoes, should fall in love with her and try to bribe her, with his great possessions, to practise renunciations of another kind—to give up her holy work and to go with him to New York, there to live as his wife, partly bullied, partly pampered, in the accustomed Burrage manner? There was as little comfort for Olive as there had been on the whole alarm in the recollection of that off-hand speech of Verena's about her preference for 'free unions.' This had been mere maiden flippancy; she had not known the meaning of what she said. Though she had grown up among people who took for granted all sorts of queer laxities, she had kept the consummate innocence of the

American girl, that innocence which was the greatest of all, for it had survived the abolition of walls and locks; and of the various remarks that had dropped from Verena expressing this quality that startling observation certainly expressed it most. It implied, at any rate, that unions of some kind or other had her approval, and did not exclude the dangers that might arise from encounters with young men in search of sensations.

XVI

M R. PARDON, as Olive observed, was a little out of this combination; but he was not a person to allow himself to droop. He came and seated himself by Miss Chancellor and broached a literary subject; he asked her if she were following any of the current 'serials' in the magazines. On her telling him that she never followed anything of that sort, he undertook a defence of the serial system, which she presently reminded him that she had not attacked. He was not discouraged by this retort, but glided gracefully off to the question of Mount Desert; conversation on some subject or other being evidently a necessity of his nature. He talked very quickly and softly, with words, and even sentences, imperfectly formed; there was a certain amiable flatness in his tone, and he abounded in exclamations—'Goodness gracious!' and 'Mercy on us!'—not much in use among the sex whose profanity is apt to be coarse. He had small, fair features, remarkably neat, and pretty eyes, and a moustache that he caressed, and an air of juvenility much at variance with his grizzled locks, and the free familiar reference in which he was apt to indulge to his career as a journalist. His friends knew that in spite of his delicacy and his prattle he was what they called a live man; his appearance was perfectly reconcilable with a large degree of literary enterprise. It should be explained that for the most part they attached to this idea the same meaning as Selah Tarrant—a state of intimacy with the newspapers, the cultivation of the great arts of publicity. For this ingenuous son of his age all distinction between the person and the artist had ceased to exist; the writer was personal, the person food for newsboys, and everything and every one were every one's business. All things, with him, referred themselves to print, and print meant simply infinite reporting, a promptitude of announcement, abusive when necessary, or even when not, about his fellow-citizens. He poured contumely on their private life, on their personal appearance, with the best conscience in the world. His faith, again, was the faith of Selah Tarrant—that being in the newspapers is a condition of bliss, and that it would be fastidious to question the terms of the privilege. He was an *enfant de la balle*, as the French say; he had begun his career, at the age of fourteen, by going the rounds of the hotels, to cull flowers from the big, greasy registers which lie on the marble counters; and he might flatter himself that he had contributed in his measure, and on behalf of a vigilant public opinion, the pride of a democratic State, to the great end of preventing the American citizen from attempting clandestine journeys. Since then he had ascended other steps of the same ladder; he was the most brilliant young interviewer on the Boston press. He was particularly successful in drawing out the ladies; he had condensed into shorthand many of the most celebrated women of his time— some of these daughters of fame were very voluminous—and he was supposed to have a remarkably insinuating way of waiting upon *prime donne* and actresses the morning after their arrival, or sometimes the very evening, while their luggage was being brought up. He was only twenty-eight years old, and, with his hoary head, was a thoroughly modern young man; he had no idea of not taking advantage of all the modern conveniences. He regarded the mission of mankind upon earth as a perpetual evolution of telegrams; everything to him was very much the same, he had no sense of proportion or quality; but the newest thing was what came nearest exciting in his mind the sentiment of respect. He was an object of extreme admiration to Selah Tarrant, who believed that he had mastered all the secrets of success, and who, when Mrs. Tarrant remarked (as she had done more than once) that it looked as if Mr. Pardon was really coming after Verena, declared that if he was, he was one of the few young men he should want to see in that connection, one of the few he should be willing to allow to handle her. It was Tarrant's conviction that if Matthias Pardon should seek Verena in marriage, it would be with a view to producing her in public; and the advantage for the girl of having a husband who was at the same time reporter, interviewer, manager, agent, who had the command of the principal 'dailies,' would write her up and work her, as it were, scientifically—the attraction of all this was too obvious to be insisted on. Matthias had a mean opinion of Tarrant, thought him quite second-rate, a votary of played-out causes. It was his impression that he himself was in love with Verena, but his passion was not a jealous one, and included a remarkable disposition to share the object of his affection with the American people.

He talked some time to Olive about Mount Desert, told her that in his letters he had described the company at the different hotels. He remarked, however, that a correspondent suffered a good deal to-day from the competition of the 'lady-writers'; the sort of article they produced was sometimes more acceptable to the papers. He supposed she would be glad to hear that—he knew she was so interested in woman's having a free field. They certainly made lovely correspondents; they picked up something bright before you could turn round; there wasn't much you could keep away from them; you had to be lively if you wanted to get there first. Of course, they were naturally more chatty, and that was the style of literature that seemed to take most to-day; only they didn't write much but what ladies would want to read. Of course, he knew there were millions of lady-readers, but he intimated that *he* didn't address himself exclusively to the gynecæum; he tried to put in something that would interest all parties. If you read a lady's letter you knew pretty well in advance what you would find. Now, what he tried for was that you shouldn't have the least idea; he always tried to have something that would make you jump. Mr. Pardon was not conceited more, at least, than is proper when youth and success go hand in hand, and it was natural he should not know in what spirit Miss Chancellor listened to him. Being aware that she was a woman of culture his desire was simply to supply her with the pabulum that she would expect. She thought him very inferior; she had heard he was intensely bright, but there was probably some mistake; there couldn't be any danger for Verena from a mind that took merely a gossip's view of great tendencies. Besides, he wasn't half educated, and it was her belief, or at least her hope, that an educative process was now going on for Verena (under her own direction), which would enable her to make such a discovery for herself. Olive had a standing quarrel with the levity, the good-nature, of the judgments of the day; many of them seemed to her weak to imbecility, losing sight of all measures and standards, lavishing superlatives, delighted to be fooled. The age seemed to her relaxed and demoralised, and I believe she looked to the influx of the great feminine element to make it feel and speak more sharply.

'Well, it's a privilege to hear you two talk together,' Mrs. Tarrant said to her; 'it's what I call real conversation. It isn't often we have anything so fresh; it makes me feel as if I wanted to join in. I scarcely know whom to listen to most; Verena seems to be having such a time with those gentlemen. First I catch one thing and then another; it seems as if I couldn't take it all in. Perhaps I ought to pay more attention to Mr. Burrage; I don't want him to think we are not so cordial as they are in New York.'

She decided to draw nearer to the trio on the other side of the room, for she had perceived (as she devoutly hoped Miss Chancellor had not), that Verena was endeavouring to persuade either of her companions to go and talk to her dear friend, and that these unscrupulous young men, after a glance over their shoulder, appeared to plead for remission, to intimate that this was not what they had come round for. Selah wandered out of the room again with his collection of cakes, and Mr. Pardon began to talk to Olive about Verena, to say that he felt as if he couldn't say all he did feel with regard to the interest she had shown in her. Olive could not imagine why he was called upon to say or to feel anything, and she gave him short answers; while the poor young man, unconscious of his doom, remarked that he hoped she wasn't going to exercise any influence that would prevent Miss Tarrant from taking the rank that belonged to her. He thought there was too much hanging back; he wanted to see her in a front seat; he wanted to see her name in the biggest kind of bills and her portrait in the windows of the stores. She had genius, there was no doubt of that, and she would take a new line altogether. She had charm, and there was a great demand for that nowadays in connection with new ideas. There were so many that seemed to have fallen dead for want of it. She ought to be carried straight ahead; she ought to walk right up to the top. There was a want of bold action; he didn't see what they were waiting for. He didn't suppose they were waiting till she was fifty years old; there were old ones enough in the field. He knew that Miss Chancellor appreci-

ated the advantage of her girlhood, because Miss Verena had
told him so. Her father was dreadfully slack, and the winter
was ebbing away. Mr. Pardon went so far as to say that if Dr.
Tarrant didn't see his way to do something, he should feel as
if he should want to take hold himself. He expressed a hope
at the same time that Olive had not any views that would lead
her to bring her influence to bear to make Miss Verena hold
back; also that she wouldn't consider that he pressed in too
much. He knew that was a charge that people brought against
newspaper-men—that they were rather apt to cross the line.
He only worried because he thought those who were no
doubt nearer to Miss Verena than he could hope to be were
not sufficiently alive. He knew that she had appeared in two
or three parlours since that evening at Miss Birdseye's, and he
had heard of the delightful occasion at Miss Chancellor's own
house, where so many of the first families had been invited to
meet her. (This was an allusion to a small luncheon-party that
Olive had given, when Verena discoursed to a dozen matrons
and spinsters, selected by her hostess with infinite consideration and many spiritual scruples; a report of the affair, presumably from the hand of the young Matthias, who naturally
had not been present, appeared with extraordinary promptness in an evening-paper.) That was very well so far as it
went, but he wanted something on another scale, something
so big that people would have to go round if they wanted to
get past. Then lowering his voice a little, he mentioned what
it was: a lecture in the Music Hall, at fifty cents a ticket, without her father, right there on her own basis. He lowered his
voice still more and revealed to Miss Chancellor his innermost
thought, having first assured himself that Selah was still absent and that Mrs. Tarrant was inquiring of Mr. Burrage
whether he visited much on the new land. The truth was,
Miss Verena wanted to 'shed' her father altogether; she didn't
want him pawing round her that way before she began; it
didn't add in the least to the attraction. Mr. Pardon expressed
the conviction that Miss Chancellor agreed with him in this,
and it required a great effort of mind on Olive's part, so small
was her desire to act in concert with Mr. Pardon, to admit to
herself that she did. She asked him, with a certain lofty coldness—he didn't make her shy, now, a bit—whether he took

a great interest in the improvement of the position of women. The question appeared to strike the young man as abrupt and irrelevant, to come down on him from a height with which he was not accustomed to hold intercourse. He was used to quick operations, however, and he had only a moment of bright blankness before replying:

'Oh, there is nothing I wouldn't do for the ladies; just give me a chance and you'll see.'

Olive was silent a moment. 'What I mean is—is your sympathy a sympathy with our sex, or a particular interest in Miss Tarrant?'

'Well, sympathy is just sympathy—that's all I can say. It takes in Miss Verena and it takes in all others—except the lady-correspondents,' the young man added, with a jocosity which, as he perceived even at the moment, was lost on Verena's friend. He was not more successful when he went on: 'It takes in even you, Miss Chancellor!'

Olive rose to her feet, hesitating; she wanted to go away, and yet she couldn't bear to leave Verena to be exploited, as she felt that she would be after her departure, that indeed she had already been, by those offensive young men. She had a strange sense, too, that her friend had neglected her for the last half-hour, had not been occupied with her, had placed a barrier between them—a barrier of broad male backs, of laughter that verged upon coarseness, of glancing smiles directed across the room, directed to Olive, which seemed rather to disconnect her with what was going forward on that side than to invite her to take part in it. If Verena recognised that Miss Chancellor was not in report, as her father said, when jocose young men ruled the scene, the discovery implied no great penetration; but the poor girl might have reflected further that to see it taken for granted that she was unadapted for such company could scarcely be more agreeable to Olive than to be dragged into it. This young lady's worst apprehensions were now justified by Mrs. Tarrant's crying to her that she must not go, as Mr. Burrage and Mr. Gracie were trying to persuade Verena to give them a little specimen of inspirational speaking, and she was sure her daughter would comply in a moment if Miss Chancellor would just tell her to compose herself. They had got to own up to it, Miss Chan-

cellor could do more with her than any one else; but Mr.
Gracie and Mr. Burrage had excited her so that she was afraid
it would be rather an unsuccessful effort. The whole group
had got up, and Verena came to Olive with her hands outstretched and no signs of a bad conscience in her bright face.

'I know you like me to speak so much—I'll try to say
something if you want me to. But I'm afraid there are not
enough people; I can't do much with a small audience.'

'I wish we had brought some of our friends—they would
have been delighted to come if we had given them a chance,'
said Mr. Burrage. 'There is an immense desire throughout the
University to hear you, and there is no such sympathetic audience as an audience of Harvard men. Gracie and I are only
two, but Gracie is a host in himself, and I am sure he will say
as much of me.' The young man spoke these words freely and
lightly, smiling at Verena, and even a little at Olive, with the
air of one to whom a mastery of clever 'chaff' was commonly
attributed.

'Mr. Burrage listens even better than he talks,' his companion declared. 'We have the habit of attention at lectures, you
know. To be lectured by you would be an advantage indeed.
We are sunk in ignorance and prejudice.'

'Ah, my prejudices,' Burrage went on; 'if you could see
them—I assure you they are something monstrous!'

'Give them a regular ducking and make them gasp,' Matthias Pardon cried. 'If you want an opportunity to act on
Harvard College, now's your chance. These gentlemen will
carry the news; it will be the narrow end of the wedge.'

'I can't tell what you like,' Verena said, still looking into
Olive's eyes.

'I'm sure Miss Chancellor likes everything here,' Mrs. Tarrant remarked, with a noble confidence.

Selah had reappeared by this time; his lofty, contemplative
person was framed by the doorway. 'Want to try a little inspiration?' he inquired, looking round on the circle with an
encouraging inflection.

'I'll do it alone, if you prefer,' Verena said, soothingly to
her friend. 'It might be a good chance to try without father.'

'You don't mean to say you ain't going to be supported?'
Mrs. Tarrant exclaimed, with dismay.

'Ah, I beseech you, give us the whole programme—don't omit any leading feature!' Mr. Burrage was heard to plead.

'My only interest is to draw her out,' said Selah, defending his integrity. 'I will drop right out if I don't seem to vitalise. I have no desire to draw attention to my own poor gifts.' This declaration appeared to be addressed to Miss Chancellor.

'Well, there will be more inspiration if you don't touch her,' Matthias Pardon said to him. 'It will seem to come right down from—well, wherever it does come from.'

'Yes, we don't pretend to say that,' Mrs. Tarrant murmured.

This little discussion had brought the blood to Olive's face; she felt that every one present was looking at her—Verena most of all—and that here was a chance to take a more complete possession of the girl. Such chances were agitating; moreover, she didn't like, on any occasion, to be so prominent. But everything that had been said was benighted and vulgar; the place seemed thick with the very atmosphere out of which she wished to lift Verena. They were treating her as a show, as a social resource, and the two young men from the College were laughing at her shamelessly. She was not meant for that, and Olive would save her. Verena was so simple, she couldn't see herself; she was the only pure spirit in the odious group.

'I want you to address audiences that are worth addressing—to convince people who are serious and sincere.' Olive herself, as she spoke, heard the great shake in her voice. 'Your mission is not to exhibit yourself as a pastime for individuals, but to touch the heart of communities, of nations.'

'Dear madam, I'm sure Miss Tarrant will touch my heart!' Mr. Burrage objected, gallantly.

'Well, I don't know but she judges you young men fairly,' said Mrs. Tarrant, with a sigh.

Verena, diverted a moment from her communion with her friend, considered Mr. Burrage with a smile. 'I don't believe you have got any heart, and I shouldn't care much if you had!'

'You have no idea how much the way you say that increases my desire to hear you speak.'

'Do as you please, my dear,' said Olive, almost inaudibly. 'My carriage must be there—I must leave you, in any case.'

'I can see you don't want it,' said Verena, wondering. 'You would stay if you liked it, wouldn't you?'

'I don't know what I should do. Come out with me!' Olive spoke almost with fierceness.

'Well, you'll send them away no better than they came,' said Matthias Pardon.

'I guess you had better come round some other night,' Selah suggested pacifically, but with a significance which fell upon Olive's ear.

Mr. Gracie seemed inclined to make the sturdiest protest. 'Look here, Miss Tarrant; do you want to save Harvard College, or do you not?' he demanded, with a humorous frown.

'I didn't know *you* were Harvard College!' Verena returned as humorously.

'I am afraid you are rather disappointed in your evening if you expected to obtain some insight into our ideas,' said Mrs. Tarrant, with an air of impotent sympathy, to Mr. Gracie.

'Well, good-night, Miss Chancellor,' she went on; 'I hope you've got a warm wrap. I suppose you'll think we go a good deal by what you say in this house. Well, most people don't object to that. There's a little hole right there in the porch; it seems as if Doctor Tarrant couldn't remember to go for the man to fix it. I am afraid you'll think we're too much taken up with all these new hopes. Well, we *have* enjoyed seeing you in our home; it quite raises my appetite for social intercourse. Did you come out on wheels? I can't stand a sleigh myself; it makes me sick.'

This was her hostess's response to Miss Chancellor's very summary farewell, uttered as the three ladies proceeded together to the door of the house. Olive had got herself out of the little parlour with a sort of blind, defiant dash; she had taken no perceptible leave of the rest of the company. When she was calm she had very good manners, but when she was agitated she was guilty of lapses, every one of which came back to her, magnified, in the watches of the night. Sometimes they excited remorse, and sometimes triumph; in the latter case she felt that she could not have been so justly vindictive in cold blood. Tarrant wished to guide her down the steps, out of the little yard, to her carriage; he reminded her that they had had ashes sprinkled on the planks on purpose.

But she begged him to let her alone, she almost pushed him back; she drew Verena out into the dark freshness, closing the door of the house behind her. There was a splendid sky, all blue-black and silver—a sparkling wintry vault, where the stars were like a myriad points of ice. The air was silent and sharp, and the vague snow looked cruel. Olive knew now very definitely what the promise was that she wanted Verena to make; but it was too cold, she could keep her there bareheaded but an instant. Mrs. Tarrant, meanwhile, in the parlour, remarked that it seemed as if she couldn't trust Verena with her own parents; and Selah intimated that, with a proper invitation, his daughter would be very happy to address Harvard College at large. Mr. Burrage and Mr. Gracie said they would invite her on the spot, in the name of the University; and Matthias Pardon reflected (and asserted) with glee that this would be the newest thing yet. But he added that they would have a high time with Miss Chancellor first, and this was evidently the conviction of the company.

'I can see you are angry at something,' Verena said to Olive, as the two stood there in the starlight. 'I hope it isn't me. What have I done?'

'I am not angry—I am anxious. I am so afraid I shall lose you. Verena, don't fail me—don't fail me!' Olive spoke low, with a kind of passion.

'Fail you? How can I fail?'

'You can't, of course you can't. Your star is above you. But don't listen to *them*.'

'To whom do you mean, Olive? To my parents?'

'Oh no, not your parents,' Miss Chancellor replied, with some sharpness. She paused a moment, and then she said: 'I don't care for your parents. I have told you that before; but now that I have seen them—as they wished, as you wished, and I didn't—I don't care for them; I must repeat it, Verena. I should be dishonest if I let you think I did.'

'Why, Olive Chancellor!' Verena murmured, as if she were trying, in spite of the sadness produced by this declaration, to do justice to her friend's impartiality.

'Yes, I am hard; perhaps I am cruel; but we must be hard if we wish to triumph. Don't listen to young men when they try to mock and muddle you. They don't care for you; they don't care for *us*. They care only for their pleasure, for what they believe to be the right of the stronger. The stronger? I am not so sure!'

'Some of them care so much—are supposed to care too much—for us,' Verena said, with a smile that looked dim in the darkness.

'Yes, if we will give up everything. I have asked you before—are you prepared to give up?'

'Do you mean, to give *you* up?'

'No, all our wretched sisters—all our hopes and purposes—all that we think sacred and worth living for!'

'Oh, they don't want that, Olive.' Verena's smile became more distinct, and she added: 'They don't want so much as that!'

'Well, then, go in and speak for them—and sing for them—and dance for them!'

'Olive, you are cruel!'

'Yes, I am. But promise me one thing, and I shall be—oh, so tender!'

'What a strange place for promises,' said Verena, with a shiver, looking about her into the night.

'Yes, I am dreadful; I know it. But promise.' And Olive drew the girl nearer to her, flinging over her with one hand the fold of a cloak that hung ample upon her own meagre person, and holding her there with the other, while she looked at her, suppliant but half hesitating. 'Promise!' she repeated.

'Is it something terrible?'

'Never to listen to one of them, never to be bribed——'

At this moment the house-door was opened again, and the light of the hall projected itself across the little piazza. Matthias Pardon stood in the aperture, and Tarrant and his wife, with the two other visitors, appeared to have come forward as well, to see what detained Verena.

'You seem to have started a kind of lecture out here,' Mr. Pardon said. 'You ladies had better look out, or you'll freeze together!'

Verena was reminded by her mother that she would catch her death, but she had already heard sharply, low as they were spoken, five last words from Olive, who now abruptly released her and passed swiftly over the path from the porch to her waiting carriage. Tarrant creaked along, in pursuit, to assist Miss Chancellor; the others drew Verena into the house. 'Promise me not to marry!'—that was what echoed in her startled mind, and repeated itself there when Mr. Burrage returned to the charge, asking her if she wouldn't at least appoint some evening when they might listen to her. She knew that Olive's injunction ought not to have surprised her; she had already felt it in the air; she would have said at any time, if she had been asked, that she didn't suppose Miss Chancellor would want her to marry. But the idea, uttered as her friend had uttered it, had a new solemnity, and the effect of that quick, violent colloquy was to make her nervous and impatient, as if she had had a sudden glimpse of futurity. That was rather awful, even if it represented the fate one would like.

When the two young men from the College pressed their petition, she asked, with a laugh that surprised them, whether they wished to 'mock and muddle' her. They went away, assenting to Mrs. Tarrant's last remark: 'I am afraid you'll feel that you don't quite understand us yet.' Matthias Pardon remained; her father and mother, expressing their perfect confidence that he would excuse them, went to bed and left him sitting there. He stayed a good while longer, nearly an hour, and said things that made Verena think that *he*, perhaps, would like to marry her. But while she listened to him, more abstractedly than her custom was, she remarked to herself that there could be no difficulty in promising Olive so far as he was concerned. He was very pleasant, and he knew an immense deal about everything, or, rather, about every one, and he would take her right into the midst of life. But she didn't wish to marry him, all the same, and after he had gone she reflected that, once she came to think of it, she didn't want to marry any one. So it would be easy, after all, to make Olive that promise, and it would give her so much pleasure!

XVII

THE NEXT TIME Verena saw Olive, she said to her that she was ready to make the promise she had asked the other night; but, to her great surprise, this young woman answered her by a question intended to check such rashness. Miss Chancellor raised a warning finger; she had an air of dissuasion almost as solemn as her former pressure; her passionate impatience appeared to have given way to other considerations, to be replaced by the resignation that comes with deeper reflection. It was tinged in this case, indeed, by such bitterness as might be permitted to a young lady who cultivated the brightness of a great faith.

'Don't you want any promise at present?' Verena asked. 'Why, Olive, how you change!'

'My dear child, you are so young—so strangely young. I am a thousand years old; I have lived through generations—through centuries. I know what I know by experience; you know it by imagination. That is consistent with your being the fresh, bright creature that you are. I am constantly forgetting the difference between us—that you are a mere child as yet, though a child destined for great things. I forgot it the other night, but I have remembered it since. You must pass through a certain phase, and it would be very wrong in me to pretend to suppress it. That is all clear to me now; I see it was my jealousy that spoke—my restless, hungry jealousy. I have far too much of that; I oughtn't to give any one the right to say that it's a woman's quality. I don't want your signature; I only want your confidence—only what springs from that. I hope with all my soul that you won't marry; but if you don't it must not be because you have promised me. You know what I think—that there is something noble done when one makes a sacrifice for a great good. Priests—when they were real priests—never married, and what you and I dream of doing demands of us a kind of priesthood. It seems to me very poor, when friendship and faith and charity and the most interesting occupation in the world—when such a combination as this doesn't seem, by itself, enough to live for. No man that I have ever seen cares a straw in his heart for what we are trying to accomplish. They hate it; they scorn it; they will try to stamp it out whenever they can. Oh yes, I know there are men who pretend to care for it; but they are not really men, and I wouldn't be sure even of them! Any man that one would look at—with him, as a matter of course, it is war upon us to the knife. I don't mean to say there are not some male beings who are willing to patronise us a little; to pat us on the back and recommend a few moderate concessions; to say that there *are* two or three little points in which society has not been quite just to us. But any man who pretends to accept our programme *in toto*, as you and I understand it, of his own free will, before he is forced to—such a person simply schemes to betray us. There are gentlemen in plenty who would be glad to stop your mouth by kissing you! If you become dangerous some day to their selfishness, to their vested interests, to their immorality—as I pray heaven every day, my dear friend, that you may!—it will be a grand thing for one of them if he can persuade you that he loves you. Then you will see what he will do with you, and how far his love will take him! It would be a sad day for you and for me and for all of us, if you were to believe something of that kind. You see I am very calm now; I have thought it all out.'

Verena had listened with earnest eyes. 'Why, Olive, you are quite a speaker yourself!' she exclaimed. 'You would far surpass me if you would let yourself go.'

Miss Chancellor shook her head with a melancholy that was not devoid of sweetness. 'I can speak to *you*; but that is no proof. The very stones of the street—all the dumb things of nature—might find a voice to talk to you. I have no facility; I am awkward and embarrassed and dry.' When this young lady, after a struggle with the winds and waves of emotion, emerged into the quiet stream of a certain high reasonableness, she presented her most graceful aspect; she had a tone of softness and sympathy, a gentle dignity, a serenity of wisdom, which sealed the appreciation of those who knew her well enough to like her, and which always impressed Verena as something almost august. Such moods, however, were not often revealed to the public at large; they belonged to Miss Chancellor's very private life. One of them had posses-

sion of her at present, and she went on to explain the inconsequence which had puzzled her friend with the same quiet
clearness, the detachment from error, of a woman whose self-
scrutiny has been as sharp as her deflection.

'Don't think me capricious if I say I would rather trust you
without a pledge. I owe you, I owe every one, an apology for
my rudeness and fierceness at your mother's. It came over
me—just seeing those young men—how exposed you are;
and the idea made me (for the moment) frantic. I see your
danger still, but I see other things too, and I have recovered
my balance. You must be safe, Verena—you must be saved;
but your safety must not come from your having tied your
hands. It must come from the growth of your perception;
from your seeing things, of yourself, sincerely and with conviction, in the light in which I see them; from your feeling
that for your work your freedom is essential, and that there is
no freedom for you and me save in religiously *not* doing what
you will often be asked to do—and I never!' Miss Chancellor
brought out these last words with a proud jerk which was not
without its pathos. 'Don't promise, don't promise!' she went
on. 'I would far rather you didn't. But don't fail me—don't
fail me, or I shall die!'

Her manner of repairing her inconsistency was altogether
feminine: she wished to extract a certainty at the same time
that she wished to deprecate a pledge, and she would have
been delighted to put Verena into the enjoyment of that freedom which was so important for her by preventing her exercising it in a particular direction. The girl was now completely
under her influence; she had latent curiosities and distrac-
tions—left to herself, she was not always thinking of the unhappiness of women; but the touch of Olive's tone worked a
spell, and she found something to which at least a portion of
her nature turned with eagerness in her companion's wider
knowledge, her elevation of view. Miss Chancellor was historic and philosophic; or, at any rate, she appeared so to Verena, who felt that through such an association one might at
last intellectually command all life. And there was a simpler
impulse; Verena wished to please her if only because she had
such a dread of displeasing her. Olive's displeasures, disappointments, disapprovals were tragic, truly memorable; she

grew white under them, not shedding many tears, as a general thing, like inferior women (she cried when she was angry, not when she was hurt), but limping and panting, morally, as if she had received a wound that she would carry for life. On the other hand, her commendations, her satisfactions were as soft as a west wind; and she had this sign, the rarest of all, of generosity, that she liked obligations of gratitude when they were not laid upon her by men. Then, indeed, she scarcely recognised them. She considered men in general as so much in the debt of the opposite sex that any individual woman had an unlimited credit with them; she could not possibly over-draw the general feminine account. The unexpected temperance of her speech on this subject of Verena's accessibility to matrimonial error seemed to the girl to have an antique beauty, a wisdom purged of worldly elements; it reminded her of qualities that she believed to have been proper to Electra or Antigone. This made her wish the more to do something that would gratify Olive; and in spite of her friend's dissuasion she declared that she should like to promise. 'I will promise, at any rate, not to marry any of those gentlemen that were at the house,' she said. 'Those seemed to be the ones you were principally afraid of.'

'You will promise not to marry any one you don't like,' said Olive. 'That would be a great comfort!'

'But I do like Mr. Burrage and Mr. Gracie.'

'And Mr. Matthias Pardon? What a name!'

'Well, he knows how to make himself agreeable. He can tell you everything you want to know.'

'You mean everything you don't! Well, if you like every one, I haven't the least objection. It would only be prefer-ences that I should find alarming. I am not the least afraid of your marrying a repulsive man; your danger would come from an attractive one.'

'I'm glad to hear you admit that some *are* attractive!' Ve-rena exclaimed, with the light laugh which her reverence for Miss Chancellor had not yet quenched. 'It sometimes seems as if there weren't any you could like!'

'I can imagine a man I should like very much,' Olive re-plied, after a moment. 'But I don't like those I see. They seem to me poor creatures.' And, indeed, her uppermost feeling in regard to them was a kind of cold scorn; she thought most of them palterers and bullies. The end of the colloquy was that Verena, having assented, with her usual docility, to her companion's optimistic contention that it was a 'phase,' this taste for evening-calls from collegians and newspaper-men, and would consequently pass away with the growth of her mind, remarked that the injustice of men might be an accident or might be a part of their nature, but at any rate she should have to change a good deal before she should want to marry.

About the middle of December, Miss Chancellor received a visit from Matthias Pardon, who had come to ask her what she meant to do about Verena. She had never invited him to call upon her, and the appearance of a gentleman whose desire to see her was so irrepressible as to dispense with such a preliminary was not in her career an accident frequent enough to have taught her equanimity. She thought Mr. Pardon's visit a liberty; but, if she expected to convey this idea to him by withholding any suggestion that he should sit down, she was greatly mistaken, inasmuch as he cut the ground from under her feet by himself offering her a chair. His manner represented hospitality enough for both of them, and she was obliged to listen, on the edge of her sofa (she could at least seat herself where she liked), to his extraordinary inquiry. Of course she was not obliged to answer it, and indeed she scarcely understood it. He explained that it was prompted by the intense interest he felt in Miss Verena; but that scarcely made it more comprehensible, such a sentiment (on his part) being such a curious mixture. He had a sort of enamel of good humour which showed that his indelicacy was his profession; and he asked for revelations of the *vie intime* of his victims with the bland confidence of a fashionable physician inquiring about symptoms. He wanted to know what Miss Chancellor meant to do, because if she didn't mean to do anything, he had an idea—which he wouldn't conceal from her—of going into the enterprise himself. 'You see, what I should like to know is this: do you consider that she belongs to you, or that she belongs to the people? If she belongs to you, why don't you bring her out?'

He had no purpose and no consciousness of being impertinent; he only wished to talk over the matter sociably with

Miss Chancellor. He knew, of course, that there was a presumption she would not be sociable, but no presumption had yet deterred him from presenting a surface which he believed to be polished till it shone; there was always a larger one in favour of his power to penetrate and of the majesty of the 'great dailies.' Indeed, he took so many things for granted that Olive remained dumb while she regarded them; and he availed himself of what he considered as a fortunate opening to be really very frank. He reminded her that he had known Miss Verena a good deal longer than she; he had travelled out to Cambridge the other winter (when he could get an off-night), with the thermometer at ten below zero. He had always thought her attractive, but it wasn't till this season that his eyes had been fully opened. Her talent had matured, and now he had no hesitation in calling her brilliant. Miss Chancellor could imagine whether, as an old friend, he could watch such a beautiful unfolding with indifference. She would fascinate the people, just as she had fascinated her (Miss Chancellor), and, he might be permitted to add, himself. The fact was, she was a great card, and some one ought to play it. There never had been a more attractive female speaker before the American public; she would walk right past Mrs. Farrinder, and Mrs. Farrinder knew it. There was room for both, no doubt, they had such a different style; anyhow, what he wanted to show was that there was room for Miss Verena. She didn't want any more tuning-up, she wanted to break right out. Moreover, he felt that any gentleman who should lead her to success would win her esteem; he might even attract her more powerfully—who could tell? If Miss Chancellor wanted to attach her permanently, she ought to push her right forward. He gathered from what Miss Verena had told him that she wanted to make her study up the subject a while longer—follow some kind of course. Well, now, he could assure her that there was no preparation so good as just seeing a couple of thousand people down there before you who have paid their money to have you tell them something. Miss Verena was a natural genius, and he hoped very much she wasn't going to take the nature out of her. She could study up as she went along; she had got the great thing that you couldn't learn, a kind of divine afflatus, as the ancients used to say, and she had better just begin on that. He wouldn't deny what was the matter with *him*; he was quite under the spell, and his admiration made him want to see her where she belonged. He shouldn't care so much how she got there, but it would certainly add to his pleasure if he could show her up to her place. Therefore, would Miss Chancellor just tell him this: How long did she expect to hold her back; how long did she expect a humble admirer to wait? Of course he hadn't come there to cross-question her; there was one thing he trusted he always kept clear of; when he was indiscreet he wanted to know it. He had come with a proposal of his own, and he hoped it would seem a sufficient warrant for his visit. Would Miss Chancellor be willing to divide a—the—well, he might call it the responsibilities? Couldn't they run Miss Verena together? In this case, every one would be satisfied. She could travel round with her as her companion, and he would see that the American people walked up. If Miss Chancellor would just let her go a little, he would look after the rest. He wanted no odds; he only wanted her for about an hour and a half three or four evenings a week.

Olive had time, in the course of this appeal, to make her faculties converge, to ask herself what she could say to this prodigious young man that would make him feel as how base a thing she held his proposal that they should constitute themselves into a company for drawing profit from Verena. Unfortunately, the most sarcastic inquiry that could occur to her as a response was also the most obvious one, so that he hesitated but a moment with his rejoinder after she had asked him how many thousands of dollars he expected to make.

'For Miss Verena? It depends upon the time. She'd run for ten years, at least. I can't figure it up till all the States have been heard from,' he said, smiling.

'I don't mean for Miss Tarrant, I mean for you,' Olive returned, with the impression that she was looking him straight in the eye.

'Oh, as many as you'll leave me!' Matthias Pardon answered, with a laugh that contained all, and more than all, the jocularity of the American press. 'To speak seriously,' he added, 'I don't want to make money out of it.'

'What do you want to make, then?'

'Well, I want to make history! I want to help the ladies.'

'The ladies?' Olive murmured. 'What do you know about ladies?' she was on the point of adding, when his promptness checked her.

'All over the world. I want to work for their emancipation. I regard it as the great modern question.'

Miss Chancellor got up now; this was rather too strong. Whether, eventually, she was successful in what she attempted, the reader of her history will judge; but at this moment she had not that promise of success which resides in a willingness to make use of every aid that offers. Such is the penalty of being of a fastidious, exclusive, uncompromising nature; of seeing things not simply and sharply, but in perverse relations, in intertwisted strands. It seemed to our young lady that nothing could be less attractive than to owe her emancipation to such a one as Matthias Pardon; and it is curious that those qualities which he had in common with Verena, and which in her seemed to Olive romantic and touching—her having sprung from the 'people,' had an acquaintance with poverty, a hand-to-mouth development, and an experience of the seamy side of life—availed in no degree to conciliate Miss Chancellor. I suppose it was because he was a man. She told him that she was much obliged to him for his offer, but that he evidently didn't understand Verena and herself. No, not even Miss Tarrant, in spite of his long acquaintance with her. They had no desire to be notorious; they only wanted to be useful. They had no wish to make money; there would always be plenty of money for Miss Tarrant. Certainly, she should come before the public, and the world would acclaim her and hang upon her words; but crude, precipitate action was what both of them least desired. The change in the dreadful position of women was not a question for to-day simply, or for to-morrow, but for many years to come; and there would be a great deal to think of, to map out. One thing they were determined upon—that men shouldn't taunt them with being superficial. When Verena should appear it would be armed at all points, like Joan of Arc (this analogy had lodged itself in Olive's imagination); she should have facts and figures; she should meet men on their own ground. 'What we mean to do, we mean to do well,' Miss Chancellor said to her visitor, with considerable sternness; leaving him to make such an application to himself as his fancy might suggest.

This announcement had little comfort for him; he felt baffled and disheartened—indeed, quite sick. Was it not sickening to hear her talk of this dreary process of preparation?— as if any one cared about that, and would know whether Verena were prepared or not! Had Miss Chancellor no faith in her girlhood? didn't she know what a card that would be? This was the last inquiry Olive allowed him the opportunity of making. She remarked to him that they might talk for ever without coming to an agreement—their points of view were so far apart. Besides, it was a woman's question; what they wanted was for women, and it should be by women. It had happened to the young Matthias more than once to be shown the way to the door, but the path of retreat had never yet seemed to him so unpleasant. He was naturally amiable, but it had not hitherto befallen him to be made to feel that he was not—and could not be—a factor in contemporary history: here was a rapacious woman who proposed to keep that favourable setting for herself. He let her know that she was right-down selfish, and that if she chose to sacrifice a beautiful nature to her antediluvian theories and love of power, a vigilant daily press—whose business it was to expose wrongdoing—would demand an account from her. She replied that, if the newspapers chose to insult her, that was their own affair; one outrage the more to the sex in her person was of little account. And after he had left her she seemed to see the glow of dawning success; the battle had begun, and something of the ecstasy of the martyr.

XVIII

VERENA TOLD HER, a week after this, that Mr. Pardon wanted so much she should say she would marry him; and she added, with evident pleasure at being able to give her so agreeable a piece of news, that she had declined to say anything of the sort. She thought that now, at least, Olive must believe in her; for the proposal was more attractive than Miss Chancellor seemed able to understand. 'He does place things in a very seductive light,' Verena said; 'he says that if I become his wife I shall be carried straight along by a force of excitement of which at present I have no idea. I shall wake up famous, if I marry him; I have only got to give out my feelings, and he will take care of the rest. He says every hour of my youth is precious to me, and that we should have a lovely time travelling round the country. I think you ought to allow that all that is rather dazzling—for I am not naturally concentrated, like you!'

'He promises you success. What do you call success?' Olive inquired, looking at her friend with a kind of salutary coldness—a suspension of sympathy—with which Verena was now familiar (though she liked it no better than at first), and which made approbation more gracious when approbation came.

Verena reflected a moment, and then answered, smiling, but with confidence: 'Producing a pressure that shall be irresistible. Causing certain laws to be repealed by Congress and by the State legislatures, and others to be enacted.' She repeated the words as if they had been part of a catechism committed to memory, while Olive saw that this mechanical tone was in the nature of a joke that she could not deny herself; they had had that definition so often before, and Miss Chancellor had had occasion so often to remind her what success *really* was. Of course it was easy to prove to her now that Mr. Pardon's glittering bait was a very different thing; was a mere trap and lure, a bribe to vanity and impatience, a device for making her give herself away—let alone fill his pockets while she did so. Olive was conscious enough of the girl's want of continuity; she had seen before how she could be passionately

serious at times, and then perversely, even if innocently, trivial—as just now, when she seemed to wish to convert one of
their most sacred formulas into a pleasantry. She had already
quite recognised, however, that it was not of importance that
Verena should be just like herself; she was all of one piece,
and Verena was of many pieces, which had, where they fitted
together, little capricious chinks, through which mocking inner lights seemed sometimes to gleam. It was a part of Verena's being unlike her that she should feel Mr. Pardon's
promise of eternal excitement to be a brilliant thing, should
indeed consider Mr. Pardon with any tolerance at all. But
Olive tried afresh to allow for such aberrations, as a phase of
youth and suburban culture; the more so that, even when she
tried most, Verena reproached her—so far as Verena's incur-
able softness could reproach—with not allowing enough.
Olive didn't appear to understand that, while Matthias Pardon drew that picture and tried to hold her hand (this image
was unfortunate), she had given one long, fixed, wistful look,
through the door he opened, at the bright tumult of the
world, and then had turned away, solely for her friend's sake,
to an austerer probation and a purer effort; solely for her
friend's, that is, and that of the whole enslaved sisterhood.
The fact remained, at any rate, that Verena had made a sacrifice; and this thought, after a while, gave Olive a greater sense
of security. It seemed almost to seal the future; for Olive
knew that the young interviewer would not easily be shaken
off, and yet she was sure that Verena would never yield to
him.

It was true that at present Mr. Burrage came a great deal
to the little house at Cambridge; Verena told her about that,
told her so much that it was almost as good as if she had told
her all. He came without Mr. Gracie now; he could find his
way alone, and he seemed to wish that there should be no
one else. He had made himself so pleasant to her mother that
she almost always went out of the room; that was the highest
proof Mrs. Tarrant could give of her appreciation of a 'gentle-
man-caller.' They knew everything about him by this time;
that his father was dead, his mother very fashionable and
prominent, and he himself in possession of a handsome patrimony. They thought ever so much of him in New York. He

collected beautiful things, pictures and antiques and objects
that he sent for to Europe on purpose, many of which were
arranged in his rooms at Cambridge. He had intaglios and
Spanish altar-cloths and drawings by the old masters. He was
different from most others; he seemed to want so much to
enjoy life, and to think you easily could if you would only let
yourself go. Of course—judging by what *he* had—he appeared to think you required a great many things to keep you
up. And then Verena told Olive—she could see it was after a
little delay—that he wanted her to come round to his place
and see his treasures. He wanted to show them to her, he was
so sure she would admire them. Verena was sure also, but she
wouldn't go alone, and she wanted Olive to go with her.
They would have tea, and there would be other ladies, and
Olive would tell her what she thought of a life that was so
crowded with beauty. Miss Chancellor made her reflections
on all this, and the first of them was that it was happy for her
that she had determined for the present to accept these accidents, for otherwise might she not now have had a deeper
alarm? She wished to heaven that conceited young men with
time on their hands would leave Verena alone; but evidently
they wouldn't, and her best safety was in seeing as many as
should turn up. If the type should become frequent, she
would very soon judge it. If Olive had not been so grim, she
would have had a smile to spare for the frankness with which
the girl herself adopted this theory. She was eager to explain
that Mr. Burrage didn't seem at all to want what poor Mr.
Pardon had wanted; he made her talk about her views far
more than that gentleman, but gave no sign of offering himself either as a husband or as a lecture-agent. The furthest he
had gone as yet was to tell her that he liked her for the same
reason that he liked old enamels and old embroideries; and
when she said that she didn't see how she resembled such
things, he had replied that it was because she was so peculiar
and so delicate. She might be peculiar, but she had protested
against the idea that she was delicate; it was the last thing
that she wanted to be thought; and Olive could see from this
how far she was from falling in with everything he said.
When Miss Chancellor asked if she respected Mr. Burrage
(and how solemn Olive could make that word she by this

time knew), she answered, with her sweet, vain laugh, but apparently with perfect good faith, that it didn't matter whether she did or not, for what was the whole thing but simply a phase—the very one they had talked about? The sooner she got through it the better, was it not?—and she seemed to think that her transit would be materially quickened by a visit to Mr. Burrage's rooms. As I say, Verena was pleased to regard the phase as quite inevitable, and she had said more than once to Olive that if their struggle was to be with men, the more they knew about them the better. Miss Chancellor asked her why her mother should not go with her to see the curiosities, since she mentioned that their possessor had not neglected to invite Mrs. Tarrant; and Verena said that this, of course, would be very simple—only her mother wouldn't be able to tell her so well as Olive whether she ought to respect Mr. Burrage. This decision as to whether Mr. Burrage should be respected assumed in the life of these two remarkable young women, pitched in so high a moral key, the proportions of a momentous event. Olive shrank at first from facing it—not, indeed, the decision—for we know that her own mind had long since been made up in regard to the quantity of esteem due to almost any member of the other sex—but the incident itself, which, if Mr. Burrage should exasperate her further, might expose her to the danger of appearing to Verena to be unfair to him. It was her belief that he was playing a deeper game than the young Matthias, and she was very willing to watch him; but she thought it prudent not to attempt to cut short the phase (she adopted that classification) prematurely—an imputation she should incur if, without more delay, she were to 'shut down,' as Verena said, on the young connoisseur.

It was settled, therefore, that Mrs. Tarrant should, with her daughter, accept Mr. Burrage's invitation; and in a few days these ladies paid a visit to his apartments. Verena subsequently, of course, had much to say about it, but she dilated even more upon her mother's impressions than upon her own. Mrs. Tarrant had carried away a supply which would last her all winter; there had been some New York ladies present who were 'on' at that moment, and with whom her intercourse was rich in emotions. She had told them all that she should be happy to see them in her home, but they had not yet picked their way along the little planks of the front yard. Mr. Burrage, at all events, had been quite lovely, and had talked about his collections, which were wonderful, in the most interesting manner. Verena inclined to think he was to be respected. He admitted that he was not really studying law at all; he had only come to Cambridge for the form; but she didn't see why it wasn't enough when you made yourself as pleasant as that. She went so far as to ask Olive whether taste and art were not something, and her friend could see that she was certainly very much involved in the phase. Miss Chancellor, of course, had her answer ready. Taste and art were good when they enlarged the mind, not when they narrowed it. Verena assented to this, and said it remained to be seen what effect they had had upon Mr. Burrage—a remark which led Olive to fear that at such a rate much would remain, especially when Verena told her, later, that another visit to the young man's rooms was projected, and that this time she must come, he having expressed the greatest desire for the honour, and her own wish being greater still that they should look at some of his beautiful things together.

A day or two after this, Mr. Henry Burrage left a card at Miss Chancellor's door, with a note in which he expressed the hope that she would take tea with him on a certain day on which he expected the company of his mother. Olive responded to this invitation, in conjunction with Verena; but in doing so she was in the position, singular for her, of not quite understanding what she was about. It seemed to her strange that Verena should urge her to take such a step when she was free to go without her, and it proved two things: first, that she was much interested in Mr. Henry Burrage, and second, that her nature was extraordinarily beautiful. Could anything, in effect, be less underhand than such an indifference to what she supposed to be the best opportunities for carrying on a flirtation? Verena wanted to know the truth, and it was clear that by this time she believed Olive Chancellor to have it, for the most part, in her keeping. Her insistence, therefore, proved, above all, that she cared more for her friend's opinion of Henry Burrage than for her own—a reminder, certainly, of the responsibility that Olive had in-

curred in undertaking to form this generous young mind, and
of the exalted place that she now occupied in it. Such revelations ought to have been satisfactory; if they failed to be completely so, it was only on account of the elder girl's regret that
the subject as to which her judgment was wanted should be
a young man destitute of the worst vices. Henry Burrage had
contributed to throw Miss Chancellor into a 'state,' as these
young ladies called it, the night she met him at Mrs. Tarrant's; but it had none the less been conveyed to Olive by the
voices of the air that he was a gentleman and a good fellow.

This was painfully obvious when the visit to his rooms took
place; he was so good-humoured, so amusing, so friendly and
considerate, so attentive to Miss Chancellor, he did the honours of his bachelor-nest with so easy a grace, that Olive, part
of the time, sat dumbly shaking her conscience, like a watch
that wouldn't go, to make it tell her some better reason why
she shouldn't like him. She saw that there would be no difficulty in disliking his mother; but that, unfortunately, would
not serve her purpose nearly so well. Mrs. Burrage had come
to spend a few days near her son; she was staying at an hotel
in Boston. It presented itself to Olive that after this entertainment it would be an act of courtesy to call upon her; but
here, at least, was the comfort that she could cover herself
with the general absolution extended to the Boston temperament and leave her alone. It was slightly provoking, indeed,
that Mrs. Burrage should have so much the air of a New
Yorker who didn't particularly notice whether a Bostonian
called or not; but there is ever an imperfection, I suppose, in
even the sweetest revenge. She was a woman of society, large
and voluminous, fair (in complexion) and regularly ugly,
looking as if she ought to be slow and rather heavy, but disappointing this expectation by a quick, amused utterance, a
short, bright, summary laugh, with which she appeared to
dispose of the joke (whatever it was) for ever, and an air of
recognising on the instant everything she saw and heard. She
was evidently accustomed to talk, and even to listen, if not
kept waiting too long for details and parentheses; she was not
continuous, but frequent, as it were, and you could see that
she hated explanations, though it was not to be supposed that
she had anything to fear from them. Her favours were

general, not particular; she was civil enough to every one, but
not in any case endearing, and perfectly genial without being
confiding, as people were in Boston when (in moments of
exaltation) they wished to mark that they were not suspicious.
There was something in her whole manner which seemed to
say to Olive that she belonged to a larger world than hers;
and our young lady was vexed at not hearing that she had
lived for a good many years in Europe, as this would have
made it easy to classify her as one of the corrupt. She learned,
almost with a sense of injury, that neither the mother nor the
son had been longer beyond the seas than she herself; and if
they were to be judged as triflers they must be dealt with
individually. Was it an aid to such a judgment to see that Mrs.
Burrage was very much pleased with Boston, with Harvard
College, with her son's interior, with her cup of tea (it was
old Sèvres), which was not half so bad as she had expected,
with the company he had asked to meet her (there were three
or four gentlemen, one of whom was Mr. Gracie), and, last,
not least, with Verena Tarrant, whom she addressed as a celebrity, kindly, cleverly, but without maternal tenderness or
anything to mark the difference in their age? She spoke to her
as if they were equals in that respect, as if Verena's genius and
fame would make up the disparity, and the girl had no need
of encouragement and patronage. She made no direct allusion, however, to her particular views, and asked her no question about her 'gift'—an omission which Verena thought
strange, and, with the most speculative candour, spoke of to
Olive afterwards. Mrs. Burrage seemed to imply that every
one present had some distinction and some talent, that they
were all good company together. There was nothing in her
manner to indicate that she was afraid of Verena on her son's
account; she didn't resemble a person who would like him to
marry the daughter of a mesmeric healer, and yet she appeared to think it charming that he should have such a young
woman there to give gusto to her hour at Cambridge. Poor
Olive was, in the nature of things, entangled in contradictions; she had a horror of the idea of Verena's marrying Mr.
Burrage, and yet she was angry when his mother demeaned
herself as if the little girl with red hair, whose freshness she
enjoyed, could not be a serious danger. She saw all this

through the blur of her shyness, the conscious, anxious silence to which she was so much of the time condemned. It may therefore be imagined how sharp her vision would have been could she only have taken the situation more simply; for she was intelligent enough not to have needed to be morbid, even for purposes of self-defence.

I must add, however, that there was a moment when she came near being happy—or, at any rate, reflected that it was a pity she could not be so. Mrs. Burrage asked her son to play 'some little thing,' and he sat down to his piano and revealed a talent that might well have gratified that lady's pride. Olive was extremely susceptible to music, and it was impossible to her not to be soothed and beguiled by the young man's charming art. One 'little thing' succeeded another; his selections were all very happy. His guests sat scattered in the red firelight, listening, silent, in comfortable attitudes; there was a faint fragrance from the burning logs, which mingled with the perfume of Schubert and Mendelssohn; the covered lamps made a glow here and there, and the cabinets and brackets produced brown shadows, out of which some precious object gleamed—some ivory carving or cinque-cento cup. It was given to Olive, under these circumstances, for half an hour, to surrender herself, to enjoy the music, to admit that Mr. Burrage played with exquisite taste, to feel as if the situation were a kind of truce. Her nerves were calmed, her problems—for the time—subsided. Civilisation, under such an influence, in such a setting, appeared to have done its work; harmony ruled the scene; human life ceased to be a battle. She went so far as to ask herself why one should have a quarrel with it; the relations of men and women, in that picturesque grouping, had not the air of being internecine. In short, she had an interval of unexpected rest, during which she kept her eyes mainly on Verena, who sat near Mrs. Burrage, letting herself go, evidently, more completely than Olive. To her, too, music was a delight, and her listening face turned itself to different parts of the room, unconsciously, while her eyes vaguely rested on the *bibelots* that emerged into the firelight. At moments Mrs. Burrage bent her countenance upon her and smiled, at random, kindly; and then Verena smiled back, while her expression seemed to say that, oh yes, she was giving up everything, all principles, all projects. Even before it was time to go, Olive felt that they were both (Verena and she) quite demoralised, and she only summoned energy to take her companion away when she heard Mrs. Burrage propose to her to come and spend a fortnight in New York. Then Olive exclaimed to herself, 'Is it a plot? Why in the world can't they let her alone?' and prepared to throw a fold of her mantle, as she had done before, over her young friend. Verena answered, somewhat impetuously, that she should be delighted to visit Mrs. Burrage; then checked her impetuosity, after a glance from Olive, by adding that perhaps this lady wouldn't ask her if she knew what strong ground she took on the emancipation of women. Mrs. Burrage looked at her son and laughed; she said she was perfectly aware of Verena's views, and that it was impossible to be more in sympathy with them than she herself. She took the greatest interest in the emancipation of women; she thought there was so much to be done. These were the only remarks that passed in reference to the great subject; and nothing more was said to Verena, either by Henry Burrage or by his friend Gracie, about her addressing the Harvard students. Verena had told her father that Olive had put her veto upon that, and Tarrant had said to the young men that it seemed as if Miss Chancellor was going to put the thing through in her own way. We know that he thought this way very circuitous; but Miss Chancellor made him feel that she was in earnest, and that idea frightened the resistance out of him—it had such terrible associations. The people he had ever seen who were most in earnest were a committee of gentlemen who had investigated the phenomena of the 'materialisation' of spirits, some ten years before, and had bent the fierce light of the scientific method upon him. To Olive it appeared that Mr. Burrage and Mr. Gracie had ceased to be jocular; but that did not make them any less cynical. Henry Burrage said to Verena, as she was going, that he hoped she would think seriously of his mother's invitation; and she replied that she didn't know whether she should have much time in the future to give to people who already approved of her views: she expected to have her hands full with the others, who didn't.

'Does your scheme of work exclude all distraction, all recreation, then?' the young man inquired; and his look expressed real suspense.

Verena referred the matter, as usual, with her air of bright, ungrudging deference, to her companion. 'Does it, should you say—our scheme of work?'

'I am afraid the distraction we have had this afternoon must last us for a long time,' Olive said, without harshness, but with considerable majesty.

'Well, now, *is* he to be respected?' Verena demanded, as the two young women took their way through the early darkness, pacing quietly side by side, in their winter-robes, like women consecrated to some holy office.

Olive turned it over a moment. 'Yes, very much—as a pianist!'

Verena went into town with her in the horse-car—she was staying in Charles Street for a few days—and that evening she startled Olive by breaking out into a reflection very similar to the whimsical falterings of which she herself had been conscious while they sat in Mr. Burrage's pretty rooms, but against which she had now violently reacted.

'It would be very nice to do that always—just to take men as they are, and not to have to think about their badness. It would be very nice not to have so many questions, but to think they were all comfortably answered, so that one could sit there on an old Spanish leather chair, with the curtains drawn and keeping out the cold, the darkness, all the big, terrible, cruel world—sit there and listen for ever to Schubert and Mendelssohn. *They* didn't care anything about female suffrage! And I didn't feel the want of a vote to-day at all, did you?' Verena inquired, ending, as she always ended in these few speculations, with an appeal to Olive.

This young lady thought it necessary to give her a very firm answer. 'I always feel it—everywhere—night and day. I feel it *here*;' and Olive laid her hand solemnly on her heart. 'I feel it as a deep, unforgettable wrong; I feel it as one feels a stain that is on one's honour.'

Verena gave a clear laugh, and after that a soft sigh, and then said, 'Do you know, Olive, I sometimes wonder whether, if it wasn't for you, I should feel it so very much!'

'My own friend,' Olive replied, 'you have never yet said

anything to me which expressed so clearly the closeness and sanctity of our union.'

'You do keep me up,' Verena went on. 'You are my conscience.'

'I should like to be able to say that you are my form—my envelope. But you are too beautiful for that!' So Olive returned her friend's compliment; and later she said that, of course, it would be far easier to give up everything and draw the curtains to and pass one's life in an artificial atmosphere, with rose-coloured lamps. It would be far easier to abandon the struggle, to leave all the unhappy women of the world to their immemorial misery, to lay down one's burden, close one's eyes to the whole dark picture, and, in short, simply expire. To this Verena objected that it would not be easy for her to expire at all; that such an idea was darker than anything the world contained; that she had not done with life yet, and that she didn't mean to allow her responsibilities to crush her. And then the two young women concluded, as they had concluded before, by finding themselves completely, inspiringly in agreement, full of the purpose to live indeed, and with high success; to become great, in order not to be obscure, and powerful, in order not to be useless. Olive had often declared before that her conception of life was as something sublime or as nothing at all. The world was full of evil, but she was glad to have been born before it had been swept away, while it was still there to face, to give one a task and a reward. When the great reforms should be consummated, when the day of justice should have dawned, would not life perhaps be rather poor and pale? She had never pretended to deny that the hope of fame, of the very highest distinction, was one of her strongest incitements; and she held that the most effective way of protesting against the state of bondage of women was for an individual member of the sex to become illustrious. A person who might have overheard some of the talk of this possibly infatuated pair would have been touched by their extreme familiarity with the idea of earthly glory. Verena had not invented it, but she had taken it eagerly from her friend, and she returned it with interest. To Olive it appeared that just this partnership of their two minds—each of them, by itself, lacking an important group of facets—made an organic whole which, for the work in hand, could not fail to be brilliantly effective. Verena was often far more irresponsive than she liked to see her; but the happy thing in her composition was that, after a short contact with the divine idea—Olive was always trying to flash it at her, like a jewel in an uncovered case—she kindled, flamed up, took the words from her friend's less persuasive lips, resolved herself into a magical voice, became again the pure young sibyl. Then Olive perceived how fatally, without Verena's tender notes, her crusade would lack sweetness, what the Catholics call unction; and, on the other hand, how weak Verena would be on the statistical and logical side if she herself should not bring up the rear. Together, in short, they would be complete, they would have everything, and together they would triumph.

XIX

THIS IDEA of their triumph, a triumph as yet ultimate and remote, but preceded by the solemn vista of an effort so religious as never to be wanting in ecstasy, became tremendously familiar to the two friends, but especially to Olive, during the winter of 187–, a season which ushered in the most momentous period of Miss Chancellor's life. About Christmas a step was taken which advanced her affairs immensely, and put them, to her apprehension, on a regular footing. This consisted in Verena's coming in to Charles Street to stay with her, in pursuance of an arrangement on Olive's part with Selah Tarrant and his wife that she should remain for many months. The coast was now perfectly clear. Mrs. Farrinder had started on her annual grand tour; she was rousing the people, from Maine to Texas; Matthias Pardon (it was to be supposed) had received, temporarily at least, his quietus; and Mrs. Luna was established in New York, where she had taken a house for a year, and whence she wrote to her sister that she was going to engage Basil Ransom (with whom she was in communication for this purpose) to do her law-business. Olive wondered what law-business Adeline could have, and hoped she would get into a pickle with her landlord or her milliner, so that repeated interviews with Mr. Ransom might become necessary. Mrs. Luna let her know very soon that these interviews had begun; the young Mississippian had come to dine with her; he hadn't got started much, by what she could make out, and she was even afraid that he didn't dine every day. But he wore a tall hat now, like a Northern gentleman, and Adeline intimated that she found him really attractive. He had been very nice to Newton, told him all about the war (quite the Southern version, of course, but Mrs. Luna didn't care anything about American politics, and she wanted her son to know all sides), and Newton did nothing but talk about him, calling him 'Rannie,' and imitating his pronunciation of certain words. Adeline subsequently wrote that she had made up her mind to put her affairs into his hands (Olive sighed, not unmagnanimously, as she thought of her sister's 'affairs'), and later still she mentioned that she was thinking strongly of taking him to be Newton's tutor. She wished this interesting child to be privately educated, and it would be more agreeable to have in that relation a person who was already, as it were, a member of the family. Mrs. Luna wrote as if he were prepared to give up his profession to take charge of her son, and Olive was pretty sure that this was only a part of her grandeur, of the habit she had contracted, especially since living in Europe, of speaking as if in every case she required special arrangements.

In spite of the difference in their age, Olive had long since judged her, and made up her mind that Adeline lacked every quality that a person needed to be interesting in her eyes. She was rich (or sufficiently so), she was conventional and timid, very fond of attentions from men (with whom indeed she was reputed bold, but Olive scorned such boldness as that), given up to a merely personal, egotistical, instinctive life, and as unconscious of the tendencies of the age, the revenges of the future, the new truths and the great social questions, as if she had been a mere bundle of dress-trimmings, which she very nearly was. It was perfectly observable that she had no conscience, and it irritated Olive deeply to see how much trouble a woman was spared when she was constructed on that system. Adeline's 'affairs,' as I have intimated, her social relations, her views of Newton's education, her practice and her theory (for she had plenty of that, such as it was, heaven save the mark!), her spasmodic disposition to marry again, and her still sillier retreats in the presence of danger (for she had not even the courage of her frivolity), these things had been a subject of tragic consideration to Olive ever since the return of the elder sister to America. The tragedy was not in any particular harm that Mrs. Luna could do her (for she did her good, rather, that is, she did her honour, by laughing at her), but in the spectacle itself, the drama, guided by the hand of fate, of which the small, ignoble scenes unrolled themselves so logically. The *dénouement* would of course be in keeping, and would consist simply of the spiritual death of Mrs. Luna, who would end by understanding no common speech of Olive's at all, and would sink into mere worldly plumpness, into the last complacency, the supreme imbecility, of petty, genteel conservatism. As for Newton, he would be more

utterly odious, if possible, as he grew up, than he was already;
in fact, he would not grow up at all, but only grow down, if
his mother should continue her infatuated system with him.
He was insufferably forward and selfish; under the pretext of
keeping him, at any cost, refined, Adeline had coddled and
caressed him, having him always in her petticoats, remitting
his lessons when he pretended he had an earache, drawing
him into the conversation, letting him answer her back, with
an impertinence beyond his years, when she administered the
smallest check. The place for him, in Olive's eyes, was one of
the public schools, where the children of the people would
teach him his small importance, teach it, if necessary, by the
aid of an occasional drubbing; and the two ladies had a grand
discussion on this point before Mrs. Luna left Boston—a
scene which ended in Adeline's clutching the irrepressible
Newton to her bosom (he came in at the moment), and demanding of him a vow that he would live and die in the principles of his mother. Mrs. Luna declared that if she must be
trampled upon—and very likely it was her fate!—she would
rather be trampled upon by men than by women, and that if
Olive and her friends should get possession of the government they would be worse despots than those who were celebrated in history. Newton took an infant oath that he would
never be a destructive, impious radical, and Olive felt that
after this she needn't trouble herself any more about her sister, whom she simply committed to her fate. That fate might
very properly be to marry an enemy of her country, a man
who, no doubt, desired to treat women with the lash and
manacles, as he and his people had formerly treated the
wretched coloured race. If she was so fond of the fine old
institutions of the past, he would supply them to her in abundance; and if she wanted so much to be a conservative, she
could try first how she liked being a conservative's wife. If
Olive troubled herself little about Adeline, she troubled herself more about Basil Ransom; she said to herself that since
he hated women who respected themselves (and each other),
destiny would use him rightly in hanging a person like Adeline round his neck. That would be the way poetic justice
ought to work, for him—and the law that our prejudices,
when they act themselves out, punish us in doing so. Olive

considered all this, as it was her effort to consider everything, from a very high point of view, and ended by feeling sure it was not for the sake of any nervous personal security that she desired to see her two relations in New York get mixed up together. If such an event as their marriage would gratify her sense of fitness, it would be simply as an illustration of certain laws. Olive, thanks to the philosophic cast of her mind, was exceedingly fond of illustrations of laws.

I hardly know, however, what illumination it was that sprang from her consciousness (now a source of considerable comfort), that Mrs. Farrinder was carrying the war into distant territories, and would return to Boston only in time to preside at a grand Female Convention, already advertised to take place in Boston in the month of June. It was agreeable to her that this imperial woman should be away; it made the field more free, the air more light; it suggested an exemption from official criticism. I have not taken space to mention certain episodes of the more recent intercourse of these ladies, and must content myself with tracing them, lightly, in their consequences. These may be summed up in the remark, which will doubtless startle no one by its freshness, that two imperial women are scarcely more likely to hit it off together, as the phrase is, than two imperial men. Since that party at Miss Birdseye's, so important in its results for Olive, she had had occasion to approach Mrs. Farrinder more nearly, and those overtures brought forth the knowledge that the great leader of the feminine revolution was the one person (in that part of the world) more concentrated, more determined, than herself. Miss Chancellor's aspirations, of late, had been immensely quickened; she had begun to believe in herself to a livelier tune than she had ever listened to before; and she now perceived that when spirit meets spirit there must either be mutual absorption or a sharp concussion. It had long been familiar to her that she should have to count with the obstinacy of the world at large, but she now discovered that she should have to count also with certain elements in the feminine camp. This complicated the problem, and such a complication, naturally, could not make Mrs. Farrinder appear more easy to assimilate. If Olive's was a high nature and so was hers, the fault was in neither; it was only an admonition that they were not needed as landmarks in the same part of the field. If such perceptions are delicate as between men, the reader need not be reminded of the exquisite form they may assume in natures more refined. So it was that Olive passed, in three months, from the stage of veneration to that of competition; and the process had been accelerated by the introduction of Verena into the fold. Mrs. Farrinder had behaved in the strangest way about Verena. First she had been struck with her, and then she hadn't; first she had seemed to want to take her in, then she had shied at her unmistakably—intimating to Olive that there were enough of that kind already. Of 'that kind' indeed!—the phrase reverberated in Miss Chancellor's resentful soul. Was it possible she didn't know the kind Verena was of, and with what vulgar aspirants to notoriety did she confound her? It had been Olive's original desire to obtain Mrs. Farrinder's stamp for her *protégée*; she wished her to hold a commission from the commander-in-chief. With this view the two young women had made more than one pilgrimage to Roxbury, and on one of these occasions the sibylline mood (in its most charming form) had descended upon Verena. She had fallen into it, naturally and gracefully, in the course of talk, and poured out a stream of eloquence even more touching than her regular discourse at Miss Birdseye's. Mrs. Farrinder had taken it rather drily, and certainly it didn't resemble her own style of oratory, remarkable and cogent as this was. There had been considerable question of her writing a letter to the New York 'Tribune,' the effect of which should be to launch Miss Tarrant into renown; but this beneficent epistle never appeared, and now Olive saw that there was no favour to come from the prophetess of Roxbury. There had been primnesses, pruderies, small reserves, which ended by staying her pen. If Olive didn't say at once that she was jealous of Verena's more attractive manner, it was only because such a declaration was destined to produce more effect a little later. What she did say was that evidently Mrs. Farrinder wanted to keep the movement in her own hands—viewed with suspicion certain romantic, æsthetic elements which Olive and Verena seemed to be trying to introduce into it. They insisted so much, for instance, on the historic unhappiness of women; but Mrs. Farrinder didn't appear to care anything for that, or indeed to know much about history at all. She seemed to begin just to-day, and she demanded their rights for them whether they were unhappy or not. The upshot of this was that Olive threw herself on Verena's neck with a movement which was half indignation, half rapture; she exclaimed that they would have to fight the battle without human help, but, after all, it was better so. If they were all in all to each other, what more could they want? They would be isolated, but they would be free; and this view of the situation brought with it a feeling that they had almost already begun to be a force. It was not, indeed, that Olive's resentment faded quite away; for not only had she the sense, doubtless very presumptuous, that Mrs. Farrinder was the only person thereabouts of a stature to judge her (a sufficient cause of antagonism in itself, for if we like to be praised by our betters we prefer that censure should come from the other sort), but the kind of opinion she had unexpectedly betrayed, after implying such esteem in the earlier phase of their intercourse, made Olive's cheeks occasionally flush. She prayed heaven that *she* might never become so personal, so narrow. She was frivolous, worldly, an amateur, a trifler, a frequenter of Beacon Street; her taking up Verena Tarrant was only a kind of elderly, ridiculous doll-dressing: this was the light in which Miss Chancellor had reason to believe that it now suited Mrs. Farrinder to regard her! It was fortunate, perhaps, that the misrepresentation was so gross; yet, none the less, tears of wrath rose more than once to Olive's eyes when she reflected that this particular wrong had been put upon her. Frivolous, worldly, Beacon Street! She appealed to Verena to share in her pledge that the world should know in due time how much of that sort of thing there was about her. As I have already hinted, Verena at such moments quite rose to the occasion; she had private pangs at committing herself to give the cold shoulder to Beacon Street for ever; but she was now so completely in Olive's hands that there was no sacrifice to which she would not have consented in order to prove that her benefactress was not frivolous.

The matter of her coming to stay for so long in Charles Street was arranged during a visit that Selah Tarrant paid there at Miss Chancellor's request. This interview, which had some curious features, would be worth describing, but I am forbidden to do more than mention the most striking of these. Olive wished to have an understanding with him; wished the situation to be clear, so that, disagreeable as it would be to her to receive him, she sent him a summons for a certain hour—an hour at which she had planned that Verena should be out of the house. She withheld this incident from the girl's knowledge, reflecting with some solemnity that it was the first deception (for Olive her silence was a deception) that she had yet practised on her friend, and wondering whether she should have to practise others in the future. She then and there made up her mind that she would not shrink from others should they be necessary. She notified Tarrant that she should keep Verena a long time, and Tarrant remarked that it was certainly very pleasant to see her so happily located. But he also intimated that he should like to know what Miss Chancellor laid out to do with her; and the tone of this suggestion made Olive feel how right she had been to foresee that their interview would have the stamp of business. It assumed that complexion very definitely when she crossed over to her desk and wrote Mr. Tarrant a cheque for a very considerable amount. 'Leave us alone—entirely alone—for a year, and then I will write you another:' it was with these words she handed him the little strip of paper that meant so much, feeling, as she did so, that surely Mrs. Farrinder herself could not be less amateurish than that. Selah looked at the cheque, at Miss Chancellor, at the cheque again, at the ceiling, at the floor, at the clock, and once more at his hostess; then the document disappeared beneath the folds of his waterproof, and she saw that he was putting it into some queer place on his queer person. 'Well, if I didn't believe you were going to help her to develop,' he remarked; and he stopped, while his hands continued to fumble, out of sight, and he treated Olive to his large joyless smile. She assured him that he need have no fear on that score; Verena's development was the thing in the world in which she took most interest; she should have every opportunity for a free expansion. 'Yes, that's the great thing,' Selah said; 'it's more important than attracting a crowd. That's all we shall ask of you; let her act out her nature. Don't all the trouble of humanity come from our being pressed back? Don't shut down the cover, Miss Chancellor; just let her overflow!' And again Tarrant illuminated his inquiry, his metaphor, by the strange and silent lateral movement of his jaws. He added, presently, that he supposed he should have to fix it with Mis' Tarrant; but Olive made no answer to that; she only looked at him with a face in which she intended to express that there was nothing that need detain him longer. She knew it had been fixed with Mrs. Tarrant; she had been over all that with Verena, who had told her that her mother was willing to sacrifice her for her highest good. She had reason to know (not through Verena, of course), that Mrs. Tarrant had embraced, tenderly, the idea of a pecuniary compensation, and there was no fear of her making a scene when Tarrant should come back with a cheque in his pocket. 'Well, I trust she *may* develop, richly, and that you may accomplish what you desire; it seems as if we had only a little way to go further,' that worthy observed, as he erected himself for departure.

'It's not a little way; it's a very long way,' Olive replied, rather sternly.

Tarrant was on the threshold; he lingered a little, embarrassed by her grimness, for he himself had always inclined to rose-coloured views of progress, of the march of truth. He had never met any one so much in earnest as this definite, literal young woman, who had taken such an unhoped-for fancy to his daughter; whose longing for the new day had such perversities of pessimism, and who, in the midst of something that appeared to be terribly searching in her honesty, was willing to corrupt him, as a father, with the most extravagant orders on her bank. He hardly knew in what language to speak to her; it seemed as if there was nothing soothing enough, when a lady adopted that tone about a movement which was thought by some of the brightest to be so promising. 'Oh, well, I guess there's some kind of mysterious law . . .' he murmured, almost timidly; and so he passed from Miss Chancellor's sight.

XX

S HE HOPED she should not soon see him again, and there appeared to be no reason she should, if their intercourse was to be conducted by means of cheques. The understanding with Verena was, of course, complete; she had promised to stay with her friend as long as her friend should require it. She had said at first that she couldn't give up her mother, but she had been made to feel that there was no question of giving up. She should be as free as air, to go and come; she could spend hours and days with her mother, whenever Mrs. Tarrant required her attention; all that Olive asked of her was that, for the time, she should regard Charles Street as her home. There was no struggle about this, for the simple reason that by the time the question came to the front Verena was completely under the charm. The idea of Olive's charm will perhaps make the reader smile; but I use the word not in its derived, but in its literal sense. The fine web of authority, of dependence, that her strenuous companion had woven about her, was now as dense as a suit of golden mail; and Verena was thoroughly interested in their great undertaking; she saw it in the light of an active, enthusiastic faith. The benefit that her father desired for her was now assured; she expanded, developed, on the most liberal scale. Olive saw the difference, and you may imagine how she rejoiced in it; she had never known a greater pleasure. Verena's former attitude had been girlish submission, grateful, curious sympathy. She had given herself, in her young, amused surprise, because Olive's stronger will and the incisive proceedings with which she pointed her purpose drew her on. Besides, she was held by hospitality, the vision of new social horizons, the sense of novelty, and the love of change. But now the girl was disinterestedly attached to the precious things they were to do together; she cared about them for themselves, believed in them ardently, had them constantly in mind. Her share in the union of the two young women was no longer passive, purely appreciative; it was passionate, too, and it put forth a beautiful energy. If Olive desired to get Verena into training, she could flatter herself that the process had already begun, and

that her colleague enjoyed it almost as much as she. Therefore
she could say to herself, without the imputation of heartless-
ness, that when she left her mother it was for a noble, a sacred
use. In point of fact, she left her very little, and she spent
hours in jingling, aching, jostled journeys between Charles
Street and the stale suburban cottage. Mrs. Tarrant sighed and
grimaced, wrapped herself more than ever in her mantle, said
she didn't know as she was fit to struggle alone, and that, half
the time, if Verena was away, she wouldn't have the nerve to
answer the door-bell; she was incapable, of course, of neglecting such an opportunity to posture as one who paid with her
heart's blood for leading the van of human progress. But Verena had an inner sense (she judged her mother now, a little,
for the first time), that she would be sorry to be taken at her
word and that she felt safe enough in trusting to her daughter's generosity. She could not divest herself of the faith—
even now that Mrs. Luna was gone, leaving no trace, and the
gray walls of a sedentary winter were apparently closing about
the two young women—she could not renounce the theory
that a residence in Charles Street must at least produce some
contact with the brilliant classes. She was vexed at her daughter's resignation to not going to parties and to Miss Chancellor's not giving them; but it was nothing new for her to have
to practise patience, and she could feel, at least, that it was
just as handy for Mr. Burrage to call on the child in town,
where he spent half his time, sleeping constantly at Parker's.

It was a fact that this fortunate youth called very often, and
Verena saw him with Olive's full concurrence whenever she
was at home. It had now been quite agreed between them
that no artificial limits should be set to the famous phase; and
Olive had, while it lasted, a sense of real heroism in steeling
herself against uneasiness. It seemed to her, moreover, only
justice that she should make some concession; if Verena made
a great sacrifice of filial duty in coming to live with her (this,
of course, should be permanent—she would buy off the Tarrants from year to year), she must not incur the imputation
(the world would judge her, in that case, ferociously) of keeping her from forming common social ties. The friendship of
a young man and a young woman was, according to the pure
code of New England, a common social tie; and as the weeks

elapsed Miss Chancellor saw no reason to repent of her temerity. Verena was not falling in love; she felt that she should
know it, should guess it on the spot. Verena was fond of human intercourse; she was essentially a sociable creature; she
liked to shine and smile and talk and listen; and so far as
Henry Burrage was concerned he introduced an element of
easy and convenient relaxation into a life now a good deal
stiffened (Olive was perfectly willing to own it) by great civic
purposes. But the girl was being saved, without interference,
by the simple operation of her interest in those very designs.
From this time there was no need of putting pressure on her;
her own springs were working; the fire with which she
glowed came from within. Sacredly, brightly single she would
remain; her only espousals would be at the altar of a great
cause. Olive always absented herself when Mr. Burrage was
announced; and when Verena afterwards attempted to give
some account of his conversation she checked her, said she
would rather know nothing about it—all with a very solemn
mildness; this made her feel very superior, truly noble. She
knew by this time (I scarcely can tell how, since Verena could
give her no report), exactly what sort of a youth Mr. Burrage
was: he was weakly pretentious, softly original, cultivated ec-
centricity, patronised progress, liked to have mysteries, sudden appointments to keep, anonymous persons to visit, the
air of leading a double life, of being devoted to a girl whom
people didn't know, or at least didn't meet. Of course he liked
to make an impression on Verena; but what he mainly liked
was to play her off upon the other girls, the daughters of
fashion, with whom he danced at Papanti's. Such were the
images that proceeded from Olive's rich moral consciousness.
'Well, he *is* greatly interested in our movement:' so much Verena once managed to announce; but the words rather irritated
Miss Chancellor, who, as we know, did not care to allow for
accidental exceptions in the great masculine conspiracy.

In the month of March Verena told her that Mr. Burrage
was offering matrimony—offering it with much insistence,
begging that she would at least wait and think of it before
giving him a final answer. Verena was evidently very glad to
be able to say to Olive that she had assured him she couldn't
think of it, and that if he expected this he had better not come

any more. He continued to come, and it was therefore to be supposed that he had ceased to count on such a concession; it was now Olive's opinion that he really didn't desire it. She had a theory that he proposed to almost any girl who was not likely to accept him—did it because he was making a collection of such episodes—a mental album of declarations, blushes, hesitations, refusals that just missed imposing themselves as acceptances, quite as he collected enamels and Cremona violins. He would be very sorry indeed to ally himself to the house of Tarrant; but such a fear didn't prevent him from holding it becoming in a man of taste to give that encouragement to low-born girls who were pretty, for one looked out for the special cases in which, for reasons (even the lowest might have reasons), they wouldn't 'rise.' 'I told you I wouldn't marry him, and I won't,' Verena said, delightedly, to her friend; her tone suggested that a certain credit belonged to her for the way she carried out her assurance. 'I never thought you would, if you didn't want to,' Olive replied to this; and Verena could have no rejoinder but the good-humour that sat in her eyes, unable as she was to say that she had wanted to. They had a little discussion, however, when she intimated that she pitied him for his discomfiture, Olive's contention being that, selfish, conceited, pampered and insincere, he might properly be left now to digest his affront. Miss Chancellor felt none of the remorse now that she would have felt six months before at standing in the way of such a chance for Verena, and she would have been very angry if any one had asked her if she were not afraid of taking too much upon herself. She would have said, moreover, that she stood in no one's way, and that even if she were not there Verena would never think seriously of a frivolous little man who fiddled while Rome was burning. This did not prevent Olive from making up her mind that they had better go to Europe in the spring; a year's residence in that quarter of the globe would be highly agreeable to Verena, and might even contribute to the evolution of her genius. It cost Miss Chancellor an effort to admit that any virtue still lingered in the elder world, and that it could have any important lesson for two such good Americans as her friend and herself; but it suited her just then to make this assumption, which was not altogether sincere. It was recommended by the idea that it would get her companion out of the way—out of the way of officious fellow-citizens—till she should be absolutely firm on her feet, and would also give greater intensity to their own long conversation. On that continent of strangers they would cleave more closely still to each other. This, of course, would be to fly before the inevitable 'phase,' much more than to face it; but Olive decided that if they should reach unscathed the term of their delay (the first of July) she should have faced it as much as either justice or generosity demanded. I may as well say at once that she traversed most of this period without further serious alarms and with a great many little thrills of bliss and hope.

Nothing happened to dissipate the good omens with which her partnership with Verena Tarrant was at present surrounded. They threw themselves into study; they had innumerable big books from the Athenæum, and consumed the midnight oil. Henry Burrage, after Verena had shaken her head at him so sweetly and sadly, returned to New York, giving no sign; they only heard that he had taken refuge under the ruffled maternal wing. (Olive, at least, took for granted the wing was ruffled; she could fancy how Mrs. Burrage would be affected by the knowledge that her son had been refused by the daughter of a mesmeric healer. She would be almost as angry as if she had learnt that he had been accepted.) Matthias Pardon had not yet taken his revenge in the newspapers; he was perhaps nursing his thunderbolts; at any rate, now that the operatic season had begun, he was much occupied in interviewing the principal singers, one of whom he described in one of the leading journals (Olive, at least, was sure it was only he who could write like that), as 'a dear little woman with baby dimples and kittenish movements.' The Tarrants were apparently given up to a measure of sensual ease with which they had not hitherto been familiar, thanks to the increase of income that they drew from their eccentric protectress. Mrs. Tarrant now enjoyed the ministrations of a 'girl'; it was partly her pride (at any rate, she chose to give it this turn), that her house had for many years been conducted without the element—so debasing on both sides—of servile, mercenary labour. She wrote to Olive (she was perpetually writing to her now, but Olive never answered), that she was conscious of having fallen to a lower plane, but she admitted that it was a prop to her wasted spirit to have some one to converse with when Selah was off. Verena, of course, perceived the difference, which was inadequately explained by the theory of a sudden increase of her father's practice (nothing of her father's had ever increased like that), and ended by guessing the cause of it—a discovery which did not in the least disturb her equanimity. She accepted the idea that her parents should receive a pecuniary tribute from the extraordinary friend whom she had encountered on the threshold of womanhood, just as she herself accepted that friend's irresistible hospitality. She had no worldly pride, no traditions of independence, no ideas of what was done and what was not done; but there was only one thing that equalled this perfectly gentle and natural insensibility to favours—namely, the inveteracy of her habit of not asking them. Olive had had an apprehension that she would flush a little at learning the terms on which they should now be able to pursue their career together; but Verena never changed colour; it was either not new or not disagreeable to her that the authors of her being should be bought off, silenced by money, treated as the troublesome of the lower orders are treated when they are not locked up; so that her friend had a perception, after this, that it would probably be impossible in any way ever to offend her. She was too rancourless, too detached from conventional standards, too free from private self-reference. It was too much to say of her that she forgave injuries, since she was not conscious of them; there was in forgiveness a certain arrogance of which she was incapable, and her bright mildness glided over the many traps that life sets for our consistency. Olive had always held that pride was necessary to character, but there was no peculiarity of Verena's that could make her spirit seem less pure. The added luxuries in the little house at Cambridge, which even with their help was still such a penal settlement, made her feel afresh that before she came to the rescue the daughter of that house had traversed a desert of sordid misery. She had cooked and washed and swept and stitched; she had worked harder than any of Miss Chancellor's servants. These things had left

no trace upon her person or her mind; everything fresh and
fair renewed itself in her with extraordinary facility, everything ugly and tiresome evaporated as soon as it touched her;
but Olive deemed that, being what she was, she had a right
to immense compensations. In the future she should have exceeding luxury and ease, and Miss Chancellor had no difficulty in persuading herself that persons doing the high
intellectual and moral work to which the two young ladies in
Charles Street were now committed owed it to themselves,
owed it to the groaning sisterhood, to cultivate the best material conditions. She herself was nothing of a sybarite, and
she had proved, visiting the alleys and slums of Boston in the
service of the Associated Charities, that there was no foulness
of disease or misery she feared to look in the face; but her
house had always been thoroughly well regulated, she was
passionately clean, and she was an excellent woman of business. Now, however, she elevated daintiness to a religion; her
interior shone with superfluous friction, with punctuality,
with winter roses. Among these soft influences Verena herself
bloomed like the flower that attains such perfection in Boston. Olive had always rated high the native refinement of her
countrywomen, their latent 'adaptability,' their talent for accommodating themselves at a glance to changed conditions;
but the way her companion rose with the level of the civilisation that surrounded her, the way she assimilated all deli-
cacies and absorbed all traditions, left this friendly theory
halting behind. The winter days were still, indoors, in Charles
Street, and the winter nights secure from interruption. Our
two young women had plenty of duties, but Olive had never
favoured the custom of running in and out. Much conference
on social and reformatory topics went forward under her
roof, and she received her colleagues—she belonged to
twenty associations and committees—only at preappointed
hours, which she expected them to observe rigidly. Verena's
share in these proceedings was not active; she hovered over
them, smiling, listening, dropping occasionally a fanciful
though never an idle word, like some gently animated image
placed there for good omen. It was understood that her
part was before the scenes, not behind; that she was not a
prompter, but (potentially, at least) a 'popular favourite,' and

that the work over which Miss Chancellor presided so effi-
ciently was a general preparation of the platform on which,
later, her companion would execute the most striking steps.

The western windows of Olive's drawing-room, looking
over the water, took in the red sunsets of winter; the long,
low bridge that crawled, on its staggering posts, across the
Charles; the casual patches of ice and snow; the desolate suburban horizons, peeled and made bald by the rigour of the
season; the general hard, cold void of the prospect; the extru-
sion, at Charlestown, at Cambridge, of a few chimneys and
steeples, straight, sordid tubes of factories and engine-shops,
or spare, heavenward finger of the New England meeting-
house. There was something inexorable in the poverty of the
scene, shameful in the meanness of its details, which gave a
collective impression of boards and tin and frozen earth,
sheds and rotting piles, railway-lines striding flat across a
thoroughfare of puddles, and tracks of the humbler, the universal horse-car, traversing obliquely this path of danger;
loose fences, vacant lots, mounds of refuse, yards bestrewn
with iron pipes, telegraph poles, and bare wooden backs of
places. Verena thought such a view lovely, and she was by no
means without excuse when, as the afternoon closed, the ugly
picture was tinted with a clear, cold rosiness. The air, in its
windless chill, seemed to tinkle like a crystal, the faintest gradations of tone were perceptible in the sky, the west became
deep and delicate, everything grew doubly distinct before taking on the dimness of evening. There were pink flushes on
snow, 'tender' reflections in patches of stiffened marsh,
sounds of car-bells, no longer vulgar, but almost silvery, on
the long bridge, lonely outlines of distant dusky undulations
against the fading glow. These agreeable effects used to light
up that end of the drawing-room, and Olive often sat at the
window with her companion before it was time for the lamp.
They admired the sunsets, they rejoiced in the ruddy spots
projected upon the parlour-wall, they followed the darkening
perspective in fanciful excursions. They watched the stellar
points come out at last in a colder heaven, and then, shuddering a little, arm in arm, they turned away, with a sense that
the winter night was even more cruel than the tyranny of
men—turned back to drawn curtains and a brighter fire and

a glittering tea-tray and more and more talk about the long martyrdom of women, a subject as to which Olive was inexhaustible and really most interesting. There were some nights of deep snowfall, when Charles Street was white and muffled and the door-bell foredoomed to silence, which seemed little islands of lamplight, of enlarged and intensified vision. They read a great deal of history together, and read it ever with the same thought—that of finding confirmation in it for this idea that their sex had suffered inexpressibly, and that at any moment in the course of human affairs the state of the world would have been so much less horrible (history seemed to them in every way horrible), if women had been able to press down the scale. Verena was full of suggestions which stimulated discussion; it was she, oftenest, who kept in view the fact that a good many women in the past had been intrusted with power and had not always used it amiably, who brought up the wicked queens, the profligate mistresses of kings. These ladies were easily disposed of between the two, and the public crimes of Bloody Mary, the private misdemeanours of Faustina, wife of the pure Marcus Aurelius, were very satisfactorily classified. If the influence of women in the past accounted for every act of virtue that men had happened to achieve, it only made the matter balance properly that the influence of men should explain the casual irregularities of the other sex. Olive could see how few books had passed through Verena's hands, and how little the home of the Tarrants had been a house of reading; but the girl now traversed the fields of literature with her characteristic lightness of step. Everything she turned to or took up became an illustration of the facility, the 'giftedness,' which Olive, who had so little of it, never ceased to wonder at and prize. Nothing frightened her; she always smiled at it, she could do anything she tried. As she knew how to do other things, she knew how to study; she read quickly and remembered infallibly; could repeat, days afterward, passages that she appeared only to have glanced at. Olive, of course, was more and more happy to think that their cause should have the services of an organisation so rare.

All this doubtless sounds rather dry, and I hasten to add that our friends were not always shut up in Miss Chancellor's strenuous parlour. In spite of Olive's desire to keep her precious inmate to herself and to bend her attention upon their common studies, in spite of her constantly reminding Verena that this winter was to be purely educative and that the platitudes of the satisfied and unregenerate would have little to teach her, in spite, in short, of the severe and constant duality of our young women, it must not be supposed that their life had not many personal confluents and tributaries. Individual and original as Miss Chancellor was universally acknowledged to be, she was yet a typical Bostonian, and as a typical Bostonian she could not fail to belong in some degree to a 'set.' It had been said of her that she was in it but not of it; but she was of it enough to go occasionally into other houses and to receive their occupants in her own. It was her belief that she filled her tea-pot with the spoon of hospitality, and made a good many select spirits feel that they were welcome under her roof at convenient hours. She had a preference for what she called *real* people, and there were several whose reality she had tested by arts known to herself. This little society was rather suburban and miscellaneous; it was prolific in ladies who trotted about, early and late, with books from the Athenæum nursed behind their muff, or little nosegays of exquisite flowers that they were carrying as presents to each other. Verena, who, when Olive was not with her, indulged in a good deal of desultory contemplation at the window, saw them pass the house in Charles Street, always apparently straining a little, as if they might be too late for something. At almost any time, for she envied their preoccupation, she would have taken the chance with them. Very often, when she described them to her mother, Mrs. Tarrant didn't know who they were; there were even days (she had so many discouragements) when it seemed as if she didn't want to know. So long as they were not some one else, it seemed to be no use that they were themselves; whoever they were, they were sure to have that defect. Even after all her mother's disquisitions Verena had but vague ideas as to whom she would have liked them to be; and it was only when the girl talked of the concerts, to all of which Olive subscribed and conducted her inseparable friend, that Mrs. Tarrant appeared to feel in any degree that her daughter was living up to the standard formed for her in their Cambridge home. As all the world knows, the opportunities in Boston for hearing good music are numerous and excellent, and it had long been Miss Chancellor's practice to cultivate the best. She went in, as the phrase is, for the superior programmes, and that high, dim, dignified Music Hall, which has echoed in its time to so much eloquence and so much melody, and of which the very proportions and colour seem to teach respect and attention, shed the protection of its illuminated cornice, this winter, upon no faces more intelligently upturned than those of the young women for whom Bach and Beethoven only repeated, in a myriad forms, the idea that was always with them. Symphonies and fugues only stimulated their convictions, excited their revolutionary passion, led their imagination further in the direction in which it was always pressing. It lifted them to immeasurable heights; and as they sat looking at the great florid, sombre organ, overhanging the bronze statue of Beethoven, they felt that this was the only temple in which the votaries of their creed could worship.

And yet their music was not their greatest joy, for they had two others which they cultivated at least as zealously. One of these was simply the society of old Miss Birdseye, of whom Olive saw more this winter than she had ever seen before. It had become apparent that her long and beautiful career was drawing to a close, her earnest, unremitting work was over, her old-fashioned weapons were broken and dull. Olive would have liked to hang them up as venerable relics of a patient fight, and this was what she seemed to do when she made the poor lady relate her battles—never glorious and brilliant, but obscure and wastefully heroic—call back the figures of her companions in arms, exhibit her medals and scars. Miss Birdseye knew that her uses were ended; she might pretend still to go about the business of unpopular causes, might fumble for papers in her immemorial satchel and think she had important appointments, might sign petitions, attend conventions, say to Doctor Prance that if she would only make her sleep she should live to see a great many improvements yet; she ached and was weary, growing almost as glad to look back (a great anomaly for Miss Birdseye) as to look forward. She let herself be coddled now by her friends of the

new generation; there were days when she seemed to want
nothing better than to sit by Olive's fire and ramble on about
the old struggles, with a vague, comfortable sense—no physical rapture of Miss Birdseye's could be very acute—of immunity from wet feet, from the draughts that prevail at thin
meetings, of independence of street-cars that would probably
arrive overflowing; and also a pleased perception, not that she
was an example to these fresh lives which began with more
advantages than hers, but that she was in some degree an
encouragement, as she helped them to measure the way the
new truths had advanced—being able to tell them of such a
different state of things when she was a young lady, the
daughter of a very talented teacher (indeed her mother had
been a teacher too), down in Connecticut. She had always
had for Olive a kind of aroma of martyrdom, and her battered, unremunerated, unpensioned old age brought angry
tears, springing from depths of outraged theory, into Miss
Chancellor's eyes. For Verena, too, she was a picturesque humanitary figure. Verena had been in the habit of meeting mar-
tyrs from her childhood up, but she had seen none with so
many reminiscences as Miss Birdseye, or who had been so
nearly scorched by penal fires. She had had escapes, in the
early days of abolitionism, which it was a marvel she could
tell with so little implication that she had shown courage. She
had roamed through certain parts of the South, carrying the
Bible to the slave; and more than one of her companions, in
the course of these expeditions, had been tarred and feathered. She herself, at one season, had spent a month in a Geor-
gian jail. She had preached temperance in Irish circles where
the doctrine was received with missiles; she had interfered between wives and husbands mad with drink; she had taken
filthy children, picked up in the street, to her own poor
rooms, and had removed their pestilent rags and washed their
sore bodies with slippery little hands. In her own person she
appeared to Olive and Verena a representative of suffering
humanity; the pity they felt for her was part of their pity for
all who were weakest and most hardly used; and it struck
Miss Chancellor (more especially) that this frumpy little mis-
sionary was the last link in a tradition, and that when she
should be called away the heroic age of New England life—

the age of plain living and high thinking, of pure ideals and earnest effort, of moral passion and noble experiment— would effectually be closed. It was the perennial freshness of Miss Birdseye's faith that had had such a contagion for these modern maidens, the unquenched flame of her transcendentalism, the simplicity of her vision, the way in which, in spite of mistakes, deceptions, the changing fashions of reform, which make the remedies of a previous generation look as ridiculous as their bonnets, the only thing that was still actual for her was the elevation of the species by the reading of Emerson and the frequentation of Tremont Temple. Olive had been active enough, for years, in the city-missions; she too had scoured dirty children, and, in squalid lodging-houses, had gone into rooms where the domestic situation was strained and the noises made the neighbours turn pale. But she reflected that after such exertions she had the refreshment of a pretty house, a drawing-room full of flowers, a crackling hearth, where she threw in pine-cones and made them snap, an imported tea-service, a Chickering piano, and the *Deutsche Rundschau*; whereas Miss Birdseye had only a bare, vulgar room, with a hideous flowered carpet (it looked like a dentist's), a cold furnace, the evening-paper, and Doctor Prance. Olive and Verena were present at another of her gatherings before the winter ended; it resembled the occasion that we described at the beginning of this history, with the difference that Mrs. Farrinder was not there to oppress the company with her greatness, and that Verena made a speech without the co-operation of her father. This young lady had delivered herself with even finer effect than before, and Olive could see how much she had gained, in confidence and range of allusion, since the educative process in Charles Street began. Her *motif* was now a kind of unprepared tribute to Miss Birdseye, the fruit of the occasion and of the unanimous tenderness of the younger members of the circle, which made her a willing mouth-piece. She pictured her laborious career, her early associates (Eliza P. Moseley was not neglected as Verena passed), her difficulties and dangers and triumphs, her humanising effect upon so many, her serene and honoured old age—expressed, in short, as one of the ladies said, just the very way they all felt about her. Verena's face brightened and grew triumphant as she spoke, but she brought tears into the eyes of most of the others. It was Olive's opinion that nothing could be more graceful and touching, and she saw that the impression made was now deeper than on the former evening. Miss Birdseye went about with her eighty years of innocence, her undiscriminating spectacles, asking her friends if it wasn't perfectly splendid; she took none of it to herself, she regarded it only as a brilliant expression of Verena's gift. Olive thought, afterwards, that if a collection could only be taken up on the spot, the good lady would be made easy for the rest of her days; then she remembered that most of her guests were as impecunious as herself.

I have intimated that our young friends had a source of fortifying emotion which was distinct from the hours they spent with Beethoven and Bach, or in hearing Miss Birdseye describe Concord as it used to be. This consisted in the wonderful insight they had obtained into the history of feminine anguish. They perused that chapter perpetually and zealously, and they derived from it the purest part of their mission. Olive had pored over it so long, so earnestly, that she was now in complete possession of the subject; it was the one thing in life which she felt she had really mastered. She was able to exhibit it to Verena with the greatest authority and accuracy, to lead her up and down, in and out, through all the darkest and most tortuous passages. We know that she was without belief in her own eloquence, but she was very eloquent when she reminded Verena how the exquisite weakness of women had never been their defence, but had only exposed them to sufferings more acute than masculine grossness can conceive. Their odious partner had trampled upon them from the beginning of time, and their tenderness, their abnegation, had been his opportunity. All the bullied wives, the stricken mothers, the dishonoured, deserted maidens who have lived on the earth and longed to leave it, passed and repassed before her eyes, and the interminable dim procession seemed to stretch out a myriad hands to her. She sat with them at their trembling vigils, listened for the tread, the voice, at which they grew pale and sick, walked with them by the dark waters that offered to wash away misery and shame, took with them, even, when the vision grew intense, the last shuddering leap. She had analysed to an extraordinary fineness their susceptibility, their softness; she knew (or she thought she knew) all the possible tortures of anxiety, of suspense and dread; and she had made up her mind that it was women, in the end, who had paid for everything. In the last resort the whole burden of the human lot came upon them; it pressed upon them far more than on the others, the intolerable load of fate. It was they who sat cramped and chained to receive it; it was they who had done all the waiting and taken all the wounds. The sacrifices, the blood, the tears, the terrors were theirs. Their organism was in itself a challenge to suffering, and men had practised upon it with an impudence that knew no bounds. As they were the weakest most had been wrung from them, and as they were the most generous they had been most deceived. Olive Chancellor would have rested her case, had it been necessary, on those general facts; and her simple and comprehensive contention was that the peculiar wretchedness which had been the very essence of the feminine lot was a monstrous artificial imposition, crying aloud for redress. She was willing to admit that women, too, could be bad; that there were many about the world who were false, immoral, vile. But their errors were as nothing to their sufferings; they had expiated, in advance, an eternity, if need be, of misconduct. Olive poured forth these views to her listening and responsive friend; she presented them again and again, and there was no light in which they did not seem to palpitate with truth. Verena was immensely wrought upon; a subtle fire passed into her; she was not so hungry for revenge as Olive, but at the last, before they went to Europe (I shall take no place to describe the manner in which she threw herself into that project), she quite agreed with her companion that after so many ages of wrong (it would also be after the European journey) men must take *their* turn, men must pay!

XXI

B ASIL RANSOM lived in New York, rather far to the eastward, and in the upper reaches of the town; he occupied two small shabby rooms in a somewhat decayed mansion which stood next to the corner of the Second Avenue. The corner itself was formed by a considerable grocer's shop, the near neighbourhood of which was fatal to any pretensions Ransom and his fellow-lodgers might have had in regard to gentility of situation. The house had a red, rusty face, and faded green shutters, of which the slats were limp and at variance with each other. In one of the lower windows was suspended a fly-blown card, with the words 'Table Board' affixed in letters cut (not very neatly) out of coloured paper, of graduated tints, and surrounded with a small band of stamped gilt. The two sides of the shop were protected by an immense pent-house shed, which projected over a greasy pavement and was supported by wooden posts fixed in the curbstone. Beneath it, on the dislocated flags, barrels and baskets were freely and picturesquely grouped; an open cellarway yawned beneath the feet of those who might pause to gaze too fondly on the savoury wares displayed in the window; a strong odour of smoked fish, combined with a fragrance of molasses, hung about the spot; the pavement, toward the gutters, was fringed with dirty panniers, heaped with potatoes, carrots, and onions; and a smart, bright waggon, with the horse detached from the shafts, drawn up on the edge of the abominable road (it contained holes and ruts a foot deep, and immemorial accumulations of stagnant mud), imparted an idle, rural, pastoral air to a scene otherwise perhaps expressive of a rank civilisation. The establishment was of the kind known to New Yorkers as a Dutch grocery; and red-faced, yellow-haired, bare-armed vendors might have been observed to lounge in the doorway. I mention it not on account of any particular influence it may have had on the life or the thoughts of Basil Ransom, but for old acquaintance sake and that of local colour; besides which, a figure is nothing without a setting, and our young man came and went every day, with rather an indifferent, unperceiving step, it is true, among the objects I have briefly designated. One of his rooms was directly above the street-door of the house; such a dormitory, when it is so exiguous, is called in the nomenclature of New York a 'hall bedroom.' The sitting-room, beside it, was slightly larger, and they both commanded a row of tenements no less degenerate than Ransom's own habitation—houses built forty years before, and already sere and superannuated. These were also painted red, and the bricks were accentuated by a white line; they were garnished, on the first floor, with balconies covered with small tin roofs, striped in different colours, and with an elaborate iron lattice-work, which gave them a repressive, cage-like appearance, and caused them slightly to resemble the little boxes for peeping unseen into the street, which are a feature of oriental towns. Such posts of observation commanded a view of the grocery on the corner, of the relaxed and disjointed roadway, enlivened at the curbstone with an occasional ash-barrel or with gas-lamps drooping from the perpendicular, and westward, at the end of the truncated vista, of the fantastic skeleton of the Elevated Railway, overhanging the transverse longitudinal street, which it darkened and smothered with the immeasurable spinal column and myriad clutching paws of an antediluvian monster. If the opportunity were not denied me here, I should like to give some account of Basil Ransom's interior, of certain curious persons of both sexes, for the most part not favourites of fortune, who had found an obscure asylum there; some picture of the crumpled little *table d'hôte*, at two dollars and a half a week, where everything felt sticky, which went forward in the low-ceiled basement, under the conduct of a couple of shuffling negresses, who mingled in the conversation and indulged in low, mysterious chuckles when it took a facetious turn. But we need, in strictness, concern ourselves with it no further than to gather the implication that the young Mississippian, even a year and a half after that momentous visit of his to Boston, had not made his profession very lucrative.

He had been diligent, he had been ambitious, but he had not yet been successful. During the few weeks preceding the moment at which we meet him again, he had even begun to lose faith altogether in his earthly destiny. It became much of a question with him whether success in any form was written there; whether for a hungry young Mississippian, without means, without friends, wanting, too, in the highest energy, the wisdom of the serpent, personal arts and national prestige, the game of life was to be won in New York. He had been on the point of giving it up and returning to the home of his ancestors, where, as he heard from his mother, there was still just a sufficient supply of hot corn-cake to support existence. He had never believed much in his luck, but during the last year it had been guilty of aberrations surprising even to a constant, an imperturbable, victim of fate. Not only had he not extended his connection, but he had lost most of the little business which was an object of complacency to him a twelvemonth before. He had had none but small jobs, and he had made a mess of more than one of them. Such accidents had not had a happy effect upon his reputation; he had been able to perceive that this fair flower may be nipped when it is so tender a bud as scarcely to be palpable. He had formed a partnership with a person who seemed likely to repair some of his deficiencies—a young man from Rhode Island, acquainted, according to his own expression, with the inside track. But this gentleman himself, as it turned out, would have been better for a good deal of remodelling, and Ransom's principal deficiency, which was, after all, that of cash, was not less apparent to him after his colleague, prior to a sudden and unexplained departure for Europe, had drawn the slender accumulations of the firm out of the bank. Ransom sat for hours in his office, waiting for clients who either did not come, or, if they did come, did not seem to find him encouraging, as they usually left him with the remark that they would think what they would do. They thought to little purpose, and seldom reappeared, so that at last he began to wonder whether there were not a prejudice against his Southern complexion. Perhaps they didn't like the way he spoke. If they could show him a better way, he was willing to adopt it; but the manner of New York could not be acquired by precept, and example, somehow, was not in this case contagious. He wondered whether he were stupid and unskilled, and he was finally obliged to confess to himself that he was unpractical.

This confession was in itself a proof of the fact, for nothing could be less fruitful than such a speculation, terminating in such a way. He was perfectly aware that he cared a great deal for the theory, and so his visitors must have thought when they found him, with one of his long legs twisted round the other, reading a volume of De Tocqueville. That was the kind of reading he liked; he had thought a great deal about social and economical questions, forms of government and the happiness of peoples. The convictions he had arrived at were not such as mix gracefully with the time-honoured verities a young lawyer looking out for business is in the habit of taking for granted; but he had to reflect that these doctrines would probably not contribute any more to his prosperity in Mississippi than in New York. Indeed, he scarcely could think of the country where they would be a particular advantage to him. It came home to him that his opinions were stiff, whereas in comparison his effort was lax; and he accordingly began to wonder whether he might not make a living by his opinions. He had always had a desire for public life; to cause one's ideas to be embodied in national conduct appeared to him the highest form of human enjoyment. But there was little enough that was public in his solitary studies, and he asked himself what was the use of his having an office at all, and why he might not as well carry on his profession at the Astor Library, where, in his spare hours and on chance holidays, he did an immense deal of suggestive reading. He took copious notes and memoranda, and these things sometimes shaped themselves in a way that might possibly commend them to the editors of periodicals. Readers perhaps would come, if clients didn't; so he produced, with a great deal of labour, half a dozen articles, from which, when they were finished, it seemed to him that he had omitted all the points he wished most to make, and addressed them to the powers that preside over weekly and monthly publications. They were all declined with thanks, and he would have been forced to believe that the accent of his languid clime brought him luck as little under the pen as on the lips, had not another explanation been suggested by one of the more explicit of his oracles, in relation to a paper on the rights of minorities. This gentleman pointed out that his doctrines were about three hundred years behind the age; doubtless some magazine of the six-teenth century would have been very happy to print them. This threw light on his own suspicion that he was attached to causes that could only, in the nature of things, be unpopular. The disagreeable editor was right about his being out of date, only he had got the time wrong. He had come centuries too soon; he was not too old, but too new. Such an impression, however, would not have prevented him from going into politics, if there had been any other way to represent constituencies than by being elected. People might be found eccentric enough to vote for him in Mississippi, but meanwhile where should he find the twenty-dollar greenbacks which it was his ambition to transmit from time to time to his female relations, confined so constantly to a farinaceous diet? It came over him with some force that his opinions would not yield interest, and the evaporation of this pleasing hypothesis made him feel like a man in an open boat, at sea, who should just have parted with his last rag of canvas.

I shall not attempt a complete description of Ransom's ill-starred views, being convinced that the reader will guess them as he goes, for they had a frolicsome, ingenious way of peeping out of the young man's conversation. I shall do them sufficient justice in saying that he was by natural disposition a good deal of a stoic, and that, as the result of a considerable intellectual experience, he was, in social and political matters, a reactionary. I suppose he was very conceited, for he was much addicted to judging his age. He thought it talkative, querulous, hysterical, maudlin, full of false ideas, of unhealthy germs, of extravagant, dissipated habits, for which a great reckoning was in store. He was an immense admirer of the late Thomas Carlyle, and was very suspicious of the encroachments of modern democracy. I know not exactly how these queer heresies had planted themselves, but he had a longish pedigree (it had flowered at one time with English royalists and cavaliers), and he seemed at moments to be inhabited by some transmitted spirit of a robust but narrow ancestor, some broad-faced wig-wearer or sword-bearer, with a more primitive conception of manhood than our modern temperament appears to require, and a programme of human felicity much less varied. He liked his pedigree, he revered his forefathers,

and he rather pitied those who might come after him. In saying so, however, I betray him a little, for he never mentioned
such feelings as these. Though he thought the age too talkative, as I have hinted, he liked to talk as well as any one; but
he could hold his tongue, if that were more expressive, and
he usually did so when his perplexities were greatest. He had
been sitting for several evenings in a beer-cellar, smoking his
pipe with a profundity of reticence. This attitude was so unbroken that it marked a crisis—the complete, the acute consciousness of his personal situation. It was the cheapest way
he knew of spending an evening. At this particular establishment the *Schoppen* were very tall and the beer was very good;
and as the host and most of the guests were German, and
their colloquial tongue was unknown to him, he was not
drawn into any undue expenditure of speech. He watched his
smoke and he thought, thought so hard that at last he appeared to himself to have exhausted the thinkable. When this
moment of combined relief and dismay arrived (on the last of
the evenings that we are concerned with), he took his way
down Third Avenue and reached his humble dwelling. Till
within a short time there had been a resource for him at such
an hour and in such a mood; a little variety-actress, who lived
in the house, and with whom he had established the most
cordial relations, was often having her supper (she took it
somewhere, every night, after the theatre), in the dim, close
dining-room, and he used to drop in and talk to her. But she
had lately married, to his great amusement, and her husband
had taken her on a wedding-tour, which was to be at the
same time professional. On this occasion he mounted, with
rather a heavy tread, to his rooms, where (on the rickety writing-table in the parlour) he found a note from Mrs. Luna. I
need not reproduce it *in extenso*; a pale reflection of it will
serve. She reproached him with neglecting her, wanted to
know what had become of him, whether he had grown too
fashionable for a person who cared only for serious society.
She accused him of having changed, and inquired as to the
reason of his coldness. Was it too much to ask whether he
could tell her at least in what manner she had offended him?
She used to think they were so much in sympathy—he expressed her own ideas about everything so vividly. She liked

intellectual companionship, and she had none now. She hoped very much he would come and see her—as he used to do six months before—the following evening; and however much she might have sinned or he might have altered, she was at least always his affectionate cousin Adeline.

'What the deuce does she want of me now?' It was with this somewhat ungracious exclamation that he tossed away his cousin Adeline's missive. The gesture might have indicated that he meant to take no notice of her; nevertheless, after a day had elapsed, he presented himself before her. He knew what she wanted of old—that is, a year ago; she had wanted him to look after her property and to be tutor to her son. He had lent himself, good-naturedly, to this desire—he was touched by so much confidence—but the experiment had speedily collapsed. Mrs. Luna's affairs were in the hands of trustees, who had complete care of them, and Ransom instantly perceived that his function would be simply to meddle in things that didn't concern him. The levity with which she had exposed him to the derision of the lawful guardians of her fortune opened his eyes to some of the dangers of cousinship; nevertheless he said to himself that he might turn an honest penny by giving an hour or two every day to the education of her little boy. But this, too, proved a brief illusion. Ransom had to find his time in the afternoon; he left his business at five o'clock and remained with his young kinsman till the hour of dinner. At the end of a few weeks he thought himself lucky in retiring without broken shins. That Newton's little nature was remarkable had often been insisted on by his mother; but it was remarkable, Ransom saw, for the absence of any of the qualities which attach a teacher to a pupil. He was in truth an insufferable child, entertaining for the Latin language a personal, physical hostility, which expressed itself in convulsions of rage. During these paroxysms he kicked furiously at every one and everything—at poor 'Rannie,' at his mother, at Messrs. Andrews and Stoddard, at the illustrious men of Rome, at the universe in general, to which, as he lay on his back on the carpet, he presented a pair of singularly active little heels. Mrs. Luna had a way of being present at his lessons, and when they passed, as sooner or later they were sure to, into the stage I have described, she interceded for her overwrought darling, reminded Ransom that these were the signs of an exquisite sensibility, begged that the child might be allowed to rest a little, and spent the remainder of the time in conversation with the preceptor. It came to seem to him, very soon, that he was not earning his fee; besides which, it was disagreeable to him to have pecuniary relations with a lady who had not the art of concealing from him that she liked to place him under obligations. He resigned his tutorship, and drew a long breath, having a vague feeling that he had escaped a danger. He could not have told you exactly what it was, and he had a certain sentimental, provincial respect for women which even prevented him from attempting to give a name to it in his own thoughts. He was addicted with the ladies to the old forms of address and of gallantry; he held that they were delicate, agreeable creatures, whom Providence had placed under the protection of the bearded sex; and it was not merely a humorous idea with him that whatever might be the defects of Southern gentlemen, they were at any rate remarkable for their chivalry. He was a man who still, in a slangy age, could pronounce that word with a perfectly serious face.

This boldness did not prevent him from thinking that women were essentially inferior to men, and infinitely tiresome when they declined to accept the lot which men had made for them. He had the most definite notions about their place in nature, in society, and was perfectly easy in his mind as to whether it excluded them from any proper homage. The chivalrous man paid that tax with alacrity. He admitted their rights; these consisted in a standing claim to the generosity and tenderness of the stronger race. The exercise of such feelings was full of advantage for both sexes, and they flowed most freely, of course, when women were gracious and grateful. It may be said that he had a higher conception of politeness than most of the persons who desired the advent of female law-makers. When I have added that he hated to see women eager and argumentative, and thought that their softness and docility were the inspiration, the opportunity (the highest) of man, I shall have sketched a state of mind which will doubtless strike many readers as painfully crude. It had prevented Basil Ransom, at any rate, from putting the dots on his *i*'s, as the French say, in this gradual discovery that Mrs. Luna was making love to him. The process went on a long time before he became aware of it. He had perceived very soon that she was a tremendously familiar little woman—that she took, more rapidly than he had ever known, a high degree of intimacy for granted. But as she had seemed to him neither very fresh nor very beautiful, so he could not easily have represented to himself why she should take it into her head to marry (it would never have occurred to him to doubt that she wanted marriage), an obscure and penniless Mississippian, with womenkind of his own to provide for. He could not guess that he answered to a certain secret ideal of Mrs. Luna's, who loved the landed gentry even when landless, who adored a Southerner under any circumstances, who thought her kinsman a fine, manly, melancholy, disinterested type, and who was sure that her views of public matters, the questions of the age, the vulgar character of modern life, would meet with a perfect response in his mind. She could see by the way he talked that he was a conservative, and this was the motto inscribed upon her own silken banner. She took this unpopular line both by temperament and by reaction from her sister's 'extreme' views, the sight of the dreadful people that they brought about her. In reality, Olive was distinguished and discriminating, and Adeline was the dupe of confusions in which the worse was apt to be mistaken for the better. She talked to Ransom about the inferiority of republics, the distressing persons she had met abroad in the legations of the United States, the bad manners of servants and shopkeepers in that country, the hope she entertained that 'the good old families' would make a stand; but he never suspected that she cultivated these topics (her treatment of them struck him as highly comical), for the purpose of leading him to the altar, of beguiling the way. Least of all could he suppose that she would be indifferent to his want of income—a point in which he failed to do her justice; for, thinking the fact that he had remained poor a proof of delicacy in that shopkeeping age, it gave her much pleasure to reflect that, as Newton's little property was settled on him (with safeguards which showed how long-headed poor Mr. Luna had been, and large-hearted, too, since to what he left *her* no disagreeable conditions, such as eternal mourning, for instance, were attached)—that as Newton, I say, enjoyed the pecuniary independence which befitted his character, her own income was ample even for two, and she might give herself the luxury of taking a husband who should owe her something. Basil Ransom did not divine all this, but he divined that it was not for nothing that Mrs. Luna wrote him little notes every other day, that she proposed to drive him in the Park at unnatural hours, and that when he said he had his business to attend to, she replied: 'Oh, a plague on your business! I am sick of that word—one hears of nothing else in America. There are ways of getting on without business, if you would only take them!' He seldom answered her notes, and he disliked extremely the way in which, in spite of her love of form and order, she attempted to clamber in at the window of one's house when one had locked the door; so that he began to interspace his visits considerably, and at last made them very rare. When I reflect on his habits of almost superstitious politeness to women, it comes over me that some very strong motive must have operated to make him give his friendly— his only too friendly—cousin the cold shoulder. Nevertheless, when he received her reproachful letter (after it had had time to work a little), he said to himself that he had perhaps been unjust and even brutal, and as he was easily touched by remorse of this kind, he took up the broken thread.

XXII

As he sat with Mrs. Luna, in her little back drawing-room, under the lamp, he felt rather more tolerant than before of the pressure she could not help putting upon him. Several months had elapsed, and he was no nearer to the sort of success he had hoped for. It stole over him gently that there was another sort, pretty visibly open to him, not so elevated nor so manly, it is true, but on which he should after all, perhaps, be able to reconcile it with his honour to fall back. Mrs. Luna had had an inspiration; for once in her life she had held her tongue. She had not made him a scene, there had been no question of an explanation; she had received him as if he had been there the day before, with the addition of a spice of mysterious melancholy. She might have made up her mind that she had lost him as what she had hoped, but that it was better than desolation to try and keep him as a friend. It was as if she wished him to see now how she tried. She was subdued and consolatory, she waited upon him, moved away a screen that intercepted the fire, remarked that he looked very tired, and rang for some tea. She made no inquiry about his affairs, never asked if he had been busy and prosperous; and this reticence struck him as unexpectedly delicate and discreet; it was as if she had guessed, by a subtle feminine faculty, that his professional career was nothing to boast of. There was a simplicity in him which permitted him to wonder whether she had not improved. The lamp-light was soft, the fire crackled pleasantly, everything that surrounded him betrayed a woman's taste and touch; the place was decorated and cushioned in perfection, delightfully private and personal, the picture of a well-appointed home. Mrs. Luna had complained of the difficulties of installing one's self in America, but Ransom remembered that he had received an impression similar to this in her sister's house in Boston, and reflected that these ladies had, as a family-trait, the art of making themselves comfortable. It was better for a winter's evening than the German beer-cellar (Mrs. Luna's tea was excellent), and his hostess herself appeared to-night almost as amiable as the variety-actress. At the end of an hour he felt, I will not say almost marriageable, but almost married. Images of leisure played before him, leisure in which he saw himself covering foolscap paper with his views on several subjects, and with favourable illustrations of Southern eloquence. It became tolerably vivid to him that if editors wouldn't print one's lucubrations, it would be a comfort to feel that one was able to publish them at one's own expense.

He had a moment of almost complete illusion. Mrs. Luna had taken up her bit of crochet; she was sitting opposite to him, on the other side of the fire. Her white hands moved with little jerks as she took her stitches, and her rings flashed and twinkled in the light of the hearth. Her head fell a little to one side, exhibiting the plumpness of her chin and neck, and her dropped eyes (it gave her a little modest air), rested quietly on her work. A silence of a few moments had fallen upon their talk, and Adeline—who decidedly *had* improved—appeared also to feel the charm of it, not to wish to break it. Basil Ransom was conscious of all this, and at the same time he was vaguely engaged in a speculation. If it gave one time, if it gave one leisure, was not that in itself a high motive? Thorough study of the question he cared for most—was not the chance for *that* an infinitely desirable good? He seemed to see himself, to feel himself, in that very chair, in the evenings of the future, reading some indispensable book in the still lamp-light—Mrs. Luna knew where to get such pretty mellowing shades. Should he not be able to act in that way upon the public opinion of his time, to check certain tendencies, to point out certain dangers, to indulge in much salutary criticism? Was it not one's duty to put one's self in the best conditions for such action? And as the silence continued he almost fell to musing on his duty, almost persuaded himself that the moral law commanded him to marry Mrs. Luna. She looked up presently from her work, their eyes met, and she smiled. He might have believed she had guessed what he was thinking of. This idea startled him, alarmed him a little, so that when Mrs. Luna said, with her sociable manner, 'There is nothing I like so much, of a winter's night, as a cosy *tête-à-tête* by the fire. It's quite like Darby and Joan; what a pity the kettle has ceased singing!'—when she uttered these insinuating words he gave himself a little imperceptible shake, which was, however, enough to break the spell, and made no response more direct than to ask her, in a moment, in a tone of cold, mild curiosity, whether she had lately heard from her sister, and how long Miss Chancellor intended to remain in Europe.

'Well, you *have* been living in your hole!' Mrs. Luna exclaimed. 'Olive came home six weeks ago. How long did you expect her to endure it?'

'I am sure I don't know; I have never been there,' Ransom replied.

'Yes, that's what I like you for,' Mrs. Luna remarked sweetly. 'If a man is nice without it, it's such a pleasant change.'

The young man started, then gave a natural laugh. 'Lord, how few reasons there must be!'

'Oh, I mention that one because I can tell it. I shouldn't care to tell the others.'

'I am glad you have some to fall back upon, the day I should go,' Ransom went on. 'I thought you thought so much of Europe.'

'So I do; but it isn't everything,' said Mrs. Luna, philosophically. 'You had better go there with me,' she added, with a certain inconsequence.

'One would go to the end of the world with so irresistible a lady!' Ransom exclaimed, falling into the tone which Mrs. Luna always found so unsatisfactory. It was a part of his Southern gallantry—his accent always came out strongly when he said anything of that sort—and it committed him to nothing in particular. She had had occasion to wish, more than once, that he wouldn't be so beastly polite, as she used to hear people say in England. She answered that she didn't care about ends, she cared about beginnings; but he didn't take up the declaration; he returned to the subject of Olive, wanted to know what she had done over there, whether she had worked them up much.

'Oh, of course, she fascinated every one,' said Mrs. Luna. 'With her grace and beauty, her general style, how could she help that?'

'But did she bring them round, did she swell the host that is prepared to march under her banner?'

'I suppose she saw plenty of the strong-minded, plenty of vicious old maids, and fanatics, and frumps. But I haven't the least idea what she accomplished—what they call " wonders," I suppose.'

'Didn't you see her when she returned?' Basil Ransom asked.

'How could I see her? I can see pretty far, but I can't see all the way to Boston.' And then, in explaining that it was at this port that her sister had disembarked, Mrs. Luna further inquired whether he could imagine Olive doing anything in a first-rate way, as long as there were inferior ones. 'Of course she likes bad ships—Boston steamers—just as she likes common people, and red-haired hoydens, and preposterous doctrines.'

Ransom was silent a moment. 'Do you mean the—a— rather striking young lady whom I met in Boston a year ago last October? What was her name?—Miss Tarrant? Does Miss Chancellor like her as much as ever?'

'Mercy! don't you know she took her to Europe? It was to form *her* mind she went. Didn't I tell you that last summer? You used to come to see me then.'

'Oh yes, I remember,' Ransom said, rather musingly. 'And did she bring her back?'

'Gracious, you don't suppose she would leave her! Olive thinks she's born to regenerate the world.'

'I remember you telling me that, too. It comes back to me. Well, is her mind formed?'

'As I haven't seen it, I cannot tell you.'

'Aren't you going on there to see——'

'To see whether Miss Tarrant's mind is formed?' Mrs. Luna broke in. 'I will go if you would like me to. I remember your being immensely excited about her that time you met her. Don't you recollect that?'

Ransom hesitated an instant. 'I can't say I do. It is too long ago.'

'Yes, I have no doubt that's the way you change, about women! Poor Miss Tarrant, if she thinks she made an impression on you!'

'She won't think about such things as that, if her mind has been formed by your sister,' Ransom said. 'It does come back to me now, what you told me about the growth of their intimacy. And do they mean to go on living together for ever?'

'I suppose so—unless some one should take it into his head to marry Verena.'

'Verena—is that her name?' Ransom asked.

Mrs. Luna looked at him with a suspended needle. 'Well! have you forgotten that too? You told me yourself you thought it so pretty, that time in Boston, when you walked me up the hill.' Ransom declared that he remembered that walk, but didn't remember everything he had said to her; and she suggested, very satirically, that perhaps he would like to marry Verena himself—he seemed so interested in her. Ransom shook his head sadly, and said he was afraid he was not in a position to marry; whereupon Mrs. Luna asked him what he meant—did he mean (after a moment's hesitation) that he was too poor?

'Never in the world—I am very rich; I make an enormous income!' the young man exclaimed; so that, remarking his tone, and the slight flush of annoyance that rose to his face, Mrs. Luna was quick enough to judge that she had overstepped the mark. She remembered (she ought to have remembered before), that he had never taken her in the least into his confidence about his affairs. That was not the Southern way, and he was at least as proud as he was poor. In this surmise she was just; Basil Ransom would have despised himself if he had been capable of confessing to a woman that he couldn't make a living. Such questions were none of their business (their business was simply to be provided for, practise the domestic virtues, and be charmingly grateful), and there was, to his sense, something almost indecent in talking about them. Mrs. Luna felt doubly sorry for him as she perceived that he denied himself the luxury of sympathy (that is, of hers), and the vague but comprehensive sigh that passed her lips as she took up her crochet again was unusually expressive of helplessness. She said that of course she knew how great his talents were—he could do anything he wanted; and Basil Ransom wondered for a moment whether, if she were to ask him point-blank to marry her, it would be consistent with the high courtesy of a Southern gentleman to refuse. After she should be his wife he might of course confess to her that he was too poor to marry, for in that relation even a Southern gentleman of the highest tone must sometimes unbend. But he didn't in the least long for this arrangement, and was conscious that the most pertinent sequel to her conjecture would be for him to take up his hat and walk away.

Within five minutes, however, he had come to desire to do this almost as little as to marry Mrs. Luna. He wanted to hear more about the girl who lived with Olive Chancellor. Something had revived in him—an old curiosity, an image half effaced—when he learned that she had come back to America. He had taken a wrong impression from what Mrs. Luna said, nearly a year before, about her sister's visit to Europe; he had supposed it was to be a long absence, that Miss Chancellor wanted perhaps to get the little prophetess away from her parents, possibly even away from some amorous entanglement. Then, no doubt, they wanted to study up the woman-question with the facilities that Europe would offer; he didn't know much about Europe, but he had an idea that it was a great place for facilities. His knowledge of Miss Chancellor's departure, accompanied by her young companion, had checked at the time, on Ransom's part, a certain habit of idle but none the less entertaining retrospect. His life, on the whole, had not been rich in episode, and that little chapter of his visit to his queer, clever, capricious cousin, with his evening at Miss Birdseye's, and his glimpse, repeated on the morrow, of the strange, beautiful, ridiculous, red-haired young *improvisatrice*, unrolled itself in his memory like a page of interesting fiction. The page seemed to fade, however, when he heard that the two girls had gone, for an indefinite time, to unknown lands; this carried them out of his range, spoiled the perspective, diminished their actuality; so that for several months past, with his increase of anxiety about his own affairs, and the low pitch of his spirits, he had not thought at all about Verena Tarrant. The fact that she was once more in Boston, with a certain contiguity that it seemed to imply between Boston and New York, presented itself now as important and agreeable. He was conscious that this was rather an anomaly, and his consciousness made him, had already made him, dissimulate slightly. He did not pick up his hat to go; he sat in his chair taking his chance of the tax which Mrs.

Luna might lay upon his urbanity. He remembered that he had not made, as yet, any very eager inquiry about Newton, who at this late hour had succumbed to the only influence that tames the untamable and was sleeping the sleep of child-hood, if not of innocence. Ransom repaired his neglect in a manner which elicited the most copious response from his hostess. The boy had had a good many tutors since Ransom gave him up, and it could not be said that his education lan-guished. Mrs. Luna spoke with pride of the manner in which he went through them; if he did not master his lessons, he mastered his teachers, and she had the happy conviction that she gave him every advantage. Ransom's delay was diplo-matic, but at the end of ten minutes he returned to the young ladies in Boston; he asked why, with their aggressive pro-gramme, one hadn't begun to feel their onset, why the echoes of Miss Tarrant's eloquence hadn't reached his ears. Hadn't she come out yet in public? was she not coming to stir them up in New York? He hoped she hadn't broken down.

'She didn't seem to break down last summer, at the Female Convention,' Mrs. Luna replied. 'Have you forgotten that too? Didn't I tell you of the sensation she produced there, and of what I heard from Boston about it? Do you mean to say I didn't give you that 'Transcript,' with the report of her great speech? It was just before they sailed for Europe; she went off with flying colours, in a blaze of fireworks.' Ransom protested that he had not heard this affair mentioned till that moment, and then, when they compared dates, they found it had taken place just after his last visit to Mrs. Luna. This, of course, gave her a chance to say that he had treated her even worse than she supposed; it had been her impression, at any rate, that they had talked together about Verena's sudden bound into fame. Apparently she confounded him with some one else, that was very possible; he was not to suppose that he occupied such a distinct place in her mind, especially when she might die twenty deaths before he came near her. Ran-som demurred to the implication that Miss Tarrant was fa-mous; if she were famous, wouldn't she be in the New York papers? He hadn't seen her there, and he had no recollection of having encountered any mention at the time (last June, was it?) of her exploits at the Female Convention. A local reputation doubtless she had, but that had been the case a year and a half before, and what was expected of her then was to become a first-class national glory. He was willing to believe that she had created some excitement in Boston, but he shouldn't attach much importance to that till one began to see her photograph in the stores. Of course, one must give her time, but he had supposed Miss Chancellor was going to put her through faster.

If he had taken a contradictious tone on purpose to draw Mrs. Luna out, he could not have elicited more of the information he desired. It was perfectly true that he had seen no reference to Verena's performances in the preceding June; there were periods when the newspapers seemed to him so idiotic that for weeks he never looked at one. He learned from Mrs. Luna that it was not Olive who had sent her the 'Transcript' and in letters had added some private account of the doings at the convention to the testimony of that amiable sheet; she had been indebted for this service to a 'gentleman-friend,' who wrote her everything that happened in Boston, and what every one had every day for dinner. Not that it was necessary for her happiness to know; but the gentleman she spoke of didn't know what to invent to please her. A Bostonian couldn't imagine that one didn't want to know, and that was their idea of ingratiating themselves, or, at any rate, it was his, poor man. Olive would never have gone into particulars about Verena; she regarded her sister as quite too much one of the profane, and knew Adeline couldn't understand why, when she took to herself a bosom-friend, she should have been at such pains to select her in just the most dreadful class in the community. Verena was a perfect little adventuress, and quite third-rate into the bargain; but, of course, she was a pretty girl enough, if one cared for hair of the colour of cochineal. As for her people, they were too absolutely awful; it was exactly as if she, Mrs. Luna, had struck up an intimacy with the daughter of her chiropodist. It took Olive to invent such monstrosities, and to think she was doing something great for humanity when she did so; though, in spite of her wanting to turn everything over, and put the lowest highest, she could be just as contemptuous and invidious, when it came to really mixing, as if she were some grand old duchess.

She must do her the justice to say that she hated the Tarrants, the father and mother; but, all the same, she let Verena run to and fro between Charles Street and the horrible hole they lived in, and Adeline knew from that gentleman who wrote so copiously that the girl now and then spent a week at a time at Cambridge. Her mother, who had been ill for some weeks, wanted her to sleep there. Mrs. Luna knew further, by her correspondent, that Verena had—or had had the winter before—a great deal of attention from gentlemen. She didn't know how she worked that into the idea that the female sex was sufficient to itself; but she had grounds for saying that this was one reason why Olive had taken her abroad. She was afraid Verena would give in to some man, and she wanted to make a break. Of course, any such giving in would be very awkward for a young woman who shrieked out on platforms that old maids were the highest type. Adeline guessed Olive had perfect control of her now, unless indeed she used the expeditions to Cambridge as a cover for meeting gentlemen. She was an artful little minx, and cared as much for the rights of women as she did for the Panama Canal; the only right of a woman she wanted was to climb up on top of something, where the men could look at her. She would stay with Olive as long as it served her purpose, because Olive, with her great respectability, could push her, and counteract the effect of her low relations, to say nothing of paying all her expenses and taking her the tour of Europe. 'But, mark my words,' said Mrs. Luna, 'she will give Olive the greatest cut she has ever had in her life. She will run off with some lion-tamer; she will marry a circus man!' And Mrs. Luna added that it would serve Olive Chancellor right. But she would take it hard; look out for tantrums then!

Basil Ransom's emotions were peculiar while his hostess delivered herself, in a manner at once casual and emphatic, of these rather insidious remarks. He took them all in, for they represented to him certain very interesting facts; but he perceived at the same time that Mrs. Luna didn't know what she was talking about. He had seen Verena Tarrant only twice in his life, but it was no use telling him that she was an adventuress—though, certainly, it *was* very likely she would end by giving Miss Chancellor a cut. He chuckled, with a certain grimness, as this image passed before him; it was not unpleasing, the idea that he should be avenged (for it would avenge him to know it), upon the wanton young woman who had invited him to come and see her in order simply to slap his face. But he had an odd sense of having lost something in not knowing of the other girl's appearance at the Women's Convention—a vague feeling that he had been cheated and trifled with. The complaint was idle, inasmuch as it was not probable he could have gone to Boston to listen to her; but it represented to him that he had not shared, even dimly and remotely, in an event which concerned her very closely. Why should he share, and what was more natural than that the things which concerned her closely should not concern him at all? This question came to him only as he walked home that evening; for the moment it remained quite in abeyance: therefore he was free to feel also that his imagination had been rather starved by his ignorance of the fact that she was near him again (comparatively), that she was in the dimness of the horizon (no longer beyond the curve of the globe), and yet he had not perceived it. This sense of personal loss, as I have called it, made him feel, further, that he had something to make up, to recover. He could scarcely have told you how he would go about it; but the idea, formless though it was, led him in a direction very different from the one he had been following a quarter of an hour before. As he watched it dance before him he fell into another silence, in the midst of which Mrs. Luna gave him another mystic smile. The effect of it was to make him rise to his feet; the whole landscape of his mind had suddenly been illuminated. Decidedly, it was *not* his duty to marry Mrs. Luna, in order to have means to pursue his studies; he jerked himself back, as if he had been on the point of it.

'You don't mean to say you are going already? I haven't said half I wanted to!' she exclaimed.

He glanced at the clock, saw it was not yet late, took a turn about the room, then sat down again in a different place, while she followed him with her eyes, wondering what was the matter with him. Ransom took good care not to ask her what it was she had still to say, and perhaps it was to prevent her telling him that he now began to talk, freely, quickly, in quite a new tone. He stayed half an hour longer, and made himself very agreeable. It seemed to Mrs. Luna now that he had every distinction (she had known he had most), that he was really a charming man. He abounded in conversation, till at last he took up his hat in earnest; he talked about the state of the South, its social peculiarities, the ruin wrought by the war, the dilapidated gentry, the queer types of superannuated fire-eaters, ragged and unreconciled, all the pathos and all the comedy of it, making her laugh at one moment, almost cry at another, and say to herself throughout that when he took it into his head there was no one who could make a lady's evening pass so pleasantly. It was only afterwards that she asked herself why he had not taken it into his head till the last, so quickly. She delighted in the dilapidated gentry; her taste was completely different from her sister's, who took an interest only in the lower class, as it struggled to rise; what Adeline cared for was the fallen aristocracy (it seemed to be falling everywhere very much; was not Basil Ransom an example of it? was he not like a French *gentilhomme de province* after the Revolution? or an old monarchical *émigré* from the Languedoc?), the despoiled patriciate, I say, whose attitude was noble and touching, and toward whom one might exercise a charity as discreet as their pride was sensitive. In all Mrs. Luna's visions of herself, her discretion was the leading feature. 'Are you going to let ten years elapse again before you come?' she asked, as Basil Ransom bade her good-night. 'You must let me know, because between this and your next visit I shall have time to go to Europe and come back. I shall take care to arrive the day before.'

Instead of answering this sally, Ransom said, 'Are you not going one of these days to Boston? Are you not going to pay your sister another visit?'

Mrs. Luna stared. 'What good will that do *you*? Excuse my stupidity,' she added; 'of course, it gets me away. Thank you very much!'

'I don't want you to go away; but I want to hear more about Miss Olive.'

'Why in the world? You know you loathe her!' Here, before Ransom could reply, Mrs. Luna again overtook herself. 'I verily believe that by Miss Olive you mean Miss Verena!'

Her eyes charged him a moment with this perverse intention; then she exclaimed, 'Basil Ransom, *are* you in love with that creature?'

He gave a perfectly natural laugh, not pleading guilty, in order to practise on Mrs. Luna, but expressing the simple state of the case. 'How should I be? I have seen her but twice in my life.'

'If you had seen her more, I shouldn't be afraid! Fancy your wanting to pack me off to Boston!' his hostess went on. 'I am in no hurry to stay with Olive again; besides, that girl takes up the whole house. You had better go there yourself.'

'I should like nothing better,' said Ransom.

'Perhaps you would like me to ask Verena to spend a month with me—it might be a way of attracting you to the house,' Adeline went on, in the tone of exuberant provocation.

Ransom was on the point of replying that it would be a better way than any other, but he checked himself in time; he had never yet, even in joke, made so crude, so rude a speech to a lady. You only knew when he was joking with women by his superadded civility. 'I beg you to believe there is nothing I would do for any woman in the world that I wouldn't do for you,' he said, bending, for the last time, over Mrs. Luna's plump hand.

'I shall remember that and keep you up to it!' she cried after him, as he went. But even with this rather lively exchange of vows he felt that he had got off rather easily. He walked slowly up Fifth Avenue, into which, out of Adeline's cross-street, he had turned, by the light of a fine winter moon; and at every corner he stopped a minute, lingered in meditation, while he exhaled a soft, vague sigh. This was an unconscious, involuntary expression of relief, such as a man might utter who had seen himself on the point of being run over and yet felt that he was whole. He didn't trouble himself much to ask what had saved him; whatever it was it had produced a reaction, so that he felt rather ashamed of having found his look-out of late so blank. By the time he reached his lodgings, his ambition, his resolution, had rekindled; he had remembered that he formerly supposed he was a man of ability, that nothing particular had occurred to make him doubt it (the evidence was only negative, not positive), and that at any rate he was young enough to have another try. He whistled that night as he went to bed.

XXIII

THREE WEEKS afterward he stood in front of Olive Chancellor's house, looking up and down the street and hesitating. He had told Mrs. Luna that he should like nothing
better than to make another journey to Boston; and it was
not simply because he liked it that he had come. I was on the
point of saying that a happy chance had favoured him, but it
occurs to me that one is under no obligation to call chances
by flattering epithets when they have been waited for so long.
At any rate, the darkest hour is before the dawn; and a few
days after that melancholy evening I have described, which
Ransom spent in his German beer-cellar, before a single glass,
soon emptied, staring at his future with an unremunerated
eye, he found that the world appeared to have need of him
yet. The 'party,' as he would have said (I cannot pretend that
his speech was too heroic for that), for whom he had trans-
acted business in Boston so many months before, and who
had expressed at the time but a limited appreciation of his
services (there had been between the lawyer and his client a
divergence of judgment), observing, apparently, that they
proved more fruitful than he expected, had reopened the affair and presently requested Ransom to transport himself
again to the sister city. His errand demanded more time than
before, and for three days he gave it his constant attention.
On the fourth he found he was still detained; he should have
to wait till the evening—some important papers were to be
prepared. He determined to treat the interval as a holiday,
and he wondered what one could do in Boston to give one's
morning a festive complexion. The weather was brilliant
enough to minister to any illusion, and he strolled along the
streets, taking it in. In front of the Music Hall and of Tremont Temple he stopped, looking at the posters in the doorway; for was it not possible that Miss Chancellor's little
friend might be just then addressing her fellow-citizens? Her
name was absent, however, and this resource seemed to mock
him. He knew no one in the place but Olive Chancellor, so
there was no question of a visit to pay. He was perfectly resolved that he would never go near *her* again; she was doubt-

less a very superior being, but she had been too rough with
him to tempt him further. Politeness, even a largely-inter-
preted 'chivalry,' required nothing more than he had already
done; he had quitted her, the other year, without telling her
that she was a vixen, and that reticence was chivalrous
enough. There was also Verena Tarrant, of course; he saw no
reason to dissemble when he spoke of her to himself, and he
allowed himself the entertainment of feeling that he should
like very much to see her again. Very likely she wouldn't seem
to him the same; the impression she had made upon him was
due to some accident of mood or circumstance; and, at any
rate, any charm she might have exhibited then had probably
been obliterated by the coarsening effect of publicity and the
tonic influence of his kinswoman. It will be observed that in
this reasoning of Basil Ransom's the impression was freely
recognised, and recognised as a phenomenon still present.
The attraction might have vanished, as he said to himself, but
the mental picture of it was yet vivid. The greater the pity
that he couldn't call upon Verena (he called her by her name
in his thoughts, it was so pretty), without calling upon Olive,
and that Olive was so disagreeable as to place that effort beyond his strength. There was another consideration, with
Ransom, which eminently belonged to the man; he believed
that Miss Chancellor had conceived, in the course of those
few hours, and in a manner that formed so absurd a sequel to
her having gone out of her way to make his acquaintance,
such a dislike to him that it would be odious to her to see
him again within her doors; and he would have felt indelicate
in taking warrant from her original invitation (before she had
seen him), to inflict on her a presence which he had no reason
to suppose the lapse of time had made less offensive. She had
given him no sign of pardon or penitence in any of the little
ways that are familiar to women—by sending him a message
through her sister, or even a book, a photograph, a Christmas
card, or a newspaper, by the post. He felt, in a word, not at
liberty to ring at her door; he didn't know what kind of a fit
the sight of his long Mississippian person would give her, and
it was characteristic of him that he should wish so to spare
the sensibilities of a young lady whom he had not found
tender; being ever as willing to let women off easily in the

particular case as he was fixed in the belief that the sex in general requires watching.

Nevertheless, he found himself, at the end of half an hour, standing on the only spot in Charles Street which had any significance for him. It had occurred to him that if he couldn't call upon Verena without calling upon Olive, he should be exempt from that condition if he called upon Mrs. Tarrant. It was not her mother, truly, who had asked him, it was the girl herself; and he was conscious, as a candid young American, that a mother is always less accessible, more guarded by social prejudice, than a daughter. But he was at a pass in which it was permissible to strain a point, and he took his way in the direction in which he knew that Cambridge lay, remembering that Miss Tarrant's invitation had reference to that quarter and that Mrs. Luna had given him further evidence. Had she not said that Verena often went back there for visits of several days—that her mother had been ill and she gave her much care? There was nothing inconceivable in her being engaged at that hour (it was getting to be one o'clock), in one of those expeditions—nothing impossible in the chance that he might find her in Cambridge. The chance, at any rate, was worth taking; Cambridge, moreover, was worth seeing, and it was as good a way as another of keeping his holiday. It occurred to him, indeed, that Cambridge was a big place, and that he had no particular address. This reflection overtook him just as he reached Olive's house, which, oddly enough, he was obliged to pass on his way to the mysterious suburb. That is partly why he paused there; he asked himself for a moment why he shouldn't ring the bell and obtain his needed information from the servant, who would be sure to be able to give it to him. He had just dismissed this method, as of questionable taste, when he heard the door of the house open, within the deep embrasure in which, in Charles Street, the main portals are set, and which are partly occupied by a flight of steps protected at the bottom by a second door, whose upper half, in either wing, consists of a sheet of glass. It was a minute before he could see who had come out, and in that minute he had time to turn away and then to turn back again, and to wonder which of the two inmates would appear to him, or whether he should behold neither or both.

The person who had issued from the house descended the steps very slowly, as if on purpose to give him time to escape; and when at last the glass doors were divided they disclosed a little old lady. Ransom was disappointed; such an apparition was so scantily to his purpose. But the next minute his spirits rose again, for he was sure that he had seen the little old lady before. She stopped on the side-walk, and looked vaguely about her, in the manner of a person waiting for an omnibus or a street-car; she had a dingy, loosely-habited air, as if she had worn her clothes for many years and yet was even now imperfectly acquainted with them; a large, benignant face, caged in by the glass of her spectacles, which seemed to cover it almost equally everywhere, and a fat, rusty satchel, which hung low at her side, as if it wearied her to carry it. This gave Ransom time to recognise her; he knew in Boston no such figure as that save Miss Birdseye. Her party, her person, the exalted account Miss Chancellor gave of her, had kept a very distinct place in his mind; and while she stood there in dim circumspection she came back to him as a friend of yesterday. His necessity gave a point to the reminiscences she evoked; it took him only a moment to reflect that she would be able to tell him where Verena Tarrant was at that particular time, and where, if need be, her parents lived. Her eyes rested on him, and as she saw that he was looking at her she didn't go through the ceremony (she had broken so completely with all conventions), of removing them; he evidently represented nothing to her but a sentient fellow-citizen in the enjoyment of his rights, which included that of staring. Miss Birdseye's modesty had never pretended that it was not to be publicly challenged; there were so many bright new motives and ideas in the world that there might even be reasons for looking at her. When Ransom approached her and, raising his hat with a smile, said, 'Shall I stop this car for you, Miss Birdseye?' she only looked at him more vaguely, in her complete failure to seize the idea that this might be simply Fame. She had trudged about the streets of Boston for fifty years, and at no period had she received that amount of attention from dark-eyed young men. She glanced, in an unprejudiced way, at the big parti-coloured human van which now jingled toward them from out of the Cambridge road. 'Well, I should like to get into it, if it will take me home,' she answered. 'Is this a South End car?'

The vehicle had been stopped by the conductor, on his perceiving Miss Birdseye; he evidently recognised her as a frequent passenger. He went, however, through none of the forms of reassurance beyond remarking, 'You want to get right in here—quick,' but stood with his hand raised, in a threatening way, to the cord of his signal-bell.

'You must allow me the honour of taking you home, madam; I will tell you who I am,' Basil Ransom said, in obedience to a rapid reflection. He helped her into the car, the conductor pressed a fraternal hand upon her back, and in a moment the young man was seated beside her, and the jingling had recommenced. At that hour of the day the car was almost empty, and they had it virtually to themselves.

'Well, I know you are some one; I don't think you belong round here,' Miss Birdseye declared, as they proceeded.

'I was once at your house—on a very interesting occasion. Do you remember a party you gave, a year ago last October, to which Miss Chancellor came, and another young lady, who made a wonderful speech?'

'Oh yes! when Verena Tarrant moved us all so! There were a good many there; I don't remember all.'

'I was one of them,' Basil Ransom said; 'I came with Miss Chancellor, who is a kind of relation of mine, and you were very good to me.'

'What did I do?' asked Miss Birdseye, candidly. Then, before he could answer her, she recognised him. 'I remember you now, and Olive bringing you! You're a Southern gentleman—she told me about you afterwards. You don't approve of our great struggle—you want us to be kept down.' The old lady spoke with perfect mildness, as if she had long ago done with passion and resentment. Then she added, 'Well, I presume we can't have the sympathy of all.'

'Doesn't it look as if you had my sympathy, when I get into a car on purpose to see you home—one of the principal agitators?' Ransom inquired, laughing.

'Did you get in on purpose?'

'Quite on purpose. I am not so bad as Miss Chancellor thinks me.'

'Oh, I presume you have your ideas,' said Miss Birdseye. 'Of course, Southerners have peculiar views. I suppose they retain more than one might think. I hope you won't ride too far—I know my way round Boston.'

'Don't object to me, or think me officious,' Ransom replied. 'I want to ask you something.'

Miss Birdseye looked at him again. 'Oh yes, I place you now; you conversed some with Doctor Prance.'

'To my great edification!' Ransom exclaimed. 'And I hope Doctor Prance is well.'

'She looks after every one's health but her own,' said Miss Birdseye, smiling. 'When I tell her that, she says she hasn't got any to look after. She says she's the only woman in Boston that hasn't got a doctor. She was determined she wouldn't be a patient, and it seemed as if the only way not to be one was to be a doctor. She is trying to make me sleep; that's her principal occupation.'

'Is it possible you don't sleep yet?' Ransom asked, almost tenderly.

'Well, just a little. But by the time I get to sleep I have to get up. I can't sleep when I want to live.'

'You ought to come down South,' the young man suggested. 'In that languid air you would doze deliciously!'

'Well, I don't want to be languid,' said Miss Birdseye. 'Besides, I have been down South, in the old times, and I can't say they let me sleep very much; they were always round after me!'

'Do you mean on account of the negroes?'

'Yes, I couldn't think of anything else then. I carried them the Bible.'

Ransom was silent a moment; then he said, in a tone which evidently was carefully considerate, 'I should like to hear all about that!'

'Well, fortunately, we are not required now; we are required for something else.' And Miss Birdseye looked at him with a wandering, tentative humour, as if he would know what she meant.

'You mean for the other slaves!' he exclaimed, with a laugh. 'You can carry them all the Bibles you want.'

'I want to carry them the Statute-book; that must be our Bible now.'

Ransom found himself liking Miss Birdseye very much, and it was quite without hypocrisy or a tinge too much of the local quality in his speech that he said: 'Wherever you go, madam, it will matter little what you carry. You will always carry your goodness.'

For a minute she made no response. Then she murmured: 'That's the way Olive Chancellor told me you talked.'

'I am afraid she has told you little good of me.'

'Well, I am sure she thinks she is right.'

'Thinks it?' said Ransom. 'Why, she knows it, with supreme certainty! By the way, I hope she is well.'

Miss Birdseye stared again. 'Haven't you seen her? Are you not visiting?'

'Oh no, I am not visiting! I was literally passing her house when I met you.'

'Perhaps you live here now,' said Miss Birdseye. And when he had corrected this impression, she added, in a tone which showed with what positive confidence he had now inspired her, 'Hadn't you better drop in?'

'It would give Miss Chancellor no pleasure,' Basil Ransom rejoined. 'She regards me as an enemy in the camp.'

'Well, she is very brave.'

'Precisely. And I am very timid.'

'Didn't you fight once?'

'Yes; but it was in such a good cause!'

Ransom meant this allusion to the great Secession and, by comparison, to the attitude of the resisting male (laudable even as that might be), to be decently jocular; but Miss Birdseye took it very seriously, and sat there for a good while as speechless as if she meant to convey that she had been going on too long now to be able to discuss the propriety of the late rebellion. The young man felt that he had silenced her, and he was very sorry; for, with all deference to the disinterested Southern attitude toward the unprotected female, what he had got into the car with her for was precisely to make her talk. He had wished for general, as well as for particular, news of Verena Tarrant; it was a topic on which he had proposed to draw Miss Birdseye out. He preferred not to broach it himself, and he waited awhile for another opening. At last, when he was on the point of exposing himself by a direct inquiry (he reflected that the exposure would in any case not be long averted), she anticipated him by saying, in a manner which showed that her thoughts had continued in the same train, 'I wonder very much that Miss Tarrant didn't affect you that evening!'

'Ah, but she did!' Ransom said, with alacrity. 'I thought her very charming!'

'Didn't you think her very reasonable?'

'God forbid, madam! I consider women have no business to be reasonable.'

His companion turned upon him, slowly and mildly, and each of her glasses, in her aspect of reproach, had the glitter of an enormous tear. 'Do you regard us, then, simply as lovely baubles?'

The effect of this question, as coming from Miss Birdseye, and referring in some degree to her own venerable identity, was such as to move him to irresistible laughter. But he controlled himself quickly enough to say, with genuine expression, 'I regard you as the dearest thing in life, the only thing which makes it worth living!'

'Worth living for—you! But for us?' suggested Miss Birdseye.

'It's worth any woman's while to be admired as I admire you. Miss Tarrant, of whom we were speaking, affected me, as you say, in this way—that I think more highly still, if possible, of the sex which produced such a delightful young lady.'

'Well, we think everything of her here,' said Miss Birdseye. 'It seems as if it were a real gift.'

'Does she speak often—is there any chance of my hearing her now?'

'She raises her voice a good deal in the places round—like Framingham and Billerica. It seems as if she were gathering strength, just to break over Boston like a wave. In fact she did break, last summer. She is a growing power since her great success at the convention.'

'Ah! her success at the convention was very great?' Ransom inquired, putting discretion into his voice.

Miss Birdseye hesitated a moment, in order to measure her response by the bounds of righteousness. 'Well,' she said, with the tenderness of a long retrospect, 'I have seen nothing like it since I last listened to Eliza P. Moseley.'

'What a pity she isn't speaking somewhere to-night!' Ransom exclaimed.

'Oh, to-night she's out in Cambridge. Olive Chancellor mentioned that.'

'Is she making a speech there?'

'No; she's visiting her home.'

'I thought her home was in Charles Street?'

'Well, no; that's her residence—her principal one—since she became so united to your cousin. Isn't Miss Chancellor your cousin?'

'We don't insist on the relationship,' said Ransom, smiling. 'Are they very much united, the two young ladies?'

'You would say so if you were to see Miss Chancellor when Verena rises to eloquence. It's as if the chords were strung across her own heart; she seems to vibrate, to echo with every word. It's a very close and very beautiful tie, and we think everything of it here. They will work together for a great good!'

'I hope so,' Ransom remarked. 'But in spite of it Miss Tarrant spends a part of her time with her father and mother.'

'Yes, she seems to have something for every one. If you were to see her at home, you would think she was all the daughter. She leads a lovely life!' said Miss Birdseye.

'See her at home? That's exactly what I want!' Ransom rejoined, feeling that if he was to come to this he needn't have had scruples at first. 'I haven't forgotten that she invited me, when I met her.'

'Oh, of course she attracts many visitors,' said Miss Birdseye, limiting her encouragement to this statement.

'Yes; she must be used to admirers. And where, in Cambridge, do her family live?'

'Oh, it's on one of those little streets that don't seem to have very much of a name. But they do call it—they do call it——' she meditated, audibly.

This process was interrupted by an abrupt allocution from the conductor. 'I guess you change here for *your* place. You want one of them blue cars.'

The good lady returned to a sense of the situation, and

Ransom helped her out of the vehicle, with the aid, as before, of a certain amount of propulsion from the conductor. Her road branched off to the right, and she had to wait on the corner of a street, there being as yet no blue car within hail. The corner was quiet and the day favourable to patience—a day of relaxed rigour and intense brilliancy. It was as if the touch of the air itself were gloved, and the street-colouring had the richenss of a superficial thaw. Ransom, of course, waited with his philanthropic companion, though she now protested more vigorously against the idea that a gentleman from the South should pretend to teach an old abolitionist the mysteries of Boston. He promised to leave her when he should have consigned her to the blue car; and meanwhile they stood in the sun, with their backs against an apothecary's window, and she tried again, at his suggestion, to remember the name of Doctor Tarrant's street. 'I guess if you ask for Doctor Tarrant, any one can tell you,' she said; and then suddenly the address came to her—the residence of the mesmeric healer was in Monadnoc Place.

'But you'll have to ask for that, so it comes to the same,' she went on. After this she added, with a friendliness more personal, 'Ain't you going to see your cousin too?'

'Not if I can help it!'

Miss Birdseye gave a little ineffectual sigh. 'Well, I suppose every one must act out their ideal. That's what Olive Chancellor does. She's a very noble character.'

'Oh yes, a glorious nature.'

'You know their opinions are just the same—hers and Verena's,' Miss Birdseye placidly continued. 'So why should you make a distinction?'

'My dear madam,' said Ransom, 'does a woman consist of nothing but her opinions? I like Miss Tarrant's lovely face better, to begin with.'

'Well, she *is* pretty-looking.' And Miss Birdseye gave another sigh, as if she had had a theory submitted to her—that one about a lady's opinions—which, with all that was unfamiliar and peculiar lying behind it, she was really too old to look into much. It might have been the first time she really felt her age. 'There's a blue car,' she said, in a tone of mild relief.

'It will be some moments before it gets here. Moreover, I don't believe that at bottom they *are* Miss Tarrant's opinions,' Ransom added.

'You mustn't think she hasn't a strong hold of them,' his companion exclaimed, more briskly. 'If you think she is not sincere, you are very much mistaken. Those views are just her life.'

'Well, *she* may bring me round to them,' said Ransom, smiling.

Miss Birdseye had been watching her blue car, the advance of which was temporarily obstructed. At this, she transferred her eyes to him, gazing at him solemnly out of the pervasive window of her spectacles. 'Well, I shouldn't wonder if she did! Yes, that will be a good thing. I don't see how you can help being a good deal shaken by her. She has acted on so many.'

'I see; no doubt she will act on me.' Then it occurred to Ransom to add: 'By the way, Miss Birdseye, perhaps you will be so kind as not to mention this meeting of ours to my cousin, in case of your seeing her again. I have a perfectly good conscience in not calling upon her, but I shouldn't like her to think that I announced my slighting intention all over the town. I don't want to offend her, and she had better not know that I have been in Boston. If you don't tell her, no one else will.'

'Do you wish me to conceal——?' murmured Miss Birdseye, panting a little.

'No, I don't want you to conceal anything. I only want you to let this incident pass—to say nothing.'

'Well, I never did anything of that kind.'

'Of what kind?' Ransom was half vexed, half touched by her inability to enter into his point of view, and her resistance made him hold to his idea the more. 'It is very simple, what I ask of you. You are under no obligation to tell Miss Chancellor everything that happens to you, are you?'

His request seemed still something of a shock to the poor old lady's candour. 'Well, I see her very often, and we talk a great deal. And then—won't Verena tell her?'

'I have thought of that—but I hope not.'

'She tells her most everything. Their union is so close.'

'She won't want her to be wounded,' Ransom said, ingeniously.

'Well, you *are* considerate.' And Miss Birdseye continued to gaze at him. 'It's a pity you can't sympathise.'

'As I tell you, perhaps Miss Tarrant will bring me round. You have before you a possible convert,' Ransom went on, without, I fear, putting up the least little prayer to heaven that his dishonesty might be forgiven.

'I should be very happy to think that—after I have told you her address in this secret way.' A smile of infinite mildness glimmered in Miss Birdseye's face, and she added: 'Well, I guess that will be your fate. She *has* affected so many. I would keep very quiet if I thought that. Yes, she will bring you round.'

'I will let you know as soon as she does,' Basil Ransom said. 'Here is your car at last.'

'Well, I believe in the victory of the truth. I won't say anything.' And she suffered the young man to lead her to the car, which had now stopped at their corner.

'I hope very much I shall see you again,' he remarked, as they went.

'Well, I am always round the streets, in Boston.' And while, lifting and pushing, he was helping again to insert her into the oblong receptacle, she turned a little and repeated, 'She *will* affect you! If that's to be your secret, I will keep it,' Ransom heard her subjoin. He raised his hat and waved her a farewell, but she didn't see him; she was squeezing further into the car and making the discovery that this time it was full and there was no seat for her. Surely, however, he said to himself, every man in the place would offer his own to such an innocent old dear.

XXIV

A LITTLE MORE than an hour after this he stood in the parlour of Doctor Tarrant's suburban residence, in Monadnoc Place. He had induced a juvenile maid-servant, by an appeal somewhat impassioned, to let the ladies know that he was there; and she had returned, after a long absence, to say that Miss Tarrant would come down to him in a little while. He possessed himself, according to his wont, of the nearest book (it lay on the table, with an old magazine and a little japanned tray containing Tarrant's professional cards—his denomination as a mesmeric healer), and spent ten minutes in turning it over. It was a biography of Mrs. Ada T. P. Foat, the celebrated trance-lecturer, and was embellished by a portrait representing the lady with a surprised expression and innumerable ringlets. Ransom said to himself, after reading a few pages, that much ridicule had been cast upon Southern literature; but if that was a fair specimen of Northern!—and he threw it back upon the table with a gesture almost as contemptuous as if he had not known perfectly, after so long a residence in the North, that it was not, while he wondered whether this was the sort of thing Miss Tarrant had been brought up on. There was no other book to be seen, and he remembered to have read the magazine; so there was finally nothing for him, as the occupants of the house failed still to appear, but to stare before him, into the bright, bare, common little room, which was so hot that he wished to open a window, and of which an ugly, undraped cross-light seemed to have taken upon itself to reveal the poverty. Ransom, as I have mentioned, had not a high standard of comfort, and noticed little, usually, how people's houses were furnished—it was only when they were very pretty that he observed; but what he saw while he waited at Doctor Tarrant's made him say to himself that it was no wonder Verena liked better to live with Olive Chancellor. He even began to wonder whether it were for the sake of that superior softness she had cultivated Miss Chancellor's favour, and whether Mrs. Luna had been right about her being mercenary and insincere. So many minutes elapsed before she appeared that he had time to remember he really knew nothing to the contrary, as well as to consider the oddity (so great when one did consider it), of his coming out to Cambridge to see her, when he had only a few hours in Boston to spare, a year and a half after she had given him her very casual invitation. She had not refused to receive him, at any rate; she was free to, if it didn't please her. And not only this, but she was apparently making herself fine in his honour, inasmuch as he heard a rapid footstep move to and fro above his head, and even, through the slightness which in Monadnoc Place did service for an upper floor, the sound of drawers and presses opened and closed. Some one was 'flying round,' as they said in Mississippi. At last the stairs creaked under a light tread, and the next moment a brilliant person came into the room.

His reminiscence of her had been very pretty; but now that she had developed and matured, the little prophetess was prettier still. Her splendid hair seemed to shine; her cheek and chin had a curve which struck him by its fineness; her eyes and lips were full of smiles and greetings. She had appeared to him before as a creature of brightness, but now she lighted up the place, she irradiated, she made everything that surrounded her of no consequence; dropping upon the shabby sofa with an effect as charming as if she had been a nymph sinking on a leopard-skin, and with the native sweetness of her voice forcing him to listen till she spoke again. It was not long before he perceived that this added lustre was simply success; she was young and tender still, but the sound of a great applauding audience had been in her ears; it formed an element in which she felt buoyant and floated. Still, however, her glance was as pure as it was direct, and that fantastic fairness hung about her which had made an impression on him of old, and which reminded him of unworldly places— he didn't know where—convent-cloisters or vales of Arcady. At that other time she had been parti-coloured and bedizened, and she had always an air of costume, only now her costume was richer and more chastened. It was her line, her condition, part of her expression. If at Miss Birdseye's, and afterwards in Charles Street, she might have been a rope-dancer, to-day she made a 'scene' of the mean little room in Monadnoc Place, such a scene as a prima donna makes of

daubed canvas and dusty boards. She addressed Basil Ransom
as if she had seen him the other week and his merits were
fresh to her, though she let him, while she sat smiling at him,
explain in his own rather ceremonious way why it was he had
presumed to call upon her on so slight an acquaintance—on
an invitation which she herself had had more than time to
forget. His explanation, as a finished and satisfactory thing,
quite broke down; there was no more impressive reason than
that he had simply wished to see her. He became aware that
this motive loomed large, and that her listening smile, innocent as it was, in the Arcadian manner, of mockery, seemed
to accuse him of not having the courage of his inclination.
He had alluded especially to their meeting at Miss Chancellor's; there it was that she had told him she should be glad
to see him in her home.

'Oh yes, I remember perfectly, and I remember quite as
well seeing you at Miss Birdseye's the night before. I made a
speech—don't you remember? That was delightful.'

'It was delightful indeed,' said Basil Ransom.

'I don't mean my speech; I mean the whole thing. It was
then I made Miss Chancellor's acquaintance. I don't know
whether you know how we work together. She has done so
much for me.'

'Do you still make speeches?' Ransom asked, conscious, as
soon as he had uttered it, that the question was below the
mark.

'Still? Why, I should hope so; it's all I'm good for! It's my
life—or it's going to be. And it's Miss Chancellor's too. We
are determined to do something.'

'And does she make speeches too?'

'Well, she makes mine—or the best part of them. She tells
me what to say—the real things, the strong things. It's Miss
Chancellor as much as me!' said the singular girl, with a generous complacency which was yet half ludicrous.

'I should like to hear you again,' Basil Ransom rejoined.

'Well, you must come some night. You will have plenty of
chances. We are going on from triumph to triumph.'

Her brightness, her self-possession, her air of being a public character, her mixture of the girlish and the comprehensive, startled and confounded her visitor, who felt that if he

had come to gratify his curiosity he should be in danger of going away still more curious than satiated. She added in her gay, friendly, trustful tone—the tone of facile intercourse, the tone in which happy, flower-crowned maidens may have talked to sunburnt young men in the golden age—'I am very familiar with your name; Miss Chancellor has told me all about you.'

'All about me?' Ransom raised his black eyebrows. 'How could she do that? She doesn't know anything about me!'

'Well, she told me you are a great enemy to our movement. Isn't that true? I think you expressed some unfavourable idea that day I met you at her house.'

'If you regard me as an enemy, it's very kind of you to receive me.'

'Oh, a great many gentlemen call,' Verena said, calmly and brightly. 'Some call simply to inquire. Some call because they have heard of me, or been present on some occasion when I have moved them. Every one is so interested.'

'And you have been in Europe,' Ransom remarked, in a moment.

'Oh yes, we went over to see if they were in advance. We had a magnificent time—we saw all the leaders.'

'The leaders?' Ransom repeated.

'Of the emancipation of our sex. There are gentlemen there, as well as ladies. Olive had splendid introductions in all countries, and we conversed with all the earnest people. We heard much that was suggestive. And as for Europe!'—and the young lady paused, smiling at him and ending in a happy sigh, as if there were more to say on the subject than she could attempt on such short notice.

'I suppose it's very attractive,' said Ransom, encouragingly.

'It's just a dream!'

'And did you find that they were in advance?'

'Well, Miss Chancellor thought they were. She was surprised at some things we observed, and concluded that perhaps she hadn't done the Europeans justice—she has got such an open mind, it's as wide as the sea!—while I incline to the opinion that on the whole *we* make the better show. The state of the movement there reflects their general culture, and their general culture is higher than ours (I mean taking the term in its broadest sense). On the other hand, the *special* condition—moral, social, personal—of our sex seems to me to be superior in this country; I mean regarded in relation—in proportion as it were—to the social phase at large. I must add that we did see some noble specimens over there. In England we met some lovely women, highly cultivated, and of immense organising power. In France we saw some wonderful, contagious types; we passed a delightful evening with the celebrated Marie Verneuil; she was released from prison, you know, only a few weeks before. Our total impression was that it is only a question of time—the future is ours. But everywhere we heard one cry—"How long, O Lord, how long?" '

Basil Ransom listened to this considerable statement with a feeling which, as the current of Miss Tarrant's facile utterance flowed on, took the form of an hilarity charmed into stillness by the fear of losing something. There was indeed a sweet comicality in seeing this pretty girl sit there and, in answer to a casual, civil inquiry, drop into oratory as a natural thing. Had she forgotten where she was, and did she take him for a full house? She had the same turns and cadences, almost the same gestures, as if she had been on the platform; and the great queerness of it was that, with such a manner, she should escape being odious. She was not odious, she was delightful; she was not dogmatic, she was genial. No wonder she was a success, if she speechified as a bird sings! Ransom could see, too, from her easy lapse, how the lecture-tone was the thing in the world with which, by education, by association, she was most familiar. He didn't know what to make of her; she was an astounding young phenomenon. The other time came back to him afresh, and how she had stood up at Miss Birdseye's; it occurred to him that an element, here, had been wanting. Several moments after she had ceased speaking he became conscious that the expression of his face presented a perceptible analogy to a broad grin. He changed his posture, saying the first thing that came into his head. 'I presume you do without your father now.'

'Without my father?'

'To set you going, as he did that time I heard you.'

'Oh, I see; you thought I had begun a lecture!' And she laughed, in perfect good humour. 'They tell me I speak as I talk, so I suppose I talk as I speak. But you mustn't put me on what I saw and heard in Europe. That's to be the title of an address I am now preparing, by the way. Yes, I don't depend on father any more,' she went on, while Ransom's sense of having said too sarcastic a thing was deepened by her perfect indifference to it. 'He finds his patients draw off about enough, any way. But I owe him everything; if it hadn't been for him, no one would ever have known I had a gift—not even myself. He started me so, once for all, that I now go alone.'

'You go beautifully,' said Ransom, wanting to say something agreeable, and even respectfully tender, to her, but troubled by the fact that there was nothing he could say that didn't sound rather like chaff. There was no resentment in her, however, for in a moment she said to him, as quickly as it occurred to her, in the manner of a person repairing an accidental omission, 'It was very good of you to come so far.'

This was a sort of speech it was never safe to make to Ransom; there was no telling what retribution it might entail. 'Do you suppose any journey is too great, too wearisome, when it's a question of so great a pleasure?' On this occasion it was not worse than that.

'Well, people *have* come from other cities,' Verena answered, not with pretended humility, but with pretended pride. 'Do you know Cambridge?'

'This is the first time I have ever been here.'

'Well, I suppose you have heard of the university; it's so celebrated.'

'Yes—even in Mississippi. I suppose it's very fine.'

'I presume it is,' said Verena; 'but you can't expect me to speak with much admiration of an institution of which the doors are closed to our sex.'

'Do you then advocate a system of education in common?'

'I advocate equal rights, equal opportunities, equal privileges. So does Miss Chancellor,' Verena added, with just a perceptible air of feeling that her declaration needed support.

'Oh, I thought what she wanted was simply a different inequality—simply to turn out the men altogether,' Ransom said.

'Well, she thinks we have great arrears to make up. I do tell her, sometimes, that what she desires is not only justice but vengeance. I think she admits that,' Verena continued, with a certain solemnity. The subject, however, held her but an instant, and before Ransom had time to make any comment, she went on, in a different tone: 'You don't mean to say you live in Mississippi *now*? Miss Chancellor told me when you were in Boston before, that you had located in New York.' She persevered in this reference to himself, for when he had assented to her remark about New York, she asked him whether he had quite given up the South.

'Given it up—the poor, dear, desolate old South? Heaven forbid!' Basil Ransom exclaimed.

She looked at him for a moment with an added softness. 'I presume it is natural you should love your home. But I am afraid you think I don't love mine much; I have been here—for so long—so little. Miss Chancellor *has* absorbed me—there is no doubt about that. But it's a pity I wasn't with her to-day.' Ransom made no answer to this; he was incapable of telling Miss Tarrant that if she had been he would not have called upon her. It was not, indeed, that he was not incapable of hypocrisy, for when she had asked him if he had seen his cousin the night before, and he had replied that he hadn't seen her at all, and she had exclaimed with a candour which the next minute made her blush, 'Ah, you don't mean to say you haven't forgiven her!'—after this he put on a look of innocence sufficient to carry off the inquiry, 'Forgiven her for what?'

Verena coloured at the sound of her own words. 'Well, I could see how much she felt, that time at her house.'

'What did she feel?' Basil Ransom asked, with the natural provokingness of a man.

I know not whether Verena was provoked, but she answered with more spirit than sequence: 'Well, you know you *did* pour contempt on us, ever so much; I could see how it worked Olive up. Are you not going to see her at all?'

'Well, I shall think about that; I am here only for three or four days,' said Ransom, smiling as men smile when they are perfectly unsatisfactory.

It is very possible that Verena was provoked, inaccessible as she was, in a general way, to irritation; for she rejoined in a moment, with a little deliberate air: 'Well, perhaps it's as well you shouldn't go, if you haven't changed at all.'

'I haven't changed at all,' said the young man, smiling still, with his elbows on the arms of his chair, his shoulders pushed up a little, and his thin brown hands interlocked in front of him.

'Well, I have had visitors who were quite opposed!' Verena announced, as if such news could not possibly alarm her. Then she added, 'How then did you know I was out here?'

'Miss Birdseye told me.'

'Oh, I am so glad you went to see *her!*' the girl cried, speaking again with the impetuosity of a moment before.

'I didn't go to see her. I met her in the street, just as she was leaving Miss Chancellor's door. I spoke to her, and accompanied her some distance. I passed that way because I knew it was the direct way to Cambridge—from the Common—and I was coming out to see you any way—on the chance.'

'On the chance?' Verena repeated.

'Yes; Mrs. Luna, in New York, told me you were sometimes here, and I wanted, at any rate, to make the attempt to find you.'

It may be communicated to the reader that it was very agreeable to Verena to learn that her visitor had made this arduous pilgrimage (for she knew well enough how people in Boston regarded a winter journey to the academic suburb) with only half the prospect of a reward; but her pleasure was mixed with other feelings, or at least with the consciousness that the whole situation was rather less simple than the elements of her life had been hitherto. There was the germ of disorder in this invidious distinction which Mr. Ransom had suddenly made between Olive Chancellor, who was related to him by blood, and herself, who had never been related to him in any way whatever. She knew Olive by this time well enough to wish not to reveal it to her, and yet it would be something quite new for her to undertake to conceal such an incident as her having spent an hour with Mr. Ransom during a flying visit he had made to Boston. She had spent hours with other gentlemen, whom Olive didn't see; but that was different, because her friend knew about her doing it and didn't care, in regard to the persons—didn't care, that is, as she would care in this case. It was vivid to Verena's mind that now Olive *would* care. She had talked about Mr. Burrage, and Mr. Pardon, and even about some gentlemen in Europe, and she had not (after the first few days, a year and a half before) talked about Mr. Ransom.

Nevertheless there were reasons, clear to Verena's view, for wishing either that he would go and see Olive or would keep away from *her*; and the responsibility of treating the fact that he had not so kept away as a secret seemed the greater, perhaps, in the light of this other fact, that so far as simply seeing Mr. Ransom went—why, she quite liked it. She had remembered him perfectly after their two former meetings, superficial as their contact then had been; she had thought of him at moments and wondered whether she should like him if she were to know him better. Now, at the end of twenty minutes, she did know him better, and found that he had rather a curious, but still a pleasant way. There he was, at any rate, and she didn't wish his call to be spoiled by any uncomfortable implication of consequences. So she glanced off, at the touch of Mrs. Luna's name; it seemed to afford relief. 'Oh yes, Mrs. Luna—isn't she fascinating?'

Ransom hesitated a little. 'Well, no, I don't think she is.'

'You ought to like her—she hates our movement!' And Verena asked, further, numerous questions about the brilliant Adeline; whether he saw her often, whether she went out much, whether she was admired in New York, whether he thought her very handsome. He answered to the best of his ability, but soon made the reflection that he had not come out to Monadnoc Place to talk about Mrs. Luna; in consequence of which, to change the subject (as well as to acquit himself of a social duty), he began to speak of Verena's parents, to express regret that Mrs. Tarrant had been sick, and fear that he was not to have the pleasure of seeing her. 'She is a great deal better,' Verena said; 'but she's lying down; she lies down a great deal when she has got nothing else to do. Mother's very peculiar,' she added in a moment; 'she lies down when she feels well and happy, and when she's sick she walks about—she roams all round the house. If you hear her on the stairs a good deal, you can be pretty sure she's very bad. She'll be very much interested to hear about you after you have left.'

Ransom glanced at his watch. 'I hope I am not staying too long—that I am not taking you away from her.'

'Oh no; she likes visitors, even when she can't see them. If it didn't take her so long to rise, she would have been down here by this time. I suppose you think she has missed me, since I have been so absorbed. Well, so she has, but she knows it's for my good. She would make any sacrifice for affection.'

The fancy suddenly struck Ransom of asking, in response to this, 'And you? would you make any?'

Verena gave him a bright natural stare. 'Any sacrifice for affection?' She thought a moment, and then she said: 'I don't think I have a right to say, because I have never been asked. I don't remember ever to have had to make a sacrifice—not an important one.'

'Lord! you must have had a happy life!'

'I have been very fortunate, I know that. I don't know what to do when I think how some women—how most women— suffer. But I must not speak of that,' she went on, with her smile coming back to her. 'If you oppose our movement, you won't want to hear of the suffering of women!'

'The suffering of women is the suffering of all humanity,' Ransom returned. 'Do you think any movement is going to stop that—or all the lectures from now to doomsday? We are born to suffer—and to bear it, like decent people.'

'Oh, I adore heroism!' Verena interposed.

'And as for women,' Ransom went on, 'they have one source of happiness that is closed to us—the consciousness that their presence here below lifts half the load of *our* suffering.'

Verena thought this very graceful, but she was not sure it was not rather sophistical; she would have liked to have Olive's judgment upon it. As that was not possible for the present, she abandoned the question (since learning that Mr. Ransom had passed over Olive, to come to her, she had become rather fidgety), and inquired of the young man, irrelevantly, whether he knew any one else in Cambridge.

'Not a creature; as I tell you, I have never been here before.

Your image alone attracted me; this charming interview will be henceforth my only association with the place.'

'It's a pity you couldn't have a few more,' said Verena, musingly.

'A few more interviews? I should be unspeakably delighted!'

'A few more associations. Did you see the colleges as you came?'

'I had a glimpse of a large enclosure, with some big buildings. Perhaps I can look at them better as I go back to Boston.'

'Oh yes, you ought to see them—they have improved so much of late. The inner life, of course, is the greatest interest, but there is some fine architecture, if you are not familiar with Europe.' She paused a moment, looking at him with an eye that seemed to brighten, and continued quickly, like a person who had collected herself for a little jump, 'If you would like to walk round a little, I shall be very glad to show you.'

'To walk round—with you to show me?' Ransom repeated. 'My dear Miss Tarrant, it would be the greatest privilege— the greatest happiness—of my life. What a delightful idea— what an ideal guide!'

Verena got up; she would go and put on her hat; he must wait a little. Her offer had a frankness and friendliness which gave him a new sensation, and he could not know that as soon as she had made it (though she had hesitated too, with a moment of intense reflection), she seemed to herself strangely reckless. An impulse pushed her; she obeyed it with her eyes open. She felt as a girl feels when she commits her first conscious indiscretion. She had done many things before which many people would have called indiscreet, but that quality had not even faintly belonged to them in her own mind; she had done them in perfect good faith and with a remarkable absence of palpitation. This superficially ingenuous proposal to walk around the colleges with Mr. Ransom had really another colour; it deepened the ambiguity of her position, by reason of a prevision which I shall presently mention. If Olive was not to know that she had seen him, this extension of their interview would double her secret. And yet, while she saw it grow—this monstrous little mystery—she couldn't feel sorry that she was going out with Olive's cousin. As I have already said, she had become nervous. She went to put on her hat, but at the door of the room she stopped, turned round, and presented herself to her visitor with a small spot in either cheek, which had appeared there within the instant. 'I have suggested this, because it seems to me I ought to do something for you—in return,' she said. 'It's nothing, simply sitting there with me. And we haven't got anything else. This is our only hospitality. And the day seems so splendid.'

The modesty, the sweetness, of this little explanation, with a kind of intimated desire, constituting almost an appeal, for rightness, which seemed to pervade it, left a fragrance in the air after she had vanished. Ransom walked up and down the room, with his hands in his pockets, under the influence of it, without taking up even once the book about Mrs. Foat. He occupied the time in asking himself by what perversity of fate or of inclination such a charming creature was ranting upon platforms and living in Olive Chancellor's pocket, or how a ranter and sycophant could possibly be so engaging. And she was so disturbingly beautiful, too. This last fact was not less evident when she came down arranged for their walk. They left the house, and as they proceeded he remembered that he had asked himself earlier how he could do honour to such a combination of leisure and ethereal mildness as he had waked up to that morning—a mildness that seemed the very breath of his own latitude. This question was answered now; to do exactly what he was doing at that moment was an observance sufficiently festive.

XXV

THEY PASSED through two or three small, short streets, which, with their little wooden houses, with still more wooden door-yards, looked as if they had been constructed by the nearest carpenter and his boy—a sightless, soundless, interspaced, embryonic region—and entered a long avenue which, fringed on either side with fresh villas, offering themselves trustfully to the public, had the distinction of a wide pavement of neat red brick. The new paint on the square detached houses shone afar off in the transparent air: they had, on top, little cupolas and belvederes, in front a pillared piazza, made bare by the indoor life of winter, on either side a bowwindow or two, and everywhere an embellishment of scallops, brackets, cornices, wooden flourishes. They stood, for the most part, on small eminences, lifted above the impertinence of hedge or paling, well up before the world, with all the good conscience which in many cases came, as Ransom saw (and he had noticed the same ornament when he traversed with Olive the quarter of Boston inhabited by Miss Birdseye), from a silvered number, affixed to the glass above the door, in figures huge enough to be read by the people who, in the periodic horse-cars, travelled along the middle of the avenue. It was to these glittering badges that many of the houses on either side owed their principal identity. One of the horse-cars now advanced in the straight, spacious distance; it was almost the only object that animated the prospect, which, in its large cleanness, its implication of strict business-habits on the part of all the people who were not there, Ransom thought very impressive. As he went on with Verena he asked her about the Women's Convention, the year before; whether it had accomplished much work and she had enjoyed it.

'What do you care about the work it accomplished?' said the girl. 'You don't take any interest in that.'

'You mistake my attitude. I don't like it, but I greatly fear it.'

In answer to this Verena gave a free laugh. 'I don't believe you fear much!'

'The bravest men have been afraid of women. Won't you even tell me whether you enjoyed it? I am told you made an immense sensation there—that you leaped into fame.'

Verena never waved off an allusion to her ability, her eloquence; she took it seriously, without any flutter or protest, and had no more manner about it than if it concerned the goddess Minerva. 'I believe I attracted considerable attention; of course, that's what Olive wants—it paves the way for future work. I have no doubt I reached many that wouldn't have been reached otherwise. They think that's my great use—to take hold of the outsiders, as it were; of those who are prejudiced or thoughtless, or who don't care about anything unless it's amusing. I wake up the attention.'

'That's the class to which I belong,' Ransom said. 'Am I not an outsider? I wonder whether you would have reached me—or waked up my attention!'

Verena was silent awhile, as they walked; he heard the light click of her boots on the smooth bricks. Then—'I think I *have* waked it up a little,' she replied, looking straight before her.

'Most assuredly! You have made me wish tremendously to contradict you.'

'Well, that's a good sign.'

'I suppose it was very exciting—your convention,' Ransom went on, in a moment; 'the sort of thing you would miss very much if you were to return to the ancient fold.'

'The ancient fold, you say very well, where women were slaughtered like sheep! Oh, last June, for a week, we just quivered! There were delegates from every State and every city; we lived in a crowd of people and of ideas; the heat was intense, the weather magnificent, and great thoughts and brilliant sayings flew round like darting fire-flies. Olive had six celebrated, high-minded women staying in her house—two in a room; and in the summer evenings we sat in the open windows, in her parlour, looking out on the bay, with the lights gleaming in the water, and talked over the doings of the morning, the speeches, the incidents, the fresh contributions to the cause. We had some tremendously earnest discussions, which it would have been a benefit to you to hear, or any man who doesn't think that we can rise to the highest

point. Then we had some refreshment—we consumed quantities of ice-cream!' said Verena, in whom the note of gaiety
alternated with that of earnestness, almost of exaltation, in a
manner which seemed to Basil Ransom absolutely and fasci-
natingly original. 'Those were great nights!' she added, between a laugh and a sigh.

Her description of the convention put the scene before him
vividly; he seemed to see the crowded, overheated hall, which
he was sure was filled with carpet-baggers, to hear flushed
women, with loosened bonnet-strings, forcing thin voices
into ineffectual shrillness. It made him angry, and all the more
angry, that he hadn't a reason, to think of the charming creature at his side being mixed up with such elements, pushed
and elbowed by them, conjoined with them in emulation, in
unsightly strainings and clappings and shoutings, in wordy,
windy iteration of inanities. Worst of all was the idea that she
should have expressed such a congregation to itself so accept-
ably, have been acclaimed and applauded by hoarse throats,
have been lifted up, to all the vulgar multitude, as the queen
of the occasion. He made the reflection, afterwards, that he
was singularly ill-grounded in his wrath, inasmuch as it was
none of his business what use Miss Tarrant chose to make of
her energies, and, in addition to this, nothing else was to have
been expected of her. But that reflection was absent now, and
in its absence he saw only the fact that his companion had
been odiously perverted. 'Well, Miss Tarrant,' he said, with a
deeper seriousness than showed in his voice, 'I am forced to
the painful conclusion that you are simply ruined.'

'Ruined? Ruined yourself!'

'Oh, I know the kind of women that Miss Chancellor had
at her house, and what a group you must have made when
you looked out at the Back Bay! It depresses me very much
to think of it.'

'We made a lovely, interesting group, and, if we had had a
spare minute we would have been photographed,' Verena
said.

This led him to ask her if she had ever subjected herself to
the process; and she answered that a photographer had been
after her as soon as she got back from Europe, and that she
had sat for him, and that there were certain shops in Boston

where her portrait could be obtained. She gave him this information very simply, without pretence of vagueness of knowledge, spoke of the matter rather respectfully, indeed, as if it might be of some importance; and when he said that he should go and buy one of the little pictures as soon as he returned to town, contented herself with replying, 'Well, be sure you pick out a good one!' He had not been altogether without a hope that she would offer to give him one, with her name written beneath, which was a mode of acquisition he would greatly have preferred; but this, evidently, had not occurred to her, and now, as they went further, her thought was following a different train. That was proved by her remarking, at the end of a silence, inconsequently, 'Well, it showed I have a great use!' As he stared, wondering what she meant, she explained that she referred to the brilliancy of her success at the convention. 'It proved I have a great use,' she repeated, 'and that is all I care for!'

'The use of a truly amiable woman is to make some honest man happy,' Ransom said, with a sententiousness of which he was perfectly aware.

It was so marked that it caused her to stop short in the middle of the broad walk, while she looked at him with shining eyes. 'See here, Mr. Ransom, do you know what strikes me?' she exclaimed. 'The interest you take in me isn't really controversial—a bit. It's quite personal!' She was the most extraordinary girl; she could speak such words as those without the smallest look of added consciousness coming into her face, without the least supposable intention of coquetry, or any visible purpose of challenging the young man to say more.

'My interest in you—my interest in you,' he began. Then hesitating, he broke off suddenly. 'It is certain your discovery doesn't make it any less!'

'Well, that's better,' she went on; 'for we needn't dispute.'

He laughed at the way she arranged it, and they presently reached the irregular group of heterogeneous buildings—chapels, dormitories, libraries, halls—which, scattered among slender trees, over a space reserved by means of a low rustic fence, rather than inclosed (for Harvard knows nothing either of the jealousy or the dignity of high walls and guarded gateways), constitutes the great university of Massachusetts. The yard, or college-precinct, is traversed by a number of straight little paths, over which, at certain hours of the day, a thousand undergraduates, with books under their arm and youth in their step, flit from one school to another. Verena Tarrant knew her way round, as she said to her companion; it was not the first time she had taken an admiring visitor to see the local monuments. Basil Ransom, walking with her from point to point, admired them all, and thought several of them exceedingly quaint and venerable. The rectangular structures of old red brick especially gratified his eye; the afternoon sun was yellow on their homely faces; their windows showed a peep of flower-pots and bright-coloured curtains; they wore an expression of scholastic quietude, and exhaled for the young Mississippian a tradition, an antiquity. 'This is the place where I ought to have been,' he said to his charming guide. 'I should have had a good time if I had been able to study here.'

'Yes; I presume you feel yourself drawn to any place where ancient prejudices are garnered up,' she answered, not without archness. 'I know by the stand you take about our cause that you share the superstitions of the old bookmen. You ought to have been at one of those really mediæval universities that we saw on the other side, at Oxford, or Göttingen, or Padua. You would have been in perfect sympathy with their spirit.'

'Well, I don't know much about those old haunts,' Ransom rejoined. 'I reckon this is good enough for me. And then it would have had the advantage that your residence isn't far, you know.'

'Oh, I guess we shouldn't have seen you much at my residence! As you live in New York, you come, but here you wouldn't; that is always the way.' With this light philosophy Verena beguiled the transit to the library, into which she introduced her companion with the air of a person familiar with the sanctified spot. This edifice, a diminished copy of the chapel of King's College, at the greater Cambridge, is a rich and impressive institution; and as he stood there, in the bright, heated stillness, which seemed suffused with the odour of old print and old bindings, and looked up into the high, light vaults that hung over quiet book-laden galleries, alcoves and tables, and glazed cases where rarer treasures gleamed more vaguely, over busts of benefactors and portraits of worthies, bowed heads of working students and the gentle creak of passing messengers—as he took possession, in a comprehensive glance, of the wealth and wisdom of the place, he felt more than ever the soreness of an opportunity missed; but he abstained from expressing it (it was too deep for that), and in a moment Verena had introduced him to a young lady, a friend of hers, who, as she explained, was working on the catalogue, and whom she had asked for on entering the library, at a desk where another young lady was occupied. Miss Catching, the first-mentioned young lady, presented herself with promptness, offered Verena a low-toned but appreciative greeting, and, after a little, undertook to explain to Ransom the mysteries of the catalogue, which consisted of a myriad little cards, disposed alphabetically in immense chests of drawers. Ransom was deeply interested, and as, with Verena, he followed Miss Catching about (she was so good as to show them the establishment in all its ramifications), he considered with attention the young lady's fair ringlets and re-fined, anxious expression, saying to himself that this was in the highest degree a New England type. Verena found an op-portunity to mention to him that she was wrapped up in the cause, and there was a moment during which he was afraid that his companion would expose him to her as one of its traducers; but there was that in Miss Catching's manner (and in the influence of the lofty halls), which deprecated loud pleasantry, and seemed to say, moreover, that if she were treated to such a revelation she should not know under what letter to range it.

'Now there is one place where perhaps it would be indeli-cate to take a Mississippian,' Verena said, after this episode. 'I mean the great place that towers above the others—that big building with the beautiful pinnacles, which you see from every point.' But Basil Ransom had heard of the great Me-morial Hall; he knew what memories it enshrined, and the worst that he should have to suffer there; and the ornate, overtopping structure, which was the finest piece of architec-ture he had ever seen, had moreover solicited his enlarged curiosity for the last half-hour. He thought there was rather too much brick about it, but it was buttressed, cloistered, turreted, dedicated, superscribed, as he had never seen anything; though it didn't look old, it looked significant; it covered a large area, and it sprang majestic into the winter air. It was detached from the rest of the collegiate group, and stood in a grassy triangle of its own. As he approached it with Verena she suddenly stopped, to decline responsibility. 'Now mind, if you don't like what's inside, it isn't my fault.'

He looked at her an instant, smiling. 'Is there anything against Mississippi?'

'Well, no, I don't think she is mentioned. But there is great praise of our young men in the war.'

'It says they were brave, I suppose.'

'Yes, it says so in Latin.'

'Well, so they were—I know something about that,' Basil Ransom said. 'I must be brave enough to face them—it isn't the first time.' And they went up the low steps and passed into the tall doors. The Memorial Hall of Harvard consists of three main divisions: one of them a theatre, for academic ceremonies; another a vast refectory covered with a timbered roof, hung about with portraits and lighted by stained windows, like the halls of the colleges of Oxford; and the third, the most interesting, a chamber high, dim, and severe, consecrated to the sons of the university who fell in the long Civil War. Ransom and his companion wandered from one part of the building to another, and stayed their steps at several impressive points; but they lingered longest in the presence of the white, ranged tablets, each of which, in its proud, sad clearness, is inscribed with the name of a student-soldier. The effect of the place is singularly noble and solemn, and it is impossible to feel it without a lifting of the heart. It stands there for duty and honour, it speaks of sacrifice and example, seems a kind of temple to youth, manhood, generosity. Most of them were young, all were in their prime, and all of them had fallen; this simple idea hovers before the visitor and makes him read with tenderness each name and place—names often without other history, and forgotten Southern battles. For Ransom these things were not a challenge nor a taunt; they touched him with respect, with the sentiment of beauty.

He was capable of being a generous foeman, and he forgot, now, the whole question of sides and parties; the simple emotion of the old fighting-time came back to him, and the monument around him seemed an embodiment of that memory; it arched over friends as well as enemies, the victims of defeat as well as the sons of triumph.

'It is very beautiful—but I think it is very dreadful!' This remark, from Verena, called him back to the present. 'It's a real sin to put up such a building, just to glorify a lot of bloodshed. If it wasn't so majestic, I would have it pulled down.'

'That is delightful feminine logic!' Ransom answered. 'If, when women have the conduct of affairs, they fight as well as they reason, surely for them too we shall have to set up memorials.'

Verena retorted that they would reason so well they would have no need to fight—they would usher in the reign of peace. 'But this is very peaceful too,' she added, looking about her; and she sat down on a low stone ledge, as if to enjoy the influence of the scene. Ransom left her alone for ten minutes; he wished to take another look at the inscribed tablets, and read again the names of the various engagements, at several of which he had been present. When he came back to her she greeted him abruptly, with a question which had no reference to the solemnity of the spot. 'If Miss Birdseye knew you were coming out to see me, can't *she* easily tell Olive? Then won't Olive make her reflections about your neglect of herself?'

'I don't care for her reflections. At any rate, I asked Miss Birdseye, as a favour, not to mention to her that she had met me,' Ransom added.

Verena was silent a moment. 'Your logic is almost as good as a woman's. Do change your mind and go to see her now,' she went on. 'She will probably be at home by the time you get to Charles Street. If she was a little strange, a little stiff with you before (I know just how she must have been), all that will be different to-day.'

'Why will it be different?'

'Oh, she will be easier, more genial, much softer.'

'I don't believe it,' said Ransom; and his scepticism seemed none the less complete because it was light and smiling.

'She is much happier now—she can afford not to mind you.'

'Not to mind me? That's a nice inducement for a gentleman to go and see a lady!'

'Well, she will be more gracious, because she feels now that she is more successful.'

'You mean because she has brought you out? Oh, I have no doubt that has cleared the air for her immensely, and you have improved her very much. But I have got a charming impression out here, and I have no wish to put another—which won't be charming, anyhow you arrange it—on top of it.'

'Well, she will be sure to know you have been round here, at any rate,' Verena rejoined.

'How will she know, unless you tell her?'

'I tell her everything,' said the girl; and now as soon as she had spoken, she blushed. He stood before her, tracing a figure on the mosaic pavement with his cane, conscious that in a moment they had become more intimate. They were discussing their affairs, which had nothing to do with the heroic symbols that surrounded them; but their affairs had suddenly grown so serious that there was no want of decency in their lingering there for the purpose. The implication that his visit might remain as a secret between them made them both feel it differently. To ask her to keep it so would have been, as it seemed to Ransom, a liberty, and, moreover, he didn't care so much as that; but if she were to prefer to do so such a preference would only make him consider the more that his expedition had been a success.

'Oh, then, you can tell her this!' he said in a moment.

'If I shouldn't, it would be the first——' And Verena checked herself.

'You must arrange that with your conscience,' Ransom went on, laughing.

They came out of the hall, passed down the steps, and emerged from the Delta, as that portion of the college precinct is called. The afternoon had begun to wane, but the air was filled with a pink brightness, and there was a cool, pure smell, a vague breath of spring.

'Well, if I don't tell Olive, then you must leave me here,'

said Verena, stopping in the path and putting out a hand of farewell.

'I don't understand. What has that to do with it? Besides I thought you said you *must* tell,' Ransom added. In playing with the subject this way, in enjoying her visible hesitation, he was slightly conscious of a man's brutality—of being pushed by an impulse to test her good-nature, which seemed to have no limit. It showed no sign of perturbation as she answered:

'Well, I want to be free—to do as I think best. And, if there is a chance of my keeping it back, there mustn't be anything more—there must not, Mr. Ransom, really.'

'Anything more? Why, what are you afraid there will be— if I should simply walk home with you?'

'I must go alone, I must hurry back to mother,' she said, for all reply. And she again put out her hand, which he had not taken before.

Of course he took it now, and even held it a moment; he didn't like being dismissed, and was thinking of pretexts to linger. 'Miss Birdseye said you would convert me, but you haven't yet,' it came into his head to say.

'You can't tell yet; wait a little. My influence is peculiar; it sometimes comes out a long time afterwards!' This speech, on Verena's part, was evidently perfunctory, and the grandeur of her self-reference jocular; she was much more serious when she went on quickly, 'Do you mean to say Miss Birdseye promised you that?'

'Oh yes. Talk about influence! you should have seen the influence I obtained over her.'

'Well, what good will it do, if I'm going to tell Olive about your visit?'

'Well, you see, I think she hopes you won't. She believes you are going to convert me privately—so that I shall blaze forth, suddenly, out of the darkness of Mississippi, as a first-class proselyte: very effective and dramatic.'

Verena struck Basil Ransom as constantly simple, but there were moments when her candour seemed to him preternatural. 'If I thought that would be the effect, I might make an exception,' she remarked, speaking as if such a result were, after all, possible.

'Oh, Miss Tarrant, you will convert me enough, any way,' said the young man.

'Enough? What do you mean by enough?'

'Enough to make me terribly unhappy.'

She looked at him a moment, evidently not understanding; but she tossed him a retort at a venture, turned away, and took her course homeward. The retort was that if he should be unhappy it would serve him right—a form of words that committed her to nothing. As he returned to Boston he saw how curious he should be to learn whether she had betrayed him, as it were, to Miss Chancellor. He might learn through Mrs. Luna; that would almost reconcile him to going to see her again. Olive would mention it in writing to her sister, and Adeline would repeat the complaint. Perhaps she herself would even make him a scene about it; that would be, for him, part of the unhappiness he had foretold to Verena Tarrant.

XXVI

'M RS. HENRY BURRAGE, at home Wednesday evening, March 26th, at half-past nine o'clock.' It was in consequence of having received a card with these words inscribed upon it that Basil Ransom presented himself, on the evening she had designated, at the house of a lady he had never heard of before. The account of the relation of effect to cause is not complete, however, unless I mention that the card bore, furthermore, in the left-hand lower corner, the words: 'An Address from Miss Verena Tarrant.' He had an idea (it came mainly from the look and even the odour of the engraved pasteboard), that Mrs. Burrage was a member of the fashionable world, and it was with considerable surprise that he found himself in such an element. He wondered what had induced a denizen of that fine air to send him an invitation; then he said to himself that, obviously, Verena Tarrant had simply requested that this should be done. Mrs. Henry Burrage, whoever she might be, had asked her if she shouldn't like some of her own friends to be present, and she had said, Oh yes, and mentioned him in the happy group. She had been able to give Mrs. Burrage his address, for had it not been contained in the short letter he despatched to Monadnoc Place soon after his return from Boston, in which he thanked Miss Tarrant afresh for the charming hour she had enabled him to spend at Cambridge? She had not answered his letter at the time, but Mrs. Burrage's card was a very good answer. Such a missive deserved a rejoinder, and it was by way of rejoinder that he entered the street car which, on the evening of March 26th, was to deposit him at a corner adjacent to Mrs. Burrage's dwelling. He almost never went to evening parties (he knew scarcely any one who gave them, though Mrs. Luna had broken him in a little), and he was sure this occasion was of festive intention, would have nothing in common with the nocturnal 'exercises' at Miss Birdseye's; but he would have exposed himself to almost any social discomfort in order to see Verena Tarrant on the platform. The platform it evidently was to be—private if not public—since one was admitted by a ticket given away if not sold. He took his in his pocket, quite ready to present it at the door. It would take some time for me to explain the contradiction to the reader; but Basil Ransom's desire to be present at one of Verena's regular performances was not diminished by the fact that he detested her views and thought the whole business a poor perversity. He understood her now very well (since his visit to Cambridge); he saw she was honest and natural; she had queer, bad lecture-blood in her veins, and a comically false idea of the aptitude of little girls for conducting movements; but her enthusiasm was of the purest, her illusions had a fragrance, and so far as the mania for producing herself personally was concerned, it had been distilled into her by people who worked her for ends which to Basil Ransom could only appear insane. She was a touching, ingenuous victim, unconscious of the pernicious forces which were hurrying her to her ruin. With this idea of ruin there had already associated itself in the young man's mind, the idea—a good deal more dim and incomplete—of rescue; and it was the disposition to confirm himself in the view that her charm was her own, and her fallacies, her absurdity, a mere reflection of unlucky circumstance, that led him to make an effort to behold her in the position in which he could least bear to think of her. Such a glimpse was all that was wanted to prove to him that she was a person for whom he might open an unlimited credit of tender compassion. He expected to suffer—to suffer deliciously.

By the time he had crossed Mrs. Burrage's threshold there was no doubt whatever in his mind that he was in the fashionable world. It was embodied strikingly in the stout, elderly, ugly lady, dressed in a brilliant colour, with a twinkle of jewels and a bosom much uncovered, who stood near the door of the first room, and with whom the people passing in before him were shaking hands. Ransom made her a Mississippian bow, and she said she was delighted to see him, while people behind him pressed him forward. He yielded to the impulsion, and found himself in a great saloon, amid lights and flowers, where the company was dense, and there were more twinkling, smiling ladies, with uncovered bosoms. It was certainly the fashionable world, for there was no one there whom he had ever seen before. The walls of the room were covered with pictures—the very ceiling was painted and framed. The people pushed each other a little, edged about, advanced and retreated, looking at each other with differing faces—sometimes blandly, unperceivingly, sometimes with a harshness of contemplation, a kind of cruelty, Ransom thought; sometimes with sudden nods and grimaces, inarticulate murmurs, followed by a quick reaction, a sort of gloom. He was now absolutely certain that he was in the best society. He was carried further and further forward, and saw that another room stretched beyond the one he had entered, in which there was a sort of little stage, covered with a red cloth, and an immense collection of chairs, arranged in rows. He became aware that people looked at him, as well as at each other, rather more, indeed, than at each other, and he wondered whether it were very visible in his appearance that his being there was a kind of exception. He didn't know how much his head looked over the heads of others, or that his brown complexion, fuliginous eye, and straight black hair, the leonine fall of which I mentioned in the first pages of this narrative, gave him that relief which, in the best society, has the great advantage of suggesting a topic. But there were other topics besides, as was proved by a fragment of conversation, between two ladies, which reached his ear while he stood rather wistfully wondering where Verena Tarrant might be.

'Are you a member?' one of the ladies said to the other. 'I didn't know you had joined.'

'Oh, I haven't; nothing would induce me.'

'That's not fair; you have all the fun and none of the responsibility.'

'Oh, the fun—the fun!' exclaimed the second lady.

'You needn't abuse us, or I will never invite you,' said the first.

'Well, I thought it was meant to be improving; that's all I mean; very good for the mind. Now, this woman to-night; isn't she from Boston?'

'Yes, I believe they have brought her on, just for this.'

'Well, you must be pretty desperate when you have got to go to Boston for your entertainment.'

'Well, there's a similar society there, and I never heard of their sending to New York.'

'Of course not, they think they have got everything. But doesn't it make your life a burden, thinking what you can possibly have?'

'Oh dear, no. I am going to have Professor Gougenheim—all about the Talmud. You must come.'

'Well, I'll come,' said the second lady; 'but nothing would induce me to be a regular member.'

Whatever the mystic circle might be, Ransom agreed with the second lady that regular membership must have terrors, and he admired her independence in such an artificial world. A considerable part of the company had now directed itself to the further apartment—people had begun to occupy the chairs, to confront the empty platform. He reached the wide doors, and saw that the place was a spacious music-room, decorated in white and gold, with a polished floor and marble busts of composers, on brackets attached to the delicate panels. He forbore to enter, however, being shy about taking a seat, and seeing that the ladies were arranging themselves first. He turned back into the first room, to wait till the audience had massed itself, conscious that even if he were behind every one he should be able to make a long neck; and here, suddenly, in a corner, his eyes rested upon Olive Chancellor. She was seated a little apart, in an angle of the room, and she was looking straight at him; but as soon as she perceived that he saw her she dropped her eyes, giving no sign of recognition. Ransom hesitated a moment, but the next he went straight over to her. It had been in his mind that if Verena Tarrant was there, *she* would be there; an instinct told him that Miss Chancellor would not allow her dear friend to come to New York without her. It was very possible she meant to 'cut' him—especially if she knew of his having cut her, the other week, in Boston; but it was his duty to take for granted she would speak to him, until the contrary should be definitely proved. Though he had seen her only twice he remembered well how acutely shy she was capable of being, and he thought it possible one of these spasms had seized her at the present time.

When he stood before her he found his conjecture perfectly just; she was white with the intensity of her self-consciousness; she was altogether in a very uncomfortable state. She made no response to his offer to shake hands with her, and he saw that she would never go through that ceremony again. She looked up at him when he spoke to her, and her lips moved; but her face was intensely grave and her eye had almost a feverish light. She had evidently got into her corner to be out of the way; he recognised in her the air of an interloper, as he had felt it in himself. The small sofa on which she had placed herself had the form to which the French give the name of *causeuse*; there was room on it for just another person, and Ransom asked her, with a cheerful accent, if he might sit down beside her. She turned towards him when he had done so, turned everything but her eyes, and opened and shut her fan while she waited for her fit of diffidence to pass away. Ransom himself did not wait; he took a jocular tone about their encounter, asking her if she had come to New York to rouse the people. She glanced round the room; the backs of Mrs. Burrage's guests, mainly, were presented to them, and their position was partly masked by a pyramid of flowers which rose from a pedestal close to Olive's end of the sofa and diffused a fragrance in the air.

'Do you call these the "people"?' she asked.

'I haven't the least idea. I don't know who any of them are, not even who Mrs. Henry Burrage is. I simply received an invitation.'

Miss Chancellor gave him no information on the point he had mentioned; she only said, in a moment: 'Do you go wherever you are invited?'

'Why, I go if I think I may find you there,' the young man replied, gallantly. 'My card mentioned that Miss Tarrant would give an address, and I knew that wherever she is you are not far off. I have heard you are inseparable, from Mrs. Luna.'

'Yes, we are inseparable. That is exactly why I am here.'

'It's the fashionable world, then, you are going to stir up.'

Olive remained for some time with her eyes fastened to the floor; then she flashed them up at her interlocutor. 'It's a part of our life to go anywhere—to carry our work where it seems most needed. We have taught ourselves to stifle repulsion, distaste.'

'Oh, I think this is very amusing,' said Ransom. 'It's a

beautiful house, and there are some very pretty faces. We haven't anything so brilliant in Mississippi.'

To everything he said Olive offered at first a momentary silence, but the worst of her shyness was apparently leaving her.

'Are you successful in New York? do you like it?' she presently asked, uttering the inquiry in a tone of infinite melancholy, as if the eternal sense of duty forced it from her lips.

'Oh, successful! I am not successful as you and Miss Tarrant are; for (to my barbaric eyes) it is a great sign of prosperity to be the heroines of an occasion like this.'

'Do I look like the heroine of an occasion?' asked Olive Chancellor, without an intention of humour, but with an effect that was almost comical.

'You would if you didn't hide yourself away. Are you not going into the other room to hear the speech? Everything is prepared.'

'I am going when I am notified—when I am invited.'

There was considerable majesty in her tone, and Ransom saw that something was wrong, that she felt neglected. To see that she was as ticklish with others as she had been with him made him feel forgiving, and there was in his manner a perfect disposition to forget their differences as he said, 'Oh, there is plenty of time; the place isn't half full yet.'

She made no direct rejoinder to this, but she asked him about his mother and sisters, what news he received from the South. 'Have they any happiness?' she inquired, rather as if she warned him to take care not to pretend they had. He neglected her warning to the point of saying that there was one happiness they always had—that of having learned not to think about it too much, and to make the best of their circumstances. She listened to this with an air of great reserve, and apparently thought he had wished to give her a lesson; for she suddenly broke out, 'You mean that you have traced a certain line for them, and that that's all you know about it!'

Ransom stared at her, surprised; he felt, now, that she would always surprise him. 'Ah, don't be rough with me,' he said, in his soft Southern voice; 'don't you remember how you knocked me about when I called on you in Boston?'

'You hold us in chains, and then, when we writhe in our

agony, you say we don't behave prettily!' These words, which did not lessen Ransom's wonderment, were the young lady's answer to his deprecatory speech. She saw that he was honestly bewildered and that in a moment more he would laugh at her, as he had done a year and a half before (she remembered it as if it had been yesterday); and to stop that off, at any cost, she went on hurriedly—'If you listen to Miss Tarrant, you will know what I mean.'

'Oh, Miss Tarrant—Miss Tarrant!' And Basil Ransom's laughter came.

She had not escaped that mockery, after all, and she looked at him sharply now, her embarrassment having quite cleared up. 'What do you know about her? What observation have you had?'

Ransom met her eye, and for a moment they scrutinised each other. Did she know of his interview with Verena a month before, and was her reserve simply the wish to place on him the burden of declaring that he had been to Boston since they last met, and yet had not called in Charles Street? He thought there was suspicion in her face; but in regard to Verena she would always be suspicious. If he had done at that moment just what would gratify him he would have said to her that he knew a great deal about Miss Tarrant, having lately had a long walk and talk with her; but he checked himself, with the reflection that if Verena had not betrayed him it would be very wrong in him to betray her. The sweetness of the idea that she should have thought the episode of his visit to Monadnoc Place worth placing under the rose, was quenched for the moment in his regret at not being able to let his disagreeable cousin know that he had passed *her* over. 'Don't you remember my hearing her speak that night at Miss Birdseye's?" he said, presently. 'And I met her the next day at your house, you know.'

'She has developed greatly since then,' Olive remarked drily; and Ransom felt sure that Verena had held her tongue.

At this moment a gentleman made his way through the clusters of Mrs. Burrage's guests and presented himself to Olive. 'If you will do me the honour to take my arm I will find a good seat for you in the other room. It's getting to be time for Miss Tarrant to reveal herself. I have been taking her into the picture-room; there were some things she wanted to see. She is with my mother now,' he added, as if Miss Chancellor's grave face constituted a sort of demand for an explanation of her friend's absence. 'She said she was a little nervous; so I thought we would just move about.'

'It's the first time I have ever heard of that!' said Olive Chancellor, preparing to surrender herself to the young man's guidance. He told her that he had reserved the best seat for her; it was evidently his desire to conciliate her, to treat her as a person of importance. Before leading her away, he shook hands with Ransom and remarked that he was very glad to see him; and Ransom saw that he must be the master of the house, though he could scarcely be the son of the stout lady in the doorway. He was a fresh, pleasant, handsome young man, with a bright friendly manner; he recommended Ransom to take a seat in the other room, without delay; if he had never heard Miss Tarrant he would have one of the greatest pleasures of his life.

'Oh, Mr. Ransom only comes to ventilate his prejudices,' Miss Chancellor said, as she turned her back to her kinsman. He shrank from pushing into the front of the company, which was now rapidly filling the music-room, and contented himself with lingering in the doorway, where several gentlemen were stationed. The seats were all occupied; all, that is, save one, towards which he saw Miss Chancellor and her companion direct themselves, squeezing and edging past the people who were standing up against the walls. This was quite in front, close to the little platform; every one noticed Olive as she went, and Ransom heard a gentleman near him say to another—'I guess she's one of the same kind.' He looked for Verena, but she was apparently keeping out of sight. Suddenly he felt himself smartly tapped on the back, and, turning round, perceived Mrs. Luna, who had been prodding him with her fan.

XXVII

'You won't speak to me in my own house—that I have almost grown used to; but if you are going to pass me over in public I think you might give me warning first.' This was only her archness, and he knew what to make of that now; she was dressed in yellow and looked very plump and gay. He wondered at the unerring instinct by which she had discovered his exposed quarter. The outer room was completely empty; she had come in at the further door and found the field free for her operations. He offered to find her a place where she could see and hear Miss Tarrant, to get her a chair to stand on, even, if she wished to look over the heads of the gentlemen in the doorway; a proposal which she greeted with the inquiry—'Do you suppose I came here for the sake of that chatterbox? haven't I told you what I think of her?'

'Well, you certainly did not come here for my sake,' said Ransom, anticipating this insinuation; 'for you couldn't possibly have known I was coming.'

'I guessed it—a presentiment told me!' Mrs. Luna declared; and she looked up at him with searching, accusing eyes. 'I know what you have come for,' she cried in a moment. 'You never mentioned to me that you knew Mrs. Burrage!'

'I don't—I never had heard of her till she asked me.'

'Then why in the world *did* she ask you?'

Ransom had spoken a trifle rashly; it came over him, quickly, that there were reasons why he had better not have said that. But almost as quickly he covered up his mistake. 'I suppose your sister was so good as to ask for a card for me.'

'My sister? My grandmother! I know how Olive loves you. Mr. Ransom, you are very deep.' She had drawn him well into the room, out of earshot of the group in the doorway, and he felt that if she should be able to compass her wish she would organise a little entertainment for herself, in the outer drawing-room, in opposition to Miss Tarrant's address. 'Please come and sit down here a moment; we shall be quite undisturbed. I have something very particular to say to you.' She led the way to the little sofa in the corner, where he had been talking with Olive a few minutes before, and he accompanied her, with extreme reluctance, grudging the moments that he should be obliged to give to her. He had quite forgotten that he once had a vision of spending his life in her society, and he looked at his watch as he made the observation:

'I haven't the least idea of losing any of the sport in there, you know.'

He felt, the next instant, that he oughtn't to have said that either; but he was irritated, disconcerted, and he couldn't help it. It was in the nature of a gallant Mississippian to do everything a lady asked him, and he had never, remarkable as it may appear, been in the position of finding such a request so incompatible with his own desires as now. It was a new predicament, for Mrs. Luna evidently meant to keep him if she could. She looked round the room, more and more pleased at their having it to themselves, and for the moment said nothing more about the singularity of his being there. On the contrary, she became freshly jocular, remarked that now they had got hold of him they wouldn't easily let him go, they would make him entertain them, induce him to give a lecture—on the 'Lights and Shadows of Southern Life,' or the 'Social Peculiarities of Mississippi'—before the Wednesday Club.

'And what in the world is the Wednesday Club? I suppose it's what those ladies were talking about,' Ransom said.

'I don't know your ladies, but the Wednesday Club is this thing. I don't mean you and me here together, but all those deluded beings in the other room. It is New York trying to be like Boston. It is the culture, the good form, of the metropolis. You might not think it, but it is. It's the 'quiet set'; they *are* quiet enough; you might hear a pin drop, in there. Is some one going to offer up a prayer? How happy Olive must be, to be taken so seriously! They form an association for meeting at each other's houses, every week, and having some performance, or some paper read, or some subject explained. The more dreary it is and the more fearful the subject, the more they think it is what it ought to be. They have an idea this is the way to make New York society intellectual.

There's a sumptuary law—isn't that what you call it?—about
suppers, and they restrict themselves to a kind of Spartan
broth. When it's made by their French cooks it isn't bad.
Mrs. Burrage is one of the principal members—one of the
founders, I believe; and when her turn has come round, formerly—it comes only once in the winter for each—I am told
she has usually had very good music. But that is thought
rather a base evasion, a begging of the question; the vulgar
set can easily keep up with them on music. So Mrs. Burrage
conceived the extraordinary idea'—and it was wonderful to
hear how Mrs. Luna pronounced that adjective—'of sending
on to Boston for that girl. It was her son, of course, who put
it into her head; he has been at Cambridge for some years—
that's where Verena lived, you know—and he was as thick
with her as you please out there. Now that he is no longer
there it suits him very well to have her here. She is coming
on a visit to his mother when Olive goes. I asked them to
stay with me, but Olive declined, majestically; she said they
wished to be in some place where they would be free to receive "sympathising friends." So they are staying at some extraordinary kind of New Jerusalem boarding-house, in Tenth
Street; Olive thinks it's her duty to go to such places. I was
greatly surprised that she should let Verena be drawn into
such a worldly crowd as this; but she told me they had made
up their minds not to let *any* occasion slip, that they could
sow the seed of truth in drawing-rooms as well as in work-
shops, and that if a single person was brought round to their
ideas they should have been justified in coming on. That's
what they are doing in there—sowing the seed; but you shall
not be the one that's brought round, I shall take care of that.
Have you seen my delightful sister yet? The way she *does* arrange herself when she wants to protest against frills! She
looks as if she thought it pretty barren ground round here,
now she has come to see it. I don't think she thinks you can
be saved in a French dress, anyhow. I must say I call it a *very*
base evasion of Mrs. Burrage's, producing Verena Tarrant; it's
worse than the meretricious music. Why didn't she honestly
send for a *ballerina* from Niblo's—if she wanted a young
woman capering about on a platform? They don't care a fig
about poor Olive's ideas; it's only because Verena has strange

hair, and shiny eyes, and gets herself up like a prestidigitator's assistant. I have never understood how Olive can reconcile herself to Verena's really low style of dress. I suppose it's only because her clothes are so fearfully made. You look as if you didn't believe me—but I assure you that the cut is revolutionary; and that's a salve to Olive's conscience.'

Ransom was surprised to hear that he looked as if he didn't believe her, for he had found himself, after his first uneasiness, listening with considerable interest to her account of the circumstances under which Miss Tarrant was visiting New York. After a moment, as the result of some private reflection, he propounded this question: 'Is the son of the lady of the house a handsome young man, very polite, in a white vest?'

'I don't know the colour of his vest—but he has a kind of fawning manner. Verena judges from that that he is in love with her.'

'Perhaps he is,' said Ransom. 'You say it was his idea to get her to come on.'

'Oh, he likes to flirt; that is highly probable.'

'Perhaps she has brought him round.'

'Not to where she wants, I think. The property is very large; he will have it all one of these days.'

'Do you mean she wishes to impose on him the yoke of matrimony?' Ransom asked, with Southern languor.

'I believe she thinks matrimony an exploded superstition; but there is here and there a case in which it is still the best thing; when the gentleman's name happens to be Burrage and the young lady's Tarrant. I don't admire 'Burrage' so much myself. But I think she would have captured this present scion if it hadn't been for Olive. Olive stands between them—she wants to keep her in the single sisterhood; to keep her, above all, for herself. Of course she won't listen to her marrying, and she has put a spoke in the wheel. She has brought her to New York; that may seem against what I say; but the girl pulls hard, she has to humour her, to give her her head sometimes, to throw something overboard, in short, to save the rest. You may say, as regards Mr. Burrage, that it's a queer taste in a gentleman; but there is no arguing about that. It's queer taste in a lady, too; for she is a lady, poor Olive. You can see that to-night. She is dressed like a book-agent, but she is more distinguished than any one here. Verena, beside her, looks like a walking advertisement.'

When Mrs. Luna paused, Basil Ransom became aware that, in the other room, Verena's address had begun; the sound of her clear, bright, ringing voice, an admirable voice for public uses, came to them from the distance. His eagerness to stand where he could hear her better, and see her into the bargain, made him start in his place, and this movement produced an outgush of mocking laughter on the part of his companion. But she didn't say—'Go, go, deluded man, I take pity on you!' she only remarked, with light impertinence, that he surely wouldn't be so wanting in gallantry as to leave a lady absolutely alone in a public place—it was so Mrs. Luna was pleased to qualify Mrs. Burrage's drawing-room—in the face of her entreaty that he would remain with her. She had the better of poor Ransom, thanks to the superstitions of Mississippi. It was in his simple code a gross rudeness to withdraw from conversation with a lady at a party before another gentleman should have come to take one's place; it was to inflict on the lady a kind of outrage. The other gentlemen, at Mrs. Burrage's, were all too well occupied; there was not the smallest chance of one of them coming to his rescue. He couldn't leave Mrs. Luna, and yet he couldn't stay with her and lose the only thing he had come so much out of his way for. 'Let me at least find you a place over there, in the doorway. You can stand upon a chair—you can lean on me.'

'Thank you very much; I would much rather lean on this sofa. And I am much too tired to stand on chairs. Besides, I wouldn't for the world that either Verena or Olive should see me craning over the heads of the crowd—as if I attached the smallest importance to their perorations!'

'It isn't time for the peroration yet,' Ransom said, with savage dryness; and he sat forward, with his elbow on his knees, his eyes on the ground, a flush in his sallow cheek.

'It's never time to say such things as those,' Mrs. Luna remarked, arranging her laces.

'How do you know what she is saying?'

'I can tell by the way her voice goes up and down. It sounds so silly.'

Ransom sat there five minutes longer—minutes which, he

felt, the recording angel ought to write down to his credit—
and asked himself how Mrs. Luna could be such a goose as
not to see that she was making him hate her. But she was
goose enough for anything. He tried to appear indifferent,
and it occurred to him to doubt whether the Mississippi system could be right, after all. It certainly hadn't foreseen such
a case as this. 'It's as plain as day that Mr. Burrage intends to
marry her—if he can,' he said in a minute; that remark being
better calculated than any other he could think of to dissimulate his real state of mind.

It drew no rejoinder from his companion, and after an instant he turned his head a little and glanced at her. The result
of something that silently passed between them was to make
her say, abruptly: 'Mr. Ransom, my sister never sent you an
invitation to this place. Didn't it come from Verena Tarrant?'

'I haven't the least idea.'

'As you hadn't the least acquaintance with Mrs. Burrage,
who else could it have come from?'

'If it came from Miss Tarrant, I ought at least to recognise
her courtesy by listening to her.'

'If you rise from this sofa I will tell Olive what I suspect.
She will be perfectly capable of carrying Verena off to
China—or anywhere out of your reach.'

'And pray what is it you suspect?'

'That you two have been in correspondence.'

'Tell her whatever you like, Mrs. Luna,' said the young
man, with the grimness of resignation.

'You are quite unable to deny it, I see.'

'I never contradict a lady.'

'We shall see if I can't make you tell a fib. Haven't you been
seeing Miss Tarrant, too?'

'Where should I have seen her? I can't see all the way to
Boston, as you said the other day.'

'Haven't you been there—on secret visits?'

Ransom started just perceptibly; but to conceal it, the next
instant, he stood up.

'They wouldn't be secret if I were to tell you.'

Looking down at her he saw that her words were a happy
hit, not the result of definite knowledge. But she appeared to
him vain, egotistical, grasping, odious.

'Well, I shall give the alarm,' she went on; 'that is, I will if you leave me. Is that the way a Southern gentleman treats a lady? Do as I wish, and I will let you off!'

'You won't let me off from staying with you.'

'Is it such a *corvée*? I never heard of such rudeness!' Mrs. Luna cried. 'All the same, I am determined to keep you if I can!'

Ransom felt that she must be in the wrong, and yet superficially she seemed (and it was quite intolerable), to have right on her side. All this while Verena's golden voice, with her words indistinct, solicited, tantalised his ear. The question had evidently got on Mrs. Luna's nerves; she had reached that point of feminine embroilment when a woman is perverse for the sake of perversity, and even with a clear vision of bad consequences.

'You have lost your head,' he relieved himself by saying, as he looked down at her.

'I wish you would go and get me some tea.'

'You say that only to embarrass me.' He had hardly spoken when a great sound of applause, the clapping of many hands, and the cry from fifty throats of 'Brava, brava!' floated in and died away. All Ransom's pulses throbbed, he flung his scruples to the winds, and after remarking to Mrs. Luna—still with all due ceremony—that he feared he must resign himself to forfeiting her good opinion, turned his back upon her and strode away to the open door of the music-room. 'Well, I have never been so insulted!' he heard her exclaim, with exceeding sharpness, as he left her; and, glancing back at her, as he took up his position, he saw her still seated on her sofa— alone in the lamp-lit desert—with her eyes making, across the empty space, little vindictive points. Well, she could come where he was, if she wanted him so much; he would support her on an ottoman, and make it easy for her to see. But Mrs. Luna was uncompromising; he became aware, after a minute, that she had withdrawn, majestically, from the place, and he did not see her again that evening.

XXVIII

H E COULD COMMAND the music-room very well from
where he stood, behind a thick outer fringe of intently
listening men. Verena Tarrant was erect on her little platform,
dressed in white, with flowers in her bosom. The red cloth
beneath her feet looked rich in the light of lamps placed on
high pedestals on either side of the stage; it gave her figure a
setting of colour which made it more pure and salient. She
moved freely in her exposed isolation, yet with great sobriety
of gesture; there was no table in front of her, and she had no
notes in her hand, but stood there like an actress before the
footlights, or a singer spinning vocal sounds to a silver
thread. There was such a risk that a slim provincial girl, pretending to fascinate a couple of hundred *blasé* New Yorkers
by simply giving them her ideas, would fail of her effect, that
at the end of a few moments Basil Ransom became aware that
he was watching her in very much the same excited way as if
she had been performing, high above his head, on the tra-
peze. Yet, as one listened, it was impossible not to perceive
that she was in perfect possession of her faculties, her subject,
her audience; and he remembered the other time at Miss
Birdseye's well enough to be able to measure the ground she
had travelled since then. This exhibition was much more complete, her manner much more assured; she seemed to speak
and survey the whole place from a much greater height. Her
voice, too, had developed; he had forgotten how beautiful it
could be when she raised it to its full capacity. Such a tone as
that, so pure and rich, and yet so young, so natural, constituted in itself a talent; he didn't wonder that they had made
a fuss about her at the Female Convention, if she filled their
hideous hall with such a music. He had read, of old, of the
improvisatrice of Italy, and this was a chastened, modern,
American version of the type, a New England Corinna, with
a mission instead of a lyre. The most graceful part of her was
her earnestness, the way her delightful eyes, wandering over
the 'fashionable audience' (before which she was so perfectly
unabashed), as if she wished to resolve it into a single sentient
personality, seemed to say that the only thing in life she cared

for was to put the truth into a form that would render conviction irresistible. She was as simple as she was charming,
and there was not a glance or motion that did not seem part
of the pure, still-burning passion that animated her. She had
indeed—it was manifest—reduced the company to unanimity; their attention was anything but languid; they smiled
back at her when she smiled; they were noiseless, motionless
when she was solemn; and it was evident that the entertainment which Mrs. Burrage had had the happy thought of offering to her friends would be memorable in the annals of the
Wednesday Club. It was agreeable to Basil Ransom to think
that Verena noticed him in his corner; her eyes played over
her listeners so freely that you couldn't say they rested in one
place more than another; nevertheless, a single rapid ray,
which, however, didn't in the least strike him as a deviation
from her ridiculous, fantastic, delightful argument, let him
know that he had been missed and now was particularly spoken to. This glance was a sufficient assurance that his invitation had come to him by the girl's request. He took for
granted the matter of her speech was ridiculous; how could it
help being, and what did it signify if it was? She was none
the less charming for that, and the moonshine she had been
plied with was none the less moonshine for her being charming. After he had stood there a quarter of an hour he became
conscious that he should not be able to repeat a word she had
said; he had not definitely heeded it, and yet he had not lost
a vibration of her voice. He had discovered Olive Chancellor
by this time; she was in the front row of chairs, at the end,
on the left; her back was turned to him, but he could see half
her sharp profile, bent down a little and absolutely motionless. Even across the wide interval her attitude expressed to
him a kind of rapturous stillness, the concentration of
triumph. There were several irrepressible effusions of applause, instantly self-checked, but Olive never looked up, at
the loudest, and such a calmness as that could only be the
result of passionate volition. Success was in the air, and she
was tasting it; she tasted it, as she did everything, in a way of
her own. Success for Verena was success for her, and Ransom
was sure that the only thing wanting to her triumph was that
he should have been placed in the line of her vision, so that

she might enjoy his embarrassment and confusion, might say to him, in one of her dumb, cold flashes—'Now do you think our movement is not a force—now do you think that women are meant to be slaves?' Honestly, he was not conscious of any confusion; it subverted none of his heresies to perceive that Verena Tarrant had even more power to fix his attention than he had hitherto supposed. It was fixed in a way it had not been yet, however, by his at last understanding her speech, feeling it reach his inner sense through the impediment of mere dazzled vision. Certain phrases took on a meaning for him—an appeal she was making to those who still resisted the beneficent influence of the truth. They appeared to be mocking, cynical men, mainly; many of whom were such triflers and idlers, so heartless and brainless that it didn't matter much what they thought on any subject; if the old tyranny needed to be propped up by *them* it showed it was in a pretty bad way. But there were others whose prejudice was stronger and more cultivated, pretended to rest upon study and argument. To those she wished particularly to address herself; she wanted to waylay them, to say, 'Look here, you're all wrong; you'll be so much happier when I have convinced you. Just give me five minutes,' she should like to say; 'just sit down here and let me ask a simple question. Do you think any state of society can come to good that is based upon an organised wrong?' That was the simple question that Verena desired to propound, and Basil smiled across the room at her with an amused tenderness as he gathered that she conceived it to be a poser. He didn't think it would frighten him much if she were to ask him that, and he would sit down with her for as many minutes as she liked.

He, of course, was one of the systematic scoffers, one of those to whom she said—'Do you know how you strike me? You strike me as men who are starving to death while they have a cupboard at home, all full of bread and meat and wine; or as blind, demented beings who let themselves be cast into a debtor's prison, while in their pocket they have the key of vaults and treasure-chests heaped up with gold and silver. The meat and wine, the gold and silver,' Verena went on, 'are simply the suppressed and wasted force, the precious sovereign remedy, of which society insanely deprives itself—the genius, the intelligence, the inspiration of women. It is dying, inch by inch, in the midst of old superstitions which it invokes in vain, and yet it has the elixir of life in its hands. Let it drink but a draught, and it will bloom once more; it will be refreshed, radiant; it will find its youth again. The heart, the heart is cold, and nothing but the touch of woman can warm it, make it act. We *are* the Heart of humanity, and let us have the courage to insist on it! The public life of the world will move in the same barren, mechanical, vicious circle—the circle of egotism, cruelty, ferocity, jealousy, greed, of blind striving to do things only for *some*, at the cost of others, instead of trying to do everything for all. All, all? Who dares to say "all" when we are not there? We are an equal, a splendid, an inestimable part. Try us and you'll see—you will wonder how, without us, society has ever dragged itself even this distance—so wretchedly small compared with what it might have been—on its painful earthly pilgrimage. That is what I should like above all to pour into the ears of those who still hold out, who stiffen their necks and repeat hard, empty formulas, which are as dry as a broken gourd that has been flung away in the desert. I would take them by their selfishness, their indolence, their interest. I am not here to recriminate, nor to deepen the gulf that already yawns between the sexes, and I don't accept the doctrine that they are natural enemies, since my plea is for a union far more intimate—provided it be equal—than any that the sages and philosophers of former times have ever dreamed of. Therefore I shall not touch upon the subject of men's being most easily influenced by considerations of what is most agreeable and profitable for *them*; I shall simply assume that they *are* so influenced, and I shall say to them that our cause would long ago have been gained if their vision were not so dim, so veiled, even in matters in which their own interests are concerned. If they had the same quick sight as women, if they had the intelligence of the heart, the world would be very different now; and I assure you that half the bitterness of our lot is to see so clearly and not to be able to do! Good gentlemen all, if I could make you believe how much brighter and fairer and sweeter the garden of life would be for you, if you would only let us help you to keep it in order! You would like so much better to walk there, and you would find grass and trees and flowers that would make you think you were in Eden. That is what I should like to press home to each of you, personally, individually—to give him the vision of the world as it hangs perpetually before me, redeemed, transfigured, by a new moral tone. There would be generosity, tenderness, sympathy, where there is now only brute force and sordid rivalry. But you really do strike me as stupid even about your own welfare! Some of you say that we have already all the influence we can possibly require, and talk as if we ought to be grateful that we are allowed even to breathe. Pray, who shall judge what we require if not we ourselves? We require simply freedom; we require the lid to be taken off the box in which we have been kept for centuries. You say it's a very comfortable, cozy, convenient box, with nice glass sides, so that we can see out, and that all that's wanted is to give another quiet turn to the key. That is very easily answered. Good gentlemen, you have never been in the box, and you haven't the least idea how it feels!'

The historian who has gathered these documents together does not deem it necessary to give a larger specimen of Verena's eloquence, especially as Basil Ransom, through whose ears we are listening to it, arrived, at this point, at a definite conclusion. He had taken her measure as a public speaker, judged her importance in the field of discussion, the cause of reform. Her speech, in itself, had about the value of a pretty essay, committed to memory and delivered by a bright girl at an 'academy;' it was vague, thin, rambling, a tissue of generalities that glittered agreeably enough in Mrs. Burrage's veiled lamplight. From any serious point of view it was neither worth answering nor worth considering, and Basil Ransom made his reflections on the crazy character of the age in which such a performance as that was treated as an intellectual effort, a contribution to a question. He asked himself what either he or any one else would think of it if Miss Chancellor—or even Mrs. Luna—had been on the platform instead of the actual declaimer. Nevertheless, its importance was high, and consisted precisely, in part, of the fact that the voice was not the voice of Olive or of Adeline. Its importance was that Verena was unspeakably attractive, and this was all the greater for him in the light of the fact, which quietly dawned upon him as he stood there, that he was falling in love with her. It had tapped at his heart for recognition, and before he could hesitate or challenge, the door had sprung open and the mansion was illuminated. He gave no outward sign; he stood gazing as at a picture; but the room wavered before his eyes, even Verena's figure danced a little. This did not make the sequel of her discourse more clear to him; her meaning faded again into the agreeable vague, and he simply felt her presence, tasted her voice. Yet the act of reflection was not suspended; he found himself rejoicing that she was so weak in argument, so inevitably verbose. The idea that she was brilliant, that she counted as a factor only because the public mind was in a muddle, was not an humiliation but a delight to him; it was a proof that her apostleship was all nonsense, the most passing of fashions, the veriest of delusions, and that she was meant for something divinely different—for privacy, for him, for love. He took no measure of the duration of her talk; he only knew, when it was over and succeeded by a clapping of hands, an immense buzz of voices and shuffling of chairs, that it had been capitally bad, and that her personal success, wrapping it about with a glamour like the silver mist that surrounds a fountain, was such as to prevent its badness from being a cause of mortification to her lover. The company—such of it as did not immediately close together around Verena—filed away into the other rooms, bore him in its current into the neighbourhood of a table spread for supper, where he looked for signs of the sumptuary law mentioned to him by Mrs. Luna. It appeared to be embodied mainly in the glitter of crystal and silver, and the fresh tints of mysterious viands and jellies, which looked desirable in the soft circle projected by lace-fringed lamps. He heard the popping of corks, he felt a pressure of elbows, a thickening of the crowd, perceived that he was glowered at, squeezed against the table, by contending gentlemen who observed that he usurped space, was neither feeding himself nor helping others to feed. He had lost sight of Verena; she had been borne away in clouds of compliment; but he found himself thinking—almost paternally—that she must be hungry after so much chatter, and he hoped some one was getting her something to eat. After a moment, just as he was edging away, for

his own opportunity to sup much better than usual was not
what was uppermost in his mind, this little vision was suddenly embodied—embodied by the appearance of Miss Tarrant, who faced him, in the press, attached to the arm of a
young man now recognisable to him as the son of the
house—the smiling, fragrant youth who an hour before had
interrupted his colloquy with Olive. He was leading her to
the table, while people made way for them, covering Verena
with gratulations of word and look. Ransom could see that,
according to a phrase which came back to him just then,
oddly, out of some novel or poem he had read of old, she
was the cynosure of every eye. She looked beautiful, and they
were a beautiful couple. As soon as she saw him, she put out
her left hand to him—the other was in Mr. Burrage's arm—
and said: 'Well, don't you think it's all true?'

'No, not a word of it!' Ransom answered, with a kind of
joyous sincerity. 'But it doesn't make any difference.'

'Oh, it makes a great deal of difference to me!' Verena
cried.

'I mean to me. I don't care in the least whether I agree with
you,' Ransom said, looking askance at young Mr. Burrage,
who had detached himself and was getting something for
Verena to eat.

'Ah, well, if you are so indifferent!'

'It's not because I'm indifferent!' His eyes came back to her
own, the expression of which had changed before they quitted them. She began to complain to her companion, who
brought her something very dainty on a plate, that Mr. Ransom was 'standing out,' that he was about the hardest subject
she had encountered yet. Henry Burrage smiled upon Ransom in a way that was meant to show he remembered having
already spoken to him, while the Mississippian said to himself
that there was nothing on the face of it to make it strange
there should be between these fair, successful young persons
some such question of love or marriage as Mrs. Luna had
tattled about. Mr. Burrage was successful, he could see that
in the turn of an eye; not perhaps as having a commanding
intellect or a very strong character, but as being rich, polite,
handsome, happy, amiable, and as wearing a splendid camellia
in his button-hole. And that *he*, at any rate, thought Verena

had succeeded was proved by the casual, civil tone, and the contented distraction of eye, with which he exclaimed, 'You don't mean to say you were not moved by that! It's my opinion that Miss Tarrant will carry everything before her.' He was so pleased himself, and so safe in his conviction, that it didn't matter to him what any one else thought; which was, after all, just Basil Ransom's own state of mind.

'Oh! I didn't say I wasn't moved,' the Mississippian remarked.

'Moved the wrong way!' said Verena. 'Never mind; you'll be left behind.'

'If I am, you will come back to console me.'

'*Back?* I shall never come back!' the girl replied, gaily.

'You'll be the very first!' Ransom went on, feeling himself now, and as if by a sudden clearing up of his spiritual atmosphere, no longer in the vein for making the concessions of chivalry, and yet conscious that his words were an expression of homage.

'Oh, I call that presumptuous!' Mr. Burrage exclaimed, turning away to get a glass of water for Verena, who had refused to accept champagne, mentioning that she had never drunk any in her life and that she associated a kind of iniquity with it. Olive had no wine in her house (not that Verena gave this explanation), but her father's old madeira and a little claret; of the former of which liquors Basil Ransom had highly approved the day he dined with her.

'Does he believe in all those lunacies?' he inquired, knowing perfectly what to think about the charge of presumption brought by Mr. Burrage.

'Why, he's crazy about our movement,' Verena responded. 'He's one of my most gratifying converts.'

'And don't you despise him for it?'

'Despise him? Why, you seem to think I swing round pretty often!'

'Well, I have an idea that I shall see you swing round yet,' Ransom remarked, in a tone in which it would have appeared to Henry Burrage, had he heard these words, that presumption was pushed to fatuity.

On Verena, however, they produced no impression that prevented her from saying simply, without the least rancour,

'Well, if you expect to draw me back five hundred years, I hope you won't tell Miss Birdseye.' And as Ransom did not seize immediately the reason of her allusion, she went on, 'You know she is convinced it will be just the other way. I went to see her after you had been at Cambridge—almost immediately.'

'Darling old lady—I hope she's well,' the young man said.

'Well, she's tremendously interested.'

'She's always interested in something, isn't she?'

'Well, this time it's in our relations, yours and mine,' Verena replied, in a tone in which only Verena could say a thing like that. 'You ought to see how she throws herself into them. She is sure it will all work round for your good.'

'All what, Miss Tarrant?' Ransom asked.

'Well, what I told her. She is sure you are going to become one of our leaders, that you are very gifted for treating great questions and acting on masses of people, that you will become quite enthusiastic about our uprising, and that when you go up to the top as one of our champions it will all have been through me.'

Ransom stood there, smiling at her; the dusky glow in his eyes expressed a softness representing no prevision of such laurels, but which testified none the less to Verena's influence. 'And what you want is that I shouldn't undeceive her?'

'Well, I don't want you to be hypocritical—if you shouldn't take our side; but I do think that it would be sweet if the dear old thing could just cling to her illusion. She won't live so very long, probably; she told me the other day she was ready for her final rest; so it wouldn't interfere much with your freedom. She feels quite romantic about it—your being a Southerner and all, and not naturally in sympathy with Boston ideas, and your meeting her that way in the street and making yourself known to her. She won't believe but what I shall move you.'

'Don't fear, Miss Tarrant, she shall be satisfied,' Ransom said, with a laugh which he could see she but partially understood. He was prevented from making his meaning more clear by the return of Mr. Burrage, bringing not only Verena's glass of water but a smooth-faced, rosy, smiling old gentleman, who had a velvet waistcoat, and thin white hair, brushed effectively, and whom he introduced to Verena under a name which Ransom recognised as that of a rich and venerable citizen, conspicuous for his public spirit and his large almsgiving. Ransom had lived long enough in New York to know that a request from this ancient worthy to be made known to Miss Tarrant would mark her for the approval of the respectable, stamp her as a success of no vulgar sort; and as he turned away, a faint, inaudible sigh passed his lips, dictated by the sense that he himself belonged to a terribly small and obscure minority. He turned away because, as we know, he had been taught that a gentleman talking to a lady must always do that when a new gentleman is presented; though he observed, looking back, after a minute, that young Mr. Burrage evidently had no intention of abdicating in favour of the eminent philanthropist. He thought he had better go home; he didn't know what might happen at such a party as that, nor when the proceedings might be supposed to terminate; but after considering it a minute he dismissed the idea that there was a chance of Verena's speaking again. If he was a little vague about this, however, there was no doubt in his mind as to the obligation he was under to take leave first of Mrs. Burrage. He wished he knew where Verena was staying; he wanted to see her alone, not in a supper-room crowded with millionaires. As he looked about for the hostess it occurred to him that she would know, and that if he were able to quench a certain shyness sufficiently to ask her, she would tell him. Having satisfied himself presently that she was not in the supper-room, he made his way back to the parlours, where the company now was much diminished. He looked again into the music-room, tenanted only by half-a-dozen couples, who were cultivating privacy among the empty chairs, and here he perceived Mrs. Burrage sitting in conversation with Olive Chancellor (the latter, apparently, had not moved from her place), before the deserted scene of Verena's triumph. His search had been so little for Olive that at the sight of her he faltered a moment; then he pulled himself together, advancing with a consciousness of the Mississippi manner. He felt Olive's eyes receiving him; she looked at him as if it was just the hope that she shouldn't meet him again that had made her remain where she was. Mrs. Burrage got up, as he bade her good-night, and Olive followed her example.

'So glad you were able to come. Wonderful creature, isn't she? She can do anything she wants.'

These words from the elder lady Ransom received at first with a reserve which, as he trusted, suggested extreme respect; and it was a fact that his silence had a kind of Southern solemnity in it. Then he said, in a tone equally expressive of great deliberation:

'Yes, madam, I think I never was present at an exhibition, an entertainment of any kind, which held me more completely under the charm.'

'Delighted you liked it. I didn't know what in the world to have, and this has proved an inspiration—for me as well as for Miss Tarrant. Miss Chancellor has been telling me how they have worked together; it's really quite beautiful. Miss Chancellor is Miss Tarrant's great friend and colleague. Miss Tarrant assures me that she couldn't do anything without her.' After which explanation, turning to Olive, Mrs. Burrage murmured: 'Let me introduce Mr. —— introduce Mr. ——'

But she had forgotten poor Ransom's name, forgotten who had asked her for a card for him; and, perceiving it, he came to her rescue with the observation that he was a kind of cousin of Miss Olive's, if she didn't repudiate him, and that he knew what a tremendous partnership existed between the two young ladies. 'When I applauded I was applauding the firm—that is, you too,' he said, smiling, to his kinswoman.

'Your applause? I confess I don't understand it,' Olive replied, with much promptitude.

'Well, to tell the truth, I didn't myself!'

'Oh yes, of course I know; that's why—that's why——' And this further speech of Mrs. Burrage's, in reference to the relationship between the young man and her companion, faded also into vagueness. She had been on the point of saying it was the reason why he was in her house; but she had bethought herself in time that this ought to pass as a matter of course. Basil Ransom could see she was a woman who could carry off an awkwardness like that, and he considered her with a sense of her importance. She had a brisk, familiar, slightly impatient way, and if she had not spoken so fast, and had more of the softness of the Southern matron, she would have reminded him of a certain type of woman he had seen of old, before the changes in his own part of the world—the clever, capable, hospitable proprietress, widowed or unmarried, of a big plantation carried on by herself. 'If you are her cousin, do take Miss Chancellor to have some supper—instead of going away,' she went on, with her infelicitous readiness.

At this Olive instantly seated herself again.

'I am much obliged to you; I never touch supper. I shall not leave this room—I like it.'

'Then let me send you something—or let Mr. ——, your cousin, remain with you.'

Olive looked at Mrs. Burrage with a strange beseechingness, 'I am very tired, I must rest. These occasions leave me exhausted.'

'Ah yes, I can imagine that. Well, then, you shall be quite quiet—I shall come back to you.' And with a smile of farewell for Basil Ransom, Mrs. Burrage moved away.

Basil lingered a moment, though he saw that Olive wished to get rid of him. 'I won't disturb you further than to ask you a single question,' he said. 'Where are you staying? I want to come and see Miss Tarrant. I don't say I want to come and see you, because I have an idea that it would give you no pleasure.' It had occurred to him that he might obtain their address from Mrs. Luna—he only knew vaguely it was Tenth Street; much as he had displeased her she couldn't refuse him that; but suddenly the greater simplicity and frankness of applying directly to Olive, even at the risk of appearing to brave her, recommended itself. He couldn't, of course, call upon Verena without her knowing it, and she might as well make her protest (since he proposed to pay no heed to it), sooner as later. He had seen nothing, personally, of their life together, but it had come over him that what Miss Chancellor most disliked in him (had she not, on the very threshold of their acquaintance, had a sort of mystical foreboding of it?) was the possibility that he would interfere. It was quite on the cards that he might; yet it was decent, all the same, to ask her rather than any one else. It was better that his interference should be accompanied with all the forms of chivalry.

Olive took no notice of his remark as to how she herself might be affected by his visit; but she asked in a moment why he should think it necessary to call on Miss Tarrant. 'You know you are not in sympathy,' she added, in a tone which contained a really touching element of entreaty that he would not even pretend to prove he was.

I know not whether Basil was touched, but he said, with every appearance of a conciliatory purpose—'I wish to thank her for all the interesting information she has given me this evening.'

'If you think it generous to come and scoff at her, of course she has no defence; you will be glad to know that.'

'Dear Miss Chancellor, if you are not a defence—a battery of many guns!' Ransom exclaimed.

'Well, she at least is not mine!' Olive returned, springing to her feet. She looked round her as if she were really pressed too hard, panting like a hunted creature.

'Your defence is your certain immunity from attack. Perhaps if you won't tell me where you are staying, you will kindly ask Miss Tarrant herself to do so. Would she send me a word on a card?'

'We are in West Tenth Street,' Olive said; and she gave the number. 'Of course you are free to come.'

'Of course I am! Why shouldn't I be? But I am greatly obliged to you for the information. I will ask her to come out, so that you won't see us.' And he turned away, with the sense that it was really insufferable, her attempt always to give him the air of being in the wrong. If that was the kind of spirit in which women were going to act when they had more power!

XXIX

MRS. LUNA was early in the field the next day, and her sister wondered to what she owed the honour of a visit from her at eleven o'clock in the morning. She very soon saw, when Adeline asked her whether it had been she who procured for Basil Ransom an invitation to Mrs. Burrage's.

'Me—why in the world should it have been me?' Olive asked, feeling something of a pang at the implication that it had not been Adeline, as she supposed.

'I didn't know—but you took him up so.'

'Why, Adeline Luna, when did I ever——?' Miss Chancellor exclaimed, staring and intensely grave.

'You don't mean to say you have forgotten how you brought him on to see you, a year and a half ago!'

'I didn't bring him on—I said if he happened to be there.'

'Yes, I remember how it was: he did happen, and then you happened to hate him, and tried to get out of it.'

Miss Chancellor saw, I say, why Adeline had come to her at the hour she knew she was always writing letters, after having given her all the attention that was necessary the day before; she had come simply to make herself disagreeable, as Olive knew, of old, the spirit sometimes moved her irresistibly to do. It seemed to her that Adeline had been disagreeable enough in not having beguiled Basil Ransom into a marriage, according to that memorable calculation of probabilities in which she indulged (with a licence that she scarcely liked definitely to recall), when the pair made acquaintance under her eyes in Charles Street, and Mrs. Luna seemed to take to him as much as she herself did little. She would gladly have accepted him as a brother-in-law, for the harm such a relation could do one was limited and definite; whereas in his general capacity of being at large in her life the ability of the young Mississippian to injure her seemed somehow immense. 'I wrote to him—that time—for a perfectly definite reason,' she said. 'I thought mother would have liked us to know him. But it was a mistake.'

'How do you know it was a mistake? Mother would have liked him, I dare say.'

'I mean my acting as I did; it was a theory of duty which I allowed to press me too much. I always do. Duty should be obvious; one shouldn't hunt round for it.'

'Was it very obvious when it brought you on here?' asked Mrs. Luna, who was distinctly out of humour.

Olive looked for a moment at the toe of her shoe. 'I had an idea that you would have married him by this time,' she presently remarked.

'Marry him yourself, my dear! What put such an idea into your head?'

'You wrote to me at first so much about him. You told me he was tremendously attentive, and that you liked him.'

'His state of mind is one thing and mine is another. How can I marry every man that hangs about me—that dogs my footsteps? I might as well become a Mormon at once!' Mrs. Luna delivered herself of this argument with a certain charitable air, as if her sister could not be expected to understand such a situation by her own light.

Olive waived the discussion, and simply said: 'I took for granted *you* had got him the invitation.'

'I, my dear? That would be quite at variance with my attitude of discouragement.'

'Then she simply sent it herself.'

'Whom do you mean by "she"?'

'Mrs. Burrage, of course.'

'I thought that you might mean Verena,' said Mrs. Luna, casually.

'Verena—to him? Why in the world——?' And Olive gave the cold glare with which her sister was familiar.

'Why in the world not—since she knows him?'

'She had seen him twice in her life before last night, when she met him for the third time and spoke to him.'

'Did she tell you that?'

'She tells me everything.'

'Are you very sure?'

'Adeline Luna, what *do* you mean?' Miss Chancellor murmured.

'Are you very sure that last night was only the third time?' Mrs. Luna went on.

Olive threw back her head and swept her sister from her

bonnet to her lowest flounce. 'You have no right to hint at such a thing as that unless you know!'

'Oh, I know—I know, at any rate, more than you do!' And then Mrs. Luna, sitting with her sister, much withdrawn, in one of the windows of the big, hot, faded parlour of the boarding-house in Tenth Street, where there was a rug before the chimney representing a Newfoundland dog saving a child from drowning, and a row of chromo-lithographs on the walls, imparted to her the impression she had received the evening before—the impression of Basil Ransom's keen curiosity about Verena Tarrant. Verena must have asked Mrs. Burrage to send him a card, and asked it without mentioning the fact to Olive—for wouldn't Olive certainly have remembered it? It was no use her saying that Mrs. Burrage might have sent it of her own movement, because she wasn't aware of his existence, and why should she be? Basil Ransom himself had told her he didn't know Mrs. Burrage. Mrs. Luna knew whom he knew and whom he didn't, or at least the sort of people, and they were not the sort that belonged to the Wednesday Club. That was one reason why she didn't care about him for any intimate relation—that he didn't seem to have any taste for making nice friends. Olive would know what *her* taste was in this respect, though it wasn't that young woman's own any more than his. It was positive that the suggestion about the card could only have come from Verena. At any rate Olive could easily ask, or if she was afraid of her telling a fib she could ask Mrs. Burrage. It was true Mrs. Burrage might have been put on her guard by Verena, and would perhaps invent some other account of the matter; therefore Olive had better just believe what *she* believed, that Verena had secured his presence at the party and had had private reasons for doing so. It is to be feared that Ransom's remark to Mrs. Luna the night before about her having lost her head was near to the mark; for if she had not been blinded by her rancour she would have guessed the horror with which she inspired her sister when she spoke in that off-hand way of Verena's lying and Mrs. Burrage's lying. Did people lie like that in Mrs. Luna's set? It was Olive's plan of life not to lie, and attributing a similar disposition to people she liked, it was impossible for her to believe that Verena had had the intention of deceiving her. Mrs. Luna, in a calmer hour, might also have divined that Olive would make her private comments on the strange story of Basil Ransom's having made up to Verena out of pique at Adeline's rebuff; for this was the account of the matter that she now offered to Miss Chancellor. Olive did two things: she listened intently and eagerly, judging there was distinct danger in the air (which, however, she had not wanted Mrs. Luna to tell her, having perceived it for herself the night before); and she saw that poor Adeline was fabricating fearfully, that the 'rebuff' was altogether an invention. Mr. Ransom was evidently preoccupied with Verena, but he had not needed Mrs. Luna's cruelty to make him so. So Olive maintained an attitude of great reserve; she did not take upon herself to announce that her own version was that Adeline, for reasons absolutely imperceptible to others, had tried to catch Basil Ransom, had failed in her attempt, and, furious at seeing Verena preferred to a person of her importance (Olive remembered the *spretæ injuria formæ*), now wished to do both him and the girl an ill turn. This would be accomplished if she could induce Olive to interfere. Miss Chancellor was conscious of an abundant readiness to interfere, but it was not because she cared for Adeline's mortification. I am not sure, even, that she did not think her *fiasco* but another illustration of her sister's general uselessness, and rather despise her for it; being perfectly able at once to hold that nothing is baser than the effort to entrap a man, and to think it very ignoble to have to renounce it because you can't. Olive kept these reflections to herself, but she went so far as to say to her sister that she didn't see where the 'pique' came in. How could it hurt Adeline that he should turn his attention to Verena? What was Verena to her?

'Why, Olive Chancellor, how can you ask?' Mrs. Luna boldly responded. 'Isn't Verena everything to you, and aren't you everything to me, and wouldn't an attempt—a successful one—to take Verena away from you knock you up fearfully, and shouldn't I suffer, as you know I suffer, by sympathy?'

I have said that it was Miss Chancellor's plan of life not to lie, but such a plan was compatible with a kind of consideration for the truth which led her to shrink from producing it on poor occasions. So she didn't say, 'Dear me, Adeline, what humbug! you know you hate Verena and would be very glad if she were drowned!' She only said, 'Well, I see; but it's very roundabout.' What she did see was that Mrs. Luna was eager to help her to stop off Basil Ransom from 'making head,' as the phrase was; and the fact that her motive was spite, and not tenderness for the Bostonians, would not make her assistance less welcome if the danger were real. She herself had a nervous dread, but she had that about everything; still, Adeline had perhaps seen something, and what in the world did she mean by her reference to Verena's having had secret meetings? When pressed on this point, Mrs. Luna could only say that she didn't pretend to give definite information, and she wasn't a spy anyway, but that the night before he had positively flaunted in her face his admiration for the girl, his enthusiasm for her way of standing up there. Of course he hated her ideas, but he was quite conceited enough to think she would give them up. Perhaps it was all directed at *her*—as if she cared! It would depend a good deal on the girl herself; certainly, if there was any likelihood of Verena's being affected, she should advise Olive to look out. She knew best what to do; it was only Adeline's duty to give her the benefit of her own impression, whether she was thanked for it or not. She only wished to put her on her guard, and it was just like Olive to receive such information so coldly; she was the most disappointing woman she knew.

Miss Chancellor's coldness was not diminished by this rebuke; for it had come over her that, after all, she had never opened herself at that rate to Adeline, had never let her see the real intensity of her desire to keep the sort of danger there was now a question of away from Verena, had given her no warrant for regarding her as her friend's keeper; so that she was taken aback by the flatness of Mrs. Luna's assumption that she was ready to enter into a conspiracy to circumvent and frustrate the girl. Olive put on all her majesty to dispel this impression, and if she could not help being aware that she made Mrs. Luna still angrier, on the whole, than at first, she felt that she would much rather disappoint her than give herself away to her—especially as she was intensely eager to profit by her warning!

XXX

MRS. LUNA would have been still less satisfied with the manner in which Olive received her proffered assistance had she known how many confidences that reticent young woman might have made her in return. Olive's whole life now was a matter for whispered communications; she felt this herself, as she sought the privacy of her own apartment after her interview with her sister. She had for the moment time to think; Verena having gone out with Mr. Burrage, who had made an appointment the night before to call for her to drive at that early hour. They had other engagements in the afternoon—the principal of which was to meet a group of earnest people at the house of one of the great local promoters. Olive would whisk Verena off to these appointments directly after lunch; she flattered herself that she could arrange matters so that there would not be half an hour in the day during which Basil Ransom, complacently calling, would find the Bostonians in the house. She had had this well in mind when, at Mrs. Burrage's, she was driven to give him their address; and she had had it also in mind that she would ask Verena, as a special favour, to accompany her back to Boston on the next day but one, which was the morning of the morrow. There had been considerable talk of her staying a few days with Mrs. Burrage—staying on after her own departure; but Verena backed out of it spontaneously, seeing how the idea worried her friend. Olive had accepted the sacrifice, and their visit to New York was now cut down, in intention, to four days, one of which, the moment she perceived whither Basil Ransom was tending, Miss Chancellor promised herself also to suppress. She had not mentioned that to Verena yet; she hesitated a little, having a slightly bad conscience about the concessions she had already obtained from her friend. Verena made such concessions with a generosity which caused one's heart to ache for admiration, even while one asked for them; and never once had Olive known her to demand the smallest credit for any virtue she showed in this way, or to bargain for an instant about any effort she made to oblige. She had been delighted with the idea of spending a week under Mrs. Burrage's roof; she had said, too, that she believed her mother would die happy (not that there was the least prospect of Mrs. Tarrant's dying), if she could hear of her having such an experience as that; and yet, perceiving how solemn Olive looked about it, how she blanched and brooded at the prospect, she had offered to give it up, with a smile sweeter, if possible, than any that had ever sat in her eyes. Olive knew what that meant for her, knew what a power of enjoyment she still had, in spite of the tension of their common purpose, their vital work, which had now, as they equally felt, passed into the stage of realisation, of fruition; and that is why her conscience rather pricked her for consenting to this further act of renunciation, especially as their position seemed really so secure, on the part of one who had already given herself away so sublimely.

Secure as their position might be, Olive called herself a blind idiot for having, in spite of all her first shrinkings, agreed to bring Verena to New York. Verena had jumped at the invitation, the very unexpectedness of which on Mrs. Burrage's part—it was such an odd idea to have come to a mere worldling—carried a kind of persuasion with it. Olive's immediate sentiment had been an instinctive general fear; but, later, she had dismissed that as unworthy; she had decided (and such a decision was nothing new), that where their mission was concerned they ought to face everything. Such an opportunity would contribute too much to Verena's reputation and authority to justify a refusal at the bidding of apprehensions which were after all only vague. Olive's specific terrors and dangers had by this time very much blown over; Basil Ransom had given no sign of life for ages, and Henry Burrage had certainly got his quietus before they went to Europe. If it had occurred to his mother that she might convert Verena into the animating principle of a big soirée, she was at least acting in good faith, for it could be no more her wish to-day that he should marry Selah Tarrant's daughter than it was her wish a year before. And then they should do some good to the benighted, the most benighted, the fashionable benighted; they should perhaps make them furious—there was always some good in that. Lastly, Olive was conscious of a personal temptation in the matter; she was not insensible to the pleasure of appearing in a distinguished New York circle as a representative woman, an important Bostonian, the prompter, colleague, associate of one of the most original girls of the time. Basil Ransom was the person she had least expected to meet at Mrs. Burrage's; it had been her belief that they might easily spend four days in a city of more than a million of inhabitants without that disagreeable accident. But it had occurred; nothing was wanting to make it seem serious; and, setting her teeth, she shook herself, morally, hard, for having fallen into the trap of fate. Well, she would scramble out, with only a scare, probably. Henry Burrage was very attentive, but somehow she didn't fear him now; and it was only natural he should feel that he couldn't be polite enough, after they had consented to be exploited in that worldly way by his mother. The other danger was the worst; the palpitation of her strange dread, the night of Miss Birdseye's party, came back to her. Mr. Burrage seemed, indeed, a protection; she reflected, with relief, that it had been arranged that after taking Verena to drive in the Park and see the Museum of Art in the morning, they should in the evening dine with him at Delmonico's (he was to invite another gentleman), and go afterwards to the German opera. Olive had kept all this to herself, as I have said; revealing to her sister neither the vividness of her prevision that Basil Ransom would look blank when he came down to Tenth Street and learned they had flitted, nor the eagerness of her desire just to find herself once more in the Boston train. It had been only this prevision that sustained her when she gave Mr. Ransom their number.

Verena came to her room shortly before luncheon, to let her know she had returned; and while they sat there, waiting to stop their ears when the gong announcing the repast was beaten, at the foot of the stairs, by a negro in a white jacket, she narrated to her friend her adventures with Mr. Burrage— expatiated on the beauty of the park, the splendour and interest of the Museum, the wonder of the young man's acquaintance with everything it contained, the swiftness of his horses, the softness of his English cart, the pleasure of rolling at that pace over roads as firm as marble, the entertainment he promised them for the evening. Olive listened in serious silence; she saw Verena was quite carried away; of course she hadn't gone so far with her without knowing that phase.

'Did Mr. Burrage try to make love to you?' Miss Chancellor inquired at last, without a smile.

Verena had taken off her hat to arrange her feather, and as she placed it on her head again, her uplifted arms making a frame for her face, she said: 'Yes, I suppose it was meant for love.'

Olive waited for her to tell more, to tell how she had treated him, kept him in his place, made him feel that that question was over long ago; but as Verena gave her no farther information she did not insist, conscious as she always was that in such a relation as theirs there should be a great respect on either side for the liberty of each. She had never yet infringed on Verena's, and of course she wouldn't begin now. Moreover, with the request that she meant presently to make of her she felt that she must be discreet. She wondered whether Henry Burrage were really going to begin again; whether his mother had only been acting in his interest in getting them to come on. Certainly, the bright spot in such a prospect was that if she listened to him she couldn't listen to Basil Ransom; and he *had* told Olive herself last night, when he put them into their carriage, that he hoped to prove to her yet that he had come round to her gospel. But the old sickness stole upon her again, the faintness of discouragement, as she asked herself why in the name of pity Verena should listen to any one at all but Olive Chancellor. Again it came over her, when she saw the brightness, the happy look, the girl brought back, as it had done in the earlier months, that the great trouble was that weak spot of Verena's, that sole infirmity and subtle flaw, which she had expressed to her very soon after they began to live together, in saying (she remembered it through the ineffaceable impression made by her friend's avowal), 'I'll tell you what is the matter with you—you don't dislike men as a class!' Verena had replied on this occasion, 'Well, no, I don't dislike them when they are pleasant!' As if organised atrociousness could ever be pleasant! Olive disliked them most when they were least unpleasant. After a little, at present, she remarked, referring to Henry Burrage: 'It is not right of him, not decent, after your making him feel how, while he was at Cambridge, he wearied you, tormented you.'

'Oh, I didn't show anything,' said Verena, gaily. 'I am learning to dissimulate,' she added in a moment. 'I suppose you have to as you go along. I pretend not to notice.'

At this moment the gong sounded for luncheon, and the two young women covered up their ears, face to face, Verena with her quick smile, Olive with her pale patience. When they could hear themselves speak, the latter said abruptly:

'How did Mrs. Burrage come to invite Mr. Ransom to her party? He told Adeline he had never seen her before.'

'Oh, I asked her to send him an invitation—after she had written to me, to thank me, when it was definitely settled we should come on. She asked me in her letter if there were any friends of mine in the city to whom I should like her to send cards, and I mentioned Mr. Ransom.'

Verena spoke without a single instant's hesitation, and the only sign of embarrassment she gave was that she got up from her chair, passing in this manner a little out of Olive's scrutiny. It was easy for her not to falter, because she was glad of the chance. She wanted to be very simple in all her relations with her friend, and of course it was not simple so soon as she began to keep things back. She could at any rate keep back as little as possible, and she felt as if she were making up for a dereliction when she answered Olive's inquiry so promptly.

'You never told me of that,' Miss Chancellor remarked, in a low tone.

'I didn't want to. I know you don't like him, and I thought it would give you pain. Yet I wanted him to be there—I wanted him to hear.'

'What does it matter—why should you care about him?'

'Well, because he is so awfully opposed!'

'How do you know that, Verena?'

At this point Verena began to hesitate. It was not, after all, so easy to keep back only a little; it appeared rather as if one must either tell everything or hide everything. The former course had already presented itself to her as unduly harsh; it was because it seemed so that she had ended by keeping the incident of Basil Ransom's visit to Monadnoc Place buried in unspoken, in unspeakable, considerations, the only secret she had in the world—the only thing that was all her own. She was so glad to say what she could without betraying herself that it was only after she had spoken that she perceived there was a danger of Olive's pushing the inquiry to the point where, to defend herself as it were, she should be obliged to practise a positive deception; and she was conscious at the same time that the moment her secret was threatened it became dearer to her. She began to pray silently that Olive might not push; for it would be odious, it would be impossible, to defend herself by a lie. Meanwhile, however, she had to answer, and the way she answered was by exclaiming, much more quickly than the reflections I note might have appeared to permit, 'Well, if you can't tell from his appearance! He's the type of the reactionary.'

Verena went to the toilet-glass to see that she had put on her hat properly, and Olive slowly got up, in the manner of a person not in the least eager for food. 'Let him react as he likes—for heaven's sake don't mind him!' That was Miss Chancellor's rejoinder, and Verena felt that it didn't say all that was in her mind. She wished she would come down to luncheon, for she, at least, was honestly hungry. She even suspected Olive had an idea she was afraid to express, such distress it would bring with it. 'Well, you know, Verena, this isn't our *real* life—it isn't our work,' Olive went on.

'Well, no, it isn't, certainly,' said Verena, not pretending at first that she did not know what Olive meant. In a moment, however, she added, 'Do you refer to this social intercourse with Mr. Burrage?'

'Not to that only.' Then Olive asked abruptly, looking at her, 'How did you know his address?'

'His address?'

'Mr. Ransom's—to enable Mrs. Burrage to invite him?'

They stood for a moment interchanging a gaze. 'It was in a letter I got from him.'

At these words there came into Olive's face an expression which made her companion cross over to her directly and take her by the hand. But the tone was different from what Verena expected when she said, with cold surprise: 'Oh, you are in correspondence!' It showed an immense effort of self-control.

'He wrote to me once—I never told you,' Verena rejoined, smiling. She felt that her friend's strange, uneasy eyes searched very far; a little more and they would go to the very bottom. Well, they might go if they would; she didn't, after all, care so much about her secret as that. For the moment, however, Verena did not learn what Olive had discovered, inasmuch as she only remarked presently that it was really time to go down. As they descended the staircase she put her arm into Miss Chancellor's and perceived that she was trembling.

Of course there were plenty of people in New York interested in the uprising, and Olive had made appointments, in advance, which filled the whole afternoon. Everybody wanted to meet them, and wanted everybody else to do so, and Verena saw they could easily have quite a vogue, if they only chose to stay and work that vein. Very likely, as Olive said, it wasn't their real life, and people didn't seem to have such a grip of the movement as they had in Boston; but there was something in the air that carried one along, and a sense of vastness and variety, of the infinite possibilities of a great city, which—Verena hardly knew whether she ought to confess it to herself—might in the end make up for the want of the Boston earnestness. Certainly, the people seemed very much alive, and there was no other place where so many cheering reports could flow in, owing to the number of electric feelers that stretched away everywhere. The principal centre appeared to be Mrs. Croucher's, on Fifty-sixth Street, where there was an informal gathering of sympathisers who didn't seem as if they could forgive her when they learned that she had been speaking the night before in a circle in which none of them were acquainted. Certainly, they were very different from the group she had addressed at Mrs. Burrage's, and Verena heaved a thin, private sigh, expressive of some helplessness, as she thought what a big, complicated world it was, and how it evidently contained a little of everything. There was a general demand that she should repeat her address in a more congenial atmosphere; to which she replied that Olive made her engagements for her, and that as the address had been intended just to lead people on, perhaps she would think Mrs. Croucher's friends had reached a higher point. She was as cautious as this because she saw that Olive was now just straining to get out of the city; she didn't want to say anything that would tie them. When she felt her trembling that way before luncheon it made her quite sick to realise how much her friend was wrapped up in her—how terribly she would suffer from the least deviation. After they had started for their round of engagements the very first thing Verena spoke of in the carriage (Olive had taken one, in her liberal way, for the whole time), was the fact that her correspondence with Mr. Ransom, as her friend had called it, had consisted on his part of only one letter. It was a very short one, too; it had come to her a little more than a month before. Olive knew she got letters from gentlemen; she didn't see why she should attach such importance to this one. Miss Chancellor was leaning back in the carriage, very still, very grave, with her head against the cushioned surface, only turning her eyes towards the girl.

'You attach importance yourself; otherwise you would have told me.'

'I knew you wouldn't like it—because you don't like *him*.'

'I don't think of him,' said Olive; 'he's nothing to me.' Then she added, suddenly, 'Have you noticed that I am afraid to face what I don't like?'

Verena could not say that she had, and yet it was not just on Olive's part to speak as if she were an easy person to tell such a thing to: the way she lay there, white and weak, like a wounded creature, sufficiently proved the contrary. 'You have such a fearful power of suffering,' she replied in a moment.

To this at first Miss Chancellor made no rejoinder; but after a little she said, in the same attitude, 'Yes, *you* could make me.'

Verena took her hand and held it awhile. 'I never will, till I have been through everything myself.'

'*You* were not made to suffer—you were made to enjoy,' Olive said, in very much the same tone in which she had told her that what was the matter with her was that she didn't dislike men as a class—a tone which implied that the contrary would have been much more natural and perhaps rather higher. Perhaps it would; but Verena was unable to rebut the charge; she felt this, as she looked out of the window of the carriage at the bright, amusing city, where the elements seemed so numerous, the animation so immense, the shops so brilliant, the women so strikingly dressed, and knew that these things quickened her curiosity, all her pulses.

'Well, I suppose I mustn't presume on it,' she remarked, glancing back at Olive with her natural sweetness, her uncontradicting grace.

That young lady lifted her hand to her lips—held it there a moment; the movement seemed to say, 'When you are so divinely docile, how can I help the dread of losing you?' This idea, however, was unspoken, and Olive Chancellor's uttered words, as the carriage rolled on, were different.

'Verena, I don't understand why he wrote to you.'

'He wrote to me because he likes me. Perhaps you'll say you don't understand why he likes me,' the girl continued, laughing. 'He liked me the first time he saw me.'

'Oh, that time!' Olive murmured.

'And still more the second.'

'Did he tell you that in his letter?' Miss Chancellor inquired.

'Yes, my dear, he told me that. Only he expressed it more gracefully.' Verena was very happy to say that; a written phrase of Basil Ransom's sufficiently justified her.

'It was my intuition—it was my foreboding!' Olive exclaimed, closing her eyes.

'I thought you said you didn't dislike him.'

'It isn't dislike—it's simple dread. Is that all there is between you?'

'Why, Olive Chancellor, what do you think?' Verena asked, feeling now distinctly like a coward. Five minutes afterwards she said to Olive that if it would give her pleasure they would leave New York on the morrow, without taking a fourth day; and as soon as she had done so she felt better, especially when she saw how gratefully Olive looked at her for the concession, how eagerly she rose to the offer in saying, 'Well, if you *do* feel that it isn't our own life—our very own!' It was with these words, and others besides, and with an unusually weak, indefinite kiss, as if she wished to protest that, after all, a single day didn't matter, and yet accepted the sacrifice and was a little ashamed of it—it was in this manner that the agreement as to an immediate retreat was sealed. Verena could not shut her eyes to the fact that for a month she had been less frank, and if she wished to do penance this abbreviation of their pleasure in New York, even if it made her almost completely miss Basil Ransom, was easier than to tell Olive just now that the letter was *not* all, that there had been a long visit, a talk, and a walk besides, which she had been covering up for ever so many weeks. And of what consequence, anyway, was the missing? Was it such a pleasure to converse with a gentleman who only wanted to let you know—and why he should want it so much Verena couldn't guess—that he thought you quite preposterous? Olive took her from place to place, and she ended by forgetting everything but the present hour, and the bigness and variety of New York, and the entertainment of rolling about in a carriage with silk cushions, and meeting new faces, new expressions of curiosity and sympathy, assurances that one was watched and followed. Mingled with this was a bright consciousness, sufficient for the moment, that one was moreover to dine at Delmonico's and go to the German opera. There was enough of the epicurean in Verena's composition to make it easy for her in certain conditions to live only for the hour.

XXXI

WHEN SHE RETURNED with her companion to the establishment in Tenth Street she saw two notes lying on the table in the hall; one of which she perceived to be addressed to Miss Chancellor, the other to herself. The hand was different, but she recognised both. Olive was behind her on the steps, talking to the coachman about sending another carriage for them in half an hour (they had left themselves but just time to dress); so that she simply possessed herself of her own note and ascended to her room. As she did so she felt that all the while she had known it would be there, and was conscious of a kind of treachery, an unfriendly wilfulness, in not being more prepared for it. If she could roll about New York the whole afternoon and forget that there might be difficulties ahead, that didn't alter the fact that there *were* difficulties, and that they might even become considerable— might not be settled by her simply going back to Boston. Half an hour later, as she drove up the Fifth Avenue with Olive (there seemed to be so much crowded into that one day), smoothing her light gloves, wishing her fan were a little nicer, and proving by the answering, familiar brightness with which she looked out on the lamp-lighted streets that, whatever theory might be entertained as to the genesis of her talent and her personal nature, the blood of the lecture-going, night-walking Tarrants did distinctly flow in her veins; as the pair proceeded, I say, to the celebrated restaurant, at the door of which Mr. Burrage had promised to be in vigilant expectancy of their carriage, Verena found a sufficiently gay and natural tone of voice for remarking to her friend that Mr. Ransom had called upon her while they were out, and had left a note in which there were many compliments for Miss Chancellor.

'That's wholly your own affair, my dear,' Olive replied, with a melancholy sigh, gazing down the vista of Fourteenth Street (which they happened just then to be traversing, with much agitation), toward the queer barrier of the elevated railway.

It was nothing new to Verena that if the great striving of

Olive's life was for justice she yet sometimes failed to arrive at it in particular cases; and she reflected that it was rather late for her to say, like that, that Basil Ransom's letters were only his correspondent's business. Had not his kinswoman quite made the subject her own during their drive that afternoon? Verena determined now that her companion should hear all there was to be heard about the letter; asking herself whether, if she told her at present more than she cared to know, it wouldn't make up for her hitherto having told her less. 'He brought it with him, written, in case I should be out. He wants to see me tomorrow—he says he has ever so much to say to me. He proposes an hour—says he hopes it won't be inconvenient for me to see him about eleven in the morning; thinks I may have no other engagement so early as that. Of course our return to Boston settles it,' Verena added, with serenity.

Miss Chancellor said nothing for a moment; then she replied, 'Yes, unless you invite him to come on with you in the train.'

'Why, Olive, how bitter you are!' Verena exclaimed, in genuine surprise.

Olive could not justify her bitterness by saying that her companion had spoken as if she were disappointed, because Verena had not. So she simply remarked, 'I don't see what he can have to say to you—that would be worth your hearing.'

'Well, of course, it's the other side. He has got it on the brain!' said Verena, with a laugh which seemed to relegate the whole matter to the category of the unimportant.

'If we should stay, would you see him—at eleven o'clock?' Olive inquired.

'Why do you ask that—when I have given it up?'

'Do you consider it such a tremendous sacrifice?'

'No,' said Verena good-naturedly; 'but I confess I am curious.'

'Curious—how do you mean?'

'Well, to hear the other side.'

'Oh heaven!' Olive Chancellor murmured, turning her face upon her.

'You must remember I have never heard it.' And Verena smiled into her friend's wan gaze.

'Do you want to hear all the infamy that is in the world?'

'No, it isn't that; but the more he should talk the better chance he would give me. I guess I can meet him.'

'Life is too short. Leave him as he is.'

'Well,' Verena went on, 'there are many I haven't cared to move at all, whom I might have been more interested in than in him. But to make him give in just at two or three points— that I should like better than anything I have done.'

'You have no business to enter upon a contest that isn't equal; and it wouldn't be, with Mr. Ransom.'

'The inequality would be that I have right on my side.'

'What is that—for a man? For what was their brutality given them, but to make that up?'

'I don't think he's brutal; I should like to see,' said Verena gaily.

Olive's eyes lingered a little on her own; then they turned away, vaguely, blindly, out of the carriage-window, and Verena made the reflection that she looked strangely little like a person who was going to dine at Delmonico's. How terribly she worried about everything, and how tragical was her nature; how anxious, suspicious, exposed to subtle influences! In their long intimacy Verena had come to revere most of her friend's peculiarities; they were a proof of her depth and devotion, and were so bound up with what was noble in her that she was rarely provoked to criticise them separately. But at present, suddenly, Olive's earnestness began to appear as inharmonious with the scheme of the universe as if it had been a broken saw; and she was positively glad she had not told her about Basil Ransom's appearance in Monadnoc Place. If she worried so about what she knew, how much would she not have worried about the rest! Verena had by this time made up her mind that her acquaintance with Mr. Ransom was the most episodical, most superficial, most unimportant of all possible relations.

Olive Chancellor watched Henry Burrage very closely that evening; she had a special reason for doing so, and her entertainment, during the successive hours, was derived much less from the delicate little feast over which this insinuating proselyte presided, in the brilliant public room of the establishment, where French waiters flitted about on deep carpets and

parties at neighbouring tables excited curiosity and conjecture, or even from the magnificent music of 'Lohengrin,' than
from a secret process of comparison and verification, which
shall presently be explained to the reader. As some discredit
has possibly been thrown upon her impartiality it is a pleasure
to be able to say that on her return from the opera she took
a step dictated by an earnest consideration of justice—of the
promptness with which Verena had told her of the note left
by Basil Ransom in the afternoon. She drew Verena into her
room with her. The girl, on the way back to Tenth Street,
had spoken only of Wagner's music, of the singers, the or-
chestra, the immensity of the house, her tremendous pleasure.
Olive could see how fond she might become of New York,
where that kind of pleasure was so much more in the air.

'Well, Mr. Burrage was certainly very kind to us—no one
could have been more thoughtful,' Olive said; and she coloured a little at the look with which Verena greeted this
tribute of appreciation from Miss Chancellor to a single
gentleman.

'I am so glad you were struck with that, because I do think
we have been a little rough to him.' Verena's *we* was angelic.
'He was particularly attentive to you, my dear; he has got
over me. He looked at you so sweetly. Dearest Olive, if you
marry him——!' And Miss Tarrant, who was in high spirits,
embraced her companion, to check her own silliness.

'He wants you to stay there, all the same. They haven't
given *that* up,' Olive remarked, turning to a drawer, out of
which she took a letter.

'Did he tell you that, pray? He said nothing more about it
to me.'

'When we came in this afternoon I found this note from
Mrs. Burrage. You had better read it.' And she presented the
document, open, to Verena.

The purpose of it was to say that Mrs. Burrage could really
not reconcile herself to the loss of Verena's visit, on which
both she and her son had counted so much. She was sure they
would be able to make it as interesting to Miss Tarrant as it
would be to themselves. She, Mrs. Burrage, moreover, felt as
if she hadn't heard half she wanted about Miss Tarrant's
views, and there were so many more who were present at the

address, who had come to her that afternoon (losing not a minute, as Miss Chancellor could see), to ask how in the world they too could learn more—how they could get at the fair speaker and question her about certain details. She hoped so much, therefore, that even if the young ladies should be unable to alter their decision about the visit they might at least see their way to staying over long enough to allow her to arrange an informal meeting for some of these poor thirsty souls. Might she not at least talk over the question with Miss Chancellor? She gave her notice that she would attack her on the subject of the visit too. Might she not see her on the morrow, and might she ask of her the very great favour that the interview should be at Mrs. Burrage's own house? She had something very particular to say to her, as regards which perfect privacy was a great consideration, and Miss Chancellor would doubtless recognise that this would be best secured under Mrs. Burrage's roof. She would therefore send her carriage for Miss Chancellor at any hour that would be convenient to the latter. She really thought much good might come from their having a satisfactory talk.

Verena read this epistle with much deliberation; it seemed to her mysterious, and confirmed the idea she had received the night before—the idea that she had not got quite a correct impression of this clever, worldly, curious woman on the occasion of her visit to Cambridge, when they met her at her son's rooms. As she gave the letter back to Olive she said, 'That's why he didn't seem to believe we are really leaving tomorrow. He knows she had written that, and he thinks it will keep us.'

'Well, if I were to say it may—should you think me too miserably changeful?'

Verena stared, with all her candour, and it was so very queer that Olive should now wish to linger that the sense of it, for the moment, almost covered the sense of its being pleasant. But that came out after an instant, and she said, with great honesty, 'You needn't drag me away for consistency's sake. It would be absurd for me to pretend that I don't like being here.'

'I think perhaps I ought to see her.' Olive was very thoughtful.

'How lovely it must be to have a secret with Mrs. Burrage!' Verena exclaimed.

'It won't be a secret from you.'

'Dearest, you needn't tell me unless you want,' Verena went on, thinking of her own unimparted knowledge.

'I thought it was our plan to divide everything. It was certainly mine.'

'Ah, don't talk about plans!' Verena exclaimed, rather ruefully. 'You see, if we *are* going to stay to-morrow, how foolish it was to have any. There is more in her letter than is expressed,' she added, as Olive appeared to be studying in her face the reasons for and against making this concession to Mrs. Burrage, and that was rather embarrassing.

'I thought it over all the evening—so that if now you will consent we will stay.'

'Darling—what a spirit you have got! All through all those dear little dishes—all through "Lohengrin!" As I haven't thought it over at all, you must settle it. You know I am not difficult.'

'And would you go and stay with Mrs. Burrage, after all, if she should say anything to me that seems to make it desirable?'

Verena broke into a laugh. 'You know it's not our real life!'

Olive said nothing for a moment; then she replied: 'Don't think *I* can forget that. If I suggest a deviation, it's only because it sometimes seems to me that perhaps, after all, almost anything is better than the form reality *may* take with us.' This was slightly obscure, as well as very melancholy, and Verena was relieved when her companion remarked, in a moment, 'You must think me strangely inconsequent;' for this gave her a chance to reply, soothingly:

'Why, you don't suppose I expect you to keep always screwed up! I will stay a week with Mrs. Burrage, or a fortnight, or a month, or anything you like,' she pursued; 'anything it may seem to you best to tell her after you have seen her.'

'Do you leave it all to me? You don't give me much help,' Olive said.

'Help to what?'

'Help to help *you*.'

'I don't want any help; I am quite strong enough!' Verena cried, gaily. The next moment she inquired, in an appeal half comical, half touching, 'My dear colleague, why do you make me say such conceited things?'

'And if you do stay—just even to-morrow—shall you be—very much of the time—with Mr. Ransom?'

As Verena for the moment appeared ironically-minded, she might have found a fresh subject for hilarity in the tremulous, tentative tone in which Olive made this inquiry. But it had not that effect; it produced the first manifestation of impatience—the first, literally, and the first note of reproach—that had occurred in the course of their remarkable intimacy. The colour rose to Verena's cheek, and her eye for an instant looked moist.

'I don't know what you always think, Olive, nor why you don't seem able to trust me. You didn't, from the first with gentlemen. Perhaps you were right then—I don't say, but surely it is very different now. I don't think I ought to be suspected so much. Why have you a manner as if I had to be watched, as if I wanted to run away with every man that speaks to me? I should think I had proved how little I care. I thought you had discovered by this time that I am serious; that I have dedicated my life; that there is something unspeakably dear to me. But you begin again, every time—you don't do me justice. I must take everything that comes. I mustn't be afraid. I thought we had agreed that we were to do our work in the midst of the world, facing everything, keeping straight on, always taking hold. And now that it all opens out so magnificently, and victory is really sitting on our banners, it is strange of you to doubt of me, to suppose I am not more wedded to all our old dreams than ever. I told you the first time I saw you that I could renounce, and knowing better to-day, perhaps, what that means, I am ready to say it again. That I can, that I will! Why, Olive Chancellor,' Verena cried, panting, a moment, with her eloquence, and with the rush of a culminating idea, 'haven't you discovered by this time that I *have* renounced?'

The habit of public speaking, the training, the practice, in which she had been immersed, enabled Verena to unroll a coil of propositions dedicated even to a private interest with the most touching, most cumulative effect. Olive was completely aware of this, and she stilled herself, while the girl uttered one soft, pleading sentence after another, into the same rapt attention she was in the habit of sending up from the benches of an auditorium. She looked at Verena fixedly, felt that she was stirred to her depths, that she was exquisitely passionate and sincere, that she was a quivering, spotless, consecrated maiden, that she really had renounced, that they were both safe, and that her own injustice and indelicacy had been great. She came to her slowly, took her in her arms and held her long—giving her a silent kiss. From which Verena knew that she believed her.

XXXII

THE HOUR THAT Olive proposed to Mrs. Burrage, in a note sent early the next morning, for the interview to which she consented to lend herself, was the stroke of noon; this period of the day being chosen in consequence of a prevision of many subsequent calls upon her time. She remarked in her note that she did not wish any carriage to be sent for her, and she surged and swayed up the Fifth Avenue on one of the convulsive, clattering omnibuses which circulate in that thoroughfare. One of her reasons for mentioning twelve o'clock had been that she knew Basil Ransom was to call at Tenth Street at eleven, and (as she supposed he didn't intend to stay all day) this would give her time to see him come and go. It had been tacitly agreed between them, the night before, that Verena was quite firm enough in her faith to submit to his visit, and that such a course would be much more dignified than dodging it. This understanding passed from one to the other during that dumb embrace which I have described as taking place before they separated for the night. Shortly before noon, Olive, passing out of the house, looked into the big, sunny double parlour, where, in the morning, with all the husbands absent for the day and all the wives and spinsters launched upon the town, a young man desiring to hold a debate with a young lady might enjoy every advantage in the way of a clear field. Basil Ransom was still there; he and Verena, with the place to themselves, were standing in the recess of a window, their backs presented to the door. If he had got up, perhaps he was going, and Olive, softly closing the door again, waited a little in the hall, ready to pass into the back part of the house if she should hear him coming out. No sound, however, reached her ear; apparently he did mean to stay all day, and she should find him there on her return. She left the house, knowing they were looking at her from the window as she descended the steps, but feeling she could not bear to see Basil Ransom's face. As she walked, averting her own, towards the Fifth Avenue, on the sunny side, she was barely conscious of the loveliness of the day, the perfect weather, all suffused and tinted with spring, which sometimes descends upon New York when the winds of March have been stilled; she was given up only to the remembrance of that moment when she herself had stood at a window (the second time he came to see her in Boston), and watched Basil Ransom pass out with Adeline—with Adeline who had seemed capable then of getting such a hold on him but had proved as ineffectual in this respect as she was in every other. She recalled the vision she had allowed to dance before her as she saw the pair cross the street together, laughing and talking, and how it seemed to interpose itself against the fears which already then—so strangely—haunted her. Now that she saw it so fruitless—and that Verena, moreover, had turned out really so great—she was rather ashamed of it; she felt associated, however remotely, in the reasons which had made Mrs. Luna tell her so many fibs the day before, and there could be nothing elevating in that. As for the other reasons why her fidgety sister had failed and Mr. Ransom had held his own course, naturally Miss Chancellor didn't like to think of them.

If she had wondered what Mrs. Burrage wished so particularly to talk about, she waited some time for the clearing-up of the mystery. During this interval she sat in a remarkably pretty boudoir, where there were flowers and faiences and little French pictures, and watched her hostess revolve round the subject in circles the vagueness of which she tried to dissimulate. Olive believed she was a person who never could enjoy asking a favour, especially of a votary of the new ideas; and that was evidently what was coming. She had asked one already, but that had been handsomely paid for; the note from Mrs. Burrage which Verena found awaiting her in Tenth Street, on her arrival, contained the largest cheque this young woman had ever received for an address. The request that hung fire had reference to Verena too, of course; and Olive needed no prompting to feel that her friend's being a young person who took money could not make Mrs. Burrage's present effort more agreeable. To this taking of money (for when it came to Verena it was as if it came to her as well), she herself was now completely inured; money was a tremendous force, and when one wanted to assault the wrong with every engine one was happy not to lack the sinews of war. She liked her hostess better this morning than she had liked her before; she had more than ever the air of taking all sorts of sentiments and views for granted between them; which could only be flattering to Olive so long as it was really Mrs. Burrage who made each advance, while her visitor sat watchful and motionless. She had a light, clever, familiar way of traversing an immense distance with a very few words, as when she remarked, 'Well then, it is settled that she will come, and will stay till she is tired.'

Nothing of the kind had been settled, but Olive helped Mrs. Burrage (this time) more than she knew by saying, 'Why do you want her to visit you, Mrs. Burrage? why do you want her socially? Are you not aware that your son, a year ago, desired to marry her?'

'My dear Miss Chancellor, that is just what I wish to talk to you about. I am aware of everything; I don't believe you ever met any one who is aware of more things than I.' And Olive had to believe this, as Mrs. Burrage held up, smiling, her intelligent, proud, good-natured, successful head. 'I knew a year ago that my son was in love with your friend, I know that he has been so ever since, and that in consequence he would like to marry her to-day. I daresay you don't like the idea of her marrying at all; it would break up a friendship which is so full of interest' (Olive wondered for a moment whether she had been going to say 'so full of profit'), 'for you. This is why I hesitated; but since you are willing to talk about it, that is just what I want.'

'I don't see what good it will do,' Olive said.

'How can we tell till we try? I never give a thing up till I have turned it over in every sense.'

It was Mrs. Burrage, however, who did most of the talking; Olive only inserted from time to time an inquiry, a protest, a correction, an ejaculation tinged with irony. None of these things checked or diverted her hostess; Olive saw more and more that she wished to please her, to win her over, to smooth matters down, to place them in a new and original light. She was very clever and (little by little Olive said to herself), absolutely unscrupulous, but she didn't think she was clever enough for what she had undertaken. This was neither more nor less, in the first place, than to persuade Miss Chan-

cellor that she and her son were consumed with sympathy for
the movement to which Miss Chancellor had dedicated her
life. But how could Olive believe that, when she saw the type
to which Mrs. Burrage belonged—a type into which nature
herself had inserted a face turned in the very opposite way
from all earnest and improving things? People like Mrs. Burrage lived and fattened on abuses, prejudices, privileges, on
the petrified, cruel fashions of the past. It must be added,
however, that if her hostess was a humbug, Olive had never
met one who provoked her less; she was such a brilliant, genial, artistic one, with such a recklessness of perfidy, such a
willingness to bribe you if she couldn't deceive you. She
seemed to be offering Olive all the kingdoms of the earth if
she would only exert herself to bring about a state of feeling
on Verena Tarrant's part which would lead the girl to accept
Henry Burrage.

'We know it's you—the whole business; that you can do
what you please. You could decide it to-morrow with a word.'

She had hesitated at first, and spoken of her hesitation, and
it might have appeared that she would need all her courage
to say to Olive, that way, face to face, that Verena was in such
subjection to her. But she didn't look afraid; she only looked
as if it were an infinite pity Miss Chancellor couldn't understand what immense advantages and rewards there would be
for her in striking an alliance with the house of Burrage.
Olive was so impressed with this, so occupied, even, in wondering what these mystic benefits might be, and whether after
all there might not be a protection in them (from something
worse), a fund of some sort that she and Verena might convert to a large use, setting aside the mother and son when
once they had got what they had to give—she was so arrested
with the vague daze of this vision, the sense of Mrs. Burrage's
full hands, her eagerness, her thinking it worth while to flatter
and conciliate, whatever her pretexts and pretensions might
be, that she was almost insensible, for the time, to the
strangeness of such a woman's coming round to a positive
desire for a connection with the Tarrants. Mrs. Burrage had
indeed explained this partly by saying that her son's condition
was wearing her out, and that she would enter into anything
that would make him happier, make him better. She was

fonder of him than of the whole world beside, and it was an anguish to her to see him yearning for Miss Tarrant only to lose her. She made that charge about Olive's power in the matter in such a way that it seemed at the same time a tribute to her force of character.

'I don't know on what terms you suppose me to be with my friend,' Olive returned, with considerable majesty. 'She will do exactly as she likes, in such a case as the one you allude to. She is absolutely free; you speak as if I were her keeper!'

Then Mrs. Burrage explained that of course she didn't mean that Miss Chancellor exercised a conscious tyranny; but only that Verena had a boundless admiration for her, saw through her eyes, took the impress of all her opinions, preferences. She was sure that if Olive would only take a favourable view of her son Miss Tarrant would instantly throw herself into it. 'It's very true that you may ask me,' added Mrs. Burrage, smiling, 'how you can take a favourable view of a young man who wants to marry the very person in the world you want most to keep unmarried!'

This description of Verena was of course perfectly correct; but it was not agreeable to Olive to have the fact in question so clearly perceived, even by a person who expressed it with an air intimating that there was nothing in the world *she* couldn't understand.

'Did your son know that you were going to speak to me about this?' Olive asked, rather coldly, waiving the question of her influence on Verena and the state in which she wished her to remain.

'Oh yes, poor dear boy; we had a long talk yesterday, and I told him I would do what I could for him. Do you remember the little visit I paid to Cambridge last spring, when I saw you at his rooms? Then it was I began to perceive how the wind was setting; but yesterday we had a real *éclaircissement*. I didn't like it at all, at first; I don't mind telling you that, now—now that I am really enthusiastic about it. When a girl is as charming, as original, as Miss Tarrant, it doesn't in the least matter who she is; she makes herself the standard by which you measure her; she makes her own position. And then Miss Tarrant has such a future!' Mrs. Burrage added, quickly, as if that were the last thing to be overlooked. 'The whole question has come up again—the feeling that Henry tried to think dead, or at least dying, has revived, through the—I hardly know what to call it, but I really may say the unexpectedly great effect of her appearance here. She was really wonderful on Wednesday evening; prejudice, conventionality, every presumption there might be against her, had to fall to the ground. I expected a success, but I didn't expect what you gave us,' Mrs. Burrage went on, smiling, while Olive noted her 'you.' 'In short, my poor boy flamed up again; and now I see that he will never again care for any girl as he cares for that one. My dear Miss Chancellor, *j'en ai pris mon parti*, and perhaps you know my way of doing that sort of thing. I am not at all good at resigning myself, but I am excellent at taking up a craze. I haven't renounced, I have only changed sides. For or against, I must be a partisan. Don't you know that kind of nature? Henry has put the affair into my hands, and you see I put it into yours. Do help me; let us work together.'

This was a long, explicit speech for Mrs. Burrage, who dealt, usually, in the cursory and allusive; and she may very well have expected that Miss Chancellor would recognise its importance. What Olive did, in fact, was simply to inquire, by way of rejoinder: 'Why did you ask us to come on?'

If Mrs. Burrage hesitated now, it was only for twenty seconds. 'Simply because we are so interested in your work.'

'That surprises me,' said Olive, thoughtfully.

'I daresay you don't believe it; but such a judgment is superficial. I am sure we give proof in the offer we make,' Mrs. Burrage remarked, with a good deal of point. 'There are plenty of girls—without any views at all—who would be delighted to marry my son. He is very clever, and he has a large fortune. Add to that that he's an angel!'

That was very true, and Olive felt all the more that the attitude of these fortunate people, for whom the world was so well arranged just as it was, was very curious. But as she sat there it came over her that the human spirit has many variations, that the influence of the truth is great, and that there are such things in life as happy surprises, quite as well as disagreeable ones. Nothing, certainly, forced such people to fix their affections on the daughter of a 'healer'; it would be very clumsy to pick her out of her generation only for the purpose of frustrating her. Moreover, her observation of their young host at Delmonico's and in the spacious box at the Academy of Music, where they had privacy and ease, and murmured words could pass without making neighbours more given up to the stage turn their heads—her consideration of Henry Burrage's manner, suggested to her that she had measured him rather scantily the year before, that he was as much in love as the feebler passions of the age permitted (for though Miss Chancellor believed in the amelioration of humanity, she thought there was too much water in the blood of all of us), that he prized Verena for her rarity, which was her genius, her gift, and would therefore have an interest in promoting it, and that he was of so soft and fine a paste that his wife might do what she liked with him. Of course there would be the mother-in-law to count with; but unless she was perjuring herself shamelessly Mrs. Burrage really had the wish to project herself into the new atmosphere, or at least to be generous personally; so that, oddly enough, the fear that most glanced before Olive was not that this high, free matron, slightly irritable with cleverness and at the same time good-natured with prosperity, would bully her son's bride, but rather that she might take too fond a possession of her. It was a fear which may be described as a presentiment of jealousy. It occurred, accordingly, to Miss Chancellor's quick conscience that, possibly, the proposal which presented itself in circumstances so complicated and anomalous was simply a magnificent chance, an improvement on the very best, even, that she had dreamed of for Verena. It meant a large command of money—much larger than her own; the association of a couple of clever people who simulated conviction very well, whether they felt it or not, and who had a hundred useful worldly ramifications, and a kind of social pedestal from which she might really shine afar. The conscience I have spoken of grew positively sick as it thought of having such a problem as that to consider, such an ordeal to traverse. In the presence of such a contingency the poor girl felt grim and helpless; she could only vaguely wonder whether she were called upon in the name of duty to lend a hand to the torture of her own spirit.

'And if she should marry him, how could I be sure that—afterwards—you would care so much about the question which has all our thoughts, hers and mine?' This inquiry evolved itself from Olive's rapid meditation; but even to herself it seemed a little rough.

Mrs. Burrage took it admirably. 'You think we are feigning an interest, only to get hold of her? That's not very nice of you, Miss Chancellor; but of course you have to be tremendously careful. I assure you my son tells me he firmly believes your movement is the great question of the immediate future, that it has entered into a new phase; into what does he call it? the domain of practical politics. As for me, you don't suppose I don't want everything we poor women can get, or that I would refuse any privilege or advantage that's offered me? I don't rant or rave about anything, but I have—as I told you just now—my own quiet way of being zealous. If you had no worse partisan than I, you would do very well. My son has talked to me immensely about your ideas; and even if I should enter into them only because he does, I should do so quite enough. You may say you don't see Henry dangling about after a wife who gives public addresses; but I am convinced that a great many things are coming to pass—very soon, too—that we don't see in advance. Henry is a gentleman to his finger-tips, and there is not a situation in which he will not conduct himself with tact.'

Olive could see that they really wanted Verena immensely, and it was impossible for her to believe that if they were to get her they would not treat her well. It came to her that they would even over-indulge her, flatter her, spoil her; she was perfectly capable, for the moment, of assuming that Verena was susceptible of deterioration and that her own treatment of her had been discriminatingly severe. She had a hundred protests, objections, replies; her only embarrassment could be as to which she should use first.

'I think you have never seen Doctor Tarrant and his wife,' she remarked, with a calmness which she felt to be very pregnant.

'You mean they are absolutely fearful? My son has told me

they are quite impossible, and I am quite prepared for that. Do you ask how we should get on with them? My dear young lady, we should get on as you do!'

If Olive had answers, so had Mrs. Burrage; she had still an answer when her visitor, taking up the supposition that it was in her power to dispose in any manner whatsoever of Verena, declared that she didn't know why Mrs. Burrage addressed herself to *her*, that Miss Tarrant was free as air, that her future was in her own hands, that such a matter as this was a kind of thing with which it could never occur to one to interfere. 'Dear Miss Chancellor, we don't ask you to interfere. The only thing we ask of you is simply *not* to interfere.'

'And have you sent for me only for that?'

'For that, and for what I hinted at in my note; that you would really exercise your influence with Miss Tarrant to induce her to come to us now for a week or two. That is really, after all, the main thing I ask. Lend her to us, here, for a little while, and we will take care of the rest. That sounds conceited—but she *would* have a good time.'

'She doesn't live for that,' said Olive.

'What I mean is that she should deliver an address every night!' Mrs. Burrage returned, smiling.

'I think you try to prove too much. You do believe—though you pretend you don't—that I control her actions, and as far as possible her desires, and that I am jealous of any other relations she may possibly form. I can imagine that we may perhaps have that air, though it only proves how little such an association as ours is understood, and how superficial is still'—Olive felt that her 'still' was really historical—'the interpretation of many of the elements in the activity of women, how much the public conscience with regard to them needs to be educated. Your conviction with respect to my attitude being what I believe it to be,' Miss Chancellor went on, 'I am surprised at your not perceiving how little it is in my interest to deliver my—my victim up to you.'

If we were at this moment to take, in a single glance, an inside view of Mrs. Burrage (a liberty we have not yet ventured on), I suspect we should find that she was considerably exasperated at her visitor's superior tone, at seeing herself regarded by this dry, shy, obstinate, provincial young woman as superficial. If she liked Verena very nearly as much as she tried to convince Miss Chancellor, she was conscious of disliking Miss Chancellor more than she should probably ever be able to reveal to Verena. It was doubtless partly her irritation that found a voice as she said, after a self-administered pinch of caution not to say too much, 'Of course it would be absurd in us to assume that Miss Tarrant would find my son irresistible, especially as she has already refused him. But even if she should remain obdurate, should you consider yourself quite safe as regards others?'

The manner in which Miss Chancellor rose from her chair on hearing these words showed her hostess that if she had wished to take a little revenge by frightening her, the experiment was successful. 'What others do you mean?' Olive asked, standing very straight, and turning down her eyes as from a great height.

Mrs. Burrage—since we have begun to look into her mind we may continue the process—had not meant any one in particular; but a train of association was suddenly kindled in her thought by the flash of the girl's resentment. She remembered the gentleman who had come up to her in the music-room, after Miss Tarrant's address, while she was talking with Olive, and to whom that young lady had given so cold a welcome. 'I don't mean any one in particular; but, for instance, there is the young man to whom she asked me to send an invitation to my party, and who looked to me like a possible admirer.' Mrs. Burrage also got up; then she stood a moment, closer to her visitor. 'Don't you think it's a good deal to expect that, young, pretty, attractive, clever, charming as she is, you should be able to keep her always, to exclude other affections, to cut off a whole side of life, to defend her against dangers— if you call them dangers—to which every young woman who is not positively repulsive is exposed? My dear young lady, I wonder if I might give you three words of advice?' Mrs. Burrage did not wait till Olive had answered this inquiry; she went on quickly, with her air of knowing exactly what she wanted to say and feeling at the same time that, good as it might be, the manner of saying it, like the manner of saying most other things, was not worth troubling much about. 'Don't attempt the impossible. You have got hold of a good thing; don't spoil it by trying to stretch it too far. If you don't take the better, perhaps you will have to take the worse; if it's safety you want I should think she was much safer with my son—for with us you know the worst—than as a possible prey to adventurers, to exploiters, or to people who, once they had got hold of her, would shut her up altogether.'

Olive dropped her eyes; she couldn't endure Mrs. Burrage's horrible expression of being near the mark, her look of worldly cleverness, of a confidence born of much experience. She felt that nothing would be spared her, that she should have to go to the end, that this ordeal also must be faced, and that, in particular, there was a detestable wisdom in her hostess's advice. She was conscious, however, of no obligation to recognise it then and there; she wanted to get off, and even to carry Mrs. Burrage's sapient words along with her—to hurry to some place where she might be alone and think. 'I don't know why you have thought it right to send for me only to say this. I take no interest whatever in your son—in his settling in life.' And she gathered her mantle more closely about her, turning away.

'It is exceedingly kind of you to have come,' said Mrs. Burrage, imperturbably. 'Think of what I have said; I am sure you won't feel that you have wasted your hour.'

'I have a great many things to think of!' Olive exclaimed, insincerely; for she knew that Mrs. Burrage's ideas would haunt her.

'And tell her that if she will make us the little visit, all New York shall sit at her feet!'

That was what Olive wanted, and yet it seemed a mockery to hear Mrs. Burrage say it. Miss Chancellor retreated, making no response even when her hostess declared again that she was under great obligations to her for coming. When she reached the street she found she was deeply agitated, but not with a sense of weakness; she hurried along, excited and dismayed, feeling that her insufferable conscience was bristling like some irritated animal, that a magnificent offer had really been made to Verena, and that there was no way for her to persuade herself she might be silent about it. Of course, if Verena should be tempted by the idea of being made so much of by the Burrages, the danger of Basil Ransom getting any kind of hold on her would cease to be pressing. That was what was present to Olive as she walked along, and that was what made her nervous, conscious only of this problem that had suddenly turned the bright day to grayness, heedless of the sophisticated-looking people who passed her on the wide Fifth Avenue pavement. It had risen in her mind the day before, planted first by Mrs. Burrage's note; and then, as we know, she had vaguely entertained the conception, asking Verena whether she would make the visit if it were again to be pressed upon them. It had been pressed, certainly, and the terms of the problem were now so much sharper that they seemed cruel. What had been in her own mind was that if Verena should appear to lend herself to the Burrages, Basil Ransom might be discouraged—might think that, shabby and poor, there was no chance for him as against people with every advantage of fortune and position. She didn't see him relax his purpose so easily; she knew she didn't believe he was of that pusillanimous fibre. Still, it was a chance, and any chance that might help her had been worth considering. At present she saw it was a question not of Verena's lending herself, but of a positive gift, or at least of a bargain in which the terms would be immensely liberal. It would be impossible to use the Burrages as a shelter on the assumption that they were not dangerous, for they became dangerous from the moment they set up as sympathisers, took the ground that what they offered the girl was simply a boundless opportunity. It came back to Olive, again and again, that this was, and could only be, fantastic and false; but it was always possible that Verena might not think it so, might trust them all the way. When Miss Chancellor had a pair of alternatives to consider, a question of duty to study, she put a kind of passion into it—felt, above all, that the matter must be settled that very hour, before anything in life could go on. It seemed to her at present that she couldn't re-enter the house in Tenth Street without having decided first whether she might trust the Burrages or not. By 'trust' them, she meant trust them to fail in winning Verena over, while at the same time they put Basil Ransom on a false scent. Olive was able to say to herself that he probably wouldn't have the hardihood to push after her into those gilded saloons, which, in any event, would be closed to him as soon as the mother and son should discover what he wanted. She even asked herself whether Verena would not be still better defended from the young Southerner in New York, amid complicated hospitalities, than in Boston with a cousin of the enemy. She continued to walk down the Fifth Avenue, without noticing the cross-streets, and after a while became conscious that she was approaching Washington Square. By this time she had also definitely reasoned it out that Basil Ransom and Henry Burrage could not both capture Miss Tarrant, that therefore there could not be two dangers, but only one; that this was a good deal gained, and that it behoved her to determine which peril had most reality, in order that she might deal with that one only. She held her way to the Square, which, as all the world knows, is of great extent and open to the encircling street. The trees and grass-plats had begun to bud and sprout, the fountains plashed in the sunshine, the children of the quarter, both the dingier types from the south side, who played games that required much chalking of the paved walks, and much sprawling and crouching there, under the feet of passers, and the little curled and feathered people who drove their hoops under the eyes of French nursemaids—all the infant population filled the vernal air with small sounds which had a crude, tender quality, like the leaves and the thin herbage. Olive wandered through the place, and ended by sitting down on one of the continuous benches. It was a long time since she had done anything so vague, so wasteful. There were a dozen things which, as she was staying over in New York, she ought to do; but she forgot them, or, if she thought of them, felt that they were now of no moment. She remained in her place an hour, brooding, tremulous, turning over and over certain thoughts. It seemed to her that she was face to face with a crisis of her destiny, and that she must not shrink from seeing it exactly as it was. Before she rose to return to Tenth Street she had made up her mind that there was no menace so great as the menace of Basil Ransom; she had accepted in thought any arrangement which would deliver her from that. If the Burrages were to take Verena they would take her from Olive immeasurably less than he would do; it was from him, from him they would take her most. She walked back to her boarding house, and the servant who admitted her said, in answer to her inquiry as to whether Verena were at home, that Miss Tarrant had gone out with the gentleman who called in the morning, and had not yet come in. Olive stood staring; the clock in the hall marked three.

XXXIII

'C OME OUT with me, Miss Tarrant; come out with me. *Do* come out with me.' That was what Basil Ransom had been saying to Verena when they stood where Olive perceived them, in the embrasure of the window. It had of course taken considerable talk to lead up to this; for the tone, even more than the words, indicated a large increase of intimacy. Verena was mindful of this when he spoke; and it frightened her a little, made her uneasy, which was one of the reasons why she got up from her chair and went to the window—an inconsequent movement, inasmuch as her wish was to impress upon him that it was impossible she should comply with his request. It would have served this end much better for her to sit, very firmly, in her place. He made her nervous and restless; she was beginning to perceive that he produced a peculiar effect upon her. Certainly, she had been out with him at home the very first time he called upon her; but it seemed to her to make an important difference that she herself should then have proposed the walk—simply because it was the easiest thing to do when a person came to see you in Monadnoc Place.

They had gone out that time because she wanted to, not because he did. And then it was one thing for her to stroll with him round Cambridge, where she knew every step and had the confidence and freedom which came from being on her own ground, and the pretext, which was perfectly natural, of wanting to show him the colleges, and quite another thing to go wandering with him through the streets of this great strange city, which, attractive, delightful as it was, had not the suitableness even of being his home, not his real one. He wanted to show her something, he wanted to show her everything; but she was not sure now—after an hour's talk—that she particularly wanted to see anything more that he could show her. He had shown her a great deal while he sat there, especially what balderdash he thought it—the whole idea of women's being equal to men. He seemed to have come only for that, for he was all the while revolving round it; she couldn't speak of anything but what he brought it back to the question of some new truth like that. He didn't say so in so many words; on the contrary, he was tremendously insinuating and satirical, and pretended to think she had proved all and a great deal more than she wanted to prove; but his exaggeration, and the way he rung all the changes on two or three of the points she had made at Mrs. Burrage's, were just the sign that he was a scoffer of scoffers. He wouldn't do anything but laugh; he seemed to think that he might laugh at her all day without her taking offence. Well, he might if it amused him; but she didn't see why she should ramble round New York with him to give him his opportunity.

She had told him, and she had told Olive, that she was determined to produce some effect on him; but now, suddenly, she felt differently about that—she ceased to care whether she produced any effect or not. She didn't see why she should take him so seriously, when he wouldn't take her so; that is, wouldn't take her ideas. She had guessed before that he didn't want to discuss them; this had been in her mind when she said to him at Cambridge that his interest in her was personal, not controversial. Then she had simply meant that, as an inquiring young Southerner, he had wanted to see what a bright New England girl was like; but since then it had become a little more clear to her—her short talk with Ransom at Mrs. Burrage's threw some light upon the question—what the personal interest of a young Southerner (however inquiring merely) might amount to. Did he too want to make love to her? This idea made Verena rather impatient, weary in advance. The thing she desired least in the world was to be put into the wrong with Olive; for she had certainly given her ground to believe (not only in their scene the night before, which was a simple repetition, but all along, from the very first), that she really had an interest which would transcend any attraction coming from such a source as that. If yesterday it seemed to her that she should like to struggle with Mr. Ransom, to refute and convince him, she had this morning gone into the parlour to receive him with the idea that, now they were alone together in a quiet, favourable place, he would perhaps take up the different points of her address one by one, as several gentlemen had done after hearing her on other occasions. There was nothing she liked so well as that, and Olive never had anything to say against it. But he hadn't taken up anything; he had simply laughed and chaffed, and unrolled a string of queer fancies about the delightful way women would fix things when, as she said in her address, they should get out of their box. He kept talking about the box; he seemed as if he wouldn't let go that simile. He said that he had come to look at her through the glass sides, and if he wasn't afraid of hurting her he would smash them in. He was determined to find the key that would open it, if he had to look for it all over the world; it was tantalising only to be able to talk to her through the keyhole. If he didn't want to take up the subject, he at least wanted to take *her* up—to keep his hand upon her as long as he could. Verena had had no such sensation since the first day she went in to see Olive Chancellor, when she felt herself plucked from the earth and borne aloft.

'It's the most lovely day, and I should like so much to show you New York, as you showed me your beautiful Harvard,' Basil Ransom went on, pressing her to accede to his proposal. 'You said that was the only thing you could do for me then, and so this is the only thing I can do for you here. It would be odious to see you go away, giving me nothing but this stiff little talk in a boarding-house parlour.'

'Mercy, if you call this stiff!' Verena exclaimed, laughing, while at that moment Olive passed out of the house and descended the steps before her eyes.

'My poor cousin's stiff; she won't turn her head a hair's breadth to look at us,' said the young man. Olive's figure, as she went by, was, for Verena, full of a queer, touching, tragic expression, saying ever so many things, both familiar and strange; and Basil Ransom's companion privately remarked how little men knew about women, or indeed about what was really delicate, that he, without any cruel intention, should attach an idea of ridicule to such an incarnation of the pathetic, should speak rough, derisive words about it. Ransom, in truth, to-day, was not disposed to be very scrupulous, and he only wanted to get rid of Olive Chancellor, whose image, at last, decidedly bothered and bored him. He was glad to see her go out; but that was not sufficient, she would come back quick enough; the place itself contained her, expressed her.

For to-day he wanted to take possession of Verena, to carry her to a distance, to reproduce a little the happy conditions they had enjoyed the day of his visit to Cambridge. And the fact that in the nature of things it could only be for to-day made his desire more keen, more full of purpose. He had thought over the whole question in the last forty-eight hours, and it was his belief that he saw things in their absolute reality. He took a greater interest in her than he had taken in any one yet, but he proposed, after to-day, not to let that accident make any difference. This was precisely what gave its high value to the present limited occasion. He was too shamefully poor, too shabbily and meagrely equipped, to have the right to talk of marriage to a girl in Verena's very peculiar position. He understood now how good that position was, from a worldly point of view; her address at Mrs. Burrage's gave him something definite to go upon, showed him what she could do, that people would flock in thousands to an exhibition so charming (and small blame to them); that she might easily have a big career, like that of a distinguished actress or singer, and that she would make money in quantities only slightly smaller than performers of that kind. Who wouldn't pay half a dollar for such an hour as he had passed at Mrs. Burrage's? The sort of thing she was able to do, to say, was an article for which there was more and more demand—fluent, pretty, third-rate palaver, conscious or unconscious perfected humbug; the stupid, gregarious, gullible public, the enlightened democracy of his native land, could swallow unlimited draughts of it. He was sure she could go, like that, for several years, with her portrait in the druggists' windows and her posters on the fences, and during that time would make a fortune sufficient to keep her in affluence for evermore. I shall perhaps expose our young man to the contempt of superior minds if I say that all this seemed to him an insuperable impediment to his making up to Verena. His scruples were doubtless begotten of a false pride, a sentiment in which there was a thread of moral tinsel, as there was in the Southern idea of chivalry; but he felt ashamed of his own poverty, the positive flatness of his situation, when he thought of the gilded nimbus that surrounded the protégée of Mrs. Burrage. This shame was possible to him even while he was conscious of what a mean business it was to practise upon human imbecility, how much better it was even to be seedy and obscure, discouraged about one's self. He had been born to the prospect of a fortune, and in spite of the years of misery that followed the war had never rid himself of the belief that a gentleman who desired to unite himself to a charming girl couldn't yet ask her to come and live with him in sordid conditions. On the other hand it was no possible basis of matrimony that Verena should continue for his advantage the exercise of her remunerative profession; if he should become her husband he should know a way to strike her dumb. In the midst of this an irrepressible desire urged him on to taste, for once, deeply, all that he was condemned to lose, or at any rate forbidden to attempt to gain. To spend a day with her and not to see her again—that presented itself to him at once as the least and the most that was possible. He did not need even to remind himself that young Mr. Burrage was able to offer her everything *he* lacked, including the most amiable adhesion to her views.

'It will be charming in the Park to-day. Why not take a stroll with me there as I did with you in the little park at Harvard?' he asked, when Olive had disappeared.

'Oh, I have seen it, very well, in every corner. A friend of mine kindly took me to drive there yesterday,' Verena said.

'A friend?—do you mean Mr. Burrage?' And Ransom stood looking at her with his extraordinary eyes. 'Of course, I haven't a vehicle to drive you in; but we can sit on a bench and talk.' She didn't say it was Mr. Burrage, but she was unable to say it was not, and something in her face showed him that he had guessed. So he went on: 'Is it only with him you can go out? Won't he like it, and may you only do what he likes? Mrs. Luna told me he wants to marry you, and I saw at his mother's how he stuck to you. If you are going to marry him, you can drive with him every day in the year, and that's just a reason for your giving me an hour or two now, before it becomes impossible.' He didn't mind much what he said—it had been his plan not to mind much to-day—and so long as he made her do what he wanted he didn't care much how he did it. But he saw that his words brought the colour to her face; she stared, surprised at his freedom and familiarity. He went on, dropping the hardness, the irony of which he was conscious, out of his tone. 'I know it's no business of mine whom you marry, or even whom you drive with, and I beg your pardon if I seem indiscreet and obtrusive; but I would give anything just to detach you a little from your ties, your belongings, and feel for an hour or two, as if—as if——' And he paused.

'As if what?' she asked, very seriously.

'As if there were no such person as Mr. Burrage—as Miss Chancellor—in the whole place.' This had not been what he was going to say; he used different words.

'I don't know what you mean, why you speak of other persons. I can do as I like, perfectly. But I don't know why you should take so for granted that *that* would be it!' Verena spoke these words not out of coquetry, or to make him beg her more for a favour, but because she was thinking, and she wanted to gain a moment. His allusion to Henry Burrage touched her, his belief that she had been in the Park under circumstances more agreeable than those he proposed. They were not; somehow, she wanted him to know that. To wander there with a companion, slowly stopping, lounging, looking at the animals as she had seen the people do the day before; to sit down in some out-of-the-way part where there were distant views, which she had noticed from her high perch beside Henry Burrage—she had to look down so, it made her feel unduly fine: that was much more to her taste, much more her idea of true enjoyment. It came over her that Mr. Ransom had given up his work to come to her at such an hour; people of his kind, in the morning, were always getting their living, and it was only for Mr. Burrage that it didn't matter, inasmuch as he had no profession. Mr. Ransom simply wanted to give up his whole day. That pressed upon her; she was, as the most good-natured girl in the world, too entirely tender not to feel any sacrifice that was made for her; she had always done everything that people asked. Then, if Olive should make that strange arrangement for her to go to Mrs. Burrage's he would take it as a proof that there was something serious between her and the gentleman of the house, in spite of anything she might say to the contrary; moreover, if she should go she wouldn't be able to receive

Mr. Ransom there. Olive would trust her not to, and she must certainly, in future, not disappoint Olive nor keep anything back from her, whatever she might have done in the past. Besides, she didn't want to do that; she thought it much better not. It was this idea of the episode which was possibly in store for her in New York, and from which her present companion would be so completely excluded, that worked upon her now with a rapid transition, urging her to grant him what he asked, so that in advance she should have made up for what she might not do for him later. But most of all she disliked his thinking she was engaged to some one. She didn't know, it is true, why she should mind it; and indeed, at this moment, our young lady's feelings were not in any way clear to her. She did not see what was the use of letting her acquaintance with Mr. Ransom become much closer (since his interest did really seem personal); and yet she presently asked him why he wanted her to go out with him, and whether there was anything particular he wanted to say to her (there was no one like Verena for making speeches apparently flirtatious, with the best faith and the most innocent intention in the world); as if that would not be precisely a reason to make it well she should get rid of him altogether.

'Of course I have something particular to say to you—I have a tremendous lot to say to you!' the young man exclaimed. 'Far more than I can say in this stuck-up, confined room, which is public, too, so that any one may come in from one moment to another. Besides,' he added, sophistically, 'it isn't proper for me to pay a visit of three hours.'

Verena did not take up the sophistry, nor ask him whether it would be more proper for her to ramble about the city with him for an equal period; she only said, 'Is it something that I shall care to hear, or that will do me any good?'

'Well, I hope it will do you good; but I don't suppose you will care much to hear it.' Basil Ransom hesitated a moment, smiling at her; then he went on: 'It's to tell you, once for all, how much I really do differ from you!' He said this at a venture, but it was a happy inspiration.

If it was only that, Verena thought she might go, for that was not personal. 'Well, I'm glad you care so much,' she answered, musingly. But she had another scruple still, and she expressed it in saying that she should like Olive very much to find her when she came in.

'That's all very well,' Ransom returned; 'but does she think that she only has a right to go out? Does she expect you to keep the house because she's abroad? If she stays out long enough, she will find you when she comes in.'

'Her going out that way—it proves that she trusts me,' Verena said, with a candour which alarmed her as soon as she had spoken.

Her alarm was just, for Basil Ransom instantly caught up her words, with a great mocking amazement. 'Trusts you? and why shouldn't she trust you? Are you a little girl of ten and she your governess? Haven't you any liberty at all, and is she always watching you and holding you to an account? Have you such vagabond instincts that you are only thought safe when you are between four walls?' Ransom was going on to speak, in the same tone, of her having felt it necessary to keep Olive in ignorance of his visit to Cambridge—a fact they had touched on, by implication, in their short talk at Mrs. Burrage's; but in a moment he saw that he had said enough. As for Verena, she had said more than she meant, and the simplest way to unsay it was to go and get her bonnet and jacket and let him take her where he liked. Five minutes later he was walking up and down the parlour, waiting while she prepared herself to go out.

They went up to the Central Park by the elevated railway, and Verena reflected, as they proceeded, that anyway Olive was probably disposing of her somehow at Mrs. Burrage's, and that therefore there wasn't much harm in her just taking this little run on her own responsibility, especially as she should only be out an hour—which would be just the duration of Olive's absence. The beauty of the 'elevated' was that it took you up to the Park and brought you back in a few minutes, and you had all the rest of the hour to walk about and see the place. It was so pleasant now that one was glad to see it twice over. The long, narrow inclosure, across which the houses in the streets that border it look at each other with their glittering windows, bristled with the raw delicacy of April, and, in spite of its rockwork grottoes and tunnels, its pavilions and statues, its too numerous paths and pavements, lakes too big for the landscape and bridges too big for the lakes, expressed all the fragrance and freshness of the most charming moment of the year. Once Verena was fairly launched the spirit of the day took possession of her; she was glad to have come, she forgot about Olive, enjoyed the sense of wandering in the great city with a remarkable young man who would take beautiful care of her, while no one else in the world knew where she was. It was very different from her drive yesterday with Mr. Burrage, but it was more free, more intense, more full of amusing incident and opportunity. She could stop and look at everything now, and indulge all her curiosities, even the most childish; she could feel as if she were out for the day, though she was not really—as she had not done since she was a little girl, when in the country, once or twice, when her father and mother had drifted into summer quarters, gone out of town like people of fashion, she had, with a chance companion, strayed far from home, spent hours in the woods and fields, looking for raspberries and playing she was a gipsy. Basil Ransom had begun with proposing, strenuously, that she should come somewhere and have luncheon; he had brought her out half an hour before that meal was served in West Tenth Street, and he maintained that he owed her the compensation of seeing that she was properly fed; he knew a very quiet, luxurious French restaurant, near the top of the Fifth Avenue: he didn't tell her that he knew it through having once lunched there in company with Mrs. Luna. Verena for the present declined his hospitality—said she was going to be out so short a time that it wasn't worth the trouble; she should not be hungry, luncheon to her was nothing, she would eat when she went home. When he pressed her she said she would see later, perhaps, if she should find she wanted something. She would have liked immensely to go with him to an eating-house, and yet, with this, she was afraid, just as she was rather afraid, at bottom, and in the intervals of her quick pulsations of amusement, of the whole expedition, not knowing why she had come, though it made her happy, and reflecting that there was really nothing Mr. Ransom could have to say to her that would concern her closely enough. He knew what he intended about her sharing the noonday repast with him somehow; it had been part of his plan that she should sit opposite him at a little table, taking her napkin out of its curious folds—sit there smiling back at him while he said to her certain things that hummed, like memories of tunes, in his fancy, and they waited till something extremely good, and a little vague, chosen out of a French *carte*, was brought them. That was not at all compatible with her going home at the end of half an hour, as she seemed to expect to. They visited the animals in the little zoological garden which forms one of the attractions of the Central Park; they observed the swans in the ornamental water, and they even considered the question of taking a boat for half an hour, Ransom saying that they needed this to make their visit complete. Verena replied that she didn't see why it should be complete, and after having threaded the devious ways of the Ramble, lost themselves in the Maze, and admired all the statues and busts of great men with which the grounds are decorated, they contented themselves with resting on a sequestered bench, where, however, there was a pretty glimpse of the distance and an occasional stroller creaked by on the asphalt walk.

They had had by this time a great deal of talk, none of which, nevertheless, had been serious to Verena's view. Mr. Ransom continued to joke about everything, including the emancipation of women; Verena, who had always lived with people who took the world very earnestly, had never encountered such a power of disparagement or heard so much sarcasm levelled at the institutions of her country and the tendencies of the age. At first she replied to him, contradicted, showed a high spirit of retort, turning his irreverence against himself; she was too quick and ingenious not to be able to think of something to oppose—talking in a fanciful strain—to almost everything he said. But little by little she grew weary and rather sad; brought up, as she had been, to admire new ideas, to criticise the social arrangements that one met almost everywhere, and to disapprove of a great many things, she had yet never dreamed of such a wholesale arraignment as Mr. Ransom's, so much bitterness as she saw lurking beneath his exaggerations, his misrepresentations. She knew he was an intense conservative, but she didn't know that being a conservative could make a person so aggressive and unmerciful. She thought conservatives were only smug and stubborn and self-complacent, satisfied with what actually existed; but Mr. Ransom didn't seem any more satisfied with what existed than with what she wanted to exist, and he was ready to say worse things about some of those whom she would have supposed to be on his own side than she thought it right to say about almost any one. She ceased after a while to care to argue with him, and wondered what could have happened to him to make him so perverse. Probably something had gone wrong in his life—he had had some misfortune that coloured his whole view of the world. He was a cynic; she had often heard about that state of mind, though she had never encountered it, for all the people she had seen only cared, if possible, too much. Of Basil Ransom's personal history she knew only what Olive had told her, and that was but a general outline, which left plenty of room for private dramas, secret disappointments and sufferings. As she sat there beside him she thought of some of these things, asked herself whether they were what he was thinking of when he said, for instance, that he was sick of all the modern cant about freedom and had no sympathy with those who wanted an extension of it. What was needed for the good of the world was that people should make a better use of the liberty they possessed. Such declarations as this took Verena's breath away; she didn't suppose you could hear any one say such a thing as that in the nineteenth century, even the least advanced. It was of a piece with his denouncing the spread of education; he thought the spread of education a gigantic farce—people stuffing their heads with a lot of empty catchwords that prevented them from doing their work quietly and honestly. You had a right to an education only if you had an intelligence, and if you looked at the matter with any desire to see things as they are you soon perceived that an intelligence was a very rare luxury, the attribute of one person in a hundred. He seemed to take a pretty low view of humanity, anyway. Verena hoped that something really bad had happened to him—not by way of gratifying any resentment he aroused in her nature, but to help herself to forgive him for so much contempt and brutality. She wanted to forgive him, for after they had sat on their bench half an hour and his jesting mood had abated a little, so that he talked with more consideration (as it seemed), and more sincerity, a strange feeling came over her, a perfect willingness not to keep insisting on her own side and a desire not to part from him with a mere accentuation of their differences. Strange I call the nature of her reflections, for they softly battled with each other as she listened, in the warm, still air, touched with the far-away hum of the immense city, to his deep, sweet, distinct voice, expressing monstrous opinions with exotic cadences and mild, familiar laughs, which, as he leaned towards her, almost tickled her cheek and ear. It seemed to her strangely harsh, almost cruel, to have brought her out only to say to her things which, after all, free as she was to contradict them and tolerant as she always tried to be, could only give her pain; yet there was a spell upon her as she listened; it was in her nature to be easily submissive, to like being overborne. She could be silent when people insisted, and silent without acrimony. Her whole relation to Olive was a kind of tacit, tender assent to passionate insistence, and if this had ended by being easy and agreeable to her (and indeed had never been anything else), it may be supposed that the struggle of yielding to a will which she felt to be stronger even than Olive's was not of long duration. Ransom's will had the effect of making her linger even while she knew the afternoon was going on, that Olive would have come back and found her still absent, and would have been submerged again in the bitter waves of anxiety. She saw her, in fact, as she must be at that moment, posted at the window of her room in Tenth Street, watching for some sign of her return, listening for her step on the staircase, her voice in the hall. Verena looked at this image as at a painted picture, perceived all it represented, every detail. If it didn't move her more, make her start to her feet, dart away from Basil Ransom and hurry back to her friend, this was because the very torment to which she was conscious of subjecting that friend made her say to herself that it must be the very last. This was the last time she could ever sit by Mr. Ransom and hear him express himself in a manner that interfered so with her life; the ordeal had been so personal and so complete that she forgot, for the moment, it was also the first time it had occurred. It might have been going on for months. She was perfectly aware that it could bring them to nothing, for one must lead one's own life; it was impossible to lead the life of another, especially when that other was so different, so arbitrary and unscrupulous.

XXXIV

I PRESUME you are the only person in this country who feels as you do,' she observed at last.

'Not the only person who feels so, but very possibly the only person who thinks so. I have an idea that my convictions exist in a vague, unformulated state in the minds of a great many of my fellow-citizens. If I should succeed some day in giving them adequate expression I should simply put into shape the slumbering instincts of an important minority.'

'I am glad you admit it's a minority!' Verena exclaimed. 'That's fortunate for us poor creatures. And what do you call adequate expression? I presume you would like to be President of the United States?'

'And breathe forth my views in glowing messages to a palpitating Senate? That is exactly what I should like to be; you read my aspirations wonderfully well.'

'Well, do you consider that you have advanced far in that direction, as yet?' Verena asked.

This question, with the tone in which it happened to be uttered, seemed to the young man to project rather an ironical light upon his present beggarly condition, so that for a moment he said nothing; a moment during which if his neighbour had glanced round at his face she would have seen it ornamented by an incipient blush. Her words had for him the effect of a sudden, though, on the part of a young woman who had of course every right to defend herself, a perfectly legitimate taunt. They appeared only to repeat in another form (so at least his exaggerated Southern pride, his hot sensibility, interpreted the matter), the idea that a gentleman so dreadfully backward in the path of fortune had no right to take up the time of a brilliant, successful girl, even for the purpose of satisfying himself that he renounced her. But the reminder only sharpened his wish to make her feel that if he had renounced, it was simply on account of that same ugly, accidental, outside backwardness; and if he had not, he went so far as to flatter himself, he might triumph over the whole accumulation of her prejudices—over all the bribes of her notoriety. The deepest feeling in Ransom's bosom in relation to her was the conviction that she was made for love, as he had said to himself while he listened to her at Mrs. Burrage's. She was profoundly unconscious of it, and another ideal, crude and thin and artificial, had interposed itself; but in the presence of a man she should really care for, this false, flimsy structure would rattle to her feet, and the emancipation of Olive Chancellor's sex (what sex was it, great heaven? he used profanely to ask himself), would be relegated to the land of vapours, of dead phrases. The reader may imagine whether such an impression as this made it any more agreeable to Basil to have to believe it would be indelicate in him to try to woo her. He would have resented immensely the imputation that he had done anything of that sort yet. 'Ah, Miss Tarrant, my success in life is one thing—my ambition is another!' he exclaimed, presently, in answer to her inquiry. 'Nothing is more possible than that I may be poor and unheard of all my days; and in that case no one but myself will know the visions of greatness I have stifled and buried.'

'Why do you talk of being poor and unheard of? Aren't you getting on quite well in this city?'

This question of Verena's left him no time, or at least no coolness, to remember that to Mrs. Luna and to Olive he had put a fine face on his prospects, and that any impression the girl might have about them was but the natural echo of what these ladies believed. It had to his ear such a subtly mocking, defiant, unconsciously injurious quality, that the only answer he could make to it seemed to him for the moment to be an outstretched arm, which, passing round her waist, should draw her so close to him as to enable him to give her a concise account of his situation in the form of a deliberate kiss. If the moment I speak of had lasted a few seconds longer I know not what monstrous proceeding of this kind it would have been my difficult duty to describe; it was fortunately arrested by the arrival of a nursery-maid pushing a perambulator and accompanied by an infant who toddled in her wake. Both the nurse and her companion gazed fixedly, and it seemed to Ransom even sternly, at the striking couple on the bench; and meanwhile Verena, looking with a quickened eye at the children (she adored children), went on—

'It sounds too flat for you to talk about your remaining unheard of. Of course you are ambitious; any one can see that, to look at you. And once your ambition is excited in any particular direction, people had better look out. With your will!' she added, with a curious mocking candour.

'What do you know about my will?' he asked, laughing a little awkwardly, as if he had really attempted to kiss her—in the course of the second independent interview he had ever had with her—and been rebuffed.

'I know it's stronger than mine. It made me come out, when I thought I had much better not, and it keeps me sitting here long after I should have started for home.'

'Give me the day, dear Miss Tarrant, give me the day,' Basil Ransom murmured; and as she turned her face upon him, moved by the expression of his voice, he added—'Come and dine with me, since you wouldn't lunch. Are you really not faint and weak?'

'I am faint and weak at all the horrible things you have said; I have lunched on abominations. And now you want me to dine with you? Thank you; I think you're cool!' Verena cried, with a laugh which her chronicler knows to have been expressive of some embarrassment, though Basil Ransom did not.

'You must remember that I have, on two different occasions, listened to you for an hour, in speechless, submissive attention, and that I shall probably do it a great many times more.'

'Why should you ever listen to me again, when you loathe my ideas?'

'I don't listen to your ideas; I listen to your voice.'

'Ah, I told Olive!' said Verena, quickly, as if his words had confirmed an old fear; which was general, however, and did not relate particularly to him.

Ransom still had an impression that he was not making love to her, especially when he could observe, with all the superiority of a man—'I wonder whether you have understood ten words I have said to you?'

'I should think you had made it clear enough—you had rubbed it in!'

'What have you understood, then?'

'Why, that you want to put us back further than we have been at any period.'

'I have been joking; I have been piling it up,' Ransom said, making that concession unexpectedly to the girl. Every now and then he had an air of relaxing himself, becoming absent, ceasing to care to discuss.

She was capable of noticing this, and in a moment she asked—'Why don't you write out your ideas?'

This touched again upon the matter of his failure; it was curious how she couldn't keep off it, hit it every time. 'Do you mean for the public? I have written many things, but I can't get them printed.'

'Then it would seem that there are not so many people—so many as you said just now—who agree with you.'

'Well,' said Basil Ransom, 'editors are a mean, timorous lot, always saying they want something original, but deadly afraid of it when it comes.'

'Is it for papers, magazines?' As it sank into Verena's mind more deeply that the contributions of this remarkable young man had been rejected—contributions in which, apparently, everything she held dear was riddled with scorn—she felt a strange pity and sadness, a sense of injustice. 'I am very sorry you can't get published,' she said, so simply that he looked up at her, from the figure he was scratching on the asphalt with his stick, to see whether such a tone as that, in relation to such a fact, were not 'put on.' But it was evidently genuine, and Verena added that she supposed getting published was very difficult always; she remembered, though she didn't mention, how little success her father had when he tried. She hoped Mr. Ransom would keep on; he would be sure to succeed at last. Then she continued, smiling, with more irony: 'You may denounce me by name if you like. Only please don't say anything about Olive Chancellor.'

'How little you understand what I want to achieve!' Basil Ransom exclaimed. 'There you are—you women—all over; always meaning yourselves, something personal, and always thinking it is meant by others!'

'Yes, that's the charge they make,' said Verena, gaily.

'I don't want to touch you, or Miss Chancellor, or Mrs. Farrinder, or Miss Birdseye, or the shade of Eliza P. Moseley, or any other gifted and celebrated being on earth—or in heaven.'

'Oh, I suppose you want to destroy us by neglect, by silence!' Verena exclaimed, with the same brightness.

'No, I don't want to destroy you, any more than I want to save you. There has been far too much talk about you, and I want to leave you alone altogether. My interest is in my own sex; yours evidently can look after itself. That's what I want to save.'

Verena saw that he was more serious now than he had been before, that he was not piling it up satirically, but saying really and a trifle wearily, as if suddenly he were tired of much talk, what he meant. 'To save it from what?' she asked.

'From the most damnable feminisation! I am so far from thinking, as you set forth the other night, that there is not enough woman in our general life, that it has long been pressed home to me that there is a great deal too much. The whole generation is womanised; the masculine tone is passing out of the world; it's a feminine, a nervous, hysterical, chattering, canting age, an age of hollow phrases and false delicacy and exaggerated solicitudes and coddled sensibilities, which, if we don't soon look out, will usher in the reign of mediocrity, of the feeblest and flattest and the most pretentious that has ever been. The masculine character, the ability to dare and endure, to know and yet not fear reality, to look the world in the face and take it for what it is—a very queer and partly very base mixture—that is what I want to preserve, or rather, as I may say, to recover; and I must tell you that I don't in the least care what becomes of you ladies while I make the attempt!'

The poor fellow delivered himself of these narrow notions (the rejection of which by leading periodicals was certainly not a matter for surprise), with low, soft earnestness, bending towards her so as to give out his whole idea, yet apparently forgetting for the moment how offensive it must be to her now that it was articulated in that calm, severe way, in which no allowance was to be made for hyperbole. Verena did not remind herself of this; she was too much impressed by his manner and by the novelty of a man taking that sort of religious tone about such a cause. It told her on the spot, from one minute to the other and once for all, that the man who could give her that impression would never come round. She felt cold, slightly sick, though she replied that now he summed up his creed in such a distinct, lucid way, it was much more comfortable—one knew with what one was dealing; a declaration much at variance with the fact, for Verena had never felt less gratified in her life. The ugliness of her companion's profession of faith made her shiver; it would have been difficult to her to imagine anything more crudely profane. She was determined, however, not to betray any shudder that could suggest weakness, and the best way she could think of to disguise her emotion was to remark in a tone which, although not assumed for that purpose, was really the most effective revenge, inasmuch as it always produced on Ransom's part (it was not peculiar, among women, to Verena), an angry helplessness—'Mr. Ransom, I assure you this is an age of conscience.'

'That's a part of your cant. It's an age of unspeakable shams, as Carlyle says.'

'Well,' returned Verena, 'it's all very comfortable for you to say that you wish to leave us alone. But you can't leave us alone. We are here, and we have got to be disposed of. You have got to put us somewhere. It's a remarkable social system that has no place for *us*!' the girl went on, with her most charming laugh.

'No place in public. My plan is to keep you at home and have a better time with you there than ever.'

'I'm glad it's to be better; there's room for it. Woe to American womanhood when you start a movement for being more—what you like to be—at home!'

'Lord, how you're perverted; you, the very genius!' Basil Ransom murmured, looking at her with the kindest eyes.

She paid no attention to this, she went on, 'And those who have got no home (there are millions, you know), what are you going to do with *them*? You must remember that women marry—are given in marriage—less and less; that isn't their career, as a matter of course, any more. You can't tell them to go and mind their husband and children, when they have no husband and children to mind.'

'Oh,' said Ransom, 'that's a detail! And for myself, I confess, I have such a boundless appreciation of your sex in private life that I am perfectly ready to advocate a man's having a half a dozen wives.'

'The civilisation of the Turks, then, strikes you as the highest?'

'The Turks have a second-rate religion; they are fatalists, and that keeps them down. Besides, their women are not nearly so charming as ours—or as ours would be if this modern pestilence were eradicated. Think what a confession you make when you say that women are less and less sought in marriage; what a testimony that is to the pernicious effect on their manners, their person, their nature, of this fatuous agitation.'

'That's very complimentary to me!' Verena broke in, lightly.

But Ransom was carried over her interruption by the current of his argument. 'There are a thousand ways in which any woman, all women, married or single, may find occupation. They may find it in making society agreeable.'

'Agreeable to men, of course.'

'To whom else, pray? Dear Miss Tarrant, what is most agreeable to women is to be agreeable to men! That is a truth as old as the human race, and don't let Olive Chancellor persuade you that she and Mrs. Farrinder have invented any that can take its place, or that is more profound, more durable.'

Verena waived this point of the discussion; she only said: 'Well, I am glad to hear you are prepared to see the place all choked up with old maids!'

'I don't object to the *old* old maids; they were delightful; they had always plenty to do, and didn't wander about the world crying out for a vocation. It is the new old maid that you have invented from whom I pray to be delivered.' He didn't say he meant Olive Chancellor, but Verena looked at him as if she suspected him of doing so; and to put her off that scent he went on, taking up what she had said a moment before: 'As for its not being complimentary to you, my remark about the effect on the women themselves of this pernicious craze, my dear Miss Tarrant, you may be quite at your ease. You stand apart, you are unique, extraordinary; you constitute a category by yourself. In you the elements have been mixed in a manner so felicitous that I regard you as quite incorruptible. I don't know where you come from nor how you come to be what you are, but you are outside and above all vulgarising influences. Besides, you ought to know,' the young man proceeded, in the same cool, mild, deliberate tone, as if he were demonstrating a mathematical solution, 'you ought to know that your connection with all these rantings and ravings is the most unreal, accidental, illusory thing in the world. You think you care about them, but you don't at all. They were imposed upon you by circumstances, by unfortunate associations, and you accepted them as you would have accepted any other burden, on account of the sweetness of your nature. You always want to please some one, and now you go lecturing about the country, and trying to provoke demonstrations, in order to please Miss Chancellor, just as you did it before to please your father and mother. It isn't *you*, the least in the world, but an inflated little figure (very remarkable in its way too), whom you have invented and set on its feet, pulling strings, behind it, to make it move and speak, while you try to conceal and efface yourself there. Ah, Miss Tarrant, if it's a question of pleasing, how much you might please some one else by tipping your preposterous puppet over and standing forth in your freedom as well as in your loveliness!'

While Basil Ransom spoke—and he had not spoken just that way yet—Verena sat there deeply attentive, with her eyes on the ground; but as soon as he ceased she sprang to her feet—something made her feel that their association had already lasted quite too long. She turned away from him as if she wished to leave him, and indeed were about to attempt to do so. She didn't desire to look at him now, or even to have much more conversation with him. 'Something,' I say, made her feel so, but it was partly his curious manner—so serene and explicit, as if he knew the whole thing to an absolute certainty—which partly scared her and partly made her feel angry. She began to move along the path to one of the gates, as if it were settled that they should immediately leave the place. He laid it all out so clearly; if he had had a revelation he couldn't speak otherwise. That description of herself as something different from what she was trying to be, the charge of want of reality, made her heart beat with pain; she was sure, at any rate, it was her real self that was there with him now, where she oughtn't to be. In a moment he was at her side again, going with her; and as they walked it came over her that some of the things he had said to her were far beyond what Olive could have imagined as the very worst possible. What would be her state now, poor forsaken friend, if some of them had been borne to her in the voices of the air? Verena had been affected by her companion's speech (his manner had changed so; it seemed to express something quite different), in a way that pushed her to throw up the discussion and determine that as soon as they should get out of the park she would go off by herself; but she still had her wits about her sufficiently to think it important she should give no sign of discomposure, of confessing that she was driven from the field. She appeared to herself to notice and reply to his extraordinary observations enough, without taking them up too much, when she said, tossing the words over her shoulder at Ransom, while she moved quickly: 'I presume, from what you say, that you don't think I have much ability.'

He hesitated before answering, while his long legs easily kept pace with her rapid step—her charming, touching, hurrying step, which expressed all the trepidation she was anxious to conceal. 'Immense ability, but not in the line in which you most try to have it. In a very different line, Miss Tarrant! Ability is no word for it; it's genius!'

She felt his eyes on her face—ever so close and fixed there—after he had chosen to reply to her question that way. She was beginning to blush; if he had kept them longer, and on the part of any one else, she would have called such a stare impertinent. Verena had been commended of old by Olive for her serenity 'while exposed to the gaze of hundreds'; but a change had taken place, and she was now unable to endure the contemplation of an individual. She wished to detach him, to lead him off again into the general; and for this purpose, at the end of a moment, she made another inquiry: 'I am to understand, then, as your last word that you regard us as quite inferior?'

'For public, civic uses, absolutely—perfectly weak and second-rate. I know nothing more indicative of the muddled sentiment of the time than that any number of men should be found to pretend that they regard you in any other light. But privately, personally, it's another affair. In the realm of family life and the domestic affections——'

At this Verena broke in, with a nervous laugh, 'Don't say that; it's only a phrase!'

'Well, it's a better one than any of yours,' said Basil Ransom, turning with her out of one of the smaller gates—the first they had come to. They emerged into the species of *plaza* formed by the numbered street which constitutes the southern extremity of the park and the termination of the Sixth Avenue. The glow of the splendid afternoon was over everything, and the day seemed to Ransom still in its youth. The bowers and boskages stretched behind them, the artificial lakes and cockneyfied landscapes, making all the region bright with the sense of air and space, and raw natural tints, and vegetation too diminutive to overshadow. The chocolate-coloured houses, in tall, new rows, surveyed the expanse; the street-cars rattled in the foreground, changing horses while the horses steamed, and absorbing and emitting passengers; and the beer-saloons, with exposed shoulders and sides, which in New York do a good deal towards representing the picturesque, the 'bit' appreciated by painters, announced themselves in signs of large lettering to the sky. Groups of the unemployed, the children of disappointment from beyond the seas, propped themselves against the low, sunny wall of the park; and on the other side the commercial vista of the Sixth Avenue stretched away with a remarkable absence of aerial perspective.

'I must go home; good-bye,' Verena said, abruptly, to her companion.

'Go home? You won't come and dine, then?'

Verena knew people who dined at midday and others who dined in the evening, and others still who never dined at all; but she knew no one who dined at half-past three. Ransom's attachment to this idea therefore struck her as queer and infelicitous, and she supposed it betrayed the habits of Mississippi. But that couldn't make it any more acceptable to her, in spite of his looking so disappointed—with his dimly-glowing eyes—that he was heedless for the moment that the main fact connected with her return to Tenth Street was that she wished to go alone.

'I must leave you, right away,' she said. 'Please don't ask me to stay; you wouldn't if you knew how little I want to!' Her manner was different now, and her face as well, and though she smiled more than ever she had never seemed to him more serious.

'Alone, do you mean? Really I can't let you do that,' Ransom replied, extremely shocked at this sacrifice being asked of him. 'I have brought you this immense distance, I am responsible for you, and I must place you where I found you.'

'Mr. Ransom, I must, I will!' she exclaimed, in a tone he had not yet heard her use; so that, a good deal amazed, puzzled and pained, he saw that he should make a mistake if he were to insist. He had known that their expedition must end in a separation which could not be sweet, but he had counted on making some of the terms of it himself. When he expressed the hope that she would at least allow him to put her into a car, she replied that she wished no car; she wanted to walk. This image of her 'streaking off' by herself, as he figured it, did not mend the matter; but in the presence of her sudden nervous impatience he felt that here was a feminine mystery which must be allowed to take its course.

'It costs me more than you probably suspect, but I submit. Heaven guard you and bless you, Miss Tarrant!'

She turned her face away from him as if she were straining at a leash; then she rejoined, in the most unexpected manner: 'I hope very much you *will* get printed.'

'Get my articles published?' He stared, and broke out: 'Oh, you delightful being!'

'Good-bye,' she repeated; and now she gave him her hand. As he held it a moment, and asked her if she were really leaving the city so soon that she mightn't see him again, she answered: 'If I stay it will be at a place to which you mustn't come. They wouldn't let you see me.'

He had not intended to put that question to her; he had set himself a limit. But the limit had suddenly moved on. 'Do you mean at that house where I heard you speak?'

'I may go there for a few days.'

'If it's forbidden to me to go and see you there, why did you send me a card?'

'Because I wanted to convert you then.'

'And now you give me up?'

'No, no; I want you to remain as you are!'

She looked strange, with her more mechanical smile, as she said this, and he didn't know what idea was in her head. She had already left him, but he called after her, 'If you do stay, I will come!' She neither turned nor made an answer, and all that was left to him was to watch her till she passed out of sight. Her back, with its charming young form, seemed to repeat that last puzzle, which was almost a challenge.

For this, however, Verena Tarrant had not meant it. She wanted, in spite of the greater delay and the way Olive would wonder, to walk home, because it gave her time to think, and think again, how glad she was (really, positively, *now*), that Mr. Ransom was on the wrong side. If he had been on the right——! She did not finish this proposition. She found Olive waiting for her in exactly the manner she had foreseen; she turned to her, as she came in, a face sufficiently terrible. Verena instantly explained herself, related exactly what she had been doing; then went on, without giving her friend time for question or comment: 'And you—you paid your visit to Mrs. Burrage?'

'Yes, I went through that.'

'And did she press the question of my coming there?'

'Very much indeed.'

'And what did you say?'

'I said very little, but she gave me such assurances——'

'That you thought I ought to go?'

Olive was silent a moment; then she said: 'She declares they are devoted to the cause, and that New York will be at your feet.'

Verena took Miss Chancellor's shoulders in each of her hands, and gave her back, for an instant, her gaze, her silence. Then she broke out, with a kind of passion: 'I don't care for her assurances—I don't care for New York! I won't go to them—I won't—do you understand?' Suddenly her voice changed, she passed her arms round her friend and buried her face in her neck. 'Olive Chancellor, take me away, take me away!' she went on. In a moment Olive felt that she was sobbing and that the question was settled, the question she herself had debated in anguish a couple of hours before.

XXXV

THE AUGUST NIGHT had gathered by the time Basil Ransom, having finished his supper, stepped out upon the piazza of the little hotel. It was a very little hotel and of a very slight and loose construction; the tread of a tall Mississippian made the staircase groan and the windows rattle in their frames. He was very hungry when he arrived, having not had a moment, in Boston, on his way through, to eat even the frugal morsel with which he was accustomed to sustain nature between a breakfast that consisted of a cup of coffee and a dinner that consisted of a cup of tea. He had had his cup of tea now, and very bad it was, brought him by a pale, round-backed young lady, with auburn ringlets, a fancy belt, and an expression of limited tolerance for a gentleman who could not choose quickly between fried fish, fried steak, and baked beans. The train for Marmion left Boston at four o'clock in the afternoon, and rambled fitfully toward the southern cape, while the shadows grew long in the stony pastures and the slanting light gilded the straggling, shabby woods, and painted the ponds and marshes with yellow gleams. The ripeness of summer lay upon the land, and yet there was nothing in the country Basil Ransom traversed that seemed susceptible of maturity; nothing but the apples in the little tough, dense orchards, which gave a suggestion of sour fruition here and there, and the tall, bright golden-rod at the bottom of the bare stone dykes. There were no fields of yellow grain; only here and there a crop of brown hay. But there was a kind of soft scrubbiness in the landscape, and a sweetness begotten of low horizons, of mild air, with a possibility of summer haze, of unregarded inlets where on August mornings the water must be brightly blue. Ransom had heard that the Cape was the Italy, so to speak, of Massachusetts; it had been described to him as the drowsy Cape, the languid Cape, the Cape not of storms, but of eternal peace. He knew that the Bostonians had been drawn thither, for the hot weeks, by its sedative influence, by the conviction that its toneless air would minister to perfect rest. In a career in which there was so much nervous excitement as in theirs they had no wish to

be wound up when they went out of town; they were sufficiently wound up at all times by the sense of all their sex had
been through. They wanted to live idly, to unbend and lie in
hammocks, and also to keep out of the crowd, the rush of the
watering-place. Ransom could see there was no crowd at
Marmion, as soon as he got there, though indeed there was a
rush, which directed itself to the only vehicle in waiting outside of the small, lonely, hut-like station, so distant from the
village that, as far as one looked along the sandy, sketchy road
which was supposed to lead to it, one saw only an empty land
on either side. Six or eight men, in 'dusters,' carrying parcels
and handbags, projected themselves upon the solitary, rickety
carry-all, so that Ransom could read his own fate, while the
ruminating conductor of the vehicle, a lean, shambling citizen, with a long neck and a tuft on his chin, guessed that if
he wanted to get to the hotel before dusk he would have to
strike out. His valise was attached in a precarious manner to
the rear of the carry-all. 'Well, I'll chance it,' the driver remarked, sadly, when Ransom protested against its insecure
position. He recognised the southern quality of that picturesque fatalism—judged that Miss Chancellor and Verena Tarrant must be pretty thoroughly relaxed if they had given
themselves up to the genius of the place. This was what he
hoped for and counted on, as he took his way, the sole pedestrian in the group that had quitted the train, in the wake
of the overladen carry-all. It helped him to enjoy the first
country walk he had had for many months, for more than
months, for years, that the reflection was forced upon him as
he went (the mild, vague scenery, just beginning to be dim
with twilight, suggested it at every step), that the two young
women who constituted, at Marmion, his whole prefigure-
ment of a social circle, must, in such a locality as that, be
taking a regular holiday. The sense of all the wrongs they had
still to redress must be lighter there than it was in Boston;
the ardent young man had, for the hour, an ingenuous hope
that they had left their opinions in the city. He liked the very
smell of the soil as he wandered along; cool, soft whiffs of
evening met him at bends of the road which disclosed very
little more—unless it might be a band of straight-stemmed
woodland, keeping, a little, the red glow from the west, or

(as he went further) an old house, shingled all over, gray and slightly collapsing, which looked down at him from a steep bank, at the top of wooden steps. He was already refreshed; he had tasted the breath of nature, measured his long grind in New York, without a vacation, with the repetition of the daily movement up and down the long, straight, maddening city, like a bucket in a well or a shuttle in a loom.

He lit his cigar in the office of the hotel—a small room on the right of the door, where a 'register,' meagrely inscribed, led a terribly public life on the little bare desk, and got its pages dogs'-eared before they were covered. Local worthies, of a vague identity, used to lounge there, as Ransom perceived the next day, by the hour. They tipped back their chairs against the wall, seldom spoke, and might have been supposed, with their converging vision, to be watching something out of the window, if there had been anything at Marmion to watch. Sometimes one of them got up and went to the desk, on which he leaned his elbows, hunching a pair of sloping shoulders to an uncollared neck. For the fiftieth time he perused the fly-blown page of the recording volume, where the names followed each other with such jumps of date. The others watched him while he did so—or contemplated in silence some 'guest' of the hostelry, when such a personage entered the place with an air of appealing from the general irresponsibility of the establishment and found no one but the village-philosophers to address himself to. It was an establishment conducted by invisible, elusive agencies; they had a kind of stronghold in the dining-room, which was kept locked at all but sacramental hours. There was a tradition that a 'boy' exercised some tutelary function as regards the crumpled register; but when he was inquired about, it was usually elicited from the impartial circle in the office either that he was somewhere round or that he had gone a-fishing. Except the haughty waitress who has just been mentioned as giving Ransom his supper, and who only emerged at meal-times from her mystic seclusion, this impalpable youth was the single person on the premises who represented domestic service. Anxious lady-boarders, wrapped in shawls, were seen waiting for him, as if he had been the doctor, on horse-hair rocking-chairs, in the little public parlour; others peered vaguely out

of back doors and windows, thinking that if he were somewhere round they might see him. Sometimes people went to
the door of the dining-room and tried it, shaking it a little,
timidly, to see if it would yield; then, finding it fast, came
away, looking, if they had been observed, shy and snubbed,
at their fellows. Some of them went so far as to say that they
didn't think it was a very good hotel.

Ransom, however, didn't much care whether it were good
or not; he hadn't come to Marmion for the love of the hotel.
Now that he had got there, however, he didn't know exactly
what to do; his course seemed rather less easy than it had
done when, suddenly, the night before, tired, sick of the city-
air, and hungry for a holiday, he decided to take the next
morning's train to Boston, and there take another to the
shores of Buzzard's Bay. The hotel itself offered few resources; the inmates were not numerous; they moved about
a little outside, on the small piazza and in the rough yard
which interposed between the house and the road, and then
they dropped off into the unmitigated dusk. This element,
touched only in two or three places by a far-away dim glim-
mer, presented itself to Ransom as his sole entertainment.
Though it was pervaded by that curious, pure, earthy smell
which in New England, in summer, hangs in the nocturnal
air, Ransom bethought himself that the place might be a little
dull for persons who had not come to it, as he had, to take
possession of Verena Tarrant. The unfriendly inn, which suggested dreadfully to Ransom (he despised the practice), an
early bed-time, seemed to have no relation to anything, not
even to itself; but a fellow-tenant of whom he made an inquiry told him the village was sprinkled round. Basil presently
walked along the road in search of it, under the stars, smoking one of the good cigars which constituted his only tribute
to luxury. He reflected that it would hardly do to begin his
attack that night; he ought to give the Bostonians a certain
amount of notice of his appearance on the scene. He thought
it very possible, indeed, that they might be addicted to the
vile habit of 'retiring' with the cocks and hens. He was sure
that was one of the things Olive Chancellor would do so long
as he should stay—on purpose to spite him; she would make
Verena Tarrant go to bed at unnatural hours, just to deprive

him of his evenings. He walked some distance without encountering a creature or discerning an habitation; but he enjoyed the splendid starlight, the stillness, the shrill melancholy of the crickets, which seemed to make all the vague forms of the country pulsate around him; the whole impression was a bath of freshness after the long strain of the preceding two years, and his recent sweltering weeks in New York. At the end of ten minutes (his stroll had been slow), a figure drew near him, at first indistinct, but presently defining itself as that of a woman. She was walking apparently without purpose, like himself, or without other purpose than that of looking at the stars, which she paused for an instant, throwing back her head, to contemplate, as he drew nearer to her. In a moment he was very close; he saw her look at him, through the clear gloom, as they passed each other. She was small and slim; he made out her head and face, saw that her hair was cropped; had an impression of having seen her before. He noticed that as she went by she turned as well as himself, and that there was a sort of recognition in her movement. Then he felt sure that he had seen her elsewhere, and before she had added to the distance that separated them he stopped short, looking after her. She noticed his halt, paused equally, and for a moment they stood there face to face, at a certain interval, in the darkness.

'I beg your pardon—is it Doctor Prance?' he found himself demanding.

For a minute there was no answer; then came the voice of the little lady:

'Yes, sir; I am Doctor Prance. Any one sick at the hotel?'

'I hope not; I don't know,' Ransom said, laughing.

Then he took a few steps, mentioned his name, recalled his having met her at Miss Birdseye's, ever so long before (nearly two years), and expressed the hope that she had not forgotten that.

She thought it over a little—she was evidently addicted neither to empty phrases nor to unconsidered assertions. 'I presume you mean that night Miss Tarrant launched out so.'

'That very night. We had a very interesting conversation.'

'Well, I remember I lost a good deal,' said Doctor Prance.

'Well, I don't know; I have an idea you made it up in other ways,' Ransom returned, laughing still.

He saw her bright little eyes engage with his own. Staying, apparently, in the village, she had come out, bareheaded, for an evening walk, and if it had been possible to imagine Doctor Prance bored and in want of recreation, the way she lingered there as if she were quite willing to have another talk might have suggested to Basil Ransom this condition. 'Why, don't you consider her career very remarkable?'

'Oh yes; everything is remarkable nowadays; we live in an age of wonders!' the young man replied, much amused to find himself discussing the object of his adoration in this casual way, in the dark, on a lonely country-road, with a short-haired female physician. It was astonishing how quickly Doctor Prance and he had made friends again. 'I suppose, by the way, you know Miss Tarrant and Miss Chancellor are staying down here?' he went on.

'Well, yes, I suppose I know it. I am visiting Miss Chancellor,' the dry little woman added.

'Oh indeed? I am delighted to hear it!' Ransom exclaimed, feeling that he might have a friend in the camp. 'Then you can inform me where those ladies have their house.'

'Yes, I guess I can tell it in the dark. I will show you round now, if you like.'

'I shall be glad to see it, though I am not sure I shall go in immediately. I must reconnoitre a little first. That makes me so very happy to have met you. I think it's very wonderful— your knowing me.'

Doctor Prance did not repudiate this compliment, but she presently observed: 'You didn't pass out of my mind entirely, because I have heard about you since, from Miss Birdseye.'

'Ah yes, I saw her in the spring. I hope she is in health and happiness.'

'She is always in happiness, but she can't be said to be in health. She is very weak; she is failing.'

'I am very sorry for that.'

'She is also visiting Miss Chancellor,' Doctor Prance observed, after a pause which was an illustration of an appearance she had of thinking that certain things didn't at all imply some others.

'Why, my cousin has got all the distinguished women!' Basil Ransom exclaimed.

'Is Miss Chancellor your cousin? There isn't much family resemblance. Miss Birdseye came down for the benefit of the country air, and I came down to see if I could help her to get some good from it. She wouldn't much, if she were left to herself. Miss Birdseye has a very fine character, but she hasn't much idea of hygiene.' Doctor Prance was evidently more and more disposed to be chatty. Ransom appreciated this fact, and said he hoped she, too, was getting some good from the country air—he was afraid she was very much confined to her profession, in Boston; to which she replied—'Well, I was just taking a little exercise along the road. I presume you don't realise what it is to be one of four ladies grouped together in a small frame-house.'

Ransom remembered how he had liked her before, and he felt that, as the phrase was, he was going to like her again. He wanted to express his good-will to her, and would greatly have enjoyed being at liberty to offer her a cigar. He didn't know what to offer her or what to do, unless he should invite her to sit with him on a fence. He did realise perfectly what the situation in the small frame-house must be, and entered with instant sympathy into the feelings which had led Doctor Prance to detach herself from the circle and wander forth under the constellations, all of which he was sure she knew. He asked her permission to accompany her on her walk, but she said she was not going much further in that direction; she was going to turn round. He turned round with her, and they went back together to the village, in which he at last began to discover a certain consistency, signs of habitation, houses disposed with a rough resemblance to a plan. The road wandered among them with a kind of accommodating sinuosity, and there were even cross-streets, and an oil-lamp on a corner, and here and there the small sign of a closed shop, with an indistinctly countrified lettering. There were lights now in the windows of some of the houses, and Doctor Prance mentioned to her companion several of the inhabitants of the little town, who appeared all to rejoice in the prefix of captain. They were retired shipmasters; there was quite a little nest of these worthies, two or three of whom might be seen lingering in their dim doorways, as if they were conscious of a want of encouragement to sit up, and yet remembered the nights in far-away waters when they would not have thought of turning in at all. Marmion called itself a town, but it was a good deal shrunken since the decline in the shipbuilding interest; it turned out a good many vessels every year, in the palmy days, before the war. There were shipyards still, where you could almost pick up the old shavings, the old nails and rivets, but they were grass-grown now, and the water lapped them without anything to interfere. There was a kind of arm of the sea put in; it went up some way, it wasn't the real sea, but very quiet, like a river; that was more attractive to some. Doctor Prance didn't say the place was picturesque, or quaint, or weird; but he could see that was what she meant when she said it was mouldering away. Even under the mantle of night he himself gathered the impression that it had had a larger life, seen better days. Doctor Prance made no remark designed to elicit from him an account of his motives in coming to Marmion; she asked him neither when he had arrived nor how long he intended to stay. His allusion to his cousinship with Miss Chancellor might have served to her mind as a reason; yet, on the other hand, it would have been open to her to wonder why, if he had come to see the young ladies from Charles Street, he was not in more of a hurry to present himself. It was plain Doctor Prance didn't go into that kind of analysis. If Ransom had complained to her of a sore throat she would have inquired with precision about his symptoms; but she was incapable of asking him any question with a social bearing. Sociably enough, however, they continued to wander through the principal street of the little town, darkened in places by immense old elms, which made a blackness overhead. There was a salt smell in the air, as if they were nearer the water; Doctor Prance said that Olive's house was at the other end.

'I shall take it as a kindness if, for this evening, you don't mention that you have happened to meet me,' Ransom remarked, after a little. He had changed his mind about giving notice.

'Well, I wouldn't,' his companion replied; as if she didn't need any caution in regard to making vain statements.

'I want to keep my arrival a little surprise for to-morrow. It will be a great pleasure to me to see Miss Birdseye,' he went on, rather hypocritically, as if that at bottom had been to his mind the main attraction of Marmion.

Doctor Prance did not reveal her private comment, whatever it was, on this intimation; she only said, after some hesitation—'Well, I presume the old lady will take quite an interest in your being here.'

'I have no doubt she is capable even of that degree of philanthropy.'

'Well, she has charity for all, but she does—even she—prefer her own side. She regards you as quite an acquisition.'

Ransom could not but feel flattered at the idea that he had been a subject of conversation—as this implied—in the little circle at Miss Chancellor's; but he was at a loss, for the moment, to perceive what he had done up to this time to gratify the senior member of the group. 'I hope she will find me an acquisition after I have been here a few days,' he said, laughing.

'Well, she thinks you are one of the most important converts yet,' Doctor Prance replied, in a colourless way, as if she would not have pretended to explain why.

'A convert—me? Do you mean of Miss Tarrant's?' It had come over him that Miss Birdseye, in fact, when he was parting with her after their meeting in Boston, had assented to his request for secrecy (which at first had struck her as somewhat unholy), on the ground that Verena would bring him into the fold. He wondered whether that young lady had been telling her old friend that she had succeeded with him. He thought this improbable; but it didn't matter, and he said, gaily, 'Well, I can easily let her suppose so!'

It was evident that it would be no easier for Doctor Prance to subscribe to a deception than it had been for her venerable patient; but she went so far as to reply, 'Well, I hope you won't let her suppose you are where you were that time I conversed with you. I could see where you were then!'

'It was in about the same place you were, wasn't it?'

'Well,' said Doctor Prance, with a small sigh, 'I am afraid I have moved back, if anything!' Her sigh told him a good deal; it seemed a thin, self-controlled protest against the tone

of Miss Chancellor's interior, of which it was her present fortune to form a part: and the way she hovered round, indistinct in the gloom, as if she were rather loath to resume her
place there, completed his impression that the little doctress
had a line of her own.

'That, at least, must distress Miss Birdseye,' he said,
reproachfully.

'Not much, because I am not of importance. They think
women the equals of men; but they are a great deal more
pleased when a man joins than when a woman does.'

Ransom complimented Doctor Prance on the lucidity of
her mind, and then he said: 'Is Miss Birdseye really sick? Is
her condition very precarious?'

'Well, she is very old, and very—very gentle,' Doctor
Prance answered, hesitating a moment for her adjective. 'Under those circumstances a person may flicker out.'

'We must trim the lamp,' said Ransom; 'I will take my turn,
with pleasure, in watching the sacred flame.'

'It will be a pity if she doesn't live to hear Miss Tarrant's
great effort,' his companion went on.

'Miss Tarrant's? What's that?'

'Well, it's the principal interest, in there.' And Doctor
Prance now vaguely indicated, with a movement of her head,
a small white house, much detached from its neighbours,
which stood on their left, with its back to the water, at a little
distance from the road. It exhibited more signs of animation
than any of its fellows; several windows, notably those of the
ground floor, were open to the warm evening, and a large
shaft of light was projected upon the grassy wayside in front
of it. Ransom, in his determination to be discreet, checked
the advance of his companion, who added presently, with a
short, suppressed laugh—'You can see it is, from that!' He
listened, to ascertain what she meant, and after an instant a
sound came to his ear—a sound he knew already well, which
carried the accents of Verena Tarrant, in ample periods and
cadences, out into the stillness of the August night.

'Murder, what a lovely voice!' he exclaimed, involuntarily.

Doctor Prance's eye gleamed towards him a moment, and
she observed, humorously (she was relaxing immensely), 'Perhaps Miss Birdseye is right!' Then, as he made no rejoinder,

only listening to the vocal inflections that floated out of the house, she went on—'She's practising her speech.'

'Her speech? Is she going to deliver one here?'

'No, as soon as they go back to town—at the Music Hall.'

Ransom's attention was now transferred to his companion. 'Is that why you call it her great effort?'

'Well, so they think it, I believe. She practises that way every night; she reads portions of it aloud to Miss Chancellor and Miss Birdseye.'

'And that's the time you choose for your walk?' Ransom said, smiling.

'Well, it's the time my old lady has least need of me; she's too absorbed.'

Doctor Prance dealt in facts; Ransom had already discovered that; and some of her facts were very interesting.

'The Music Hall—isn't that your great building?' he asked.

'Well, it's the biggest we've got; it's pretty big, but it isn't so big as Miss Chancellor's ideas,' added Doctor Prance. 'She has taken it to bring out Miss Tarrant before the general public—she has never appeared that way in Boston—on a great scale. She expects her to make a big sensation. It will be a great night, and they are preparing for it. They consider it her real beginning.'

'And this is the preparation?' Basil Ransom said.

'Yes; as I say, it's their principal interest.'

Ransom listened, and while he listened he meditated. He had thought it possible Verena's principles might have been shaken by the profession of faith to which he treated her in New York; but this hardly looked like it. For some moments Doctor Prance and he stood together in silence.

'You don't hear the words,' the doctor remarked, with a smile which, in the dark, looked Mephistophelean.

'Oh, I know the words!' the young man exclaimed, with rather a groan, as he offered her his hand for good-night.

XXXVI

A CERTAIN PRUDENCE had determined him to put off his visit till the morning; he thought it more probable that at that time he should be able to see Verena alone, whereas in the evening the two young women would be sure to be sitting together. When the morrow dawned, however, Basil Ransom felt none of the trepidation of the procrastinator; he knew nothing of the reception that awaited him, but he took his way to the cottage designated to him overnight by Doctor Prance, with the step of a man much more conscious of his own purpose than of possible obstacles. He made the reflection, as he went, that to see a place for the first time at night is like reading a foreign author in a translation. At the present hour—it was getting towards eleven o'clock—he felt that he was dealing with the original. The little straggling, loosely-clustered town lay along the edge of a blue inlet, on the other side of which was a low, wooded shore, with a gleam of white sand where it touched the water. The narrow bay carried the vision outward to a picture that seemed at once bright and dim—a shining, slumbering summer-sea, and a far-off, circling line of coast, which, under the August sun, was hazy and delicate. Ransom regarded the place as a town because Doctor Prance had called it one; but it was a town where you smelt the breath of the hay in the streets and you might gather blackberries in the principal square. The houses looked at each other across the grass—low, rusty, crooked, distended houses, with dry, cracked faces and the dim eyes of small-paned, stiffly-sliding windows. Their little door-yards bristled with rank, old-fashioned flowers, mostly yellow; and on the quarter that stood back from the sea the fields sloped upward, and the woods in which they presently lost themselves looked down over the roofs. Bolts and bars were not a part of the domestic machinery of Marmion, and the responsive menial, receiving the visitor on the threshold, was a creature rather desired than definitely possessed; so that Basil Ransom found Miss Chancellor's house-door gaping wide (as he had seen it the night before), and destitute even of a knocker or a bell-handle. From where he stood in the porch

he could see the whole of the little sitting-room on the left of
the hall—see that it stretched straight through to the back
windows; that it was garnished with photographs of foreign
works of art, pinned upon the walls, and enriched with a
piano and other little extemporised embellishments, such as
ingenious women lavish upon the houses they hire for a few
weeks. Verena told him afterwards that Olive had taken her
cottage furnished, but that the paucity of chairs and tables
and bedsteads was such that their little party used almost to
sit down, to lie down, in turn. On the other hand they had
all George Eliot's writings, and two photographs of the Sistine Madonna. Ransom rapped with his stick on the lintel of
the door, but no one came to receive him; so he made his
way into the parlour, where he observed that his cousin Olive
had as many German books as ever lying about. He dipped
into this literature, momentarily, according to his wont, and
then remembered that this was not what he had come for and
that as he waited at the door he had seen, through another
door, opening at the opposite end of the hall, signs of a small
verandah attached to the other face of the house. Thinking
the ladies might be assembled there in the shade, he pushed
aside the muslin curtain of the back window, and saw that
the advantages of Miss Chancellor's summer-residence were
in this quarter. There was a verandah, in fact, to which a
wide, horizontal trellis, covered with an ancient vine, formed
a kind of extension. Beyond the trellis was a small, lonely
garden; beyond the garden was a large, vague, woody space,
where a few piles of old timber were disposed, and which he
afterwards learned to be a relic of the shipbuilding era described to him by Doctor Prance; and still beyond this again
was the charming lake-like estuary he had already admired.
His eyes did not rest upon the distance; they were attracted
by a figure seated under the trellis, where the chequers of sun,
in the interstices of the vine-leaves, fell upon a bright-
coloured rug spread out on the ground. The floor of the
roughly-constructed verandah was so low that there was virtually no difference in the level. It took Ransom only a moment to recognise Miss Birdseye, though her back was turned
to the house. She was alone; she sat there motionless (she had
a newspaper in her lap, but her attitude was not that of a

reader), looking at the shimmering bay. She might be asleep; that was why Ransom moderated the process of his long legs as he came round through the house to join her. This precaution represented his only scruple. He stepped across the verandah and stood close to her, but she did not appear to notice him. Visibly, she was dozing, or presumably, rather, for her head was enveloped in an old faded straw-hat, which concealed the upper part of her face. There were two or three other chairs near her, and a table on which were half a dozen books and periodicals, together with a glass containing a colourless liquid, on the top of which a spoon was laid. Ransom desired only to respect her repose, so he sat down in one of the chairs and waited till she should become aware of his presence. He thought Miss Chancellor's back-garden a delightful spot, and his jaded senses tasted the breeze—the idle, wandering summer-wind—that stirred the vine-leaves over his head. The hazy shores on the other side of the water, which had tints more delicate than the street-vistas of New York (they seemed powdered with silver, a sort of midsummer light), suggested to him a land of dreams, a country in a picture. Basil Ransom had seen very few pictures, there were none in Mississippi; but he had a vision at times of something that would be more refined than the real world, and the situation in which he now found himself pleased him almost as much as if it had been a striking work of art. He was unable to see, as I have said, whether Miss Birdseye were taking in the prospect through open or only, imagination aiding (she had plenty of that), through closed, tired, dazzled eyes. She appeared to him, as the minutes elapsed and he sat beside her, the incarnation of well-earned rest, of patient, submissive superannuation. At the end of her long day's work she might have been placed there to enjoy this dim prevision of the peaceful river, the gleaming shores, of the paradise her unselfish life had certainly qualified her to enter, and which, apparently, would so soon be opened to her. After a while she said, placidly, without turning:

'I suppose it's about time I should take my remedy again. It does seem as if she had found the right thing; don't you think so?'

'Do you mean the contents of that tumbler? I shall be

delighted to give it to you, and you must tell me how much you take.' And Basil Ransom, getting up, possessed himself of the glass on the table.

At the sound of his voice Miss Birdseye pushed back her straw-hat by a movement that was familiar to her, and twisting about her muffled figure a little (even in August she felt the cold, and had to be much covered up to sit out), directed at him a speculative, unastonished gaze.

'One spoonful—two?' Ransom asked, stirring the dose and smiling.

'Well, I guess I'll take two this time.'

'Certainly, Doctor Prance couldn't help finding the right thing,' Ransom said, as he administered the medicine; while the movement with which she extended her face to take it made her seem doubly childlike.

He put down the glass, and she relapsed into her position; she seemed to be considering. 'It's homœopathic,' she remarked, in a moment.

'Oh, I have no doubt of that; I presume you wouldn't take anything else.'

'Well, it's generally admitted now to be the true system.'

Ransom moved closer to her, placed himself where she could see him better. 'It's a great thing to have the true system,' he said, bending towards her in a friendly way; 'I'm sure you have it in everything.' He was not often hypocritical; but when he was he went all lengths.

'Well, I don't know that any one has a right to say that. I thought you were Verena,' she added in a moment, taking him in again with her mild, deliberate vision.

'I have been waiting for you to recognise me; of course you didn't know I was here—I only arrived last night.'

'Well, I'm glad you have come to see Olive now.'

'You remember that I wouldn't do that when I met you last?'

'You asked me not to mention to her that I had met you; that's what I principally recall.'

'And don't you remember what I told you I wanted to do? I wanted to go out to Cambridge and see Miss Tarrant. Thanks to the information that you were so good as to give me, I was able to do so.'

'Yes, she gave me quite a little description of your visit,' said Miss Birdseye, with a smile and a vague sound in her throat—a sort of pensive, private reference to the idea of laughter—of which Ransom never learned the exact significance, though he retained for a long time afterwards a kindly memory of the old lady's manner at the moment.

'I don't know how much she enjoyed it, but it was an immense pleasure to me; so great a one that, as you see, I have come to call upon her again.'

'Then, I presume, she *has* shaken you?'

'She has shaken me tremendously!' said Ransom, laughing.

'Well, you'll be a great addition,' Miss Birdseye returned. 'And this time your visit is also for Miss Chancellor?'

'That depends on whether she will receive me.'

'Well, if she knows you are shaken, that will go a great way,' said Miss Birdseye, a little musingly, as if even to her unsophisticated mind it had been manifested that one's relations with Miss Chancellor might be ticklish. 'But she can't receive you now—can she?—because she's out. She has gone to the post-office for the Boston letters, and they get so many every day that she had to take Verena with her to help her carry them home. One of them wanted to stay with me, because Doctor Prance has gone fishing, but I said I presumed I could be left alone for about seven minutes. I know how they love to be together; it seems as if one *couldn't* go out without the other. That's what they came down here for, because it's quiet, and it didn't look as if there was any one else they would be much drawn to. So it would be a pity for me to come down after them just to spoil it!'

'I am afraid I shall spoil it, Miss Birdseye.'

'Oh, well, a gentleman,' murmured the ancient woman.

'Yes, what can you expect of a gentleman? I certainly shall spoil it if I can.'

'You had better go fishing with Doctor Prance,' said Miss Birdseye, with a serenity which showed that she was far from measuring the sinister quality of the announcement he had just made.

'I shan't object to that at all. The days here must be very long—very full of hours. Have you got the doctor with you?' Ransom inquired, as if he knew nothing at all about her.

'Yes, Miss Chancellor invited us both; she is very thoughtful. She is not merely a theoretic philanthropist—she goes
into details,' said Miss Birdseye, presenting her large person,
in her chair, as if she herself were only an item. 'It seems as if
we were not so much wanted in Boston, just in August.'

'And here you sit and enjoy the breeze, and admire the
view,' the young man remarked, wondering when the two
messengers, whose seven minutes must long since have expired, would return from the post-office.

'Yes, I enjoy everything in this little old-world place; I
didn't suppose I should be satisfied to be so passive. It's a
great contrast to my former exertions. But somehow it
doesn't seem as if there were any trouble or any wrong round
here; and if there should be, there are Miss Chancellor and
Miss Tarrant to look after it. They seem to think I had better
fold my hands. Besides, when helpful, generous minds begin
to flock in from *your* part of the country,' Miss Birdseye continued, looking at him from under the distorted and discoloured canopy of her hat with a benignity which completed
the idea in any cheerful sense he chose.

He felt by this time that he was committed to rather a dishonest part; he was pledged not to give a shock to her optimism. This might cost him, in the coming days, a good deal
of dissimulation, but he was now saved from any further expenditure of ingenuity by certain warning sounds which ad-
monished him that he must keep his wits about him for a
purpose more urgent. There were voices in the hall of the
house, voices he knew, which came nearer, quickly; so that
before he had time to rise one of the speakers had come out
with the exclamation—'Dear Miss Birdseye, here are seven
letters for you!' The words fell to the ground, indeed, before
they were fairly spoken, and when Ransom got up, turning,
he saw Olive Chancellor standing there, with the parcel from
the post-office in her hand. She stared at him in sudden horror; for the moment her self-possession completely deserted
her. There was so little of any greeting in her face save the
greeting of dismay, that he felt there was nothing for him to
say to her, nothing that could mitigate the odious fact of his
being there. He could only let her take it in, let her divine
that, this time, he was not to be got rid of. In an instant—to

ease off the situation—he held out his hand for Miss Birdseye's letters, and it was a proof of Olive's having turned rather
faint and weak that she gave them up to him. He delivered
the packet to the old lady, and now Verena had appeared in
the doorway of the house. As soon as she saw him, she
blushed crimson; but she did not, like Olive, stand voiceless.

'Why, Mr. Ransom,' she cried out, 'where in the world
were *you* washed ashore?' Miss Birdseye, meanwhile, taking
her letters, had no appearance of observing that the encounter
between Olive and her visitor was a kind of concussion.

It was Verena who eased off the situation; her gay challenge rose to her lips as promptly as if she had had no cause
for embarrassment. She was not confused even when she
blushed, and her alertness may perhaps be explained by the
habit of public speaking. Ransom smiled at her while she
came forward, but he spoke first to Olive, who had already
turned her eyes away from him and gazed at the blue sea-
view as if she were wondering what was going to happen to
her at last.

'Of course you are very much surprised to see me; but I
hope to be able to induce you to regard me not absolutely in
the light of an intruder. I found your door open, and I
walked in, and Miss Birdseye seemed to think I might stay.
Miss Birdseye, I put myself under your protection; I invoke
you; I appeal to you,' the young man went on. 'Adopt me,
answer for me, cover me with the mantle of your charity!'

Miss Birdseye looked up from her letters, as if at first she
had only faintly heard his appeal. She turned her eyes from
Olive to Verena; then she said, 'Doesn't it seem as if we had
room for all? When I remember what I have seen in the
South, Mr. Ransom's being here strikes me as a great
triumph.'

Olive evidently failed to understand, and Verena broke in
with eagerness, 'It was by my letter, of course, that you knew
we were here. The one I wrote just before we came, Olive,'
she went on. 'Don't you remember I showed it to you?'

At the mention of this act of submission on her friend's
part Olive started, flashing her a strange look; then she said
to Basil that she didn't see why he should explain so much
about his coming; every one had a right to come. It was a

very charming place; it ought to do any one good. 'But it will have one defect for you,' she added; 'three-quarters of the summer residents are women!'

This attempted pleasantry on Miss Chancellor's part, so unexpected, so incongruous, uttered with white lips and cold eyes, struck Ransom to that degree by its oddity that he could not resist exchanging a glance of wonder with Verena, who, if she had had the opportunity, could probably have explained to him the phenomenon. Olive had recovered herself, reminded herself that she was safe, that her companion in New York had repudiated, denounced her pursuer; and, as a proof to her own sense of her security, as well as a touching mark to Verena that now, after what had passed, she had no fear, she felt that a certain light mockery would be effective.

'Ah, Miss Olive, don't pretend to think I love your sex so little, when you know that what you really object to in me is that I love it too much!' Ransom was not brazen, he was not impudent, he was really a very modest man; but he was aware that whatever he said or did he was condemned to seem impudent now, and he argued within himself that if he was to have the dishonour of being thought brazen he might as well have the comfort. He didn't care a straw, in truth, how he was judged or how he might offend; he had a purpose which swallowed up such inanities as that, and he was so full of it that it kept him firm, balanced him, gave him an assurance that might easily have been confounded with a cold detachment. 'This place will do me good,' he pursued; 'I haven't had a holiday for more than two years, I couldn't have gone another day; I was finished. I would have written to you beforehand that I was coming, but I only started at a few hours' notice. It occurred to me that this would be just what I wanted; I remembered what Miss Tarrant had said in her note, that it was a place where people could lie on the ground and wear their old clothes. I delight to lie on the ground, and all my clothes are old. I hope to be able to stay three or four weeks.'

Olive listened till he had done speaking; she stood a single moment longer, and then, without a word, a glance, she rushed into the house. Ransom saw that Miss Birdseye was immersed in her letters; so he went straight to Verena and stood before her, looking far into her eyes. He was not smiling now, as he had been in speaking to Olive. 'Will you come somewhere apart, where I can speak to you alone?'

'Why have you done this? It was not right in you to come!' Verena looked still as if she were blushing, but Ransom perceived he must allow for her having been delicately scorched by the sun.

'I have come because it is necessary—because I have something very important to say to you. A great number of things.'

'The same things you said in New York? I don't want to hear them again—they were horrible!'

'No, not the same—different ones. I want you to come out with me, away from here.'

'You always want me to come out! We can't go out here; we *are* out, as much as we can be!' Verena laughed. She tried to turn it off—feeling that something really impended.

'Come down into the garden, and out beyond there—to the water, where we can speak. It's what I have come for; it was not for what I told Miss Olive!'

He had lowered his voice, as if Miss Olive might still hear them, and there was something strangely grave—altogether solemn, indeed—in its tone. Verena looked around her, at the splendid summer day, at the much-swathed, formless figure of Miss Birdseye, holding her letter inside her hat. 'Mr. Ransom!' she articulated then, simply; and as her eyes met his again they showed him a couple of tears.

'It's not to make you suffer, I honestly believe. I don't want to say anything that will hurt you. How can I possibly hurt you, when I feel to you as I do?' he went on, with suppressed force.

She said no more, but all her face entreated him to let her off, to spare her; and as this look deepened, a quick sense of elation and success began to throb in his heart, for it told him exactly what he wanted to know. It told him that she was afraid of him, that she had ceased to trust herself, that the way he had read her nature was the right way (she was tremendously open to attack, she was meant for love, she was meant for him), and that his arriving at the point at which he wished to arrive was only a question of time. This happy consciousness made him extraordinarily tender to her; he couldn't put enough reassurance into his smile, his low murmur, as he said: 'Only give me ten minutes; don't receive me by turning me away. It's my holiday—my poor little holiday; don't spoil it.'

Three minutes later Miss Birdseye, looking up from her letter, saw them move together through the bristling garden and traverse a gap in the old fence which inclosed the further side of it. They passed into the ancient ship-yard which lay beyond, and which was now a mere vague, grass-grown approach to the waterside, bestrewn with a few remnants of supererogatory timber. She saw them stroll forward to the edge of the bay and stand there, taking the soft breeze in their faces. She watched them a little, and it warmed her heart to see the stiff-necked young Southerner led captive by a daughter of New England trained in the right school, who would impose her opinions in their integrity. Considering how prejudiced he must have been he was certainly behaving very well; even at that distance Miss Birdseye dimly made out that there was something positively humble in the way he invited Verena Tarrant to seat herself on a low pile of weather-blackened planks, which constituted the principal furniture of the place, and something, perhaps, just a trifle too expressive of righteous triumph in the manner in which the girl put the suggestion by and stood where she liked, a little proudly, turning a good deal away from him. Miss Birdseye could see as much as this, but she couldn't hear, so that she didn't know what it was that made Verena turn suddenly back to him, at something he said. If she had known, perhaps his observation would have struck her as less singular—under the circumstances in which these two young persons met—than it may appear to the reader.

'They have accepted one of my articles; I think it's the best.' These were the first words that passed Basil Ransom's lips after the pair had withdrawn as far as it was possible to withdraw (in that direction) from the house.

'Oh, is it printed—when does it appear?' Verena asked that question instantly; it sprang from her lips in a manner that completely belied the air of keeping herself at a distance from him which she had worn a few moments before.

He didn't tell her again this time, as he had told her when, on the occasion of their walk together in New York, she expressed an inconsequent hope that his fortune as a rejected contributor would take a turn—he didn't remark to her once more that she was a delightful being; he only went on (as if her revulsion were a matter of course), to explain everything he could, so that she might as soon as possible know him better and see how completely she could trust him. 'That was, at bottom, the reason I came here. The essay in question is the most important thing I have done in the way of a literary attempt, and I determined to give up the game or to persist, according as I should be able to bring it to the light or not. The other day I got a letter from the editor of the "Rational Review," telling me that he should be very happy to print it, that he thought it very remarkable, and that he should be glad to hear from me again. He shall hear from me again—he needn't be afraid! It contained a good many of the opinions I have expressed to you, and a good many more besides. I really believe it will attract some attention. At any rate, the simple fact that it is to be published makes an era in my life. This will seem pitiful to you, no doubt, who publish yourself, have been before the world these several years, and are flushed with every kind of triumph; but to me it's simply a tremendous affair. It makes me believe I may do something; it has changed the whole way I look at my future. I have been building castles in the air, and I have put you in the biggest and fairest of them. That's a great change, and, as I say, it's really why I came on.'

Verena lost not a word of this gentle, conciliatory, explicit statement; it was full of surprises for her, and as soon as Ransom had stopped speaking she inquired: 'Why, didn't you feel satisfied about your future before?'

Her tone made him feel how little she had suspected he could have the weakness of a discouragement, how little of a question it must have seemed to her that he would one day triumph on his own erratic line. It was the sweetest tribute he had yet received to the idea that he might have ability; the letter of the editor of the 'Rational Review' was nothing to it. 'No, I felt very blue; it didn't seem to me at all clear that there was a place for me in the world.'

'Gracious!' said Verena Tarrant.

A quarter of an hour later Miss Birdseye, who had returned to her letters (she had a correspondent at Framingham who usually wrote fifteen pages), became aware that Verena, who was now alone, was re-entering the house. She stopped her on her way, and said she hoped she hadn't pushed Mr. Ransom overboard.

'Oh no; he has gone off—round the other way.'

'Well, I hope he is going to speak for us soon.'

Verena hesitated a moment. 'He speaks with the pen. He has written a very fine article—for the "Rational Review." '

Miss Birdseye gazed at her young friend complacently; the sheets of her interminable letter fluttered in the breeze. 'Well, it's delightful to see the way it goes on, isn't it?'

Verena scarcely knew what to say; then, remembering that Doctor Prance had told her that they might lose their dear old companion any day, and confronting it with something Basil Ransom had just said—that the 'Rational Review' was a quarterly and the editor had notified him that his article would appear only in the number after the next—she reflected that perhaps Miss Birdseye wouldn't be there, so many months later, to see how it was her supposed consort had spoken. She might, therefore, be left to believe what she liked to believe, without fear of a day of reckoning. Verena committed herself to nothing more confirmatory than a kiss, however, which the old lady's displaced head-gear enabled her to imprint upon her forehead and which caused Miss Birdseye to exclaim, 'Why, Verena Tarrant, how cold your lips are!' It was not surprising to Verena to hear that her lips were cold; a mortal chill had crept over her, for she knew that this time she should have a tremendous scene with Olive.

She found her in her room, to which she had fled on quitting Mr. Ransom's presence; she sat in the window, having evidently sunk into a chair the moment she came in, a position from which she must have seen Verena walk through the garden and down to the water with the intruder. She remained as she had collapsed, quite prostrate; her attitude was the same as that other time Verena had found her waiting, in New York. What Olive was likely to say to her first the girl scarcely knew; her mind, at any rate, was full of an intention of her own. She went straight to her and fell on her knees before her, taking hold of the hands which were clasped together, with nervous intensity, in Miss Chancellor's lap. Verena remained a moment, looking up at her, and then said:

'There is something I want to tell you now, without a moment's delay; something I didn't tell you at the time it happened, nor afterwards. Mr. Ransom came out to see me once, at Cambridge, a little while before we went to New York. He spent a couple of hours with me; we took a walk together and saw the colleges. It was after that that he wrote to me—when I answered his letter, as I told you in New York. I didn't tell you then of his visit. We had a great deal of talk about him, and I kept that back. I did so on purpose; I can't explain why, except that I didn't like to tell you, and that I thought it better. But now I want you to know everything; when you know that, you *will* know everything. It was only one visit—about two hours. I enjoyed it very much—he seemed so much interested. One reason I didn't tell you was that I didn't want you to know that he had come on to Boston, and called on me in Cambridge, without going to see you. I thought it might affect you disagreeably. I suppose you will think I deceived you; certainly I left you with a wrong impression. But now I want you to know all—all!'

Verena spoke with breathless haste and eagerness; there was a kind of passion in the way she tried to expiate her former want of candour. Olive listened, staring; at first she seemed scarcely to understand. But Verena perceived that she understood sufficiently when she broke out: 'You deceived me—you deceived me! Well, I must say I like your deceit better than such dreadful revelations! And what does anything matter when he has come after you now? What does he want—what has he come for?'

'He has come to ask me to be his wife.'

Verena said this with the same eagerness, with as determined an air of not incurring any reproach this time. But as soon as she had spoken she buried her head in Olive's lap.

Olive made no attempt to raise it again, and returned none of the pressure of her hands; she only sat silent for a time, during which Verena wondered that the idea of the episode at Cambridge, laid bare only after so many months, should not have struck her more deeply. Presently she saw it was because the horror of what had just happened drew her off from it. At last Olive asked: 'Is that what he told you, off there by the water?'

'Yes'—and Verena looked up—'he wanted me to know it right away. He says it's only fair to you that he should give notice of his intentions. He wants to try and make me like him—so he says. He wants to see more of me, and he wants me to know him better.'

Olive lay back in her chair, with dilated eyes and parted lips. 'Verena Tarrant, what *is* there between you? what *can* I hold on to, what *can* I believe? Two hours, in Cambridge, before we went to New York?' The sense that Verena had been perfidious there—perfidious in her reticence—now began to roll over her. 'Mercy of heaven, how you did act!'

'Olive, it was to spare you.'

'To spare me? If you really wished to spare me he wouldn't be here now!'

Miss Chancellor flashed this out with a sudden violence, a spasm which threw Verena off and made her rise to her feet. For an instant the two young women stood confronted, and a person who had seen them at that moment might have taken them for enemies rather than friends. But any such opposition could last but a few seconds. Verena replied, with a tremor in her voice which was not that of passion, but of charity: 'Do you mean that I expected him, that I brought him? I never in my life was more surprised at anything than when I saw him there.'

'Hasn't he the delicacy of one of his own slave-drivers? Doesn't he know you loathe him?'

Verena looked at her friend with a degree of majesty which, with her, was rare. 'I don't loathe him—I only dislike his opinions.'

'Dislike! Oh, misery!' And Olive turned away to the open window, leaning her forehead against the lifted sash.

Verena hesitated, then went to her, passing her arm round her. 'Don't scold me! help me—help me!' she murmured.

Olive gave her a sidelong look; then, catching her up and facing her again—'Will you come away, now, by the next train?'

'Flee from him again, as I did in New York? No, no, Olive Chancellor, that's not the way,' Verena went on, reasoningly, as if all the wisdom of the ages were seated on her lips. 'Then how can we leave Miss Birdseye, in her state? We must stay here—we must fight it out here.'

'Why not be honest, if you have been false—really honest, not only half so? Why not tell him plainly that you love him?'

'Love him, Olive? why, I scarcely know him.'

'You'll have a chance, if he stays a month!'

'I don't dislike him, certainly, as you do. But how can I love him when he tells me he wants me to give up everything, all our work, our faith, our future, never to give another address, to open my lips in public? How can I consent to that?' Verena went on, smiling strangely.

'He asks you that, just that way?'

'No; it's not that way. It's very kindly.'

'Kindly? Heaven help you, don't grovel! Doesn't he know it's my house?' Olive added, in a moment.

'Of course he won't come into it, if you forbid him.'

'So that you may meet him in other places—on the shore, in the country?'

'I certainly shan't avoid him, hide away from him,' said Verena, proudly. 'I thought I made you believe, in New York, that I really cared for our aspirations. The way for me then is to meet him, feeling conscious of my strength. What if I do like him? what does it matter? I like my work in the world, I like everything I believe in, better.'

Olive listened to this, and the memory of how, in the house in Tenth Street, Verena had rebuked her doubts, professed her own faith anew, came back to her with a force which made the present situation appear slightly less terrific. Nevertheless, she gave no assent to the girl's logic; she only replied: 'But you didn't meet him there; you hurried away from New York, after I was willing you should stay. He affected you very much there; you were not so calm when you came back to me from your expedition to the park as you pretend to be now. To get away from him you gave up all the rest.'

'I know I wasn't so calm. But now I have had three months to think about it—about the way he affected me there. I take it very quietly.'

'No, you don't; you are not calm now!'

Verena was silent a moment, while Olive's eyes continued to search her, accuse her, condemn her. 'It's all the more reason you shouldn't give me stab after stab,' she replied, with a gentleness which was infinitely touching.

It had an instant effect upon Olive; she burst into tears, threw herself on her friend's bosom. 'Oh, don't desert me— don't desert me, or you'll kill me in torture,' she moaned, shuddering.

'You must help me—you must help me!' cried Verena, imploringly too.

XXXVII

BASIL RANSOM spent nearly a month at Marmion; in announcing this fact I am very conscious of its extraordinary character. Poor Olive may well have been thrown back into her alarms by his presenting himself there; for after her return from New York she took to her soul the conviction that she had really done with him. Not only did the impulse of revulsion under which Verena had demanded that their departure from Tenth Street should be immediate appear to her a proof that it had been sufficient for her young friend to touch Mr. Ransom's moral texture with her finger, as it were, in order to draw back for ever; but what she had learned from her companion of his own manifestations, his apparent disposition to throw up the game, added to her feeling of security. He had spoken to Verena of their little excursion as his last opportunity, let her know that he regarded it not as the beginning of a more intimate acquaintance but as the end even of such relations as already existed between them. He gave her up, for reasons best known to himself; if he wanted to frighten Olive he judged that he had frightened her enough: his Southern chivalry suggested to him perhaps that he ought to let her off before he had worried her to death. Doubtless, too, he had perceived how vain it was to hope to make Verena abjure a faith so solidly founded; and though he admired her enough to wish to possess her on his own terms, he shrank from the mortification which the future would have in keeping for him—that of finding that, after six months of courting and in spite of all her sympathy, her desire to do what people expected of her, she despised his opinions as much as the first day. Olive Chancellor was able to a certain extent to believe what she wished to believe, and that was one reason why she had twisted Verena's flight from New York, just after she let her friend see how much she should like to drink deeper of the cup, into a warrant for living in a fool's paradise. If she had been less afraid, she would have read things more clearly; she would have seen that we don't run away from people unless we fear them and that we don't fear them unless we know that we are unarmed. Verena feared

Basil Ransom now (though this time she declined to run); but now she had taken up her weapons, she had told Olive she was exposed, she had asked *her* to be her defence. Poor Olive was stricken as she had never been before, but the extremity of her danger gave her a desperate energy. The only comfort in her situation was that this time Verena had confessed her peril, had thrown herself into her hands. 'I like him—I can't help it—I do like him. I don't want to marry him, I don't want to embrace his ideas, which are unspeakably false and horrible; but I like him better than any gentleman I have seen.' So much as this the girl announced to her friend as soon as the conversation of which I have just given a sketch was resumed, as it was very soon, you may be sure, and very often, in the course of the next few days. That was her way of saying that a great crisis had arrived in her life, and the statement needed very little amplification to stand as a shy avowal that she too had succumbed to the universal passion. Olive had had her suspicions, her terrors, before; but she perceived now how idle and foolish they had been, and that this was a different affair from any of the 'phases' of which she had hitherto anxiously watched the development. As I say, she felt it to be a considerable mercy that Verena's attitude was frank, for it gave her something to take hold of; she could no longer be put off with sophistries about receiving visits from handsome and unscrupulous young men for the sake of the opportunities it gave one to convert them. She took hold, accordingly, with passion, with fury; after the shock of Ransom's arrival had passed away she determined that he should not find her chilled into dumb submission. Verena had told her that she wanted her to hold her tight, to rescue her; and there was no fear that, for an instant, she should sleep at her post.

'I like him—I like him; but I want to hate——'

'You want to hate him!' Olive broke in.

'No, I want to hate my liking. I want you to keep before me all the reasons why I should—many of them so fearfully important. Don't let me lose sight of anything! Don't be afraid I shall not be grateful when you remind me.'

That was one of the singular speeches that Verena made in the course of their constant discussion of the terrible question, and it must be confessed that she made a great many. The strangest of all was when she protested, as she did again and again to Olive, against the idea of their seeking safety in retreat. She said there was a want of dignity in it—that she had been ashamed, afterwards, of what she had done in rushing away from New York. This care for her moral appearance was, on Verena's part, something new; inasmuch as, though she had struck that note on previous occasions—had insisted on its being her duty to face the accidents and alarms of life— she had never erected such a standard in the face of a disaster so sharply possible. It was not her habit either to talk or to think about her dignity, and when Olive found her taking that tone she felt more than ever that the dreadful, ominous, fatal part of the situation was simply that now, for the first time in all the history of their sacred friendship, Verena was not sincere. She was not sincere when she told her that she wanted to be helped against Mr. Ransom—when she exhorted her, that way, to keep everything that was salutary and fortifying before her eyes. Olive did not go so far as to believe that she was playing a part and putting her off with words which, glossing over her treachery, only made it more cruel; she would have admitted that that treachery was as yet unwitting, that Verena deceived herself first of all, thinking she really wished to be saved. Her phrases about her dignity were insincere, as well as her pretext that they must stay to look after Miss Birdseye: as if Doctor Prance were not abundantly able to discharge that function and would not be enchanted to get them out of the house! Olive had perfectly divined by this time that Doctor Prance had no sympathy with their movement, no general ideas; that she was simply shut up to petty questions of physiological science and of her own professional activity. She would never have invited her down if she had realised this in advance so much as the doctor's dry detachment from all their discussions, their readings and practisings, her constant expeditions to fish and botanise, subsequently enabled her to do. She was very narrow, but it did seem as if she knew more about Miss Birdseye's peculiar physical conditions—they were *very* peculiar—than any one else, and this was a comfort at a time when that admirable woman seemed to be suffering a loss of vitality.

'The great point is that it must be met some time, and it will be a tremendous relief to have it over. He is determined to have it out with me, and if the battle doesn't come off to-day we shall have to fight it to-morrow. I don't see why this isn't as good a time as any other. My lecture for the Music Hall is as good as finished, and I haven't got anything else to do; so I can give all my attention to our personal struggle. It requires a good deal, you would admit, if you knew how wonderfully he can talk. If we should leave this place to-morrow he would come after us to the very next one. He would follow us everywhere. A little while ago we could have escaped him, because he says that then he had no money. He hasn't got much now, but he has got enough to pay his way. He is so encouraged by the reception of his article by the editor of the "Rational Review," that he is sure that in future his pen will be a resource.'

These remarks were uttered by Verena after Basil Ransom had been three days at Marmion, and when she reached this point her companion interrupted her with the inquiry, 'Is that what he proposes to support you with—his pen?'

'Oh yes; of course he admits we should be terribly poor.'

'And this vision of a literary career is based entirely upon an article that hasn't yet seen the light? I don't see how a man of any refinement can approach a woman with so beggarly an account of his position in life.'

'He says he wouldn't—he would have been ashamed—three months ago; that was why, when we were in New York, and he felt, even then—well (so he says) all he feels now, he made up his mind not to persist, to let me go. But just lately a change has taken place; his state of mind altered completely, in the course of a week, in consequence of the letter that editor wrote him about his contribution, and his paying for it right off. It was a remarkably flattering letter. He says he believes in his future now; he has before him a vision of distinction, of influence, and of fortune, not great, perhaps, but sufficient to make life tolerable. He doesn't think life is very delightful, in the nature of things; but one of the best things a man can do with it is to get hold of some woman (of course, she must please him very much, to make it worth while), whom he may draw close to him.'

'And couldn't he get hold of any one but you—among all the exposed millions of our sex?' poor Olive groaned. 'Why must he pick you out, when everything he knew about you showed you to be, exactly, the very last?'

'That's just what I have asked him, and he only remarks that there is no reasoning about such things. He fell in love with me that first evening, at Miss Birdseye's. So you see there was some ground for that mystic apprehension of yours. It seems as if I pleased him more than any one.'

Olive flung herself over on the couch, burying her face in the cushions, which she tumbled in her despair, and moaning out that he didn't love Verena, he never had loved her, it was only his hatred of their cause that made him pretend it; he wanted to do that an injury, to do it the worst he could think of. He didn't love her, he hated her, he only wanted to smother her, to crush her, to kill her—as she would infallibly see that he would if she listened to him. It was because he knew that her voice had magic in it, and from the moment he caught its first note he had determined to destroy it. It was not tenderness that moved him—it was devilish malignity; tenderness would be incapable of requiring the horrible sacrifice that he was not ashamed to ask, of requiring her to commit perjury and blasphemy, to desert a work, an interest, with which her very heart-strings were interlaced, to give the lie to her whole young past, to her purest, holiest ambitions. Olive put forward no claim of her own, breathed, at first, at least, not a word of remonstrance in the name of her personal loss, of their blighted union; she only dwelt upon the unspeakable tragedy of a defection from their standard, of a failure on Verena's part to carry out what she had undertaken, of the horror of seeing her bright career blotted out with darkness and tears, of the joy and elation that would fill the breast of all their adversaries at this illustrious, consummate proof of the fickleness, the futility, the predestined servility, of women. A man had only to whistle for her, and she who had pretended most was delighted to come and kneel at his feet. Olive's most passionate protest was summed up in her saying that if Verena were to forsake them it would put back the emancipation of women a hundred years. She did not, during these dreadful days, talk continuously; she had long periods of pale, intensely anxious, watchful silence, interrupted by outbreaks of passionate argument, entreaty, invocation. It was Verena who talked incessantly, Verena who was in a state entirely new to her, and, as any one could see, in an attitude entirely unnatural and overdone. If she was deceiving herself, as Olive said, there was something very affecting in her effort, her ingenuity. If she tried to appear to Olive impartial, coldly judicious, in her attitude with regard to Basil Ransom, and only anxious to see, for the moral satisfaction of the thing, how good a case, as a lover, he might make out for himself and how much he might touch her susceptibilities, she endeavoured, still more earnestly, to practise this fraud upon her own imagination. She abounded in every proof that she should be in despair if she should be overborne, and she thought of arguments even more convincing, if possible, than Olive's, why she should hold on to her old faith, why she should resist even at the cost of acute temporary suffering. She was voluble, fluent, feverish; she was perpetually bringing up the subject, as if to encourage her friend, to show how she kept possession of her judgment, how independent she remained.

No stranger situation can be imagined than that of these extraordinary young women at this juncture; it was so singular on Verena's part, in particular, that I despair of presenting it to the reader with the air of reality. To understand it, one must bear in mind her peculiar frankness, natural and acquired, her habit of discussing questions, sentiments, moralities, her education, in the atmosphere of lecture-rooms, of *séances*, her familiarity with the vocabulary of emotion, the mysteries of 'the spiritual life.' She had learned to breathe and move in a rarefied air, as she would have learned to speak Chinese if her success in life had depended upon it; but this dazzling trick, and all her artlessly artful facilities, were not a part of her essence, an expression of her innermost preferences. What *was* a part of her essence was the extraordinary generosity with which she could expose herself, give herself away, turn herself inside out, for the satisfaction of a person who made demands of her. Olive, as we know, had made the reflection that no one was naturally less preoccupied with the idea of her dignity, and though Verena put it forward as an excuse for remaining where they were, it must be admitted that in reality she was very deficient in the desire to be consistent with herself. Olive had contributed with all her zeal to the development of Verena's gift; but I scarcely venture to think now, what she may have said to herself, in the secrecy of deep meditation, about the consequences of cultivating an abundant eloquence. Did she say that Verena was attempting to smother her now in her own phrases? did she view with dismay the fatal effect of trying to have an answer for everything? From Olive's condition during these lamentable weeks there is a certain propriety—a delicacy enjoined by the respect for misfortune—in averting our head. She neither ate nor slept; she could scarcely speak without bursting into tears; she felt so implacably, insidiously baffled. She remembered the magnanimity with which she had declined (the winter before the last) to receive the vow of eternal maidenhood which she had at first demanded and then put by as too crude a test, but which Verena, for a precious hour, for ever flown, would *then* have been willing to take. She repented of it with bitterness and rage; and then she asked herself, more desperately still, whether even if she held that pledge she should be brave enough to enforce it in the face of actual complications. She believed that if it were in her power to say, 'No, I won't let you off; I have your solemn word, and I won't!' Verena would bow to that decree and remain with her; but the magic would have passed out of her spirit for ever, the sweetness out of their friendship, the efficacy out of their work. She said to her again and again that she had utterly changed since that hour she came to her, in New York, after her morning with Mr. Ransom, and sobbed out that they must hurry away. Then she had been wounded, outraged, sickened, and in the interval nothing had happened, nothing but that one exchange of letters, which she knew about, to bring her round to a shameless tolerance. Shameless Verena admitted it to be; she assented over and over to this proposition, and explained, as eagerly each time as if it were the first, what it was that had come to pass, what it was that had brought her round. It had simply come over her that she liked him, that this was the true point of view, the only one from which one could consider the situation in a way that would lead to what she called a *real* solution—a permanent rest. On this particular point Verena never responded, in the liberal way I have mentioned, without asseverating at the same time that what she desired most in the world was to prove (the picture Olive had held up from the first), that a woman *could* live on persistently, clinging to a great, vivifying, redemptory idea, without the help of a man. To testify to the end against the stale superstition—mother of every misery—that those gentry were as indispensable as they had proclaimed themselves on the house-tops—that, she passionately protested, was as inspiring a thought in the present poignant crisis as it had ever been.

The one grain of comfort that Olive extracted from the terrors that pressed upon her was that now she knew the worst; she knew it since Verena had told her, after so long and so ominous a reticence, of the detestable episode at Cambridge. That seemed to her the worst, because it had been thunder in a clear sky; the incident had sprung from a quarter from which, months before, all symptoms appeared to have vanished. Though Verena had now done all she could to make up for her perfidious silence by repeating everything that passed between them as she sat with Mr. Ransom in Monadnoc Place or strolled with him through the colleges, it imposed itself upon Olive that that occasion was the key of all that had happened since, that he had then obtained an irremediable hold upon her. If Verena had spoken at the time, she would never have let her go to New York; the sole compensation for that hideous mistake was that the girl, recognising it to the full, evidently deemed now that she couldn't be communicative enough. There were certain afternoons in August, long, beautiful and terrible, when one felt that the summer was rounding its curve, and the rustle of the full-leaved trees in the slanting golden light, in the breeze that ought to be delicious, seemed the voice of the coming autumn, of the warnings and dangers of life—portentous, insufferable hours when, as she sat under the softly swaying vine-leaves of the trellis with Miss Birdseye and tried, in order to still her nerves, to read something aloud to her guest, the sound of her own quavering voice made her think more of that baleful day at Cambridge than even of the fact that at that very moment Verena was 'off' with Mr. Ransom—had gone to take

the little daily walk with him to which it had been arranged
that their enjoyment of each other's society should be reduced. Arranged, I say; but that is not exactly the word to
describe the compromise arrived at by a kind of tacit exchange of tearful entreaty and tightened grasp, after Ransom
had made it definite to Verena that he was indeed going to
stay a month and she had promised that she would not resort
to base evasions, to flight (which would avail her nothing, he
notified her), but would give him a chance, would listen to
him a few minutes every day. He had insisted that the few
minutes should be an hour, and the way to spend it was obvious. They wandered along the waterside to a rocky, shrub-
covered point, which made a walk of just the right duration.
Here all the homely languor of the region, the mild, fragrant
Cape-quality, the sweetness of white sands, quiet waters, low
promontories where there were paths among the barberries
and tidal pools gleamed in the sunset—here all the spirit of a
ripe summer-afternoon seemed to hang in the air. There were
wood-walks too; they sometimes followed bosky uplands,
where accident had grouped the trees with odd effects of
'style,' and where in grassy intervals and fragrant nooks of rest
they came out upon sudden patches of Arcady. In such places
Verena listened to her companion with her watch in her hand,
and she wondered, very sincerely, how he could care for a girl
who made the conditions of courtship so odious. He had recognised, of course, at the very first, that he could not inflict
himself again upon Miss Chancellor, and after that awkward
morning-call I have described he did not again, for the first
three weeks of his stay at Marmion, penetrate into the cottage
whose back windows overlooked the deserted ship-yard.
Olive, as may be imagined, made, on this occasion, no protest
for the sake of being ladylike or of preventing him from putting her apparently in the wrong. The situation between them
was too grim; it was war to the knife, it was a question of
which should pull hardest. So Verena took a tryst with the
young man as if she had been a maid-servant and Basil Ransom a 'follower.' They met a little way from the house; beyond it, outside the village.

XXXVIII

O LIVE THOUGHT she knew the worst, as we have perceived; but the worst was really something she could not know, inasmuch as up to this time Verena chose as little to confide to her on that one point as she was careful to expatiate with her on every other. The change that had taken place in the object of Basil Ransom's merciless devotion since the episode in New York was, briefly, just this change—that the words he had spoken to her there about her genuine vocation, as distinguished from the hollow and factitious ideal with which her family and her association with Olive Chancellor had saddled her—these words, the most effective and penetrating he had uttered, had sunk into her soul and worked and fermented there. She had come at last to believe them, and that was the alteration, the transformation. They had kindled a light in which she saw herself afresh and, strange to say, liked herself better than in the old exaggerated glamour of the lecture-lamps. She could not tell Olive this yet, for it struck at the root of everything, and the dreadful, delightful sensation filled her with a kind of awe at all that it implied and portended. She was to burn everything she had adored; she was to adore everything she had burned. The extraordinary part of it was that though she felt the situation to be, as I say, tremendously serious, she was not ashamed of the treachery which she—yes, decidedly, by this time she must admit it to herself—she meditated. It was simply that the truth had changed sides; that radiant image began to look at her from Basil Ransom's expressive eyes. She loved, she was in love—she felt it in every throb of her being. Instead of being constituted by nature for entertaining that sentiment in an exceptionally small degree (which had been the implication of her whole crusade, the warrant for her offer of old to Olive to renounce), she was framed, apparently, to allow it the largest range, the highest intensity. It was always passion, in fact; but now the object was other. Formerly she had been convinced that the fire of her spirit was a kind of double flame, one half of which was responsive friendship for a most extraordinary person, and the other pity for the sufferings of women in general. Verena gazed aghast at the colourless dust into which, in three short months (counting from the episode in New York), such a conviction as that could crumble; she felt it must be a magical touch that could bring about such a cataclysm. Why Basil Ransom had been deputed by fate to exercise this spell was more than she could say—poor Verena, who up to so lately had flattered herself that she had a wizard's wand in her own pocket.

When she saw him a little way off, about five o'clock—the hour she usually went out to meet him—waiting for her at a bend of the road which lost itself, after a winding, straggling mile or two, in the indented, insulated 'point,' where the wandering bee droned through the hot hours with a vague, misguided flight, she felt that his tall, watching figure, with the low horizon behind, represented well the importance, the towering eminence he had in her mind—the fact that he was just now, to her vision, the most definite and upright, the most incomparable, object in the world. If he had not been at his post when she expected him she would have had to stop and lean against something, for weakness; her whole being would have throbbed more painfully than it throbbed at present, though finding him there made her nervous enough. And who was he, what was he? she asked herself. What did he offer her besides a chance (in which there was no compensation of brilliancy or fashion), to falsify, in a conspicuous manner, every hope and pledge she had hitherto given? He allowed her, certainly, no illusion on the subject of the fate she should meet as his wife; he flung over it no rosiness of promised ease; he let her know that she should be poor, withdrawn from view, a partner of his struggle, of his severe, hard, unique stoicism. When he spoke of such things as these, and bent his eyes on her, she could not keep the tears from her own; she felt that to throw herself into his life (bare and arid as for the time it was), was the condition of happiness for her, and yet that the obstacles were terrible, cruel. It must not be thought that the revolution which was taking place in her was unaccompanied with suffering. She suffered less than Olive certainly, for her bent was not, like her friend's, in that direction; but as the wheel of her experience went round she had the sensation of being ground very small indeed. With her light, bright texture, her complacent responsiveness, her genial, graceful, ornamental cast, her desire to keep on pleasing others at the time when a force she had never felt before was pushing her to please herself, poor Verena lived in these days in a state of moral tension—with a sense of being strained and aching—which she didn't betray more only because it was absolutely not in her power to look desperate. An immense pity for Olive sat in her heart, and she asked herself how far it was necessary to go in the path of self-sacrifice. Nothing was wanting to make the wrong she should do her complete; she had deceived her up to the very last; only three months earlier she had reasserted her vows, given her word, with every show of fidelity and enthusiasm. There were hours when it seemed to Verena that she must really push her inquiry no further, but content herself with the conclusion that she loved as deeply as a woman could love and that it didn't make any difference. She felt Olive's grasp too clinching, too terrible. She said to herself that she should never dare, that she might as well give up early as late; that the scene, at the end, would be something she couldn't face; that she had no right to blast the poor creature's whole future. She had a vision of those dreadful years; she knew that Olive would never get over the disappointment. It would touch her in the point where she felt everything most keenly; she would be incurably lonely and eternally humiliated. It was a very peculiar thing, their friendship; it had elements which made it probably as complete as any (between women) that had ever existed. Of course it had been more on Olive's side than on hers, she had always known that; but that, again, didn't make any difference. It was of no use for her to tell herself that Olive had begun it entirely and she had only responded out of a kind of charmed politeness, at first, to a tremendous appeal. She had lent herself, given herself, utterly, and she ought to have known better if she didn't mean to abide by it. At the end of three weeks she felt that her inquiry was complete, but that after all nothing was gained except an immense interest in Basil Ransom's views and the prospect of an eternal heartache. He had told her he wanted her to know him, and now she knew him pretty thoroughly. She knew him and she adored him, but it didn't make any difference.

To give him up or to give Olive up—this effort would be the greater of the two.

If Basil Ransom had the advantage, as far back as that day in New York, of having struck a note which was to reverberate, it may easily be imagined that he did not fail to follow it up. If he had projected a new light into Verena's mind, and made the idea of giving herself to a man more agreeable to her than that of giving herself to a movement, he found means to deepen this illumination, to drag her former standard in the dust. He was in a very odd situation indeed, carrying on his siege with his hands tied. As he had to do everything in an hour a day, he perceived that he must confine himself to the essential. The essential was to show her how much he loved her, and then to press, to press, always to press. His hovering about Miss Chancellor's habitation without going in was a strange regimen to be subjected to, and he was sorry not to see more of Miss Birdseye, besides often not knowing what to do with himself in the mornings and evenings. Fortunately he had brought plenty of books (volumes of rusty aspect, picked up at New York bookstalls), and in such an affair as this he could take the less when the more was forbidden him. For the mornings, sometimes, he had the resource of Doctor Prance, with whom he made a great many excursions on the water. She was devoted to boating and an ardent fisherwoman, and they used to pull out into the bay together, cast their lines, and talk a prodigious amount of heresy. She met him, as Verena met him, 'in the environs,' but in a different spirit. He was immensely amused at her attitude, and saw that nothing in the world could, as he expressed it, make her wink. She would never blench nor show surprise; she had an air of taking everything abnormal for granted; betrayed no consciousness of the oddity of Ransom's situation; said nothing to indicate she had noticed that Miss Chancellor was in a frenzy or that Verena had a daily appointment. You might have supposed from her manner that it was as natural for Ransom to sit on a fence half a mile off as in one of the red rocking-chairs, of the so-called 'Shaker' species, which adorned Miss Chancellor's back verandah. The only thing our young man didn't like about Doctor Prance was the impression she gave him (out of the crevices of her reticence he hardly knew how it leaked), that she thought Verena rather slim. She took an ironical view of almost any kind of courtship, and he could see she didn't wonder women were such featherheads, so long as, whatever brittle follies they cultivated, they could get men to come and sit on fences for them. Doctor Prance told him Miss Birdseye noticed nothing; she had sunk, within a few days, into a kind of transfigured torpor; she didn't seem to know whether Mr. Ransom were anywhere round or not. She guessed she thought he had just come down for a day and gone off again; she probably supposed he just wanted to get toned up a little by Miss Tarrant. Sometimes, out in the boat, when she looked at him in vague, sociable silence, while she waited for a bite (she delighted in a bite), she had an expression of diabolical shrewdness. When Ransom was not scorching there beside her (he didn't mind the sun of Massachusetts), he lounged about in the pastoral land which hung (at a very moderate elevation), above the shore. He always had a book in his pocket, and he lay under whispering trees and kicked his heels and made up his mind on what side he should take Verena the next time. At the end of a fortnight he had succeeded (so he believed, at least), far better than he had hoped, in this sense, that the girl had now the air of making much more light of her 'gift.' He was indeed quite appalled at the facility with which she threw it over, gave up the idea that it was useful and precious. That had been what he wanted her to do, and the fact of the sacrifice (once she had fairly looked at it), costing her so little only proved his contention, only made it clear that it was not necessary to her happiness to spend half her life ranting (no matter how prettily), in public. All the same he said to himself that, to make up for the loss of whatever was sweet in the reputation of the thing, he should have to be tremendously nice to her in all the coming years. During the first week he was at Marmion she made of him an inquiry which touched on this point.

'Well, if it's all a mere delusion, why should this facility have been given me—why should I have been saddled with a superfluous talent? I don't care much about it—I don't mind telling you that; but I confess I should like to know what is to become of all that part of me, if I retire into private life, and live, as you say, simply to be charming for you. I shall be like a singer with a beautiful voice (you have told me yourself my voice is beautiful), who has accepted some decree of never raising a note. Isn't that a great waste, a great violation of nature? Were not our talents given us to use, and have we any right to smother them and deprive our fellow-creatures of such pleasure as they may confer? In the arrangement you propose' (that was Verena's way of speaking of the question of their marriage), 'I don't see what provision is made for the poor faithful, dismissed servant. It is all very well to be charming to you, but there are people who have told me that once I get on a platform I am charming to all the world. There is no harm in my speaking of that, because you have told me so yourself. Perhaps you intend to have a platform erected in our front parlour, where I can address you every evening, and put you to sleep after your work. I say our *front* parlour, as if it were certain we should have two! It doesn't look as if our means would permit that—and we must have some place to dine, if there is to be a platform in our sitting-room.'

'My dear young woman, it will be easy to solve the difficulty: the dining-table itself shall be our platform, and you shall mount on top of that.' This was Basil Ransom's sportive reply to his companion's very natural appeal for light, and the reader will remark that if it led her to push her investigation no further, she was very easily satisfied. There was more reason, however, as well as more appreciation of a very considerable mystery, in what he went on to say. 'Charming to me, charming to all the world? What will become of your charm?—is that what you want to know? It will be about five thousand times greater than it is now; that's what will become of it. We shall find plenty of room for your facility; it will lubricate our whole existence. Believe me, Miss Tarrant, these things will take care of themselves. You won't sing in the Music Hall, but you will sing to me; you will sing to every one who knows you and approaches you. Your gift is indestructible; don't talk as if I either wanted to wipe it out or should be able to make it a particle less divine. I want to give it another direction, certainly; but I don't want to stop your activity. Your gift is the gift of expression, and there is nothing I can do for you that will make you less expressive. It won't gush out at a fixed hour and on a fixed day, but it will irrigate, it will fertilise, it will brilliantly adorn your conversation. Think how delightful it will be when your influence becomes really social. Your facility, as you call it, will simply make you, in conversation, the most charming woman in America.'

It is to be feared, indeed, that Verena was easily satisfied (convinced, I mean, not that she ought to succumb to him, but that there were lovely, neglected, almost unsuspected truths on his side); and there is further evidence on the same head in the fact that after the first once or twice she found nothing to say to him (much as she was always saying to herself), about the cruel effect her apostasy would have upon Olive. She forbore to plead that reason after she had seen how angry it made him, and with how almost savage a contempt he denounced so flimsy a pretext. He wanted to know since when it was more becoming to take up with a morbid old maid than with an honourable young man; and when Verena pronounced the sacred name of friendship he inquired what fanatical sophistry excluded him from a similar privilege. She had told him, in a moment of expansion (Verena believed she was immensely on her guard, but her guard was very apt to be lowered), that his visits to Marmion cast in Olive's view a remarkable light upon his chivalry; she chose to regard his resolute pursuit of Verena as a covert persecution of herself. Verena repented, as soon as she had spoken, of having given further currency to this taunt; but she perceived the next moment no harm was done, Basil Ransom taking in perfectly good part Miss Chancellor's reflections on his delicacy, and making them the subject of much free laughter. She could not know, for in the midst of his hilarity the young man did not compose himself to tell her, that he had made up his mind on this question before he left New York—as long ago as when he wrote her the note (subsequent to her departure from that city), to which allusion has already been made, and which was simply the fellow of the letter addressed to her after his visit to Cambridge: a friendly, respectful, yet rather pregnant sign that, decidedly, on second thoughts, separation didn't imply for him the intention of silence. We know a little about his second thoughts, as much as is essential, and especially how the occasion of their springing up had been the windfall of an editor's encouragement. The importance of that encouragement, to Basil's imagination, was doubtless much augmented by his desire for an excuse to take up again a line of behavior which he had forsworn (small as had, as yet, been his opportunity to indulge in it), very much less than he supposed; still, it worked an appreciable revolution in his view of his case, and made him ask himself what amount of consideration he should (from the most refined Southern point of view), owe Miss Chancellor in the event of his deciding to go after Verena Tarrant in earnest. He was not slow to decide that he owed her none. Chivalry had to do with one's relations with people one hated, not with those one loved. He didn't hate poor Miss Olive, though she might make him yet; and even if he did, any chivalry was all moonshine which should require him to give up the girl he adored in order that his third cousin should see he could be gallant. Chivalry was forbearance and generosity with regard to the weak; and there was nothing weak about Miss Olive, she was a fighting woman, and she would fight him to the death, giving him not an inch of odds. He felt that she was fighting there all day long, in her cottage-fortress; her resistance was in the air he breathed, and Verena came out to him sometimes quite limp and pale from the tussle.

It was in the same jocose spirit with which he regarded Olive's view of the sort of standard a Mississippian should live up to that he talked to Verena about the lecture she was preparing for her great exhibition at the Music Hall. He learned from her that she was to take the field in the manner of Mrs. Farrinder, for a winter campaign, carrying with her a tremendous big gun. Her engagements were all made, her route was marked out; she expected to repeat her lecture in about fifty different places. It was to be called 'A Woman's Reason,' and both Olive and Miss Birdseye thought it, so far as they could tell in advance, her most promising effort. She wasn't going to trust to inspiration this time; she didn't want to meet a big Boston audience without knowing where she was. Inspiration, moreover, seemed rather to have faded away; in consequence of Olive's influence she had read and studied so much that it seemed now as if everything must take form before-hand. Olive was a splendid critic, whether he liked her or not, and she had made her go over every word of her lecture twenty times. There wasn't an intonation she hadn't made her practise; it was very different from the old system, when her father had worked her up. If Basil considered women super-ficial, it was a pity he couldn't see what Olive's standard of preparation was, or be present at their rehearsals, in the eve-ning, in their little parlour. Ransom's state of mind in regard to the affair at the Music Hall was simply this—that he was determined to circumvent it if he could. He covered it with ridicule, in talking of it to Verena, and the shafts he levelled at it went so far that he could see she thought he exaggerated his dislike to it. In point of fact he could not have overstated that; so odious did the idea seem to him that she was soon to be launched in a more infatuated career. He vowed to him-self that she should never take that fresh start which would commit her irretrievably if she should succeed (and she would succeed—he had not the slightest doubt of her power to pro-duce a sensation in the Music Hall), to the acclamations of the newspapers. He didn't care for her engagements, her cam-paigns, or all the expectancy of her friends; to 'squelch' all that, at a stroke, was the dearest wish of his heart. It would represent to him his own success, it would symbolise his vic-tory. It became a fixed idea with him, and he warned her again and again. When she laughed and said she didn't see how he could stop her unless he kidnapped her, he really pitied her for not perceiving, beneath his ominous pleasant-ries, the firmness of his resolution. He felt almost capable of kidnapping her. It was palpably in the air that she would be-come 'widely popular,' and that idea simply sickened him. He felt as differently as possible about it from Mr. Matthias Pardon.

One afternoon, as he returned with Verena from a walk which had been accomplished completely within the pre-scribed conditions, he saw, from a distance, Doctor Prance, who had emerged bareheaded from the cottage, and, shading her eyes from the red, declining sun, was looking up and down the road. It was part of the regulation that Ransom should separate from Verena before reaching the house, and they had just paused to exchange their last words (which every day promoted the situation more than any others), when Doctor Prance began to beckon to them with much animation. They hurried forward, Verena pressing her hand to her heart, for she had instantly guessed that something terrible had happened to Olive—she had given out, fainted away, perhaps fallen dead, with the cruelty of the strain. Doctor Prance watched them come, with a curious look in her face; it was not a smile, but a kind of exaggerated intimation that she noticed nothing. In an instant she had told them what was the matter. Miss Birdseye had had a sudden weakness; she had remarked abruptly that she was dying, and her pulse, sure enough, had fallen to nothing. She was down on the piazza with Miss Chancellor and herself, and they had tried to get her up to bed. But she wouldn't let them move her; she was passing away, and she wanted to pass away just there, in such a pleasant place, in her customary chair, looking at the sunset. She asked for Miss Tarrant, and Miss Chancellor told her she was out—walking with Mr. Ransom. Then she wanted to know if Mr. Ransom was still there—she supposed he had gone. (Basil knew, by Verena, apart from this, that his name had not been mentioned to the old lady since the morning he saw her.) She expressed a wish to see him—she had something to say to him; and Miss Chancellor told her that he would be back soon, with Verena, and that they would bring him in. Miss Birdseye said she hoped they wouldn't be long, because she was sinking; and Doctor Prance now added, like a person who knew what she was talking about, that it was, in fact, the end. She had darted out two or three times to look for them, and they must step right in. Verena had scarcely given her time to tell her story; she had already rushed into the house. Ransom followed with Doctor Prance, conscious that for him the occasion was doubly solemn; inasmuch as if he was to see poor Miss Birdseye yield up her philanthropic soul, he was on the other hand doubtless to receive from Miss Chancellor a reminder that *she* had no intention of quitting the game.

By the time he had made this reflection he stood in the presence of his kinswoman and her venerable guest, who was sitting just as he had seen her before, muffled and bonneted, on the back piazza of the cottage. Olive Chancellor was on one side of her, holding one of her hands, and on the other was Verena, who had dropped on her knees, close to her, bending over those of the old lady. 'Did you ask for me—did you want me?' the girl said, tenderly. 'I will never leave you again.'

'Oh, I won't keep you long. I only wanted to see you once more.' Miss Birdseye's voice was very low, like that of a person breathing with difficulty; but it had no painful nor querulous note—it expressed only the cheerful weariness which had marked all this last period of her life, and which seemed to make it now as blissful as it was suitable that she should pass away. Her head was thrown back against the top of the chair, the ribbon which confined her ancient hat hung loose, and the late afternoon-light covered her octogenarian face and gave it a kind of fairness, a double placidity. There was, to Ransom, something almost august in the trustful renunciation of her countenance; something in it seemed to say that she had been ready long before, but as the time was not ripe she had waited, with her usual faith that all was for the best; only, at present, since the right conditions met, she couldn't help feeling that it was quite a luxury, the greatest she had ever tasted. Ransom knew why it was that Verena had tears in her eyes as she looked up at her patient old friend; she had spoken to him, often, during the last three weeks, of the stories Miss Birdseye had told her of the great work of her life, her mission, repeated year after year, among the Southern blacks. She had gone among them with every precaution, to teach them to read and write; she had carried them Bibles and told them of the friends they had in the North who prayed for their deliverance. Ransom knew that Verena didn't reproduce these legends with a view to making him ashamed of his Southern origin, his connection with people who, in a past not yet remote, had made that kind of apostleship necessary; he knew this because she had heard what he thought of all that chapter himself; he had given her a kind of historical summary of the slavery-question which left her no room to say that he was more tender to that particular example of human imbecility than he was to any other. But she had told him that this was what *she* would have liked to do—to wander, alone, with her life in her hand, on an errand of mercy, through a country in which society was arrayed against her; she would have liked it much better than simply talking about the right from the gas-lighted vantage of the New England platform. Ransom had replied simply 'Balderdash!' it being his theory, as we have perceived, that he knew much more about Verena's native bent than the young lady herself. This did not, however, as he was perfectly aware, prevent her feeling that she had come too late for the heroic age of New England life, and regarding Miss Birdseye as a battered, immemorial monument of it. Ransom could share such an admiration as that, especially at this moment; he had said to Verena, more than once, that he wished he might have met the old lady in Carolina or Georgia before the war—shown her round among the negroes and talked over New England ideas with her; there were a good many he didn't care much about now, but at that time they would have been tremendously refreshing. Miss Birdseye had given herself away so lavishly all her life that it was rather odd there was anything left of her for the supreme surrender. When he looked at Olive he saw that she meant to ignore him; and during the few minutes he remained on the spot his kinswoman never met his eye. She turned away, indeed, as soon as Doctor Prance said, leaning over Miss Birdseye, 'I have brought Mr. Ransom to you. Don't you remember you asked for him?'

'I am very glad to see you again,' Ransom remarked. 'It was very good of you to think of me.' At the sound of his voice Olive rose and left her place; she sank into a chair at the other end of the piazza, turning round to rest her arms on the back and bury her head in them.

Miss Birdseye looked at the young man still more dimly than she had ever done before. 'I thought you were gone. You never came back.'

'He spends all his time in long walks; he enjoys the country so much,' Verena said.

'Well, it's very beautiful, what I see from here. I haven't been strong enough to move round since the first days. But I am going to move now.' She smiled when Ransom made a gesture as if to help her, and added: 'Oh, I don't mean I am going to move out of my chair.'

'Mr. Ransom has been out in a boat with me several times. I have been showing him how to cast a line,' said Doctor Prance, who appeared to deprecate a sentimental tendency.

'Oh, well, then, you have been one of our party; there seems to be every reason why you should feel that you belong to us.' Miss Birdseye looked at the visitor with a sort of misty earnestness, as if she wished to communicate with him further; then her glance turned slightly aside; she tried to see what had become of Olive. She perceived that Miss Chancellor had withdrawn herself, and, closing her eyes, she mused, ineffectually, on the mystery she had not grasped, the peculiarity of Basil Ransom's relations with her hostess. She was visibly too weak to concern herself with it very actively; she only felt, now that she seemed really to be going, a desire to reconcile and harmonise. But she presently exhaled a low, soft sigh—a kind of confession that it was too mixed, that she gave it up. Ransom had feared for a moment that she was about to indulge in some appeal to Olive, some attempt to make him join hands with that young lady, as a supreme satisfaction to herself. But he saw that her strength failed her, and that, besides, things were getting less clear to her; to his considerable relief, inasmuch as, though he would not have objected to joining hands, the expression of Miss Chancellor's figure and her averted face, with their desperate collapse, showed him well enough how *she* would have met such a proposal. What Miss Birdseye clung to, with benignant perversity, was the idea that, in spite of his exclusion from the house, which was perhaps only the result of a certain high-strung jealousy on Olive's part of her friend's other personal ties, Verena had drawn him in, had made him sympathise with the great reform and desire to work for it. Ransom saw no reason why such an illusion should be dear to Miss Birdseye; his contact with her in the past had been so momentary that he could not account for her taking an interest in his views, in his throwing his weight into the right scale. It was part of the general desire for justice that fermented within her, the passion for progress; and it was also in some degree her interest in Verena—a suspicion, innocent and idyllic, as any such suspicion on Miss Birdseye's part must be, that there was something between them, that the closest of all unions (as Miss Birdseye at least supposed it was), was preparing itself. Then his being a Southerner gave a point to the whole thing; to bring round a Southerner would be a real encouragement for one who had seen, even at a time when she was already an old woman, what was the tone of opinion in the cotton States. Ransom had no wish to discourage her, and he bore well in mind the caution Doctor Prance had given him about destroying her last theory. He only bowed his head very humbly, not knowing what he had done to earn the honour of being the subject of it. His eyes met Verena's as she looked up at him from her place at Miss Birdseye's feet, and he saw she was following his thought, throwing herself into it, and trying to communicate to him a wish. The wish touched him immensely; she was dreadfully afraid he would betray her to Miss Birdseye—let her know how she had cooled off. Verena was ashamed of that now, and trembled at the danger of exposure; her eyes adjured him to be careful of what he said. Her tremor made him glow a little in return, for it seemed to him the fullest confession of his influence she had yet made.

'We have been a very happy little party,' she said to the old lady. 'It is delightful that you should have been able to be with us all these weeks.'

'It has been a great rest. I am very tired. I can't speak much. It has been a lovely time. I have done so much—so many things.'

'I guess I wouldn't talk much, Miss Birdseye,' said Doctor Prance, who had now knelt down on the other side of her. 'We know how much you have done. Don't you suppose every one knows *your* life?'

'It isn't much—only I tried to take hold. When I look back from here, from where we've sat, I can measure the progress. That's what I wanted to say to you and Mr. Ransom—because I'm going fast. Hold on to me, that's right; but you can't keep me. I don't want to stay now; I presume I shall join some of the others that we lost long ago. Their faces come back to me now, quite fresh. It seems as if they might be waiting; as if they were all there; as if they wanted to hear. You mustn't think there's no progress because you don't see it all right off; that's what I wanted to say. It isn't till you have gone a long way that you can feel what's been done. That's what I see when I look back from here; I see that the community wasn't half waked up when I was young.'

'It is you that have waked it up more than any one else, and it's for that we honour you, Miss Birdseye!' Verena cried, with a sudden violence of emotion. 'If you were to live for a thousand years, you would think only of others—you would think only of helping on humanity. You are our heroine, you are our saint, and there has never been any one like you!' Verena had no glance for Ransom now, and there was neither deprecation nor entreaty in her face. A wave of contrition, of shame, had swept over her—a quick desire to atone for her secret swerving by a renewed recognition of the nobleness of such a life as Miss Birdseye's.

'Oh, I haven't effected very much; I have only cared and hoped. You will do more than I have ever done—you and Olive Chancellor, because you are young and bright, brighter than I ever was; and besides, everything has got started.'

'Well, you've got started, Miss Birdseye,' Doctor Prance remarked, with raised eyebrows, protesting drily but kindly, and putting forward, with an air as if, after all, it didn't matter much, an authority that had been superseded. The manner in which this competent little woman indulged her patient showed sufficiently that the good lady was sinking fast.

'We will think of you always, and your name will be sacred to us, and that will teach us singleness and devotion,' Verena went on, in the same tone, still not meeting Ransom's eyes again, and speaking as if she were trying now to stop herself, to tie herself by a vow.

'Well, it's the thing you and Olive have given your lives to that has absorbed me most, of late years. I did want to see justice done—to us. I haven't seen it, but you will. And Olive will. Where is she—why isn't she near me, to bid me farewell? And Mr. Ransom will—and he will be proud to have helped.'

'Oh, mercy, mercy!' cried Verena, burying her head in Miss Birdseye's lap.

'You are not mistaken if you think I desire above all things that your weakness, your generosity, should be protected,' Ransom said, rather ambiguously, but with pointed respectfulness. 'I shall remember you as an example of what women are capable of,' he added; and he had no subsequent compunctions for the speech, for he thought poor Miss Birdseye, for all her absence of profile, essentially feminine.

A kind of frantic moan from Olive Chancellor responded to these words, which had evidently struck her as an insolent sarcasm; and at the same moment Doctor Prance sent Ransom a glance which was an adjuration to depart.

'Good-bye, Olive Chancellor,' Miss Birdseye murmured. 'I don't want to stay, though I should like to see what you will see.'

'I shall see nothing but shame and ruin!' Olive shrieked, rushing across to her old friend, while Ransom discreetly quitted the scene.

XXXIX

HE MET Doctor Prance in the village the next morning, and as soon as he looked at her he saw that the event which had been impending at Miss Chancellor's had taken place. It was not that her aspect was funereal; but it contained, somehow, an announcement that she had, for the present, no more thought to give to casting a line. Miss Birdseye had quietly passed away, in the evening, an hour or two after Ransom's visit. They had wheeled her chair into the house; there had been nothing to do but wait for complete extinction. Miss Chancellor and Miss Tarrant had sat by her there, without moving, each of her hands in theirs, and she had just melted away, towards eight o'clock. It was a lovely death; Doctor Prance intimated that she had never seen any that she thought more seasonable. She added that she was a good woman—one of the old sort; and that was the only funeral oration that Basil Ransom was destined to hear pronounced upon Miss Birdseye. The impression of the simplicity and humility of her end remained with him, and he reflected more than once, during the days that followed, that the absence of pomp and circumstance which had marked her career marked also the consecration of her memory. She had been almost celebrated, she had been active, earnest, ubiquitous beyond any one else, she had given herself utterly to charities and creeds and causes; and yet the only persons, apparently, to whom her death made a real difference were three young women in a small 'frame-house' on Cape Cod. Ransom learned from Doctor Prance that her mortal remains were to be committed to their rest in the little cemetery at Marmion, in sight of the pretty sea-view she loved to gaze at, among old mossy headstones of mariners and fisher-folk. She had seen the place when she first came down, when she was able to drive out a little, and she had said she thought it must be pleasant to lie there. It was not an injunction, a definite request; it had not occurred to Miss Birdseye, at the end of her days, to take an exacting line or to make, for the first time in eighty years, a personal claim. But Olive Chancellor and Verena had put their construction on her appreciation of the

quietest corner of the striving, suffering world so weary a pilgrim of philanthropy had ever beheld.

In the course of the day Ransom received a note of five
lines from Verena, the purport of which was to tell him that
he must not expect to see her again for the present; she
wished to be very quiet and think things over. She added the
recommendation that he should leave the neighbourhood for
three or four days; there were plenty of strange old places to
see in that part of the country. Ransom meditated deeply on
this missive, and perceived that he should be guilty of very
bad taste in not immediately absenting himself. He knew that
to Olive Chancellor's vision his conduct already wore that
stain, and it was useless, therefore, for him to consider how
he could displease her either less or more. But he wished to
convey to Verena the impression that he would do anything
in the wide world to gratify *her* except give her up, and as he
packed his valise he had an idea that he was both behaving
beautifully and showing the finest diplomatic sense. To go
away proved to himself how secure he felt, what a conviction
he had that however she might turn and twist in his grasp he
held her fast. The emotion she had expressed as he stood
there before poor Miss Birdseye was only one of her instinctive contortions; he had taken due note of that—said to himself that a good many more would probably occur before she
would be quiet. A woman that listens is lost, the old proverb
says; and what had Verena done for the last three weeks but
listen?—not very long each day, but with a degree of attention of which her not withdrawing from Marmion was the
measure. She had not told him that Olive wanted to whisk
her away, but he had not needed this confidence to know that
if she stayed on the field it was because she preferred to. She
probably had an idea she was fighting, but if she should fight
no harder than she had fought up to now he should continue
to take the same view of his success. She meant her request
that he should go away for a few days as something combat-
ive; but, decidedly, he scarcely felt the blow. He liked to think
that he had great tact with women, and he was sure Verena
would be struck with this quality in reading, in the note he
presently addressed her in reply to her own, that he had determined to take a little run to Provincetown. As there was

no one under the rather ineffectual roof which sheltered him to whose hand he could intrust the billet—at the Marmion hotel one had to be one's own messenger—he walked to the village post-office to request that his note should be put into Miss Chancellor's box. Here he met Doctor Prance, for a second time that day; she had come to deposit the letters by which Olive notified a few of Miss Birdseye's friends of the time and place of her obsequies. This young lady was shut up with Verena, and Doctor Prance was transacting all their business for them. Ransom felt that he made no admission that would impugn his estimate of the sex to which she in a manner belonged, in reflecting that she would acquit herself of these delegated duties with the greatest rapidity and accuracy. He told her he was going to absent himself for a few days, and expressed a friendly hope that he should find her at Marmion on his return.

Her keen eye gauged him a moment, to see if he were joking; then she said, 'Well, I presume you think I can do as I like. But I can't.'

'You mean you have got to go back to work?'

'Well, yes; my place is empty in the city.'

'So is every other place. You had better remain till the end of the season.'

'It's all one season to me. I want to see my office-slate. I wouldn't have stayed so long for any one but her.'

'Well, then, goodbye,' Ransom said. 'I shall always remember our little expeditions. And I wish you every professional distinction.'

'That's why I want to go back,' Doctor Prance replied, with her flat, limited manner. He kept her a moment; he wanted to ask her about Verena. While he was hesitating how to form his question she remarked, evidently wishing to leave him a little memento of her sympathy, 'Well, I hope you will be able to follow up your views.'

'My views, Miss Prance? I am sure I have never mentioned them to you!' Then Ransom added, 'How is Miss Tarrant to-day? is she more calm?'

'Oh no, she isn't calm at all,' Doctor Prance answered, very definitely.

'Do you mean she's excited, emotional?'

'Well, she doesn't talk, she's perfectly still, and so is Miss Chancellor. They're as still as two watchers—they don't speak. But you can hear the silence vibrate.'

'Vibrate?'

'Well, they are very nervous.'

Ransom was confident, as I say, yet the effort that he made to extract a good omen from this characterisation of the two ladies at the cottage was not altogether successful. He would have liked to ask Doctor Prance whether she didn't think he might count on Verena in the end; but he was too shy for this, the subject of his relations with Miss Tarrant never yet having been touched upon between them; and, besides, he didn't care to hear himself put a question which was more or less an implication of a doubt. So he compromised, with a sort of oblique and general inquiry about Olive; that might draw some light. 'What do you think of Miss Chancellor—how does she strike you?'

Doctor Prance reflected a little, with an apparent consciousness that he meant more than he asked. 'Well, she's losing flesh,' she presently replied; and Ransom turned away, not encouraged, and feeling that, no doubt, the little doctress had better go back to her office-slate.

He did the thing handsomely, remained at Provincetown a week, inhaling the delicious air, smoking innumerable cigars, and lounging among the ancient wharves, where the grass grew thick and the impression of fallen greatness was still stronger than at Marmion. Like his friends the Bostonians he was very nervous; there were days when he felt that he must rush back to the margin of that mild inlet; the voices of the air whispered to him that in his absence he was being outwitted. Nevertheless he stayed the time he had determined to stay; quieting himself with the reflection that there was nothing they could do to elude him unless, perhaps, they should start again for Europe, which they were not likely to do. If Miss Olive tried to hide Verena away in the United States he would undertake to find her—though he was obliged to confess that a flight to Europe would baffle him, owing to his want of cash for pursuit. Nothing, however, was less probable than that they would cross the Atlantic on the eve of Verena's projected *début* at the Music Hall. Before he went back to

Marmion he wrote to this young lady, to announce his reappearance there and let her know that he expected she would come out to meet him the morning after. This conveyed the assurance that he intended to take as much of the day as he could get; he had had enough of the system of dragging through all the hours till a mere fraction of time was left before night, and he couldn't wait so long, at any rate, the day after his return. It was the afternoon-train that had brought him back from Provincetown, and in the evening he ascertained that the Bostonians had not deserted the field. There were lights in the windows of the house under the elms, and he stood where he had stood that evening with Doctor Prance and listened to the waves of Verena's voice, as she rehearsed her lecture. There were no waves this time, no sounds, and no sign of life but the lamps; the place had apparently not ceased to be given over to the conscious silence described by Doctor Prance. Ransom felt that he gave an immense proof of chivalry in not calling upon Verena to grant him an interview on the spot. She had not answered his last note, but the next day she kept the tryst, at the hour he had proposed; he saw her advance along the road, in a white dress, under a big parasol, and again he found himself liking immensely the way she walked. He was dismayed, however, at her face and what it portended; pale, with red eyes, graver than she had ever been before, she appeared to have spent the period of his absence in violent weeping. Yet that it was not for him she had been crying was proved by the very first words she spoke.

'I only came out to tell you definitely it's impossible! I have thought over everything, taking plenty of time—over and over; and that is my answer, finally, positively. You must take it—you shall have no other.'

Basil Ransom gazed, frowning fearfully. 'And why not, pray?'

'Because I can't, I can't, I can't, I can't!' she repeated, passionately, with her altered, distorted face.

'Damnation!' murmured the young man. He seized her hand, drew it into his arm, forcing her to walk with him along the road.

That afternoon Olive Chancellor came out of her house and

wandered for a long time upon the shore. She looked up and down the bay, at the sails that gleamed on the blue water, shifting in the breeze and the light; they were a source of interest to her that they had never been before. It was a day she was destined never to forget; she felt it to be the saddest, the most wounding of her life. Unrest and haunting fear had not possession of her now, as they had held her in New York when Basil Ransom carried off Verena, to mark her for his own, in the park. But an immeasurable load of misery seemed to sit upon her soul; she ached with the bitterness of her melancholy, she was dumb and cold with despair. She had spent the violence of her terror, the eagerness of her grief, and now she was too weary to struggle with fate. She appeared to herself almost to have accepted it, as she wandered forth in the beautiful afternoon with the knowledge that the 'ten minutes' which Verena had told her she meant to devote to Mr. Ransom that morning had developed suddenly into an embarkation for the day. They had gone out in a boat together; one of the village-worthies, from whom small craft were to be hired, had, at Verena's request, sent his little son to Miss Chancellor's cottage with that information. She had not understood whether they had taken the boatman with them. Even when the information came (and it came at a moment of considerable reassurance), Olive's nerves were not ploughed up by it as they had been, for instance, by the other expedition, in New York; and she could measure the distance she had traversed since then. It had not driven her away on the instant to pace the shore in frenzy, to challenge every boat that passed, and beg that the young lady who was sailing somewhere in the bay with a dark gentleman with long hair, should be entreated immediately to return. On the contrary, after the first quiver of pain inflicted by the news she had been able to occupy herself, to look after her house, to write her morning's letters, to go into her accounts, which she had had some time on her mind. She had wanted to put off thinking, for she knew to what hideous recognitions that would bring her round again. These were summed up in the fact that Verena was now not to be trusted for an hour. She had sworn to her the night before, with a face like a lacerated angel's, that her choice was made, that their union and their work were more to her than any other life could ever be, and that she deeply believed that should she forswear these holy things she should simply waste away, in the end, with remorse and shame. She would see Mr. Ransom just once more, for ten minutes, to utter one or two supreme truths to him, and then they would take up their old, happy, active, fruitful days again, would throw themselves more than ever into their splendid effort. Olive had seen how Verena was moved by Miss Birdseye's death, how at the sight of that unique woman's majestically simple withdrawal from a scene in which she had held every vulgar aspiration, every worldly standard and lure, so cheap, the girl had been touched again with the spirit of their most confident hours, had flamed up with the faith that no narrow personal joy could compare in sweetness with the idea of doing something for those who had always suffered and who waited still. This helped Olive to believe that she might begin to count upon her again, conscious as she was at the same time that Verena had been strangely weakened and strained by her odious ordeal. Oh, Olive knew that she loved him—knew what the passion was with which the wretched girl had to struggle; and she did her the justice to believe that her professions were sincere, her effort was real. Harassed and embittered as she was, Olive Chancellor still proposed to herself to be rigidly just, and that is why she pitied Verena now with an unspeakable pity, regarded her as the victim of an atrocious spell, and reserved all her execration and contempt for the author of their common misery. If Verena had stepped into a boat with him half an hour after declaring that she would give him his dismissal in twenty words, that was because he had ways, known to himself and other men, of creating situations without an issue, of forcing her to do things she could do only with sharp repugnance, under the menace of pain that would be sharper still. But all the same, what actually stared her in the face was that Verena was not to be trusted, even after rallying again as passionately as she had done during the days that followed Miss Birdseye's death. Olive would have liked to know the pang of penance that *she* would have been afraid, in her place, to incur; to see the locked door which *she* would not have managed to force open!

This inexpressibly mournful sense that, after all, Verena, in her exquisite delicacy and generosity, was appointed only to show how women had from the beginning of time been the sport of men's selfishness and avidity, this dismal conviction accompanied Olive on her walk, which lasted all the afternoon, and in which she found a kind of tragic relief. She went very far, keeping in the lonely places, unveiling her face to the splendid light, which seemed to make a mock of the darkness and bitterness of her spirit. There were little sandy coves, where the rocks were clean, where she made long stations, sinking down in them as if she hoped she should never rise again. It was the first time she had been out since Miss Birdseye's death, except the hour when, with the dozen sympathisers who came from Boston, she stood by the tired old woman's grave. Since then, for three days, she had been writing letters, narrating, describing to those who hadn't come; there were some, she thought, who might have managed to do so, instead of despatching her pages of diffuse reminiscence and asking her for all particulars in return. Selah Tarrant and his wife had come, obtrusively, as she thought, for they never had had very much intercourse with Miss Birdseye; and if it was for Verena's sake, Verena was there to pay every tribute herself. Mrs. Tarrant had evidently hoped Miss Chancellor would ask her to stay on at Marmion, but Olive felt how little she was in a state for such heroics of hospitality. It was precisely in order that she should not have to do that sort of thing that she had given Selah such considerable sums, on two occasions, at a year's interval. If the Tarrants wanted a change of air they could travel all over the country—their present means permitted it; they could go to Saratoga or Newport if they liked. Their appearance showed that they could put their hands into their pockets (or into hers); at least Mrs. Tarrant's did. Selah still sported (on a hot day in August), his immemorial water-proof; but his wife rustled over the low tombstones at Marmion in garments of which (little as she was versed in such inquiries), Olive could see that the cost had been large. Besides, after Doctor Prance had gone (when all was over), she felt what a relief it was that Verena and she could be just together—together with the monstrous wedge of a question that had come up between them. That was company enough, great heaven! and she had not got rid of such an inmate as Doctor Prance only to put Mrs. Tarrant in her place.

Did Verena's strange aberration, on this particular day, suggest to Olive that it was no use striving, that the world was all a great trap or trick, of which women were ever the punctual dupes, so that it was the worst of the curse that rested upon them that they must most humiliate those who had most their cause at heart? Did she say to herself that their weakness was not only lamentable but hideous—hideous their predestined subjection to man's larger and grosser insistence? Did she ask herself why she should give up her life to save a sex which, after all, didn't wish to be saved, and which rejected the truth even after it had bathed them with its auroral light and they had pretended to be fed and fortified? These are mysteries into which I shall not attempt to enter, speculations with which I have no concern; it is sufficient for us to know that all human effort had never seemed to her so barren and thankless as on that fatal afternoon. Her eyes rested on the boats she saw in the distance, and she wondered if in one of them Verena were floating to her fate; but so far from straining forward to beckon her home she almost wished that she might glide away for ever, that *she* might never see her again, never undergo the horrible details of a more deliberate separation. Olive lived over, in her miserable musings, her life for the last two years; she knew, again, how noble and beautiful her scheme had been, but how it had all rested on an illusion of which the very thought made her feel faint and sick. What was before her now was the reality, with the beautiful, indifferent sky pouring down its complacent rays upon it. The reality was simply that Verena had been more to her than she ever was to Verena, and that, with her exquisite natural art, the girl had cared for their cause only because, for the time, no interest, no fascination, was greater. Her talent, the talent which was to achieve such wonders, was nothing to her; it was too easy, she could leave it alone, as she might close her piano, for months; it was only to Olive that it was everything. Verena had submitted, she had responded, she had lent herself to Olive's incitement and exhortation, because she was sympathetic and young and abundant and fanciful; but it had been a kind of hothouse loyalty, the mere contagion of example, and a sentiment springing up from within had easily breathed a chill upon it. Did Olive ask herself whether, for so many months, her companion had been only the most unconscious and most successful of humbugs? Here again I must plead a certain incompetence to give an answer. Positive it is that she spared herself none of the inductions of a reverie that seemed to dry up the mists and ambiguities of life. These hours of backward clearness come to all men and women, once at least, when they read the past in the light of the present, with the reasons of things, like unobserved finger-posts, protruding where they never saw them before. The journey behind them is mapped out and figured, with its false steps, its wrong observations, all its infatuated, deluded geography. They understand as Olive understood, but it is probable that they rarely suffer as she suffered. The sense of regret for her baffled calculations burned within her like a fire, and the splendour of the vision over which the curtain of mourning now was dropped brought to her eyes slow, still tears, tears that came one by one, neither easing her nerves nor lightening her load of pain. She thought of her innumerable talks with Verena, of the pledges they had exchanged, of their earnest studies, their faithful work, their certain reward, the winter-nights under the lamp, when they thrilled with previsions as just and a passion as high as had ever found shelter in a pair of human hearts. The pity of it, the misery of such a fall after such a flight, could express itself only, as the poor girl prolonged the vague pauses of her unnoticed ramble, in a low, inarticulate murmur of anguish.

The afternoon waned, bringing with it the slight chill which, at the summer's end, begins to mark the shortening days. She turned her face homeward, and by this time became conscious that if Verena's companion had not yet brought her back there might be ground for uneasiness as to what had happened to them. It seemed to her that no sail-boat could have put into the town without passing more or less before her eyes and showing her whom it carried; she had seen a dozen, freighted only with the figures of men. An accident was perfectly possible (what could Ransom, with his planta-

tion-habits, know about the management of a sail?), and once
that danger loomed before her—the signal loveliness of the
weather had prevented its striking her before—Olive's imagination hurried, with a bound, to the worst. She saw the boat
overturned and drifting out to sea, and (after a week of nameless horror) the body of an unknown young woman, defaced
beyond recognition, but with long auburn hair and in a white
dress, washed up in some far-away cove. An hour before, her
mind had rested with a sort of relief on the idea that Verena
should sink for ever beneath the horizon, so that their tremendous trouble might never be; but now, with the lateness
of the hour, a sharp, immediate anxiety took the place of that
intended resignation; and she quickened her step, with a heart
that galloped too as she went. Then it was, above all, that she
felt how *she* had understood friendship, and how never again
to see the face of the creature she had taken to her soul would
be for her as the stroke of blindness. The twilight had become
thick by the time she reached Marmion and paused for an
instant in front of her house, over which the elms that stood
on the grassy wayside appeared to her to hang a blacker curtain than ever before.

There was no candle in any window, and when she pushed
in and stood in the hall, listening a moment, her step awak-
ened no answering sound. Her heart failed her; Verena's staying out in a boat from ten o'clock in the morning till nightfall
was too unnatural, and she gave a cry, as she rushed into the
low, dim parlour (darkened on one side, at that hour, by the
wide-armed foliage, and on the other by the veranda and trellis), which expressed only a wild personal passion, a desire to
take her friend in her arms again on any terms, even the most
cruel to herself. The next moment she started back, with another and a different exclamation, for Verena was in the
room, motionless, in a corner—the first place in which she
had seated herself on re-entering the house—looking at her
with a silent face which seemed strange, unnatural, in the
dusk. Olive stopped short, and for a minute the two women
remained as they were, gazing at each other in the dimness.
After that, too, Olive still said nothing; she only went to Verena and sat down beside her. She didn't know what to make
of her manner; she had never been like that before. She was

unwilling to speak; she seemed crushed and humbled. This was almost the worst—if anything could be worse than what had gone before; and Olive took her hand with an irresistible impulse of compassion and reassurance. From the way it lay in her own she guessed her whole feeling—saw it was a kind of shame, shame for her weakness, her swift surrender, her insane gyration, in the morning. Verena expressed it by no protest and no explanation; she appeared not even to wish to hear the sound of her own voice. Her silence itself was an appeal—an appeal to Olive to ask no questions (she could trust her to inflict no spoken reproach); only to wait till she could lift up her head again. Olive understood, or thought she understood, and the wofulness of it all only seemed the deeper. She would just sit there and hold her hand; that was all she could do; they were beyond each other's help in any other way now. Verena leaned her head back and closed her eyes, and for an hour, as nightfall settled in the room, neither of the young women spoke. Distinctly, it was a kind of shame. After a while the parlour-maid, very casual, in the manner of the servants at Marmion, appeared on the threshold with a lamp; but Olive motioned her frantically away. She wished to keep the darkness. It was a kind of shame.

The next morning Basil Ransom rapped loudly with his walking-stick on the lintel of Miss Chancellor's house-door, which, as usual on fine days, stood open. There was no need he should wait till the servant had answered his summons; for Olive, who had reason to believe he would come, and who had been lurking in the sitting-room for a purpose of her own, stepped forth into the little hall.

'I am sorry to disturb you; I had the hope that—for a moment—I might see Miss Tarrant.' That was the speech with which (and a measured salutation), he greeted his advancing kinswoman. She faced him an instant, and her strange green eyes caught the light.

'It's impossible. You may believe that when I say it.'

'Why is it impossible?' he asked, smiling in spite of an inward displeasure. And as Olive gave him no answer, only gazing at him with a cold audacity which he had not hitherto observed in her, he added a little explanation. 'It is simply to have seen her before I go—to have said five words to her. I want her to know that I have made up my mind—since yesterday—to leave this place; I shall take the train at noon.'

It was not to gratify Olive Chancellor that he had determined to go away, or even that he told her this; yet he was surprised that his words brought no expression of pleasure to her face. 'I don't think it is of much importance whether you go away or not. Miss Tarrant herself has gone away.'

'Miss Tarrant—gone away?' This announcement was so much at variance with Verena's apparent intentions the night before that his ejaculation expressed chagrin as well as surprise, and in doing so it gave Olive a momentary advantage. It was the only one she had ever had, and the poor girl may be excused for having enjoyed it—so far as enjoyment was possible to her. Basil Ransom's visible discomfiture was more agreeable to her than anything had been for a long time.

'I went with her myself to the early train; and I saw it leave the station.' And Olive kept her eyes unaverted, for the satisfaction of seeing how he took it.

It must be confessed that he took it rather ill. He had decided it was best he should retire, but Verena's retiring was another matter. 'And where is she gone?' he asked, with a frown.

'I don't think I am obliged to tell you.'

'Of course not! Excuse my asking. It is much better that I should find it out for myself, because if I owed the information to you I should perhaps feel a certain delicacy as regards profiting by it.'

'Gracious heaven!' cried Miss Chancellor, at the idea of Ransom's delicacy. Then she added more deliberately: 'You will not find out for yourself.'

'You think not?'

'I am sure of it!' And her enjoyment of the situation becoming acute, there broke from her lips a shrill, unfamiliar, troubled sound, which performed the office of a laugh, a laugh of triumph, but which, at a distance, might have passed almost as well for a wail of despair. It rang in Ransom's ears as he quickly turned away.

XL

IT WAS Mrs. Luna who received him, as she had received him on the occasion of his first visit to Charles Street; by which I do not mean quite in the same way. She had known very little about him then, but she knew too much for her happiness to-day, and she had with him now a little invidious, contemptuous manner, as if everything he should say or do could be a proof only of abominable duplicity and perversity. She had a theory that he had treated her shamefully; and he knew it—I do not mean the fact, but the theory: which led him to reflect that her resentments were as shallow as her opinions, inasmuch as if she really believed in her grievance, or if it had had any dignity, she would not have consented to see him. He had not presented himself at Miss Chancellor's door without a very good reason, and having done so he could not turn away so long as there was any one in the house of whom he might have speech. He had sent up his name to Mrs. Luna, after being told that she was staying there, on the mere chance that she would see him; for he thought a refusal a very possible sequel to the letters she had written him during the past four or five months—letters he had scarcely read, full of allusions of the most cutting sort to proceedings of his, in the past, of which he had no recollection whatever. They bored him, for he had quite other matters in his mind.

'I don't wonder you have the bad taste, the crudity,' she said, as soon as he came into the room, looking at him more sternly than he would have believed possible to her.

He saw that this was an allusion to his not having been to see her since the period of her sister's visit to New York; he having conceived for her, the evening of Mrs. Burrage's party, a sentiment of aversion which put an end to such attentions. He didn't laugh, he was too worried and preoccupied; but he replied, in a tone which apparently annoyed her as much as any indecent mirth: 'I thought it very possible you wouldn't see me.'

'Why shouldn't I see you, if I should take it into my head? Do you suppose I care whether I see you or not?'

'I supposed you wanted to, from your letters.'

'Then why did you think I would refuse?'

'Because that's the sort of thing women do.'

'Women—women! You know much about them!'

'I am learning something every day.'

'You haven't learned yet, apparently, to answer their letters. It's rather a surprise to me that you don't pretend not to have received mine.'

Ransom could smile now; the opportunity to vent the exasperation that had been consuming him almost restored his good humour. 'What could I say? You overwhelmed me. Besides, I did answer one of them.'

'One of them? You speak as if I had written you a dozen!' Mrs. Luna cried.

'I thought that was your contention—that you had done me the honour to address me so many. They were crushing, and when a man's crushed, it's all over.'

'Yes, you look as if you were in very small pieces! I am glad I shall never see you again.'

'I can see now why you received me—to tell me that,' Ransom said.

'It is a kind of pleasure. I am going back to Europe.'

'Really? for Newton's education?'

'Ah, I wonder you can have the face to speak of that—after the way you deserted him!'

'Let us abandon the subject, then, and I will tell you what I want.'

'I don't in the least care what you want,' Mrs. Luna remarked. 'And you haven't even the grace to ask me where I am going—over there.'

'What difference does that make to me—once you leave these shores?'

Mrs. Luna rose to her feet. 'Ah, chivalry, chivalry!' she exclaimed. And she walked away to the window—one of the windows from which Ransom had first enjoyed, at Olive's solicitation, the view of the Back Bay. Mrs. Luna looked forth at it with little of the air of a person who was sorry to be about to lose it. 'I am determined you shall know where I am going,' she said in a moment. 'I am going to Florence.'

'Don't be afraid!' he replied. 'I shall go to Rome.'

'And you'll carry there more impertinence than has been seen there since the old emperors.'

'Were the emperors impertinent, in addition to their other vices? I am determined, on my side, that you shall know what I have come for,' Ransom said. 'I wouldn't ask you if I could ask any one else; but I am very hard pressed, and I don't know who can help me.'

Mrs. Luna turned on him a face of the frankest derision. 'Help you? Do you remember the last time I asked you to help me?'

'That evening at Mrs. Burrage's? Surely I wasn't wanting then; I remember urging on your acceptance a chair, so that you might stand on it, to see and to hear.'

'To see and to hear what, please? Your disgusting infatuation!'

'It's just about that I want to speak to you,' Ransom pursued. 'As you already know all about it, you have no new shock to receive, and I therefore venture to ask you——'

'Where tickets for her lecture to-night can be obtained? Is it possible she hasn't sent you one?'

'I assure you I didn't come to Boston to hear it,' said Ransom, with a sadness which Mrs. Luna evidently regarded as a refinement of outrage. 'What I should like to ascertain is where Miss Tarrant may be found at the present moment.'

'And do you think that's a delicate inquiry to make of *me*?'

'I don't see why it shouldn't be, but I know you don't think it is, and that is why, as I say, I mention the matter to you only because I can imagine absolutely no one else who is in a position to assist me. I have been to the house of Miss Tarrant's parents, in Cambridge, but it is closed and empty, destitute of any sign of life. I went there first, on arriving this morning, and rang at this door only when my journey to Monadnoc Place had proved fruitless. Your sister's servant told me that Miss Tarrant was not staying here, but she added that Mrs. Luna was. No doubt you won't be pleased at having been spoken of as a sort of equivalent; and I didn't say to myself—or to the servant—that you would do as well; I only reflected that I could at least try you. I didn't even ask for Miss Chancellor, as I am sure she would give me no information whatever.'

Mrs. Luna listened to this candid account of the young man's proceedings with her head turned a little over her shoulder at him, and her eyes fixed as unsympathetically as possible upon his own. 'What you propose, then, as I understand it,' she said in a moment, 'is that I should betray my sister to you.'

'Worse than that; I propose that you should betray Miss Tarrant herself.'

'What do I care about Miss Tarrant? I don't know what you are talking about.'

'Haven't you really any idea where she is living? Haven't you seen her here? Are Miss Olive and she not constantly together?'

Mrs. Luna, at this, turned full round upon him, and, with folded arms and her head tossed back, exclaimed: 'Look here, Basil Ransom, I never thought you were a fool, but it strikes me that since we last met you have lost your wits!'

'There is no doubt of that,' Ransom answered, smiling.

'Do you mean to tell me you don't know everything about Miss Tarrant that can be known?'

'I have neither seen her nor heard of her for the last ten weeks; Miss Chancellor has hidden her away.'

'Hidden her away, with all the walls and fences of Boston flaming to-day with her name?'

'Oh yes, I have noticed that, and I have no doubt that by waiting till this evening I shall be able to see her. But I don't want to wait till this evening; I want to see her now, and not in public—in private.'

'Do you indeed?—how interesting!' cried Mrs. Luna, with rippling laughter. 'And pray what do you want to do with her?'

Ransom hesitated a little. 'I think I would rather not tell you.'

'Your charming frankness, then, has its limits! My poor cousin, you are really too *naïf*. Do you suppose it matters a straw to me?'

Ransom made no answer to this appeal, but after an instant he broke out: 'Honestly, Mrs. Luna, can you give me no clue?'

'Lord, what terrible eyes you make, and what terrible

words you use!' "Honestly," quoth he! Do you think I am so fond of the creature that I want to keep her all to myself?'

'I don't know; I don't understand,' said Ransom, slowly and softly, but still with his terrible eyes.

'And do you think I understand any better? You are not a very edifying young man,' Mrs. Luna went on; 'but I really think you have deserved a better fate than to be jilted and thrown over by a girl of that class.'

'I haven't been jilted. I like her very much, but she never encouraged me.'

At this Mrs. Luna broke again into articulate scoffing. 'It is very odd that at your age you should be so little a man of the world!'

Ransom made her no other answer than to remark, thoughtfully and rather absently: 'Your sister is really very clever.'

'By which you mean, I suppose, that I am not!' Mrs. Luna suddenly changed her tone, and said, with the greatest sweetness and humility: 'God knows, I have never pretended to be!'

Ransom looked at her a moment, and guessed the meaning of this altered note. It had suddenly come over her that with her portrait in half the shop-fronts, her advertisement on all the fences, and the great occasion on which she was to reveal herself to the country at large close at hand, Verena had become so conscious of high destinies that her dear friend's Southern kinsman really appeared to her very small game, and she might therefore be regarded as having cast him off. If this were the case, it would perhaps be well for Mrs. Luna still to hold on. Basil's induction was very rapid, but it gave him time to decide that the best thing to say to his interlocutress was: 'On what day do you sail for Europe?'

'Perhaps I shall not sail at all,' Mrs. Luna replied, looking out of the window.

'And in that case—poor Newton's education?'

'I should try to content myself with a country which has given you yours.'

'Don't you want him, then, to be a man of the world?'

'Ah, the world, the world!' she murmured, while she

watched, in the deepening dusk, the lights of the town begin to reflect themselves in the Back Bay. 'Has it been such a source of happiness to me that I belong to it?'

'Perhaps, after all, I shall be able to go to Florence!' said Ransom, laughing.

She faced him once more, this time slowly, and declared that she had never known anything so strange as his state of mind—she would be so glad to have an explanation of it. With the opinions he professed (it was for them she had liked him—she didn't like his character), why on earth should he be running after a little fifth-rate *poseuse*, and in such a frenzy to get hold of her? He might say it was none of her business, and of course she would have no answer to that; therefore she admitted that she asked simply out of intellectual curiosity, and because one always was tormented at the sight of a painful contradiction. With the things she had heard him say about his convictions and theories, his view of life and the great questions of the future, she should have thought he would find Miss Tarrant's attitudinising absolutely nauseous. Were not her views the same as Olive's, and hadn't Olive and he signally failed to hit it off together? Mrs. Luna only asked because she was really quite puzzled. 'Don't you know that some minds, when they see a mystery, can't rest till they clear it up?'

'You can't be more puzzled than I am,' said Ransom. 'Apparently the explanation is to be found in a sort of reversal of the formula you were so good, just now, as to apply to me. You like my opinions, but you entertain a different sentiment for my character. I deplore Miss Tarrant's opinions, but her character—well, her character pleases me.'

Mrs. Luna stared, as if she were waiting, the explanation surely not being complete. 'But as much as that?' she inquired.

'As much as what?' said Ransom, smiling. Then he added, 'Your sister has beaten me.'

'I thought she had beaten some one of late; she has seemed so gay and happy. I didn't suppose it was *all* because I was going away.'

'Has she seemed very gay?' Ransom inquired, with a sinking of the heart. He wore such a long face, as he asked this question, that Mrs. Luna was again moved to audible mirth, after which she explained:

'Of course I mean gay for her. Everything is relative. With her impatience for this lecture of her friend's to-night, she's in an unspeakable state! She can't sit still for three minutes, she goes out fifteen times a day, and there has been enough arranging and interviewing, and discussing and telegraphing and advertising, enough wire-pulling and rushing about, to put an army in the field. What is it they are always doing to the armies in Europe?—mobilising them? Well, Verena has been mobilised, and this has been headquarters.'

'And shall you go to the Music Hall to-night?'

'For what do you take me? I have no desire to be shrieked at for an hour.'

'No doubt, no doubt, Miss Olive must be in a state,' Ransom went on, rather absently. Then he said, with abruptness, in a different tone: 'If this house has been, as you say, headquarters, how comes it you haven't seen her?'

'Seen Olive? I have seen nothing else!'

'I mean Miss Tarrant. She must be somewhere—in the place—if she's to speak to-night.'

'Should you like me to go out and look for her? *Il ne manquerait plus que cela!*' cried Mrs. Luna. 'What's the matter with you, Basil Ransom, and what are you after?' she demanded, with considerable sharpness. She had tried haughtiness and she had tried humility, but they brought her equally face to face with a competitor whom she couldn't take seriously, yet who was none the less objectionable for that.

I know not whether Ransom would have attempted to answer her question had an obstacle not presented itself; at any rate, at the moment she spoke, the curtain in the doorway was pushed aside, and a visitor crossed the threshold. 'Mercy! how provoking!' Mrs. Luna exclaimed, audibly enough; and without moving from her place she bent an uncharitable eye upon the invader, a gentleman whom Ransom had the sense of having met before. He was a young man with a fresh face and abundant locks, prematurely white; he stood smiling at Mrs. Luna, quite undaunted by the absence of any demonstration in his favour. She looked as if she didn't know him, while Ransom prepared to depart, leaving them to settle it together.

'I'm afraid you don't remember me, though I have seen you before,' said the young man, very amiably. 'I was here a week ago, and Miss Chancellor presented me to you.'

'Oh yes; she's not at home now,' Mrs. Luna returned, vaguely.

'So I was told—but I didn't let that prevent me.' And the young man included Basil Ransom in the smile with which he made himself more welcome than Mrs. Luna appeared disposed to make him, and by which he seemed to call attention to his superiority. 'There is a matter on which I want very much to obtain some information, and I have no doubt you will be so good as to give it to me.'

'It comes back to me—you have something to do with the newspapers,' said Mrs. Luna; and Ransom too, by this time, had placed the young man among his reminiscences. He had been at Miss Birdseye's famous party, and Doctor Prance had there described him as a brilliant journalist.

It was quite with the air of such a personage that he accepted Mrs. Luna's definition, and he continued to radiate towards Ransom (as if, in return, he remembered *his* face), while he dropped, confidentially, the word that expressed everything—' "The Vesper," don't you know?' Then he went on: 'Now, Mrs. Luna, I don't care, I'm not going to let you off! We want the last news about Miss Verena, and it has got to come out of this house.'

'Oh murder!' Ransom muttered, beneath his breath, taking up his hat.

'Miss Chancellor has hidden her away; I have been scouring the city in search of her, and her own father hasn't seen her for a week. We have got his ideas; they are very easy to get, but that isn't what we want.'

'And what do you want?' Ransom was now impelled to inquire, as Mr. Pardon (even the name at present came back to him), appeared sufficiently to have introduced himself.

'We want to know how she feels about to-night; what report she makes of her nerves, her anticipations; how she looked, what she had on, up to six o'clock. Gracious! if I could see her I should know what I wanted, and so would she, I guess!' Mr. Pardon exclaimed. 'You must know something, Mrs. Luna; it isn't natural you shouldn't. I won't inquire any further where she is, because that might seem a little pushing, if she does wish to withdraw herself—though I am bound to say I think she makes a mistake; we could work up these last hours for her! But can't you tell me any little personal items—the sort of thing the people like? What is she going to have for supper? or is she going to speak—a—without previous nourishment?'

'Really, sir, I don't know, and I don't in the least care; I have nothing to do with the business!' Mrs. Luna cried, angrily.

The reporter stared; then, eagerly, 'You have nothing to do with it—you take an unfavourable view, you protest?' And he was already feeling in a side-pocket for his notebook.

'Mercy on us! are you going to put *that* in the paper?' Mrs. Luna exclaimed; and in spite of the sense, detestable to him, that everything he wished most to avert was fast closing over the girl, Ransom broke into cynical laughter.

'Ah, but do protest, madam; let us at least have that fragment!' Mr. Pardon went on. 'A protest from this house would be a charming note. We *must* have it—we've got nothing else! The public are almost as much interested in your sister as they are in Miss Verena; they know to what extent she has backed her: and I should be so delighted (I see the heading, from here, so attractive!) just to take down "What Miss Chancellor's Family Think about It!" '

Mrs. Luna sank into the nearest chair, with a groan, covering her face with her hands. 'Heaven help me, I am glad I am going to Europe!'

'That is another little item—everything counts,' said Matthias Pardon, making a rapid entry in his tablets. 'May I inquire whether you are going to Europe in consequence of your disapproval of your sister's views?'

Mrs. Luna sprang up again, almost snatching the memoranda out of his hand. 'If you have the impertinence to publish a word about me, or to mention my name in print, I will come to your office and make such a scene!'

'Dearest lady, that would be a godsend!' Mr. Pardon cried,

enthusiastically; but he put his note-book back into his pocket.

'Have you made an exhaustive search for Miss Tarrant?' Basil Ransom asked of him. Mr. Pardon, at this inquiry, eyed him with a sudden, familiar archness, expressive of the idea of competition; so that Ransom added: 'You needn't be afraid, I'm not a reporter.'

'I didn't know but what you had come on from New York.'

'So I have—but not as the representative of a newspaper.'

'Fancy his taking you——' Mrs. Luna murmured, with indignation.

'Well, I have been everywhere I could think of,' Mr. Pardon remarked. 'I have been hunting round after your sister's agent, but I haven't been able to catch up with him; I suppose he has been hunting on his side. Miss Chancellor told me—Mrs. Luna may remember it—that she shouldn't be here at all during the week, and that she preferred not to tell me either where or how she was to spend her time until the momentous evening. Of course I let her know that I should find out if I could, and you may remember,' he said to Mrs. Luna, 'the conversation we had on the subject. I remarked, candidly, that if they didn't look out they would overdo the quietness. Doctor Tarrant has felt very low about it. However, I have done what I could with the material at my command, and the "Vesper" has let the public know that her whereabouts was the biggest mystery of the season. It's difficult to get round the "Vesper."'

'I am almost afraid to open my lips in your presence,' Mrs. Luna broke in, 'but I must say that I think my sister was strangely communicative. She told you ever so much that I wouldn't have breathed.'

'I should like to try you with something you know!' Matthias Pardon returned, imperturbably. 'This isn't a fair trial, because you don't know. Miss Chancellor came round—came round considerably, there's no doubt of that; because a year or two ago she was terribly unapproachable. If I have mollified her, madam, why shouldn't I mollify you? She realises that I can help her now, and as I ain't rancorous I am willing to help her all she'll let me. The trouble is, she won't let me enough, yet; it seems as if she couldn't believe it of me. At any rate,' he pursued, addressing himself more particularly to Ransom, 'half an hour ago, at the Hall, they knew nothing whatever about Miss Tarrant, beyond the fact that about a month ago she came there, with Miss Chancellor, to try her voice, which rang all over the place, like silver, and that Miss Chancellor guaranteed her absolute punctuality to-night.'

'Well, that's all that is required,' said Ransom, at hazard; and he put out his hand, in farewell, to Mrs. Luna.

'Do you desert me already?' she demanded, giving him a glance which would have embarrassed any spectator but a reporter of the 'Vesper.'

'I have fifty things to do; you must excuse me.' He was nervous, restless, his heart was beating much faster than usual; he couldn't stand still, and he had no compunction whatever about leaving her to get rid, by herself, of Mr. Pardon.

This gentleman continued to mix in the conversation, possibly from the hope that if he should linger either Miss Tarrant or Miss Chancellor would make her appearance. 'Every seat in the Hall is sold; the crowd is expected to be immense. When our Boston public *does* take an idea!' Mr. Pardon exclaimed.

Ransom only wanted to get away, and in order to facilitate his release by implying that in such a case he should see her again, he said to Mrs. Luna, rather hypocritically, from the threshold, 'You had really better come to-night.'

'I am not like the Boston public—I don't take an idea!' she replied.

'Do you mean to say you are not going?' cried Mr. Pardon, with widely-open eyes, clapping his hand again to his pocket. 'Don't you regard her as a wonderful genius?'

Mrs. Luna was sorely tried, and the vexation of seeing Ransom slip away from her with his thoughts visibly on Verena, leaving her face to face with the odious newspaper-man, whose presence made passionate protest impossible—the annoyance of seeing everything and every one mock at her and fail to compensate her was such that she lost her head, while rashness leaped to her lips and jerked out the answer—'No indeed; I think her a vulgar idiot!'

'Ah, madam, I should never permit myself to print that!' Ransom heard Mr. Pardon rejoin, reproachfully, as he dropped the *portière* of the drawing-room.

H E WALKED ABOUT for the next two hours, walked all
over Boston, heedless of his course, and conscious
only of an unwillingness to return to his hotel and an inability
to eat his dinner or rest his weary legs. He had been roaming
in very much the same desperate fashion, at once eager and
purposeless, for many days before he left New York, and he
knew that his agitation and suspense must wear themselves
out. At present they pressed him more than ever; they had
become tremendously acute. The early dusk of the last half of
November had gathered thick, but the evening was fine and
the lighted streets had the animation and variety of a winter
that had begun with brilliancy. The shop-fronts glowed
through frosty panes, the passers bustled on the pavement,
the bells of the street-cars jangled in the cold air, the newsboys hawked the evening-papers, the vestibules of the theatres, illuminated and flanked with coloured posters and the
photographs of actresses, exhibited seductively their swinging
doors of red leather or baize, spotted with little brass nails.
Behind great plates of glass the interior of the hotels became
visible, with marble-paved lobbies, white with electric lamps,
and columns, and Westerners on divans stretching their legs,
while behind a counter, set apart and covered with an array
of periodicals and novels in paper covers, little boys, with the
faces of old men, showing plans of the play-houses and offering librettos, sold orchestra-chairs at a premium. When from
time to time Ransom paused at a corner, hesitating which
way to drift, he looked up and saw the stars, sharp and near,
scintillating over the town. Boston seemed to him big and full
of nocturnal life, very much awake and preparing for an evening of pleasure.

He passed and repassed the Music Hall, saw Verena immensely advertised, gazed down the vista, the approach for
pedestrians, which leads out of School Street, and thought it
looked expectant and ominous. People had not begun to enter yet, but the place was ready, lighted and open, and the
interval would be only too short. So it appeared to Ransom,
while at the same time he wished immensely the crisis were

over. Everything that surrounded him referred itself to the idea with which his mind was palpitating, the question whether he might not still intervene as against the girl's jump into the abyss. He believed that all Boston was going to hear her, or that at least every one was whom he saw in the streets; and there was a kind of incentive and inspiration in this thought. The vision of wresting her from the mighty multitude set him off again, to stride through the population that would fight for her. It was not too late, for he felt strong; it would not be too late even if she should already stand there before thousands of converging eyes. He had had his ticket since the morning, and now the time was going on. He went back to his hotel at last for ten minutes, and refreshed himself by dressing a little and by drinking a glass of wine. Then he took his way once more to the Music Hall, and saw that people were beginning to go in—the first drops of the great stream, among whom there were many women. Since seven o'clock the minutes had moved fast—before that they had dragged—and now there was only half an hour. Ransom passed in with the others; he knew just where his seat was; he had chosen it, on reaching Boston, from the few that were left, with what he believed to be care. But now, as he stood beneath the far-away panelled roof, stretching above the line of little tongues of flame which marked its junction with the walls, he felt that this didn't matter much, since he certainly was not going to subside into his place. He was not one of the audience; he was apart, unique, and had come on a business altogether special. It wouldn't have mattered if, in advance, he had got no place at all and had just left himself to pay for standing-room at the last. The people came pouring in, and in a very short time there would only be standing-room left. Ransom had no definite plan; he had mainly wanted to get inside of the building, so that, on a view of the field, he might make up his mind. He had never been in the Music Hall before; and its lofty vaults and rows of overhanging balconies made it to his imagination immense and impressive. There were two or three moments during which he felt as he could imagine a young man to feel who, waiting in a public place, has made up his mind, for reasons of his own, to discharge a pistol at the king or the president.

The place struck him with a kind of Roman vastness; the doors which opened out of the upper balconies, high aloft, and which were constantly swinging to and fro with the passage of spectators and ushers, reminded him of the *vomitoria* that he had read about in descriptions of the Colosseum. The huge organ, the background of the stage—a stage occupied with tiers of seats for choruses and civic worthies—lifted to the dome its shining pipes and sculptured pinnacles, and some genius of music or oratory erected himself in monumental bronze at the base. The hall was so capacious and serious, and the audience increased so rapidly without filling it, giving Ransom a sense of the numbers it would contain when it was packed, that the courage of the two young women, face to face with so tremendous an ordeal, hovered before him as really sublime, especially the conscious tension of poor Olive, who would have been spared none of the anxieties and tremors, none of the previsions of accident or calculations of failure. In the front of the stage was a slim, high desk, like a music-stand, with a cover of red velvet, and near it was a light ornamental chair, on which he was sure Verena would not seat herself, though he could fancy her leaning at moments on the back. Behind this was a kind of semicircle of a dozen arm-chairs, which had evidently been arranged for the friends of the speaker, her sponsors and patrons. The hall was more and more full of premonitory sounds; people making a noise as they unfolded, on hinges, their seats, and itinerant boys, whose voices as they cried out 'Photographs of Miss Tarrant—sketch of her life!' or 'Portraits of the Speaker—story of her career!' sounded small and piping in the general immensity. Before Ransom was aware of it several of the arm-chairs, in the row behind the lecturer's desk, were occupied, with gaps, and in a moment he recognised, even across the interval, three of the persons who had appeared. The straight-featured woman with bands of glossy hair and eyebrows that told at a distance, could only be Mrs. Farrinder, just as the gentleman beside her, in a white overcoat, with an umbrella and a vague face, was probably her husband Amariah. At the opposite end of the row were another pair, whom Ransom, unacquainted with certain chapters of Verena's history, perceived without surprise to be Mrs. Burrage and her insinuating son. Apparently their interest in Miss Tarrant was more than a momentary fad, since—like himself—they had made the journey from New York to hear her. There were other figures, unknown to our young man, here and there, in the semicircle; but several places were still empty (one of which was of course reserved for Olive), and it occurred to Ransom, even in his preoccupation, that one of them ought to remain so—ought to be left to symbolise the presence, in the spirit, of Miss Birdseye.

He bought one of the photographs of Verena, and thought it shockingly bad, and bought also the sketch of her life, which many people seemed to be reading, but crumpled it up in his pocket for future consideration. Verena was not in the least present to him in connection with this exhibition of enterprise and puffery; what he saw was Olive, struggling and yielding, making every sacrifice of taste for the sake of the largest hearing, and conforming herself to a great popular system. Whether she had struggled or not, there was a catch-penny effect about the whole thing which added to the fever in his cheek and made him wish he had money to buy up the stock of the vociferous little boys. Suddenly the notes of the organ rolled out into the hall, and he became aware that the overture or prelude had begun. This, too, seemed to him a piece of claptrap, but he didn't wait to think of it; he instantly edged out of his place, which he had chosen near the end of a row, and reached one of the numerous doors. If he had had no definite plan he now had at least an irresistible impulse, and he felt the prick of shame at having faltered for a moment. It had been his tacit calculation that Verena, still enshrined in mystery by her companion, would not have reached the scene of her performance till within a few minutes of the time at which she was to come forth; so that he had lost nothing by waiting, up to this moment, before the platform. But now he must overtake his opportunity. Before passing out of the hall into the lobby he paused, and with his back to the stage, gave a look at the gathered auditory. It had become densely numerous, and, suffused with the evenly distributed gaslight, which fell from a great elevation, and the thick atmosphere that hangs for ever in such places, it appeared to pile itself high and to look dimly expectant and formidable. He had a throb of uneasiness at his private purpose of balking it of its entertainment, its victim—a glimpse of the ferocity that lurks in a disappointed mob. But the thought of that danger only made him pass more quickly through the ugly corridors; he felt that his plan was definite enough now, and he found that he had no need even of asking the way to a certain small door (one or more of them), which he meant to push open. In taking his place in the morning he had assured himself as to the side of the house on which (with its approach to the platform), the withdrawing room of singers and speakers was situated; he had chosen his seat in that quarter, and he now had not far to go before he reached it. No one heeded or challenged him; Miss Tarrant's auditors were still pouring in (the occasion was evidently to have been an unprecedented success of curiosity), and had all the attention of the ushers. Ransom opened a door at the end of a passage, and it admitted him into a sort of vestibule, quite bare save that at a second door, opposite to him, stood a figure at the sight of which he paused for a moment in his advance.

The figure was simply that of a robust policeman, in his helmet and brass buttons—a policeman who was expecting him—Ransom could see that in a twinkling. He judged in the same space of time that Olive Chancellor had heard of his having arrived and had applied for the protection of this functionary, who was now simply guarding the ingress and was prepared to defend it against all comers. There was a slight element of surprise in this, as he had reasoned that his nervous kinswoman was absent from her house for the day—had been spending it all in Verena's retreat, wherever that was. The surprise was not great enough, however, to interrupt his course for more than an instant, and he crossed the room and stood before the belted sentinel. For a moment neither spoke; they looked at each other very hard in the eyes, and Ransom heard the organ, beyond partitions, launching its waves of sound through the hall. They seemed to be very near it, and the whole place vibrated. The policeman was a tall, lean-faced, sallow man, with a stoop of the shoulders, a small, steady eye, and something in his mouth which made a protuberance in his cheek. Ransom could see that he was very strong, but he believed that he himself was not materially less so. However, he had not come there to show physical fight—a public tussle about Verena was not an attractive idea, except perhaps, after all, if he should get the worst of it, from the point of view of Olive's new system of advertising; and, moreover, it would not be in the least necessary. Still he said nothing, and still the policeman remained dumb, and there was something in the way the moments elapsed and in our young man's consciousness that Verena was separated from him only by a couple of thin planks, which made him feel that she too expected him, but in another sense; that she had nothing to do with this parade of resistance, that she would know in a moment, by quick intuition, that he was there, and that she was only praying to be rescued, to be saved. Face to face with Olive she hadn't the courage, but she would have it with her hand in his. It came to him that there was no one in the world less sure of her business just at that moment than Olive Chancellor; it was as if he could see, through the door, the terrible way her eyes were fixed on Verena while she held her watch in her hand and Verena looked away from her. Olive would have been so thankful that she should begin before the hour, but of course that was impossible. Ransom asked no questions—that seemed a waste of time; he only said, after a minute, to the policeman:

'I should like very much to see Miss Tarrant, if you will be so good as to take in my card.'

The guardian of order, well planted just between him and the handle of the door, took from Ransom the morsel of pasteboard which he held out to him, read slowly the name inscribed on it, turned it over and looked at the back, then returned it to his interlocutor. 'Well, I guess it ain't much use,' he remarked.

'How can you know that? You have no business to decline my request.'

'Well, I guess I have about as much business as you have to make it.' Then he added, 'You are just the very man she wants to keep out.'

'I don't think Miss Tarrant wants to keep me out,' Ransom returned.

'I don't know much about her, she hasn't hired the hall.

It's the other one—Miss Chancellor; it's her that runs this lecture.'

'And she has asked you to keep me out? How absurd!' exclaimed Ransom, ingeniously.

'She tells me you're none too fit to be round alone; you have got this thing on the brain. I guess you'd better be quiet,' said the policeman.

'Quiet? Is it possible to be more quiet than I am?'

'Well, I've seen crazy folks that were a good deal like you. If you want to see the speaker why don't you go and set round in the hall, with the rest of the public?' And the policeman waited, in an immovable, ruminating, reasonable manner, for an answer to this inquiry.

Ransom had one, on the instant, at his service. 'Because I don't want simply to see her; I want also to speak to her—in private.'

'Yes—it's always intensely private,' said the policeman. 'Now I wouldn't lose the lecture if I was you. I guess it will do you good.'

'The lecture?' Ransom repeated, laughing. 'It won't take place.'

'Yes it will—as quick as the organ stops.' Then the policeman added, as to himself, 'Why the devil don't it?'

'Because Miss Tarrant has sent up to the organist to tell him to keep on.'

'Who has she sent, do you s'pose?' And Ransom's new acquaintance entered into his humour. 'I guess Miss Chancellor isn't her nigger.'

'She has sent her father, or perhaps even her mother. They are in there too.'

'How do you know that?' asked the policeman, consideringly.

'Oh, I know everything,' Ransom answered, smiling.

'Well, I guess they didn't come here to listen to that organ. We'll hear something else before long, if he doesn't stop.'

'You will hear a good deal, very soon,' Ransom remarked.

The serenity of his self-confidence appeared at last to make an impression on his antagonist, who lowered his head a little, like some butting animal, and looked at the young man from beneath bushy eyebrows. 'Well, I *have* heard a good deal, since I've ben in Boston.'

'Oh, Boston's a great place,' Ransom rejoined, inattentively. He was not listening to the policeman or to the organ now, for the sound of voices had reached him from the other side of the door. The policeman took no further notice of it than to lean back against the panels, with folded arms; and there was another pause, between them, during which the playing of the organ ceased.

'I will just wait here, with your permission,' said Ransom, 'and presently I shall be called.'

'Who do you s'pose will call you?'

'Well, Miss Tarrant, I hope.'

'She'll have to square the other one first.'

Ransom took out his watch, which he had adapted, on purpose, several hours before, to Boston time, and saw that the minutes had sped with increasing velocity during this interview, and that it now marked five minutes past eight. 'Miss Chancellor will have to square the public,' he said in a moment; and the words were far from being an empty profession of security, for the conviction already in possession of him, that a drama in which he, though cut off, was an actor, had been going on for some time in the apartment he was prevented from entering, that the situation was extraordinarily strained there, and that it could not come to an end without an appeal to him—this transcendental assumption acquired an infinitely greater force the instant he perceived that Verena was even now keeping her audience waiting. Why didn't she go on? Why, except that she knew he was there, and was gaining time?

'Well, I guess she has shown herself,' said the door-keeper, whose discussion with Ransom now appeared to have passed, on his own part, and without the slightest prejudice to his firmness, into a sociable, gossiping phase.

'If she had shown herself, we should hear the reception, the applause.'

'Well, there they air; they are going to give it to her,' the policeman announced.

He had an odious appearance of being in the right, for there indeed they seemed to be—they were giving it to her.

A general hubbub rose from the floor and the galleries of the hall—the sound of several thousand people stamping with their feet and rapping with their umbrellas and sticks. Ransom felt faint, and for a little while he stood with his gaze interlocked with that of the policeman. Then suddenly a wave of coolness seemed to break over him, and he exclaimed: 'My dear fellow, that isn't applause—it's impatience. It isn't a reception, it's a call!'

The policeman neither assented to this proposition nor denied it; he only transferred the protuberance in his cheek to the other side, and observed:

'I guess she's sick.'

'Oh, I hope not!' said Ransom, very gently. The stamping and rapping swelled and swelled for a minute, and then it subsided; but before it had done so Ransom's definition of it had plainly become the true one. The tone of the manifestation was good-humoured, but it was not gratulatory. He looked at his watch again, and saw that five minutes more had elapsed, and he remembered what the newspaper-man in Charles Street had said about Olive's guaranteeing Verena's punctuality. Oddly enough, at the moment the image of this gentleman recurred to him, the gentleman himself burst through the other door, in a state of the liveliest agitation.

'Why in the name of goodness don't she go on? If she wants to make them call her, they've done it about enough!' Mr. Pardon turned, pressingly, from Ransom to the policeman and back again, and in his preoccupation gave no sign of having met the Mississippian before.

'I guess she's sick,' said the policeman.

'The public'll be sick!' cried the distressed reporter. 'If she's sick, why doesn't she send for a doctor? All Boston is packed into this house, and she has got to talk to it. I want to go in and see.'

'You can't go in,' said the policeman, drily.

'Why can't I go in, I should like to know? I want to go in for the "Vesper"!'

'You can't go in for anything. I'm keeping this man out, too,' the policeman added genially, as if to make Mr. Pardon's exclusion appear less invidious.

'Why, they'd ought to let *you* in,' said Matthias, staring a moment at Ransom.

'May be they'd ought, but they won't,' the policeman remarked.

'Gracious me!' panted Mr. Pardon; 'I knew from the first Miss Chancellor would make a mess of it! Where's Mr. Filer?' he went on, eagerly, addressing himself apparently to either of the others, or to both.

'I guess he's at the door, counting the money,' said the policeman.

'Well, he'll have to give it back if he don't look out!'

'Maybe he will. I'll let *him* in if he comes, but he's the only one. She is on now,' the policeman added, without emotion.

His ear had caught the first faint murmur of another explosion of sound. This time, unmistakably, it was applause—the clapping of multitudinous hands, mingled with the noise of many throats. The demonstration, however, though considerable, was not what might have been expected, and it died away quickly. Mr. Pardon stood listening, with an expression of some alarm. 'Merciful fathers! can't they give her more than that?' he cried. 'I'll just fly round and see!'

When he had hurried away again, Ransom said to the policeman—'Who is Mr. Filer?'

'Oh, he's an old friend of mine. He's the man that runs Miss Chancellor.'

'That runs her?'

'Just the same as she runs Miss Tarrant. He runs the pair, as you might say. He's in the lecture-business.'

'Then he had better talk to the public himself.'

'Oh, *he* can't talk; he can only boss!'

The opposite door at this moment was pushed open again, and a large, heated-looking man, with a little stiff beard on the end of his chin and his overcoat flying behind him, strode forward with an imprecation. 'What the h—— are they doing in the parlour? This sort of thing's about played out!'

'Ain't she up there now?' the policeman asked.

'It's not Miss Tarrant,' Ransom said, as if he knew all about it. He perceived in a moment that this was Mr. Filer, Olive Chancellor's agent; an inference instantly followed by the reflection that such a personage would have been warned against him by his kinswoman and would doubtless attempt to hold him, or his influence, accountable for Verena's unexpected delay. Mr. Filer only glanced at him, however, and to Ransom's surprise appeared to have no theory of his identity; a fact implying that Miss Chancellor had considered that the greater discretion was (except to the policeman) to hold her tongue about him altogether.

'Up there? It's her jackass of a father that's up there!' cried Mr. Filer, with his hand on the latch of the door, which the policeman had allowed him to approach.

'Is he asking for a doctor?' the latter inquired, dispassionately.

'You're the sort of doctor he'll want, if he doesn't produce the girl! You don't mean to say they've locked themselves in? What the plague are they after?'

'They've got the key on that side,' said the policeman, while Mr. Filer discharged at the door a volley of sharp knocks, at the same time violently shaking the handle.

'If the door was locked, what was the good of your standing before it?' Ransom inquired.

'So as you couldn't do that;' and the policeman nodded at Mr. Filer.

'You see your interference has done very little good.'

'I dunno; she has got to come out yet.'

Mr. Filer meanwhile had continued to thump and shake, demanding instant admission and inquiring if they were going to let the audience pull the house down. Another round of applause had broken out, directed perceptibly to some apology, some solemn circumlocution, of Selah Tarrant's; this covered the sound of the agent's voice, as well as that of a confused and divided response, proceeding from the parlour. For a minute nothing definite was audible; the door remained closed, and Matthias Pardon reappeared in the vestibule.

'He says she's just a little faint—from nervousness. She'll be all ready in about three minutes.' This announcement was Mr. Pardon's contribution to the crisis; and he added that the crowd was a lovely crowd, it was a real Boston crowd, it was perfectly good-humoured.

'There's a lovely crowd, and a real Boston one too, I guess, in here!' cried Mr. Filer, now banging very hard. 'I've handled prima donnas, and I've handled natural curiosities, but I've never seen anything up to this. Mind what I say, ladies; if you don't let me in, I'll smash down the door!'

'Don't seem as if *you* could make it much worse, does it?' the policeman observed to Ransom, strolling aside a little, with the air of being superseded.

XLII

Ransom made no reply; he was watching the door, which at that moment gave way from within. Verena stood there—it was she, evidently, who had opened it—and her eyes went straight to his. She was dressed in white, and her face was whiter than her garment; above it her hair seemed to shine like fire. She took a step forward; but before she could take another he had come down to her, on the threshold of the room. Her face was full of suffering, and he did not attempt—before all those eyes—to take her hand; he only said in a low tone, 'I have been waiting for you—a long time!'

'I know it—I saw you in your seat—I want to speak to you.'

'Well, Miss Tarrant, don't you think you'd better be on the platform?' cried Mr. Filer, making with both his arms a movement as if to sweep her before him, through the waiting-room, up into the presence of the public.

'In a moment I shall be ready. My father is making that all right.' And, to Ransom's surprise, she smiled, with all her sweetness, at the irrepressible agent; appeared to wish genuinely to reassure him.

The three had moved together into the waiting-room, and there at the farther end of it, beyond the vulgar, perfunctory chairs and tables, under the flaring gas, he saw Mrs. Tarrant sitting upright on a sofa, with immense rigidity, and a large flushed visage, full of suppressed distortion, and beside her prostrate, fallen over, her head buried in the lap of Verena's mother, the tragic figure of Olive Chancellor. Ransom could scarcely know how much Olive's having flung herself upon Mrs. Tarrant's bosom testified to the convulsive scene that had just taken place behind the locked door. He closed it again, sharply, in the face of the reporter and the policeman, and at the same moment Selah Tarrant descended, through the aperture leading to the platform, from his brief communion with the public. On seeing Ransom he stopped short, and, gathering his waterproof about him, measured the young man from head to foot.

'Well, sir, perhaps *you* would like to go and explain our hitch,' he remarked, indulging in a smile so comprehensive that the corners of his mouth seemed almost to meet behind. 'I presume that you, better than any one else, can give them an insight into our difficulties!'

'Father, be still; father, it will come out all right in a moment!' cried Verena, below her breath, panting like an emergent diver.

'There's one thing I want to know: are we going to spend half an hour talking over our domestic affairs?' Mr. Filer demanded, wiping his indignant countenance. 'Is Miss Tarrant going to lecture, or ain't she going to lecture? If she ain't, she'll please to show cause why. Is she aware that every quarter of a second, at the present instant, is worth about five hundred dollars?'

'I know that—I know that, Mr. Filer; I will begin in a moment!' Verena went on. 'I only want to speak to Mr. Ransom—just three words. They are perfectly quiet—don't you see how quiet they are? They trust me, they trust me, don't they, father? I only want to speak to Mr. Ransom.'

'Who the devil is Mr. Ransom?' cried the exasperated, bewildered Filer.

Verena spoke to the others, but she looked at her lover, and the expression of her eyes was ineffably touching and beseeching. She trembled with nervous passion, there were sobs and supplications in her voice, and Ransom felt himself flushing with pure pity for her pain—her inevitable agony. But at the same moment he had another perception, which brushed aside remorse; he saw that he could do what he wanted, that she begged him, with all her being, to spare her, but that so long as he should protest she was submissive, helpless. What he wanted, in this light, flamed before him and challenged all his manhood, tossing his determination to a height from which not only Doctor Tarrant, and Mr. Filer, and Olive, over there, in her sightless, soundless shame, but the great expectant hall as well, and the mighty multitude, in suspense, keeping quiet from minute to minute and holding the breath of its anger—from which all these things looked small, surmountable, and of the moment only. He didn't quite understand, as yet, however; he saw that Verena had not refused, but temporised, that the spell upon her—thanks to which he should still be able to rescue her—had been the knowledge that he was near.

'Come away, come away,' he murmured, quickly, putting out his two hands to her.

She took one of them, as if to plead, not to consent. 'Oh, let me off, let me off—for *her*, for the others! It's too terrible, it's impossible!'

'What I want to know is why Mr. Ransom isn't in the hands of the police!' wailed Mrs. Tarrant, from her sofa.

'I have been, madam, for the last quarter of an hour.' Ransom felt more and more that he could manage it, if he only kept cool. He bent over Verena with a tenderness in which he was careless, now, of observation. 'Dearest, I told you, I warned you. I left you alone for ten weeks; but could that make you doubt it was coming? Not for worlds, not for millions, shall you give yourself to that roaring crowd. Don't ask me to care for them, or for any one! What do they care for you but to gape and grin and babble? You are mine, you are not theirs.'

'What under the sun is the man talking about? With the most magnificent audience ever brought together! The city of Boston is under this roof!' Mr. Filer gaspingly interposed.

'The city of Boston be damned!' said Ransom.

'Mr. Ransom is very much interested in my daughter. He doesn't approve of our views,' Selah Tarrant explained.

'It's the most horrible, wicked, immoral selfishness I ever heard in my life!' roared Mrs. Tarrant.

'Selfishness! Mrs. Tarrant, do you suppose I pretend not to be selfish?'

'Do you want us all murdered by the mob, then?'

'They can have their money—can't you give them back their money?' cried Verena, turning frantically round the circle.

'Verena Tarrant, you don't mean to say you are going to back down?' her mother shrieked.

'Good God! that I should make her suffer like this!' said Ransom to himself; and to put an end to the odious scene he would have seized Verena in his arms and broken away into the outer world, if Olive, who at Mrs. Tarrant's last loud challenge had sprung to her feet, had not at the same time thrown herself between them with a force which made the girl relinquish her grasp of Ransom's hand. To his astonishment, the eyes that looked at him out of her scared, haggard face were, like Verena's, eyes of tremendous entreaty. There was a moment during which she would have been ready to go down on her knees to him, in order that the lecture should go on.

'If you don't agree with her, take her up on the platform, and have it out there; the public would like that, first-rate!' Mr. Filer said to Ransom, as if he thought this suggestion practical.

'She had prepared a lovely address!' Selah remarked, mournfully, as if to the company in general.

No one appeared to heed the observation, but his wife broke out again. 'Verena Tarrant, I should like to slap you! Do you call such a man as that a gentleman? I don't know where your father's spirit is, to let him stay!'

Olive, meanwhile, was literally praying to her kinsman. 'Let her appear this once, just this once: not to ruin, not to shame! Haven't you any pity; do you want me to be hooted? It's only for an hour. Haven't you any soul?'

Her face and voice were terrible to Ransom; she had flung herself upon Verena and was holding her close, and he could see that her friend's suffering was faint in comparison to her own. 'Why for an hour, when it's all false and damnable? An hour is as bad as ten years! She's mine or she isn't, and if she's mine, she's all mine!'

'Yours! Yours! Verena, think, think what you're doing!' Olive moaned, bending over her.

Mr. Filer was now pouring forth his nature in objurgations and oaths, and brandishing before the culprits—Verena and Ransom—the extreme penalty of the law. Mrs. Tarrant had burst into violent hysterics, while Selah revolved vaguely about the room and declared that it seemed as if the better day was going to be put off for quite a while. 'Don't you see how good, how sweet they are—giving us all this time? Don't you think that when they behave like that—without a sound, for five minutes—they ought to be rewarded?' Verena asked, smiling divinely, at Ransom. Nothing could have been more tender, more exquisite, than the way she put her appeal upon the ground of simple charity, kindness to the great good-natured, childish public.

'Miss Chancellor may reward them in any way she likes. Give them back their money and a little present to each.'

'Money and presents? I should like to shoot you, sir!' yelled Mr. Filer. The audience had really been very patient, and up to this point deserved Verena's praise; but it was now long past eight o'clock, and symptoms of irritation—cries and groans and hisses—began again to proceed from the hall. Mr. Filer launched himself into the passage leading to the stage, and Selah rushed after him. Mrs. Tarrant extended herself, sobbing, on the sofa, and Olive, quivering in the storm, inquired of Ransom what he wanted her to do, what humiliation, what degradation, what sacrifice he imposed.

'I'll do anything—I'll be abject—I'll be vile—I'll go down in the dust!'

'I ask nothing of you, and I have nothing to do with you,' Ransom said. 'That is, I ask, at the most, that you shouldn't expect that, wishing to make Verena my wife, I should say to her, "Oh yes, you can take an hour or two out of it!" Verena,' he went on, 'all this is out of it—dreadfully, odiously—and it's a great deal too much! Come, come as far away from here as possible, and we'll settle the rest!'

The combined effort of Mr. Filer and Selah Tarrant to pacify the public had not, apparently, the success it deserved; the house continued in uproar and the volume of sound increased. 'Leave us alone, leave us alone for a single minute!' cried Verena; 'just let me speak to him, and it will be all right!' She rushed over to her mother, drew her, dragged her from the sofa, led her to the door of the room. Mrs. Tarrant, on the way, reunited herself with Olive (the horror of the situation had at least that compensation for her), and, clinging and staggering together, the distracted women, pushed by Verena, passed into the vestibule, now, as Ransom saw, deserted by the policeman and the reporter, who had rushed round to where the battle was thickest.

'Oh, why did you come—why, why?' And Verena, turning back, threw herself upon him with a protest which was all, and more than all, a surrender. She had never yet given herself to him so much as in that movement of reproach.

'Didn't you expect me, and weren't you sure?' he asked, smiling at her and standing there till she arrived.

'I didn't know—it was terrible—it's awful! I saw you in your place, in the house, when you came. As soon as we got here I went out to those steps that go up to the stage and I looked out, with my father—from behind him—and saw you in a minute. Then I felt too nervous to speak! I could never, never, if you were there! My father didn't know you, and I said nothing, but Olive guessed as soon as I came back. She rushed at me, and she looked at me—oh, how she looked! and she guessed. She didn't need to go out to see for herself, and when she saw how I was trembling she began to tremble herself, to believe, as I believed, we were lost. Listen to them, listen to them, in the house! Now I want you to go away—I will see you to-morrow, as long as you wish. That's all I want now; if you will only go away it's not too late, and everything will be all right!'

Preoccupied as Ransom was with the simple purpose of getting her bodily out of the place, he could yet notice her strange, touching tone, and her air of believing that she might really persuade him. She had evidently given up everything now—every pretence of a different conviction and of loyalty to her cause; all this had fallen from her as soon as she felt him near, and she asked him to go away just as any plighted maiden might have asked any favour of her lover. But it was the poor girl's misfortune that, whatever she did or said, or left unsaid, only had the effect of making her dearer to him and making the people who were clamouring for her seem more and more a raving rabble.

He indulged not in the smallest recognition of her request, and simply said, 'Surely Olive must have believed, must have known, I would come.'

'She would have been sure if you hadn't become so unexpectedly quiet after I left Marmion. You seemed to concur, to be willing to wait.'

'So I was, for a few weeks. But they ended yesterday. I was furious that morning, when I learned your flight, and during the week that followed I made two or three attempts to find you. Then I stopped—I thought it better. I saw you were very well hidden; I determined not even to write. I felt I *could* wait—with that last day at Marmion to think of. Besides, to leave you with her awhile, for the last, seemed more decent. Perhaps you'll tell me now where you were.'

'I was with father and mother. She sent me to them that morning, with a letter. I don't know what was in it. Perhaps there was money,' said Verena, who evidently now would tell him everything.

'And where did they take you?'

'I don't know—to places. I was in Boston once, for a day; but only in a carriage. They were as frightened as Olive; they were bound to save me!'

'They shouldn't have brought you here to-night then. How could you possibly doubt of my coming?'

'I don't know what I thought, and I didn't know, till I saw you, that all the strength I had hoped for would leave me in a flash, and that if I attempted to speak—with you sitting there—I should make the most shameful failure. We had a sickening scene here—I begged for delay, for time to recover. We waited and waited, and when I heard you at the door talking to the policeman, it seemed to me everything was gone. But it will still come back, if you will leave me. They are quiet again—father must be interesting them.'

'I hope he is!' Ransom exclaimed. 'If Miss Chancellor ordered the policeman, she must have expected me.'

'That was only after she knew you were in the house. She flew out into the lobby with father, and they seized him and posted him there. She locked the door; she seemed to think they would break it down. I didn't wait for that, but from the moment I knew you were on the other side of it I couldn't go on—I was paralysed. It has made me feel better to talk to you—and now I could appear,' Verena added.

'My darling child, haven't you a shawl or a mantle?' Ransom returned, for all answer, looking about him. He perceived, tossed upon a chair, a long, furred cloak, which he caught up, and, before she could resist, threw over her. She even let him arrange it and, standing there, draped from head to foot in it, contented herself with saying, after a moment:

'I don't understand—where shall we go? Where will you take me?'

'We shall catch the night-train for New York, and the first thing in the morning we shall be married.'

Verena remained gazing at him, with swimming eyes. 'And what will the people do? Listen, listen!'

'Your father is ceasing to interest them. They'll howl and thump, according to their nature.'

'Ah, their nature's fine!' Verena pleaded.

'Dearest, that's one of the fallacies I shall have to woo you from. Hear them, the senseless brutes!' The storm was now raging in the hall, and it deepened to such a point that Verena turned to him in a supreme appeal.

'I could soothe them with a word!'

'Keep your soothing words for me—you will have need of them all, in our coming time,' Ransom said, laughing. He pulled open the door again, which led into the lobby, but he was driven back, with Verena, by a furious onset from Mrs. Tarrant. Seeing her daughter fairly arrayed for departure, she hurled herself upon her, half in indignation, half in a blind impulse to cling, and with an outpouring of tears, reproaches, prayers, strange scraps of argument and iterations of farewell, closed her about with an embrace which was partly a supreme caress, partly the salutary castigation she had, three minutes before, expressed the wish to administer, and altogether for the moment a check upon the girl's flight.

'Mother, dearest, it's all for the best, I can't help it, I love you just the same; let me go, let me go!' Verena stammered, kissing her again, struggling to free herself, and holding out her hand to Ransom. He saw now that she only wanted to get away, to leave everything behind her. Olive was close at hand, on the threshold of the room, and as soon as Ransom looked at her he became aware that the weakness she had just shown had passed away. She had straightened herself again, and she was upright in her desolation. The expression of her face was a thing to remain with him for ever; it was impossible to imagine a more vivid presentment of blighted hope and wounded pride. Dry, desperate, rigid, she yet wavered and seemed uncertain; her pale, glittering eyes straining forward, as if they were looking for death. Ransom had a vision, even at that crowded moment, that if she could have met it there and then, bristling with steel or lurid with fire, she would have rushed on it without a tremor, like the heroine that she was. All this while the great agitation in the hall rose and fell, in waves and surges, as if Selah Tarrant and the agent were talking to the multitude, trying to calm them, succeeding for the moment, and then letting them loose again. Whirled down by one of the fitful gusts, a lady and a gentleman issued from the passage, and Ransom, glancing at them, recognised Mrs. Farrinder and her husband.

'Well, Miss Chancellor,' said that more successful woman, with considerable asperity, 'if this is the way you're going to reinstate our sex!' She passed rapidly through the room, followed by Amariah, who remarked in his transit that it seemed as if there had been a want of organisation, and the two retreated expeditiously, without the lady's having taken the smallest notice of Verena, whose conflict with her mother prolonged itself. Ransom, striving, with all needful consideration for Mrs. Tarrant, to separate these two, addressed not a word to Olive; it was the last of her, for him, and he neither saw how her livid face suddenly glowed, as if Mrs. Farrinder's words had been a lash, nor how, as if with a sudden inspiration, she rushed to the approach to the platform. If he had observed her, it might have seemed to him that she hoped to find the fierce expiation she sought for in exposure to the thousands she had disappointed and deceived, in offering herself to be trampled to death and torn to pieces. She might have suggested to him some feminine firebrand of Paris revolutions, erect on a barricade, or even the sacrificial figure of Hypatia, whirled through the furious mob of Alexandria. She was arrested an instant by the arrival of Mrs. Burrage and her son, who had quitted the stage on observing the withdrawal of the Farrinders, and who swept into the room in the manner of people seeking shelter from a thunder-storm. The mother's face expressed the well-bred surprise of a person who should have been asked out to dinner and seen the cloth pulled off the table; the young man, who supported her on his arm, instantly lost himself in the spectacle of Verena disengaging herself from Mrs. Tarrant, only to be again overwhelmed, and in the unexpected presence of the

Mississippian. His handsome blue eyes turned from one to the other, and he looked infinitely annoyed and bewildered. It even seemed to occur to him that he might, perhaps, interpose with effect, and he evidently would have liked to say that, without really bragging, *he* would at least have kept the affair from turning into a row. But Verena, muffled and escaping, was deaf to him, and Ransom didn't look the right person to address such a remark as that to. Mrs. Burrage and Olive, as the latter shot past, exchanged a glance which represented quick irony on one side and indiscriminating defiance on the other.

'Oh, are *you* going to speak?' the lady from New York inquired, with her cursory laugh.

Olive had already disappeared; but Ransom heard her answer flung behind her into the room. 'I am going to be hissed and hooted and insulted!'

'Olive, Olive!' Verena suddenly shrieked; and her piercing cry might have reached the front. But Ransom had already, by muscular force, wrenched her away, and was hurrying her out, leaving Mrs. Tarrant to heave herself into the arms of Mrs. Burrage, who, he was sure, would, within the minute, loom upon her attractively through her tears, and supply her with a reminiscence, destined to be valuable, of aristocratic support and clever composure. In the outer labyrinth hasty groups, a little scared, were leaving the hall, giving up the game. Ransom, as he went, thrust the hood of Verena's long cloak over her head, to conceal her face and her identity. It quite prevented recognition, and as they mingled in the issuing crowd he perceived the quick, complete, tremendous silence which, in the hall, had greeted Olive Chancellor's rush to the front. Every sound instantly dropped, the hush was respectful, the great public waited, and whatever she should say to them (and he thought she might indeed be rather embarrassed), it was not apparent that they were likely to hurl the benches at her. Ransom, palpitating with his victory, felt now a little sorry for her, and was relieved to know, that, even when exasperated, a Boston audience is not ungenerous. 'Ah, now I am glad!' said Verena, when they reached the street. But though she was glad, he presently discovered that, beneath her hood, she was in tears. It is to be feared that with the union, so far from brilliant, into which she was about to enter, these were not the last she was destined to shed.

Chronology

1843 Born April 15 at 21 Washington Place, New York City, the second child (after William, born January 11, 1842, N.Y.C.) of Henry James of Albany and Mary Robertson Walsh of New York. Father lives on inheritance of $10,000 a year, his share of litigated $3,000,000 fortune of his Albany father William James, an Irish immigrant who came to the U.S. immediately after the Revolution.

1843–45 Accompanied by mother's sister, Catharine Walsh, and servants, the James parents take infant children to England and later to France. Reside at Windsor, where father has nervous collapse ("vastation") and experiences spiritual illumination. He becomes a Swedenborgian (May 1844), devoting his time to lecturing and religious-philosophical writings. James later claimed his earliest memory was a glimpse, during his second year, of the Place Vendôme in Paris with its Napoleonic column.

1845–47 Family returns to New York. Garth Wilkinson · James (Wilky) born July 21, 1845. Family moves to Albany at 50 N. Pearl St., a few doors from grandmother Catharine Barber James. Robertson James (Bob or Rob) born August 29, 1846.

1847–55 Family moves to a large house at 58 W. 14th St., New York. Alice James born August 7, 1848. Relatives and father's friends and acquaintances—Horace Greeley, George Ripley, Charles Anderson Dana, William Cullen Bryant, Bronson Alcott, and Ralph Waldo Emerson ("I knew he was great, greater than any of our friends")—are frequent visitors. Thackeray calls during his lecture tour on the English humorists. Summers at New Brighton on Staten Island and Fort Hamilton on Long Island's south shore. On steamboat to Fort Hamilton August 1850, hears Washington Irving tell his father of Margaret Fuller's drowning in shipwreck off Fire Island. Frequently visits Barnum's American Museum on free days. Taken to art shows and theaters; writes and draws stage scenes. Described by father as "a devourer of libraries." Taught in assorted private schools and by tutors in lower Broadway and Greenwich Village. But father claims in 1848 that American schooling fails to provide "sensuous education" for his children and plans to take them to Europe.

1855–58   Family (with Aunt Kate) sails for Liverpool, June 27. James is intermittently sick with malarial fever as they travel to Paris, Lyon, and Geneva. After Swiss summer, leaves for London where Robert Thomson (later Robert Louis Stevenson's tutor) is engaged. Early summer 1856, family moves to Paris. Another tutor engaged and children attend experimental Fourierist school. Acquires fluency in French. Family goes to Boulogne-sur-mer in summer, where James contracts typhoid. Spends late October in Paris, but American crash of 1857 returns family to Boulogne where they can live more cheaply. Attends public school (fellow classmate is Coquelin, the future French actor).

1858–59   Family returns to America and settles in Newport, Rhode Island. Goes boating, fishing, and riding. Attends Reverend W. C. Leverett's Berkeley Institute, and forms friendship with classmate Thomas Sergeant Perry. Takes long walks and sketches with the painter John La Farge.

1859–60   Father, still dissatisfied with American education, returns family to Geneva in October. James attends a pre-engineering school, Institution Rochette, because parents, with "a flattering misconception of my aptitudes," feel he might benefit from less reading and more mathematics. After a few months withdraws from all classes except French, German, and Latin, and joins William as a special student at the Academy (later the University of Geneva) where he attends lectures on literary subjects. Studies German in Bonn during summer 1860.

1860–62   Family returns to Newport in September where William studies with William Morris Hunt, and James sits in on his classes. La Farge introduces him to works of Balzac, Merimée, Musset, and Browning. Wilky and Bob attend Frank Sanborn's experimental school in Concord with children of Hawthorne and Emerson and John Brown's daughter. Early in 1861, orphaned Temple cousins come to live in Newport. Develops close friendship with cousin

Mary (Minnie) Temple. Goes on a week's walking tour in July in New Hampshire with Perry. William abandons art in autumn 1861 and enters Lawrence Scientific School at Harvard. James suffers back injury in a stable fire while serving as a volunteer fireman. Reads Hawthorne ("an American could be an artist, one of the finest").

1862–63   Enters Harvard Law School (Dane Hall). Wilky enlists in the Massachusetts 44th Regiment, and later in Colonel Robert Gould Shaw's 54th, the first black regiment. Summer 1863, Bob joins the Massachusetts 55th, another black regiment, under Colonel Hollowell. James withdraws from law studies to try writing. Sends unsigned stories to magazines. Wilky is badly wounded and brought home to Newport in August.

1864   Family moves from Newport to 13 Ashburton Place, Boston. First tale, "A Tragedy of Error" (unsigned), published in *Continental Monthly* (Feb. 1864). Stays in Northampton, Massachusetts, early August–November. Begins writing book reviews for *North American Review* and forms friendship with its editor, Charles Eliot Norton, and his family, including his sister Grace (with whom he maintains a long-lasting correspondence). Wilky returns to his regiment.

1865   First signed tale, "The Story of a Year," published in *Atlantic Monthly* (March 1865). Begins to write reviews for the newly founded *Nation* and publishes anonymously in it during next fifteen years. William sails on a scientific expedition with Louis Agassiz to the Amazon. During summer James vacations in the White Mountains with Minnie Temple and her family; joined by Oliver Wendell Holmes Jr. and John Chipman Gray, both recently demobilized. Father subsidizes plantation for Wilky and Bob in Florida with black hired workers. The idealistic but impractical venture fails in 1870.

1866–68   Continues to publish reviews and tales in Boston and New York journals. William returns from Brazil and resumes medical education. James has recurrence of back ailment and spends summer in Swampscott, Massachusetts. Begins friendship with William Dean Howells. Family moves to 20 Quincy St., Cambridge. William, suffering from nervous ailments, goes to Germany in spring 1867. "Poor Richard," James's longest story to date, published in *Atlantic Monthly* (June–Aug. 1867). William begins intermittent criticism of Henry's story-telling and style (which will continue throughout their careers). Momentary meeting with Charles Dickens at Norton's house. Vacations in Jefferson, New Hampshire, summer 1868. William returns from Europe.

1869–70   Sails in February for European tour. Visits English towns and cathedrals. Through Nortons meets Leslie Stephen, William Morris, Dante Gabriel Rossetti, Edward Burne-Jones, John Ruskin, Charles Darwin, and George Eliot (the "one marvel" of his stay in London). Goes to Paris in May, then travels in Switzerland in summer and hikes into Italy in autumn, where he stays in Milan, Venice (Sept.), Florence, and Rome (Oct. 30–Dec. 28). Returns to England to drink the waters at Malvern health spa in Worcestershire because of digestive troubles. Stays in Paris en route and has first experience of Comédie Française. Learns that his beloved cousin, Minnie Temple, has died of tuberculosis.

1870–72   Returns to Cambridge in May. Travels to Rhode Island, Vermont, and New York to write travel sketches for *The Nation*. Spends a few days with Emerson in Concord. Meets Bret Harte at Howells' home April 1871. *Watch and Ward*, his first novel, published in *Atlantic Monthly* (Aug.–Dec. 1871). Serves as occasional art reviewer for the *Atlantic* January–March 1872.

1872–74   Accompanies Aunt Kate and sister Alice on tour of England, France, Switzerland, Italy, Austria, and Germany from May through October. Writes travel sketches for *The Nation*. Spends autumn in Paris, becoming friends with James Russell Lowell. Escorts Emerson through the Louvre. (Later, on Emerson's return from Egypt, will show him the Vatican.) Goes to Florence in December and from there to Rome, where he becomes friends with actress Fanny Kemble, her daughter Sarah Butler Wister, and William Wetmore Story and his family. In Italy sees old family friend Francis Boott and his daughter Elizabeth (Lizzie), expatriates who have lived for many years in Florentine villa on Bellosguardo. Takes up horseback riding on the Campagna. Encounters Matthew Arnold in April 1873 at Story's. Moves from Rome hotel to rooms of his own. Continues writing and now earns enough to support himself. Leaves Rome in June, spends summer in Bad Homburg. In October goes to Florence, where William joins him. They also visit Rome, William returning to America in March. In Baden-Baden June–August and returns to America September 4, with *Roderick Hudson* all but finished.

1875   *Roderick Hudson* serialized in *Atlantic Monthly* from January (published by Osgood at the end of the year). First book, *A Passionate Pilgrim and Other Tales*, published January 31. Tries living and writing in New York, in rooms at 111 E. 25th Street. Earns $200 a month from novel installments and continued reviewing, but finds New York too expensive. *Transatlantic Sketches*, published in April, sells almost 1,000 copies in three months. In Cambridge in July decides to return to Europe; arranges with John Hay, assistant to the publisher, to write Paris letters for the New York *Tribune*.

1875–76   Arriving in Paris in November, he takes rooms at 29 Rue de Luxembourg (since renamed Cambon). Becomes friend of Ivan Turgenev and is introduced by him to Gustave Flaubert's Sunday parties. Meets Edmond de Goncourt, Émile Zola, G. Charpentier (the publisher), Catulle Mendès, Alphonse Daudet, Guy de Maupassant, Ernest Renan, Gustave Doré. Makes friends with Charles Sanders Peirce, who is in Paris. Reviews (unfavorably) the early Impressionists at the Durand-Ruel gallery. By midsummer has received $400 for *Tribune* pieces, but editor asks for more Parisian gossip and James resigns. Travels in France during July, visiting Normandy and the Midi, and in September crosses to San Sebastian, Spain, to see a bullfight ("I thought the bull, in any case, a finer fellow than any of his tormentors"). Moves to London in December, taking rooms at 3 Bolton Street, Piccadilly, where he will live for the next decade.

1877   *The American* published. Meets Robert Browning and George du Maurier. Leaves London in midsummer for visit to Paris and then goes to Italy. In Rome rides again in Campagna and hears of an episode that inspires "Daisy

Miller." Back in England, spends Christmas at Stratford with Fanny Kemble.

1878   Publishes first book in England, *French Poets and Novelists* (by Macmillan). Appearance of "Daisy Miller" in *Cornhill Magazine*, edited by Leslie Stephen, is international success, but by publishing it abroad loses American copyright and story is pirated in U.S. *Cornhill* also prints "An International Episode." *The Europeans* is serialized in *Atlantic*. Now a celebrity, he dines out often, visits country houses, gains weight, takes long walks, fences, and does weightlifting to reduce. Elected to Reform Club. Meets Tennyson, George Meredith, and James McNeill Whistler. William marries Alice Howe Gibbens.

1879   Immersed in London society (". . . dined out during the past winter 107 times!"). Meets Edmund Gosse and Robert Louis Stevenson, who will later become his close friends. Sees much of Henry Adams and his wife, Marian (Clover), in London and later in Paris. Takes rooms in Paris, September–December. *Confidence* is serialized in *Scribner's* and published by Chatto & Windus. *Hawthorne* appears in Macmillan's "English Men of Letters" series.

1880–81   Stays in Florence March–May to work on *The Portrait of a Lady*. Meets Constance Fenimore Woolson, American novelist and grandniece of James Fenimore Cooper. Returns to Bolton Street in June, where William visits him. *Washington Square* serialized in *Cornhill Magazine* and published in U.S. by Harper & Brothers (Dec. 1880). *The Portrait of a Lady* serialized in *Macmillan's Magazine* (Oct. 1880–Nov. 1881) and *Atlantic Monthly*; published by Macmillan and Houghton, Mifflin (Nov. 1881). Publication both in United States and in England yields him the then-large income of $500 a month, though book sales are disappointing. Leaves London in February for Paris, the south of France, the Italian Riviera, and Venice, and returns home in July. Sister Alice comes to London with her friend Katharine Loring. James goes to Scotland in September.

1881–83   In November revisits America after absence of six years. Lionized in New York. Returns to Quincy Street for Christmas and sees ailing brother Wilky for the first time in ten years. In January visits Washington and the Henry Adamses and meets President Chester A. Arthur. Summoned to Cambridge by mother's death January 29 ("the sweetest, gentlest, most beneficent human being I have ever known"). All four brothers are together for the first time in fifteen years at her funeral. Alice and father move from Cambridge to Boston. Prepares a stage version of "Daisy Miller" and returns to England in May. William, now a Harvard professor, comes to Europe in September. Proposed by Leslie Stephen, James becomes member, without the usual red tape, of the Atheneum Club. Travels in France in October to write *A Little Tour in France* (published 1884) and has last visit with Turgenev, who is dying. Returns to England in December and learns of father's illness. Sails for America but Henry James Sr. dies December 18, 1882, before his arrival. Made executor of father's will. Visits brothers Wilky and Bob in Milwaukee in January. Quarrels with William over division of property—James wants to restore Wilky's share. Macmillan publishes a collected pocket edition of James's novels and tales in fourteen volumes. *Siege of London* and *Portraits of Places* published. Returns to Bolton Street in September. Wilky dies in November. Constance Fenimore Woolson comes to London for the winter.

1884–86   Goes to Paris in February and visits Daudet, Zola, and Goncourt. Again impressed with their intense concern with "art, form, manner" but calls them "mandarins." Misses Turgenev, who had died a few months before. Meets John Singer Sargent and persuades him to settle in London. Returns to Bolton Street. Sargent introduces him to young Paul Bourget. During country visits encounters many British political and social figures, including W. E. Gladstone, John Bright, and Charles Dilke. Alice, suffering from nervous ailment, arrives in England for visit in November but is too ill to travel and settles near her brother. *Tales of Three Cities* ("The Impressions of a Cousin," "Lady Barbarina," "A New England Winter") and "The Art of Fiction" published 1884. Alice goes to Bournemouth in late January. James joins her in May and becomes an intimate of Robert Louis Stevenson, who resides nearby. Spends August at Dover and is visited by Paul Bourget. Stays in Paris for the next two months. Moves into a flat at 34 De Vere Gardens in Kensington early in March 1886. Alice takes rooms in London. *The Bostonians* serialized in *Century* (Feb. 1885–Feb. 1886; published 1886), *Princess Casamassima* serialized in *Atlantic Monthly* (Sept. 1885–Oct. 1886; published 1886).

1886–87　Leaves for Italy in December for extended stay, mainly in Florence and Venice. Sees much of Constance Fenimore Woolson and stays in her villa. Writes "The Aspern Papers" and other tales. Returns to De Vere Gardens in July and begins work on *The Tragic Muse*. Pays several country visits. Dines out less often ("I know it all—all that one sees by 'going out'—today, as if I had made it. But if I had, I would have made it better!").

1888　*The Reverberator*, *The Aspern Papers*, *Louisa Pallant*, *The Modern Warning*, and *Partial Portraits* published. Elizabeth Boott Duveneck dies. Robert Louis Stevenson leaves for the South Seas. Engages fencing teacher to combat "symptoms of a portentous corpulence." Goes abroad in October to Geneva (where he visits Miss Woolson), Genoa, Monte Carlo, and Paris.

1889–90　Catharine Walsh (Aunt Kate) dies March 1889. William comes to England to visit Alice in August. James goes to Dover in September and then to Paris for five weeks. Writes account of Robert Browning's funeral in Westminster Abbey. Dramatizes *The American* for the Compton Comedy Company. Meets and becomes close friends with American journalist William Morton Fullerton and young American publisher Wolcott Balestier. Goes to Italy for the summer, staying in Venice and Florence, and takes a brief walking tour in Tuscany with W. W. Baldwin, an American physician practicing in Florence. Miss Woolson moves to Cheltenham, England, to be near James. *Atlantic Monthly* rejects his story "The Pupil," but it appears in England. Writes series of drawing-room comedies for theater. Meets Rudyard Kipling. *The Tragic Muse* serialized in *Atlantic Monthly* (Jan. 1889–May 1890; published 1890). *A London Life* (including "The Patagonia," "The Liar," "Mrs. Temperly") published 1889.

1891　*The American* produced at Southport has a success during road tour. After residence in Leamington, Alice returns to London, cared for by Katharine Loring. Doctors discover she has breast cancer. James circulates comedies (*Mrs. Vibert*, later called *Tenants*, and *Mrs. Jasper*, later named *Disengaged*) among theater managers who are cool to his work. Unimpressed at first by Ibsen, writes an appreciative review after seeing a performance of *Hedda Gabler* with Elizabeth Robins, a young Kentucky actress; persuades her to take the part of Mme. de Cintré in the London production of *The American*. Recuperates from flu in Ireland. James Russell Lowell dies. *The American* opens in London, September 26, and runs for seventy nights. Wolcott Balestier dies, and James attends his funeral in Dresden in December.

1892   Alice James dies March 6. James travels to Siena to be near the Paul Bourgets, and Venice, June–July, to visit the Daniel Curtises, then to Lausanne to meet William and his family, who have come abroad for sabbatical. Attends funeral of Tennyson at Westminster Abbey. Augustin Daly agrees to produce *Mrs. Jasper*. *The American* continues to be performed on the road by the Compton Company. *The Lesson of the Master* (with a collection of stories including "The Marriages," "The Pupil," "Brooksmith," "The Solution," and "Sir Edmund Orme") published.

1893   Fanny Kemble dies in January. Continues to write unproduced plays. In March goes to Paris for two months. Sends Edward Compton first act and scenario for *Guy Domville*. Meets William and family in Lucerne and stays a month, returning to London in June. Spends July completing *Guy Domville* in Ramsgate. George Alexander, actor-manager, agrees to produce the play. Daly stages first reading of *Mrs. Jasper*, and James withdraws it, calling the rehearsal a mockery. *The Real Thing and Other Tales* (including "The Wheel of Time," "Lord Beaupré," "The Visit") published.

1894   Constance Fenimore Woolson dies in Venice, January. Shocked and upset, James prepares to attend funeral in Rome but changes his mind on learning she is a suicide. Goes to Venice in April to help her family settle her affairs. Receives one of four copies, privately printed by Miss Loring, of Alice's diary. Finds it impressive but is concerned that so much gossip he told Alice in private has been included (later burns his copy). Robert Louis Stevenson dies in the South Pacific. *Guy Domville* goes into rehearsal. *Theatricals: Two Comedies* and *Theatricals: Second Series* published.

1895   *Guy Domville* opens January 5 at St. James's Theatre. At play's end James is greeted by a fifteen-minute roar of boos, catcalls, and applause. Horrified and depressed, abandons the theater. Play earns him $1,300 after five-week run. Feels he can salvage something useful from playwriting for his fiction ("a key that, working in the same *general* way fits the complicated chambers of *both* the dramatic and the narrative lock"). Writes scenario for *The Spoils of Poynton*. Visits Lord Wolseley and Lord Houghton in Ireland. In the summer goes to Torquay in Devonshire and stays until November while electricity is being installed in De Vere Gardens flat. Friendship with W. E. Norris, who resides at Torquay. Writes a one-act play ("Mrs. Gracedew") at request of Ellen Terry. *Terminations* (containing "The Death of the Lion," "The Coxon Fund," "The Middle Years," "The Altar of the Dead") published.

1896–97 Finishes *The Spoils of Poynton* (serialized in *Atlantic Monthly* April–Oct. 1896 as *The Old Things;* published 1897). *Embarrassments* ("The Figure in the Carpet," "Glasses," "The Next Time," "The Way It Came") published. Takes a house on Point Hill, Playden, opposite the old town of Rye, Sussex, August–September. Ford Madox Hueffer (later Ford Madox Ford) visits him. Converts play *The Other House* into novel and works on *What Maisie Knew* (published Sept. 1897). George du Maurier dies early in October. Because of increasing pain in wrist, hires stenographer William MacAlpine in February and then purchases a typewriter; soon begins direct dictation to MacAlpine at the machine. Invites Joseph Conrad to lunch at De Vere Gardens and begins their friendship. Goes to Bournemouth in July. Serves on jury in London before going to Dunwich, Suffolk, to spend time with Temple-Emmet cousins. In late September 1897 signs a twenty-one-year lease for Lamb House in Rye for £70 a year ($350). Takes on extra work to pay for setting up his house—the life of William Wetmore Story ($1,250 advance) and will furnish an "American Letter" for new magazine *Literature* (precursor of *Times Literary Supplement*) for $200 a month. Howells visits.

1898 "The Turn of the Screw" (serialized in *Collier's* Jan.–April; published with "Covering End" under the title *The Two Magics*) proves his most popular work since "Daisy Miller." Sleeps in Lamb House for first time June 28. Soon after is visited by William's son, Henry James Jr. (Harry), followed by a stream of visitors: future Justice Oliver Wendell Holmes, Mrs. J. T. Fields, Sarah Orne Jewett, the Paul Bourgets, the Edward Warrens, the Daniel Curtises, the Edmund Gosses, and Howard Sturgis. His witty friend Jonathan Sturges, a young crippled New Yorker, stays for two months during autumn. *In the Cage* published. Meets neighbors Stephen Crane and H. G. Wells.

1899 Finishes *The Awkward Age* and plans trip to the Continent. Fire in Lamb House delays departure. To Paris in March and then visits the Paul Bourgets at Hyères. Stays with the Curtises in their Venice palazzo, where he meets and becomes friends with Jessie Allen. In Rome meets young American-Norwegian sculptor Hendrik C. Andersen; buys one of his busts. Returns to England in July and Andersen comes for three days in August. William, his wife, Alice, and daughter, Peggy, arrive at Lamb House in October. First meeting of brothers in six years. William now has confirmed heart condition. James B. Pinker becomes literary agent and for first time James's professional relations are systematically organized; he reviews copyrights, finds new publishers, and obtains better prices for work ("the germ of a new career"). Purchases Lamb House for $10,000 with an easy mortgage.

1900 Unhappy at whiteness of beard which he has worn since the Civil War, he shaves if off. Alternates between Rye and London. Works on *The Sacred Fount*. Works on and then sets aside *The Sense of the Past* (never finished). Begins *The Ambassadors*. *The Soft Side*, a collection of twelve tales, published. Niece Peggy comes to Lamb House for Christmas.

1901 Obtains permanent room at the Reform Club for London visits and spends eight weeks in town. Sees funeral of Queen Victoria. Decides to employ a woman typist, Mary Weld, to replace the more expensive overqualified shorthand stenographer, MacAlpine. Completes *The Ambassadors* and begins *The Wings of the Dove*. *The Sacred Fount* published. Has meeting with George Gissing. William James, much improved, returns home after two years in Europe. Young Cambridge admirer Percy Lubbock visits. Discharges his alcoholic servants of sixteen years (the Smiths). Mrs. Paddington is new housekeeper.

1902   In London for the winter but gout and stomach disorder force him home earlier. Finishes *The Wings of the Dove* (published in August). William James Jr. (Billy) visits in October and becomes a favorite nephew. Writes "The Beast in the Jungle" and "The Birthplace."

1903   *The Ambassadors, The Better Sort* (a collection of twelve tales), and *William Wetmore Story and His Friends* published. After another spell in town, returns to Lamb House in May and begins work on *The Golden Bowl*. Meets and establishes close friendship with Dudley Jocelyn Persse, a nephew of Lady Gregory. First meeting with Edith Wharton in December.

1904–05   Completes *The Golden Bowl* (published Nov. 1904). Rents Lamb House for six months, and sails in August for America after twenty years absence. Sees new Manhattan skyline from New Jersey on arrival and stays with Colonel George Harvey, president of Harper's, in Jersey shore house with Mark Twain as fellow guest. Goes to William's country house at Chocorua in the White Mountains, New Hampshire. Re-explores Cambridge, Boston, Salem, Newport, and Concord, where he visits brother Bob. In October stays with Edith Wharton in the Berkshires and motors with her through Massachusetts and New York. Later visits New York, Philadelphia (where he delivers lecture "The Lesson of Balzac"), and then Washington, D.C., as a guest in Henry Adams' house. Meets (and is critical of) President Theodore Roosevelt. Returns to Philadelphia to lecture at Bryn Mawr. Travels to Richmond, Charleston, Jacksonville, Palm Beach, and St. Augustine. Then lectures in St. Louis, Chicago, South Bend, Indianapolis, Los Angeles (with a short vacation at Coronado Beach near San Diego), San Francisco, Portland, and Seattle. Returns to explore New York City ("the terrible town"), May–June. Lectures on "The Question of Our Speech" at Bryn Mawr commencement. Elected to newly founded American Academy of Arts and Letters

(William declines). Returns to England in July; lectures had more than covered expenses of his trip. Begins revision of novels for the New York Edition.

1906–08   Writes "The Jolly Corner" and *The American Scene* (published 1907). Writes 18 prefaces for the New York Edition (twenty-four volumes published 1907–09). Visits Paris and Edith Wharton in spring 1907 and motors with her in Midi. Travels to Italy for the last time, visiting Hendrik Andersen in Rome, and goes on to Florence and Venice. Engages Theodora Bosanquet as his typist in autumn. Again visits Mrs. Wharton in Paris, spring 1908. William comes to England to give a series of lectures at Oxford and receives an honorary Doctor of Science degree. James goes to Edinburgh in March to see a tryout by the Forbes-Robertsons of his play, *The High Bid*, a rewrite in three acts of the one-act play originally written for Ellen Terry (revised earlier as the story "Covering End"). Play gets only five special matinees in London. Shocked by slim royalties from sales of the New York Edition.

1909   Growing acquaintance with young writers and artists of Bloomsbury, including Virginia and Vanessa Stephen and others. Meets and befriends young Hugh Walpole in February. Goes to Cambridge in June as guest of admiring dons and undergraduates and meets John Maynard Keynes. Feels unwell and sees doctors about what he believes may be heart trouble. They reassure him. Late in year burns forty years of his letters and papers at Rye. Suffers severe attacks of gout. *Italian Hours* published.

1910   Very ill in January ("food-loathing") and spends much time in bed. Nephew Harry comes to be with him in February. In March is examined by Sir William Osler, who finds nothing physically wrong. James begins to realize that he has had "a sort of nervous breakdown." William, in spite of now severe heart trouble, and his wife, Alice, come to England to give him support. Brothers and Alice go to Bad Nauheim for cure, then travel to Zurich, Lucerne, and Geneva, where they learn Robertson (Bob) James has died in America of heart attack. James's health begins to improve but William is failing. Sails with William and Alice for America in August. William dies at Chocorua soon after arrival, and James remains with the family for the winter. *The Finer Grain* and *The Outcry* published.

1911 Honorary degree from Harvard in spring. Visits with Howells and Grace Norton. Sails for England July 30. On return to Lamb House, decides he will be too lonely there and starts search for a London flat. Theodora Bosanquet obtains two work rooms adjoining her flat in Chelsea and he begins autobiography, *A Small Boy and Others*. Continues to reside at the Reform Club.

1912 Delivers "The Novel in *The Ring and the Book*," on the 100th anniversary of Browning's birth, to the Royal Society of Literature. Honorary Doctor of Letters from Oxford University June 26. Spends summer at Lamb House. Sees much of Edith Wharton ("the Firebird"), who spends summer in England. (She secretly arranges to have Scribner's put $8,000 into James's account.) Takes 21 Carlyle Mansions, in Cheyne Walk, Chelsea, as London quarters. Writes a long admiring letter for William Dean Howells' seventy-fifth birthday. Meets André Gide. Contracts bad case of shingles and is ill four months, much of the time not able to leave bed.

1913 Moves into Cheyne Walk flat. Two hundred and seventy friends and admirers subscribe for seventieth birthday portrait by Sargent and present also a silver-gilt Charles II porringer and dish ("Golden Bowl"). Sargent turns over his payment to young sculptor Derwent Wood, who does a bust of James. Autobiography *A Small Boy and Others* published. Goes with niece Peggy to Lamb House for the summer.

1914 *Notes of a Son and Brother* published. Works on "The Ivory Tower." Returns to Lamb House in July. Niece Peggy joins him. Horrified by the war ("this crash of our civilisation," "a nightmare from which there is no waking"). In London in September participates in Belgian Relief, visits wounded in St. Bartholomew's and other hospitals; feels less "finished and useless and doddering" and recalls Walt Whitman and his Civil War hospital visits. Accepts chairmanship of American Volunteer Motor Ambulance Corps in France. *Notes on Novelists* (essays on Balzac, Flaubert, Zola) published.

1915–16   Continues work with the wounded and war relief. Has occasional lunches with Prime Minister Asquith and family, and meets Winston Churchill and other war leaders. Discovers that he is considered an alien and has to report to police before going to coastal Rye. Decides to become a British national and asks Asquith to be one of his sponsors. Receives Certificate of Naturalization on July 26. H. G. Wells satirizes him in *Boon* ("leviathan retrieving pebbles") and James, in the correspondence that follows, writes: "Art *makes* life, makes interest, makes importance." Burns more papers and photographs at Lamb House in autumn. Has a stroke December 2 in his flat, followed by another two days later. Develops pneumonia and during delirium gives his last confused dictation (dealing with the Napoleonic legend) to Theodora Bosanquet, who types it on the familiar typewriter. Mrs. William James arrives December 13 to care for him. On New Year's Day, George V confers the Order of Merit. Dies February 28. Funeral services held at the Chelsea Old Church. The body is cremated and the ashes are buried in Cambridge Cemetery family plot.

Note on the Texts

This volume of the novels of Henry James presents the texts of three novels: *Washington Square* (1880), *The Portrait of a Lady* (1881), and *The Bostonians* (1886). All of these novels appeared first in serial form; two of them ran concurrently in England and the United States. Each appeared in book form on both sides of the Atlantic, following the conclusion of the serial appearance by only a few weeks. *The Portrait of a Lady* was later included in the New York Edition of 1907–09.

James's journal entry of February 21, 1879, recounting a story told him the evening before by Fanny Kemble, contains the germ of the story of *Washington Square*. The composition of the novel, however, waited at least until September 1879, when he had finished both *Confidence* and his "little book" on Hawthorne. According to a letter to his father, the novel was finished by March 1880, when he left England for Italy, intending to work on *The Portrait of a Lady*. James arranged, probably as early as July 1879, to have the work serialized in England in *Cornhill Magazine*, edited by Leslie Stephen. For the first time in his career, he also arranged for a simultaneous American serialization. His contract with Harper & Brothers (signed on May 19, 1880) providing for American book publication included a hand-written codicil specifying the appearance of the work in *Harper's New Monthly Magazine*.

Washington Square began in *Cornhill Magazine* in June and ran through six issues, until November 1880. The text was set from manuscript supplied by James; this manuscript is not known to survive. George du Maurier prepared twelve illustrations to accompany the text, but James was not involved with these illustrations and in general disapproved of any illustrations in his novels. Two sets of proofs were provided by *Cornhill Magazine* and proofread by James, who sent one set back to *Cornhill* and one set to *Harper's New Monthly Magazine* in New York, where the novel was serialized from July through December of 1880. Harper & Brothers published its first book edition with a few further corrections on December 1, 1880 (although the title page bears the imprint

1881). This edition reprinted the Du Maurier illustrations from the *Cornhill Magazine*. James supervised the book's publication in England, where it was issued by Macmillan & Co. on January 26, 1881, in two volumes, the second also containing the stories "The Pension Beaurepas" and "A Bundle of Letters." Macmillan & Co. reprinted the novel in August 1881, in one volume, and again in 1889, but James was not involved in the preparation of either of these printings.

All the texts of *Washington Square* therefore derive from the one first published in *Cornhill Magazine*, and all of them show differences in house-style editing. James did, however, make about thirty significant alterations in the periodical text for the Macmillan edition, among them changing "queer corners" to "far-away lands" at 20.10; "talkative guest" to "anecdotical idler" at 39.27; "quiet" to "formally submissive" at 81.4; "sadly" to "wearily" at 107.31; "with her unexploded bomb in her hands" to "primed, to repletion, with her apology, but unable to bring it to light" at 149.31–32; "passion" to "passive grief" at 155.2; "grief" to "misery" at 155.5; and "some solemnity" to "much expression" at 164.9–10. Because of these revisions, the edition by Macmillan & Co. is the best of the available texts and is the one reprinted here.

James wrote to William Dean Howells, editor of the *Atlantic Monthly*, in August 1879 to propose publishing his longer novel, *The Portrait of a Lady*, in the *Atlantic Monthly* simultaneously with its publication in England in *Macmillan's Magazine*. Howells accepted this arrangement in September 1879, and the novel was scheduled to begin in the July 1880 issues of the two magazines, but was delayed several months in both cases. James wrote to his father in March 1880 that he was "taking a holiday, pure and simple—before settling down to the daily evolutions of my 'big' novel." He began to write the novel in Florence in April 1880, reworking "an old beginning made long ago." By arrangement with Macmillan & Co., James sent the manuscript in installments to Clay and Taylor, the publisher's printer. This manuscript is not known to survive. The printer sent two sets of proofs back to James, who revised and corrected them and returned one set to *Macmillan's Magazine* and the other to the *Atlantic Monthly* (the first installment went to Howells July 20, 1880). *The Portrait of a Lady* appeared in *Macmillan's Magazine* from October 1880 through November 1881 and in the *Atlantic Monthly* from November 1880 through December 1881. James continued to correct and forward proofs to both periodicals while staying in France and Italy from March through June of 1881.

Upon his return to London, James made an agreement with Houghton, Mifflin and Company to publish an American edition and set about revising sheets from *Macmillan's Magazine*. The revisions between periodical and book versions are not numerous; some are merely corrections of typographical errors, and others are stylistic. Examples of these revisions are his changing "thirteenth year" to "eleventh year" at 224.3; "forces, the most important being an excitable pride and a restless conscience," to simply "forces" at 224.38; "Her head was full of premature convictions and unproportioned images," to "Her thoughts were a tangle of vague outlines," at 241.7–8; and "if a certain impulse should be stirred" (in *Macmillan's*) or "if a certain impulse were stirred" (in the *Atlantic*) to "if a certain light should dawn" at 244.5.

Type was set for Macmillan & Co. by Clay and Taylor, and molds for plates were sent to Houghton, Mifflin and Company in Boston, who published a one-volume first printing in October 1881 (with a title-page date of 1882). Therefore, the text of the first American book printing, having been set in England, contains British spelling and usage. Clay and Taylor then added three-point leading to the standing type and re-broke lines in order to make the novel fill three volumes. The first English book edition, printed directly from this re-leaded type, was published by Macmillan & Co. on November 8, 1881. It was not until twenty-seven years later that James extensively revised *The Portrait of a Lady* for the New York Edition (Charles Scribner's Sons, 1908), using the Houghton, Mifflin and Company version, making this final version a very different book from the one that first appeared in 1881. The present volume reprints the 1881 text of Houghton, Mifflin and Company, because its revisions were made soon after composition, and because it represents James's earlier intentions better than the periodical texts.

James first outlined the plot of *The Bostonians* in a letter of April 8, 1883, to his American publisher James R. Osgood, who bought a five-year contract for serial and book publication rights (English and American) for $4,000, to be paid upon completion of the manuscript. Osgood in turn sold the serial rights to the *Century Magazine*. James returned to England from America in September 1883, but did not begin writing the novel at once, having committed himself to finishing a number of short stories first. After meeting this commitment he returned to the novel. He sent typewritten copy (he had begun using a public typist soon after his return to London) of the first installment to Richard Watson Gilder at the *Century Magazine* before October 1, 1884. The novel eventually filled thirteen installments in the *Century*, from February 1885 through February 1886. Neither James's manuscript nor the typescript is known to survive. In late April 1885, James wrote to Osgood that he had "sent to the *Century* all the copy for the *Bostonians* . . . with the exception of 70 or 80 pages in the total ms. of 950." On May 5, 1885, however, he learned that James R. Osgood and Company had failed, still owing him all the money for *The Bostonians* and royalties on his other volumes. After first investigating the possibility of renegotiating the contract with Osgood's successor, Benjamin Ticknor, James sold the work to his English publisher, Macmillan & Co., for an advance of £500 ($2500) against a fifteen percent royalty for English and American book publication.

James's revisions for the book publication of *The Bostonians* were extensive. There had been no opportunity to correct proofs for the *Century Magazine*, and he had complained of its "vile misprints." He corrected most of them, and made other revisions as well. Some examples of these changes are: at 805.19, "and radicals" was changed to "and roaring radicals"; at 809.27, the sentence "It will be seen that she, at least, did not wish to be personal." was deleted following "individuals."; at 816.26, "single" was corrected to "signal"; at 821.1, "I guess" was changed to "I reckon"; at 837.6, "for two years" was changed to "for nearly a year"; and at 840.36, "pathology" was changed to "physiology."

Macmillan & Co. published *The Bostonians* on February 15, 1886, in London, in an impression of 500 three-volume sets. Macmillan then removed the leading from the standing type, produced a one-volume impression of 5,000 copies, and shipped 3,000 of them to New York, where the book was published on March 19, 1886. *The Bostonians* was not revised again and was not included in the later New York Edition. Since James was not involved in the production of the one-volume printing, the original three-volume English printing, published by Macmillan & Co., furnishes the last text of *The Bostonians* that James revised, and it provides the text reprinted in this volume.

The standards for American English continue to fluctuate and in some ways were different in earlier periods from what they are now. In nineteenth-century writings, for example, a word might be spelled in more than one way, even in the same work. Commas could be used expressively to suggest the movements of voice, and capitals were sometimes meant to give significances to a word beyond those it might have in its uncapitalized form. Since modernization would remove such effects, this volume has preserved the spelling, punctuation, capitalization, and wording of the editions reprinted. The present edition is concerned only with representing the texts of these editions; it does not attempt to reproduce features of their typographic design—such as the display capitalization of chapter openings.

Some changes, however, have been made. Typographical errors, many of them due to imperfect plates, have been corrected; the following is a list of those errors by page and line number: 8.35, women; 15.37, palate,; 15.38, abroad;; 19.10, them; 22.6, him; 29.15, you!"; 39.4, real,; 39.37, claret?; 49.33, tutor; 56.8, money.; 72.3, doctor; 76.37, Your; 82.2, imagination; 86.25, hands,; 92.15, sometime; 98.23, case have; 98.26, Townsend; 102.8, cried,; 106.2, you?; 111.9, "Well; 112.15, a; 119.26, Catherine; 125.11, am,; 128.29, dressmaker's; 131.8, implacable!; 136.19, him; 136.23, brilliant,; 136.28, laugh,; 143.32, them.; 144.17, was an; 146.1, you.; 150.27, on,; 150.34, rich?; 151.14, said,; 151.40, do?; 152.10, go?; 152.15, that?; 161.20, aunt; 161.36, Catherine; 161.40, Orleans!; 162.16, me!; 162.32, him!; 166.39, out,; 167.18, cheerful,; 177.23, of property; 177.36, shools; 189.24, hard!; 198.4, himself"; 209.3, you; 218.6, besides"; 219.14, resentment,; 220.30, husband; 251.23, upon father's; 255.37, conversation; 258.12, wait?; 272.11, designs?;

279.31–32, his cousin; 282.36, her mysterious; 295.25, Lord's; 296.4, likes; 298.40, Gardencourt; 322.32, are gone; 323.11, beyond.; 343.37, twenty; 346.6, darkness; 349.39, uncle?; 356.5, that; 363.23, Bedfordshire."; 380.17, but her; 391.9, flat?; 392.26, whereever; 395.24, tender; 406.5, had; 412.27, it?——; 431.26, answered; 443.16, them?; 448.38, She; 454.13, bibelots; 458.4, Osborne; 459.4, aunt; 460.22, Countess of; 507.23, seem; 524.28, own; 525.33, Florence; 540.36, would; 556.4, sister-in-law; 561.27, *bibelots*; 567.19, bibelots; 577.15, then; 581.13, insulted; 620.35, Piazza; 648.24, him.; 648.39, If; 683.2, imprudence; 702.20, she; 720.32, has; 722.12, contradiction; 754.30, "So; 764.25, me"; 776.9, two; 794.27, admired; 796.32, different.; 796.38, If; 797.14, life?; 806.23, he; 819.12, thought; 819.12, indeed; 819.13, Yet; 819.15, news; 819.20, sympathy; 820.3, instant; 820.21, Why; 820.22, radiant; 820.40, proceeded; 821.37, undulations; 822.3, defiance; 822.5, of; 822.7, advances; 839.17, side,; 847.39, added,; 850.11, rejoinded; 862.34, can; 868.5, definit; 879.28, *entsagen!* "; 907.20, precuniary; 911.13, "fam'ly"; 921.39, You; 940.28, t; 959.1, he; 964.14, discussions; 977.23, he; 999.23, deliciously!; 1002.14, ladies?; 1010.11, ours,; 1039.20, 'sympathising friends.'; 1062.24, Mrs; 1091.13, Burrages; 1192.9, Rasil; 1198.26, place,; 1201.30 whereever. Errors corrected second printing: 676.16, the (Library of America error); 1198.27, unique. (*LOA*); 1201.18, oppsite (*LOA*).

Notes

In the notes below, the reference numbers denote page and line of the present volume (the line count includes chapter headings). No note is made for material included in a standard desk-reference book. For more detailed notes, references to other studies, and further biographical information than is contained in the Chronology, see: *The Art of the Novel: Critical Prefaces by Henry James*, with an Introduction by Richard P. Blackmur (New York: Charles Scribner's Sons, 1934); *The Notebooks of Henry James*, ed. by F. O. Matthiessen and Kenneth B. Murdock (New York: Oxford University Press, 1961); *Henry James Letters*, ed. by Leon Edel, 4 vols. (Cambridge: Harvard University Press, 1974–84); *The Portrait of a Lady: An Authoritative Text / Henry James and the Novel / Reviews and Criticism*, ed. by Robert D. Bamberg (New York: W. W. Norton and Company, 1975); *The Bostonians*, ed. by Alfred Habegger (Indianapolis: The Bobbs-Merrill Company, 1976); and *The Bostonians*, ed. by Charles R. Anderson (London: Penguin Books, 1984).

WASHINGTON SQUARE

15.22   the Fifth Avenue]   A common idiom of the period.

15.39   ailantus-trees]   Spelled "ailanthus" in *Webster's Third New International Dictionary*, but *The Oxford English Dictionary* describes that spelling as a "corruption." In the *Cornhill Magazine* the word was spelled "alanthus-trees."

26.28   *Excelsior!*]   Henry Wadsworth Longfellow's famous poem (1842) wherein the unnamed youth perishes in a snowstorm while carrying a banner up a mountainside.

81.26–27   to . . . say]   In French, *ciel*, the word for "sky," also denotes heaven and God.

114.14   only]   The word "only" is used here in the British sense to mean "except" or "but."

160.14   'the . . . speak!']   *Macbeth*, IV, i, 98.

171.22   *Il fait le mort.*]   He shams death.

THE PORTRAIT OF A LADY

314.4, 18   Caliban . . . Prospero]   Three characters in Shakespeare's *The Tempest*.

334.39   that . . . art]   The reference here is to the South Kensington Museum, which opened in 1857; now called the Victoria and Albert Museum.

363.32   good . . nods]   This common phrase, meaning "even the best makes mistakes," is thought to have originated in Horace's *Ars Poetica*, 359.

367.20   Beethoven's]   In the New York Edition (1908), James changed this to "Schubert's."

367.35–36   *du . . . doigts*]   At the tips of my fingers; that is, softly.

390.12   Wallachia]   Sometimes spelled "Walachia," a region in southern Romania. Changed to "Malta" in the New York Edition.

390.28   Serena]   Madame Merle's given name was Geraldine in the *Atlantic Monthly* version.

392.11–12   *je . . . loin*]   I come from far back.

392.31–32   *je . . . peu*]   I only ask you.

409.27–28   the government . . . France]   A reference to the Third Republic, proclaimed September 4, 1870, on the overthrow of the Second Empire of Napoleon III.

410.34   "defended"]   Play on the French word *défence*, in the sense of "to prohibit."

411.5   *Almanach de Gotha*]   Famous European social register begun in 1763.

411.14   Pau]   Tourist area in southwest France.

411.30–31   Hôtel Drouot]   The French government's official auction house for works of art, located in Paris.

411.39–40   *sans blague*]   Without fooling.

412.2   *je . . . ça!*]   That is all I am saying.

426.15–16   *Ce . . . partie.*]   That is not my part; or, that is not what I do.

428.16   *Le couvent . . . monde,*]   The convent is not like the world.

428.36–37   *Le monde y gagnera.*]   The world will be better for it.

429.28–29   *là-bas*]   There or over there.

429.33–34   *Que . . . fille.*]   God protect you, my daughter.

431.13   *Je . . . mesdames.*]   I greet you, ladies.

439.38   "*En . . . comptés?*"]   In carefully counted money?

444.27   modicity]   This use of the word (defined as "moderateness") is cited as its single example in *Webster's Third New International Dictionary* (1961).

448.16–17   *de confiance*]   With confidence.

449.11   Athenian . . . Just]   Aristides (c.530–468 B.C.), statesman and general of Athens, was ostracized in 482 B.C. According to Plutarch, one citizen explained that he had voted to banish Aristides because he was tired of hearing him called "the Just."

450.14   *négociant*]   Merchant, trader.

451.11   superurban]   James apparently coined this word to establish the location of the piazza over the city.

457.10–11   *à fond*]   To the bottom, i.e. thoroughly.

473.18   *soupirant*]   Suitor, wooer.

484.35   *Dame*]   Italian interjection meaning "indeed" or " well."

485.27   "Murray."]   A reference to the well-known and respected travel guides published in London by John Murray.

492.39   Saint . . . Constantinople]   Also Hagia Sophia, famous cathedral, later converted to a mosque, supreme example of Byzantine architecture.

499.17   Dying Gladiator]   Known also as *The Dying Gaul*, this statue is probably by Epigonos of Pergamon (c.250 B.C.).

505.34   Bellaggio]   A popular resort near Lake Como.

506.21   Ampère]   Jean Jacques Ampère (1800–64), French writer and scholar, author of a history of Rome, and subject of a review by James in the *Galaxy* in 1875.

513.26   *"Ah, . . . trouve!"*]   Ah, it can happen like that!

518.7   *portone*]   Main entrance.

541.24   Cascine]   Large park near Florence.

562.3   *belle-mère*]   Stepmother.

564.37   *"Gardez-vous en bien!"*]   Be very careful!

566.30   *piazzetta*]   Small public square.

566.40   *piano nobile*]   First story above the mezzanine.

567.9   Limoges]   Enamel produced in Limoges, France, since the twelfth century.

569.33   Capo di Monte]   Locale near Naples that produced hard porcelain in rococo style widely imitated by French manufacturers in the nineteenth century.

575.13   *salottino*]   Small sitting room.

586.5   Catania]   Sicilian port and winter resort.

597.36   *in petto*]   To himself.

599.37   Campagna]   Picturesque lowlands near Rome.

601.8   *vous . . . trop*]   You demand too much of me.

605.10   Pincian]   Section of Rome favored by the aristocracy.

614.35   *Je . . . moi!*]   There is nothing I can do about it!

620.27   famous grist-tax]   A tax on the grinding of food grains introduced in Italy in 1868 and considered unfair to the poor.

647.29   *prétendant*]   Suitor.

660.26   *c'est bien gentil*]   It is very nice.

663.3   Medicean Venus]   Celebrated Greek statue, sometimes called the
Medicean *Aphrodite*, probably derived from Praxiteles's *Aphrodite of Cnidus*.

690.8   Posilippo]   A suburb of Naples.

710.40   *à . . . heure*]   A good hour, that is, grand.

724.20   St. John Lateran]   San Giovanni in Laterano, seat of the Bishop
of Rome, has the oldest Christian basilica (fourth century) in the city. Its
famous façade by Allessandro Galilei was built in 1733–36.

727.11   "*Eh moi, donc!*"]   And me, then? (i.e. what about me?).

732.12   Baths of Titus]   One of the famous ruins of the Esquiline Hills.

737.29   "*En . . . pose!*"]   There you are, my dear, what a pose!

761.23–24   *Elle . . . maison*]   She brightens the house.

765.25   "*Eh . . . pensez-vous?*"]   Well, dear Madam, what do you think?

THE BOSTONIANS

805.17   Brocken]   A peak in the Harz Mountains in Germany, the most
famous of the sites where witches were said to gather on Walpurgis Night,
April 30.

805.23–24   Whatever . . . wrong]   A reversal of Pope's epigrammatic
"Whatever is, is right" (*Essay on Man*, I, 289).

816.23   Back Bay]   The name given to the fashionable residential area that
had been reclaimed since 1856 from the mudflats along the Charles River.

821.6   South End]   Unfashionable end of Boston at the other side of
town from Back Bay.

831.10   Beacon Street]   The center of old Boston where its most respected families lived.

831.23   Mill-dam]   Embankment running along Back Bay.

831.33   Roxbury]   Suburb south of Boston.

833.17   State Street]   Financial center of Boston.

840.17   'Transcript.']   *The Boston Evening Transcript*, a daily newspaper representing the conservative New England tradition.

854.24   Esmeralda]   The gypsy heroine of Victor Hugo's *Notre Dame de Paris* (1831).

865.9   Cayuga community]   An allusion to the Oneida community (1848–81), a famous Utopian group in central New York State that believed in communal property and the abolition of marriage.

866.25   'Summer-land,']   The after-life.

879.28   *"Entsagen . . . entsagen!"*]   A misquotation of Goethe's *Faust*, I, 1549: "Entbehren sollst du! sollst entbehren!"

880.4   "Thou . . . abstain!"]   This free verse translation by the American poet, novelist, and traveler Bayard Taylor (1825–78) was made in 1870–71.

884.31–32   Empress . . . last war]   Eugénie, consort of Napoleon III, considered to have contributed to the outbreak of the Franco-Prussian War in July 1870.

891.33   Tremont Temple]   Founded in 1839 as the First Baptist Free Church, it was the first integrated congregation in Boston and had a long association with radical causes. Its large auditorium was frequently rented for public events.

903.10   *portée*]   Significance, bearing.

905.7   *à la Chinoise*]   In the Chinese manner.

915.11   Mount Desert]   Maine's Mount Desert Island had several fashionable resorts, most notably Bar Harbor.

916.1   *enfant . . . balle*]   One who is born to the trade.

916.15   *prime donne*]   Italian plural form of prima donna.

917.19   gynecæum]   Inner part of Grecian house where women lived. Usually spelled *gynæceum* or *gynæcium*.

919.32   new land]   The fashionable Back Bay area, which was built on new land. See note 816.23.

931.30   *vie intime*]   Intimate life.

957.26   Parker's]   The well-known Parker House in Boston.

958.29   Papanti's]   Boston dancing academy for children of the upper class; private balls were sometimes given in its large hall.

959.8–9   Cremona violins]   This Italian city was famous for the violins made there from the sixteenth through the eighteenth century.

960.17   Athenæum]   Large private library in Boston, founded in 1807.

962.13   Associated Charities]   A well-known charitable association in Boston.

966.6   Music Hall]   The largest auditorium in Boston at the time, built before the Civil War.

968.1   the age . . . thinking]   The complete phrase is "plain living and high thinking are no more," in Wordsworth's sonnet "O Friend! I Know Not Which Way I Must Look," from his *Poems Dedicated to National Independence and Liberty* (1802).

968.19   Chickering piano]   Built in Boston and named after the founder of the pianoforte company, James Chickering (1798–1853).

968.20   *Deutsche Rundschau*]   German literary monthly founded in 1874.

974.25   Astor Library]   Founded by John Jacob Astor (1763–1848) and his son William (1792–1875), it later became the nucleus of the New York Public Library.

976.12   *Schoppen*]   German beer glasses.

977.35   Messrs. Andrews and Stoddard]   Editors of *A Copious and Critical Latin-English Lexicon* (1850), a Latin grammar still in use.

991.19   *gentilhomme de province*]   A country gentleman.

1001.33   Framingham and Billerica]   Towns near Boston.

1023.36–37   Memorial Hall]   Built between 1870 and 1878 as a memorial to Harvard students and alumni who died fighting for the Union in the Civil War.

1035.28   under the rose]   From the Latin *sub rosa*, indicating covertness or concealment.

1038.31   like Boston]   The Wednesday Evening Club had long been established in Boston.

1039.38   Niblo's]   Niblo's Garden Theater in New York.

1043.5   *corvée*]   Unpleasant duty or task.

1050.12   cynosure . . . eye]   Probably an allusion to Milton's line "the Cynosure of neighboring eyes," from "L'Allegro," or Carlyle's "the cynosure of all eyes," from *The French Revolution*, I, ii.

1060.18–19   *spretæ . . . formæ*]   The offense of despising her beauty.

1064.21   Delmonico's]   Famous restaurant in New York.

1084.34   *éclaircissement*]   Clarification.

1085.12–13   *j'en . . . parti*]   I have chosen sides.

1086.6   Academy of Music]   The principal opera house in New York from its opening in 1854 until the completion of the Metropolitan in 1883.

1120.16   Marmion]   James's name for Marion, a small town on Buzzards Bay, which is at the southwestern end of Cape Cod.

1132.11–12   Sistine Madonna]   By the Italian painter Santi Raphael (1483–1520).

1159.37–38   'Shaker' species]   Plain furniture was designed and made by this ascetic religious sect.

1161.10   poor . . . servant]   See the parable of the talents, Matthew 25:14–30.

1175.23   Provincetown]   Then a small village at the northeast end of Cape Cod.

1191.22–23   *Il . . . cela!*]   That is all that is lacking.

1199.4–5   *vomitoria*]   Entrances to the Colosseum in Rome.

1204.16   Boston time]   Time zones were not standardized until 1884.

1217.28   Hypatia]   Alexandrian Neo-Platonic philosopher and mathematician renowned for her teaching and her beauty. She was barbarously murdered by a Christian mob incited by St. Cyril of Alexandria in 415 and was the subject of Charles Kingsley's historical novel *Hypatia* (1853), which James knew.

LIBRARY OF CONGRESS CATALOGING IN PUBLICATION DATA

James, Henry, 1843–1916.
  Novels 1881–1886.

  (The Library of America; 29)
  Edited by William T. Stafford.
  Contents: Washington Square—The portrait of a lady—The Bostonians.
  I. Stafford, William T.   II. Title.   III. Series.
PS2112   1985   813'.4   85-5207
ISBN 0–940450–30–5

This book is set in 10 point Linotron Galliard,
a face designed for photocomposition by Matthew Carter
and based on the sixteenth-century face Granjon. The paper
is acid-free Olin Nyalite and meets the requirements for permanence of the American National Standards Institute. The binding
material is Brillianta, a 100% woven rayon cloth made by
Van Heek-Scholco Textielfabrieken, Holland. The composition is by Haddon Craftsmen, Inc., and The
Clarinda Company. Printing and binding
by R. R. Donnelley & Sons Company.
Designed by Bruce Campbell.

South-5-96